JACK WINDRUSH COLLECTION

BOOKS 5-8

MALCOLM ARCHIBALD

Copyright (C) 2023 Malcolm Archibald

Layout design and Copyright (C) 2023 by Next Chapter

Published 2023 by Next Chapter

This book is a work of fiction. Names, characters, places, and incidents are the product of the author's imagination or are used fictitiously. Any resemblance to actual events, locales, or persons, living or dead, is purely coincidental.

All rights reserved. No part of this book may be reproduced or transmitted in any form or by any means, electronic or mechanical, including photocopying, recording, or by any information storage and retrieval system, without the author's permission.

For Cathy

WINDRUSH - JAYANTI'S PAWNS

JACK WINDRUSH BOOK 5

PRELUDE

Lucknow, India, March 1858

'Welcome to Lucknow!' Lieutenant Elliot ducked behind the embankment as an enemy cannon ball screamed overhead. 'When I'm an old man, I'll bore my grandchildren with tales of this campaign.'

'If we live to have grandchildren.' Jack leaned against the trunk of a *gul-mohur* tree beside the sunken track. 'These mutineers are giving us harder fighting than the Ruskies did at Inkerman.'

'Aye, that's for sure.' Elliot cautiously peered over the embankment. 'They never give up, do they? We beat them again and again, and still they come back.'

'Sir Colin will sort them out,' Jack said. 'We have thirty-one thousand men now, and over a hundred guns, ten times the number we had with Havelock last year. This time we'll capture Lucknow and hold it against all comers.'

The mutineers' artillery opened up in a frenzy of flame and smoke, hammering at the British positions. Jack glanced at his men. He didn't need to order them to keep their heads down; they were veterans of a score of battles and skirmishes from the earlier campaigns of Lucknow and Cawnpore, while some had been with him through the nightmare of Crimea. Two or three had even fought in Burma, six years ago. They looked back at him with steady eyes in nut-brown faces, tobacco-chewing professionals in this vicious game of war.

'Bloody pandies,' Private Thorpe muttered as a roundshot landed among the Sikh infantry to their right. 'Why don't they give up now? They know they haven't a hope with old Campbell against them.'

'It's because they're scared, Thorpey.' Coleman ejected a stream of tobacco juice onto the ground, narrowly missing a column of ants. 'Remember how General Neill treated them, even before Cawnpore?'

'He hanged the bastards,' Thorpe said. 'He hanged every one he caught.'

'That's why they're still in the field.' Coleman lifted his Enfield rifle and sighted at the walls of the Little Imambarra. 'They know what will happen if they surrender.'

'We'll hang them all.' Thorpe spoke with savage satisfaction. 'We'll hang all the murdering, backstabbing women-raping bastards.'

Jack listened without emotion. He understood the men's venom. His veterans had witnessed the well at Cawnpore where the mutineers had thrown the mutilated bodies of the British women and children they had murdered. Men such as Coleman, Riley and Thorpe had ensured the replacements were aware of the full horror of that atrocity, adding as many embellishments as they felt suitable. At a time when British men often treated their women with veneration, the Cawnpore murders created intense hatred.

'The boys are still angry,' Jack said.

Elliot nodded. 'They haven't forgotten.'

Jack checked his revolver, chamber by chamber. 'Nor have you.'

'I never will.' Elliot touched the hilt of his sword. 'I never will. The Lord tells us to forgive us our enemies, but I'll never forgive what the pandies did at Cawnpore.'

'I doubt any of us will fully trust them again.' Jack inched to the lip of the embankment, lifted his binoculars and scanned the enemy positions. He could see the heads and smoking cannon-muzzles of the defenders. Despite the British numbers, their impending attack would be a bloody experience.

'Can I take the Colours now, please, sir?' Ensign Green looked as if he should still be sitting at a school desk, rather than commanding men in battle. His face was too smooth to have felt the kiss of a razor while his long eyelashes would undoubtedly endear him to a plethora of girls.

'Not yet, Green. Wait until Sir Colin orders us forward,' Jack said.

'Yes, sir.' Green hesitated. 'This is my first battle, sir.'

'I know, ensign.' Jack forced a smile he didn't feel. 'I'm sure you'll be a credit to your family. Follow orders and do your duty.' He tapped Green's sword. 'You might have the opportunity to use that.'

'Yes, sir!' Green looked eager.

'Good luck, ensign,' Jack said. 'Now get back to your men. They need your leadership.' He watched as Green's slim figure darted back to the men. 'Sometimes, Arthur, I feel very old.'

'You are very old, respected captain, sir,' Elliot said. 'You must be all of twenty-four now.'

'I was twenty-five last month,' Jack said. 'I feel like eighty-five when I see children like Green all keen to go to war.'

'We were like that once,' Elliot said.

'It seems a long time ago.' Jack lifted his binoculars again and studied the triple row of earthworks that protected their objective, and the mutineers that waited for them.

The Little Imambarra loomed ahead, another palace within a walled garden. If the British took the Little Imambarra, there would be nothing between them and the palace of the Kaisarbagh. Beyond the Kaisarbagh lay Lucknow, with its army of mutineers and rebels that defied the right of the British to own India.

Elliot lifted a battered silver hip flask to his lips, swallowed, and offered Jack a drink.

'No, thank you.' Jack concentrated on the Kaisarbagh. In common with nearly all the palaces that adorned the ancient city of Lucknow, a massive wall surrounded a rectangular enclosure in which was a series of gardens and once-beautiful buildings of marble. Although the elite had built the compounds for their pleasure, each made a natural defensive position that the British had to assault on their slow advance. The mutineers had added earthworks and ranks of cannon.

'Thirty thousand trained mutineers are inside Lucknow, they say,' Elliot murmured, 'with another fifty thousand volunteers.'

Jack didn't ask where Elliot obtained his figures. 'It's the volunteers that bother me,' he said. 'We can beat the mutineers; after all, we trained and armed them, so we know how they fight. These matchlock-men and warriors, the Indian soldiers loyal to a native Rajah, or to Oudh.' He shook his head. 'They're not fighting for some fancied grievance over greased cartridges or some such. They're fighting for their monarchs, much as we are fighting for the queen. They're patriots, and that makes them more dangerous.'

'As long as our men are even more dangerous,' Elliot said, 'I won't worry too much about the pandies.'

A trio of British rockets whooshed off, each leaving a trail of red sparks. One veered off course and soared straight into the sky, while the others exploded before they reached their target, leaving a smudge of white powder smoke drifting in the air.

'That'll scare the birds,' Elliot said. 'It certainly won't do anything else.'

'I hope Sir Colin gives the order to attack soon.' Jack slid back onto the track and bit the tip of a cheroot. 'The longer we wait, the less daylight we'll have to fight in.'

'He's not the fastest of commanders.' Elliot scratched a Lucifer and lit Jack's cheroot. 'He is the most thorough, though. He won't attack until he's certain of victory.'

'Windrush!' Colonel Grey strode along the 113th's position, not deigning to duck when the mutineers fired a salvo of grapeshot.

'Yes, sir.' Jack hid his irritation. He needed to concentrate on the impending attack; he did not wish his commanding officer to distract him.

'I want you to take Number Two Company to the left flank.' Grey stroked his whiskers as the enemy musketeers fired a volley. One musket ball raised a tiny puff of dust as it hit the embankment between Jack and the colonel.

'Yes, sir.'

'You'll know that Nana Sahib led the uprising at Cawnpore,' Grey said.

'Yes, sir.' *Why do senior officers state the obvious?*

'Nana Sahib's bodyguard is said to be in the Little Imambarra.' Grey said. 'If you see them, destroy them.'

'Yes, sir,' Jack said. 'How will I recognise them?'

'You'll know them when you see them.' Grey nodded and strode away.

'He's a queer beggar,' Elliot said. 'We've to destroy Nana Sahib's bodyguard. So what do we do?'

'We take the left flank and destroy everything that opposes us,' Jack said. 'As we always do.'

Jack lifted his head as a bugle blared in the rear. 'That's it! We're going in.' He raised his voice. 'Ready, Number Two Company of the 113th!'

The bugle sounded again, its brassy notes clear against the batter of artillery. There was no hesitation as the British and Sikhs rose to the attack.

'Oh Lord, I shall be very busy this day,' Elliot whispered. 'I may forget thee, but do not forget me, a sinner.' Taking another quick pull at his silver hip flask, he stood up and drew his sword. 'Follow me, lads!'

'Cry Havelock!' Coleman gave the battle cry that Elliot had created the previous year when they formed part of Havelock's small army that battered its way to Cawnpore. 'And let loose the dogs of war!'

'Let loose the dogs,' Thorpe echoed and looked at Coleman for approval.

Ensign Green held the Colours high, the yellow-buff fly with the number 113 faded by sun and damp, torn by musket balls but still proud. Two yards away, rangy Sergeant Greaves held the Queen's Colours. The multi-crosses of the Union Flag announced that Queen Victoria's fighting men were returning to reclaim the city.

After days when the British artillery had thundered to breach the defences, and the mutineers' guns had responded with a will, now the bayonets of the British and Sikhs and the kukris of the Nepalese would contest the issue with the matchlocks and tulwars of the defenders.

Mutineers and warriors lined the wall of the Little Imambarra, firing muskets at the advancing British lines. White powder smoke jetted out to lie thick in the dense air, so the British seemed to be moving towards a fog that partially concealed the first defensive wall. Orange muzzle flares flashed through the smoke and men began to fall. The Sikhs forged forward, with the 10th Foot – the Lincolnshires, matching them step for step.

'Keep moving!' Jack yelled. 'Leave the wounded for the doolie-bearers.' He spoke for the benefit of the replacements. The veterans didn't need instructions. Jack flinched as a musket ball whizzed past his head, swore and increased the pace. His men followed, cursing and stumbling, with Riley singing a soft song.

'Wait there, you bastards,' Logan muttered. 'Wee Donnie's coming for you. Don't run away, you pandy buggers.'

'They won't run,' Riley said. 'They'll still be there.'

'I hate crossing open ground under fire.' Thorpe ducked as something flicked at his shako. 'Bloody hell!'

'Think of it as penance for all those sins and crimes you've committed,' Coleman said. 'And the reward will be killing these murdering buggers.'

Twenty yards now, with the mutineers' musketry increasing. A six-pounder cannon roared, spreading grapeshot among the Sikhs, who raised their pace, stepped over the dead and writhing wounded and yelled their war cry.

Jack grunted as he heard '*Jai Khalsa Ji*' – "Victory to the Khalsa", the old battle cry when the Sikhs had been an independent nation.

'Follow me, lads or the Sikhs will beat us to it!' Jack broke into a run, tripped over a loose rock, staggered, recovered and swore as Elliot overtook him.

'Come on, sir!' Riley hesitated. 'Are you hit?'

Shaking his head, Jack ran on.

Logan, the smallest man in the regiment, was first to the wall. 'I cannae get up!' Logan glared upwards jabbing uselessly with his bayonet, until Riley threw himself up the wall, lay along the top and extended a hand downward.

'Come on Logie and watch you don't stick your bayonet in me!'

Scrambling up, Logan slashed at the defenders, using his bayonet as a sabre to clear a space. 'Come on you bastards; wee Donnie's here!'

In front of Jack, the artillery had done its job and tumbled in a section of wall, with sword-wielding warriors waiting in the breach. They looked like something from the Middle Ages – lithe, dark-skinned men with turbans and round shields.

Jack shot one, staggered as another slammed at him with a shield, fired again and missed. A warrior lifted his sword, screaming his hatred, and doubled over as Ensign Green thrust the staff of the Regimental Colour into his stomach.

'Good man, Green.' Jack rolled away, aimed and fired. The bullet smashed into the warrior's chest, knocking him backwards.

'Thank you, sir.' Green looked shocked at the carnage around him.

'Come on, ensign!' Jack saw Elliot exchanging sword strokes with a long-bearded Rajput as the Sikhs surged onward to his right and the 10th Foot charged at a second defensive line.

'To me, 113th!' Jack ran on. 'Don't let the Poachers get in front of us!'

Mutineer infantry clustered around a small battery of artillery, firing muskets in support of the six-pounders. A sudden roar from the rear alerted Jack, and he saw the Sikhs burst open an arched gate and charge into the enclosure. A slender, active man rallied the defenders with shouts in a high, if muffled, voice. Rough grey cloth covered the lower half of his face, while he had pulled a black turban low over his forehead, emphasising the intensity of his eyes.

'That man looks dangerous,' Elliot gasped. 'He might be Nana Sahib's body-guard that Colonel Grey told us to look for.'

'In that case, he should be with Nana Sahib.' Jack levelled his revolver, fired and missed. 'Damn the man.'

The man in the black turban lifted his tulwar high and shouted something Jack couldn't understand. The mutineers gathered around him, facing the advancing British, panting, some yelling, bayonets and swords held ready.

Something plucked at Jack's sleeve as he looked around for his men. They followed Ensign Green with the Colours, khaki-clothed, sweat-stained and swearing.

'Come to me and keep your discipline, lads!' Jack roared. 'We'll hit them together, not as a mob of individuals.'

The 113th stopped for a moment to dress their lines and pushed on, bayonets levelled.

The man in the black turban brandished his tulwar. '*Maro Firinghi Soor*' – "kill the foreign pigs", and his followers repeated his words.

'*Maro Firinghi Soor!*'

'Remember Cawnpore!' the British replied.

'*Bole so nihal Sat siri Akaal*' – "The one who believes in the truth of God is immortal" the Sikhs shouted as they rushed forward.

The defenders were fighting hard, with warriors clashing swords against the bayonets of the 10th and 113th Foot, firing their clumsy matchlocks while the mutineers, the men who had recently been sepoys in the Honourable East India Company's Bengal Army, fired and withdrew in sullen discipline. Jack saw the man in the black turban lead a counter-attack to check the advance of the 10th Foot.

Jack lunged forward, only for a surge of desperate warriors to halt him. 'Get that fellow!' He pointed to Black Turban. 'He's rallying the enemy.'

'Yes, sir!' Green shouted.

'Logan! Riley – go with the ensign!' Jack motioned two of his veterans forward.

The fighting intensified as the mutineers once more rallied behind the man with the black turban. Jack levelled his revolver and fired, missing again. 'Damn this thing!' Running closer, he saw Logan shoot at a mutineer and then lunge forward with the bayonet as Riley knelt and aimed at a desperate farmer armed with a crude hoe.

The man in the black turban man swapped his tulwar from his right hand to his left and slashed sideways. One of the British replacements fell, staring as his intestines tumbled out in a pink and white coil. He opened his mouth in a silent scream, trying to replace his insides as the man in the black turban parried the swing of a Sikh sword, disarmed his adversary with a twist of the wrist and decapitated the man. The Sikh's head lifted on a jet of blood and landed on the ground.

'Jesus, that fellow is good,' Jack said.

'I'll get him, sir!' Holding the Colours as a lance, Green charged forward.

'No, Green!' Jack knew the youngster would have little chance against a man who was so expert. Aiming his revolver, Jack fired again, to see his target immediately duck. *Who the devil are you?*

'Green! Come back!'

The man in the black turban man straightened up, saw Green with the Colours and stepped forward. As if in slow motion, Jack saw Green swing the staff, miss, and Black Turban slice forward with his tulwar. The blade took Green across the face. He screamed shrilly as a child and fell, dropping the Colours.

'Save the Colours!' Jack yelled, jumping forward. The Colours were the soul of the regiment and to lose them was a major disgrace. He felt sympathy for Green, but the lad had signed on as a soldier and had to take his chance.

Black Turban shouted something, and a rush of mixed warriors and mutineers charged between the 113th and the Colours. One lifted the staff and held it high, with the yellow-buff fly crushed and stained with Green's blood. A surge of mutineers came to help, cheering at their psychological triumph.

'Come on, lads!' Logan led the counter-charge, sliding under a mutineer's bayonet to gut him, roll across the ground and rise in the middle of the enemy ranks. When Riley followed, with Coleman and Thorpe at his back, all the fight left the mutineers, and they fled in disorder. The warriors remained, standing around their leader, clashing their tulwars on round shields and flaunting their prize. The man in the black turban stepped to their front, lithe, slim and undoubtedly in command.

Jack aimed at Black Turban and fired his final round, cursed as he hit a retreating mutineer, holstered his pistol and drew his sword. 'You and me, Black-hat!'

Black Turban waited for him, tossing his tulwar from hand-to-hand, his eyes focused on Jack. The sun glinted blood red on a ruby ring on the index finger of his left hand.

Sergeant Greaves was at the forefront of the charge that smashed into the warriors' flank, and a melee began, bayonet and rifle butt against sword and shield. The force of the 113th pushed the enemy back, and the wiry man holding the Colours staggered as Logan smashed his rifle butt into his face.

'Sir!' Jack didn't see who shouted, he remained intent on facing Black-Turban. 'The Sikhs are in the Kaisarbagh!'

The man in the black turban glanced down at the writhing Green and slid his tulwar into the ensign's groin, twisted and stepped back into the mass of the warriors as a corporal lifted the Colours.

'You monster!' Jack roared as Green's screams redoubled. 'I'll find you!'

A bank of powder smoke momentarily obscured the enemy as Jack knelt beside the writhing ensign.

'Let's have a look at you,' Jack said and flinched. The tulwar had destroyed Green's face, splitting one eye, cutting off his nose and leaving a bleeding gash across his mouth. No girl would look at him again. Jack only glanced at the bloody horror of Green's groin and looked away quickly. 'It's not too bad,' he said. 'The surgeons will soon put you right.'

Patting Green's shoulder, Jack stood up. In the few seconds he'd spent with Green, the battle had moved on. The 113th was roaring over the walls of the Kaisarbagh, in company with the 10th and the Sikhs.

Without time to reload his revolver, Jack drew his sword and ran, jumping over the dead and wounded of both sides. He had two objectives in his head: lead his men to victory and find the man in the black turban.

Once over the Kaisarbagh wall, he found himself in a series of magnificent gardens with fruit trees and marble arbours, sparkling canals and tinkling fountains.

'We're in paradise.' The sheer beauty of his surroundings forced Elliot to stop in admiration. The whine of a bullet passing close by brought him back to reality.

'Keep after the pandies,' Jack ordered, 'there will be time for sight-seeing later.' He ran into a sequence of courtyards overlooked by Venetian windows and with mutineers appearing on the roof above to fire and then disappear.

'Stand and fight!' Jack yelled.

'*Maro Firinghi Soor*! somebody shouted with another voice adding,'*Allah Akbar! Angrez kaffirs!*'

Jack stepped sideways as a tall, shaven-headed Pathan appeared in a doorway and fired a *jezzail*. The Pathan shouted something, half drew the long cleaver known as a Khyber knife, held Jack's gaze for an instant and then slid away.

'Stand and fight!' Jack slashed uselessly with his sword and ran on, with a press of the 113th and Sikhs at his back. The Pathan vanished into the maze of courtyards and gardens, and Jack tried to follow, brandishing his sword as he burst into the palace itself. Men of the 113th were behind him, exclaiming at the treasures that surrounded them. There was more wealth in one room than they would ever see in ten lifetimes.

'This is more like it!' Private Armstrong, saturnine and predatory, said. 'Bugger the pandies.'

'Leave the loot!' Jack warned. 'There are still mutineers around!'

Soft carpets deadened the sound of their feet; silk hangings decorated the walls, mirrors reflected their images so for a second Jack prepared to strike at a wild-eyed swordsman before he realised it was himself.

'They're running!' Elliot sounded amazed. He stood with his pistol in his left hand and his sword in his right, panting as the mutineers and warriors began a fighting withdrawal from the Kaisarbagh.

'Stand and fight, you pandy bastards!' Logan waved his rifle at them; blood dripped from the bayonet. 'Remember Cawnpore!'

After the massacres at Cawnpore and Meerut, the British had no mercy. They killed anybody who did not immediately surrender. Jack watched without emotion. The penalty for mutiny and treason had always been death, and the mutineers had murdered British women and children. In this war, there was little mercy on either side.

'Loot!' somebody else shouted, and the cry spread among the British and Sikhs. As the enemy fled, the attackers realised that they were safe and within a selection of buildings that held immense wealth. 'Loot, boys, gold and jewels for us all!'

With those words, the drive eased from the attack as men turned their attention to rapaciousness rather than soldiering. What they couldn't steal, they destroyed, so in minutes the Kaisarbagh became an orgy of pointless vandalism and theft.

'Stick together, 113th!'

Men ignored Jack's shout as they delved into rooms to see what loot they could find.

'113th! To me!' Jack roared. He didn't want his men scattered around the Kaisarbagh where they could be vulnerable to enemy ambush. Capturing a town or palace was the most testing time for any military unit. Regiments held together in battle or on the parade ground, but British soldiers were prone to the temptations of loot or drink.

'Sir!' Riley ran up with small, ugly Logan at his side.

'I thought you'd be first at the looting, Riley.' Jack knew that Riley had been a cracksman, a professional thief before he joined the army.

Riley shrugged. 'There's as much smashing as stealing, sir. These lads have got no idea.'

Jack glanced around. Most of the veterans were with him, together with some of the replacements, the Johnny Raws who hadn't yet recovered from their first sunburn. Armstrong was missing, which didn't surprise him. 'Well done, lads.'

The black-turbaned leader appeared from behind a fountain. He looked directly at Jack, raised his tulwar in salute and vanished. Jack did not see where.

'Who was that sir?' Logan was on one knee, aiming his rifle. 'I cannae see the bastard.'

'I don't know who he was,' Jack said, 'but I think we will see him again.' He replaced his sword in its scabbard. *And when we do, I will kill him.*

CHAPTER ONE

Lucknow, April 1858

'We have trouble, sir.' Sergeant Greaves came to attention and saluted.

'What sort of trouble, sergeant?' Jack asked.

'We have two men missing, sir.'

Jack sighed. Sergeant O'Neill would have sorted such a thing out himself without recourse to an officer. 'Let me guess – Thorpe and Coleman.' Two old soldiers with a liking for drink and women, Thorpe and Coleman were nothing but trouble when the 113th was in cantonments and worth their weight in gold when the bayonets were out.

'No, sir,' Greaves said. 'Riley and Logan.'

'That's unusual,' Jack responded. 'Have you asked Mrs. Riley where her husband might be?' Charlotte Riley was a sensible woman who usually kept her husband out of trouble.

'No, sir.'

'Come on then, sergeant.'

Charlotte Riley was washing clothes in a wooden tub. She looked up when Jack arrived, drew the back of her hand across her forehead and nodded acknowledgement. Behind her, a group of women similarly engaged stopped work to listen. Three children, dressed in clothes inappropriate to the weather, scampered back inside the native huts the 113th had appropriated for temporary married quarters.

'Good morning, Captain Windrush.' Charlotte Riley spoke guardedly, with her eyes bright and wary.

'Good morning, Mrs. Riley. We seem to have mislaid your husband.'

'Have you?' Charlotte's eyes widened.

'We have, and that other reprobate, Donald Logan.'

'Wee Donnie?' Charlotte Riley smiled. 'Now there's a surprise.' She eyed Jack. 'It must be important for you to be involved, captain. How long have they been gone for?'

'Two hours, Mrs. Riley.' Sergeant Greaves replied at once.

'Oh, is that all?' Charlotte sounded relieved. 'Don't concern yourselves, gentlemen, they'll be back.'

'How do you know?' Sergeant Greaves asked.

'Riley wouldn't leave me behind.' Charlotte returned to her washing. 'He's not deserted.'

'That is true.' Jack knew that Riley was close to Charlotte. 'Do you have any idea where they might be, Mrs. Riley? I'd like to find them before they end in serious trouble.'

Charlotte pondered for a moment. 'Well, Captain Windrush, Riley is not interested in other women, so don't think of brothels. Neither he nor Wee Donnie drinks much, so it's not that.' She shrugged. 'They'll turn up. I can't think what else interests them.'

I can. Jack remembered that neither Riley nor Logan looted the Kaisarbagh. *Why not? Riley had been a professional cracksman, a high-class thief, and Logan was a street Arab from Glasgow, always on the lookout for what he could take for nothing. The only reason they would not join in the general orgy was if they had something else in mind.* 'They haven't deserted,' Jack agreed. 'Thank you, Mrs. Riley. Sergeant Greaves, go and find Thorpe. He can help us.'

'Thorpe, sir? Yes, sir.' Greaves was too much of an old soldier to reveal his surprise.

Thorpe was on guard duty, standing outside the regimental lines with his rifle in his hands. He slipped a stubby clay pipe inside his mouth as Jack and Greaves approached.

'Stand at attention when an officer is present, Thorpe!' Greaves roared.

'I am, sir,' Thorpe mumbled.

'It's all right, Thorpe, you're in no trouble,' Jack said. 'And you'd better take the pipe out of your mouth before you burn your tongue.'

'Yes, sir. Thank you, sir.' Thorpe looked uneasily from Greaves to Jack.

'We have come to you,' Jack said, 'because you are an old soldier, a veteran of battle and siege.' He could feel Greaves staring at him, wondering what he was doing. Officers didn't normally speak to private soldiers in such a friendly manner.

'Yes, sir,' Thorpe was equally suspicious.

'You know all that's going on,' Jack continued. 'Where everybody is and who has secrets.'

'Yes, sir.' Thorpe gave a little smile.

'I thought I could rely on you, Thorpey.' Jack clapped him on the shoulder. 'We fought together in Burma, remember?'

'Yes, sir,' Thorpe said.

'Now, I need your help. I have to tell Riley something, and I can't find him. Do you know where he is?'

'Yes, sir.' Thorpe didn't remove the pipe from his lips, so a puff of foul smoke accompanied every word. 'He's down by the River Goomtee for a little swim. Remember when we evacuated Lucknow last year, sir? They were the days, eh?'

'They were, Thorpey, they were indeed. Whereabouts by the river is Riley?'

'He's where we evacuated the city, sir, last time we was here.' Thorpe frowned, evidently thinking he had made that plain. 'Do you want a smoke, sir?' He produced a sweaty handful of something vaguely resembling tobacco. 'Me and

Coley make it with cow dung and weeds, sir and a bit of real baccy when we can find any.'

'No thank you, Thorpe. You might need it.' Jack hastily withdrew before Thorpe began patting his shoulder and calling him Jack.

'Down by the river Goomtee.' Greaves repeated. 'Why the devil would he be down by the river? And it's not for a swim.'

'I agree with you, sergeant, and we'll soon find out. Come on.'

'I'll bring a picket, sir.'

'No need, sergeant.' Jack shook his head. 'I know these men.'

'That's what I mean, sir. So do I.' Greaves grimaced. 'Riley is a smooth-tongued blackguard, and I can feel Logan watching me every time I turn my back. He's gallows bait, that one, sir.'

Jack smiled. 'You'll get used to them, Greaves. You only joined us a few months ago, didn't you?'

'Yes, sir. Three months ago. I was in Number Three Company in Malta when this mutiny blew up.'

'You'll get to know the men. Come on, sergeant.'

Jack saw the flash of white skin in the water as he marched along the muddy bank of the Goomtee. 'Riley!' He roared the name.

Riley started, and Logan appeared from behind a ruined building, rifle in hand.

'What are you doing, Riley?'

'Swimming sir.' Riley was the picture of innocence as he stood stark naked and thigh deep in water. 'It's hot.'

'Swimming!' Greaves raised his voice to a roar. 'You should be on duty, Riley! By God, I'll have you two at the triangle before I'm through.'

Jack saw Riley's expression alter. Once before, Major Snodgrass had ordered Riley flogged and neither he nor Charlotte had ever forgiven the major. Now his eyes narrowed at the threat.

'Aye, would you?' Logan shifted his rifle enough to cover Greaves.

'There won't be any of that if you're back on duty within the hour.' Jack hardened his voice. 'And you'll remain under Sergeant Greaves direct supervision until I say otherwise. Logan!' Jack turned around. 'Your tunic is not buttoned properly, and your rifle is loaded. You're on extra guard duty tonight once the sergeant finishes with you! Now get back to camp, the pair of you!'

Jack watched as Greaves force-marched both men away. He looked back at the river where sad trees dipped their branches into the slow-swirling waters, and colourful birds hunted for insects. If he had Sergeant O'Neill with him, rather than Greaves, he would have found out more, but Greaves didn't know his men. Now it was unlikely he would ever discover what Riley and Logan had been doing at this river.

Lighting a cheroot, Jack sauntered back to the 113th's lines, glad that the campaign was nearly over. He had been fighting since the previous summer, battle after battle and march after toiling march. He had lost count of the number of actions he'd survived and only knew that he needed rest, a period of peace. Surely now that Lucknow had fallen, the pandies would throw in the towel.

Please God, let this nightmare end soon. I have had enough of killing and death for a while.

'Soldiers? You're not soldiers! You're babes just out of the crib! You ain't a pukka soldier until you've had a nap hand.' Sergeant Greaves paced slowly along the line of replacements, meeting the gaze of each man and saying nothing until he reached the end. 'Soldiers? I've seen Sawnies fresh from the heather who knew more about soldiering, Paddies straight from the bogs who could march better and Cockneys from the stews who had more brains.'

'He's not bad.' Watching from the side-lines, Coleman gave his professional opinion as he sucked on the stem of his pipe. 'Not as good as O'Neill, but not bad.'

'I wonder if he can fight as well as he can talk.' Thorpe dealt out the greasy playing cards.

'He did no' bad at the Kaisarbagh,'Logan said. 'He never ran away, anyway.'

'Let's see how he is when we're not winning,' Coleman grunted at his cards.

Riley examined his hand. 'Did you shuffle the pack, Thorpey? You've given me five aces.'

Logan grunted. 'Aye, me too. You're a cheating bastard Thorpey.'

'No I'm not,' Thorpe looked up, 'I'm not a cheating bastard, sir.'

'They're pulling your leg, Thorpe. Ignore them and get on with the game.' Jack eased the sudden tension.

'He's right, Thorpey. Concentrate on the cards.' Coleman said. 'That blustering sergeant will pull the beer trick soon. See if he doesn't.'

'All right,' Sergeant Greaves returned to the centre of the line. 'Step forward two paces, all those who drink beer.'

The replacements glanced at each other in wonderment, deciding what trick the sergeant was playing. Greaves waited, with the sun drawing the sweat from his face and evaporating it nearly simultaneously. Two men took a deep breath, and one stepped forward.

'They always fall for it,' Coleman said.

Logan glanced at Riley. 'Aye. Bloody fools.'

'So you drink beer, do you?' Sergeant Greaves thrust his face close to that of the lone volunteer.

'Yes, sergeant.' The man looked about twenty, with neatly shaped black whiskers and red skin peeling from his nose. Jack couldn't place which part of Scotland his accent was from, although it was vastly different from the harsh gutter Glasgow of Logan.

'Do you eat bread and cheese?' Greaves asked.

'Sometimes, sergeant,' the private said.

'Well, that's nice. You eat bread and cheese and drink beer. You'll need that for you are about to become a soldier. Now, what's your name?'

'MacKinnon, sergeant. Alexander Mackinnon from the Island of—'

'Well MacKinnon, we have a Sergeant's Mess here. I want you to trot along and tell them that nice Sergeant Greaves has sent you to have one bottle of beer with his compliments.' Greaves watched as MacKinnon hurried away.

'The rest of you,' Greaves spoke in a conversational tone, 'are lying dogs. You lied to your friendly sergeant about not drinking beer, and for that, you will double around the square with your *bundooks* above your head, until I tell you to stop. Now move, you lying bastards! Don't drink beer eh? By the living Christ! If you're the army, thank God we've got a navy.'

'Stupid buggers,' Thorpe said with neither malice nor sympathy. 'I'm having three cards.'

'An officer is coming,' Riley warned.

The officer was tall and slender, with black hair slicked back and lapping his neck and a moustache that drooped past the ends of his mouth. He wore the insignia of a lieutenant colonel.

'Stand up, lads,' Jack said quietly as Sergeant Greaves called his section to attention and slammed an immaculate salute.

'Oh, don't bother with that nonsense,' the officer spoke to Greaves. 'I'm looking for Captain Windrush. Captain Jack Windrush.'

'That's me, sir,' Jack stepped forward.

The colonel subjected Jack to prolonged scrutiny. 'You're Captain Jack Windrush?'

'I am, sir.' Jack knew it was highly unusual for an officer to associate so closely with the men and wondered if the colonel would comment.

'I am Charles Hook, Lieutenant-Colonel Charles Hook.'

Jack nodded. 'Yes, sir.'

'You knew my brother, Lieutenant Hook. You served together in Burma.' Hook held Jack's gaze. 'He mentioned you in the last letter he ever wrote to me.'

'He was a good man.' Jack couldn't think what else to say. He'd been a very young and inexperienced griffin when he fought beside Lieutenant Hook.

'Come with me, Windrush. Your men will be all right without you for a few moments.' Hook nodded to the Dilkusha palace which was still magnificent, despite the battering it had received during this final assault on Lucknow. 'I've found a modest apartment in the Dilky.'

Hook's idea of modest differed from Jack's. Two burly Sikhs stiffened to attention as Hook approached the studded doorway to his requisitioned apartment. He entered with a nod, and Jack followed him into a room lit by pointed latticed windows and cooled by an invisible *punkah-wallah*.

'Some minor prince or other lived here,' Hook said casually. 'I sent in my lads to ensure it was untouched during the general looting.'

'They did a good job.' Jack looked around him. He had been in half a dozen Indian palaces and forts during the present conflict, but only during the attack, or after the British had captured them from their previous owners. This room had the furnishings undamaged and the drapery intact. Jack stared at the silks and satins, the inlaid furniture and the exquisite wall hangings, with carpets from Afghanistan and Bokhara and a display of jewelled weapons on the wall. The two chairs appeared like thrones, broad and semi-circular with deeply padded seats and armrests carved into the likeness of snarling tigers.

'It will do for now.' Hook sounded nonchalant. 'Take a seat, Windrush.'

Jack sat on the smaller of the two thrones, sinking into the luxurious cushion.

'Now, Windrush,' Hook remained on his feet, pacing back and forth from one of the windows to the door, 'I believe that you've seen quite a bit of action in India.'

'A bit, sir. I was with General Havelock's column in the relief of Cawnpore and Lucknow, and then with Sir Colin Campbell.'

'You participated in both of Campbell's campaigns against Lucknow,' Hook said. 'And before the Mutiny, you were in the Crimea and Burma.'

'That's correct, sir.' Jack wondered how Hook knew so much about him.

'Colonel Maxwell told me you were a useful man.' Hook answered Jack's unspoken question. 'He suggested that you were a little unorthodox and less regimental than most officers. When I saw you playing cards with your men, I knew that to be correct.'

Jack was unsure how to reply.

'Would you agree with our assessment, Windrush?' Hook didn't halt his pacing, yet his gaze never strayed from Jack's face.

'Colonel Maxwell knew me well, sir,' Jack said.

'I heard you were involved in some interesting escapades against the Plastun Cossacks around Sevastopol,' Hook said.

'Yes, sir.' Jack remembered the biting cold and nervous strain when he had led his men against the best irregular infantry in the Russian army.

Hook's sudden stop took Jack by surprise. 'You were successful.'

'Some we won and some we lost, sir, like the campaign itself.'

'You killed your adversary,' Hook said. 'The object of war is to outmanoeuvre and destroy the enemy, which is what you did. You are a soldier, Windrush.' His smile was genuine. 'And I am looking for a soldier who is not hide-bound by tradition and regulations.'

'There are many more experienced soldiers than me in the army.' Jack avoided Hook's last statement. 'Lieutenant Elliot was with me most of the time, and he is a fine officer and a gentleman.'

'I am fully aware of Lieutenant Arthur Elliot's abilities,' Hook said. 'As I am aware you have acted the spy on occasion.'

'I had no choice, sir.' Jack knew that most officers thought spying was dishonourable. He decided to end the colonel's game. 'What do you wish me to do, sir?'

'Good man. Take the direct approach and hang the consequences, eh?' Hook sat on the larger throne. 'I want you to work for me.'

Jack felt the increased patter of his heart. 'Doing what, sir?'

'Whatever I wish you to do.' Hook's gaze was level. 'Well? I could make it an order, captain Windrush.'

'You'll have to, sir. My duty is with the 113th, beside my men.' Jack knew it was foolish to argue with a superior officer.

'Maxwell was right about you. He said that as well as being unorthodox and less regimental than most officers, you have loyalty to your men.'

'We've been through a lot together,' Jack said.

Hook's smile faded slightly. 'I suspect that you have more to go through before this war is over.' He sat on the larger throne. 'You saw the well at Cawnpore.'

'Yes, sir.' Jack would never forget the horror of the well at Cawnpore. Heads, torsos, arms and legs of women and children had filled the well in a sickening scene that still haunted him. The massacre at Cawnpore had put new savagery to an already terrible war, with atrocities and retaliation on both sides.

'Do you know who was responsible?'

'I heard it was Nana Sahib, sir, or his lover, Hussaini Khanum.'

'Hussaini Khanum is a fascinating woman.' Hook took a long cheroot from an inside pocket and tapped the end on the arm of his chair. 'Do you think that women can be as ruthless in war as men?'

Not expecting the question, Jack had no ready answer. 'I haven't thought about it, sir. I suppose I always think of women as the gentler sex.'

Hook lit the cheroot, leaned back in his throne and exhaled blue smoke. 'That is what most people seem to think,' he said. 'Have you heard of Uda Devi?'

'No, sir.' Jack shook his head, wondering where Hook was leading him with these seemingly disassociated questions.

'No? That surprises me, considering you were involved in the battle where we killed her.' Hook drew on his cheroot. 'You must remember the affair at Sikandrabagh when the Highlanders shot a female in a papal tree?'

'I do, sir,' Jack said. 'The woman had killed some of our men.'

'That woman was Uda Devi.' Hook paused for effect. 'She was not the only woman warrior, but allegedly the leader of a company of female fighters, many of whom died in the battle for Lucknow.'

'I see, sir. She was a brave woman, whoever she was.'

'Our intelligence informs us that she was trained in guerrilla tactics, martial arts and espionage. She was much more than an angry woman killing British soldiers but… we don't know what she was.'

Jack waited. It was not politic to rush a senior officer.

'You are wondering what the connection is between Uda Devi and you.' A slow smile spread across Hook's face.

'I am, sir,' Jack said.

'We believe that another woman has taken Uda Devi's place,' Hook said. 'Our informants are very vague. They tell us that they have heard the name "Jayanti".'

'Jayanti.' Jack ran the name around his mouth. 'That's evocative.'

'The name is interesting,' Hook said. 'It means "victorious".'

'Victorious?' Jack raised his eyebrows. 'We have defeated the mutineers wherever they have made a stand.'

'Orientals don't view time as we do,' Hook said. 'They may view this war as only the first round in a prolonged struggle.' He shrugged. 'Now that they've given us fair warning, we'll take the appropriate action. More important for the present, this Jayanti may be planning to raise another army of women.' He exhaled blue smoke. 'If they are as skilled as Uda Devi, or as ruthless as Hussaini, then they could cause us a devil of a lot of trouble.'

'The Mutiny is all but over now, sir, is it not?' Jack suffered a prickle of unease. 'We've recaptured Delhi, defeated every army they raised and taken Cawnpore and Lucknow. There is only Central India to pacify and the ragtag and bobtail to mop up.'

'If only it were that easy.' Hook's laughter lacked any mirth. 'This is India, Windrush. We are sitting on the lid of a cauldron while the devil stokes the fire. You know what happens when a boiler has no outlet, don't you? It explodes. This mutiny was an outlet, and now we must ensure any future outbreaks are small and quickly subdued. We might not find Jayanti easy to control if we don't stop her soon.'

'By we, do you mean me, sir?'

Hook nodded. 'Why else would I be telling you all this? I want you to find Jayanti, and either capture her and bring her to trial, or kill her.' He stretched out on his chair. 'If she even exists. All we have is rumour and speculation.'

Nausea rose in Jack's gut. The army was once again using him for the unorthodox. 'I'm sure other officers know India better than I do, sir. Perhaps somebody from John Company with a more intimate knowledge of the native peoples would be more suitable.'

'Maxwell told me you were an argumentative sort of fellow, Windrush.' Hook examined the end of his cheroot. 'In case you have forgotten, John Company's sepoys have just mutinied. How can I trust one of their officers after that? You are Indian-born and have more experience than most in irregular warfare.'

Jack knew there was no point in arguing further. 'How many men can I have, sir?'

'I leave that up to you, Windrush. You know what is best. Remember that too many men will make you conspicuous and too few and you'll be vulnerable to every band of badmashes and broken pandy unit in India.'

'Yes, sir,' Jack said.

Hook's grin was as reassuring as a tiger stalking its prey. 'Here is what you are going to do, Windrush. Have you heard of the Rohilkhand Field Force?'

'I've heard the name included in a hundred shaves, sir.'

'Well, here is what is happening. Rohilkhand, as you know, is a large province northeast of Delhi, and near Meerut, where this entire horrible business began.'

'Yes, sir.'

'It appears that Rohilkhand is a rallying place. The survivors from Delhi have fled there, and the local Rohillas joined them. The Rohillas are a tough crowd, descended from Afghans. Their leader, Khan Bahadur Khan is a formidable presence. As if that was not sufficient, the Nawab of Farukhabad has raised the standard of rebellion as has the Maulvi of Faizabad.'

'All the disaffected clans,' Jack murmured. 'All we need is Bonny Prince Charlie.'

'Or Bonnie Princess Jayanti,' Hook said. 'I think you are beginning to understand. The Mutiny is not yet over; it has assumed a new form, that's all.'

'Yes, sir.' Jack resigned himself to another summer's campaigning in the heat of India.

'Sir Colin is sending four columns against Rohilkhand. General Penny is marching from Meerut; Brigadier Coke is leading a division from Rurki, Seaton will advance from Fatehgarh and Brigadier-General Robert Walpole from Lucknow.'

'Yes, sir.'

'You will join Walpole's column until you hear news of Jayanti. After that, you either strike out on your own or report your intelligence to me, if I am available.'

'Yes, sir.'

'Oh, and Windrush; keep an ear and eye open for Nana Sahib and Major Snodgrass, would you? You know that Snodgrass and his entire command vanished.'

'I'll do that, sir.' The senior major of the 113th, Snodgrass had been in charge of an escort for the regiment's women and children when the Mutiny began the previous year. He and the escort had disappeared one night, leaving the women to find their own way to safety.

'I know you didn't always see eye-to-eye with Major Snodgrass,' Hook again revealed his thorough knowledge of Jack, 'but he is a British officer.'

'Yes, sir.'

'After all this time, I doubt you'll find him alive,' Hook said. 'The mutineers probably ambushed the poor fellow.' Hook finished his cheroot and immediately lit another. 'However, I'm telling all the searching columns to look out for him, and I'll tell you too.'

'Is there anything else, sir?'

'Yes, Windrush. At present, we don't know much about Jayanti, and we don't want any false rumours to spread across the army. God knows there are sufficient lies and exaggerations already. Keep the object of your search between yourself and Elliot.'

'Yes, sir.'

'I think that's all, Windrush. You have your orders. Find this Jayanti woman and look out for poor Major Snodgrass. Good luck.' He held out his hand.

'Thank you, sir.'

Hook's hand was as hard and cool as his eyes.

CHAPTER TWO

'You know Jack', Elliot uncorked his silver hip flask. 'We've been in India for centuries, yet we're less part of it now than we ever were. We exist in a regimental cocoon while India lives outside us.'

'We're not in a regimental cocoon for much longer, Arthur, we're on the road again.' Jack leaned against the wall of their shared quarters.

Elliot held out the flask. 'I guessed that when Hooky wanted you.'

'Do you know him?'

Elliot shook the flask to attract Jack's attention. 'I know that he's a man best avoided. Where is he sending us?'

Jack took the flask and sipped at the contents. 'God that's rough! What's it meant to be?'

'Whisky. Campbell's 79th make their own.'

'What do they make it from? Dead horses?' Jack choked down the fiery liquid. 'Thanks Arthur, I needed that, and you'll need the rest when you hear what Colonel Hook wants us to do.' He looked around their bare chamber, comparing it to Hook's luxurious quarters and sighed. 'We're after a woman named Jayanti. She's said to be the head of a regiment of female warriors.'

'Amazons by Jove.' Elliot swallowed more of his whisky, coughed and wiped a hand across his mouth. 'And where does Jayanti live when she's at home?'

'That's the interesting part,' Jack retrieved the flask for another swallow. 'We don't know.' He explained the situation.

'I had thought the 113th had redeemed its reputation after Inkerman and Lucknow,' Elliot said. 'Apparently not. It seems that the powers-that-be still use us for the dirty jobs that other units don't want.' He shook his head. 'A British regiment hunting down a woman. What would Wellington have said?'

'He would have said, "do your duty".'

'Probably.' Elliot downed some more whisky. 'So we wander about India knocking on doors and enquiring politely if a woman named Jayanti is inside?'

'We are part of a large column,' Jack said. 'We march and fight, gather intelligence and listen.'

'You'll have to say your goodbyes to Mary.' Elliot eyed Jack over the mouth of his flask. 'What are your intentions with that woman, Jack?'

'Honourable.' Jack kept his voice neutral. He'd met Mary when the mutineers attacked the 113th cantonment at Gondabad the previous year. They'd forged a close friendship despite the fact that Mary was Anglo-Indian, with a British father and an Indian mother, and therefore not a woman that a respectable British officer should know.

'How honourable?' Elliot didn't allow Jack to wriggle off his hook.

'I will not dishonour her,' Jack said. 'I'm not my father.'

Elliot passed across the flask. 'I remember that your father had a friendship with a Eurasian woman.'

'He fathered me to a native of the country,' Jack said. 'I'm a half-breed.'

'Your mother was only half-Indian,' Elliot said, 'making you three-quarters white and anyway, you are a British officer.' He kept his voice quiet.

'If the queen learned of my antecedents, she would revoke my commission.' Jack held Elliot's gaze.

'Not our Victoria.' Elliot said. '*If* the queen did such a thing, and it's a big if, Her Majesty would be losing one of her finest officers. However, that is not likely to happen, and you are avoiding my question. What are your intentions with the delightful Mary?'

'I don't know,' Jack said. 'I like her.'

'The whole regiment knows that you *like* her.' Elliot couldn't hide his smile. 'And also, that she likes you. The question is, how *much* do you like her?'

'I don't know,' Jack said again.

'For your sake, Jack, find out,' Elliot said. 'I'm your friend, I hope, so when I speak, I'm only thinking of your happiness. Keep Mary as a friend, by all means, but no more than that. Don't, for God's sake, contemplate matrimony.'

Until that moment, Jack hadn't seriously considered marrying Mary. However, as soon as Elliot gave his advice, Jack frowned. 'I'll do as I damn well please, Arthur.'

'Will you?' Elliot said. 'Best consider the future, Jack. Jack!' He raised his voice as Jack rose from the chair and stormed away.

'Damned cheek,' Jack grumbled to himself as he lit a cheroot. 'Telling me what I can and can't do and who I can and can't marry. Bloody cheek of the man.'

Mary had found lodgings in a small chamber near the Dilkusha palace. She looked up from her small charpoy when Jack tapped on the door.

'Come in.'

'You look tired.' Jack stepped inside the bleak chamber.

'I'm a lot better than most in here.' Mary sat up and ran her hands through her thick black hair.

'You're acting as a nurse, aren't you?' Jack sat on the woven *mooda* stool that was one of the few pieces of furniture in the room.

'No.' Mary shook her head. 'I'm not *acting* as anything. I *am* a nurse. There are a lot of badly injured men who need help.'

'I've heard,' Jack said. 'The pandies have left powder stores all over the city, and our men light their pipes and throw away the Lucifers.'

'Exactly so.' Mary reached for the chapatti that lay on the small table beside her charpoy. Tearing it in half, she passed one piece to Jack and bit into the other. 'Some of the poor devils lie there and pray for death, and no wonder with most of their bodies burned to a crisp. All we can do is try to soothe their pain.'

'You're a good woman, Mary Lambert,' Jack said.

Mary washed down the chapatti with a drink of water from a brass bowl. 'No, Jack, I'm only a woman.'

'You're one of the best,' Jack told her.

'What can I do for you?' Mary's smile only highlighted the tired lines around her eyes.

'I've come to tell you that I'll be leaving Lucknow shortly,' Jack said.

'Are you allowed to tell me where you are heading?'

'Into Rohilkhand,' Jack said.

'Rebel territory.' Mary put out a hand. 'Be careful, Jack, please be careful.'

'I will,' Jack said.

'No.' Mary shook her head. 'I know you. You will charge into whatever danger there is and end up with more wounds and more scars, or worse.'

'That's part of the soldier's bargain,' Jack said.

'It's a poor bargain,' Mary responded. She waved her hand to fend off a circling fly. 'I'll be thinking of you.'

Jack nodded. He tried to think of something reassuring to say. 'I'll be thinking of you, too.'

'You know where liars go,' Mary said with her mouth full of half-masticated chapatti. 'You won't think of me at all, only of your beloved regiment.'

'I will think of you,' Jack said quietly. He wanted to touch her.

Mary held his gaze for a long minute before she replied. 'I know you will.' Her voice was equally quiet. 'I do.'

Jack knew that she was still watching as he left the chamber. He wished he could have said more as he stalked away with his temper growing fouler by the minute. *What am I going to do about that woman?*

'We are joining Walpole's column with orders to remove any rebels from the left bank of the Ganges and bring British rule and justice into the districts through which we pass.' Jack addressed his junior officers. 'Our goal is Bareilly, one hundred and fifty or so miles away.'

'Another long march.' Elliot glanced upwards. 'And the hot season is reaching its zenith.'

'Check the boys fill their water bottles,' Jack said, 'and ensure the bullock waggons have extra water. I don't trust these *bullock-wallahs* any more than I would trust a pandy.'

'Sergeant Greaves has already checked,' Elliot said.

'Well, do it again,' Jack ordered. 'I'm not going to depend on the word of a sergeant to look after my men.' He knew he was bad-tempered this morning and Elliot was doing his best. However, junior officers were there to assuage the wrath of their superiors. Jack looked at his men, some marching, others riding six-a-piece on bullock-daks. They were relaxed, jesting and fit. He had no real worries with them. He glanced back toward Lucknow, hoping to see Mary.

Damn the woman. She could at least spare a few moments to wave goodbye. So much for her protestations of thinking about me. Bloody woman.

'We have a decent little army here,' Jack forced his mind onto other things. 'A Highland Brigade, two battalions of the Rifle Brigade, the Company's 1st Bengal

Europeans, two sepoy regiments, two regiments of Queen's cavalry, three Punjab cavalry regiments, seamen from HMS *Shannon* and a gaggle of engineers and artillery.'

'And us,' Elliot said, 'two companies of the 113th Foot. The pandies won't stand against this lot so it will be a wasted expedition.'

'They might not have to stand,' Jack said. 'All they have to do is keep mobile and let us chase them across India. They can live on rice, water and burned corn and they ignore the sun while we'll lose men by the score with heat exhaustion.'

'It's better being on the move than waiting in Lucknow,' Elliot said. 'The quicker we beat the rebels, the sooner this war will be over. Anyway,' he shrugged, 'I've had more than enough of Lucknow with its dead bodies putrefying in the streets, mines waiting to explode and murderers hiding in the alleys.'

'The men are still keen,' Jack said.

'They want to kill pandies,' Elliot agreed. 'They won't forget Cawnpore.'

Jack took a last look at Lucknow, the city of palaces where he had met Mary and lost his mother. There was no familiar, friendly face waiting to wave him off.

'Come on Arthur, let's find this Jayanti woman and finish this blasted war.'

* * *

The searing wind raised a mist of dust that hid the sun, coated every surface and scoured every face. The column marched through waist-high dust, spat out dust-filled phlegm and narrowed their eyes to protect sensitive pupils. When the men drank, they swallowed dust-tasting water, and they tried not to scratch at the dust that seeped inside their clothes and made walking a chafing nightmare. India had indirect methods of fending off invaders.

'Tell me again, Coley, why do we want India?' Thorpe took off his hat, shook off the dust and replaced it, as dusty as before.

'India,' Coleman said, 'is the jewel in the Empire's crown, the glory of the nation and a money-spinning gem for the Honourable East India Company.'

'Oh.' Thorpe thought about Coleman's words for a few moments. 'That might be right, Coley, but why do *we* want it. It's a cesspit.'

Coleman sighed. 'It brings money to the East India Company,' he said. 'It's all about money for the nobs.'

'So how come we're fighting here and the nobs aren't?' Thorpe asked. 'We don't want the bloody place.'

'I don't want it either,' Parker said.

'Can we not just tell the East India Company that we don't want their country and give it back to the Indians?' Thorpe said.

'That's what we'll do!' Hutton said. 'We'll all go to the East India Company and tell them that. You go first Thorpey, as it's your idea.'

'Will you come with me?' Thorpe asked.

'We'll all come with you,' Hutton said. 'You lead us Thorpey, and we'll follow.'

'Thanks lads,' Thorpe said. 'Where is this East India Company?'

'In London,' Coleman said. 'We can go after the war.'

Thorpe grinned and straightened up. 'All of us?'

'All of us, Thorpey. The whole regiment, band, Colours, colonel and all.'

'Thanks, lads,' Thorpe said. 'You're real mates, you are.'

Jack watched them as they marched on into the dust, weary men with no future except fighting, disease and poverty, living on false hopes and the prospect of a few hours oblivion through alcohol and cheap prostitutes. 'It's strange, Arthur, that ultimately the Empire depends on these men. Without them, there would be nothing.'

'Aye,' Elliot nodded. 'They're the base of the pyramid and the directors of John Company are at the top.'

'Surely the Queen is at the top,' Jack said.

'Is she?' Elliot looked away. 'I wonder if money is not more important than monarchy now.'

After Havelock's lightning marches of the previous year, Walpole's advance seemed interminably slow. There were few roads in this part of India, so they had to move in the full heat of the day, sheltering in *topes* of trees at night. With the cavalry scouting ahead, there was little for the infantry to do except march and curse or sit in the dusty wagons and curse.

'I hope the pandies stand and fight,' Logan muttered. 'If they fight, we can smash them.'

Jack peered through the curtain of dust that screened the surrounding countryside. 'When I lived in England, I thought India was a land of romance and jungles, with tigers and princes and fabled cities. Now I see it as a land where anybody can be an enemy.' He preferred being in charge of his own destiny, rather than obeying the orders of a superior officer he didn't know.

The British moved slowly, dragging the guns through the dust, frequently stopping to allow the column to keep together, tormented by flies and heat. The bullocks proved more trouble than expected, lying down at their leisure and refusing to move until their drivers taught the soldiers a simple trick. While one man held the tail out straight, another placed a stick on each side and rubbed vigorously up and down.

'That makes the bugger jump,' Thorpe said.

'It's cruel sore on the animals,' Parker said in his broad Liverpool accent.

'I'll be cruel sore on you, unless you shut up and march on,' Sergeant Greaves snarled.

Soldiers and syces, horses and camels, elephants that smelled of pigs, servants of every variety, doolie bearers and warriors marched, cursed, swore, and laughed as they crawled across the vast Indian countryside. Some villages were deserted, others were full of huge-eyed, scared people. There were empty fields and the occasional temple or mosque. Cavalry cantered to check every copse of mango or peepul trees, infantry scouted every village for a sight of the enemy, and Walpole's column advanced to reclaim India for the Honourable Company and its shareholders in London's Leadenhall.

On the 14th April, only fifty miles from Lucknow, Walpole ordered a halt, and the long, straggling column stopped.

'What's happening?' Jack asked. Elliot seemed to have some hidden power, which enabled him to garner intelligence from unknown sources.

Elliot didn't let him down. 'There's a fort in that patch of jungle.'

'How the deuce do you know that?' The heat was making Jack irritable.

Elliot shrugged. 'You'll know more than me, soon, the general's runner is coming for you.'

'I'm sure you're psychic,' Jack said.

'Captain Windrush.' The cornet of the 7th Hussars had a peeling red face and the enthusiasm of youth. 'General Walpole sends his regards and requests—'

'I'm coming.' Jack pulled his reins aside and kicked in his heels.

As the most junior officer in the group which formed around Walpole, Jack stood at the back and listened without giving any comment. Dust had rendered the kilts of the Highlanders as khaki as most of the uniforms, while there was a grim determination among the whiskered, bearded faces that listened to the general.

'We cannot yet see it, gentlemen,' Walpole said, 'but inside that patch of jungle is Fort Ruhya. We have to take it before we continue.'

The circle of officers nodded. Most had seen action before and knew what to expect. A naval officer caught a fly and flicked the dead body onto the ground.

Walpole continued, his voice more hesitant than Jack had expected from a general. 'Nirpat Singh holds the fort, with some fifteen hundred men. He is an adherent of Nana Sahib, so we can expect a resolute defence.'

'How are the approaches, sir?' a major of the 42nd asked.

'There is a belt of jungle around the fort,' Walpole replied.

'On all four sides, sir?' Brigadier Adrian Hope of the 93rd Highlanders asked. 'That is unusual. The garrison must have some method of entry – I suggest we send in a party to have a look. It will certainly be hard to drag the guns through the jungle.'

Jack decided to keep silent. It must have been difficult for Walpole to command men with so much more experience, for Hope had fought in the Kaffir Wars in Africa, as well as the Crimea.

'Then we go without artillery,' Walpole decided. 'It's only a small fort. It won't present any difficulties.'

Hope looked at the officers of the 42nd, raised his eyebrows and tried again. 'I believe that a trooper of Hodson's Horse was a prisoner in the fort, sir and escaped. He said that Nirpat Singh would put up token resistance and then surrender.'

'That's the story, sir,' a deeply tanned Company major agreed. 'If we roll up to the gate with artillery and infantry, Nirpat Singh will fire a few shots for honour's sake and run. We'll take the fort without any casualties.'

'Nonsense,' Walpole dismissed the idea. 'The infantry go in on the north.'

'Sir Colin's instructions are clear, sir,' one of the Highland officers said. 'We are to bombard any fort with artillery and then send in the infantry to storm the breach. The commander-in-chief has ordered that we should not attack any fort without at least two heavy pieces of artillery.'

Jack nodded. Although some of the more fire-eating officers of the army termed Sir Colin Campbell "Old Khabardar" or "Old Be-Careful" for his caution and lack of speed, he had far fewer casualties than most commanders in this war. Havelock's final advance to Lucknow had been prolific in British lives compared to Sir Colin's approach.

'We don't need to do that,' Walpole said. 'We will advance immediately. Brigadier Hope, take four companies of the 42nd, with the 4th Punjab Infantry. Windrush, your company of the 113th will be in support. Once the 42nd and the Sikhs are in, you follow up.'

'Yes, sir,' Jack said as the Highlanders glanced at each other.

Brigadier Hope was a Scottish peer and a typical leader of Highlanders. Once Walpole had issued the orders, he did his best to follow them to a conclusion. 'Follow me Windrush,' he was laughing, 'and we'll have the British flag flying over this fort within the hour, with or without the artillery.'

'We're going in,' Jack said on his return to the 113th. 'Extended order, boys, fixed bayonets and keep your heads down.'

'Where are the guns, sir?' Greaves asked.

'No guns this time, Sergeant. We're doing this the old-fashioned way, straight through the jungle and over the walls.'

'Hugh Gough style, eh?' Greaves had been in the army longer than Jack had and remembered the battle of Chillianwala, where the 113th had first seen action. To the shame of the regiment, they had turned and run before the Sikh artillery.

'We're a better regiment now than we were under General Gough,' Jack said.

Greaves nodded. 'Yes, sir.'

Jack raised his voice. 'Make sure you have ammunition in your pouches, boys, and water in your canteens. 'Thorpe, you stay close to Coleman. You Johnny Raws, do as the sergeants and officers tell you and don't mind the shine. It will be noisier than anything you've ever heard before, and you will see things that will make you sick. That's all part of the soldier's bargain. Don't linger and if you're hit, lie quiet and wait for the doolie bearers to pick you up.'

The veterans had heard it all before. The replacements, pale under their tan, listened. Some tried bravado in an attempt to impress their new comrades, who said nothing.

'Do your duty, boys,' Elliot said quietly, 'that's all that the regiment expects.'

They moved forward in extended order, Highlanders and Sikhs and a company of the 113th, walking toward an unknown number of rebels in a fort they could not yet see. Jack's 113th was in the second line, with the kilts of the Black Watch rustling in front.

'The scouts say it's only a small fort, with a high mud wall and bastions at each angle,' Jack instructed as they began the advance. 'There are two gates; we'll go for the one on the left unless the 42nd or the Sikhs force an entrance elsewhere.'

'I don't like this,' Elliot said. 'We've no skirmishers out in front, no flank guards and no artillery. This Walpole fellow is a bit casual, is he not?'

Jack grunted. Although he agreed, it was unprofessional to croak about superior officers.

'How many defenders are there, sir?' Young Ensign Wilden asked.

'The general thinks there are fifteen hundred,' Jack said.

'I heard there were only a couple of hundred.' Elliot's information was usually accurate.

"We'll gut the bastards, however many there are,' Logan said.

With their feet trampling the dry grass and snapping stray twigs, the British and Sikhs moved into the thorny undergrowth of the jungle. A flight of birds exploded from above them and insects buzzed around their faces, probing into ears and eyes, biting the sweat-softened skin of necks and wrists, distracting them from the job at hand.

'I hate bloody India,' Thorpe said. 'There are too many flies.'

'Face your front,' Greaves snapped. 'Don't worry about the insects. You'll have enough to occupy you when we attack the fort.'

'Which bloody fort?' Hutton complained. 'There's no bloody fort here.'

'Shut your mouth.' Armstrong made a rare contribution to the conversation. 'You know nothing, you.'

The jungle grew thicker, with thorns hindering their advance and tree branches cutting the view of the sky. The 113th advanced through a dense green dimness, silent now as they expected to see the fort, holding their Enfield rifles in brown, calloused hands and careful of every footfall. Jack gripped his revolver, called encouragement and watched the Black Watch, ten yards in front, vanish into an even denser patch of woodland.

'Remember Burma?' Coleman grumbled. 'They dacoits would love this. They would have a hundred ambushes waiting for us here. These pandy bastards don't know how to fight.'

'They know how to run though,' Logan said. 'Cry Havelock!' He raised the 113th battle cry, extending the final vowel of Havelock's name.

'Let loose the dogs of war!' the 113th responded.

'There it is!' Thorpe pointed ahead. 'There's the fort!'

The first line pushed through the jungle fringe to a clearing, a *maidan*, in the centre of which stood the khaki-coloured walls of Fort Ruhya. Compared to the splendid palaces of Lucknow it wasn't impressive, a low walled, mundane-looking building with irregular bastions – the lair of a robber baron rather than the abode of a rajah.

Although Jack had expected the rebels to defend the fort, the volume of musketry took him by surprise. Muzzle-flares lit up the loop-holed walls, the bastions, the tops of the gate and the bushes on either flank.

'That's not a token defence,' Elliot said.

'Steady, 113th!' Jack shouted. Firm leadership was required as men dropped from all three regiments. The first volley could test even the staunchest of troops.

'With me, Highlanders!' Brigadier Hope pushed himself forward, tall, urbane, distinguished and as brave as any regiment would expect. 'Follow me, the Black Watch.' For one minute, he strode in front of the army, a smiling Scottish aristocrat and a veteran commander and then he staggered, threw up his hands and crumpled to the ground.

'Jesus, they've shot the brigadier!'

'They'll shoot you too, Hutton, if you don't get under cover!' Greaves said. 'Find a tree, boys and wait for orders!'

The musketry continued, sweeping the open ground in front of the fort and felling everybody who tried to advance. Crumpled bodies littered the *maidan*, some lying still, others writhing and moaning in pain.

'It's the Redan, all over again,' Elliot said.

'We can take them, sir,' Logan said.

'Get down!' Jack didn't see who gave the order. Officers and men slumped to the ground, to seek whatever cover they could find. One replacement hesitated, looking forward at the fort until Riley hauled him unceremoniously to the ground.

'Get your bloody head down, you stupid bastard!'

The rebel musketry continued, joined by artillery that swept iron grapeshot across the *maidan*.

'That's a killing ground.' Greaves gave his professional opinion. 'Who's in charge of the fort, sir?'

'Nirpat Singh,' Elliot said. 'He's one of Nana Sahib's merry men.'

'Fire at them!' Ensign Wilden lifted his revolver and loosed three shots.

'Hold your fire!' Jack countermanded. 'Men lying on the ground can't reload and if the enemy sally, I don't want our boys to face them with empty rifles.'

As the British slid under whatever shelter they could find, the firing from the fort eased. Unable to find any targets, Nirpat Singh's musketeers waited behind the walls, ready for movement.

The rising sun scorched the British while busy insects feasted on their sweat. Every so often, the rebels fired a volley that cut through the branches above the attackers' heads and dropped leaves and twigs on their prone bodies. Between the gunfire, there was birdsong and the occasional scream of a monkey. Always, there was the buzz of flies and the moaning of the wounded.

A few yards from Jack a man yelled and grabbed his leg. 'Snake!' He half rose, there came the sharp crack of a rifle, and he fell without another sound.

'Shot right through the head,' Armstrong said. 'Good shooting by the pandies.'

'That came from above,' Riley said. 'They've got sharpshooters in the treetops.'

Jack frowned. Uda Devi, the woman who had killed so many men in the second relief of Lucknow, had sheltered in the top of a tree. Perhaps the mysterious Jayanti woman used the same technique.

'Don't stand up,' Jack ordered, 'try and scan the trees.' He shifted slightly, heard the crack of a rifle and flinched as a shot thumped into the tree at his side. *That was too close.*

'I see him, sir,' Whitelam, the ex-poacher whispered. 'Don't move an inch.'

'Where is he?'

'About sixty yards to your right, halfway up a tall peepul tree. For God's sake, don't move sir, he's watching you.' Whitelam's words brought cold sweat to Jack's forehead despite the baking heat. To know that an expert sharpshooter was waiting for him was unnerving.

'I'm going after him,' Jack decided. *Better moving than lying as a target.*

'He's pointing his rifle right at you, sir.' Whitelam spoke in broad Lincolnshire as the strain worked on his nerves. 'You won't be able to move fast enough before he fires.'

'I'll catch the bastard's eye, sir,' Logan said. 'I'm no' lying here all bloody day just to keep some pandy bugger happy.'

'You keep your head down, Logan!'

'Aye, right sir. So I will.' Logan was moving on the last word. Rolling from his cover, he ran back to distract the sharpshooter. Jack was on his feet before the rifle's echo reached him. He had to run the sixty yards to the rebel's tree before he or she could reload, and then climb up the bole without either the sharpshooter or the defenders of the fort shooting him. It was a tall order.

Another shot sounded, followed by Logan's voice. 'Missed the bugger! He moved.'

Jack glanced up and saw a drift of white gun smoke from a peepul tree. That must be the one. He hurried towards it, unfastening his sword belt as he did. The sabre was long and would be cumbersome as he climbed. He felt a bullet whiz past him as somebody fired from the fort, but hitting a moving figure at over a hundred yards amidst waist-deep scrub was nearly impossible.

The lower few feet of the peepul's trunk was smooth, without handholds, so Jack had to throw himself upward to grasp the lowest protruding bough. He climbed quickly, hoping the sharpshooter had not yet reloaded.

There was more shooting from the fort, and another bullet knocked splinters from the bole of the tree. Jack looked upwards, gasping. He could see only a tracery of branches and foliage; there was no sign of the sniper. Grabbing for the next handhold, he hauled himself up. As a boy, Jack had enjoyed birds nesting in the woodland around the Malvern Hills and the grounds of his school. He had never expected to use his tree-climbing skills hunting rebels in Rohilkhand.

'He's searching for you, sir!' Whitelam's voice floated to him. 'I'll try a shot.'

'No! You can't reload!' Jack shouted.

Something dropped from above, rustling through the leaves and missing Jack's shoulder by a few inches. He looked down and saw a spear quivering in the ground, swore, pointed his revolver upwards and fired a single shot. He didn't expect the bullet to take effect but hoped to unsettle the sharpshooter. This situation was unnerving, playing hide-and-seek with a sniper while climbing a peepul tree.

Jack knew that after he'd fired the six chambers in his revolver, he had no weapon. Without time to reload, he had to hit the sharpshooter or rely on his strength and experience to defeat him. That could be interesting, as many rebels were veteran warriors with more skill in close-quarter fighting than he had.

Jack cursed as a dense clump of branches blocked his view up the tree. 'Can anybody see him?'

'Twenty feet, sir!' Whitelam shouted. 'He's twenty feet above you!'

The musketeer fired as Whitelam spoke, with a puff of white smoke giving his position away. Jack dragged himself upward into the thick foliage, hoping to catch his quarry while he reloaded.

Thrusting his head between two branches and uncaring of the scrapes and scratches, Jack saw a small timber platform above him. The sharpshooter squatted on top, wearing a black turban, with a grey cloth covering the lower half of his face. *Is that the same man who mutilated Ensign Green?*

The man looked down, and for a moment, Jack stared straight into his eyes. They were brown and strangely gentle, without any of the viciousness he had expected. Jack lifted his revolver, took quick aim and swore as the sharpshooter moved to the side.

Inching higher, Jack tried to climb onto the platform, pulling back as the sharpshooter kicked at his head. Firing involuntarily, Jack had no idea where his shot went. The sharpshooter vanished.

He must be somewhere on the platform. Jack crouched immediately beneath the rough timber. He wondered if a bullet from his revolver had the power to bore through the platform and hit the man, and if so, would it be able to inflict a telling wound? He had four shots left, should he try, and maybe waste a bullet?

The spear point crashed through a gap between the planks, grazing Jack's shoulder. He flinched and yelled, and the spear withdrew, to plunge down again, harder than before. Simultaneously, a bullet thudded into the tree a few inches from Jack's leg.

Jack jerked his leg aside, swearing. *Jesus! There's more than one sniper!* There was another somewhere, firing at him. Jack glanced around, saw only the tops of trees and launched himself upward. If he remained where he was, he would be a target for the second sharpshooter. If he kept moving, he would be harder to hit.

Dragging himself over the edge of the platform, Jack rolled on the timber as the sharpshooter lunged at him with a spear. He was a lithe man, clothed in baggy green. As the spear thudded into the platform, an inch from his groin, Jack pointed his revolver at the sharpshooter and squeezed the trigger. The shot sent the man staggering backwards. Jack fired again, and again, seeing the bullets smack into the sharpshooter's body, seeing the flower of blood as each shot pushed the man further back. Jack squeezed the trigger again, realised that the hammer was falling on empty chambers and rose to a crouch.

The sharpshooter tottered on the edge of the platform, stared at Jack, made a last ineffectual lunge with the spear and fell backwards. Jack watched him bounce through the branches and land on the ground far below.

'You were a brave man,' Jack said. 'You were worthy of a far better cause than rebellion and mutiny.'

Sitting on the platform and hoping that he was out of the vision of any more snipers, Jack began the laborious process of reloading his revolver. He had to place each round down the muzzle and into the chamber and then fit the percussion cap. As he worked, he looked around. A jezzail lay on the platform, the old-fashioned but accurate musket used by Afghan tribesmen. There was also Minié rifle with a quantity of ammunition. Four spears, a long steel dagger and a tulwar, completed the weapons. His erstwhile opponent had prepared well for the fight.

'Captain Windrush!' Riley's voice floated from below. 'Are you all right, sir?'

'All right, Riley,' Jack called down. 'Keep under cover. There are other sharpshooters.' Replacing his revolver in its holster, Jack lifted the Minié, remembering using the weapon in the desperate action at Inkerman where the 113th rediscovered their soul. He loaded it quickly and scanned the trees for movement.

The jets of smoke from the fort attracted Jack's eye an instant before he heard the reports, and a dozen musket balls hummed around his tree, flicking off leaves and crashing through the branches. None came close. Jack knew that the mutineers would be lucky to hit him with the weapons they had, yet with so many men firing it would only be a matter of time before one found its mark. He moved to the northern side of the tree, so the bole afforded some protection. Even from here, the forest concealed most of the British and Sikh force although Jack could see men and officers cowering on the ground, under bushes and behind trees. The rebels had stalled the British advance and held the upper hand. Jack grunted; Sir Colin had been right about the use of cannon.

Ignoring the fort, Jack studied the trees, spotting an occasional spurt of white smoke where other sharpshooters fired at the British lines. Distance or foliage concealed the majority of the snipers, so only one was visible. Jack steadied himself and aimed the Minié. The rebel wore the same baggy green clothing, black turban and drab veil as the man Jack had killed.

Jack's shot splintered the timber at the man's feet, making him leap aside but doing no further damage. Jack grunted and rolled away as the sniper scanned the trees to see who had shot at him. Knowing his gun smoke would reveal his position, Jack lay prone for a few moments as flies explored his face. As soon as a bullet sprayed chips from the bole of the tree, Jack stood to reload.

Looking towards his adversary, Jack saw him doing the same, and it became a race between the two as they hammered bullets down the rifle muzzle and placed the caps on with nervous, desperate fingers. Jack was a fraction slower and saw the enemy's Minié rise. He flinched as the muzzle flared orange and he felt the passage of the bullet, and then he steadied himself, took a deep breath and fired.

The bullet took the sharpshooter high in the chest. He staggered, fell and dragged himself to his feet, looking for his adversary. Jack reloaded with desperate haste, fired again and missed. Despite his wound, the sharpshooter began to load a jezzail. The superbly balanced weapon was lighter than the British rifles and had a more extended range. Jack threw himself down, rolled away and lifted the jezzail that lay beside him. He'd never fired one before, hoped it was loaded, aimed and fired in a single movement. The kick was less than he expected, and he didn't see where the shot went.

For a moment, Jack stared at his opponent across the intervening foliage, and then both moved together, scrabbling to load. Jack chose the rifle, the enemy lifting the jezzail and both concentrating on their weapon and oblivious to anything else. Jack knew that he was faster than most at loading, yet his wounded enemy was first and was aiming the jezzail while Jack lifted his Minié.

Both shots merged in a double crack. Jack felt the tug on his right sleeve even as he saw the opponent stiffen and fall. He took a deep breath to still the hammer of his heart. That had been close. These black-turbaned musket men were expert. Now he should leave his perch before another targeted him. *I've been lucky twice; if luck deserts me, I'll be dead.*

Kicking the weapons to the ground, Jack swung over the edge of the platform and slithered down the tree, swearing as he hit half a dozen branches on his descent.

'Welcome back, sir,' Whitelam said, 'and keep your head down. The pandies are angry at you.'

Jack agreed as a cannon fired from the fort, spraying grapeshot all around. Throwing himself to the ground, he rolled to the back of the tree and lay still as the enemy used him as a target. *How old am I? Twenty-five? If I was a cat, I'd already have used up all my lives.*

'We've to withdraw, sir,' Elliot reported. 'The general's ordered in the artillery.'

'Bloody General Walpole!' Jack heard one of the 42nd shouting. 'He cannae organise a simple assault. Look at the dead – Walpole's a murdering sot, so he is.'

Others seemed to agree, to judge by the comments. With their unblemished record of victories now spoiled, the Highlanders were incensed, blaming Walpole for their defeat.

'The Sawnies are right,' Thorpe said. 'Walpole's a murdering sot.'

'Enough of that!' Jack shouted. 'Get back to the camp and leave the moaning to others.' Jack knew that he should nip any criticism of the higher command in the bud, for criticism led to disobedience and then mutiny, and this war started with mutinous soldiers. The 113th trudged back with their heads down and murder in their hearts, and as they withdrew, artillerymen pushed forward two eighteen-pounders and a pair of mortars.

'Leave it to the artillery.' Jack looked at the dead and wounded that the abortive attack had cost. *Ordinary soldiers always pay the price of a bad commander's folly.*

'People laugh at Sir Colin for his caution,' Elliot said. 'He's a far better commander than Walpole or a hundred Walpole's will ever be.'

Jack didn't respond directly. 'Take command of the men.'

'Where are you going, sir?'

'To look at those sharpshooters I killed,' Jack said. 'Do you remember Uda Devi, the woman the Highlanders shot outside Lucknow?'

'I do,' Elliot said.

'She fought the same way, shooting from the top of a tree. I wonder if either of those snipers were women.' Jack realised he was shaking. 'I hope one was Jayanti. It was only good fortune that they didn't kill me.'

'Good luck, sir.' Elliot handed over his hip flask.

Not caring if Elliot saw him trembling or not, Jack took a deep draft. The taste no longer mattered; he needed the alcohol to settle his nerves. 'Thank you, Arthur. Get the men safely back.' He returned to the jungle.

The eighteen-pounders began their bombardment, shaking the ground and pouring acrid smoke through the trees. There were no birdcalls now, and even the insects seemed subdued as Jack searched for the peepul where the first sniper had been. There were so many trees, and all looked so similar that it was ten minutes before he located the peepul and another five before he found the body. It lay a few yards from the foot of the peepul, face down and already furred by flies.

'Sorry, my brave enemy.' Bending over the crumpled, bloody mess, Jack turned him on his face and pulled off the veil.

'Oh, dear God, I was right.'

The face of a young woman stared sightlessly up at him. She was darker skinned than most indigenous people of the area, lithe and wiry. Jack guessed her to be around twenty years old.

'Why?' Jack asked, 'why must a girl like you die?' He sighed. 'Rest easy, warrior woman. You fought bravely for what you believed.'

The second markswoman had fallen into a tangle of vegetation. Jack eventually saw a leg sticking up and cleared the undergrowth until he found the body. Kneeling down, Jack gently unrolled the veil that covered the lower face. Again, young features stared at him, twisted in death.

'Go with your God,' Jack said, 'or rather, your Gods.' He unfolded the veil and replaced it over the woman's face to protect her from the questing flies.

'So now we know,' Elliot said when Jack passed on his information. 'Colonel Hook was correct, and we're on the right track.'

'I wish we had some spies we could trust.' Jack lit a cheroot. 'General Walpole doesn't seem to favour our normal information gathering techniques. We can't plan anything based on two dead women.'

'Could we not ask the trooper who escaped from Ruhya Fort?' Elliot asked. 'He seems like a handy sort of fellow.'

'I think he's gone back to Hodson's Horse.' Jack was pleased that for once he knew more than Elliot did.

'That's a shame.' Elliot passed across his hip flask. 'We must carry on blind then, and hope for a break.'

'At least we know a little more.' Jack sipped at the flask. 'We know that female warriors are fighting for the rebels and the fact that they all dress the same indicates they're in the same unit. I wish we knew how many of them we have to face.'

Elliot retrieved his flask. 'Could you imagine a whole army of Uda Devis? The women here are every bit as dedicated as the men.'

Jack thought of his stepmother's calculating years-long wait to unleash her vengeance on him. 'That could be true for women in general. We place them on a glass pedestal, we call them weak and emotional, we claim they lack common sense, and we say we have to look after them.' He shook his head. 'Except for a couple of fleeting encounters in Hereford and on the boat to India back in '51, I had never spoken to a woman until I met Myat in Burma. I knew nothing of them.'

Elliot grinned. 'I know what you mean. Public schools aren't the best preparation for mixing with women. Some of the officers I've met seem genuinely afraid of them.' He laughed.

'You never talk about women,' Jack said.

'I've got four sisters.' Elliot sipped at his flask. 'I know they are neither angels nor demons.' He grinned. 'Some days they are a mixture of both! Now your Mary—'

'She's not *my* Mary,' Jack denied at once.

'Methinks you doth protest too much.' Elliot's grin returned. 'Your Mary has more of the angel than the demon in her.' His expression became serious. 'Be careful there, Jack, my lad. While your old *amour* Helen may have enhanced your career, what with her being a colonel's daughter and all, Mary will not, however delightful a woman she might be.'

'We are not here to discuss Mary Lambert,' Jack said.

'Of course not.' Elliot switched the subject with ease. 'Did you hear about poor Colonel Grey?'

'Colonel Grey? What about him?' Jack asked.

'He's dead. Dysentery.' Elliot grunted. 'That's another colonel the 113th has lost.'

'This regiment is hard on colonels,' Jack said. 'We hardly get to know them and then they're gone.'

'That is so.' Elliot shrugged. 'Death is common out here.'

'Too common,' Jack said. 'And it comes too young. That woman I shot was about twenty years old, and a Dalit, I think. That's an untouchable, the lowest caste in India.

'I know what a Dalit is, Jack, damn it!' Elliot said.

'One in every six people in India is untouchable.' Elliot shook his head. 'I can understand why the Rajahs fight us. They want control over their lands again. I can also see the sepoys' point in mutinying if they believed that we were interfering with their religion. But I don't understand why the untouchables fight. Every other caste despises them and condemns the untouchables to the lowest and most menial jobs. One would think they would welcome British help, and maybe wish us to end Hinduism and the caste system.'

'One would think that,' Jack agreed cautiously. 'Religion is a strange thing.'

Elliot sighed. 'I once believed that the Indians liked us because we bring fair justice and some security. If even the untouchables don't want us, perhaps I was wrong.'

Jack nodded. 'I thought that we belonged here. I was born here, after all. People always say that as India was never a single nation, there are no foreigners and we, the British, are viewed as just another caste by the Hindus.' He shrugged. 'Now, with this rebellion, I'm not sure.'

'I don't know anymore,' Elliot said. 'Then you think of our Indian allies, Gurkhas, Sikhs and the camp followers, and you remember the loyal sepoys of the Madras and Bombay Presidencies. These men fight beside us and share all the danger we face. If they ever combined against us, they would so vastly outnumber us that we couldn't hope to stand against them.'

'Let's pray that doesn't happen,' Jack said.

They sat in silence for a moment as the heat built up and the regular batter of the eighteen-pounders reminded them that the battle for Fort Ruhya continued on the other side of the belt of jungle.

'I used to think that we had more morality than the native peoples,' Jack said at last. 'After we hanged hundreds or thousands of people on our rampages through the countryside, I'm not sure that we are superior.'

Elliot grunted. 'I wonder how things will be after this war.' He looked sideways at Jack. 'I don't know if I should ask this again, Jack.'

'Ask,' Jack said. 'We've been friends long enough.'

'Mary,' Elliot said. 'And Jane. How do you feel about things?'

Jack took Elliot's hip flask without asking and drank deeply. 'If you ever send in your papers, Arthur, don't consider a career in the diplomatic corps.'

'Sorry, Jack.'

'How do I feel about being a quarter Indian, my father having an affair with a Eurasian woman and my liking for another Eurasian?' Jack handed back the flask. 'That's a lot to ask in one sentence, Arthur.'

'I know,' Elliot said.

'I am glad to have friends who are still my friends despite my mixed blood,' Jack admitted. 'And that is not to say that I'm ashamed of my mother and her line.'

'Jane was a fine woman,' Elliot agreed, 'a true Christian and one of the best.'

Jack thrust an unlit cheroot into his mouth. He could talk to Elliot about such matters. There was nobody else on Earth, except perhaps Mary, in whom he would confide. 'As soon as I arrived in India, I felt as if I belonged,' he said. 'That feeling hasn't disappeared. The pandies, the massacres and the battles haven't altered anything. Sometimes I hate the heat and the poverty, the flies and the disease, and other times I love the colour and the friendliness, the generosity and the beauty, but I never feel like a stranger here, as I did in Burma or the Crimea, or Malta even.'

'I hate the place,' Elliot admitted. 'I hate the cruelty and the poverty and the heathen gods. I'm counting the days until I leave.' He nursed his flask. 'And now the big question, Jack. Again: what about Mary?'

'I wish I knew the answer to that,' Jack decided to light his cheroot. His hand was still shaking. *I don't want to go into battle again.*

CHAPTER THREE

When the 42nd Highlanders, the Black Watch, learned that some of their wounded remained in front of Fort Ruhya, Quarter-Master Sergeant John Simpson led a patrol of four volunteers who returned carrying severely injured men. Simpson won the Victoria Cross for rescuing men under heavy fire. The eighteen-pounders continued their pounding as the infantry wondered why Walpole had so casually put these men's lives at risk.

With his memories unsettling him, Jack patrolled the lines, speaking quietly to those men who acknowledged him and allowing the others to relax.

'Good lads, the Sawnies,' Riley said. 'They'll hate being stopped by the pandies.'

Logan gave a sour grin. 'Dinnae worry about the Forty-Twa. They'll get their ain' back, and God help any pandy that gets in their way. There'll be bloody bayonets before this campaign is over.' Leaning back on the ground, he pushed a short pipe into his mouth. 'You and me though, Riles, we've got plans, eh?'

Riley saw Jack passing. 'So we have, Logie, and we'll keep them to ourselves.'

'That we will,' Logan said. He unsheathed his bayonet and began to sharpen it. 'Nae bastard will stop us, eh?'

Did Logan intend that last phrase as a threat to me? Jack wondered. Although he and Logan had fought through two wars together, he knew that the little Glaswegian had his own unique code of morality. If Logan took a dislike to him, Jack knew he would have to watch his back, officer or not. The threat of hanging wouldn't deter Logan if he believed somebody had wronged him.

That night's camp was dismal with dispirited men slumped in the heat.

'I heard why the pandies beat us,' Elliot said.

'Why was that?' Jack was still wondering what Logan and Riley had been discussing.

'We were meant to have supports,' Elliot said. 'They never came, and the reserves went to the wrong place completely.' He shook his head. 'We took Havelock and old Sir Colin for granted. If either of them had been here, we would be inside that fort now.'

'The Sawnies are cursing,' Lieutenant Bryce said. 'They're calling Walpole for everything under the sun. It's the first defeat they've experienced since Culloden. What a blasted shambles.' Bryce was in his thirties and had transferred to the 113th in the hope of action and promotion.

'Enough of that croaking,' Jack said. 'Even Wellington had the occasional reverse. We dust ourselves down and carry on.'

'Defeated by the pandies over a blasted mud-walled fort.' Lieutenant Bryce ignored Jack. 'And the 113th was involved again. It's like Chillianwala, all over again.'

'Nobody will even notice we were there.' Elliot calmed Bryce down. 'The Highland Brigade will get all the attention.'

'As you choose not to take my orders, Lieutenant Bryce, you can take a patrol out to the fort.' Jack kept his voice level. 'See what's happening and report back.'

'Sir.' Bryce gave a formal salute to show his displeasure.

Jack watched him march stiffly away. 'He'll learn,' he said. 'I just hope he learns quickly and doesn't lose any of my men in the process.'

'I remember hearing about a keen young ensign disobeying orders to attack a Burmese stockade,' Elliot said.

'He was a bloody fool.' Jack looked back at his younger self without pleasure.

When Bryce reported that the rebels had abandoned the fort, the column marched on in sullen anger, stamping their feet on the hard ground and glowering forward. At that moment, Jack thought, the infantry hated General Walpole more than they hated the enemy.

'I hope the pandies make a stand,' Logan said. 'Then we can smash them.'

'I hope they don't,' Armstrong grumbled. 'Bloody Walpole will get us all killed for nothing again.'

On the 22nd April, Logan had his wish as the rebels' halted their retreat at a small village called Sirsa.

Jack scanned the enemy positions with his binoculars. 'Cavalry, infantry and artillery,' he reported. 'Nirpat Singh is going to fight.'

'Come on, boys!' Logan hefted his rifle.

'Not this time,' Riley said. 'Walpole's discovered he has guns. He won't need us.'

'Does Walpole even know what infantry are for?' Logan asked as the British artillery pounded the enemy camp.

'If he doesn't use us, Logie, then we've more chance of surviving,' Riley said. 'And we've something to live for, remember?'

'Aye.' Logan sounded surly. 'I still wanted to fight them.'

Jack noted snatches of the conversations between the crashes as Walpole's artillery pounded the enemy. Only when the guns had weakened the defences did Walpole send in the cavalry. After a brief, if bloody skirmish, the rebels ran, abandoning their artillery and, more important, leaving the bridge over the River Rāmgangā intact.

'Well,' Jack said, 'Walpole won that battle efficiently enough.'

'There's no glory for us in this campaign,' Lieutenant Bryce said.

'If you're looking for glory, Lieutenant, you've come to the wrong regiment. In the 113th, we don't look for glory. We do our duty. Now check your men.' Jack turned away, aware he sounded pompous.

Walpole's column marched on, until twelve days after the affair at Fort Ruhya, they merged with Sir Colin Campbell's main army and continued towards Bareilly.

With elephants and camels, hordes of camp followers and thousands of men in the reinforced column, Jack guessed that only a significant rebel army would face them and any possibility of gathering intelligence was limited.

'I wish I spoke the language better,' Jack said after a fruitless day asking the pickets if they had any sign of men or women in black turbans and dropped the name Jayanti among the scurrying servants with no success at all.

'Yes.' Elliot pulled at a cheroot. 'I think all officers in India should learn at least one of the languages. Especially us, with the strange assignments we get.' He gave a twisted grin. 'Or at least Hooky could have provided us with a translator. Mary, perhaps.'

'That's enough,' Jack said. 'We're not discussing Mary again, and I'm not putting her in any danger. We had enough of that in the last campaign.'

'Yes, sir,' Elliot said. 'I won't mention Mary again.'

'Best not, Lieutenant Elliot.' Jack adopted his captain's tone.

At the beginning of May, Brigadier Penny's column reinforced Campbell's force. They marched relentlessly onward along a raised roadway with the ground on either side flat and featureless, dotted with *topes* of trees and the occasional village. As they neared the old British cantonments at Bareilly, the terrain altered, with a small river hiding within a deep bed and a hundred *nullahs* in which the rebels could hide, to pounce on any part of the unwieldy British column.

As always, Sir Colin Campbell made detailed preparations, so the army was ready for the final march and the capture of Bareilly. With unknown numbers of rebel cavalry on the prowl, Sir Colin ordered a strong guard for the straggling supplies and ensured the sick in their doolies were on the right side of the column, where the enemy was least likely to attack.

'Sir Colin's doing his best,' Elliot said.

'He's very slow,' Bryce complained. 'He should leave the sick and supplies behind and attack with the fighting men.'

'If he did,' Elliot murmured, 'the rebels would have a soft target, and then the army would lack food, tents and ammunition.'

On the 5th May, they left camp as dawn splintered the horizon and the heat of the day was already mounting.

'When do the rains come?' A replacement asked as he staggered under the force of the sun.

'Not yet,' Coleman said. 'It's maybe a month until the monsoon. You'll notice when the rain starts.'

'I hope they come before that.' The man wiped a hand across his forehead.

'I don't care about the heat,' Logan said. 'I wish we could march without all these bloody halts to allow the artillery and baggage to catch us. Havelock didn't need all that rubbish.'

'Havelock lost more men through heat exhaustion,' Coleman said. 'I'll have old Sir Colin any time.'

'I'd have old Sir Colin any time,' Thorpe echoed.

Riley gave Coleman a searching look. 'You're not as stupid as you look, Coley. Bonaparte had the right idea planting trees for shade. We've nothing here except some scrub.'

The British moved on in a jolting procession, half-blinded by the dust and with uncountable flies tormenting them, seeking moisture in eyes and mouths and nostrils. The sound of boots on the road was a monotonous drumbeat, augmenting the thunder of elephants and occasional snort of camels.

'It's like travelling with a circus,' Riley said.

'You would know about that.' Armstrong said and spat a mouthful of dust-filled phlegm on the ground. 'You and that actress woman you call a wife.'

Jack intervened before Logan retaliated for Charlotte's honour.

The landscape altered as they came closer to Bareilly. The open country gave way to small but thick woods of peepul and mango trees, with the occasional straggling village or lonely house, mostly abandoned in the face of the squabbling armies.

A sweating cornet reined in his horse beside Jack. '113th to go to the front!'

'Give me a proper report, Cornet!' Jack snapped.

The cornet took a deep breath. 'Sorry, sir. Sir Colin sends his respects, sir, and could the 113th take up a position at the front of the infantry.'

'That's better, Cornet. Please convey my respects to Sir Colin and inform him that we will be there directly.'

It was good to have the men stretch their legs and march past the other regiments, good to hear the shouted insults and catcalls of the Black Watch as they gave ribald encouragement.

'Go on, the 113th; soften them up for the real soldiers!'

'Away, you teuchter bastards,' Logan replied in uncompromising Glaswegian. 'Make way for the 113th.' He grinned. 'That told them, eh, Riley?'

'Aye, Logie, you told them,' Riley said. 'Remember to keep your head down.'

There was marginally less dust at the front of the column, with only the cavalry screen between the 113th and any possible enemy. Jack revelled in the relative freedom. *Here we are, the once-despised 113th, leading Sir Colin Campbell's army against the rebels. Much as I hate the bloodshed and agony of war, this is the reason I became a soldier, and for the minute there is nowhere in the world I would rather be. Here our peers accept us as soldiers and men; here we matter.*

The cannon broke Jack's reverie, and the solid iron shot bounded past the cavalry screen to roll along the pukka road.

'Ready boys.' Jack knew that his veterans would be alert. The replacements might need some encouragement.

'It's mid-day,' Riley said. 'That's the pandy's dinner gong.'

'Is that what it was?' Thorpe said. 'I thought they were firing at us.'

'Nah, they wouldn't do that, Thorpey,' Coleman said. 'They're going to welcome us with beer and cheese.'

'Are they?' Thorpe thought for a moment. 'I don't think they will, Coley. I think they were firing at us.'

Whitelam pointed ahead. 'You're right, Thorpe. There's a pandy gun on the road, and it's firing at us.'

Jack lifted his binoculars. The rebels had built a small earthwork beside the road, with the muzzle of a single cannon protruding through an embrasure. 'One cannon won't halt the army,' Jack said. 'The best it can do is delay us a little.'

'Here's Sir Colin's reply.' Elliot brushed a questing fly from his eyebrow.

Two pieces of artillery galloped past with the gunners whipping the horses and laughing at the prospect of action. 'Make way for the guns, 113th!' They unlimbered two hundred yards in front and fired a few rounds at the enemy emplacement.

When the British cannonballs bounced around them, the rebels abandoned their cannon and fled in apparent panic.

'They didn't stand for long,' Elliot said. 'What are they planning, I wonder?'

'They weren't in sufficient force to halt us,' Jack said. 'I think they fell out with Nana Sahib and he ordered them here as punishment. I can't think of any other reason.' *Unless they're trying to entice us into a trap.* Jack scanned the surroundings with the binoculars, searching for anything that might indicate an enemy ambush. He saw nothing except drifting dust and a heat haze.

Jack lowered the binoculars. 'The pandies have to make a stand at Bareilly, or they're admitting defeat. Their little victory at Fort Ruhra will have heartened them, and they'll think they have our measure.'

'Thank God that Sir Colin's in command again and not that fool, Walpole,' Elliot said. 'I hear that Khan Bahadar Khan is in charge at Bareilly.'

Jack looked at his men. It didn't matter to them who led the enemy. They were marching through the dust, staggering under the heat and cursing fluently. *Good.* If British soldiers ever stopped swearing, he would know something was seriously wrong. 'Who is this Khan Bahadur Khan fellow, Arthur?'

'The descendant of a long line of Rajput rulers,' Elliot said. 'He's the grandson of Hafiz Rahmat Khan if that helps.'

'Not in the slightest,' Jack confessed.

Elliot smiled. 'Well, I only know the name. Khan Bahadur Khan took over Bareilly when the Mutiny began. He is about thirty-five, a bearded, dignified fellow. I don't know how good he is as a soldier.'

'We'll find out soon enough,' Jack said.

As they marched, Jack surveyed his surroundings. Bareilly was not as exotic as Lucknow, as evocative as Cawnpore or as politically vital as Delhi, yet it was significant in its own right as the capital of Rohilkhand. The city sat on the level, with a gentle slope toward the south, from where Campbell led the British army. Bareilly was straggling rather than compact, with groves of trees scattered over a plain intersected by gulleys and a few defensible streams. Jack lifted his binoculars again, searching for enemy cavalry.

'Bareilly's rather beautiful,' Elliot said. 'Why do we have to destroy it?'

'Ask this Khan Bahadur Khan fellow.' Jack continued to eye the terrain. The atmosphere was tense, as if the land was waiting for something. 'Or ask Jayanti and her young warriors. All the pandies have to do is stop fighting, and we can all have peace again.'

Elliot nodded. 'The rebels might view it differently. They might say that all we have to do is leave India and they can live without us. They might prefer their heathen gods, their wife-burning suttee, their thugee, their castes and all the rest.'

'Once we've defeated them, we can ask.' Jack lifted his binoculars. 'There go the cavalry.' He watched as the Company sowars cantered forward to investigate the plain.

'The shave says Khan Bahadur has 30,000 infantry in Bareilly,' Elliot said, 'with 6,000 cavalry and forty guns.'

'Is that what the shave says?' Jack watched the Company cavalry spread out across the plain. 'Where did he get that many men? We've smashed the main rebel armies and broken the mutineers. Cut the figures in half, and we'd be more accurate.'

Elliot grunted. 'There'll still be plenty of them.'

'We won't argue with that,' Jack said. He saw the Company sowars congregate around a ford of one of the rivers. There was a jet of white smoke and sowars reined back. 'It looks as if we've made contact with the enemy. That was cannon fire.'

'Here we go again,' Elliot said.

'Captain Windrush!' Jack recognised the sun-reddened cornet that approached him. 'I have a message from Sir Colin for you, sir.

'Thank you, Cornet.' Jack read the note the cornet handed him. 'Please convey my respects to Sir Colin and inform him that I will act immediately.'

Elliot watched as the cornet galloped away. 'That young Griff needs his bottom kicked. What does Sir Colin say?'

'We've to patrol ahead of the column and see if there are any enemy in the *topes*.'

'Is that not what the cavalry are meant to do?' Elliot asked.

'Aye, but we do it better,' Jack said. 'Right Elliot, take the right flank, Bryce, take the left. I have the centre with Ensigns Wilden and Peake.' Jack gave unhurried orders. 'Advance in extended order lads, loaded rifles and bayonets fixed. If in doubt, shoot.'

'What if they're civilians, sir?' Elliot asked.

'Do you think any civilians will still be here, with two armies about to do battle?' Jack paused. Elliot had made a valid point. 'Don't shoot any civilians and look out for Jayanti and her women.' By now, everybody in the 113th knew the real purpose of their mission. 'If you kill any of them, mark the spot. I want to see the bodies later.' *I want that woman who mutilated Ensign Green.*

The 113th moved forward slowly, probing every *tope* for signs of the enemy and stopping to drink at the streams. The heat was punishing, pounding them into the Indian soil, making every movement torture while each man moved with a circlet of flies around his head, and dust in his boots.

The first *tope* was of bamboo, crackling in the heat, tall and serene. Logan swore as a colourful snake slithered away. 'It's bad enough with the bloody pandies, let alone the buggering wildlife.' He stepped back to allow the creature to escape.

The 113th moved on, checking the treetops, probing the undergrowth, wary of an ambush.

'Sir,' Greaves spoke quietly. 'Something is moving in front. I don't know what.'

Jack nodded. Too experienced to show any alarm, he peered to his left. 'Whereabout, Sergeant?'

'There's a dip in the ground sir, and I swear I saw a shadow move. There's no wind.'

'I'll have a look. Be ready to support me.'

'Yes, sir.'

Patrolling alone was unprofessional. Leaving his men was wrong. Jack didn't care. He could not send a man to do a job he would not do himself; no proper officer would. With the dry grass brittle under his boots, he stepped forward, one hand on the butt of his revolver. Every yard took him further from his men and closer to the enemy. The notion came that at that moment he may well be the most advanced infantry soldier in the British Army.

A single bird rose from a *tope* two hundred yards to his left, and then another. The second bird called, the sound harsh in the oppressive air. Jack shook away the memory of the melancholic beauty of the blackbirds calling around the Malvern Hills. The ground dipped, as Greaves had said, and Jack felt the handle of his revolver slippery with sweat.

One moment Jack was walking over an empty landscape and the next the woman in the black turban was in front of him, watching. She was medium height with the bottom half of her face veiled and she had the most intense eyes Jack had ever seen.

Jack loosened his revolver in its holster. The woman wore similar clothing to the other female warriors, with green baggy clothes, black turban and the khaki veil over the lower part of her face. She also wore a studded leather glove on each hand and didn't carry any weapons.

'Who are you?' Her voice had the musical intonation of most Indians. To Jack, raised in Herefordshire, it sounded nearly Welsh.

'I am Captain Jack Windrush of Her Majesty's 113th Foot.' The woman seemed unconcerned by either the heat that hammered down on them or the circling flies. 'Who are you?' He'd already guessed the answer.

'I am Jayanti,' the woman said. She held Jack's gaze as if challenging him.

The rumours are correct, Jayanti exists. 'I've heard of you.' Jack felt the butt of his revolver slip a little in his hand. He contemplated lifting it, firing and ending this quest here and now.

'I would not try.' Jayanti seemed to read his mind. 'At this moment I have five rifles pointed directly at you. All I have to do is raise my hand, and they will fire.'

'I could still kill you,' Jack pointed out. 'A life for a life and your life is more important to your cause than mine is to Her Majesty.'

Gauging Jayanti's feelings was hard. Her eyes remained as intense as ever. 'I am unarmed,' Jayanti said. 'You are a British gentleman. Your code prevents you from killing me.'

'You're a clever woman, Jayanti,' Jack said. 'Sufficiently clever to realise that you cannot win this war. My Queen can send out many more regiments of professional fighting men with the most modern equipment.'

'You are a clever man, Captain Windrush,' Jayanti echoed his words. 'Sufficiently clever to realise that although you may win this campaign, you ultimately cannot win this war. India will wait until the time is right and then overwhelm you. Britain is many thousands of miles away. India is here.'

'Why are you telling me this?'

'Because you are different from the others,' Jayanti said.

'I am no different from any other British officer.' *What does she mean?*

Jayanti stepped back. 'Think about what I said, Jack Baird Windrush. You are different. And look out for your men. There are others very close by who do not wish to merely talk.'

'Come back!' Jack shouted, just as the rifle cracked and a spurt of dust rose a yard in front of him.

'Five rifles, Captain,' Jayanti reminded. She took another step back and vanished as suddenly as she had appeared.

'Sir!' Sergeant Greaves shouted. 'Cavalry!'

They erupted from the riverside, a horde of irregular cavalry with flowing robes and flashing swords. Jack swore. Spread out in the open, his men would be easy prey to these superb Indian horsemen.

'Form square!' He shouted as he ran back, all thought of Jayanti forgotten in his sudden concern for his men. 'Form a square!'

The 113th ran toward him, with the officers and NCOs hectoring the men, pushing the few laggards and watching the fast-approaching cavalry through nervous eyes.

'By platoon!' Jack ordered. 'Remember your training!'

The cavalry advanced at a canter, their hooves kicking up a curtain of dust through which only their heads, shoulders and waving swords were visible. A walnut-faced private, limping from an old Crimean wound, stumbled as he ran for the square, and sprawled in the dust. As if in slow motion, Jack saw the veteran rise and stare at his fellows, now fifty yards away. The veteran's rear-rank-man hesitated and ran to help, arm outstretched. Three rebel cavalrymen galloped free from the press toward the lone private. With one leg injured, the veteran fell to one knee and levelled his rifle. Then the cavalry was on him, a sword flashed in the sunlight, and the private's head rose in the air. His comrade turned and ran toward the rapidly-forming square.

One minute the injured private was alive and the next he was dead. He had been some mother's son, reared in the hell's kitchen of an English industrial slum, or in an Irish cabin or Scottish clachan. Some months from now the private's family would learn of his death and would mourn him for a day or a month or perhaps dismiss his memory with a shrug. He would have been born with hope and love only to die in a pointless skirmish many thousands of miles from home.

Rule Britannia. The poorest always paid the price of Empire to ensure profit for the richest.

Jack's men formed around him, taking their positions as automatically as they had done on a score of training exercises and field days.

'Front rank, kneel!' Jack ordered. There were no more stragglers out on the *maidan*, and already the charging cavalry was past the private's decapitated body.

'Second rank, cap!'

The men fitted their percussion caps, the replacements with shaking hands, the veterans with studied calmness.

'Ready!' The rifles came to the present on all sides of the square, a hundred British Enfield rifles ready to blast the approaching cavalry. It was the same formation that Wellington had used at Waterloo and not much different from the schiltrons that King Robert the First had used at Bannockburn over five centuries previously.

The cavalry increased their pace from a trot to a canter, half-seen in the dust, hundreds of fierce warriors, some of the best horsemen in the world, veterans of battle and skirmish.

The 113th faced them, the old soldiers' expressionless and the replacements white under their sunburn, wide-eyed, scared. Tongues licked dry lips; hands shook on the stocks of Enfields.

'Steady, lads,' Jack said. 'It's only men sitting on horses.'

'Come on you bastards.' Logan gave his ubiquitous invitation. 'Wee Donnie's waiting for you!'

'Cry Havelock!' somebody shouted, prolonging the final vowel so the others could join in. 'Let loose the dogs of war!'

'Ready!' Jack glanced to his right and left. His men were holding, the replacements drawing strength from the veterans. 'Second rank, on my word, fire a volley... Ready... Fire!' The Enfields cracked; the bullets sped toward the advancing cavalry. Unable to see for the dust, Jack could only imagine the chaos, the fallen horses, the injured men, the blood and agony and death.

'Second rank, cap and load! First rank, present!'

The cavalry emerged from the dust, wild men from the plains wielding curved swords, professional warriors ready to savage these northern invaders from across the *kala pani*, the black water.

'First rank, fire! Second rank, present!'

The rifles hammered again, and this time the cavalry were so close that Jack could see the havoc. Horses fell, screaming, torn by lead bullets. The riders immediately following trying to get past them, leaping over the kicking legs and writhing bodies. Men shouted, struggling to control their mounts.

'First rank, cap and load. Second rank, fire a volley!'

The bullets hammered in, remorseless, maiming, killing, wounding. The leading horses turned away, nostrils flaring, terrified, some falling under the hooves of the cavalry immediately behind.

'Second rank, cap and load! First rank, fire a volley!'

The 113th acted like a machine, firing and loading, aiming into the mass, professional soldiers doing their job, the cutting edge of Empire, the ultimate tool in Queen Victoria's arsenal, the little men at the sharp end who enforced the politicians' snake-tongued words.

'They're breaking, sir!' Greaves shouted.

'First rank, cap and load. Second rank, fire a volley!'

The 113th was unsupported. Cavalry could have charged into the enemy's flanks and completed the rout or artillery could have fired grapeshot into the retreating enemy horse. As it was, the 113th could only stand in their square and watch their enemy ride away.

'Come back and try again!' Logan roared.

Only a few yards in front of the square, thirty men and horses lay in a tangle, some dead, others writhing or groaning. The rebels had paid the price for attacking the 113th.

'Keep in formation,' Jack ordered. 'March back to camp.' The incident was over, and it would be foolish to remain out on the *maidan* in case more cavalry appeared, this time backed by musket-carrying infantry or artillery to blast his small square to bloody fragments.

Only when Jack returned to camp did he realise the full implications of what had occurred.

'Jayanti called me Jack *Baird* Windrush. How the devil did she know that? How does she know my full name?'

Elliot shrugged. 'I'm blessed if I know, Jack. These Indian fellows have spies everywhere. I wouldn't be surprised if half the bearers and doolie carriers in the column were giving information to the enemy. Why, they'd cut their granny's throat for a rupee and hand back the change.'

Jack nodded and tried to shake off the feeling that something was very wrong. How would a leader of irregular Indian low-caste warriors know his full name? Why would she approach him and, if she had five rifles aimed at him, why did she not kill him where he stood? There was more to Jayanti than he knew.

What sort of pickle has Colonel Hook landed me in?

The 113th didn't have much time to recover. That evening, 4th May 1858, Khan Bahadur Khan prepared to defend Bareilly. The British Army buckled its collective belt, checked its powder was dry and sharpened its bayonets for the test ahead.

'Here we go again.' Elliot loaded his revolver, tamping each bullet down the barrel and checking his percussion caps. 'Lord, I shall be very busy this day. I may forget thee, but do not forget me.' He looked up. 'And may God have mercy on us all.'

Jack couldn't muster a smile. 'I hope He has, Arthur, I do hope He has sufficient mercy for us all.'

The senior officers gathered around Sir Colin Campbell with the heat bouncing from the ground and the smell of men's sweat potent in the air. Jack glanced around the stern, bearded faces and the uniforms that spoke of glory and triumph, and wondered what the public back home would think if they ever experienced the reality of war.

'Windrush.' Campbell always muted his Glasgow growl when he explained his plans for a forthcoming battle. 'I know your men are expert in skirmishes and ambushes, scouting and picket work. It's time they made their name in a major encounter.' Campbell's dour, moustached face glared at Jack.

'My boys were at Inkerman, sir, and with General Havelock's advance on Cawnpore and Lucknow.'

'I am aware of that, Windrush.' Campbell gave what he probably believed was a smile. 'That's why I'm putting your 113th on the front line.'

'Thank you, sir.'

'Khan Bahadur Khan means to fight,' Campbell said. 'He has positioned his artillery on a range of sand hills directly on our line of advance. He also has cavalry on the flanks, so we have to keep formation, or he'll ravage our infantry.'

Jack wondered if he had thanked Campbell too soon. Glory and honour were all very well for the officers and the reputation of the regiment, but all too often it came at the price of maimed and broken men.

'We will advance in two lines,' Campbell informed the gathered officers. 'In the front line will be the Highland Brigade, the 113th, the 4th Punjab Rifles and the Baluch battalion. I will place a heavy field battery in the centre to counter the enemy artillery, and we'll have horse artillery and cavalry on the flanks. If Khan Bahadur Khan unleashes his horse, our guns will shatter them from a distance, and our cavalry will destroy what remains.'

There was nothing original about Sir Colin's plan. It was methodical, practical and sound.

'The second line will include everybody else,' Sir Colin said. 'Nobody will be left behind. The siege train, the baggage and the camp followers, the wounded and the sick will follow the fighting men.'

Elliot checked that his hip flask was full, pulled his sword from his scabbard to ensure it didn't stick and gave a weak smile. 'Good luck, Jack.'

'Good luck, Arthur.' They shook hands, and Elliot lifted his flask in salute.

'Here's to the next to die.'

'The next to die,' Jack echoed. He couldn't think of life without Elliot. After years of bloody campaigning, they were closer than brothers. 'Try to stay alive, Arthur. If you fell, I would have to tell your father what a rotten soldier you are and how little chance you ever had of becoming a captain, let alone a general.'

'And I want to see Helen again and tell her she married the better brother.'

During the Crimean War, Helen had left Jack for his half-brother, William, an officer in the far more prestigious Royal Malvern regiment and heir to the family house and fortune.

The men were also making their preparations for the forthcoming battle.

'If I die, Thorpie, make sure you see me buried, eh? Don't leave me for the wild beasts to eat.'

Thorpe shook his head. 'I won't Coley. I'll see you buried decent. You do the same for me, too.'

'I will.' Coleman sharpened his bayonet on a stone. 'Don't leave me, Thorpey, not out here. Swear that by the Book will you?' He produced a very battered Bible. 'Swear it, Thorpey.'

Thorpe recoiled slightly. 'I can't read, Coley.'

'That doesn't matter. Just swear. God won't mind that you can't read.'

Putting his hand on the Bible, Thorpe mumbled, 'I swear not to leave your body for the beasts to eat.'

Coleman did the same. 'Thanks, Thorpey. You're all right.' He returned to sharpening his bayonet.

Jack saw Thorpe look away to hide the tears in his eyes. Men such as Thorpe, orphaned at a young age and deprived of familial affection, prized any sort of relationship.

'That's the way, lad.' Sergeant Greaves marched up to them. 'Use that bayonet properly mind, Coleman, and you too, Thorpe. I don't want you poking like an old woman with a knitting needle. When you see an angry pandy, you think of me, yell *bastard*, stick it right in him, twist and withdraw.'

'Yes, Sergeant,' Thorpe said. 'I always say bastard when I think of you.'

'Good lad, Thorpe. I knew you weren't as stupid as Coleman looks.' Greaves marched away to spread his words of encouragement.

At seven in the morning, the advance began, a slow march across the stream-seamed plain with the sun already hammering at the men. Within a few minutes, Khan Bahadur Khan's artillery opened up.

'Maybe if we kick up enough dust, they won't see us,' Thorpe began to shuffle his feet.

'Good idea, Thorpey,' Coleman said. 'The pandies will think the dust is a mist and all the noise is the monsoon starting. They'll all go home and let us win.'

'Do you think so, Coley?' Thorpe shuffled harder.

'Try and see,' Coleman said as a roundshot crashed into the ground in front of them, bounced once and rolled toward the extended khaki line.

'Jump over that ball! Don't try and block it!' Although the iron ball looked slow and cumbersome as it growled along the ground, it had tremendous momentum. In previous battles, Jack had seen raw soldiers try to stop a rolling roundshot with their feet, only to lose their entire leg. Somewhere to their right, the Highland pipes sounded, high and wild in the Eastern air.

'There are the pipes,' Logan said. 'Come on the tartan!'

The British advance continued, the slow, purposeful, remorseless march of professional infantry with a tradition of near-unbroken victory behind them. British, Sikhs and Baluchis marching side by side, bayonets and Enfields, turbans and the feather bonnets of the Highlanders mere specks on the dusty Indian plain.

'The pandies are moving.' Elliot peered through the screen of dust and powder smoke. 'I think they're coming out to attack us!'

Jack took a deep breath. The rebel infantry liked little better than a face-to-face battle with swords and shields against the British bayonets. They were ferocious fighting men, skilled and brave. Jack drew his sword. He didn't relish the massive, bloody melee that would occur if thousands of rebel warriors met the British in the open.

'Come on, you bastards!' Logan had his own opinion. 'Wee Donnie's waiting for you!'

'They're not coming out,' Greaves said. 'They're withdrawing.'

'They're on the run!' Thorpe said. 'You were right, Coley, the pandies thought we were mist!'

'That's what it was, Thorpey, that's just what it was.' Coleman spat a mouthful of dust and phlegm onto the ground. 'Your kicking up dust won us the battle. You'll get another Victoria Cross for that!'

As the British advanced, most of Khan Bahadur Khan's forward defensive line withdrew inside the city. Always careful with his men, Campbell ordered a halt when the British reached the stream that coursed between the advance and the suburbs of Bareilly. Those units of the rebels that had not retreated stood on the far side of the river, waiting in silence with the sun glinting on the steel of swords and the long barrels of jezzails. A thin wisp of smoke drifted from the muzzle of their cannons, positioned on the British side of the bridge.

'We'll have to get over the river.' Jack eyed the single bridge and the rebels who crowded on the far side.

'That's the Nukutte Bridge,' Elliot said. 'If the pandies decide to stand here they can do us damage. Their positions are a bit amateur though, with their guns at this side of the bridge and that *nullah* behind them.'

'Maybe not. The pandy artillery can fire without damaging the bridge.' Jack swept his binoculars across the enemy position. 'If they had decent leadership, they could have made a fine stand there. It's like the Alma, and on their day the Indians are as doughty fighters as any Russian.'

The rebel cannon opened up as soon as the British came within range, orange spurts of flame splitting the smoke.

'For what we are about to receive,' Elliot murmured, 'may the Lord make us truly thankful.'

'Bloody pandy bastards.' Logan was less philosophical.

Before the first enemy cannonball landed, Campbell sent forward the British artillery, and a gun duel began. The infantry watched in interested impotence as British and rebel artillery exchanged shots across the sun-hot *maidan*. After less than an hour, the rebel guns stopped firing.

'They're running,' Bryce said as the enemy fired a few final shots and then pulled out, toward Bareilly.

'Not all of them.' Elliot pointed towards the nearest *tope*. 'See over there?'

Jack focused his binoculars on the trees. Sunlight flashed on the helmets and swords of cavalry. He couldn't tell how many. 'Aye, they're waiting for the infantry to advance. Once we break formation to cross the river, they will pounce.'

'What's happening?' Lieutenant Bryce asked.

'Khan Bahadur Khan has placed his cavalry in the *topes*. Sir Colin will bring up the guns to scatter them,' Jack said. 'Here we go! We're moving again. Keep together, 113th!'

As the wary British crossed the bridge and forded the stream, Campbell sent the artillery forward to bombard the enemy cavalry. The steady hammer of the guns and the black streaks of cannon balls arcing overhead punctuated the advance.

Elliot thrust a cheroot into his mouth. 'Bahadur's taken over the old cantonments, where the Company sepoys were stationed before they mutinied.' *Trust Elliot to know what is happening.* 'Thank God Sir Colin's using the artillery. Old Havelock would have us rushing straight down their throat.'

Jack surveyed the British lines, with the kilted Highlanders, the turbaned Sikhs and his 113th in faded khaki. 'Sir Colin is a bit more careful of his men's lives, thank goodness.'

'There's no glory in that,' Bryce said.

Jack marshalled his men over the bridge and checked they were ready to repel any attack, but Campbell's caution ensured the rebel cavalry didn't have the opportunity to mass and charge. When the second British line was over the stream, Campbell's methodical advance began again, with the artillery bombarding every *tope* and every building.

'We're just crawling along.' Bryce removed his hat to wipe the sweat from his forehead.

'We're making progress.' Jack focused his binoculars on the left. 'Something's happening over there.' He watched as the 4th Punjab Rifles doubled forward to the old sepoy cantonments, turbans bobbing and rifles held ready.

'That's our Sikhs,' Elliot said.

'Beyond them,' Jack pointed to a mass of white-and-green clothed men waiting in and around the outer suburbs of Bareilly. 'Those men are not ours. It looks like they're going to try and turn our left flank.' He raised his voice. 'Ensign Peake! Convey my compliments to Sir Colin and inform him that there is a large force of rebels about to threaten our left flank. Have you got that?'

'Yes, sir!' Peake looked eager as he began to move away. Jack grabbed the sleeve of his jacket. 'Say it back to me, Peake.'

'Captain Windrush sends his compliments, and there is a large force of rebels about to threaten our left flank.'

'Off you go and be quick about it!' Jack watched Peake jink through the British lines to Campbell. The ensign returned a few moments later, red-faced and eyes bright with excitement.

'He sends his—'

'Who sends his? Report properly, Ensign Peake!' Jack fixed the boy with a hard glare.

'Sorry, sir! Sir Colin sends his compliments and could the 113th please support the 42nd in helping the Punjabi Rifles in repelling the enemy.'

'That's better, Peake.' Jack spared the boy a few moments of his time. 'Always repeat a message exactly, Ensign. You could miss out some small word that alters the meaning and causes disaster.'

'Yes, sir.' Peake looked crestfallen. 'Sorry, sir.'

'You'll know next time, Peake. Now off you go to your men and do your duty.'

Jack watched Peake for a moment, thinking that it was only a year or so ago that the youngster's greatest worry was his headmaster's cane. Now he was responsible for the lives of grown men.

Jack raised his voice. 'Form two lines, boys! Lieutenant Bryce, take the left flank, Lieutenant Elliot, command the second line!' Jack gave them time to form up and then strode forward, revolver in hand. As always, he felt the mixed surge of elation and fear, with the excitement of knowing he was doing what generations of his forbears had been born to do, leading men into battle.

On his right, he saw the 42nd Foot marching forward with the élan and confidence for which all Highland regiments were famous. The officers walked or rode in front, kilts swinging as the men's bayonets gleamed wickedly in the sun. In the middle, grizzled face as calm as if he was strolling through his native Glasgow, Sir Colin Campbell encouraged his men.

'Come on 113th!' Jack roared. 'Don't let the Sawnies beat us to the enemy!'

A bank of powder smoke rolled ahead, punctured by orange and yellow muzzle flashes and the rattle of musketry.

'The rebels are in those houses.' Bryce pointed to a clump of single-storey buildings in the Bareilly suburbs. White smoke spurted as the enemy fired into the Punjabi Rifles, the moment they moved into the old sepoy cantonments. Taken by surprise, the Punjabis recoiled and began to retreat toward the advancing 113th and 42nd.

'Prepare to open ranks and allow the Punjabis through,' Jack said. He didn't want his men to remain in a close formation when a mob of retreating Sikhs crashed into them. Jack remembered the opening phase of the battle of the Alma in the Crimean War, when one unit had fallen back, disorganising the regiments immediately to their rear. The 113th would have to maintain their discipline as the Punjabis withdrew through them.

'Jesus!' Parker blasphemed. 'The barrel of my rifle is red hot!'

Other men were having the same experience as the sun heated anything metal until it was too hot to the touch.

'India is fighting back,' Elliot said. 'The Russians may talk about General Winter; over here India has General Summer, Colonel Monsoon and Major Disease.'

'What the devil?' Bryce drew his sabre as hundreds of sword-wielding men burst from the half-ruined houses and ran at the withdrawing Punjabis, screaming '*deen, deen!*'

'Ghazis!' These were the men Jack had seen gathering on the flank. Muslim fanatics, they wore white robes with green cummerbunds and charged with their heads down, protected by small, circular shields. As they ran, they slashed and hacked with their wickedly sharp tulwars, turning the Punjabi's withdrawal into a rout.

'Stand, the 4th Rifles,' Jack shouted, knowing the tumult of battle drowned his voice. 'Don't let them see your backs! Steady, the 113th!'

'Sir!' Bryce looked at Jack. 'What are your orders, sir?'

Jack swore. If his men fired, they could as easily hit the Punjabis as the Ghazis. If they held their fire, the Ghazis would chase the Punjabis into the 113th, disorganising them so they would be in no position to face the enemy. It was the sort of quandary that no officer liked.

'*Deen! Deen!*' The yells of the Ghazis were clear above the screams of the wounded and the fear of the now-panicking Punjabi Rifles. '*Bismillah! Allah Akbar!*'

Sir Colin Campbell, vastly experienced, solved the dilemma. 'Fire away, men! Shoot them down. Shoot every man jack of them!' The gruff Scottish voice gave confidence to all who heard. 'Bayonet them as they come on!'

The 42nd fired at once, the kilted Highlanders trying to avoid the Punjabis and aimed for the charging Ghazis.

'Come on 113th! You heard Sir Colin! Fire!'

Jack had expected some hesitation, but he'd been mistaken. The 113th fired the second he gave the order, with some of the replacements stepping forward in their eagerness to be involved. The situation had altered now. If the 113th retained their open formation, the Ghazis would break in and cause havoc. 'Close ranks!'

'Steady there, men!' Greaves' voice sounded above the crackle of musketry. 'Keep in line! Close up the ranks!'

'Close up, men!' Bryce added his orders. 'Don't leave gaps for the pandies to get through!'

'First rank, cap and load. Second rank, fire a volley!' Jack used the old, familiar phrases, knowing that hours of training on the parade ground now proved their worth as the men worked by instinct, following orders as if by numbers and the whole company working together on the word of command.

The Enfield rifles crashed out, the bullets hammering into the charging Ghazis and hitting some Punjabis.

'Stupid buggers!' Logan gave his philosophical thoughts. 'They should have fought, then we wouldn't be shooting them. Stand and fight you bastards!'

'The Ghazis are getting close!' Bryce balanced his sabre against his right shoulder. 'It'll be hand to hand in a minute.'

Bent almost double to make themselves as small a target as possible, the Ghazis sheltered behind the illusive protection of their shields, raised their tulwars high and circled them in the air, yelling as they raced on. For a second Jack wondered if his great-grandfather had seen something similar as he stood with the Royal Malverns at Killiecrankie, when Bonny Dundee's Highlanders had poured down the hillside to smash the redcoats. That was the only battle where the Royal Malverns had ever broken and fled, he remembered, and vowed that his 113th would not follow that example.

As they neared the British lines, the Ghazis bent even lower, ducking under the jabbing bayonets and slashing at the legs of the 113th and 42nd.

'Aye, would you, you bastard!' Logan blocked a swinging sword with the barrel of his rifle.

'I've got him,' Riley sidestepped and jabbed his bayonet into the neck of the Ghazi. The man tried to straighten up, and Logan finished him with a thrust through the heart.

'Close up!'

While the sustained, regular volley fire had been the result of hundreds of hours of drill on the parade ground, the clash of steel on steel as the Ghazis closed with the 113th and 42nd proved something more primeval. The British Army taught basic techniques of bayonet fighting to its men, but there was something instinctive about the way the 113th and 42nd faced the tulwars of the Ghazis. The men parried and thrust as their training dictated, while adding boots and fists, rifle butts and knees in a more primitive manner that the men had learned on the back streets of Dundee and Newcastle, Cardiff and Dublin. Gaelic slogans combated the Ghazis calls of '*Din, din*!' and '*Allah Akbar*!'

'They've outflanked us!' Elliot shouted.

A body of Ghazis had come from the left, having hidden in one of the *topis* of trees. Ignoring the 113th, the Ghazis charged at Colonel Cameron of the 42nd. Cameron dragged free his sword and fought a snarling Ghazi on the right side when another two on the left grabbed his tunic and pulled him from his horse.

'They've got the colonel!' Colour-sergeant William Gardener of the 42nd shouted and ran forward, kilt flying. He bayonetted two of Ghazis as they prepared to hack Cameron to death while a private swivelled and shot the third.

'We're holding them!' Greaves said, and then it was over. The Punjabis streamed through the British lines to reform. Rifle fire and bayonets of the 42nd and 113th ensured that no Ghazis got through the line, while cold-eyed privates from both regiments stepped forward and plunged their bayonets into any of the fanatics who showed signs of life.

'That's not right,' Bryce objected. 'We don't murder the wounded.'

'Would you rather they waited until you stepped over their prone bodies and they slashed at your privates with their tulwars?' Jack asked. 'Any Indian veteran has seen that. This is not European warfare, Lieutenant. There are no civilised conventions here.'

Bryce glowered, shook his head and said nothing.

'Forward!' Sir Colin ordered, and the line advanced over the carpet of dead Ghazis, staggering under the heat as the sun reached its zenith.

'Jesus, but it's hot,' Hutton said.

'This is the killing time.' Greaves looked upwards. 'I've seen it so often out East; men survive a bloody battle and then die of heat exhaustion when we chase the retreating enemy. If India doesn't get you one way, it'll get you another.'

Sir Colin was equally aware of the perils of the Indian summer. As soon as the British reached the outskirts of Bareilly, he ordered a halt.

'We should pursue the pandies,' Bryce said. 'Harass and push them until they have to stand and fight. We can break them and win this war.'

Jack nodded to the 113th, as they staggered with exhaustion after their day's exertions. 'I am sure all the breakfast table strategists back in Britain would agree with you, but India is a place where practicalities outweigh theories, and the laws of European warfare do not apply. An Indian Army will move faster across India than any British Army, especially in hot weather and Khan Bahadur Khan will not stop to fight unless he has overwhelming force. A rapid pursuit will cost us many casualties even without any fighting.'

'It would be worth the risk,' Bryce insisted.

'The longer we march,' Jack said, 'the more men we'll lose to the sun, and therefore the weaker our army will be. The rebels could gather forces at any time, so when Khan Bahadur Khan thinks that the balance has tipped sufficiently in his favour, he would turn and rend us. No, Lieutenant Bryce, Sir Colin is correct.'

A rising tumult from the rear disrupted the conversation. Jack focused his binoculars. 'Pandy cavalry!' He swore. 'They're attacking the baggage train.'

'We have to do something.' Elliot looked suddenly agitated. He checked his revolver. 'Could I take out a platoon, sir?'

'They've got an escort,' Bryce frowned. 'We're not here to babysit grooms and syces and camel drivers.'

'We'd best help them, sir.' Elliot ignored Bryce.

'What's to do, Elliot?' Jack knew by Elliot's tone of voice that something was wrong.

Elliot hesitated, glanced at Bryce and made a formal request. 'May I have your permission to take a party to help the baggage train, sir?'

'Yes, if you think it necessary,' Jack said.

'Thank you, sir.' Elliot ran at once, shouting: 'Greaves, bring the Lucknow veterans. *Jildi!*'

'What the devil?' Jack watched as Elliot led a file of fifteen men at the double, bayonets fixed. 'Oh, damn it to hell. Bryce, take over here. Corporal Hunter, select ten more men and come with me.' He followed Elliot, ignored a gaggle of bearers who ran in the opposite direction yelling 'Sowar! Sowar!' and examined the baggage train.

Chaos, he thought. There was no other word to describe it other than chaos. A mob of animals and camp followers covered the road and the surrounding fields, all dashing for the security of the British encampment, with a few score rebel cavalrymen slashing and hacking at them. Defeated or not, the rebels had proved yet again that they could strike back.

Ignoring a panicking, splay-legged camel and the fleeing camp followers, Elliot led his men straight through the middle of the confusion and around a trio of rebel cavalry that circled a terrified elephant. The cavalry sliced at the tendons at the back of its legs until the beast trumpeted in agony.

Without waiting for orders, Private Parker dropped to one knee, aimed and fired in a single fluid movement. One of the horsemen staggered, and Parker immediately reloaded. 'Look at them,' he said. 'Torturing that poor elephant.'

'Oh, for God's sake,' Elliot said. 'Help Parker, somebody, and then join us.'

Elliot led his men to a bullock cart labouring at the rear of the scattered column. 'Guard this wagon with your lives, men. The cargo is invaluable.'

'Yes, sir.' The men spread out around the cart.

What is that man doing? Jack asked himself. 'Come on Greaves!' he increased his speed.

A group of sowars galloped toward the wagon, saw the determined men of the 113th and reined away. They were there to kill and spread panic, not to fight professional soldiers.

'What's happening, Elliot?' Jack left Greaves and Corporal Hunter to arrange the wagon's defence.

'We're just protecting the convoy, sir,' Elliot said.

'Why this particular wagon? What are you hiding, Lieutenant?' Without waiting for a reply, Jack vaulted onto the back of the vehicle and pulled back the canvas cover. 'Oh, dear God in heaven.'

'Hello, Jack.' Mary looked up at him.

CHAPTER FOUR

'Do you mean you knew that Mary was travelling with the column?' Jack stared at Elliot.

'Yes, sir.' Elliot stood at attention inside the tent. Sweat glistened on his face.

'Why the devil did you not tell me?'

'I thought you had enough worries,' Elliot said. 'I kept an eye on her.'

'Dear God, man – she could have been killed!'

'Yes. That's why I kept an eye on her.' Elliot remained stubbornly unrepentant.

'Go and find her and bring her here,' Jack ordered.

'No need for that, Captain. I'm already here.' Mary pushed back the flap and entered the tent. 'Arthur is not to blame, Jack. I made him swear not to tell you.'

About to blast her, Jack took a deep breath to control his temper. *This woman drives me to distraction.* 'Why are you here?'

'Sir Colin needed an interpreter,' Mary said.

'Did he ask for you?' Jack asked.

'I volunteered my services.' Mary held Jack's glare with impressive composure.

'Have you any idea how dangerous that could be?'

'Why no, Captain Windrush,' Mary said. 'I thought it would be as safe as strolling in the cantonment at Gondabad.'

Jack opened his mouth and closed it again. The previous year, he had helped rescued Mary from the mutineers at Gondabad. 'You should have told me.'

'Lieutenant Elliot was correct in what he said. If you'd known, you would have worried about me. That might have impaired your ability to do your duty, and I do not wish that on my conscience.'

'Leave us, Elliot,' Jack said.

'Yes, sir,' Elliot said. 'Sir—'

'Leave us!' Jack glowered at Elliot until he hurried out of the tent.

'Now, Miss Lambert,' Jack said, and realised that Mary was laughing at him. Although her face was immobile, her eyes were alive with bright mischief.

'Before you shout at me, Captain Jack,' Mary said. 'I have one thing to say.'

'And what is that, pray?'

'This.' Leaning forward, Mary gave him a single kiss on the forehead. 'I'm glad that we are both still alive, Jack.'

Jack touched her arm, his anger completely gone. 'I wish you would keep yourself out of danger, Mary. Battlefields are no place for a woman.'

'Battlefields are no place for *anybody*,' Mary said. 'Every night I pray to the Lord that there are no more battles, and every day I learn that the Lord has desires contrary to my wishes.'

'There will be another battle tomorrow,' Jack said. 'Khan Bahadur Khan will fight to defend Bareilly, and that will be ugly. I saw street fighting in Lucknow, and we lost far too many men.'

'Let's hope that the Lord helps him see sense and surrender.'

'Khan Bahadur Khan will not surrender,' Jack said. 'We hang our prisoners or blow the poor fellows from a cannon. They have nothing to gain from surrender.'

'I have never found Sir Colin to be particularly bloodthirsty,' Mary said. 'He is a good soldier and a humane man.'

Jack shook his head. 'He's the most humane commander I've ever known.' He frowned as a sudden thought struck him. 'Have you been here ever since we left Lucknow?'

Mary shook her head. 'No. I watched you march away with Walpole, and I felt sick, frankly.'

Jack frowned again. British gentlewomen should not be so forthcoming about their emotions.

'Thank you,' Jack said, aware how inadequate his words sounded. 'I didn't like leaving you behind. I would have liked it less to have you come with us.'

'Oh?' Mary's eyebrows rose. 'Don't you like my company?'

Jack frowned. 'I do like your company. I don't like to think of you being in danger.'

Mary couldn't hide her smile as she looked away. 'In India, Captain Jack, we are in danger all the time. Until this war is over, nowhere is safe.'

'I'll do my best to finish it quickly for you.' It was not hard for Jack to alter his frown into a smile.

'Take care, Jack,' Mary said seriously. 'I also like *your* company.' She deliberately repeated Jack's words. 'I don't like to think of you being in danger.'

'Danger is part of the soldier's bargain,' Jack said. 'We know that when we accept the Queen's shilling or the Queen's commission. You have done neither. It's my job to try and protect the civilian population.' He lowered his voice. 'On the other hand, I *want* to protect you.'

Mary nodded, once. Her eyes didn't stray from Jack's face. 'I know,' she said.

'Captain Windrush!' The educated voice came from outside the tent.

Jack sighed. 'Somebody wants me.'

'So it seems.' Mary rose from her seat. 'We never have time together. I'll leave you to your duty.' Her hand lingered on his arm for longer than was necessary.

'Thank you.' Jack watched her leave the tent before he raised his voice. 'I'm Captain Windrush!'

The ensign was red-faced, as they all seemed to be this season, and fair-haired. 'Colonel Hook sends his compliments, sir and requests your presence in his tent at your earliest convenience.'

Colonel Hook? How did he get here?

'That means now,' Jack said with a wry smile. 'Thank you, ensign. Pray convey my respects to Colonel Hook and inform him that I will be along directly.' He hesitated. 'Or I will when you tell me where his tent might be.'

Hook's tent was in the centre of the British encampment, with two heavily bearded Sikhs on guard at the flap. They moved aside when Jack announced himself.

'Ah, Windrush. What have you to report?' Hook sat at an ornately carved bureau, half hidden behind a pile of paperwork.

'I met Jayanti,' Jack said and described what had happened. Hook listened, nodding where necessary.

'Interesting woman,' Hook said. 'I wonder why she didn't kill you. Indeed, I wonder why she spoke to you at all.'

'I wonder how she knew who I was, sir,' Jack reminded. 'She even knew my middle name.'

'That's even more interesting.' Hook selected a long cheroot from a silver case. 'There's a lot more here than we know about.'

'Yes, sir.'

'You have done better than I expected, Windrush. I thought you might find some intelligence about Jayanti and here you have succeeded in contacting her.'

'She contacted me, sir and I would like to know why,' Jack said. *There are two women in my life now, and both are trouble.*

'I'll have to check with my colleagues and see if they can enlighten us.' Hook gave a sudden smile. 'As you're part of the organisation now, Windrush, you should know who they are. We have William Muir, the magistrate fellow in Agra, and Major Herbert Bruce. Have you heard of Bruce?'

'No, sir,'

'He used to work in the Punjab police and served under General Neill and Havelock as well as Sir Colin. He's a good man.'

'I see, sir.' Jack realised that there were layers of British rule about which he knew nothing.

Hook tapped his cheroot on his bureau, his gaze never straying from Jack's face. 'You'll know about Raja Nahr Singh, of course.'

'No, sir. I've never heard of that gentleman.'

Hook lit the cheroot, allowing smoke to spiral around the tent. 'He was our spymaster in Delhi. He kept William Muir informed of everything that happened inside Delhi.'

'He is a loyal man, sir.'

'No.' Hook shook his head. 'Or rather, not loyal to the Queen, if that's what you mean.'

Jack frowned. 'Do you mean he was loyal to John Company?'

Hook's smile was as intriguing as anything Jack had ever seen. 'Not exactly, Windrush. He and John Company were both loyal to the same thing.'

'The Empire?'

Hook laughed. 'Not quite.' Reaching into a small bureau that stood behind his chair, Hook unlocked the top drawer and pulled out a small leather draw-bag. 'They are both loyal to this.' Opening the bag, he poured out a golden cascade of guineas, sovereigns and mohurs. 'Money, Windrush. Wealth. This country runs on two things, information and wealth. It is a venal society with professional intelligence gatherers such as Mukhdum Baksh. Poor Mukhdum worked for us in Delhi and latterly was my agent in Bareilly.'

Jack wished he had never asked. He didn't recognise this India. 'You say that Mukhdum *was* your agent?'

'Correct. Nana Sahib found him and had him executed.' Hook waved his cheroot around his head. 'You don't wish to know the details.'

Jack shook his head. 'No, sir.' Indian executions could be gruesome.

Hook scooped all the golden coins back into the bag and lifted it in the air. 'This,' he jingled the bag, 'is what India is all about. Money. The Company wants to increase its profits, and the rajahs and princes want the wealth that comes from power. The mutineers buy recruits, the rebel princes pay their followers, and we give our sepoys regular pay. If we stop paying the sepoys, they have no reason to be loyal to us. The British, as John Company, are in here for profit, while Britain needs the revenue, and the prestige.'

'I thought this mutiny was about religion, sir.' Jack thought of the fanatical Ghazis, sacrificing themselves against the bayonets of the 42nd and 113th.

'It is, in part,' Hook said. 'The men who run it manipulate the sepoys with stories of threats, real or fanciful, to their religion, and the Ghazis and so on are genuine in their hatred of our missionaries and their fear that we are trying to Christianise the whole country.' He shrugged. 'But the men – and women – at the top want their positions back, and the wealth that goes along with it.' Hook threw the leather bag in the air and caught it one-handed. 'Wealth and power, Windrush; that's what everything comes down to, here and elsewhere.'

'The love of money is the root of all evil.' Jack gave one of the few Biblical quotes he remembered.

'Timothy, chapter six, verse ten. Simplistic but true to an extent,' Hook said. 'Add the love of power to that, and I would agree.' He examined the tip of his cheroot, flicked off the excess ash and replaced it in his mouth. 'Now, you have made some progress with Jayanti, Windrush – continue with the search.'

'Yes, sir.' Jack paused. 'Do you wish me to take out my company and search the Terai to the north?'

'No, you can start in Bareilly,' Hook said. 'We'll have some rebel prisoners who may wish to help in exchange for their lives.'

'We have to capture it first,' Jack reminded.

'The rebels will run,' Hook said casually. 'They won't fight.'

'Are you sure, sir?'

'Quite sure.' Hook smiled. 'Information and wealth, Windrush. Trust me, we'll have Bareilly in two days with the minimum of fuss, and then you will have some prisoners to interview.'

'Yes, sir,' Jack said. An order was an order.

CHAPTER FIVE

On the 6th May, British artillery started bombarding suspected insurgent strongpoints in Bareilly. Next day, with the dust and smoke still drifting across the city, Campbell drove in his column without resistance. The enemy had fled.

'We're still chasing Jayanti.' Jack lit another cheroot, coughed, and sat on the chair next to Elliot. A servant salaamed and brought a brass bowl, brimming with water.

'Do we know where she is?'

'Not yet, Arthur. Colonel Hook suggests that we ask the prisoners.'

Elliot snorted. 'I'm sure they will willingly tell all before we hang them.' He looked up. 'How's your Pushtu? Alternatively, will they speak Hindustani? I can speak about a dozen words in total.'

'I know a few words, and I know good translator,' Jack said.

'Do you mean Mary?' Elliot lifted the flask again.

'I do,' Jack said.

Elliot swallowed. 'It could be difficult for her.'

'I won't force her,' Jack said. 'I'll give her a choice.'

'I know your choices.' Elliot took another pull at his silver flask. 'Take it or take something worse.'

'I won't be like that with Mary.' Jack smiled. 'I like her.' Jack waited for Elliot's reaction.

'Only *like* the woman, or do you more than like the woman? Do you like her as much as you liked Helen?'

Jack considered. 'I think Mary is a better person than Helen.'

'That is not what I asked, my verbally elusive Captain Windrush,' Elliot said.

Jack smiled. 'I know it's not. I will tell you the answer when I know it myself.'

Elliot nodded. 'Be careful, Jack, that is all I ask.'

'At present, I need Mary as a translator,' Jack said.

'You could ask one of the Company wallahs. They work with the natives; they have to speak their languages.'

'The sepoys mutinied against the Company,' Jack said. 'I doubt they would talk to a Company officer.'

Elliot nodded. 'Will they be any more willing to talk to a woman? How will you convince your prisoners to talk?'

Jack shrugged. 'I've seen the Sikhs burning their prisoners alive. I could offer to hand the sepoys over to them.'

'Others might do that, Jack. You wouldn't.' Elliot leaned back in his cane chair. 'We're supposed to be officers and gentlemen, representatives of the most civilised nation on earth, and here we are condoning murder and torture. Thank God that Sir Colin is against such slaughter. Our men want blood though. To them, any native could be a pandy, and the only good pandy is a dead pandy.'

Jack nodded. 'You're right there. We may pay for this brutality later.' He thought of the black-turbaned woman slicing at the injured Green. 'The trouble is, the enemy can be every bit as barbaric, so atrocity leads to retaliation.'

'They are very like us, and we are very like them,' Elliot said. 'That's what worries me. We announce our progressive civilisation and Christianity and then act as badly as the enemy.' He shrugged and poured more whisky down his throat. 'It's enough to drive a man away from drink.'

'I've allocated a permanent sentry for Mary and placed her in a tent in the centre of the camp, between our lines and the 42nd. No pandy will dare try attacking her.' Jack stood up. 'I'll see if she agrees to translate.'

'Be careful, Jack.' Elliot raised his flask in salute. 'Don't get too attached to her. A girl like Mary will only ruin your career.'

Jack nodded. He knew Elliot was correct.

Hutton saluted as Jack approached the tent. 'Good afternoon, sir.' He kept his face immobile.

'Good afternoon, Hutton. Is the lady at home?' Jack scratched on the canvas and waited for Mary to invite him in.

'Of course, I'm at home!' Mary answered. 'Come in, Captain Jack.'

'I need your help,' Jack said as he entered.

Mary smiled. 'You should never try to be a diplomat, Jack. You're too blunt for that.' She stood up from her charpoy and stretched her arms. 'What can I do for you?'

'I need your language skills.' Jack explained the situation.

'These prisoners you want me to question.' Mary was frowning. 'When you've questioned them, what will happen to them?'

'Oh, they'll be hanged.'

'I thought so.' Mary sat back down. 'I've seen enough suffering in this war, Jack.'

'I'm not asking you to torture them.'

'No, you're asking me to help interrogate people who know we're going to hang them.'

'They're traitors and rebels.' Jack fell back on traditional beliefs.

'Or patriots and men whom our actions forced to rebel.' Mary countered him without losing her patience. 'Do you think they will help you, knowing their death is inevitable whatever they say?'

'You have something up your sleeve, Mary,' Jack said. 'Come on now, out with it!'

'Freedom,' Mary said. 'Offer them their freedom if they co-operate.'

'They might lie to save themselves.' Jack sat cross-legged on the floor, not caring how undignified a position it was.

Mary's smile always took him by surprise. 'They might lie anyway, knowing it doesn't matter what they say.'

'Yes.' Jack tried to retain his patience. 'But how can we trust them? They'll tell us anything for freedom.'

Mary's smile broadened. 'If any of them know where Jayanti is, make him guide you there, and you will only free him when you know he's not lying.'

'You are a cunning lady.' Jack sighed. 'You have all the answers.'

'Why, thank you, kind sir.' Mary sunk into a graceful curtsey. Jack was unsure if her eyes were friendly or mocking.

Even with the offer of freedom, few of the prisoners were willing to be helpful. Most sat in silence as Mary asked questions, with some replying with shouted slogans and threats. Only three responded to Jack's request; one was a Pathan from the Khyber, and the other two had been sowars in the Company's cavalry, high-class Hindus with land and families.

'We'll speak to these three,' Jack decided, 'and ignore the others.'

The sowar mutineers were proud men, defiant despite their capture. They answered Jack's questions with short, sharp answers and glared at him.

'Of course, I know of Jayanti,' the first sowar said.

'Everybody knows about the devil woman,' the second replied, 'except the proud sahibs.'

'Only Shiva can catch her,' the first sowar said. 'The sahibs will need my help.'

'I can lead you to her lair,' the second offered, 'for a thousand rupees and a fast horse.'

'Why are you helping?' Jack asked the final question.

'To get back to my family,' the first mutineer said.

'To get back to my family,' the second sowar gave an identical answer.

Jack sent both away. 'I don't trust them,' he said.

'Would you prefer to see the Pathan?' Mary sounded amused. 'Pathans kill for fun and rob as a matter of course.'

'Bring him in,' Jack said. 'The mutineers have already broken their faith and now say they are willing to betray one of their own. I would trust them as far as a wooden threepenny bit.'

The Pathan was tall and lean, with a face that would give Satan nightmares and even in chains, he looked as if he would murder his brother for a handful of gold mohurs.

'Your name?' Jack had sufficient experience with the men of the 113th to recognise a rogue.

'Batoor.' The Pathan held Jack's gaze without fear. Jack had heard that if a Pathan met Queen Victoria, he would look her in the eye and shake hands as if to say, "I'm as good a person as you are". People also reckoned Pathans as faithless, thieving and predatory, while their mothers prayed that their sons became famed robbers. With this fellow Batoor, all these stereotypes appeared to be correct.

'So you claim to know the whereabouts of Jayanti, even though she is a Hindu and you are a Pathan?'

Batoor grunted. 'I know where she may be,' he said.

That's the most honest answer so far. One point for the Pathan.

'You were captured fighting against us; why would you help us now?'

'I was fighting for money,' Batoor said. 'I have reasons for being here, and if I help you, I will be free again.'

Jack glanced at Mary, who nodded. 'That makes sense,' she said. 'I would love to know what his reasons were.' She gave a half smile. 'Being a Pathan, it will be something to do with money or *Pashtunwali*.'

'What in God's name is *Pashtunwali*?'

Mary smiled. 'Aren't you glad I'm here to educate you, Captain Jack? *Pukhtunwali* is the Pathan code of honour. They must give fugitives refuge and protection, they must give hospitality, even to an enemy, and they have to avenge any insult to the family or the tribe.'

Jack eyed Batoor and nodded. The Pathan held his gaze. With his shaven head and long beard, he looked every inch a warrior. 'I've seen you before,' Jack said. 'You fired a jezzail at me at the Kaisarbagh!' He waited for Mary to translate.

Batoor smiled. 'I was at the Kaisarbagh, and I fired at many British soldiers. You might have been one of them.'

'Good God, man!' Jack shook his head. 'Why are you at Bareilly now? Do you hate us so much?'

Batoor's smile didn't waver. 'As the woman says, it has something to do with *Pashtunwali*.'

Jack was beginning to respect this man. In a different world, he would have fitted into the 113th without difficulty. 'If you are free, would you fight against us again?'

Batoor rattled his chains. 'I might. I might not.'

'He's honest by his own lights,' Mary added after she translated.

'You're a lying, treacherous murdering blackguard, Batoor,' Jack stood up, 'and I can't think of any reason why I should trust you.'

Batoor rattled his chains again. 'You don't trust me, but you need me. Who else can lead you to the devil woman who plans to destroy your Company?'

'Nobody, damn you.'

'Will you keep your word, Captain Windrush?' Batoor turned the conversation around, with Mary hiding her smile as she translated.

'Of course, I will, I'm a British officer!' Jack had to control his temper.

Batoor's laugh was high pitched, and as cynical as anything Jack had ever heard. 'Only the British believe their own lies. I am asking you, Captain Windrush, man to man – will you keep your word?'

Mary raised her eyebrows as she translated. 'He's not wrong, Jack, Lord Dalhousie is not the only British official to distort the truth to the native peoples of India.'

Jack frowned. Brought up to believe that a British gentleman always honoured his word, he still found it hard to believe that some broke that code.

Batoor spoke again, and Mary translated. 'Batoor is asking the same question, Jack. Will you keep your word? Will you free him if he leads you to this woman?'

'Of course I will, damn it!' Jack felt his anger rise again. Taking a deep breath, he faced Batoor. 'Yes, Batoor, I will keep my promise. You have my word on it as a British officer and…' Jack extended his hand. 'I do not know what crimes you have committed in the past or who you have killed or why, but if you take my hand, we will shake on it, man to man.'

Batoor looked to Mary for the translation before he slid his hand hesitantly into

Jack's. They shook, and Jack knew that whatever happened, he would keep his word to Batoor.

'One more thing.' Jack had come prepared. Taking a small packet from his pocket, he drew his sword and emptied the contents onto the blade. The white powder formed a little pyramid on the steel.

'Take the salt, warrior, and swear your loyalty to me.'

Batoor's grin was white behind his beard. He put his hand on the blade, lifted a pinch of salt and placed it on his lips. Mary translated his words. 'I am your man, Captain Windrush.'

'If you let me down,' Jack said, 'I will hunt you down and kill you.'

Batoor grinned. 'Yes, Captain Windrush. And if you let me down, I will kill the woman and then you.'

Mary's expression didn't alter as she translated Batoor's words. 'Accept that Jack,' Mary added. 'I'm in no danger as long as you are true.'

Jack fought down his recurring anger. 'We understand each other,' he said to Batoor. Raising his voice, he called in the guards and had the Pathan taken back to confinement.

'When are we leaving?' Mary asked.

'We?' Jack said. 'You are not coming.'

'You took me last time,' Mary said. 'When you were searching for the regiment's missing women.'

'This is different,' Jack said. 'This is a military operation, and there are still pandies around.'

'There were more pandies around last time,' Mary reminded. 'And you'll need a translator if you are wandering around the countryside, or have your language skills improved in the last few minutes?' Her smile was as sweet as a hunting cobra.

'We'll manage,' Jack growled at her. He sighed and admitted the truth. 'You know that I'd prefer to have you along, Mary, but it's too dangerous.'

She stood up. 'It will be a lot more dangerous for you to blunder around not able to talk to anybody. Is Lieutenant Elliot able to speak Urdu or Pushtu? No! How about Sergeant Greaves or any of your men? Goodness, Jack, most of them can hardly speak English.'

Jack matched her temper with the anger he had been trying to control all day 'It's too damned dangerous, Mary!'

'My, my.' Mary's sudden smile took Jack by surprise. 'Is that how British officers and gentlemen talk to women?'

Jack stopped in mid-tirade. About to say "only when they care for them", he stopped and stood erect. 'You are correct,' he said. 'I should not have shouted at you. I do apologise, madam.' He gave a stiff, formal bow, turned around and marched out of the room. He knew that he was retreating from a conflict that he couldn't possibly win. He hoped that Mary didn't realise the same but knew she would. *Damn that woman. One thing is sure; she's not coming with my column.*

CHAPTER SIX

'O'Neill's back!' Riley was first with the news, and soon the words spread around the company. Jack looked up as Sergeant O'Neill marched in, gaunt-faced but as erect as ever, with his uniform clean and his rifle in his hand.

'Sergeant O'Neill reporting for duty, sir!' O'Neill gave a smart salute.

'Good to have you back, Sergeant,' Jack said. 'How's the wound?' O'Neill had been injured during the fighting in the tunnels underneath Lucknow, when Campbell had relieved the siege earlier in the war.

'The medical men saved my arm, thank you.'

Jack nodded. 'Are you fit for a long march? Don't say you are, if you're not.'

'I'm fit, sir. I could outmarch any Johnny Raw.'

'Aye, you probably could, O'Neill. Sheer bloody determination would see you through.' Jack looked around. He had moved his company of the 113th outside the walls of Bareilly, away from the temptation of looting and the dangers of women and drink. The men had grumbled at first and, being British soldiers, many had tried to sneak back into the city. Now they were panting in the heat, or under fatigues, or cleaning their rifles. 'I hope so, O'Neill because we're on the march soon.'

'Where are we going, sir?'

'I'm not sure, sergeant,' Jack said. 'Have you ever heard of a woman called Jayanti?'

'I can't say that I have, sir.' O'Neill looked suddenly defensive. 'Has she been asking for me, sir?'

'No.' Jack had no desire to ask about O'Neill's amorous adventures. 'She is the leader of a band of fighting women, like Uda Devi.'

'I remember that name, sir. That's the bint that hid up a tree and shot some of our lads.' O'Neill stamped his feet. 'I hoped we didn't meet others like her.'

'There are others, sergeant, and this Jayanti woman is their leader. We've been ordered to find her.'

'And kill her, sir?'

'If we can, sergeant.' Jack waited for O'Neill's reaction. 'What do you think of that?'

'I don't normally hold with killing women, sir.' O'Neill gave the reply Jack would expect from any British soldier. 'But if this Jayanti is anything like Uda Devi, well, she killed some of ours, sir, so she's fair game.'

Jack asked O'Neill a question he would never have asked Greaves. 'How will the men react to being ordered to kill or capture a woman?'

O'Neill screwed up his face as he considered the question. 'I'm not sure, sir. Our lads won't be too happy about it, sir. They won't want to kill a woman, even that one. Some of the others, though,' he shrugged, 'they'd kill their grannies for the price of a drink.'

Jack nodded. He understood what O'Neill meant. By "our lads", O'Neill meant the Burma and Crimea veterans that bloody battles had bonded together. Jack shared O'Neill's opinion of others that the Army had recruited from the criminal class, the lowest of the low, men rejected by other regiments to end up in the 113th.

'When do we leave, sir?'

'In two days, sergeant,' Jack said. 'I'm taking fifty men and a Pathan prisoner who claims to know where Jayanti may be based.'

'Oh, does he claim that, sir?' O'Neill looked sceptical. 'And who told him? Some fellow down the public, or maybe his granny heard it when she was washing her clothes in the river?'

Jack smiled. 'I share your disbelief, sergeant. That's why he'll be under close guard all the time, and if he tries to bolt, we'll shoot him like a dog.'

O'Neill grunted. 'He's a Pathan, you say? They are the most devious devils under the sun, sir. He'll cut a few of our throats at night, steal half a dozen rifles and slip back to the Khyber.'

'He won't' Jack said. 'Not with you watching him.'

'Yes, sir.' There was a hint of a smile on O'Neill's face. 'I thought you were coming to that.'

Both men stopped to watch a regiment of Gurkhas march past, small, stocky men resplendent in red coats and blue pantaloons, very much like the Zouaves the 113th had known in the Crimea.

'Cocky little buggers,' O'Neill said. 'I'm told there are 16,000 of them with us now.'

'They fight well, I've heard,' Jack said.

O'Neill eyed them sourly. 'Aye; we'll see. Since the sepoys turned traitor, I have little time for native troops. I won't trust them again, and that's the truth.'

'There's a lot of people think like that,' Jack murmured. 'Nothing will be quite the same in India after the Mutiny.'

An hour before dawn they marched out of Bareilly, heading north and east. Jack led with Elliot and Lieutenant Bryce behind him, and Ensigns Wilden and Peake at the rear. In between marched fifty men with Sergeants Greaves and O'Neill. All were in khaki, with handkerchiefs to protect their necks from the sun and Enfield rifles at their shoulders.

'You'd better not be leading us into an ambush,' O'Neill warned Batoor. 'If you try any funny stuff, I'll ram six inches of steel up your arse.'

Batoor replied in Pushtu and spread his hands in an expression of innocence that would have made Jack smile in other circumstances.

'Try it once, son, just try it once.' The diminutive Logan was a full head shorter than Batoor. 'I'll gut you.'

Batoor only grinned, with his shaven head bobbing above Logan's hat and his wrists chained together.

Jack stepped aside and watched his men march past. As well as Logan, the truculent Glasgow man, there was Riley, the gentleman-thief, Coleman and Thorpe, forever arguing until the fighting started. There was the ex-poacher Whitelam, Parker from Liverpool with his love of animals, and the Welshman Williams who had done sterling work during the defence of Lucknow the previous year. Hutton was next, a quiet man, steadier than the majority of the 113th, and beside him slouched Armstrong. Jack didn't like Armstrong, the one-time deserter who had been inside the army's detention centre at Greenlaw and harboured resentment against authority, but he was useful in a fight.

Jack kept them marching until the sun grew too hot and then they camped in the shade of a small clump of trees, with the men dropping to the ground and gasping for air.

'There's still pandies around!' O'Neill and Greaves kicked them back to their feet. 'Get this camp in order! Hutton, Armstrong, Smith, Monaghan, you're on picket duty! The rest of you, get the tents up!'

'Leave it to the sergeants,' Jack advised the ensigns. 'They know what they're doing, and the men listen to them.'

'Yes, sir,' Wilden said. 'But I'm an officer, I hold the Queen's commission. I outrank the sergeant.'

Jack stared at the boy while Elliot looked away to hide his smile. 'Sergeant O'Neill fought in Burma against dacoits and faced the Russians at the battle of Inkerman and the Redan. He was in the first relief of Lucknow; he fought at Cawnpore and was wounded defending Lucknow. What have you done?'

Ensign Wilden coloured.

'Exactly,' Jack said. 'Now take two men and patrol back the way we have come. March one mile, check to see if there are any pandies and return. Move!'

'What was that for?' Elliot asked.

'To get the young Griff out of my way,' Jack replied.

'We were young too, once.' Elliot said.

'I'm sure we were never that young,' Jack said with a smile.

The officers had a tent each, while a dozen men had to share. When the heat reached its zenith, officers and men not on duty would lie near naked on their charpoys, struggling for breath in the scorching atmosphere and wishing the monsoon would come. With pickets posted and the men eating and drinking, Jack could relax a little. He checked his half company. A few years ago, the 113th had been the worst regiment in the British Army, and now they were slowly gaining a reputation as a hard-fighting unit able to take care of itself.

'We're still at the bottom of the pile, Jack.' Elliot had known him long enough to gauge what he was thinking.

'Are we, Arthur?'

'We'll never be socially acceptable like the Brigade of Guards or the Royals.' Elliot lit a cheroot and allowed the aromatic smoke to coil around them. 'We'll always be the regiment that generals turn to for the dirty jobs.' He passed over a cheroot to Jack.

'Could you imagine the Guards or the Royal Malverns tracking a woman across

India?' Jack shook his head. 'It would be far beneath their dignity. You're right, Arthur. We're here for the tasks nobody else wants.'

'Or the tasks nobody else can do,' Elliot said. 'Our men have skills the Guards or Royals may lack.'

Jack glanced over at Riley and Whitelam. 'We have thieves, housebreakers and poachers. Yes, we have a fine collection of men; they are quite the pick of the country.'

'You're in a bad mood,' Elliot said. 'What's bothering you, Jack?'

'Where are we headed, Arthur? What is all this about? We've broken the back of this mutiny, killed God-only-knows how many pandies and civilians, and lost thousands of our men and women. What then? India carries on, and the Army will send you, the 113th, and me somewhere else to squash another trouble spot, lose more men to disease and the bullet. What's it all about, Arthur?'

'I'm damned if I know,' Elliot said. 'This was the only career open to a duffer like me. I'm the third son, with no money and no prospects.' He shrugged. 'What else can I do? I haven't the head for business or the inclination to follow my father into the church.'

Jack pulled on his cheroot. 'I know your people wish you to be a general,' he said. 'General Sir Arthur Elliot. That sounds good. I was always intended to be a career soldier, as you know.'

'I know,' Elliot said. 'Like your father and your grandfather.'

'And my great grandfather and great-great grandfather and as far back as records go.' Jack blew out a perfect smoke ring and watched as it wavered in the heat. 'I do not doubt that there was a Windrush at the Battle of Hastings, although God knows which side he was on, and when Boadicea faced the Romans, there was probably a Windrush in her army as well.'

'The Romans must have viewed her as we view Jayanti or Hussaini Khanum or the Rani of Jhansi,' Elliot lay back and contemplated a pair of hunting birds high amidst the clouds. 'And now we are the foreigners invading other countries to bring civilisation. How times change.'

'Except India was not a country when we came here, so we are not foreign,' Jack said. 'Or at least, we're no more foreign than the Sikhs or Ghurkhas or Pathans.'

'And we're better rulers.' Elliot watched as one of the birds swooped down on its prey. 'We are benevolent, kindly and honourable.'

'Tell that to all the mutineers we've hanged or blown from guns,' Jack said. 'Or the hundreds of men General Neill executed without trial.'

'I was being sarcastic,' Elliot said. 'Halloa, something's up. Whitelam's all of an agitation there.'

Jack looked up. Whitelam was talking to O'Neill, his arms flapping and his voice raised. 'I'd better go and see before he talks himself into trouble. You stay here and rest, Arthur. All that deep thinking must be very tiring for you.'

'I'm telling you, sergeant, that's what I saw!' Whitelam was shouting, nearly pressing his face against that of O'Neill.

'And I am telling you, Whitelam, that you will not be disturbing Captain Windrush with any of your nonsense. Now go and dig a latrine trench like I told you.'

'What's the trouble, sergeant?' Jack had a final pull on his cheroot and flicked the stub away.

'It's nothing to worry about, sir.' O'Neill gave a smart salute. 'Private Whitelam here is just leaving.'

'What did you see, Whitelam?' Jack asked.

'Somebody is dogging us, sir. I swear there is. I saw him twice on the march, and again ten minutes ago.'

'What was he like?' Jack knew that Whitelam was not a man to speak out of turn. He had been a poacher before he took the Queen's Shilling and after a lifetime spent dodging gamekeepers, he would know if somebody was following him.

'I can't rightly say, sir.' Whitelam screwed up his face with the effort of thought. 'He was a slim fellow, keeping to the shadows and the dead ground.'

'Was he wearing green clothing and a black turban?'

Whitelam refused to be drawn. 'I don't know, sir. As I said, he was in the shadows.'

'Right.' Jack thought quickly. 'Where did you see him last?'

'Over there, sir, past that grove of babul trees. He was walking slowly and ducked into cover, sir.' Whitelam gestured to a small group of acacia trees a few hundred yards to the south.

'Has he moved since?' Jack asked.

'Not that I've seen, sir, and I've been watching for him.'

If Whitelam hadn't seen him – or her – move, then he was still there.

'Sergeant O'Neill,' Jack said. 'I don't want this man or woman alarmed. It might be Jayanti or one of her women. Take a picket out and see if you can round him up. Be careful, if it's Jayanti she is very dangerous.'

'Aye, sir.' O'Neill screwed up his eyes as he peered through the glare of the sun. 'It might be best if I flushed him, sir, drove him towards the camp.'

'Good man, O'Neill. I'll wait for him. I'll give you ten minutes and then form a cordon with a dozen men. We'll catch him, or her, in a net.'

'I'll leave Greaves in charge of the Pathan, sir,' O'Neill said.

'Wilden!' Jack motioned to the ensign. 'You're with me.'

'Where are we going, sir?' Wilden couldn't disguise his smile.

'We're going to catch a mutineer. Do as you're told and don't ask fool questions. Whitelam, take a position a hundred yards out and to the right. Hutton, do the same on the left. Find dead ground and don't be seen.'

Both men were veterans and needed no further orders.

Jack watched as O'Neill led a dozen men well to the right of the babul trees, and then ordered them into an extended line five yards apart. The sergeant headed left for a hundred yards, turned and walked back. At his crisp order, each man fitted and lowered his bayonet, moving behind the viciously pointed blades.

'That should chase him out,' Jack said. His picket waited at the fringe of the camp, with Coleman and Thorpe watching, stony-faced.

'Do you want us to kill him, sir?' Thorpe asked.

'I want to see who he is,' Jack said, 'and why he's following us.' *He might be scouting for a larger body or merely a curious bystander.*

'That means we take him alive, Thorpey,' Coleman explained. 'Dead men can't talk.'

Thorpe nodded. 'Yes, Coley. I won't kill him, sir, unless Captain Windrush wants me to.' He stamped his feet. 'You could have let me go in, sir. I would have set fire to the trees and got him that way.'

'Thank you, Thorpe,' Jack said. 'Maybe next time.'

O'Neill's men were at the fringes of the *tope* now, advancing cautiously in case of an ambush. O'Neill gave a sharp order, and four men remained outside, watching while the others entered.

'Here he comes, flushed like a partridge.' Thorpe raised his rifle.

The lone man emerged at a run, holding a hood over his head as he scurried free of the trees.

No black turban. It's not Jayanti or one of her women.

'With me, lads, and be careful.' Drawing his sword, Jack strode forward, knowing his men would follow.

The fugitive saw the soldiers ahead, turned, saw O'Neill's men behind and stopped.

'He's surrendering, sir,' Coleman said. 'Either that or he's up to something. You've got to watch these pandies, sir. They're tricky devils. Best let me and Thorpey get him.'

Ignoring the advice, Jack broke into a run. 'Drop your weapon and get your hands in the air, you blackguard!' Although the man wouldn't understand the words, the tone and menace would be evident.

The fugitive raised his hands and stood still as the British net closed. He was small and slight, dressed in a hooded cape that extended from his head to the ground.

'Right, you.' Jack sheathed his sword. 'Who the devil are you, and why are you following us?' Grabbing the man's hood, he hauled it off the fugitive's face.

'Why, Jack, don't you recognise me?' Mary smiled at him. 'And do you need all these men to capture a single woman?'

'What?' Jack stared at her. 'What are you doing here?' He signalled with his hand, and the circle of soldiers lowered their bayonets. Some were openly grinning.

'I told you that you needed a translator.' Mary sounded as calm as if she was sitting sewing in the British cantonment.

'I ordered you to stay behind!' Jack felt his temper rising.

'I know you did, Jack, but I'm not one of your soldiers.' Mary smiled serenely. 'You have no power to order me around.'

Jack realised that he had an interested circle of listeners, most of whom were now nudging each other, highly amused at their officer's discomfiture. 'O'Neill, get these men back to camp.'

'Yes, sir! You heard the order, lads!'

Was O'Neill's use of "order" a deliberate echo of Mary's words? Jack glowered at the sergeant until he doubled away with his men.

Mary raised her eyebrows. 'Well, Captain Jack, or should that be Captain Windrush? Now you have me, what are you going to do with me?'

Jack took a deep breath as a sequence of images flashed through his mind. 'I know what I would like to do with you,' he began and shook his head as Mary raised her eyebrows in mocking interest. 'I should send you back to Lucknow under an escort.'

'But then who would translate for you?' Mary asked sweetly. 'And wouldn't you look a bit silly? And you would be depleting your force, just for one weak woman.'

'You're about as weak as Genghis Khan.' Jack's anger was reducing as Mary smiled at him. 'This will be a dangerous mission, you know.'

'I know,' Mary said.

'I don't like to put you in danger.'

'I know that, too,' Mary said. 'You're not putting me in danger. I'm putting myself in danger, and I'm probably safer with you and your *badmashes* than anywhere else in India.' Her smile broadened. 'Come on now, Jack, we both know that you and your men will look after me.'

'You're an irritating woman, Mary,' Jack said.

'So your mother used to say.' Mary deliberately reminded Jack of their family connection.

'You'd best stay with us,' Jack said, grudgingly. 'You might be useful. If any of my men bother you—'

'Your men have never bothered me,' Mary said quickly.

Jack thought of Armstrong and some of the handful of replacements he had brought with him. 'I'll find you a tent and post a sentry at the flap.' *I'll also warn O'Neill and Greaves to keep an extra eye on you, as if they didn't have enough to do.*

'If you think it best.' Mary agreed without a protest.

'All right, Mary, if you're sure, then welcome aboard.' Jack considered for a minute. 'In fact, you can start now.'

'I knew you needed me.' Mary didn't disguise her smug smile.

Batoor was sitting with his back to a tree when they approached.

'Stand up!' Jack ordered, adding *jildi* to prove to Mary that he had mastered at least one word of the native languages.

Logan helped by yanking Batoor to his feet. 'Up you get, you, when the officer tells you.'

'Where are you taking us, Batoor?' Jack asked, with Mary putting his words into Pushtu.

'Northward, Captain Windrush.' Batoor rattled his chains. 'And then westward.'

'How far to the north?'

'If I told you, Captain Windrush, you would not need me, and you may kill me.' Batoor smiled. 'I'm not yet ready to be a martyr. I have things to do.'

'You mean you have throats to cut in the Khyber country,' Jack said.

'A woman betrayed me to the British.' Batoor rattled his chains again. 'Else I would not be wearing these.'

'You gave me your word,' Jack said, 'and I gave you mine so we should trust each other.' He tapped the chains. 'It appears that neither of us trusts the other.'

Batoor smiled and said nothing.

'Well then,' Jack unlocked Batoor's chains and threw them into the darkness. They clattered against something hard. 'There is a sign of my trust.' He was aware of Mary watching him, her eyes quizzical while Logan lifted his bayonet, ready to thrust it into Batoor's belly.

Batoor rubbed the raw marks the manacles had left on his wrists. 'You are a strange man, Captain Windrush.'

'I'm taking a chance on you,' Jack said.

Batoor looked at Logan before he replied. 'I'd like a weapon before this man tries to kill me.'

'He'll only kill you if you try to escape, or attack one of us.'

Batoor spread his arms. 'I've eaten your salt.'

'Where are you taking us?' Jack asked again.

'Gondabad,' Batoor said. Even Jack understood that name without Mary having to translate. Jack took a deep breath. That was where he'd been born and where the Mutiny had started for him.

'I know the way.'

Batoor nodded as Mary translated.

'Are you sure that Jayanti is there?' Jack asked.

'I am not sure she is there. I think she may be there.' Batoor answered before Mary translated. 'Yes, Captain Windrush, I speak English.'

'Well, that is truthful for a Pathan,' Jack said. 'My men will still watch you.'

'I believe you.' Batoor eyed Logan, who ran a calloused thumb up the length of his bayonet.

* * *

Jack heard the gunfire from deep in his sleep. Rolling on his side, he grabbed his revolver and sword and was outside his tent before the echoes of the second shot died away. The third came an instant later, followed by an irregular fusillade.

'What's happening? Jack buckled his sword belt around his naked waist. 'Elliot! Bryce!'

'Somebody fired into the camp, sir!' Bryce was fully dressed and had his revolver in his right hand. 'I had the sentries fire back.'

'Cease fire!' Jack ordered. There was a single shot and then the eerie silence of the night, broken only by the buzz of insects and the chirping of frogs. 'Did anybody see anything?'

'I did, sir.' Parker said. 'I saw a muzzle flash over to the left.'

'Is anybody hit?'

'No, sir,' O'Neill said.

'Elliot, take Sergeant Greaves, Parker and ten men, search in the area from where the shot came.'

'Sir.' Elliot detailed nine veterans and a replacement named Mahoney. He vanished into the night.

'Who was it, sir?' Ensign Peake asked.

'We don't know, Peake,' Jack said. 'We won't know until Lieutenant Elliot returns, and we might not know even then.'

'Shall I go and look, sir?'

'No! Go and attend to your men.' Jack glowered at Peake until he disappeared.

'You were a little harsh on that boy,' Mary said.

'He has to learn his duty,' Jack said. 'If he went out there,' he nodded into the night, 'the pandies would cut him to pieces.'

'I see.'

'And God only knows what they'd do to you. Get back inside the camp, get into your tent and keep your head down.'

Mary opened her mouth to protest, saw the determination in Jack's face and nodded. 'Yes, sir.' She took three steps and turned around. 'You know, it might be better if you put some clothes on next time you gave me an order. It would be more dignified for both of us.'

'What?' Jack realised that he was wearing nothing except his sword belt. 'I was in bed,' he said. 'A real lady would not comment on such things.' His retaliation was too late for Mary was ten paces away, striding for her tent. *Blasted woman. Only Mary can drive me to such irritation.*

. . .

'Nothing, sir,' Elliot reported when he returned. 'We found nothing at all, not a sign of anybody.'

'All right, I didn't think you would. It might have been a stray mutineer trying his luck, or just a passing *badmash* causing trouble. Double the sentries.'

'Yes, sir.' Elliot lowered his voice. 'Is Mary all right, Jack? And the Pathan?'

'Mary's in her tent,' Jack said. 'I've posted a sentry, and I want him relieved every two hours.'

'Yes, sir,' Elliot said.

'The Pathan is still here,' Batoor's deep voice sounded. 'He did not take advantage of your confusion to escape.'

Jack gave a small smile. 'I didn't think he would.'

Jack didn't try to sleep again that night. Dressing quickly, he spent the hours until midnight patrolling the camp perimeter, quietly talking to the pickets and peering into the dark. He roused the camp three hours before dawn, supervised breakfast, loaded the camels and had everybody on the march within the hour.

The men stumbled through the dark, swearing quietly, alert for any ambush, holding loaded rifles and wondering if they should have thrown back the shilling they'd accepted from a smooth-tongued recruiting sergeant.

'Sir,' Sergeant Greaves saluted Jack. 'One of my men reports we're being watched.'

'I'm sure most of the men think that, Greaves.'

'Yes, sir. This time it's a bit different,' Greaves said. 'This man is certain, sir.'

Jack sighed. 'Bring him up, sergeant.'

The private gave a hurried salute. 'I know you,' Jack said. 'You were the lad MacKinnon, for whom Sergeant Greaves bought beer.'

'Yes, sir,' Mackinnon said.

'What do you have to say then, MacKinnon?'

'There's somebody out there in the dark, sir.'

'What have you seen?'

'Nothing, sir.' MacKinnon hesitated. 'I can feel them, sir, out there.'

'Do you know where, MacKinnon?'

'No, sir. I do know though, sir.' It was evident that the man couldn't explain further.

'Thank you, MacKinnon.' Jack frowned. 'Where are you from?'

'Skye, sir. It's an island in the Hebrides, off Scotland.'

'I see.' Jack wondered if he had just experienced an example of Hebridean second sight. 'Keep me posted, will you?'

'Yes, sir.' MacKinnon seemed relieved to escape.

'Greaves, send out strong pickets on either flank and double the rear guard, at least until day-break.' Jack saw Wilden watching nervously and called him over.

'Wilden,' Jack spoke quietly. 'How long have you held a commission in the army?'

'Nearly nine months, sir,' Wilden said proudly.

'And how much of that time have you been with the men?'

'One month, sir. The rest of the time I was travelling from England.'

'Well ensign, here is some free advice. These men come from bad backgrounds. Many are orphans, or their parents were drunkards, jailbirds or walked away and left them. Some are petty criminals; others are not so petty. As you see, they are a mixture of old soldiers and young lads very much like you, except without your education.'

'Yes, sir.' Wilden was sensible enough to realise that Jack was speaking from his own experience.

'If you treat the men decently, listen to their problems and help them, they will follow you to the gates of Hell and beyond. All they want is somewhere to belong. The regiment is their family. We, the officers, are surrogate parents. Do your duty, help them to do theirs, guide them and watch over them.'

'Yes, sir,' Wilden nodded eagerly. 'Like us, sir, they joined for queen and country.'

Jack grunted. 'Patriotism is said to be the last refuge of the scoundrel, ensign. For most men, this regiment is the last refuge of the desperate.' He passed over a cheroot, as if to a friend. 'Belonging to the regiment is vital. Officers can transfer or buy their way into other regiments; the men cannot. The 113th is their home. The more pride they have in the regiment, the better their morale and the better they will fight.'

'Yes, sir.'

Jack nodded. 'When it comes to action, lead from the front. It's the only place for a British officer.'

'Of course, sir!' Wilden said.

Jack smiled. 'In plain speaking, Wilden, just do your duty, and you'll be fine.' He patted the boy's shoulder. 'Now off you go and look after your section. Make sure their water bottles are full of water and not gin, make sure their rifles are not rusty, make sure their bayonets slide free from the scabbard and they have ammunition in their pouches and not loot or whisky.'

'Yes, sir.'

'Drink is the sin of the soldier, Wilden. Drink and women. I'm sure you have experience with the latter; your duty is to ensure the men don't cause themselves disease.' Jack winked and walked away, lighting a cheroot. The column trudged on, rifles slung, boots kicking up dust.

'That was kindly,' Mary said.

'I feel like a grandfather,' Jack said.

'How old are you, Jack?' Mary asked.

'Twenty-five,' Jack said. 'I feel about fifty-five.'

Mary smiled. 'How long have you been a soldier?'

'Since 1851 – coming up for seven years.' Jack looked back on himself. 'I was like Wilden then, young, keen and stupid.'

'How many battles have you been in?' Mary walked at Jack's side, matching him stride for stride.

Jack thought of Rangoon and Pegu, Inkerman and the Redan and the battles for Cawnpore and Lucknow. 'I don't know,' he said. 'Too many, Mary, too many.'

'Once this campaign is over the army may give you a rest.'

'Maybe they will,' Jack said. *That won't happen. The army will use the 113th for the dirty jobs, the unpleasant tasks without glamour or glory. My future is one of constant fighting until the grave, a soldier's life and a soldier's death.* He realised that Mary was looking at him with her head slightly to one side and her eyes thoughtful.

'You don't believe that, do you?' Mary asked.

'No.' Jack looked up as a flock of birds exploded from a tamarind tree. 'Wilden, take your men and see what disturbed these birds.'

Mary withdrew. 'I'll leave you to your duty.'

They marched on, more wary, with men gripping their rifles and peering into the fading grey of the early morning. India could be indescribably beautiful, tragically poor or insufferably hot. There was a combination of colour and dust, obscene cruelty and nonstop kindness, loyalty beyond reason and always variety. Jack pulled aside as the men slogged past.

'Did you find anything Wilden?'

'No, sir.'

'Carry on. How about you, Sergeant Greaves?'

'All well, sir. All present.'

The first shot came just as dawn silvered the sky, followed by a screaming charge on the 113th's left flank. One minute the column was marching solidly through a seemingly empty countryside, the next they were under attack by an unknown number of men. Jack had a nightmare vision of glaring eyes and gaping mouths, gleaming blades and flowing robes as the enemy rushed in. The flanking picket took the first shock and withdrew, firing and cursing, as Jack shouted for the central column to form a square around the transport camels.

'Hold your fire until ordered!' Jack glanced at his men, trying to ensure they were all in the square. 'Fire!' White and acrid, powder smoke drifted across the perimeter as the yelling subsided. Men peered into the half-light, sweaty hands slippery on the stocks of their rifles.

'Where are they?' Bryce fingered the trigger of his revolver. 'They've gone. We've beaten them off.'

'Keep quiet!' Jack snarled. 'Can anybody see anything?'

'They're still there, sir,' O'Neill said. 'I can smell them.'

'They're on this side, sir!' MacKinnon gave the warning. 'I know they are.'

Jack nodded. 'Left flank, load and cap. Right flank, aim low, fire a volley, fire!'

The Enfields crashed out with fleeting muzzle flares and spurts of smoke, a scream from the dark and then shocking silence. Powder smoke caught dry throats; a man coughed.

'Right flank, load and cap!' Jack ordered. 'Keep quiet and listen.'

The music began so softly that Jack thought he was hearing things, Indian music, rhythmic and subtly beautiful, with undertones that unsettled him.

'What the devil are they doing?' Bryce asked.

'Serenading us,' Elliot said.

'They're trying to unnerve us,' Jack said.

'They might be trying to mask the sounds of an attack,' Elliot said.

'Good thinking, Elliot. Everybody keep quiet, ignore the music and listen.' Jack glanced over his shoulder. Mary was amidst the camel drivers in the centre of the square, squatting. He lifted a hand, and she acknowledged with a wave. She was as safe there as anywhere in the square.

'It's getting lighter.' Jack was used to the speed of the tropical dawn. 'We can see them now if they come.' He relaxed a little, confident in the ability of his fifty men to defeat an attack by many times their number. After serving with Havelock and Sir Colin Campbell, he knew the fighting prowess of the British soldier. His 113th was as good as any soldiers in the world and better than most.

'They've gone sir,' MacKinnon said.

'The music is still playing,' Bryce pointed out.

'Sir!' O'Neill gave a quick salute. 'Packer's missing.'

Packer was one of the replacements, a thin, undersized youth from London.

'Has he fallen out?' It was common for Johnny Raws to collapse on long marches, from either exhaustion or heat.

'No, sir,' O'Neill said. 'He was with us ten minutes ago. I think the pandies grabbed him in that first rush.'

'Oh, dear God almighty.' Jack took a deep breath. 'We'll have a look. O'Neill, you're with me. I want Coleman, Thorpe, Riley and Logan.'

'Where are you going, sir?' Ensign Wilden asked. 'Can I come?'

'Not this time, Wilden.' Although officers needed to blood Griffs and Johnny Raws, there was a time and place, and this was neither.

'Elliot, take command.'

'Yes, sir,' Elliot said and lowered his voice. 'I'll take care of her, sir.'

'Come on, O'Neill.' Jack slipped through the square and into the growing light outside. They were in an area of extensive fields, small *topes* of trees and abandoned villages. A hanged man swung from the bough of a tree; victim of mutineer, vengeful British or local lawmaker, Jack did not know.

'Sir,' Coleman knelt on one knee. 'Over here. Blood.'

A cluster of flies rose from the bloodstain as Jack examined it. 'We got one of them, then, whoever they were.'

'Yes, sir,' Coleman agreed. 'Unless that's Packer's blood.'

'I hope it was quick.' Riley said what they were all thinking.

'They've gone now.' O'Neill scanned the open terrain. 'There's no sign of anybody.'

'They'll be there, watching us,' Jack led them in a wide circle around the 113th position, searching for Packer and the enemy and finding nothing.

'We'll stay put for a couple of hours,' Jack ordered when he returned. 'Greaves, Elliot, Bryce, take out patrols and look for Packer.' He could only afford a couple of hours. Any more and he would be marching in the afternoon and would lose more men to the heat. In this sort of expedition, they moved from water to water, sought the shade or died.

'Now we wait,' he said to Mary.

'And Packer?' Mary asked.

'We hope.'

Mary nodded, touched his arm and searched for the closest shade. She knew he was worried about his missing man.

One by one, the patrols returned, all with grim faces and a shake of the head. 'The pandies have gone,' they reported.

'And Packer?' Jack asked, already aware what the reply would be.

'There is no sign of Packer.'

Jack swore. He hated leaving a man behind.

'We beat them off, sir!' Wilden put a more optimistic slant on the encounter.

'You did well,' Jack said. 'You stood with your men and did your duty. That's what soldiers are supposed to do.' He turned away, knowing that his few words would have boosted Wilden's morale more than a hundred brass bands or long speeches.

'Forward!' Taking his place in front of the column, Jack waved them on. Already the heat was intolerable. Within fifteen minutes, the men would be sodden with sweat, made prickly by the dust of the road sticking to them. Within another half-hour they would be flagging, some staggering as the heat smote them like a brass fist. He looked ahead, knowing there was a village two miles along the road that would have a well.

'Wilden; take a picket ahead, find water. Take five men, three old soldiers and two Johnny Raws.'

That was an easy enough mission that would improve the lad's confidence and give him and the replacements some experience of acting outside the regimental framework.

'You'll really need to learn some languages.' Mary seemed comfortable sitting inside a pannier, slung at the side of one of the baggage camels. With a scarf shading her head, she looked as if she belonged in this environment.

'Why?' Jack was preoccupied with scanning the surrounding countryside. 'I have you.'

'I won't be here forever,' Mary said. 'You didn't want me here this time.'

Jack frowned, wondering if Mary was hinting at something. 'You'd better teach me, then.'

'Now?'

'Not now! I'm leading a column in hostile territory! Damn it, woman!' He thought of Packer, wondering if he could have done more to find the missing man.

We can start when we camp then.' Mary ignored his irritability.

'Yes,' Jack said, 'when we camp, unless the mutineers attack.'

'Oh?' Mary raised her eyebrows, a habit she seemed to have. 'Surely you would not allow the mutineers to interfere with your education.'

Only the slightest twitch at the corner of her mouth indicated that Mary was pulling his leg. Jack shook his head. 'You'd better get back in the middle of the column in case the pandies come.'

'Yes, Captain Windrush, sir,' Mary gave a mock salute that raised a smile on the faces of the nearest men.

Aware he was watching her rather than concentrating on his duty, Jack looked away abruptly. *Duty, duty, first and last. Duty to the death.*

'Penny for them,' Elliot said.

'What?'

'Penny for your thoughts,' Elliot said.

'I was wondering if the pandies would try to attack us again.'

'You're a lying hound, Jack Windrush,' Elliot said pleasantly. 'You were thinking of Mary Lambert.'

'I was doing nothing of the kind!'

'Another lie!' Elliot said. 'You'd better be careful, Jack, or Saint Peter will bang the pearly gates in your face and kick you downstairs with the thieves, robbers and blackguards.' He grinned. 'And I'll be waiting with the 113th to welcome you.'

'Watch your blasphemy, lieutenant, and you a clergyman's son.'

'She's a good woman, Jack,' Elliot said.

'As good as any other.' Jack tried to sound grudging in his praise.

'You risked your life to save her in the evacuation of Lucknow,' Elliot reminded. 'And she nursed you when you were wounded.'

'She knew my mother,' Jack said.

'There's more than that.' Although he was talking, Elliot never ceased to survey the countryside through which they passed. 'You know there is.'

'She's a useful woman with her language skills, and she's a pleasant companion.' Jack eased off a little.

'Is that all?' Elliot raised his binoculars to study a ruined village on the horizon. He grunted. 'Something is moving over there. Could be pandies.'

'Riley and Logan are on the flank picket. If there's anything out there, they'll pick it up.'

'She likes you, too.' Elliot accepted Jack's opinion on the distant village. 'And more than likes you, or she wouldn't have followed you here. Be careful, Jack.'

'I know what I'm doing.' Jack was becoming used to Elliot's warnings of doom where Mary was concerned.

'She'll be bad for your career,' Elliot said. 'She's Anglo-Indian, or Eurasian or whatever you wish to call it. Could you imagine introducing her into the Mess? What would the officers say? How would the other wives react?'

Jack felt his temper rising. 'Who the hell cares what the officers say, or how the other wives react? Surely any decision would be between Mary and me, and I'm not saying that I have any idea about marriage or anything else.'

'Mary might care,' Elliot said quietly. 'Could you imagine what sort of life she would have, especially if the Army posted us home? The wives would shun her, and the other officers would treat her like dirt. It's not fair on Mary to lead her on, Jack, and as for you...' Elliot shrugged. 'You could whistle for your next step. No matter what heroics you did, a man with a Eurasian wife would never get promotion. You would remain a captain, Jack until you were in your dotage and Horse Guards would find some excuse to put you on half pay so you would rot in Eastbourne or Brighton or some other nowhere.'

'Thank you for your advice, Lieutenant,' Jack said stiffly. 'And now if you could return your attention to your duty, we would all be grateful.' Jack had been watching Ensign Wilden hurry back from his patrol.

'There is a village ahead, sir, with a working well.'

'Good man, Wilden,' Jack encouraged. 'Now take ten men forward and secure the village perimeter until we get there.'

'Yes, sir!' Wilden looked excited as he called together the nearest ten men and rushed forward again.

'Poor lad.' Elliot was not the slightest abashed by Jack's rebuke. 'He'll learn.'

'Let's hope he has time to learn and the pandies don't get him,' Jack said. 'Or the cholera.'

The village centred on a well and a babul tree. In peacetime, elderly men would gather under the tree, exchanging gossip and watching the world go by, but in the present war, the place was deserted.

'Water the camels first,' Jack ordered, 'then the men and the officers last.' There was an order of priority in the army and any officer who drank before his men would soon learn of his mistake.

'This place is eerily quiet.' Mary dismounted with a single fluid movement and stretched her limbs before walking toward Jack.

'It's the war,' Jack said. 'We're marching through a land accursed by God.'

'It's more than that,' Mary said.

'Something's wrong.' MacKinnon held his rifle ready. 'Something's wrong here, sir. There are no birds or anything.'

'He's right,' Mary said. 'There are no birds, not even in the tree.'

Jack frowned. Even if the villagers were absent, the babul tree should be swarming with birds. Where were they?

'That camel, what's wrong with it?'

The camel was swaying from side to side as if drunk. As Jack watched, it fell to one side, spilling its load of tents and water-canteens.

'What the devil?' Jack jumped forward. 'What's happening here?' He grabbed the camel driver. 'What have you done to the beast?'

The man stared at him, terrified.

'He's done nothing,' Mary said. 'You can't blame him! Look at that other camel!'

A second camel was also swaying, staggering from side to side.

'The blasted things were all right a minute ago,' Jack said.

'They were all right until they drank from the well,' Elliot pointed out.

'Bad water!' Jack yelled in near panic. 'The pandies have poisoned the well. Get the animals back! Nobody touch the blasted water!'

'The foul bastards!' Elliot was not normally prone to swearing. 'Get back, lads! Don't touch the water! Get away from the well!' He extended his arms and pushed back thirsty camels and thirsty men. 'Back!' They retreated, swearing.

'That's a new trick,' Jack said. 'It's a dirty thing to do in a hot climate.'

'We need water.' Elliot pushed back a thirsty camel. 'Neither the men nor the animals will last another day without it.'

Unfolding his map, Jack spread it on the ground, weighed down the corners with stones and pored over their position. 'It's the dry season' he said as if speaking to Griffs, 'so there is little standing water in this part of the world. We have to find a well.'

'Yes, sir.' Elliot agreed.

'We passed close by a deserted village a mile or two down the road,' Jack reminded. 'They'll have a well.'

'The pandies could have poisoned that one too,' Lieutenant Bryce said.

'Take out a strong picket out and find out, Bryce,' Jack decided. 'Be careful.'

'Yes, sir.' Bryce selected a dozen men and marched off. Jack posted sentries around the village as the remaining men sought shade, cursing the enemy and the climate.

'What do we do now?' Mary asked.

'You keep away from the sun,' Jack said. 'I'll do my duty.'

'You're worried.' Mary touched his arm.

'The men can't see that. They must think their commander is confident of success at all times.' Jack checked his revolver was loaded and looked around the village once more. Both camels that had drunk at the well were now dead, and Jack gave orders to redistribute their loads among the others.

'What's taking Bryce so long?' Jack scanned the distant village through his binoculars.

The rifle fire was flat and vicious under the pressing sun.

'Ambush,' Jack said. 'The pandies have ambushed Bryce. Form up, men! We're heading out!'

For a moment, Jack wondered if he should leave his camels and Mary behind with an escort, but decided that further splitting his force when facing an unknown number of the enemy would be foolish.

'Keep together. Elliot, take the right flank, Wilden, and O'Neill, take the left, Peake, command the rear guard. Follow me.'

As Jack doubled back toward the village, he saw that Bryce and his men had gone to ground, lying in an extended line to fire at an invisible enemy.

75

Jack ducked as a bullet flicked his forage hat, and then Bryce was rising beside him.

'They're firing at us, sir,' Bryce reported.

'Get down, man!' Jack ordered. 'There's no sense in making yourself a target. How many of them are there?'

'I don't know, sir,' Bryce said. 'Maybe a hundred or so.'

'Very good, Bryce.' Jack didn't need to ask where the enemy was; he could see powder smoke rising from the village and various points on either side.

The village was no different from a thousand others in India, with a peepul tree near the centre of a straggle of houses of different sizes. Jack knew the rules when ambushed. He could find cover and try to fight it out, knowing that the ambushers held all the advantages of position and surprise, he could withdraw, or he could charge for the throat and hope to unsettle them. In this case, retreat was not an option.

'Hutton, Smith; stay with the translator and don't let her come to harm. The rest of you, follow me! Come on the 113th!' Jack charged forward. Cheering and swearing, his men followed. There was no time to think of tactics. He had to rely on force and speed.

'Cry Havelock!' Elliot used the old battle cry. 'And let loose the dogs of war!'

The dogs were loose.

Smoke jetted from the windows of the nearest house, and Jack felt something flick past his face. Lifting his revolver, he fired back. A mutineer appeared at the upper window, his scarlet jacket now faded with sun and exposure. For a moment, Jack stared right into his face. He was a havildar – a sergeant of native infantry – with greying hair and impressive whiskers, a man who had grown middle-aged in the service of John Company and now had lost his pension and his reputation by turning against his old employers.

Weaving from left to right, Jack ran forward and fired again, knowing he had little chance of hitting the havildar. The door of the house crashed open, and a press of men rushed out, some were mutineers, other warriors in white clothes and twisted red turbans with curved tulwars and round shields. Jack shot the leading man, dropped his revolver as it jammed and drew his sword.

There was no time for hesitation now. For the next few moments, all Jack saw was screaming faces and darting bayonets, slashing tulwars and round metal shields. He thrust, parried and swore, felt the shock of impact as his sword entered a man's chest, and then something heavy crashed on the side of his head, and he staggered, falling to the ground.

He lay there, dazed, seeing only the white trousers of the mutineers and the bare brown legs of a swordsman. A mutineer in a faded scarlet tunic and loincloth straddled him and poised a bayonet.

Here is death, Jack thought. He wasn't scared. He was a soldier, and this was a soldier's death. The mutineer snarled at him and lifted the bayonet, ready to plunge it into his chest. The man's face twisted in hatred, his eyes wide open and his teeth bared. Jack wondered why an NCO had not pulled the sepoy up for having a rusty blade and then a naik pulled the man away. Jack rolled to his feet and grabbed his sword.

'Sir!' O'Neill and a press of men arrived with sweating faces and thundering boots. Logan dispatched the sepoy with a casual thrust of his bayonet. 'Are you all right, sir?'

'I'm all right,' Jack said. 'What happened?'

'You were on the ground sir, and an old naik saved you, sir,' O'Neill said.

'Why?' Still dazed, Jack felt the side of his head. 'Why did the naik save me?'

'Dunno, sir.' O'Neill shook his head. 'Rum fellows, these sepoys. You never know what's going on in their heads.'

'Where is the naik now?'

'He's gone, sir,' O'Neill said. 'He shoved Jack Pandy aside and fled.'

Jack wiped sweat from his forehead and looked around. There was a litter of bodies on the ground, but after the brief skirmish outside the houses, the mutineers had not fought. Only three of the enemy remained, standing in the open with tulwars and round shields.

'They think they're in the middle ages.' Elliot fired two rounds from his revolver, and the tallest of the enemy spun and fell, gasping and holding his shoulder. Armstrong stepped forward and casually bayoneted the wounded man.

'Don't kill them!' Jack shouted. 'I want them for questioning!'

He was almost too late as Logan ducked the swing of a tulwar and thrust his bayonet into the stomach of the next man. 'There's a Cawnpore breakfast, you pandy bastard!'

The third man stood alone, clashing his sword against his shield and shouting what Jack took to be a challenge.

'Come on!' Ensign Peake drew his sabre and dashed forward. 'Single combat, old man!'

'Get back, you stupid boy!' Jack shouted. 'He'll chop you to pieces!'

The rebel parried Peake's slash with his shield and sliced sideways. Peake leapt back, so the tulwar missed him, and then O'Neill arrived with a clubbed musket and battered the rebel to the ground.

'I was winning, sergeant,' Peake said. 'It was a fair fight!'

'This is war, not the school playing fields.' Jack looked at the rebel. 'Well done, O'Neill.'

'Aye. That was too easy, sir.' O'Neill kicked away the tulwar and shield. 'Look at this bugger; look at his scars.'

Dressed in a loincloth that revealed numerous scars on his upper body, the rebel was about thirty-five, with a small beard.

'He's a warrior, that one,' O'Neill said. 'He would have easily killed Ensign Peake, sir.'

'Maybe he wanted to be a martyr,' Jack said. 'More importantly, sergeant, form a defensive perimeter around the village. Keep this man for now; we'll question him later. Greaves, check the well is sweet.'

'It's as sweet as Irish honey, sir!' Greaves reported.

'Thank God for small mercies; get the camels and men watered.'

'That was too easy, sir,' O'Neill said. 'They outnumbered us, and they were in a strong position.'

'I know.' Jack retrieved his pistol and slowly reloaded. 'Make sure the pickets stay alert, sergeant.'

They heard the first scream an hour later, as the men were trying to sleep in the shade of the deserted houses.

'What's that?' Mary asked.

'It could be anything.' Jack tried to concentrate. Ever since the blow to his head, he'd been dizzy, and his thoughts were unclear.

'That's Packer,' Jackson said. 'I know his voice. That's Packer, I tell you.'

Another scream sounded, longer than before, ending in a long, drawn-out howl that raised the small hairs on the back of Jack's neck.

'They're torturing him!' Jackson said. 'We have to do something, sir!'

Jack considered. He could send out a patrol, but the rebels would expect that and would have an ambush waiting. By now, they knew his numbers and disposition; they held all the cards. On the other hand, if he sat and did nothing, the morale of his men would drop, and they would think he had no care for their lives.

'Elliot! Take charge of the camp. O'Neill, I want you, Coleman, Thorpe, Logan and Riley.' He had chosen his veterans, men who had threaded through the Burmese jungles and out-foxed the Plastun Cossacks in their homeland. 'We're looking for Packer. Hutton, you and Smith, guard the translator.' He felt Mary's gaze on him and didn't look around.

The dark closed around them, hot and humid. Jack took a deep breath. A few years ago, he had revelled in these night expeditions as he sought opportunities to make his name, while the excitement had driven him to deeds that now made him shudder. Now, these patrols were routine, something he had to do, although he could not deny the flutter of nervousness in the pit of his stomach and the dryness of his mouth. He closed his eyes for a few seconds, trying to control his bouts of dizziness.

Am I turning into a coward? Or have I already stretched my nerves past their limit?

The ground was hard under his feet. In six weeks or so, the rain would come, and this area would be a morass. That was India, his second home – perhaps his first home.

The screaming subsided into agonised sobbing that lasted for minutes. Jack sensed the anger of the men. They had witnessed more suffering in three years than most men would see in their lifetimes. Experience had added callouses to their skins and taught them to value friendship and loyalty above all. Now a friend was being tortured within their hearing, and they were powerless to help.

'Spread out,' Jack whispered. 'Not too far. Keep within two yards.' He didn't want the enemy to capture any more of his men.

They moved slowly, not putting their boots down until they had checked for dry twigs or loose stones that could rattle and give their position away, controlling their breathing, listening for any sound that did not belong.

O'Neill raised his hand, and they all halted, listening, peering into the dark. Jack felt the sweat slide down his back and loosened his grip on his revolver. He could hear nothing except the expected night sounds. They moved on, step by slow step.

The attack came suddenly, a rush of men from the dark straight for the centre of their line. Logan fired first, with O'Neill and Thorpe half a second later. The muzzle-flares erupted, and then there were a few furious moments of bayonets, rifle butts and boots hammering against semi-visible opponents. Jack felt hands grab him and fired, with the revolver bucking in his hand. One man fell, a second took his place, and somebody dragged him forward, struggling desperately.

Coleman and Riley came in from the flanks, swearing, bayonets plunging.

Something hard and heavy crashed on Jack's right wrist. He gasped and dropped his pistol, kicked out with his right foot, felt a surge of satisfaction as he contacted something soft, and tried to draw his sword. He swore as his numbed fingers failed to grip the hilt.

'Sir!' Coleman fired as he approached with the bullet taking one of Jack's attackers in the chest. The force threw the man back and then Riley was there, dapper and dangerous. The mutineers melted into the dark, leaving Jack gasping and holding his injured wrist.

'Are you all right, sir?'

'I think so. Nothing is broken anyway.' Jack flexed his wrist. 'What happened there?'

'They tried to kidnap you, sir,' Riley said.

'Why would they do that?' *That was a stupid question. I'm not thinking straight.*

'Information maybe, sir,' Riley said. 'Or a ransom. It is quite common in parts of Europe, kidnapping people for ransom.' Trust Riley to know the criminal practices of other countries.

'This isn't Europe, Riley, and they would get nothing by ransoming me.' Jack shook his head. 'I'm blessed if I know. Thank you for rescuing me, men.'

Riley turned away. Coleman grinned in embarrassment.

Having achieved nothing, Jack led the patrol back. There was no more screaming that night. He didn't try to sleep.

'That's twice something strange has happened,' he said to Elliot. 'First, the naik stopped a man from killing me and then an attempt to capture me.'

Elliot lit a cheroot. 'Your guardian angel is looking after you.' He smiled through the smoke. 'Seriously though, Jack, it's a rum do. I can't think what it is. This entire war has been strange, like a civil war against our friends and with the men running wild. Have you ever seen British soldiers behave in such a manner? Have you ever heard of them wanting to hang and execute like they are now?'

'I haven't,' Jack said. 'And I want to know why that naik saved my life and these pandies tried to capture me.'

'To question you, I guess,' Elliot said.

'I'm only a captain.' Jack shook his head. 'I don't know what's to do at all.'

'Well,' Elliot patted his shoulder. 'You're alive, your wrist is unbroken, and that's all that matters. Don't let the men hear that you're uncertain. They need a confident commander, not a worried one. Now if you'll excuse me, I have my rounds to make.'

'Aye, off you go, Arthur. Thank you.' Jack lit a cheroot and stared at the sweltering countryside. He felt as if India was playing with him, patting his mind and body back and forward like a shuttlecock. He would be glad when this campaign was over, and peace returned to this tortured land.

Jack gasped at the sudden pain in his head. He didn't know what was happening; he only knew that something was wrong. He closed his eyes as another dizzy spell came to him. Grasping the bole of a tree, he held on. He couldn't let anybody see this new weakness. He was the commander, he must always appear strong and confident, or the men would lose faith in him. He must do his duty.

CHAPTER SEVEN

'There's something on the road ahead, sir.' Sergeant Greaves reported. 'Shall I go and see what it is?'

'Yes, sergeant.'

Greaves trotted ahead and returned at the double. 'It's a head, sir! A human head!'

Jack sighed. *With how many more horrors will India torture me?*

Somebody had severed the head at the neck and thrust it onto the end of a stake. They had gouged out the eyes and placed something in the mouth.

'That's Packer!' Jackson hurried forward, only to stop as he reached the head. 'No, it's not.'

'No,' Jack said. 'It's not Packer. It's a European, though.'

'It's Keay, sir, of Number One Company,' Greaves said. 'How did he get here?'

'He was with Major Snodgrass,' Jack struggled to remember. 'They were escorting the women to Cawnpore from Gondabad last year.' Colonel Hook asked me to keep an eye out for them.

'I remember, sir,' Greaves said. They all vanished, if I recall.'

'That's right. And now Keay has turned up here, or part of him has.' Jack carefully detached the head and removed the contents of the mouth. 'It's a note.' He read it out.

British soldiers, why fight for a shilling a day when you can earn twenty times that amount fighting for a better cause? Why fight for the shareholders of the Honourable East India Company when you can fight for yourselves and have beautiful Indian women as your companions?

All you have to do is walk away and join us. Welcome bhaiya! Welcome, brother!

Realising that his men were listening to every word, Jack forced a laugh, screwed the paper into a ball and threw it away. 'Well, that's a lot of moonshine. Who would believe the word of a rebel?'

'Somebody might,' Greaves said. 'Not all our men are blessed with strong minds. Some might believe the lies. Others might want the money and women.'

Jack grunted and raised his voice so that everybody could hear. 'Not in this regiment. We are the 113th. Our lads have more sense than to believe that nonsense. Now, let's bury what's left of this poor fellow.'

'Why would they do that?' Elliot asked. 'Why torture the poor soul?'

Jack grunted. 'Why do we blow mutinous sepoys from the mouths of cannon, or make them lick up the blood of our women and children before we hang them?' He hardened his voice. 'Bring the prisoner to me. And fetch Mary.'

Armstrong and Hutton dragged across the man they'd captured at the village. He stood there, erect and semi-naked, unemotional.

'Ask him what's the meaning of this?' Jack demanded. 'Why did they torture and murder poor Private Keay?'

When Mary translated, the prisoner looked at Keay's head, smiled and said nothing.

'Ask him again,' Jack said to Mary. 'Tell him that we'll hang him in pigskin unless he tells us what it's all about.'

Mary shook her head. 'He's a Hindu,' she said. 'Pigskin is no threat to him.'

'Tell him we'll hang him with a cowhide rope then,' Jack said. 'Tell him any damned thing you like as long as it helps us find out why they tortured Private Keay.'

Mary spoke to the prisoner for a few moments, with his answers coming calmly. 'He says that Jayanti ordered it,' Mary said at last. 'Jayanti ordered the foreigner to be put to death to frighten us.'

'Frighten us?' Jack stared at the prisoner. 'Disgust us, maybe. Damn it, we have beaten the rebels and the mutineers; we're not going to be frightened by a rag-tag mob of broken men. Ask him where Jayanti is, Mary.'

A circle had formed around the prisoner, angry men listening to the questioning and offering unwanted advice regarding what to ask and how to treat him.

The prisoner ignored the shouts from the onlookers as he replied.

'He says that Jayanti is going to destroy the British,' Mary reported.

'Is that not what they said last year?' Jack snorted. 'They should try something original, the murdering hounds.' He frowned and took a deep breath. 'Ask him where Jayanti is.' He looked up. 'You men, get about your duty or by God, I'll find you something to do! Bryce! Elliot! Don't you have duties to perform? Check the pickets, send out patrols!' He glowered until the men moved back, giving him more space with the prisoner.

'You're getting out of temper,' Mary told him.

'I have to think,' Jack said. 'Ask him where Jayanti is and how she has so much power over men.'

'He says she is the great woman who is going to blow the British out of India.'

Jack nodded. 'Ask her real name, for by Christ, I don't believe it's Jayanti.' He waited as Mary exchanged words with the prisoner.

'He does not know, and please do not blaspheme, Jack.'

'Or he says that he doesn't know,' Jack said. 'All right. How many men does she have?' *Am I blaspheming?*

'He says ten thousand.'

Jack grunted. 'Ten thousand pandies and they're scared to attack a handful of the 113th? No wonder their mutiny failed.' He gestured to Armstrong. 'Take this liar away and keep him secure until I decide what to do with him.'

The screams of the night and the incident of Keay's head had unsettled Jack, and he was silent as he led the column on the road to Gondabad. Now that he knew his destination, he didn't need Batoor. He could send the Pathan back to Lucknow under escort, bring him along with the column or release him.

Although he had promised Batoor liberty in exchange for information, Jack was reluctant to release a man who knew his numbers and destination. He grunted; the mutineers' intelligence service was so efficient they probably knew where he was bound before he did himself.

'Bring Batoor to me,' he ordered.

The Pathan stood erect in front of Jack, his eyes level.

'We had a deal,' Jack said. 'If you helped us find Jayanti, you would be released.'

'That is correct, Captain Windrush,' Batoor said.

'I have already released you from your chains, and you have not run, so we trust each other to an extent. If Jayanti is in Gondabad, I will free you entirely and inform the authorities that you are not a rebel.'

'Yes, Captain Windrush.'

'If she is not in Gondabad, I will hang you.'

'Yes, Captain Windrush.' Batoor gave no visible sign of emotion at either his liberty or death.

'Now answer me this, Batoor,' Jack said, 'why are you still here? You could slip past my sentries any time.'

Batoor smiled. 'I have my reasons for helping you find Jayanti, Captain Windrush. I am using you as much as you are using me.'

Jack nodded. 'Thank you, Batoor. That was an honest answer. When we find this woman in Gondabad, I will give you a tulwar and a horse.'

Batoor smiled. 'If we do not find her you will give me a rope. If you can hold me.'

'That is what will happen.'

'Then we understand each other,' Batoor said.

As they marched on, the days grew hotter and the ground dustier. Jack led them off the main roads and onto bullock tracks, the network of paths that bound all the villages and towns of India together. Dust rose as they marched, irritating their eyes, entering their noses and ears, coating their uniforms. They greeted the occasional river like manna, leading in the camels and drinking their fill.

'Avert your eyes,' Jack advised Mary as he allowed the men to bathe, and forty naked men gambolled like children in the water. The remaining ten were on guard duty, cursing their luck and enviously waiting their turn in the river.

'Yes, Captain Jack.' Rather than obeying, Mary turned towards the river and watched, smiling.

'Gentlewomen would not look at such things,' Jack said.

'Then I am thankful to be Anglo-Indian and not included in any gathering of gentlewoman,' Mary said. 'I nursed sick and wounded men, Jack. I have seen everything there is to see, and I have survived.'

'I would prefer that you looked elsewhere,' Jack said.

'There is little to see elsewhere. Watching your men is more amusing.' When she smiled at him, Jack wondered if Mary was genuinely interested, or if she found teasing him more entertaining. 'When your men are finished splashing around,' Mary said, 'you could send one or two to the shallows upstream, near that tamarind tree. There will be shoals of rohu fish at that spot, not great eating perhaps, but they would make a change in diet for everybody.'

'You are an interesting woman, Mary.' Jack decided he couldn't force her away from watching the men bathing. *If I had the opportunity to watch forty naked young women, would I watch? Yes, I would.* 'Indeed,' he said, 'I think you are the most honest woman I have ever met.'

'Why, thank you, Captain Jack.' Mary's mocking curtsey did not match the thoughtful expression in her eyes.

The country gradually changed, so they marched through a vast landscape of ochre-yellow earth, scrub and clumps of dark rock, interspersed with groups of thorn trees and stretches of pampas grass.

'Captain Windrush.' Mary pointed from her pannier. 'Best warn your men to avoid these *datura* plants.' She pointed them out. 'They look pretty, but they are poisonous.'

'Thank you, Mary, I'll pass that on.' Jack lifted his binoculars and scanned an outcrop of rock. He raised his voice. 'Lieutenant Bryce, take a patrol out to those rocks there, I think I saw movement.'

'We haven't seen the pandies for days, sir.'

'We haven't seen God either, but we both know he's there!' Jack snapped.

The days continued one very much like another, with the occasional flurry of activity to investigate a village or *tope* of trees. Twice a musket man fired at them, and each time Jack sent out a patrol. Each time they returned empty-handed.

'These pandies are like smoke,' Elliot smeared sweat across his forehead. 'They vanish into the country.'

They marched past an area of dark ravines where men pointed out mirages that floated above the land like castles from an Arthurian romance, and they stopped at settlements where the inhabitants had never seen a European before, let alone heard about the Mutiny. One village set above a river opposite a small temple was like an Elysian scene, with naked little boys and handsome men bathing, some smacking the water, so it rose in diamond-bright showers. When they left, a score of women took their place, laughing and quarrelling as they beat their saris in the water and spread them around the rocks. A few waded deep into the water to bathe, while the 113th watched, willing the women to undress. The women did not comply and emerged with streaming unbound hair and the saris plastered to their bodies. The barking of pi-dogs and the smell of cooking enhanced the scene.

'That is the real India,' Jack said. 'India without armies and killing and plunder.' He led his men on, leaving the village and temple and the peaceful people behind.

In other villages, watchmen guarded studded doors in the mud walls and stared at them from behind the protection of a large stick while little naked children laughed at these exciting strangers invading their world.

There were stretches of country where the incessant noise of crickets rattled around Jack's head until he wanted to cover his ears, and where the Johnny Raws pointed to snakes on the track.

'Here, you!' Jack pointed to a man who staggered in the heat and dropped his water bottle. 'Pick that up! You'll need it later.' He rationed the water and ensured each man wore his hat and neck-flap. He positioned O'Neill or Greaves at the back of the column to stop anybody falling by the wayside. He made sure his men camped in the shade, and he took every precaution he could to preserve their health.

When Jack accepted the hospitality of isolated villages, he paid generously for chapattis from the hands of wide-eyed women, filled up the men's water bottles from wells, picked ripe tamarind fruit from the trees, and ensured nobody interfered with the local women or killed the village animals. Always, Mary asked for Jayanti and Major Snodgrass.

They heard nothing about Snodgrass, but on three occasions they heard rumours of Jayanti, a woman the locals swore had risen in the ashes of the Mutiny. Each time the intelligence was vague, with only one evident fact resulting.

'The people are certain that Jayanti is powerful,' Mary said.

'Her fame is spreading, with nothing ever definite.' Jack rubbed his head. He had been experiencing headaches ever since the mutineer had cracked him over the skull.

'Are you all right, Jack?' Mary sounded concerned.

'It's just a headache. It will pass.'

'You've had headaches for days now,' Mary said.

'It's nothing, I tell you. It will pass!'

'You've been more irritable since you left Bareilly as well.' Mary placed her hand on Jack's head. 'You have to take better care of yourself.'

'It's more important that I take care of Jayanti.' Jack closed his eyes, as he felt suddenly dizzy. He thought of that strange meeting with Jayanti outside Bareilly. *I should have killed her there and then. I neglected my duty through fear of his life. I failed. Duty should come first, last and always. Duty, duty, duty.*

Only vaguely aware that Mary was watching him, Jack walked away. *I must catch Jayanti. I have to kill her before she murders anybody else. It's my duty. Oh, God, I wish it were cooler.*

CHAPTER EIGHT

A full moon glossed the countryside, shining on the *topes* of trees and the patches of jungle. In the distance, the city of Gondabad sat under its protective fort, with the now abandoned British cantonment a mile away.

Jack lit a cheroot and slowly inhaled. He had been born in Gondabad in 1833. Now, in 1858, he was going back with fifty hard-bitten men of the 113th Foot, a Pathan, a prisoner, a rag-tag of camel-drivers and servants and one woman. Of them all, that lone woman concerned him most.

Apart from his stepmother and his mother, there had been two women in his life. Myat had been the first. He had been a very raw ensign, a Griffin, during the Second Burmese War in 1852. Had that only been six years ago? It seemed like a lifetime when he had rushed into every action in his hope to make a name for himself and gain promotion. He had taken a fancy to Myat until he learned that she was the wife of one of his sergeants. It had been a sickening disappointment, alleviated when he met Helen, the daughter of Colonel Maxwell, the then commander of the 113th.

Jack inhaled, watching the tip of his cheroot glow bright red. He tried to ignore the constant thumping of his head.

Jack had harboured high hopes of Helen. She had been everything that a woman should be, beautiful, shapely, intelligent and incredibly courageous. Her family connections helped, of course. If he had married a colonel's daughter, he would have almost guaranteed a smoother passage to promotion. Fate decreed otherwise.

The dirty copper coin clattered onto the stony ground at Jack's feet.

'There's another penny, Jack. Now you have to share your thoughts.' Elliot had his silver flask in his hand.

'I was thinking about Helen.' Jack didn't need to hide his recent past from Elliot.

'Ah, the delectable Helen of dubious intentions,' Elliot said. 'The woman you intended to marry who scrambled off with your esteemed brother.' He sipped from his flask. 'Your best view of Helen was her backside, as she wriggled farewell.'

'Indeed.' Jack said no more.

'You're better without her,' Elliot said. 'And now you have Mary, another woman with no future.' His voice hardened. 'As I have already told you, more than once.'

'Thank you for your advice,' Jack said. 'Which I will completely ignore.'

'I thought you would,' Elliot said. 'You're too fat-headed to listen to the truth. You know the old army maxim about women, don't you? Catch them young, treat them rough, tell them nothing and leave them.'

'Not my style,' Jack smiled.

'I know.' Elliot passed over his flask. 'You're going to talk to Mary, aren't you?'

'I am.' Jack took a swallow and coughed. 'By thunder, Arthur, what is this muck you're forcing me to drink?'

'I've no idea. Riley found it for me. We were much better in the Crimea; Campbell's Highlanders always had a supply of the real Ferintosh.'

'Well, Arthur.' Jack handed back the flask. 'Thank you for the Indian courage. I am off to speak to that woman of whom you disapprove.'

'I don't disapprove of the woman,' Arthur said. 'Only of the effect she might have on your career.'

'To the devil with my career,' Jack said.

CHAPTER NINE

'I wonder how old that place is.' Elliot sipped at his flask as they surveyed the ancient fort of Gondabad. 'And what sort of terrible things have happened there.'

The fort squatted on top of a hillside, its red walls sprawling along the summit, with circular towers every hundred yards and the sun flashing on the steel points of spears and helmets on the battlements. It looked sinister, a massive place that dominated the sprawling acres of flat-roofed buildings and alleyways at its base.

'I'm less concerned about its age than its security,' Jack said, 'and whether or not Jayanti is inside.'

'The Rajah and Rani of Gondabad live in there,' Elliot continued. 'They are two of the most mysterious rulers in the country.' He borrowed Jack's binoculars to scan the walls. 'They're the most northerly Hindu rulers in this part of India, I think, scions of the Rajputs and nobody knows if they are loyal to the mutineers or us.'

Jack grunted. 'That will depend on who looks like winning.' He signalled to Batoor. 'Right, Batoor, this is where you prove your worth.'

The Pathan grinned through his beard. 'Yes, Captain Windrush.'

'Don't let me down,' Jack said.

'I would not trust him.' Bryce was openly sceptical.

'He's eaten our salt,' Jack wasn't as confident as he tried to sound. 'And he's not betrayed our trust yet.'

Bryce grunted. 'That means nothing.'

'All right Batoor, I want you to go into Gondabad and discover if Jayanti is there,' Jack said. 'Then you return and tell me. We are here on your word.' As Batoor walked away, Jack called him back. 'Batoor!'

'Captain Windrush?'

'Take this.' Jack threw across the tulwar he had taken from the prisoner. 'You might need it.'

The Pathan caught the sword one-handed, smiled and stalked away, his stride long and confident.

'That's the last we'll see of him,' Bryce said.

'You could be right,' Jack said. *I have taken my men to Gondabad on the word of an enemy, and now I have allowed him to walk away. Am I stupid?*

Mary was sitting outside her tent, watching the moon when Jack arrived.

'Good evening Jack,' she said, 'or is it Captain Windrush?'

'It's Jack.' Jack cursed his bluntness.

'What can I do for you, Captain Jack?'

'Just a social call,' Jack said. 'Elliot is looking after the camp.'

'It's in good hands, then,' Mary said.

They looked at each other, with a distant jackal breaking the silence. Moonlight cast quiet shadows across Mary's face as Jack stood under a banyan tree.

'I would offer you tea, but I haven't any,' Mary said at last.

Jack forced a smile. He couldn't think what to say. 'I thought this would be a simple search expedition to find Jayanti. It seems it might be something more, something I don't understand. First, that naik saved my life and then Jayanti knew my name. There was also the attempt to kidnap me.'

'You're an important man, Jack Windrush,' Mary said.

'I think we're putting the lid on a boiler,' Jack said. 'Unless we do something fundamentally different, India will simmer and boil, and we'll sit on top, smiling and smug until it explodes again.' He sat at Mary's side, watching the moon. 'Oh, we'll defeat them this time. With men such as Campbell and Sir Hugh Rose, we'll scatter their armies. My lads of the 113th won't get beaten by any number of pandies.' He lit a cheroot. 'We were lucky though. If they had a couple of decent leaders, things could have turned out completely differently.'

Mary sat on a small *mooda* stool that somebody had found for her. 'Do you think the sepoys can be trusted any more, Jack?'

Jack considered for a moment as he studied the familiar sky. 'I don't know, Mary and that's worrying. The sepoys are good soldiers. I would say they are equally brave as our lads and careless of dying. They don't have our Christian doubts or humanitarian sentiment, and scenes of slaughter and mutilation don't concern them.'

'In that case, how do we always defeat them? Is it all down to leadership?'

'We don't always defeat them,' Jack said. 'They have inflicted quite a few reverses on us.'

Mary nodded. 'How then are we *usually* successful? Is that only due to our superior generals?'

'Not only better leadership.' Jack said. 'I said that the sepoys, or the pandies, match us in bravery and are less concerned about casualties. We have other qualities.' He pointed to the pickets, where Coleman and Thorpe were walking a few steps outside the perimeter of the camp. 'See these two there?'

'Coleman and Thorpey?' Mary gave a little smile. 'An odd couple, they are always quarrelling.'

'They are, yet when things are tough, they will never let each other down. They use dark humour to get through even the worst of situations. These two things, plus their innate determination never to get beat helps us win. Even after a defeat, our men don't *think* they're the best. They *know* they're the best.'

'That's very arrogant,' Mary said.

'It may be.' Jack pulled at his cheroot. 'If so, then thank God for arrogance. If we lose the humour and the comradeship, we'll be like any other army.' He stopped as he heard somebody shouting.

'Listen.' Mary held up her hand.

'We are the 113th!'

'That's something else we have.' Jack couldn't restrain his smile. 'We have regimental pride.'

'I noticed.' Mary was also smiling, but whether at him or with him, Jack couldn't tell.

Jack realised he was having an intelligent conversation with Mary, unlike the light nonsense he had exchanged with Helen. Had the Mutiny altered him that much, or was Mary a different kind of woman? He looked at her anew, seeing the light lines around her eyes and the determined set of her mouth.

She was a woman, rather than the half-child that Helen had been. Jack took a deep breath. 'Oh, dear God,' he said softly.

'What's the matter, Jack and do you have to blaspheme?'

'It's nothing.' Jack suppressed his sudden desire to reach across and kiss her. 'It does not matter.'

'I see.' Mary said. 'You can tell me when you're ready.'

They sat side-by-side in the now-comfortable silence.

'I'm scared, Jack. If we lose India, where will we – people like me – go?' Mary continued to gaze at the sky.

'We won't lose India. Not this time anyway,' Jack said.

'We will sometime,' Mary spoke quietly. 'And then there is nowhere.'

Jack saw the opening and opened his mouth to speak. Mary was faster of speech and forestalled his words.

'Your mother used to tell me that I could marry an officer. I thought about it, Jack and I looked after their children and spoke to them. Some officers treated me as an equal – nearly. Most treated me as a servant. I found their lives to be excessively boring.'

'Boring?' Jack started. 'Don't you think it would be fun to have female company, with regimental parties, afternoon teas and a change of scenery every time the army posts the regiment elsewhere? You would see the world, with guaranteed accommodation and friends.'

'No.' Mary's headshake was emphatic. 'It's a trivial life centred on the husband's work and sport. All the wives must do is look respectable, dress decently and not say anything outrageous at the endless dinner parties and balls. It would be claustrophobic and confining, wasting one's time and only being an appendage to one's husband. I need more than that, Jack. I want to be useful in my own right.'

'Oh,' Jack felt something sink inside him. He wasn't sure what to say.

'I have two skills that may help.' Mary seemed unaware of Jack's discomfiture. 'I have many languages, and I'm happy with children. I could be a language teacher at a school somewhere, if they would have me.'

'Why would they not have you?'

'Because I'm Anglo-Indian,' Mary said. 'Eurasian, a half-caste, a part blacky, I've a touch of the tar-brush.'

'All right.' Jack stopped her. 'That's enough of that.'

Mary smiled as if all her troubles had suddenly vanished. 'So, I promised I would teach you languages, Jack and there's no time like the present. Come on!'

* * *

'Batoor's not coming back.' Elliot tipped back his hip flask.

Jack nodded. He was disappointed in Batoor, he had thought the Pathan would remain true to his word. It was a full thirty hours since Batoor had entered Gondabad and there was no sign of him. *What should I try next?*

'He probably has some private business in Gondabad.' Elliot passed over the flask, shaking it to encourage Jack to partake. 'He'll have a throat to cut or a horse to steal.'

'That will be it.' Jack was in no mood to argue. Was their entire journey wasted? Had he been following a will-o-the-wisp on no more evidence than the word of an enemy?

'I'm going in myself,' Jack announced. He had no choice, he couldn't return without having achieved anything.

'Don't be a fool, man!' Elliot nearly dropped his hip flask. 'You'll never get away with it.'

'I'm not coming all this way to turn back right at the gates,' Jack said. He would search for Jayanti. Warrior women would inevitably be prominent. When he found her, he would kill her. The decision wasn't hard. A British officer and gentleman would not kill a woman, he knew. He also knew that it would ruin his reputation and his career. That didn't matter if it saved India from more bloodshed and more carnage.

India was as much his home as Britain was. Killing Jayanti might save his homeland much bloodshed. After all, what reason had he to live? He couldn't afford the next step to major, he couldn't afford to leave the army, and with Mary determined not to marry an officer... *There, I've admitted that I had contemplated marriage to that blasted woman.*

'They'll spot you right away,' Elliot said.

'We got away with it in the Crimea,' Jack reminded.

'You could look Russian,' Elliot pointed out. 'You don't look Indian.'

Jack's smile was more ironic that Elliot realised. 'I should,' he said. 'I'm part Indian, remember?'

'I remember,' Elliot said. 'You're also a British officer. Are you certain you wish to act the spy?'

'I've done it before,' Jack said.

Elliot sighed. 'If you want to risk your fool neck, then I'll come with you.'

'No, you won't,' Jack said. 'You'll look after the men until I get back.'

'Yes, sir!' Elliot gave a smart salute. 'You're a blasted fool, sir.'

'Thank you, Lieutenant Elliot.' Jack returned the salute. 'Now you can help me prepare.'

Naturally dark haired and with a complexion that easily tanned, Jack, didn't have to apply blacking. Dressed in a flowing white robe that descended to his ankles and with a dirty white turban on his head, he concealed his revolver next to his skin and thrust a long Khyber knife through the green cummerbund around his waist.

'There you go,' Elliot said. 'You look every inch a bazaar badmash.'

'What's this?' Mary peeped inside the tent. 'What's happening here?'

'Captain Windrush is going into Gondabad,' Elliot said.

Jack could feel Mary's sudden anger.

'Why?' Her voice was like ice.

'To search for Jayanti,' Jack said.

'Is there nobody else who can do that job?' Mary's eyes were smouldering. 'You're meant to command this force, not swan about acting the spy.'

'It's because I am in command that I have to go,' Jack said.

'You can hardly speak a word of any native language,' Mary said.

'I'll grunt a lot,' Jack said.

'I'm coming too,' Mary told him.

'You are not!' Jack said. 'I order you to remain behind.'

Mary's laugh may have been genuine. 'I'm a civilian, Captain Windrush. You can't order me to do anything.'

'By the living Christ, I can!' *This woman can make me angry with only a few words.* 'I can send you back to Lucknow.'

'I wish you would stop blaspheming, Jack! And would you send me back on my own?' Mary asked sweetly. 'With so many pandies around? Oh, Captain Jack Windrush, how could you be so cruel?'

'You little minx!' Jack's glare bounced off Mary without effect as Elliot began to whistle a little song and walked away to study the bark of a tree as if he had never seen such a thing before.

Jack took a long deep breath. *Why do we always argue?* 'If you come,' he conceded inevitable defeat, 'you do as I say and keep out of trouble.'

'Yes, Captain Windrush,' Mary said meekly.

'I don't like the idea.'

'Yes, Captain Windrush,' Mary said again. 'You do forget something. I have been walking through Indian towns all my life, and I grew up around Gondabad. I know the city and the people far better than you do, or anybody in your little army.'

Jack had no answer to that. 'I plan on going into the fort as well.'

'All right,' Mary said. 'I'll talk to the women. They will know more than the men do. Where will you start?'

'In the bazaar,' Jack said.

'That's as good a place as any,' Mary approved.

'We'll leave after dark,' Jack said. He wasn't happy to take Mary into danger once more. 'Maybe you'll be glad to have a boring and claustrophobic cantonment life after this trip.'

He felt Mary's eyes surveying him and wondered what she was thinking.

CHAPTER TEN

The city of Gondabad had long outgrown its walls, sprawling into the surrounding countryside in an array of slum housing and the more impressive dwellings of merchants. Pi-dogs barked at irregular intervals.

With her head covered and a green and red sari extending to her ankles, Mary walked a few steps behind Jack as he walked boldly toward one of the city's side gates. As a warrior, he adopted a swagger, snarling at anybody who tried to speak to him and spitting betel-nut juice at infrequent intervals. Only when he approached the gate did Jack realise how difficult it might be to get into the city.

Three guards lounged at the gates, two wearing the uniform of Bengal Army sepoys and the third sporting a spiked helmet and a breastplate. The sepoys stepped forward, Brown Bess muskets extended.

'Don't say a word,' Mary gave a quiet order. 'I'll say you're mute.'

Jack nodded, placed a hand on the hilt of his Khyber knife and increased his swagger. He walked right up to the muzzle of the closest sepoy and grunted as Mary spoke in Hindi. Within a few moments, the guards stepped aside, and Jack marched into the city.

Last time he'd been in Gondabad, he had been removing a private from a brothel in the days before the utiny. Now the mutineers and their allies held the city and possibly the vast fort above, with any British expelled or dead. The loyalists in Gondabad would be sitting quietly, waiting for the British to return, while the majority would wait to support whichever side turned out to be stronger.

'This way,' Mary took over, leading Jack through the twisting narrow passageways of the ancient town. Avoiding the sewers that bisected the streets, they passed shuttered windows and walked underneath overhanging balconies. The smell, as always, was strong, a mixture of filth and exotic spices, camels and other animals, and crowded humanity. They passed windowless houses with deeply inset ornate doors, heard evocative Indian music and hurried past the large *havelis* – townhouses – of merchants before they stopped at a wide, pointed gateway.

'The bazaar is through here.' Mary appeared more relaxed than Jack felt. She frowned. 'I'm interested in knowing how you expected to question people when you can hardly speak a word of any Indian language.'

'Remember that we're looking for Jayanti.' Jack ignored her sarcasm. 'She might be conspicuous.'

'I won't forget,' Mary said.

The bazaar was crowded with men and women, all talking and shouting, buying and selling and living their lives. Jack had thought the war would have created poverty, but the shops in the bazaar were full. Wherever he looked, he saw custard apples and mangoes, guavas and vegetables, with the aroma of hot sweets enticing little boys, while little girls sported glass-bead bangles or eating sticks of sugar cane while their parents haggled with goldsmiths who worked on tiny scales. It was a scene of vibrant colour and life, with itinerant merchant and a dancing bear, children darting everywhere and rangy dogs snarling and fighting amongst the crowds. A handful of sepoys merged with the rest, talking and laughing as if they belonged. Jack stilled the anger he felt when he saw the mutineers.

'Your time will come,' he promised himself. 'We'll round you up and have you dancing at the end of a rope.'

'What was that, Jack?' Mary asked.

'I didn't say anything.'

'You were talking to yourself in English. Be careful.'

A wounded warrior limped past, with bloody bandages around his head and leg. Jack nodded in satisfaction. He didn't like human suffering but listening to the pandies torturing and mutilating one of the 113th had killed any lingering sympathy he had held for the mutineers. In some way, it had been worse than the well at Cawnpore.

'I can't see any woman warriors,' Jack said.

'Did you think Jayanti would come to the bazaar to buy her bread and fruit?' Mary's sharp tones revealed her inner strain. 'Now stay with me and keep quiet.'

Walking to a crowd of woman around a stall, Mary began to talk to them, with Jack feeling out of place. A passing sepoy glanced at him, and Jack glared back, hoping to intimidate. The sepoy spat on the ground and walked on.

Mary took hold of his arm. 'It's all right, Jack, they will think I'm your wife, or at least your woman.' She kept her voice low.

'Did you learn anything?'

Mary guided Jack to a corner of the wall, stinking with urine and spices. 'I said that I was glad there were some female warriors and not only men, who seemed to run away every time the British fired their guns.'

'Did it work?'

'Oh, yes,' Mary smiled. 'If one wants to make friends with a woman, all one has to do is insult men. It creates an instant bond that transcends race, religion or nationality. It's an international sisterhood.'

'What did you find out?'

'They are only low caste women, so they're not highly educated,' Mary began. 'They told me that Jayanti is in the fort and will drive the British away without any help from the men.'

'That was quick work,' Jack said. He sighed. 'You did well, Mary.'

'Speaking the language helps,' Mary said. 'Honestly, Jack, I don't know what you were thinking of trying to come here alone.'

Jack grunted, ignoring his blinding headache and the dizzy spells that were becoming more frequent by the hour. He found it hard to do anything, let alone think. 'I was doing my duty,' he said. 'Let's have a look at the fort.'

From the outside, Gondabad Fort was ugly, with granite walls twenty feet thick pierced by ten gates and a deep moat. On the north side, the wall rose perpendicular from its granite base, while on the south the gates opened directly into the city.

'It's strong.' Jack had passed the fort many times when the 113th had garrisoned Gondabad. 'I hadn't realised how big it is.'

'It's fifteen acres in area.' Mary surprised him with her knowledge. 'The Chandela kings were here for centuries, and the Rajputs strengthened it centuries ago, and then the Moghuls captured it. I heard that thousands died in the siege and sack of the city.'

'And then we took it,' Jack said.

'No, we didn't,' Mary said. 'We always had an agreement with the Rajah, so he retained power as an ally or rather a client, of the British.'

'I hadn't realised that.' Jack gave her a little bow to acknowledge her scholarship. 'We were not allowed to approach the fort. The Rajah had an arrangement with the army.' He shrugged. 'It was all very mysterious.'

'I don't know what happened when the mutineers took the city,' Mary said.

'Whatever happened, Sir Colin or Hugh Rose will capture the fort and city.' Jack swayed as another bout of dizziness swept over him.

'Jack? Are you all right?' Mary sounded concerned.

'I'm fine.' Jack tried to concentrate on the fort. With its defended gateways and round towers, even Sir Colin's well-equipped army would have difficulty storming such a place.

'Are we going in?' Mary stared at the imposing walls.

'What is there that a bold man will not dare?' Jack misquoted the Bold Buccleuch. 'I'm going in. You are going back to the camp to tell Lieutenant Elliot what you've discovered.'

'No.' Mary shook her head. 'I'm not leaving you alone here. You're not well.'

'I'm fine,' Jack said.

'Don't lie to me, Jack Baird Windrush,' Mary hissed. 'You're not thinking straight. The best thing for you would be to get back to the camp and let Elliot take over.'

'No!' Shaking his head increased the pain. 'I'm going into the fort.'

'And what will you do when you get there?'

'Kill Jayanti.' The words were out before Jack could stop them.

Mary stared at him. 'Jack! You are not thinking at all! Even if you get in, you'll never get close to her, and the second you kill her they'll kill you!'

Jack shrugged. 'That's all right. Elliot is quite capable of getting you and the men back safely. He's a better officer than I am.'

'And how about me when you are gone?' Mary asked.

'I said that Elliot would get you back safely.' Jack was unsure what point Mary was trying to make.

'How about us, Jack?'

'Us?' Jack hadn't expected that question.

'Us – you and me?'

Jack stared at her. 'I thought you didn't wish to marry a soldier.'

'Oh, for goodness sake, Jack!' Mary visibly controlled her temper. 'All right, we'll discuss this later, not in a bazaar full of mutineers.'

Even Jack saw the sense of that. He winced as his dizziness returned. 'You get back to camp,' he said.

'No, Jack. We will stay together. Somebody has to look after you.' Mary shook her head, muttering about men who wanted to be spies without knowing a single word of the language.

'We'll try up here.' Mary indicated a long narrow street. 'It leads to one of the smaller gates into the fort.' She gave a half smile. 'Come along, Captain Jack.' Turning, Mary smiled over her shoulder and stepped ahead.

Jack saw the hand reach from a doorway to wrap around Mary's mouth. He lunged forward, just as a tall sepoy appeared from an alley and blocked his view. Pushing the man aside, Jack saw another, and then a naik with greying hair and neat whiskers stood in his path.

'No, Windrush sahib,' the naik said.

Momentarily forgetting his role, Jack stared at the naik. 'You saved my life back in that village. How the devil do you know my name? Get out of my way!' Producing his revolver, Jack aimed directly at the man's face. 'Move aside, damn you!'

There were other men around him, sepoys with brown eyes and oiled whiskers, some wounded, others in smart uniforms. Jack struggled to get through. He saw someone drag Mary backwards and swore, squeezed the trigger and heard the shot.

The darkness was sudden and complete as somebody dropped a hood over his head. Jack shouted and felt somebody grab his wrist. He fired again, unable to see anything, aware that he was in the midst of a group of mutineers and only concerned for the safety of Mary.

Not sure what was happening, he kicked out as somebody lifted him. Many hands closed on him, carrying him away from the alley. Jack shouted into the stifling darkness, squeezed the trigger and heard only a frustrating click as the hammer fell on an empty chamber.

The next few minutes were a blur as the mutineers carried him inside some large building. He heard the different sound as their footsteps echoed from stone and felt the jerky movement as they ran up a flight of steps.

'Put me down, damn you!' Jack shouted. The hood muffled his words. He sensed a change in atmosphere and guessed that they were indoors, and then whoever carried him lowered him gently onto a soft surface.

'You are safe, sahib,' the naik's voice sounded and the bag removed from his head.

'What the devil?' Jack looked around him. The naik and his sepoys were withdrawing through an arched door, and he was alone in the most luxurious bedroom he had ever seen in his life.

The bed was lower than Jack was used to, and much larger, with a padded silk coverlet in vibrant red and gold. Persian carpets covered the floor while rich silks covered the walls, except for the four small pointed windows. Scented candles infused the air with a heady perfume that Jack couldn't help but inhale.

Cringing at the pain any movement caused him Jack stood up and moved to the windows. They were too small to allow him to leave and too high up even if he did. He looked out on the city of Gondabad far below.

'What the deuce is going on?' He asked himself. 'I'd expected to be taken to some dungeon or a torture chamber.' *Where is Mary?*

A bottle stood on a small table at the side of the bed, with a single crystal glass and a bowl of fruit. Suspecting poison, Jack ignored both bottle and fruit. He tried the door. It was locked, and his captors had taken away his pistol and Khyber Knife.

What do I do now? More importantly, where is Mary?

The door opened, and a small man with a neat beard, silk robes and a large turban stepped in.

'Who are you?' Jack backed away, searching for a weapon.

'Muhammed Khan,' the man answered at once. 'Who are you?'

'I think you already know that,' Jack said. 'I am Captain Jack Windrush of the 113th Foot.'

Khan's smile would have shamed a hunting tiger. 'Thank you, Captain Windrush. What is your full name?' He had a soft, cultured voice.

'What has that to do with you?' Jack asked. 'You've captured me, a British officer; now do whatever it is you do to prisoners.' He remembered the screams outside the camp and Keane's mutilated head and felt sick.

'If it was up to me,' Khan spoke with hardly a trace of an accent, 'I would hand you to the women to be castrated and burned alive. However, it is not up to me.'

'Who is it up to?' Jack asked.

'What is your full name?' Khan repeated. 'Be careful how you answer for your future depends on your words. If you give the right answer, then your treatment will be kind. If you give the wrong answer, then I will have charge of you. What is your full name?'

Fighting the pain in his head, Jack stood to attention. 'Captain Jack Baird Windrush, 113th Foot.'

Khan smiled again. 'Good. We have the right man. I will send in a doctor in a minute.'

'Wait!' Jack said. 'How about Mary?'

'I don't know a Mary.' Khan closed the door.

'You kidnapped her!' Jack shouted in frustration. He kicked the door, swearing. 'Let me out of here!'

'What's all the noise, Captain Sahib?' The man who entered was young, with almond-shaped eyes and a wispy beard. He carried a small leather bag.

'You have Mary,' Jack said. 'You kidnapped my woman.'

'No,' the young man said. 'Nobody kidnapped your woman. The half-caste who came with you is not in the fort.'

Jack took a deep breath. It seemed that the mutineers knew all about him. 'Who are you?'

'I am Khitab Gul,' the man said. 'Doctor Khitab Gul.'

'You speak excellent English.'

'I know. I also speak French, Spanish and Italian as well as native languages. Call me Doctor Khitab and lie back.'

'Why?'

'You have been wounded twice recently,' Doctor Khitab said. 'Once on your right wrist and once on your head.'

'How the deuce do you know that?' Jack tried to sit up, only for Doctor Khitab to push him back down on the bed.

'We've been watching you, Captain Windrush. Lie still please.' The doctor's hands were gentle as they examined Jack's head. 'Have you experienced any headaches, captain? Dizziness? Lack of concentration?'

'All of those,' Jack said.

'Yes. That was a nasty crack on the head. Your skull is not broken, fortunately. You also suffer from much nervous tension. You need rest and sleep, which you will not find inside the camp of the 113th. It's all right, captain, Lieutenant Elliot is taking good care of your men although Private Carruthers has gone down with dysentery.'

'How…?'

'Oh, we know far more than you realise, captain. Now lie still and drink this.' The doctor poured a small glass of something. 'It's all right, captain. It's just to help you sleep.'

'I don't want to sleep, damn it!'

'I know you don't want to captain, but you do need to.' Doctor Khitab held the glass to Jack's lips. 'It is all right, captain. It will help you and when you wake you will feel much better.'

Jack drank the liquid. He saw the doctor's smile broaden and then fade.

When Jack awoke, his headache was gone. He stretched on the bed, looked around at the room and felt better than he had for weeks. 'I could get used to this,' he told himself as sunlight seeped through the small windows to land on the beautiful carpets.

'You are feeling better.' Doctor Khitab was sitting at the side of the bed. 'Good. You do not rest enough, Captain Windrush. You need weeks of rest and sleep, not merely one day and one night. First, you need a wash, a barber and a change of clothes.'

'I'm fine,' Jack said. 'What is all this for? I'm your prisoner, where am I, and where is Mary?'

'Oh, no, Captain Windrush, sahib.' The doctor salaamed. 'So many questions! You are not a prisoner. On the contrary, you are our most honoured guest in the Fort of Gondabad.'

'I'm your enemy, damn it,' Jack said.

The doctor's laugh would have been heart-warming in different circumstances. 'Would you rather we treated you like the British treat their enemies? Do you wish us to hang you, sahib? Or blow you from the muzzle of a cannon, perhaps?'

'I'm no mutineer,' Jack defended what he knew to be the truth. 'I was never disloyal to the Queen.'

The doctor salaamed again. 'That, at least, is correct, Windrush sahib. You are no mutineer, and you were never disloyal to your queen. Now if you will follow me, please?'

'Why? Is Mary there?'

'Please, sahib.' Doctor Khitab's smile didn't waver. 'I assure you we mean you no harm. On the contrary, we can help you find everything your heart desires.'

Jack tensed himself, ready to try and escape. The doctor opened the door wider, to reveal two muscular Rajputs, with long pistols thrust through sashes and tulwars held ready. They looked as if they knew what they were doing.

'Lead on, MacDuff,' Jack said. 'I suppose there's no help for it.'

'There is no help at all, Windrush, sahib,' Doctor Khitab said.

With an armed Rajput warrior a few yards in front and another at his back, Jack knew that escape would be impossible as the doctor led him through a succession of corridors. From his impressions of the exterior, he had expected the fort to be a bare, bleak place of stone walls and austerity. Instead, the interior was more luxurious than anything he had seen in his life. Silk hangings decorated the painted walls, sticks of incense wafted perfume through the air, oil lamps provided light between the ornate windows, and he walked on Afghan and Persian carpets that would cost more than a humble captain earned in five years. There were cushions of Bokhara silk, bed covers of Sind cotton and decorations of the Tree of Life with capering monkeys. All was light, gaiety, and colour.

'In here, Windrush, sahib.'

After the splendour of the corridor, the chamber was surprisingly bare, with a small drain in the middle of a stone-flagged floor and arched glazed windows with little décor. Three wiry old men stood beside three tubs of water.

'What's this?' Jack asked. 'Some form of torture?'

'No, Sahib. It is some form of washing.'

As the Rajput warriors took up positions on either side of the door, the elderly men stepped forward and gently removed Jack's clothes. Smiling, they led him to the centre of the room.

'What's to do?'

'We don't sit in a tub to bathe, Captain Windrush sahib.' The doctor shook his head. 'We think that is strange, having one's dirt splashing all around us. Stand still.'

One by one, the three elderly men dipped beakers of water into the tubs and emptied cool water over Jack. He stood there, determined not to admit that this Indian bathing method was superior to the British.

'Now you are cleansed for the day. Do you wish to pray?' Doctor Khitab asked. 'It is an Indian custom.'

'Maybe later.' Jack looked for his clothes. A white-coated servant presented him with a new set, with white cotton trousers and jacket and a simple yellow turban.

'Put them on, Windrush sahib,' Doctor Khitab said. 'When the *Angrez* first came to this land, they adopted our dress and our customs, and many married our women. We were like one people. Now there is a gulf between us.'

The clothes were soft, clean and very comfortable compared to Jack's habitual stiff uniform.

'Good, Windrush sahib. Now follow me.'

Once more into the corridor with the silent Rajput escort, the doctor led Jack down a flight of marble stairs into a large room. Brought up believing that England was the pinnacle of civilisation and that his family home of Wychwood Manor compared to anywhere in the world, Jack could only stare at the majesty of the room. He had been in a few Indian palaces and forts during this war, but only in the aftermath of cannon fire and siege. The shambles of a palace during wartime could not remotely compare to the splendour of this room.

'This is the minor Durbar room,' the doctor said. 'You may know that the name durbar can mean a state reception, or the hall in which such events take place.'

Jack ignored the lecture as he gazed at the Durbar room. Ornate plasterwork embellished every surface of the walls and ceiling, dominated by symbols of Ganesha, the elephant god that brought good fortune. One wall carried three depictions of peacocks while sticks of incense and masses of flowers sweetened the air. As with the corridor, a carpet covered the floor, so luxurious that Jack felt his slippered feet sinking into it. An ivory screen hid the furthest corner of the room, behind which an orchestra played evocative Indian music.

These details barely distracted from the two people who sat at the head of the room, watching Jack as he walked in. Five marble steps led to their ornate thrones, with their armrests carved into the likeness of leopards, whose snarling faces intimidated those who approached. The seat and back were of padded silk, while on either side sat marble tigers, so realistic that Jack wondered at the skill of the sculptor.

'The Rajah and Rani of Gondabad,' the doctor spoke in hushed tones.

The Rajah sat upright, with long robes from neck to ankles and a sarpech set with diamonds and emeralds in his turban. His fourteen-strand necklace of natural pearls must have weighed ten pounds while his clothes glittered with gold, and rings gleamed on his fingers. His face was serene, with a neat white beard and mobile brown eyes that never strayed from Jack.

Beside him, the Rani was quieter and much plainer in a simple white silk sari, while a plain muslin dupatta covered her head. Jack guessed her age at about twenty-eight, much younger than her husband, and she stared at Windrush without expression. Smoke from the incense created a slight haze around the thrones, so the faces and persons of the Rajah and Rani were blurred, nearly ethereal as if lesser mortals should not view them.

Jack hesitated, feeling very much out of place. If he had been in uniform, he would have known how to act. In his Indian clothes, he was a stranger, a part-Indian foreigner, an interloper in a world about which he knew nothing.

'Approach.' The Rani spoke in a low clear tone.

As Jack walked forward, he became aware of the guards. The opulence of this Durbar room had astonished him, so he had not seen the dozen or so stalwart men in chain mail and steel helmets that stood against the walls.

'I am Captain Jack Windrush of the 113th Foot.' Jack announced. He bowed, straightened up and waited to see what would happen next. If what he had heard of Indian royalty was correct, they could order him trampled by elephants, immured forever in a dungeon or any other sort of horror.

'Why are you here, Captain Windrush?' The Rani spoke in English, with an attractive singsong accent.

'I am searching for a murderer.' Jack decided to speak the truth. These people already knew all about him so it would be foolish to lie. He straightened his back. Whatever clothes he happened to be wearing, he was a British officer and gentleman, and he was damned if any foreign princeling would intimidate him. 'Her name is Jayanti, and she has murdered British soldiers.'

'Why did you not come through official channels?' the Rani asked. 'Why did you choose to come sneaking into our home like a thief?'

'I did not think you would see me,' Jack said. 'India is disturbed at present with the misguided actions of some of our sepoy regiments. I was unsure whether you wished to compromise your security by accepting a message from a junior British officer.'

The Rajah and Rani exchanged a private conversation for a few moments before the Rani spoke again. 'Where should our loyalties lie, Captain Windrush?'

'Your loyalties should lie with the British,' Jack said.

'Why?' Although the Rani's voice was gentle, there was no mistaking the steel behind her question.

'To ensure peace and stability and a fair system of justice.' Jack couldn't think of any other answer. He wished that Elliot were here, with his quick mind and capacity for more profound thought.

'The British have been in India for two hundred and fifty years,' the Rani said. 'During that time there have been wars and conquest and a lack of stability.'

Jack thought quickly. 'There was warfare and conquest and instability before the British arrived,' he said. 'And beyond the British frontier, there is still warfare and conquest and instability. Better to retain British protection than to return to anarchy, where states fought states, Muslim fought Sikh and Hindus and the law depended on bribery rather than legality.'

The Rajah and Rani conferred again, both glancing at Jack from time to time before the Rani spoke again. 'Then why is there war again within the British area of peace, stability and justice?'

'The sepoys, the Indian soldiers of Britain, have broken their oath,' Jack said. 'They have believed lies told against their masters and have attacked the hand that fed them. Others have joined in, the malcontents, evil men and women.' He paused. 'I believe that Jayanti, one of those evil women, a murderess of the worst kind, is within your Majesty's dominions now. I think she is hiding, ready to cause trouble and spread violence among your loyal subjects.'

Are these two playing with me? Jack wondered. *Are they teasing me, before they kill me? Or are these questions genuine?* The scent of the incense was more powerful now, making Jack's head swim so that he saw the Rajah and Rani through a thickening haze, while the Indian music was a distraction.

'If we help the British, how will the British reward us?' the Rani asked.

'You will have done your duty.' Jack gave the answer that would most appeal to a British officer and then paused to consider what an Indian prince most wished. 'The British would ensure that you maintain your position as Rajah and Rani of Gondabad.'

What more can I say?

'If we help the enemies of the British, what will happen?' The Rani's voice was unemotional, as if she was discussing a menu with her servants.

'The British will surely quell this mutiny,' Jack said what he believed. 'The British have already reconquered Delhi and put the rebels to the sword. Sir Colin Campbell has recaptured Lucknow and wreaked vengeance on the mutineers and rebels there. The British know that your majesties are loyal and that the troubles in Gondabad were against your wishes. They will not blame you for what has happened. However, if your majesties join the forces of evil and discontent, Sir Colin Campbell or Hugh Rose will surely capture your city and lay siege to your fort. There will be death and disaster and much slaughter, as there was in Delhi and Lucknow.'

Jack took a deep breath. He hadn't spoken so much in his life. *Am I too forceful with my threats?*

The Rajah and Rani conferred again, and the Rani flicked her finger. 'You may go now, Captain Windrush.'

Doctor Khitab took hold of Jack's arm and ushered him to a side door, with the two Rajputs a few steps behind him. The Rani's voice followed him. 'Take him to the other one.'

'The other one? Who is the other one? Is that Mary? Do you have Mary here?' When Jack tried to ask questions, one of the Rajputs shoved him onward.

'Keep quiet, Captain Windrush, sahib. It is rude to question royalty,' Doctor Khitab said. 'All will be revealed for he who is patient.'

'What is this all about?'

'Have patience, Captain Windrush sahib.' Doctor Khitab patted his shoulder. 'Everything is as it should be; you are a guest among friends.'

Leaving the Durbar room, they marched along what seemed like miles of passages, along which an army of servants hurried without a word or a sound. The luxury gradually faded until Jack's surroundings were merely lavish and there were warriors among the servants. There was no mistaking the two different types of people, with men carrying swords and shields, spears and muskets. One or two were bandaged or scarred, veterans of skirmish, siege or battle.

'In here, Captain Windrush, sahib.' Doctor Khitab stopped before a massive door studded with iron. 'I hope your mind is clear.'

'My mind? What do you mean?'

The doctor didn't respond to Jack's questions as one Rajput opened the door and the other propelled Jack inside the chamber.

CHAPTER ELEVEN

While the Durbar room had been about opulence and luxury, only warriors occupied this room. The floor was stone-flagged and the walls bereft of any decoration except an array of spears and fearsome looking daggers. A rack of tulwars sat beneath unglazed windows while another of long jezzails stretched to a plain wooden table around which sat a group of men.

They watched Jack step in.

They were warriors with quick movements and smooth muscles, hard eyes and the direct stare of men who were not afraid to act. Three reached for swords, and another with a spiked helmet lifted a long pistol that he had been loading.

'*Ram ram*,' Jack said and waited for a response. Alone and unarmed, he knew he would not stand a chance if these men attacked him. He also knew that he would fight and neither run nor surrender.

The warriors spoke quietly as the man with the spiked helmet pointed his pistol at Jack. Suspecting that they were discussing his immediate death, Jack marched toward them.

One man stood up. In his early thirties, he was round-faced and black haired, slightly overweight with a small beard and sharp, round eyes. Shaking his head, he pushed the pistol back on the table and turned over a large hourglass. Sand began to trickle from the upper to the lower container. The man's smile was friendlier than Jack had expected as he spoke in perfect English.

'You are welcome, Captain Jack Baird Windrush of Her Majesty's 113th Foot.'

Jack nodded. 'Thank you. You have the advantage of me. I do not know to whom I am speaking.'

'I am Dhondu Pant, a Peshwa of the old Maratha Empire. You may know me better as Nana Sahib.'

'Dear God!' Jack reached for the sword he no longer had. 'Nana Sahib!'

Nana Sahib was the warrior and aristocrat who had fostered and led the rebellion in Cawnpore, the man ultimately responsible for the murder of hundreds of

British men, women and children. This smiling, urbane man was the arch-enemy of British rule in India.

The others at the table jumped to their feet, most reaching for swords or pistols.

'Peace, *bhaiyas*, peace, brothers,' Nana Sahib calmed them down in Urdu and English. 'Captain Windrush is no threat to me or you. He has no weapons and has even adopted our way of dress.'

The warriors sat back down, with only the man in the spiked helmet continuing to glare at Jack. '*Barnshoot Firinghi*' – "incestuous foreigner", he said, until Nana Sahib waved him to silence.

'You seem surprised to see me, Captain Windrush, and I do not know why. After all, this is my land, and these are my people.'

'Gondabad is not part of the old Maratha Empire.' Jack forced aside his hatred.

'It was once,' Nana Sahib said.

'You are a traitor, a rebel and a murderer.' Jack wondered if he could jump across and strangle Nana Sahib before his followers chopped him to pieces. *No, these warriors are alert and experienced. I would merely throw away my life.*

Nana Sahib smiled. 'Insults from an enemy are as sweet as compliments from a friend. Are you an enemy, Captain Windrush?'

'You became the enemy of my people the moment you turned against us.' Jack tried to remain calm. He watched the slowly emptying hourglass and wondered what its function might be.

'I could say that your people became my enemy the moment they turned against me,' Nana Sahib countered.

'Why am I here?' Jack asked.

'To learn.' Nana Sahib's smile faded. 'Sit down, captain,' he indicated a chair opposite him at the table.

'Why me?'

'There are reasons,' Nana Sahib said. 'Now listen.'

Jack sat down, acutely aware that the man in the spiked helmet moved the position of his pistol so that the muzzle pointed directly at his chest.

'I'm listening.'

'You think I am a monster,' Nana Sahib said.

'I think you are a treasonous murdering traitor.' Jack guessed that Nana Sahib would shortly order his death. He had nothing to gain by attempting to be pleasant.

'Listen to my story.' Nana Sahib did not appear in the slightest annoyed by Jack's reaction. 'You will know about Badgee Rao, the old Peshwa of the Mahrattas?'

'I know the name,' Jack admitted. 'He was a good man and a loyal friend of the British.'

'And how did the British repay that loyalty?' Nana Sahib's voice remained calm and smooth. 'They repaid it with deceit and robbery. Badgee Rao gave his assistance to the East India Company when they warred with Tippoo Sahib, the Tiger of Serangipatam in 1799. The East India Company won that war, and how did they reward Badgee Rao?'

'I do not know,' Jack admitted.

'Then allow me to educate you.' Nana Sahib's voice remained calm. 'The Company made treaties with Badgee Rao, broke their word on many occasions and in 1817, they grabbed his lands. After fighting against the might of the Company, Badgee Rao eventually led his army to face General Sir John Malcolm's force, with the Deccan as the prize. Malcolm sent in a flag of truce and proposed that Badgee

Rao should renounce his sovereignty and surrender with his family and some adherents and attendants.'

'That would save needless slaughter.' Jack defended the British general.

'The British offered to respect Badgee Rao and his people and locate them in Benares or any other holy city. They offered a pension to Badgee Rao and his family and promised to provide for his attached adherents. The pension for Badgee and his family was to be at least eight lacs of rupees a year.'

Jack did a rapid calculation. 'That's about £80,000, a very fair offer.'

'Quite a sizeable sum,' Nana Sahib agreed. 'However, when he was an old man, Badgee Rao was still childless.' He stopped. 'Badgee Rao adopted me as his son and heir. He died in 1851 and immediately the Governor-General, Lord Dalhousie cancelled the pension the Honourable East India Company had guaranteed. My family and I were reduced to poverty.'

'I see.' Jack wondered how a man reduced to poverty could be as plump and sleek as Nana Sahib. 'So your revolt and all the deaths and suffering are due to your desire for more British money.'

For the first time, Nana Sahib showed some emotion. A flicker of anger crossed his face. He continued.

'I asked the Lieutenant Governor of the North West Provinces to reconsider Lord Dalhousie's judgement. In return, the Company granted me a few acres of land for life. The British Commissioner of Bithoor, an honest man, issued an urgent appeal on my behalf and the Company severely reprimanded him. I contacted the Court of Directors in Leadenhall Street. They issued a reply a year later, telling me to try the Indian government. I did that with no response.'

Jack said nothing. Having lost any title to his lands in England through illegitimacy, he could understand some of Nana Sahib's sense of injustice. The lower section of the hourglass was now three-quarters full.

'The lands that Badgee Rao ceded in 1802, 1817 and 1818 gave the East India Company a million pounds a year in revenue.' Nana Sahib continued. 'I have a few paltry rupees.'

'So your rebellion is about money, then,' Jack said. 'It isn't about religion or Indian nationalism or race.'

'I am protesting about British injustice,' Nana Sahib said.

Jack nodded. Do you mean British injustice to those who would like to rule or British injustice to those who the old rulers oppressed? Do you mean the injustice of suppressing suttee and of ending thugee, the injustice of not accepting bribes and of one law for rich and poor?' Jack knew he was playing with fire.

Nana Sahib sat down. 'Your family connections led me to believe there was hope for you, Captain Windrush. I see I was wrong.' He grasped the hourglass just as the top section emptied. 'Take him away!'

What family connections? Jack was about to speak when three Rajput guards entered the room and hustled him away into the corridor outside.

CHAPTER TWELVE

Jack tried to follow their route as the Rajputs dragged him out of the chamber and down a flight of stairs. The walls were bare of decoration, the steps worn by the passage of many feet and the air progressively fouler. They stopped at a long corridor poorly lit by torches, barged through a narrow door and plunged downward again to a vast area with what seemed a score of open arches. One of the guards had taken a torch from the wall, and its flickering light illuminated a series of stone chambers, some large, some small.

The guards moved in silence, not responding to Jack's demands that they release him until they arrived at a weighty, iron-studded door. One Rajput turned the key in the lock, and the others dragged him inside. The guards shoved Jack against a granite wall and fastened manacles around his ankles and wrists. Checking his chains to ensure they were secure, the Rajputs left, slamming the door. Jack heard the key rasp in the lock.

Oh, dear God, what happens now?

Jack lay against the wall, hearing something rustle in his dungeon, a rat or insect maybe, and closed his eyes. A few hours ago, he had woken in a luxurious apartment with a gentle doctor treating his injuries. Since then he had met a Rajah and a Rani and then, one of the deadliest enemies of British India. Now his enemies had entombed him in a filthy dungeon. Had they tested him in some way? If so, he must have failed.

The mysteries remained. Jack wondered how the rebels knew his name and so much about him. Why had they singled out him for attention? There were many far more distinguished officers than him, men who had made their name in half a dozen campaigns, men who were famous far outside the often-claustrophobic confines of the British Army. Why had the rebels not captured one of them? Was he merely more vulnerable because he led a small party? Jack shook his head. By walking into Gondabad he had virtually placed himself into their hands, and now – he rattled the chains in futility – he must pay the price.

I wonder what fate they have in mind for me. Will they have elephants trample me to death? Will I be tortured with tiger-claws and blinded?

Jack took a deep breath. Whatever happened, he had tried to do his duty. That was his only consolation for an abortive campaign to remove Jayanti, and his failure to care for Mary.

The rustling continued, and something ran over his legs. Jack started and jerked aside. The creature fled with sharp claws scraping him. Jack closed his eyes, trying to garner strength through sleep.

He didn't know how much time had elapsed before another three Rajput guards arrived with a torch. While one man held the torch high, another released Jack from his chains. The second Rajput grunted and pointed to Jack, indicating that he should follow them.

'By God,' Jack said. 'Not until you tell me where we are going.'

The Rajputs said nothing, merely prodded at Jack with the point of a tulwar, which was a sufficiently strong hint to follow. 'I am a British officer,' he said. His guards didn't look impressed as they shoved him toward the door, helping him along with repeated jabs with the tulwar.

After what seemed an interminable journey along dark passages and up flights of stone steps, the Rajputs stopped at a heavily studded door, outside which stood one of Jayanti's female warriors. Jack eyed her, noting the black turban and the veil across the lower part of her face. She scrutinised him in return, touching the tulwar she wore at her waist. When Jack saw that she didn't wear a ruby ring on her left hand, he lost interest.

The Rajputs stepped aside, and the female warrior rapped on the door and pushed it open.

Jack stepped inside, into a different world.

He didn't know what he'd expected, either a torture chamber or a military barracks. Instead, he entered a light and airy room where birds flew around a tracery of foliage and sunlight dappled the Persian carpet on the floor. A mirror on one wall enhanced the size of the room, while the crystal chandelier hung like draping diamonds from the high ceiling.

Two more female guards stood against a wall of light bamboo, and directly opposite him, sitting at a beautifully carved ivory table, Jayanti sat on an armed chair, with her veil in place and her turban pulled low over her forehead.

'Welcome, Captain Windrush.' She indicated a chair on the other side of the table. 'Please join me. Would you care for a drink? I can offer you wine, whisky, rum, *nimbu pani, aam pani,* coconut water, *toddy* or water.'

Jack became aware of his thirst, and for some reason, he wished he'd washed and shaved before meeting Jayanti. 'Just water, please.' He watched as Jayanti clapped her hands and gave quiet instructions to a smooth-faced servant, who returned in a few moments with a brass jug and two small brass cups. Jayanti filled both cups with water.

'Take one,' she invited, 'and I will drink the other.'

Jack selected one at random. 'I doubt you have brought me here only to poison me,' he said. 'You could have killed me at any time from the moment you had me kidnapped.'

Jayanti lifted her veil sufficiently to drink.

The water was sweet, cool and very welcome. 'Is Mary safe?' Jack asked.

'I do not know,' Jayanti said. The veil muffled her voice slightly.

'You kidnapped her,' Jack accused.

'I did not,' Jayanti responded.

'Why have you brought me here?'

Jayanti eyed Jack across the table. 'Have you heard of the game of chess, Captain Windrush?'

'I have,' Jack responded.

'Have you ever played chess, Captain Windrush?'

'I played chess when I was at school,' Jack said. *Those days seem so far away.*

'We shall play.' Jayanti clapped her hands, and two female servants carried in a low marble table and a yellow ivory box. As Jack watched, one servant placed the table on the ground. Skilled hands had carved the ivory into the familiar black-and-white squares of a chessboard. The second servant opened the box and set up pieces that resembled the chess with which Jack was familiar, except that a chariot replaced the rook and an elephant the bishop. Small rubies adorned the crown of the king and queen; tiny emeralds shone for the elephant's eyes.

Jayanti walked across with her trousers rustling and a long dagger in a jewelled sheath at her waist. 'Did you know that chess was invented in Northern India, twelve hundred years ago?'

'I didn't know that,' Jack admitted.

'It spread to Persia and then when the Muslims overran the Persian Empire, they carried the game all over the Islamic world and into Europe.' Jayanti nearly whispered the explanation as she lifted the carved ivory pieces, one by one. 'The rules and the names and function of the pieces have altered through time.' She looked up. 'We will play with Indian pieces, but European rules.'

'I have no desire to play chess,' Jack said.

Jayanti lifted the king. 'This piece was known as the rajah; you know him as the king. In chess, captain, the object is to capture the king. He is the figurehead, while the most powerful player is the queen.' She held the queen in her left hand. 'In the original game, there was no queen, and the equivalent piece was called the *mantri*, or minister. In this case, the Europeans may have improved matters. Ministers, like other politicians, cause trouble while a queen will make a better ruler than any rajah.'

'Gondabad has a Rajah and a Rani,' Jack pointed out.

'I know,' Jayanti said. 'You will sit opposite me, captain, and we will play. Chess is like war, a contest of manoeuvre, nerve and skill, with casualties when one player makes a mistake or a successful gambit.' She sat down gracefully. 'We called chess *chaturaṅga*, which means four divisions, infantry, cavalry, elephantry, and chariotry.'

Jack eyed the pieces. Despite the Indian shapes, he could recognise their function. 'Thank you for the history lesson. I have not played for a long time.'

'Think of it as a battlefield, Captain Windrush,' Jayanti said. 'Now step with me to the window.'

The window overlooked a courtyard where a fountain tinkled, and tamarisk trees provided shade from the sun. Jayanti clapped her hands. 'Bring them in.'

Two lithe female warriors entered, followed by a tall, muscular man grotesquely dressed in what seemed like medieval armour, covered in metal spikes. He balanced a massive curved sword on his right shoulder.

'The man with the sword is my executioner,' Jayanti said casually.

Jack heard the rattle of chains, and then a procession of sixteen tattered men came in, all wearing the scarlet uniforms of British soldiers. He stiffened as more female warriors marched at the rear, pushing at the prisoners until they were all within the courtyard.

'Do you recognise them?' Jayanti asked.

Jack shook his head. 'I can see that they are British soldiers,' he said. 'I expect they are survivors of some garrison the mutineers overran.'

'Look closer, captain.'

Jack frowned, hoping that they weren't the men he'd led this far. He started when he saw the familiar yellow facings. 'They are from the 113th,' he said.

'These are the men from your missing Number One Company,' Jayanti confirmed. 'These are the proud British soldiers of the Queen. They are not proud now, are they? They are not proud after a few months' captivity. Not proud when they surrendered to the pandies that they despised so much.' Her bitterness was evident.

'The British are trying to bring peace to this land.' Even as Jack spoke, he knew it was a lie. He remembered Hook's words about money and power and saw the East India Company in another light, a place for faceless men in London to grow wealthy while British and Indians sweated and suffered and died fighting each other in wars that neither side understood.

'The British.' Jayanti injected scorn into the name. 'I will tell you what it means to live under British rule. It is to eat cows and drink wine. It is to bite greased cartridges and to mix pig's fat with sweetmeats. It is to destroy Hindu and Moslem temples on the pretence of making roads, to build churches and to send clergymen into the streets to preach the Christian religion. It is to institute English schools, and pay people a monthly stipend for learning the English sciences.' She stopped. 'These are not my words, but I believe them to be true.'

Jack nodded. 'I do not believe that the British plan to destroy the native religions of India.'

'Do you not?' Jayanti turned on him. 'And do you believe in British justice?' She nodded to the shackled British soldiers. 'Your generals hanged any prisoners they captured, or blew them from the muzzle of a cannon. As you see, we kept our prisoners alive. Who is the more civilised, Captain Windrush?'

Jack pursed his lips.

'You say nothing, I see.' Jayanti smiled. 'Then let us play, captain. She sat cross-legged at the table, and Jack copied her position.

The board sat between them, with the sun easing through the windows into the pleasant room, and the British prisoners standing in the baking heat of the courtyard, round-shouldered and bareheaded.

'I have not played for years,' Jack said.

'You may start,' Jayanti offered.

'Why are we playing chess?'

'Play,' Jayanti ordered.

Jack moved forward the pawn diagonally to the left of the queen, intending to free her to act as a mobile strike force, rather like the 113th.

Jayanti moved her queen's knight, taking a quick offensive. 'You are cautious, captain, like your commander-in-chief.'

'I hope I am as successful in defeating the enemy.' Jack moved the queen three spaces.

'Yet you are my prisoner, captain.' Jayanti moved her king's knight.

'Temporarily, in a war you have already lost.' Jack moved his king's pawn one space.

'The war is not over.' Jayanti moved her king's knight's pawn.

'Hugh Rose and Colin Campbell will finish it shortly.' Jack moved his king's pawn one space.

Jayanti's smile was as sincere as a hunting cat. She moved another pawn. 'Your British army sneers at General Colin Campbell, saying he is too slow, too cautious.'

Jack frowned. 'He has never lost a battle.' He moved his queen's knight.

'He allowed our men to escape from Lucknow and Bareilly.' Jayanti held Jack's eye and deftly captured a pawn. 'That is one pawn you have lost.' She held it up. 'The first casualty of our little campaign.' Standing up, Jayanti walked to the window. 'Join me, captain.'

Jack didn't see the two warrior-women move. One stood on his right, the other behind him, with a knife pressed against his spine.

The prisoners still stood in the broiling sun.

Jayanti leant out of the window. 'One pawn.'

The women in the courtyard shifted slightly. One lifted a hand in acknowledgement.

'Choose a private, captain,' Jayanti said and only then did Jack realise that the body of men below were divided into two halves. Eight were privates, and eight were NCOs and junior officers.

'Why?'

'You have lost a pawn,' Jayanti said patiently. 'Which private will you take out of the sun?'

'Oh.' Jack pointed to a man at random. 'That fair-haired fellow.'

Jayanti shouted something, and two of her warriors released the fair-haired private to a small space, away from the others. Without a word, they forced him to his knees.

'What the devil...' Jack said, as the executioner stepped forward with his sword still balanced on his shoulder. 'You murdering bitch, Jayanti!'

With a supreme effort, the private jerked to his feet. He saw the executioner approach with the gigantic sword, waited and spat straight in the man's face. Chained hand and foot, he could manage no other gesture of defiance. The executioner waited as two more female warriors helped drag the soldier down to a kneeling position. One woman grabbed the soldier's hair with both hands and pulled his head forward, and another tore back his uniform, exposing the neck.

Jack watched, feeling sick as the executioner rested the blade of his sword on the soldier's neck, swung the weapon back, braced himself and sliced down. The soldier's head sprung clear from his body and blood jetted from his neck.

'And you lose a pawn,' Jayanti said. 'Shall we return to the game?'

Shaken, Jack sat back down. 'Was that murder necessary?'

'We are both soldiers, as was that private. He knew that a soldier's life ends in death. What difference is it, if he dies in glorious battle or at the edge of an executioner's sword? All our decisions have consequences, Captain Windrush. If you play badly, then you lose a man.'

'And if I play well? Do I watch your chief murderer decapitate one of your warriors?'

Jayanti shook her head. 'No, Captain Windrush. If you capture one of my pieces, I free one of your men from today's possibility of death.'

Jack nodded. 'I see. And if I win the game?'

'If you defeat me, all your surviving men return to their cell for today. It is quite simple.' Jayanti's smile was calm. 'And tomorrow we start again, with the same rules.'

'You're a murdering, evil blackguard,' Jack said.

'Perhaps. Even so, I give your men a chance. Your army executes their prisoners, innocent or not. It is your move, I believe.'

After another three moves, it was evident that Jayanti was the better player. Jack sat in a fever of anxiety as he tried to block her attacks, watched her effortlessly blunt his offensives and hoped desperately to capture some of her pieces to save at least a few of the prisoners.

'Another pawn.' Jayanti lifted the piece in triumph. 'Would you like to accompany me, captain?'

'I would not,' Jack said.

'Then my soldiers will persuade you.'

Sword in hand, the two female warriors closed around Jack, and he rose and stepped to the window. The procedure was the same as before, except that the private seemed resigned to his death as the women forced him to kneel. The executioner used the same apparently casual swing, and the man's head rolled on the stone-flagged floor. The tinkling cheerfulness of the fountain was almost an insult to the men who remained.

Jack made two more trips to the window before he saw an opening and managed to capture one of Jayanti's pawns.

'Well played, captain.' Jayanti applauded with a soft handclap. 'Now choose which man will live for another day.'

It was as hard to select a man to live, as it was to point to a man for the executioner to kill. 'Oh, God forgive me,' Jack breathed as he chose a red-haired, snub-nosed youngster. 'That fellow there,' he said.

Thinking he was about to be executed, the man struggled desperately as two women grabbed him. Jack could not watch as the women dragged him away.

'Now, shall we continue?' Jayanti sounded nonchalant.

Knowing Jayanti outmatched him, Jack dispensed with caution and threw himself recklessly into the attack. By a minor miracle, he managed to capture Jayanti's queen's knight.

'You have my knight,' Jayanti said. 'That will save the life of a sergeant.'

Jack captured two more pawns and the king's rook before Jayanti put him into checkmate.

'I am sure you will try to improve by tomorrow.' When Jayanti clapped her hands, a servant tidied away the chess pieces. 'Or you will lose more of your men.' She looked up, her eyes gleaming. 'We will raise the stakes tomorrow, I think. Your Major Snodgrass will act as king.'

Jack said nothing. The thought of the slaughter in the courtyard sickened him. 'Now I can understand Hussaini Begum,' he said. 'Before I met you, I wondered how a woman could order the murder of innocents, could allow children to be dismembered and stuffed into a well. Now, having seen the cold-blooded manner in which you ordered the murder of these men, I understand. You are devoid of humanity.'

Jayanti salaamed. 'Thank you, captain. The insult of an enemy is a compliment indeed. If you give me your word of honour not to escape, I shall order guest apartments to be prepared for you, with all the comforts your heart and body could desire.'

'I will do no such thing, damn you,' Jack said.

'I rather thought you would say that.' Jayanti salaamed again. 'In that case, I am afraid we shall place you in the same rather more austere surroundings from which we fetched you.' She clapped her hands and spoke rapidly. Half a dozen of the female warriors filed in, grabbed hold of Jack and hustled him away. 'Until tomorrow, Captain Windrush,' Jayanti said. 'And let us hope your play is better, for the execution of a king or a major will be, shall we say, more colourful than that of a pawn?'

Back in his chains, Jack relived the executions in the courtyard, the sinister hiss of the sword, the clump of the head landing on stone slabs and the subdued gasp of the other prisoners. He wondered what horror Jayanti had in mind for Major Snodgrass. He remembered Jayanti's quiet, refined voice as she spoke to him and the click of ivory chess pieces on the board. He remembered the babble of voices and the chaos of colour in the bazaar. One image over-rode all others. He found himself reaching forward and mouthing "no" as he thought of the moment that hand snaked out and wrapped around Mary's mouth.

'Mary, where are you?' Jack rattled his chains in frustration. 'I wish to God that I could help you.'

He looked up as his cell door opened and two of the warrior-women entered. As one held up a torch, the other tossed a heavy bag toward him. The door closed with a bang.

'Is that my lunch?' Jack shouted. Only echoes replied.

As his eyes became accustomed to the dark, Jack realised that there was a tiny window, no larger than his hand, high up in the wall. The thin beam of light that entered showed nothing cheerful, only grim granite and rusty chains. Jack stretched forward, lifted the bag that his guards had left, opened the mouth and peered inside. The face of the fair-haired executed man stared at him; blue eyes open and tongue slightly protruding.

'Oh, dear God!' Jack pushed the bag away, and more heads rolled out, some to face the far wall and others to stare at him, as if accusing him of the sin of being a weak chess player.

Jack could not think of a worse time in his life. He had lost Mary. He had allowed the enemy to chain him inside a dungeon. He had watched helplessly as Jayanti's executioner murdered men of the 113th. Jack closed his eyes. *I'm a failure as an officer, and I have failed Mary, leading her into this terrible place.*

The scratching started again, and something ran over his legs. 'Get away!' He kicked out violently, hearing the chains rattle. For a moment he wondered who had been here before, wearing these rusted chains, and what had happened to them. He felt weary; he needed to sleep and closed his eyes. The scratching intensified and something bit at his leg.

'Get away!' He kicked out again. 'What foul things have these rats been feeding on? They're not going to eat me next.' At the same time, Jack knew that if he did not sleep, he would be stupid with weariness the following day and unable to concentrate on the chess game. He would be responsible for the death of more men. He closed his eyes, started as something with sharp claws crawled over his legs and swore softly.

Damn it all; I'm not thinking straight. I am Captain Jack Baird Windrush of the 113th

Foot, I hold the Queen's Commission, and I am not going to die in some damned Indian dungeon. I'm going to get out of here, find Mary, get back to my men and raze this bloody fort to the ground.

Forcing himself upright, Jack inspected his chains. Although the metal was rusty, the links were still too strong to break, and the lock that held them required a key. He traced the chains back to the staple in the wall. Whoever had anchored it knew his business; it didn't budge when he yanked at it. He wouldn't give up though and began to shove the staple this way and that, trying to loosen it from the surrounding stone.

'Captain Windrush!'

The word echoed through his dungeon. Jack jerked his head from side to side. *What new torment is this?* 'Who's there?'

'Captain Windrush! Look up!'

Jack looked up. The sun had sunk so there was no light from the small window. 'Who's that?'

'Look up!'

Jack was wrong. There was a minuscule light flickering at the window. It hovered for a second and then slowly descended, swinging slowly back and forth. Jack watched and reached out when it came close. It was a small lantern on the end of a long rope.

'Got it?' The voice echoed in the granite chamber.

'I have it, thank you.' The echo distorted the sound. 'Who is that?'

'It's Batoor, Captain Windrush.'

'I thought you had deserted!' Jack felt a lift of pleasure. 'What are you doing here?'

'I'm trying to get you out of the dungeon,' Batoor said.

'I'm chained to the wall,' Jack said.

'Take the light and send back the rope.'

When Jack untied the lantern and put it on the ground, Batoor flicked the rope away. The lantern-light reflected on a dozen eyes as the rats withdrew. One gnawed on a soldier's head until Jack rattled the chains and frightened it away.

The rope returned a few moments later, with the end tied around a long knife. Jack held it gratefully. 'Thank you!' he said. There was no reply. 'Batoor? Batoor, have you seen anything of Mary?'

Only silence replied. Jack wished he'd asked about Mary first.

Perhaps Batoor considered his duty done by delivering the knife. Jack felt more like a soldier with a weapon in his hand. He tried the blade in the manacle lock, hoping it had a simple catch that the knife could spring. After a few minutes, he gave up in disgust. The blade was too broad to enter the keyhole. Instead, Jack returned to the staple in the wall. He scraped at the granite, pulling and twisting the iron until his hands were bleeding raw. With no method of judging the passing of time, except by glancing at the stars in the tiny square of sky through the window, Jack worked on, dislodging minuscule flakes of stone without making any headway.

He heard the rasp of the key in the door, pulled desperately at the staple and found it as secure as ever. Swearing silently, he snuffed the lantern, hid it in a corner and backed to the wall, trying to conceal his knife. When the door opened, three warrior women stepped in. Without a word, one drew her tulwar and held it to

Jack's throat while the others released the chains and pushed him to the door. Jack slid the knife up his sleeve, wondering if he could fight all three at once.

No. That would be a quick and pointless suicide. Better to attack Jayanti instead. Jayanti was more valuable to the mutineers than he was to the British. Holding the blade of the knife in his folded fingers, Jack allowed the warriors to push him out of the dungeon and into the darkness.

CHAPTER THIRTEEN

'Get down, Captain Windrush!' The voice came from nowhere as Batoor erupted from the shadows. Jack barely heard the hiss of his tulwar, and the first of his guards crumpled, her throat slashed wide open. The second woman turned, and Batoor thrust his blade into her breast and twisted it. Her scream echoed as the third woman swung at Batoor with her sword.

Jack threw himself forward, knocking the woman sideways, so her blade missed Batoor by a handspan. Dropping the knife into his hand, Jack reversed it and stabbed, catching her at the side of the throat. Warm blood spurted as he ripped the blade sideways, ignoring the woman's gurgling screams.

'Glad to see you, Batoor,' he said as the Pathan wiped his blade clean on the clothes of his first victim.

'You were not hard to find,' Batoor said. 'The first person I asked knew all about the Windrush sahib prisoner.'

Jack thought it best not to ask about Batoor's methods of asking questions.

'Batoor,' Jack asked the question that had been uppermost in his mind for many hours. 'Do you know what happened to Mary?'

Batoor's smile was as broad as ever. 'Yes, I know, Captain Windrush.'

'Is she alive? Is she a prisoner in this fort?'

'Yes, she is alive, and no, she is not a prisoner in this fort.' Batoor's answers only created more questions. 'We'll have to get away now, Captain Windrush. The Jayanti woman will soon miss her soldiers, and then they'll search for you.'

'How will we get out?'

'We walk out the front door,' Batoor said. Bending down, he tested each of the female warrior's tulwars and handed one to Jack. 'Strap that around your waist, Windrush, and swagger like a warrior.' He shoved a dozen betel nuts into Jack's hand. 'Chew these and say nothing.' He stepped back. 'You don't look much like a sahib.'

For the first time, Jack blessed his part-Indian heritage. 'Thank you.' He knew Batoor intended his words as a compliment.

'Follow me.' Batoor strode through the gloomy dungeons as though he owned the place. He kicked open a door, snarled to a man who tried to stop him and mounted a steep flight of steps two at a time.

'You were never an English public-school man, were you?' Jack asked.

'What is that?' Batoor asked.

'You have the same arrogance in your manner,' Jack said. 'As if the whole world belongs to you and damn anybody who tries to deny it.'

'I am an English sahib then.' Batoor increased his swagger.

Jack gripped the hilt of his tulwar as they passed the sentries at one of the minor gates and took a deep breath as they stepped outside. Freedom smelled good. 'Mary?'

'Come with me, Captain Windrush.' Batoor led Jack into the crowded, narrow streets until Jack found himself in a maze of small, flat-topped houses. 'In here.' He pushed open a surprisingly elaborate door.

The interior was much as Jack had expected, a bare, hot room with a minimum of furniture and an Indian woman sitting on a low stool, her head shrouded and her sari covering her from shoulder to ankles. The flame of a single *diya* lantern provided all the light there was.

'Good evening, Ma'am,' Jack said. '*Ram ram.*'

'Good evening, Captain Jack.' Mary threw back her head covering. 'I'm glad my teachings were effective, and you've finally learned a word of the language.'

CHAPTER FOURTEEN

'Dear God in heaven.' Jack stared at Mary for a long time, shaking his head. He was aware of Batoor in the room, or he would have folded her in his arms. 'You're safe,' he said.

'So are you.' Mary's eyes were huge.

'I'm glad.' Jack didn't know what to say.

'So am I.'

'I saw you grabbed,' Jack said. 'I saw somebody pull you into a building.'

'That was Batoor.' Mary looked at the Pathan. 'He saved me, and we have been trying to find you ever since.'

'There are other British prisoners.' Jack didn't know how to thank her, or Batoor. More used to the abrupt manners of soldiers and the code of gentlemen, he was unsure how to act with a woman such as Mary. He frowned as he realised what he was thinking. *A woman such as Mary? What do I mean by that? Is Mary different from any other woman he had known? Is she different from Myat, or Helen or that young barmaid back in Hereford? Yes, yes, she is.*

Why? Was it because she was Eurasian?

No.

Jack breathed out in relief. He didn't think differently about Mary because she was half-Indian. *There is quite another reason.*

'We know about the British prisoners.' Mary had been watching him, waiting until his mind had cleared. 'They are chained in a dungeon and guarded by Jayanti's warriors.'

'Can we get them out?'

Batoor and Mary exchanged glances. 'Batoor thinks not,' Mary said. 'They are too well guarded.'

'I'll come back with the 113th.' Jack didn't mention the chess game and the executions. He could feel Mary's eyes on him. 'I'll tear this place apart to rescue these men.'

'There may be another way,' Mary said. 'We could try to get the Rajah to help.'

'I don't understand.' Jack fought his tiredness. He had no idea what time, or even what day it was.

'The commander of the Rajah's army is British,' Mary said. 'If we approach him, he may help us.'

In this time of confusion and divided loyalties, Jack wasn't surprised to hear the nationality of the Rajah's commander. 'It was the Rajah who handed me to Nana Sahib,' he said. 'He's thrown in his lot with the rebels.'

'I'm not sure that he has,' Mary said. 'Nana Sahib and Jayanti are at one end of the fort, and the Rajah is at the other.' She sighed. 'Are you game to try him?'

Jack considered. His first inclination had been to return with his 113th, storm the fort and free the prisoners. On reflection, he knew that his handful of infantry, without artillery or cavalry, could never reduce the fort. His second thought was to take Riley, the cracksman, find the prisoners and release them, but Batoor had said that Jayanti's warriors guarded them too well, and he respected the Pathan's judgement.

'I'll have a look at this commander fellow first,' Jack said. 'And then I'll decide.'

'He drills his troops every day,' Batoor said. 'Left, right, left, right, attention, stand at ease.' He laughed. 'It provides the people with endless amusement.'

'Where does he drill them?' Jack had a sudden dread of returning to the fort.

'On the *maidan*, the parade ground, under the walls to the north of the fort, with trees all around for shade.' Mary explained. 'When I was young, we watched the army training.'

'What's this man's name?' Jack asked. 'I mean, who is he?'

'Commander-sahib,' Mary said. 'That's what everybody calls him.' She smiled. 'He's no youngster, Jack.'

'Show me,' Jack demanded.

If Mary had not told Jack that the Commander-sahib was British, Jack would never have known. He stood in front of his men dressed in the full uniform of a commander of native infantry, with a steel breastplate and a spiked helmet as he gave orders in fluent Hindi, while a dozen shrill-voiced rissaldars – officers – ensured their men obeyed.

'They're smart,' Jack approved, as the Gondabad Army marched and counter-marched to the word of command. 'They could match up to any regular British line regiment for drill. It is as well that their weapons are outdated.'

The infantry carried the old Brown Bess India pattern musket, an excellent weapon in its day but outclassed by the British Army's modern Enfields.

'There must be three thousand men on parade,' Jack said. 'The Commander-sahib has drilled them well. Does he have any cavalry?'

'Over there.' Batoor pointed with his chin.

As the infantry marched into the fort in columns of four, ten squadrons of cavalry took their place on the maidan, each man dressed in a splendid blue and silver uniform and carrying a curved sabre.

'They look as impressive as the infantry.' Jack wondered if they had the discipline to advance into Russian guns, like the Light Brigade at Balaklava only four years previously. 'How good are they in battle?'

'The Rajah of Gondabad does not like battles,' Batoor said with a sneer. 'He keeps his army intact by ignoring everything that happens. His soldiers are children's toys, pretty to look at and nothing else. They would run at the sight of blood.'

Standing under the shade of the trees with a scattering of local men and women,

Jack watched the Commander-sahib. He was undoubtedly elderly, with a neat white beard and grizzled face, yet he stood erect, and his commands dominated the parade ground. 'Yes, Mary. I will speak to that man.'

'He has the ear of the Rajah,' Mary agreed.

Batoor spat betel juice onto the ground. 'It will do no good, Captain Windrush. The Rajah will whine to the rebels, and they will ignore him. He is a man with no teeth and no courage.'

'Perhaps you are correct,' Jack said. 'I'll try anyway. Where can I find the Commander-sahib?'

'Over there.' Mary nodded to a walled enclosure beside the parade ground. 'He lives and works in the same building.'

'When he goes in, I shall follow him,' Jack said.

'I'll come as well,' Mary said at once.

'I want you to stay with Batoor,' Jack said. 'It might be dangerous.'

'Oh, Jack, will you stop singing that same old song?'

Sometimes even the bravest soldier has to admit defeat. 'If there's any trouble, Mary, turn and run. You can merge into the city far more easily than I can.'

'I know that, Jack.' Mary spoke as patiently as she would to a child.

'I will come too, Windrush,' Batoor said. 'In case the enemy chooses to fight.'

'You and Private Logan would get on well together,' Jack said sourly. 'He's also a bloodthirsty rascal.'

Two acres of gardens surrounded the Commander-sahib's house, created in a mixture of British and Indian styles, with flowerbeds wilting under the sun, small groves of trees and the ubiquitous fountains. The two sentries at the door looked efficient and bored.

'I'll talk,' Batoor said. 'I'll tell them we want an audience with the Commander-sahib.' He walked up to the sentries, speaking rapidly. They reacted at once, crossing their muskets in front of him to bar any entrance.

'I'll try,' Mary said and smiled as she addressed the sentries. One man laughed, and the other eyed Batoor with dislike before they stepped aside. 'I told them that I had two recruits for the Commander-sahib,' Mary explained.

One sentry shouted something over his shoulder, and a rissaldar appeared.

'He's demanding to know who we are.' Mary translated the officer's words.

'Use the same story,' Jack was aware of Batoor resting a hand on the hilt of his tulwar. *Can we fight our way clear of here?*

The rissaldar glared at Mary, evidently wondering why two stalwart men should have a woman with them. He jerked his head inside the building and shook a finger at Mary. They spoke for a while, and he grimaced and allowed her to enter.

'I told them you are dumb, Jack, and need somebody to speak for you.'

The interior of the house boasted a mixture of British and Indian styles, with beautiful carpets on the ground, and pointed and arched doorways. Hunting prints hung incongruously on the wall, together with a black and white etching of Robert Burns the poet, and a statue of Skanda, the Hindu god of war.

'The Commander-sahib is undoubtedly confused about his nationality,' Jack murmured.

The rissaldar brought them up a flight of stairs to a large room that overlooked the garden at the front. Nodding to the single sentry, he tapped on the door and thrust it open, closing it before Jack, and the others could follow. The sentry stood immobile, both hands on his musket. His eyes swivelled over them, disregarded

Jack, lingered on Mary's breasts for a few seconds and settled on Batoor. His hands tightened on his musket, and Jack guessed he had no love for Pathans.

After a few moments, the door opened again, and the rissaldar beckoned them inside.

The first thing Jack noticed was the mixture of European and Indian styles that made up the vast room. The next was the array of tulwars and Brown Bess muskets decorating the wall and the Commander-sahib sitting behind a teak bureau at the end of the room.

The Commander-sahib beckoned them closer and dismissed the rissaldar with a casual wave.

Mary salaamed politely, while Jack stood to attention, purely out of habit while in the company of a superior officer. Batoor was a few paces behind, right leg forward and his hand on the hilt of his tulwar. The Commander-sahib leaned back and contemplated them through narrow eyes, while the single ruby in the centre of his turban reflected the light that poured through the windows.

Mary spoke first, saying that she had brought two possible recruits for the Rajah's army.

'Enough of that nonsense,' the Commander-sahib interrupted her in gruff English. 'Don't perjure your soul with a lot of lies. You were taught better than that at the missionary school, Mary Lambert.'

It was the first time Jack had seen Mary truly astonished. 'Do you know me?' she asked at last.

'I do.' The Commander-sahib seemed pleased that he had caught her by surprise. 'And I knew your father, Major Lambert of the Bengal Fusiliers.'

'Oh!' Mary put a hand to her mouth. 'How did you know him?'

'The Fusiliers were based at Gondabad for a season or two,' the commandant-Sahib said. 'I don't know this Pathan fellow.'

'I am Batoor.'

'One name and no history,' the Commander-sahib said. 'There is a long untold story there, I wager. Whose throat have you cut, my man, or whose daughter have you ravaged to bring the wrath of the clan on you?'

The wrath of the clan? What Indian, however educated, would use that type of language? This man is indeed British.

Batoor smiled. 'It is better than I do not go back home for a while,' he said.

'And you.' The Commander-sahib eventually looked directly at Jack. 'I always wondered how you would turn out. I heard about your arrival with the 113th, although why you are with that bunch of blackguards and ne'er-do-weels, I can't imagine.'

'It's a long story.' Jack didn't wish to say too much until he knew more about this man. 'We have come to ask your advice, sir.' *"I always wondered how you would turn out." What the devil does that mean?*

'Have you now?' The Commander-sahib scratched his head under the turban. 'Well, I have a proposal for you, Captain Jack Baird Windrush, and as I considerably outrank you in both seniority and years, I will say my piece first.'

'Yes, sir.' Jack couldn't restrain his curiosity. 'How do you know who I am, sir?'

'You'll damn well listen to me first, boy!' the Commander-sahib snapped.

'Yes, sir.'

'I am in command of the Rajah's army,' the Commander-sahib said. 'As such, I train it, equip it and discipline it.'

Jack wondered if he should comment. 'Yes, sir.'

'My knowledge is thirty years out of date,' the Commander-sahib said. 'I need an officer with recent experience of British equipment and tactics. That could be you.'

Jack stared at him. 'I am an officer of the British Army, sir. I will not renounce my allegiance to Her Majesty.'

The Commander-sahib continued as if Jack hadn't spoken. 'I can offer you a position for life, taking over command from me after I die, with unlimited power and as many women as you desire.'

Jack knew that Mary was watching him. 'I have no desire for unlimited power, sir, and no desire for a harem of women.'

The Commander-sahib rested both hands on the top of his desk. 'I could have you killed,' he mused. 'I could have you trampled to death by elephants, thrown from the highest tower or blown from a cannon's mouth.'

'I am sure you could, sir.' Jack tried not to quail before the Commander-sahib's range of possible executions.

'I won't, of course,' the Commander-sahib mused. 'Damn it; one does not treat one's own family that way.'

Jack said nothing until he absorbed the full impact of the words. 'I am sorry, sir. I don't understand.'

'I think you do, Jack. Might I call you Jack? You are my grandson, after all.'

'Oh, dear God.' Jack stared at the Commander-sahib in disbelief. 'Who are you?'

'I am the Commander-sahib of his majesty, the Rajah of Gondabad. In a previous life, I was Major Jack Baird of the Bengal Fusiliers. I am your grandfather, Jack.'

'Oh, dear God.' Jack could only stand and stare at the old man. 'Oh, dear God in heaven.' He felt Mary's arm slide into his and was glad of her support. 'How did that happen?'

'The usual way,' Baird said. 'Man meets woman—'

'No, I mean, how did you become Commander of the Rajah's army? How long have you been here?'

'I was stationed here with the Fusiliers,' Baird said, 'and I loved the place and the people. The old Rajah, the present Rajah's father, offered me the position and I took it, about thirty years ago.'

Jack tried to work out the timeline. 'My grandmother? When did you meet her?'

'Long before that, Jack. I met her when I was in the Company's employ. We were together for years, it was no fly-by-night affair. We were legally married; such things between Briton and Indian were much more common then, than they are now.' Baird was smiling; his eyes warm as they probed Jack's. 'She was the reason I left the Company's employ, you see. The regiment was posted to Calcutta, and I wished to stay here, so when the old Rajah offered me the post, I took it.'

'My mother?'

'Your grandmother and I decided it would be better for her to grow up within the British sphere. The British star was on the ascendancy. It tore your grandmother's heart to hand her over.'

Jack nodded. Most British residents in India sent their children 'home' to be educated for much the same reason. Life was hard for British families in India.

My grandfather. This man is my grandfather. Jack's mind whirled with the new knowledge. *I have this man's name. Dear God, help me. I knew that I felt at home in India and now I have more family here.*

'We will talk about family matters later,' Baird said. 'You must know that I've been searching for you for some time. I gave out the word that nobody was to harm you.' His smile revealed perfect teeth. 'I even offered a reward if somebody could bring you to me, unharmed.'

Jack remembered the naik saving his life and the attempt to kidnap him, as well as Jayanti's surprising behaviour. 'I wondered what was happening,' he said. 'But other British prisoners have been murdered.'

Baird nodded. 'They are not my grandsons.'

'You are British,' Jack reminded. 'Don't you have any loyalty to Her Majesty?'

'My wife was Indian,' Baird said gently. 'My only daughter was half Indian. My grandson is part Indian. My employer is Indian. I have many more Indian than British friends. Am I more British or Indian? Who means more to me? Loyalty is not something to be assumed, taken for granted, or based on place of birth. Out here, whoever pays the most buys allegiance, while friendship has to be earned.' He glanced at Batoor. 'Our Pathan companion dances to a different tune with his loyalty to his clan.'

Jack remembered Colonel Hook saying something similar about money. 'I presume that the Rajah of Gondabad is in the pay of the rebels, then? Does Jayanti or Nana Sahib pay his wages?'

'The Rajah is neither for nor against Britain,' Baird said. 'Nana Sahib has little money. Oh, Nana taxes the lands he travels through, and his men rob the rich merchants, but he lost the loot of Lucknow, and when Campbell chased him out of Bareilly, he had no time to rob the treasury. My Rajah is waiting to see who is the stronger, and he will join that side. Like many out here, he is a pragmatist.'

'Jayanti and the rebels are sheltering in his fort,' Jack reminded.

'Yes,' Baird said, 'and if Sir Colin Campbell arrived, the Rajah would also give shelter to the British. You will notice that you're still alive, and the Rajah has confined the rebels – as you term them – to one area of the fort. My Rajah has not chosen yet, and although his army is small – well, three thousand well-trained men might turn a battle.'

'That is true,' Jack agreed. 'So the Rajah could be persuaded to join us?'

'He could,' Baird said. 'If the Company came up with a sizeable pension and could be trusted to keep its word.'

'I cannot promise a pension, but perhaps the British could muster up a single large payment,' Jack said, his mind working furiously. 'Perhaps the British could find payment enough to buy the Rajah and ransom the British prisoners from Jayanti.' He was aware of Mary staring curiously at him and continued, recklessly. 'Would that do the trick?'

Baird's smile was slow. 'It might. How would the British manage to find such a payment in the middle of a war?'

'I'm not certain that they could,' Jack said, 'but I think it might be worth trying.' He paused and held the old man's gaze. It had been a shock to meet his grandfather, and he hadn't yet analysed how he felt. 'The longer I take, the more chance there is that Jayanti will tire of the prisoners and kill them off.' He grunted. 'I'm surprised she has kept them so long.'

'Thank the Rajah for that,' Baird said. 'He was angry when Jayanti decapitated so many of the prisoners.'

Jack gave a slow nod. 'If I'd been a better chess player, more men would be alive today.' He knew that Mary was confused.

Baird nodded. 'Jayanti enjoys her little games.'

Now that the idea was in Jack's mind, he wished to get started. 'Commander-sahib... grandfather.' He paused. 'What should I call you?'

'Whatever you wish,' Baird said.

Jack avoided the issue. 'Thank you for your help, sir,' he said. 'I will leave at once, with your permission.'

'I've searched for you for years, Jack, and now you wish to run away?'

'Duty calls, sir,' Jack said.

'Wait!' Mary put a hand on Jack's arm. 'Commander-sahib. My father – could you tell me about him?'

'Next time, perhaps, Mary,' Baird said. 'Your man lacks his mother's patience. He is a soldier.'

Only when Jack left the room did he wonder if he would ever see the Commander-sahib again. He wished he'd spent more time with the old man. *No.* Jack pushed that thought aside. *I have my duty to do. I have to try to save as many of the 113th as I can and persuade the Rajah to support the British. My desires must take second place to my duty as an officer of the Queen.*

CHAPTER FIFTEEN

Elliot shook his head when he heard Jack's news. 'Your grandfather is the Rajah's military commander? We can surely use that.'

'Only if the Rajah decides to join us,' Jack said. 'If the Rajah is on our side, Jayanti and her warriors can't stay in the fort.'

'What's your plan, Jack?'

'Do you remember back at Lucknow, when Riley and Logan were absent for a while and Sergeant Greaves reported them?'

'I remember,' Elliot said. 'You caught them swimming, as I recall.'

'That was their story. Now, you and I know Riley better than that. He was after something more interesting than a face full of Indian river water.'

Elliot nodded. 'I thought it strange at the time.'

'Cast your mind back to when Campbell evacuated Lucknow, and there was a convoy of tumbrels and wagons carrying treasure and the crown jewels.'

Elliot glanced at Mary. 'I remember. We were a bit busy, what with escorting the civilians out of the city.' He didn't mention that Jack's mother had died during the evacuation.

'Riley and Logan disappeared for a while there, as well,' Jack said.

'I can't remember that.'

Jack saw that Mary was listening intently. She had been in a convoy of refugees, easing out of the besieged Residency while the outnumbered British tried to fend off the mutineers and rebels.

'At the same time, an entire treasure wagon went missing,' Jack said. 'Thirty-seven wagons left the city, and only thirty-six arrived safely. I had more important matters on my mind at the time.' Jack didn't refer directly to the death of his mother. That was still an intensely painful memory.

'Do you think Riley and Logan stole it?' Mary asked.

'I do,' Jack said. 'That's why they returned to the river a few weeks ago.'

'What are you planning, Captain Jack?' Mary narrowed her eyes.

'The Rajah of Gondabad might be bribed. The British prisoners, our men of the

113th, can be ransomed and we may know the location of a treasure wagon,' Jack said. 'Put them all together, and we can do a power of good.'

'There is a huge step from pure speculation to fact,' Mary cautioned.

'Would it not be better to ask Sir Colin first?' Elliot asked. 'Or even Colonel Hook? We're taking a lot of responsibility dabbling in such things.' He hesitated. 'If it comes out that we acted without authority from above, it won't do our careers much good.'

'Sir Colin is the best general in the army,' Jack agreed, 'but he's not renowned for his speed. He would as likely send a full expedition to find the wagon or rescue the prisoners, and by that time, it would be too late. As for Hooky – I beg your pardon, Colonel Hook – where is he? He jumps around so much.'

'With fifty of us, we'll make better time than Sir Colin.' Elliot looked worried.

'I'm not taking fifty men,' Jack said. 'This is a quick expedition. I will take ten men, mostly to act as porters, including Riley and Logan. You'll stay here in charge of the remainder.'

Mixed expressions of relief and disappointment crossed Elliot's face. 'If you don't mind me saying so, sir, this is not the best defensive site. The locals already know that we're here, so it won't be long before Jayanti and her women come probing, or maybe even Nana Sahib if he's still around.'

'That's true,' Jack said. 'The pandies would like nothing better than to snap up an isolated British garrison. It would hearten their supporters and increase their prestige. Do you have anywhere else in mind?'

'Yes, sir.' Elliot had evidently given his situation some thought. 'Do you remember that old Hindu temple we camped at last year, after the Gondabad massacre? It's a bit further away and much more defensible. I think we should move there.'

* * *

It was strange to return to the temple where they'd found refuge the previous year. It was strange to have the old Hindu gods watching over them and the exotic carvings staring at them through a green screen of vegetation. The war could have been on a different continent as child-sized monkeys capered and screeched, butterflies rose in clouds from the grass, and in the distance, a deer barked. Although the heat bounced from the stonework, the spring of bright water that bubbled in the centre of the temple was welcome, and the men relaxed in the shade, swatted flies and mosquitoes and set to work preparing defensive positions.

'This is familiar.' Mary looked around her, smiling. 'I'm going to explore and renew old memories.'

Jack nodded. 'Take care.' He called over Riley and Logan. 'You two, I want you.'

Logan came with his usual swagger while Riley was more cautious, suspecting trouble. Jack took them to a secluded area between two heavily carved pillars as Hanuman the Monkey God gazed down on them. 'Now, I want the truth, Riley.'

'Always, sir,' Riley lied.

'When we left Lucknow last year, you two hid some treasure.' Jack didn't try to be subtle. 'Don't deny it.'

'What makes you think that, sir?' Riley asked.

'Your behaviour, Riley, and your character,' Jack said.

'Could you explain, sir?' Riley asked.

That was sufficient fencing. 'When Sir Colin evacuated Lucknow last year,' Jack faced Riley directly, 'you two stole one of the treasure wagons. That wagon is the property of Her Majesty. You could be hanged.'

The silence confirmed what up until then had only been a strong suspicion.

'It is my duty to place you both under arrest,' Jack said.

'Yes, sir,' Riley said. 'What are you planning?'

'What do you mean, Riley?'

'We know each other, sir. You have something in mind that doesn't concern a noose.'

Jack hid his amusement. 'You're a clever man, Riley. Now listen.' He explained the situation as Riley and Logan nodded.

'So, you want us to go to Lucknow, retrieve this alleged treasure and hand it all over to some Indian Rajah,' Riley said.

'That's right,' Jack agreed.

'And if there's no treasure and we object?' Riley asked.

'There is a treasure, and you won't object.' Jack spoke softly. 'I know you, Riley, and I know Charlotte. You won't let her down.'

Jack knew that threats wouldn't work with Logan and appeals to patriotism would be a waste of breath. Men with the bitter-hard background that most of the 113th shared had little cause to love their homeland. However, while Pathans had *Pashtunwali*, loyalty to clan and family, British soldiers had loyalty to their regiment and Jack used that as a lever to persuade Logan to join him.

'I know you as well, Logan. You're not a thief.' That last part wasn't entirely accurate for like many British soldiers, Logan had the idea that anything not nailed down was fair game. 'That money will buy the lives of a score or more soldiers of the 113th.'

'Aye,' Logan said. 'We cannae let the pandies kill they lads, Riles.'

'We'll leave before dawn tomorrow.'

Logan grunted reluctant agreement and Riley could only nod.

'Very good. Get yourselves prepared.' Jack watched them walk away.

'Jack,' Mary touched his arm. 'Come with me.'

She led him through the temple building, past the statue to Hanuman and pushed past a tangle of creepers to an inner chamber that Jack had not noticed before. The sudden coolness surprised Jack.

'Where are you taking me?'

She put a finger to his lips. 'Shush Jack. Trust me.'

'I do,' he said.

A single shaft of sunlight permeated the chamber, highlighting strange carvings of copulating couples.

'A young man such as you should not look at these statues,' Mary linked her arm with that of Jack, 'unless he wishes to see.'

'I am always surprised how open Indian people are about such matters.' Jack felt a twinge of embarrassment at Mary's casual acceptance of the explicit images.

Mary smiled. 'Despite being brought up in a missionary school, I am always surprised how *closed* British people are about such matters.' She squeezed his arm. 'Come on Jack, you and I are both here because our parents made love, and the same goes for everybody else.'

'Yes, but there's no need to show such things,' Jack said.

'Why not?' Mary laughed again. 'Is it such a big secret that most of us need and desire love, physical as well as emotional?'

'No, of course not.' Jack watched as Mary lit a small *diya* lantern and placed it on a handy shelf. Yellow light pooled around them, illuminating the carvings, so they seemed almost alive.

'Are they not interesting?' Mary's fingertips traced the outline of a plump woman, following her curves with relish. 'Look at her, waiting to receive him, look at her anticipation, Jack. Is she not attractive?'

'Yes, she is, I suppose.' Jack agreed as Mary teased him, cupping a stone breast in her hand.

'And is this fellow here not impressively masculine?' Mary allowed her hand to drift to the woman's partner, a handsome young man evidently ready for the act of love. 'Don't they look happy there?'

'They do.' Jack couldn't hide his discomfort as Mary's hand stroked the man.

'Jack,' Mary said. 'Why are Englishmen such cold fish?'

'Are we?'

'Yes,' Mary said. 'I was taught, again and again, to hide my emotions, not to cry, to be phlegmatic like a true Englishwoman. You know that I am not a true Englishwoman, Jack. I am half-Indian. I am sure that English women share my passions and I think that Englishmen do as well, underneath that chilling exterior.'

'Do I have a chilling exterior?' Jack asked.

'Yes, sometimes,' Mary said. 'Not always. At present, you look embarrassed, bemused and lost. Here, let me help you.' Reaching over, she kissed him on the cheek. 'There, Captain Jack. Is that not better?'

'What are you doing?' Jack touched his cheek. 'I have a unit of men to command.'

'Lieutenant Elliot is more than capable of organising them, Captain Jack, and I am seducing you. Or did you believe I brought you here to admire the artwork?'

'Mary!' Jack said.

She stepped back. 'Jack Baird Windrush,' she said sternly. 'Are you rejecting me?'

'Heaven forbid,' he said.

'That is just as well for you, Captain Jack.' Mary stepped forward again, cupped his face in her hands and kissed him soundly. 'There now, that was a proper kiss for you.' Suddenly Jack allowed his growing desire to triumph. *Hang duty, Mary is right; Elliot and Bryce are more than capable of looking after the men, and O'Neill and Greaves are there if required. I am here, with Mary, we have survived a whole raft of dangers, and God only knows when we will get another chance to be alone together. Indeed, either of us might catch a fever and die tomorrow, or the rebels could kill us. India may be a place of death, but it's also a place of vivacious life and love.*

'Do you call that a proper kiss?' He looked into her brown eyes. 'Try this.'

Her lips parted beneath his, their tongues intertwined, and Jack eased his hands around her, caressing her back and smoothing downward to the plump swell of her bottom. He withdrew for breath, half expecting her to protest. Instead, she pressed against him, cupping his buttocks in both hands.

Before Jack realised what had happened, they were on the ground, using soft foliage as a bed as they slipped off their clothes.

'The men?' Mary asked once.

'They won't come in here.' Jack was no longer concerned about the men. Elliot would have them under control.

'Jack,' Mary whispered in his ear. 'I've only done this once before. Remember that time?'

Jack paused as the memories flooded back. 'I'll never forget. You're doing very well, again,' he said. 'Are you sure you wish—'

'Oh, Heavens, Jack! You know I do.'

The lantern cast their shadows across the carved couples, showing the living reality and a continuity of human desire in that chamber dedicated to love. There was no sound except their deep breathing and the soft tinkle of the spring outside. They could have been alone in the world, separate from the turmoil and horror of the war that still tore India apart. Nothing mattered but each other, and then nothing mattered at all. Jack rolled away and looked at Mary, as she lay naked and with her breasts softly undulating with each breath. 'You're beautiful,' he said.

She opened her eyes. 'We needed that,' she said.

'Did you do that because we needed it?' Jack asked.

There was a short pause before Mary replied. 'No.' She shook her head. 'No, I did *that*,' she emphasised the last word, 'because I wanted it.' She held his eyes for a long moment. 'I wanted you.'

'You got me,' Jack said.

'You're covered with scars.' Reaching forward, Mary touched the barely-healed white ridge that ran across his ribs. 'What was that?'

'That was in Lucknow,' Jack said. 'Bayonet or sword, I never knew which.'

'And that?' She touched the raised scar on his thigh.

'A pointed stake in Burma.'

'And this?' She touched a circular white mark on his arm.

'A Burmese decoit chewed me.' Jack didn't explain further.

'And this one?'

'Crimea.' Jack tired of the game and touched her face. 'Where do we go from here, Mary?'

'You go off to find some mythical treasure,' Mary said, 'and I either go with you or stay here with Elliot.'

Jack briefly wondered which would be safer for her. Should he take Mary on a long march through India, or leave her in this isolated garrison knowing that the enemy was only a few miles away? 'That's not what I meant.'

'What did you mean?' Mary's face was full of innocence.

'I mean, where do *we* go from here – you and I.' Jack hesitated for a moment. 'Us.'

Mary's head jerked up at the last word. 'Is there an *us*, Jack? Or are we just using each other because of this terrible war.'

Jack realised that although Mary was naked and lying within a few inches of him, he was concentrating on her face and her words rather than on her body. She meant more to him than merely a few moments pleasurable relief. Was there an *us*? Could there be an *us*? Did he wish an *us*? Alternatively, was Elliot correct and would any relationship with Mary, beyond the mere physical, wreck his military career?

'Would you like there to be an *us*?' Jack temporised by handing the question and the responsibility back to Mary.

'It's not my place to decide,' Mary replied at once. 'You know the difficulties that marrying a Eurasian would bring to you if it's marriage that you're thinking of. Or rather, if it is marriage of which you are thinking.' She smiled. 'There's my missionary school upbringing coming to the fore, Captain Jack.'

There had been no reason to ask the question. Mary lying there naked provided all the proof required that she cared for him. She was not the sort of woman to invite such intimacy with a mere acquaintance.

'No,' Jack said. 'You're right.' He looked around at the no-longer shocking carvings. 'I wonder how many people have come here to make love.'

'Hundreds probably, over the years,' Mary said. 'Perhaps even thousands.'

Jack had a sudden recollection of something his mother had said. 'My mother and father met in this temple,' he said. 'I wonder if they were in this chamber.' He had hardly known his true mother while his few memories of his father were of a loud, confident man. Yes, he could believe that they'd met in here, surrounded by images of long-gone lovers. It was something that would appeal to his mother's romantic side. His father? He would probably have found it quite amusing, perhaps even stimulating.

'Continuity,' Mary said. 'That's nice.' Reaching forward, she took hold of his hand. 'I'm not trying to put pressure on you, Jack. I know I am only a Eurasian, a *chee-chee*, a half-caste, a *teen pau* rather than a *pukka* British woman. I am country-born and country-bred. I didn't entice you here to force the issue, Jack.'

'The thought never entered my head,' Jack said truthfully. 'Anyway, I am country-born as well, not four miles from this temple.'

'Nor do I wish to be thought of as your bit of *khyfer*.'

'My bit of skirt?' Jack smiled. 'That's hardly the language an officer would use, Mary, or his lady.' He ran his hand down the length of her body, from her throat to her knees, enjoying the sensation.

'I'm yours, Jack,' Mary said simply. 'If you want me.' She took hold of his hand and pressed it into her groin. 'I want you, Captain Jack and I want to know you want me.'

For a brief, betraying moment, Jack wondered if Helen Maxwell, or other British women, would be as forward once they disposed of the outer veneer. He pushed the thought away. Helen had no place in his mind and certainly no place in this enchanted chamber. This place belonged to Mary and him, and no other, however many couples had been here before, and however many would be here in the future. They didn't matter. Only the present mattered, only what was happening between him and Mary at this moment.

'I want you,' Jack said.

Mary's smile was somehow wistful. She spread her arms. 'Then come and get me, Captain Jack.'

CHAPTER SIXTEEN

As Jack inspected his ten-man patrol, he wondered how many departures he'd endured. How often had he marched out of an encampment or cantonment with the knowledge that he might never return, that he could leave his bones in some foreign place, the cold uplands of Inkerman, the fever-jungles of Burma or the baking plains of India? Jack thought this time felt worse, perhaps because he was leaving behind somebody he knew cared for him. He patted his pocket, with the emergency medical bag that had been Mary's parting gift.

'You know how you always hurt yourself,' she had said and kissed him. 'Take care, Captain Jack.'

Do your duty. The stern words brought Jack back to the present.

'All set, O'Neill?' Jack had selected his men with care. As well as Riley and Logan, he was taking Batoor, Coleman and Thorpe, MacKinnon and Mahoney, Whitelam and Armstrong. Jack had chosen Coleman and Thorpe for their long experience, while Whitelam had a poacher's instincts, Mahoney was a quiet, steady Irishman and MacKinnon had some inner gifts that Jack didn't understand but guessed could be valuable. Armstrong was a thoroughly unpleasant man whom Jack personally disliked, yet he valued him as an efficient fighting man.

'All set, sir.' O'Neill threw a smart salute.

'*Shabash*, sergeant.' Jack glanced back at the temple. He would never forget this place with its special chamber and sweet memories. Mary was standing in the shade of Hanuman's pillar, trying to catch his eye. Jack lifted a hand in salute, still in an inner turmoil. Was their relationship only a brief episode in his life of campaigning and blood-letting?

He couldn't say.

Mary's gaze remained on him as he turned away. He knew she would watch as long as he was in sight, and probably a lot longer than that. He steeled himself. He had his duty to do, and Mary would have to wait.

He didn't want to leave her.

'We march fast and hard,' Jack said. 'We stop for nobody and nothing. We ignore trouble and don't get involved.'

The men looked at him, bitter eyes in hard sun-browned faces, Enfields held casually in calloused hands, uniforms a dozen shades of khaki and bayonets, buttons and all things metal browned to ensure they didn't reflect the sun.

'Bring double water bottles.' Jack had requisitioned a camel and loaded the panniers with *mussocks* – leather water bags – and ammunition. 'You look after the water,' he told the uncomprehending driver, 'and don't let me down.'

'Batoor,' Jack said, 'you watch this fellow. If he tries to run or does anything except what I tell him, you cut his throat.'

Batoor grinned and touched the Khyber knife with which he had replaced his tulwar. 'Yes, Captain Windrush.'

'We'll need transport on the return.' Riley sounded surly, unhappy to lose his prize.

I will have to watch him, and Logan. Logan lived by loyalty to the regiment and to his friends, of which Riley was the foremost. If Riley decided that Jack's throat should be cut, Logan would wield the blade – not out of any dislike of Jack, but through loyalty to Riley.

'We'll deal with that when we need it.' Jack decided he'd come too far to have scruples. If he needed more transport than one camel, he would find it, somehow.

When Jack had lived in his bungalow in the Gondabad cantonment, back in the far-off days of peace, there had been measures to cope with the hot season. The servants had placed hurdles of dried straw – *khas-khas tatties* – against the verandah and the open doors and had thrown water on the straw. This procedure cooled the air that entered the house, and incidentally, created a sickening smell of mildew. In common with other officers, Jack would sleep naked on his charpoy, with a mosquito net above and a table at his side complete with a brass bowl of water and a revolver. On some nights, he would sleep outdoors on the lawn, naked under his mosquito net.

Out here on the plains, he couldn't take such precautions, and from the moment the sun cracked over the horizon, the heat was intolerable and the glare so intense, it was impossible to move with eyes fully open.

'Keep moving!' Jack pushed the 113th on, following the road, with the heat rising from the ground beneath, burning the soles of their feet and coming up the legs of their trousers in unbelievable waves. The hot-weather birds were calling, with koels and brain fever birds, the latter with a rising call that ended in an irregular high pitch. 'I don't mind these birds so much,' Coleman said. 'It's the tin-pot bird that I hate. It goes hammer-hammer-hammer all the bloody time. Hammer-hammer-bloody-hammer.'

'We should shoot the bugger,' Thorpe said. 'It'll be working for the pandies.'

'If it was only one, I wouldn't mind,' Coleman said, 'but they're everywhere.'

'It's only a bird,' Armstrong said.

They marched on, avoiding settlements wherever possible, covering the ground twice as fast as Havelock's column had managed. Jack drove them hard, knowing their capabilities as well as their weaknesses. He posted sentries when they halted and ignored the terrifying howling of jackals. Twice they heard outbreaks of distant shooting, and each time Jack altered direction to avoid the trouble.

'We're British soldiers,' Logan said. 'We should go and see what's happening.'

'We've more important things to do,' Riley told him. 'Like giving away our treasure.'

Jack inched closer to the two men, trying to hear their conversation and gauge Riley's intentions. Logan saw him, grunted something to Riley and they marched in silence except for the monotonous drumbeat of boots on the pukka road.

'These jackals are like banshees,' Mahoney said. 'But quieter.'

'Have you ever heard a banshee?' MacKinnon asked. 'I mean a real one, back in Ireland?'

'No,' Mahoney said. 'I never have. I heard the old people talking about them though.'

MacKinnon nodded slowly. 'We don't have them in Skye,' he said. 'We have other things, especially up in the Cuillin Mountains.'

Mahoney looked over to MacKinnon. 'I've heard of Skye. It's a weird place for those with the power to understand.' He waited for a second as their boots hammered on the ground. 'You've got the power, haven't you?'

Jack moved fractionally closer, wondering what MacKinnon's answer might be until O'Neill interrupted the conversation.

'Sir!' O'Neill pointed north. They were on a track in a level plain, with small *topes* of trees and wide areas of grassland. 'Something is moving out there.'

Jack levelled his binoculars. 'The grass is certainly moving,' he said.

'Rebels? Dacoits?' O'Neill ran a hand along the barrel of his rifle.

'Something's coming this way,' Jack said. 'And it's coming fast.' He raised his voice. 'Form square lads! There's something or someone coming from the north.'

'There are only eleven of us,' Armstrong said. 'How can we form a square?'

'Follow orders, you grousing bastard!' O'Neill shoved him into place.

'Here it comes,' O'Neill said as the grass parted.

'It's only a dog!' Thorpe said. 'A little mangy dog.'

'Shoot it,' Jack ordered. 'Open fire!'

Veteran soldiers who had fought in a dozen battles and could uncaringly shoot at Burmese or mutineers or Russians, hesitated when ordered to fire at an animal. 'It's only a dog,' MacKinnon said.

As O'Neill lifted his Enfield to fire, Logan shifted sideways and nudged his elbow, sending the sergeant's shot wide.

'Oh, sorry, Sergeant!' Logan said.

'You bloody idiot!' Jack grabbed Logan's rifle, shoved him aside and aimed. The dog was running toward them, its mouth open and its course undeviating. Jack kept the dog in his sights, took a deep breath and let it out slowly. He measured the distance, waiting until he knew he could not miss. A bead of sweat formed on his right eyebrow, hovered for a second and dropped. Jack squeezed the trigger.

The dog jerked backwards as the bullet made contact. Its head exploded in a shower of blood and bones.

'You've killed it!' Logan said.

Jack handed back the rifle. 'That dog could have killed at least one of us.'

'It was only a dog.' Logan automatically reloaded his rifle.

'Running like that, it was rabid,' Jack said. 'It only had to lick one of us to give us rabies. Have you ever thought about rabies, Logan?'

'No, sir.'

'You'll go mad, Logan, and froth at the mouth. You'll be scared of water, and you'll howl. You've heard the jackals howling at night. You'll sound the same, before you convulse and bend backwards until you break your spine and die.'

'Yes, sir.'

'And the next time you disobey my order or disrupt my sergeant when he's about to shoot, I won't save your life, Logan. I'll leave you for a rabid dog, or Sergeant O'Neill – whichever is most dangerous.'

'That would be me, Logan. That would be me,' O'Neill said quietly. 'When we get back to camp, I will deal with you.'

'Yes, sergeant. I thought—'

'You thought?' O'Neill shook his head. 'You're a soldier, Logan; you're paid to fight, not to think!'

They smelled the village an hour before dawn and came to it within fifteen minutes. The first body sprawled on the road, a woman lying on her back, legs and arms splayed out.

'Somebody's outraged that woman,' Riley said, as Logan used a more obscene expression and added what he would do to the men responsible.

The second body was a plump matron who must have been in her forties. She lay under a tree, naked and mutilated.

'Bastards,' Thorpe said. 'What had that woman ever done to hurt anybody? She's probably somebody's ma.'

'Maybe hers.' Coleman pointed to the body of a small child, who lay huddled beside a burned out hut.

'What're they killing babies for?' Thorpe asked. 'What harm can a little baby do to anybody? These rebels aren't human!'

'Sergeant,' MacKinnon said. 'Somebody's watching us.'

'Don't look in his direction, MacKinnon,' O'Neill said. 'Where is he?'

'I don't know,' MacKinnon said. 'I can feel it.'

'All right, son, keep moving and tell me as much as you can.' O'Neill slipped his finger onto the trigger of his rifle. He raised his voice slightly. 'Keep alert men; we're not alone here.'

'Probably another bloody dog,' Logan said.

'Probably another bloody dog,' Thorpe repeated. 'One with scabies.'

'Rabies,' Coleman corrected.

'Same thing,' Thorpe said. 'Except scabies is *worse* than rabies.'

They walked on, eyes mobile and the rear guard walking backwards, watching every ruined house in the village, checking every crumpled body to ensure it was dead and not waiting to pounce on them.

'Sergeant!' MacKinnon hissed. 'Something's wrong.'

'I can see that, MacKinnon. All the people are dead.'

'It's coming! Something's coming!' MacKinnon lifted his rifle.

'Halt!' Jack gave the order out of instinct a second before the house exploded. Flames and smoke rose ten yards in front of them, with pieces of blazing thatch and fragments of wood rising high, to fall on them in a burning shower. The patrol scattered, with some diving to the ground and others running for shelter. Batoor pulled the camel away from the danger.

'It's an ambush!' Jack said as a rush of people came from the abandoned houses. Deafened by the sound, Jack could hear nothing as a mob attacked them. Perhaps thirty men with swords, spears, sticks and unwieldy agricultural implements charged from all around, mouths open in yells that Jack couldn't hear. Drawing his revolver, he fired into the mass, shouting orders as his veterans met the attackers with bullet, bayonet and rifle butt.

Although the British were outnumbered, they were veterans of battle and brawls, trained soldiers, while the attackers were not. After just a few moments, it was evident that the fight was one-sided. The 113th hacked down all who opposed them and stood, panting, as the remainder of the enemy turned and fled, dropping their weapons in panic.

'What was that all about?' Logan cleaned his bayonet on the loincloth of a man he had killed. 'They lads were not even soldiers.'

'No, 'Jack agreed. 'They were villagers. They must have thought we were the men who killed their women and children.'

'Maybe so, sir,' O'Neill said. 'Either that, or they don't like the British. Anyway, they got that gunpowder from somewhere. Ordinary villagers don't have explosions. This country is a mess.'

They moved on, leaving the village behind them. 'That noise will have woken up half the countryside,' Jack said. 'We'll find a safe spot to hide up for a few hours and move through the night.'

'Is anywhere safe in this cursed country?' O'Neill asked.

'Some of the natives must think that we are the curse,' Jack said softly. That thought remained with him for the remainder of their journey. Perhaps if the British left India, peace would return.

CHAPTER SEVENTEEN

The River Goomtee flowed turgid and brown between parched banks, with many of the surrounding buildings still in ruins from the previous year's siege. Women washed clothes and gossiped while children laughed and played in the water.

Jack shivered, remembering the terrible days of Havelock's relief and the evacuation. Not far from here, he had acknowledged his mother, and over there – he altered his angle of vision – she had died at the hands of a Pathan. He glanced at Batoor and wondered anew at his loyalty. He had so many memories of Lucknow, good and bad, for Mary was also here, in his mind.

'Are you all right, sir?' O'Neill asked.

'Yes, sergeant.' Jack concentrated on the task at hand. 'Well, Riley, this is where you lead the pack. You know where this treasure wagon is hidden.'

Riley glanced at Logan. 'I know where somebody hid a wagon last year, sir,' he said slowly. 'They may have returned for it since then.'

'Let's hope not,' Jack said and hummed the first few bars of Chopin's *Funeral March*.

'We'll look for it, sir,' Riley said.

'I'm sure you'll remember where to find it.' Jack glanced along the riverbank. 'Perhaps a good place to start would be where you chose to go swimming a few weeks ago.'

'Yes, sir.' Riley sounded frustrated. 'That might be a good place to start.'

'Sergeant O'Neill will make sure you don't get lost,' Jack said. 'And in case you're worried about Charlotte, she is very well.'

'Thank you, sir.' Riley saluted.

Jack posted four sentries along the banks of the river and sent all the others into the river with Riley.

'I believe that the wagon was submerged around here.' Riley looked around, searching for any familiar landmarks. 'It was a bit hectic at the time, what with the pandies attacking and General Campbell trying to get everybody out safely.'

'I remember,' Jack said.

'Over here.' Logan pointed to a tree that overhung the riverbank. 'I remember that crooked tree. Somebody had hanged a pandy from it, and he was swinging back and forward.'

'We'll work at night,' Jack decided. 'If we search through the day, we'll attract too much attention.' He was breaking every rule in the book. *By rights, I should contact my superior officer, Colonel Hook, wherever he may be, or Sir Colin Campbell.* By making this decision to search for and hand over a treasure wagon that by rights belonged to the East India Company, Jack knew he was far exceeding his authority. The Army could cashier him, or charge him with theft. On the other hand, if he waited for orders, Jayanti might execute her prisoners. It was a choice between his career and the life of an unknown number of soldiers of the 113th.

Most of the outskirts of that part of Lucknow were in ruins, with a gaggle of refugees huddling in whatever shelter they could find. Jack found a battered house within a walled garden, posted sentries at the only gate and settled his men in until dusk. Used to the tedium of army life, the men accepted their lot without demur, while Jack fought his frustration at the inactivity and led them back to the riverside as soon as the light faded.

'How did you come to find the treasure in the first place, Riley?'

'The last wagon in the column broke a wheel,' Riley said. 'The driver ran away, and a couple of men drove it into the river to hide it.'

'You and Logan would be the two men.' Jack smiled when Riley shrugged. 'It's all right, Riley. Carry on with your story.'

'The wagon was in a bad state, sir,' Riley said. 'It might have broken up in the river.'

'If that happened, the current would take the contents downstream,' Jack said. 'Whatever was inside could be anywhere, miles away.'

'Maybe, sir,' Riley knew more about treasure than Jack ever would. 'The river would take away the wood and any documents, any light stuff. It was last November, sir, after last year's rains, and this year's rains are not due for a couple of months yet.'

'I am aware of the seasons, Riley,' Jack said.

'Yes, sir. I mean that the current is not strong enough to shift anything heavy, or not far. If we look downstream from where these men – whoever they were – left the wagon, we should find at least some of the golden or silver items.'

Jack hid his smile. 'Can you remember where these mysterious men left the wagon?'

'Opposite that tree, sir,' Riley said. 'Logie and I were watching them and wondering what they were doing.'

'Yes, sir,' Logan added. 'We thought they looked a right pair of blackguards, sir, and wondered if we should tell you.'

'I'm sure you considered that, Logan.'

Jack spread the men downstream from the tree, with orders to scour the bed of the river and hand him anything they found. He sat on the bank and prepared to supervise. A lot had happened since he had been last in Lucknow. He had met his grandfather and played chess with Jayanti. He had also made love to Mary. Jack smiled at the memory. Now life had moved on again, and he was back in this city of palaces, watching his men wade in the river.

There was something surreal about this task, with eight men splashing about in an Indian river by the light of a sickle moon, dipping and cursing as they searched for a Rajah's treasure. Jack grunted; he hadn't expected to do this when he accepted the Queen's commission. The life of an officer in the British Army was full of variety and interest, although he could never tell his grandchildren about this particular experience.

'I've found something.' Mahoney held up a glittering object.

'Bring it here.' Jack stepped into the river.

It was a small golden cup with a single band of rubies. 'Well done, Mahoney.' That cup would be worth more money than Mahoney would pocket in ten years. Jack placed it in the canvas sack he'd brought. It was a start. 'Keep looking, lads, Mahoney's cup might be the first.' Alternatively, the Sikhs could have found everything months ago. Jack gave a rueful smile; the Sikhs were reputed to be the most expert looters in India.

As dawn lightened the horizon, he called in the men and checked what they had brought him. Among the assorted rubbish he collected was one human skull, a few miscellaneous bones and a silver coin with Arabic script.

'Well done lads,' Jack said when his men straggled ashore, dripping wet and slightly furtive. 'Now strip.'

They stared at him. 'What?'

'Strip,' Jack repeated. 'Why so shy, boys? I've seen you unclad before.' He raised his voice slightly. 'Shall I ask the sergeant to help you?'

Slowly, one-by-one, they began to take off their sodden uniforms, with Jack searching each piece of clothing and removing the items he found. Within minutes, he had a sizeable collection of golden artefacts, pieces of jewellery and coins.

'Good hunting, lads.' Jack bundled his treasure into a sack. 'We'll do the same tomorrow night and onward until we have sufficient treasure to free our colleagues.' He felt their eyes on him, the suspicious, predatory, bright eyes of some of the most desperate soldiers in the world. These were his men, yet he would not sleep easy until he had handed the treasure over. As Colonel Hook had said, the love of money, as well as power, was the root of all evil.

'Sergeant O'Neill,' Jack said. 'I want this treasure guarded. Its presence is a great temptation to some of the men. Batoor will help you.'

'The Pathan? They're the greatest thieves in the East!'

'Set a thief to catch a thief,' Jack said. 'Besides, he has eaten my salt.' He was aware that Batoor was listening and knew he need say no more.

Jack joined the men in the water on the second night, probing further down river and finding an elegant brass chest adorned with emeralds, and a jewelled knife scabbard that must have been worth a small fortune. On the third night, Riley handed over an ivory chess set.

'Thank you,' Jack said. The set with its exotic pieces brought back memories of his deadly game with Jayanti. It was a reminder why he was here.

'Keep working lads,' Jack encouraged. 'We have lives to save.' He drove them harder after that, starting earlier, keeping them longer in the water and taking more risks of discovery. He set Batoor as a permanent guard of their haul, with the Pathan sleeping on top of the treasure by night and remaining in their base house through the stupefying heat of the day.

When any locals came too close, Jack had Armstrong or Logan scare them away, and on the only occasion that a British picket looked curiously at these men in the river, Jack pulled rank on the sergeant in charge. With so many of the British garrison engaged in chasing after the remaining rebels in Oudh, the Central Provinces and Rohilkhand, there were insufficient soldiers to spare in Lucknow, to investigate his small party.

Twice MacKinnon reported that something was wrong. Each time Jack sent him out with Coleman and Thorpe to scout the surrounding area, and they returned without incident.

'It's just the general tension, MacKinnon,' Jack said. 'We'll only be one more day.'

The one more day stretched into two, and then three, and although Jack's store of Lucknow's royal wealth mounted, it was not sufficient to bribe a rajah. Every day at least one of the men would approach him with the suggestion that they could divide the loot between them and desert en masse. Each time Jack thanked the man for his idea and ordered him back to work. Such a reaction was inevitable when a collection of desperadoes such as the 113th collected treasure.

At the back of Jack's mind was the worry that the men might decide to slit his throat and run with the loot. Despite their valour in battle, the men of the 113th were still the dregs of the British Army. Jack slept with his revolver to hand and his sword loose in the scabbard.

'Sir!' Thorpe held up his hand as if he were a schoolboy. 'I've found something.'

'Well bring it over, Thorpe,' Jack kept his patience – Thorpe was doing his best.

'I can't, sir. It's too big.'

Jack splashed through the river. 'What do you have, Thorpe?' He grunted as he stubbed his toe on something hard and delved into the water. His hands encountered a wooden frame, and then something circular.

A wheel. Thorpe had found the remains of the wagon. He'd discovered the mother lode.

'They must have driven the wagon into a hole in the river bed, sir, and it's broke up.' Thorpe gave his opinion.

'Well done, Thorpe,' Jack said, raised his voice and gathered all the men together. 'Up here, men.'

Jack agreed with Thorpe's assessment. The thieves had driven the wagon into the river, aiming for the deep central area, but only quarter way across must have lurched into a hidden depth. *That was lucky for us.* After months in the river, the wooden body of the wagon had rotted, and it was the work of five minutes to tear a sizeable hole and reveal the contents. Jack organised the men, with the best swimmers diving under the surface to lift the booty and the others forming a human chain, handing the objects to one another until they reached the riverbank, where Jack took final delivery. The pile of golden objects and jewelled clothing, shining cups and strings of pearls and rubies grew by the minute.

Dawn was threatening before they finished, and the heap of treasure littered the bank.

'That will do,' Jack decided at last.

'There's more left, sir.' Thorpe had enjoyed looting the wagon.

'I'm sure there is, Thorpe. When you leave the Army, you can return here and take what remains.'

'No, sir,' Thorpe said. 'I would never do that. It's stealing sir.'

This was a new side to Thorpe. 'Well said, Thorpe.'

'You go to Hell for stealing, sir,' Thorpe informed him.

They carried the loot to their base in relays, with Jack leaving honest Private Thorpe in charge of the collection at the riverside. 'If anybody tries to take anything, Thorpe, shoot him. Whoever it is.'

'Yes, sir,' Thorpe said and happily pointed his rifle at Armstrong.

'Not one of us, Thorpey,' Coleman pushed the rifle barrel aside. 'Captain Windrush didn't mean that.'

'I was only jesting,' Thorpe said.

Jack wasn't sure. He should know by now to ensure his orders were explicit for men such as Thorpe. Armstrong didn't seem amused at the joke either.

'That's us,' Jack said when the last of the treasure was deposited inside their base house. 'Now we have to get this to Gondabad.'

'We have one camel,' Riley said. 'We'll need at least six, or a wagon.'

'No wagon,' Jack decided. 'They move too slowly, and we won't be on pukka roads most of the time. We'll use camels.'

'Where the hell will we find camels?'

'Batoor.' Jack tossed over half a dozen gold mohurs from the pile on the floor. 'You're the expert. Take our camel driver and find us half a dozen camels. Don't get caught, and if you cut anybody's throat, make sure he's not important.'

'Yes, Captain Windrush.' Batoor gave a mock salaam.

'Now we prepare and wait for Batoor,' Jack said. The fate of the British captives in Gondabad and the possible allegiance of the Rajah of that city depended on the loyalty of a Pathan who had lately fought against them. For some reason he couldn't understand, the thought made Jack smile.

Even inside the thick walls of the house, the heat was intense. The men of the 113th lay there, sweltering, aware that their future would be one of poverty and danger despite the king's ransom that lay at their feet. Jack leaned against the wall with his hand never far from the butt of his revolver. He hated himself for distrusting his men after all they'd been through together.

'Something's not right,' Mackinnon said. 'I feel it.'

'*You're* not bloody right,' O'Neill growled, 'and you'll feel my boot up your arse unless you shut your mouth.'

Flies buzzed around them, seeking sweat. The men swatted ineffectually.

'I hope Batoor isn't long,' Coleman said.

'He'll be as long as it takes,' O'Neill said. 'You go to the window and keep watch.'

'What am I watching for?'

'Anything that could be suspicious, Coleman. You heard MacKinnon; something's not right.'

'Why not send Mac, then?' Coleman asked.

'Because I sent you.'

'Get the loot into sections.' Jack gave the men work to reduce the tedium of waiting. 'We better be ready to load up when Batoor arrives.'

Jack let the day's routine continue, wondering if he was right to trust Batoor. It would be easy for the Pathan to whistle up a dozen unscrupulous rogues in Lucknow, descend on his small party at night and slaughter them for the treasure.

'Sir.' Coleman's voice awoke him from a heat-induced doze. 'Somebody's coming.'

'Stand to,' Jack said quietly. He'd convinced himself that Batoor would betray them and now expected nothing else. 'Load and cap, have your bayonets ready.'

'It's Batoor,' Coleman said.

Here we go. Jack unbuttoned his revolver.

'He's brought camels,' Coleman said, 'and some camel drivers.'

'Anybody else?' Jack asked.

'No, sir.'

Jack breathed out in relief and fastened the button of his holster. His initial faith in Batoor had been justified.

* * *

They moved out an hour after sunset, with flitting clouds reflecting the blossoming light of the moon.

'Sergeant.' Jack called O'Neill over. 'Keep alert.'

'Yes, sir.' O'Neill put just enough emphasis on the phrase to inform Jack he didn't need an officer to instruct him in the obvious.

'Watch Riley and Logan,' Jack kept his voice low. 'I wouldn't be surprised if they decided to slip away with a camel load of loot.'

'Aye, sir.' O'Neill nodded. 'I had thought that as well, although it's Armstrong that's been wandering recently.'

'Armstrong?'

'Yes, sir,' O'Neill said. 'Twice this week he's left the house to go into Lucknow.'

'I'm sure you can handle him, sergeant. In the meantime, take care of Logan and Riley.'

O'Neill raised his hand. 'Can you hear that tinkling? That's camel bells. I made sure each driver has them. It will make us more audible, but the locals know the sound anyway. If I hear bells from anywhere except in our convoy, I'll know somebody's running off with them.'

'Good man, sergeant.'

Leaving Lucknow behind, they headed into the darkness, with Jack watching for trouble from his men as much as from an enemy. The camels walked in single file, not hurrying but covering the ground at a steady pace and easing over the road with no apparent effort. The men marched alongside the camels; rifles slung over shoulders, hats pulled low and boots kicking up dust. Jack checked each man, trying to gauge his mood. Thorpe and Coleman marched side by side, not speaking much but as relaxed as veteran soldiers should be. MacKinnon and his rear rank man, Mahoney, were slouching a little, while Armstrong and Whitelam were a little apart. Jack turned his attention to Logan and Riley.

Riley remained very close to the rearmost camel, nearly touching the driver, while Logan looked wary, turning to look behind him every few steps. *What are you waiting for, Logan?*

The quarter moon revealed the road stretching ahead across the plains. Even in the night, sweat soaked through Jack's uniform tunic, forming beads on his eyebrows and easing down his face. He felt as if he had been journeying across India for years, marching through the hot darkness, worrying about his men, waiting for the sudden ambush, listening for the cry of *"Din, din!"* or *"Allah Akbar!"* or the crisp orders of the British-trained mutineers.

As they approached a grove of palm trees, something rustled above Jack's head, a night hunting bird or a bat perhaps. He quickened his pace. He must have passed a hundred such *topes* in the past few weeks, with each one a possible site for an ambush. Hurrying to the front of the convoy, he stepped beside MacKinnon.

'Is everything all right, here?'

'Yes, sir,' Mahoney answered at once.

'I'm not sure, sir.' MacKinnon was eyeing the palm trees. 'I've got that queer feeling again.'

'So have I, Mackinnon,' Jack said. 'Careful now, lads.'

The column speeded up, with Jack watching until the last camel passed the *tope*. Palm fronds hissed slightly in the oven-hot breeze, with a host of insects descending on the marching men and lizards watching them through stony eyes. There was no ambush, and Jack breathed his relief as they moved on over a featureless plain.

'My camel's lame, sir,' Armstrong shouted. 'The brute's limping.'

There is always something. Jack hurried over, shouting for Batoor to join him.

'Here, sir.' Armstrong pointed to the camel's front left leg. 'He must have injured it somehow.'

'Let me see,' Jack knelt beside the camel. 'I can't see anything.' He sensed movement and shifted sideways. Armstrong's blow crashed into his shoulder rather than the back of his head. Even so, the force was sufficient to knock him face-down into the dust as Armstrong fired his rifle.

That shot was a signal for a high-pitched yell as a mass of men rose from hiding in the surrounding grass and rushed onto the convoy.

'Fire!' O'Neill took command. 'Shoot the buggers flat!'

Jack tried to rise, staggered and fell again when Armstrong smashed him a second time with the butt of his rifle. He heard the irregular crackle of musketry as his men fired, then the patter of many feet on the ground and the calling of camels.

Logan's voice shouted, 'Would ye, you dirty bastard?' and then came the hammer of hooves.

'Fight them,' Jack shouted. He rose again, dazed, and pulled his revolver from its holster.

In the few moments that he'd been on the ground, the raid had finished. Only one camel remained, with Thorpe holding grimly onto the reins. Mahoney was thrashing on the ground, cursing as he clutched the gaping wound in his chest, and Riley lay still.

'Roll call!' Jack shouted. 'O'Neill, is everybody accounted for?' Still dizzy from the blow to his head, Jack peered around him.

'No, sir.' O'Neill was wiping blood from the blade of his bayonet. 'Mahoney is wounded, sir, Riley is down, and Logan and Armstrong are missing, as well as five camels and their drivers.'

'Armstrong was part of whatever happened,' Jack said. 'He knocked me down and fired a signal shot.' *You warned me, O'Neill. You told me that Armstrong was wandering in Lucknow and MacKinnon knew something was wrong. I'm to blame. I have to make amends. Has Logan joined Armstrong?*

Jack knelt beside Mahoney. 'Let me see that wound.'

Mahoney shook his head, pressing his hand against his chest. His eyes were huge. 'No, sir.'

'Let me see!' Jack eased Mahoney's hand away. Blood seeped from a long if shallow, gash across Mahoney's chest. 'It's not bad,' he said. 'We'll soon have that sorted out.'

'Logan!' O'Neill's yell split the night. 'Where are you, Logan, you Sawney dwarf!'

'I'm here!' Logan emerged from the dark. 'I couldnae catch the murdering, treasonous bastard. How's Riley?'

Logan wasn't part of it. Only Armstrong, then.

'Dead,' O'Neill said at once.

Jack felt a delayed thrill of horror. He was used to death, to losing men by bullet or disease but Riley was one of his old soldiers, a man who had survived the worst the Crimea had to offer as well as the battles for Cawnpore and Lucknow. Jack and he had shared hardships and adventures in and around Sebastopol.

'No, he isnae,' Logan said at once. 'There isnae a pandy born that could kill Riley.' He knelt beside the body. 'Come on, Riley man, up ye get.'

Unable to help Logan and Riley, Jack said, 'Bring me light.' He examined Mahoney's wound by the beam of a bulls-eye lantern. 'I'm going to have to stitch that, Mahoney.'

'It'll be all right, sir,' Mahoney said.

'If I don't, you'll bleed to death,' Jack said. *And if I do, the wound will probably become infected, and you will die anyway.*

Jack blessed Mary for giving him an emergency medical kit as they removed Mahoney's shirt and laid him face up on a doolie.

'Who has some alcohol?' Jack asked. 'Something to help this lad?'

'I have sir.'

'Good lad, MacKinnon. Help him drink it and then take hold of him. Make sure he lies still.'

'I'll be all right, sir,' Mahoney said.

'I know you will, Mahoney,' Jack said. 'But it's best to be sure.'

Taking a deep breath, Jack began to stitch the wound together. He had no skill in such procedures so relied on the number of times he had seen army surgeons working with the wounded. Mahoney flinched under the initial prick of the needle and then lay as still as he could under Jack's cumbersome attention.

'I'm sorry,' Jack said as he probed too deep with the needle.

'It's all right, sir.' Mahoney's eyes were huge.

'There,' Jack said. 'That will do you, Mahoney. A fine scar to impress your girl.'

'Yes, sir.' White under his tan, Mahoney managed to raise a smile. 'Thank you, sir. You will have to leave me behind, sir. I'll slow you down.'

'No, Mahoney. We'll take you with us.' Jack had no illusions what would happen to a lone, wounded British soldier left alone in this part of India.

O'Neill had organised the men into a defensive perimeter. 'What happened sir?'

'Armstrong knocked me down and fired a shot as a signal to whoever attacked us.'

'The dirty bastard. Do you know who it was, sir?'

'No.' Jack shook his head. He had never liked Armstrong, but hadn't expected anything like this. He'd lost his treasure, lost a good man in Riley, and had another wounded.

'See?' Logan's harsh voice sounded again. 'I telt ye that Riley wasnae deid. Come on, Riles, up on your feet.'

'What was that?' Jack looked over.

'It's Riley, sir. I'm telling you, he's no deid.'

Jack stepped over. Riley lay on his side with ants already exploring the blood that pooled under him.

'Who gave you permission to lie down, Riley?' Jack asked. 'Get up! We've a job to do!'

Riley opened his eyes, closed them again and groaned. 'I think I'm dead, sir.'

'Nonsense.' Jack could feel Logan's relief. 'It's an offence for a man of the 113th to die on the road. Get better at once, and that's an order.' Jack saw amusement on O'Neill's face. 'And when you report for duty, Riley, get a haircut.'

'Yes, sir.' Riley held up a hand, and Logan helped him up. The cut on his head was already congealing.

'Wash that scratch and get a bandage on it, Riley.' It was all Jack could say. 'Are you able to walk?'

'Yes, sir,' Riley said.

'We'll need a doolie for Mahoney,' Jack said.

'Are we heading back to Gondabad, sir?' O'Neill asked.

'No,' Jack said. 'We're going to chase whoever took our treasure. Whitelam! You're our best *shikari*. Follow the spoor.'

'Yes, sir.' Whitelam accepted the order as calmly as he did everything else. 'It won't be hard, sir. Half a dozen camels and God knows how many men will leave a deep trail.'

'MacKinnon, Batoor, you two have the first stint at carrying Mahoney. Whitelam, you take the lead. O'Neill, you're rear guard. Logan, look after Riley.' Jack gave rapid orders. 'I am damned if we'll allow some rebels to attack us and get away with it. They won't get the better of the 113th, and we need that gold.'

CHAPTER EIGHTEEN

Whitelam was correct. Even in darkness, the trail was easy to follow, with the camels having churned up the dry ground and left plenty other evidence of their passing.

'Sir,' Mahoney said. 'We'll slow you down. Leave Riley and me behind. We'll look after each other.'

Logan glared at Jack. 'I'm not leaving Riley behind.'

'Nor am I,' Jack assured him. However, he agreed that Mahoney had a point. Carrying a doolie and helping the injured Riley was slowing them down. 'O'Neill!'

'Sir.'

'Take Batoor and run ahead. Find our camels, find out how many men we're up against and report back to me.'

'Yes, sir,' O'Neill said.

With O'Neill's dust receding in the distance, Jack pushed on with the remainder of his party.

Within an hour, they found a village, shuddering under the relentless onslaught of the sun. 'Maybe this is where the badmashes came from.' Coleman readied his rifle.

'No,' Jack said. 'These are poor people; farmers, not warriors. Even if they got gold and jewels, they wouldn't know what to do with them.'

They stopped at the well, with the men drinking all they could and filling their water bottles. Jack tried his meagre Urdu on the staring villagers.

'*Ram ram*,' he said and indicated Mahoney on his doolie. 'Medicine man? Doctor?' He asked hopefully. The villagers stared at him, and he wondered if they had ever seen a white man before, let alone a whole patrol complete with rifles.

'Hey, Johnnie!' Logan decided to take a hand. 'We need a doctor. A medical man, right?' He pointed to Riley's head. 'My mate's hurt, see? And so is Mahoney.' He lifted Mahoney's tunic, so the wound was visible.

The villagers gathered around and called to one old woman, who limped forward and poked painfully at Mahoney's chest. Lifting her finger, she gestured toward the nearest of the huts.

'She wants us to go in there,' MacKinnon said.

'It could be an ambush.' Coleman was sceptical.

'It's not,' MacKinnon said. 'Come on Mahoney, and the old biddy will sort you out.' One of the more active of the villagers took hold of the rear of the doolie and helped MacKinnon into the hut.

'You lads stay here,' Jack ordered, 'keep in the shade and be careful. Coleman, take over out here. Let me know if anything happens.'

The inside of the hut was dark and surprisingly cool. Noticing that Jack had his hand on the butt of his revolver, the old woman shook her head angrily at him, the caste marks between her eyes seeming to dance as she wrinkled her forehead. Chattering at Jack, she pointed to the ground.

'Put Mahoney down there.' Jack tried to appear as if he was in charge of the situation. 'And bring in Riley. The old witch may as well look at him as well.'

'She might kill him,' Logan said.

'No.' MacKinnon shook his head. 'She will help.' He salaamed to the woman. '*Jai ram*,' he said, and spoke to her in Gaelic.

'*Jai ram, sahib*.' Another voice spoke from a gloomy corner of the hut, and an old man appeared, nearly toothless and with silver-white hair.

'And who are you, grandfather?' MacKinnon salaamed again.

'Naik Abhi Basu.' The old man slammed to attention and threw an impressive salute. '31st Bengal Native Infantry Regiment! Bhurtpore!'

'He's a bloody pandy!' Logan lifted his rifle.

'No, he's not!' MacKinnon stepped between Logan and the naik. 'He's a veteran. Did you not hear him?'

Jack breathed out and returned the salute. He hadn't realised he was nervous. 'At ease, Naik. I am Captain Jack Windrush of the 113th Foot. These are Privates MacKinnon and Logan, and the wounded are Privates Mahoney and Riley.'

Naik Basu's smile could not have been more extensive. While Logan lowered his rifle, MacKinnon held out his hand and greeted the naik in Gaelic. Within seconds, the two were talking like old friends, both in their native tongue and neither understanding a word the other was saying.

'This naik was at Bhurtpore with Lake back in 1805,' MacKinnon said at length.

'How the devil do you know that?' Jack asked.

'He told me,' MacKinnon said.

'You don't speak Urdu or Hindustani.' Jack shook his head.

'He still told me.' MacKinnon looked puzzled as if astonished that Jack hadn't followed the drift of the naik's words.

Jack nodded. 'I believe you. Can the old woman help Mahoney and Riley?'

'Oh, yes,' MacKinnon answered at once. 'She's a wise woman; she'll know what herbs and plants to use. She knows the *Unani* treatment, sir, that's normally Islamic, but it's spread to the Hindu areas. We could not have come to a better house. We can leave them here, sir, and they'll be safe,' MacKinnon said.

'We won't.' Jack hardened his voice. 'I'm not leaving any of my men in the middle of India.' He watched as the old woman fussed over his wounded. She examined their wounds with surprisingly gentle hands and then gave sharp orders that had half a dozen younger women running around the village finding herbs while the old naik boiled a copper pot over a small fire.

'You lie still, Riley,' Logan said. 'The old besom will sort you out.'

When O'Neill returned from his solo patrol, he was hot, dusty and exhausted. 'They've stopped for the day, sir,' he reported. 'About a hundred and twenty men and some women, with a few looking as if they know what they're doing and the rest only to make up the numbers.'

'Is Armstrong among them?'

'Yes, sir.' O'Neill touched the lock of his Enfield. 'I had him in my sights. He's with the leaders.'

'Right, Sergeant. Keep them under observation and report back.'

'Yes, sir.' O'Neill immediately turned around.

With both wounded stripped to the waist, the old woman created poultices from the gathered herbs.

'You take care of them, granny,' Logan said as MacKinnon helped the woman to apply the poultices. The woman gave MacKinnon instructions in Hindi, and he obeyed with an instinctive grasp of what she needed.

'How long will this take?' Jack asked.

'Not long, sir.' MacKinnon looked up from Mahoney's chest. 'I've seen old witchy-women like this before. They leave the herbs on for a day or a night, and it sucks out all the poison.'

Jack glanced outside. Time was precious. He wanted to recover the stolen treasure and get back to Gondabad before Jayanti executed her prisoners. He could ill-afford even a day, yet if he left these men unattended, they might well die.

'We can spare one day,' he said, hoping that was sufficient time for his men to recover. He glanced at the sun, thought of Mary back at the temple and wondered if the burden of command was prematurely turning his hair grey.

Would I have it any other way? No. Jack gave a rueful smile and stepped across to Riley. These were his men, and he would care for them every way he could. *I will wait until these men are fit, and then I will regain our treasure.*

CHAPTER NINETEEN

'Sir,' O'Neill panted. 'They're still moving.'

They waited on the crest of the ridge with the trees baking around them, looking down at the convoy. The five camels swayed as they walked, with the escort a straggling crowd carrying more sticks and spears than firearms.

Jack frowned, embarrassed that this rabble had bested his professional soldiers. Lifting his binoculars, he scanned the mob until he found Armstrong, riding a small horse near the head. 'I see you, you back-stabbing bastard.'

'Is that Armstrong, sir?' O'Neill asked.

'Yes.' Jack passed over the binoculars.

'He's talking to somebody,' O'Neill said. 'I can't see who for the dust.'

'Nor can I.' Jack glanced over his men. 'We'll find out tomorrow when we get our loot back.'

O'Neill's chuckle contained little humour. 'How shall we do it, sir?'

Jack watched as Armstrong leaned closer to the man at his side. 'We'll do it the old way, O'Neill. We'll hit them as we hit the Plastun Cossacks in Crimea. We are the 113th, and we'll fight like the 113th.'

'Eight of us and two sick against one hundred and twenty badmashes,' O'Neill said. 'It'll be a massacre.'

'It will,' Jack said softly. 'And I want Armstrong taken alive. I want to know why he turned traitor and I want to see him hang.'

'It's either because of a woman, sir, or money.' O'Neil said,

'You could be right, Sergeant.' Jack took back the binoculars and tried to focus through the heat-haze. The camels seemed distended, as if they had legs thirty feet in length and extra-long necks. 'We'll take them tomorrow.'

They moved through the night, jogging across the plain with the air clear and the jackals howling like damned souls. They stopped twice for water and overtook the convoy at half-a-mile distance as they searched for a suitable ambush spot. Nobody spoke. Nobody wasted breath, and nobody complained. They might be

British soldiers, but they were also the 113th Foot, despised by everybody and with perverse pride that pushed them past the borders of endurance.

'Here.' Drenched with sweat and with his chest heaving to drag oxygen from the blistering air, Jack halted.

'There's nothing here.' O'Neill glanced around the featureless landscape. They stood on a bare plain that stretched as far as they could see, with only small copses of trees to break the monotony.

'That's the idea,' Jack said. 'When we march, we expect an ambush at every wood, village or bridge. We are more relaxed in this kind of country. Armstrong's badmashes will be the same.'

'Yes, sir.' O'Neill looked doubtful.

'Thorpe, I want you and Coleman to gather dry wood, grass, anything that can burn.'

'Are we making a fire, sir?' Thorpe looked eager. Before he joined the army, Thorpe's arsonist tendencies had brought him trouble with the law.

'You are, Thorpe. I want a broad stretch of dry wood, tinder, anything that burns, across the road and along that side, opposite us. Don't make it high, so the badmashes won't wonder what it is. I want it deep, tangled and hard to cross. In this climate, it shouldn't take you long.'

When Thorpe hurried away, giving instructions to Coleman how best to gather combustible material, Jack spoke to the remainder of his men.

'Right lads, dig rifle pits, deep enough to lie in, shallow enough so you can watch the road. Look out for snakes and scorpions and other creeping nasties.'

Tired and hot, the men struggled to make an impression on the sun-hard ground until Logan laughed. 'Come on, boys; remember digging on Inkerman Ridge when we shovelled frozen rocks and corpses under Russian artillery fire. This dirt is nothing compared to that.'

Jack hid his smile. It was unlike Logan to cheer anybody up.

Scraping out holes in the ground, they used some of the earth to form a slight ridge in front of them and the remainder they sprinkled over their prone bodies.

'Good.' Jack inspected them from a distance. 'I can't see you until I reach this point.' He thrust a stick into the ground. 'So as soon as the enemy reach this, we open fire. Who's the best with camels here?'

'Batoor,' O'Neill said at once.

'Batoor,' Jack called over the Pathan. 'I want you three hundred paces over there,' he pointed in the opposite direction to the dried kindling.

'Yes, Captain Windrush.' Batoor looked uncertain as he stepped the distance.

Jack nodded. 'Good. Now we wait.'

Lying prone proved a tougher ordeal than Jack had expected. The sun hammered their backs and legs, burning through the worn material of their uniforms. 'Stick it, men,' he said. 'We're the 113th.'

'Stick it, men,' Thorpe repeated. 'We're the 113th.'

As the sun rose, the heat increased, turning rifle-barrels to heated tubes and raising blisters on any exposed flesh.

'Bloody India,' Logan said. 'This is all Armstrong's fault.'

'Here they come,' Whitelam murmured at last, and Jack felt the tremble of the ground. He took a deep breath as the familiar sensations of fear and excitement danced somersaults in his stomach. He had heard that a man only had a certain amount of luck and when he had used that up, death was almost certain. So far, luck had been with him. He'd fought in battles where thousands had formed up on either side and in skirmishes of a few dozens and had escaped with only minor injuries. He knew that someday, perhaps today, he would finish his store of luck and a bullet or bomb would end his career and his life. Worse, he could be maimed, to exist as a crippled wreck for the remainder of his life. *Please God for a quick death, a soldier's death rather than that lingering hopelessness.*

The enemy convoy was thirty yards from the marking stick, a ragged mass surrounding the treasure camels. Jack searched for Armstrong.

'Ready, boys,' O'Neill's low voice carried along the British line.

Jack unfastened the flap of his holster. The steel of his revolver was hot enough to burn his hand. He wrapped his fingers around the butt, feeling the wood slippery with his sweat.

Twenty-five yards to the marking stick. The enemy straggled across both sides of the road rather than marching in military precision. Jack cursed; that made his job more difficult. He still couldn't see Armstrong among the mass.

Twenty yards now, with the mob seething toward the marking stick, talking, some singing and all pleased with themselves. Jack readied his revolver, feeling the excitement mount.

A group of the enemy surged forward, past the marking stick. One hauled it from the ground and waved it around his head, shouting.

'Sir?' O'Neill's whisper carried through the air.

'Now!' Jack yelled. 'Fire! 113th, Fire and keep firing!'

The rifles cracked out, seemingly few against the mass of enemy. At the first volley, there were screams and yells, and men began to fall, dead or wounded. A few ran toward the rifles, most cowered away or turned and fled. Jack watched the camels, guessing that Armstrong would be with his prize.

'Thorpe!' Jack yelled. 'Do your stuff!'

He saw Thorpe emerge from the cover of his trench and scrape a Lucifer.

'Come on Thorpe!'

'My matches are damp with sweat, sir!'

Swearing, Jack watched as some of the enemy ran past the kindling and into the plain beyond. Rising from his trench, he pulled a packet of Lucifers from his pocket and threw them over to Thorpe. 'Try these!'

'Thank you, sir!' Thorpe waved, struck a match and applied it to the kindling. A flame flickered, wavered nearly colourless and blossomed. 'That's it, sir.' Ignoring the enemy horde, Thorpe watched the flame spread until the kindling was ablaze in near smokeless fury. 'Isn't that beautiful?'

'Get down, you bloody fool!' Leaping forward, Jack dragged Thorpe down as enemy shots whistled around. They lay side by side on the hot ground, watching in horror as burning men screamed and writhed.

'Oh, dear God, what have I done?' Jack stared, unable to look away as man after man caught fire and ran, howling, in a blaze of flames. A woman screamed terribly as her hair exploded in a fiery ball.

Jack felt sick.

'The camels, sir!' O'Neill shouted.

Longer-legged than the men, the camels, had turned at the first whiff of smoke and loped in the opposite direction to the fire, bearing their helpless drivers with them.

'Leave them,' Jack trusted to Batoor to round up the fleeing animals. 'Concentrate on the enemy.'

With their retreat blocked by the flames, the surviving enemy realised they had no choice but to fight. They stood and fired, or gathered in small clumps preparing to charge, and the 113th shot them down like targets at a fairground.

'Keep firing!' Jack searched for Armstrong. 'Leave Armstrong alive!'

Jack flinched when something hissed past his head. Another bullet raised a fountain of dust at his feet. 'Somebody's aiming at me,' he said and rolled sideways for a better look. 'Is that you, Armstrong?'

A random gust of furnace-hot wind cleared the smoke, and Jack saw Armstrong with his Enfield in his hands, staring at him.

'Surrender, Armstrong, and I'll ensure you have a fair trial.'

Armstrong said nothing as he hurriedly reloaded his rifle, with his gaze never straying from Jack's face.

Somebody shouted, the sound high pitched and despite their losses and the hideous screams from the burning men, the enemy began to rally. Jack aimed his revolver at Armstrong, reluctant to shoot one of his 113th. 'Put the rifle down, Armstrong.'

'I have him covered, sir,' Logan said. 'Say the word, and I'll blow the bastard's heid right off.'

Jack shook his head. 'Not yet, Logan.'

As Armstrong lifted his rifle, the enemy charged. The mob covered the ground at an astonishing speed, screaming as they waved tulwars and spears, knives and iron-tipped staffs.

The 113th met them with a rolling volley that felled the leading half dozen and then it was down to the bayonet, boot and rifle butt. The enemy was brave, tough and hardy but they faced veteran professional soldiers whose business was fighting. Jack emptied his revolver, dropped it and drew his sword. The slither of steel from its scabbard thrilled him, perhaps with an inherited folk memory or some half-hidden desire to test himself blade-to-blade.

For a moment, the press of bodies concealed Armstrong. Jack stepped forward and thrust at the leading man, who dodged and ran on. Jack had a glimpse of the black turban and partial face-veil of one of Jayanti's warriors. As Jack hesitated, firelight flickered on the ruby ring on her left hand.

'You!' Jack shouted and rushed towards her. 'You murdering witch.' He slashed at a loin-clothed peasant who swung a staff at him, barged the man aside and squared up to the black-turbaned woman.

For a moment, they glared at each other until Batoor roared up behind Jack, slicing his Khyber knife into a luckless spearman. He shouted in Pushtu at the black-turbaned warrior and thrust with his blade. The warrior parried without seeming effort, and for a minute they fenced, slashing, thrusting and parrying with speed and skill that Jack could only admire. Only when the 113th rushed forward did Black-turban vanish, leaving Batoor panting.

'I ordered you to catch the camels, Batoor, not get mixed up in the fighting.'

'The camels are safe, Captain Windrush, and that woman would have killed you. Would you have me stand and watch when you die?' Batoor sounded amused.

'Where are the camels?'

'Knee haltered, sir,' O'Neill gasped. Sweat dripped down his face.

'I see.' Jack glanced over his shoulder to see six camels standing together. He swallowed his pride. 'Thank you, Batoor.'

'He's dead, sir,' O'Neill said.

'Who?' Jack's mind was on the warrior with the ruby ring.

'Armstrong, sir.'

Jack swore. 'A pity. I would have liked to question him.'

'That woman killed him,' O'Neill nodded to Armstrong's body, crumpled between two near-naked men on the plain with his face twisted in agony. Black-turban had emasculated him. 'There's something in his mouth.'

Jack prised open Armstrong's jaw and removed the crumpled sheet of paper.

British soldiers, why fight for a shilling a day when you can earn twenty times that amount fighting for a better cause? Why fight for the shareholders of the Honourable East India Company when you can fight for yourselves and have beautiful Indian woman as your companions?

All you have to do is walk away and join us. Welcome bhaiya! Welcome, brother!

'So much for brotherhood,' Jack said. 'Armstrong must have kept this note and contacted the enemy.'

'Yes, sir,' O'Neill said. 'I did report that he went missing a couple of times when we were in Lucknow.'

'Indeed you did,' Jack agreed. *And I did nothing about it.*

'These black-turbaned women use people and kill people, Captain Windrush,' Batoor said. 'Once Armstrong told them about the treasure he would not be of any further use.'

'Do you know the woman?' Jack cleaned blood from his sword. 'Do you know the woman who wears the ruby ring?'

Batoor looked away. 'We have met.' His voice was lower than normal, and Jack wondered if he was witnessing the real Batoor. 'And I also know Jayanti. Jayanti killed my wife and my son. I will hunt her.' He kissed the bloodied blade of his Khyber knife in a dramatic gesture. 'And I will kill her.'

'Why did she do that?' Jack was curious.

Batoor sheathed his knife. 'Who knows the workings of a woman's mind?'

He's not going to tell me anything more.

'The woman with the ring mutilated a young friend of mine,' Jack said. 'I want her dead.'

'Then we both follow *Pashtunwali*,' Batoor said. 'I thought you had Pathan blood.'

Perhaps I have.

'We have the camels under orders, sir.' O'Neill brought them back to the present. 'MacKinnon got himself slightly wounded. All the others are present and fit, sir.'

That was O'Neill's subtle method of asking for orders.

'The lads did well,' Jack said. 'We'll water at the last village; rest up until dark and head for Gondabad.'

We won the battle, and I learned something new. India gets more complicated by the day.

CHAPTER TWENTY

Gondabad rose from the shimmering heat like a ship appearing over the horizon. For a while, the fort seemed to float by itself with the haze hiding the houses below, and then, one by one, minarets and temples appeared. The city itself was last, with the homes of the people barely seen and gold mohur trees eye-catching bright, as the coppersmith birds clattered relentlessly.

'There we are again,' O'Neill said as they halted. 'Gondabad.'

Jack nodded. 'I hope Elliot is safe.' He pushed aside the thought of Mary. He knew she was used to the company of soldiers, but he didn't like to think of her surrounded by the desperate men of the 113th.

'Lieutenant Elliot is a fine officer, sir,' O'Neill said. 'He'll take care of your men.' He hesitated for only a second. 'Miss Lambert will be safe as well sir. She's a brick, that one.'

'Thank you, sergeant,' Jack said. 'Yes, she is a brick. Now we have to find some way of getting this treasure to the Rajah. It's a shame Jayanti already knows about it.'

O'Neill relapsed into silence. He was a first-class sergeant, but nature had not blessed him with much imagination.

'We'll find somewhere safe to halt the convoy,' Jack decided, 'and I'll take Batoor into the fort and find the Commander-sahib.' *It will be more like Batoor taking me into the fort.*

'Yes, sir.'

They halted in a small *tope*, with the trees for shade and a sluggish stream for water. Jack sent Whitelam up the tallest tree to act as lookout and trusted O'Neill to post pickets.

'We'll be back soon, sergeant,' Jack said. 'Or we'll be dead.' He could speak quite cheerfully of his possible demise. In India, death was so prevalent and came in so many guises, that it was senseless to ignore it.

'Yes, sir.'

'If we're not back in three days, make your way to Lieutenant Elliot, give him my compliments and advise him that he is to act as he thinks best.'

'Very good sir.'

There was no need to advise O'Neill to watch the men. He would do that as a matter of course, and not one single *anna* of the treasure would be missing when Jack returned.

Jack and Batoor left an hour before dusk, sliding out of the *tope* and across the *maidan* to the city with the night sounds eerie and the crackle of distant musketry.

'Something's happening,' Jack said.

'Yes, Captain Windrush,' Batoor said. 'It could be Sir Colin Campbell, or perhaps something much closer. The land is very disturbed.'

'It is.' Jack hoped that Elliot and Mary were safe.

'Captain Windrush,' Batoor broke a long silence. 'How will you bribe this cow-worshipping Rajah to support the British?'

'Why, Batoor, with the treasure of course.'

'Yes, Captain Windrush, but what is to stop the Rajah from taking your treasure and then cutting all our throats?'

'I know the commander of his army,' Jack said.

'And I knew that devil with the ruby ring. We were lovers, she and I. It did not stop her from murdering my wife and son.'

'Do you have a plan, Batoor?' Jack thought it best not to comment on Batoor's ideas of morality, or on his angry disclosure. Batoor was gradually revealing himself as trust grew.

'I have a plan, Captain Windrush.'

'Let's hear it then, Batoor.' Jack nodded as Batoor explained.

The Rajput sentries at the fort entrance looked askance at Batoor, who pushed past them as if he belonged. Jack heard the words "Commander-sahib", and the Rajputs allowed them passage. Once more in the interior of the fort, Jack felt the claustrophobia clutch at him and tried to appear nonchalant.

'In the den of Shaitan.' Batoor tapped the hilt of his Khyber knife, looking a bit like the devil himself.

Jack forced a smile. 'Well, Batoor, let's show the devil what we can do.'

'God is great,' Batoor said, 'and all things are His will.'

'I hope His will coincides with our desires,' Jack said softly.

As Jack entered Baird's office, he saw a furtive figure slide behind a screen at the far side of the room and guessed that one of the Rajah's servants was listening to everything he said. *Well then*, Jack thought in a sudden devil-damn-you-all flash, *let's give him something worth reporting to his master.*

'Good evening, Commander-sahib.' Jack saluted his grandfather.

'Jack my boy, and Batoor.' Baird was all geniality as he stood up to greet them. 'Did your mission to Lucknow succeed? I know all about it, you see.'

'I thought you might,' Jack said.

'You don't look as if you've suddenly come into a fortune,' Baird said.

'I have hidden my fortune outside the walls of Gondabad, and there it will remain until I have assurances of its safety.'

'You're thinking like an Indian now, Jack,' Baird approved. 'What kind of assurances do you want? I can willingly give you my word.'

'It is not your word I doubt,' Jack said. 'It is the word of your Rajah.'

'Ah,' Baird nodded. 'He could not send out the army without asking me. I am their commander, after all.'

'Would you fight against the British if he ordered you?' Jack remained on the offensive.

'I hope it never comes to that,' Baird temporised.

'If it came to a choice, Commander-sahib, where would your loyalty lie?'

Baird didn't reply directly. 'How do you intend to encourage the Rajah to back the British, and keep his word?'

'With a hostage.' Jack saw Baird start. Batoor's suggestion had at least caught the Commander-sahib's attention. It might also work with the Rajah.

'Asking for a hostage will show your distrust of the Rajah.' Baird sat back down, with his fingers tapping on his bureau.

'I know,' Jack said.

'There is nothing to stop the Rajah from taking your fortune – if it exists – and then supporting the rebels.' Baird seemed to be thinking aloud.

'Yes, there is,' Jack said. 'I will arrange for the hostage to be sent to Calcutta. If the Rajah reneges on his word, then the hostage will be hanged.' Jack was lost in the murky waters of Indian and Imperial politics now, so far out of his depth that he felt as if he was drowning.

Baird lay back in his chair. 'The Rajah might not agree to that condition.'

'Then the treasure goes directly to John Company in Calcutta, less the cut that I will take to ransom the British prisoners from Jayanti.' He put an edge to his voice. 'I will take my men to Sir Colin Campbell and inform him that the Rajah of Gondabad has sided with the mutineers and has given shelter to Nana and Jayanti. I will say that Jayanti murdered British prisoners in this fort. Sir Colin will be incensed and will march here with his army.'

Jack stopped talking for a moment to emphasise his next words. 'Sir Colin will storm Gondabad and raze this fort to the ground. He will hang the Rajah and ensure his family lose any rights to British protection or British money. The Company will take over the lands, and that will be the end of the Rajah of Gondabad and his line.'

Although Jack had no authority to issue any of these threats, he had enjoyed acting the tyrant. Perhaps it was because of the strain of the last few months, or the abject poverty of so many people in India when compared to the gross luxury of the princes. He waited for a reaction.

Baird nodded slowly. 'I will pass on your message.'

'There is no need.' Jack felt more reckless than he had for months. 'The Rajah's spy is behind the screen in this room, so he will soon relate all that I said. Here is more for him. I wish the Rajah's sons as hostages. I know how important it is to Hindus to leave an heir, so I will promise the British will care for them, as long as the Rajah remains loyal. On the other hand, if we so much as sniff disloyalty, they will be hanged without mercy.'

That was a pure bluff, Jack knew. The British government and especially the Queen would never countenance such treatment. Once the Rajah's sons were in British custody, they would be as safe as any public schoolboy in England.

Baird breathed out slowly. Jack heard slight movement in the room and guessed that the spy had left, presumably by some hidden doorway. These old Indian forts were rumoured to be full of secret tunnels and entrances.

'The Rajah won't like the British threatening him,' Baird said.

'I'm not here to be nice to the Rajah,' Jack said. 'As somebody told me recently, I'm not a diplomat; I'm a soldier. How long will I have to wait here before I get an answer?'

'The Rajah might order you killed out of hand,' Baird said. 'I've never known anybody talk like that in this fort.'

'If the Rajah has me killed,' Jack said, 'then Sir Colin will undoubtedly destroy the place. My men know where I am and have orders to report to Sir Colin if I don't return within a specified time.'

'You're a brave man,' Baird said.

Jack shrugged. Nobody would ever know how untrue Baird's statement was. For all Jack's bluff, he was shaking inside, and the prospect of the Rajah killing him in some hideous manner was terrifying.

When the door opened a file of tall Rajputs in breastplates and helmets entered, each one carrying a tulwar.

'The Rajah's guard,' Baird said. 'Your fate is now out of my hands.'

Jack forced a smile. 'Well, grandfather, it has been interesting meeting you once more. I hope there is a third time, but if not,' he shrugged, 'look after yourself.'

As the guard pushed Batoor aside and formed around Jack, he wondered if the Rajah would call his bluff. *Think well of me, Mary. I tried to do my duty.*

The durbar room was much as before, with the Rajah and Rani sitting on their thrones as if they did nothing else. The Rajah still sported his jewels and finery while the Rani remained plainly dressed.

The escort pushed Jack inside.

'Good evening,' Jack said as he entered the room. He contemplated salaaming and decided not to. He was not here on a diplomatic mission. 'You will remember me – Captain Jack Windrush of the 113th Foot.'

'We remember you.' The Rani's voice was low.

'I believe that you are considering joining the rebels.' Jack thought it politic not to mention the rebel warriors already ensconced within the fort.

The Rajah looked at him as if he were some form of lower insect that he should squash underfoot, while the Rani raised a single finger.

'The wind blows this way and that,' the Rani said. 'If it blows from the north, it may blow the British into the sea. If it blows from the south, it may bring more British across the *Kala Pani.*'

'That is very cryptic,' Jack said. The Rajah looked away. The Rani lifted a small brass bell and rang it, once. A soft-footed servant appeared holding a silver tray on which stood a bottle and one glass.

'Have a drink, Captain Windrush.'

'Thank you.' Was the Rani offering him the last drink of a condemned man? It was impolite to refuse hospitality, so he poured himself a small glass of a milky white liquid and tasted it. 'Very nice.'

'I know how much British soldiers like to get drunk,' the Rani said.

'Some do,' Jack agreed.

'I hear that you have tribute for us.'

Tribute? That's one way of describing a bribe. 'I have some wealth that the British government may wish to exchange in return for the privilege of looking after your majesty's sons.' *That sounded good.*

'My sons are happy here,' the Rani said.

'If the war continues,' Jack spoke slowly, 'and Sir Colin Campbell or General

Rose learn that Nana Sahib and Jayanti have taken refuge in Gondabad, they will believe that you are siding with the rebels. They will undoubtedly destroy this fort, and there will be no safe place for your sons. If I take them with me, they will be safe.'

'Will they?' Jack thought there was genuine concern in the Rani's face.

'You have my word as a British officer,' Jack said.

The Rani's smile was as cynical as anything Jack had ever seen. 'Even with that assurance from a captain in the 113th Regiment of Foot, will they be safe?'

'I believe so.'

Leaning across to the Rajah, the Rani whispered something, to which he replied. They spoke for a few moments, and the Rani returned her attention to Jack. 'How much tribute do you have for us?'

'I have five camel loads,' Jack said. 'I have not counted the value.'

'Will there be more tribute later?' The Rani held Jack's gaze.

'If you confirm your support to the British, I am sure that the Honourable East India Company will show its appreciation.'

The Rani leaned back in her throne as if exhausted by the conversation. She flicked her fingers as if in dismissal.

'There is one more thing, Your Majesty.' Jack didn't know the correct term of address for a Rani so used the same as he would for the queen. 'The outlaw Jayanti holds some British prisoners in another section of your fort. Perhaps they sneaked in without your knowledge.' He watched the Rani for some sign of emotion, either satisfaction or guilt. He saw neither. 'Could Your Majesty use her authority to free these prisoners?'

The Rani looked bored, if anything. She spoke quietly to her husband for some time while Jack waited for an answer. 'We know nothing of these matters,' she said at last and spoke to the guards.

As Jack opened his mouth to continue the conversation, he saw the guards approaching him. Without a word, they formed around him and marched out of the durbar room. It seemed that their majesties had no interest in helping the British prisoners.

CHAPTER TWENTY-ONE

Batoor was waiting for Jack at the camp. 'I thought the Rajah would throw you to the elephants,' he said.

'So did I.' Jack forced a smile.

'What happens now, sir?' O'Neill asked.

'We try to ransom the prisoners.' Jack lifted his head. 'Can you hear firing?'

'Yes, sir. It's been going on half the night. Not constant, just every half hour or so and then it fades away again, maybe depends on the wind.'

'That might be our boys,' Jack said. 'I heard musketry earlier but thought nothing of it. As far as I'm aware, the only British unit near here is Elliot. Forget the prisoners for the present, O'Neill. We're heading to the temple.'

'Yes, sir. How about the camels?'

'We're taking them too; I'll be damned before I give the pandies a present of our loot.'

O'Neill grinned. 'Yes, sir. The pandies already know we're here, sir.'

'I thought they might,' Jack said. 'We're moving right away before the Rajah sends his army after our treasure.'

'There are about thirty men on that ridge to the south,' O'Neill said.

'As long as they remain on the ridge, they can number three hundred and thirty.' Jack patted the neck of the nearest camel. 'Come on, sergeant. We're on the road again.'

They headed north towards the jungle and the temple, keeping the camels in the centre of their small column and watching their surroundings.

'They're following us, sir,' MacKinnon reported.

Jack swore when he heard a spatter of firing ahead. Whoever was following him, he had no desire to lead them to the temple, yet his handful of men was too weak to fight off a determined attack.

'Go and find out what's happening, O'Neill. Don't get involved.'

'Yes, sir.'

Jack glanced around. 'We'll wait on that knoll there.' The small hillock would provide a decent all-round field of fire.

O'Neill slipped ahead, moving as silently as any jungle-dweller as he vanished into the trees. Jack led the others to the knoll, settled the camels down and formed a defensive perimeter. He sighed. None of his plans was working out in this campaign. He had made no progress with the Rajah, the enemy seemed to have discovered Elliot's position, and Jayanti still held the British prisoners. Colonel Hook had ordered him to find and destroy her, and she was as strong as ever.

'They're coming closer,' Whitelam warned.

'Good.' Logan hefted his rifle.

Jack scanned the now-nearby enemy. 'That's the same bunch that stole our camels.' He searched for the woman with the ruby ring.

The mob yelled at them, waving swords, spears and sticks.

'If shouting is the best they can do, we've nothing to worry about,' Coleman said. 'Bloody raggy-arsed blackguards, them.'

'They're bloody raggy-arsed blackguards,' Thorpe repeated. 'Aren't they, Logie, raggy-arsed blackguards?'

'Aye, that's right, Thorpey. A bit like you, eh?'

'They're nothing like me,' Thorpe objected. 'Eh, they're nothing like me, Coleman? I'm not a raggy-arsed blackguard; I'm a soldier.'

'Yes, you're a soldier Thorpe,' Jack said. 'Now act like one and have a decko around the perimeter. Take Coleman with you in case you get lost.'

A single shot ran out, and Jack flinched as the bullet thudded into the tree a few inches from his head. He ducked, swearing, and searched the surrounding forest. A betraying puff of smoke drifted high up and to his right.

'There's a sniper,' Riley reported.

'It'll be one of Jayanti's women,' Jack said. 'Do you remember Fort Ruhya?'

'How can I forget?' Riley scanned the treetops.

'There she is,' Whitelam aimed his rifle. 'She's in that palm, hidden behind a bunch of fronds. Can I fire, sir?'

'Yes, Whitelam.' Jack sighed. Sometimes he found it irritating working with men who needed an order for the simplest thing.

Whitelam's rifle cracked out. 'That's one less,' he said, as a body hurtled from the tree to swing upside down from the end of a rope. 'She was tied in.'

'There will be more.' Jack wondered if the marksmoman wore a ruby ring. 'Keep your heads down and watch the tree tops.'

A figure appeared, weaving through the jungle. Hatless and dishevelled, O'Neill ducked as a musket roared out, jumped over something Jack couldn't see and threw himself into the 113th position.

'Trouble, sir,' he said. 'There must be fifty of the enemy around us, with these crazy women amongst them, and Lieutenant Elliot's under siege.'

Jack nodded, trying to assimilate the information. 'Thank you, sergeant. How is Elliot holding out?'

'He's doing all right, sir. I don't know how many men are besieging him, I couldn't get close enough to count.'

'A hundred? Two hundred? A thousand?' Jack asked. 'Take a guess, sergeant.'

'I can't tell sir. Maybe two hundred, maybe three.'

'We'll join Elliot,' Jack said. 'We're doing no good here.'

The temple was still a mile away through the forest, with narrow tracks perfect for ambush and overhanging trees on which sharpshooters could perch.

'Move fast,' Jack ordered. 'O'Neill, lead us, and I will be rear guard.' In situations such as this, the last man was in most danger, and Jack wished to ensure that all his men were safe. 'Drive those camels fast!'

Batoor grinned at Jack. 'We are now camel drivers as well as warriors.'

'I don't care what they call us, as long as we get through safely.'

The enemy was waiting, with men and women dodging through the trees, firing at them, throwing spears and shouting slogans that they may have been intended to intimidate.

'Push on!' Jack slapped the rump of a reluctant camel. 'Don't stop for anything!'

A half-naked man sprang from the trees in front of O'Neill, who barely broke stride as he thrust his bayonet into the man's stomach, ripped sideways and tossed him aside like a sack of meal. Somebody fired from the right, and another from the left, with Thorpe yelping as a shot grazed his leg.

'Hey! You dirty blackguards! Come and fight fair!'

'Never mind that scratch,' Jack yelled. 'Keep moving!'

Driving camels was never easy, and when the drivers were scared and the path narrow, the task was much more difficult. After another quarter of a mile, the enemy began to target the camels.

A black-turbaned woman emerged from a stand of bamboo, fired point-blank and ran away before Coleman could react. The leading camel spat blood, tried to recover and fell in a tangle of legs and tumbling panniers.

'Coleman, Thorpe! Lift these panniers; put them on the nearest two camels!' Jack fired his revolver in the direction the warrior woman had fled. He looked around. His convoy spread over twenty-five yards of the path, with the escort very thin to guard the five remaining camels. 'Close up!'

The enemy was getting bolder now, standing at the jungle edge to try to slash escort and camels with swords and spears. Jack saw Logan step sideways and thrust with his bayonet, and heard him curse as his attacker melted into the trees.

'Keep moving!' Jack said. 'We're nearly there.'

There was still a quarter of a mile to go, uphill and with the sun hammering down on them. 'One last push,' Jack yelled, and then a second camel fell.

Jack saw it happen. A red-turbaned man lunged from the jungle and pressed a long musket to the chest of the camel driver. MacKinnon, the nearest escort, was a second too late in swinging his rifle butt at the man's head. Red-turban fired the musket, the driver screamed and fell, and three more men burst from the trees at the opposite side of the track.

Lifting his revolver, Jack hesitated as the camel shifted, coming between him and his target. The men hacked at the animal with long knives before vanishing between the trees. MacKinnon began to follow until Jack grabbed hold of his arm. 'No, MacKinnon, they'll be waiting for you in there.' He fired a pointless shot after them and knelt by the camel. It was not dead but severely wounded, thrashing around on the ground beside its prone driver.

'Poor bugger,' MacKinnon said. 'Why do we have to bring animals to war?'

'Parker would agree,' Jack said. Placing his revolver against the animal's head, he pressed the trigger. 'Best to end its suffering.'

'Yes, sir,' MacKinnon said.

'Take the camel's gear and spread it around,' Jack said. 'Hurry man!' He could hear the rustlings in the forest and knew the enemy was gathering. If he had been their commander, he would launch an attack now, while part of the British force was struggling to unload the camel and they were still some distance from the temple.

'Come on, lads!' Jack helped MacKinnon carry the panniers to the next animal, which still walked with its characteristic slow lope along the jungle path.

'Not far now, sir!' O'Neill shouted.

As the remaining camels struggled with the increased loads, their speed dropped further. Jack sympathised with the animals, yet knew he had no alternative. He fired a shot when a face appeared in the jungle, swore as he tried another shot, and the hammer clicked on an empty chamber.

'Sir!' O'Neill's voice. 'We're at the temple!'

O'Neill's claim was slightly premature as the convoy emerged from the jungle to the hundred-yard-wide *maidan* that separated them from the temple, and intermittent firing on both sides. Mysterious small humps littered the *maidan*, and the acrid reek of gunpowder drifted among the trees.

'The lads won't know who we are,' Jack said. 'Tell them that we're the 113th!'

'Cry Havelock!' Coleman elongated the last vowel. 'Cry Havelock!'

'Cry Havelock!' The shout echoed from the temple.

'And let loose the dogs of war!'

Between the heat and the powder smoke, the outskirts of the temple were hazy. Although Jack knew that Mary, Elliot and the bulk of his men were there, he could see only the vague shapes of men darting among the ruins and the occasional orange flashes of muzzle-flares.

The small humps in the *maidan*, Jack realised, were the dead bodies of men, some recent and furred with flies, others older and already decomposing in the heat. The sweet smell of purification hit him.

'We'll have to run for it,' Jack said. 'A hundred yards with the pandies firing at us.'

'Yes, sir.' O'Neill showed no emotion.

'Right lads!' Jack shouted. 'There's the temple and the rest of our force. It's a little bit to cover, and then we're home. On the count of three, up on your hind legs and run.' He felt the tension and waited until Batoor translated his words to the camel drivers. 'Go!'

The men reacted at once, haring toward the temple ruins, yelling 'Havelock' as if the old general's name was a talisman that would protect them from enemy fire. The defenders of the temple responded in kind, shouting and laying down suppressing fire into the surrounding forest.

'Come on, Batoor!' Jack smacked the rump of the nearest camel. The animal gave him an imperious look and ambled forward, with the driver shouting encouraging sounds and ducking from the passing shots.

'Good man!' Jack said. Two of the three remaining camels were nearly across the *maidan* with only the last taking its time. Jack lingered to help any casualties to safety. He saw a bullet hit the camel in the neck, saw the spurt of blood and the animal twist its head. The second shot whistled past Jack and smashed into the body of the camel. The animal staggered, spraying blood.

'Make it move!' he shouted to the driver. The man stared at him, yelled something and ran for the shelter of the ruins.

'Run!' Elliot's voice was clear above the hammer of the guns. 'Run, Jack!'

'I'm damned if I'll run before a pack of bloody rebels,' Jack said to himself. He took hold of the camel's reins. 'Come on, boy,' he said. 'Try.'

Another bullet slammed into the animal, and it collapsed, kicking on the ground. Jack looked behind him, where the jungle fringe was about sixty yards away, dotted with little orange flares where the enemy was firing, and he looked forward the forty yards to the temple, where similar orange flashes showed the British response.

Without thinking, Jack began to unfasten the panniers. The buckles were stiff, the leather iron-hard and he struggled, trying to ignore the bullets that struck the camel and raised angry fountains of dust on either side of him.

'Run, Jack!'

Elliot was shouting again, with others joining in.

'Sir! We'll cover you!'

A bullet thudded into the pannier beside Jack's hand, numbing his fingers with the impact and ringing on the metal inside.

'Jack!' That was Mary's voice. *Thank God, she's still alive.* 'Run, you idiot!'

Jack looked up, suddenly realising that Mary was correct. He was acting like a complete fool offering himself as a target for every pandy and rebel gun in the jungle. And all for what? A few basket-loads of treasure that the Rajah had rejected, and John Company would take for its already bloated shareholders. *Is it worth dying to make other people rich?*

The rebel bullet had ripped open the pannier, exposing some of the contents. Grabbing what treasures he could reach, Jack huddled them close to his body and ran toward the temple. He heard the crackle of musketry behind him and the cheer of men in front.

Elliot shouted, 'Give him covering fire for Heaven's sake,' and then bullets whistled past his head.

Something slammed into the heel of his boot, spinning him around and throwing him to the ground. He lay there, dazed as the musketry continued. He heard somebody screaming – a woman – *please God, not Mary! Please, God, don't let her be hurt.*

Jack looked up. He was twenty yards from the British lines. Mary stood there, hands over her mouth with somebody – MacKinnon – holding her, preventing her from coming to his aid. Scrabbling to gather the items he'd dropped, Jack dashed forward, limping as the numbness in his heel spread to his foot and lower leg. There would be a beautiful bruise there tomorrow if he lived that long.

Then he was passing gaunt-faced Private Smith who grinned at him with a pipe at the side of his mouth. Elliot was giving brisk orders, O'Neill was raising a hand in salute and Mary was running toward him, arms outstretched.

Mary embraced him, held him close and then pushed him away. 'You could have been killed!'

Jack nodded. 'We could all be killed yet.'

'Sir!' Elliot's voice dragged him away from Mary. 'Glad you're back, sir.'

Jack nodded and tried to collect his senses. 'What's happening, Elliot?'

'We're surrounded, sir. I think it's a splinter of Nana Sahib's men.'

'How many?'

'I'm not sure, sir. I estimate three or four hundred.'

Jack grunted, trying to think. 'That's plenty. Do they have artillery?'

'No, sir.' Elliot shook his head. 'So far they've tried a couple of assaults and a lot of musketry. Their sharpshooters are accurate though.'

'They've no artillery, and they can't use cavalry in this terrain,' Jack looked around. 'We can hold out as long as the water and ammunition last, or we can break out and head for the nearest British garrison.'

'That's Bareilly, as far as we know,' Elliot said. 'Did you succeed in your mission, sir?'

Jack shook his head. 'No, Elliot. We recovered the treasure, but the Rajah won't play ball, and I didn't get a chance to try and ransom the prisoners.'

'At least you tried, sir, and you got the treasure. John Company will be pleased.'

'I'm sure they will,' Jack nodded to the dead camel lying in the open. 'That beast's loaded with gold trinkets, and I don't want to hand it to the enemy.'

'Yes, sir,' Elliot said. 'Parker, Hutton, watch that camel. Shoot any pandies that come close.'

'Yes, sir.'

Jack nodded. Elliot had matured in his few days of independent command. 'I want the treasure recovered. In rebel hands, it could buy hundreds of men.'

'Shall we send out a party after dark, sir?'

'I'll lead it,' Jack said.

Elliot shook his head. 'With respect, sir, you will be in command here. It's not the commander's place to take foolhardy risks.'

Elliot certainly had changed. Jack looked at him with increased respect. 'Whose place is it to take foolhardy risks, lieutenant?'

'The second in command sir, or a junior officer,' Elliot replied at once.

'That could mean Lieutenant Bryce,' Jack said. 'He'll be glad of the chance to have his name noticed.'

'Lieutenant Bryce is dead, sir. He died of fever three days ago.'

'How many other casualties, Elliot?' *I should have asked that first.*

'We have three dead, sir, including Lieutenant Bryce and Sergeant Greaves. We have two wounded and three down sick with heat exhaustion.'

'What's our strength now?'

'We're down to forty effectives, sir, including your men.' Elliot knew the numbers at once.

'Ammunition?'

'We've been conserving it. We still have fifty rounds a man.' Elliot pulled Jack aside. 'Excuse me, sir, the pandies like to wait until we stand still for a few minutes and then shoot.'

'Nasty little devils.' Jack glanced upward. 'It'll be dark soon. I want the treasure unloaded from the camels and put inside the temple, with a reliable guard. With Sergeant Greaves dead, that will be Ensign Wilden.'

'Wilden is sick with fever,' Elliot said at once.

Jack cursed. 'A pity. We'll have Ensign Peake then, and two privates.' *Soldiering to protect the Empire is like that. Men you knew and served with were hale and hearty one day and gone the next. India may be the jewel in Queen Victoria's crown, but she demanded a high price from the men who filled the ranks of the army and the woman and children who accompanied them. Even in a time of peace, cholera and fever, malaria and the heat can kill a little child or a strong man in a few hours.*

'I want you to take a party out to that camel as soon as the sun sinks,' Jack said. 'Bring back the panniers and all they contain.'

'I'll take three men,' Elliot decided at once.

'Be careful. I'd hate to write a letter to your father, lying about how good a soldier you were.'

Elliot lifted his hip flask. 'Here's to the next to die.' He took a swallow and handed the flask over.

'May his passage be swift and easy.' Jack sipped in turn.

'And may Saint Michael welcome him into his band of martial angels.' Elliot closed his eyes. 'That's what we are you know, Jack, guardian angels fighting the good fight against evil and ignorance. We are the sword and armour of the Lord.'

Jack said nothing. He wondered if the Lord agreed with mass hangings and destruction. Then he remembered that sack of soldier's heads in his dungeon and wondered if any side was right in this war, or in any war. Only a soldier could know the true obscenity of warfare, the mad game kings and governments played with the lives of men. Jayanti with her chess had been only a pawn in this ultimate sport.

'Let's hope that our swords are sharp and our armour strong,' Jack said. 'May the Lord protect you, Arthur.' He had never been more sincere.

'May the Lord protect us all,' Mary spoke from behind them.

Jack looked at her, unable to admit to his feelings. 'I hope He does,' he said. *Especially you.* For a moment, he was back in Herefordshire, with the blackbirds singing in a bright morning and a host of butterflies rising as he walked the gentle slopes of the Malvern Hills. The grass was soft underfoot, cattle were lowing softly in the fields, and the sky above was crystalline blue. He was walking toward a smiling woman in a long dress. He was home, far from India with its heat and diseases, ever-present flies and the threat from dangerous men.

That was only a dream. Without money, Jack knew he could never return home. He was destined to live out his life fighting for Queen and country. Only promotion could realistically bring him sufficient wealth to get back to Herefordshire. *Within fifty yards is a Rajah's ransom.*

For the first time in years, Jack was tempted. As a young, inexperienced ensign, he had looted two golden Buddhas from a Burmese temple. He'd intended then to buy his way back to Herefordshire until Myat, a Burmese woman, had persuaded him to return his loot. Since then he'd deliberately avoided temptation. Now it sprang to life, fully formed.

Why? What has altered?

'Are you all right, Jack?' Mary placed a hand on his sleeve.

'Thank you,' Jack said. 'I'm fine.'

'I'll leave in an hour, sir.' Elliot had been busy collecting men while Jack had been thinking.

'I'll arrange covering fire,' Jack said.

Mary patted Jack's arm and stepped back. She didn't say anything.

* * *

Clouds obscured the moon as Elliot led O'Neill, Williams and Parker beyond the thin British line and into the open ground beyond. Somewhere a leopard coughed, the sound sinister, and Jack wished he were in Elliot's place. It was hard to remain behind, hard to stand and wait while men, particularly friends, risked their life. Was a load of gold worth a soldier's life, or any life? Jack took a deep breath.

He knew the answer. He would pay a hundred Rajah's ransoms to keep Elliot alive, or Mary, or any of his men. He also knew that the world did not view a soldier's life as important compared to gold or silver or jewels. *We are expendable; we are Jayanti's pawns, that the nation can discard for the sake of wealth.*

Lifting his binoculars, Jack tried to penetrate the darkness. He could make out the dim shapes of Elliot's party as they crept forward, and he could hear the occasional crackle of dry grass.

'I can't see them,' Logan said.

'Good.' Riley had his Enfield at his shoulder. 'If we can't see them, then neither can the pandies.'

A bat flicked past them, hunting for insects, and somewhere a jackal howled.

'Bloody India.' Mahoney lay stiffly, favouring his still-raw wound.

'Sir!' Ensign Peake saluted. 'Permission to help Lieutenant Elliot.'

'Denied!' Jack hissed. 'You were ordered to guard the treasure. Get back to your post, Peake!'

'Sir, I want to help!'

'Your duty is to guard the treasure.' Jack knew he didn't have to explain. 'You eat, sleep and live there until relieved! Now move!'

'Yes, sir,' Peake turned away.

'Bloody Griffs,' Logan grunted.

'He's keen,' Riley said. 'You were like that once.' He considered. 'Maybe not.'

'Bad *cess* to you, Riley,' Logan said.

Musketry came from ahead, followed by a yell and then another shot.

'Elliot's hit trouble,' Jack said. 'Reserve party!' He called to the six men he had waiting. 'Over you go!'

Newly promoted Corporal Hutton led the other five forward, bayonets blackened to avoid reflecting any moonlight, boots thudding on the hard ground. Jack watched them go, cursing the responsibilities of command, praying that Elliot was all right.

'Dear God, look after that man.'

He had never actively prayed for another soldier, but it seemed natural to do so for Elliot. Jack desperately wanted to go out into the dark himself, yet knew that he could not. If the enemy killed him and Elliot, the command would devolve to Peake, who was too inexperienced. Jack knew that a few months ago he would not have hesitated to take the risk. What had changed?

Mary, of course.

There was a shout from the dark, more musketry and then an Indian voice, chanting something. Somebody was sobbing in pain.

'Sir!' Logan had his Enfield at his shoulder as he glared into the dark. 'I cannae see anything. Can I go out there?'

'Stand fast, Logan,' Jack said.

The silence lengthened, stretching Jack's nerves. He felt himself trembling. *Is it through fear or excitement? I don't know. Jesus, this is hard. Maybe Elliot and all his men are lying on the maidan, dead or wounded.*

'Somebody's moving out there, sir,' Riley said. 'I hear something.'

They listened, trying to ignore the natural night sounds and focus on Elliot's party. There was a definite sound, a shuffling, with the occasional clink. *Somebody is moving the treasure, but whom? Is it Elliot or the pandies?*

'Sir, I can go forward,' Logan said.

'Damn it, man!' Jack could take no more. 'I'm going myself.' Unbuckling his sword belt, he handed it to Riley. 'Look after that; it's too clumsy.' Drawing his revolver, he crawled forward.

There were shadowy shapes ahead, men coming toward him.

'Cry Havelock,' he whispered. 'Cry Havelock.'

'And let loose the dogs.' The welcome words returned to him.

'Evening, sir,' Elliot said calmly. 'The pandies thought the same as us. We have the treasure.'

'Any casualties.'

'Williams is slightly wounded, nothing serious.'

The musketry began then, a fusillade from the rebel lines.

'The pandies have woken up,' Elliot said.

They returned to the temple, keeping low as the enemy shots crackled and screamed above their heads. One bullet hit the ground an inch from Jack's arm, raising a furrow of dust. He watched it dispassionately. *I'm no longer scared.* The defenders fired back, with Jack's party between the opposing ranks of rifles.

'Come on, sir!' O'Neill shouted. 'We've left a gap for you.'

Jack waited until his men were safe before rolling over the defences and into the welcome shelter of the temple. *I'm shaking again. Is that just reaction?*

'You did well,' Jack said. 'Get that treasure to the storehouse and make sure Peake looks after it.'

'Yes, sir.'

Jack couldn't control his shaking. Waiting while others put themselves in danger was more of a strain than being in the field. He reached for a cheroot, remembered he had none left and swore, softly.

'They'll come tomorrow morning,' he said. 'I know these pandy lads, and I'm beginning to know Jayanti's women. They'll come for their wealth, and they'll want a victory to hearten the others. Well, I'm not Wheeler, and this is not Cawnpore. There will be no surrender and no negotiating.'

'Yes, sir.' Elliot dabbed at a scratch on his face. The blood was black in the darkness. 'They come most mornings, sir, a frontal charge with no finesse.'

Jack nodded. 'You've done well to hold out so long.'

Elliot shrugged.

'Post O'Neill and six men on the right flank, Elliot, and when we hold them in front, he can unsettle them. As long as they have no artillery, and our ammunition holds, we can last.'

'Aye, sir.' Elliot said. 'And we'll pray to the Lord for relief.'

'I hope He listens,' Jack said. He remembered Jayanti's executioner. 'I hope to God that He listens.'

CHAPTER TWENTY-TWO

The attack came an hour before dawn when the guards were tired and waited for their relief. There was little warning. One minute the sentries were staring into the darkness and the next the enemy was before them.

'Careful, lads!' Logan shouted. 'The bloody pandies are here!' He fired once and then backed off, bayonet busy.

'What's happening?' Jack ran toward the sudden noise, revolver in hand. A black mass of men emerged along the British front, screaming their war cry and swinging tulwars.

'Meet them!' Elliot led the counter-attack, firing his revolver as he ran, dropping it and drawing his sword. 'Cry Havelock!'

'O'Neill!' Jack shouted. 'Take them in the flank!' He slashed with his sword, feeling the blade slice through human flesh and bone, saw a screaming face before him, fired the revolver he held in his left hand and saw a man fall. He heard O'Neill's party fire a volley from his right and knew that the enemy would be taking casualties. There were more men in front, contorted faces and frantic swords, the flicker of baggy clothes and the crash of musketry.

And then silence.

As quickly as it had started, the attack ended. The enemy turned and ran, leaving their dead and dying in the *maidan* and the drift of white powder smoke across the temple ruins.

'As long as they don't learn new tactics,' Jack said, 'we can hold out here indefinitely.'

Privately, he wasn't so sure about the strength of their position. With a limited supply of ammunition and food, and with every day bringing casualties, the defenders were slowly weakening. Even a minor wound could put a man out of action, and the heat and strain were taking their toll. In India, every British army suffered more from disease and climate than from enemy shot and shell. The rebels wouldn't give up. They would know that this small party of the 113th was isolated, with no method of sending for help. The rebels seemed to have unlimited man and womanpower, so it was only a matter of time, of waiting and creating casualties among the defenders, before they weakened the British sufficiently to win.

'We normally hear them coming,' Elliot said. 'They must have crawled across the *maidan*.'

'They're using new tactics,' Jack said. 'Even so, that attack was not pressed home as hard as it could have been.'

'They're not the same quality as the men we faced on the march to Lucknow,' Elliot agreed.

Jack inspected the temple's defences, a range of rifle pits along the perimeter and lookout positions giving all-around visibility.

'You've done well here,' Jack said.

'Sir,' MacKinnon called down. 'There's movement in the jungle sir. I can hear lots of noises, like men dragging something heavy.'

Jack exchanged glances with Elliot. 'Artillery,' he said.

* * *

With enemy artillery advancing toward them, Jack knew that it was only a matter of time before the temple became untenable. He ordered the men to dig the rifle pits deeper, with sloping banks of earth in front to absorb the impact of the solid shot and loopholes through which the defenders could fire without exposing themselves. He altered the position of the strong points to enable interlocking fields of fire, ensuring that any advancing enemy would pass through a fearful fire-zone. He had small parties go into the *maidan* and collect enemy weapons, firearms or swords so that even if his men ran out of ammunition, they would have something with which to fight.

'Make sure you lift any powder horns or wherever the pandies carry the powder,' Jack said.

'Yes, sir.' The inflexion of O'Neill's voice indicated that he didn't need an officer to tell him the obvious.

With the outer defences as formidable as they could make them, Jack created an inner ring, centred on the ornate ruins around the chamber where he had made love to Mary, and where the wounded and sick were presently under her care.

'This will be where we make our last stand,' he said.

'Aye.' Elliot pulled on a home-made cheroot. 'And then it's the end.'

'There is no surrender,' Jack said. 'I'm not handing my men to these people as hostages or worse.'

'And Mary?' Elliot asked.

That question had worried Jack ever since he had arrived at the temple. *What about Mary? What would happen to her once the enemy destroyed the 113th's position?*

'She might be able to merge into their army,' Elliot said. 'She is half Indian, so she could disguise herself without difficulty.'

'She might do that,' Jack said.

'Or…'

'Exactly.' Jack knew what was in Elliot's mind. 'Or.'

'If they capture her,' Elliot spoke slowly, 'God only knows what they will do. Remember Cawnpore.'

'I'll never forget Cawnpore as long as I live.'

'Who will perform the act?' Elliot asked.

'I'll have to,' Jack said. 'She's my woman. I have the responsibility.'

'Sweet Heavens,' Elliot whispered. 'How have we descended to such a thing?'

'It's this war,' Jack said. 'Crimea was bad. This mutiny is infinitely worse. We are fighting our own people. I know you see it as a war against superstition and evil, and you're right to an extent. I see it as a struggle against ourselves; we're reaping the whirlwind of our own bad decisions, fighting people who are our friends and our blood.'

Elliot sipped at his silver hip flask. 'It's beyond a nightmare, Jack. How will you do it?'

'I'll keep the last two bullets for Mary,' Jack said.

'Two?'

'In case of a misfire.'

Elliot nodded. 'You won't use one on yourself though.' He raised tired eyes to Jack's face. 'If they capture you and torture you, Jack, whatever they do, your soul is safe. You fought the good fight, and you'll die a Christian.'

Jack sighed. 'Aye, maybe. I hope so.'

'If you kill yourself, Jack, that's a mortal sin. You'll lose your soul.'

'I won't do that,' Jack said.

'Good man.' Elliot held out his hand. 'What if the pandies get you while Mary is still alive?'

'Would you do the necessary for me, Arthur?'

Elliot nodded, wordless.

'What are you two talking about so quietly?' Mary's eyes were red-rimmed with lack of sleep while stress had carved new lines around her mouth.

'Our future.' Jack told the truth as he mustered a smile.

'Well, we have another two sick men,' Mary said, 'and I could use a hand with the washing. There are many soiled clothes in here. My sick need clean linen.'

'I'll send one of the men.' Jack calculated who he could best spare from the defence. 'Corporal Hutton's a steady fellow, and Parker has a kind heart.'

Mary sighed and sat on a broken pillar at their side. 'I hardly see you, Jack. Here we are penned up in a few square yards, and it's like we're in different worlds.'

'There will be other times,' Jack said, as Elliot made polite excuses and walked away.

'Will there, Jack?' Mary leaned closer to him. 'How will we get away from here? Nobody knows where we are and the enemy is all around us.'

Jack tried to smile. 'We'll hold out,' he said. 'The pandies know that they're defeated. Sir Colin and Hugh Rose are smashing their armies and capturing their last strongholds. They will not last forever. The longer we hold out, the weaker they'll get.'

The deep boom of cannon fire and the passing howl of roundshot interrupted Jack's words.

'Sorry, Mary, I'll have to go. It seems that the enemy artillery is in range.'

'You be careful now, Jack.' Mary put a hand on his shoulder.

'You too, Mary,' Jack said. He kissed her quickly, felt her briefly press against him and then they parted. He watched her return to the hospital chamber and turned away.

CHAPTER TWENTY-THREE

'I think the pandies have only one cannon in position, sir,' Elliot said. 'I'll take a patrol and have a look.'

'No,' Jack shook his head. 'I'll take a patrol as soon as it's dark. You take over here.'

Elliot frowned. 'No, sir. I protest. The men need you here.'

He's right, damn it!

'All right, Elliot. Take who you think best.' Jack ducked as the cannon barked again and a large calibre shot crashed against a stone pillar. 'You'd think they'd have some respect for one of their own temples.'

Elliot chose O'Neill, Coleman and Thorpe, three Burmese veterans who had experience of fighting in the jungle. They slipped away as the sun set in an orange blaze.

'Arthur can look after himself,' Mary murmured.

'I know, but I worry so.' Jack admitted his fears.

'I know you do.' Mary touched his arm and withdrew to her patients.

It had been only a brief meeting, yet Jack felt better for it. He scanned the *maidan* for signs of Elliot and breathed his relief when the patrol returned.

'How close are the pandies?'

'They've set up firing positions about twenty yards inside the jungle perimeter,' Elliot reported. 'They've only two light guns in position so far, and they've cleared the trees in front to give themselves a field of fire. Heavier guns are still on their way, hacking and banging through the jungle.'

'We'll take them tomorrow night,' Jack decided.

'A raiding party?' Sweat dripped off Elliot's face as he looked back across the *maidan*.

'A strong one,' Jack said. 'If they get heavy artillery up, they can batter us to pieces, and we won't be able to do a thing about it.'

'How many men shall I have?'

'I'll lead this one,' Jack said.

About to protest, Elliot saw the determination in Jack's face. 'Yes, sir. How many men?'

'I'll take twenty,' Jack said. 'If we fail, we're lost. If we succeed, we'll buy ourselves another few days, or sting them into a massed attack we can deal with.'

Elliot didn't argue. 'What will you do?'

'Damage the guns and kill as many pandies as possible,' Jack said. 'It must be a decisive blow.' He shook away the image of Mary sitting in her chamber. *I can't think of her. I must concentrate on my duty.*

But he knew he needed to see her.

* * *

They sat side-by-side, leaning against a pillar while the sun eased downward. It was a moment of rare peace in the temple, with the monkeys chattering in the background and the jungle alive with nature's sounds.

'India can be incredibly beautiful,' Mary said. 'Sometimes I feel so blessed to live here, although I was brought up to think of Britain as home.'

Jack edged slightly closer. 'I don't know how I feel,' he said. 'Back in England, we thought we were the centre of the world and that all that is civilised rotated around London. Now,' he gestured to the surrounding temple, 'I find architecture that surpasses anything in Europe, a culture that predates us by a thousand years and people who have never heard of Great Britain. My little island seems so small and cold, somehow.'

Mary laughed. 'You're turning Indian, Jack!'

'Maybe I am,' Jack said. 'I still miss England. I miss the coolness and safety, without the constant threat of disease. I miss the long-drawn-out sunsets and the crisp winter frosts. I miss the old inns and fishing in the rivers.'

'I'd like to visit England sometime,' Mary said. 'I've always wanted to go Home.'

Putting an arm around Mary's shoulder, Jack pulled her close. 'You will do,' he said. 'You'll love the greenness of summer and the yellow fields of wheat in the autumn, the apple orchards of Herefordshire and Worcestershire and the soft slopes of the Malvern Hills.'

'I want to visit the libraries.' Mary snuggled closer. 'I want to see the great abbeys and the cathedrals, the River Thames and Wordsworth's Tintern Abbey, even although that's in Wales.' Her voice lowered. 'I don't only wish to see England, Jack. I grew up with the novels of Sir Walter Scott, so I want to see Scotland as well, the places Sir Walter wrote about; Edinburgh and the Eildon Hills, the Border Country, Loch Katrine and the Trossachs.'

'I've never been to Scotland,' Jack said. 'I've never been so far north.'

'You've read Walter Scott's novels though.' Mary pulled away slightly. 'Every educated person must have read Walter Scott's novels!'

'I've read some,' Jack said. 'His *Waverley*. The Jacobite one.'

'Scott wrote three Jacobite novels,' Mary corrected. 'Oh, Jack, we have so much to talk about and explore! I wish we could spend more time together.'

We have our whole lives. Jack bit off the words before they reached his lips. *Damn the woman. She is trying to trap me.* 'I'll have to read the others some time.'

Mary sensed his change of mood and pulled away. 'I'm sure you will, Jack, if you ever release yourself from your *duty*.' Tossing her hair, she stood up and walked away.

Jack watched the swing of her hips and swore repeatedly. *Damn, damn, damn, damn, damn! We never have sufficient time!*

* * *

Even in the dark, it wasn't hard to find the rebel convoy. There was no attempt to minimise the noise as busy labourers worked with axes and saws and scores of men hauled at the ropes.

'They have six pieces of artillery,' Jack noted. 'Two six-pounders in position, three eighteen-pounders pulled by bullocks and another eighteen-pounder pulled by hand. There must be four hundred men with the column, about two hundred of them warriors.'

'We have thirty-seven fit men,' O'Neill said. 'We're a bit outmatched.'

'We could delay them a bit, sir.' Coleman lifted his rifle. 'They won't expect it.'

Jack imagined the damage twenty rifles could do against such a large number of men. He would delay the advance by a few minutes or a few hours at best. What chance would all his men have of returning safely against so many? *Not much.*

My men are soldiers, Jack told himself. *They had known the dangers when they took the Queen's shilling. Soldiers?* He shook his head. *Thorpe was an arsonist, sent to the army as an alternative to jail. Coleman was an orphan and joined the army rather than shivering to death in the bitter winters of the 1840s. The potato blight forced O'Neill to take the Queen's shilling. Technically, they are volunteers, yet it was not for love of a queen about whom they knew nothing or a country that failed them, that enticed them into the scarlet uniform.*

They are soldiers. They have their duty to perform.

'Thorpe. I need your special expertise.'

'Yes, sir.' Thorpe paused. 'What does that mean, sir?'

'The two six-pounders in position must have ammunition,' Jack explained. 'They must have a powder store.'

'Yes, sir,' Thorpe said.

'Sergeant O'Neill will take you, Coleman and a two-man escort to blow it up. Do whatever you do, Thorpe, and make me a big bang and a huge fire.'

'Yes, sir!' Thorpe's enthusiasm was evident.

'Sergeant.' Jack didn't need to lower his voice with all the noise the enemy was making. 'Set fire to the powder and take the men back. Don't wait for us. Let Thorpe take charge where he can; he's the expert.'

'Yes, sir.' O'Neill nodded.

'I'll give you fifteen minutes to prepare, and then I'll have a crack at the column.' Jack watched as O'Neill led his men away.

Lying in the forest within a hundred yards of an enemy column was amongst the most nerve-wracking experiences Jack had ever had. He lay prone, ignoring the insects that investigated his body and hoping that his men retained their patience as the enemy crept ever closer to the temple. The hands of his watch seemed to crawl, with each minute a seeming eternity.

The enemy was working hard, widening the path they had already made for the small six-pounders to drag through the much larger eighteen-pounders. Jack watched them, admiring their energy even as he knew he must kill as many as he could. There was a swirl among the enemy, with men stepping aside to salaam as a disciplined unit arrived. *Please, God, that's not the Rajah's army.*

'Trouble.' Jack mouthed the word as he saw the black turbans and veiled faces, with every woman bearing a musket and tulwar. They marched in silence, purposeful and dangerous. 'That's Jayanti and her warriors. There must be sixty of them.'

And then the black turbans were past, sliding into the forest.

Forget them; concentrate on the artillery.

'Right lads.' The larger hand of his watch approached the fifteenth minute. 'Get ready. On my word, aim for the bullocks.' He knew that was an unpopular decision, but each bullock could do the work of ten men. 'If anybody misses, I'll put them on a charge.' He ignored the frowning looks, knowing that some of his men would deliberately miss rather than hurt an animal.

'Cap... On my word... Aim... Fire!'

They fired together, with the sharp crack of the rifles echoing in the jungle. Three of the bullocks fell at once while two others bellowed in pain. War was every bit as hard on animals as it was on men.

The effect was instantaneous with the bullock drivers running into the forest and the accompanying men staring around them or cowering on the ground.

'One more volley,' Jack said. 'Aim for the men on the leading gun this time. That tall fellow giving orders.' He pointed to a bearded man with an ornate turban.

The men loaded quickly, too experienced to panic, aimed with steady hands and fired on Jack's command. The officer staggered and fell, and two men nearby crumpled at once.

'That's enough, now. The pandies will have men after us in a second. Reload and back to the temple.'

They obeyed at once, sliding between the trees. Corporal Hutton led the way, and Jack was rear-marker, turning every few steps to see if the enemy was following. Behind him, he heard the noise from the enemy column increase as they assessed what had occurred.

After a hundred yards, Jack halted the rearmost five men. 'We'll hold them here and allow the others time to escape.'

Logan grunted, 'Aye, sir,' and slid behind a tree. The others followed, calm-eyed and controlled, levelling their Enfields and waiting.

'There, sir,' Whitelam gestured into the darkness. 'I saw movement.'

'Right, lads, give them a volley,' Jack said. A second later, the rifles crashed out. 'Load and withdraw.'

The 113th ran through the forest with scattered shots following them, bringing down leaves and pieces of branches. The men jinked and weaved to spoil the enemy's aim, with every step taking them closer to the relative safety of the temple.

The explosion was louder than anything Jack had heard since the siege of Sebastopol, an ear-pounding crash that blasted down trees and illuminated the night sky. Pieces of debris and fragments of men rose a hundred feet in the air, hovered for a moment amidst the white cloud of smoke and descended in a terrible rain that had the patrol diving for shelter.

'Dear God!' Jack lay prone and tried to burrow into the ground as pieces of burning wood and shattered men fell all around him.

After the explosion came the silence; a hush so intense it seemed unreal. Jack dragged himself up, winced as something stabbed in his leg and looked around at his men. Most were still lying, stunned by the noise, one or two were attempting to rise.

'Come on, lads!' Jack didn't hear his words and knew that the explosion had temporarily robbed him of his hearing. He shook Smith, the man nearest to him and gestured towards the temple. Hutton was swearing and patting at his trouser leg, which was ablaze from the falling debris. One man stood to stare at the flames and colossal tower of white smoke. That was Thorpe, of course, admiring his handiwork.

'I told you to get back to the temple, sergeant!' Jack shouted to O'Neill, whose words were lost in Jack's deafness. 'Seventeen, eighteen,' he counted his men. 'There are two missing.'

Dragging them up and pushing them towards the temple, Jack found his missing men. Both were dead; one lay crushed under the carriage of a gun that the explosion had lifted and dropped on top of him. Bromley, his name had been, a freckle-faced youngster from the London stews with a sharp wit and a foul tongue. He would never see the Thames again. A mass of burning powder had landed on the second man. Pinthorpe had been a drunken scoundrel, a wastrel although popular with his colleagues, now he was nearly unrecognisable, a blackened crisp. These men would join the tens of thousands of British dead in India, only remembered by their colleagues and possibly by their families, if they had any.

Staggering, each man holding his rifle, the surviving men crossed the *maidan* at a rush. Jack hurried the laggards, pushing them forward, roaring words he knew they couldn't hear. He saw the little fountain of dust by the reflected light of the fire, the mark of a bullet hitting the ground. The enemy had recovered far quicker than he had expected and were firing at the withdrawing British party.

'Move lads!'

The temple's outer defences were a few yards ahead, the earth banking dotted with men and Elliot standing tall, waving in the raiding party.

Corporal Hutton was lagging, limping and clutching his burned leg. 'Come on, Hutton,' Jack pushed him onward, 'get into the temple.'

Hutton stopped and put a hand to his ear. He mouthed something Jack couldn't hear.

'Come on!' Jack grabbed him at the same instant as the enemy fired. The bullet hit Hutton squarely in the back of the head, distorting it and exiting from the right temple. Hutton died immediately.

Elliot pulled Jack over the barrier. 'Are you all right, sir?'

Jack guessed at Elliot's words.

'We destroyed their powder store,' he began to shake with reaction, 'and we lost three men.'

'That's a success.' Jack's hearing eased. He could hear Elliot's voice as though through water, distorted and unclear.

'Jayanti has arrived,' Jack said. 'With scores of her women.'

Elliot lit one of his foul-smelling cheroots. 'Things are coming to a head.' His smile lacked any humour. 'With luck, we'll send Jayanti to Gehenna, where she belongs.'

Jack stared toward the jungle where the smoke was dissipating although orange flames still illuminated the sky. 'It looks as if she is already there.'

'If you wish, I'll take out a patrol and make sure.' Elliot sucked on his cheroot. 'Well, this is vile.' He walked away, leaving Jack to wonder if he meant that the war was vile or the cigar. *Probably both*, he decided.

I'll check on Mary and get back to duty. God, I'm tired.

The firing increased minutes later. *Are the pandies attacking again?* Jack raised his voice. 'Stand to!'

The 113th hurried to their positions, tired men with ragged uniforms and limited ammunition. They faced outward, bayonets loose in their scabbards.

'They'll come again,' Smith said, 'and again and again.'

'And we'll send them back, again and again,' Whitelam said.

'Each time they come we're a bit weaker,' Smith pointed out.

'And each time we repel them, we get their guns and powder to make us stronger,' Whitelam countered. 'Come on, lads, we've been in worse spots. Captain Windrush will see us through.'

As his hearing slowly returned, Jack heard the words and wondered. *Captain Windrush is nearing the end of his tether,* he said to himself. *He is running out of ideas.*

'Take positions,' Jack shouted. 'Peake, take the right flank, Elliot, the left, Wilden, I know you're just off your sick bed, but take charge of the rear.' He didn't wait for their response. 'Everyone get where he belongs!'

The men obeyed, sliding into rifle-pits or behind barriers, peering into the darkness for a sight of the enemy. Most of the defenders were in the front-line positions around the perimeter of the temple, with six waiting as a reserve. If the enemy broke through at any point, those six men were all Jack had to counter-attack.

'Ready, lads!' Jack roared. 'Here they come,' Jack saw the mass rushing across the *maidan.* 'Cap, lads, wait for my command... steady.'

He waited until the enemy was close, knowing the psychological effect of the first volley.

'Steady...'

The enemy was close now. The timing had to be right, wiping out the foremost men, disheartening the others yet still leaving sufficient time for his men to reload. Jack could make out the features on each attacker's face; he could see every detail of their clothing and weapons. *That is close enough, damn it.*

'Fire! Cap, ready, present, Fire!'

The front rank of the attacks disappeared as if swept by a scythe. The second rank wavered, until the men behind pushed them on, where the British Enfields felled them in turn.

'Keep coming and we'll keep shooting you,' Logan loaded and shouted at the same time.

'They never learn,' Riley said.

'Sir!' Peake called. 'They're over here, sir.'

'They've broken in, sir!' Elliot yelled. 'Jayanti's women!'

'Reserves! Bayonet men, throw them out!' Concentrating on the mob in front, Jack could only spare a second to glance behind him. He saw the six bayonet men rise from their position and charge Jayanti's women.

'Keep firing,' Jack ordered. 'I'll be back in a minute.'

The bayonet men were struggling. Already one was down, with a warrior woman hacking at his body. Swearing, Jack ran into the melee. He fired his revolver, hitting the closest woman, fired again to ensure she remained down and ran on. The fighting was desperate, with gasps and grunts, and the clatter of steel on steel as tulwar met bayonet. Jack saw another soldier fall as a woman sliced underhand into his belly, heard the man's despairing scream and fired at the woman, missing her.

The perimeter firing grew intense, and Jack knew that the enemy had launched another attack. They were pressing hard, slashing and thrusting with sword, bayonet and spear. The woman he had missed turned on him, her eyes gleaming above the veil, her tulwar slicked with soldier's blood.

For a second they faced each other, the British officer and the Indian warrior, a clash of cultures and beliefs in the midst of a ruined Hindu temple, and then Jack saw the ring on her left hand. 'You!' he said and fired his revolver at her. The hammer clicked uselessly.

'Misfire by God!' Jack threw the pistol, catching the woman on the side of her head and making her flinch. That half-second was all Jack needed to draw his sword. He parried as the woman slashed at his legs, swore at the force of the blow and hacked back, missing.

'You murdering witch.'

The woman said nothing, recovered her blade and aimed for his groin. Jack met her swing, followed through with a thrust at her throat and saw her block with almost casual skill. This woman was no ordinary cut-and-thrust soldier but a skilled warrior. For a minute, all Jack's world concentrated on the duel with this warrior woman. He could not think of the attack on the perimeter or the progress of the siege. The only thing that mattered was survival. If he relaxed for a fraction of a second, she would kill him. He feinted left, thrust to her face, felt her parry, and knew her retaliation would be swift and deadly. He saw her eyes, dark, unyielding and very familiar.

I know you!

'They've broken through!' Peake's voice was full of despair. 'Fight them, men! Push them out!'

Jack saw the flash of triumph in the woman's eyes. She shouted something in a voice that was high and clear despite her veil, and her warriors pushed on. Another of Jack's bayonet men fell, with two women chopping at him in a frenzy of blood and fury.

'To me!' Jack shouted. He could see seven of the warrior-women remaining, with others lying prone or thrashing on the ground. 'Cry Havelock!'

There was no answering roar from his men. The perimeter had collapsed, with soldiers in tattered khaki withdrawing, firing, fighting with bayonet and rifle butt against the attackers.

'Get to the inner defences!' Jack shouted. 'Withdraw, boys!'

The black-turbaned women had gone, leaving his surviving bayonet men gasping and bloodied, too exhausted even to swear. 'We'll hold them at the inner defences, lads,' Jack said.

Elliot was down, crawling through the temple with blood on his head and one hand clutching his left leg. Jack saw O'Neill lift a wiry attacker with his bare hands and throw him into a crowd of others. Logan was roaring, holding his rifle like a club as he fought. His bayonet lay at his side with the blade broken. Whitelam was writhing on the ground as a pandy thrust a bayonet into his belly, again and again, laughing with each blow.

'On me, the 113th!' Jack shouted. Grabbing Elliot by the collar of his tunic and ignoring his yells, he hauled him behind the second line of defence. '113th!'

The survivors were reeling back, wild-eyed or cursing, firing or stabbing at the mass of white-clad, scarlet-uniformed or bare-chested rebels that pursued them.

Jack thrust forward to where the mutineer continued to hack at the now-dead Whitelam. 'He's one of my men, you bastard!' Jack purposefully slid his sabre into the mutineer's belly, twisting the blade so there could be no hope of survival.

'113th!' That was Wilden's young voice.

'Good man, ensign,' Jack slashed at the back of a passing rebel, cutting the man wide open. 'Fight the bastards. Form a line, lads!'

Shocked, exhausted, reeling from the heat – the surviving men of the 113th took positions in the rifle pits and behind the shattered masonry.

'Cap!' Jack gave the familiar orders, relying on the discipline learned on the parade ground to bring his men back. They obeyed automatically, with hundreds of hours of drill having imprinted the words and movements into their minds.

'Aim!'

The rifles levelled. The sight of the menacing black muzzles gave pause to the attackers.

'Fire!'

The volley crashed out, felling half a dozen of the attackers.

'Number your ranks,' Jack ordered. 'One, two three!'

The men looked to left and right, shouting out numbers.

'Every odd number is the front rank, every even number is the rear rank,' Jack roared. 'Load!'

The attackers were recovering, rallying for another assault with Jayanti's warrior women adding steel in their midst. Jack saw Jayanti among them, talking to the woman with the ring. He frowned for a second; it seemed as if the ring-woman was giving Jayanti orders, rather than the other way around. *What's to do?*

'Both ranks cap and present!' Jack shouted. He could worry about the details of command among the enemy later, if he survived. *I wish I had kept my revolver and not thrown it away.* 'First rank, fire!'

The diminished volley crashed out. 'First rank load and cap. Second rank fire!'

The rifles crashed, the enemy reeled and withdrew a step, leaving casualties on the ground.

'Come on you bastards!' Logan yelled.

'First rank fire! Second rank, load and cap!'

Jack kept them firing. With a much smaller perimeter to defend, there were no gaps. The enemy couldn't approach without facing the muzzle of at least one rifle.

'Keep it up, boys!' That was Elliot's voice.

Jack glanced backwards. Elliot was leaning against a pillar with blood streaming down his face, using a branch for support and looking every inch a hero. His father would be proud of him.

'Second rank fire! First rank load and cap.'

They were using ammunition at a prodigious rate, with men scrabbling for caps and bullets.

'Second rank, load and cap. First rank fire!'

Some of the men had rags around their hands to protect them from the insufferable heat of the rifle barrels. Others held the weapons by the wooden stocks. What with the heat of the sun and the constant firing, the Enfields were becoming too hot to hold, the bores were foul and the accuracy impaired. How many rounds had the men fired? How long had they been fighting? Jack didn't know. It seemed his life consisted only of the crash of rifles and the screams of agonised men, the sight of yelling, distorted faces and the gleam of tulwars and bayonets, the acrid sting of powder smoke and the sick raw stench of human blood.

'First rank cap and load! Second rank fire!'

The volleys were less regular now as the some of the more fouled rifles fired before the men were ready. It would be bayonets and rifle butts soon, and then the end as the pandies swarmed over their dead bodies.

And what about Mary? Jack remembered his pledge to leave two cartridges to save her from the hellish fate of capture by the rebels. Unless he could recover his revolver, he had broken that promise. He could see his pistol lying on the ground between the bodies of a warrior woman and Private Gallacher.

'Second rank, cap and load! First rank, fire!'

'They're breaking, sir!' O'Neill said.

The sergeant was correct. The rebels were not pressing forward with anything like the same vigour. As long as the 113th had ammunition, the enemy could not penetrate their defences without taking unacceptable casualties. The enemy line was further back, beyond what had been the original British perimeter.

'Cover me, lads,' Jack said. Taking a deep breath, he stepped clear of the inner defences and walked forward. He didn't run, hoping to maintain his dignity as an officer. Ignoring the crack of musketry, Jack stooped to lift his revolver, turned and marched back to the 113th position.

'What were you thinking of, sir?' Pale-faced with pain and loss of blood, Elliot stared at him.

'Fetching my gun.'

'You could have been killed!'

Jack felt a mad desire to laugh. He indicated the surrounding carnage. 'We're in the middle of a battle, Elliot; the enemy could kill any of us at any time. Have you had Mary see to your leg?'

'Not yet,' Elliot admitted.

'Then do so,' Jack ordered. 'I'll need you when the pandies come again, and you're no good to me if you collapse. Sergeant O'Neill!'

'Sir!' O'Neill arrived at Jack's side.

'What are our casualties?'

'Five dead sir, six wounded, two seriously.' O'Neill listed the names. 'The less seriously wounded are fit to fight.'

Jack did a quick calculation. 'We're down to twenty-nine fit men then, plus four walking wounded. How about ammunition?'

O'Neill frowned. 'Not so good, sir. We've about fifteen rounds a man.'

'That will see off one major attack,' Jack said. With the reduced perimeter, he didn't have to raise his voice. 'Remember, men, no firing unless an officer or NCO orders it, and take the ammunition from the casualties.'

The men nodded silently, faces tired and lined. They knew the end was near.

'We have a smaller area to defend now,' Jack tried to encourage them. 'They can't get in.'

'Is there a relief column coming for us, sir?' Coleman asked.

'I don't think so, Coleman.' Jack had resolved not to lie to his men. 'We're on our own here. We stand here, and we may die here.'

The 113th nodded; they understood. Even the replacements were veterans now. They tried their best to emulate the old soldiers' nonchalance.

'I wish we had the Colours, sir,' Coleman said.

Jack agreed. It would be good to make a last stand under the yellow-buff regimental Colours, the same flag that had fluttered above them at Inkerman. However, the Colours remained with the regimental headquarters wherever that may be. 'We're still the 113th, Coleman, with or without the Colours. There is no surrender.'

'Aye.' Logan spat on the ground. 'No surrender. Remember Cawnpore. They'll have to kill us first.'

'Cawnpore,' Thorpe repeated. 'Remember Cawnpore.'

Some of the men shouted the word as if it were a battle cry. 'Cawnpore! Cawnpore!'

'That's not our slogan,' MacKinnon said. 'Cry Havelock!'

Elliot was first to repeat the cry. 'Cry Havelock!'

The men shouted it, roaring defiance with all their remaining might. The reply came within a few minutes, Indian music sounding from all around the temple.

In between the music, another chant echoed that of the 113th *'Raja ram Chandra Ki Jai!'*

'What's that?' Elliot asked. 'Is that a threat?'

'That's the Karkha,' Batoor answered. 'It's the war cry of the Rajputs.'

'Fuck them.' Logan spat on the ground.

'The Rajputs are a warrior race,' Batoor said.

'So is the 113th.' Logan was cleaning his rifle. 'Let them come.'

'They will,' Batoor said. 'They will.'

'Water.' Mary walked from man to man, filling up their canteens. 'Drink your fill; water is one thing we have plenty of.'

'Thank you, Mary.' Jack touched her arm. 'We'll get out of this.'

'Yes, I know we will.' Mary spoke with such certainty that for a moment Jack wondered if she had information that he lacked. 'You always get us out.'

Jack tried to smile, thought of the two revolver rounds he was saving and turned away. *Maybe not this time, Mary.* On an impulse, he turned back and hugged her.

'What was that for?'

'Your faith,' Jack said. *I wish I could think of a way out.*

'We could send a man through the forest,' Elliot suggested as the sun swooped down and there were a few moments of lesser heat. 'We could send one of the Burma veterans who could vanish among the trees.'

Jack considered. 'There are only four Burma men left. There's me, O'Neill, Thorpe and Coleman. I won't leave, O'Neill is the best NCO we have, and I doubt if any officer of sufficient seniority would listen to Thorpe or Coleman.'

Elliot nodded. 'You've given this some thought, I see.'

'I have,' Jack said. 'I wondered if we could give the messenger a written message.'

'If the pandies caught them…'

'They'd know how desperate our position is.' Jack finished Elliot's sentence. 'We have no choice. We sit and wait and die together.'

They exchanged glances and looked away. Jack wished he could spirit Mary to safety.

CHAPTER TWENTY-FOUR

'Something's happening.' Elliot looked up. 'It's all gone silent.'

Elliot was right, Jack realised. The music and the Rajput war cry had stopped. 'Jayanti is up to something. Come on Elliot.'

Dragging his wounded leg, Elliot followed Jack to the defensive positions. Only insects disturbed the oppressive silence, with all the bird sounds stilled. Heat rebounded from the stones of the temple, forcing sweat from suffering bodies, causing men to gasp for every breath.

'What's happening, sergeant?'

'Dunno, sir,' O'Neill stood behind one of the carved pillars, surveying the outworks and the *maidan* beyond. 'There's movement in the forest.'

'Keep your eyes open.' Jack spoke loudly enough for all the defenders to hear. 'Jayanti is a tricky devil.'

The men grunted, wiped sweat from their faces, swatted away insects and gripped their rifles.

'Sir,' O'Neill murmured. 'Over there.'

The woman who emerged from the jungle fringe carried a white flag and moved slowly.

'They're surrendering,' Thorpe said. 'The pandy buggers are surrendering to us.'

'Aye, that's right, Thorpey. They heard that you're here with your Victoria Cross and they're scared.' Coleman grunted. 'It's a flag of truce, you bloody moonraker. They want to talk.'

'Why?'

'How should I know? I'm not a bloody pandy.' Coleman shifted his rifle and settled the stock against his chin. 'Come closer, you murderous bitch, and I'll blow your bloody head off.'

'Hold your fire.' Jack knew the mood of his men. After so long on campaign, they would shoot anything that they even suspected of being an enemy. 'We'll hear what she has to say. Watch the rear and flanks. It could be a trick.'

'It could be a trick,' Thorpe repeated. 'Watch in case it's a trick, lads.' His laugh was unsettling, and Jack wondered if nervous strain had unhinged his mind even more.

'That's Jayanti.' Jack recognised the woman as she approached them. 'What devilish thing is she planning now?' He stepped out of cover. 'If they shoot me, you take charge, Elliot.' He handed over his revolver. 'You know what to do with that.'

'Yes, sir,' Elliot said. 'Take care.'

Feeling acutely vulnerable, Jack stepped beyond the defences and into the outer temple. He knew that the enemy would be aiming at him, as his men were aiming at Jayanti. Taking a deep breath that seemed to scorch his lungs, he straightened his shoulders and marched forward.

The dry grass crackled beneath his boots and a dozen insects buzzed around his head.

'Well, Jayanti?' Jack stepped twenty paces into the *maidan*. He could run that distance if the enemy tried to shoot or capture him.

'*Jai ram*.' Jayanti salaamed politely.

'What do you want?' Jack was as curt as possible.

'Here we are again, Captain Windrush.' Jayanti held her flag aloft. 'You and I, in the midst of my country.'

'Here we are again,' Jack kept his voice firm. 'You and I in British India. Do you wish to surrender to me now, or are you going to wait until General Rose or General Campbell arrives to smash your army?'

'General Rose is deep in the south, tied up before the walls of Jhansi,' Jayanti said. It was impossible to see Jayanti's expression behind her veil, yet Jack sensed some humour in her voice. If they had met as anything except enemies he could have liked, or at least admired, this woman. 'And as for Sir Colin, he is so slow that he would take months to reach you, even if he knew or cared about your existence. You and your men – how many? Forty? Thirty? You are all alone, Captain Windrush.'

Jack was not surprised at Jayanti's words. 'Do you wish to surrender to me, then, Jayanti?'

'We have a proposition, captain.'

Jack smiled. 'We? Who is commanding your army, Jayanti? Is it Nana Sahib, who Sir Colin Campbell and General Havelock have defeated so often? Or is it some other failed leader?'

'We have a proposition, captain.' Jayanti ignored Jack's probes. 'I advise you to listen and consider before you decide. We surround you, we outnumber you, and your men face defeat, disgrace and death.'

'We hold a strong position, we have plenty of food, water and ammunition and we have defeated every attack you have made,' Jack countered.

'Your wounded are suffering, your food and ammunition are running out, and you will not survive another three days,' Jayanti replied easily. 'Now listen, Captain Windrush. You have something we want, and we are prepared to be generous to obtain it.'

'Oh?' Jack placed a hand on the hilt of his sword. 'What do we have that you want?'

'You have the treasure of Lucknow,' Jayanti said, 'and you have the man Batoor.'

Jack couldn't hide his surprise. 'Batoor?' he repeated. 'Why the devil do you want a stray Pathan?' He recovered. 'As for the treasure, we only hold a small portion of it. The Honourable East India Company possesses the bulk.'

'Our reasons are our own,' Jayanti said. 'Hand over Batoor and the Lucknow treasure, and in return, we will allow you passage to the nearest British garrison. We will provide an escort to ensure your safety.'

Jack laughed openly. 'We have heard such promises before,' he said. 'General Wheeler at Cawnpore accepted such an offer. Where is he now? He's dead, with all his men and women. The word of a mutineer is not to be trusted.'

'Then I have another proposition.' Jayanti didn't seem surprised that Jack had rejected her offer. Her voice hardened. 'We hold some prisoners of your regiment. Hand over Batoor and our treasure, or we will execute them.'

Despite the heat, Jack felt a chill creep over him. Remembering the game of chess he'd played with her, he knew Jayanti was not bluffing.

'I will not hand over any of my men,' Jack said.

'Batoor is not one of your men,' Jayanti reminded. 'Batoor is a prisoner you recruited to find me. You have no further use for him.'

'I will not hand him over.' Jack was no longer surprised at the efficiency of the enemy's intelligence service.

'As you wish, Captain Windrush.' Jayanti took a single step back. 'My offer stands. If you choose to reconsider, come out under a flag of truce, or send out the brave Lieutenant Elliot. I hope he survives the wound in his leg. We will arrange an escort to take all your men to safety and even release our British prisoners in return for Batoor and our Lucknow treasure.' Her eyes were brown and sincere. 'It is a more generous offer than any British general would grant an Indian force in your position.'

Jack said nothing to that, he knew Jayanti was correct. 'If you wish to surrender to me,' he countered, 'I will speak to Sir Colin on your behalf.'

'Thank you, captain. That will not be necessary. You may return in peace to your men. Hostilities will restart in five minutes.'

Tempted to hurry back, Jack forced himself to stroll, pausing to light one of Elliot's disgusting cheroots to show his contempt for the enemy.

'What's happening?' Elliot's omission of the word "sir" proved his disquiet.

Jack explained what Jayanti had said.

'Bastards.' Elliot shook his head. 'Will they kill their prisoners?'

'Without a doubt,' Jack said.

'Is there anything we can do to stop them?'

'We could hand over the loot and Batoor.' Jack was glad when Elliot didn't even consider that option.

'We could use sharpshooters against them,' Elliot said. 'Our Crimea men were trained in shooting. I know they used the old Minié rifles, but they're still better shots than the average soldier.'

'Who are our best shots?'

'Whitelam, MacKinnon, Riley and Coleman,' Elliot said at once.

'Whitelam is dead,' Jack said. 'Tell the others to select a firing position, and we'll see what happens.' He drew on Elliot's cheroot. 'God, this is foul.'

'I know,' Elliot said with a grin. 'We might be poisoned to death even before the pandies get us.'

'Sir,' O'Neill called out. 'I see movement.'

First out were a group of men carrying muskets or rifles, followed by a dozen of Jayanti's women, and then three men in battered British uniforms.

'Oh, dear God,' Jack said.

'You were right.' Elliot tipped back his hip flask. 'Jayanti has kept her word.'

'That's our men!' Thorpe shouted. 'Look, that's Higginthwaite, Peter Defford and O'Malley from Number One Company. O'Malley still owes me a shilling.' He half rose from his rifle-pit until Logan shoved him back down.

'Keep your heid down, you stupid bastard! The pandies have got sharpshooters waiting for us.'

As if in confirmation, two rifles cracked out from the jungle and a bullet thudded into the earth a few inches from Thorpe's head.

'Missed!' Thorpe jeered. 'You couldn't hit a bull's arse with a broomstick!'

'Sir,' Coleman whispered. 'Can I fire? I can hit the sharpshooter or these devil women.'

'Not yet,' Jack said. 'Jayanti might only be bluffing.'

Behind Jayanti's women, a file of men trotted out with a selection of lengths of rough-hewn timber. As the 113th watched, the rebels built a triangular structure with three uprights connected at the uppermost point by three crosspieces.

'That's a gallows,' Jack said.

'It's a copy of the Tyburn Tree,' Elliot agreed.

'Ready your rifles, boys,' Jack ordered. 'Shoot any pandies that try to hang our men.'

'Yes, sir,' Riley answered.

The enemy sharpshooters took positions at the 113th's old front line.

Jack watched as a group of white-clad men threw ropes over the crossbars; each rope had a noose on its end.

'The pandies are going to strangle the prisoners.' Thorpe sounded interested in the proceedings. 'I thought they might break their necks.'

'That's too merciful,' Logan said. 'They pandy bastards will do things the cruellest way.'

Jayanti's women pushed forward the three British prisoners.

'Ready lads,' Jack said. 'Make sure you hit the executioners and not our men.'

The hush was so intense, Jack could almost taste it as the white-clad men placed the ropes around the necks of the prisoners.

'Get the bastards.' Logan fitted his bayonet with a metallic snick.

'Take that blade off, Logan,' Jack ordered. He knew that Logan was quite capable of launching a solo attack on the entire enemy army, getting himself killed in the process and losing Jack a valuable rifleman.

'Permission to fire, sir?' Coleman asked.

'Yes, if you can get a clear shot,' Jack said.

MacKinnon was first to fire, with the crack of the rifle startlingly loud and the echoes resounding around the temple. One of the white-clad men staggered backwards and fell, kicking on the ground. Coleman fired half a second later, with one of the executioners grabbing at his arm and spinning around.

'Winged the bastard,' Coleman said.

'I can't fire, sir,' Riley said. 'Our boys are in the way.'

The enemy reply came at once as their musket men began a rapid fire. Bullets pinged and whined from the stonework, spreading chips of masonry around the ducking defenders.

Jack slid behind a pillar, flinched as a bullet smacked against the stone and breathed out slowly. He inched back around the opposite side and swore as another bullet landed a few inches from his face. One of the rebels evidently had him in his sights. Dropping low, Jack rolled away and into the nearest rifle-pit. He crouched beside the occupant – a dapper man named Flynn – and peered through the embrasure.

'Murdering blackguards!'

The three British prisoners swung and kicked from the gallows, trying to grasp at the ropes that slowly tightened around their throats.

'Bastards!' Logan roared the word. 'Dirty pandy bastards!'

'If the pandies want us to surrender,' Flynn murmured, 'they don't know much about the 113th, do they, sir?'

'Give me your rifle.' Jack thrust the Enfield through the embrasure. He wanted to kill. He wanted to kill Jayanti and all her warriors. He wanted to kill everybody who murdered his men in such a foul manner.

Jayanti was not among the group of women at the base of the gallows. Jack selected a victim at random. He didn't sufficiently trust his marksmanship to hit her head so aimed for her belly, the widest part of her body. He grunted with satisfaction when she staggered and clutched her middle.

'Suffer, you witch,' he said and handed back the rifle. 'Load that, Flynn.'

'Can we fire back, sir?' Logan asked.

'No,' Jack said. 'Nobody fire, except the designated marksmen. Jayanti wants us to waste our ammunition.'

'You fired, sir.' Thorpe sounded indignant.

'I did,' Jack admitted.

Two of the prisoners had stopped struggling and were motionless at the end of their ropes, with the third still kicking. Even as Jack watched, the white-clad men dragged another three British soldiers forward.

'Sir!' Thorpe pleaded, 'can we fire now?'

'Fire be buggered,' Logan said. 'We should charge forward and free the poor buggers.'

Jayanti's strategy is working. My men are unsettled. 'You lads facing the gallows,' he said, 'fire, only if you have a clear target. Don't waste ammunition. The others sit still and face your front. The pandies could be using these murders as a distraction.'

Thorpe was first to fire, with Logan a moment afterwards. Jack nodded when he saw one of the white-clad men crumple. At least the executioners were paying a hefty price.

'Sir!' O'Neill called. 'Flag of truce!'

The enemy's firing ended as Jayanti stepped forward under the white flag.

'What does that woman want now?' Jack wondered. Again, he handed his revolver to Elliot, checked his sword was secure and walked forward onto the *maidan*.

'Well, captain,' Jayanti gestured to the gallows and the three dead men, 'you can see that we were not bluffing.'

'You are a murdering blackguard,' Jack told her.

'Your General Neil regularly hanged his prisoners.'

'The penalty for mutiny and treason is death.' Jack was in no mood for games.

'Fighting against foreign oppression is not treason,' Jayanti said.

'I am no foreigner.' Jack realised that Jayanti was drawing him into another discussion. 'Why do you walk under a flag of truce? Are you going to surrender?'

'Look.' Jayanti stepped aside to reveal the identity of the three British prisoners.

Two were stony-faced privates that Jack didn't know. The third was Major Snodgrass, the commander of Number One Company.

For an instant, Jack met Snodgrass's gaze and then he looked away. As an officer, he should think that the life of Major Snodgrass was worth more than two anonymous privates. As a human being, and a man who had spent much of his career with the ordinary infantrymen of the 113th, he no longer believed that was true. Every single man of the regiment mattered as much as any other, no matter what the rank. *Besides, I don't like Snodgrass.*

'Windrush!' Major Snodgrass shouted. 'For God's sake, get us free!'

'Now will you agree on the exchange?' Jayanti asked. 'I guarantee you safe passage and the lives of these men. In return, all you have to do is surrender your Pathan and the treasure, which we will gain in time anyway.'

'Come and get them,' Jack said. 'If you dare.'

'Windrush!' Snodgrass shouted. 'I order you to free us! Hand over the damned Pathan and the gold.'

'We already are coming, and we already are daring,' Jayanti said and laughed when firing broke out at the temple. 'You see?'

Jack swivelled around. 'You treacherous hussy!' Jayanti had used the flag of truce to distract the defenders' attention and then launched an attack. Drawing his sword, Jack pounced forward, to see Jayanti withdrawing, with a dozen of her warriors running towards him. He hesitated for a moment, calculated the odds and ran back to the British positions.

The enemy had attacked three fronts at once, crawling through the long grass to the original British front line and then charging forward. Elliot must have been alert, for the defenders were firing regular volleys. Jack swore as a group of sepoys in the battered scarlet tunics of a Bengal Native Infantry regiment ran to cut him off. Jack glanced behind him, where Jayanti's warriors had spread out; there was no escape in that direction.

'Don't shoot the captain!' Jack heard O'Neill's roar through the clamour of battle.

'Fire away, lads!' Jack shouted. 'Shoot the bastards flat!'

The mutineers were closing, rifles levelled and bayonets glittering. Jack dodged right and left as if on the football field, slashed with his sword, missed, and ran on. A mutineer appeared in front of him, presented his bayonet and collapsed as a bullet crashed into his back. Jack ran on, jinking, and slashing with his sword whenever anybody came close.

He reached the old British outer perimeter, parried the wild swing of a tulwar, thrust his sword into the arm of a careless mutineer, withdrew, ducked a clumsy spear, dodged left and ran.

'Don't shoot! It's the captain!'

Jack leapt over the outer wall and landed inside a rifle-pit where Logan was firing and swearing with equal skill.

'Glad you could make it, sir,' Logan said.

'Thank you, Logan.' Jack looked around. The enemy was pressing the flanks harder than in front or rear. 'Number yourselves!' He waited until the men had intoned their numbers, one to twenty-four. *So few!* 'Every third man on the front move to the right flank, every third man on the rear move to the left flank.'

The reinforcements wouldn't add much firepower, but every bullet counted.

'Elliot! Revolver!' He caught it by the belt and buckled it around his waist.

'Here they come!' That was O'Neill's roar.

The attack came heaviest on the right flank, a mixed horde of men, some in near-mediaeval uniforms with steel helmets and chain breastplates, others wearing loincloths and carrying spears, a few with white clothes and wicked tulwars. They came at a rush and hesitated before the disciplined fire of the 113th.

'These are not soldiers,' O'Neill said. 'Most aren't even warriors. They don't know how to fight.' He shot a tall man with a red turban. 'Look at that poor fellow, he just stood there waving his spear.'

'Don't complain, sergeant,' Jack said. 'Shoot and keep shooting until they run.'

'Left flank!' Elliot shouted. 'They're on the left flank!'

Jack swivelled. While he'd been concentrating on the right flank, the real attack had developed on the left. The enemy came in two columns, one composed of Jayanti's women, trotting forward with musket and sword, and the other comprising a company of sepoys, still wearing their scarlet uniforms and fighting under their regimental colours.

'Another feint, by God,' Jack said. 'Jayanti's good, I'll grant her that. She's very good.'

'Fire!' Elliot ordered. The Enfields crashed out, knocking down half a dozen of the attackers, but they were Company-trained soldiers and dedicated warriors, rather than the unhappy peasants on the right flank. Ignoring their losses, they pushed on and clashed with the defenders, sword to rifle butt and bayonet to bayonet.

Jack saw Elliot shoot one of the sepoys; he saw two women hack down a private and neatly cut off his head, he saw a havildar heft his regimental colours and lead a section of three sepoys onto the parapet. By sheer force and pressure of numbers, the attackers drove the 113th back, fighting, swearing and stabbing.

'They've broken through!' Jack shouted. 'Form a square!'

It was the last line of defence, the solid British square that had withstood the test of time. The surviving men of the 113th formed around Jack; panting, bleeding, cursing but still fighting, still soldiers.

There is no retreat from here, and no hope of relief.

Jack looked around. Mary stood at the entrance to the carved chamber. He wanted her with him.

'Mary!' he roared. 'Come into the square!'

Mary shook her head. She replied, but Jack couldn't hear her words above the clamour of the battle.

'Damn you, woman, come here, it's safer inside the square!'

Mary shook her head slowly and lifted a hand in farewell before she returned to her patients. Jack swore. *Damn the woman and her sense of duty. Does she not know that the pandies will rape and kill her? Yes,* he told himself, *yes, she knows that only too well, just as she knows the wounded will feel better with her there.*

At that instant, Jack admitted what he had long known. *Damn you, Mary Lambert, I love you.*

Then there was no time to think of Mary. There was only the enemy, the crash of rifles and slash and thrust of bayonets and swords. The pressure of numbers forced back the right of the square until the 113th stood in a clump, fighting with all their strength.

'Well, Jack, it looks like this is it.' Elliot had a cheroot in his mouth. He dropped his revolver and drew his sword. 'It's been a pleasure to serve with you.'

'And with you, Arthur.' Jack spared him a smile. 'Your father will be proud of you.'

'Fucking kill the pandy bastards!' Logan interrupted their brief conversation.

'Logan has the rights of it,' Jack said. 'Come on, Elliot! Come on, 113th! One last effort!'

Perhaps the enemy heard Jack's words for they seemed to hesitate. The mob at the right flank pulled back, some dropped their weapons, and they began to drift away. The mutineers stepped back to straighten their ranks, with havildars and naiks shouting hoarse orders.

'What are they doing now?' Jack began. 'Never mind. Reform the square lads! Load and cap. Take any ammunition you can from the casualties. The rebels have given us a breathing space.' *We have a few more moments to live. Run, Mary, run and live your life.*

The ground was damp and slippery with blood, littered with dead and dying men and women. Jack crouched beside a young wounded private. 'Hold on, Preston. This battle will all be over soon, and we'll get you all sorted out.'

'Did we win, sir? Did we lick them?'

Jack looked at the odds against them. There were nineteen of his men still on their feet, and around fifty sepoys, plus forty or so of Jayanti's women warriors. Even without the armed rabble, the enemy still vastly outnumbered them. 'Not yet Preston, but we will.'

'That's good sir. We fought well, didn't we? The 113th fought well.'

'We fought like heroes, Preston. Now you lie quiet and let us finish this off. Close your eyes and think of home.'

'Sir! Look!' Bleeding from a gash across his face,' O'Neill pointed to the *maidan*.

'Oh, dear Lord!' Jack said.

A fresh army was marching toward the temple. Hundreds strong, there were scarlet-coated soldiers with Brown Bess muskets over their shoulders, led by men on horseback with yellow uniforms and ornate turbans. Their column stretched as far into the jungle as Jack could see, with a band carrying Indian musical instruments.

'That's the Rajah of Gondabad's army.' Jack recognised Baird at their head. 'The Rajah must have made his decision to join the rebels.' He balanced his sabre across his right shoulder. *I've failed. I failed to capture or kill Jayanti. I failed to save Snodgrass and his men, and I failed to turn the Rajah to support the British. Here I stand, Jack Baird Windrush, grandson of a traitor, bastard half-breed, rejected by my family and an officer who has led his men to defeat and massacre. It ends here at the ruined Hindu temple where my parents created me. I've travelled full circle.*

'We could surrender,' thin-faced Private Smith said.

'Bugger that.' Logan spat on the ground. 'We're the 113th, not some bloody Hyde Park Strollers.' He raised his voice. 'We're the 113th! Come and get us, you bastards!'

'Cry Havelock!' Coleman shouted.

'Let loose the dogs of war!' the 113th chorused.

Jack straightened his back. He may be a failure, but he led men. These were his men, and he would be proud to die alongside them. *How about Mary?*

'Sir!' O'Neill spoke softly. 'Look.'

The Rajah of Gondabad's army had formed into three long columns and was advancing toward the temple with slow, measured steps.

'Here they come, boys,' Jack said softly. 'Everybody take their position. How much ammunition do we have left?'

'Seven rounds a man, sir,' O'Neill said, 'and then it's bayonets and belt-buckles.'

'Don't waste ammunition.' Jack looked for Jayanti and the warrior with the ruby ring. He hoped he could kill them before he died himself. That was his final ambition. *Look after yourself Mary; please look after yourself.*

'Come on, you bastards!' Logan yelled. '113th!'

The Rajah's band began to play, with the music strange to Jack's ears. He frowned as the tune altered. 'What's that they're playing?'

'It's *Rule Britannia*,' Elliot said. 'Or it's meant to be.'

'The cheeky bastards!' O'Neill sounded more surprised than angry. 'Play your own tunes!'

'They are, sergeant,' MacKinnon said. 'They're not joining the pandies.'

'Sweet Lord,' Elliot pointed. 'Would you look at that?' The Rajah's army unfurled two flags. One was the Rajah's standard, and the other was the Union Flag.

'They've joined us,' Jack said. 'The Rajah of Gondabad has joined the British side.'

On sight of the British flag, the mutineers had begun an orderly, if rapid withdrawal. Jayanti's warriors lingered longer before they trotted away toward the jungle.

'After them!' Jack made rapid decisions. 'I want Jayanti dead! Elliot, try and find the prisoners, find our men!' In that few moments, the entire situation had altered. Jack led his 113th out of their positions to chase after the retreating enemy. Diplomacy dictated that he should wait to greet the Commander-sahib of the Rajah's army, but Jack had never considered himself a diplomat. Keeping his eye on Jayanti, he chased after her, leaping over dead bodies and ignoring everybody else in his pursuit.

'Jayanti!' he yelled. 'Stand and fight me, you murdering witch!'

When the warrior women reached the edge of the jungle, Jayanti paused, turned and raised her sword in salute.

'This battle is over, Captain Windrush. The war will continue.' Turning, she ran light-footed into the trees.

'Stand and fight!' Jack roared, knowing he wouldn't catch her in the jungle. *I've still failed. Jayanti will escape and return to cause more trouble and murder more British soldiers.* He saw the bullet catch Jayanti high in the thigh. She spun around, grabbing at her leg, and the second bullet smacked into her chest. Jayanti lifted her tulwar, glared at Jack and jerked backwards as a third bullet took off the top of her head.

Ensign Peake held his revolver in slack fingers and stared at the body. 'I killed her,' he said. 'I killed that woman.'

'You did,' Jack said. 'And you were right to kill her.'

'I killed a woman.' Peake dropped his revolver. 'Oh, what will happen to me?'

Jack stopped for a moment as the battle continued around them. 'It's all right, ensign. The first is always the worst.' He patted the boy's shoulder. 'You'll never forget it, but the memory will fade.'

As Peake began to cry, another voice sounded, educated, calm and feminine.

'I will fight you.'

'What?' Jack looked up. The woman stared at him with her black turban low over her forehead, and the veil pulled up until it touched her nose. Jack saw the gleam of the ruby ring.

'You!'

'Me.' The woman drew her tulwar. Sunlight glittered on the emerald in the pommel. No ordinary warrior could afford a weapon of that quality. *Who are you? I saw you give orders to Jayanti. Who are you?*

'If you surrender,' Jack said. 'I will guarantee you a fair trial.' *I hope you fight. I haven't forgotten Ensign Green.*

In response, the woman ran at him, swinging her tulwar like an amateur. Jack easily fended off the blow and cut backhanded, until the blade of his sabre tangled in the woman's loose clothing.

Unspeaking, the woman attacked again, her tulwar a blur of steel as she pressed Jack back.

'We may have lost this battle,' the woman said, 'but I will kill you, Captain Windrush.' She clashed her tulwar against Jack's sabre, scraped down the blade and twisted. Jack gasped as his blade snapped. Throwing the handle at her, he dodged backwards, reaching for his revolver. As he dragged it free, the woman thrust at him, with the point of her sword nicking the top of his thigh.

Jack swore at the pain and fired without aiming. He missed, and the woman advanced again.

'You will die slowly, captain, a screaming eunuch, like your ensign friend.'

Jack fired a second time, missed again and threw the revolver. The woman advanced, circling her blade, taunting as Jack backed away.

'Let me fight her, Captain Windrush.' Batoor stepped from between the trees. He was smiling as he drew his Khyber knife.

For a moment, the woman and Batoor spoke in Pushtu. Their voices rose and then they fought. Jack had never seen such fury or such skill. He knew that he wasn't a swordsman and watched as two experts traded blows, parrying, thrusting and swinging with a force that had both reeling.

Batoor parried one of the woman's swings and kicked her full in the stomach. She fell, shouted something and threw her sword. It missed Batoor by a yard and clattered uselessly on the ground. Jack lifted it and stepped forward.

'I promised this woman a fair trial,' he said.

'I made no such promise,' Batoor said, and thrust his Khyber knife into the woman's belly, slowly twisting as she writhed in pain.

'Batoor!' Jack tried to push the Pathan away.

'Leave us, Captain Windrush. This woman sent Jayanti to murder my wife and child.' Batoor twisted his blade, easing it slowly down her belly.

The woman died in front of Jack's eyes.

'That was murder,' Jack said.

'That was *Pashtunwali*.' Batoor flicked off the woman's veil. The Rani of Gondabad stared sightlessly upward. 'This is the Rani.'

Jack took a deep breath. 'I thought I saw her giving orders to Jayanti.' He looked up. 'Now tell me why you two hated each other?'

'We were lovers once,' Batoor said, 'when I was the captain of her bodyguard. Then she found out I was married and sent Jayanti and her warriors to kill my wife and my family.' He faced Jack. 'Did you think that the British are the only power in India? Many things happen without your knowledge, Captain Windrush.'

Jack looked at the twisted body of the Rani. 'The Rajah won't like you killing his wife.'

'The Rani has controlled the Rajah for years,' Batoor said. 'She supported the mutineers while the Rajah thought the British would win. Now she is dead; he is free to make up his own mind, so he will do the opposite of what she wanted.'

'I see,' Jack said. 'What a tangled country this is.'

Batoor smiled and wiped his blade on the Rani's clothes. 'Good-bye, Captain Windrush,' he said. 'We have completed our agreement.'

'We have not,' Jack said. 'I owe you a horse.'

'You can pay me if we meet again,' Batoor said, 'either as friends or enemies.'

'Hopefully in friendship,' Jack said. 'I would not like you as an enemy.' He picked up the Rani's tulwar and thrust it through his belt. When he looked up, Batoor was already walking into the jungle. *Now I'd better find the Commander-sahib.*

Baird was sitting on a gleaming brown horse, calmly directing his men to scour the jungle for Jayanti's black-turbans and the remnants of the mutineers. 'Ah, Jack, my boy.' Baird looked down at him. 'I believe we have something to pick up for the Rajah.'

'It's good to see you, commander,' Jack said, 'and I believe you are correct, in exchange for a couple of hostages.'

'Your Lieutenant Elliot rescued the British prisoners,' Baird spoke casually. 'And now that we're on the same side, you may wish to know that I know of another military position opening soon.'

'Is that right, sir?' Jack was still trying to recover from the strain of the battle.

'I'll come and talk to you when the dust settles,' Baird said. 'Now, where is the tribute for my Rajah?'

CHAPTER TWENTY-FIVE

Gondabad, January 1859

The notes of the bugle faded as the 113th settled down for the night in their cantonments at Gondabad. Jack sat in a corner of the Officers' Mess, enjoying the noise and bustle of peace. Glancing out the window, Jack saw the tall bamboos casting shade over a patch of grass while half a dozen *ayas* looked after the regiment's children. Charlotte Riley was in the midst of the *ayas*, laughing as she lifted a small boy in a sailor suit.

God is in his Heaven; Queen Victoria is on her throne and peace, thank the Lord, has returned to India. Jack looked up when the door opened, and Elliot limped in, favouring his recently-healed leg and with a romantic scar on his left temple.

'Congratulations, Captain Elliot.' Jack held out his hand. 'Not that you deserve promotion, of course. Imagine you, gazetted captain for your services throughout the campaign! Well done.'

'There's more.' Elliot looked embarrassed. 'They're talking of giving me the Victoria Cross as well.'

Jack shook his head. 'They hand those out to anybody, nowadays.' He smiled. 'Nobody deserves it more, Arthur.'

'It's not right, Jack. You led us, you found Jayanti, and you convinced the Rajah to support the British.'

Jack asked a servant for a whisky and sank into one of the cane chairs. 'You held the temple, Arthur, and you rescued the prisoners.'

Elliot shook his head. 'I didn't *have* to rescue them; they were running loose. It's not right.'

Jack grinned. 'It *is* right. Besides, our new colonel doesn't like me much.'

'Our new colonel doesn't like you at all,' Elliot said. 'Here he is now. Mind your manners, Jack.'

Colonel Snodgrass stepped through the doorway and surveyed his kingdom. Still gaunt from his long captivity, he was greyer of hair and whiskers than he had been, and even shorter of temper. He snapped his fingers for brandy and stalked to his favourite seat, with the servants scurrying to avoid him and the officers stepping out of his way.

'I have to ask him,' Jack said. 'He won't like it.'

'Don't do it, Jack,' Elliot said quietly. 'You'll ruin your career. You'll never get your step, and you'll remain a captain forever.'

Jack sipped at his whisky. 'This Ferintosh is better than the kill-me-deadly you forced me to drink.'

'Don't do it, Jack,' Elliot repeated. 'You'll alienate yourself and lose all your friends in the regiment.'

'Did your Highland colleagues distil that stuff from dead elephants?' Jack took a final drink before rising. *Do I need Scotch courage? Or am I only putting off the evil moment?* Jack shrugged. He and Snodgrass had never been the best of friends.

'May I have a word please, colonel?'

'If you must.' Colonel Snodgrass gave a curt nod.

'I have a request to make.'

'What is it, Windrush?'

'I wish to get married.'

'Who is the woman?' Snodgrass didn't smile. 'Is she suitable?'

'Mary Lambert,' Jack said. 'Her father was an officer in the Company's service.'

'And her mother?'

'A native of India.'

'You may marry her if you wish,' Snodgrass said. 'And then you may leave my regiment. There is no place for half-castes in the 113th.'

Jack imagined his fist landing on Snodgrass's jaw. He could see the colonel rising from the chair and landing on the floor. He could also envisage the resulting court martial that would cashier him and leave him penniless and unemployed. He would be unable to provide for himself, let alone anybody else. Punching the colonel would grant instant satisfaction and long-term misery. It wouldn't help Mary in the slightest.

'No, sir. We only have a place for officers who surrender themselves and all their men.' Jack gave a little bow as a sudden hush descended on the mess. 'You will have my resignation in writing within the hour.' He could feel the tension and hear the shuffle as nearly every officer present moved further away from him. He'd expected such a reaction from men who were desperate to enhance the reputation of the regiment and advance up the career ladder.

'Captain Windrush,' Elliot's voice was loud in the subdued Mess. 'I hope I may have the honour of acting as your best man.'

Although Elliot had been at his side through a score of battles and skirmishes, Jack had never appreciated his friendship more than at that moment. 'The honour would be mine, Captain Elliot.'

Thank you, Arthur. I hope your loyalty has not damaged your career.

Jack paced to his bungalow and nodded to the bored watchman at the door. 'Do I have a visitor?'

'Yes, sahib.'

Pushing open the outer door, Jack walked into his front room. 'Good evening, Grandfather.' He poured them both a drink.

'How did the good colonel react?' Baird was lounging on Jack's chair.

'Predictably.' Jack balanced on the table. 'I hope I'm doing the right thing here.'

'You had a choice,' Baird said. 'You can remain in the 113th under Colonel Snodgrass and try and keep friendly with Mary Lambert as long as you are in India, or you can marry the blasted woman and leave the regiment.'

'I have chosen the latter course.'

'Women can do that to you.' Baird was smiling. 'That's how your mother came about.' His chuckle could have come from a man forty years younger. He held out his glass for a refill and smiled when Jack obliged. 'And I don't regret it in the slightest.'

'I'll miss the 113th,' Jack admitted. He liked his grandfather, although he recognised that he was a rogue. 'I'll miss the men.' He thought of Riley and Coleman, Thorpe and O'Neill, even the murderous Logan. Most of all he thought of Arthur Elliot.

'You could be too busy to even think of them,' Baird said. 'Our mutual friend can be very demanding.'

'How do you know him?'

'He contacted me,' Baird admitted. 'We discussed you.'

'Did you indeed?'

'We did,' the voice came from the outer door as Colonel Hook walked in. 'I am glad you chose to join me, Windrush. We have much work to do.'

'Yes, sir.' Jack knew that his world was about to change again. He smiled as Mary stepped into the room. Whatever happened, he knew he would never be alone, not with Mary beside him.

I have made my choice and have no regrets.

'Where are you sending me, sir?'

'To the furthest side of the world, Windrush.' Hook said.

HISTORICAL NOTE

The Indian Mutiny was arguably the most bitter of the British 19th-century colonial campaigns. Although the fighting spluttered on into 1859, the Mutiny effectively finished in 1858. The days of the Honourable East India Company ended, and those of the British Raj began as the Crown took control of India. The old Company armies merged into a new Indian Army, with the so-called 'martial races' as its backbone, with Sikhs and Gurkhas dominant and justly famed as fighting men.

The Mutiny left some British paranoid about the possibility of further outbreaks, with warnings to incoming officers to maintain their vigilance. The British never found Nana Sahib, although expeditions sought him and rumours and speculation abounded.

British rule survived another ninety years and two world wars, finally ending with the independence of India, Pakistan, Burma and Ceylon in 1947. Historians disagree about the events of 1857-58, and the real causes of the war. Nobody can disagree that all sides fought with incredible bravery.

In Britain, people have largely forgotten the generals and men who fought in that war and the battles of Lucknow, Cawnpore, Delhi and all the rest are barely known. Indian historians often brand the conflict as the First War of Independence and portray it as a national uprising against British rule. History rolls on; attitudes alter, what one generation accepts as a fact, the next will scorn. Jack Windrush, Arthur Elliot, Mary Lambert, Riley, Logan, Thorpe and all their colleagues lived within their own timeframe, with the attitudes and perceptions of the mid-nineteenth century. Their lives and adventures continued.

Malcolm Archibald

WINDRUSH - WARRIORS OF GOD

JACK WINDRUSH BOOK 6

First comes one Englishman, as a traveller or for shikar; then come two and make a map; then comes an army and takes the country. Therefore, it is better to kill the first Englishman.
   Pashtun proverb

PRELUDE

Daffadar Habib Khan heard the tiny click through the sinister blanket of night. It could have been nothing, a stone dislodged by the wind, the noise made by a nocturnal animal, but Habib Khan was instantly alert. Born and bred to *Pakhtunwali*, the Pashtun way of life, he touched the shoulder of the sowar to his right, nodding in the direction of the sound. Immediately understanding, the sowar passed on the message until every man of the Guides patrol was alert.

A chill wind blew from the unseen heights of the Spin Ghar, the range of mountains otherwise known as the Safed Koh. Here, in Pakhtunkhwa, the unstable North-West Frontier between British India and the independent land of Afghanistan, every sound could mean danger.

When Habib Khan heard the slither of cloth on rock, he knew that a man was approaching. When he caught the slight whiff of gun oil, he knew that the man was armed. Every single sound or smell added to his knowledge so that within minutes Habib Khan had a complete picture of what was out there in the dark. He did not have to think; the instincts of generations of hillmen had been bred into him.

Twenty men, he told himself. *Ghilzais; they are moving into an ambush position.*

Lying prone, Habib Khan nestled his rifle behind a rock and got ready to fire. He did not have to load; any man who carried an empty firearm in Pakhtunkhwa was either a fool or dead. Habib Khan was not the former and had no desire to be the latter. There was no sound from his colleagues; they knew the danger as well as he did.

A horse whinnied behind them, the sound carrying far in the dark. It was a tiny incident but enough to preempt the Ghilzai tribesmen's attack. They rose as one, moving onto what they hoped would be a sleeping camp. Instead they walked into the fire of a dozen Guides' rifles.

The shots shattered the silence, echoing from the surrounding hills as each muzzle flash gave a tiny vignette of the scene. Habib Khan had a partial picture of a score of Ghilzais advancing through the night with Khyber Knives or pulwars naked in their hands and rifles slung across their backs. Then came sudden darkness as the firing stopped. The acrid reek of powder smoke drifted in the sharp air.

'What the devil…' Lieutenant Beattock, back with the main body of the Guides, shouted. 'What's happening up there, Daffadar?'

With no time to explain, Daffadar Habib Khan ordered his men to fix bayonets. The metallic snicks sounded sinister on the hushed hillside.

'Ready?' Habib Khan had no need to ask.

The Guides followed, feet silent in the dark as Habib Khan led them forward to meet the Ghilzais, men of their blood, men every bit as adept in hill-craft as themselves, men eager to meet their attack.

Bayonet to Khyber Knife, rifle butt to pulwar, the skirmish lasted only five minutes and ended with the Ghilzais melting back into the dark. Lieutenant Beattock scrambled up in time to see the final few seconds. 'Well done, Daffadar.' He looked around at the crumpled bodies of three Ghilzais while a single wounded Guide tried to hold his entrails in place. 'Take Khazi back down the hill and we'll get him attended to.'

'Yes, Beattock Sahib,' Habib Khan said.

'Halloa now.' Beattock turned over one of the Ghilzai dead. 'What have we here?' Removing the rifle from the man's back, Beattock held it up. 'Now here's mischief. Where did you get this from, my fine fellow?' Lifting the rifle to his shoulder, Beattock sighted along the barrel. 'You did very well, Daffadar, even better than you think.' He looked again at the dead Ghilzai, swore softly, and crouched down. 'We have trouble,' he said, pulling at the red cord the man sported on his right wrist. 'We could have major trouble.'

CHAPTER ONE

Gondabad, India, June 1863

'Have you seen this, Jack?' Mary tapped the relevant paragraph of the *Times* with her forefinger. 'It's about your brother.'

Captain Jack Windrush looked up from the fishing fly he was tying. 'I didn't know the papers had arrived. What's William doing now? Winning the Victoria Cross for bravely parading down Pall Mall?'

'He's making more babies,' Mary said. 'I'll read it out to you: "We are pleased to announce that Captain William Windrush of the Royal Malverns has been blessed with a child. The new arrival, William Crimea Windrush, came into this world on the 13th of January 1862. Mother and baby are both well. Captain William Windrush is already the proud father of a three-year-old girl, Helen Sevastopol Windrush." '

'I'm glad they are both well,' Jack said.

'You are glad that William's Helen is well even though Helen transferred her affections from you to William?' Mary reminded sweetly.

'That was a long time ago.' Jack did not enjoy the memory.

'Well, I am glad she did,' Mary said. 'It left you open for me.'

Jack grunted as he missed the knot. He began to tie the fly again. 'That was fortunate.'

Mary put the newspaper down. 'What does William's male child mean for your position, Jack?'

Jack considered for a moment, sighed, and put the fly aside. He knew he would not get any peace until Mary had exhausted the subject. 'I grew up thinking I was the heir to Wychwood Manor, as you know. It was not until my father died that I learned that, although I was the oldest, I was also illegitimate, with William the oldest legitimate son and, therefore, the heir.'

'I know that,' Mary said patiently.

Jack leaned back in his chair, swatting at a circling mosquito. 'When my mother, or rather my step-mother, told me that I was illegitimate, I was devastated.'

'I can imagine.' Mary did not remind Jack she had heard the story before. 'Your mother must be a cruel woman. Was she cruel?'

'No.' Jack shook his head. 'I have had years to think about this. When my step-mother first told me that I was illegitimate and would lose what I thought was my inheritance, I did believe she was cruel.' He looked away, reliving those dark days. 'I thought it was unfair that I should not join the family regiment, the Royal Malverns. I thought it wrong that I was only commissioned into the 113th, the lowest regiment in the army, with what I considered a pittance to live by.'

Mary listened. 'Do you still think the same, twelve years later?'

'No.' Jack shook his head. 'The family is not anything like as rich as I once thought we were. The Windrushes are only country gentry with a handful of acres, not some great landowners with a vast estate. With two legitimate sons to support as well as me, our land was insufficient to grant me a large allowance. In fact, Mother was more than generous giving me what she did. She could legally have thrown me out without a penny.'

'Did you ever speak to a lawyer about your position, Jack?'

'Not right away,' Jack said. 'I was young, foolish and angry. I wanted to make my name and get rapid promotion to show the world how clever I was.' He shook his head. 'When I think now of the risks I took!' He looked away. 'I despair of some of the young griffins I meet now, but I was worse than any of them.'

'Did you speak to a lawyer eventually?' Mary kept the subject on topic.

'Eventually,' Jack said. 'I consulted a Mr Stark in Calcutta. He told me that an illegitimate child, which I was, was not entitled to inherit anything unless the parents married each other after the child was born. In that case, the child could legally inherit wealth – movable assets.'

'I don't understand,' Mary said. 'What are movable assets?'

'Movable assets are money or possessions. The land or the house would only come to me if my father had specifically mentioned me in his will.'

'Did he?'

'He did not leave a will. He died of disease. I presume that he expected to live longer and may have intended to write a will later. As it happens...' Jack shrugged. 'I got nothing, as you are well aware. My father did not marry my mother. My half-brother William got the estate, and the commission into the Royal Malverns, with my other half-brother Adam having the right to live here plus inheriting half the movable assets.'

Mary sighed. 'It would have been good to have a base in England, somewhere to go Home when you retire from the Army.'

Jack said nothing until Mary prompted him. 'Do you miss Wychwood Manor?'

'I miss it because I always thought of it as Home, despite not being there much,' Jack said. 'I was in India until I was about five, although my memories are a bit vague. Father sent me to England, but I was at boarding school most of the time.' He leaned back as the memories returned. 'It's strange. I used to think that Wychwood Manor was huge until I went to India. Now I see that it's only a small country house, unpretentious and rather ugly, really.'

Mary patted his arm. 'I'm sure it's a lovely house. Will you show me sometime?'

'I'd like to,' Jack said. 'I'm due leave; in fact, I'm overdue leave.' Lighting a cheroot, he blew a slow cloud of smoke toward the mosquito, which reacted with an angry whine. 'I need a change, Mary. When I took this job with Colonel Hook, I believed it would be interesting. All I've done for the past four years has been routine and, quite frankly, dull.'

'I know what you have been doing,' Mary said. 'You've helped reorganise the country after the Mutiny; you've learned Pushtu and Urdu and some Persian; you've improved your horse-riding immeasurably.' Leaning forward, Mary took the cheroot from him and drew on it, smiling. 'Most importantly, you've been married to me, and we've created a child together.'

'I certainly don't regret that part of it.' Jack thought of young Andrew, sleeping in his cot with the ayah looking after him whenever Mary allowed. He did not mention to Mary that it would soon be time to send the lad back Home to be properly educated. After surviving the horrors of childhood disease, such partings of mother and child were the most heart-wrenching in the world. Taking his Home leave would enable them all to travel together and ease some of the pain.

'It was a wonderful day.' Mary handed back the cheroot, still smiling. Jack knew she was reliving the day of their marriage.

Jack had intended the wedding to be low-key affair, knowing that Mary was not a woman who sought to be the centre of attention. With his half-Indian mother, Jack was on the very margin of British respectability, while Mary as a Eurasian was on the opposite side of that definite social divide. He had not expected many guests.

They had married in the garrison church at Gondabad, with newly promoted Captain Arthur Elliot as best man and one of the mission teachers as maid of honour. Few of the officers of the 113th attended, for Colonel Snodgrass had made his disapproval evident. Only Ensigns Peake and Wilden, men who had marched with Windrush in the latter part of the Mutiny campaign, accompanied Elliot.

'The church is nearly empty.' Mary had tried to hide her disappointment as she surveyed the echoing interior.

'Your presence fills it all for me.' Jack was insufficiently skilled with words for his attempt at gallantry to succeed.

'Thank you, Jack.' Mary had looked beautiful dressed in white, with her veil pushed back and the white gloves extending almost to her elbows. She forced a smile for him. They had both turned around as the church door crashed open, with Jack instinctively reaching for his sword.

Mary had taken hold of his wrist. 'It's all right, Jack.'

'Sorry,' Jack had said. 'Old habits.'

Mary had released him. 'The Mutiny is over now. We're all at peace.'

'Sorry we're late, sir!' Dressed in his Number One uniform, Sergeant O'Neil had stridden into the church with a squad of men at his back. Jack had known who they would be even before he looked at them. There were Thorpe and Coleman, the Burma veterans, Riley the gentleman thief, and Logan, the diminutive Glaswegian with his face split into an uncharacteristic smile. There was Williams, limping from his recent wound, and Mackinnon who possessed some instinct that enabled him to sense danger. At the back was Parker, the quietly kind-hearted Liverpudlian.

'Thank you for coming, lads.' Jack had felt his words were inadequate. He knew his men would understand. 'I hope you don't get into any trouble for coming here.'

'No, sir.' Riley had said.

Jack had said no more. He could trust Riley to have thought of some dodge to subvert authority.

Mary had patted Jack's arm. She did not have to say anything. Her smile wrapped around the grinning men.

'Sir.' Sergeant O'Neill had thrown a thunderous salute as his boots crashed onto the paving stones that floored the church. 'We don't have much time, sir, but we all want to wish you and Mary ... the future Mrs Windrush the best of all possible happiness, sir.'

'Thank you, Sergeant.' Jack had looked over his men. He could not quite believe that he was leaving the 113th. After sharing years of trials and bloody war, he would probably never see them again. *I'm getting foolishly emotional. Such partings are a soldier's lot.*

'The Church is quite full now with all your men there.' Mary's bright words had chased away his momentary gloom.

The ceremony had been brief. Elliot played his part with his usual efficiency, producing the ring at the required moment, and organising everything and everybody to an inch of their lives. Jack and Mary exchanged their vows without hesitation, with Jack wondering at the speed he transferred from a single man to a husband with responsibilities.

'I do,' he had said, and that was that. He was married for evermore. Looking at Mary, he had no regrets. It felt right, and there was no more to be said.

When Jack and Mary had marched back down the aisle as man and wife, their footsteps sounded hollow in the nearly empty church. O'Neill and his men had already left. Mary bit back her renewed disappointment.

'They probably had their duty to attend,' Jack had whispered. 'They would be here for you if it was humanly possible.' *All the same, I thought Elliot would have organised something.*

Mary's hand had squeezed his arm, gently reassuring. 'I know.'

All the same, I'd prefer the lads to be here for Mary's sake. She'll only have one wedding in her life. I hope.

The second they had stepped outside the gloom of the church into the bright Indian sunlight, Jack knew that he should have trusted Elliot. His men waited in a double row with their bayoneted rifles forming a triumphal arch under which Jack and Mary had to walk.

'Oh!' Mary had put a hand to her mouth. 'Oh, Jack!'

'All Elliot's doing.' Jack had renounced all responsibility. He resolved to buy Elliot a bottle of something suitable at the first opportunity. No price could adequately compensate for Mary's pleasure.

As they had marched beneath the glittering steel arch, Jack tried not to think of the times he had seen these same bayonets dripping with blood. Instead, he concentrated on the delight on Mary's face, and the loyalty of these rogues and badmashes he had fought beside for so many years.

'It's not the same without you, sir.' O'Neill had spoken awkwardly, as if he had not seen Jack in every state of dress and undress for the past decade.

'You have Elliot as Company Commander,' Jack had said. 'He's a good man.'

'Yes, sir,' O'Neill had agreed. He glanced at Mary, who gave an encouraging smile. 'Well, sir, me and the boys had a bit of a collection to help your marriage, sir, you and Mrs Windrush of course.'

'There's no need,' Jack had begun until Mary forestalled him by stepping forward.

'How delightful!' Mary had said. 'You are good men, all of you. Forgive me,

Jack.' Without another word she planted a kiss on O'Neill's craggy face, following that by doing the same to each of the men. Jack watched in amazement as his bitter-eyed veterans responded with smiles, and even blushes.

'I'll never forget this,' Mary had said. 'Thank you, gentlemen.'

Elliot had marched up, caught Jack's eye and winked. 'I could not find a spare carriage,' he said. 'I'm sorry, Mrs Windrush. I had to get a native form of transport.'

'Oh, that's all right,' Mary had said. 'A bullock dak is fine by me.'

'There were no bullocks available,' Elliot had said. 'Forgive me.' Putting both fingers in his mouth, he gave a loud whistle.

Jack had not seen from where the elephant thundered. He only knew it was large and grey, with an elaborately decorated howdah. 'Well done, Arthur!'

With the grinning mahout dressed in splendid gold and red and tassels of the same colour swinging from the howdah, the elephant had been an impressive sight as it came to a halt in front of them. Mary's smile could not have been broader as the beast knelt down, to the cheers of O'Neill and the men of the 113th.

Feeling slightly self-conscious with so many people watching, Jack had helped his new wife into the howdah.

'General Baird supplied the elephant,' Elliot had said. 'That's the Rajah of Gondabad's general, in case you have forgotten.'

'My grandfather,' Jack had murmured. 'I'm hardly likely to forget.'

Elliot had nodded. 'The elephant will take you on a tour of the camp and city. It's not quite a carriage ride, I'm afraid, Mrs Windrush.'

'It's wonderful.' Mary had been nearly in tears with pleasure. 'Thank you, Arthur.'

'Thank you, Arthur,' Jack had echoed.

It had been strange to see Gondabad from the back of an elephant. It was not strange to have his new wife sitting opposite. Jack smiled across to her; it seemed perfectly natural to have Mary there, as if they had always belonged together and always would. There was no feeling of awkwardness, no embarrassment, just a sense of completion as if he had always known that Mary would come along, with his previous romantic encounters merely preparing him for the real thing. It had taken the blood and slaughter of the Mutiny to bring them together, so one good thing came out of that nightmare. Jack's eyes darkened for a moment, then he realised Mary was watching him and smiled. Pushing away the memories of the horrors the recent Mutiny had unleashed on India, Jack tried to contemplate the future.

With Mary being half-Indian, many regiments would not accept her in their Mess. Colonel Snodgrass of the 113th had given him an ultimatum: Mary or the regiment. Jack knew that by choosing Mary, he might have made himself an outcast, with his prospects of promotion blocked. He could be a captain forever, fortunate for any post that kept him from surviving on half pay in some dreary English coastal town.

'Jack?' Mary had leaned forward. 'We're here.'

The elephant had brought them back to their home, outside the lines of the 113th yet still within the British cantonment. Standing within its own grounds, the bungalow had no bad memories. It was a fresh start for their new life together.

'Come on, Mary.' Lifting her in both arms, Jack had carried her past the bewildered servants and over the threshold to deposit her on one of the broad wickerwork chairs. 'Welcome to our home, lady of the house.'

Mary had looked up at him, her eyes concerned. 'I hope you don't regret marrying me.'

'Don't be silly.' Jack had said with a grin. 'Anyway, it's too late now. There's no going back.' He gestured to the room next door. 'The wedding presents are in there. I suppose you want to wait a day or two before you look at them?' He grinned as Mary scampered across the floor.

Mary had no need to open Elliot's wedding present. The huge bed stood in the centre of the room. 'Oh.' She put a hand over her mouth.

'Well, even Arthur knows that we have to sleep somewhere,' Jack had said.

'It's a bit suggestive.' Mary had touched the carved footboard. 'I wonder where he got it.'

'He had it made especially for us,' Jack had said. 'What else is there?'

Smiling, Mary had turned to the large ivory chess set with its elephants and rajahs. 'That's unexpected. I did not know you were keen on chess, Jack.'

'That was Jayanti's chess set.' As the memories had rushed back, Jack pushed the set to one side. 'That should not be here. It's too soon.'

'Too soon?' A small frown had puckered Mary's forehead.

'I'll tell you sometime. What else can you find?'

With the colonel's displeasure hanging over them, the officers of the 113th had not been generous with their gifts. Mary sifted through the small pile of simple offerings. 'It was very good of them to give anything,' she said. 'They know what Colonel Snodgrass thinks of us.'

Jack grunted. 'We won't spoil the day by thinking of such things.'

'What's this?' Mary had walked to a chest that sat in the corner of the room. 'Is this yours? I haven't seen it before.'

'It's not mine.' Jack had guessed who it was from.

Heavily carved with elephants and monkeys, the chest was of teak, bound with brass. Turning the key in the lock, Mary had opened it and gasped. 'Who sent this?'

The chest was packed with clothes in the finest silk and cotton. Jack had stepped back as Mary lifted them out, one by one, exclaiming in wonder with each item.

'That should keep you going for a while,' Jack had said.

At the very bottom of the chest, the document had been folded into an oblong of parchment, yellowed with age and heavily sealed. Red ribbon crossed and re-crossed the parchment, enclosing a square of white paper with a short note in shaky handwriting.

'What's that?' Mary had taken her attention from the clothes long enough to glance at the document.

'I do not know.' Jack had read the note and handed it over. 'See what you think.'

'Dear Mary and Jack,' Mary had read. 'You know that I would have loved to attend your wedding, but circumstances did not allow. I do thank you for the very thoughtful invitation. As you know, I head the army of the Raja of Gondabad, a position which has a surfeit of prestige, but little in the way of portable remuneration.'

Mary had sighed. 'That means the rajah does not pay your grandfather very well,' she explained. 'Probably in case he returns Home.'

'Yes, Mary.' Jack had understood the letter when he read it. 'Carry on.'

'On the credit side, I have a fine group of women who are friendly with me.' Mary had frowned. 'Does that mean your grandfather has a harem?'

'I would think so,' Jack had said.

Mary had shaken her head. 'I would have thought he was a little old for that sort of thing.'

'I'll remind you of that when we are his age,' Jack had said.

Mary had lifted her eyebrows. 'I might hold you to that, Mister.'

'Each of my women has a clothing allowance, so it was an easy matter to obtain the enclosed for the use of Mary.'

Mary had lifted the clothes again. 'So these are clothes from a harem.' Her voice was thick with disapproval.

'Quality clothes from my grandfather,' Jack had said.

'I'm at the final two paragraphs.' Even as she read, Mary had not relinquished hold of the clothing. 'You will see that I have sealed the attached document. I have put it in your case and ask you not to open it until the event of my death. My days on this earth have been full, and it cannot be long before they come to an end. I will meet my Maker in a much happier frame of mind knowing that my only grandson has had the sense to marry such a beautiful lady as you, Mary.

I close this missive with the assurance of all the love I am capable of giving, and my blessings for a long, happy and fruitful marriage.

Yours aye

Jack Baird, Major, Bengal Fusiliers,

General, the Rajah of Gondabad's army.'

Mary's hand had shaken as she read the letter a second time and then lifted the sealed document. 'Should we open it?'

'No.' Jack had shaken his head. He took the parchment away. 'It will be the general's will and testament. We will honour his desire.'

Mary had snapped shut the chest. 'As you wish, Jack. There is also this.' She lifted the packet that O'Neill had handed over in the church.

'This means a lot to me.' Jack had lifted the packet. 'These men only get paid one shilling and a penny a week, and they have so many stoppages it's amazing they have anything left, let alone a surplus to raise money for us.'

'They have good hearts,' Mary had said. 'Rough tongues but good hearts.'

'They can have.' Jack had thought of all the dangers he had faced with the 113th. At that moment he despised the class system and the innate snobbery of Colonel Snodgrass and his kind. He handed over the sealed packet to Mary. 'You open it, Mary. They meant it for you anyway.'

'I feel guilty taking the men's money.' Mary had broken the simple seal. 'The parable of the widow's mite comes to mind.' She emptied the contents onto the table.

Half a dozen silver coins had clattered out, with three golden sovereigns and a thumb-nail sized packet.

'That's a lot of money from the men.' Jack had read the writing on the final packet. 'This has your name on it.'

'I'll open it later.' Mary had tucked it away inside her pocketbook. 'We have other things to do.'

'What's that?' Jack had asked.

'It's our wedding night.' Mary had extended her hand. 'And we have Arthur's bed to test out. Come with me, husband.'

* * *

Jack jerked back to the present. Marriage had undoubtedly hindered his advancement. When the war in China had broken out, Jack had applied to go, for success in active service was the best step towards promotion. With the troops sent from India, Sir Colin Campbell, now elevated to the peerage as Lord Clyde, chose the staff officers.

Jack's hopes had risen when Lord Clyde had sent for him.

'I know you, Windrush,' Lord Clyde had said, glowering through his crinkled, kindly face. 'You are a fair officer. Why the devil did you get married?'

'Because I fell in love, sir.'

'Hmm.' Lord Clyde surveyed Jack from under his bushy eyebrows. 'Well, congratulations on your marriage, Windrush. Permission to join the Chinese expedition withheld.'

'Sir?'

'I said permission withheld, Windrush. I'm not going to deny Mrs Windrush the pleasure of your company so soon after your wedding. I'll give the poor woman some happiness; God knows there are enough departures and loneliness in the life of a soldier's wife.'

Aye, Jack thought, *trust kind-hearted old Sir Colin to think of the women as well as the men. He is a one-off, is Sir Colin, but he has not done my career much good. I could have been a major by now if things had gone well in China. There is a lot of truth in the saying that marriage is ruinous to the prospects of a young officer. What was the mantra? A subaltern cannot marry, a lieutenant must not marry, a captain should not marry, a major may marry, and a colonel must marry. Well, I married as a captain, and my career has stalled as a result.*

'Jack?' Mary noticed his preoccupation. 'Are you all right?'

'Never better,' he said truthfully. He looked at Mary. He did not regret his decision. Lighting another cheroot, Jack discarded the memories and handed the cheroot to his wife. 'I have spent sufficient time being a glorified clerk. I am not suited to pushing papers around.'

'What's in your mind, Jack?' Mary puffed on Jack's cheroot.

'One of two things.' Jack leaned forward in his chair. 'Either I take the leave I'm due, or I look for a vacancy in a regiment, either British or one of the native pultans. The latter surely won't object to me having a half-Indian wife.'

'Why not do both?' Mary said.

'I could,' Jack mused. 'How do you fancy a trip Home? I could show you Wychwood Manor, London, Bath, maybe travel up to Scotland to see all the places Sir Walter Scott wrote about. When we're over there, I can visit Horse Guards and see about transferring.'

'I'd love to see Home,' Mary said.

'Good.' Jack kissed her on the forehead. 'I'll speak to Colonel Hook tomorrow.' He leaned back. He felt as if this peaceful chapter of his life was about to end. He had enjoyed his time with Mary but knew that it was false; something was missing. He had been waiting for his career to begin again.

CHAPTER TWO

Gondabad, India July 1863

'Ah, Windrush!' Lieutenant-Colonel Hook marched forward with his hand extended, his hair still unfashionably long but his face remarkably unlined. 'I was about to send for you. I need your services for something more interesting than administration.'

'Yes, sir.' Jack saw his hopes of home leave begin to fade. 'What's happened, sir?'

'Now.' Hook perched on the edge of the table, sipping at a glass of brandy. He continued as if Jack had never spoken. 'You'll be wondering what this is all about, Windrush.'

'I am, sir.' Jack glanced around. Hook had taken up his quarters in the great fort of Gondabad, where the Rajah had become a staunch ally of Britain since the failure of the Mutiny. The room was empty except for the desk, a small, glass-fronted drinks cabinet, two deep leather armchairs, and what looked like a couple of brass-bound arms chests. A large map of North West India covered one wall, with hand-written annotations in various places.

'You'll find out in a minute or two.' Hook looked no older than he had when Jack had first met him. 'Ah, here he comes now.'

A short, heavily bearded major entered behind Jack.

'Ah, Kerr, do you know Windrush?'

'No, sir.' The major nodded to Jack.

Hook made the introductions. 'Major Kerr of the Guides, meet Captain Windrush, late of the 113th, now working for me. For the past few years, Kerr, Windrush has been busy reorganising India under the Queen's, rather than the Company's, rule.'

Standing with his back to the door, Kerr looked anything but impressed. His eyes bored into Jack with the intensity of gimlets.

Hook put down his brandy. 'Now I have another task for you, Windrush. One perhaps more fitted to your peculiar talents.'

Glancing at Kerr, Jack took a deep breath. He had promised Mary he would mention home leave to Hook. 'I am due home leave, sir.'

'I am aware of that,' Hook said. 'I'm afraid you'll have to wait. Duty comes first. Mary will understand.'

Jack nodded. He knew that Mary would understand, but that did not mean he wished to disappoint her. He hoped that Colonel Hook's task, whatever it was, would not take too long.

Hook stood up. 'The job I have in mind may be more important than any military post you have ever held, however distinguished your service may have been.'

'What is this job, sir?' Jack was acutely aware that the silent Kerr was listening to every word.

'I'll come back to that in a minute, Windrush. You know the northern Indian plains as well as any officer of your rank. How well do you know the North West Frontier?'

'Not at all, sir.' Jack looked past Hook to the giant map that was spread across the wall. Most of the annotations were along the North West. He wondered what they signified.

'Have you ever read Clausewitz, Windrush?'

'Yes, sir.' As a young ensign, Jack had striven to learn all he could about military theory. The book *On War* by the Prussian Carl Von Clausewitz had introduced him to the moral and political aspects of warfare. A decade of the reality, peppered by three wars and five savage campaigns, had taught him that theory and reality did not often coincide.

Hook grunted. He was not used to young officers who had spent time reading books. 'You'll be familiar with Clausewitz's phrase: "War is an act of violence pursued to the utmost." '

'Yes, sir.'

'Could you describe that, Windrush?'

Jack blinked. 'I am not sure what you mean, sir.'

'Could you describe an act of violence pursued to the utmost?' Hook sipped again at his brandy.

Jack considered for a minute. 'I presume Clausewitz was referring to a battle, sir.'

'What would you think of a people – and I choose that term carefully – what would you think of a people whose entire culture is based around violence? What would you think of a people who have resisted invasion for not hundreds but thousands of years, who have never been completely conquered, and who control the gateway to India?'

'They must be an impressive people, sir.' Jack felt Kerr stir behind him.

'They have been called many things, Windrush, usually by their enemies. They are a Semitic people, more devoutly Muslim than the Crusaders were Christian. They speak Pushtu, and we know them as Pathans, Paythans, Pakhtuns or Pashtuns.' Hook's smile should have acted as a warning to Jack. 'You are going to get to know them very well.'

Jack had already guessed that. 'Yes, sir.'

'Pour yourself a drink, sit back, and let me educate you,' Hook said. 'Major Kerr, please be seated and join in whenever you wish.'

'Whisky for me, sir, please.' Jack chose a Glenfiddich before he settled into one of the armchairs.

'Good choice,' Hook approved. 'Glenfiddich is her Majesty's tipple, I believe. Now, let me take you back in time a couple of hundred years or more to when the British first came to this land. We came as traders to Madras, Calcutta and Surat.'

Jack nodded. His family had been involved with India for generations.

'When the major local power, the Moghul Empire, gradually disintegrated, other Indian states rose in importance, some friendly to us, some friendly to our trade rivals, the French, some not caring about either, and everybody out for what they could get.' Hook paused, presumably to see how Jack was accepting his version of Indian history.

Jack nodded, wordless.

Hook continued. 'With so many rival states marching and counter-marching their armies across India, Britain, or rather the Honourable East India Company, needed to protect their trading posts. The Company recruited local forces, well, you know the pattern. What had begun as a simple trading operation ended up in one of the most successful companies in the world. Our often less-than-Honourable Company expanded to control much of the Indian sub-continent. The Company's final war of expansion was against the Sikhs, which brought Company rule to this point here.'

For the first time, Hook stepped to the map of India. Lifting a pointer, he stroked it down the northwest of the sub-continent. 'Now that the Company has gone and the Crown has taken over India, the British Army is responsible for this North West Frontier.'

Jack felt a shiver run through him. The name seemed redolent of an ending, as if the ancient civilisations of India stopped at that frontier, and something much wilder, something dangerously untamed, began.

Hook tapped the map with his pointer. 'Here we have hundreds of miles of mountains, from beyond the Khyber Pass in the north to Baluchistan and the Bolan Pass in the south.' Hook stopped, ostensibly to sip at his brandy, but Jack suspected more likely for dramatic effect.

Jack stepped forward to examine the map. Although he had been born in India and Indian blood flowed through his veins, he had never served west of the Indus. The North West Frontier was unknown to him. 'It looks like an interesting area, sir.'

'These mountains are bleak beyond your imaginings, Windrush, with some of the wildest, most independent-minded, intractable people in the world.' Hook leaned back in his chair. 'It is certainly the most dangerous frontier of the Empire; it is arguably the most dangerous in the world.'

'Yes, sir.'

'It is a land of savage, bare mountains interspaced with narrow passes, like sabre slashes between high peaks. It has some green, beautiful valleys but more often is stark and bare beyond description, tormented by dust storms, bitter cold with snow in winter, scorched by the sun in summer.' Lifting his pointer, Hook pushed Jack out of the way and indicated the map. 'There are avenues into this area. We have the Kabul River, the Khyber Pass, the Kurrum River, the Tochi River, the Gomal River, and the Bolan. As a student of military history, which you are, Windrush, you will be aware that a British Army came badly unstuck in these passes back in '41.'

'I have heard of General Elphinstone's misfortune, sir.'

'Bear it in mind. It was undoubtedly the worst defeat the British Army has ever suffered in the East.' Hook continued his lecture. 'There are fertile valleys where crops are grown, there are fast-running rivers, there are ancient forts, hill villages, and there are the Pashtuns.' He looked up then, catching Jack's gaze. 'I believe you have a little experience of these gentlemen.'

'Yes, sir. A Pathan, sorry, a Pashtun named Batoor helped me during our last campaign in the Mutiny. I was glad he was on our side and not against us.'

Hook gave an enigmatic smile. 'The Pashtuns are the most obliging fellows imaginable, as long as it suits them. I am not sure if the Pashtuns are ever on anybody's side except their own. It might have happened that his needs coincided with yours on that occasion.'

'I believe that was the case, sir,' Jack agreed.

'Let's talk about these people.' Hook spoke so casually that Jack knew he was hiding something. 'The Pashtuns occupy a large area between British India and the independent nation of Afghanistan, spilling into both territories. They are divided into tribes who are as often as not mutually hostile, rather like the Scottish Highland clans or even more like the old reiving families of the Scottish-English Border. If you have read your Walter Scott, you'll know what I mean.'

'I am working my way through Scott's novels, sir, when I have free time.'

Hook gave a bleak smile. 'I am sure that Mary will guide you there.'

'Yes, sir.'

'Back to the Pashtuns,' Hook said. 'From the north, we have the Yusufzai, then the Mamunds, the Mohmand, the Afridi, the Waziri, and the Mahsud and Baluchis, who are slightly different but associated.'

Jack listened, wishing he had thought to bring a notepad and pencil. He guessed that such information was going to be important.

'Each tribe is divided into sub-tribes, which for the sake of clarity I will call clans. For example, the Yusufzai have the Bunerwals, the Ado Khel, the Babuzai, the Hassanzai, and many others. Often the clans are further split into family units. Do you get the idea?'

Jack nodded. 'Yes, sir.' He heard Kerr shift behind him.

Hook sipped at his brandy before continuing. 'Throughout history, the Pashtuns have existed, never thrived, by being semi-nomads, trying to farm their thin soil, grazing livestock in summer and raiding the richer plains of India to the East. The men are brought up to robbery, fighting and feuding; I'll come to that later.'

Jack nodded. No British soldier serving in India could fail to hear about the tribes of the North West Frontier.

'If the Pashtun families fall out, they live by the blood feud, again like the Scottish clans or Border reiving families.' Hook refilled his glass, offered Jack more whisky, and nodded when Jack refused. 'Very wise. You'll need all your faculties where I am sending you.'

'I gather that I'm going to the Frontier, sir.'

'Don't jump the gun, Windrush.' Hook sipped at his brandy again. 'The Pashtuns are adept at using their jezzails, their long muskets, as our men will all testify to. They live by Pakhtunwali, the way of the Pashtuns, and are dedicated to Islam.'

'Yes, sir.' Jack was beginning to feel as if he sat in a lecture theatre.

'Have you heard of the Five Pillars of Islam, Windrush?' Hook asked.

'I have, sir,' Jack said.

'Good. What are they?'

Jack had expected the question. 'They are: shahada, which is faith, salah or prayer, zakat or charity, sawm or fasting, and hajj, where every follower of Islam should endeavour to make the pilgrimage to Mecca at least once in his life.'

'Good man.' Hook approved. 'Well, there is an unofficial sixth to which the Pashtun can become addicted. That is Jihad: Holy War. It is a concept that sits on their shoulder at all times.'

'They sound like a formidable if quarrelsome people, sir. Yet I rather liked Batoor, the Pashtun I worked with.'

'I respect them beyond all other peoples I have ever met, Windrush, except perhaps the Sikhs. They have no mercy to the loser, offer hospitality to any traveller, follow blood feuds to the death, and keep their code. If you have a Pashtun for a friend, you have a friend for life, or until he decides otherwise.' Hook finished his brandy, looked at the decanter, shook his head in sorrow, and pushed it away. 'Now, you will be wondering what all this has to do with you.'

'I am, sir.'

'Open that first case.' Hook indicated the brass-bound case that sat on the floor.

The padlock was already open. The case contained a dozen Enfield rifles.

'Enfields, sir.'

'Exactly what we don't wish the Pashtun to own. Our patrols have been picking them up the length and breadth of the frontier; the Ghilzais of the Kurrum Valley, the Afridis of the Khyber, the Mohmands, and even the Bunerwals, who are a fairly peaceful tribe, by Frontier standards. In fact, they think themselves superior to all others, being religious and surprisingly honest.'

'Do we know how the Pashtuns are getting these weapons, sir?'

'No, Windrush.' Hook shook his head. 'We all know that the tribesmen are amongst the greatest thieves in the world. They can take a rifle from a man's hands while he is asleep, but that would only account for a few weapons. We have found dozens of these Enfields.'

'It's a bit worrying, sir.' Jack knew that the British Army had dominance over the native armies they had met through three things: discipline, strong leadership, and more modern arms and tactics. The wars with the Sikhs had been amongst the hardest fought in India because the Sikh Khalsa had both discipline and modern weapons. If they'd had better leadership, the wars could have taken quite another turn. The Pashtun had a plethora of capable commanders; with modern weapons, they represented a significant threat to the security of North West India.

'It is worrying,' Hook agreed. 'I've put notice out to all our political agents, the men who live with the tribes, to look out for these rifles. I have also sent a few trusted men into Pakhtunkhwa, tribal territory, to see what they can find.'

'To let you understand,' Hook pressed his point, 'some of our sepoy battalions still carry the Brunswick Rifle, which has a range of 250 yards. The Pashtuns' normal firearm is the locally manufactured jezzail, with a range of up to 400 yards. Our Enfield is sighted to over a thousand yards.'

'There was a problem with the cartridges, sir,' Jack reminded him.

'There was a problem with the grease that coated the cartridges,' Hook corrected. 'The sepoys believed the paper cartridges were coated with pig and cow fat, which was abhorrent to their religion. Now the cartridges are coated with *ghee*, butter, so are quite acceptable. However, that is not your problem.'

'Yes, sir.' Jack waited to find out his fate.

'I have an important role for you, Windrush.' Hook offered Jack a cheroot.

'Thank you, sir.' *Sugar to sweeten bitter medicine*, Jack thought. *I hope Mary is alright when she hears my leave is indefinitely postponed.*

'How are your language lessons coming along?' Hook's smile appeared genuine.

'Not bad, sir. I've had plenty of practice in Hindi, and my Pushtu is passable. Not so great in Persian.'

'Good man. You'll need all three.' Hook drew on his cheroot. 'Concentrate on Pushtu just now, Windrush, because you're going to the Frontier.'

'Yes, sir.' All prospect of going Home disappeared.

'I want you to find out where these Enfields are coming from. Do we have a rogue supplier in Britain? Do we have a gun runner on the Frontier? Or is there a regiment somewhere with a quartermaster who is storing up his pennies for a comfortable retirement, based on the blood of British soldiers and Indian civilians?'

'I'll see what I can do, sir.'

'Up to this point, Windrush, you have worked nearly exclusively with British infantry. Well,' Hook said and smiled, blowing smoke into the air, 'Major Kerr will introduce you to the Guides. You'll no longer be plodding along at the pace of a snail; you will be with the cream of the Indian Army, and that means you will be working with the best soldiers in the world. Is that not so, Kerr?'

'We like to think so, sir,' Kerr said. His accent was pure Ulster. 'We have the best soldiers. We need the best officers to command them. Not all make the grade.'

Is that a warning? Or a challenge?

'All right. Windrush, report to Major Kerr in Peshawar as soon as you can.'

'Yes, sir.' Windrush glanced at Kerr, who responded with a cold nod.

'Oh, there is one more thing, Windrush.' When Hook spoke in that casual tone, Jack knew that he was about to introduce something particularly unpleasant. 'Some of the Pashtuns who have been active against our men were wearing these on their right arms.' Opening the top drawer of his desk, Hook lifted a twisted red cord, which he dropped into Windrush's extended hand. 'Do you know what it is?'

Jack's mind leapt back to the advance on Bareilly during the Mutiny, when hundreds of swordsmen in green cummerbunds had charged at them. The swordsmen had broken the redoubtable 4th Punjab rifles before the 42nd and 113th had mown them down. Each swordsman had worn such a red cord.

'It's the mark of a Ghazi, sir, a fanatical Muslim fighter.'

'The Warriors of God,' Hook said softly. 'Warriors with modern weapons.' Something in his voice sent shivers down Windrush's spine.

'I'll watch out for them,' Jack promised.

'Well, the best of luck to you, Windrush.' Hook held out his hand. 'You'll be glad to be doing something active after so much desk work.'

As Jack left the room, he thought of Mary, sitting in their bungalow full of hope for their leave back Home.

CHAPTER THREE

Peshawar July 1863

Peshawar. The last city before the Frontier and the final outpost of British rule; East of Peshawar stretched the hot Indian plains; West of Peshawar spread some of the most dangerous territory on the face of the Earth. The very name meant Frontier Town.

Jack reined up Colwall, his brown gelding, to survey the city. Allowing the dust of his passage to settle, he watched as a long caravan of camels plodded majestically out of the city gate. The caravan headed into India, with the camel bells tinkling, and the merchants eyeing Windrush with bold curiosity. If this had been India proper, Jack would have expected a salaam or two, an obsequious greeting. Here, so close to the Frontier, such things did not happen. These men were not inclined to be servile to anybody, much less a lone British officer travelling without a single servant.

As the caravan passed in choking dust, Windrush looked at Peshawar. Set in the fertile Vale of Peshawar with its orchards of plum, apple, peach and pear trees, its canals and its gardens, Peshawar had a wall some five miles long to protect it from the predators of the surrounding mountains. Jack was immediately aware of the aura of menace. Even the names were harsh. The range to the north was the Hindu Kush, the killer of Hindus, allegedly named for the thousands of Indians who had died on the passage west as captured slaves of Islamic conquerors. From Peshawar the road stretched westward to the Khyber Pass, built by the Mughal Babur, who had conquered northern India, updated only a few years previously by Lieutenant Alexander Taylor. That was the road of merchants, holy men, poets and conquerors. Beyond the Khyber was Kandahar, Kabul, and all of Afghanistan.

'Let's get on, boy,' Jack whispered to Colwall. He passed through the Lahori Gate with the atmosphere closing about him and the heat punishing as it rebounded from the pukka-brick walls of the houses. Three storeys high, with the lowest storey used as a shop, the building created channels of streets crowded with traders and women, beggars and water carriers. Jack pushed through, noting everything he could. He saw tall, rangy hill men in hairy poshteens with long jezzails slung across their backs. He saw clean-shaven Hazaurehs with conical hats, a handful of burqa-clad women, and a single patrol of sweating British soldiers in red serge tunics and a more wary air than Jack had experienced since the end of the Mutiny.

Hailing the officer who commanded the patrol, Jack enquired for the address Hook had given him.

'Just outside the Bala Hissar.' The lieutenant's eyes were never still, inspecting every man that passed. 'There is a Guide on duty outside.'

'Thank you, Lieutenant.'

'Are you new to the Frontier, Captain?'

'Is it that obvious?'

'Yes, Captain, with all due respect.' The lieutenant glanced over his shoulder as somebody shouted. One of his men shifted his rifle to the ready position until the sergeant snarled at him. 'British soldiers are not always made welcome here. Sometimes it's not best to travel alone.'

'I know India, if not the Frontier,' Windrush said. 'I am not a Griffin.' A Griffin was a man new to the East.

'Yes, Captain.' The lieutenant did not press the subject. 'Peshawar is not quite India, but the best of luck, Captain.' The patrol walked warily, the rear marker turning every few steps to check behind him. Jack watched them for a moment and then walked deeper into the city.

Jack saw the sentry standing at attention. He wore the khaki uniform of the Guides, with a blue turban, and did not move when Jack approached.

'I am Captain Jack Windrush. Is the sahib in?' Jack asked.

'Yes, sahib.' The Guide remained at his post, his face impassive.

'I wish to see him.'

'Kerr sahib may not wish to see you.' The Guide appeared less than impressed with Windrush's travel-battered uniform.

'Please tell him I am here.'

Without moving, the Guide bellowed something, and a young servant appeared at his elbow.

'Please tell Kerr Sahib that a Captain Windrush sahib is here,' Jack said.

Within a minute the young servant was back. He salaamed. 'Kerr Sahib will see you, Captain Windrush, sahib.'

The Guide edged aside to allow Jack bare access to the two-storey house.

'You made it then, Windrush?' Major Kerr surveyed Windrush through the hardest eyes Jack had ever seen.

'Yes, Major.'

'Don't Major me, off duty, Windrush. I'm Kerr.' The handshake was firm as Kerr's glance took in Windrush from his forage cap with the havelock to protect his neck to the dust on his boots. 'My boys will take care of your horse. How do you like Peshawar?'

'It's unlike any other city I've been in,' Jack said. 'Your guard at the gate was not keen to let me in. I am used to having sepoys jump to attention at even the sight of me.'

Kerr nodded. 'He is an Afridi, as different to the normal sepoy as a mountain is to a hill. You have to earn the respect of an Afridi. Have you had any dealings with them before?'

Jack thought of Batoor. 'I knew one Afridi very well.'

Kerr's level gaze did not falter. 'In that case, you will know that they are not a people to take lightly.'

'I found that out.'

'Do you know why Colonel Hook sent you here?' Kerr stood four-square in the centre of the room.

'Gun running, Major.' Jack did not remind Kerr he had been present at the interview.

'That is part of it,' Kerr said, 'and only for the servants. Anything said in Gondabad will be repeated in Kabul before the echo dies, and probably St Petersburg and Washington I shouldn't wonder.'

Jack waited.

'This is the Frontier, Windrush; there is always trouble brewing here.' Kerr walked to the window, which afforded him a fine view over Peshawar and to the west. 'You're going to be working for me out there.' He nodded towards the hills. 'I will warn you that it is the most dangerous posting in the British Empire. You will face extreme heat and chilling cold; you will be up against an enemy that can be your friend one minute and an enemy the next, with no thought of mercy or pity. If you are captured, they will certainly kill you and most probably torture you in ways so hideous even the thought will make your skin crawl.'

'Yes, Major,' Jack said.

'Do you now wish you had remained with the 113th?' Kerr asked.

Jack's anger was beginning to rise at this bitter-eyed major. 'Duty is duty, Kerr. Danger is part of the soldier's bargain.'

Kerr grunted. 'We will see if you still think that in six months if you are still alive.'

'I'll do my best to live,' Jack said.

'I have arranged for you to be temporarily transferred to the Guides.' Kerr's gaze never left Jack's face. 'If I feel, even for an instant, that you will disgrace the regiment or put any of my men in danger, I will send you back to Hook.'

'As you wish.' Jack was not offended at the suggested slight; he knew how protective good officers could be of their men.

'Are you wishing you could strike me?' Kerr's question took Jack by surprise. 'Come, man. Be honest! We have no room for fabrications in the Guides!'

'You are my superior officer, Kerr,' Jack said.

'If I were not your superior officer?' Kerr asked.

'In that case, the situation would not have arisen.'

When Kerr stepped abruptly forward, Jack put himself in a position of defence.

'Ah! So you are ready to fight me!' Kerr's grin further unbalanced Jack. 'Can you shoe a horse?'

'Major?' Jack did not hide his confusion.

'Can you shoe a horse? Come, man, it's a simple enough question. Well?'

'Yes, Kerr. I can,' Jack said.

'Good man. In the Guides, you will have to be more independent than in the Queen's regiments.' Kerr sat down, offering a cheroot. 'That's why I picked you. You have a reputation for operating with small, hard-hitting units. You are an unconventional officer, Windrush.'

'Yes, Kerr. I had not realised that you picked me.'

'I was looking for an officer who is not scared to operate outside the regimental system,' Kerr said. 'Colonel Hook made me aware of your exploits in the Crimea, and more recently in the Mutiny.'

'What am I to do?' Jack asked.

'I'll tell you en route to Hoti Mardan. I hope you are fit to travel. We don't count much on weariness in the Guides.' Kerr's eyes were still basilisk, but there was an underlying humour that Jack had not noticed before. 'Your horse has been fed and watered, so we will leave immediately.'

It was a forty-mile ride to Mardan, the headquarters of the Guides, with the sun hot above.

'You see, Windrush.' Kerr rode his horse as if he had been born to it, with an easy grace that ignored the miles. He spoke through the scarf that protected his mouth from the constant dust. 'We think there is something serious brewing on the Frontier, something much more dangerous than the usual raiding and feuding.'

'Why is that, Kerr?'

'When you've been out here for a few years, you get a feeling for that sort of thing.' Kerr lifted a hand to acknowledge two men with a string of camels. They met his eyes, tall, rangy men with twisted turbans on their heads. Both walked with long, lifting strides that covered the ground without apparent effort. One had a jezzail strapped across his back, the other a Minie rifle that could only have come from a British soldier, alive or dead.

'Have you heard about the Hindustani Fanatics?' Kerr asked.

'Only vague rumours,' Jack said.

'Forget the rumours,' Kerr said. 'They are as desperate a threat as we have faced since the Mutiny. We know them as the Hindustani Fanatics, while the Muhammadans call them the Mujahidin, the Warriors of God.'

'That's an interesting name.' Jack remembered that Hook had used the same phrase.

'You might know them better as Ghazis.'

'I've met them.' Jack mentioned the fight outside Bareilly as Kerr listened, nodding.

'Pray to the Lord you never meet them again,' Kerr said. 'Now imagine the Pashtuns joining the Ghazis. What a ferocious combination that would be.'

Jack watched a family group pass by. The men stared through kohl-rimmed eyes, each with a jezzail on his back and a ferocious Khyber knife at his belt. The women wore the long burqas that hid them entirely from view, except for a slit around the eyes. Only the young pre-pubescent female children had their faces uncovered. They watched the two British horsemen with curious eyes and big smiles.

'I can see the dangers,' Jack said.

'I am going to give you a history lesson,' Kerr said. 'Listen carefully. Back in the 1820s, a Ghazi named Sayyid Ahmad visited Mecca; you are aware that visiting Mecca is one of the pillars of Islam.'

'I am,' Jack said.

'Good. Inspired by his visit, Sayyid Ahmad came to Pakhtunkhwa with about a hundred followers and began preaching holy war, a jihad, to the Yusufzai.' Kerr lifted his hand to a bullock cart before he continued. 'In the 1820s, you will remember, the Sikhs controlled all this area. We were not involved. Sayyid Ahmad gathered thousands of Pashtun tribesmen to his standard. He was able to push back the Sikhs, besiege and capture Peshawar.'

Jack looked around. The mountains surrounded them, seeming to dominate everything. 'The Sikhs would not be pleased.'

'They were not,' Kerr said. 'Can you think of two more dangerous people to cross swords than the Sikhs and the Pashtuns? The Sikhs waited for a couple of years then sent an army from Lahore. They recaptured Peshawar, killed Sayyid Ahmad and a thousand or so of his Ghazis, and chased the rest into the hills.'

Jack nodded to show he was still listening.

'Those Mujahidin that remained settled in a small village named Sitana, hard by the Mahabun Mountains, on the west bank of the Indus maybe seventy-five miles northwest of Peshawar.'

Kerr moved aside to allow a string of mules to file past, each one attached to the beast behind. The two mule drivers neither looked up nor acknowledged the British officers.

'We're not in the India I know now,' Jack said.

'It's better not to even think that you are,' Kerr said. 'This is Pakhtunkhwa. The British are merely the next wave of invaders. To continue with my history lesson: a follower of Sayyid Ahmad by the name of Sayyid Akbar Shah owned the village of Sitana. Within a short time, the number of Mujahidin swelled. They amused themselves by looting and raiding the more settled lands. By the time the British came to this area, these Mujahidin Ghazis were a damned nuisance.'

Jack nodded. After the battles of the Mutiny and the Crimea, the antics of a few hundred fanatics did not seem as dangerous to him as they did to Kerr.

Kerr noticed Jack's air of scepticism. 'In 1852, after we had defeated the Sikhs and annexed the Punjab, Colonel Mackeson took a force to the Sitana area, captured the Mujahidins' Fort Kotla and withdrew. Before the last British soldier had left, the fanatics returned to their raiding ways, kidnapping merchants for ransom and making a general nuisance of themselves. The Mutiny was a boom time for them as hundreds if not thousands of malcontents joined them.'

'Were these new recruits defeated Mutineers?' Jack asked.

'Possibly, or just the usual ragtag and bobtail that wars throw up.'

Jack nodded as Kerr continued his story. 'With the end of the Mutiny we had time to sort them out again, and in 1858 Sir Sydney Cotton led five thousand men to scatter the Mujahidin. They ran to Malka, which is on the north of the Mahabun Mountains.'

'Are they still there?' Jack asked.

'The Mujahidin have reorganised once more,' Kerr said. 'Now they are infesting a mountain at Siri. We are at present blockading the tribes that allowed them to pass through their lands.' Kerr reined up. 'That's where you come in, Windrush.'

The hills were closer now, frowning upon them, seeming to listen to everything they said.

'What am I doing, Kerr?'

'There is an Afridi clan we know as the Rahmut Khel not too far from the Khyber. We know that they have a new Khan, a new leader; we don't know who he is. We think that the Rahmut Khel have allowed these Mujahidin through their lands.'

'I see.' Jack nodded.

'You are taking a patrol to the new Khan of the Rahmut Khel, Windrush, and you are going to persuade him not to allow these fanatics through his territory. While you are there, search for any sign of gun-runners.'

Jack nodded. 'Yes, Kerr.' He was back in the saddle again, going into the heart of Pakhtunkhwa to see an unknown Pashtun Khan. Mary and the prospect of Home leave seemed very far away.

CHAPTER FOUR

Mardan, India, July 1863

Jack was unsure what to expect at Hoti Mardan, the headquarters of the famous Guides. His first view of the squat, star-shaped fort that sat on the Yusufzai Plain was not inspiring. Shimmering under the frontier heat, it was functional rather than dramatic. A score of Guides infantry drilled on the *maidan* in front of the gate, marching back and forth with their khaki smocks and pyjama trousers looking slightly shabby, while their khaki turbans were untidy. The jemadar in charge was screaming at them in Pushtu, the words very similar to those any British sergeant would use to a platoon of privates.

The infantry stepped aside to allow a patrol of cavalry to return from the hills, indigo blue turbans bobbing above horses that seemed better cared for than the riders. The men were handy enough, Jack allowed, remembering the British cavalry he had seen in the Crimea.

After they had eaten, Kerr showed Jack to his quarters, a tiny cubicle within the walls of Mardan, with an orderly with a face like Satan to cater for him.

'Early reveille tomorrow,' Kerr said. 'Hassan will look after you.'

Hassan glowered at Jack through narrow eyes.

'I'll be all right,' Jack dismissed him.

Grunting something that might have been a curse or a blessing, Hassan withdrew, leaving Jack alone with Kerr. 'One thing, Kerr,' Jack said. 'Do my men know how to fire Enfields? I want the best available if we are to go into Afridi country.'

'They will carry Enfields,' Kerr promised. 'And bayonets as well as their favoured sidearm.'

With his head spinning from days of travel, Jack barely undressed before throwing himself on his charpoy. The Pashtun voices seemed alien, with high-pitched laughter echoing around the fort. Although Jack had lived in India for six years, he was used to a British cantonment with British voices around him. He felt slightly uncomfortable spending the night surrounded by armed Pashtuns, whatever the colour of their uniforms.

Well, Mary, here we go again. Jack unpacked the Bible that Mary had handed him before he left Gondabad. *Once this mission is over, I will apply for leave and show you Home.* The thought of the soft green Malvern Hills brought a wistful smile. Jack shook his head, wishing that he was back with Mary.

Marriage has softened you, he told himself, placing his revolver under the pillow. He was sleeping before he closed his eyes.

* * *

Kerr inspected the men who were lined up outside the walls of Mardan. They stared back impassively, tall, bearded men with narrow eyes who looked capable of anything from murder to storming the Redan.

'Captain Windrush is going up the Khyber. Hassan is going with him.'

Jack tried to read the expression in Hassan's face. It was a mixture of disgust and resignation. *Now there's a man I will not trust.*

'I want another five volunteers. That's you, Zaman, Sawan, Ursulla, Fatteh and Alladad.'

All willing volunteers then, Jack thought. The names meant nothing to him.

'The rest of you, dismiss,' Kerr said.

The six picked men remained standing. They returned Jack's scrutiny, no doubt wondering who this officer was and why he was taking them into hostile territory when there were experienced Guides officers who could do the same job.

'Say a few words,' Kerr ordered. 'Let them hear your voice.'

'Well volunteered, men,' Jack said. 'I have heard good things about the Guides.' There was no reaction from the men. They stared at him, stone-faced. 'I'll soon see how good you are.' Still no reaction. 'We are going to Torkrud to speak to the Rahmut Khel.'

One man started at that.

'That troubles you, I see.' Jack focussed on the man. He was in his mid to late twenties, he judged, with a neat beard and bright brown eyes.

'I may not be welcome at Torkrud,' the man said.

'Why is that, Zaman?' Kerr was frowning.

'It is a family matter.' Zaman clamped shut his mouth. 'It is nothing.'

Kerr's frown deepened. 'I take it you have cut the wrong throat or slept with the wrong woman, Zaman.'

'It is of no importance,' Zaman said.

'I could leave you behind,' Jack offered. 'Many men would be willing to take your place.'

'No, sahib.' Zaman shook his head. 'It was Allah's will that Major Kerr sahib volunteered me.'

'Good man, Zaman,' Kerr said. 'You are a soldier of the queen and a trooper of the Guides. If anybody attacks you, they attack all of us.'

That might not be much consolation to Zaman if he is killed, Jack thought. *I'll keep an eye on that man.* This expedition showed signs of having as many complications as any other he had been on. All the same, Jack could not deny his tingle of excitement. He had lived all his life to be a soldier; maybe it was this thrill he had missed while enjoying the ease of married life.

'Hassan,' Kerr said. 'I've promoted you to daffadar.'

Although Hassan nodded, Jack was not sure if he looked pleased or not.

'Look after Windrush sahib,' Kerr said. 'He is not used to our ways yet.'

'Yes, Kerr sahib.' Hassan's glance at Windrush may have been meaningful or merely instinctive. Jack fought back his irritation. It was unusual for a major to ask a daffadar, the equivalent of a corporal, to look after an officer of Jack's experience, but the Guides were a unique formation.

'Captain Windrush.' Kerr dropped his voice. 'I've known Hassan for years. I would advise you to be guided by him. He knows the Frontier far better than you and I. Even if you don't agree with his advice, or it goes against the grain, trust him.'

Jack nodded. 'I will remember that, Major.'

'Good luck, gentlemen.' Kerr raised his voice again. 'May Allah guide you.'

That was the first time that Jack had heard a British officer say such a thing. He could only nod in return, check each man's equipment, and ensure they had food, water and ammunition for the expedition ahead.

***

They rode out of Mardan in the black of the pre-dawn with the air brisk and the horses lively beneath them. Jack looked over his men. He was unsure if Kerr had chosen them as willing volunteers or they had grudgingly accepted him. Either way, the die had been thrown; they were stuck with each other. Jack wondered if the evil-looking Hassan could be trusted and what secret Zaman was hiding. Moonlight glinted on the bugle that bounced at Fatteh's thigh. Jack grinned. *I wonder how Fatteh can use that with only half a dozen troopers? He must be proud of his position to display his bugle so prominently.*

Even a mile from Mardan, the tension was tangible. Jack felt as though the very air was electric, brittle with suspense. His Guides rode quietly, without the subdued chatter he would have expected from a similar patrol of British soldiers. Glancing over his shoulder, he saw that each man was alert, with their heads up and eyes never still as they constantly examined their surroundings.

Jack touched a hand to the butt of his revolver then checked the hilt of his sword. Although India was at peace since the repression of the Mutiny, he felt very much that he was on active service. Peace was relative on the Frontier.

They entered the Khyber exactly as the dawn rose angry-red in the east, tinging the harsh mountains to the colour of dark blood. Immediately, Jack felt the atmosphere alter once more. The air seemed harder, the Guides waiting for something to happen.

I have left India far behind now, Jack thought. *This is a different world to the sultry heat of my homeland.* He felt the tension in his men. They rode more alert, spread out slightly, and kept their rifles handy. Even the steady clump-clump of their horses' hooves seemed to echo, mocking their progress, while the vultures that circled above were hardly reassuring.

The road ascended, twisting in front of them. As the sun rose, the heights on either side became clearer, gaunt, dark-shadowed, like the bones of the earth shed of all flesh.

'When Allah made the world,' Hassan murmured in his ear, 'He had a pile of rocks left. "What shall I do with these?" he asked himself and fashioned them into Afghanistan, with Pakhtunkhwa as the remnants.'

Jack smiled. 'Is Afghanistan your country?'

'No, sahib. It is Pakhtunkhwa, the land of the Pashtun, who are watching us now.'

Jack peered into the dark. 'I can't see them.'

'No, sahib,' Hassan said. 'But they can see us.' He touched the lock of his Enfield. 'Although the British pay tribute to the tribes, a wayward youth may still take a shot at a British soldier just for *shikar*, for sport, or an old man to recall the pleasures of his youth.'

A string of camels passed them, walking toward India with the camel bells tinkling musically.

'*Salaam Alaikum* – greetings, good day,' the camel driver said with his gaze level with Jack's.

'*Salaam Alaikum*,' Jack replied.

'May you never tire.' The camel driver did not drop his gaze.

'May you never see poverty.' Jack had been schooled in the correct reply.

The camels swayed on, each one with two panniers full of fruits and Afghan carpets. The dust settled. Jack continued deeper into the pass.

At the defile of Bagiari, the heat was oppressive as it bounced from the cruel rocks. A small British garrison challenged their progress, with the Dogra sepoys holding rifles in sweating hands.

'Captain Windrush with a patrol of Guides.' Jack reined up, brushing dust from his uniform.

The lieutenant in charge of the post was about twenty-five, with the eyes of an old man. He looked wearily over the Guides. 'Be careful out there, Windrush. The Afridi are getting a bit restless these past few weeks.'

'We'll be careful,' Jack said.

'Where are you headed?' Lines of responsibility were deeply etched around the lieutenant's mouth.

'Torkrud,' Jack said, 'to speak to the new Khan of the Rahmut Khel.'

The lieutenant stiffened, glancing over Jack's escort. 'You might need to reconsider. That's bad country for such a small force, Windrush, if you don't mind me saying so.'

'Thank you for your advice, Lieutenant, but orders is orders.'

The lieutenant gave a faint smile. 'That's true, Windrush. Well, good luck, and may the Lord look after you.' He gestured to the west. 'We're the last British outpost. After us, you are all alone.'

That was not a comforting thought as Jack looked forward to the route to Afghanistan and the heartland of Pakhtunkhwa. He grinned. *Come on, Jack, I'm letting my imagination carry me away here. Nothing has happened, and probably nothing will happen.*

The pass narrowed as they approached Ali Masjid, where the fort glowered at them from its steep-sided hill.

'Sahib.' Hassan approached with more diffidence than usual. 'Some of the men have a request.'

'What is that, daffadar?'

'This is a holy place, sahib. There is a shrine here to Ali ibn Abi Talib, who was Mohammed's cousin and son-in-law. Some of the men wish to pray.'

Jack hesitated for only a moment. *Don't interfere with the men's religion.* 'As long as you're careful, Hassan. Keep two men on watch at all times.'

'Yes, sahib.' For the first time, Jack thought he saw a glimmer of respect in Hassan's face. He stood aside as his Guides prayed at the shrine. It was an example of the devotion of the Pashtun people that Jack had never experienced with ordinary British soldiers. He was unsure how he felt, but he knew that every little bit he learned about the Pashtun might help. Unsure how the Guides would feel if he watched, he rode fifty yards away to survey the route ahead.

The horseman appeared at the back of the shrine, an unkempt, bare-chested, shaggy-haired figure astride a horse that looked in no better condition than the rider. Jack watched the rider for a moment, saw he had a tabla drum but no weapon, and lost interest. India was full of strange people; it seemed that they also seeped into the Khyber Pass. A man with a drum was no threat to him.

'Captain Windrush, sahib.' Hassan threw a salute. 'We are ready.'

'Thank you, daffadar.'

Leaving Ali Masjid with its holy shrine and grim fortress, Jack led them through a narrow gorge and upward to the summit of the pass. He halted there, with the hills of Tirah to the south, and a valley on the north, gradually rising toward the Inzar Kandao Pass.

'Now we leave the Khyber,' he said.

'Yes, sahib.' Hassan said no more.

Jack glanced over his men. Most looked impassive. Zaman looked a little edgy, his eyes continually roving to the surrounding hills. Jack wondered what he was thinking. Until he earned the trust of these Guides, they would never open up their fears to him. Jack accepted that: British soldiers were the same.

Spread out and moving in a zig-zag to ensure they were a more difficult target for the jezzail men who Jack guessed would be watching them from the crags around, the Guides rode on. Fatteh was softly singing, his voice surprisingly melodious. Slightly off the road, tribal villages sheltered behind stone-and-mud walls, each village with a watchtower or fort. Men stood or sat on the flat roofs of each tower, watching Jack's patrol ride past. Some lifted a hand in acknowledgement. Most did not.

Jack consulted his map, trying to make sense of his surroundings. He noticed the riders cantering away to their right.

'Three men, moving fast,' Hassan said. 'Afridis.'

When the riders came within a few hundred yards of Jack, they abruptly altered direction, heading at right angles to their original route.

'They are nervous of us,' Jack said. 'They've seen that we are the Guides.'

'Yes, sahib,' Hassan said. 'Why should that make them nervous? Half a dozen Guides in the midst of Afridi territory? They could call on a hundred men in minutes.'

'That is true,' Jack agreed. 'Hassan, take a couple of men and bring these fellows to me. I want to know what they are afraid of.'

'Sahib!' Hassan signalled to Sawan and Fatteh to join him.

'Come on, lads.' Jack gave them a moment to draw ahead. 'This way.' Kicking in his heels, he followed the galloping Hassan.

The chase did not last long. Like many Pashtuns, Hassan was a superb horseman, while the fugitives evidently rode tired horses. Within ten minutes Hassan rounded them up and herded them back to Jack. For a moment, Jack thought the men would show fight, so he rode forward with what he hoped was a smile, removing the rifle from the man who appeared to be their leader.

'Salaam Alaikum,' he said, 'greetings, good day.'

'Salaam,' the man replied with ill grace, watching the Guides through nervous eyes.

'I wanted to apologise for frightening you.' Jack disarmed the man with an apology.

'We are not frightened,' the man denied.

'I am glad to hear that,' Jack said. 'You were riding so sedately until you saw us, and then you galloped away. What are you scared of?'

'This one is hiding something.' Hassan took hold of the oldest of the three men. 'What are you hiding?'

The man said nothing, while his hand slid toward the T-shaped *Choora* dagger at his waist. 'You will not need that.' Hassan took the dagger away. 'I will find out what you're hiding, cousin. Get off that horse.'

'Don't hurt the man,' Jack said. 'He has done us no harm.' He glanced around the surrounding heights, hoping the incident was not attracting too much attention. The flash of sunlight on steel confirmed that at least one man was watching them.

'Here.' Hassan pulled a folded note from inside the man's clothing. 'He is carrying a message. Who is this for, fellow?'

'Gulbaz of the Rahmut Khel,' the man said at once, spreading his hands in a gesture of innocence. 'It is only a message. It is of no importance to anybody except Gulbaz and the man who sent it.'

'Then why did you run and try to hide it?' Jack asked. 'Give it here.' The note was written in flowing Persian, the language used by the more educated of the Afghan and Pashtun tribal leaders.

Jack's language lessons had included basic Persian, but even so, he struggled with the terminology. 'This seems to be a legal document,' he said. 'It mentions a lawsuit, with the law agent being the most important person.'

'Yes, sahib,' the elderly man nodded eagerly. 'It is from a lawyer to Gulbaz of the Dagger Hand.'

'Can you read Persian, Hassan?' Jack wondered about Gulbaz's nickname.

'No, sahib.' Hassan shook his head.

'It seems perfectly innocent.' Jack handed back the note. 'I am sorry to break your journey.'

'He's not innocent, Windrush sahib,' Zaman said. 'Whatever he is, he is not innocent.'

'He is no threat to us,' Jack decided. 'Let these men go.'

Zaman grunted, stepping back.

Jack watched as the released men smiled and rode on in the same direction as Jack's party. 'I agree they are suspicious,' he said. 'But they have not attacked us, and the note seemed innocuous.'

Hassan frowned. 'They are trouble, sahib. I can feel the menace on them.'

'We should have asked them further.' Zaman touched the hilt of his bayonet. 'I know Gulbaz.'

'You know more about Torkrud than you are saying,' Jack said. 'Tell me about Gulbaz.'

'Gulbaz wishes to be Khan of the Rahmut Khel,' Zaman said.

'Tell me more,' Jack insisted.

'He is not a man you wish to cross.' Zaman again touched the hilt of his bayonet. 'If he wishes to meet you, he will come. If he does not, he will not.' Zaman pulled his horse around a prominent rock. 'He is watching us right now.'

'Where?' Jack looked around.

'Up there, just below the skyline.' Zaman nodded to the left. 'He is beside that group of pine trees.'

Lifting his binoculars, Jack focussed on the trees. Gulbaz made no attempt to hide. He sat astride a black horse with his left hand at his side. As soon as he saw Jack looking at him, he rode free of the pines and walked his horse slowly along the ridge.

'He's ensuring that we can see him,' Jack said.

'He is showing us that he is not afraid of us.' Hassan tapped the hilt of his sabre. 'I would be happier if Gulbaz was short of a head as well as his hand.'

'We cannot kill people merely because we don't like them,' Jack said. Perhaps these Pashtun can do that. What did Hassan mean, short of his hand? Moving his binoculars, Jack studied Gulbaz again. He grunted: Hassan was correct. Gulbaz had no right hand, which explained the strange way he rode his horse. He had a hook in place of his hand, with what looked like the sheath of a dagger protruding. The hook and dagger were attached to his stump by long strips of steel.

'Gulbaz looks like a formidable man,' Jack said. Gulbaz was a bear of a man with a great beard, a steel skull cap, and boots like a Cossack, from which thongs and rings dangled.

'He is,' Zaman said. 'I will kill him someday.'

Jack felt a chill run through him at the matter-of-fact way that Zaman said the words. He looked back over the rump of Colwall. 'Are you at feud with him?'

'Not yet.' Zaman's smile was a promise of future violence.

'Keep your feuding away from your duty,' Jack growled. 'You are a Guide before anything else.'

'Yes, Windrush, sahib.' Zaman's attempt to look innocent was a ludicrous failure. 'Torkrud is about half an hour's ride ahead,' Zaman said quietly. 'The khan of the Rahmut Khel will welcome us, or he will try to kill us.' His grin suggested he did not mind whichever choice the khan made.

'Thank you, Zaman. I suspect that you know Torkrud well.'

'I know it, sahib,' Zaman said.

The village was much like any of the others they had passed, except it was larger, with an arched doorway behind an array of dusty fields. The watchtower was taller and adorned with battlements.

Feeling like an alien in this environment, Jack took a deep breath. *I have my duty to do. Act as though you own the place.* 'Halloa!' He reined up outside the walls. 'I am Captain Jack Windrush of the Guides! I seek an audience with the Khan of Torkrud.' Even as he said them, Jack knew the words sounded melodramatic, as if he were playing a part in a pantomime rather than holding Her Majesty's commission. He stifled his smile. This whole place seemed like something out of the Arabian Nights, except the dust was real, as was the danger. The man in the watchtower looked down at him, spat betel-nut juice, and fired his jezzail into the air.

The shot set a dozen dogs barking.

'Now we will see.' Zaman lifted his rifle to a more comfortable position.

Hassan grunted. 'If Allah wills.'

As there seemed no response from Torkrud, Jack flicked his reins and walked

Colwall through the arched gate. The Guides followed in single file, each man with his rifle held across the crupper of his horse.

Children crowded to watch the visitors, with a motley array of dogs emerging from corners to bark and snap at the horses. Jack kicked one persistent mongrel away as his Guides spoke to the children. An old man, his beard dyed bright red, came to the door of his house with a curved pulwar, the Pashtun sword, balanced across his shoulder. One woman in a white burqa scurried to the safety of a walled enclosure. A tall man in a twisted red turban watched from the corner of one of the high walls that delineated each family house. He fingered the pulwar that he wore around his waist, saying nothing as his eyes, kohl-rimmed, studied each of the Guides in turn before settling on Jack. The muzzle of a jezzail protruded from behind his left shoulder.

'There is trouble,' Hassan said quietly. 'Watch that man, sahib.'

'I see him,' Jack murmured, feeling for the butt of his revolver. He could nearly taste the suspicion in the air. *Any moment now the inhabitants of this place will attack us en masse.*

'Windrush!' The name boomed out across the village.

Jack saw the familiar figure striding towards him. The Pashtun wore a pakul, a woollen hat above a face with high cheekbones and a long beard. Alone of all the men who had appeared in doorways, the man did not carry a rifle, only a long Khyber knife at his belt, while a long-legged, hairy dog loped at his side. Despite his surroundings, Jack could not control the smile that spread across his face. 'Batoor! What are you doing here?'

'Did you bring my horse, Windrush?'

Batoor and Jack had fought together in the latter stages of the Mutiny when Batoor had freed Jack from captivity.

'I did not know you would be here, Batoor.' Jack dismounted at once, extending his hand in friendship. 'I wish I had! Do we meet in friendship or in war?'

'What's the difference?' Batoor asked. 'The Pashtun are only at peace when they are at war. You are welcome, Windrush, whatever your government says!' He raised his voice to a shout. 'Captain Windrush and his Guides are my guests!' The words echoed around the village.

Jack nodded. 'Thank you, Batoor.' He knew that by the laws of Pakhtunwali, the code by which the Pashtun people lived their lives, he and his men were now protected. If anybody attacked or even insulted them, Batoor was bound by his honour to avenge them. 'I hope your khan does not object. It is he I have come to see.'

Batoor looked suddenly solemn. 'Have you come to Torkud to meet the Khan of the Rahmut Khel?' He touched a hand to the hilt of his Khyber Knife in a gesture that Jack remembered well.

'I have.' Jack felt his Guides mustering behind him. He wondered if they would have to shoot their way out of Torkud, despite his having met an old friend here. He noticed Batoor's eyes narrow as he saw Zaman. *These two know each other.*

'Zaman is with me,' Jack spoke quietly. 'He is now one of your guests.'

Batoor's expression lifted as he looked about him. 'Have you heard about our new khan, Windrush? Have you heard how he came to power?'

'I know little about him,' Jack said. 'I have heard he is a powerful man.'

'Come with me, and I will introduce you,' Batoor said. 'He is a badmash indeed, a man with no scruples, a killer born to the saddle, a master of raid and rapine.'

Jack thought of Gulbaz of the dagger hand. Please God that Gulbaz is not the khan! 'A badmash and a killer? He sounds as if he would fit well in the 113th Foot!'

Batoor laughed again. 'He might, Windrush. Come with me and see for yourself.'

Jack knew that his men were listening to every word. 'My Guides will come with me.' He looked for the tall man with the red turban, but he had vanished.

'Your men will find their entertainment in Torkud,' Batoor said. 'They will be as safe in our *hujrah*, our guest house, as they would be in Mardan. Perhaps safer indeed, as the wicked Afridis of the Rahmut Khel will not snipe at them.'

Jack smiled at Batoor's roar of laughter. This was a new side to the highly efficient warrior that Jack had come to rely on. Batoor at home was a much more jovial man.

'Come with me, Windrush.' Taking Jack by the arm, Batoor led him into the heart of the village. 'Don't worry; your horse will be as well cared for as your men. Trust me.'

'I do trust you.' Jack told the truth. It was the unknown khan that he did not trust.

'The Khan lives in that building.' Batoor pointed to a walled compound, slightly larger than any of the others in the village. 'As you see, the gate is open. I will go ahead to announce you, Windrush. Follow me at a distance, and you will meet the Khan.' He paused for a significant moment. 'Be careful, Windrush. The Khan is a man of short temper and a long sword. Only he wears the silver sword of the Rahmut Khel.'

'The what?' Jack asked, but Batoor was already striding away. Wondering why most of the men of Torkud were laughing at him, Jack followed Batoor's instructions. Remembering the formidable appearance of Gulbaz, Jack felt his heartbeat increase. He touched the butt of his revolver for reassurance as he strode through the gate.

The walls must have been ten feet high, without a single window on the outside. Jack knew they were only partly for security; they were also to ensure the women were in *purdah*, privacy. The door was narrow, but once inside Jack saw there were three courtyards, one for animals, one for women and another for ordinary family life. The accommodation backed against the external mud walls, square and simple, while trees within the compound afforded shade.

'Halloa!' Jack stood within the first courtyard. 'I am Captain Jack Windrush of the Guides. I am looking for the Khan of the Rahmut Khel!' He heard various rustlings from the buildings behind him. 'Is there anybody here?'

'Only me, Captain Windrush.' Batoor strode in behind him, still grinning as if at a private joke. He had replaced his pakul with a karakul hat of Astrakhan fur, headgear often worn by a man of position.

Jack hid his irritation. 'I don't believe that your Khan wishes to talk to me.'

'The Khan of the Rahmut Khel is already talking to you,' Batoor said. He extended both hands. 'I am Batoor Khan, Windrush! I am the Khan of the Rahmut Khel!'

CHAPTER FIVE

'Batoor!' For a moment Jack was nonplussed. 'You are the Khan?'

Batoor placed his arm around Windrush's shoulder. 'Come, Windrush. Come into my home.'

'I am here on official business,' Jack reminded.

'Pleasure first, business later,' Batoor said. 'It must be four, five years since we parted outside the walls of Gondabad. Much has happened in that time. You have left your *pultan*, and I have become a Khan.' He touched the silver hilt of the pulwar that protruded from an ornate scabbard at his waist. 'As you see, I wear the silver sword of the Khan of the Rahmut Khel.'

'It is a beautiful sword.' Jack tried to make sense of this new development as Batoor led him toward the nearest building.

'Only the Khan can wear it.' Batoor seemed as proud of his sword as he was of his position as Khan. Drawing it with a single gesture, he rested the long, slightly curved blade on the palm of his left hand. The hilt was of ivory, inlaid with semi-precious stones, and the guard of chased silver. Sunlight gleamed on the flowing Persian inscriptions on the steel. 'It is at least two hundred years old, an example of Pashtun culture.'

Jack compared the pulwar with his own Wilkinson's blade. It looked longer and lighter. 'Is it sharp?'

In answer, Batoor took a square of silk from inside his loose perahan top. Lifting it high, he altered the angle of the pulwar so the blade was uppermost and allowed the silk to drop. The blade sliced the silk in half. 'You see, Windrush? Can you do the same with your Wilkinson's sword?'

Jack laughed. 'I won't even try,' he said. 'It's good to see you again, Batoor Khan! You can put your sword away now.'

'Batoor!' The red-turbaned man overtopped Batoor by two inches as he strode into the compound. 'This man is a feringhee.'

'This man is my guest, Ayub.' Batoor faced him, one hand on the hilt of his sword.

'A feringhee is not welcome in the lands of the Rahmut Khel.' Ayub ignored Jack. His gaze fixed on the silver sword of the Rahmut Khel.

Batoor straightened his shoulders. 'This man is my guest,' he repeated. 'He is under my protection, by Pakhtunwali.'

'There are more than you in the Rahmut Khel,' Ayub said.

'Ayub, my friend,' Batoor said, 'you do not wish to fall out with me over a solitary feringhee. There are many more in the world.'

Ayub glared at Jack through startlingly blue eyes. 'If I had my way,' he said, 'the skins of the feringhee and his companions would cover my floor, and their heads would decorate spikes along the wall of my house.'

Jack looked away. A private conversation between two old friends was none of his business. Turning aside, he flicked open the button of his holster.

'I will call a *Jirga* about this matter.' Ayub threw Jack a final baleful glare before storming out of the compound. 'Gulbaz will need to know about this.'

There is that name again. Gulbaz must be a man of some note.

'That was Ayub Beg,' Batoor said. 'He is a man with a large mouth and a small brain. You need not worry about him.'

'I won't,' Jack said. 'I might worry about somebody else. I have heard the name Gulbaz mentioned more than once. He watched us approach Torkud.'

'Gulbaz of the dagger hand, one of my last surviving cousins.' Batoor dismissed Gulbaz with a shrug. 'If he has offended you, tell me, and I will kill him. His absence will make the world a more pleasant place.'

'He seems a very forceful fellow.' Jack knew that Batoor's offer was genuine. 'You said Gulbaz was one of your last *surviving* cousins. What happened to your other cousins?'

'They did not survive.' Batoor's smile broadened. 'Come inside my house. I have warned my women.'

Unsure what to expect, Jack followed Batoor through a simple arched doorway into his house. It was neat, clean and comfortable rather than luxurious, with a gaggle of young children waiting to stare at the feringhee. Two women in full white burqas greeted Jack politely. Their eyes were friendly as they scrutinised him.

'Two of my wives,' Batoor explained, 'and some of my children.'

'You've been busy.' Jack counted five children. 'Two wives?'

'I have another somewhere.' Batoor sat down, inviting Jack to do the same. 'She will be organising the household, no doubt, ensuring that everybody does as she wishes. You know what women are like.'

Thinking of Mary, Jack nodded. 'They control us with their smiles.'

'And other things,' Batoor said. 'You will have heard the saying, a woman for business, a boy for pleasure, and a goat for choice?'

'I have heard people say that of the Pashtun,' Jack agreed cautiously.

'That is not my nature.' Batoor thanked the taller of his two wives for handing him a pipe. 'I prefer women to boys or goats.' He eyed Jack with an amused smile. 'Did you marry that woman of yours? Or shall I sing you the Zakhmi Dil?'

Jack knew the gist of that song: *There's a boy across the river with a bottom like a peach but alas I cannot swim.* He shook his head. 'There is no need to torment me with your singing, Batoor. And yes, I married Mary.'

'Good!' Batoor roared his delight. 'How many children has she borne you?'

'One. We have a son. Andrew.'

'Only one? You must marry another woman and get more sons,' Batoor gave his opinion.

'We are only allowed one wife,' Jack said.

Batoor was suddenly serious. 'You are strange people, feringhee. What will happen if she becomes barren?'

'More children will come in their own time.' It was something that Jack had often discussed with Mary, who hoped for a large family.

'It is the will of Allah the all-merciful.' Batoor clapped his hands. 'You'll be hungry, Windrush. Let's eat.'

A smooth-faced young man brought in a tray of tea, which was served to Jack first, as a guest, and then to Batoor and a group of elders who arrived with grave greetings and bright eyes. Jack tasted the mixture of milk, sugar and tea leaves that the youngest man carefully poured into small bowls. The sweet biscuits were delicious, as were the rice-flour-and-ghee cakes.

After the tea came the main meal. Jack was surprised at the quality of the food, chicken and eggs, flat leavened bread with a variety of vegetables including onions and spinach. As the Pashtun only ate meat on special occasions, Jack knew the chicken had been killed especially for him.

After the meal, the elderly men told stories, laughing as they recounted tales of fights against the British, scowling as they mentioned the far more bitter feuds with other Pashtun clans. 'The British are feringhees; they will pass in time. Our enemies of the Adam Khel will be here forever.'

'If you will excuse me, Batoor.' Jack stood. 'I had better leave you.'

'You must hear more, Windrush,' Batoor insisted. 'We have singing, dancing and stories.'

'Thank you, Batoor, but I will have to check on my men.' Jack gave a little bow. 'You know what trouble soldiers can get into.'

The Guides were in the hujra, sitting in a loose group, smoking, singing and talking, while their rifles were close at their sides. The building was large and airy, with a score of charpoys, wooden-framed beds, lining the walls.

When Hassan shouted an order, they leapt to attention.

'Stand easy, men,' Jack said. 'How are you being treated?'

'All well, Windrush sahib,' Hassan reported. He nodded to the tray of tea that sat on the ground.

'Keep your rifles handy.' Jack gave advice he knew the men did not need.

'Yes, Windrush sahib.'

Zaman wiped breadcrumbs from his beard. 'If Gulbaz comes in the night, do I have your permission to kill him, Windrush sahib?'

'If I don't give permission, you would kill him anyway,' Jack said. 'However, Zaman, he will not come. You are under the protection of Batoor Khan.' He could not read the expression on Zaman's face.

'Fatteh,' Jack spoke quietly. 'There will be no need for you to sound the last post with your bugle. It might irritate our hosts.' He saw the disappointment on the young man's face. 'There will be other opportunities.'

The Guides told stories or sang softly, with Fatteh producing a rubab, the Pashtun lute. His young voice had a certain beauty that Jack had not previously associated with these hills.

In some ways, Jack thought, the Pashtun were unlike any people he had met before, while in others, they were very similar. He shrugged: people were people with good and bad points. Today had been a success; tomorrow, when he discussed gun runners and the Mujahidin, things might be different.

As Jack settled to sleep, he heard the drumming, a slightly unsettling low throbbing that came from outside the village. He touched the butt of the revolver under his pillow and returned to sleep.

* * *

They stood in the middle of the village with Batoor stroking the throat of the laggar falcon that perched on his wrist. 'When I have this bird trained, Windrush, we can go hunting, you and I. Shikar is as good as war.'

'I would like that,' Jack said. 'I used to follow the hounds back in England when I had the chance.'

'Let me show you Torkud.' Batoor sounded as proud of his village as Fatteh was of his bugle. Within the outer barrier, a score of compounds rose, each one with high walls and a solid tower, eighteen or twenty feet tall.

'Why are the walls mainly of mud?' Jack asked. 'There is plenty of stone around.'

'The main watchtowers are of stone,' Batoor said. 'But in times of feud or war, the tribes destroy their enemy's houses. It is easier to rebuild a mud wall than one of stone.'

Jack nodded. He had heard the same sort of story from the Border wars between England and Scotland. The people along both sides of the Border had their peel-towers for defence, much like the watchtowers of these Pashtun villages. They built dry-stone cottages which could be replaced after the invaders of whichever nation returned over the Border. Jack understood the Pashtun point of view.

Wherever Batoor led Jack, women either scurried away from them or watched boldly through the slits in their burqas, while children laughed, joked and pointed to the strange feringhee. Groups of bare-chested boys played a hopping game, trying to knock each other down while balancing on one leg. Other boys, as young as five or six, played with large cleavers or eyed their elder brothers' rifles with real envy. *These are a martial people indeed.* Jack knew that the more he learned of them, the better, but he had his duty to do. 'How did you rise to become Khan, Batoor?'

'When I was with the feringhees,' Batoor seemed pleased to explain, 'I heard them talk about a process of elimination. That is how I became Khan.'

'Tell me more.'

'When I got back here after killing Jayanti, my uncle, the old Khan was dead. There was a Jirga, a meeting of the elders, to decide who should replace him.'

'Should it not be the eldest son?' Jack remembered the complications surrounding his own family.

'Perhaps,' Batoor said. 'My father had many sons by many women. It was hard to know who the eldest was. The Jirga decided that one of my brothers named Dilawar should be the khan, although Gulbaz and I pleaded our case, along with another man.'

Jack noted Batoor's reticence with the third name. 'Where is Dilawar now?'

Batoor stopped outside the ruins of what had once been a substantial house. Shattered stones lay amidst a heap of dry earth, with splinters of timber and pieces of what looked like rags. 'I accepted the Jirga's decision and invited Gulbaz, Dilawar, and his supporters to a peace meeting at my house.'

'That was the most honourable thing to do.' Jack knew that Batoor had more to add to his story.

Batoor pushed at one of the stones with his foot. 'They did not all come. Gulbaz turned down my kind offer.' Batoor's eyes were as calm as Jack had ever seen them. 'When Dilawar and his men arrived, I had two kegs of gunpowder waiting beneath the building, and I blew them all up!' Batoor roared with laughter at his cleverness. He indicated the ruined building beside him. 'There is the result. What remains of Dilawar is under there somewhere. Dig for him if you wish, Windrush.'

Jack nodded. 'I'll leave the digging to somebody else. Now you are the undisputed Khan except for Gulbaz and the third claimant you did not name.'

'Yes.' Batoor nodded. 'It is a pity that they were not here when I eliminated the others.' Batoor seemed to like that idea. 'Since Gulbaz returned, he has tried to depose me. I will have to kill him eventually.'

The cold-blooded statement shook Jack a little. 'Could the two of you not discuss things without bloodshed?'

'He wishes to be Khan,' Batoor said. 'I wish to be Khan. One of us will succeed, one will die.' He moved on, long-striding. 'There is another possibility, my other cousin, who may also return to stake his claim.'

Jack frowned. He guessed who this cousin might be. 'Where is this fellow now?'

'In the hujrah.' Batoor spoke without emotion.

'My Guides are in the hujrah,' Jack said.

'I know,' Batoor said softly.

'Is one of my men your cousin?' Jack wondered if Batoor's hospitality would extend to a rival for his position.

'Zaman.' Batoor confirmed Jack's suspicions.

'Is he safe? Will you harm him?' Jack stepped aside to give space to a smiling young man herding two buffalo.

'He is my guest. He is safe.' Batoor smiled. 'As long as he is within my lands, he is under my protection, unless he tries to kill me.'

Jack remembered Zaman's reluctance to come to Torkrud. 'He will not do that.'

'Then he is safe from me.' Batoor touched the silver hilt of his sword.

Every so often, Batoor stopped to talk to one of the many children or nod to a rifle-carrying man. All the time, Jack was looking at the rifles, checking for Enfields or any other British-made weapons.

'Could you not call a Jirga to decide who is khan?'

'We have, and the Jirga chose me. If they had not...' Batoor indicated the ruins behind him. 'That was in the past. More important for you, Gulbaz has called a Jirga over you and your Guides.'

'Has he? Why?'

'The British are not liked here. Many of our older men fought when the British invaded Afghanistan.'

'That was twenty years ago,' Jack said.

Batoor smiled. 'Twenty years, two hundred years, two thousand years. It does not matter. Our concepts of time are different from yours, Windrush.'

'The Pashtuns fought with us during the Mutiny,' Jack reminded him. 'You fought with us against the Mutineers.'

'I fought for my own hand, Windrush, as you know,' Batoor said. 'It happened that my cause coincided with yours at the time.'

'When is the Jirga?'

'Tomorrow,' Batoor said. 'They will decide if you and your men are guests, as I wish, or enemies, as Gulbaz wishes.'

So soon! Jack glanced around Torkrud. Armed men stood at every doorway, watching him, unsmiling. Some tapped the butts of their rifles; others had a hand on the hilt of Khyber knife or pulwar. 'What will happen if they decide as Gulbaz wants?'

'They will kill you,' Batoor said. 'It will be the will of the elders.' He lowered his voice. 'It will be the will of Allah. Come now, and we will try out my falcon.'

I will have to warn the men. I will have them prepared for any eventuality. What has Colonel Hook landed me in this time?

CHAPTER SIX

Torkrud, north-west frontier July 1863

Jack heard the slow throbbing of the drum as he rode to the Jirga. He did not know if the drums were part of the proceedings or purely coincidental. He only knew that the sound added to his tension as he left the village for the knoll outside, where the elders of the Rahmut Khel gathered around a gnarled group of pine trees.

The men sat cross-legged in a great circle, some chewing betel-nuts, others smoking from hookahs or merely listening to the speeches. They looked dignified and serious, as befitted men who had survived many years in Pakhtunkhwa, men accustomed to making decisions for the benefit of their community. Jack stood some way apart with one hand on the butt of his revolver, aware that his life was being decided. In one way this seemed a very primitive method of determining what course to take, but in another, it was real democracy at work as each man had his say, while the others listened without interruption. Jack nodded, comparing proceedings to the bear-garden that was the House of Commons. *This Jirga is more polite than Westminster,* he thought. *It is similar to the Thinga parliaments of the Norse. People are far more alike than different.* Then he remembered that if the decision of the Jirga went against him, he could be dead before nightfall.

I've warned my Guides; they know what to do if things go wrong, but I'm damned if I will hide away.

'I have fought beside Windrush in the war with the mutinous sepoys.' Batoor was on his feet, talking. 'He is a man like us. He lives by the concept of *nang*, of honour. As Khushal Khan Khattak said: "I despise the man who does not guide his life by honour." Windrush keeps his word and defends his men. He is Pashtun in everything except blood and religion.'

There was a ripple of assent at that. As Jack had learned, the Pashtuns considered personal honour one of the highest virtues.

Ayub was no elder, but he stood next, pointing at Jack. 'This man is a feringhee. He cannot be trusted. We all know the proverb. First comes one Englishman, as a traveller or for shikar; then come two and make a map; then comes an army and takes the country. Therefore it is better to kill the first Englishman.' He sat down again, giving Jack a poisonous glare. He tapped the Khyber knife at his belt.

Some of the assembled men nodded ominous approval. One wiry old man with a henna-dyed beard stood next.

'I know the proverb. I also know Pakhtunwali, the way of the Pashtun. We have given this feringhee hospitality. By the law of *melmastia,* we are bound to shelter any traveller arriving at our village. If we break that tradition, we damage our *nang* and will forever be dishonoured. The feringhee and his men should stay in peace.'

Some of the assembled men mumbled agreement, others looked annoyed. Jack could not tell which feeling was in the majority. He stiffened when Gulbaz stood, with the sun catching the steel of his wickedly curved hook.

'I have no disagreement with Batoor over the feringhee's nang.' Gulbaz spoke quietly, with intensity. He pointed a finger at Batoor. 'I have no argument that Windrush and his men may be honourable, as far as a feringhee can have honour, and a Pashtun may retain his honour, while still accepting a feringhee's salt.'

There was a murmur of assent from the gathered elders. Jack wondered what the follow-up would be. He suspected that he and his Guides would have to fight their way clear of this village. He fingered his revolver once more. He was meant to find out about gun-running and the fanatics, not get involved in a firefight.

Gulbaz paused to give more weight to his words. 'I am sure that Batoor found Windrush a brave man while fighting those who eat pork and worship cattle.'

Gulbaz is going to try the religious angle, Jack thought. *That is clever.* He waited as Gulbaz paused, giving intensity to his next words.

'Why should we give hospitality to feringhees? We should wage jihad on them, as the Mujahidin wish!'

Jack grunted. Any mention of holy war or Mujahidin was troubling, especially with these Mujahidin now carrying modern rifles. He did not know how many Muhammadans there were in India, but many millions, surely. If they rose simultaneously and called on their religious brothers in Afghanistan, Persia or central Asia to join them, the under-strength British Army in India could be overwhelmed. The Waziris alone were said to have over a hundred thousand warriors.

'Why should we give hospitality?' An old man used a stick to help himself to his feet. A deep scar ran from his empty eye socket to the corner of his mouth. 'We are Pashtun. We follow Pakhtunwali. That is why we give hospitality to Windrush and his Guides. If we fail in our law, we fail as Pashtuns.'

Another ancient man rose, his face seamed by countless years but his eyes bright. His beard was white, streaked with red. 'Am I not a Pashtun?' he said and sat back down again with his contribution to the Jirga made.

Other men rose, some speaking in favour of Batoor, others arguing for Gulbaz. Jack noted who supported whom, while he mentally worked out his route of escape if Gulbaz won the day.

At last Batoor stood. 'Windrush and the Guides are my guests,' he stated. 'They are under my protection by our law of melmastia.' He stopped, looking around the Jirga, meeting the gaze of every man there. 'If anybody wants to dispute my right to have them as my guests, let him do so now.'

Jack held his breath as silence fell over the Jirga. Even Gulbaz held his peace.

'Very good,' Batoor said. 'We shall now vote.'

Jack slid a hand onto the butt of his revolver. He had told his Guides that he would fire three spaced shots if the Jirga decided against them. Now he wondered if he would have time to send such a warning.

The voting was surprisingly orderly, with a small majority of men agreeing with Batoor. Jack released his breath with relief as Batoor nodded.

'Windrush and the Guides are our guests,' Batoor said. 'That saves us the trouble of killing them.' Some of the assembled men smiled at that. 'It also saves us from fighting off another British column as it marches through the passes. If the feringhee come in peace, we should welcome them and learn all we can of their intentions. If they come in war…' He spread his arms. 'Well, "The Pashtun is never at peace, except when he is at war." '

'Will you accept the decision of the Jirga, Gulbaz?' the one-eyed oldster asked, stroking his beard.

'I will accept it as long as Batoor extends his hospitality, and I am not expected to be friendly to the feringhee.'

The one-eyed man smiled. 'Nobody expects you to share your bed with the feringhee; only to spare him your blade.'

The gathering laughed as the men returned to their homes. Only Gulbaz remained. He faced Jack, nodded slowly, touched the hilt of his knife, and strode away.

'You see?' Batoor said. 'You are welcome.'

'Gulbaz does not think so,' Jack said.

'Gulbaz will obey the will of the Jirga,' Batoor spoke softly. 'It is Pakhtunwali.'

'You did not obey the will of the Jirga,' Jack reminded. 'I will sleep with my revolver under my pillow.'

Batoor's laugh was as loud as Jack had ever heard it. 'That also is Pakhtunwali!'

Jack looked up. The drumming he had heard before the Jirga had started again, or perhaps it had never stopped. He saw a lone horseman riding along the hill flank to his right, near naked and with a tabla drum in front of him on the saddle. *I have seen that man before, at Ali Masjid.* 'Who is that?'

Batoor looked and frowned. 'That is a mullah, Windrush, an itinerant holy man. He could be doing good, or he could be doing evil. I will tell my sentinels to watch him.'

* * *

They sat inside Batoor's house with sunlight streaming through the open door to dapple the floor around them. Batoor grunted and passed over the hookah. 'I have asked about these Mujahidin. They have not come here yet, Windrush.'

'My Colonel Hook believes that you have allowed them through your tribal lands.' Jack smoked the hookah, finding it milder than most cheroots he used.

'It is worrying, Windrush,' Batoor said. 'Jihads are always worrying. They are started by holy men, mullahs such as you saw earlier. They do not understand the concept of war. They do not listen to the words of generals or warriors who have experience of fighting. They think that belief and the words of the Koran alone will win battles against rifles and artillery.'

'We have Christians with equal faith,' Jack said.

'Some of these mullahs tell the young men that if they wear the words of the Koran around their neck, the infidel's bullets will not harm them.' Batoor spoke quietly. 'Many young men die that way.' He shrugged. 'Maybe it is true. I have not tried it.'

'I would not advise it, Batoor. Would you let me know if you hear anything about a mullah talking Jihad?'

'I will watch for him,' Batoor said. 'I don't wish a Jihad. In our own hills, we can defeat you. In the plains, against your artillery and discipline, I am not so sure.' He lowered his voice. 'Do not tell my people I said that.'

'I won't,' Jack promised. 'You have not allowed these fanatics, or Mujahidin, to cross your lands, then?'

'I have not,' Batoor said.

'There is another thing.'

'With the British, there is always another thing.' Batoor was smiling. 'You are always pushing, striving, altering. What is it, Windrush?'

'Rifles,' Jack said. 'There have been many British Enfield rifles turning up all along the Frontier. I noticed that two of your men carried such rifles. Do you know where they got them?'

Batoor smiled. 'I am not their father. If two of my men have modern rifles, then that is their concern.'

Jack nodded. He knew better than to press further. If Batoor knew more, then he was keeping his knowledge to himself. 'Tonight,' he said, 'I will sleep in the hujrah with my men. I do not wish them to think I am neglecting them.'

That night, Jack heard the drumming again, insistent through the dark. Leaving the hujrah, he walked around the village, ignoring the barking of the dogs and the occasional noise from within the compounds. A scimitar moon shone above, with myriad stars pricking the void of the sky, showing the ragged edges of the surrounding mountains.

There is a rare beauty out here, Jack thought, *a wildness that the Romantic poets would find attractive. It is like the people, raw, untamed, and perhaps untameable.* Climbing to the flat roof of the hujrah, he peered over the walls of Torkrud, seeing the land ghost-lit by the moon. A shaft of moonlight caught the mullah as he rode his horse around the village. *That's three times I have seen that tabla mullah. He is trouble.* The mullah was nearly naked, with a mane of matted hair that descended past his shoulders. Using his knees to guide the horse, he beat his tabla drum with a monotonous rhythm as he slid out of the moonlight into the dark. The throbbing of the mullah's drum continued long after he was out of sight.

Pliny the Elder said Semper aliquid novi Africam adferre, Africa always brings something new, Jack said to himself. *Well, India is the same. What surprises is this fragmented sub-continent going to spring next?*

When a cloud slid across the moon, darkness closed down the landscape. Jack could see nothing. The drumming continued, wrapping its sound around all within the walls of Torkrud.

'Dear Lord in Heaven.' Jack touched the Bible that Mary had given him. 'Guide me in my hours of need.'

'Windrush sahib.' Hassan had appeared at his side. 'You are talking to yourself.'

'I am praying, Hassan,' Jack said.

'Ah.' Hassan nodded in complete understanding. 'I will leave you in peace. May Allah guide your words.'

'I hope He does, Hassan. I really hope that He does.'

Jack remained on the roof of the hujrah for another half hour, listening as the drumming continued. Eventually, he returned to bed with the throbbing of the drum constant in his head. *There is trouble in the wind. I can feel it.*

* * *

'Windrush sahib.' Hassan stood at the side of Jack's charpoy. 'Batoor Khan is leaving.'

Jack struggled awake. He could hardly make out Hassan's shape in the darkness. 'What's happening, Hassan?'

'The Khan is leaving.'

'The devil he is.' Jack got up and pulled on his trousers and jacket. 'Where is he?'

'This way, Windrush sahib.' Hassan was at the door with the other Guides behind him. Fully dressed, they all carried their rifles.

'Follow me.' Diving into the darkness, Jack nearly ran to Batoor's compound. The village was awake, with men on horse and on foot trotting in the same direction as Jack, muted voices through the night, and the ubiquitous barking of dogs.

'Batoor Khan!' Jack did not hesitate. 'What is happening, Batoor?'

'We have intruders on Rahmut Khel land,' Batoor said. 'They did not ask our permission, so we are going to challenge them. It is nothing to do with you, Windrush, or your Guides.'

Jack paused for a second. 'We are your guests, Batoor. Your enemies are our enemies.' That sounded very melodramatic. Jack wondered how Colonel Hook would react if he got involved in a private war, but being friends with the British had to be seen to have some advantages for the Rahmut Khel.

'I do not know who they are.' Batoor was not smiling as he checked the Khyber knife at his belt. As he spoke, he strapped a Minie rifle across his back. 'It may be your Mujahidin, or the Adam Khel. We will find out. This is not your quarrel.'

'We'll come with you,' Jack said. 'We'll help.'

'You are British soldiers,' Batoor said. 'If you fight alongside us, we may be seen as your allies.' His grin gleamed through the night. 'You have your duty to do. Stay safe, Windrush, and God save the Queen.' His laugh broke the tension.

'How long will you be?' Jack viewed the growing number of Rahmut Khel warriors. 'We still have much to discuss.'

Batoor touched the hilt of his Khyber knife. 'I will be back as soon as I have removed these intruders.' He raised his voice. 'Men of the Rahmut Khel, we belong to God, and unto God do we return!'

Lifting his hand, he trotted out of the village with his men following in disciplined silence. A band of horsemen led, and then a larger group of warriors on foot, running at the same speed as the cavalry.

When the dust cleared, Jack looked at his Guides. 'This could alter things.'

'Torkrud is stripped of fighting men,' Zaman said. 'Batoor Khan has taken them all with him except a handful of elders.' He took a deep breath. 'And those who still follow Gulbaz.'

'It would be a good time for a rival to try to become Khan.' Hassan looked at Zaman. 'Unless he was an honourable man, a man of nang.'

Zaman smiled. 'It is all right, daffadar. I am true to my salt. Where would you be without me? I am the best fighting man in the unit.'

'If not the most modest,' Jack said.

'You boast like a Sikh.' Hassan punctured Zaman's ego. 'This would also be a good time for the Adam Khel or the Yusufzai to raid, sahib. Unless it is them that Batoor is riding against.'

'I don't think it was the Yusufzai.' Jack remembered the mullah of the previous night. 'I believe it was the Mujahidin.' Suddenly he felt very isolated. He was in an Afridi village in the heart of tribal territory with a handful of men of a vastly different culture. All around were tribes who waited on a hair-trigger to take offence, start a feud or otherwise create mayhem. He shook the depression away, trying to use Hassan's words to his advantage.

'Whoever it was, Hassan, if they raid, we will defend this village to repay Batoor Khan's hospitality.' Jack looked around. The rising sun cast long shadows from the peaks to the east, darkening the village. 'You know the culture better than I do; will we be insulting the Rahmut Khel if we mount guard on Torkrud?'

Hassan grunted. 'Gulbaz will not like it, but Gulbaz will not approve of us until we are dead.'

'That is all the more reason to get ourselves in a defensive position,' Jack said. 'Everybody ensure they have their ammunition pouches to hand, full water bottles and as much food as they can carry. Alladad, go and check the horses, make sure they are fed, and ensure the saddles, bridles and reins are close to hand. We may have to mount and ride in a hurry.'

'Yes, Windrush sahib.' Alladad strode away.

'Windrush sahib.' Hassan lifted his head. 'He may not have time.'

'Why is that?'

'Listen, sahib.'

The chanting came from outside the walls of Torkrud, a low babble that steadily increased in volume.

'What's that all about?' Jack could not make out any of the words.

'They want you.' Hassan did not sound agitated. 'They want the feringhee, the foreigner.'

'Ah.' Jack felt the old familiar tension rise within him. He usually experienced that mixture of fear, apprehension and excitement before a battle, but always he had been supported by the men of his regiment. He did not know how these Guides would react. Could he trust Pashtuns, even if they wore the Queen's uniform, to fight alongside him against men of their own religion and race? The old memories of the Mutiny increased his tension, now augmented by a thrill of elation he had not expected. He was a soldier again, facing danger. Some small part of him was enjoying this sensation.

'I'd better speak to them.'

'They don't want to talk,' Zaman said. 'They want to kill you, sahib.'

'Well,' Jack said. 'Let's see, shall we? I'll go and talk to them, for I'm damned if I'll run from a mob I haven't even seen yet!' He felt, rather than saw, Hassan motion the Guides onward. 'I'll go myself. There's no sense any of you men putting yourself in danger.'

Stepping onward, Jack did not have far to go before he saw the mob. They walked slowly, fifty or sixty strong, with a variety of weapons from iron-shod lathes to pulwars and jezzails. Jack stood still with one hand on the butt of his revolver.

'I am Captain Jack Windrush of the Guides!' He had to shout to be heard above the roar of the crowd.

The first stone rattled off the ground a foot to his left. The next whizzed past his head.

'I am a guest of Batoor Khan!' Jack tried again.

'They know that, sahib.' Hassan had followed him. 'Gulbaz has gathered men from the villages all around. With Batoor's warriors away from Torkrud, Gulbaz is the next most important man in the Rahmut Khel.' The other Guides lined up behind Hassan.

Jack glanced over his shoulder at the Guides. How would Zaman react to this situation? Would he try his hand at becoming Khan?

Jack refused to duck as another stone flicked past. The crowd was getting closer, swelling by the minute. He saw Gulbaz in the centre, taller than most of the others, encouraging them on with his metal claw held high. While the majority of the mob seemed to be old men, boys, and badly armed farmers, the men who surrounded Gulbaz were undoubtedly warriors, tall, rangy, fully armed men.

The mob continued to advance. Jack could make out their chant: 'Kill the feringhee' – kill the foreigner. 'Kill the Guides.'

'Load.' Jack snapped the order as he drew his revolver.

'We're already loaded, sahib.' Hassan sounded calm. 'Shall we kill them?'

'No! Aim into the air. Shoot above their heads.' Jack had no wish to cause civilian casualties, particularly in Batoor's home village.

'That's a waste of ammunition, sahib,' Zaman reproved. 'Kerr Sahib does not like us to waste ammunition.'

'Above their heads!' Jack ignored the complaints. 'Fire!'

When all six rifles crashed out, the mob halted. The chanting died away. Gulbaz stepped forward, the sun glinting on his steel hook.

'Reload.' Jack had no need to give the order as the Guides quickly reloaded and capped their rifles. Somewhere above, a bird called, the sound strangely sweet in the crisp air.

'Kill the feringhee!' Gulbaz voice grated through the bird call. 'Before the Guides reload.'

The mob surged forward again. Swearing, Jack fired his revolver in the air, knowing he had to make a rapid decision. He could stay put and fight it out, six Guides and himself against an armed mob that was now a hundred strong, or he could run for a defensive position and hold them off.

'Sahib…' Hassan glanced at Jack. 'Shall we fire?'

'To the watchtower, lads,' Jack decided. 'We'll hold them off there.'

Jack was too experienced to sit in any place without having a plan of escape, while he knew the reputation of the Pashtun too well to not guard his back. He had reconnoitred the village as soon as he arrived, looking for escape routes and defensive sites. Twenty feet tall, the watchtower was at the northern side of Torkrud, grimly overlooking the valley. Once there, Jack knew they could hold out until he decided on their ultimate course of action. Also, the watchtower gave them a splendid field of fire over the village, while denying that advantage to the enemy.

The Guides withdrew in good order, but their retreat encouraged the mob, which followed at a run, stopping only to throw rocks.

Sawan staggered as a stone crashed above his ear. He swore, lifted his rifle to aim, changed his mind when Jack growled at him, and continued the withdrawal with a trickle of blood down the side of his head. Ursulla stopped to lift a stone and throw it back.

'Don't delay.' Jack acted as rearguard. 'Keep moving, lads.' He pointed his revolver in the general direction of the crowd, tempted to shoot at Gulbaz, knowing he would not fire at stone-throwing civilians.

Were these civilians? They were certainly not uniformed soldiers such as the Cossacks or mutinous sepoys he had faced previously. He could not fire at them unless they fired first. That would be against everything he stood for. Jack grunted as a fist-sized stone thudded on the ground at his side. An increasing number of armed men had joined the crowd, no different from the tribesmen he would meet in the passes. Remembering the attack on the British at Kabul that began the terrible retreat of 1841, Jack was well aware of the danger.

The fusillade of stones increased, bouncing from the road and the walled compounds on either side. Jack heard women's voices from the houses, screaming to encourage the men. A boy about eight years old appeared, wielding a long Khyber knife and gesticulating toward the Guides. Jack had never seen such an evil expression on the face of a child.

A single shot sounded, followed by another. Jack saw a man kneel to fire his jezzail, with the long barrel swinging to aim at him.

That's enough, fellow! Stones are one thing, bullets something else! Swearing, Jack levelled his revolver and fired a quick shot. The jezzail man did not flinch; he levelled his weapon, but before he could shoot a surge of the mob obstructed his aim.

'Nearly there, Sahib!' Fatteh was first to reach the watchtower. 'There's no door!'

'There's a ladder in that house.' Jack indicated the nearest compound. *Fatteh should know that many of these towers had no internal stairs. The man is not thinking straight.* 'Fatteh, with me. The rest of you, fix bayonets. Form a defensive line, lads; only fire if they fire!' He knew the sobering effect that a glittering line of bayonets had on any crowd. Most of the mob would be willing for others to charge forward; few would want to be at the forefront when a soldier of the Guides waited with his bayonet poised.

'Afridi pigs!' Alladad was a Yusufzai, no friend of the Afridi. He grinned across the sight of his rifle. 'Come and try a real man.' His finger curled over the trigger.

The mob had halted, threatening with words and gestures, gesticulating with pulwars, waiting for any sign of weakness from the Guides.

Unlike most of the buildings in Torkrud, the watchtower was mostly stone-built, loose boulders crudely put together with mud in place of mortar. Decorative architecture was not one of the qualities of the Pashtun people. Pragmatic building was.

Don't run, Jack told himself. *If you run, the rabble will think you are panicking. Walk.*

Jack marched to the door of the compound that held the ladder. For a moment he had an impulse to knock politely, and ask to borrow their ladder, but instead, he booted the door in and burst inside. A woman, minus her Burqa, shrieked in horror at the sight of an unrelated man. Ignoring her, Jack grabbed the simple ladder that lay on the ground and withdrew, dragging it behind him.

'Come on, Fatteh! Daffadar, take charge of the men!'

Jack and Fatteh propped the ladder against the wall of the tower. Although it did not quite reach the crenellated top, Jack knew it was the best they could do. A group of young boys ran forward, each one throwing stones that bounced from the wall. A shot rang out from the flat roof of one of the houses, with the drift of powder smoke the only sign of the shooter.

Jack returned to the short line of bayonets. 'Up the ladder with you, lads! Hassan, you go first! Guides, if you see anybody aiming at us, shoot him.'

The Guides swarmed up one at a time, with Jack last. He heard the deep boom of a jezzail and saw the heavy splash as a bullet thudded into the wall two feet from his side.

'Fire!'

An instant before Jack gave the order, the Guides opened up. Four rifles fired at once, followed by a deep laugh from Alladad. 'That's one Afridi who won't be raiding my village!'

'Good man!' Jack rolled onto the roof of the tower. 'Haul the ladder up!'

Jack looked around. The roof of the tower was flat, with a low, crenellated wall as a defence against attack. In the centre of the floor, a square hatch allowed access to whatever lay beneath. Stones were piled at various places on the roof. Like most things in Pakhtunkhwa, it was functional but basic.

'Keep watch,' Jack ordered.

The Guides were safe for the present, Jack reasoned. He did not wish to think of the reverse; although Gulbaz's men could not get up, neither could the Guides get down. The watchtower could only be a temporary refuge.

'Sawan! Check down below; see if there is any food or water stored.'

'Yes, Sahib.' Sawan moved on Jack's final word.

With the Guides all in the same place, Gulbaz stepped forward from the mob. He lifted his metal hook, urging the crowd to the attack. They swirled ahead, throwing missiles.

'How many are there, sahib?' Zaman asked.

'I'm not sure.' The crowd was growing by the minute as men swarmed to Torkrud from the surrounding villages. 'At least a couple of hundred.'

'We can shoot them until our ammunition runs out.' Zaman sounded calm.

'They are your people.' Jack was surprised at Zaman's callousness.

'They are attacking us.' Zaman showed the pragmatism of the Pashtun.

'Don't fire unless they fire first.' Jack raised his voice. 'Check your ammunition! How many rounds do you have?'

'Seventy rounds each, sahib,' Hassan said. 'We are the Guides. We carry seventy rounds and eighty-five percussion caps.'

'Good man.' Jack was learning why the Guides were considered an elite fighting force. They were ready for whatever emergency the Frontier threw up.

Sawan swarmed up from the chamber below. 'There is neither food nor water, sahib,' he reported. 'Only some old clothes fit for rags, a few bits of broken weapons, some rubbish and barrels of mouldy gunpowder.'

We're sitting on barrels of explosives. That's not healthy. 'We can't stay here for long, then.' Jack had wondered if he could remain on the tower until Batoor returned. 'We only have whatever water is in our water bottles.'

'They're coming, sahib!' Hassan warned.

Now swollen to over 300 men, the mob surged forward, some firing at the Guides and others throwing stones.

'Fire at the men with muskets,' Jack ordered as a ball chipped the parapet beside him. Aiming his revolver, he loosed two shots without hitting his man. Rather than fire wildly as inexperienced men might have done, the Guides leant their rifles on the parapet, took careful aim, and squeezed their triggers. Two of the jezzail men crumpled, one to lie still as the other writhed, holding his stomach. A crowd of young boys began to clamber up the wall of the tower.

'Get rid of them, Sawar!' Jack ordered. 'Try not to hurt them. They're only children.'

'Yes, sahib.' Lifting one of the loose rocks that were scattered about the flat roof, Sawar leaned over the parapet. 'Here!' He dropped the rock. Three boys fell to the ground.

'I said don't hurt them.' Jack ducked as a bullet whined past his head. He saw a large part of the mob surge to the base of the tower and charge around, searching for an entry. Yelling and shaking crude weapons, they milled around the base.

'Leave them,' Jack said. 'I have no intention of starting a blood feud by killing virtually unarmed men. They can't do us any harm down there.'

'They can try,' Hassan said. 'Look. Gulbaz has them organised.'

With Gulbaz giving loud orders, dozens of men were hacking at the stonework at the base of the tower, sliding the blades of Khyber knives and pulwars between the stones to prise them free.

Jack swore. 'You're right, Hassan. If they take out enough stones, the tower will collapse.' He pointed to the closest pile of rocks. 'Copy Sawar; save ammunition by dropping stones on them.'

Hassan nodded. 'Yes, sahib.'

Laying aside their rifles, Hassan, Sawar and Fatteh rolled the largest of the rocks over to the edge of the roof. Beneath them, the crowd continued to work at the wall, cheering whenever they managed to work loose one of the stones.

'Ready?' Jack ducked as one of Gulbaz's men fired his jezzail. The sound was like a miniature cannon as a massive spurt of smoke jetted from the barrel. The shot crashed against the parapet, crumbling the solid mud. 'Drop!'

Grinning, Hassan toppled the rock.

The men working on the wall glanced up; one pointed upwards, too late. The rock landed in the middle of the pack, killing one man outright and injuring three others. One crawled away with his leg at a terrible angle; another held a shattered arm. The others scattered, shouting.

'Now fire!' Jack said softly. Gulbaz and his men were serious; it was time to properly retaliate. 'Try and drop Gulbaz.'

It was only an hour or so since Jack had doubted the loyalty of the Guides when facing fellow Pashtuns. He no longer had any misgivings as they opened rapid fire on Gulbaz's men so for a few moments the watchtower was the centre of a firefight. With their elevated position and better weapons, the Guides had the advantage, so their attackers withdrew to the cover of the various compounds. Glaring over his shoulder, Gulbaz joined them.

'Cease fire,' Jack ordered.

Powder-smoke drifted over the four Pashtun dead on the ground and the half dozen staggering or crawling wounded. The small boys continued to jeer; hiding behind a wall, they threw stones at the watchtower.

'We beat them back,' Hassan said.

'For now,' Jack agreed. 'But we can't stay up here forever. They will come again at night.'

'They will.' Hassan gave a small smile. 'The Guides can also fight at night.'

Jack hid his smile. It seemed that the Pashtun were as liable to regimental pride as any British regiment. 'Of course we can.' He emphasised the use of 'we.'

The day passed slowly, with Gulbaz's men keeping their distance but sniping when they could. Jack watched for the return of Batoor while trying to work out a plan to withdraw safely from the village. They ate half the bread they had brought with them drank from their water bottles, baked in the sun, and waited.

Evening came with its usual rush. The crisp darkness of the Frontier descended, brittle with tension as if the world held its breath. The chanting began again.

'They are saying, "kill the feringhee," ' Hassan said.

'They'll have to catch me first,' Jack said. "We'll take shifts. Two on watch, the others resting.' He raised his voice slightly. 'You men on watch; keep moving so the enemy cannot aim at you.'

'We know how to fight, sahib,' Hassan rebuked gently.

'I'm sure you do.' Jack glanced upward, where clouds obscured the night sky. 'No stars tonight, so we'll need artificial lights in case Gulbaz attacks.' He lowered his voice, knowing how far sound travelled at night. 'Fatteh: I have been told that you can find anything; find me a length of cloth. The rest of you, give me one of your cartridges.'

'Sahib?' The Guides looked confused.

'One cartridge from each man,' Jack said. 'Fatteh, have you found me that cloth yet?'

'There are old clothes below,' Sawan reminded him as Fatteh disappeared down the hatch.

Collecting the cartridges, Jack split them open and ground the gunpowder into the cloth Fatteh brought him. 'Fatteh; cut that into four, and put one piece on each side of the tower. Those are our lanterns if we need them.'

'Yes, sahib.' Sawan sounded confused.

'Now, unless you are on watch, grab as much sleep as you can. Either stay up here or go into the chamber below.' Jack contemplated remaining awake but knew he needed to keep alert, which meant resting while he could. Lying in the shadow of the parapet, Jack closed his eyes. Despite his best intentions, he could not sleep. He lay still, with ideas and images chasing each other through his mind. He saw the tabla mullah, and Batoor's friendly face, the children climbing up the wall of the tower, and Gulbaz with his iron claw, the long puff of smoke from a jezzail, and the scared face of the woman without a burqa.

He heard the noises an hour later, the furtive pad of feet on hard ground.

Jack nudged Zaman, the nearest Guide. There was no need to say anything. Zaman understood immediately, waking the man next to him. Moving more quietly than even Jack expected, the Guides took their posts behind the battlements of the tower.

The first of Gulbaz's men slid over the parapet in complete silence. A young, lithe man wearing a pakul hat and carrying a naked pulwar, he had only time to look around him before Zaman thrust his bayonet into his chest, so he died without a sound. The second man was naked except for a loin-cloth, and with a knife between his teeth. Alladad slit his throat, catching the sword he carried before it clattered onto the ground. The attackers climbed two sides at once, with the Guides disposing of them immediately as they arrived. Within three minutes there were five dead men on the top of the tower. Zaman had disposed of the final two men; they lay on top of the bloody pile with the Guides grinning at each other, satisfied with a job well done.

'Shall we throw the bodies over the wall, sahib?' Hassan asked.

About to give assent, Jack remembered their lack of water. 'No, Hassan,' he said. 'We'll hold on to them just now.'

'They'll stink when the sun rises,' Hassan said.

'They might come in useful.' Jack did not elaborate. His idea was still embryonic.

'I hear something,' Zaman whispered.

The Guides fell silent, listening. Zaman lifted his hand, fingers outstretched. He closed his fist and opened it again three times. *Fifteen men approaching*, Jack guessed.

Taking a packet of Lucifer matches from inside his jacket, Jack scratched one alight and placed the flame on the nearest length of cloth. The gunpowder sparked immediately, casting darting shadows across the roof of the tower.

Lifting the end of the cloth furthest from the flame, Jack threw it over the parapet. The burning rag floated down, twisting as the fire caught hold. The light flitted across the ground, revealing half a dozen men lying prone with lethal pesh-kabz daggers or Khyber knives in their hands. As soon as the light revealed them, they rose, moving swiftly forward.

'Shoot them,' Jack ordered. 'Don't waste ammunition. Only fire if you're certain of a hit.'

'Hassan, Alladad; check the other sides.' Jack sounded calmer than he felt. He moved around the roof, setting fire to the rags he had prepared. The Guides were firing, the time between each shot informing Jack they were carefully aimed.

'They're all around us.' Hassan's voice was calm.

'How many?' Jack did not have to ask. Zaman had reported fifteen attackers, so fifteen attackers there would be.

'There were fifteen,' Hassan said. 'We've killed some.' There was the sound of a shot. 'I think eleven now.'

The attackers broke before the Guide's rifle fire, running back to the shelter of the dark village.

'Cease fire.' Jack waved his hand to clear some of the powder-smoke. He ducked at the thud of a jezzail, the bullet slamming into the parapet. 'It's going to be a long night.'

The sobbing of a wounded man disturbed the hush.

CHAPTER SEVEN

Torkrud, north-west frontier July 1863

Dawn brought little relief as the heat rose with the sun, baking the handful of men who sheltered behind the stone-and-mud parapets on the lookout tower. With the sun came the flies, attracted by the blood on the pile of dead bodies. The sobbing of the wounded Pashtun had ceased. He lay a few yards from the tower, his twisted body furred with flies.

'We should throw them over the side.' Hassan nodded to the corpses. 'Soon they will stink.'

'Don't your people hold their dead in high esteem?' Jack asked. 'Don't they value men killed in battle?'

'That is true, sahib, but these men are not Guides.' Hassan dismissed the bodies as if they were so much carrion.

'We could cut off their heads.' Zaman added various other anatomical details that Jack preferred not to contemplate.

'Gulbaz may want his dead back.' Jack had noticed that parties of Gulbaz's men were creeping out to retrieve the dead from the previous night's skirmish.

'Is it your intention to give succour to the enemy?' Hassan looked unbelieving. 'It is not the Pashtun way.'

'I intend to barter with them,' Jack said. Raising his voice to a shout, he called out: 'Gulbaz! Can you hear me?'

After a few minutes, an answering hail came. 'I hear you, Windrush. If you surrender, I will supply an escort to take you and your men away from the lands of the Rahmut Khel.'

'Elphinstone sahib agreed to such terms,' Jack reminded him. 'The Afghans murdered all his men, with twelve thousand camp followers. I have another proposal for you.'

The silence was broken by the deep thud of a jezzail and the crunch of a bullet against the parapet.

'Speak, Windrush.' Gulbaz's voice was strangely musical.

'I propose that you surrender to me, and I will not desecrate the bodies of the men we have here.' Jack knew that Gulbaz would never agree to such a suggestion. He also knew that the relatives of the dead men would wish the bodies returned, so with luck he might spread dissension among the enemy.

Before Jack continued, Zaman shouted: 'We will castrate them, cut off the heads, and pour bacon grease into the mouths and bodies.'

Pigs were anathema to the followers of Islam. Zaman had given one of the worst insults he could imagine. He glanced at Jack, grinning.

'We have no bacon grease, sahib.' Ursulla was not the brightest of the Guides.

'Gulbaz does not know that.' Jack did not approve of Zaman's interference, but given the circumstances, he decided to say nothing. He expected Gulbaz's renewal of activity as half a dozen jezzails fired at once, with the bullets crashing into the battlements or whistling through the embrasures.

'We've got him angry, sahib.' Zaman was still grinning. 'Shall I throw him the head of one of his men?'

'Not yet,' Jack said.

'Shall I throw him something else, then?' Zaman made several suggestions, each one cruder than the previous.

'Not yet,' Jack repeated. 'Let's wait until he thinks about my proposal.'

'What do you have in mind, sahib?' Hassan asked.

'A trade,' Jack said. 'We need water and food; Gulbaz will want the bodies back.'

Hassan nodded. 'You are not as stupid as I thought you were, sahib.'

'Thank you, Hassan.'

The firing sputtered to a stop. 'Windrush!' Gulbaz shouted again. 'Leave us our dead, and you can go free.'

'I won't even answer that,' Jack said softly.

'Zaman had the best idea,' Hassan said. 'Throw Gulbaz a head or two, sahib.'

'Not yet,' Jack said. 'Ursulla, wrap up a rock in a piece of cloth. Make it look like a human head in cloth.'

'Yes, sahib.' Ursulla was apparently confused but was too good a soldier to question a direct order. He handed Jack a covered bundle that was roughly the size of a human head.

'Gulbaz!' Jack made to stand up until a marksman took a shot with a jezzail. Fortunately firing upward at a moving target seen through the aperture between irregular battlements did not help the marksman's aim. The shot flicked past Jack's shoulder. 'Here is a present for you, Gulbaz!' He threw the bundled rock as far as he could, watched it thud onto the hard ground, bounce once and roll. Almost immediately a man scurried out of cover to retrieve the bundle.

'Don't shoot him,' Jack ordered as Zaman levelled his rifle. He watched as Gulbaz's man scurried away with the bundle.

'That's a rock!' Gulbaz said a moment later.

'The next one won't be,' Jack promised.

'What do you want, Windrush?' Gulbaz did not appear from behind his sheltering wall.

'Water and food.' Jack decided to end the guessing game. 'Unless you wish to surrender.'

'You wish water and food in exchange for what?'

'I wish water and food in exchange for the return of your dead,' Jack said.

There was a pause. Jack guessed that Gulbaz was consulting his elders. 'I agree. Lower our dead, and we will bring you water and food.'

Jack grunted. He was making some progress. 'You bring out food and water, Gulbaz, and I will have some of your dead lowered.' He raised his voice. 'To show that I trust you, for I know an Afridi will never damage his honour by breaking his word, I will have one man lowered first.' He signalled to Hassan and Ursulla, who took hold of the hands and ankles of the topmost corpse.

'Lower him carefully,' Jack ordered.

'Yes, sahib.' Hassan hoisted the dead man above the parapet and let him go.

Ten minutes later, two of Gulbaz's men staggered into the open. Both carried heavy goatskin containers and baskets of bread.

'Stop there!' Jack commanded. 'Both of you.' The men were thin, nearly gaunt, and large-eyed. They stared as Jack stood with one foot on top of the battlements. 'Take a drink from the water.'

They stared at him. One lifted the skin to his mouth, dropped it, and ran away. The second followed quickly.

With his throat already parched from lack of water, Jack shouted, 'Try again, Gulbaz! Bring us water that you have not poisoned. This is your last chance!'

'Throw him a head, sahib,' Hassan urged.

'No,' Jack said. 'I won't stoop to such barbarity.'

'It may save all our lives,' Hassan said.

About to refuse permission, Jack remembered Kerr's advice to be guided by Hassan. 'All right, Hassan.'

God forgive me for the sacrilege.

Jack did not watch as Zaman cheerfully sawed off the head of the nearest fly-covered corpse.

'Here, Gulbaz. A gift for you.' Lifting the head by its hair, Zaman swung it back and forth before throwing it in a high, blood-spraying arc over the battlements. Jack saw the head bounce once before it rolled towards the nearest house.

'The feringhee officer is pouring pig fat over the body!' Zaman laughed as somebody in the village began to wail, a cry that was soon taken up by others.

After the expected fusillade of musketry, Gulbaz shouted again, 'Here is clean water, Windrush, and the bread is fresh.'

This time three veiled women brought the water and bread. When they appeared, Zaman aimed his rifle.

'Don't fire.' Jack pushed the barrel up.

The women stopped at the foot of the tower, placed the water-skins and baskets of bread on the ground, and gracefully returned with their long white burqas brushing the dirt.

Jack manoeuvred the ladder over the wall. 'I'll go down. Cover me.'

With his heart thumping inside his chest, Jack swarmed down the ladder and carefully sampled the water. 'It's sweet,' he announced. His head was throbbing from dehydration.

Expecting the thump of a jezzail bullet, Jack carried the water and food up the ladder. 'Throw the bodies over. Throw them as far as you can to clear the flies away.'

It was a relief to get the corpses with their buzzing cargo from the tower. Jack watched, licking dry lips as the men drank from the water-skins. When at last it was his turn, the goat-scented liquid tasted like nectar.

'We don't appreciate how precious water is back in England,' he said. The Guides looked at him, not comprehending.

'This bread is delicious.' Jack had not realised how hungry he had been.

Hassan nodded at that. 'We have a saying that Pashtun women make bread and children. They need do no more. They make the best bread and the strongest children.' He laughed, pointing to the surrounding landscape. 'They have to be the strongest, or they would not survive in a land such as ours.'

The moments the bodies were removed, the sniping began again. Every time one of the Guides showed his head in one of the embrasures a jezzail would fire. Fatteh swore as a splinter nicked the side of his face.

'Permission to fire back, sahib?'

'Only if you are certain of your target,' Jack said. 'Don't waste ammunition.' He kept careful watch over the village, seeing a steady trickle of men come in from the surrounding hills. 'The enemy's numbers are growing all the time.'

'They will starve us out,' Hassan said. 'Now we have nothing left to bargain with, and they know we are short of water and food. They will wait until we are weak and then charge the tower. Patience is a Pashtun virtue.'

Jack nodded. 'I have heard that your people can wait for days to ambush a single man.'

Hassan nodded. 'The feringhees hurry here, and hurry there; they do everything at a rush. Among the Pashtun, we have a proverb. The Pashtun who took revenge after a hundred years said: I took it quickly.'

Jack nodded. 'We have different ideas about time, Daffadar.'

With his 113th Foot, Jack would have not hesitated to ask the advice of an experienced sergeant. He did not know how the Guides would respond. Again, he remembered Kerr telling him to take Hassan's advice. 'We have choices to make, gentlemen. You all know the Pashtun better than I do, so I will welcome any comments, although I will make the final decision.'

The Guides nodded their acceptance. *Good.*

'Our first choice is that we remain on this tower in the hope that Batoor Khan returns soon. Our second choice is to slide away at night and hope to escape unseen. Our third is to fight our way out, hoping to cause so many casualties that Gulbaz is unwilling to follow us.'

The Guides listened, nodding. 'We do not know where Batoor Khan is,' Hassan pointed out. 'He could be defending the lands of the Rahmut Khel as he said, but if so, we have heard no gunfire.'

'That is true,' Jack conceded the point.

'In that case, Batoor Khan is far away, and we do not know how long he will be.'

Jack nodded. 'That is also true. The option of waiting for him is closed.' He ducked as a jezzail roared. The bullet smacked into the parapet, chipping away a sizeable chunk of stone.

'Gulbaz will expect us to sneak away at night,' Zaman pointed out. 'His men will be alert for that.'

Jack nodded. He knew that his Guides were expert at silent night movement, but so were the warriors of Gulbaz's Rahmut Khel.

Zaman patted the lock of his rifle. 'A break out will be honourable.'

'It will also be suicidal,' Hassan said.

Jack ducked as another jezzail bullet crashed into the parapet at his side. 'Sawan, you said there was no food or water stored below. Remind me what else there was.'

'Gunpowder, sahib,' Sawan replied at once. 'A few rusty pulwars that my grandfather would have thrown away, some old clothing...'

'Gunpowder? I forgot you mentioned that.'

'I said it was mouldy, sahib. It is not of good quality.'

'I'll have a look,' Jack said. 'Daffadar, you take over here. I'm going down below.'

The chamber was dark and dusty, with scorpions that scuttled away, tails erect, as Jack used a flaming rag for light. Wary of the gunpowder, he peered around. Sawan's assessment of the stores was correct. The pulwars were rusted and fragile-bladed, the clothing mostly rotted, and only a few of the barrels of gunpowder in reasonable condition.

Jack inspected the three best of the barrels; the British government markings stamped on the outside suggested that they had been stolen from some garrison, possibly during the Mutiny. Jack remembered his mission to search for stolen Enfields, briefly wondered if there was a connection, and dismissed the thought. His priority now was to get his men to safety. All other considerations were secondary.

He started as something crashed against the wall, realised that it was only a jezzail bullet, and rolled the powder kegs immediately beneath the hatch.

'Sawan! Drop me your bayonet!'

Using the tip of the blade, Jack made a hole in each of the barrels. The coarse-grained powder inside was dry but probably more volatile than he would have liked. Casting around for a fuse, he grabbed at the bundle of old clothes, swearing at the swarm of crawling insects that he released.

'That'll do.' He sliced a long strip of cloth, scattered gun powder over the top, and coiled it around the barrels. As an afterthought, he part-emptied each barrel, pouring the gunpowder into one of the small half-rotted goatskin bags that lay in an untidy pile in one corner of the chamber.

One can never have too much gunpowder, he told himself. *Although I do not at present know how I can use it.*

Aware of the Guides looking quizzically at him when he emerged from below, Jack took a quick swig from the already warm water. 'We're leaving an hour after sundown,' he said.

'Yes, sahib.' Having already voiced their concerns, the Guides would obey Jack's orders without question.

'We'll leave Gulbaz's men with a little souvenir of our visit,' Jack said. 'I'm afraid Batoor Khan will have to build another watchtower, as we're going to blow this one up.' He saw the glimmer of humour in the eyes of his men. 'We need a diversion.'

Splitting the remaining bread into two unequal portions, Jack spread around the smaller pile. 'Eat that,' he said. 'We'll need to keep our strength up.' The rest he divided into seven pieces and handed out to his men. 'This will have to feed us until we find a friendly village.'

'Yes, sahib.'

'Who amongst you is best at moving silently at night?' Jack knew that all Pashtun were expert at the arts of concealment and ambush, so the best of this patrol of Guides would be an expert.

'Alladad,' Hassan said without hesitation. 'He can walk through a thunderstorm disguised as a drop of rain without getting wet.'

Alladad was a supremely handsome man with kohl-rimmed eyes. He stroked his immaculate beard, evidently pleased at the praise.

'I have a job for you, Alladad, if you are willing,' Jack said. 'It is not an order; think of the implications before deciding.' Jack knew that his style of leadership, developed with the rogues of the 113th, was not what the Guides were used to. He hoped they would not take advantage of his flexibility.

'Speak, Sahib.'

'Could you slip through Torkud to retrieve our horses?'

Ignoring the almost obligatory jezzail shot, Alladad stood up, moving from side to side to put any marksman off his mark. He scanned the village, passing his gaze across the walled houses to where the horses were stabled. 'Yes, sahib.'

'The men of Torkud will be waiting for you.'

Alladad smiled. 'If Allah wills, I will succeed.'

'Can you all ride without saddles and bridles?' Jack asked.

'We are Pashtun.' Hassan's reply was calm as ever. 'And we are the Guides.'

'I expected nothing else,' Jack said with immense satisfaction. He bit back his concern for Alladad. The man was a soldier; he must accept danger.

The loud report startled Jack. The entire tower shook as something heavy crashed into the wall. 'That was no jezzail.' *Has Gulbaz found some artillery? Is the gun-runner dealing with more than just rifles?*

'That was a jingal.' Zaman sounded calm.

Jack saw the rising coil of smoke from deep inside Torkrud. *Of course, it was a jingal.* Jingals were large-calibre muskets or small, smooth-bore cannons, with a greater range than hand-held firearms. The deep boom sounded again, and another jingal ball crashed into the parapet, raising a great cloud of dust. 'I've faced them before,' Jack said. 'I thought they were normally mounted on the back of camels or elephants.'

'Gulbaz must have one somewhere in Torkrud.' Hassan pushed Fatteh further down. 'Keep down, Fatteh. I'm not going to kiss you better if Gulbaz puts a bullet through your arse.'

The jezzail ball crashed into the ground between Jack's feet, spreading splinters of rock. One sliced into his calf, tearing open a small cut. He grunted; that was another scar to add to his collection.

'Lie down,' Jack ordered. 'If you see any targets, shoot.' The Guides had been lucky so far, but with the volume of fire increasing, it was only a matter of time before they began to take casualties.

'The jingal is well concealed,' Hassan said quietly. 'Luckily it takes time to load. I hope they don't have much powder.'

I wonder if the powder kegs in this tower were for the jingal.

'We'll survive the day,' Jack said. 'Keep under cover as much as you can.' He ducked as the deep thud of the jingal sounded again. The ball crashed against the top of the parapet, destroying the stonework. 'I wish we could do something about that.'

Hassan nodded toward the drifting smoke. 'I could take two men across to find it.'

'In daylight?' Jack shook his head. 'Gulbaz will be waiting for that. Roll over the rocks to form a second barrier behind the parapet. Gulbaz is firing from a lower level, so hopefully, the jingal won't be able to reach us.'

It was the work of ten minutes to create a second barricade and pull the Guides behind it. The sniping continued, punctuated by the heavier boom of the jingal every fifteen minutes. 'There's no need for us all to lie so exposed,' Jack said. 'I'll stay up here with two men on watch. The rest go down below. It's safer. For God's sake, don't cause any sparks."

'Sahib,' Hassan said. 'It is best if you go below. We are used to the heat.'

'Thank you, Daffadar, but I'll stay here.' Jack knew the old adage that an officer should not order a man to do what he would not do himself. He would not leave men in danger while he hid below.

The jingal concentrated on one section of the tower, very slowly crumbling away the parapet and the corner of the roof that faced the village.

'They are trying to weaken us,' Jack said. 'They'll come at night with scaling ladders.'

'Yes, sahib,' Hassan said.

'We'll have to ensure that Alladad moves first,' Jack decided. He did not admit how worried he was. *A good officer must appear confident at all times, or his men will lose faith in him. Sometimes, only sometimes, I wish I was a ranker with no responsibilities except to myself. How easy a life a private soldier's must be, following orders and allowing others to make all the decisions.*

No! Jack shook his head. *I cannot think like that. I do have responsibilities; I have to look after these men, and I have Mary and Andrew waiting for me.* For a moment Jack thought what Mary's life would be like as the wife of an ordinary soldier. She would share a barrack room with a score of men with only a tattered blanket for privacy, with no security, half a man's rations, and always the possibility of being left behind when the regiment moved.

No.

'We have to stick it, Hassan.' Jack forced a grin.

We have to stick it.

CHAPTER EIGHT

Torkrud, north-west frontier July 1863

Lying behind a makeshift barricade under the sun, Jack watched as the jingal balls slowly crumbled their parapet away. He could do nothing except watch and wait.

I do not want Andrew to join the Army. Jack thought of his young son, helpless in his cot. *No, I want him to be a solicitor, or a banker, or a doctor, anything but a soldier. I don't want him to put himself in danger on a daily basis. I must tell Mary that when I get back. But first I have to get back.*

'Get ready, Alladad. It's nearly time.'

Stripped to only a loincloth, Alladad slipped through an embrasure at the back of the tower and vanished. Although Jack was only a few feet from him, he did not see him move. He peered into the dark.

The night was still. No wind; no sound, not even the barking of a dog or bleating of a goat. Jack felt the tension rise. Gulbaz had made a mistake; he should have kept the jezzail-men firing if only to keep the Guides occupied. He should have sent his storming party forward in the half-light before full dark when men were unsure what was real and what was not. That hesitation gave the attackers the advantage. *It's too late now, Gulbaz, too late now.*

Taking out his watch, Jack counted the seconds. Alladad had said he would need only five minutes to reach the stables. Jack allowed six, with each second hanging heavy as the minute hand slowly hovered above the next mark. He disliked sending a man into danger, for he firmly believed that an officer should never send a man to do what he would not do himself. However, Jack knew that Alladad was far better suited at freeing the horses than he would ever be. *God speed, Alladad, or Allah speed, if you prefer.*

'Time,' Jack said. Dropping through the hatch to the chamber below, he scratched a Lucifer and watched the flame grow for a moment before applying it to the end of the rag and scrambling back up.

'We've got less than three minutes.'

'We belong to God,' Hassan said, 'and to God do we return.'

Rather than everybody crowding on one ladder, Jack had them tie the old clothes together into makeshift ropes. With the top end fastened to the battlements where Alladad had climbed down, he dropped the ropes over the side, and the Guides slithered down, landing on the hard ground without a sound. They moved silently across to the corner of the building opposite, taking up defensive positions.

'Where's Alladad?' Jack thought of the fuse within the tower, quickly fizzing toward the kegs of gunpowder. He wished he had given it longer to burn.

'He's not here yet.' Hassan was as calm as if he was in barracks at Mardan.

The whole operation depends on Alladad. I should have gone myself, rather than sending a trooper. Jack glanced over his shoulder, thinking of the sparking fuse at the gunpowder. *Dear God, hurry, Alladad!*

'He's coming,' Zaman said. 'I heard the stable door open.'

Jack heard the horses' hooves a moment later, accompanied by a high yell that could only have been Alladad.

'Here he comes.' Jack swore as he heard the crackle of musketry. 'Get ready, lads!'

The horses erupted from the darkened village, a confusion of tossing manes and pounding hooves, with flaring nostrils and the occasional fearful high whinny.

'Grab your horse,' Jack ordered. 'Make for the gate! Hurry!' Waiting until all his men were mounted, Jack threw himself onto the last horse in the pack. He saw Colwall among the loose horses but had no time to reach for him. 'Well done, Alladad! Move now!'

Without glancing at his watch, Jack knew that time was up. The kegs of powder should have blown by now; the tower should be ablaze, giving them cover from the pursuit that was bound to occur. He hoped he had not taken too much powder from the kegs; he needed a massive explosion.

A horse whinnied shrilly as a bullet hit it. Blood spurted, half seen in the dark. Men rose beside them, slashing with pulwars and Khyber knives. Zaman roared, parried a pulwar swing with his Enfield, fired, and rode on.

The yelling increased as a hundred men burst from the buildings. Gulbaz must have timed his attack for that moment, for each man was armed and ready. Jack had time to fire a single round from his revolver before the mob was surging behind him.

'Spur, lads!'

That was when the gunpowder kegs blew up. Jack had experienced louder explosions during the siege of Sevastopol, and at Lucknow, but rarely had he been so close to a building that was so thoroughly destroyed. The gunpowder threw out the unmortared stones of the tower, so they splintered into small, deadly fragments that sprayed across the village, adding to the mayhem. Half a dozen of Gulbaz's men fell at once, with others ducking or throwing themselves to the ground to escape the flying debris. Fatteh fell from his horse, shook his head, and threw himself onto the nearest mount.

'Spur!' Temporarily deafened by the blast, Jack did not hear himself shout. As a youth, Jack had occasionally ridden bareback on the swelling slopes of the Malvern Hills. Back then it had been fun, an innocent feat of daring. Now, with scores of Pashtun warriors behind him, riding without a saddle, bridle or reins was far harder than he remembered. Clutching a handful of the horse's mane, Jack held on, shouting 'gallop, lads!' as loudly as he could.

The Guides did not have to be ordered to gallop. Jack was a good horseman; he had ridden point-to-point across Herefordshire and along the ridge of the Malvern Hills, yet he was awed by the skill of his men. Even without saddles or stirrups, they rode their horses like trained jockeys, ducking away from the flying splinters, driving onwards to the exit of the village.

Glancing over his shoulder, Jack saw Gulbaz's men as a mass of fierce, shouting faces and waving pulwars. He could not pick out individuals, even if he had wished to. By sheer determination, Jack forced himself to the front of his Guides to arrive at the gate a length ahead of his men.

The gate was closed and barred, with the white-bearded watchman staring in confusion at the flaming watchtower and the mass of horses charging towards him. Sensibly, he moved out of the way as Jack leapt from his horse, staggered, rolled and recovered. Grabbing the beam that closed the gate, Jack lifted it, poised, and threw it aside, nodding as Hassan joined him.

'Good man, Hassan!'

Working together, they thrust open the gate, with Jack waving through the Guides.

'I'll join you, Hassan!' Jack heard his voice as a distant croak. 'Get on your horse!'

'I won't leave you behind, sahib.' Hassan lifted his Enfield to cover Jack.

'I'm just coming!' Jack looked back at Torkrud. He had been welcomed here, yet left it a scene of smoking carnage. Othere than surrender, to face a grisly death by torture, there was nothing else he could have done.

Ten horses lay on the ground amidst the rubble of the watchtower and the bodies of men. In the dark, Jack was unsure if they were his Guides or the enemy. He hesitated, wondering if he had time to check. He saw Gulbaz's warriors surging forward and knew he had not.

'Come on, sahib. Your men are waiting for you.'

Jack looked around. Hassan was correct. His men were waiting, sitting astride their horses in line abreast. 'Come on, lads!' Kicking in his heels, he held on to the mane of his horse as they cantered into the dark with Gulbaz's men sending them away with a fusillade of shots.

Jack counted his men. By some miracle, they were all there, although one or two nursed minor wounds. That was on the credit side. On the debit side, his mission had ended in inglorious failure. He was no further forward in discovering the gun smugglers and had only gathered scanty information about the Mujahidin. Now he may have turned a potential British ally into an enemy. Jack pushed the black thoughts from his head. *No. He must concentrate on getting his men home. That was his principal duty; all the rest had to wait.*

'Kick on, boys, let's get away from here.'

That mad careen along the dark valley was something that Jack would long remember. His Guides took it all in their stride; riding bareback through potentially hostile territory without knowing the track seemed not to bother them. After fifteen minutes, Jack eased their pace and called them together.

'Well done, men,' he said. 'Now I have only one plan: get back to Mardan. We're stuck deep in tribal territory here, so it might be a bit sticky.'

'Every man's hand will be against us.' Fatteh looked around. Patchy clouds concealed the moon, but starlight glowed dimly behind the ragged peaks.

'We will have to fight our way through.' Zaman looked pleased with the prospect.

'If it is Allah's will, we will survive.' Alladad was struggling into his uniform.

'That is so.' Hassan nodded.

'We will ride faster with saddles,' Jack said. 'We can double back and pick up our own, or raid a village for them, although I don't like to take from innocent people.'

'These are only Afridis.' Alladad spoke with the contempt that the Yusufzai had for all other peoples. 'We need the saddles more than they do.'

'We double back.' Jack made his decision. 'We will lose distance, but Gulbaz won't expect that.'

'We will have to fight,' Hassan said.

'We have the advantage of surprise,' Jack reminded him. 'Ride hard, hit them, and return.'

There were no arguments. The Guides accepted Jack's decision. Leaving the spare horses tethered within a small copse of wind-stunted pines, they turned at once, galloping through the dark towards Torkrud. Jack knew he had no need to order the Guides to load their rifles; these men had been carrying weapons since they could walk.

'Look ahead, sahib!' Hassan pointed into the dark.

Jack had already heard the drumbeat of hooves on the path. Gulbaz had organised the pursuit with impressive speed, so now a score of mounted men hammered towards them.

Fight or flee? We are the Guides; we need saddles.

'Blast your way through,' Jack ordered. 'Fire when you have a target!' He knew that surprise was half the battle. Despite Gulbaz's men having the advantage of numbers and saddles, he knew that a sudden rush would catch them unawares. Movement always stimulated his brain; the idea came to him immediately.

'Fatteh! Do you have your bugle with you?'

'Yes, sahib!' Fatteh produced the instrument.

'When we are closer, play it. Sound the charge. Everybody, the instant that Fatteh plays, make as much noise as you can. Make Gulbaz believe that the entire Guides cavalry is here, aye and the Household Brigade and the Enniskillen dragoons as well. On my word, Fatteh!'

It was an old trick that Jack had used before in the fighting around Sebastopol. At best it could unsettle the enemy; at worst it was only a waste of Fatteh's breath.

A few of Gulbaz's horsemen slowed as they tried to ascertain who was charging towards them. A hail or two sounded through the dark. Somebody fired a shot in the air. With a curtain of dust adding to the darkness, Jack drew his revolver, hoping he could retain his seat without stirrups.

'Now, Fatteh! Sound the charge!'

The brassy notes cut through the night, joined by the yells and cheers of the Guides.

'Forward the Guides!' Jack added his own voice to the noise. 'Number One troop, to the right. Number Two troop, guard the flanks! Number Three Troop, act as rearguard!' Leaning forward over his horse's neck, he fired two shots at the now confused Rahmut Khel. 'Follow me, Guides!'

The Guides hit Gulbaz's men hard, slicing into the hesitating horsemen and pushing through without pausing. Jack fired, seeing the mass part before him, heard a confusion of rifle fire in his wake, and kicked his horse on. He saw men turn aside, heard Zaman's high-pitched laugh, and then burst through to open ground with the Guides in arrowhead formation behind him.

Unsure of the number of men who had appeared so suddenly, the Rahmut Khel had little time to retaliate. Most of them scattered into the night, preferring the security of the dark to the uncertainty of fighting an unknown force.

As soon as they were clear of the Rahmut Khel, Jack pulled up. 'Is anybody missing?'

'No, sahib.' Hassan was not even out of breath.

'Kick on.' Jack guided his horse aside to count his men. *All present! Thank you, God.* He pushed onward, feeling the muscles of the horse between his legs. The gates of Torkrud were open, with a gaggle of ancient men and burqa-clad women clustered to see what the shooting meant. Riding through them without a word of explanation, Jack passed the smoking, still burning remnants of the watchtower to head straight for the stables.

'Zaman, you and Sawan guard the doors. The rest, grab saddles and bridles, get the horses ready.' Jack knew he had only minutes before Gulbaz reorganised his men. He had no wish to be trapped inside Torkrud. 'I'll have Colwell back.' He exchanged horses with Sawan, wasting a few seconds to fondle his animal.

There was no resistance in the village. The men of Torkrud were either with Batoor or Gulbaz, while the women had scattered as soon as Jack rode into the village. The Guides stared as Jack grabbed half a dozen horse-blankets. 'We might need these,' he said.

'Yes, sahib.' Their expressions indicated their disbelief.

'Get the saddles on.' Jack decided that the time spent in putting on the saddles would be well-spent. If they had a serious encounter with Gulbaz, having the men properly mounted would be a major advantage. Only when he was satisfied that everybody was ready did he glance around the stable, with his men's bearded, hard faces half-seen in the dim light. 'Does anybody know this area well?'

'I know it.' Ursulla spoke after a few moments' hesitation. He was the quietest of Jack's men. 'I have raided here.'

'Is there another way out, one we can get back to the Khyber or Mardan?'

Ursulla considered carefully before replying. 'Yes, sahib. Over the hills.'

'Could you find it in the dark?'

Again Ursulla paused before replying. 'Yes, sahib.'

'Take us.' Jack made an instant decision. 'You lead; we will follow.'

Filling their water bottles from the well, the Guides followed Ursulla out of Torkrud.

'Watch for Gulbaz,' Jack said.

Ursulla did not hesitate as he led them around the walls of the village and up the slope behind, at right angles and to the north of the direction they rode previously. Ursulla did not speak; he rode at a slow trot, concentrating on his route.

After the first mile, the path faded, so the horses had to pick their way over a rough hillside in the dark. Jack glanced behind them. The flames from the watchtower had faded to a dull glow, barely seen through the night. Listening for sounds of pursuit, he heard nothing but the clack of the horses' hooves on loose stones.

'How far is it, Ursulla?'

'We will circle around the main path,' Ursulla said. 'We have to climb a bit later.'

'How far?'

Ursulla screwed up his face. 'About thirty miles before we reach the Khyber.' His grin highlighted the brightness of his brown eyes. 'You will see what other areas of Pakhtunkhwa are like, sahib.'

Jack nodded; he was gradually unravelling the mysteries of this land. 'That can only be a good thing, Ursulla.'

With the horses slowly picking their way up a hillside of slithering scree and broken rock, the Guides were silent, concentrating on moving rather than thinking about Gulbaz and his men. When Colwell began to struggle, Jack dismounted and walked beside him, wondering at the sure-footed Afghan horses his men rode.

'Kabul ponies,' Hassan told him. 'They are stout and strong horses, not fast, but surer-footed than anything the British have. They are best in the hills.' He shook his head. 'They are not good on the plains, though.'

After another two hours climbing, the sky began to lighten, with grey-orange bands streaking behind the mountains. Jack heard the low whinny of a horse behind them. 'I think we're being followed.'

'Shall I go and check, sahib?' Zaman tapped his rifle.

'No.' Jack did not want his men straggled all across the hills of Pakhtunkhwa. 'We'll stick together. Muffle the horses.' He showed them how to fasten cloth around the horse's hooves. Fast learners, the Guides understood at once.

'Is that why you brought the horse blankets?' Hassan asked.

'It is one reason,' Jack said.

The Guides moved on, as silently as possible through the lessening dark. Every time they stopped, Jack listened for the sounds of pursuit. An eagle called, high, shrill and thrilling. Jack glanced up; nature did not care about the stupid manoeuvrings of mankind. Each animal and bird lived its own life without any process of politics, religion or race. They were even more pragmatic than the Pashtun.

'Sahib,' Hassan said softly. 'There is one man very close behind us. Gulbaz will have sent his fastest man to ensure he does not lose us. That man will follow, leaving signs for the others to follow.'

'That's a neat trick.' Jack approved of Gulbaz's professionalism. He tapped Zaman on the shoulder. 'Did you hear all that, Zaman?'

'Yes, sahib. I know Gulbaz's methods.'

'Could you kill the man who is following us?' That seemed a very cold-blooded question.

'Yes, sahib.' Zaman's teeth gleamed behind his beard.

'Do you want somebody with you?'

'No, sahib.'

'Don't drop too far behind.' Jack contained his doubts about separating his command.

They moved on, slightly slower, with Jack leading Colwell and the Guides riding. Nobody spoke. Everybody listened for sounds of pursuit or the resounding thud of a jezzail. Only the call of the eagle disturbed the night.

It was half an hour before Zaman ghosted beside them. Grinning, he handed Jack a bloody package. 'Here are the man's ears, sahib. He was a youngster with no more guile than a feringhee.'

Jack shook his head at the gift. 'Do with them what you wish, Zaman.'

'I will make them into a necklace,' Zaman said.

'You'll not disgrace your uniform.' Hassan spoke first. 'Throw these things away, trooper.'

Zaman, the prospective Khan of the Rahmut Khel, glared at Daffadar Hassan, then at Jack before he tossed away the dripping ears.

'Enough time wasted,' Jack said. 'Come on.'

They moved on as dawn burst out in the east. They had reached an area of stark mountains, with razor-edged ridges and a plethora of crevasses and chasms. Their route took them to where a hand-wide ridge soared above perpendicular slopes that descended to shadow. The roar of a distant river rose and fell with the wind. 'Is this the best road, Ursulla?'

'Yes, sahib.'

The ridge led to a slope too steep even for Kabul ponies to ascend, so the Guides dismounted and led them, uncomplaining. Jack looked down into the dark crevasses, wiped sweat from his forehead, and carried on with the muscles of his legs screaming in protest and hunger gnawing at his stomach. As they reached each crest, he checked behind him, seeing nothing except a wilderness of rocky hills, the hammering sun reflecting on the rocks to increase the heat. The first time that a stone cracked in the heat, Jack started, believing that one of Gulbaz's men was firing at them. After the third occurrence, he accepted the sound as part of the landscape of the Frontier.

This is different soldiering from the humid heat of India. I have tales to tell my grandchildren if I survive that long.

Above them, a second eagle had joined the first; both circled, looking for something to kill.

'Are we still being followed?'

Hassan nodded. 'Yes, sahib. Gulbaz lost us when Zaman killed his scout, but he is back now. He must know this area as well as Ursulla.'

'I can't see anybody.' Jack peered over the route they had come.

'Forgive me, sahib.' Hassan took Jack by the shoulder. 'Do you see that rock? Use your binoculars.'

Jack did so. The rock looked no different from a thousand others.

'Look closely, sahib.'

Jack focussed. 'It's moving!'

'That is Gulbaz. Look for the sun reflecting on his hook. The rock to his right? Do you see?'

Jack altered the angle of his binoculars. 'Yes, I see. That is also a man.'

'They all are, sahib. When we passed that way, there were no rocks. Now there are a hundred. Gulbaz knows we are watching, so he has ordered his men to lie still and cover themselves with their *kameez*, their long shirts. With these and the *shalwar*, the baggy trousers, being the same colour as the hill from this distance, they appear like rocks.' Hassan was very patient with his explanation.

'By God, that man is clever.' Jack calculated the distance. In the clear mountain air, Gulbaz's men looked closer than they were. 'They are out of range. Push on.'

Leading the horses up inclines that had Jack panting for breath, the Guides continued, exchanging banter as Jack checked behind him every few moments. Now that he knew what he was looking for, he saw Gulbaz's men every time, flitting behind them, closing the gap.

'The horses are slowing us down, sahib,' Hassan said. 'If we release them, we can outpace these pigs.'

'We'll need them later,' Jack pointed out. 'I don't intend us to walk through the Khyber Pass.'

'If Gulbaz catches us, we won't be alive to walk through the Khyber.'

'We'll have to make sure he does not catch us, then. Increase the speed.' Jack ignored Hassan's frown. 'Come on, lads! Gulbaz is nearly on our heels!'

They negotiated another narrow ridge with the horses' hooves kicking at loose stones that clattered down a nearly vertical slope to an unseen valley hundreds of feet below. Beyond the ridge, a mountain rose, sun-tortured to the unforgiving sky.

'We have to cross that hill,' Ursulla said.

Jack looked up, his mind busy. The horses were flagging. 'Hassan, take the men on. Leave signs, so I know in which direction you have gone.'

'What are you going to do, sahib?'

Jack took Ursulla's rifle and ammunition. 'I am going to slow down Gulbaz.'

'It would be better if I did that,' Hassan said. 'I am faster in the mountains. I won't get lost.'

'I gave you an order, Hassan.' Although Jack knew that Hassan was correct, he would not order one of his men to remain in danger while he walked away.

The sun was high now, pouring its heat from a bright sky. Jack felt the sweat breaking out on his forehead, soaking his back. He grunted; he had experienced worse in the Indian plains.

Lying prone on the baking ground, Jack placed his cartridges and percussion caps handy beside him and built a crude sangar with a single aperture through which to shoot. This low position limited his view of the ridge, so Gulbaz's men would be closer than he liked when he opened fire, but on the other hand, they could not see him. Settling down to wait, Jack thought of the days he and the 113th had skirmished with the Cossacks outside Sevastopol. *I must be getting old*, he told himself, *living on past memories*.

A monitor lizard scurried past, eyed him curiously for a second, and moved on. The eagles above continued to circle. The overall silence magnified every sound, so Jack heard his men toiling up the hillside. When that sound faded, the quiet was oppressive. Jack remained still, trying to regulate his breathing. He did not know how much time had elapsed before he heard the soft slither of feet on the rocks.

The leading Afridi approached, moving frighteningly fast over the tortured ground. He was a young man with a twisted dun turban on his head and his mouth gaping open. Jack aimed for the centre of his body, the most extensive target, took a deep breath, let it out slowly and squeezed the trigger. The Enfield kicked, white smoke spurted, and the man fell.

It was as easy as that. It was eleven years since Jack first killed a man. The sensation was no more pleasant now than it had been then. It was so simple to end a life, so final. There was no glamour, no glory, only an ending. The echoes of the Enfield rebounded from the hills, gradually fading. One of the eagles called again.

Gulbaz's Rahmut Khel had vanished. Jack could only see the man he had shot, lying like an untidy bundle of rags with flies already exploring the blood. Jack knew that the others were there watching him with the uncanny patience of the Pashtun, waiting for him to move, perhaps crawling unseen across that stark landscape. He had had the advantage in that first shot; now the pendulum had swung. The shot and the drift of powder smoke gave away his position to the Afridis. At that moment there were a dozen or more jezzails waiting for him to move. He was as trapped as Gulbaz's men.

The monitor lizard ran past, heading for the new corpse. The powder smoke drifted away slowly. The sun tortured Jack, baking him as he lay unmoving amidst the rocks. *The longer I delay them, the further away my Guides would travel. Every minute increases their chances of success.*

Jack felt the sun scorching his back. He thought back to the Crimea again. The

Cossacks had been a dangerous enemy; if anything these Rahmut Khel Afridis were more patient, even more skilled at moving unseen through a broken landscape. Using all his training from these days in the Crimean War, Jack peered through the tiny gap he had left in his sangar. The ridge looked empty of men. He could not see a single one of the hundred or so Rahmut Khel he knew were there. *I must use an old trick.*

Lifting a loose stone, and ensuring he remained behind the shelter of the sangar, Jack tossed it to his right. The stone landed with a distinct clatter that drew fire from a score of positions. Jack nodded, noting from where the white smoke jetted. The men of the Rahmut Khel were still there, watching, waiting for him to make a mistake, but now he knew where some of them lay. Jack snuggled his cheek beside the stock of his Enfield. The Afridi may well be patient stalkers of men; well, so was he. He had learned his trade in the jungles of Burma, in the biting cold of Inkerman Ridge, and on the humid plains of India.

Come on, lads. Let's be having you.

Flies already clustered around the man Jack had shot. They were like a black-furred blanket, rising and falling as they feasted. Jack lay still, trying to ignore the insects that explored him. A palm-sized spider emerged from a crack in the rocks at his elbow, scuttled toward him, walked across the stock of his rifle, and moved on to search for more interesting prey.

The man moved so slowly that Jack was unsure if it was his imagination. At first, he thought it might be a shimmer caused by the heat of the sun, then he knew it was not. One of the Rahmut Khel was crawling toward him, oh-so-slowly. Jack knew that if he altered his aim, even that tiny movement would alert the enemy. He schooled himself in patience, ignored the bead of sweat that hung on his left eyelid, and waited until the enemy moved into his line of sight.

I can see one. How many more are there? How many of the most devilish warriors in the world are creeping toward me at this second? Please God that they don't take me alive.

Jack remembered the tales he had heard of the Pashtun's treatment of prisoners. How they would routinely castrate their captives, skin them alive or hand them over to the women for prolonged torture.

Dear Lord, if I must die, make it clean and quick.

Waiting until the Afridi was in his direct line of fire, Jack squeezed the trigger. He saw the man jump as the bullet struck him full on the head, and then the Rahmut Khel responded. Half a dozen bullets slammed around Jack, spraying vicious splinters of stone. He rolled away, loading as rapidly as he could, replaced the percussion cap with his thumb, and returned to his position. Enfield rifles were not designed to be loaded from a prone position, so the time Jack had taken allowed a dozen of the Rahmut Khel to rise from cover. They advanced quickly, leaping across the broken rocks of the ridge.

I can shoot one. After that?

Unable to see Gulbaz in the press of faces, Jack sighted on the closest man. He fired, saw the man fall, and wished he had thought to borrow a bayonet as well as the rifle. Struggling to load, he knew he might get in another shot, with luck, and then it was the wildly inaccurate revolver and his sword.

Goodbye, Mary; I hope you find a better man. Goodbye, Andrew; I would have loved to see you grow up.

'Come on, you bastards! I am Jack Windrush of the Guides!' And then Jack yelled the old battle cry of the 113th, elongating the final syllable. 'Cry Havelock!'

The triple crack of Enfield rifles, so different from the deeper boom of the jezzail, startled him. Jack saw the puffs of smoke from higher up the slope, wondered how the Rahmut Khel had got behind him and heard Hassan's voice. 'Shoot them, brothers!'

Two of the Rahmut Khel fell. When two more Enfields fired, another Afridi fell, halting the advance. The nature of the ridge meant that they could only move in single file. With dead and dying men blocking their route, the Rahmut Khel lost their enthusiasm and took to ground.

'What the devil are you doing here, Hassan?' Jack greeted his rescuers with abuse. 'I ordered you to take the horses away!'

'We did, sahib.' Hassan looked as hurt as a Pashtun could. 'We took the horses away, and then came back for you.'

'I ordered you to get away!'

'Yes, sahib.' Hassan pulled Jack's head lower as Gulbaz's men began to snipe at them. 'But you must remember that Kerr sahib ordered me to look after you. He outranks you, so his orders are more important.' His grin was of pure triumph.

There was no arguing with a Pashtun. 'So now you have effectively trapped all my men here, Hassan, what do you plan next?' Jack hoped the sarcasm was evident.

'The horses are safe, sahib,' Hassan said. 'Fatteh is in charge of them. We have a surprise prepared for these Rahmut Khel further up the hill. All we need do is climb a little and not get shot.'

'Is that all?' Jack asked.

'Follow me, sahib, and ensure you keep a rock between your body and the sights of an Afridi jezzail. Gulbaz thinks he is only chasing a feringhee. He forgets that now you are one of the Guides.'

'Move in stages,' Jack ordered. 'I want one man to remain behind, watching Gulbaz's men. He will shoot at any movement. After five minutes, he moves up, and another man watches.'

Using all the skills he had learned stalking Cossacks in the Crimea, Jack traversed the hillside. The Guides had a natural ability at moving unseen, gliding uphill without a sign, moving from cover to cover.

Once Jack heard the crack of an Enfield, with every Guide remaining static until the echoes had died away. Twice Jack heard the sonorous thud of a jezzail, with a bullet flattening itself on the rocks a few inches from his head. He lay still, watching a small lizard scurry past his face until Hassan motioned him to continue.

'Come on, sahib. If you stay there much longer, you will grow roots.'

The slope seemed to stretch forever into the hard heat. Knowing that his men must think him a weak feringhee, Jack ignored the screaming agony of his muscles as he forced himself upward and ever upward.

'Be careful, sahib,' Hassan whispered. Jack had not seen Fatteh until he nearly stood on him. They had reached the summit plateau, with the horses tethered in the slight shade of an outcrop of rock. Flicking sweat from his forehead, Jack looked downward. He could not see the Rahmut Khel.

'Where are they?'

'Still on the ridge,' Hassan said. 'Zaman shot one who tried to leave. Now Gulbaz will have them wait until we are over the summit. He knows that you will station a man here to kill any who move.'

Jack grunted at Hassan's less-than-subtle advice. He had a lot to learn about fighting in this type of country. 'How long will Gulbaz have them follow us?'

'Until they have killed us all,' Hassan said.

That's reassuring. Thank you, Hassan.

'It is a long way to Mardan,' Jack said, 'through some very hostile country.' He glanced down the slope. 'It would be better to stop these Rahmut Khel now, so our rear is secure.'

'That is true, sahib,' Hassan agreed.

'Are there any villages at the base of this mountain?'

'Did you see any sahib? I did not.' Hassan was not smiling. 'There is no fertile land for crops or livestock.'

'There are no villages, then.' Jack accepted the implied rebuke. 'There are also plenty of loose boulders here.' He indicated the side of the plateau, which was lined with rocks of various sizes.

'Yes, sahib,' Hassan said patiently.

'We could wait until Gulbaz's men are part way up the slope, and then roll these boulders down. They might cause an avalanche and rid us of Gulbaz.'

'Yes, sahib. I said that we have a surprise waiting for them. We moved the rocks ready to drop on the Rahmut Khel.'

Still not used to the independent thinking of the Guides, Jack grunted his approval. 'Good thinking, Hassan, you exceeded your orders.'

'No, Windrush sahib. Kerr sahib ordered me to look after you.'

Jack hid his smile; he expected that Hassan would roll out that excuse for everything he did. 'Good man, Hassan. However, as you seem incapable of following my orders, I'll keep you under my direct command. We'll all stay together and roll rocks down the hill.'

Although Hassan nodded solemnly, Jack detected a gleam of humour in his eyes.

'Teach me how to spot them,' Jack asked. 'Continue with my lessons.'

Nodding, Hassan pointed to a rock a few yards up from the edge of the ridge. 'You see that rock, sahib?'

Jack nodded.

'Its neighbours are shimmering in the heat. It is not.'

'That's right,' Jack agreed.

'That is no rock, sahib. That is a man. Look for what is not there.'

Jack listened as Hassan explained the basics of fighting on the Frontier. 'Patience, sahib. A Pashtun can wait in one place for three days to make a single shot at a target. A British sahib,' he grinned and shook his head, 'he will rush. If we are in ambush, we sit still. If any young man makes a single move that might be seen, we leave.'

'That man has moved.' Jack indicated the man he had thought was a rock.

'Six men have moved since you joined me, sahib.' There was no expression on Hassan's face.

'We will wait until they are halfway up the slope,' Jack decided. 'That way there is less chance that any will escape.' *I have become more callous with every campaign I fight.*

The Guides sat, quite relaxed, behind the barrier of rocks. While most British soldiers might have played cards, or spoken in forced whispers, the Pashtuns were motionless, without speech or visible communication. Jack could not help but admire them.

These men are unlike any I have met before. Oh, they are thievish and predatory, fierce and bloodthirsty, but while they are reckless of the lives of others, they do not spare their own. They possess gallantry and courage; they are like us in so many ways. As our immediate enemy are also of this calibre, we will be up for a hard fight if anything significant develops on this Frontier.*

After Hassan's schooling, Jack looked for small signs that he may have missed. *Is that a rock or a man? Is it different from its neighbours?* Jack focussed. He saw a hint of movement, concentrated and realised that what he had thought was a pebble was the end of a man's sandal. Gulbaz's men were moving much faster than Jack had expected, sliding up the slope virtually unseen. He could not make out faces yet. Far above, three vultures had replaced the eagles circling, as if they knew there would soon be pickings. Jack looked up, already hating these birds. He imagined what it must feel like to be lying injured on the ground with one of these devilish creatures swooping down, all beak, talons and predatory eyes. This Frontier certainly stimulated the imagination.

'It is time, Hassan,' Jack decided.

The Guides were at his side as soon as Jack spoke the last word. They looked at him, each man behind a rock, awaiting his order. Jack braced himself. 'Now.' He whispered the word even as he pushed.

Jack's rock teetered slightly on the edge of the plateau and then swung back toward him. He pushed again, harder, heard a small shower of stones slither down the slope, and the rock moved forward, nearly overbalancing him. He saw it begin a slow, lumbering roll, gathering a collection of small stones in its journey. The Guides had been busy, with their boulders also shifting downhill, accumulating others on their descent, so within thirty seconds a miniature avalanche was powering toward Gulbaz's men.

'Dear God,' Jack said. 'I had not realised it would be so bad.'

'It will sweep Gulbaz away.' Zaman sounded pleased.

The distinctive boom of a jezzail was unexpected among the rumble of the avalanche. Jack did not see where the shot went as his men ducked into cover.

'Even in death, the Afridi wolves bite,' Hassan said. 'They are men. They are true Pashtun.' He did not hide the respect in his voice.

'They are brave men,' Jack agreed. 'Now, we have a long way to go yet.'

The plateau ended in a long, shallow slope descending to another of the fast-flowing rivers that seamed this countryside. The Guides picked their way down cautiously, watching for ambush or stray herdsman who might give their position away.

There was no need to tell the Guides to water the horses first. They were born equestrians, as skilled horsemen as the Cossacks.

Jack looked around. The landscape was bleak beyond description, with areas of grey scree and shattered rocks that could provide cover for a score of marksmen. 'Zaman, keep on watch,'

'Yes, sahib.'

Only when the horses were filled did the Guides drink. Fortunately, there were a few patches of rough grass beside the river, so the horses could also feed.

'How far to the Khyber?' Jack asked.

'About twenty miles.'

Jack checked the sky. It was later than he thought, with the light already beginning to fade. 'We'll cross this river and find a place to bed down for the night. The horses need a rest. So do the men.'

'The men are hungry,' Hassan said. 'They have not eaten since Gulbaz's bread.'

'Are there fish in that river?' Jack's mind was working rapidly, searching for possibilities.

Hassan looked confused for a second. 'We have no nets to catch them with.'

'We have these.' Jack held out his hands. It was many years since he had poached fish as a boy, but he was sure he remembered the technique. The food at school had been as basic as the accommodation, so the boys had often resorted to the local river, chancing the trouble they would get into if the gamekeeper had caught them.

'Watch for Gulbaz's men, or anybody else.' Jack slipped off his tunic so he was in his shirt. Despite the heat of the sun, when he slid his arms into the water, it felt as if he was dipping into ice. All the same, he persevered, teaching the watching Guides the subtle art of fish-tickling, or guddling, as one of his classmates had called it.

'Not only have the Pashtuns had patience,' Jack said. The river was innocent of human presence, so within a few minutes a decent-sized fish swam between his fingers. He hauled it out with an impulsive shout. 'Kill it!'

He caught two more before his hands were too numb with cold to perform their task.

'What kind of fish are they?' One looked like a large catfish but with a pointed head and both eyes in front rather than on the side of its head. Jack glanced at its sharp teeth and decided not to try that method of fishing again. 'Never mind. Cook them; I'm not eating raw fish.'

The Guides looked at him with new respect. Hassan nearly smiled.

Posting a man high up the hillside, Jack had the fish gutted and cooked, with every man eating his share. It was not the best meal he had ever tasted, but far better than nothing.

Hassan provided the words of caution. 'The smell may warn Gulbaz if he is still alive.'

'Then we will keep the campfire burning,' Jack said. 'If he is around, it will attract him like a moth to a flame.' He pointed up the hillside. 'We'll stay the night up there and watch.' He took Hassan's nod as a sign of approval. Perhaps the Guides no longer looked on him as a Griffin in this type of warfare.

CHAPTER NINE

Pakhtunkhwa, July 1863

Jack had them moving before dawn, with horses and men rested and fed. Ursulla still led with Jack on his shoulder and some of the hills becoming familiar as they neared the Khyber.

'We have a tributary of the Kabul River to ford,' Ursulla said, 'and the Zargun Pass to get through before we are above Mardan.'

Jack nodded his satisfaction. Although he could never relax on this Frontier, his understanding was increasing daily. He no longer felt a novice amongst these hills.

'How far to the Zargun Pass?' Jack consulted his map. The pass was marked, but he knew that Ursulla knew the area better than any western mapmaker.

'Two hours,' Ursulla said.

The sound of the drumming came to Jack first.

'Tabla drum.' Hassan listened for a moment. 'I've heard that rhythm before.'

'At Torkrud,' Jack said. 'The mullah played it. And at Ali Masjid.'

Hassan glanced at Jack. 'That's correct, sahib.'

'I can remember a rhythm and a mullah.' Jack knew he had no reason to explain. He raised his voice slightly. 'Right, lads; muffle the horse's hooves again. There might be trouble ahead.'

Now in single file, they moved on, keeping a space between each man to reduce their mass as a target, watching the surrounding tree-dotted heights, keeping a finger on the trigger of their rifles.

'Sahib.' Fatteh saw them first, a group of men just below the skyline, flitting from tree to tree.

'Ursulla.' Jack called him over. 'How far now to the Zargun Pass?'

'When we round the spur of this hill,' Ursulla said, 'we'll find a ford of the river, with the pass rising on the far side. Once we are over the pass, we are only a half day's ride to Mardan.'

Taking out his binoculars, Jack focussed on the men on the hill slope. They looked like typical Pashtuns, with pakol hats, baggy clothing, and the ubiquitous jezzail strapped across their backs. Each man had a red cord on his right arm. 'Oh, dear God.'

'What is it, sahib?' Hassan was quick to detect Jack's change of mood.

'Take a look, Hassan.' Jack passed over the binoculars.

'Mujahidin,' Hassan said at once.

'Do they know who we are?' Jack wondered.

'He will know.' Hassan used his chin to point ahead, where the mullah sat on his horse. As Jack watched, the mullah began to play on his tabla drum.

Jack nodded. 'That fellow gets everywhere,' he said quietly. 'Move on, lads. There is no point in keeping silent now. That tabla mullah is staring straight at us.'

'Ride at attention!' Hassan ordered. 'Show them that we are the Guides.'

The mullah remained still until Jack's men were within fifty yards when he wheeled his horse and rode slowly back, beating his tabla drum. The group of men on the hill cantered toward him, forming a loose escort.

As they passed the hill spur, the mullah and his escort increased speed. 'Follow,' Jack ordered. 'Let's see what their hurry is.'

The Guides cantered around the spur, with Fatteh singing a Pashtun song, and the sound of the horses' hooves echoing from the rugged slopes. Within a few moments, the ground opened up to a small clearing. The Zargun Pass lay ahead, a definite cleft between two groups of hills with the slender thread of a track winding upwards into a mist. Between Jack's Guides and the pass, a broad river churned between surprisingly fertile grassland. In any other time, the area would have been noted as a place of beauty; the milling groups of armed men made it a place of extreme danger.

The mullah had stopped to address the men who gathered around him.

'Wait.' Jack held up his hand. 'The mullah is talking. I wish to hear.'

'Oh, Muslims.' The mullah had a surprisingly strong voice for such a scrawny man. 'I am not asking you to fight Afghans or Pashtuns, who are true believers, but to make ghaza. Therefore it is necessary that you should all obey my commands, which are those of God and his prophets. We are all God's slaves, but ghaza is the duty of us all.'

Jack looked at his Guides. They were listening, watching the mullah without expression.

'I inform you that I have come to release Pakhtunkhwa from the hands of the British. We should not let the country of true believers fall into the hands of the feringhees. If they gain our country, our reputation and honour will go, too. Hearken to my advice; if you will not listen, it is plainly my duty to make ghaza against you as infidels. Make up your mind either to be supporters of God and Mohammed or to be prepared for war against those who are.'

Jack looked over his men, wondering how they were taking the mullah's rhetoric. The mullah tapped his drum for a few moments and then continued.

'The kafirs have taken possession of all Islamic countries and, owing to the lack of spirit on the part of the people, are conquering every region. They have now reached the land of the Pashtuns. These people attack the kafirs day and night. Help from God awaits us, and victory is at hand. God willing, the time has come when the kafirs should disappear.'

The Guides listened in silence with the horses snorting, tails flicking.

'That looks unpleasant.' Jack scanned the waiting men with his binoculars. The mullah trotted over the river in a great show of spray, wheeling his horse on the far side to face Jack's men. The throbbing of his drum began again. 'Is there another way across?'

'No,' Hassan said. 'This is the only ford for twenty miles, and the Zargun Pass the only route. The Mullah has chosen well.'

'Well, they've seen us now, so there is no point in trying to hide.' Jack pointed to a small knoll. 'We'll form a camp there, build up sangars, and work out what to do next.' The Guides did not argue. Jack guessed that they were as bereft of ideas as he was himself. After escaping from Gulbaz, it seemed cruel fate to run across the mullah and his Mujahidin.

The slopes to the knoll were littered with rocks, while two wind-tormented pines surmounted the summit. Fortunately, there was a little grazing for the horses, if nothing for the men.

Hassan took charge of building the sangar as Jack surveyed the Mujahidin through his binoculars.

'Why don't they attack?' Jack asked. 'They far outnumber us.'

'They have no need to attack,' Hassan said. 'They know we are trapped. We cannot go back to Gulbaz, and we cannot go forward. All they have to do is wait as we weaken through lack of food.'

Jack nodded. There was that Pashtun pragmatism again. These people were a strange mixture of incredible bravery, patience and fanaticism. 'The mullah will tell them who we are.'

Hassan gave a small smile. 'They already know, Windrush sahib. The whole of Pakhtunkhwa will be aware that a British officer and a patrol of Guides are trying to get back to British territory.'

'I see.' Jack did not ask how they knew; he was already impressed by the efficiency of the Pashtun intelligence service. 'Keep strengthening our defences.' *I need time to think.*

Rain began to fall, grimly grey, shading the hills, slowly dripping from the turbans of the Guides. It continued into the night, part-shielding the campfires of the Mujahidin. Ascending one of the pines, Jack studied the enemy, listening to the drumming of the mullah and watching the figures flitting around the campfire.

'You must sleep, Windrush sahib,' Hassan said. 'The Mujahidin will be there tomorrow and the next day.'

Hassan was correct. Next morning the Mujahidin still waited at the ford of the river, the pass rising behind them between the twin hills. As the sun rose, hundreds of warriors scrambled up the slopes. The tabla mullah and a few men remained at the ford, inviting the Guides to cross.

'How many of them are there, would you say?' Jack asked.

'One hundred, two hundred,' Hassan said. 'Perhaps more. They will have more men that we cannot see.'

'That's a lot of men to deal with half a dozen Guides. They must have a very high opinion of us,' Jack said. *Either that or their presence here is pure bad luck. They must be here for another reason.*

Jack could see the Mujahidin's strategy. They would remain on the hillside during the day, with all the advantages of height and visibility, and return to ground level in the evening to cook their evening meal, blocking any access to the pass. Jack knew that if he led his men through the pass in daylight, the Mujahidin on the hillside would pick them off in minutes. At night, the hundreds of Mujahidin beside the ford made crossing impossible. The hills on either side were inaccessible to even the sure-footed Kabul ponies, while the longer he delayed, the more danger they were in from Gulbaz, if he had survived, and however many of the Rahmut Khel he had managed to collect.

Jack looked at his half-dozen Guides. He was responsible for the lives of these men. He had to get them back to Mardan.

We have to get over that pass. To do that we have to get past the enemy. We cannot force through, so we must either sneak through or remove them from our path. As they are Pashtuns, they will be alert to every move we make, which makes the first option nearly impossible. I have to resort to trickery; the old ways from the Crimea.

'Whoever is in charge does not know his job. They should attack us,' Jack said. 'They would overrun us by sheer numbers.'

'Yes, sahib,' Hassan agreed. 'The Pashtun are patient men, but if the mullah decides it is time, he will lead the Mujahidin across the ford and then...' He passed a finger across his throat.

'Strengthen the sangar,' Jack said. 'Dig a trench behind it, so we have more cover, and clear a field of fire all around; create a killing ground,' Jack ordered. 'I want to make them scared to attack us.'

Understanding at once, the Guides worked with a will, with Jack lending his muscles to the labouring. Officers should lead by example, not drive by words. They rolled boulders from the slopes to strengthen the sangar, hacked down the scrub, and placed sticks every fifty yards to act as range markers. Across the ford, the mullah beat his drum in a constant rhythm that got inside Jack's head. When he felt his position was as secure as he could make it, Jack nodded.

'That's better. Now if they come across the river to attack us, we can at least account for some of them.' Jack glanced at the hillside opposite, where the Mujahidin would be watching. 'They think they have trapped us,' Jack said. 'Let's make things hot for them.' Pouring half the gunpowder he had carried from the watchtower at Torkrud into spare water bottles, Jack made half a dozen small bombs.

'What are you planning, sahib?' Hassan asked.

'We bury these under an inch or so of dirt and mark the spot. When the enemy reaches our marker, we shoot the flask and boom, we blow them up.'

Hassan gave another of his bleak smiles. 'They will still kill us, sahib.'

'Perhaps,' Jack said. He would not merely wait to be attacked. He would take a more aggressive approach. Everybody had their weakness, and the Mujahidin were no exception. Swarming back up the tree, Jack stared across the ford, noting everything that was happening. After an hour, he saw a small group of men descend the hill, occasionally turning around as if to argue, with some of the Mujahidin shouting at them, brandishing their jezzails. As Jack watched, one of the Mujahidin slit the throat of a sheep. Focussing his binoculars, Jack saw the first group carried no weapons except stout staffs.

'Daffadar!' Jack called Hassan up the tree. 'Who are these men? They don't look like warriors to me.'

Hassan took the binoculars. 'Shepherds,' he said casually. 'They are shepherds without goats or sheep.'

'I thought they might be.' Jack's mind was working overtime. 'Now these lads up there,' Jack said to Hassan. 'The Mujahidin. What do they eat?'

Hassan looked puzzled. 'They eat whatever they carry with them.'

'I see.' Jack pointed to a thread of Mujahidin, negotiating the hill slopes. 'And what are these fellows carrying down the hill?'

'Dead sheep. You saw the shepherds.' Hassan was staring at Jack as if he was an imbecile.

'Exactly,' Jack said. 'We may be able to use that.'

Hassan frowned. 'The Mujahidin will not share their sheep with us, sahib.'

'No,' Jack said. 'Nor will they share with the proper owners.' He raised his voice. 'Sawan, bring these shepherds to me. I want to talk to them.'

'They're only shepherds, sahib.' Sawan looked as confused as Hassan was. 'Herdsmen. They are not of any interest.'

'Just do it,' Jack said. 'Will they cross by the ford?'

'Probably.' Sawan sounded doubtful.

'Wait until they cross and then grab them,' Jack said. 'Don't hurt them, and don't let the Mujahidin see you.'

The shepherds stared at Jack when Sawan brought them over. They were gaunt-faced men, perhaps in their late teens, one with kohl-rimmed eyes and lovelocks, the other with a tattered pakol decorated by an eagle's feather.

'They did not cross by the ford,' Sawan said. 'They used this.' He held up an inflated goatskin.

'Keep it,' Jack said briefly. 'You men.' Jack tried not to sound like an imperious British officer as he addressed the shepherds. 'Are you friends with the warriors on the hill?'

The shepherds glanced at Hassan, who ordered them to tell the truth. 'The sahib will not be pleased if you lie to him,' Hassan said. 'I will know, and I will tell him.'

Jack waited for a reply. 'No,' the shepherd with the lovelocks said. 'They are not our friends. They stole our sheep.' There was no hiding the bitterness in his voice.

'I thought not.' Jack played his hands slowly, one at a time. 'How much was your flock worth?'

The shepherds looked even more confused.

'Would this pay for them?' Producing a sovereign from his pocket-book, Jack held it up to the light.

The shepherd reached for the golden coin.

Jack pulled it away. 'How about two of them?' He pulled out another sovereign, holding them between his fingers, aware that Hassan was staring at him.

The shepherd looked disappointed when Jack closed his fist over the coins. 'We can make a deal,' he said. 'You have known these hills all your life, I think.'

The shepherd agreed, his gaze never straying from Jack's hand.

'You will know the best ways to the top.'

Again the shepherd agreed.

'Can you get to the summit of the hill in the dark without the warriors seeing you?'

The shepherd did not hesitate. 'Yes, if Allah wills.'

'Good. If you lead two of my men to the summit without being detected, I will give you one gold coin. If you lead two men to the summit without being detected and leave without the warriors knowing, I will give you both gold coins.'

The shepherd's looked pleased. 'That will be easy work.' They spoke to Hassan rather than Jack. 'If the men we lead are Pashtun.' The kohl-rimmed man glanced furtively at Jack. 'The feringhee are too clumsy. They make too much noise with their big feet and bands blowing.'

Jack frowned. He had intended to go up himself, yet the shepherd's words made sense. He might jeopardise everybody's life by the simple act of kicking a loose stone or gasping too loudly.

'The shepherd is correct,' Jack admitted, grudgingly. 'It is better if he takes up two Guides.' He felt his men give a silent sigh of relief. 'Are there any volunteers for what will be a hazardous mission?' He felt a surge of pride as all the Guides volunteered.

'Thank you, gentlemen,' Jack said. 'I only need two men: Fatteh, you and your bugle, and Alladad.' He had contemplated sending Hassan but knew that Alladad was the most skilled at night movement, while he had a use for Fatteh.

The two men looked pleased to be selected. Fatteh stepped forward. 'What do you wish us to do, sahib?'

'When it is dark, the Mujahidin will come down from the hill to the river. The shepherds will take you over the river with the goatskin and up the hill byways that only they know. The Mujahidin might leave a few men on the slopes; avoid them. I want no noise, nothing to alert the enemy of our presence.' Jack waited to ensure Fatteh and Alladad understood.

'Yes, sahib.' They nodded.

'When you get to the summit, make a sign; nothing large, just a single light to say you have arrived. We will be watching for it.' Again Jack waited.

'We understand, sahib.'

The Guides were quicker in the uptake than the majority of British soldiers would have been. The Pashtun could have been born for this type of guerrilla warfare, while even the 113th had to be trained.

'When I reply to your signal, I want you, Fatteh, to blow your bugle as hard as you can. I want you to blow every regimental call you know, and any others you think you know. Make the enemy think the entire Brigade of Guards is on top of the hill. You, Alladad, I want you to set off explosives to sound like artillery. I want the Mujahidin to believe the British Army has got behind them.'

Both men nodded, enjoying the deception. 'Yes, sahib,' Alladad said, 'except we don't have any explosives.'

'Yes, we do. I brought some from the watchtower in Torkrud, remember?'

'Yes, sahib. We used that to make these bombs in the ground.'

'I held some back for emergencies,' Jack said. 'All we need is a suitable receptacle.'

One of the shepherds carried a little earthenware pot of snuff, which Jack bought for half a rupee. 'That's a thief's bargain, my friend.' Filling the pot with gunpowder, he held it up. 'Can you find anything else suitable?'

Grinning, the shepherds unearthed more earthenware pots, although Jack did not want to think in what part of their filthy clothing they had been hidden. 'You'll have me destitute before this day's work is done,' Jack said as he tipped the last of the gunpowder into the pots before handing them to Alladad.

'Now we wait for dark,' he said. 'Hassan, make sure the shepherds stay with us and don't run off to warn the enemy.'

'Zaman is looking after them,' Hassan said. 'He has told them what he will do if they betray us.'

'I can imagine.' Jack did not ask any more. The Guides had their own way of doing things, not always in accordance with the wishes of the gentlemen at Horse Guards and perhaps all the more effective for that.

As on the previous day, the Mujahidin began to move half an hour before dark. Jack watched them descend the hill, so confident of their superiority in numbers they made no attempt at concealment.

'I've never seen Pashtuns so careless.'

'They know we are trapped,' Hassan said. 'They could destroy us if they wished.'

'I still don't understand why they don't,' Jack said.

Hassan tapped the stock of his rifle. 'Pashtuns enjoy shikar, the hunt. They treat us like sport. They are playing with us.'

'Not for long,' Jack said grimly. 'As soon as it's full dark, send up Alladad and Fatteh.'

'The shepherds will want to see their gold,' Hassan said.

Calling Fatteh over, Jack handed him one of his sovereigns, knowing the shepherds were watching. 'Give that to the shepherds when you reach the summit safely and undetected. If they seem likely to betray you to the Mujahidin, kill them.'

'Yes, Sahib,' Fatteh said without a trace of emotion.

'Tell the shepherds that they will get the second sovereign either when they return to me, or when we join them at the top.' Jack paused for a moment. 'Not a moment before.'

Already the Mujahidin were setting great fires on the other side of the river, while sounds of singing and merriment accompanied the scent of roasting mutton that tortured the hungry Guides.

'There's your sheep, boys,' Jack said to the shepherds. 'Don't forget.' He showed the second sovereign before replacing it in his pocketbook. 'Good luck, lads.' Jack sent Alladad and Fatteh up the hill. The love-locked shepherd led the way with the other herding the Guides as if they were sheep.

Jack watched as the two Guides padded upstream and launched themselves into the fast current, one at a time, with each man paying out a cord from the goatskin so it could be retrieved for the next. Remembering the night-time encounters with the Plastun Cossacks outside the walls of Sevastopol, Jack wondered how his Guides would have fared. *Probably very well*, he thought. He looked up to the hill, unseen in the dark. *I hope these lads are all right up there. I hope this plan works.*

Time always passed slowly when Jack waited for something to happen. Even the river seemed to run slower, with the rippling louder, and the occasional splash of a fish making his nerves jump. The Mujahidin were singing, bouts of loud laughter reaching across the ford. Jack glanced at his watch for the fifth time. Each minute seemed an eternity.

'Your watch will not speed the passage of time, sahib,' Hassan said. 'It is Allah that decides our fate, not the ticking of a clock.'

'On that, we must agree, Hassan.' Jack checked the men. Hassan was on sentry duty, his eyes roving through the darkness. The others were asleep as if two of their number were not at that minute climbing a mountain in the face of the enemy, risking hideous torture if they were caught. These Pashtun were the most philosophical soldiers Jack had ever met.

The singing from across the river increased, with the figures of warriors silhouetted against the campfires. Jack wondered what would happen if he led his men into a night attack. The idea appealed, but the odds were too heavy even for the Guides. No, he had made his plan and must abide by it.

'Sahib.' Hassan touched his arm. 'Up on the hill.'

Jack looked up, unsure if Hassan was warning him of disaster or notifying him of success. The gleam of light showed, distinct in the dark. It flickered, flared up for a second, then died so completely that Jack wondered if he had ever seen it.

'They've made it.' Jack felt a surge of relief. 'Wake up the men, Hassan.' He heard the grimness in his voice as he struck a Lucifer and applied it to the torch of dried grass he had ready.

The sudden flare would be visible for miles. The men on the summit of the mountain could not fail to see it, while the Mujahidin across the river might wonder what he was doing.

Let them wonder, Jack thought. *With luck, they will have more on their minds in a minute than a handful of fugitive Guides.* 'Come on, Fatteh. You've wanted to blow that blasted bugle since I first met you; do your stuff.'

Shrill and distinctive, the bugle rang out a moment later. Jack stood upright. 'Well done, Fatteh!' Call followed call, with the sound echoing around the mountains. Jack peered across the ford, seeing increased movement against the flaring bonfires. The next stage took longer than Jack had expected, but eventually, he heard the sharp crack of an explosion as the first of his gunpowder flasks erupted.

Jack had not known what to expect from the Mujahidin. He heard the rising clamour from across the river as the second gunpowder flask exploded, followed by the third. He saw the muzzle flares as some of the enemy began firing wildly up the hill, then the Mujahidin's bonfires grew larger.

'They don't know what's happening, sahib,' Zaman said.

'That's the idea,' Jack said. 'Let's make things a little worse. Fire into them. Give them a few casualties to worry about.'

The Guides needed no encouragement. Lining the parapet of the sangar, they fired across the river as another of the gunpowder flasks exploded. That was followed by a familiar rumble.

'Avalanche.' Hassan sounded mildly excited. 'That last explosion has caused an avalanche.'

An avalanche was frightening in the day. At night, with the sound increasing, yet the extent invisible, it was terrifying. Jack nearly felt sorry for the enemy on the far side of the river.

'Ceasefire,' he said. 'Save our ammunition. Only shoot if any of the Mujahidin try to get across the ford.'

Fatteh's bugle sounded again, the notes thin against the rumble of shifting rocks. It faded away and died.

'They're coming back down,' Hassan said.

'They've done well,' Jack approved. 'Better than I had anticipated.'

The Mujahidin continued to fire, although in what direction Jack was not sure. A couple of stray shots whistled overhead, with one splintering the facing rock of the sangar. The rumble of the avalanche subsided. *Patience, Jack, wait for your men to return.*

'Sahib!' Fatteh was hardly out of breath despite his climb up and down two thousand feet of rugged rock in the dark and a double crossing of the river. Water dripped from him to puddle on the ground. 'We did it, sahib.'

'You did well, Fatteh. You, too, Alladad; your explosions were successful.'

'Yes, sahib. I planted the flasks under loose rocks, remembering the avalanche we caused at the ridge.'

'Good thinking, Alladad. There's a daffadar in you, at least. I will inform Kerr sahib when we get back to Mardan.'

'Sahib,' Fatteh reminded him, 'the shepherds may expect their gold now. They led us well.'

Jack handed over the second sovereign. 'Thank you, gentlemen,' he said solemnly. 'I hope these coins are sufficient recompense for your lost sheep.'

The shepherds grabbed the money with hardly a glance before scurrying away into the dark in case Jack changed his mind.

'That is more gold than they have ever seen in their lives,' Hassan said. 'They are richer than they ever dreamed.'

'Good,' Jack said. 'Now let's see what's happening across the river. Ursulla, wait here with the horses.' He had another idea. 'Zaman: blow up a couple of these bombs we made. With luck, the Mujahidin will think we are firing artillery at them. The rest come with me.'

CHAPTER TEN

Pakhtunkhwa, July 1863

The firing from the mujahidin had increased, joined by high-pitched shouts and the occasional scream. Jack led his Guides into the cold rushing water of the ford. He moved slowly, checking every step, holding his revolver ready, feeling very vulnerable in the open. The water was deeper than he expected, reaching to his waist in the middle before receding again.

It was a relief to step onto dry ground, even though he was closer to the enemy. The revived campfires sent flickering light across the ground, revealing groups of men milling around, some firing upwards at the mountain in the belief that the British were there, others not sure what to do. When Zaman's mines crashed out, more of the Mujahidin started firing across the ford, with the bullets whistling past the ears of the Guides. *That was a bad idea I had.*

'They are different tribal levies.' Hassan reeled off half a dozen names that Jack did not recognise. 'This must be a gathering place.'

'That tabla mullah must be calling them all together. I wondered how there were so many armed men at the pass. There are certainly too many for our little group.'

Hassan looked around, holding his Enfield ready. 'Some may not be hostile to the British.'

'Lie down,' Jack ordered. 'We'll watch for a few moments. As far as I am concerned, they all opposed a party of the Guides. That makes them equally hostile.'

'Yes, sahib,' Hassan said.

'That group there,' Jack indicated a large body of men who looked more aggressive than the others. 'On my word, open fire on them.'

Settling down, the Guides aimed, waiting for Jack's command. There was another outburst of firing from higher up the pass.

'The tribal groups are shooting at each other,' Hassan said. 'They don't know who the enemy is.'

Jack grunted. He had seen even the best-trained soldiers fire on their allies in the confusion of battle. He could not expect these tribal levies to maintain their brittle discipline when under pressure at night. That was the weakness of tribal fighters; they may be as brave as hunting lions, but they lacked discipline. That, more than anything else, was what gave the British their advantage in the wars out here. It was not only superiority of arms and equipment; it was not better leadership, although that tipped the balance in the late Mutiny; it was discipline and the knowledge that each soldier could count on the men and the units on either side to keep their position. With tribes who were often mutually hostile, such trust could not exist.

'Fire.'

The four Guides fired on Jack's order. Between the flickering light and drifting smoke, Jack could not see the full effects, although at least one man fell. The others seemed undecided who to blame, with some pointing to another group, while others fired up the hill at the non-existent British army.

'Wait,' Jack ordered. 'Reload.'

His men lay still. They knew as well as he that a man lying still is hard to spot even in the daylight. At night he is next to impossible to see. The Guides watched as the tribal group argued among itself what to do. Jack waited until the argument was at its height. Seeing the Tabla Mullah ride past the fire, Jack took the rifle from Sawan, waited until he had a clear shot, and fired.

His bullet took the mullah full in the chest. The man slumped down on his horse. *Good! That's you out of the way. You won't cause us any more trouble.*

'Fire,' Jack ordered. Two other men fell. Jack could sense the frustrated anger of the warriors as they searched for their attackers, eventually deciding that a group beyond the Guides must be responsible. Jack had no need to order his men to lie still as the various tribes fired on each other. He watched as the gathering broke up in confusion, with individuals and small parties of men running back over the pass, still shooting.

'That leaves the way clear for us.' Jack felt neither satisfaction nor remorse at the scattering of bodies on the ground. If these men had not opposed him, he would have no quarrel with them. 'Sawan, fetch Ursulla, Zaman and the horses. The rest of you, fill the water bottles, and search the bodies for food.'

'There are many dead sheep, sahib,' Hassan pointed out. 'Plenty of mutton.'

'Good thinking, Hassan. We will eat as much as we can before we set off.'

That will give the tribes time to get out of our way, while men do not operate efficiently with empty bellies. Bonaparte was right in that; an army marches on its stomach.

'Has anybody seen the body of that damned mullah I shot?'

'No, sahib.'

Jack grunted. He would have liked to confirm his kill. He had thought that somebody had been rallying the tribes; it must have been that mullah. With luck, the mullah's death would end some of the threat; perhaps it would even end the entire Jihad. It was too early for such speculation. He had his men to feed and to get home to Mardan.

The mutton was a treat for hungry men; augmented by the pieces of bread they found scattered with the other debris of a broken army, Jack's Guides felt they had feasted in the hour before they moved. By that time the night was fading, the sky a leaden grey, streaked with bands of pink that enhanced the rugged beauty of the mountains. Ignoring the weariness that seemed to accompany any military unit in any campaign, Jack ordered that every Mujahidin weapon should be collected. Knowing how much the Pashtun valued their rifles, he would not leave them to be used against the British at a later date.

'Sahib,' Hassan called. 'This Waziri has an Enfield.'

Jack's had not forgotten the original purpose of his mission. He hurried across. 'Show me, Hassan.'

The Waziri was not dead. He lay apart from the main body with both legs trapped under a huge rock. His eyes glared hatred as Jack approached, and he lifted his rifle threateningly. The Guides formed a circle around him, mocking.

'You have no bullets in your gun, Waziri,' Zaman said. 'What are you going to do, wave it at me?'

'Where did you get that from?' Jack saw the man was in pain. 'Tell me, and we will remove the rock and splint your legs.'

Unable to do anything else, the Waziri spat at Jack. 'If I were able, I would gut you, feringhee!'

'Yet you are not able,' Zaman mocked. He stepped closer, with the tone of his voice becoming more urgent. 'That sword, Waziri; where did you get that sword?'

Jack frowned. The Waziri's silver-hilted pulwar had fallen half out of his scabbard to lie at his side. Light from the rising sun highlighted the flowing Persian script along the blade. 'That is Batoor's sword,' he said. 'The sword of the Khan of the Rahmut Khel.'

Zaman nodded. 'It is, sahib.' Ignoring the Waziri's curses, he lifted the pulwar, holding it reverently in both hands.

'How did you come by that?' Jack asked the Waziri.

'I shall ask him, sahib,' Zaman said. 'He will not talk to a feringhee. He will talk to me.'

'That may be true.' Jack stepped back to listen. 'Find out about Batoor as well as the rifle.'

'It might be better if you are not here, sahib,' Zaman suggested tactfully.

'All right, Zaman.' Jack lit a cheroot and withdrew. One thing he had learned as an officer was when it was best not to notice things. He had no illusions about the methods of persuasion that Zaman would use. Once, as an idealistic young Griffin, Jack would not have believed that British officers would sanction such ungentlemanly practices. The reality of war on the frontiers of Empire had taught him differently.

Leaving Zaman to interrogate the Waziri, Jack checked the horses. He heard the odd muffled moan from behind him, a grunt or two and one stifled scream.

If that mullah was the man rallying the tribes, perhaps we have indeed broken the back of the trouble already? Did I kill him? I saw my shot strike, but there is no sign of the body. Jack tried to concentrate on his duty, while his mind wavered. Batoor had been so proud to show his sword; he would never have willingly parted with it. *Is Batoor dead? I can't think of that laughing, vital man dying.*

'Sahib.' Zaman marched toward him, smiling. He handed Jack the Enfield. 'Our Waziri was most co-operative.'

'I'm glad to hear it.' Jack tried not to notice the blood on Zaman's hands. 'What did he tell you?'

'He bought the rifle from a small village named Tazhak, further to the north.'

'Tazhak.' Jack frowned. 'I have never heard of that place. Do you know it, Zaman?'

'I know where it is, sahib.'

Jack grunted. 'Thank you, Zaman.' He noticed that Zaman had Batoor's sword around his waist. 'And the sword?'

'The Waziri told me he took the sword from a dead Afridi,' Zaman said. 'A tall man with a skull cap. He said the Mujahidin asked a body of Afridis to join the jihad. The Afridis refused and were killed.'

Jack fought his instant distress. He could nearly picture the scene, with Batoor facing up to the Mujahidin on Rahmut Khel land, the altercation followed by a vicious fight.

'Batoor Khan would be happy to die in such a way,' Zaman said.

Jack was numb at the thought of Batoor's death. 'You are right, Zaman.' He shook away his sadness; there would be time to mourn later. Now he had a party of Guides to get to safety and new intelligence to digest. 'We'll put splints on the Waziri's legs and leave him here with food and water. His friends may come back for him.'

'There is no need for the splints, Windrush sahib, or the food and water.'

Jack shook his head. 'The man is injured, Zaman. We must try to help him.'

'The Waziri died, sahib.' Zaman's face was expressionless.

'That is unfortunate.' Jack was not surprised. Suddenly he did not care; that Waziri had killed Batoor. 'How far away is this Tazhak?'

'About two days' ride, sahib.'

Could he take his Guides as far as that? 'Is it rough country?'

'Yes, sahib.'

Jack already knew that he must visit Tazhak. 'Which tribe is there?'

'Tazhak is in Yusufzai territory.'

'Call a Jirga, Zaman.' What Jack had in mind was not exactly a Jirga, but he could think of no other term to describe the meeting he convened.

The six Guides sat around him with the sun fast rising and the inevitable fur of flies covering the bodies of the dead. The vultures that seemed to follow them hovered patiently, aware that they would move on, waiting for their absence to feast on human flesh.

'So far, gentlemen, we have been lucky,' Jack told them. 'We have escaped siege and ambush without taking a single casualty, largely because of your skill in this sort of country.'

The Guides looked at him, nodding sagely as they waited for him to have his say. Jack knew that he was not behaving like an officer of the British Army, but these men were not ordinary British soldiers. He was determined to respect their methods as far as was compatible with his duty to the Queen.

'As you know, we were sent out to gather information about gun smuggling and these Mujahidins. So far, we have not been very successful, until today.' Jack held up the Enfield. 'This is the first example of a British Enfield rifle that we have found.'

The Guides waited patiently. They knew all this already.

'Zaman asked the Waziri where it came from. He said it was from Tazhak, in Yusufzai country. Now, what was a Waziri from the south doing in Yusufzai territory far to the north?'

'Buying a rifle.' Hassan gave the answer Jack had been expecting.

'Exactly,' Jack said. 'These Enfields have been appearing up and down the Frontier. How do they get to Tazhak? Who brings them there? Who supplies them?'

The Guides waited, perhaps wondering if Jack was going to answer his questions.

'I do not know the answer,' Jack said. 'Zaman's discovery of Tazhak may clear up the mystery, it may be the next link in the chain, or it may lead nowhere. We are going to march to Tazhak before we return to Mardan.'

He waited for the groans of protest that his 113th would have emitted. The Guides merely nodded. Hassan took a pinch of snuff.

'Do you know the way, sahib?' Hassan asked.

'No,' Jack admitted. 'But you will.'

'We have to pass through Mohmand and Mamund territory,' Hassan said. 'I have blood feuds with both.'

'We will travel with care.' Jack looked up. 'If we stay here much longer, we will grow roots, or Gulbaz will catch us.'

'That is true,' Hassan agreed. 'Windrush sahib...'

'Yes, Hassan?'

'What are we going to do when we get to Tazhak?'

Jack considered for a moment. 'I'm not sure, Hassan. We'll have a look around and see what there is to see.'

'We look like British soldiers, sahib,' Hassan pointed out. 'I don't think that British soldiers have ever been in the valley of Kot, where Tazhak sits. It would be better if we dressed like Pashtuns.'

'You are right, Hassan. Strip some of these bodies.' Jack could be every bit as pragmatic as his men. Wearing a uniform in Pakhtunkhwa was an invitation to every roaming tribesman to try his marksmanship. 'You're going to turn me into a Pashtun warrior.'

The Pashtun clothes were comfortable and warmer than Jack had expected. He slipped a woollen pakol on his head, adjusted it, and grinned. 'Now I am as Pashtun as you are.' He had not expected the genuine laughter from his men. 'Right, lads, destroy all the old weapons and toss them into the river.'

Acts of destruction seemed as popular with the Pashtun as they were with British soldiers. The Guides worked with a will, laughing as they smashed up the old jezzails. Only when he was satisfied did Jack give orders to move out.

'Alladad, ride ahead to scout. Sawan, you are our rearguard; watch for pursuit or any sign of Gulbaz.'

The two men left at once. Jack felt slightly happier now that he had found an Enfield and knew the location where it was bought. He had justified his mission to an extent. Now he wished to find this Tazhak, riding through hostile territory with a tired group of men he still did not wholly understand.

Jack sighed. He had wanted to be a soldier; now he had to accept the tribulations of a soldier's lot. 'Keep alert boys; we are the Guides.'

CHAPTER ELEVEN

Pakhtunkhwa, July 1863

Tazhak stood on a prominent rise within the confines of the Valley of Kot. Protected by a ten-foot-high earthen wall, there was a tall arched gate for entry, with two sturdy watchmen on guard. A stone tower nailed down each corner of the village, manned by armed warriors in skull caps. Under a low, leaden sky, the village looked uncompromisingly hostile. Every so often the distinctive crack of a rifle sounded from within the walls.

'They evidently don't want strangers to enter unseen,' Jack said.

'The Yasufzai take care of their own.' There was pride in Hassan's voice. 'Are we not the sons of Joseph?'

Jack reined up on a ridge overlooking the valley. 'We'll wait here a bit,' he said. 'I want to see how many people enter and leave Tazhak.'

There was a steady stream of visitors, far more than Jack would have expected from a village of that size in such a remote location. He watched as the ubiquitous caravans of camels or strings of mules arrived, together with men in groups or individually. He saw no families, no children. 'It's like a trading entrepot,' he said. 'A place of men. What are the people buying?'

Weapons, he told himself as one mule left with four Brunswick rifles strapped to its sides. *They are buying rifles. How the devil did the rifles get here? I must find the source. I have to find the seller first and then trace the supplier.*

Jack looked over his men. They were as handy a bunch of soldiers as he had ever known, quick in the uptake, expert at mountain warfare and always ready to fight. If he had a company of Guides, he could surround the village to stop ingress and egress, and then search the place house by house until he found the Enfields. With only half a dozen men, such a move was not possible. He would have to think of something else.

The solution was evident if nerve-wracking. During the latter stages of the Indian Mutiny, Jack had disguised himself as a native to enter Gondabad, a city the

Mutineers then controlled. It helped that he was naturally swarthy, possibly because he was one-quarter Indian, while since then he had learned some of the languages of the country. All the same, entering a walled village in the heart of Yusufzai territory was akin to putting his head in a tiger's mouth while simultaneously pulling its tail.

Jack took a deep breath. 'I need two volunteers,' he said quietly. 'It will be very dangerous, with little chance of survival.'

'We are all volunteers,' Hassan said at once. Weary as they were, the Guides nodded their agreement.

'I am going into Tazhak to find the gun seller,' Jack said. 'I want two men as escorts. I am going in disguise, but if the locals find out I am a feringhee, we will all be killed.' He waited to see the impact of his words. 'Although I speak Pushtu, my accent may give me away.'

'Yes, sahib,' Hassan said. 'You speak like a feringhee. The moment you speak, the Tazhak people will know what you are. They will flay us alive and decorate the gate with our heads.'

'I'll need your help to look like a tribesman,' Jack said.

While Hassan looked grave, Zaman and Fatteh laughed, as if it was a colossal joke. 'The Yusufzai will spot you right away,' Zaman said. 'You walk like a feringhee, all tense, with your feet nearly scuffing the ground.'

'Teach me,' Jack said. 'I want to find this gun seller.'

Looking at each other, the Guides shook their heads. 'You can't learn to be a Pashtun,' Hassan said. 'You have to suck the milk of a Pashtun mother.' He was the only man who was not smiling.

'I must go in,' Jack said. 'I cannot learn enough by simply observing. If nobody wishes to accompany me, then I shall go alone.' *I won't send a man into danger while I stand in the shadows.*

'If you go alone, we will salute your head as it grins to us from above the entrance gate,' Hassan said. 'I'll come with you.'

'I'd prefer you remain with the men, daffadar,' Jack said. 'You are the best suited to get them to Mardan.'

'No, sahib,' Hassan said. 'You are best suited to get the men to Mardan. That is why I must go with you.' He gave a rare smile. 'Kerr sahib ordered me to look after you, remember? I cannot disobey the orders of a superior officer.'

Opening his mouth to blast Hassan for his insolence, Jack closed it with a snap. 'There is nobody I would rather have at my side, Hassan.' *Except for Batoor, wherever he is, heaven or hell.* 'We will take Zaman as well. He is a good man in a fight.' *He is also liable to cause a war if left unsupervised,* Jack thought. *Zaman is the sort of soldier one wants in one's unit during a battle, but he would be a handful in peacetime.*

Dressed in a shaggy poshteen, and with his pakol pulled low over his head, Jack hoped he looked like a bedraggled tribesman with sufficient funds to buy a rifle as he approached the gate of Tazhak. He rode a Kabul pony rather than the larger Colwell. Hassan rode at his side, erect as always, although his usually steady eyes strayed continually to Jack. A few yards behind them, Zaman held an old fashioned jezzail as if ashamed of the weapon, which he possibly was, Jack thought.

The two watchmen at the gate stepped forward on their approach. One must have been well over six feet, and broad as anybody Jack had ever seen, with a French rifle across his back and a Khyber knife at his waist. 'Your business?'

'We come to buy rifles,' Hassan said.

'You don't look as if you could afford them.' The watchman's eyes were busy on Jack's face.

'That is our business, not yours.' Zaman would not be intimidated by anybody, whatever his size.

'We can afford them.' Hassan pushed past without another word. Jack followed, keeping his head down. Fortunately, his beard had developed over the past few weeks, so he looked the part. Grabbing hold of Zaman's poshteen, he pulled him away from the watchman. 'Come, Zaman, before that fellow decides to cut off your head.'

The watchman laughed, as Jack had intended.

'I will trim his beard,' Zaman growled.

'Not today, Zaman,' Jack whispered savagely. 'We have more important things to do than disposing of an arrogant fool.'

At first, Tazhak appeared like any other large Pakhtunkhwa village that Jack had visited. There was the usual array of walled houses, and the conventional well, with the typical street of small shops and merchants. However, he realised that there was a great preponderance of warriors between the houses, and a constant rattle of metal on metal replaced the usual chatter of children and bleating of sheep.

'Tazhak seems to specialise in metal work,' Jack said. 'And warriors.'

'Yes, sahib.' Hassan looked around. 'I used to know this village before I joined the Guides. It has changed since then. Where are the children? Where are the women? There is no life in a village without them.'

Jack agreed. Tazhak was a place of men. Warriors from seemingly all the tribes of the Frontier plus some from Afghanistan and even further afield wandered the streets, bearing an assortment of clothes and armaments. Buffaloes trundled as if they belonged there, with the occasional small herd of cattle. The main street seemed composed entirely of shops, emblazoned with bright hand-lettered signs, with each one depicting a firearm. Jack glanced at Zaman, swaggering a few paces to the rear. He hoped he could control the Afridi's aggression. Hassan had been correct; he should have left Zaman behind. There was nobody better in a fight, but his hair-trigger temper could make him a liability.

'Ask somebody where we can buy an Enfield rifle, Hassan.' Jack decided to fulfil his mission and get out of Tazhak fast.

'That should not be hard, sahib.' Hassan pointed to the street that stretched ahead of them. 'Every workshop here is making guns.' Between the shops were dirty alleys, too narrow for two people to pass each other, sufficiently dark to make even a brave man hesitate to enter. The sound of hammer on metal was distinct, a background to everything else. Jack flinched as a shaven-headed man emerged from a shop ten yards away, lifted a jezzail and fired it into the air. Grinning, he returned inside.

Jack grunted. 'I don't want somebody to make me a jezzail, Hassan. We're here to find out who is buying British rifles and from where they come.'

Hassan nodded. 'I know, sahib.' He nodded to the nearest workshop. 'Look at that Mohmand, who is leaving the shop, sahib.'

The man was in his early thirties with a ragged turban carelessly tied on his head and a round shield across his back. He emerged from the workshop looking pleased, with an Enfield rifle in the crook of his arm.

'Well done, Hassan.' Dismounting, Jack stalked toward the workshop, with Hassan at his side. 'Look after the horses, Zaman.'

'It may be best if I do the talking, sahib,' Hassan said.

Jack nodded. 'That is true. Enfield rifles, remember, Hassan.'

'I know, sahib.'

Jack did not know what to expect as he entered the workshop. There were four men inside; one was an Afridi customer, another was a man with a red-dyed beard who was apparently the salesman, and the other two were working with a lathe and file. As Jack watched, a grey-bearded craftsman used a hammer and chisel to expertly create the lock of a replica Tower musket. On the wall at the back, the workshop displayed examples of their skill, with four different weapons including a jezzail, an Enfield and a Brown Bess musket.

When the Afridi left, muttering darkly about high prices, Hassan approached the salesman.

'*Salaam alaikum* – greetings, good day.'

'*Salaam alaikum*,' the salesman returned politely. He looked directly at Hassan as he spoke and then took in both Jack and Zaman with a single sweep of his eyes.

'Your fame as a gunsmith has spread from Tashkent to Delhi.' Hassan had a smooth tongue. 'We came from the Vale of Peshawar.'

'I know the accent, Yusufzai.' The salesman glanced at Jack, who said nothing. 'Your friend is not a Yusufzai.'

'No.' Hassan lowered his voice. 'He would prefer not to be known.'

'Ah; blood feud.' The salesman understood at once. 'That is why the Afridi waits outside watching everything. What kind of rifle do you wish?'

'I heard that you have British-made Enfields.' Jack decided to cut short the rhetoric.

The salesman looked confused. 'We have no British-made weapons here. Everything we sell, we make ourselves.'

Stepping to the wall, Jack lifted down the Enfield. 'You did not make this yourself,' he said.

'Yes, we did.' The salesman was hurt by the accusation. 'Am I a liar?'

'No.' Jack had no intention of impinging the man's honour by such an accusation. 'No, you are a Yusufzai, and Yusufzais never lie.'

The salesman accepted Jack's near-apology with good grace. 'That is so. My sons and I made that weapon.'

'You are a skilled man.' Jack examined the weapon, noting the British government stamp and serial number. 'My companion was right to come to you first. Could you make others like this?'

'We do make others.' The salesman nodded to his sons. 'We are making one now.'

Jack wandered over to the two younger men, who had not looked up from their labours. One was punching at the metal of the rifle.

'Forgive me.' Jack lifted the weapon. The stamp and serial number were identical to the first he had handled. 'Thank you. What do you charge for a new Enfield?'

The salesman looked from Jack to Hassan and back, obviously assessing them, working out how much they were worth. When he mentioned a figure, Hassan grunted. 'Too much,' he said. 'You might cheat my colleague; you will not cheat a fellow Yusufzai. Come, cousin.' Tapping Jack on the shoulder, he stalked out of the shop.

'Did you know that fellow made Enfields?'

Hassan gave a small smile. 'Not until I entered the workshop. You must know that the Pashtun are renowned for their skill in copying firearms.'

'So I see,' Jack said. 'One man could not make all the weapons that have been recovered the length and breadth of the Frontier. He is not the man for whom we are looking.'

'No, sahib,' Hassan said.

Jack guessed that Hassan was hiding something. 'We'll keep looking.'

The next workshop was much like the first, with a small group of men busy with simple tools. Again, Hassan made the introductions as Jack studied the weapons on display. He lifted down the Enfield to see the identical serial number. 'Do you have other Enfields?'

The salesman gave Jack a hard look as he produced another Enfield. When Jack lifted the rifle, he thought it was fractionally lighter than the weapons he was used to. A quick check revealed the same serial number.

'I can see a pattern developing here.' Jack looked along the busy street. 'I imagine that most of these workshops produce Enfields?'

'Yes, sahib.' Hassan sounded very patient. 'Are we still searching for the warriors of God? The Ghazi?'

'I hope that we scattered them at the Zargun Pass,' Jack said.

'We defeated some, sahib,' Hassan said. 'But can you not see the men with the red cords around their right arm?' Hassan asked.

Jack had been too busy concentrating on the rifles to notice much else.

'They are Ghazis,' Hassan reminded him.

Jack took a deep breath. Now that he looked, he could see more red cords, with every fourth man sporting one. He felt his tension increase. He had been strolling around Tazhak without thought. 'This village is a hotbed of the Mujahidin.'

'It may be so, sahib,' Hassan said.

'Dear God in Heaven,' Jack said softly, measuring the distance to the gate. *No, he told himself. I am here to look for the gun-runner. I cannot allow personal danger to interfere with my mission.* In normal circumstances, he would have lit a cheroot to still his jangling nerves. A Pashtun would not do such a thing. 'Thank you, Hassan. I will watch for them. In the meantime, I still hope to find who sells British-made rifles.'

They spent the morning visiting the workshops, with Jack becoming increasingly alarmed at the skill shown by the gunsmiths. 'These weapons are first class,' he said. 'They are nearly as good as the rifles we make in Britain.'

'Yes, sahib.'

Every workshop they visited displayed a variety of weapons, with about half having the capability to create an Enfield. Jack checked the weapons, finding most had the same serial number. There were only two different numbers, proving to Jack that the weapons had been copied from two originals.

'How many gunsmiths are there in Tazhak, Hassan?'

Hassan glanced along the street. 'About a hundred, sahib.'

'Was it always like this?'

Hassan shook his head. 'When I lived in the valley of Kot, Tazhak was like any other village.'

Somebody has changed it. Somebody is deliberately making modern rifles here and selling them to the Mujahidin. There can only be one reason for that. I must tell Colonel Hook what we have found.

'I don't believe that there is a man smuggling guns to the tribes,' Jack decided.

'Nor do I believe that they have stolen scores of Enfields. I think this village of Tazhak is churning them out like a factory.'

'Yes, sahib,' Hassan agreed.

'If we wish to stop the tribes gaining modern rifles,' Jack said, 'we'll have to shut down this village.'

'These men are only doing what their forefathers have done for generations,' Hassan pointed out. 'They are not breaking any law, Pashtun or British.'

'I know.' Jack could not think of a solution. If the British decided to stop the workshops making weapons, they would be interfering with a centuries-old tradition, which in itself would cause unrest. 'Let's get away, Hassan. We must pass the information on to the authorities.' Colonel Hook would be most interested to hear about the gun-making village of Tazhak. Although it was a relief to know there was no traitor on the British side, it was worrying to realise how skilled the local gunsmiths were.

There was another question: who was behind the gun-making? Who had the power to turn a traditional Yusufzai village into a gun-making powerhouse? Had it been that mullah with the tabla drum?

'I have seen three men that I should kill.' Zaman interrupted Jack's thoughts. 'My family is at feud with them.'

'Not today, Zaman,' Jack said. 'You can have your sport when you are off duty.'

'Sometimes the Queen's service is hard,' Zaman said.

'With that, we can all agree.' Jack thought of Mary, so far away. 'Right, Hassan, we've discovered what we set out for. Let's get back to Mardan as quick as Allah will let us.'

As they neared the gate, a shambling group of mixed horsemen and warriors on foot approached. Even from a distance, Jack could see they were travel-weary, with some limping or carrying injuries.

'Ride round these lads,' Jack said as he came closer.

'Sahib. These are from the Rahmut Khel.' Zaman was a second too late as a tall man pushed forward.

Jack saw the man's hook. 'Gulbaz!' It was too late to escape detection.

'You!' Gulbaz pointed to Jack. 'What are you doing here?' He raised his voice into a roar. 'This is a British officer, a feringhee!'

Swearing, Jack contemplated reaching for his revolver, realised that they were too outnumbered to put up a fight, dug in his heels and thrust forward.

'With me, Guides!'

Now they had been recognised, there was no point in further pretence. Jack hit the Rahmut Khel at an angle, barged one limping footman over, avoided a yelling horseman by luck rather than skill, and at last managed to pull his revolver clear. 'Come on, lads!'

Jack heard a rising tumult of shouts behind him as Gulbaz and his men pressed closer, with some drawing pulwars as they tried to block the Guides' passage. Laughing, Zaman swung his sword at Gulbaz, who parried by lifting his arm. Zaman's blade clattered on the steel bands that held the hook secure. He laughed again and wheeled his horse just outside the ranks of the Rahmut Khel.

'Come on, sahib!'

Glancing over his shoulder, Jack saw Hassan jinking through the mob. 'Come on, Hassan!'

'Ride, sahib!' Hassan said.

'Gallop, lads!' Jack ordered. 'Get out of here.' He kicked in his heels, wishing he had Colwall rather than the sure-footed but slower Kabul pony. A glance over his shoulder revealed that Gulbaz's men had quickly re-organised. He pushed Zaman on. 'The lads will have seen the commotion, and they'll be ready to go.' *I hope.*

The Guides did better than Jack expected. They rode out with rifles in their hands, and the spare horses trotted beside them.

'Well done, Guides!' Even at that emergency, Jack thought how good it was to work with such professional soldiers. 'Fatteh, Ursulla, Alladad, fire on the mob. Try and slow them down.'

'Spur!' He gave the unnecessary order as the Guide's Enfields cracked out. 'Hassan, take the lead; you know the route better than I do!'

Slowing slightly, Jack ensured that all his men were together with no stragglers. Twisting in the saddle, he levelled his revolver and fired two rapid shots. He did not expect to hit anybody, only to unsettle the pursuit. The men of the Rahmut Khel were already far behind. Riding tired horses or on foot, they had not expected to run into the Guides, and the accurate shooting of the Enfields must be discouraging.

'Fatteh, Ursulla, Alladad, reload! Zaman, Hassan, Sawan, fire!' That was all Jack needed to say. Three more shots cracked out with the sounds echoing and fading. The men of the Rahmut Khel were shooting more in anger rather than a serious attempt to hit anything.

Jack organised their fighting withdrawal for another half mile, with the Guides alternately shooting and riding. He could not see any casualties among Gulbaz's men, but they did fall even further behind.

That was unpleasant. I had hoped that Gulbaz had given up the chase.

'Slow to a trot,' Jack ordered. 'Save the horses. Hassan, take us back to Mardan by the fastest safe route.'

'Yes, sahib.' Hassan gave a wry smile. 'This is Pakhtunkhwa, sahib. There is no safe route.'

'So I have learned,' Jack said. 'That firing will have alerted the locals.'

'No, sahib.' Hassan shook his head. 'Listen.'

Jack slowed down his horse. He heard the intermittent crackle of gunfire, single shots interspersed with what could nearly be regular volleys. 'Are they still trying to fire at us?'

Hassan lifted his head a fraction to listen. 'No. That is the gunsmiths testing their new weapons, or those men who have bought a rifle firing it in the air.' He smiled. 'The locals will be used to gunfire. They will pay no heed to a few more shots.'

'I hope you are right, Hassan.' Jack glanced at the surrounding heights. He could plainly see the figures of men, some against the skyline, others sitting on rocks, watching the small body of Guides riding along the valley floor.

'Men are coming, sahib,' Hassan warned. 'Riding fast from the north.'

A minute later Jack felt the slight tremble of the ground. 'Leave the track.' He indicated a group of loose boulders amongst scattered pines. 'We'll wait there.' If the approaching men were hostile, he wanted some solid rocks to shelter behind; they could not hope to run forever.

Within a few minutes, Jack heard the steadily increasing sound of horses' hooves. He glanced over his men; they were well hidden behind boulders, holding their horses close. There was no need to order them to keep alert.

A rising cloud of dust marked the passage of the unknown horsemen. Jack watched them slow down as they neared the rocks where the Guides waited. The dust cleared, leaving the riders visible. There were twenty or so with rifles strapped across their backs and round shields bouncing from their saddles. Jack felt for the butt of his revolver.

'Ghazis.' Hassan placed a percussion cap on his rifle. 'See the red cords?'

'I see the red cords.' Jack felt the tension rise within the Guides. If the Ghazis saw them, they would attack without mercy.

'Cap and load,' Jack said quietly.

'We already have, sahib.' Hassan was equally quiet.

Jack nodded. 'Fatteh, look after the horses. Try and keep them from moving around.'

The Ghazis remained still, looking around as if they suspected that the Guides were nearby. Jack could sense the menace. They were wild-looking men, some with long hair exploding from beneath their pakols, and unkempt, ragged beards, one in chainmail and with a steel helmet. They carried long pulwars and round shields as well as some modern rifles strapped across their backs.

'Allah Akbar!' one of the ghazis shouted. The others joined in, 'Allah Akbar!' One lifted his Enfield into the air and fired it. 'Allah Akbar!'

'God is great indeed,' Hassan said. He breathed out slowly when the Ghazis trotted away. 'He saved us from death there.'

'Were they so dangerous?' Jack wished to hear the opinion of this veteran of the Frontier.

'The men who followed Gulbaz were warriors, yes, but also farmers or craftsmen or herders. These men, these Ghazis, are holy warriors. They know no fear. They fight for Allah, for God, so if they die, they go to paradise. If they kill a feringhee, a kafir, a non-believer, they are assured a place in paradise.' Hassan watched the Ghazis ride away with dust rising in their wake.

'They sound like men it is best to avoid.'

'If the Ghazis take a dislike to you,' Hassan said, 'you have three choices: run forever, for they will hunt you to the end of the earth, allow them to kill you, or kill them.'

'Such men with modern weapons will be dangerous enemies,' Jack said.

'A Ghazi will not stop until he is dead,' Hassan said.

'We have to close down this village of Tazhak,' Jack decided. 'Ghazis with pulwars and jezzails are bad enough, Ghazis with rifles...' he allowed his words to drift away. 'Let's get to Mardan.'

CHAPTER TWELVE

Mardan July–August 1863

'Report, Captain.' Hook sat in the room he had requisitioned, overlooking the parade ground outside Mardan. He had aged in the past few weeks, with new lines of worry engraved on his face. He listened carefully as Jack told him about the situation in Torkrud, the growing numbers of Mujahidin and the gunsmiths of Tazhak.

'Batoor Khan of Torkrud is dead, you say?'

'Yes, sir. We found a Waziri with his sword.'

'He was a friend of yours, I believe. That is a pity; we need every friend we can get out here.' Hook sighed. 'Can't be helped; we'll cope. Now, about these Enfields. Every weapon had the same serial number, you say?' Hook had been scribbling notes as Jack spoke.

'There were two serial numbers, sir. Most had the same.'

'What was the number?'

'771,' Jack said at once.

'771?' Hook took two strides to the rifle that was chained to the wall. 'Even in the heart of Mardan,' he said as he unfastened the chain, 'I keep things secure. We are no distance from the Khyber, and the Khyberies are the best thieves in Afghanistan, and the Afghans are the best thieves in the world.' Tossing over the rifle, he told Jack to check the serial number.

'771,' Jack said.

'Another copy then,' Hook said. 'That is disturbing. We can trace a gun smuggler and plug the leak. It will be more difficult to stop the tribesmen copying. We are dealing with some very skilled men, Windrush.'

'I wonder if we should not destroy Tazhak.'

'A bit draconian, don't you think?' Hook looked amused. 'Technically, the gunsmiths are doing nothing wrong.'

'I can't think of any other solution.' Jack felt his anger rise. 'My men risked their lives a dozen times to get this intelligence, sir.'

'They are soldiers,' Hook said. 'It is their job to risk their lives. They are Guides, so they would enjoy pitting themselves against the wild Pashtuns.'

Jack swallowed his anger. He knew that the colonel was correct, but it seemed foolish to allow gunsmiths to manufacture weapons that would undoubtedly be used against soldiers of the queen.

'There will always be gunsmiths on the Frontier, Windrush.' Hook tapped his fingers on the desk. 'I'll have to think about this village. More importantly, we have to deal with these fanatics, these so-called Warriors of God, the Mujahidin. You have one point, though, Windrush; the Mujahidin will be even more dangerous with modern weapons.' Hook slammed a hand on his desk. 'Damn! If it had been a gun-runner, we could have stopped the supply at source. Your intelligence alters everything!'

'Yes, sir.' Jack did not pursue what he still believed was the most logical course of action. 'I also believe that one man had been organising them.' Jack explained about the mullah with the tabla drum.

Hook grunted. 'You may be correct. We have been plagued by these mad mullahs in the past. As you know, religion is a powerful thing. Even the most sensible of men can become turbulent when somebody taps into his religion.'

'Yes, sir.'

Hook perused Jack over the rim of his brandy glass. 'What we don't wish to do, Windrush, is stir up the tribes. The Pashtun are much like us. They have deep religious beliefs and will defend their land with tenacity and courage.'

'I agree, sir. My own worry is that our own people will become affected. We don't want a second Mutiny.'

'Indeed, Windrush, indeed.' Colonel Hook sighed, looking older than ever. 'I'll see what I can find out about this tabla mullah you think you shot. As always, you have given me worries, Windrush.' He tapped his finger on the desk again. 'With Batoor Khan dead, then this Gulbaz fellow leads the Rahmut Khel.'

'Yes, sir, and he's no friend of ours.'

Hook grimaced. 'That's a shame, Windrush. Again, it can't be helped. We'll deal with him if the need arises. Now, what do you make of this?' He handed over a crushed fragment of paper.

Jack read the ornate Persian script. 'It's like a note from a lawyer,' he said. 'It mentions a lawsuit and a law agent.' He reread it. 'Something about the law agent being the most important person.' Jack looked up. 'That's an interesting coincidence; we picked up a small group of fellows outside Torkrud with a very similar message for Gulbaz. It had the same Persian script and nearly the same message.'

'What sort of fellows, Windrush?'

Jack tried to remember. 'So much has happened since then. There were three of them, one elderly fellow with a dyed beard and two younger men. If they had not tried to run when they saw us, we would not have even noticed them.'

'Were they Mujahidin? Did they have the red cord?'

Jack shook his head. 'Not that I noticed, sir. My lads thought them suspicious, but as they did not try to harm us, I let them go.'

'That is disturbing, but not unique, unfortunately.' Hook opened a drawer of his desk to produce another square of paper. 'Tell me what you think about this one, then?'

Jack scanned the message, translating it from Urdu. 'They seem to say the same thing, sir. I am guessing that they were not all sent to the same person?'

'Your guess is correct.' Hook's fingers began to tap again. 'These messages have been turning up all across North West India, particularly in the Frontier area. These last two I gave you were carried by Fanatics.'

'So they are not from lawyers then,' Jack said.

'I think they are messages from the Fanatics to their supporters,' Hook said. 'Although I cannot think what they mean.'

'Nor can I, sir,' Jack said. 'It reminds me of the start of the Mutiny when chapattis were sent around India to warn that something was about to happen, except these notes seem to contain a more specific message.'

'Carry on, Windrush.'

'Before the Mutiny, the chapattis were general; nobody knew what they meant or who sent them, while these messages are sent to individuals from an individual. Presumably, the recipient knows the sender, or at least knows of him, or what the message might mean.'

Hook poured himself another brandy. 'You are leading up to something, Windrush.'

'I think these messages prove that there is one man behind all this agitation, sir.' Jack reread the notes. 'This word "lawsuit" comes up in all of these messages.' He laid the letters side by side. 'As does the name "the law agent." ' He sat back in his chair. 'I would hazard that the law agent is somebody high up; not a lawyer but somebody much higher in the Mujahidin hierarchy.'

'I see your point,' Colonel Hook said. 'The law agent may be the leader of the whole movement, one of those crazed preachers who spread hate and the idea of a holy war against us and anybody else who does not share their ideas. Perhaps the law agent is that mad tabla mullah that you shot.'

Jack frowned. 'Perhaps, sir. I hope so. The Pashtun are as devout to their religion as we are to Christianity, sir.'

'I know that, Windrush.'

'I tend to think of our militant Christians, sir, Cromwell and the like.' Hook's expression did not offer much comfort to Jack, who continued. 'They have their own laws that are different from ours, Sharia law.'

'I know that, damn it!'

'Yes, sir. I am thinking as I speak.' Jack tried to order his thoughts. 'As far as I understand it, Sharia is based on the Koran, and Sharia law must respect life, family, intellect property and honour.'

'Carry on, Windrush. Where are you taking me?'

'Mohammed is the prophet and wrote down the Koran on God's instructions, with the archangel Gabriel acting as intermediary. In that case, sir, Sharia law, based on the Koran, would be the law of God, of Allah.' Jack waited for Hook's nod.

'I know all this, Windrush.' Hook's fingers began to tap again. 'Do you have a point to make?'

'Yes, sir,' Jack said. 'These notes all mention the law agent. I suggest that the law agent, the man who makes the law, is not merely a mullah, but Allah Himself.'

Hook's fingers stopped tapping. He drained his glass, stood up, poured two glasses of brandy, and handed one to Jack. 'That might make sense, Windrush, although I cannot see how it advances our case.'

Jack lifted the brandy. 'Thank you, sir, that is most kind of you. This other word, sir, lawsuit, is also used a lot.'

'Do you have a theory for that, too, Windrush?'

'I may have, sir,' Jack said. 'Is a lawsuit not a legal argument, where one lawyer argues with another?'

Hook nodded carefully. 'I believe so.'

'Then, if we accept that the law agent is what these fanatics call Allah – which is a bit of an insulting term for the great Creator, reducing him to a mere lawyer – then a lawsuit would be a dispute in which he might be expected to adjudicate?' Jack swirled the brandy within its glass.

'You are tiresomely wordy today, Windrush. Carry on.'

Windrush swallowed some brandy to fortify himself. 'As the Mujahidin wish to dispute Pakhtunkhwa, their country, with us over religious grounds, perhaps a lawsuit is their code word for a dispute, or perhaps a battle?'

'We have not had a battle with these fanatics,' Hook said.

'No, sir,' Jack agreed. 'Not yet.' He looked up. 'Perhaps the Mujahidin, or rather the man who leads them, are planning one. Once again, sir, the situation is very much like the prelude to the Mutiny, when all sorts of omens and portents flew about the countryside.'

'Ye shall hear of wars and rumours of wars.' Hook murmured. 'Matthew 24, Verse six. See that ye be not troubled: for all these things must come to pass, but the end is not yet.'

'I hope not, sir.'

'We have spoken of a major rising,' Hook said. 'Yet I have had my finger on the pulse of India for some time. I don't feel any desire to cause upset; the aftermath of the Mutiny with its hangings and blowing-from-cannon seems to have quite dampened the ardour of even the most anti-British agitator. The huge majority wish peace and stability under the rule of the crown.'

'I agree sir, but religion is a powerful motivator.' Jack felt as if they were repeating the same arguments to no purpose. 'A minority will follow any eloquent orator.'

'For the peace of India and the security of the people, let's hope that it is only a small minority.' When Hook looked up, Jack saw the genuine concern behind his eyes. 'This country has seen more than sufficient bloodshed in its history, Windrush, what with petty kingdoms fighting one another, Hindus fighting Moslems, Marathas and Pindaris slaughtering everybody, Moslems slaughtering Sikhs, Sikhs butchering Moslems, Afghan raids, Nepalese raids and the Mutiny. The last thing it needs is a new religious war. Please God, Windrush, any god, that we can have peace now.'

'That would be the prayer of most people,' Jack agreed.

'Well then, let's nip this thing in the bud before it grows even uglier,' Hook said. 'I will paraphrase your intelligence of this tabla mullah and this village of gunsmiths and send it to the Earl of Elgin, our august Viceroy.' He looked up. 'I expect some reaction from the Viceroy. We cannot afford to let this thing grow until we have another situation like the Mutiny on our hands.'

'Yes, sir.'

'In the meantime, you and your men have earned yourselves a bit of a rest.' Hook gave a bleak smile. 'You did well.'

'I'm not sure that I did, sir.'

'You got your men into Torkrud and back out without a single casualty,

Windrush. On this Frontier, that is a success. Your Guides are also talking of some very unorthodox tactics. Coming from them, that means a lot.'

'Thank you, sir.' For one moment, Jack contemplated requesting permission to go to Gondabad to see Mary. He knew he could not. He was too deeply involved in this new situation on the Frontier. It was his duty to see it through to its conclusion. At present, he wanted a long bath and a longer sleep.

CHAPTER THIRTEEN

Mardan, September 1863

'Did you hear the news, Windrush?' The cheroot seemed incongruous as it thrust from Major Kerr's heavily bearded face. Dressed in an Afghan poshteen and boots, a puggaree adorning his head, he looked more like a Pashtun than anything else. The pulwar at his side completed the image. Sometimes Jack wondered if the Pashtuns were converting the British to their culture rather than the other way around. That idea became stronger when Kerr swore in Pushtu as he barked his shin against the edge of the table.

'Language, Kerr,' Jack rebuked mildly. 'I heard the Mujahidin attacked our camp at Topi.'

'That's right. Damned cheek, attacking a Guides camp.' Rubbing his shin, Kerr perched himself on the edge of the table. He puffed out smoke. 'Impudent beggars! I would not mind if they attacked a Queen's regiment, but not the Guides!'

'We'll have to do something about them,' Jack said. After his expedition into the Frontier, he felt part of the regiment. He knew Hassan, Fatteh, Alladad and the others; they were his men now.

'Oh, we are doing something about them.' Kerr gave a smile that promised bad news for the Mujahidin. 'It's taken time, but that attack has, at last, stirred us up into sorting out these Fanatics once and for all. They'll find that it's one thing to raid and rob unarmed farmers and merchants and quite another when they attack the Guides!'

'What are we doing?' After a period of relative peace on the Frontier, Jack had harboured some aspirations that he might be able to go on his long-delayed leave with Mary. Now that the Mujahidin had caused further trouble, that faint hope withered and died.

Kerr adjusted his pulwar. 'Last time we moved against the Fanatics, Sir Sydney Cotton took five thousand men and chased them from their base at Sitana, burning their villages.'

'You told me that already. That was back in '58, wasn't it?' Jack asked.

'That's right.'

'I was a little busy in Oudh at the time.' Jack did not go into detail.

'I thought that would get you going.' Kerr's granite eyes nearly relaxed into a smile. 'From Malka, the Fanatics have been recruiting again, as you know.'

'I saw some of them,' Jack agreed cautiously.

Kerr nodded. 'When they realised that we would not bother them, the Fanatics moved to a splendidly fortified hill near Siri, but rather than attack them, we only blockaded the tribes that permitted them access.' Kerr shifted on the table, blowing more smoke. 'And sent warnings to those we suspected. That included your friend Batoor Khan, and the Rahmut Khel, of course.'

'I'm not sure if the Rahmut Khel did help them.' Jack tried to defend Batoor.

Kerr raised his eyebrows, pulled on his cigar, and did not pursue that subject. 'Now the Fanatics have returned to Sitana, raiding, plundering and murdering once more. We've had enough, so we have arranged a punitive expedition.' Kerr smiled again, with his eyes softening a little.

'Something seems to be amusing you, Kerr.'

'Something certainly is amusing me, Windrush.' Sliding off the table, Kerr stalked to the far side and opened the drawer. 'Colonel Hook sent this for you.' He held up a folded, sealed document. 'I already know the contents.'

'Thank you.' Jack guessed that the document would not be good news. Breaking the seal, he unfolded the stiff paper and scanned the contents. 'I am to report to Brigadier General Sir Neville Chamberlain as a staff officer with expertise on the Frontier,' he said.

Kerr lit another cheroot. 'That's right, Jack me boy. You, a virtual griff on the Frontier, are to give local help and advice to General Sir Neville Bowles Chamberlain, the bravest of the brave, a man who has fought the length and breadth of the land from Kabul to Baluchistan. Chamberlain, who has collected more wounds than Alexander the Great; why, Captain, once Chamberlain dies, they are going to smelt his body for the lead, he has so many bullets in it. The man is a veritable legend, and you have to give him advice.' Kerr did not laugh often, but when he did, he did not hold back. He roared with laughter at the thought of Jack, with one Frontier expedition to his name, advising one of the most experienced men in the army.

Jack could not help his rueful smile. He had not asked for the posting. He did not want the posting, but orders were orders. He had no choice except to do his duty as best he could.

'My darling wife,' Jack penned a hurried note to Mary. *'I am off on my travels again. This time I am posted to the staff of General Chamberlain, who is, I am sure you know, one of the most distinguished officers in India. I still hold out hope of leave once this present emergency is over, so do not despair. As soon as we dispose of the threat of these Warriors of God, I should be back to your loving arms.'*

Jack paused to nibble the end of his pen. He was never very good at voicing his emotions, let alone writing them down. What would Mary wish to hear? What could he tell her about his experiences that would allow her into his life without unduly alarming her?

'I have had some interesting times out here, which I will tell you about more fully when next we meet. The Pashtun people are entirely different from those we know so well. You will be pleased to know that I was entertained by our old friend Batoor for a while.

I must close now, as I am due to meet General Chamberlain soon and must get washed and brushed up to look my best.
Give young Andrew a hug from his father, and I send all my love to you.
Your affectionate husband,
Jack.'

Reading the letter, Jack knew it was hardly adequate to express even a tenth of the love he held for Mary. He also knew that she would understand; she was Mary. She always understood. Making a decision, he pressed the blotter over the damp ink, folded the paper, sealed and addressed it.

Please, God, I see her in person soon and don't have to write any more letters. Yet he knew that was a vain hope. The government would not send out a man such as General Chamberlain unless they had a full-blown expedition in mind.

As Kerr had intimated, Chamberlain was a vastly experienced soldier. Wounded five times in the first Afghan War alone, he had since fought through the Gwalior War and the second Sikh War, doing great execution at the battle of Gujerat. More recently he had been wounded again during the terrible fighting around Delhi during the Mutiny. Jack had never met him, although his name had been mentioned on numerous occasions.

* * *

'Well, Windrush.' Looking far older than his forty-three years, Chamberlain had recently fought off a bout of malaria, as the yellowish tinge of his skin proved. 'You are to be on my staff as an advisor.' He smoothed a finger across his neat little moustache. 'Damned nonsense, of course; I have forgotten more about this Frontier than you will ever know.'

'I do appreciate that, sir,' Jack said. 'However, I may have some pertinent information.'

'You may,' Chamberlain said. 'We will discuss that later.' Although he sighed like an old man, Jack saw bright humour behind the weariness. 'I really hoped for a less demanding post, but it looks as if my last days in India are to be spent in fatigue and exposure. I would much rather turn my sword into a shepherd's crook. However, if duty really requires the sacrifice, I cannot repine.' He sighed deeply. 'All right, Windrush, if you are to be on my staff, then you should share the intelligence we have.'

Chamberlain glanced around the room as if fearing one of the Mujahidin may be listening under the table. 'You know that the fanatics are back at Sitani. Evidently, I need to take a more forceful approach if we are to eradicate this poison once and for all.'

'Yes, sir.' Jack studied the map of North West India and the Frontier that Chamberlain unrolled on the table.

'We must attack them from the north.' Chamberlain stabbed down his finger with some force. 'That way the Fanatics have two choices. They can stand and fight us when we will slaughter them to the last man, or they can run across the Indus, where our army in Hazara can destroy them.'

'Having seen some Ghazis, sir; I am sure that they will fight.'

Chamberlain stroked his moustache again. 'You've met our Ghazis, have you? I hope they do fight, Windrush. There can only be one outcome for any native force standing against a British Army; inevitable defeat.'

'The Afghans destroyed Elphinstone's army, sir,' Jack dared to remind the general. 'And the Sikhs gave us plenty hard knocks.'

'I was present at both, and we were ultimately successful.' Chamberlain treated Jack to a chilling stare.

'Yes, sir.' Having said his piece, Jack thought it diplomatic to let the general have the last word.

'We will base our Yusufzai Field Force here, in the Chamla Valley.' Chamberlain indicated a valley about twenty miles north of Mardan, deep in the northern hills. 'Although they can muster some ten thousand fighting men, the Bunerwal tribe there has shown no hostility to us.'

'Yes, sir. I have heard they are a warlike bunch toward other Pashtuns, though. If they are pressed, they retaliate.'

'Yes, indeed. You are holding something back, Captain. Say what you think.' Chamberlain's voice was sharp. 'Your duty is to advise me!'

'Have we ever had an expedition there, sir? I've never heard of one.'

Chamberlain shook his head. 'Not that I am aware of, Windrush. As I said, they have shown no hostility to us.'

'I think they may be friendly because we have left them in peace, sir. From what I have seen of the Pashtun, they want the freedom to live their own lives without any outside interference.'

'You're an opinionated beggar, aren't you, Windrush? What you say may be correct,' Chamberlain allowed. 'However, there is no help for it. We must chance a smaller evil in the hope of averting a greater.' Chamberlain glanced at Jack to ensure he was paying attention. 'To get to the Chamla Valley, we have to cross this range of hills that stretches from the south-western spurs of the Mahabun Mountains to the Guru Mountains.'

Jack studied the map. He was growing used to the tangle of rocky hills that made up the Frontier. 'I can see three passes, sir.' He marked them with his finger. 'There is the Ambela, the Kanpoor and the Daran.'

'That's correct, Windrush,' Chamberlain agreed. 'We know virtually nothing about the Kanpoor; certainly, we lack sufficient knowledge to march an army through it. When Cotton explored the Daran, he thought the tribes extremely hostile and the road impossible for artillery, so that only leaves the Ambela. A two-day forced march should see us through the pass.'

'Which tribe claims the Ambela Pass, sir?' Jack studied the map again. 'Is it the Bunerwals again?'

'It is,' Chamberlain said. 'My local informants tell me that the Bunerwals dislike the Fanatics as much as we do. I presume that they suffer from their raiding; neighbours on the Frontier are seldom the best of friends.'

'That is certain, sir. Most feuds seem to be among neighbours.'

'Quite so, Windrush.' Chamberlain nodded. 'I will command some five thousand men, including one hundred sabres of the Guides and the 11th Bengal Cavalry, plus the 71st Highlanders, the 101st Royal Bengal Fusiliers, six battalions of the Frontier Force, Sikh Pioneers and artillery.'

Jack nodded. 'That is a formidable force, sir.'

'I hope it is sufficiently formidable to overawe the tribes and smash the Fanatics,' Chamberlain said. 'I will advance with two separate columns. I'll send a column to protect the Indus; we'll call that the Hazara column. I will lead the main force, which we'll call the Peshawar column.' Lifting a stick, Chamberlain traced his planned route on the map.

'While the Hazara column ensures the tribes around the Indus remain quiet, the Peshawar column will march to Nawakili, a few miles from the Daran Pass. The Fanatics will think we are emulating Cotton's route and prepare to receive us there. Once we reach the Daran, we will swing around and march for the Ambela Pass.'

'The Pashtuns can move faster than us, sir,' Jack reminded him.

'I am well aware of that, Windrush. We must do what we can. Now, make yourself useful. I want you to collate all the intelligence reports that our spies and agents hand in. I doubt you'll find anything out of the ordinary, but it will keep you occupied. Oh, and find us sufficient transport for 5,600 men plus guns.'

In the Army, Jack knew, he could be attacking a heavily defended position one day and acting as nursemaid to the officers' wives the next. It was typical of the Army to casually order him to do two jobs at once, both vitally important, and one utterly time-consuming. Cursing the gods of fate that had sent him to the Frontier, Jack took a deep breath, reminded himself that he must do his duty, begged Major Kerr to lend him Hassan to do the legwork, and buckled down.

Finding transport for such a large force on the North West Frontier was not easy. Now more experienced in the reality of travelling in Pakhtunkhwa, the first thing Jack did was buy himself a stout Khyber pony that could carry him over all except the sternest of mountains. After that, Jack immersed himself in the commissariat aspect of soldiering. He was aware that although fighting was the ultimate object of a soldier's job, the Army had to get him to his destination and ensure he was adequately fed, watered and equipped at all times.

Just as Jack was getting to grips with the transport situation, the intelligence reports began to arrive. Most were of a routine nature, talking of the difficulties of the different routes, the lack of fodder, and the population of the various villages which the British columns would have to pass. Every so often, Jack found himself reading something more interesting. He placed his reports into two classifications: Group A, which were the mundane, and Group B, which were the significant.

The first of the Group B reports came from a Guide patrol, mentioning a sighting of Mujahidin in the Ambela Valley. Jack put that report to one side. When a second Guide report spoke of a mullah with a tabla drum, Jack became more concerned. *Damn! I thought I had killed that man! He must have only been wounded.* Where that mullah appeared, trouble invariably followed.

Sending an account of the two pieces of intelligence to Chamberlain, Jack ordered the patrols to look for more activity by the Mujahidin in the Ambela Valley, and particularly to watch for the tabla mullah.

It was Hassan who made the next breakthrough. 'I happened to be passing through the villages, sahib,' he said smoothly, 'and spoke to one of the men here.'

Jack translated that as meaning Hassan was engaged in a personal blood feud, and his enemy had given him information under some compulsion. 'What did you learn, Hassan?'

'There is a Jirga planned in the Chamla Valley, sahib.' Hassan stood at attention beside the battered plank table that Jack used as a desk. 'The Mujahidin have sent envoys to the Bunerwals.'

'Do you know why, Hassan? Do you know what they are going to talk about?'

'Yes, sahib,' Hassan said. 'The Mujahidin wish to persuade the Bunerwals to join them in a jihad.'

Jack had expected nothing else. 'I'd like to be a fly on the wall at that Jirga.' He smiled at Hassan's confusion. 'I mean I would like to hear what they say, Hassan.'

Hassan nodded, wordless, but Jack wondered what thoughts were behind his expressionless blue eyes.

Chamberlain's frown deepened as he listened to Jack's report. 'Thank you, Windrush.'

'I could go along to the Jirga, sir.' Jack felt the usual mixture of sick despair and high elation as he volunteered to venture into one of the most dangerous places on earth.

'That would be suicidal.' Chamberlain turned down the idea without a second thought. 'Who do you think you are? Sekundar Burnes? Remember what happened to him?'

'Yes, sir.' Captain Sir Alexander Burnes was a Scottish explorer and diplomat who surveyed the Indus and explored Afghanistan. He was the first British diplomat to Bokhara and advised the British to support Dost Mohammed on the Afghan throne rather than Shah Shuja. If Lord Auckland had listened to Burnes, the disaster of the First Afghan War might have been avoided. As it was, Burnes died heroically when the Afghans rose against the British and the ruler they imposed.

'So we'll have no more clandestine operations among these people, Windrush.' Chamberlain closed the subject. 'There is sufficient evidence to warn us to alter our plans. As you are aware, we were originally informed that the Bunerwals were more inclined to support us than the Fanatics. Now you have found out that the Fanatics are working with the Bunerwals, spreading their idea of jihad.' Chamberlain's grin did not fool Jack for a moment. 'It would be more sensible to restrict our movements.'

Jack nodded. He knew it would be foolish to offer advice to a general. He had already learned that on the Frontier; the situation was always fluid. While part of him was relieved that he would not be venturing into the Chamla Valley, he also felt that the situation was not yet proven. Although he trusted Hassan's information, he would have preferred to hear the mullah's words for himself.

Chamberlain continued: 'Rather than attacking the Fanatics in their valley fastnesses, we will attack the villages they infest.'

'Yes, sir.'

Chamberlain looked older than ever. 'We will rid the country of this particular poison, Windrush, although knowing the Pashtun as I do, there will be other mullahs coming along in their wake.'

Jack nodded. He knew that Chamberlain had made up his mind. Nothing a mere captain said would influence the general's decision.

'We will advance by the Ambela Pass into the Chamla Valley.'

The die was cast, the cards were dealt; now the soldiers, the ultimate expression of Queen Victoria's imperial will, would march. Jack took a deep breath. He was going to war once more. *We belong to God, and unto God do we return.* Jack shook his head. No, he would use the old 113th slogan: *Cry Havelock and let loose the dogs of war.*

CHAPTER FOURTEEN

North west frontier 19th October 1863

'It's a shambles,' Jack said. They stood at the base camp with the mountains of the Frontier rising before them. All around, the land seethed with activity, with infantry preparing to march, the artillery checking their equipment, and the cavalry feeding their horses. Great elephants trumpeted as their mahouts fastened the carts and artillery they would have to pull. Camels spat, roared, bubbled and refused to move while the discordant braying of mules sounded everywhere. A host of soldiers, British, Gurkha and Indian, waited in increasing impatience for the order to move. Jack walked over to have a word with the Guides.

'Halloa there, Windrush.' Major Kerr fixed him with his gimlet stare. 'Are you joining us?'

'I don't know what I'm doing,' Jack said honestly. 'I seem to be a bit of everything and a lot of nothing.'

'That's life on the staff for you,' Kerr said. 'Take my advice, man, and get back into regimental duty.'

'I doubt that a Queen's regiment would have me,' Jack said. Not many officers' messes would accept a man with a half-Indian wife, while Mary would live an isolated and uncomfortable life with the other wives.

'Try the Guides, Windrush. My lads liked you, and they are particular who they serve with.'

Jack appreciated the compliment. The Guides did not take to every officer. 'Thank you, Major. I may do that.' He missed the men of the 113th, his old regiment. He would relish that personal contact with soldiers again, being part of the minutiae of their lives, their daily problems and triumphs. With the Guides, he would be part of the Punjab Frontier Force, permanently stationed on or near the Frontier. He would belong. But did he want to belong to a sepoy regiment? Try as he might, Jack could not shake away the memory of the opening weeks of the Mutiny, when regiments who had been part of the Company's forces for a century and more attacked their British officers. He remembered the horrors of the sack of Gondabad where he and Elliot had rescued Mary from the rampaging sepoys. Could he ever fully trust a sepoy regiment again, let alone serve in one and have Mary and young Andrew at their mercy?

'Think about it.' Kerr puffed on his cheroot. 'You look a trifle agitated, Windrush. What's bothering you?'

'I've never been on the commissariat side of the army before,' Jack said. 'It's a blasted shambles. We're advancing into the Frontier, and half the artillery pieces are useless. The general has ordered them sent back, as well as the five-and-a-half-inch mortars.'

'We're weak in artillery then,' Kerr said. 'Not good when we're out here.' He glanced at the heights that frowned down on them. 'Let's hope the Bunerwals have resisted the Mujahidin advances and remain friendly to us. If they turn hostile, we'll have to fight our way through some very ugly territory.'

Jack nodded. 'The general used to think the Bunerwals preferred us to the Mujahidin. Now he is not so sure.'

'My boys are convinced that the Mujahidin have infiltrated the Bunerwals,' Kerr said. 'As Hassan told you, there have been mullahs parading around the Chamla Valley, including your famous tabla mullah.'

'I thought I had killed that man,' Jack said. 'I shot him clear.' He shook his head. 'I have often wondered if one man is behind all this unrest, and that fellow seems to turn up wherever there is trouble.'

Kerr nodded. 'He certainly seems to be a man to watch.' Kerr watched as a troop of Guides cavalry formed up, each man riding proud. 'Religion is a unifying force with the Pashtun. Please, God, it can be a force for good.' He gave a wry smile. 'Did you realise that Caspar, one of the Three Wise Men, was from this part of the world?'

'I did not.' Jack wondered if Mary knew about Caspar.

'The Acts of Thomas in the Apocrypha call him Gudapharasa, and local legend says he founded Kandahar, just a few miles away in Afghanistan.'

Trust an Ulsterman to know his Bible and all facts related to it. Jack looked around. The army was forming up, the Guides Cavalry at the forefront, as was right and proper, with the 11th Bengal Cavalry backing them up. Jack looked at their faces, pushing away the memory of the sepoys running amok in Gondabad, killing civilians. That black day was passed now; these men had proved their loyalty. Hassan, Zaman and the others had not put a foot wrong when they had accompanied him to Torkrud and on that tortuous journey back. He was wrong to doubt them, yet he knew that the shadow of distrust remained.

As officers and NCOs began to bark orders, the infantry formed up, blocks of scarlet and khaki with rifles held ready. The Guides Infantry were there, stolid, proud of the red piping on their uniforms that highlighted the part they played in the Siege of Delhi. Beside the Guides were the 20th (Punjabi) Native Infantry including the Sikhs, to Jack's mind some of the most stolid infantry in the world. The British infantry was nearby, lean, with the nut-brown faces of long-term professionals, eyeing the mountains with neither fear nor favour.

After a single, searching scrutiny of his Guides cavalry, Kerr signalled for his horse. 'Have you been to Taxila, near Islamabad, Windrush?'

'No.' Jack had never heard of the place.

'Take your Mary there, she'll be interested,' Kerr said. 'It was on the old Silk Road. There's a tradition that one of the Magi passed through on the way to the Holy Land.' He mounted his horse. On foot he was a stocky, slightly cumbersome man; mounted, he looked like a centaur, an extension of the horse. 'We won't be as famous as the three wise men, Windrush, but let's try and make a bit of a name for ourselves!' When he grinned, his basilisk eyes brightened with the crazed joy of soldiering. 'You already have a reputation from Sevastopol and Lucknow, Jack-my-lad. Now you can add to it on the Frontier. Ho, now; here's mischief coming our way.'

'So I see.' Jack watched as the galloper pushed through a section of Sikh infantry, and reined up, his face alight with excitement. 'Are you Captain Windrush?'

'I am.'

'General Chamberlain wants you.'

'Who are you?' Jack grabbed hold of the galloper's reins before he rode off.

'Cornet Aubrey Cheshire.' The cornet looked down at Jack.

'You call me sir, cornet.' Jack spoke softly but with an edge to his voice.

About to kick in his spurs, the cornet looked into Jack's eyes, and quickly changed his mind. 'Yes, sir.'

'Now report properly.' Jack knew that the members of some Queen's regiments thought themselves superior to men who served in units of the Indian Army, even the Guides. He made it his business to alter that misconception.

'Yes, sir.' Cornet Cheshire coloured as Kerr also stared at him. 'General Chamberlain sends his respects, sir, and could you attend to him at your earliest convenience.'

'That's better, cornet. You're only a Griff. Don't give yourself airs and graces out here; they won't last long. And you rode through the Sikhs as if they were unimportant. Don't ever treat the Sikhs like that again; they are better men and finer soldiers than you will ever be. Now cut along and try to look like you're useful.'

Red-faced, Cornet Cheshire trotted away.

'Well said, Windrush.' A Sikh officer nodded to Jack. His men were all watching, their bearded faces impassive, yet Jack knew they had heard every word. 'Some of my men were in the Khalsa.'

Jack included the Sikh infantry as he returned the nod. 'I thought they looked like true soldiers.' He saw the grins; the Sikhs recognised his appreciation. 'I fought beside Sikhs in the Mutiny. Few better.'

'None better,' the officer corrected. He shook his head. 'These young ringtail griffs now; they are not the same quality as they used to be.' He lowered his voice. 'Nor are the British regiments, I fear.'

Jack said nothing to that. He had heard similar concerns voiced before. Thinking of the quality of the Highlanders at Lucknow and the Connaught Rangers outside Sevastopol, he wondered if any soldiers could reach these heights again. 'I hope we are both wrong in thinking that.'

'Aye; well, you'd better report to the general, Captain.'

Jack turned to say his farewells to Kerr, but the major had already ridden to join his Guides. Once again, Jack realised that he wished to belong to a regiment.

'Windrush.' Chamberlain looked younger now the campaign had properly started. There was bright humour in his eyes. 'Ride with the advance column; when they meet with the men I have sent to guard the Daran Pass, send a galloper to inform me.'

'Yes, sir.'

'Pray inform the advance column they have to halt at the entrance to the Ambela Pass. They must wait there for the main body to arrive.'

'Yes, sir.' Jack prepared to kick in his heels. 'Sir, Major Kerr informs me that his Guides also believe the Mujahidin have been attempting to suborn the Bunerwals.'

Chamberlain nodded. 'That confirms the intelligence you gathered, Windrush. Let's hope that the Bunerwals have enough sense not to listen to them. The last thing we need is to have to fight our way through the passes.' He straightened his shoulders. 'But if we have to, then we shall.'

'Yes, sir.' Jack rode on. To his mind, cornets carried messages, not captains with a dozen years of experience behind them. However, orders were orders, like it or not.

'General Chamberlain sends his respects,' he reported to Colonel Wilde, in command of the advance force. 'Could you halt the advance body at the entrance to the Ambela Pass?'

Wilde barely nodded. 'Will do, Windrush.' He nodded to the surrounding hills. 'The locals look a bit agitated.'

From the glowering heights, parties of lean men with jezzails sat or stood, watching Wilde's advance force move toward the Ambela Pass. Jack trotted over to the Guides cavalry, at the front of Wilde's men. 'Hassan,' he called. 'Who are these men?'

'Bunerwals,' Hassan said without hesitation. 'They have not fired on us yet. They will if we enter the Pass.'

'Thank you, Hassan.' Wheeling his horse, Jack thought it best to report himself, so galloped back to Chamberlain. 'The Bunerwals have pickets out to watch us, sir.'

'They will have.' Chamberlain accepted the information. 'Do they look hostile?'

'They are all armed, sir, but nobody has fired on us yet. The Guides believe they might if we enter the Pass.'

'Very good, Windrush. Let's hope our main body can get a blasted move on. We have to penetrate the pass by noon, for God's sake.' Chamberlain hesitated only a moment. 'Bunerwals or no Bunerwals.'

'Yes, sir.'

Chamberlain's main body was three hours behind the advance force, struggling to haul the artillery over the ever-worsening road. Jack watched as the elephants failed to find sufficient space, with the mahouts who sat behind the elephant's ears urging them on with the pointed sticks they carried.

'Wilde's men will be isolated unless we push along,' Chamberlain said. 'I don't like to leave a small body alone on the Frontier.'

To Jack, it was evident that Chamberlain's experiences during the Afghan War haunted him. 'Wilde's a good man, sir, with good quality troops.'

'That I don't doubt,' Chamberlain said. 'We'd get on faster if we leave the guns behind, but we need all the firepower we can get out here.'

Remembering his earlier conversation about the failing quality of British infantry, Jack studied the men as they marched past. The 71st Highland Light Infantry moved at a fair pace. Lithe, gaunt-faced men in tartan trews and scarlet jackets, they looked as capable as any infantry Jack had ever seen. But this was a veteran regiment; they had fought in Crimea and in the latter parts of the Mutiny, although Jack had not been associated with them in either of these wars. Looking at their grim, set faces, Jack was glad he was not facing them in battle.

Then came the 101st Royal Bengal Fusiliers, a regiment that the Honourable East

India Company had raised in 1652, and which had been transferred to the British Army after the demise of that company. The regiment had a proud history, having fought at Plassey, the first Afghan war and in Burma in 1852 as well as distinguishing itself in the terrible actions around Delhi during the Mutiny. With many experienced men having left in protest at the transfer to crown control, hundreds of ringtails, young recruits now filled the ranks. Jack was unsure whether griffins could cope with the conditions on the Frontier.

Pulling aside Sharbat, his Kabul pony, Jack watched as three battalions of Punjab infantry, stolid, professional and mainly Sikh, marched past. They would fight, whatever the odds. Jack had every respect for the Sikhs. They had not joined in the Mutiny, and nor had the Gurkhas, who came next.

Jack spent the remainder of that day passing on messages or gathering intelligence from unit commanders and scouts. He spoke to the ranking soldiers as well as the officers. The men may have had a limited view of events, and were often starved of information from the top, but an experienced NCO could gauge what was happening. Their comments had always given Jack an insight into their morale, helping him decide what was possible. It was the ordinary men who provided the sharp edge of any army and without them, there was only hot air and ideological rhetoric.

As the main body pushed on, the road petered into nothingness as the surrounding hills increased in size. Jack realised that leading a small body of very mobile horsemen in this terrain was vastly different from forcing through an army. The Frontier could have been designed specifically for defence, with every rock a possible hiding place and every ridge a potential ambush spot.

'Windrush.' Chamberlain seemed determined to use Jack at every opportunity. 'Ride ahead; see if Colonel Wilde has secured the head of the pass yet.'

Once again, Jack kicked his heels, and Sharbat responded willingly. She was not as fast or as attractive as Colwall, but there was no doubt she had a stout heart. Jack waited for the ribald comments that the 113th or Campbell's Highlanders would have shouted as he passed, but neither the 71st nor the 101st responded. Jack frowned, wondering if the Sikh officer had been correct. He hoped that British infantry had not lost their spirit.

The Ambela pass rose before him, narrow, craggy and stern, with towering pine trees straggling up the rocky slopes. When a picket of Guides infantry challenged him, Jack responded with a wave.

'Captain Windrush, sometimes attached to the Guides. I'm off to find Colonel Wilde.'

'He's about a mile ahead, making a secure base for the general sahib.' The Guide was a Mohmand with deep brown eyes. 'Watch for snipers, sahib. The Bunerwals can be treacherous.'

'Thank you, I will.' Jack rode on.

Wilde looked concerned when Jack reined up. 'Pray inform the general that the Bunerwals do not appreciate our presence, Windrush.' He pointed to the crags that lowered over them. 'The Guides have reported an ominous number of them in small parties and large.'

'Have they attacked you, sir?' Jack asked.

'Not yet, Windrush. I think it's only a matter of time.' Wilde looked behind him. 'In this terrain, it's essential we control the heights, and for that we need artillery. I believe we sent some back.'

'Yes, sir. The guns were not functional.'

'Guns that don't work are no blasted good to me.' Wilde preened his whiskers. 'I don't know what this army is coming to. Don't report that to General Chamberlain though, Windrush; he knows what he is doing.'

Jack could feel the brittle tension in the air. Fir trees dotted the slopes, affording cover to any Bunerwal, with date trees and wild figs lower down. To Jack, the combination of vegetation encompassed the region, a mixture of near-Alpine and sub-tropical that typified the Pashtun people themselves, an amalgam of intense fierceness and deep family loyalty. His time with the Guides had heightened his ability to spot movement, so he could observe the tribesmen on the hills. He saw a patch of shade on the wrong side of a rock, a flash on sunlight on metal, the branch of a tree shifting against the breeze. 'This is the most fascinating place in the world.' Jack had not intended to voice his thoughts.

'Aye, and the most dangerous.' Wilde did not flinch at the deep thud of a jezzail. 'Here we go. The Bunerwals have opened the ball; it could be a typical Pashtun shot for shikar or the beginning of something much bigger.' He looked at Jack through jaundiced eyes. 'You'd better warn the general that I expect trouble here.'

By the time Jack returned to the main body, he knew the road between Wilde's force and the main army very well.

Chamberlain grunted at Jack's news. 'If Colonel Wilde expects trouble, then trouble there will be.' He looked backwards, where the elephants were toiling to find space on the narrow track. 'Get these blasted guns moving, Windrush!'

Feeling more like a messenger than a soldier, Windrush carried Chamberlain's instructions.

'Please inform the general that we're as quick as we can be,' the reply came. 'Does he want us to carry the damned things on our backs?'

'Do that.' Chamberlain had followed Jack. 'Do anything that is necessary. I won't have my men exposed to long-range fire without the ability to retaliate.' He turned to Jack. 'I saw enough of this business back in '41, Windrush. The Pashtun are not people you can give an inch to. They are the most perfect warriors.'

'We have better rifles now, sir. Back in '41, the Afghans jezzails outranged our old Brown Bess muskets. Now our rifles are better than theirs.'

Chamberlain replied with one word: 'Tazhak.'

'Indeed, sir,' Jack said.

'Get the artillery moving, Windrush.'

'Yes, sir.' Jack could understand Chamberlain's agitation. Having seen one British army with all its camp followers massacred, he had no wish to preside over the loss of another.

The guns struggled onwards, with the men pushing, carrying what they could, sweating until their uniforms were stained black. Still, the main body made painfully slow progress, so they were much later than planned when the two forces finally merged. Chamberlain called a meeting of his senior officers and staff with Jack, as a lowly captain, standing on the outside of the ring.

Chamberlain surveyed his officers and the surrounding hills. 'Gentlemen, I have decided on a change of plan. With our present slow rate of progress, I no longer intend to penetrate into the Chamla Valley. Tonight we will set up camp at the summit of the Ambela Pass.'

Jack nodded approval. With night fast approaching, it would be foolish to push a cumbersome column into the territory of a tribe that was appearing more hostile by the hour.

'Colonel Wilde, send out pickets to secure these heights.' Chamberlain pointed to surrounding hills.

'I have already done so, sir.' Wilde was an experienced man. Jack saw the khaki turbans of the Guides infantry bobbing among the pine trees and rocks.

'I'll post the mountain guns on the high ground in the morning,' Chamberlain said. 'At present, the gunners are too exhausted to do anything.'

The British camp was just to the right, the south, of the ridge of the Ambela Pass, at the head of a couple of small streams that flowed into a river, presumably the Chamla, Jack thought. On the right was ridge after wooded ridge that climbed to the peaks of the Mahabun Mountains. To their left, the five-thousand-feet-high Guru Mountains frowned over them, appearing sinister in the gathering dark, with a British piquet occupying an outlying spur.

'That place is like an eagle's nest,' Kerr said.

'That's as good a name for it as any.' Jack was busy with his binoculars.

To the northeast, at the tip of the roughly oval British camp, was Standard Point, from where the multi-crossed Union flag would be hoisted at daybreak. Beyond that, to the southeast, another knoll rose, covered with pines and rocks. The British soldiers had already christened it Crag Piquet, with Water Piquet slightly to the south, and less well-protected. To the south, east of these hills, was a double-peaked conical hill. By the time Jack focussed his binoculars on that hill, the light had faded away.

When the meeting broke up, Jack mounted Sharbat once more and rode to the summit of the Ambela Pass. To the south, dim in the distance, glittering lights sugared the plain of Yusafzai.

I stand on the border between one civilisation and another. On one side I have a gradually improving land of trade and industry under British protection. On the other, there are tribes, wild and free. I am like a Roman legionnaire guarding Hadrian's Wall from the Picts, but what did Calgagus say when he opposed Agricola's army at Mons Graupius? The Romans make a desert and call it peace. Are we seeking to make a desert of Pakhtunwali? Are we attempting to alter a culture that is happier to be left alone?

Riding back into camp, Jack saw Chamberlain frowning at him. 'Windrush, first thing tomorrow I want you to accompany Colonel Taylor of the Engineers and Lieutenant Sandeman on a reconnaissance.'

'Yes, sir.' *It seems that life on the staff does not mean beer and skittles. At least I am being useful.*

Although he knew he might be riding into the open jaws of a tiger, Jack was glad to go. Anything was better than being used as a glorified runner. As he lay on his charpoy, Jack wrote another letter to Mary, sealing it with a sigh. He did not say much, but he felt closer to her when he wrote.

I have no idea when you will get this. I hope this is a short campaign, but I must do my duty.

As always on the Frontier, Jack did not undress and tied his revolver to his wrist. Even deep in the British camp, with guards patrolling the perimeter, he knew that the local thieves could sneak in if they chose to. He sighed; was this what he had missed when working in Gondabad?

Lieutenant-Colonel Dighton Probyn commanded the escort for the reconnaissance. A handsome man wearing the obligatory beard, he stood with his head slightly down and looked to Jack like a brooding eagle. 'So you're Windrush,' he said when Jack reported to him.

'Yes, sir,' Jack admitted. He surveyed the straight-nosed, steady-eyed man who had won the Victoria Cross for acts of incredible bravery during the late Mutiny. *This is another of these iron men we throw up so casually.*

'You did good work at Lucknow,' Probyn said. 'I didn't know you were on the Frontier.'

'I'm fairly new here, sir.'

Probyn nodded. 'Aye; you'll find it's not the same as fighting under Colin Campbell.'

'I've found that already,' Jack said.

Probyn's eyes softened a little. 'We both know that you should be more advanced in rank, Windrush, after your exploits.'

Jack knew he could not afford to purchase promotion. 'Perhaps I have reached my ceiling, Colonel.'

Probyn frowned. 'Perhaps the Bunerwals will welcome us with open arms and psalms of praise, but I doubt that, too, Windrush. Come on.' Kicking in his heels, he inspected his men and took up a position at the head of the reconnaissance force.

With Probyn's green-turbaned 1st Sikh Irregular Cavalry, known as Probyn's Horse, riding loosely around the column, Colonel Taylor led them down the pass and into the Chamla Valley. Jack kept one hand near the hilt of his revolver as he saw the Bunerwals watching from behind rocks, or occasionally standing in the open, not responding to any greetings from Taylor's men.

'They're just watching us,' Probyn said, 'as if they are waiting for something to happen. What do you think, Windrush?'

'I think they're counting our numbers,' Jack said. 'They're wondering how strong we are, and if we are likely to fight, or run.'

'We'll know soon enough.' Probyn pointed to a ridge. 'That saddle-back is what we know as the Kotal. On the opposite side is Buner, which these lads call home. If the Bunerwals are as friendly as we hope, it will be nearly empty. If they distrust us, the warriors will have occupied it to prevent us from coming too close.'

Jack saw the flash of sunlight on steel. He focussed his binoculars. 'They're there.' He saw an array of turbans and long robes as the warriors stood on the ridge, making no attempt to hide from the small British patrol. A slight wind ruffled the dun clothes of the Bunerwals, giving a rippling effect to the men who stood watching.

'How many?' Probyn's casual tone did not fool Jack.

'A couple of hundred,' Jack said. 'They are shifting around. Capable-looking lads, however many there are. They're making sure that we can see them.'

'All the Pashtuns are capable lads,' Probyn said. 'Two hundred, eh? And ensuring they're visible. The Bunerwals are sending us a message, Windrush. It's like our gamekeepers, they are saying: Keep out, no trespassing.'

Jack lowered his binoculars. 'Perhaps we should have sent a note asking permission first. "Please Mr Bunerwal, please may we crash through your valley with thousands of men, guns and elephants so we can attack your neighbours." '

'There's no perhaps about it, Windrush. That's exactly what we should have done. I fear that we have turned a neutral tribe into an enemy when God knows we have more than sufficient enemies in this part of the world.' He touched the hilt of his sword. 'Pray that Chamberlain does not do an Elphinstone and lead us to disaster.'

'He seemed to know what he is doing,' Jack said. 'He's very experienced.'

Probyn released his sword. 'Let's hope so, Jack, let's hope so. Pass over your binoculars. There's a good lad.'

The even more casual use of his Christian name alerted Jack to Probyn's concern. He handed over the binoculars without a word as he continued to scan his surroundings. Somewhere on the Kotal, a drum began to throb.

'I thought so.' Probyn spoke without emotion. 'While we've been riding around showing the flag, the Bunerwals have been busy. Do you see that broken ground between us and the head of the pass? Look at that area of rocks and ravines that overlooks the camp.'

'I see it.' Jack felt the sudden surge of mixed fear and excitement that always marked the prelude to action. He wished that the men of his old 113th were around him. He missed the stolid security of O'Neill, the foul-mouthed aggression of Logan, the banter of Thorpe and Coleman. He drew a deep breath. They were not here; with service in the army being what it was, he would probably never see them again.

'The Bunerwals are there, waiting for us. I hope you are ready to fight, Windrush.'

'Oh, aye, always ready.' Jack tried to sound as casual as Probyn. The drumming was louder now. Was the tabla mullah with the Bunerwals? Or was there another drummer?

'Ride in front, Jack, while I get the lads ready.' Probyn's grin was of pure delight. The elemental warrior was at home in this sort of situation. 'Now you'll see why Probyn's Horse is the best in the business.'

Did every unit in the army believe it was the best? Jack did not speak his thoughts as Probyn wheeled away to attend to his men. Jack knew that the Guides considered themselves to be the elite, as did the Guards, while every regiment knew that they were superior to every other. Even his own 113th had boosted their credentials at the battle of Inkerman and during the Mutiny.

Glancing over his shoulder, Jack saw Probyn's Horse forming up, the bearded faces eager as they drew their swords. Taylor and Sandeman pulled back. Probyn kissed the guard of his sword in a melodramatic gesture that belonged to the Middle Ages rather than the industrialised nineteenth century. 'Are you with us, Jack?'

That was a challenge Jack could not refuse without damaging his reputation. 'I've never been in a cavalry charge.' He had to raise his voice above the increasing pounding of the horses' hooves. 'I'll just follow your lead.'

'Good man!' There was sheer joy in Probyn's face as he gave the next order. 'Remember, Jack, slash and cut, don't thrust. If your blade gets deep into somebody, it's hard to disengage unless you twist your wrist and ride on. You are vulnerable at that time. There is nothing a Pashtun warrior likes better than a vulnerable British soldier.' He grinned again. 'If you run a man through on the move, you either break your sword or are unhorsed because you can't get the damned thing out.'

'I'll remember.' Holding the reins in his left hand, Jack clutched the hilt of his sword. It felt rough and clumsy.

'Try to remember. It might save your life.' Probyn raised his voice. 'Bugler, sound the advance.'

Jack remembered watching the Heavy Brigade advance at Balaclava and the headlong charge of the Light Brigade into a valley where Russian artillery dominated on three sides. He had never thought to take part in such an event himself.

The bugle sounded again, the shrill notes raising the small hairs on the back of Jack's neck. He heard the increasing drumming of hooves behind him, the jingle of bridles, the quick snort of a horse, and the subdued laugh of a nervous trooper. 'Let the horse lead, Jack.' Probyn spoke quietly.

Jack did not need to force his smile. 'We're fine, Probyn. We're just waiting for your orders.'

'Canter!' Probyn commanded. The bugler blew again, and the horsemen increased their speed. Now Jack was aware of nothing except the men around him, the feel of the horse beneath, and the land speeding past. Somebody was shouting, the words formless in the air. With the reins in his left hand, Jack tightened his grip on the hilt of his sword.

This exhilaration was different from the slow, impersonal advance of British infantry, or even the terrifying frenzy of a bayonet charge. It felt mediaeval, as if he were a Crusader knight charging the Saracens, or one of William the Conqueror's Normans advancing against the Saxon shield-ring at Hastings. For the first time, he could understand the attraction of the cavalry.

'Sound the charge!' Probyn yelled. 'Follow me, lads! Show them the best regiment in the world!'

The bugler called again, the cords of his neck standing out as he blew the charge. Jack drew his sword. He did not know what he yelled as Sharbat bounded forward with the other horses. *I wish I had Colwall rather than this pony, but too late now.* Riding at his best speed, Jack hardly saw the Bunerwals as they fired their jezzails or rose from cover to face Probyn's Horse, pulwar and circular shields in hand.

As Probyn had said, the ground was broken, with outcrops of rock amidst rough grass, the occasional tree or group of trees and small holes that would trap the ankles of a horse. Jack saw a Bunerwal appear from behind a boulder to lunge at him with a Khyber knife, parried with a swing of his sabre, felt the shock of steel on steel, and then he was past, with the force of the exchange having driven the Bunerwal back a pace. Jack had to tug madly at the reins to avoid a shattered rock, flinched as something buzzed past his ear, heard the deep thump of a jezzail being fired, and swore as the ground fell abruptly away in front of him.

'Steady, Sharbat!' He hauled at the reins as his exhilaration altered to anxiety. He was an infantry soldier, not a cavalryman; neither he nor his horse was trained in this form of warfare.

The Bunerwal rushed at him from the left, pulwar in one hand, shield in the other. Still fighting to control Sharbat, Jack raised his sabre just in time to parry the Bunerwal's swing at his leg. Balancing on the stirrups, Jack twisted his blade, hoping to disarm the Bunerwal, but the warrior was skilled, withdrew his pulwar, and lunged with the point. Jack shifted sideways to avoid the blow, altered his grip on his sabre, and struck back-handed. The point sliced at the warrior's face, opening a long if shallow gash that sent the man reeling backwards. Jack seized the opportunity to steer Sharbat away from the ravine.

'They're running.' Probyn wiped blood from his sword. 'My boys have taken the position.' He looked around. 'I'll leave a few of the lads here and report to the general.'

'I wasn't much help, I'm afraid,' Jack said.

'You fought,' Probyn said. 'In your first cavalry action, nobody can ask more than that. Now you can tell your grandchildren that you rode with Probyn's Horse.'

Jack nodded. Suddenly he felt intensely weary, and that damned drumming had started again.

CHAPTER FIFTEEN

Ambela Pass September 1863

General Chamberlain sat on the folding camp chair behind his travelling desk, listening to Probyn's account of the patrol.

'You say the Bunerwals are guarding the Kotal.'

'Yes, sir,' Probyn said. 'They tried to prevent us from returning to camp, as well. I have left a strong picket at the point of action.'

'I'll send a couple of companies of infantry to relieve them.' Chamberlain gave the orders to a fresh-faced runner. 'That way if the Bunerwals try to return they'll find a hot reception waiting for them.' He stood up, stroking his moustache. 'The Bunerwals won't like being pushed aside in their own territory. They'll seek retribution.'

'I agree, sir. They'll attack us,' Probyn said. 'As sure as death, the Bunerwals will come at us either tonight or early tomorrow morning.'

'Then we'll have to be ready for them.' Chamberlain shouted for another runner. 'I'll order that the sentries are doubled and warn the men to keep alert.'

The precautions seemed sensible, although Jack would have preferred a more robust response. With the Pashtun, doubling the sentries hardly seemed sufficient.

'Well, Windrush.' Chamberlain noticed Jack at last. 'What intelligence can you add to what Colonel Probyn has already relayed to me?'

'I heard more drumming, sir. I wondered if the tabla mullah was with the Bunerwals.'

'Did you see him?' Chamberlain asked. 'Did you see him, Probyn?'

'No, sir, but we do know that the Mujahidin have been busy among the Bunerwals. Captain Windrush believes that one man is behind this outbreak and has seen this tabla fellow in various places.'

'You are the only man to have seen him, Windrush. Keep a lookout for him. Do you have anything else?' Chamberlain leaned forward to study the map that was spread out in front of him.

'The patrol proved that the Bunerwals are out in force, sir,' Jack said. 'Hassan, one of the Guides, told me that the Bunerwals believe we are here to annex their lands. That is what the Mujahidin have told them. I wonder if there is still time to talk to their khans, hold a Jirga to explain our actions, or we could have the whole tribe attacking us.'

Chamberlain glanced at Probyn and back to Jack. 'That may be an idea, Windrush, except it would delay us. Anyway, who is to say that the Fanatics have not already influenced them past the point of reason?' He nodded. 'No, Windrush, we will stick to our original plan.'

'Yes, sir.'

'Now, you get some rest.' Chamberlain said. 'I suspect that this campaign is just beginning. That little skirmish you had today will only be a preamble to what is to come.'

Jack thought of the man he had wounded. How many more men will be maimed or killed before this new horror is completed?

'You're looking pensive, Jack me boy!' Probyn appeared outside Jack's tent. 'I have a bottle to kill and nobody to help me drink it.' He looked at Jack closely. 'You're not one of these deeply religious temperance fellows, are you?'

'Not at all.' Jack knew that he should rest but also knew that he would not sleep that night.

'Good man!' Probyn grinned. 'You'll help me then? It's whisky of some sort. I got it from that Sawney regiment, the 71st Highlanders.'

'Trust the Sawneys to find whisky,' Jack said. 'They were the same outside Balaclava, while Campbell's boys at Lucknow used to make their own; only God knows how.'

'Turning water into wine, were they?' Probyn grinned at his weak joke.

'Come into my tent,' Jack invited.

'I sometimes wonder why we're here,' Jack said as he lounged on a basketwork chair with Probyn opposite, the level of whisky in the bottle fast diminishing. 'Oh, I know the theories about bringing civilisation to the heathen and all that sort of stuff, but the Indians had a civilisation when we still lived in caves, and these Pashtuns are happy with their own culture. They will never accept ours.'

'Perhaps not.' Probyn poured himself another glass. 'Would you prefer that we allowed them to raid into India, steal Hindu women and force them to be wives, capture merchants for ransom, burn, rape and plunder at will?' He raised his eyebrows. 'That was a rhetorical question, old boy. We both know that you would not like that. No; we're here, and we have to keep the peace, although history tells us that nobody has ever done that before.' He grinned again. 'Well, these Pashtun fellows have never met Probyn's Horse before, or the Guides.'

'We do our duty,' Jack said. 'As always.'

Probyn sipped at his whisky. 'Could you imagine yourself doing anything else, Jack? Maybe farming back in England, or working in a bank, God help you?'

Jack shook his head. 'I've no lands to farm unless I became a tenant. And as for working in an office, banking, lawyer or what have you.' He shivered. 'I would go out of my mind with boredom.'

'As would I,' Probyn said. 'What do you think of the Frontier, Jack?'

'Hard and hostile,' Jack said. 'I suppose it is necessary to hold it, although I think the best way would be to allow the indigenous peoples to get on with their lives with a minimum of interference from us.'

'You don't agree with the Forward Policy then,' Probyn said.

'No, I don't believe we should keep pushing, just in case Russia may decide to move into Afghanistan sometime.' Jack wondered why Probyn sounded him out in this manner. Most young officers would never talk shop, preferring to discuss hunting, women or simply pass the time over cards. 'I think we should leave Afghanistan and its environs severely alone. God help the Russians if they ever decide to invade. The Pashtun would wipe the floor with them.'

'Ah.' Probyn took a deep drink from his bottle. The sound of a single shot interrupted whatever he was about to say. He looked at Jack with the glass still to his mouth. 'One shot is merely a man on shikar or having fun with our sentries.'

A second shot sounded, the resounding thud of a jezzail.

'Two shots could be more meaningful.' Probyn's smile broadened if anything.

The third and fourth shots were so close together they merged into a single sound, followed quickly by a high-pitched yell that seemed to encompass the entire camp while penetrating the thin canvas walls of Jack's tent.

'Allah Akbar!'

Then there was silence so intense that Jack thought he could hear the wings of each individual insect humming as they vibrated.

'I think that they're playing on our nerves.' Probyn's smile had not altered.

'If they are, it's working.' Jack felt his breath coming in short gasps.

'Stand to!' That was Chamberlain's voice. 'Bugler! Sound the stand to!'

'That's our call.' Placing the glass on the ground, Probyn stood up, reached for his sword belt, and buckled it in place. 'No rest for the wicked, is there? And they don't come much more wicked than a soldier of the queen on this frontier.'

'Allah! Allah!' The words came clearly through the bustle of men hurrying to their posts. 'Allah! Allah!'

'Here they come, boys!' Chamberlain mounted a rocky knoll to peer around the perimeter of the camp. 'Fire on your officers' command.'

Moon and starlight glittered on the circling blades of swords as the Bunerwals screamed their war cry. With the jezzails giving their hefty thump, the Bunerwals emerged from the trees a hundred yards from the camp.

'Fire!' The command was laconic, followed by the sharp crack of rifles. Muzzle flares revealed brief vignettes of charging tribesmen, of twisted turbans and long robes, of men ducking behind round shields, of waving pulwars and screaming mouths. The Bunerwals covered the ground at an amazing pace, charging straight for the pickets and lines of British and Indian infantry.

Jack heard the calm words of command.

'Fire!'

'Cap and load!'

'Present!'

'Mark your target: fire!'

'Fix bayonets, 71st!'

The British response came with the controlled, calculated volleys of professional soldiers. The same musketry that had smashed the French at Waterloo, that had defeated the Americans at the battle of Camden, that had repelled the Russians at Inkerman and Balaclava. Powder smoke smeared the camp, lay heavy on the men in their scarlet serge, stung eyes, and bit acrid into twitching nostrils.

'Fire!'

The volleys rolled out. Without a company to command, Jack drifted to the nearest body of infantry, the 71st Highland Light Infantry. He heard them mutter to themselves, the lithe, high-cheekboned men in tartan trews who reminded him so much of Logan of the 113th.

Dear Lord! That was a thought! An entire regiment of Logans. Jack shivered at the prospect.

'Captain Windrush requesting permission to join your regiment, sir.' Jack saluted a hard-faced major with a splendid set of whiskers.

'Oh, do join us, Windrush. Glad to have you aboard.' The man's voice was as gravelly as General Colin Campbell's. *Lord Clyde now,* Jack reminded himself. 'I'm Girvan. Find yourself a spot and help yourself. Plenty of the enemy to go around, don't ye know?' Girvan jerked a calloused thumb at the advancing Bunerwals.

'Thank you, Major.' Jack slotted in behind a forward company of the 71st. Two of the men glanced at him, wondering who this stranger was in their midst.

'Who's he?' the nearest man, a gaunt-faced private, asked.

'How should I know? As long as he's on our side.' The second man was red-haired, with china-blue eyes.

'Here they come again!' A wiry sergeant with a sprig of fir in his checked bonnet said. 'Ready with your bayonets, lads.'

'They'll no' get that close, Sergeant Dalgleish,' the gaunt-faced private said. He was clean-shaven, unlike most of his moustached colleagues.

'If they do, I'll blame you, Rougvie.'

The gaunt-faced man spat tobacco juice onto the ground. 'Thank you, Sergeant. I didnae know I was that important.'

'Dinnae worry, Rougie. You're no' important.' The red-haired private assured him. 'Naebody'll miss you when the Paythans slice you up.'

'You'll miss me, Dougie. I owe you a fill of baccy.' Rougvie faced the sergeant again. 'Here, sergeant, what's oor orders when we're on picket duty again?'

'You're not on picket duty, Rougvie. The general doesn't trust you.'

'Aye, but when we are, sergeant.'

'Simple, Rougvie. You don't leave your post til you're killed, and if you see anybody else leaving, you've to shoot them.'

'Aye, that's what I heard. So I can shoot Dougie here.'

'I wish somebody would shoot you, Rougvie, and spare me the bother.'

Jack hid his grin. It was reassuring to hear the black humour of British infantrymen. It made him feel at home. *God, I miss the 113th.*

The Bunerwals had been reinforced for their second charge. Again the cry 'Allah! Allah!' announced their coming as they left the shadowed shelter of the trees to rush directly at the British camp.

'Nae finesse, they lads.' Rougvie shook his head in disapproval. 'Just making themselves targets, that's what they're doing. They think we cannae hear them in the dark.'

Sergeant Dalgleish kicked Rougvie's leg. 'Stop yacking, and start firing, Rougvie; you're meant to be a soldier, not a comedian.'

Unfastening his holster, Jack hauled out his revolver. A few moments ago he had felt fear. Now, in the company of men such as Probyn and Private Rougvie, he did not. For a moment he wondered if more people were like that, bolstering their courage with the bravery of others. Perhaps that was how armies worked, collective courage that made men perform actions that they would never attempt alone. Then the Bunerwals were closing, and he had no time for abstract theories.

Jack flinched at the roar of artillery; grapeshot and canister ripped into the charging Bunerwals, tossing up gravel to add to the confusion as the infantry augmented the guns with rifle fire.

'Fire!' the whiskered major roared.

The Highland Light Infantrymen responded, ignoring the brutal kick of their rifles as they fired into the teeth of the advancing Bunerwals. Again smoke clouded, dense, white and acrid. The yells of 'Allah' ended, replaced by the piteous howling of wounded men.

'Cease fire.' Standing on his knoll, silhouetted against the moon, Chamberlain no longer looked like a tired man. Rather, he was some classical warrior surveying the scene of his latest triumph. 'They've gone. See to the wounded; our lads first, and then the enemy.'

Somebody began to sing, the words and voice unfamiliar to Jack, although he suspected Rougvie was the singer. *Fatteh would approve.*

'When first I went to soldier
With rifle on my shoulder
There wasn't no-one braver
In the Corps boys'

Others joined in, humming the tune or mumbling the words they did not know, and roaring those they did.

'And when I walked abroad
All the pretty girls would wink at me
The ladies can't resist a jolly soldier.'
The words died away as Sergeant Dalgleish glared at them.

'A jolly soldier? You lot? You're about as jolly as a cold November in Airdrie!' The sergeant clamped shut his mouth as Major Girvan lifted a hand.

'That's the spirit, lads!' Girvan roared. 'Sing out! Show the Paythans that we care nothing for their pulwars!'

Most of the regiment joined in the chorus, with men from the 101st Fusiliers also doing their bit, so the valley echoed with the stentorian, if virtually tuneless, bellow of the invading army.

'Bang upon the big drum, clash upon the cymbal
We'll sing as we go marching along boys, along
And although on this campaign there's no whisky or Champaign
Still, we'll keep our spirits flowing with a song, boys.'

Chamberlain remained on his knoll, watching, no doubt listening, remembering the Afghan War as his army yelled out the last verse of their song.

'Then we marched from Chalazan
And we met the wild Afghan
And made him crazy for to run boys, oh
And we marched into Kabul
And we took the Bala Hissar
And we made them to respect the British soldier.'

As the brave words faded away into the dark, Jack saw Chamberlain jump down from his knoll.

'Now we know the Bunerwals mean business,' he said. 'We're a bit isolated out here, so we'll fortify the camp. I'm not marching into their territory to be ambushed and sniped to pieces.'

Jack nodded; Chamberlain was a cautious commander, which was needed out on this wild frontier.

'We'll let them come to us and mow them down. If it was good enough for Wellington at Waterloo, it's good enough for me.'

Jack looked around the already greying heights, wondering how many predatory eyes were watching them and how many messengers were gathering warriors to come to the party. The drumming was soft in the background, a sinister reminder that the Pashtun would not give up after one encounter. Jack knew that they were still out there, watching and waiting, their eyes probing for any weakness to exploit.

'That was round one.' Probyn sounded as laconic as ever. He toured the field of the skirmish, looking at the dead. 'These are all Bunerwals, as far as I can see, but look at this.' Kneeling down, he pointed to the right wrist of one white-bearded man. 'This fellow is wearing a red cord; he is a Ghazi.'

'So is this fellow.' Jack turned over a man whose face had been obliterated by grapeshot.

Probyn stood up. 'It seems that our intelligence was correct. The Fanatics have influenced the Bunerwals. This fight will be like nothing you have seen before.' Jack was unsure if his grin was forced or natural.

CHAPTER SIXTEEN

Ambela Pass October 1863

'So it has happened.' Chamberlain stood on his knoll, scrutinising the valley through his binoculars. 'Well, my tactics will not alter. As I said last night, we'll hold here and let them come to us.' He gestured to the pinnacle of the Eagles Nest that stood prominently between the British camp and the Guru Mountains. 'We only sent a piquet there. I want it properly occupied and fortified.'

Chamberlain's staff officers scribbled notes as the general spoke.

'Over there, on the right' Chamberlain pointed to a series of rocky, forested hills. 'I want each of these peaks occupied and strengthened right up to the Crag Piquet. That will see our flanks guarded. Colonel Wilde, you take command of the Crag Piquet, and Colonel Vaughan, take over the Eagle's Nest.'

'Sir.'

Chamberlain continued: 'Where's the artillery? I want it positioned as high as possible, so when the Bunerwals and Fanatics attack, the guns can support the men. We need every advantage we can get out here.'

That day was one of bustle and sweated labour as Chamberlain's force fortified their position. Artillery from the Peshawar Mountain Battery was manhandled up the slithering rocks, with mules giving up halfway up the slope and men swearing as they slogged up with wheels, gun-barrels and ammunition. Jack carried messages from one post to the other and lent a hand where he could.

'I don't think I like these screw guns,' Rougvie said as he fell on his face for the third time. 'They're bloody heavy.'

'You'll bless the guns when the Paythans attack,' Sergeant Dalgleish told him. 'We'll all bless them then.'

'Why are they called screw-guns?' a very young-looking Griffin asked.

'I'll tell you,' Rougvie said until Sergeant Dalgleish silenced him.

'Ignore Rougvie,' Dalgleish said. 'His mind is like a sewer, and his actions are worse. No, it's simple son. If you look closely, you'll see that the muzzle and the breech screw together. That makes them easier to carry and more mobile.'

The sepoys who operated the guns grinned at the young soldier. 'You'll thank us soon,' they said. 'We save your lives.'

Jack fought off his vague feeling of discomfort when he heard the accent of low-country sepoys. He could not rid himself of the prejudices the Mutiny had created.

With the screw-guns finally in position, the 71st looked around, no doubt hoping for a respite, for despite the lateness of the season, sweat coursed down their faces and darkened their tunics.

'Thank God for that.' Rougvie threw himself down behind a rock.

'Don't relax yet,' Jack said. 'I want scouts out to watch in case the Bunerwals creep up on us.' He ordered half a dozen men a hundred yards in front. 'And we'll need sangars if the Bunerwals attack.'

Rougvie looked at Jack, then at the sergeant. 'Is this officer in the 71st, Sergeant Dalgleish?'

'Do as the captain says,' Dalgleish ordered. 'Don't mind him, sir, his mouth works faster than his brain. He means nothing by it; he just speaks before he thinks.'

'As long as he works as fast as he speaks,' Jack said. *There is that regimental pride again. The 71st Highlanders only take orders from their own officers.* 'From what I've seen of the Pashtuns, the more protection we have between them and us the better.'

'Excuse me, sir.' Dalgleish threw a smart salute. 'Are you *the* Captain Windrush?'

'*The* Captain Windrush?' Jack repeated. 'There are at least two officers of my rank and name in the army, sergeant.'

'Yes, sir. Are you the Captain Windrush who was with the 113th at Lucknow, sir? If you don't mind me asking.'

'I am he.' Jack wondered what the sergeant was going to say.

'I thought so.' Sergeant Dalgleish nodded. 'I've heard of you, sir.'

'Then you'll know that I make my men work,' Jack said. 'I want these sangars built above breast height, with loopholes in the rocks to fire through. The Pashtuns are crack shots; they can kill a man at four hundred yards with their jezzails, so make the loopholes small. The less of a target we give them, the better.'

'Yes, sir,' Dalgleish said. 'I'll make sure the lads do it right.'

There was a hush around Eagles Nest Picket, broken only by the click of stone on stone as the 71st built their sangars, the low breastworks that they would shelter behind if the Bunerwals attacked. The hills around seemed to be watching, waiting. *I know this atmosphere,* Jack told himself. *It is the hush before the storm, the lull before the hurricane. The Bunerwals are observing everything we do.*

'I can see them.' Dalgleish placed a head-sized rock on top of a sangar. 'Over there at the fringe of the trees.' A veteran of Crimea and the Mutiny, he had never ceased to study his surroundings, searching for the enemy.

Jack nodded. He could also see the hint of movement within the trees. The Bunerwals were there, watching.

'Why don't the ghastlies attack?' Rougvie asked. 'They could come when we're still building the sangar.'

'They're assessing us,' Sergeant Dalgleish said. 'They're working out how many of us there are, where the weak points are, and how they are going to come.'

'Good,' Jack said. 'The longer they are doing nothing, the stronger we can make the defences. Scoop a little hollow behind each sangar, lads; it gives you a little bit extra protection. Rougvie, you have a lot to say for yourself; go to the Fusiliers and the Punjabis, use your silver tongue to scrounge some more water canteens. Fighting is a thirsty business, so we can never have too much water.' He looked up as Probyn strolled up, his feet making no noise on the stony surface.

'What date is it, Jack?' Probyn lit an oversized cheroot as he perched on a flat rock. Above him, a pine tree shivered as a jezzail bullet smacked into the trunk.

'25th October.' Jack glanced at his now sadly scratched watch. 'Four-thirty in the afternoon.'

Probyn nodded. 'It'll be dark in an hour and a half. Time for the Bunerwals to come again.' He sighed. 'This is a lovely spot; far too pretty for a battle. It's far more picturesque than Gandamak or Jalalabad or any of these other places we've fought along this frontier.' He drew on his cheroot. 'I think that politicians and kings and queens and what-nots should all gather together in a big room somewhere and decide where to have their wars. They should choose the ugliest places they can find, where nobody lives. That way nobody will care when it gets torn to pieces by shell fire or battered by bullets.'

'If only things were that simple,' Jack said.

'They could be,' Probyn said. 'I mean to say, just look at this valley.' He waved his cheroot around, so a thin trail of blue smoke followed his hand. 'It's as romantically picturesque as the Lake District or Switzerland or the Trossachs. If this were in Europe, there would be a road, and every day a charabanc would unload its cargo of visitors to admire the scenery and gawp at the picturesque locals.'

'The picturesque locals here would shoot them,' Jack said.

'That is a drawback, I admit,' Probyn said with one of his characteristic grins. 'We can't have dead bodies cluttering up our romantic scenery, can we?'

'Windrush,' Chamberlain interrupted them. 'There's a Sikh officer sick with dysentery on Crag Piquet. Take his place.'

'Yes, sir.' *Probyn is correct: there is no rest for the wicked.*

'Look after yourself, Jack,' Probyn said. 'The Bunerwals will come again tonight.'

It was about a mile of rough country from one extreme flank of the British position to the other. Refreshed after her rest, Sharbat took Jack across to Crag Piquet in fifteen minutes, where the Sikhs of the Punjab Infantry welcomed him with solemn nods.

The Crag was a tall, narrow knob of ground, overlooked by higher hills, shielded by open woodland. The Crag itself was so small that it could only hold ten men, with the main Punjabi lines below, and a couple of forward pickets up the south-eastern slopes among the pine trees.

It's not the most secure position in the world, Jack told himself. *The Bunerwals will know that we must hold the Crag, so they will want it back, while the trees give them plenty of cover.*

'Captain, sahib.' A solemn-faced naik gave a smart salute. 'Welcome to the Punjab Infantry and to Kutlghar, the place of slaughter.'

'Thank you,' Jack said.

'Now you will see how the best soldiers in India fight.' Turning away, the naik shouted a string of orders in Punjabi, a language with which Jack had no familiarity. He could only watch with admiration as the Sikhs formed a defensive perimeter and pushed forward a number of piquets.

'Do you know Johnny Sikh?' The major was long, lanky and laconic. He offered Jack a cheroot, lit it from his own and shouted a string of orders in fluent Punjabi.

316

'I saw them a few times during the Mutiny,' Jack said. 'I fought beside them outside Lucknow.'

'Best soldiers in the world.' The major could not have been more enthusiastic. 'They'll soldier seven days a week, never say die, and kill you for a threepenny bit. If you're lucky, you'll see them in action. God help the Pashtun if Johnny Sikh gets off the leash. They hate each other. What did you say your name was?'

'I didn't, but it's Windrush. Jack Windrush. I'm replacing a man who has dysentery.'

'I know. I sent for a replacement officer. I'm Sinclair by the by,' the major said. 'I met a Windrush once. I was attached to the Cameronians during the Sebastopol business. A fellow named William Windrush serving with the Royal Malverns. I can't recollect his rank. Any relation?'

Jack nodded. 'My half-brother.'

Sinclair raised his eyebrows. 'Was he indeed? He won the Victoria Cross, I believe, for doing something or other. Damned if I remember what. It would be suitably heroic no doubt. So he is your half-brother, is he?' The languid look did not fool Jack. Sinclair was assessing him to see if he was suitable material to serve with his Sikhs, even temporarily.

'He is,' Jack said.

'Ah.' Sinclair peered into the growing dark. 'Are you like him?'

'Not in the slightest,' Jack said. 'I'm no hero.'

Sinclair's eyes ran over Jack from the crown of his head to his feet and back. 'No, perhaps not. Which unit were you with before you became a staff man and general factotum?'

'113th Foot,' Jack said. 'Not quite the esteemed Royal Malverns.'

'No,' Sinclair said. 'The 113th are not the Royal Malverns.' He blew blue smoke into the chill evening air. 'I'd better make sure my lads are all right. My Sikhs can be a little over-enthusiastic at times.' He waved his cheroot around, dropped it and ground out the glowing end under the heel of his boot. 'I wouldn't put it past them to attack the Bunerwals just for the fun of the thing.'

'I'll bear that in mind,' Jack said.

'It's been interesting chatting to you, Windrush.' Touching the brim of his forage cap, Sinclair ambled off into the dusk. He stopped after a dozen paces. 'They'll come tonight, you know. The Bunerwals will come tonight. That's what they do. You'd better get some sleep while you can, old man. Oh, and don't let my Sikhs down. I wouldn't like that one bit.'

Jack's weariness descended on him without warning. Sliding down in the lee of a rock, he slept in a crumpled bundle, with dreams haunted by the throbbing of a tabla drum, and Mary warning him to look after himself.

The drumming continued after the deep chill of pre-dawn woke him. Jack stretched, groaned and breakfasted by lighting a cheroot until Sinclair knocked it from his mouth and stamped the glowing end out.

'The Bunerwals can see the gleam,' he said in a fierce whisper. 'Their marksmen will kill you.'

Jack nodded. Tiredness had made him careless. The Sikh sentries were alert, with the others sleeping in various positions. He heard the whisper of wind in the trees, smelled the sweet scent of pine, and sighed. Probyn had been correct; why did humanity spoil beauty with bloodshed? Thank goodness there was no sound of the tabla drum.

A few minutes before dawn, the Bunerwals attacked. This time there was no warning. They came in a rush, silent except for the swift pad of their feet on the ground and the rustle of their blue cloaks.

The first Jack knew of it was a crackle of musketry through the dark and a shrill cry of 'Allah Akbar!'

'Sahib!' The naik stood at attention as Jack stepped toward the sangar. The naik spoke first in Punjabi and then, realising that Jack did not understand, tried Urdu. 'Major Sinclair Sahib asks that you come to the central sangar.'

Jack was moving before the naik finished speaking. 'Thank you, naik. Please inform Sinclair Sahib that I am on my way.'

The sound of musketry increased, now backed by the rhythmic thunder of war-drums, and the high screech of 'Allah!' Something thudded into the ground near Jack's foot.

The Punjabis were at their posts, waiting for the order to fire. So far the Bunerwals were only attacking the piquets at the summit of the Craig.

'Everything all right?' Sinclair loomed up.

Jack nodded. 'What's happening out there?'

'They've overrun our forward piquets.' Sinclair sounded as calm as if he were discussing the price of tea. 'Damned nuisance in the dark.' He did not flinch as two of the screw-guns opened up, sending grapeshot spattering in front of the Sikh's position.

A messenger ran to Sinclair, speaking in rapid Punjabi. Sinclair replied, sending the man away. 'Change of plan, but this is the Frontier, dear boy,' Sinclair said. 'One must be prepared for anything at any time.' He gestured to the left. 'Take the left flank, could you, Windrush? We have a wounded officer.'

'That was rather silly of him.' Jack tried to emulate Sinclair's nonchalance.

'Rather.' Sinclair sauntered away, exchanging cheerful banter with his Sikhs as the artillery fired again. At night the extended muzzle flares were always spectacular. To the Bunerwals, unused to such sights, they must have been terrifying. *If anything can terrify the Pashtun,* Jack thought as he strode to the left flank.

The Bunerwal came through the dark in a screaming mob, pulwars raised above their heads and circular shields in front of them.

'Fire,' Jack ordered. Perhaps it was the influence of these stolid soldiers, but he felt amazingly calm. He stalked behind his men, speaking in Urdu, wishing he had learned Punjabi, and watching the Sikhs load, cap and fire with a precision that would rival the Brigade of Guards.

The Bunerwal attack slowed, and then the artillery hit them. The screw-guns may only have been lightweight compared to the siege artillery Jack had seen in the Crimea, but their effects on charging men were devastating. Each shot sliced great swathes into the dim shapes of the Bunerwals, cutting men down in ones, twos and groups. The Bunerwals learned quickly, ducking into cover each time they heard the bark of the guns, hiding behind trees and firing their jezzails at the sepoy artillerymen. Jack saw a horseman moving through the fringes of the forest. When he came closer, Jack realised that the man had a long drum in front of him and was beating each side to encourage the Bunerwals. The tabla mullah was back.

Right, you bastard. I missed the last time. I won't miss again.

'Cease fire!' Jack ordered. The space in front of the sangar was empty except for the dead and dying. The Bunerwals had withdrawn to the trees, taking the drummer with them. The reek of burnt powder smoke drifted to Jack, with that incessant drumming in the background. Jack waited, single-minded in his search. The tabla mullah appeared, a vague figure with the smoke veiling his horse, and only his upper body visible.

'Give me a rifle.' Jack lay prone. He placed the cap very carefully, adjusted the ladder rear sight for four hundred yards, and aimed. *I won't miss this time.* A drift of smoke covered the tabla mullah; when it cleared, he had gone.

Damn.

The rifles remained silent. The Sikhs waited. One man began to sing, the words and tune unfamiliar to Jack, whose calmness evaporated. He felt very alien out here with these men whose language and culture he did not understand in this place on the very fringe of Empire. What lay beyond these mountains? There was Afghanistan and then the mysterious lands of Central Asia, the great Steppes that reached all the way to Russia.

Dear God, I am a long way from Herefordshire.

The drumming continued, now joined by the lilting strains of a shpelai, the Pashtun flute.

The tabla mullah appeared again, riding slowly through the fringe of trees. Taking a deep breath, Jack waited until the man's head was squarely in his sights. He slowly squeezed the trigger. The kick of the recoil bruised his shoulder, and when the smoke cleared the mullah's horse was empty. *Got you! At last, I've got you! There was no mistake that time, you trouble-making bastard.*

Jack's shot seemed to activate the Bunerwals into activity. They exploded from the forest, yelling with pulwars raised and shields held in front of them.

'Here they come again.' Jack felt the familiar rush of excitement and fear. 'Fire!' Dropping his rifle, he gave an example by firing two shots from his revolver, with no noticeable effect on the blue-clad mass that erupted from the trees.

Sinclair appeared at Jack's shoulder. 'They've taken the Crag Piquet!' His words permeated the crackle of musketry.

'That's a bugger.' The piquet dominated the sharp point of the hill. With quality infantry and an excellent field of fire, the piquet should have been able to hold out against any number of attackers.

'These lads don't fight like the Russians or even the Mutineers.' Sinclair was as calm as ever as he peered upwards toward the Crag. 'I would not be surprised if they used the frontal attack on us as a cover to take the Crag Piquet. I don't like to think of my lads being overwhelmed.'

'We have to get the Crag back.' Jack knew he was stating the obvious. 'The Bunerwals can overlook our whole position from there. Imagine a dozen sharp-shooters with jezzails shooting down.'

'We'll get it back,' Sinclair said. 'Johnny Sikh is the best in the business at hand to hand fighting.'

Finding a small knoll to stand on, Sinclair made a short speech in Punjabi. He ended with a quote, repeating it in English for Jack's sake:

'O Power of Akaal, give me this boon. May I never ever shirk from doing good deeds.

That I shall not fear when I go into combat. And with determination, I will be victorious.

That I may teach myself this greed alone, to speak only of Thy Almighty Lord Waheguru praises.

And when the last days of my life come, I may die in the might of the battlefield.'

'That is powerful.' Jack had listened, trying to pick up the rhythm of the words.

'So are my Sikhs.' Sinclair jumped from his knoll. 'Don't let my men down, Windrush.'

The attack faded away. The Bunerwals withdrew to the trees. The music of the shpelai continued without any drumming.

Dawn cracked the eastern sky, bringing light that gleamed like blood through the drifting powder-smoke. As Jack held the flank against intermittent Bunerwal probes and the occasional more determined attack, Major Keyes of the Guides consulted with Sinclair to organise a counterattack to retake the Crag.

'I spoke to the naik from the Crag Piquet,' Sinclair said. 'He told me that there's a ridge running right up to the summit. The Bunerwals crawled up there at night, and when the piquet was lending its fire to repel the frontal assault, the Bunerwals slid behind them.'

'Clever men, these Bunerwals,' Jack said.

'Aye, sneaky is another word. The Bunerwals have reinforced the Crag.' Sinclair nodded upwards. 'They've jammed it solid with men.'

In the gathering light, Jack saw a horde of Bunerwals beneath the summit peak, busily reinforcing the sangars between them and the Punjabi positions.

'Major Keyes and I are taking up half a company of men to recapture it,' Sinclair said. 'I want you to take command of a platoon to come in support.'

'Yes, sir.' Jack looked up the precipitous slope of the Craig. He wished he knew the men better; he knew the capabilities of his own 113th and had learned the skills of the Guides. He had no idea how to talk to these Sikhs. 'I hope they speak Urdu, sir. I have no Punjabi.'

'Lead by example, Windrush.' Sinclair thrust a cheroot into his mouth. 'My lads will always follow a good officer.'

As soon as it was full daylight, Keyes and Sinclair led the 1st Punjabis in a counter attack. Clad in rifle-green, the Punjabis, mainly Sikhs but with some Pashtuns among them, clambered up the shifting slope to avenge the loss of their position, while Major Brownlow led the 20th Punjabis in support.

Still with the unlit cheroot between his teeth, Sinclair strode to the front of his men. Shouting in Punjabi, he pushed upwards, a distinctively tall figure. As they neared the Crag, the hill became steeper, so the men had to climb up in single file, with the Bunerwals firing down at them from above. As so often in battle, the powder smoke soon concealed the action, so Jack was left fretting with little idea what was happening up there in the trees.

The sound of musketry increased, joined by shouts of 'Allah Akbar' and *Jo Bole so Nihaal, Sat Shri Aka,l*' the Sikh battle cry.

Knowing that this was the largest operation since the Mutiny, Jack was professionally interested to see how the new Indian Army performed. Until 1857 there had been three separate armies of the now dissolved East India Company. Now there was one army, with a new focus on manpower from the so-called 'martial races' of the northern sub-continent rather than the traditional recruiting grounds of Bengal, Oudh and Madras.

Jack saw the Sikhs advance with the bayonet as the Bunerwals and Mujahidin put their backs to rocks and trees to face them with sword and shield. He saw Keyes stagger and fall, with a young ensign leading a determined attack on a group of Ghazis, but then the Bunerwal musketry began to fall on his own position.

We're doing no good here, Jack told himself. 'Come on, Punjabis! Let's get up there!'

Jack clambered up the slope, trying to keep ahead of the Punjabis. They were not natural hill men like the Pashtun or Gurkhas, but what they lacked in agility they made up for in sheer determination, climbing without any outward sign of fatigue. Within a few moments, Jack felt the breath rasping in his throat and his lungs burning. A sudden hammer-blow to his left leg made Jack cry out and fall. He looked down, expecting to see the limb hanging by a frayed thread of skin. However, his leg seemed perfectly normal save for a slight trickle of blood halfway up the thigh.

I've been hit. Jack inspected the wound. A spent bullet had slammed into his thigh on precisely the same spot that a stake had injured him in Burma a decade previously. The skin was hardly broken, yet when Jack tried to stand, the leg would not take his weight.

He slipped, swore and began to slither back downhill again with his arms flailing to help him try to regain his balance.

'Sahib!' A very young Sikh ran across the slope, eyes full of concern. Speaking in rapid Punjabi, he took hold of Jack's arm and hauled him to his feet, deliberately placing his body between Jack and the Bunerwal's fire.

'Thank you,' Jack spoke in Urdu. 'What is your name?'

'Ishar Singh, sahib.' The Sikh stood to attention despite the Bunerwal bullets that pattered down.

'Thank you, Ishar Singh. You'd better leave me now.' Jack saw that his Sikhs were now yards ahead, climbing up with incredible energy. He tried to catch up, staggered again and found Ishar Singh at his side, still smiling.

The youngster stepped backwards, put his shoulder to Jack's backside, and pushed.

'I'll be all right.' Jack hated to look undignified. *I am a British officer, damn it!*

Ishar Singh either did not understand or chose not to as he shoved all the harder until Jack was propelled up the hill at a greater speed than was comfortable. He passed through his men, ignored their undisguised amusement, and drew his sword. 'Come on, Punjabis! *Jo Bole so Nihaal, Sat Shri Akal!*'

As the tree cover thinned, Jack found himself in a battle as desperate as any he had ever seen. Sikh Bayonets and Pashtun pulwars clashed over the tumbled stones of a succession of sangars. As the attackers pushed to the summit, the Bunerwals withdrew, barrier by barrier, and began hurling down rocks. Jack saw a boulder crash into a British lieutenant; the Punjabis shuddered, regrouped and renewed their attack.

'*Jo Bole so Nihaal, Sat Shri Akal!*' Without waiting for orders, Jack's platoon threw themselves up the final few yards of the slope and onto the Bunerwal position.

'Leave me!' Jack ordered Ishar Singh. Drawing his revolver and using his sword as a makeshift crutch, Jack clambered upward into the melee.

The Sikhs were gradually pushing the Bunerwals back, taking sangar after sangar and tree after tree. One of Jack's platoon ducked under the swing of a Bunerwal pulwar, yelled, and thrust with his bayonet. The blade entered the Bunerwal's chest, killing him instantly.

'Sahib!' Ishar Singh was on the ground, his rifle dropped from his hand. One muscular Bunerwal held him down by sheer weight, while another poised ready to lunge with his pulwar.

Levelling his revolver, Jack took quick aim at the warrior with the pulwar. He squeezed the trigger, cursing when nothing happened. 'It's jammed,' he said, tried again, and swore once more.

'Hold on, Ishar!' Jack shouted, balanced on his sword, and vaulted forward. In that instant, nothing else mattered except to save the life of the beleaguered Sikh who had helped him. Using his pistol as a club, Jack swung it at the head of the pulwar-wielding Bunerwal. The warrior staggered, turned around with the pulwar in his hand, and slashed overhand.

Jack did not hear the shot that killed the Bunerwal. He only saw the effects as the bullet hit the man in the head, smashing it open and throwing him two yards back.

'Thank you, somebody.' With the pain in his thigh easing, Jack put his left foot back on the ground.

'Up you get!' Helping Ishar Singh to his feet, Jack handed him his rifle. 'Look after this,' he said. In the few moments he had spent rescuing the youngster, the skirmish had been won and the Punjabis had retaken the Crag. Jack had a momentary vision of the Bunerwals retreating, running down the opposite slope at great speed and then up to the hills beyond, blue cloaks flying.

Sinclair appeared, cleaning his sword as he gave orders in rapid Punjabi. 'Windrush, take your platoon back to camp. I'll leave a strong piquet here. That was a warm morning's work.' He sheathed his sword with a flourish. 'I remember now what your brother was saying about you.'

Jack stiffened. 'What was that, sir?' Whatever William said would not be good.

'He said you were born on the wrong side of the blanket.' Sinclair faced Jack squarely. 'Is that correct?'

'It is, sir.' Jack expected instant sneering.

'Me too, old man, me too,' Sinclair said. 'Your old man was a philanderer, was he? I mean no offence.' He stopped to shout orders at an NCO, waved to a lieutenant, and began to saunter back down the hill. 'Mine was a regular womaniser who chased any filly with a skirt. My mother was one of his captures.' He pulled two cheroots from his breast pocket and handed one to Jack. 'She was a good woman. Too good for him.' He stopped to acknowledge the salute as a platoon of Sikhs filed past, one with his left arm in a bloody sling. 'Did you know your mother?'

'I met her briefly.' Jack was reluctant to give too much away.

'I know it's not done to smoke while in uniform,' Sinclair said, lighting up, 'but I don't give much of a fig for conventions. Oh, I'm all for the traditions of the regiment and all that, of course.'

'Yes, sir.' Jack remained cautious.

'Your brother spoke at some length about you, now I recall,' Sinclair said. 'He said there was an officer of the 113th that shared his name. He also said that that officer had an Indian mother.'

'My mother was Eurasian.' Jack felt his chin lift in defiance.

Sinclair drew on his cheroot. 'So is your wife, if the stories are to be believed.'

'She is.' Again, Jack waited for the mockery. He knew he would respond with anger if anybody, British officer or not, insulted Mary. He wondered if he should challenge Sinclair to a duel or just punch him in the jaw. Either would see him in front of a court martial.

Sinclair jumped from a rock onto scree below, slithered down a few yards, and waited for Jack to catch up. 'Not many British officers would marry a Eurasian,' Sinclair said. 'Woo them, yes, bed them, certainly, and then discard them as if they were nothing like my father did to my mother.'

It took a few moments for Sinclair's words to sink in. 'I see,' Jack said.

'There are more of us around than people think,' Sinclair said.

They walked in silence for a few moments, with the Sikhs passing them on their return to the camp.

'Before this action,' Sinclair jerked his head back to indicate the Crag, now bright with autumn sunlight, 'we were discussing your brother.'

'We were,' Jack agreed.

'There must be Windrush blood in both of you,' Sinclair said. 'Yet you're nothing like William Windrush. He is undoubtedly a brave man, but he would never stop to help an ordinary ranker, as you did with young Ishar.' Sinclair did not look at Jack as he spoke. 'My men won't forget. If you ever wish to transfer into the 1st Punjab Infantry, mention my name.'

'Thank you,' Jack said. That was an honour, as the Sikhs reckoned themselves an elite regiment. Jack hid his smile; every Indian Army regiment considered themselves elite. They were fighting men with as much pride as any regiment in the British Army, and with reason.

'You were with the 113th, you said,' Sinclair said.

'They were known as the Baby Butchers,' Jack said. That seemed a very long time ago now.

'Were they?' Sinclair shrugged. 'I did not know that. I knew of them as the regiment that fought at Inkerman and marched with Havelock.'

'They did that, too,' Jack said softly. If he had helped the 113th wipe clean their old sordid reputation, then he had done something positive with his life. He breathed out. He was just beginning to relax when he heard his name called.

'Windrush, is that you?' Chamberlain shouted from the back of his horse. 'The 71st need an officer, and you're unattached. Grab yourself something to eat then report to the 71st's colonel. They're on the Eagle's Nest.'

'Yes, sir,' Jack said. He was again moving from one flank of the British position to the other, but at least he was useful, and the 71st Highlanders spoke English, of a fashion. He might be able to understand something that they said.

CHAPTER SEVENTEEN

Ambela Pass October 1863

The Eagle's Nest was a more extensive scale model of the Crag, an isolated peak at the opposite flank of the British camp, with rugged hills overlooking it. Pine trees, knolls, and a plethora of rocks and boulders provided cover for the enemy. By the time Jack struggled to the 71st's position, it was nearly noon.

'Welcome back, Girvan.' The major greeted him with a sour grin. 'Well, now you're here, you'd better stay, but our lads are not very susceptible to officers from other units.'

'So I've heard, but I'll see what I can do.'

'Aye.' Girvan glanced over his men. 'They're a decent enough bunch. They can fight. The Bunerwals are gathering in the trees over there.' He pointed to the fringe of the encroaching pine forest. 'This country could be made for them.'

'Where do you want me?' Jack agreed with Girvan. The terrain was perfect for the sort of irregular warfare the Pashtun's favoured.

'In reserve,' Girvan was blunt. 'It's a job for an ensign, maybe a lieutenant, but the best I can offer.' He nodded to a platoon of fifteen men. 'There is your command. If any section of the line is hard pressed, I want you to take over.'

The men surveyed Jack without a pretence of respect. The sergeant in charge gave a reluctant salute. 'Sergeant Dalgleish, sir.'

Jack remembered him. 'As you were, Dalgleish. What are the men doing?'

The privates had relapsed into small groups, stuffing small items into glass bottles.

'Making Ambela Pegs, sir. We're a bit short of artillery, so we must make do.'

Crouching beside one of the groups, Jack studied the procedure. While three of the infantrymen ignored him, the third, the red-haired, freckle-faced man in his early twenties that Jack had heard called Dougie, shifted aside to make room.

'I've never heard of them before,' Jack said. 'Are they a sort of grenade?'

'That's right, sir. We got gunpowder from the gunners and added small stones and anything else that might be useful, so when the Paythans come, we can lob the pegs among them.'

'I see you've a pipe in your mouth,' Jack said. 'You'd best be careful not to drop hot ash into the gunpowder.'

'Oh, aye, we'll be careful sir.'

'What's your name?'

'Douglas Lennox, sir,' the freckle-faced man said. 'That's Connor, Rougvie and Burnes.'

'I remember you and Rougvie,' Jack said quietly as the other three privates glanced up briefly. Connor, a broad-faced ruffian in his thirties, gave a brief nod. His eyes were grey and steady.

'Well, if the Bunerwals come, I'm sure these Ambela pegs will come in very handy.'

'Yes, sir.'

The drums started then, fast and low, gradually increasing until the sound seemed to throb around the entire valley. Jack could not hear the distinctive throb of the tabla drum.

'That's their encouragement,' Dalgleish said quietly. 'The pipes will start soon, lads; nothing for you to worry about.'

'Who's worried?' Rougvie wore a fir sprig in his bonnet. 'They should be bloody worried, not us.'

Burns gave a weak grin. He was the youngest man there, an auburn-haired youth with a pencil-faint moustache. 'Will they attack, sergeant? The Sikh lads just cleared them from the Crag Piquet.'

'That they will, lad.' Dalgleish said. 'Their mullahs, their holy men, tell them that our bullets can't hurt them, but if they die they go to Paradise with hordes of virgin women.'

Burns spat on the ground. 'What good is a bloody virgin? You want a woman who kens what she's doing.'

'As if you would know,' Connor said, as the privates jeered.

'Women are not much bloody good if they're deid,' Rougvie said. 'Do the virgins want to be in a paradise with all these beardy Bunerwals? Or is paradise only for dead warriors?'

'You can ask them that yourself,' Dalgleish said. 'Here they come now.'

Don't these Bunerwals ever give up? They are launching one attack after another, probing our defences.

As the Bunerwals surged from the tree cover, the 71st opened fire. Massed rifles, backed by the screw-guns once again created great gaps in the attackers, but sheer numbers saw them reach the British line. All the time, Pashtun marksmen fired at the British, hitting a man here and there, so the defences were weakened by the time the Bunerwals reached the sangars.

Jack saw that some of the Bunerwals carried standards that flapped and flowed above them. One brave man leapt on to the British parapet, thrusting the staff of his red standard between two of the rocks.

'Allah Akbar!' he yelled, seconds before a man of the 71st thrust a bayonet into his belly, twisted and withdrew. The standard bearer slowly crumpled. The bayonet man hauled down the standard, stiffened and fell as a Bunerwal bullet thumped into his chest. He passed the standard to another man, spat blood and died.

Behind Jack, the sepoys of the artillery fired the screw-guns, angling the barrels so the shot passed over the heads of the defenders. He saw one blast mow down a dozen of the attackers as a second Bunerwal wave erupted from the trees. The drumming continued, with the distinctive roll of a tabla as a sonorous background.

You're back, are you? That's twice I've killed you. Maybe there is something in the idea that a sacred charm protects these Mujahidin warriors.

Girvan was on the front line of the 71st, giving orders and fighting with his sword. In their tartan trews and stained scarlet jackets, the men of the 71st appeared like Highland ghosts as they alternately appeared and disappeared in the powder smoke.

'The lads at the sangars are hard-pressed,' Jack addressed his platoon. 'Fix your bayonets. We might be needed soon.'

The platoon left their peg-making, fixed bayonets, hitched up their trews and stamped their feet, getting ready for work.

'Rougvie, your bayonet's rusty!' Dalgleish yelled. 'I've told you before about that! A rusty bayonet can stick in the scabbard, delaying your draw and giving the enemy time to plunge their pulwar into your guts. Do you want that, Rougvie?'

'No, thank you, Sergeant.'

'I thought not. Next time, you'll be on a charge.'

'Yes, Sergeant.' Rougvie did not sound concerned.

'Captain Windrush!' Girvan's voice floated above the clamour of battle.

'That's us.' Jack saw that Girvan was stepping back as a horde of Bunerwals was pushing over the sangar. 'Follow me, lads!'

However reluctant they had been to acknowledge Jack's authority, the platoon ran forward on the word of command. There was no need to give any more orders; these men of the 71st were born rough-house soldiers. They smashed into the Bunerwals without hesitation, fighting with plunging bayonets and flailing butts to meet the pulwars and shields of the Pashtuns.

After his recent experience with his revolver jamming, Jack left it in its holster and drew his sword, although he knew that the Bunerwals were experts with that weapon. He clashed blades with a tall man in a filthy red turban, gasped as the man rammed a shield against his chest, kicked up, missed, swore, and lunged with his sword. The Bunerwal twisted to catch Jack's blade on his shield, grunted, and crumpled with a bayonet in his side.

Jack saw the flare of explosion an instant before he heard the bang. The peg had landed in the midst of a group of Bunerwals, the flash of gunpowder and scatter of small pebbles knocking one man down and injuring three others. As the Bunerwals hesitated at this unexpected twist, a second peg exploded among them, enveloping one man in flames. Jack had not expected the high-pitched screams.

'They're going!' Rougvie shouted, smashing the butt of his rifle on the bearded face of a bright-eyed man. 'Chase them, lads!'

'Stand fast.' Grabbing hold of Rougvie's shoulder, Jack dragged him back. 'Our job is to wear them out, not get ourselves killed.' He saw the tabla mullah emerge from the fringe of the woodland. As before, the man was naked except for a loincloth and a dirty turban. He sat astride a Kabul pony with the drum across his waist, pattering his hands steadily as his gaze roamed along the British sangars. For a moment, he looked directly at Jack, his eyes smoky, and then his horse took him away, the Bunerwals streaming past him into the shelter of the trees.

'Who's the best shot here?' Jack asked.

'The lads with the fir sprigs in their bonnets are our marksmen.' Sergeant Dalgleish touched the fir in his bonnet.

'See that fellow on the horse?' Jack pointed to the tabla mullah. 'He is goading the tribes to attack us. Wherever there is trouble, he appears.' *I've shot that man twice. Does he have some divine protection, as some Pashtun claim?*

Dalgleish nodded. 'Yes, sir. Rougvie, Connor, did you hear that?'

'We're ready, sir,' Connor replied for them both.

'Kill that mad mullah,' Dalgleish said.

'Yes, sir.' While Rougvie lay down, Connor took a stance behind a tree with his rifle resting on a branch. The two shots rang out as one. Jack saw the horse fall, taking the mullah with it. 'Good shooting, lads.'

'We missed,' Connor said laconically as the mullah rolled free from the horse, stood up, and stared at the powder-smoke drifting British lines.

'Try again.' Taking out his binoculars, Jack focussed on the tabla mullah. He was not as old as Jack had supposed, perhaps in his late thirties, with a tinted beard and long hair that straggled around his head. He looked directly at Jack through kohl-lined eyes, his stare more direct than anything Jack had seen before. 'That man is dangerous.'

As Jack watched, a group of Pashtuns ran to the mullah, surrounding him. Precisely at that moment, Rougvie fired. One of the Pashtuns crumpled. Another took his place, standing as a human shield between the mullah and the British lines. A man in a dun pakol lifted the tabla drum, faced the 71st, and spat his contempt on the ground.

'That mullah bears a charmed life,' Jack said.

'If kind Sergeant Dalgleish gives me a sixpence I'll melt it into a silver bullet,' Rougvie said. 'It worked for Bluidy Claverhouse at Killiecrankie'

Jack knew the story. When Claverhouse led the Highland charge at Killiecrankie, the British soldiers thought he was in league with the devil, so one of the redcoats shot at him with a silver bullet.

'Maybe his Allah is looking after him,' Connor murmured.

'Maybe he is at that.' British other ranks always could surprise him.

Girvan nodded. 'Keep trying.'

Rougvie settled down again. Taking a cartridge from his pouch, he ripped it open with his teeth, poured the gunpowder down the barrel, licked the bullet to aid lubrication, and rammed it home. Placing the percussion cap in place, he adjusted the back sight. 'Right, you scruffy bastard,' he said softly. 'Let's have another shot at you.' Lying behind the sangar, he rested his rifle on a boulder, aimed carefully at the mullah, and fired just as one of the mullah's guardians moved.

The mullah staggered and fell.

'Got you, you dirty old bastard.' Rougvie immediately began to reload.

Jack focussed his binoculars. Two of the guardians lifted the mullah, who was bent double, holding his thigh. 'He's wounded, Rougvie. You hit him.'

'I want him dead.' Rougvie returned to his previous position as a dozen Pashtuns fired at the 71st's sangars, narrowly missing Jack. 'They've taken him away.'

'With any luck, he'll bleed to death.' Jack was shocked at his own callousness.

'We have forty casualties,' Girvan said. 'That's a heavy price. Only God knows how many men the Bunerwals lost. If they carry on like this, we'll denude the whole tribe of its manhood.'

Jack nodded. Chamberlain's strategy was paying off. When adequately equipped British troops held a defensive position, heaven and earth would not shift them, let alone a few thousand ill-armed tribesmen. The Tabla Mullah, if he survived Rougvie's bullet, would have to recruit many times the number of men. Or find them better weapons. Jack remembered the gunsmiths of Tazhak. *We should destroy that place.*

Probyn joined them, dismounting and stepping elegantly across the camp. He ignored the sniping from the Bunerwal jezzails.

'We might decimate the Bunerwal tribe as Major Girvan says,' Probyn said, 'if it was only the Bunerwals who opposed us. I saw Afridis, Mahmuds, Swats, Hazaras, and even Waziris from the Baluchistan border among the enemy. Some were wearing the Ghazis' red cord on their right wrists. Others,' he shrugged, 'others are just here for the love of the thing or their dislike of us.'

'It's a gathering of the clans,' Girvan said. 'Our presence is acting as a magnet. The longer we are here, the more Pathans will come. This valley will be a permanent battlefield until we smash them, or they overrun us.'

'Let's hope it's not the latter,' Jack said. 'All the Pashtuns need is one decisive victory over us for all the clans to rise en masse, with God knows what effect on India.'

'I wouldn't worry about India, Jack,' Probyn said.

'Why not?' Jack pressed his point. 'Some of the Sikhs will remember the good old days of the Khalsa when they were independent, there are plenty of sepoys who joined the Mutiny ready to take up arms again, and I would not trust some of these rajahs and maharajas as far as I could spit.'

'Still no reason for you to worry.' Probyn was smiling as if at a rare joke.

'Why the devil not?'

'Because you'll be dead, old boy, along with the rest of us!' Probyn burst into roaring laughter. 'Remember Elphinstone's disaster at Kabul? Well, we may be in line to be the next, unless Chamberlain has something very clever up his sleeve.'

Probyn's laugh was so infectious that Jack and Girvan both joined in. *What must the Bunerwals think of us, laughing in the face of death? Batoor would understand.*

Jack had a vision of Batoor lying dead, killed by the tabla mullah and his Mujahidin. *Well, Tabla, I can follow the Pashtun code of badal, as well. Batoor gave me hospitality. I will take retaliation on his behalf, even if that means coming back to the Frontier myself and hunting you down, wounded as you are.* The feeling was so strong that Jack felt himself shaking with anger. He straightened up, staring beyond the British camp to the fringe of pine trees where he had last seen the tabla mullah. *Batoor was a friend. If you are still alive, Tabla, then I will kill you.* Jack shook his head. *Dear God, the Pashtun have converted me to their culture.*

Scattered firing disrupted the night when the Bunerwals and Ghazis tried to infiltrate the British positions, and the Guides and Gurkhas met them on their own terms in the broken terrain of the slopes. In the game of stalk and counter-stalk, the Bunerwals were gradually pushed back. Jack heard the Bunerwals' complain that the British were not fighting in the same fashion they had during the Afghan War. The voice came clearly to the British camp.

'Where are the *lal pagriwalas* (red-turbaned Sikhs) or the *goralog* (Europeans)? They are better sport!'

Jack could not hide his smile. *We are not the Khalsa, boys. We can match anything you can do.*

Chamberlain had his ideas of creating a better understanding that did not include badal. The next day, 27th October, he arranged a ceasefire so that the Bunerwals could collect and dispose of their dead.

'It shows good faith,' the general said. 'The Pashtun people do not like to leave their dead in the hands of unbelievers. More importantly for us, if we leave piles of dead around our camp perimeters, it will attract predators and flies.'

Remembering his ruse at the Torkrud watchtower, Jack could not argue with that. Those corpses which were not already the target of vultures or other creatures were a mass of flies.

The tribesmen were cautious at first as they came to collect their casualties, but when they realised that the British were acting honesty, they became more confident. Men arrived in small groups, with jezzails ready if the British proved hostile. Under strict orders, the British and Indian soldiers held their fire.

Jack wandered over to the Guides position, where Alladad was happily talking to one of the Pashtun.

Jack waited until the conversation ended. 'Do you know that man, Alladad?'

'That is my brother,' Alladad said. 'I told him I would kill him next time he attacked.' Alladad was laughing, as if at a colossal joke.

'What did he say to that?'

'He said he would kill me first.' Alladad laughed all the louder.

Chamberlain waited until the Pashtun trusted the truce then invited them to a Jirga. A group of grey-bearded elders considered the proposal and then agreed.

'We trust your nang, General Chamberlain,' their spokesman said.

'As I trust yours.' Chamberlain gave a stiff little bow. 'You come along, too, Windrush. I want you to identify this tabla mullah fellow if he is still alive.' He nodded. 'You don't have to say anything.'

That was as firm an order to keep my mouth shut as any Chamberlain has ever given, Jack thought as he positioned himself at the edge of the Jirga, looking at the men who he had so recently been fighting and listened to what was being said. As always, the Pashtuns who attended were elderly, dignified men with grey or henna-dyed beards. They all wore their pulwars or Khyber knives.

'Salaam Alaikum.' They greeted Chamberlain gravely as if they had not been trying to destroy his army only the previous day.

'Salaam Alaikum.' Chamberlain was equally polite. He got down to business at once. 'You have lost many men,' Chamberlain said. 'You cannot possibly win against British infantry fighting behind stone walls. All you will do is incur needless casualties among your people.'

The Bunerwal tribal leaders nodded courteously, long beards wagging, intelligent eyes fixed on Chamberlain or examining the British defences. 'We have lost many men,' they agreed. 'We have lost too many for us to give up the fight against invaders who defile our holy land.'

Holy land? Jack remembered the Russians using similar language when they fought the British in the Crimea.

'Our land, like our women, is kept in purdah,' a man with his beard dyed henna-red explained. 'We cannot allow infidels to trespass here.' He tapped his jezzail to emphasise his words. 'We cannot allow feringhees to take our land.'

'We did not come to make war on the Bunerwals,' Chamberlain said. 'I know your holy men have told you that we came to take away your land. That is not true.'

'Then leave,' the tribesmen said. 'You did not seek our permission before you came with an army. We know the British; they come with smiles and promises of friendship, then they take over and tell us they are doing us a favour by being here. We do not wish such favours. Leave our land, and leave us in peace.'

Chamberlain shook his head. 'I can assure you that we have no intention of taking your land.'

'We have a proverb.' The man looked about seventy, still fit and wiry, with bright, predatory eyes. 'First comes one Englishman, as a traveller or for shikar; then come two and make a map; then comes an army and takes the country. Therefore it is better to kill the first Englishman.' He sat down again, his gaze fixed on Chamberlain.

In that spirit, the Jirga broke up. Proud and defiant, the Bunerwals lifted their dead and departed, leaving the British with a feeling of foreboding. Standing in the shadows, Jack saw the tabla mullah sitting astride his horse unhurt. As long as that man was present, Jack knew there would be no peace on the Frontier. *I have tried to kill him on two occasions, and Rougvie shot him clean, yet here he is. Perhaps he does have a charmed life.* Jack shook his head. *Don't be stupid; that is rank superstition. At least Gulbaz is not here,* Jack thought. *He was sent these notes about the law agent. Perhaps I was wrong in my assessment?*

Probyn pulled his horse beside Jack. 'The worst is yet to come.' He passed over a cheroot to Jack. 'I can feel it.'

'So can I,' Jack said. 'I felt like this before the Mutiny broke out. It is as if the land is waiting.' He looked around at the surrounding hills. 'This is a harsh country, quite unlike the lush plains of India. As that Bunerwal elder said, the Pashtun keep Pakhtunkhwa in purdah against everybody. We have no right here.'

'None at all,' Probyn agreed. 'Yet here we are, and the minute we leave, the tribes will debouch onto the Peshawar Valley, over the Indus to raid and kidnap, rape and plunder to their hearts' content. The Sikhs held them in check for a generation. Now that we've broken the power of the Khalsa, it is up to us to act as guardians of India, whether India likes it or not.'

'Do you think there will ever be peace in this land?' Jack asked.

Probyn shook his head. 'There may be peace sometime in the far distant future when man's attitude has changed to peace-mongering, and all the swords are made into ploughshares.' He grinned. 'I think some fellow said that hundreds and hundreds of years ago. His message has not reached this part of the world yet.'

'Evidently.'

'Not to worry.' Probyn slapped Jack's shoulder. 'Think of the bright side; this is a grand place for soldiering, and that's the life we chose. Could not be better for the likes of you and me, eh? A stern landscape, a bold and worthy foe, brave soldiers as comrades, and all the world before us. What more could we want?'

'What more indeed.' Jack thought of himself as a young ensign, when he sought glory and advancement above all. Back then he would have asked for nothing more than a posting to the Frontier. Now, with a decade of experience, he was not so sure. Experience and marriage had altered him.

'Probyn,' Chamberlain interrupted them. 'Take out a patrol of your badmashes; see what's happening to the east. Windrush; you're at a loose end just now. Do the same on the west. My compliments to Major Kerr, and could he lend you half a dozen of his men.'

'Yes, sir.' If nothing else, this expedition was keeping him from boredom or moping for Mary.

Kerr's beard seemed bushier than ever as he nodded to Jack. 'Take the same lads you had last time, Windrush. You got back in one piece without losing a man. That is unusual out here.' He lowered his voice, his Ulster accent seemingly quite at home amidst the brittle tension of the Frontier. 'Don't push your luck, man. I value my Guides, and this place is waiting to explode.'

'I'll look after them,' Jack promised. *Or they'll look after me.*

The Guides welcomed him as if he were one of their own. Jack looked over them, from grave Hassan, the volatile, dare-devil Zaman, young musical Fatteh, to handsome Alladad with his kohl-rimmed eyes, they were nearly as familiar to him as the men of the 113th.

'Where are you taking us this time, Windrush sahib?' Ursulla asked.

'Only on a short patrol; the general sahib wishes us to see what the Bunerwals are up to on the west.'

'They are up to mischief,' Hassan said. 'The Bunerwals are always up to mischief.'

'Then it's up to us to see what that mischief is, and stop it,' Jack said. 'You men are the shield and sword of India.' Although those words sounded like trite rhetoric, the men seemed to appreciate them.

'We are the Guides,' Fatteh said simply.

Although Jack led his patrol out before dawn, the Bunerwals were already alert. A jezzail thumped the moment the Guides left the camp, with the muzzle flare distinct against the dark. Others followed.

'Ride fast and hard,' Jack ordered.

'We know, sahib,' Hassan murmured.

Jack grunted; he was giving orders to men who had lived in this environment all their lives. As the shrill bugle calls of reveille from the camp faded behind him, he felt the old mixture of excitement and apprehension. He was outside the security of the camp, away from senior officers and all the familiar apparatus of order. Out here in the wild lands, a man had to be able to stand on his own merits, especially if he did not have the framework of clan or tribe as support. Was that the appeal of this kind of life? Or was the British army the equivalent of the family? He had heard it said that British officers were more than a class, yet not quite a caste or a military order like the old Knights Templar. They were a select society of their own. Yet often Jack felt more comfortable with his ranking soldiers than his fellow officers. He shook his head; he was not here to indulge in philosophical debates with himself, yet something about this untamed landscape awoke that desire within him.

He had been aware of the party of Bunerwals moving alongside them in the decreasing dark for the past ten minutes. Although Jack's patrol was mounted, while the Bunerwals were on foot, they kept pace without trouble.

'Sawan, drop back a little and see if they are trying to cut us off.'

'Sahib.' Sawan needed no further instructions. He cantered back a few moments later. 'No, sahib. They are quite content to watch. They are observing us, as we are observing them.' Only a Pashtun trooper would have added the unnecessary words to instruct his feringhee officer.

'Thank you, Sawan. Now it is your job to observe them observing us. If you think they pose a threat, inform me immediately.'

'Yes, sahib.'

They rode on cautiously, with their swords loose in their scabbards, alert for any possible attack. The air had a decided chill, a foretaste of the harsh winter that would soon sweep upon them. Jack remembered his boyhood dreams of India, of heat and jungles and balmy nights. He had no thought of this frontier with its extremes of climate and a population every bit as martial as the British. Jack gave a wry smile; when he was a boy, the Sikhs controlled this frontier.

Jack saw something thrusting from a ridge to his left, with the cold rays of morning sun glinting on the tasselled green. At first, he thought it was a tree, dimly seen in the half-light, but as he drew closer, he realised that it was a standard on a tall pole.

'Something's happening over there, lads. Let's have a look.' Guiding Sharbat to the left, Jack realised that their escorting Bunerwals were moving closer. One levelled his jezzail and fired a shot. The bullet whistled close to Jack. 'They don't want us to find out what that standard means,' he said. 'What do you think, Hassan?'

'I think that if we ride towards the standard, the Bunerwals will attack us.'

'I agree.' Jack peered at the body of Bunerwals still keeping pace with his patrol. His attempts at counting them gave different totals as the Bunerwals ducked behind cover, sheltered behind trees or showed themselves openly, depending on their mood. 'They seem to be playing with us.'

'Yes, sahib.' Hassan sounded patient, like a schoolteacher with a stupid pupil. 'They don't wish us to know how many of them there are.'

'Let's see what they are hiding,' Jack decided. 'We were sent out here to gather intelligence. Perhaps these Bunerwals are only a screen to fool us while the rest retreat, so we will be shadow-boxing nobody as the whole of Pakhtunkhwa mocks us.'

He knew that the opposite might also be true; the Bunerwals could be luring them into a trap.

'Be prepared for anything,' Jack ordered. 'Follow me!'

Veering left, he increased his speed to a trot, with Sharbat's hooves kicking up clods of earth. He saw the Bunerwals spread out, a score of turbans and blue cloaks, with gesticulating arms and the flash of early sunlight on pulwars. He heard the deep roar of a jezzail, but where the shot went, he could not tell.

'Fatteh! Sound the canter!'

This was exhilarating, riding forward towards an unknown number of the enemy on the farthest frontier of the empire. Was this why he had joined? To fight the foes of Victoria, Queen of Great Britain? Or was it to follow the family tradition, as these Pashtuns were doing? Or was it just for the excitement?

The Bunerwals had spread out; some were levelling their jezzails, others holding the long, curved pulwars as they ducked behind the circular shields.

'Charge!' Jack roared, knowing that he would be more sensible to observe and withdraw. *To the devil with that*! He was a soldier, not a spy; his job was fighting, not skulking. With the adrenaline surging inside him, Jack drew his sword. 'Come on the Guides!'

As the thin notes of the bugle sounded out and the Guides galloped forward, the Bunerwals melted away. One or two fired, the shots going nowhere; the others vanished, making use of the plentiful cover the terrain provided. Jack found himself charging nothing except broken ground and the fringes of a steep tree-crowned ridge.

'Canter,' he ordered, 'trot and walk.' He was unsure of the correct commands for cavalry, but the Guides were unconventional at least. They would understand what he meant.

The ridge ran north and south with uneven, rock-and-pine-tree slopes. In a gap on the summit between two clumps of trees, the green standard swayed slightly in the breeze.

'Do you recognise that flag, Hassan?'

'Yes, Sahib. That is the banner of the Akhund of Swat.' Hassan's voice was neutral, although Jack sensed the tension behind the words.

'Forgive my ignorance, Hassan. I do not know the name.'

'May I explain, Windrush Sahib?' Hassan was uncharacteristically diffident.

'Please do, Hassan.'

'He is also known as Akhund Abdul Ghaffur, sahib. You might know that name?'

Jack shook his head. He could see men flitting among the trees. 'No, I don't. Keep moving, boys. We don't know how many of the enemy are there.'

'The Akhund is the Emir of Swat, away up there, deep in the mountains.' Hassan indicated the north.

'Why have I not heard of him?'

'He has been a peaceful man for many years,' Hassan said. 'The British have had no reason to make war on Swat.'

Jack accepted that. He was a soldier; his attention was taken by military matters. Peaceful Emirs did not interest him.

'What is he like?'

Hassan screwed up his face. 'He is an elderly man,' he said. 'Over sixty, maybe even seventy.'

'What is he doing here?'

'He will not be here for his military prowess,' Hassan said. 'He is a mullah, a religious leader, and sahib, although he has been quiet for years, he is no friend to the British. In 1836 he called for a Jihad. He opposed the Sikhs and supports Dost Mohammad Barakzai of Afghanistan.'

Jack absorbed the information. 'Is the Akhund of Swat influential? Would men, Pashtuns, follow him?'

'The Pashtun would follow the Akhund to Paradise or to Jahannam, sahib, to heaven or hell.' Hassan's voice shook slightly.

'I did not know the Pashtun believed in hell.' Jack wondered if the Akhund could influence Hassan's loyalty.

'Some do, some do not. Some say that the entrance to hell is in Wadi Jahannam in Afghanistan.'

Jack nodded. From what he had heard of Afghanistan, the entrance to hell might well be there. 'I want to see what's behind that ridge. I want to see this Akhund fellow.'

Hassan shook his head. 'The Bunerwals will stop us.' He looked shaken.

'I'll go alone,' Jack decided. He had no intention of taking his Guides into danger.

'Then the Bunerwals will kill you.'

'Perhaps.' Jack wondered at his sudden recklessness. 'I want you to create a diversion.'

'Ah,' Hassan nodded. 'The sahib is not quite as stupid as he pretends.'

'The sahib does not appreciate being spoken about in such a manner,' Jack responded, knowing that Pashtuns had their own way of dealing with foolish British officers. 'I want you to take the men and ride north at great speed as if you had discovered something. Give me a full hour. If I'm not here when you return, get back to camp. Inform Kerr Sahib what happened. Tell him I ordered you to leave me.'

'He won't be pleased,' Hassan said.

'You must obey a direct order,' Jack said. 'Major Kerr Sahib understands that.'

Sliding off Sharbat, Jack jettisoned his sword, which would slow him down when he climbed the ridge. Fastening his scabbard over the saddle and carrying only his revolver, he slid into cover as Hassan rode off. Jack understood the magnitude of the risk he was taking; he knew that if he was captured he faced a horrendous death by torture, but the rewards might be worth the risk. Either the Bunerwals were retreating, or the Akhund of Swat had arrived. The news could be very good or very bad; he had to find out which.

Lying still for five minutes, Jack surveyed his surroundings. He saw his Guides trot north with much hallooing and waving of hands. A moment later a dozen Pashtun footmen followed. Jack allowed them another few moments, before sliding from his cover and moving up the hill. Wearing khaki and a turban, he was not dressed much differently from the average tribesman, so from a distance, he would be safe. If anybody came close, it would be another story. Jack felt his heart hammer as he thought again of the consequences. What would Mary think if he was killed?

No; Jack shook his head. Thinking like that would weaken him. He could not think like that. He must concentrate on climbing this hill.

The tree cover grew thinner as Jack climbed with little undergrowth to either hide him or impair his progress. Twice his feet slipped under him, and he fell; once he heard the mutter of conversation and lay still as a couple of Pashtun warriors walked easily up the steep slope. One carried a jezzail in his hand; the second had a Minie rifle, or a copy of a Minie rifle, across his back.

At the summit of the ridge, a length of bleak scrubland stretched between two belts of trees. In the middle of the gap, thrust into a pile of loose stones, the Akhund's green banner ruffled unattended in the breeze.

Why is that there? Jack thought. *Is it a challenge to us? Is it to lure us here?*

Avoiding the bare area, Jack moved cautiously within the trees until he had a clear view of the opposite side of the hill. He stopped, taking a deep breath.

Oh, dear Lord. Oh, dear Lord in heaven. All the Pashtuns in Pakhtunkhwa have gathered here.

On the reverse slope of the ridge, Jack counted scores of different standards flapping in the breeze. Predominately green or black, each thrust proudly above an encampment of Pashtun warriors. Some of the Pashtuns were smoking from hookahs, others talking together, cleaning their rifles or sharpening their swords. Music drifted to Jack from shpelai, sitar or sarinda, or a combination of all three.

Jack tried to count the assembled army, maybe twelve thousand, maybe fifteen thousand men, each one a warrior, each one at home in this rugged country. Chamberlain had encamped and invited the Pashtuns to the ball. They had responded with a vengeance.

'We asked for a piper,' Jack said. 'Now we must pay the bill.'

As he watched, each man stopped what he was doing, knelt on the ground and bowed in prayer. Thousands of men praying together was an impressive sight, something that Jack had never expected to see. He watched, not even sure what to think until the Pashtuns resumed their previous occupations. The music began again, softly.

The sound of drums alerted him, and he swivelled his binoculars. Riding among the different groups was the tabla mullah. *I have shot you twice. I saw Rougvie's bullet hit you clean as a whistle, yet there you are,* he said to himself, *the indestructible mullah, spreading mayhem wherever you appear. Do I need a silver bullet?*

'It is a fine sight, is it not, Windrush Sahib?'

The words made Jack start. The point of the knife pricking the back of his neck forced him to keep still. 'I know that voice.'

'Rise slowly, Captain Windrush, in case your sense of duty compels you to do something so foolish that I will be forced to use this blade, which would deny your lady Mary the man she misses so much.'

Jack obeyed, feeling somebody remove the revolver from his holster. 'I know that voice very well.'

'So you should, Windrush Sahib. We have fought side by side.'

When Jack turned slowly around, he found himself facing the humorous eyes of Batoor.

CHAPTER EIGHTEEN

Ambela Pass October 1863

'Batoor?' Jack stared at him. 'I thought you were dead!' Unable to hide his pleasure, he lunged forward, grabbing hold of Batoor's upper arms. 'How are you? What are you doing here?'

Jack's initial surge of pleasure faded at sight of the red cord tied around Batoor's right arm.

'I am watching you crawling around.' Batoor pulled back his Khyber knife without replacing it in the scabbard. 'You are a brave man, Windrush. Not many would place their heads in the tiger's mouth. I heard that you had escaped from Gulbaz at Torkrud.' He nodded, stepping back slightly. 'I did not know you were with Chamberlain Sahib until a few days ago.' He grinned. 'Once I learned you were with Chamberlain Sahib, I set this trap for you.'

'For me?'

'Probyn Sahib would come with all his horsemen. Only Windrush would come with a small band of men.' Batoor laughed at his own cleverness.

'I did not know you were here at all. You were going to chase intruders from your land, Batoor. What happened?'

Batoor did not smile. 'I met the Akhund of Swat.'

Jack touched the red cord. 'Why are you with these fanatics? I thought you were dead.'

'Why did you think I was dead?' Batoor asked.

'We found your sword, the sword of the Rahmut Khel. A Waziri told us he had taken it from the dead body of the owner.'

'Ah,' Batoor nodded. 'The khan's silver sword. I did not take that with me, Windrush. It belongs in Torkrud.' He shook his head slowly. 'Ayub always had eyes for that sword. He must have taken it and fallen foul of the Mujahidin.'

'I see.' Jack remembered Ayub eyeing the sword. 'But why did you join the Mujahidin, Batoor? You are not a Ghazi.'

'I am now.' Batoor sounded surprised at the question. He indicated the red cord around his wrist. 'The Akhund of Swat asked me to join the Jihad.'

'You could have said no.'

'You cannot say no to the Akhund.' Batoor spoke seriously.

'Does he ride a horse and beat a tabla drum? Is that the Akhund of Swat?'

Batoor shook his head. 'No, Windrush. Once you meet him, you will know that there is nobody like him.'

The indestructible tabla mullah is not the Akhund, then. Is the Akhund more powerful than a man who cannot be killed?

'Are you going to kill me?' Jack dropped his guard to look as vulnerable as possible. Batoor had saved his life in the past, so Jack gambled that their friendship was stronger that Batoor's new found religious enthusiasm.

'No, Windrush.' Batoor kept the knife in his hand. 'I am going to show you how impossible it is for you to win this fight. I am going to send you back to General Chamberlain with a message from Allah, and from the Akhund of Swat.'

'I would like to meet this man who convinced you to turn against us,' Jack said.

'You shall.' Batoor slid his knife into its scabbard. 'If you try to overpower me, there are a hundred men nearby. They would give you to the women to blind, castrate, and flay alive.'

'I will not try to overpower you.' Jack knew that Batoor was a master of the sword and knife.

Sliding Jack's revolver into his cummerbund, Batoor nodded. 'Come to the standard, Windrush Sahib, and tell me what you see.'

Feeling very vulnerable, Jack stepped to the open space where the green standard fluttered in the breeze.

Previously hidden by a dip in the ground, an elderly, white-bearded man appeared beside the standard, flanked by two large, heavily bearded men who could only have been his bodyguards. On their own, either of the large men would have been distinctive. When next to the elderly man, they were insignificant.

'Is this your Captain Windrush, Batoor?' The elderly man turned his gaze to Jack. 'Salaam Alaikum, Captain Windrush.'

'Salaam Alaikum, sir,' Jack responded. 'Do I have the honour of addressing the Akhund of Swat?'

'Some men call me that. Others know me as Saidu Baba. Only Allah knows my true name, as only Allah knows yours.' The Akhund gave a small smile, his gaze never leaving Jack's face. Jack was immediately aware of the force of the man's personality. Although he must have been about seventy years of age and well past his physical prime, his eyes held Jack's attention like few men he had met. Suddenly Jack knew who had organised this rising against the British. It had not been the tabla mullah. It was this quiet, unassuming man with the serene eyes.

'Stand beside me, Captain Windrush.'

Jack found himself, a British officer, obeying without thought. 'From here we can see right across to the British camp on one side of the ridge and over the massed warriors of the Pashtun on the other. It is a good vantage point, don't you think?' The Akhund's smile was like a benign doctor, not like a man who had raised half of Pakhtunwali against the British. 'I like to think that both sides can view my standard.'

'It is a good vantage point,' Jack agreed. Once more he heard the drift of music on the wind and saw men gathered around campfires. He saw the glitter of sunlight on arms and accoutrements and the constant movement of men. The Akhund must have tremendous influence to gather so many warriors from different tribes together in one spot. It could not only be his personality unless he had visited each tribe individually.

'We have fifteen thousand men gathered here.' There was no pride in the Akhund's voice. He was merely stating facts. 'And more are coming from all across Pakhtunkhwa. Most are Ghazis or *Taliban-ul-ilm*, religious devotees, men dedicated to the cause of Allah.'

'I can see the red cord on Batoor's arm,' Jack said.

'My messages are going out all across Pakhtunwali,' the Akhund continued as if Jack had not spoken. 'Gathering men to the lawsuit, the battle between Allah, the law agent, may his name be praised, and the breakers of Allah's law, the feringhees.'

Jack nodded. So he had been right. The letters were for a gathering of the clans, with religion the unifying force.

'I have issued orders for a jihad against the infidels. We have men from all the tribes between the Kabul River and the Indus; I brought a hundred standards, each capable of rallying forty men. Pashtun warriors are coming from as far as Bajour, the Mullazyes of Dher, and others from the furthest reaches of Pakhtunkhwa.'

'It is a large army for a *lashkar*, a tribal force.' Jack decided to throw in a little dissent. 'Until they remember their blood feuds and start squabbling with each other.'

The Akhund's gaze did not waver. There was wisdom there, as well as infinite sadness, yet there was iron behind all. 'It may look large to you, Windrush, but this is only the beginning. My messengers are everywhere. Soon all the Afridi will join us, and the Waziri, the most fierce and most numerous of the Pashtun. The Waziri can raise 150,000 men, ten times the number you see here.'

Jack tried not to look shaken. He drew on his experiences with the Commissariat for Chamberlain's much smaller force. 'That number of men will need supplied, fed, transported, and cared for.'

'We are not a European army, Windrush, nor yet an Indian one.' The Akhund did not raise his voice, yet every word was clear despite the blustery wind. 'We do not need large baggage trains and thousands of servants. We are the Pashtun.'

'Indeed you are, sir.' Jack tried to find a way to weaken the Akhund's confidence. He remembered the chaos at the Zargun Pass. 'Sooner or later, Akhund, the various tribes in your army will turn against each other. It is not in the Pashtun's nature to stay united for long.'

'That has been the way of the Pashtun in the past. Not this time.' The Akhund gave his gentle smile. 'It is manifest to me that the British have a grudge against Islam.'

'We do not.' Jack tried to break the Akhund's chain of words. 'We have millions of the Faithful living peacefully under British rule.'

Again the Akhund continued as if Jack had not spoken. 'The British, in common with the other feringhee nations, have never forgiven Islam for their humiliation in the Crusades. They cannot bear to see Islam become powerful again.'

Jack could not control his anger. 'Islam attacked Christianity long before the Crusades, and in the shape of the Ottoman Empire and the Barbary corsairs, long after, as well.'

The Akhund looked directly into Jack's eyes. His power was so nearly hypnotic that Jack was forced to jerk his gaze away. *This is the most dangerous man I have ever* met. *The Tabla Mullah is nothing compared to him. The Pashtun have found their leader, their Saladin, their Montrose, their Washington.*

'There are many good followers of Islam in Chamberlain's army,' Jack said gently. 'They worship the Prophet as devoutly as any in your army.'

The Akhund gave another gentle smile. 'They have been deceived into following a feringhee general who represents the infidels. They would be welcome if they chose to change sides, as your friend Batoor has been welcomed.'

Batoor had been listening intently, nodding at all the right places. 'How many men does your general have, Windrush? We estimate six thousand.'

'You are facing the British army, Akhund.' Jack did not directly reply to Batoor's question. 'You know that no gathering of tribal levies will defeat us. Oh, you may gain a victory here, or ambush a column there, but we will always be back with a larger and more powerful force.'

'Large forces starve in the valleys of Pakhtunkhwa.' The Akhund spoke without emotion. 'And small forces are ambushed. This is our holy land. Allah has given this land to his people. Although all lands belong to Allah, Pakhtunkhwa is especially blessed.'

That was twice Jack had heard that phrase, our holy land. It was troubling, this infusing of religion, nation and the military power of the Pashtuns. He knew enough about human nature to know it was dangerous to interfere with anybody's religion, let alone the belief of a people as warlike as the Pashtun.

'Even so, Akhund.' Jack tried to defend a position he knew was becoming untenable. 'An essentially guerrilla army, however large, cannot defeat a modern nation of trained soldiers with modern weapons.'

'Don't you know your own history, Captain?' The Akhund's gaze never left Jack's face. 'Great Britain lost thirteen of their North American colonies to what you call an essentially guerrilla army.'

Jack hid his surprise; he had not expected a tribal leader from the Frontier to know about British military history. About to mention the French influence in the American war, he closed his mouth. Perhaps it was not wise to argue with a man who could kill him in a second.

'General Elphinstone's army was also defeated by similar tactics.' The Akhund was not finished yet. 'Even the armies of the great Napoleon Bonaparte suffered huge losses by such warfare in Spain and Russia.'

Jack swallowed his pride. 'You are right, Akhund. One must never underestimate one's enemies. I know that General Chamberlain does not, and neither, I am sure, do you. Batoor here knows how dangerous the British Army can be.'

The Akhund gave a grave nod. 'We will prevail if it is Allah's will. Only Allah understands everything.'

'We agree there, Akhund,' Jack said. 'We have different names for the same God.'

The Akhund gave a grave bow. 'That is also the will of Allah.'

Even as Jack spoke, he glanced at Batoor, one of the most dynamic men he knew. The Akhund had turned Batoor into a Ghazi seemingly without any trouble. His calm certainty was unsettling, yet strangely reassuring. Despite the fact the Akhund was an enemy, Jack could not help respecting, even liking, the man.

Batoor tapped the butt of the Enfield rifle that was strapped across his back. 'So far, Captain Windrush, the Pashtun have faced your army with outdated weapons. Now Allah has seen fit to supply us with rifles as good as anything the British

Army carries. In a short time, General Chamberlain will face thousands of Mujahidin armed with modern rifles.'

'Oh?' Jack raised his eyebrows. He hoped he would survive to pass this information on to Chamberlain. *In a short time? What does that mean?*

'I think you have seen sufficient, Captain Windrush,' the Akhund said. 'It is the will of Allah that I use you as my messenger for General Chamberlain. Tell him that if he withdraws at once, I will hold back my men from attacking him. If he and his army depart from Pakhtunkhwa and promise that no British Army will return, I will call off the Jihad.' He sighed. 'I am a spiritual leader, Captain Windrush, not a man of war. When I wanted a messenger that General Chamberlain would listen to, Batoor Khan suggested you.' The Akhund permitted himself a small smile. 'His deception was successful. We know the British, you see.'

Jack did not respond to Batoor's smile. He had been very neatly trapped.

The Akhund continued. 'Neither of us wish any more blood spilt on this land, Captain Windrush. Pray tell that to the good general.' He bowed and spoke to Batoor. 'Ensure that Captain Windrush returns safely to the infidel's encampment, Batoor Khan.'

Batoor took hold of Jack's shoulder. 'Your men will be back for you shortly. Remember to inform General Chamberlain that the Akhund of Swat orders him out of Pakhtunkhwa in the name of Allah. If the general remains, the forces of Allah will descend upon him.'

'I will pass the message on.' Jack's mind struggled to process all this new intelligence. He had to tell Chamberlain that the Pashtuns expected modern arms soon. He had a last look at the Akhund, who remained standing beneath his banner, his face grave.

'Come on, Windrush.' Batoor guided Jack away from the Akhund and along the ridge.

'I am glad you are alive, Batoor.' Jack spoke the truth. 'Although I am saddened you have joined the Mujahidin. You can still come back to us. You know you would be welcome.'

Shaking his head, Batoor gave a small smile. 'Will General Chamberlain take heed of the Akhund's warning, Captain Windrush?'

'He is a general, Batoor. Who knows how a general thinks?'

Before he began the descent, Jack glanced again at the Pashtun forces with their flapping banners, drifting smoke and hordes of warriors. For a moment he felt an overwhelming sadness about the futility of war. He was beginning to know these people. They only wanted to be left to pursue their own way of life. He also knew that the average British soldier had no interest in Pakhtunkhwa.

Ill-used men from the back slums of industrial towns, plodding ploughmen from the broad English fields, half-starved Irishmen from impoverished cabins or freckle-faced sons of Highland crofters were not warriors. Oh, they were brave and hardy, but they had not been brought up to war and fighting as these Pashtun had. In some ways, it was unfair to pitch the two peoples and cultures together. In a straight contest, without the army training, weapons and discipline, the British soldier would be no match for these warriors. If the Pashtun had weapons and leadership equal to those of the British soldiers, then the balance tilted in their favour. In the Akhund, they had a charismatic leader. In the village of Tazhak, they had the source of better rifles.

'Come, Captain.' Batoor was watching as the thoughts ran through Jack's head. 'Or your men will return without you.'

Small groups of Pashtun warriors watched as Batoor escorted Jack down the wooded ridge to his agreed rendezvous with his Guides. None tried to interfere, although some shouted insults.

'You cannot defeat the Akhund,' Batoor said solemnly. 'He is favoured by Allah. Every morning, when rising from prayers, Allah deposits gold under the Akhund's praying mat, sufficient gold to fund him through the day.'

Jack grunted. 'Is that true, Batoor? Do you believe it is true?'

'It does not matter if I believe it, Windrush.' Batoor balanced on the steep slope without difficulty. 'What matters is that the warriors of God believe it.'

Jack nodded. For a moment he wondered how sincere Batoor's faith was and why he had told him about the rifles. 'You know you cannot win, Batoor. We will wear down the Bunerwals and smash the Mujahidin.'

Batoor's smile taunted Jack. 'We think of time differently, Windrush. We have patience; to us, a wait of a hundred years is a snap of Allah's finger.'

'What does that mean?'

'It means that you must hustle and bustle and think today's deeds are all that matters. Allah has granted us infinity. A battle lost today can be gained in a year or a hundred years.' Batoor kept his smile. 'I am glad you are still alive, Windrush.' He escorted Jack to the lowest fringe of trees, so the valley was open before them. 'There are your men,' Batoor said as the six-strong Guides patrol trotted along the flank of the hill. 'It is all right; the Akhund has given orders that they are not to be harmed.'

'That was kind of him.' Jack kept the irony from his voice. Remembering the force of the Akhund's personality, he could imagine that the orders would be obeyed.

'Come on, Captain Windrush.' Batoor increased his pace, so he ran down the final slope of the hill, disappearing behind a rocky spur. Jack kept up as best he could, stumbling in Batoor's wake.

Jack heard the voice as a Bunerwal hailed the Guides from within the trees. 'Why are you here, fighters for the feringhee?'

Zaman shouted back. 'We are true to our salt. Run away, Bunerwal, lest true men come for you.'

'Do you seek the infidel officer Windrush?'

Jack started to hear his name so well known among the enemy.

'We seek him,' Hassan answered for the Guides. Although the words carried quite clearly to Jack, the angle of the hill spur prevented him from seeing what was happening.

'He's dead!' The Bunerwal sneered. 'We caught him and killed him.'

'He's alive!' A gust of wind blew away Batoor's words. He slowed slightly. 'Hurry, Windrush, or your men will leave without you.'

'If you have killed Windrush,' that was Hassan's voice, 'we will kill all of you.'

Half a dozen Bunerwals joined in the laughter. 'Run back to the British, servants of the feringhees.'

'Come on, Windrush.' Drawing his Khyber knife, Batoor ran, leaping downhill without any regard where he placed his feet. He stopped at the base of the slope, where a party of some dozen Bunerwals were still jeering at the withdrawing Guides.

'We are too late,' Batoor said as Jack's patrol trotted away, taking Sharbat with them. The Bunerwals watched, sneering.

'Who told the Guides that Windrush was dead when the Akhund ordered him let alone?' Batoor asked mildly.

A young man stepped forward. His kohl-rimmed eyes and lovelocks beneath his pakul contrasted with the pulwar at his belt and jezzail across his shoulder. 'Who are you to ask?'

'I am Batoor Khan of the Rahmut Khel.' Drawing his Khyber knife, Batoor plunged it deep into the man's chest.

The other Bunerwals watched without interfering. Jack wondered if Batoor had just started a new blood feud.

'I will take you to the British camp,' Batoor said. 'You will be safe with me. I am known by both the Bunerwals and the Mujahidin as a friend of Akhund.'

About to refuse the offer, Jack realised that Batoor spoke sense. On his own, he could be a target for any hot-headed young Pashtun or any sharpshooter with a jezzail.

'You might wish this back.' Batoor handed over his revolver. 'I don't like these weapons. They jam too easily and are hard to reload.' He touched the hilt of his Khyber knife. 'I prefer my old friend here.'

'I still owe you a horse,' Jack said. 'And I know where the sword of the Rahmut Khel is.'

Batoor nodded. 'The sword will return to Torkrud when the time is right. Come on, Windrush. You have a message to deliver.'

CHAPTER NINETEEN

Ambela Valley October 1863

'My men told me you were dead.' Major Kerr seemed angry that Jack proved his men to be wrong.

'I'm not.' Jack could see Hassan staring at him as if he had risen from the grave. 'I must see General Chamberlain.'

Kerr touched him with a thick forefinger. 'You are a hard man to kill, Windrush. I've never heard of a man being escorted to safety by a Ghazi before.'

Jack grinned. 'That was Batoor Khan. My one-time host.'

'I see,' Kerr grunted. 'You lead an interesting life, Jack, I'll grant you that. Come on, and we'll see what the general makes of all this.'

Chamberlain shook his head as Jack repeated what Akhund had told him. 'Fifteen thousand men to my six thousand, and more coming. This Akhund; is he a military leader, would you say, Windrush?'

Jack shook his head. 'I would say that the Akhund is more of a spiritual leader, a man who inspires his men.'

'The Ghazis are among the most formidable opponents we have faced,' Chamberlain said. 'They are as courageous as the Sikhs. If they had half the discipline of the Khalsa, they would be a very dangerous force indeed.'

'I can't answer for their discipline,' Jack said. 'I do know that they will soon be better armed.'

Chamberlain grunted. 'A few gunsmiths, even a score of gunsmiths, won't make sufficient rifles to arm 15,000 men.'

'No, sir, although I would calculate there were about a hundred gunsmiths in Tazhak, maybe more.'

'Even a hundred, creating say, one, maybe two rifles a week at most?' Chamberlain shook his head. 'I think we can disregard the Akhund's warning. He was trying to frighten us into withdrawal. That is what happened with Elphinstone in '41. He accepted the word of the Afghans.'

Jack nodded; it was evident that memories of that disastrous campaign still haunted Chamberlain.

'No.' Chamberlain made his decision. 'Thank you for your information, Windrush. I will think about what to do about these rifles. In the meantime, I will stick to my original strategy and stand fast here. We will let the Fanatics and Bunerwals take casualties when they attack us.' Standing up, Chamberlain paced the few paces that his tent allowed. 'However, I will send for reinforcements. The Pioneers have been building roads from here, one forward to the village of Ambela, the other giving us better communications over the lower slopes of the Mahabun Mountains to the Peshawar Plain. I entertain no fear as to the final result if we are supported by more infantry and kept in supplies and ammunition.' He smiled. 'That is what I shall tell the Commander-in-Chief, Sir Hugh Rose. The tribes are losing men and will tire first. In the meantime, when you have rested and eaten, I want you to trot over to the Punjabis. They are still an officer short.'

'Yes, sir.' Once again Jack wished he had the continuity of a regimental officer, rather than being sent to whichever spot he might be useful.

* * *

Major Sinclair welcomed him with a faint smile and a handshake. 'I heard you were killed and came back from the dead.'

'That's right, Major.'

'Useful trick, that. You'll have to teach it to me sometime.'

'I hope I never have to use it again.'

Sinclair nodded. 'Can't say I blame you. Now, I'll give you a company to command. The Bunerwals and all those other interesting chaps have not forgotten about us. They keep things lively with sniping and the occasional raid.'

'I'm sure your Sikhs can cope with that, sir.'

'Oh, it's all meat and potatoes to my boys.' Sinclair nodded. 'We are the best there has ever been.'

'So I've heard, sir.'

'You get settled in with my lads,' Sinclair said. 'You know them now.'

It was next morning before the Bunerwals and Mujahidin attacked again, just as dawn greyed the sky. The first Jack knew was a sinister noise he instantly recognised. 'Can you hear that?' He asked the nearest man, the young Ishar Singh.

'I hear it, sahib,' Ishar Singh said. 'It's a tabla drum.'

I will have to kill that mullah yet again. 'Rouse the men,' Jack said. 'The enemy is coming.'

There was no need to say more. The Sikhs rose willingly, forming up in near-silence with their bearded faces showing a variety of emotions from eagerness to impassivity.

'Here they come, lads! Hundreds of the buggers!'

The Bunerwals and Ghazis came with a rush, heads down and pulwars held high.

Ishar Singh levelled his rifle. The other Sikhs did the same, waiting for the order to fire.

'They're not coming on this front,' Jack said. 'Hold your fire.'

'Ready!' Kerr's Guides were on Jack's left flank, with Hassan closest to Jack. 'Here they come!'

'Stand ready, 5th Gurkhas!' A powerful voice came from the Punjabi's left flank. A dozen standards fluttered above the mass of Ghazis that advanced on the stone breastwork guarding the eastern end of the pass. Unseen behind the warriors, pipes and tabla drum urged them on.

The Ghazis split, with hundreds charging for the Guides, the British infantry and the Gurkhas, yet none approaching Jack's section of the line. He felt his Sikhs fretting with frustration, eager to join in.

'They're scared of us!' Sinclair said.

'Sahib,' Ishar Singh pleaded, 'can we go and help?'

'No. Stand fast,' Jack said.

'Ready, cap, aim, fire!' The precise commands rang out as the men of the 71st Highlanders and 101st Regiment fired volleys into the charging masses, felling Mujahidins and Bunerwals in small piles. Ignoring their casualties, the Pashtun charged on to be met by the stabbing bayonets and clubbed muskets of the 71st and 101st.

'There's my father!' Hassan shouted on Jack's left. Without hesitation, he aimed and fired. 'Missed you that time!'

Jack shivered. What sort of men were these to fire at their own kin? Would he ever understand the Pashtun?

The Pashtun attack faltered at the British line, with warriors at the rear trying to push forward the more reluctant men at the front.

General Chamberlain recognised the hesitation. 'Now, 5th Gurkhas!' he ordered. 'Now's your time! Let them see the blades of your kukris!'

Jack saw the delight on the Gurkhas' faces as they unsheathed their wickedly sharp kukris and vaulted over the sangar.

'Sahib, can we join them?' Ishar Singh said. 'The Gurkhas are having all the glory.'

'Stand still,' Jack ordered.

In an instant the Gurkhas who had lightened the camp with their cheerful good humour altered into one of the most efficient fighting machines that Jack had ever seen. Disregarding the bullets that pattered among them from the Pashtun's jezzails, they charged with their kukris held high.

Although Jack had experienced many hand-to-hand encounters in his career, he had never seen anything like the charge of the 5th Gurkhas. Yelling, they used only their kukris as they pursued the suddenly fleeing Pashtuns. Heads and arms flew in the air; others of the Pashtun were disembowelled or simply slashed to pieces as the Gurkhas chased them hundreds of yards from the British positions. Even when the recall sounded, some of the Gurkhas continued, so that the officers and NCOs had to physically pull the men back.

'Go on, Johnnie Gurkha!' The 71st Highlanders roared their approval.

The firing continued as the 5th Gurkhas returned to the British positions, with jezzails thumping from the Pashtun side and the British sharpshooters and artillery replying.

Sighing, the Sikhs settled back down, evidently disappointed that they had not been allowed to share in the fighting.

'Better luck next time, lads.' Sinclair seemed to share their dissatisfaction. 'There are plenty more of the enemy out there.'

General Chamberlain loomed up, looking as weary as ever. 'I hope you enjoyed your rest with the Punjabis, Windrush. Come with me, please.'

The general had set up his tent in the lee of a small ridge in the centre of the British camp, with a stalwart Sikh sentry standing like a granite statue. Ushering Jack inside, Chamberlain seated himself behind his desk.

'You have been fairly successful in your information gathering so far, Windrush.'

'Thank you, sir.' Jack was unsure what else to say.

'Judging by the casualties and the banners, Windrush, we have tribesmen from half the Frontier opposing us. Until our reinforcements arrive, we will continue to invite the enemy onto our defences and fend off all their attacks.'

'Indeed, sir.' Jack was too experienced to think that Chamberlain had brought him into his tent to keep him apprised of the military situation. The general was merely laying the foundations for some ugly news.

'Now, sir.' Reaching under his desk, Chamberlain produced an Enfield rifle. 'What do you make of this, eh?'

'It's an Enfield.' Jack checked the serial number. 771, complete with crown and cypher. 'With the same number as the weapons copied by the Pashtuns in Tazhak.'

'A patrol of the Guides picked up this from one of the dead out there. It seems that your rifles are indeed filtering through to the enemy.'

'Yes, sir.' Jack thought it diplomatic not to say any more.

'Your Akhund fellow mentioned that his army would soon be supplied with modern weapons, Windrush.'

'Yes, sir.'

'We can take that to mean a shipment from Tazhak,' Chamberlain said.

'I believe so, sir.' *Why are generals so pedantic? Get to the point, man!*

'Very well,' Chamberlain said. 'You know more about Tazhak than anybody else. I want you to take a small force, find and destroy the arms, and make sure there are no more made at Tazhak.'

'Yes, sir.' Jack spoke before the practicalities of the mission struck him. 'How small a force, sir? I'll have to move at night to get past the Bunerwals and Mujahidin, so I'll need men used to clandestine operations.' Once more he wished for his men of the 113th with their vast experience in this type of operation.

'You know best, Windrush. You can have your pick as long as you don't weaken me too much.'

'Thank you, sir.' Mentally scanning the garrison, Jack discarded them regiment by regiment. The British infantry was expert at attacking or defending fixed positions or fighting a conventional battle in the open. In Jack's opinion, there were none better anywhere. They were not as good in irregular warfare or in moving silently in the dark. The Sikhs had the same attributes and failings as British infantry. That left the Gurkhas, Probyn's Horse or the Guides. He had no doubt of the Gurkhas' courage or skill and had recently seen their fighting prowess, but his lack of Gurkhali would be a disadvantage.

'The Guides, sir. I would like a score of the Guides cavalry.'

'I'll speak to Kerr,' Chamberlain agreed at once.

Jack's mind was racing. Now that Chamberlain had finally agreed to his request, he seemed to have a thousand questions and things to do with little time in which to do them. 'Could you set up a diversion, sir, something to attract the enemy's attention while we slip out of camp?'

Chamberlain gave a single nod. 'I'm fully aware of the magnitude of your task, Windrush. I am ordering you into the jaws of a very dangerous leopard. You can take more men if you wish; say, two hundred with a couple of screw guns.'

Jack remembered the Akhund's words. 'That would be a small army, sir, and in the Frontier, small armies are ambushed. No; I'll take the Guides I had before if they are available, and another dozen of the same.' He grunted. 'There are certain things I wish done before we leave, sir. The men might not like them.' He explained what he wanted as Chamberlain nodded.

CHAPTER TWENTY

Pakhtunkhwa, November 1863

The artillery barrage started two hours after dark, cracking open the silence of the night as the guns targeted the ridge on which the Akhund's standard flew. For a moment Jack watched the yellow-white explosions highlighting the ragged pines and wondered how many men would die or be maimed merely to provide a cover for his Guides.

'Right, lads.' Jack had insisted that rather than Guides uniform, the men should wear the local loose top and trousers, with whatever headgear they preferred, and a poshteen against the cold. Even so, his men looked distinctly military as he led them out of the camp and into the valley. All sported the red cord of the Ghazis on their right arm.

'Spread out,' Jack ordered. 'Try to look less like soldiers. You're a mob of Mujahidin, not a troop of Guides cavalry!'

The men grinned at him, teeth white through the dark. For some, years of training in the Guides had become second nature, while others quickly reverted to the less disciplined habits of their previous existence.

After ten minutes the artillery fire died away. Only a few isolated rifle shots punctuated the silence, and when they faded there was silence except for the keen of the wind.

Jack had ordered each man to muffle his equipment, so there was nothing to jingle or rattle as they rode. The horses' hooves were padded to make no sound on the ground, while no man carried anything that might mark them down as fighting for the British. Even their weapons were altered so rather than Enfields, they carried an assortment of captured Pashtun firearms, with Khyber knives or pulwars as side arms.

I've done all I can. Let's see if we can dent these Mujahidin.

Hassan took the lead when they passed close to a Bunerwal outpost. He shouted out a greeting before the Bunerwals challenged.

'Salaam Alaikum,' Hassan said. 'Allah Akbar.'

Jack kept riding as his Guides responded to the Bunerwals with obscene jests. Their combined laughter rose.

'Stop.' Jack turned around in the saddle, removed his Minie rifle from its holster, and fired a round in the direction of the British camp. At this distance, it was unlikely he could do any damage, while the gesture might help bolster an image of a group of Fanatics.

The other Guides followed Jack's example, with the result that one of the British piquets fired back.

'Hey! You Mujahidin are all the same!' One of the Bunerwals complained. 'You start the trouble and leave it to men like us to finish it off! You get away back to Swat and leave us in peace. I've got two wives to support; I've no time for a war with the feringhee!'

Raising a hand in acknowledgement, Jack said quietly: 'Ride on. Hassan, you know this country far better than I ever will. Could you guide us?'

'Yes, sahib.' Hassan pushed forward without any fuss.

They rode until dawn and camped in an abandoned caravanserai that a troop of vultures had made their home. The well contained sweet water for the horses, but the accommodation was timeworn, and alive with insects. Shuddering, Jack stamped on one of the enormous spiders the British knew as jerrymungulums. *What a country; even the spiders want to kill you.*

As he lay on the ground, looking up at the quickly fading stars, Jack wondered anew what he was doing here. *It's like a roundabout,* he told himself. *One of the tribes raids the part of India we protect. We retaliate by attacking that tribe; we burn their crops and kill some of their young men. They need food so raid their neighbours, who then ride into India to plunder for food, and we retaliate. It is a Pashtun blood feud on a larger scale. We are not solving anything by being here; we have been caught up in the local way of life. Am I tired of being a soldier? Has marriage softened me?*

Jack heard the familiar drumming before he was properly awake. He opened his eyes to see Zaman standing over him with an old Brunswick rifle in his hand. The silver hilt of the Rahmut Khel sword glinted at his waist. 'There is trouble, Windrush, sahib.'

'Get the men up.' Jack reached for his Minie. He kicked Fatteh awake. 'Come on, lads. Where is the drummer, Zaman?'

'About a hundred paces from the caravanserai entrance, sahib.'

'Is he the same mullah?' Jack knew the answer before Zaman nodded. Somehow he knew that wherever he travelled, the indestructible tabla mullah would arrive. He sighed. 'Come on then, lads.'

Jack's Guides were still getting ready when the Mullah's men rode into the caravanserai, with two dozen men surrounding him.

I'll kill you yet, Tabla.

For a second the two groups of men eyed each other with hands twitching toward their weapons and eyes wary. At last, supposing Hassan to be the leader of the group, the Mullah reined up in front of him. Jack glanced at his thigh; there was no wound, no sign at all that Rougvie had shot him. What sort of man was this?

'I am gathering warriors for the Jihad against the infidels,' the tabla mullah said.

Hassan indicated the scarlet cord on his right arm, saying nothing.

The mullah turned his smoky eyes on the Guides, studying them one by one. 'You claim to be Ghazi, yet here you are sheltering miles away from the feringhee.'

'We are in the same place as you.' Hassan was calm as he rested his hand on his sword.

The mullah turned until his gaze settled on Jack.

'We have met already, cousin,' the mullah said.

Knowing that he would reveal himself as soon as he spoke, Jack merely grunted. The mullah dismounted, stepping closer. Jack held his gaze, hoping to mirror the confidence of a Pashtun. The mullah scrutinised Jack for what seemed hours, but was probably only a couple of minutes, then looked away. Jack could not read the expression of his eyes.

Jerking his head to his men, Jack made for the entrance of the caravanserai and the covering darkness of the night. He felt the frantic hammer of his heart gradually slow.

'I thought that mullah had recognised me,' he said.

Hassan nodded. 'If he had, we would all be dead by now, or wishing that we were.'

'Let's put some distance between him and us.'

With Hassan in the lead, they rode into the night, following some obscure track that Jack could barely see. Twice he heard a grey wolf howl, the sound bringing some repressed folk memory that sent a cold chill down his spine. Once he heard the rustle of wings overhead and wondered if the vultures were following them, sensing death.

'How far are we from Tazhak?' They had been riding for hours, stopping only to rest the horses.

'We'll reach there at dawn.' Hassan sounded quite comfortable in his role of guide.

Jack looked over his men, wondering if he should have brought more. Twenty men, even such formidable fighters as the Guides, was a tiny force to capture and destroy an entire village as well as a caravan. Ever since he had been given the task, he had cudgelled his mind trying to think of some stratagem to even the odds. He had nothing. His once-fertile brain was blank. He would have to camp nearby, observe the target, and hope for inspiration — that was not reassuring while operating in very hostile territory.

And as for the caravan? Jack took a deep breath. Was the Akhund's information inaccurate? He shook his head: *I was never in worse humour for anything in my life. What's wrong with me?*

With the onset of dawn, Jack recognised his surroundings. They were in the Valley of Kot, only a couple of miles from Tazhak. He looked around; the valley was quiet, with only a few herds of sheep on the lower slopes and no discernible inhabitants. He had to make his decision soon.

'We'll find somewhere overlooking Tazhak.' Jack tried to sound more confident than he felt. 'And observe the village.' As a young officer, he would have ridden straight there and attacked bald-headed. Now, with more than a decade of experience including three wars under his belt, he had learned caution.

Circling around Tazhak and being careful to keep out of sight, the Guides found a position in the hills and settled down. They were in a saucer-like depression, with a fringe of rocks and trees to provide cover from casual travellers. Jack focussed his binoculars on the village. There were some small groups of men arriving but less than there had been on his last visit, which he found odd, given that Chamberlain's campaign should ensure brisk business for gun makers.

'What do you think, Hassan?' Jack passed over the binoculars.

'It is very quiet,' Hassan said.

Jack swept his gaze along the guard towers. The sentinels watched as intently as they had last time, yet he sensed that something was wrong. If anything, the sentinels looked too alert.

'I'm going down for a closer look,' Jack decided. 'If I don't come back, you are in charge, Hassan. Get the men back safely.'

'Yes, sahib.' Hassan accepted the possibility of Jack's death with disturbing equanimity. He hesitated for a moment. 'Sahib, it may be best if you take one of the Guides with you in case you have to talk. Your accent is terrible.'

Jack nodded. 'Thank you, Hassan. I'll take Sawan. You're needed here. Come on, Sawan!'

Slipping down the hill on foot, they sauntered close to Tazhak's only gate. Sawan hummed a little song, fingering his jezzail with more nervousness than Jack had expected. It was quite reassuring to know that the Pashtun were human, with the same fears and emotions as everybody else.

'Steady, Sawan,' Jack murmured as they approached the entrance. A warrior leant against the open gate, sharpening his pulwar on a stone. He gave Jack and Sawan a hard glance before returning to his sharpening.

'Salaam Alaikum,' Sawan said quietly.

'Salaam,' the guard replied.

'Where are you going, cousin?' A second guard looked up from his position inside the gate. His indigo-black clothes and steel cap suggested he came from the Indus Valley, while the buckler across his back was of untanned buffalo-hide. Jack put his age as anything between thirty and forty.

'To look at the rifles,' Sawan patted his jezzail, 'this one was old when your grandfather was a young man.'

'You are wearing the red cord of a Ghazi,' the Indus Valley guard observed. 'Should you not be fighting the feringhees?'

'I shall,' Sawan said, 'as soon as I get a better weapon.'

'You might be a day late.' Grunting, the guard spat betel-juice on the ground, and returned to his post, his hooded eyes never straying from Sawan's face.

A day late? Has the caravan already departed?

Feeling as if he was passing through the gates of hell, Jack stepped inside the village. Only half a dozen steps later he realised why the guards had been so wary. Filling the main street, thirty camels stood patiently, some decorated with colourful cloths and little bells, others old and dull. Their drivers stood at their sides, wiry bare-legged men in dusty turbans and open sandals. Each camel was laden with panniers. As Jack watched, a man emerged from one of the gunsmith's workshops carrying an Enfield in each hand. Without hesitation, he placed the rifles inside the pannier of the nearest camel. Jack had a glimpse of another score of Enfields before the man closed the pannier.

We're not too late.

'That's our caravan.' Jack stopped a few paces within the village.

'Yes, sahib,' Sawan said. 'There are thirty camels, each with two panniers. If each pannier holds twenty rifles, that's forty for each camel, twelve hundred in total.'

The Akhund must have made these craftsmen work flat out. Twelve hundred Enfield copies!

Jack had a mental image of twelve hundred Ghazis armed with modern rifles.

Added to their huge preponderance of numbers and their martial skill, that made them an incredibly formidable enemy. If Chamberlain were defeated, the blow to British prestige would be as immense as the Kabul disaster of 1841, weakening the British position in India. 'We have to stop them.'

'Yes, sahib,' Sawan said.

'We can't leave here yet,' Jack said. 'Let's see if they have any Enfield rifles in the first workshop.'

Jack led them in, knowing that every minute could be vital yet aware that if they left Tazhak after only a few moments without purchasing anything, the sentries at the gate would be instantly suspicious, which could jeopardise the entire mission. The gunsmith inside the workshop looked at him without recognition or expression.

'How much are your Enfields?' Jack allowed Sawan to do the talking.

The smith spread his hands. 'Alas, we have only just now sold the last one. Can I interest you in a Brunswick, perhaps? Or a Minie?'

'I only want an Enfield.' Sawan was too forthright for Jack, who wished to purchase something, anything, as an excuse to leave the village.

'The Minie is a fine weapon,' the gunsmith said. 'Your colleague carries one. Do you find that it suits, cousin?' He faced Jack directly.

'Yes,' Jack said shortly. 'We'll take the Minie.'

'I want an Enfield,' Sawan protested.

'You'll take a Minie and like it.' Jack cursed the bloody-mindedness of these Pashtuns. *They're as bad as the blasted Scots.* He glowered at the gunsmith, daring him to make any comment.

Sawan grabbed the Minie with ill grace as Jack parted with far too much money for the weapon.

'My younger brother,' Jack explained as the gunsmith peered at him.

'Family.' The gunsmith shook his head. 'He is a Yusufzai, yet you speak like a feringhee. How is that?'

Jack felt the tension rise within the workshop. 'I was in the feringhee's army,' he said. 'And his jail.'

The gunsmith laughed. 'No wonder you became a Warrior of God.'

The caravan was still in the street when they left the workshop, Sawan holding his Minie as if it was diseased.

'That was a short visit.' The Indus Valley sentinel at the gate recognised them.

'We had it on order.' Sawan was quicker-witted than Jack had expected. He held the Minie up for inspection.

The sentinel spat more betel-juice. 'You'd be better with an Enfield.'

'Next time,' Sawan said over his shoulder as he examined the Minie. 'They're too expensive, with this jihad.'

* * *

'There is a caravan of thirty camels lined up in the main street,' Jack explained to the Guides. 'I think each camel carries about forty copies of the Enfield rifle. That will be a significant boost to the Mujahidin's firepower, so they will be able to do more damage, kill more farmers, kidnap more merchants and attack more posts of the Guides.'

The Guides watched him impassively. Zaman stood up, his right hand on the silver pommel of the Rahmat Khel pulwar that never left his side. 'We know these things, Windrush Sahib. When are we going to attack them?'

'We will attack two hours before sunset when there is still sufficient light for us to see,' Jack said softly. 'If the caravan leaves the village, we will attack earlier. Make sure your weapons are oiled. Make sure your swords are sharp. We are going straight through the front door. Half of us,' he split the Guides in two, ensuring some of his veterans were in each party, 'will cut out the caravan and take it out of the village. The rest will destroy the workshops and wreck the tools.'

The Guides nodded eagerly, understanding at once. Jack knew there was no need to explain further. To such men, bred to the blood feud, a raid on a village came as naturally as breathing. He wished again that he had brought more men.

'Zaman, I want you to command the destruction party.' As the most aggressive of the Guides, Zaman was the obvious choice.

Zaman nodded, grinning. 'Yes, sahib.'

'Don't kill any civilians,' Jack reminded him. 'We are on the Queen's business, not a tribal raid.'

'Yes, sahib,' Zaman agreed, far too readily.

The rest of that afternoon, Jack kept an anxious watch on Tazhak in case the caravan should leave. A few men walked into the village with a single train of mules, but the caravan remained within the walls. Nothing else changed. The guards on the towers were as alert as ever, swivelling this way and that while the sentinels at the gate questioned all who came in.

Jack checked his watch; three in the afternoon. 'That caravan will not leave today,' he said with satisfaction. 'There is not sufficient daylight remaining for it to get anywhere.'

The Guides readied themselves for the raid, sharpening swords, checking and re-checking their firearms. They prayed twice, kneeling on the stony ground to face Mecca. Jack wondered what Mary would say when she learned that he had neglected the worship that she demanded.

I won't tell her, he decided, knowing that she would ask, worming the truth out of him within ten minutes. He grinned, missing her. *I hope that a relief column reaches Chamberlain soon. I hope he can smash the Mujahidin, so we get something like peace in Pakhtunkhwa.*

Jack knew that peace was a false hope as long as the Pashtun held to Pakhtunwali, and the British Empire abutted onto Pakhtunkhwa. He sighed, wondering about the as-yet-unborn generations of British soldiers who would have to guard this Frontier. In the unthinkable future, when the British Empire disappeared, as it would, as every Empire always did, their successors in India would inherit the same clutch of problems, and the same circle of raids and reaction would continue.

Jack sighed. *I hope Mary is right and sometime, somehow, there is a Second Coming to bring peace to this troubled world.*

'Sahib.' Hassan was beside him, proffering a hunk of bread and chicken. 'You have not eaten today.'

Jack looked up. 'Thank you, Hassan. I was just thinking of the future. I was wondering if there would ever be peace in this land.'

'All lands belong to Allah,' Hassan said. 'If He wills there to be peace, then peace will come. If His will is for war, then there will be war. All blessings to Allah.'

Jack spoke through a mouthful of bread. 'I hope His will is for peace, Hassan.'

Hassan smiled. 'Then you and I will both be unemployed, Windrush sahib. Who then will look after our families? Allah's timing is perfect in every matter. We don't understand the wisdom behind it, but we have to learn to trust it.'

Jack nodded. 'The ways of Allah are wonderful.' Mary would have substituted God for Allah with identical sentiments. 'Mount up, Guides.'

'We belong to God, and unto God we do return,' Hassan said, with the others murmuring the words.

Jack led his Guides on a wide detour, so they approached the gate from the valley floor. He had them ride in a casual group, laughing as if they had not a care in the world.

Both sentinels stepped forward, the man from the Indus Valley raising his hand. Without stopping, Jack rode through the gates, barging the men aside, knowing his Guides would follow his orders.

For one moment everything seemed right. The camel caravan stood precisely as Jack had left it, a few people walked around the workshops, and some men turned to stare as Jack's Guides crashed into the village.

'Right, lads!' Jack ordered, just before the world exploded around him.

As soon as the last of the Guides clattered into the village, half a dozen Pashtun warriors raced from the nearest compound to slam shut the gates and drop in the massive securing beam. One shouted, 'Allah Akbar,' and fired his rifle in the air.

The shot was a signal. The men who had been standing casually beside the camels suddenly produced rifles, while more warriors appeared on the watchtowers and poured from the workhouses.

'It's a trap!' Jack yelled. He saw the tabla mullah appear at the tail of the caravan. Jack fired, missed, and swore as the mullah began to thunder at his drum, bringing forth an eruption of warriors, some shooting at once, others levelling their rifles at the Guides. Jack saw one of his men fall, sliding sideways from the saddle. A Yusufzai Mujahidin immediately pounced on him, repeatedly stabbing with a long *pesh-kabz* dagger.

'Get out of here!' Jack drew his sword, wishing it was his own sabre rather than the less familiar pulwar. He slashed at an advancing warrior, missed utterly, felt something crash into his leg, looked down to see a massive warrior with a clubbed rifle, kicked in his spurs, and yelled for his men to join him.

'Come on, Guides! Back to the gate.' There were some recommended responses to an ambush, from sitting tight to charging straight for the centre of the ambushers, but none were possible in such an enclosed space. Slashing at a warrior with an upraised pulwar, Jack rode for the door, cursing to see four Pashtuns standing in front of the massive beam that held it closed.

The tabla mullah was encouraging the Pashtun with his drum, so more warriors surged onto the wall and around the gate.

'Allah Akbar!' It was a call that Jack knew would come to him in his nightmares, the same cry that the Ottoman Turks had used in their assault on Christian Europe, the same cry the Moors had used as they invaded Spain. Richard, the Lion Heart, would have known that call, and now it was his turn to be out-thought and out-manoeuvred by the Warriors of God.

No, by God! The Mujahidin are not quite as smart as they think. They acted too fast; they should have waited until we were split further apart.

'Stick together, lads!'

Jack's Guides mustered around him, firing, slashing with their swords, some with gritted teeth, Fatteh singing, Zaman cursing the attackers, striking with the sword of the Rahman Khel. Jack saw Fatteh fall from the saddle, to be immediately dragged away by two warriors. His eyes were huge.

'Sahib! Help!'

Jack reached out. 'Fatteh!'

A group of the Mujahidin got in his way, angry bearded faces intent on killing. *So this was what defeat felt like.* 'Get away from that man!' Jack slashed right and left, swearing.

'Hassan! Take the men to the gate!' Jack made another push for Fatteh, knowing he could not leave anybody in the hands of the enemy. Wishing he was astride Colwall rather than the lighter Sharbat, he tried to thrust through the mass, feeling his sword-cuts parried by a skilful enemy. Another Guide fell, cut down by a swinging pulwar. More Mujahidin warriors appeared at the gate, blocking the Guides' exit.

What's happening here? Jack asked himself. *They could have stayed in the shelter of the houses and shot us down like targets at a shooting gallery. I have to lead my men clear.*

More shots sounded, and two horses fell, throwing their riders onto the ground. Jack saw a tall man vault down from the gate, land on his feet and shout orders. The man looked directly at Jack.

'Batoor!' Jack said.

Zaman turned his horse, kicked in his spurs, and burst through the Pashtun ranks, cutting down a skull-capped Mahmud. Jack barged into one of the Pashtun warriors, knocking him out of the way. Dismounting, he wrestled with the heavy bar. 'Keep out of the way, Batoor. I don't want to kill you!'

Batoor strode forward, pressing his Khyber knife against Jack's throat. 'I can kill you and all your men,' he said softly, 'or you can surrender.'

Jack looked around. The Mujahidin had his men surrounded, with knives, swords and rifles pointed at each man. Only Hassan and Zaman continued to fight, Hassan shouting some slogan and Zaman screaming in frustrated fury as three men parried his blows. *They are containing Zaman's attack. They could easily kill him. What is this?*

'No!' Lifting his sword high, Zaman thrust it into the logs of the gate, used it as a lever, and threw himself upwards. Without looking back, he vaulted to the top of the gate, reached down, retrieved his sword, and vanished outside.

'Surrender, Windrush,' Batoor said. 'I cannot hold my men back much longer.'

'There will be no surrender, Batoor! You're not torturing my men.'

'You have my word, Windrush. None of your men will be tortured. We will treat you with honour.' Batoor eased the pressure of his knife. 'You know me, Windrush.'

Surrender meant captivity and humiliation. Not to surrender meant death for all his men. Jack could see that the Mujahidin were eager to kill the Guides, arguably the most effective regiment that the British had on the Frontier.

'If you break your word to my men, Batoor, you will have lost your honour forever.'

'I despise the man who does not guide his life by honour,' Batoor quoted Khushal Khan Khattak, the Pashtun warrior poet. 'I do not wish to kill you, Windrush. What would Mary think of me then?'

'You're a bastard, Batoor.' Jack felt the frustration of defeat. He raised his voice. 'Sorry, lads. Drop your weapons. We have Batoor's word that they will treat us well.'

One by one, the Guides threw down their weapons, most with a curse. 'It is the will of Allah.' Hassan stood quietly, counting his men. 'We have lost three men, Windrush. I saw you try to rescue Fatteh.'

'Try and stick together,' Jack said. He could only watch in numb despair as Batoor had his men remove the Guides' weapons. The tabla mullah rode around them, smiling, his drum stilled for once.

'Where is Zaman?' Batoor asked. 'Where is my cousin?'

'He got away.' Jack felt bitter about Zaman's desertion, yet pleased that at least one of his men had escaped.

'A pity,' Batoor said. 'I was going to hand him to my women.'

'You gave your word,' Jack said.

'I gave my word that none of the Guides would be tortured or killed. I did not give my word that my cousin would live. We are at feud, as you know. That is Pakhtunwali.'

Jack grunted, understanding why Zaman escaped. It was not cowardice or treason but simple self-preservation, the pragmatism of a man who lived with the realities of life in Pakhtunkhwa.

As the Mujahidin herded the Guides into one of the compounds, Batoor led Jack away to another of the houses. Three sturdy Mujahidin followed, never taking their gaze off Jack.

'Chain him.' Batoor gave rapid orders. 'This is Captain Windrush of the 113th Foot, and now of the Guides. He is a most dangerous man.'

'Was this trap your idea, Batoor, or was it that madman with the drum?'

Batoor smiled. 'We knew that the British knew about the rifle making, so they would eventually decide to end it. We thought it better to tell you about the caravan so that your General Chamberlain would send a column to stop it. I guessed he would either send Probyn or you.' Batoor gave a small frown. 'Allah heeded our wishes, although I had hoped for a larger force to weaken the British position.'

'You were right, Batoor,' Jack admitted grudgingly. 'Your trap worked perfectly.' He lifted his arms, not resisting as the warriors placed heavy manacles on his wrists. *Keep him talking. Learn all you can. There will be a way to escape. Don't give up hope. Find out why they want us captive when they could easily have killed us.* 'You're a clever man, Batoor.'

'I know how you work, Windrush, so setting an ambush was easy.'

Jack grunted. *Am I so predictable? I will have to change my methods if I survive this ordeal.* 'What are your plans with us now, Batoor?'

Leaning over, Batoor checked to ensure Jack's chains were secure. 'The Akhund will convert your men. If you had brought me British, Gurkhas or Sikhs, we would execute them. British-trained men will help us to understand the enemy even better.'

Jack nodded. *That made sense. Why kill men when they could be persuaded to join the Jihad?* 'My Guides are not so easily converted,' Jack said.

'The Akhund will guide them to the truth,' Batoor dismissed Jack's words. 'You, Windrush, I will hand as a gift to the Akhund of Swat. I do not know what he will do with you.'

Jack did not pursue that line of thought. 'Your camels will soon tire of standing here waiting for Probyn or whoever General Chamberlain sends to find what's happened to us.'

Batoor shook his head. 'No, Windrush. I will take the caravan to our forces opposite Chamberlain. I will also send a message to him from you that the village and caravan are destroyed in case he decides to send a larger column.' Batoor frowned. 'Why only bring twenty men, Windrush? We hoped for a much larger number.'

'If I had, Batoor Khan,' Jack rattled his chains, 'we would have burned your village to the ground and destroyed your caravan. As it is, nobody will believe your message.'

'Perhaps they will. Perhaps they will not. Allah will decide,' Batoor said. 'It is no longer your concern.'

'Perhaps it is not. Perhaps it is.' Jack returned Batoor's words. 'Why have you joined these fanatics, Batoor? You know that they cannot win. Your position of Khan was secure; now it is under threat from Gulbaz. He moved against you the moment you left Torkrud.'

'It is Allah's will,' Batoor said. 'Position in this world does not matter when compared with the paradise of the next.'

'You have been smitten with religion, haven't you? Well, that's probably the will of Allah as well.' Jack forced a smile. 'We were friends once, Batoor.'

'We are still friends.' Batoor sounded surprised at Jack's statement. 'We are friends on opposite sides of a war.' He stepped up to Jack, crouching at his side, speaking urgently. 'If you embrace Islam, Windrush, what a team we would make. I would ensure you had all the earthly things a man could want, while Allah would take care of you in Paradise.'

'I thought you religious types did not believe in such material matters,' Jack tried to test Batoor's commitment to the Jihad.

'I can ensure you have horses and hawks for shikar.' Batoor's eyes were bright. 'We can hunt every day, Windrush, you and me, and talk about old campaigns. We can raid for women if you wish, or boys if you prefer.'

'I have Mary,' Jack reminded him. 'My wife. I have no use for boys or other women.'

Batoor was not affected by Jack's attempts to unsettle him. 'You could send for Mary, Windrush. If she does not come, I will send men to bring her here as your senior wife. She will soon become used to our culture.'

This man, my captor, wishes to remain my friend. Our concept of war is vastly different. 'I do not think that Mary would wish to be kidnapped, Batoor. Nor would she be willing to share me with other women.' For a moment Jack toyed with the idea.

'She would be with you,' Batoor said simply. 'Would you not do the same for her?'

Jack closed his mouth. *Would I? Would I change my religion for Mary, if she embraced Islam?*

'I can see you are considering that.' Batoor stood up. 'I do not like to see you in chains, Windrush. Think what times we could have! Think what campaigns we could wage, what stories we could tell our children!' He stepped to the door. 'Your men will be well cared for, Windrush, whatever they decide.' He left, closing the door behind him.

Although it was not the first time that Jack had been held prisoner, it was the first time that he had been captured by a man who considered him a friend. Unsure what to think, Jack leaned back. He knew that sleep and hope were vital to a prisoner. *Without rest, I will be gradually worn down; without hope, I will descend into a slough of despond, as Bunyan would say. So sleep and allow your mind to recover, Jack, my boy. Things look bad, but you're not dead yet.*

Calming himself down with thoughts of Mary, Jack heard the drum of the tabla mullah. He knew his men would remain loyal. They were Guides.

What a mess.

Sleep was fitful with the chains dragging at Jack's wrists and ankles and the sounds of the village now more alien. After a while, the hypnotic drumming of the Tabla faded away, to be replaced by the snorting of camels.

The door opened with a crash. Two unsmiling Mujahidin handed a hunk of fresh bread and a leather bottle of water to Jack. 'Eat and drink, feringhee.' They waited until Jack was finished before unfastening his chains and leading him outside the compound.

'Salaam Alaikum.' Batoor was waiting in the main street. 'I hope you have reconsidered your position, Windrush.'

'You know I won't change, Batoor.' Jack watched the tabla mullah lead the caravan out of Tazhak, the shuffling of feet and tinkling of bells replacing the beating of the drum.

'There, you see?' Batoor touched Jack's arm. 'Some of your Guides have already embraced Mujahidin; they are now Warriors of God.'

Jack lifted his head. He felt a twist of despair when he saw Hassan and Ursulla among the escort of the caravan. Ursulla looked directly at him, then away again, quickly.

'Aye, you should feel guilty,' Jack shouted. 'You have betrayed your salt!'

Hassan faced Jack. 'It is the will of Allah,' he said quietly. 'You could join us, Windrush Sahib.' His eyes were pleading. 'Join us, sahib.'

For an instant, Jack contemplated singing God Save the Queen but decided that such a display would be crass and clamped shut his mouth. As he watched the caravan leave the village at a steady pace with a dozen of his Guides among the escort, he felt as if his world was collapsing. If even the Guides, the elite of the Indian Army, could be suborned to the Mujahidin cause, how vulnerable was India to such attacks?

The camels glided past, each one with its laden panniers, each one holding rifles that could kill British or Indian soldiers, each one carrying a cargo that could end the fragile peace in India and allow the Mujahidin to debouch from the mountains into the vulnerable plains to rape, raid, kidnap and kill. He had been sent to end such occurrences, and he had failed.

The tabla mullah rode up to him, now tapping lightly on his drum. He circled Jack three times, staring at him through these strange smoky eyes. 'Embrace Islam,' he advised. 'Come to Allah.'

Jack said nothing. He held the gaze of the mullah, seeing nothing there except contempt. 'I am going to kill you,' he said flatly. There was no bullet wound on the mullah's chest or thigh.

'If Allah wills.' The mullah circled Jack again, always beating his drum. 'You will be welcome in our ranks, Captain Windrush.'

'Damn you for a troublemaker,' Jack said.

The mullah rode away, following the caravan.

'You can join us, Windrush,' Batoor said. 'You are more like us than you know.'

'I am an officer in the British Army,' Jack reminded him. 'I cannot join you, even if I wanted to.' He knew that his refusal probably meant he was consigning himself to a very unpleasant death.

Batoor looked genuinely sorry. 'Then I must leave you, Windrush. I am taking the caravan to its destination. We may meet again, in peace or war.'

'If it is in war, Batoor,' Jack said, 'I hope you choose the right side next time. If it is in peace, then I shall shake your hand and give you the horse I owe you.'

'May Allah go with you.' Batoor raised his voice. 'Take this man away! Keep him secure until the Akhund gives orders what to do with him.' He sighed. 'Your jailors are not warriors, Windrush.' He tapped his forehead significantly. 'I have given them orders to look after you. I have done all I can for you.'

Jack nodded. 'If we meet in war, Batoor, I will try to kill you. I hope we meet in peace.'

'It will be as Allah wills.' Turning around, Batoor strode away. He did not turn back.

Two burly Pashtuns grabbed hold of Jack and marched him back into the compound he had just left. Within minutes he was pushed to the ground, his chains were looped around a staple in the wall, and both men had landed a couple of hefty kicks that left him in no doubt that he was not a welcome guest.

'I hope the Akhund wants you dead,' the younger man said. He spoke slowly as if forming the words was a great effort.

'The women will castrate you,' the older man added, equally ponderously. 'Then slowly flay you as you scream for mercy.' He seemed to enjoy the idea, for he hovered over Jack, savouring his words. 'They will peg out what is left of you and urinate in your mouth until you drown.'

'I will take your skin and make it into a coat,' the younger man said.

Jack forced a smile, although he knew that nothing these men said was exaggerated. *Don't let them see that I am scared. Bullies feed on the fear of their victims.* 'Come closer,' he said. 'Help me up.'

'Help you up?' The first man said.

'Yes, I have something to tell you.' Jack waited until both men hauled him roughly to his feet. 'Do you want this jacket I am wearing?' He indicated his poshteen. 'It is a very special jacket. It is an English jacket.'

'An English jacket?' The second man repeated. 'It looks Afghan.'

'Help me take it off.' Jack had worked out that these men were the Pashtun equivalent of the village idiots. They were not sufficiently sharp-witted to join a raiding party.

'He is trying to escape,' the first man said. 'It is a trick.'

'It is no trick,' Jack said. 'It is a special English jacket.' His hope that he may escape as they released his chains died as one held a knife to his throat as the other stripped him of the poshteen.

'It's not made from goatskin or sheepskin,' he said. 'It is made from an animal that only lives in England. You will know by the smell.' He hid his satisfaction as the younger man grabbed a handful of his coat and inhaled.

'What is it?' The older man asked.

'The great Malvern swine,' Jack said. 'Our own brand of pig.' He laughed openly as both men recoiled from the skin of an unclean animal. 'What's wrong, lads? You have both pawed my pigskin coat.'

The older man kicked at him, while the younger contented himself with a mouthful of oaths foul enough to earn him praise in any barrack room in the British Army. Jack was still laughing as his guards left the house, slamming shut the door. It was only a tiny victory but one that raised his morale slightly.

Keep your head up, Jack. There are rough times ahead, but I'm not defeated yet.

Waiting until he was sure he was alone, Jack began to work at his chains. After searching them for any weakness, Jack scraped the links of his chain against each other, hour after hour until his fingers bled with the strain. *I have little chance of releasing myself, but I'm damned if I'll just give up without a struggle.* With no window in the room, and Batoor having helped himself to his watch, Jack was unable to keep count of time. He worked on until fatigue overcame him, then he dozed, to wake with a start, unsure where he was. At one time he thought he was back in Jayanti's dungeon; at another he thought he was in that hellish Burmese hut.

I've been in worse positions in the past. Work on. I'll get home to you, Mary, somehow.

As time passed, Jack became weaker. With nobody checking on him or feeding him, he thought he would be left to die of hunger and thirst. He scraped on, making little impression on the links but keeping some hope alive.

When the door eventually opened, Jack blinked in the unexpected light. 'Who's there?' He lifted his hands to shield his eyes.

'You're going to meet the Akhund. He wants you alive.' The older man had returned, bringing a third jailor with him.

'Best take care of me, then.' Jack heard the rasp of his own voice.

'Drink.' The third man, heavily bearded, thrust the end of a leather bottle into Jack's mouth. The water was warm, flavoured with goatskin, and tasted like nectar. Jack gulped it down greedily until the bearded man took the goatskin away.

'Take him outside.'

A bevy of Mujahidin hustled Jack into full daylight, where cold rain washed some of the filth from him. He looked up, blinking, to see a dozen horsemen waiting, their predatory faces glowering at him. One man brought forward a horse.

'I can't ride with these on.' Jack indicated the chains around his ankles.

'You aren't going to ride.'

When two of the Mujahidin grabbed his arms, Jack made a clumsy swing at them with his chained arms. Weak from lack of food, he missed completely. Lifting him bodily, the men threw him face-down over the saddle.

After a few moments, Jack knew he was in for a supremely uncomfortable ride. He only hoped that the Akhund was not too far away. Unable to move with the chains weighing him down, bouncing up and down on the back of a horse, Jack gritted his teeth as cramps hit him. He endured, thinking of Mary. What would she think of him now? He saw himself, the once-proud British officer, chained and helpless across a Pashtun's horse. There was no dignity in this position. There was only pain. Jack drifted into the abyss of agony, only dimly aware what was happening around him. Every part of him screamed for release, yet he refused to make a noise. His captors would love to hear him moan; he would not give them that satisfaction.

Jack did not know how long that ride lasted. He was drifting into unconsciousness when the motion finally ended. The pain continued. He heard men talking, a gruff laugh, then the sound of men at prayer. Twisting his head, he could see his captors on their knees, praying. If Jack had not been chained, he would have slipped off the horse and tried to run. As it was, he could not move. After a while, the Mujahidin stood up. One approached him, hauling him casually off the horse so he fell in an untidy bundle onto the ground. The man stepped over him as if he was a bale of straw and led the horse away. Somebody kicked him, grabbed his hair, pulled back his head, and shoved a hunk of what tasted like mouldy bread into his mouth.

'Eat, feringhee. The Akhund wants you alive.'

Jack chewed. It was so long since he had eaten that he found it difficult to swallow. Struggling onto his side, he forced himself to sit upright. They were in a bowl of the hills with a rapid river running between bare rocks. Pine trees straggled close by, some sprinkled with slowly falling sleet. Jack closed his eyes; he remembered snow coating the gentle slopes of the Malvern Hills back home. He remembered the square tower of Mathon Church and the squeak of the gate as he entered the hushed graveyard. He recalled the reassuring sound of carols ringing out on the Sunday before Christmas and suddenly felt very homesick. What was he doing in this alien land so far from home?

'Water.' The Pashtun dropped a goatskin bag in Jack's lap and walked away. Jack lifted it clumsily. The water was fresh and cold. He choked, spewed out water, and drank some more, looking around, trying to assess his position. The geography was unfamiliar; the faces less so. He could be anywhere from Kabul to Chitral; somewhere in the north of Pakhtunkhwa to judge by the pine trees. If he was being taken to the Akhund, he might be returning to the Ambela Pass. The thought of being close to British troops was heartening.

Perhaps the idea stimulated Jack's mind, for he heard the crackle of distant musketry. He killed his initial surge of hope that it could be British troops; on this Frontier, it could be any two rival tribal groups fighting among themselves, or even a wedding party celebrating by firing in the air, or at each other. Captivity had sullied Jack's growing liking for the Pashtun.

'Here they come now,' one of the Mujahidin warriors said. He tipped back his skull cap and spat on Jack. 'The Akhund will know how to treat the feringhee.'

'He is a Christian, isn't he?' a young man with a skimpy beard and liquid brown eyes said. 'Maybe the Akhund will order him crucified. I've never seen a crucifixion.'

Jack said nothing, although the horror crept through him. He remembered the mild eyes of the Akhund. Surely that man would not order the torture and death of a British officer? Then Jack remembered that nobody knew where he was or even if he were still alive. To General Chamberlain, he was only another junior officer, one of the hundreds he had seen killed in his career. Jack knew his life or death depended on the humanity of the Akhund.

'That's not the Akhund coming.' The young man reached for his pulwar. 'There's no standard.'

'Maybe he's sent some riders to take the kafir.' The second man gave a wide grin. 'The feringhee would not ride here.'

The Guides, Jack thought. *Kerr has heard about my predicament and has sent a squadron of horse to rescue me.* He looked up as a large troop of horsemen clattered into the Mujahidin's camp. The leader dismounted without hesitation and strode up to Jack.

'I know this man. Give him to me.'

Jack looked up with all his hope quickly draining away. Gulbaz Khan stared down at him with no expression in his vicious eyes.

CHAPTER TWENTY-ONE

Pakhtunkhwa, November 1863

'You are Captain Jack Baird Windrush.' Gulbaz lifted his hook.

'You are Gulbaz Khan.' Jack tried to show no fear, although he knew his life with Gulbaz was likely to be short and agonising.

Gulbaz's stare did not falter. 'You blew up my watchtower.'

'Your men tried to kill me.'

'It seems that they failed,' Gulbaz said.

'Yes.' There was little else that Jack could say. He saw Gulbaz's men clustering around, some looking curiously at him as they fingered their weapons, others watering the horses or talking to the Mujahidin who had brought him this far.

Jack grunted as one of Gulbaz's followers strode up to him. 'Zaman! So you made your choice.' He injected venom into his words.

'I did, Windrush sahib.' Zaman stood at attention out of pure habit. 'I had a choice to remain with the Guides and have Batoor Khan hand me to the women, or escape and bring Gulbaz an end to his feud with Batoor once and for all.'

'And your oath of allegiance?' Jack could not hide his contempt. 'Do you remember that you took an oath of loyalty to the Guides?'

Zaman grinned. 'You don't understand us yet, Windrush Sahib.'

Gulbaz grunted. 'Take off his chains.'

The Mujahidin guards protested, until Zaman lifted his Khyber knife and killed the first. After that, the Mujahidin obeyed Gulbaz's order. Jack raised his wrists, surprised how light they felt with the shackles off them. He kicked out as the guard unfastened the chains from his ankles. 'Thank you, Gulbaz.' *He must have some trick planned. Keep alert.*

'I would kill you.' Gulbaz touched the hilt of his pulwar. Jack noted with surprise that it was the silver-mounted sword of the Rahmut Khel. 'I am honour-bound by a pledge to your man Zaman.'

Jack grunted. 'What's this all about, Zaman?'

Gulbaz spoke before Zaman could open his mouth. 'Zaman has renounced all claim to be Khan of the Rahmut Khel in return for your freedom.'

Dear God! Zaman did not betray his allegiance. These Pashtuns can always have the capacity to astonish me. Suddenly humble, Jack bowed to Zaman. 'You have my gratitude, Zaman.' It was a new situation for Jack. *Indeed*, he told himself, *it was probably a new situation for any British officer.* Bending, Jack lifted the dead guard's pulwar and jezzail. The sword was well balanced with an ornate handle. The jezzail was of poor quality, but better than nothing.

'The river is there, Windrush Sahib,' Zaman wrinkled his nose. 'Your scent is offending the horses.'

Jack nodded. Unable to wash for the past days, he would stink. 'Thank you, Zaman.'

The river water was so cold that it stung Jack's skin. He emerged, discarded his old clothes, and stripped the dead guard, wondering if he probably had fleas, lice or both. *I don't care. I can deal with that later.*

Gulbaz had been watching, wordless.

'What happens now?' Jack fastened the pulwar around his waist.

'Now we find Batoor Khan.' Gulbaz lifted his metal hook. 'You can ride the horse that carried you, Windrush. If you endanger my men or fail to keep up, I will have you killed.'

Grabbing a stale loaf from the baggage of the dead man, Jack adjusted the saddle and mounted his horse. Surrounded by men who would kill him in a heartbeat, riding through a hostile country without any idea what he was doing or where he was going, Jack felt helpless. Only Gulbaz's honour and his word to Zaman kept him alive.

'What's happening, Zaman?'

'Gulbaz is going to find Batoor,' Zaman said quietly. 'When Batoor took his followers to join the Mujahidin, Gulbaz chased us out of Torkrud, as you know.'

Jack nodded.

'We lost him in the hills, so Gulbaz returned to Torkrud and called for a Jirga of the Rahmut Khel. He showed them the message he got from the Akhund of Swat, the one we intercepted when we first came here.'

'I remember,' Jack said.

'Gulbaz told them that he had rejected the jihad and questioned if Batoor Khan should lead the Rahmut Khel. The Jirga decided that the Rahmut Khel should not join Akhund's Jihad, although individuals could do so if they wished. They removed Batoor from his position.' Zaman dropped his voice to a whisper as one of the Rahmut Khel inched suspiciously closer. 'Or rather Gulbaz persuaded the elders he was the better man.'

Jack tried to grasp the tangled skein of Pashtu politics, where religion and Pakhtunwali struggled for supremacy. 'I see. How did you know where Gulbaz would be?'

'I didn't,' Zaman admitted. 'When I left Tazhak I rode to Torkrud to see what I could do.'

There is so much left out there, so much I will never know. 'You gave up your hope of being Khan for me.'

Zaman grinned. 'I've not given up anything yet, sahib. Gulbaz is temporarily using my sword. The future is unwritten.'

'The future depends on Allah's will and the hands of the Pashtun,' Jack murmured. He felt rather than saw Zaman's sideways look.

'That is so, sahib.'

Jack jerked his head up as Gulbaz lifted his hook. 'What's happening?' The Rahmat Khel slowed down as more riders erupted from the pine trees on the slopes above. The men galloped down towards them with swords and rifles raised, yelling and firing.

Zaman stopped Jack from reaching for his sword. 'It's all right, sahib. These are also the Rahmat Khel.'

Jack estimated a hundred warriors were charging down the hill. 'I thought that Batoor took the bulk of the fighting men with him.'

'No, sahib.' Zaman shook his head. 'Batoor only brought the men of Torkrud who followed him. Gulbaz has raised men from all the lands of the Rahmat Khel.'

'I hope they all know that we are on their side,' Jack said.

'You are a guest of the Khan,' Zaman reminded him.

'Now we will remove Batoor, the man who claims to be Khan,' Gulbaz shouted. 'Come with me, men of the Rahmat Khel!'

Carried along with the Rahmut Khel, Jack could do nothing except ride. The Mujahidin had defeated his Guides; he had failed in his mission. He was only alive because of Zaman's selfless act and the Pashtun code of honour. Fighting away the wave of self-pity, Jack lifted his chin. *I am still alive, damn it. I am still a British officer. All is not lost. Fight on!*

'We're in the Chamla Valley,' Zaman said. 'The caravan is ahead.'

Peering through the dust haze raised by the Rahmat Khel, Jack nodded. 'I see them.'

'Batoor must be a hard taskmaster to push them so hard.' Jack heard respect in Zaman's voice. 'Camels are slow animals.' The caravan was at the inner lip of the Ambela Pass, within a couple of miles of the scattered Bunerwal position. From where he stood, Jack could see the Akhund's standard flying proud on its ridge, a host of supporting standards on either side. The head of the caravan was on the final rise leading to the pass, each camel toiling under its load, while the escort looked casual, not expecting any trouble so close to the Akhund's army.

'Oh, Batoor.' Jack shook his head. 'I thought you were better than that.' He felt a lift of hope. Even the best of the Pashtuns could make mistakes.

Gulbaz did not waste any time. Forming his riders into a rough vee formation with Jack near the tail, Gulbaz gave brief instructions. 'Come on, Rahmut Khel, follow me, get rid of the false Khan, and take these Enfields for ourselves.' Folding the reins around his hook, Gulbaz headed straight for the caravan. Still weak, Jack sat his horse with difficulty, unsure how he should act when he met Batoor. *Is he an enemy or a friend? I do not know.*

The caravan escort looked stunned as Gulbaz's cavalry appeared over the ridge. While some of the guards tried to wave, others realised their danger and drew their swords. Jack noted with some satisfaction that his Guides were among the latter. Only when he was about ten yards from the caravan did Jack shake off his intense weariness.

'Guides!' Jack croaked the name. 'To me, Guides!' At last, drawing his pulwar, he slashed at the nearest of the Mujahidin. The man parried Jack's weak blow and stared open-mouthed in complete incomprehension. 'To me, Guides!'

This situation was the ultimate test of the Guides' loyalty when their officer was virtually helpless beside them and three rival forces competed for their swords. Would they follow Batoor and the Akhund, would they choose to fight for Gulbaz in his private war with Batoor, or would they return to their salt? If they chose either of the first two options, Jack knew that his life was precarious, at best.

'To me, Guides!'

'Captain Windrush!' Hassan pulled toward Jack. 'It's Captain Windrush!'

Sawan and Ursulla were next, with the other Guides rallying as the news spread.

'Shabash, Windrush Sahib!' Alladad shouted, waving his pulwar. 'Shabash the Guides!'

As Gulbaz's Rahmut Khel crashed into the escort in a welter of bodies, slashing swords and yelling, bearded faces, Jack gave rapid orders to his men. 'Scatter the camels! Drive them towards the British lines.' Levelling his jezzail, Jack fired it at one of the Mujahidin escorts. The noise was deafening, the kick nearly unhorsing him. He had no idea where the shot went, except it did not hit his target.

It was a three-way battle with nobody sure who the enemy was. Jack slashed sideways at one of the escorts, roared at a camel driver, who fled in terror, and smacked the flat of his sword against a camel's rump to make it increase its speed. With the Mujahidin more intent on facing Gulbaz's warriors than tending to their caravan, Jack's Guides could concentrate on the camels.

'Come on, Guides!' Jack encouraged. 'Herd the camels!' He looked for Batoor in the mass, dodged a riderless horse, cut loose the reins of a camel, and kicked out at another.

One by one, the camels began to break their formation and lope forward, grouping together as they covered the ground. A steel-helmeted tribesman pushed his horse in front of the group until Sawan shot his horse. The man fell, screaming as the now panicking camels trampled him underfoot on their mad dash onwards.

'Drive the camels; forget the rest!' Jack ordered. The two factions of the Rahmut Khel were fighting, the Mujahidin supporting Batoor or standing aside to watch. Jack left them to it; his duty lay with the camel caravan. Batoor and Gulbaz were no longer relevant.

'Come on, Guides! Drive them to the camp!' Jack could see British soldiers lining the sangars, their forage caps and puggarees bobbing as they tried to make sense of this new force galloping toward them.

'Hold your fire!' Jack roared, knowing the thunder of feet and the noise from the battle would drown out his words. 'We're the Guides!'

'Fire!' Somebody shouted. The 101st Foot greeted Jack's onrushing camels with a spatter of musketry. The forward piquets in their circular sangars fell back, thinking they were under attack, with support coming from the main wall until a hirsute major roared an order.

'Stand fast, damn you! It's only a bunch of camels. Shoot the damned Pathans.'

'You leave the damned Pathans alone,' Jack shouted. 'We are the Guides!'

'What?' The major mounted the wall, waving his hand in front of him in a futile attempt to clear the dust. 'Cease firing!'

'Bring the camels in,' Jack ordered as lack of food caught up with him and he collapsed on the British side of the wall. 'They're carrying rifles.'

Ten of the camels had died in the crazed rush to the British lines. The Guides rounded up the remainder, bringing them to Jack as if to apologise for their earlier defection.

'Here are your camels, sahib,' Alladad said.

The 101st watched, some with amusement, others alarm, as if they would have to dispose of these unruly beasts.

For the first time, Jack had the opportunity of counting his men. Of the original twenty he had taken out, he had lost Fatteh and five of the new men. Two of the fourteen who remained had been wounded.

Jack glanced beyond the wall. The battle between Batoor and Gulbaz had ended, leaving a score of casualties on the ground. Jack could not tell which faction had been the victor. At that second he did not care.

'I've sent a runner to the general,' the hirsute major said. 'Windrush, isn't it?'

'Yes, sir.'

'You'd better get yourself and your badmashes cleaned up. You look like a bunch of scallywags rather than soldiers of the queen. My men nearly shot you flat.'

'We are the Guides,' Jack retorted. 'We don't need to dress in scarlet to look like soldiers. We are soldiers.'

The major gave a small nod. 'Windrush, eh? I'll remember that name.' Turning on his heel, he stalked away.

More trouble in the future, Jack thought. *That can wait. I have things to sort out here first.*

'Before we go any further,' Jack glared at his men, 'you had better decide where your loyalties lie.' He spoke Pushtu, guessing that few, if any, of the watching 101st spoke that language. 'You deserted your salt in Tazhak.'

'We did not, sahib. We are Guides.' Hassan seemed more puzzled than hurt.

'You joined the Mujahidin,' Jack said flatly.

Hassan raised his hands to still the Guides protests. 'Captain Windrush, what would you have us do? By pretending to join the Mujahidin, we saved our lives so we could return to our duty.' The other Guides nodded.

That was plausible. But was it true? Jack pondered. He wanted to believe these men. He had ridden and fought beside them; he had trusted them with his life, and they had not let him down until Tazhak. He had already heard Zaman's story and seen the proof with the arrival of Gulbaz with the sword of the Rahmat Khel.

Jack took a deep breath. Were these men lying to him? Was there a cultural difference that he did not understand, or was he being too hard on them because of his lingering distrust of sepoys since the Mutiny? These Guides had certainly rallied to him in the skirmish around the camels, and Zaman had probably saved his life with his agreement with Gulbaz.

'All right.' Jack counted his men. 'Including me, we have thirteen fit men. I don't know how many of us died in Tazhak, but I believe that we have left some behind as prisoners.' He nodded grimly. 'That will be the men who did not join the Mujahidin. I don't like leaving men behind. We're not finished with Tazhak yet.' He turned and walked away.

'Where are you going, sahib?' Hassan asked.

'I am going to report to the general,' Jack said. 'And if he agrees, we are going back. We failed in our mission. I dislike failure.'

* * *

Chamberlain listened to Jack's story, scribbling the occasional note on a pad of thick paper. 'How well do you know this fellow Batoor Khan?'

'I thought I knew him very well, sir. We fought side by side in the Mutiny. He was the Khan of Torkrud before he joined the Akhund of Swat. Until this last incident, I would have trusted him with my life.'

'Religious fervour is a terrible thing,' Chamberlain said. 'Whatever religion it is.'

'Yes, sir. Can I have permission to return to Tazhak, sir? I'll take a larger force this time.'

'You brought back the Enfields, Windrush.'

'Yes, sir, but I did not destroy the workshops, and I left some of my men behind.'

'They'll be dead by now,' Chamberlain said. 'If they are lucky.'

'I'd like to see for myself, sir.'

When Chamberlain looked up, his eyes were dark with compassion. 'I understand your concern for your men, Windrush, but we are under siege by thousands of Pashtun warriors here. Why should I send you again to try what you already failed to do?'

Jack lifted his chin. 'I don't like failure, sir. I want to redeem myself and try to rescue my men.'

Chamberlain sighed, stood up and paced the interior of the tent. 'You are a bit of a loose cannon, Windrush. I don't know what to make of you. Your men like you, but Colonel Snodgrass of the 113th got shot of you, and only an hour ago another officer complained about your attitude to him. Perhaps you are not officer material.' He stopped. 'I knew your father when he was out here. He was a good man.'

'I hardly met him, sir.' Jack saw any hopes of career advancement sliding away. He was destined to remain a captain for the remainder of his life.

'No?' Chamberlain shook his head. 'That's a pity, Windrush. You could have learned a lot from him.' He sat down again. 'All right, Windrush. You may have another opportunity to do what you failed to do the first time.' When he looked up, Chamberlain looked very old. 'I am doing this for your father's memory and for the sake of these poor men who may still be in Pashtun captivity.'

'Thank you, sir.'

'Get your men together,' Chamberlain ordered. 'Get rested and re-equipped, then wait for my command. Don't let me down.' He mused for a moment. 'I won't tell you not to let your men down, Windrush. That is one thing of which you are not guilty.'

Was that back-handed praise? Unfortunately, the opinion of rankers did not win an officer promotion.

CHAPTER TWENTY-TWO

Ambela Pass 20th November 1863

The runner arrived at Jack's side. 'The general wants you, Captain Windrush.' He was gone before Jack could reply.

Leaving his position behind the 1st Punjabi's ranks, Jack strode to the mound on which General Chamberlain stood. 'You sent for me, sir?'

Ignoring the odd bullet that whistled past, Chamberlain scanned the entire perimeter before he replied. 'Since we moved our camp to the south side of the pass two days ago, the tribesmen have attacked with even greater ferocity, but our men will hold them.'

'Yes, sir,' Jack agreed. From Chamberlain's knoll, he could see the ebb and flow of battle, with long clouds of grey-white smoke where the defenders were firing volleys in response to the massed charges of the Bunerwals and their Mujahidin allies.

'We expect reinforcements any day; the 7th Fusiliers, 93rd Highlanders, 3rd Sikhs, and 23rd pioneers; all good fighting men. How many of my Guides Cavalry are you taking?'

'Thirty, sir.'

'More than last time.' Chamberlain nodded. 'How long will it be before they are ready?'

'My men are waiting for your word, sir.'

'You have it. Take them out the moment this present attack wanes.' Chamberlain turned to a runner, giving him explicit orders to carry to the left flank.

'Yes, sir.' Fighting his lift of elation, Jack called together his Guides. Deliberately parading them inside the British camp, he walked along their ranks.

'All right, Guides. Conditions out here may be different to anywhere else, but the basics remain the same. There is us, the Army, the Guides, and there is the enemy. We stay together, fight together and support each other. Rank, race, religion is secondary to our bond within the regiment.'

The firing was increasing. Jack knew he would have to lead his men out soon after the defenders had repelled the attack. With Chamberlain in command, watching everything, the Bunerwals and Mujahidin would never overrun the British positions. Chamberlain might look old, but his mind was acute, and his military intellect as sharp as the point of a rapier.

'We're going back to Tazhak. Make sure you are ready.' Jack ignored a stray shot that whined overhead. 'I'm taking a chance on you all. Don't let me down. Regain your nang. Rescue our colleagues.'

Jack could feel the hurt from the Guides. He had insulted them in the worst possible way by hinting they were dishonourable. They could react by killing him once they were clear of the British camp, or they could attempt to prove him wrong. He did not yet understand the Pashtuns well enough to know which avenue they would choose.

The firing increased, volley after volley crashing out.

'Cease fire!' That was Sinclair's voice. 'They're on the run!'

'Sir!' A breathless Cornet Cheshire nearly tugged at Jack's sleeve. 'General Chamberlain's orders, sir, and could you ride out directly.'

'Thank you, Cornet. You delivered that message very well.' Jack added a wink to his words. There was no harm in being friendly to this youngster now that he had learned how to deliver a message.

'Mount up, Guides.' Jack kept his voice deliberately hard. 'Follow me.'

Leading from the front, Jack rode out of the British camp. He ignored the spatter of musketry; there were sufficient British, Gurkha and Sikh soldiers to take care of any number of tribesmen. Having seen them in action, Jack now had no doubts about the loyalty or fighting prowess of the Sikhs or Gurkhas. It was only his Guides, the elite, he questioned. Well then, he would give them a chance to prove themselves.

With Sharbat sturdy underneath him, Jack increased his speed from a walk to a trot.

'The men are faithful, sahib.' Hassan rode beside him, his face concerned.

'We'll see, daffadar.' Jack had not forgotten the time that Hassan had rescued him on the ridge when Gulbaz's men were pressing hard. 'I hope that you are right.'

'You insulted their honour.' Hassan did not give up. 'My honour, too.'

Jack did not immediately reply. He remembered too well the carnage at Gondabad when the sepoys mutinied. He recalled the horror of the well at Cawnpore where the mutineers thrust the mutilated bodies of the murdered women and children of the British garrison. He could never forget such things; the actions of the Guides at Tazhak had not been a hundredth as bad, yet they had awakened that niggle of distrust.

'Keep up with me,' Jack snarled.

Riding hard, they pushed through the retreating Mujahidin and Bunerwals and ignored any shouted challenges. Jack watched his men as they passed the Akhund's banner, flying from the summit of its ridge, the green fabric now tattered and stained with powder smoke. He was glad to see his Guides barely glanced at it as they passed out of the valley, and into the semi-wooded hills beyond.

That's one test passed. Well done, lads.

Twice marksmen fired at them, the shots going nowhere. The wind was keen now, biting into them as a harbinger of the bitter winter to come. Jack pulled his poshteen closer, hauled his pakol over his forehead, and spurred on. After his previous visits to Tazhak, he knew the way as well as any of his Guides.

They camped at night, lighting a small fire close to one of the many rivers, and moving a quarter of a mile away to sleep. On this Frontier, only a fool would advertise where they camped.

'Sahib,' Hassan said. 'The men are unhappy.'

'Are they indeed?' Jack was in no mood to pander to the *nang i pukhtana*, the honour of the Pashtun. He listened to the rush of the river and the distant howl of a wolf. He also fought a gnawing headache.

'They wish me to speak for them.'

'Then speak, Hassan.' Jack spoke shortly. With his head pounding and sweat soaking his clothes, he found it hard to concentrate.

'They want you to know that they were always faithful.'

'Thank you, Hassan.'

The next day Jack would lead these men back to Tazhak, where his missing men may be held captive, or they could be dead. The men of Tazhak might expect his arrival; if Batoor had survived the battle with Gulbaz Khan, then he would undoubtedly expect Jack to return. There could be a great deal of tough fighting ahead. He could not fight with men he did not trust. Jack closed his eyes; he had to forget the Mutiny. These men had not been involved in that old war. Their behaviour at Tazhak had been unusual from a British perspective, but perhaps not from a Pashtun point of view.

I have no choice; I must put aside my distrust. If I am wrong, well, death is a soldier's lot. Fight this feeling of lethargy.

Sighing, Jack stepped over to the Guides. They sat in a circle with their eyes the only mobile things in the dim. Jack squatted among them.

'Right, gentlemen,' he said quietly, very aware that his voice could carry far in the night. 'I have already said my piece about disloyalty. I will not repeat my words.'

'Do you no longer trust us, Windrush sahib?' Hassan asked the direct question.

In answer Jack unbuckled his sword belt, handing the weapon to Hassan. He took the revolver from its holster next to his skin and placed it on the ground at Zaman's feet. 'I am now unarmed,' he said. 'I am standing without a weapon in the midst of the biggest collection of rogues and badmashes between Kabul and the Khyber.'

Some of the Guides smiled at that, as Jack had intended.

'If I did not trust you, would I do such a foolish thing?'

The gesture appealed to the Pashtuns' sense of drama. Zaman was first to laugh, with the others following soon after.

'All right then. Now we have to destroy the gunsmiths of Tazhak,' Jack said. 'More importantly, we have to rescue any Guides still in the village.'

'They will be dead,' Hassan said. Jakub, the second daffadar that Jack had brought, nodded his agreement.

'They might be. We won't know until we get there. If we rest for three hours now, we should reach Tazhak just before dawn.' Jack took a deep breath. 'I want every workshop destroyed and every Enfield copy located.'

'Shall we kill the gunsmiths too, sahib?' Zaman asked the question that Jack most wanted to avoid.

'No.' Remembering the elderly men and their sons who made the guns in the first workshop he had visited, Jack shook his head. Even though he was aware the smiths were every bit as dangerous to the British as warriors were, he could not condone killing civilians.

'They will merely set up shop elsewhere.' Hassan was always the pragmatist.

'I know.' Jack remembered the aftermath of the Mutiny when furious British soldiers had hanged anybody who might have been a mutineer. Hundreds of innocent men had died in that orgy of vengeance. Jack swore he would never be guilty of such practices. 'Destroy all their tools and equipment.' It was not a perfect solution but the best that Jack could devise... 'If there are any warriors...'

'There will be few warriors,' Hassan said. 'The mullahs have swept the Kot Valley clear for the jihad.'

Jack nodded. He had noticed the lack of men in the valley. The Akhund and his mullahs were gathering everybody they could to defeat Chamberlain. 'Shoot only if you have to. Try and take the craftsmen alive.'

Tazhak was in darkness. Even knowing where the village was, Jack could hardly make out the walls against the dark of the overcast night. He knew his Guides were behind him, watching from the same bowl in the hills that they had occupied on their previous visit.

'You know what to do,' Jack said. 'We belong to God, and unto God we do return.'

'Yes, sahib.' Hassan spoke for the Guides.

With the horse's hooves and all loose equipment muffled, Jack led them slowly downhill. He had no idea of knowing how large the garrison was or if the Mujahidin had set another trap. He only knew he had to succeed.

As the gate was on the eastern side of the village, the sentinels on the watchtower would face into the rising sun, giving Jack's men a slight advantage. 'Halt.' He spoke in a whisper. 'Zaman, Alladad: Kill the sentries, and open the gate.'

Without a word, the two Guides dismounted and moved toward the village. Jack felt his tension mount, knowing that he had sent the two men best suited for the task, fighting his guilt at not accompanying them. Commanding men was never easy; sending men into danger while one waited in comparative safety was harder than advancing into enemy fire.

'Sahib.' Alladad's voice was soft at Sharbat's shoulder. 'The sentries are gone, and the gate is open.'

'Well done, Alladad. Mount up.' Jack walked on with the Guides a few steps behind. Sharbat stepped delicately over the body of one guard just within the doorway. Zaman stood casually a few paces deeper into the village.

'There were three guards,' Zaman said.

'Well done, Zaman.' Already the light was increasing, making Jack's job slightly easier. 'You four.' He pointed to Jakub and four Guides. 'Take over the watchtower and gate. Don't let anybody in or out.'

Jakub nodded. 'Yes, sahib.'

'Shut and bar the gate.' On their previous visit, Jack's men were trapped when the Mujahidin slammed the gate on them. Now that he controlled the entrance, he had a secure escape route.

'Sahib.' Hassan touched his arm. 'Up there. Fatteh is watching us.'

'What?' Jack's surge of hope ended when he looked up. Fatteh's head adorned the top of a stake, staring out of empty eye sockets, his genitals thrust into his mouth. At his side were the heads of the other Guides that Jack had hoped to rescue. The Mujahidin had treated them all in the same manner.

'Bastards,' Jack said. 'The dirty, murdering, torturing bastards.' He tried to fight the anger that sought to take over from his rational mind. 'Destroy this place,' he said. 'Tear it to the ground.'

'Hassan, take fifteen men to the far side of the village, evict the gunsmiths, and destroy the workshops. If anybody shows fight, shoot them.'

'Yes, sahib.' Hassan understood Jack's anger.

'You have three minutes to reach the far side, and we'll start at this end.' Those three minutes seemed to stretch to eternity before Jack gave the order to start work. By then the light had strengthened so he could see what he was doing.

'Two men to each workshop,' Jack ordered. 'Bring the people out, break all the equipment, and burn the place down.' He did not need to give any more orders. The Guides were naturals, zestfully kicking the doors down before thrusting into the workshops, smashing up all the tools, and throwing any gunsmiths who lived there into the street, where Jack had five men waiting to keep them under control. The occasional gunshot showed that some of the smiths resisted. Jack grunted; he could trust his Guides to deal with them.

The prisoners were restive, protesting to their captors, waving their hands in the air as they saw their livelihoods destroyed before their eyes.

'Who killed these men?' Jack asked, pointing to the heads of Fatteh and his companions. 'Who murdered my men?'

Shocked at the destruction of their homes and businesses, the men gave the same response. 'The mullah ordered it.'

'Which mullah?' Jack already guessed the answer.

'The mullah with the drum.'

The tabla mullah. The man I have already killed twice. That man is the epitome of evil. I must hunt him down. My mission is not complete as long as that murderer is loose.

The explosion took Jack by surprise. He looked up as one of the workshops at the far end of the village blew up, coiling smoke into the sky. 'What the devil has happened?'

Gunpowder! Each of the workshops would have a supply of gunpowder. A second explosion followed the first, and then a third as the flames spread from building to building. By now the entire village was awake, with crowds of men running back and forward, unsure in which direction to run.

'Gather the gunsmiths,' Jack shouted. 'Get all the others out of the village.' He gave rapid orders that saw his Guides clearing the streets as workshop after workshop exploded in a welter of fire and fury. He had not intended to blow Tazhak up; the destruction was far more significant than he expected. *There will be no more guns made in this village. That is fitting for the murder of Fatteh. Sleep easy, my friend. I have extracted badal for your murder. I will extract more.*

'Get out, lads!' Jack shouted. 'Leave the village.' He waited, counting his men out one by one. Some carried loot in the shape of rifles or food. He said nothing. Looting had been the perquisite of soldiers since time began. No doubt the men who followed Darius of Persia or Alexander the Great had scoured this very valley. *The people of Tazhak watched while the tabla mullah murdered Fatteh; they deserve no pity.*

'That's us.' Jack counted the last of his men. He had brought thirty in, and he would bring thirty out. That was a success. Now there was only that blasted indestructible mullah. Jack swayed, holding a hand to his thumping head. 'Zaman!'

'Yes, sahib.' Zaman was smoke-blackened but smiling.

'That mullah is not here. One of these men will know where.'

'The mullah that had Fatteh killed?' Zaman nodded. 'I will find out, sahib.'

'Daffadar!' Jack roared. Hassan and Jakub appeared.

'I want you to check the prisoners. Hold the master gunsmiths, but let the apprentices go.'

'Yes, sahib,' Jakub said.

'Why, sahib?' Hassan had served with Jack long enough to ask questions.

'You will be taking the master gunsmiths to General Chamberlain,' Jack said. 'He can decide what to do with them. I have other business to attend to.'

Hassan gave Jack a sidelong look. 'You are going after the mullah who killed Fatteh.'

'I am,' Jack said. 'I am leaving the Guides in the hands of one of the most capable NCOs I have ever met.' Jack did not often give praise. He thought this was an excellent time to break his habit.

'You do not know Pakhtunkhwa as we do,' Hassan said. 'You will die on your own.'

'That is my choice.' Jack gave a twisted smile. 'It is Allah's will if I live or die.'

Hassan looked away. 'That is true.'

'Windrush Sahib.' Zaman marched over, smiling. 'The very first man I spoke to was accommodating.'

'What did he tell you, Zaman?'

'The mullah has his headquarters in a cave near the Chamla Valley.' Zaman cleaned blood from the blade of his pesh-kabz knife. 'The cave is at the Jaromgar waterfall.'

'Chamla?' Jack tried to order his chaotic thoughts. 'That's in Bunerwal territory.'

'It is the heart of Bunerwal territory,' Hassan confirmed. 'You will never get in alone, sahib.'

'I can only try.' Jack knew that his smile was crooked. 'I want badal for Fatteh.'

'You are not Pashtun,' Hassan said.

'Fatteh was Pashtun, and he was one of my men,' Jack said. *I wonder if I should try a silver bullet to kill the tabla mullah, as Rougvie had suggested. Nothing else seems to work. The Tabla Mullah's wounds even miraculously heal.*

'How about the prisoners, sahib?'

'We will bring them to Chamberlain sahib,' Jack said. He could accompany the Guides as far as he could before striking off alone. 'He can decide what to do with the master gunsmiths. I am sure he will find jobs for such skilled men in the armoury.'

Taking a deep breath to combat his growing dizziness, Jack kicked in his heels, with Sharbat responding willingly. Leaning forward, Jack caressed the horse's ears. 'Well done, thy good and faithful servant. You can rest soon. When we get back to Mardan, you will get a long rest.'

'Somebody is following us,' Hassan said.

'I know.' Jack had been aware of the small body of horsemen ever since they left Tazhak. 'Let them follow.' Out here on the Frontier, he expected nothing less.

CHAPTER TWENTY-THREE

Ambela Valley December 1863

'This is where we part company,' Jack said. They stood at the head of the Ambela Valley with the British encampment in the far distance, hazed by powder smoke. The intermittent rattle of musketry informed Jack that the siege continued. 'You are as capable as I am of taking the men in, Hassan.'

'That is so, sahib,' Hassan agreed.

'Then do so,' Jack said. 'Pray convey my respects to Major Kerr, and tell him that I will join him at my earliest convenience. No, hang it all, I'll write this down.'

Finding a scrap of paper, Jack wrote that he had ordered Hassan to bring the men home while he pursued the Tabla Mullah, who he considered too much of a threat to India to leave alive.

'Thank you, sahib.' Hassan held the scrap of paper as if it were gold dust. 'I will ensure this reaches Major Kerr.'

'I know you will, Hassan.' Jack returned Hassan's precise salute. *Hassan does not expect to see me alive again.* Turning Sharbat, Jack checked he had ammunition and caps for his Enfield rifle and touched the revolver inside his poshteen and the pulwar at his waist. He was as prepared as circumstances permitted.

All right, tabla mullah. I've seen you shot at least three times before. If bullets cannot hurt you, I will cut off your blasted head. You murdered my men. Swaying slightly in the saddle, Jack allowed the sure-footed Sharbat to pick her own way along the rough terrain. He did not know where he was going; he only knew that the Chamla Valley was over the ridge on which he rode and that the Tabla Mullah lived in a cave in a small valley near the Jaromgar waterfall.

Ridge followed ridge, with a keen wind biting at Jack's face. He shivered, delving into his poshteen.

I will exact badal on this mullah. Jack repeated the words as Sharbat plodded on, upwards to the summit of the ridge and over to the opposite side. *I will extract badal on this mullah.* Jack swayed again. *What the devil is wrong with me? I am a British offi-*

cer; I cannot give in to weakness. He halted there, overlooking a broad valley with the path stretching before him, a huge drop below, and copses of pines scattered all around.

'Sahib.' The voice came as from a fog. 'Sahib.'

Zaman caught Jack before he fell. 'Sahib.'

'Zaman?' Jack peered into Zaman's face. 'What are you doing here?'

'You are not going alone into the Chamla valley, sahib.' Zaman looked concerned.

'I ordered you to take the prisoners to General Chamberlain.' Even saying these few words was exhausting.

'Yes, sahib,' Zaman said. 'You have a fever. You must rest.'

'Damned if I will,' Jack said. *I won't give in to fever!* 'Do you know this cave, Zaman?'

'I know a cave near the Jaromgar waterfall,' Zaman said.

'Take me,' Jack ordered. 'Take me quickly before this damned fever takes full control.'

'Can you keep up?' Zaman sounded genuinely concerned.

'Take me, damn it.'

'You are not well…'

The rider galloped from the shelter of a group of trees, long sword raised in his left hand, yelling. With the fever dulling his reactions, Jack barely registered the man before Zaman pushed Sharbat away.

'Gulbaz!' Zaman reined his horse to one side, drawing his pulwar in the same movement. The blades clashed, held, and parted as Gulbaz spurred on. Zaman laughed. 'I wondered who was following us!'

'I'll kill you,' Gulbaz roared, 'and then the feringhee.'

'We were allies once,' Zaman reminded him.

'Of necessity, not choice!' Gulbaz attacked again, riding his horse directly at Zaman, who waited until the two animals were nearly touching before jinking aside in a display of horsemanship as neat as any Jack had ever seen.

Swearing, Gulbaz clattered by, the hooves of his horse kicking loose stones from the path into the fearful abyss below.

Drawing his pistol, Jack aimed at Gulbaz until Zaman shouted, 'No, sahib! This is about honour. The best warrior will win.'

Lowering his pistol, Jack nodded. It was the Pashtun equivalent of a duel, man against man. He understood, although he had not expected such chivalry on the Frontier.

Turning on the very edge of the precipice, Gulbaz sheathed his sword, lifted an old-fashioned single-barrel pistol, and fired. The bullet crashed into Zaman's horse, sending it staggering. As Gulbaz quickly dropped the pistol and drew his sword, Zaman leapt agilely from the stricken horse, landed on his feet, and parried Gulbaz's slash.

Again Gulbaz trotted past, but this time Zaman followed. As Gulbaz turned, Zaman leapt on the back of his horse, thrust his sword into Gulbaz's side, twisted the blade, withdrew, and jumped back down. Gulbaz turned, his eyes wide.

'Zaman Khan of the Rahman Khel,' he said. Wordless, Zaman thrust his sword through Gulbaz's chest.

'Now I am Khan.' Lifting the silver-hilted sword of the Rahman Khel, Zaman removed the scabbard from the body of Gulbaz and attached it to his belt. 'I will take better care of this than the previous two owners.' Tipping Gulbaz's body over the edge of the ravine, he adjusted the stirrups of Gulbaz's horse and mounted. It had taken less than two minutes for the Rahmat Khel to lose and gain a khan.

'Are you still fit to continue, Windrush Sahib?'

'I am still fit,' Jack said.

'Then let's find this mullah.'

Jack nodded, barely able to sit his horse, let alone register all that was happening. He allowed Zaman to lead him down the dizzying slope into a surprisingly fertile valley.

'Where are we?'

'In the Chamla Valley, the heart of Buner.' Zaman looked around. 'Normally this place would be filled with people and animals. As you see, it is empty. The men are either fighting Chamberlain Sahib or are already dead.'

'So much the better for us.' Jack fought waves of dizziness. 'How far is this waterfall, Zaman?'

'About an hour's journey,' Zaman said. 'Can you manage that?'

'Take me.'

Jack gripped the reins tightly, fighting to stay in the saddle as Zaman led him through the most fertile valley he had yet seen in Pakhtunkhwa. Around them, snow-smeared mountains soared above the line of dense pine trees, reminding Jack of pictures he had seen of Switzerland. Perhaps the tabla mullah had discovered his paradise while still alive.

'Sahib.' Zaman put out a hand to prevent Jack from falling. 'We are nearly there, sahib. It would be better if I met this man.'

Jack shook his head. 'No, Zaman. I must do this. It is my duty. I must get badal for Fattah.'

Zaman looked at him sideways. 'This way, sahib.'

Jack heard the rush of the waterfall before they crossed the spur of a hill to a dell that would have delighted the most demanding of Romantic artists. A thread of water eased over a rocky ledge to plummet toward a small pool, from where it overflowed into a dramatic drop of some hundred feet into a turquoise lake. Even Zaman stopped to appreciate the beauty.

'This is the Jaromgar Waterfall,' Zaman said.

'Where is the cave? Where is the tabla mullah?' Jack felt for the hilt of his pulwar. 'Show me.' He felt his strength draining minute by minute. He had to act quickly before he was too weak. 'Take me to him, Zaman.'

'Down here, sahib.' The track was pencil thin as it spiralled down the side of a grass-and-scrub slope towards the lake.

'Come on, Sharbat.' Jack allowed the horse to take control, concentrating on remaining in the saddle. The further down the slope they rode, the more the noise of the waterfall dominated until all he could hear was the hammer of falling water. In his head, the sound altered to the rolling of the Tabla drum, so the two sounds became indistinguishable.

The mullah belonged to this place; perhaps both his holiness and his drumming came from the waterfall? Jack shook his head. *No. That was the fever talking. Keep rational, Jack; fight this thing.*

'Over here, sahib.' Zaman dismounted.

'I can't see a cave.' Jack nearly fell from the saddle. He recovered, took hold of the hilt of his sword, and looked around.

'The spray from the waterfall hides it.' Zaman stepped forward. 'Look.' He pointed to a group of Kabul ponies standing under an overhang of rock. 'This way, sahib.'

The entrance was little more than one man wide with a muddy puddle underfoot. Jack blinked into the darkness, trying to ignore the sickeningly familiar stench as he entered. Handing his rifle to Zaman, he drew his pulwar. 'Bullets don't work with this mullah,' he muttered. 'Unless they are made of silver.'

Zaman also drew his sword. 'May Allah guide our steps.' His voice trembled. 'We belong to God, and unto God we do return.'

Jack stumbled over the uneven surface. 'I am Captain Jack Baird Windrush of the Guides!' The echo of his voice mocked him. 'Show yourself, if you are here.'

'I should go ahead, sahib.' Zaman's voice was weaker than Jack had ever heard.

'No, Zaman.' Jack pushed on, nearly gagging at the stink of death. 'What is happening in here?'

'There's light ahead,' Zaman said. 'And the smell of smoke.'

'I see it,' Jack said. 'Somebody has lit a fire.'

The light diffused from a crack high in the roof of the cave, spreading out as the cave itself widened into a cavern. Jack stopped. In front of him, the tabla mullah sat beside a small fire that was as smoky as his eyes as he looked up.

'Salaam Alaikum, Captain Windrush.' He remained sitting.

'You murdered my men,' Jack said.

The mullah stood up. Stark naked, snakes of lank hair coiled past his shoulders. 'Everything is the will of Allah.'

'You had him murdered.' Jack's sword felt so heavy he had difficulty in lifting it. Swaying, he tried to thrust, slipped, and crumpled to the ground. He lay still for a moment, gathering his strength to push himself to his feet.

'You cannot kill me,' the mullah said. 'Allah has blessed me. Your bullets cannot hurt me; your blade will not part my flesh.'

'Mine will.' Lifting the sword of the Rahmat Khel, Zaman sliced sideways, taking the Mullah's head clean from his shoulders. 'That was for Fatteh,' he said. The firelight gleamed from the sword's silver hilt.

Jack pushed himself upright. 'He might come back to life. He's already been killed twice and wounded once.'

'No.' Zaman shook his head. 'That is impossible. Only the Yusufzai would believe that.' Lifting a brand from the fire, he stepped into the darker recesses of the cavern. 'Here, sahib. Here is your answer.'

Using his sword as a makeshift walking stick, Jack followed.

'Here, sahib.' When Zaman lifted the burning brand higher, the light showed three bodies lying on the floor of the cave. Each man was identical, a copy of the Tabla Mullah. One had been shot in the head, one in the chest, and the third in the leg. The stink from the rotting bodies was appalling.

'Quadruplets,' Jack said. 'I did kill them after all.'

'Yes, sahib. That was how this mullah could appear after you killed him. There were four of them, each identical.'

Jack nodded. 'Let's get back to the camp, Zaman. I can do no more here.'

There had been no need for a silver bullet. The tabla mullahs had been mortal, like everybody else. Jack sat astride Sharbat, barely aware of his surroundings as they rode to the Ambela Valley. He heard the firing as if in a dream.

'Who is shooting, Zaman? Wait! That's British artillery — screw-guns!'

'I don't know what's happening yet.' Zaman had a hand on Jack's reins, leading him slowly onward. 'Something is burning, as well. I can smell the smoke.'

The first of the fleeing warriors arrived a moment later, running along the floor of the Chamla valley. The drift of smoke increased, together with the high crack of the screw-guns. The musketry continued, both in regular, controlled volleys and the heavy thumping of jezzails.

'There's a regular battle going on.' Jack's sense of military duty surfaced through the lassitude of his fever. He saw a retreating tide of warriors, some in organised units, others individually. 'I think the British have advanced from the camp at last.'

'Be careful, sahib.' Zaman pulled Sharbat's reins, trying to take Jack away from the valley floor.

'No, hang it, Zaman.' Jack fought the fever. 'Leave me be.'

The horsemen rode in a purposeful group, ignoring the chaos around them. The green banner fluttering above them told its own story. 'It's the Akhund of Swat,' Jack said.

'This way, sahib.' Zaman's voice was urgent as he attempted to guide Jack away from the oncoming Akhund. 'Stay still, sahib, and say nothing.' Zaman stopped when a horde of fleeing warriors blocked their way, some firing over their shoulders, others intent on escape. 'He's seen us!'

The Akhund's horsemen slowed as they approached Jack. Their banner was in the centre, still proud despite the fly being faded and frayed.

Drawing his sword, Zaman edged closer to Jack. 'Stay with me, sahib.' Holding the pulwar across his chest, he faced the Akhund's two huge bodyguards.

The Akhund pushed closer with a third man close behind. 'Salaam Alaikum, Captain Windrush.'

'Salaam Alaikum, Akhund.' Jack gave a little bow from the saddle. He fought to clear his fever-muddled brain. 'It seems that the tide of war has turned against you.'

The Akhund was as calm as ever. 'Allah willed that British reinforcements should bring victory to them, this time.'

Jack realised that the Akhund's third escort was Batoor. 'Do you intend to raise another army, Akhund? Batoor Khan there will be a good general.' He heard the exhaustion in his voice.

The Akhund gave a small smile. 'It seems that Allah intends me to be a spiritual leader rather than a man of war, Captain Windrush. Without the modern rifles, my warriors fought at a disadvantage.'

Jack felt Batoor's gaze on him. 'Perhaps it is not yet the Pashtun's time.'

'Time does not end, Windrush. Empires, even the British Empire, always do. Allah is with the patient.' The Akhund glanced at Batoor and back to Jack. 'We will not meet again, Captain Windrush. Peace be upon you.'

The words came into Jack's head from some half-forgotten text. *Respect the enemy; he is a man doing what he believes is right.* 'Peace be upon you, Akhund.' Despite all that had happened, Jack could not bring himself to dislike this courteous, dignified man.

The musketry continued with a shell exploding fifty yards away, scattering dust and pebbles in a wide diameter. Jack saw a charge of Probyn's Horse and Guides scatter a force of Mujahidin. At the call of a bugle, Probyn's men headed for Jack, no doubt attracted by the Akhund's green banner.

'Akhund.' Jack pointed to Probyn's approaching horsemen.

'Thank you, Captain Windrush,' the Akhund said gravely. 'Batoor, I wish you to remain with Captain Windrush. Your time with me is at an end. You and Zaman Khan have things to discuss.' Unhurried, the Akhund cantered away with his two bodyguards close behind. Jack watched his standard for a moment. He felt as if he had gone back in time and met a great man. He knew he would never see his like again.

Batoor and Zaman glared at each other, each with his hand on the hilt of his sword. Jack pushed between them.

'I will fight the first man to draw his sword.'

'You, Windrush?' Batoor laughed. 'You are as weak as a day-old kitten! You are sick with fever.'

'Then you will have to kill me.' Jack knew that Batoor was correct. He could barely lift his sword, let alone fight with it.

'Zaman Khan. One of us will be Khan of the Rahmut Khel.' Batoor did not flinch as Probyn's horsemen closed around him. Hassan was in their midst, with Alladad Ursulla and Sawan slightly further back.

'Hold!' Jack lifted his hand. He did not want any of his Guides to start a blood feud. He did not wish any of his men to face Batoor.

'I killed Gulbaz Khan.' Zaman tapped the hilt of his sword.

Batoor smiled. 'You will find me harder to kill, Zaman. I have two hands.'

'I want no killing.' Jack forced Sharbat between the two men.

'There will be none, sahib,' Zaman said gently. 'I have no need to kill you, Batoor. You are the Khan of the Rahmat Khel, and I am a trooper of the Guides. A sword for a sword.' Zaman drew the sword of the Rahmat Khel, reversed it, and presented the hilt to Batoor. 'Take care of your sword, Batoor, and the people of the Rahmat Khel.'

Unbuckling his sword belt, Batoor handed over the Khyber knife he carried, replacing it with the sword of the Rahmut Khel.

Jack stared, unsure what he had just witnessed. 'Next time we meet, Batoor,' Jack said, 'I hope it is in peace. Go now, before my Guides decide you are an enemy.' Then he fell from Sharbat.

CHAPTER TWENTY-FOUR

Gondabad February 1864

Jack lay on his charpoy, fighting the last of the malaria germs that had racked his body. He looked around his world. Mary was sitting with Andrew on her lap and a book in her hand, her eyes stern with concentration. Jack took a deep breath, knowing he wanted nothing else. He read the official letter that a smart Rajput had handed into the bungalow. 'That's my home leave confirmed, Mary.'

'That cheered you up,' Mary said. 'You've been lying there feeling sorry for yourself for weeks.'

Jack scanned the letter again before handing it to Mary. 'We're going Home, Mary. You'd better dust down your list of where you want to go.'

Holding young Andrew in her arms, Mary stepped to the side of Jack's charpoy. 'Before I do, Captain Jack, there are things you should know.'

'Oh? What sort of things?'

'Do you remember that Sergeant O'Neill gave us a wedding gift?' Mary said.

'I do.' Jack smiled at the memory. 'I think it was four pounds ten shillings.'

'That's right,' Mary agreed. 'Do you remember there was also a small packet with my name on it?'

'No,' Jack said. 'That was years ago, Mary. A lot has happened since then.' He fondled Andrew's blond hair. 'Like this little chap.'

'I know. I was there at the time,' Mary said. 'That small packet was a wedding gift to us, and it was very kind of the sergeant. You should remember such things, Jack. Anyway, here it is.' Mary lifted the packet. 'Do you want to open it, or shall I?'

'We both know that you opened it years ago.' Jack did not hide his smile. 'The seal's already broken. You haven't stuck it back very well.'

'Of course I opened it.' Mary re-broke the seal with her fingernail and emptied the packet. 'Look.' Lantern light sparkled from the small shower of jewels that cascaded downward onto Jack's charpoy.

'Now that's interesting.' Jack lifted the closest jewel. 'That's a fine ruby, Mary.'

'Yes, indeed. All these jewels are of top quality. I wonder where Sergeant O'Neill got these.'

'He didn't,' Jack said dryly. 'O'Neill had nothing to do with these. I'd wager a thousand pounds to a pinch of tea these came from Private Riley. He and Logan tried to steal a wagon of loot from Lucknow. I'll have a word with him if ever I meet him again.'

'They were stolen?' Mary said.

'Yes. How else would a ranking soldier get anything like this?'

'We can't keep them of course,' Mary said. 'That would be dishonest. We should return them to the legal owner if you know who that is.'

Jack saw his jewels sliding away from him. 'The convoy was bound for the coffers of the Honourable East India Company,' Jack said, 'so as the government took over John Company, and India indeed, I presume that they should go to the Crown or the governor general, whoever that may be.'

'Sir John Lawrence is the present governor general.' Mary pursed her lips. 'He doesn't need the money, and nor does the government.'

'We need the money,' Jack said. 'We could sell one of the rubies and buy my majority. I can't see any other way of me getting my step.'

'I like you fine as a Captain,' Mary said.

'A major has more responsibility and higher wages.' Jack indicated the walls of their bungalow. 'We could get a better house, maybe a promotion to lieutenant-colonel in time.' That exalted rank seemed an impossible dream.

'No.' Mary shook her head. 'The Book says we should not build our house on sand, and stolen jewels are not a good foundation for anybody's life. If we sell these, the money could fund an orphanage.'

'They could pay for a house back Home.' Jack tried to regain the jewels.

'No.' Mary replaced the jewels in their packet, folding it up securely. 'Jack, did you not hear the other news when you were out on the Frontier?'

'I was a little bit busy.' Jack had been too fever-stricken to tell Mary about Pakhtunkhwa. 'What news should I have heard?'

'We already have a house back home.' Mary put a hand on Jack's shoulder. 'Your grandfather, old General Baird, died when you were away.'

Jack nodded, saddened but not surprised. 'That's a shame. He was a decent old stick.'

'He was.' Mary allowed Jack a moment to absorb the news. 'You'll miss him.'

'I will miss him,' Jack said. 'But he lived his life as he wanted to. He was the last of his kind, I think, a British man settling in India, taking Indian wives and living like the natives. That's all changing now.'

'We live in unsettling times.' Mary was watching Jack closely. 'I read the general's will. I know I should have waited for you.'

Jack did not have to force his smile. 'It's as much for you as for me. What does it say?'

'It says that your grandfather has left you just about everything, including his properties back home.' Mary pushed Jack back down onto the charpoy. 'You own two modest houses, Captain Jack, a small house and a slightly larger house.'

'Oh.' Jack stared at her. 'I did not think that the general had anything back home. What are our houses like?'

'The smaller one is in the north somewhere. The larger one is smack in your area. It's in Herefordshire, Jack, at the Malvern Hills.'

'Oh, dear God.' Jack felt the increased hammer of his heart. 'We'd better start packing, Mary. I want to see our house.' He was going Home. After twelve years abroad, he was going back to Herefordshire.

HISTORICAL NOTES

PASHTUNS AND THE NORTH WEST FRONTIER

Many historians have written about the Pashtuns of the North West Frontier. They were, and are, a uniquely independent people occupying one of the most hostile pieces of land in the world. The Pashtun know their land as Pakhtunkhwa, while their preferred way of life was Pakhtunwali, a strict code of hospitality and revenge.

Harry Lumsden, one of the great early British commanders of the Guides, said of the Pashtun: 'Everywhere family is arrayed against family, and tribe against tribe, in fact, one way and another every man's hand is against his neighbour.'

In 1898, the Army believed there were around 200,000 tribal warriors with approximately 48,000 rifles. Ownership of a rifle gave a Pashtun warrior great prestige, and the British tried all they could to stem the flow of modern weapons to the area, including a naval blockade of the Persian Gulf.

The North West Frontier was a constant source of trouble to the British, who launched scores of expeditions to try to keep the peace. Even as late as the 1930s, the British Army was active here, with mixed success.

THE AMBELA CAMPAIGN

The Ambela or Umbeyla campaign of 1863 against the Mujahidin, or so-called Hindustan Fanatics, was one of the larger expeditions on the North West Frontier between the First Afghan War of 1839-1842 and the Second Afghan War of 1879-1881. General Chamberlain led 5,600 men on to the Ambela Pass, camped there and endured wave after wave of Bunerwal attacks. When Chamberlain was wounded attacking a Bunerwal position, Major General John Garnock took command of the expedition. With the expedition now reinforced to 9,000 men, he advanced out of the Ambela Pass into the plain of Chamla. He moved in two columns, taking the fanatic stronghold of Conical Hill and the village of Lalu.

With the infantry having cleared the way, the vastly experienced Probyn led 400

HISTORICAL NOTES

horsemen to attack the Mujahidin in Chamla Valley with the infantry close behind. During this set-piece victory over the fanatics, the Bunerwals watched without getting involved. Realising they could not defeat the British in open warfare, they asked what the British wished of them. The British asked them to destroy the headquarters of the Mujahidin. The Bunerwals did so, not without drama, and the British withdrew.

The campaign had lasted three months but is largely forgotten now. It cost the lives of 15 British officers, 34 British and 189 Indian, Sikh, Pashtun and Gurkha soldiers, with another 24 British officers, 118 British soldiers and 541 Sikh, Pashtun, Indian and Gurkha wounded. The casualties among the enemy are not known but probably run into several hundred.

THE GUNSMITHS OF TAZHAK

Tazhak is purely fictitious but based on a real village. Darra Adam Khel near Peshawar is a village whose primary industry is making copies of commercial firearms. Working with primitive machinery, the thousands of craftsmen of Darra Adam Khel can produce a copy of virtually any firearm within a few days. The weapons are useable but lack the quality of the originals.

THE AKHUND OF SWAT

In his day, the Akhund of Swat was one of the most respected spiritual leaders of northern India. In 1835 he led a small army of Yusufzais against the Sikhs, who brushed him aside. Returning to Swat, the Akhund reverted to a peaceful, religious life of piety to Islam. It was not until 1863 that he returned to military action against Chamberlain's force. The Akhund was said to feed the poor, cure the sick, and work miracles. As early as the 1850s, the Akhund was calling for an Islamic state that would stand against the British, who he said were 'fast laying the foundations of their rule deep in our homelands.'

The Akhund lived to the age of 84, dying in 1871, with his tomb becoming an important Pashtun shrine.

SIR NEVILLE CHAMBERLAIN

Born on 10th January 1820 in Rio de Janeiro where his father was consul-general, Chamberlain was one of four brothers. Educated at Woolwich, he was commissioned in the Bengal Native Infantry at the age of 17. He fought in the First Afghan War of 1839-1842 where he was wounded at least four times and took part in the 1843 Gwalior Campaign. He was also present in the Sikh Wars, being notably active at the battle of Gujerat.

In 1849 he was Assistant Commissioner at Rawalpindi, then Hazara. In 1852 he relaxed by hunting lions in South Africa, following this by becoming brigadier of the Punjabi Irregulars, watching the North West Frontier. Never idle, in 1855 he led two expeditions against the Pashtun, and another the following year. He was active in the Mutiny, being wounded in front of Delhi. In 1858 he was back on the Frontier to stop a Sikh rebellion, with another expedition on the Frontier in 1859, this time against the Waziris. In 1860 he was facing the Mahsuds, and then in 1863, he commanded the Ambela expedition, his final duty, where he was wounded for the ninth time.

After he retired, honours came to Chamberlain. He became KCSI in 1866, GCB in 1875, and a Field Marshal when he was eighty years old. More curiously, he is perhaps better remembered for inventing the game of snooker than for all his fighting prowess.

WINDRUSH - AGENT OF THE QUEEN

JACK WINDRUSH BOOK 7

PRELUDE

Dartmoor, England, November 1862

Ignoring the jagged splinters that thrust into his emaciated body, Markovic lay rigid beneath the rough planking of the cart, with filth dripping on him from above and the wheels jolting over the cobbles beneath. Clear above the pattering rain, he heard the wardens questioning the driver, their voices crisp and suspicious.

"Are you alone, driver?"

"Of course I'm bloody alone. You can see that."

Markovic felt the slight jerk as a warden probed a pointed stick into the human excrement piled on the cart.

"What the hell are you doing?" The driver asked.

"Making sure nobody is hiding in there."

"Good God, man, they'd suffocate, sure as death." The driver sounded angry. "Let me pass, so I can dump this muck and get home."

"You'd be surprised what some prisoners will do to try to escape Her Majesty's free hotels." The warden shoved his stick in again and the steel tip penetrated the bottom boards of the cart. Markovic did not flinch as the point jabbed into his thigh.

"Right," said the warden, withdrawing his stick, "on you go."

Markovic hung on grimly as the cart lurched out of the prison gate, seemingly finding every bump and pothole in the track. He heard the wheels grind over the uneven road, with the driver alternatively cursing and singing, as the mood took him, until, after what seemed an eternity, the cart ground to a halt.

"Out you come."

Markovic heard the nerve-shredding screech of iron nails on wood as the driver prised away the planks that held him in his mobile coffin. A blast of chill air welcomed the passenger to freedom, as the driver's rough hands grabbed his shoulders and hauled him out. He lay on the ground for a moment, stretching his cramped muscles, very aware that the reeking dung-cart with its hack of a horse was beside him, while the driver watched through impassive eyes.

"Here you are, Mr Markovic." The driver did not offer to help his erstwhile passenger to his feet. "You said there would be a reward."

Markovic spared a glance at the narrow compartment under the base of the cart in which he had travelled. "I am to meet people here."

"There's nobody here yet." The driver looked around. He had pulled the cart off the road to a small disused quarry, where wind-stunted trees wept rainwater into spreading puddles, and jagged rocks thrust upward to an uncaring sky. "Who's coming, anyway?" Broad-featured with suspicious eyes, he gripped a cudgel in his right hand. "If I get caught with you, I'll get the jail."

"You won't get caught," Markovic said. "I promise you. Here are my friends now."

"Where?" As the driver turned to look, Markovic slipped both hands around his neck and twisted sharply until he heard a crack. He dropped the driver's lifeless body on to the ground as a soft hail came from the quarry entrance.

"Markovic?"

"That's me." Markovic lifted the driver's cudgel. "Give me your name."

"Reilly."

"And who is with you, Reilly?" Markovic withdrew a pace to the shelter of the cart.

"Flaherty." The second voice sounded as two men emerged from the shadows. Neither even glanced at the body of the driver. "Come on, Markovic. Here are some clean clothes for you."

"I'll wash first," Markovic said.

"Fine. We'll get you cleaned up and then we have work to do."

"Take me to a river," Markovic ordered. "Now!"

Flaherty shrugged. "As you wish."

Markovic followed the two men over the wastes of the moor, keeping pace with them step for step even after his years of imprisonment. When they reached a small stream between two steep sloping banks, Markovic stripped naked. Gaunt to the point of starvation, his body was ridged and scarred, white with prison pallor. Indifferent to the biting wind and freezing water, he plunged into the stream, submerging himself entirely and emerging again, scrubbing at himself with sand from the river bed.

Only when his skin was red-raw did Markovic step out of the stream. "Clothes!" he demanded. He pulled on the rough trousers and jacket before hauling on the heavy navvy boots.

"Weapon," he commanded. He took the revolver that Reilly handed him, automatically checked that the chambers were loaded and thrust it into the waistband of his trousers. "Now tell me how the war is progressing."

"The war?" Reilly looked confused.

"The war in the Crimea," Markovic replied. "I have been in kept in solitary confinement for years with the silent system. I have not heard any news."

"That war ended six years ago, Markovic," Reilly said. "The Allies captured Sebastopol."

Markovic thrust out his chin, with the white scar above his left eye pulsating. "Did they, by God?" He touched the butt of his revolver. "Take me to the leader of the Brotherhood."

Reilly grinned. "I heard you were keen."

"I have an Empire to destroy." When Markovic looked up, Reilly shivered at the cold madness in his eyes.

CHAPTER ONE

Malvern Hills, England, October 1865

"It's beautiful." Mary Windrush stood on the terraced slope of the Herefordshire Beacon, looking down at the pass through the Malvern Hills. She grabbed her hat as a gust of wind threatened to blow it from her head. "Is that the house in which you grew up?"

"That's the house in which I grew up." Nearly 14 years ago, Jack left Wychwood Manor under a cloud of illegitimacy. Now, a married man with a son, he was a captain in the British Army with three campaigns and other operations under his belt. "That's where my half-brother now lives, with his wife and my mother."

"Shall we visit them?" Mary threw Jack a quizzical glance. "Surely they won't still bear a grudge after all this time."

Lighting a cheroot, Jack took a long draw as the memories crowded into his brain. "I don't know," he said. "William is not the most pleasant of men and, as for my mother…" He gave a wry smile. "My stepmother, rather. She said that if I ever set foot on Windrush ground again, she would cut off my allowance."

"We no longer need an allowance from your mother," Mary said. "You're no longer a penniless ensign. You're a captain with property and some money of your own."

"Our own," Jack corrected.

Taking Jack's cheroot, Mary drew on it, blew out smoke and gave a sudden, devil-may-care grin. "Come on, Captain Jack, let's bell the cat."

"What?"

"Oh, did you not get educated at your fancy school?" Mary laughed. "Let's beard the lion in his den, let's singe the King of Spain's beard. Let's go and see what brother William says."

"Brother William won't be pleased," Jack said.

"All the more reason to meet him, then." Mary passed back the cheroot. "I've taken a great dislike to your half-brother, Jack." Slapping Jack's arm, Mary lifted the hem of her skirt and mounted Katrine, her brown mare. "Come along, Captain Jack."

"You might regret meeting them," Jack pointed out.

"I might," Mary agreed cheerfully. "We won't know until we try."

They negotiated the slope down to the pass, with Mary a few yards in front and Jack following on Cedric, his stallion. He felt the old familiar mixture of apprehension and excitement as if he were going into battle rather than merely riding to see his brother. While sheltering in the bitter trenches outside Sebastopol, sweltering in the Burmese jungles, facing the Pandies at Lucknow or confronting the Pashtuns of the Frontier, Jack had thought of his boyhood home; now he hoped the reality would not destroy his dreams.

"Come along, Jack." Mary spoke over her shoulder. "You're hideously slow back there."

"I'm coming," Jack said.

The gateway to Wychwood Manor was the same as he remembered, if a little the worse for wear, with weeds easing beneath the stone tigers that surmounted the pillars guarding the driveway. Out of old habit, Jack leaned from his saddle to touch the pillars, as he had done as a child.

"For luck," he explained, seeing Mary's quizzical expression.

"It's strange to think that you grew up here," Mary stretched to copy him. "I always think of you as belonging to India rather than England."

"I do, in a way," Jack agreed. "I am as much Indian as English, anyway."

Riding slowly to allow news of their arrival to reach the house, Jack reined Cedric in as they negotiated the final curve of the drive. He caught his breath as Wychwood Manor came into view. Once, Jack had thought this place magnificent, the equal of any ancestral home in England, which to his youthful mind meant the equal to anywhere in the world. Now, after service in Malta, Crimea and across India from the Frontier to Burma, Jack could see Wychwood for what it was, the dwelling place of a minor country gentleman, no more and no less.

The manor's central wing dated from the 14th century. From then on, a succession of Windrush owners had added whatever took their fancy over the following generations. The result was a sprawling building of contrasting architectural styles. Lawns that Jack remembered as stretching for many acres now appeared cramped in comparison to the grounds of the Indian palaces he knew so well.

"Wychwood Manor seems to have shrunk," Jack commented.

"No, Jack. You have grown."

Jack eyed the weathered Windrush arms that challenged all comers from above the main door. For the first 18 years of his life, he had imagined he would own this house until his stepmother told him that he was illegitimate, and his half-brother William was the true heir. Now he was returning as a visitor with his Eurasian wife.

"If they're unkind," Jack murmured as he dismounted. "We won't stay long."

"I have had British people being unkind to me all my life," Mary said quietly. "I have grown thick skin." As Mary slid off Katrine, a woman emerged from the side of the house with a hat holding her dark hair in place. She was singing softly, the words familiar to Jack, the marching song of the Royal Malverns, the regiment of his brother, father and ancestors.

*"Always victorious
Glorious and more glorious,
We followed Marlborough through battle and war
We're the Royal Malverns, the heroes of Malplaquet."*

The woman stumbled over the last word, repeated it with as little success, said: "Oh, damn," and looked up. "Good morning," she said brightly and stopped. "Oh, good God!" Her right hand rose to her mouth. "Jack."

"Good morning, Helen." Jack gave a little bow. "May I introduce you to Mary, my wife? Mary, this is Helen, William's wife and the lady to whom I was once engaged."

Jack expected the awkward pause as the women sized each other up. On one side was Helen, the attractive daughter of Colonel Maxwell, daring, yet calm in a crisis, a woman Jack had known during the Crimean campaign. On the other was Mary, the half-Indian daughter of a British officer, a woman who had endured many adventures with Jack during the Indian Mutiny.

"Mrs Windrush." Mary was first to dip into a curtsey.

Helen responded with a little twitch of her lips as she glanced from Mary to Jack and back. "How do you do, Mrs Windrush? Imagine, three Mrs Windrushes all in the same house. What fun."

"You're looking well, Helen," Jack said. "You've hardly changed."

"Thank you." Helen dropped in a slight curtsey. "You are looking very well yourself." She eyed him up and down. "You got your captaincy, I heard. William is a major now."

"Is William at home?"

"He's in the stables, I believe." Helen had gained about half a stone, which suited her well. Her mouth was tighter than Jack remembered, and she had tiny lines around her eyes, yet Jack could sense the old devil-damn-you spirit under her matronly veneer. "I'll send a servant to fetch him." Helen signalled to a young lad who was watching from a safe distance. "Get the master! Tell him we have guests!"

The boy scampered away.

After her first extended look at Mary, Helen concentrated on Jack, holding his gaze. "Won't you come inside? One of the boys will care for your horses."

"Thank you," Mary replied for them both. "That's most kind of you."

Jack found it strange to return to the outer hall with its Corinthian columns, oak panelling and an array of portraits of long-deceased Windrush men in their bold scarlet uniforms. He noted that a black curtain still hid the picture of Uncle George. "He married a native woman, according to the story," Jack explained when Mary frowned at the curtain. "In reality, he became a dacoit in Burma."

"Oh."

"One of my men, Sergeant Wells, killed him." Jack remembered those desperate days when he had been a young ensign enduring his first campaign.

"So this is where you grew up." Mary looked around her as if trying to catch the essence of her husband. "I can nearly imagine you here, running up and down the stairs, shouting and getting into all sorts of mischief."

"Actually, I spent most of my time at school." Jack tried to shake away the ghosts of his past. "I was at home only during the holidays, and even then I was outside most of the time." The inner hall was smaller than he remembered, with the furniture more worn and the light dimmer. Everything seemed less grand, drabber, almost colourless after the vitality of India. Were all homecomings like this after long service out East? Or was he merely torn between his two homes, England and India?

"What the devil are you doing here?" Two years younger but a stone heavier than Jack, William Windrush strode into his house with a frown on his face, his white shirt open and his arms bare to the elbows. Wisps of straw sticking to his trousers suggested he had been working in the stables. "I did not invite you, and I'm certain that Mother never would." He glowered at Helen before looking away with a snort of contempt. "It's bad enough having blasted poachers infesting the place without bastards and half-castes."

"Good morning, William," Jack replied coolly. "Your wife has been very welcoming."

"Is that so?" William's glare at Helen promised hot words when they were alone. "I'm sure you remember what Mother said when she threw you out, Jack." William stood with his hands on his hips, half a head taller than Jack, master of all he surveyed. "She said the second you resign your commission or set foot on Windrush land, your money stops."

"I remember." Jack had to lean back to meet William's poisonous gaze. He failed to control his rising temper. "You made quite a name for yourself in the Crimea, William, basking in reflected glory. Now I hear that you swan about London, toadying to the nobs while the real soldiers do the fighting. What's the matter? Was one campaign one too many for you?" Jack had not come for an argument, but he would not allow his younger brother to bully him, especially with Mary present. He could almost feel the women watching, wondering what would happen next.

When William clenched his fists, Jack stepped back, prepared to defend himself and partially welcoming a confrontation.

"Boys, boys!" Helen stepped forward with her hands upraised. "Behave yourselves!" Despite her show, Helen's eyes were bright with mischief, and Jack knew she was enjoying the drama.

"If you were a gentleman, Jack," William sneered, "I'd call you out, even if we do share my father's blood."

"If you were brave enough to do so," Jack replied, trying to force down his anger, "I'd shoot you like a rabid dog."

"What's all the noise?" Time had been kind to Mrs Elizabeth Windrush. She hardly looked a month older than she had when she banished Jack from Wychwood Manor some 14 years previously. Now she stood partway down the stairs, calm-faced and ready to take control. "William? Who are these people?" Mrs Windrush frowned when she saw Mary. "Who is this?" She looked at Jack, gasped and looked away quickly.

"Hello, Mother," Jack said.

"I am not your mother." Elizabeth Windrush pulled herself more erect. "Who is this dark woman, William?"

"This woman is my wife." Jack kept his emotions under control. "Her name is Mary."

"You inherited your father's tastes, I see." Elizabeth Windrush stared at Mary as if at some mortal enemy.

"Only the best ones, Mother." Again, Jack forced down his temper. He edged closer to Mary, who attempted to hold Elizabeth's gaze.

"Get this blackamoor out of my house, William," Elizabeth Windrush commanded, turning away. "Instruct her to take my husband's bastard with her."

Jack waited until his step-mother was three yards distant before he spoke again. "I thought you'd be pleased to greet your new neighbours," he said. "You see, Mary and I have inherited the adjacent estate." He saw Elizabeth Windrush falter. "The old Baird house of Netherhills."

"Inherited?" William's voice sounded strangled.

"From my grandfather," Jack said pleasantly. "My blood mother's father, don't you know." He smiled at the shocked expression on William's face. "As neighbours, William, we'll be able to keep in touch. Mary and I intend to be frequent guests in my family home."

"Get out of my house!" William raised his voice. "By God, I'll have the servants turn the dogs on you and your nigger woman."

"You won't talk about my wife like that!" Jack's temper snapped. Without conscious thought, he swung a punch that caught William full on the mouth. As William staggered away, Mary took hold of Jack's arm and guided him out the front door.

"Enough now, Jack. We're not here to cause trouble." She propelled him down the steps to the gravel path outside. "Come on now!"

Reluctant to leave a job half-done, Jack turned back, stabbing a finger towards his half-brother. "I won't forget this, William, I'm telling you! You'll not insult my wife again, by God!"

"Enough, Jack!" Mary hustled him away. "You're not a schoolboy any more." She lowered her voice. "There are other ways."

"What?" Blinded by his anger, Jack had failed to see the light in Mary's eyes. "What do you mean?"

"I said: 'There are other ways.'" Mary gripped his arm. "We've been married for years, and I've never seen you like that before." Her smile was sudden and unexpected. "That was as good a punch as any prizefighter's. Now, where are our horses?"

"I must apologise for my family's behaviour," Jack started until Mary pushed him again.

"Don't be a pompous ass, Jack; you're not responsible for your family. Come on; let's get out of here."

Back on his feet, William glowered at them silently from his front door as a trickle of blood ran down his chin.

Jack stormed past the belt of trees that screened the stable block, now anxious to get away from Wychwood Manor as quickly as he could.

"Lad!" Jack shouted as he entered the coolness of the stable. "Where are our horses?" He looked around, muttering: "Damn the boy, what's he done with them?"

"There they are." Mary walked to Katrine. "Your Cedric is two stalls down."

"Lad!" Jack roared again. He heard a rustle in the hayloft above. "Stop skulking up there and come and do your duty! Saddle our horses, you young scoundrel!"

"Jack!" Mary admonished him, "calm yourself!"

"This place makes me angry."

"William made you angry," Mary corrected.

"Not just William, Mary. Mother made me angry as well." Jack raised his voice again. "Get down here, you young rogue, or I'll come up and it'll be the worse for you."

"The poor lad's probably terrified of you," Mary remarked. "Leave him alone. We can get the horses ourselves. Can't we, Katrine?" She soothed her horse, fondling its ears and blowing in its nostrils. "Yes, of course, we can."

Halfway up the ladder, Jack paused. Expecting to see one of the stable-lads, he found himself staring into the wide eyes of a maidservant. "What the devil are you doing here?"

"What is it, Jack?" Mary asked, looking up curiously.

"Oh, nothing important." Jack descended again. "Not our business. Come on, Mary, let's get away."

* * *

"It's a funny thing," Mary said as they lay in bed that night, "Helen rather enjoyed you punching her husband. I was watching her."

Jack reached out for her, caressing the comfortable swell of her stomach. "I rather enjoyed it, too."

"So, did I, Jack, so did I." Mary slid towards him. "And tomorrow we see Netherhills, our new home."

"As long as the neighbours are friendly," Jack said, "we'll be all right."

It had not been the homecoming of which Jack had dreamed. He hoped tomorrow would be better.

* * *

The gates of Netherhills, between their plain stone pillars, greeted them with a display of rusted neglect. Jack dismounted to push them open, fighting past the tangle of nettles that choked the entrance to the grounds. "I don't believe anybody has lived in this place for years!"

"We'll have fun putting it to rights." Mary walked Katrine gently through the gates and on to the weed-infested driveway. "I'm quite excited to see our first English home."

Jack said nothing, desperately hoping that Mary would learn to love Herefordshire as much as he did. Glancing across to her, he saw she was studying everything from the ancient trees to the blackbirds that chattered in sudden panic at this intrusion into their territory.

Jack grinned as a colony of rabbits scurried for shelter in front of them. "Poachers' paradise," he said, "but grandfather certainly had good taste in timber." He gestured towards the oak, elm, and beech trees that lined the drive.

"Come on, Jack, race you to the house!" Mary kicked in her heels and trotted around the final bend, stopping when Netherhills House came into view. "Oh, my word."

"Indeed." Jack reined in at her side. "Oh, our word. Grandfather Baird, what have you left us?"

With the front door securely locked and half-covered with ivy, vegetation growing from the gutters and weathered and peeling shutters at all the windows, Netherhills House looked neglected, an architectural orphan.

"It only needs love," Mary said. "How old is the house, do you think?"

Jack surveyed the building style. "It's Georgian, I think, so not all that old; maybe 100 years at most." He nodded to the Italianate tower that protruded two storeys above the bulk of the house. "I doubt the tower is more than 50 years young."

"Come on, Jack," Mary dismounted. "Let's explore. Will the horses be all right?"

"Leave them here. They won't go far."

"You have the key?" Mary looked up in sudden alarm.

"I picked it up from the lawyers, remember?" On an impulse, Jack handed the key to Mary. "Go on – you first." He watched as she opened the door, stepped into their house and stopped.

"Come on, Jack."

They walked in together, side by side and hand in hand.

Despite the length of time that Netherhills had been empty, the house smelled sweet, although cobwebs hung heavy from every corner and the dust stood half an inch deep on each surface. Leaving the front door open, Mary and Jack explored slowly, unfastening the shutters to allow in light and with Mary making little comments in every room.

"This will be the withdrawing room. I can entertain here."

"I don't know what I'll use this room for."

"We'll have a piano in the corner there, and bookcases on three walls. Come on, Captain Jack, let's go upstairs."

As they mounted the stone stairs, Mary patted the wooden balustrade. "This walnut will polish up nicely."

"I can already see you as the lady of the manor," Jack said.

Mary pushed open another door. "Now this, Jack," she said, holding his arm tightly, "will be our bedroom. I want a four-poster bed in the centre and a cheval glass in that corner so that I can make sure I look my best each morning." She stepped into the middle of the room. "I like this room with these big windows overlooking the grounds. We can happily make more babies here."

Jack raised his eyebrows. Although he had no objections to the baby-making process, he was not sure if he wanted to add to their family. "Babies grow into children, which means the expense and worry of schooling for boys and marriage for girls," he pointed out.

"And schooling for girls and marriage for boys, too," Mary replied sharply. "I'm not having any girls of ours growing up uneducated, or allowing my sons to live without a wife to guide them."

"I'll leave the schooling of any daughters in your hands," Jack said at once.

Mary acknowledged his words with a nod.

"Somebody's been in here," Jack said the minute they entered the west wing, from where the tower rose in Italianate splendour. Chairs stood in a circle around a burn-scarred table, while cigar butts and broken clay pipes littered the floor.

Mary frowned at this intrusion at her home. "And more than once, too. Vagabonds, do you think?"

"Vagabonds who smoke cigars?" Jack said. "Poachers perhaps; William mentioned he had problems with poachers. Well, whoever they are, they won't be back once we're in residence."

"They'd better not come back," Mary said grimly.

"Do you like your house, then?" Jack asked when they had completed their initial survey.

"I did not expect to find furniture." Mary swept a hand over the dust covers that shrouded the furniture. "And it needs a good clean and a lot of redecoration. We'll need servants, too."

Jack nodded, quite happy for Mary to take over the running of the house. "One worry I have, Mary. Will you be all right here when I'm posted away again? My leave won't last for ever."

"What do you mean, will I be all right here? I'm coming with you." Mary lifted her chin. "I didn't marry you to rattle around in an empty house while you travel the world having fun."

"If it is possible, then you shall accompany me." Jack forestalled any looming argument.

Mary accepted her victory. "I shan't like leaving David behind, or any other children we may have."

"If we're lucky, I might be posted somewhere in the British Isles." Clearing a windowpane of dust and cobwebs, Jack saw movement outside. "I thought there were no servants left in this place."

"That's what the lawyer said."

"Then we have an intruder in the outbuildings. It'll be those blasted poachers. Wait here!" Bounding outside, Jack raced across to the modest stables and pushed open the unfastened door. "Halloa!"

Darkness closed around him, thick with dust. "Who's here?"

Jack was not surprised when there was no reply. Wishing he had a pistol with him, he shouted again. "Halloa! Is anybody there?" He heard the sudden scuffle of feet, turned and swore when somebody barged into him. Punching out, Jack felt contact and grunted as something slammed into his stomach, knocking him to the ground. He had a glimpse of a broad-shouldered man in moleskins running from the stables, but by the time he regained his feet, the man had gone.

"Jack?" Mary was running from the house.

"He got away from me." Jack smiled ruefully. "I can catch Pashtun tribesmen on the most volatile frontier in the world, but I can't catch a single poacher in my own house."

"Never mind," Mary said. "Nobody's hurt, and I doubt he'll be back now we're here." She looked around with her eyes gleaming. "Right then, Captain Jack, we have a house to put to rights, servants to hire and a statue of Kali to find."

Jack flinched. "Why the devil do we want a statue of Kali? She's that Hindu goddess with a multitude of arms."

"Exactly so," Mary said. "And we're going to put her on the most prominent place we can find, facing Wychwood Manor."

"Why?" Jack shook his head. "You're Christian, not Hindu."

"I know that, and you know that," Mary said, "but your beloved brother and his mother don't know that!" Her grin was pure mischief. "I told you there were other ways to get even with them." She pointed to the Italianate tower. "And I want a large telescope up there, Jack, the biggest and best that we can get, for I'm going to spy on everything that your brother does. Call me a blackamoor and a nigger, will they? We'll see who sets the dogs on whom before this is over."

"You might pick up a statue of Kali in London." Jack hoped his wife would change her mind. "We have a lot of travelling to do before we settle here and Hooky asked me to visit Horse Guards, remember."

"Horse Guards." Mary's expression of distaste said more than her words. "Stuff and nonsense, Jack. You're on leave! Colonel Hook had no right to ask that."

"I know, but duty is duty."

"We'll stay here tonight," Mary told him. "I know it's not properly habitable yet, but we've survived a lot worse."

Lighting a cheroot, Jack nodded. "I'm going for a stroll around the grounds while you familiarise yourself with Netherhills."

"Yes, you keep out of my way." Mary's eyes gleamed with the prospect of an empty house to organise from scratch.

Netherhills had 20 acres of badly overgrown land, with a tangle of undergrowth blocking access to a stone-built folly and dense weeds infesting what had once been smooth lawns.

We'll need a decent head gardener, with a couple of boys to help him, Jack thought to himself. He found he was enjoying planning out his grounds. Puffing on his cheroot, he frowned as he saw a definite trail through the long grass. "These damned poachers think they own the place," he muttered to himself. "I would expect the odd poacher, but that looks as if it's a regular path." Following the trail, he came to the dry-stone wall that marked the boundary of Netherhills and looked up in surprise.

The woman sat astride her horse with her bonnet at an acute angle and both hands on her reins.

"I thought I might find you patrolling your boundaries." Helen's smile was as wide as Jack remembered. He noticed the triangular Tartar amulet around her neck, remembered her buying it in Balaclava and knew she wore it specifically for him.

"Is William with you?" Jack enquired, looking around.

"No." Helen shook her head. "Is Mary with you?"

"She's planning out our house."

"We're all alone then." Helen fingered her amulet. "Like the old days in the Crimea."

"It would seem so." Jack waited to see what Helen wanted.

"I miss you, Jack," Helen said quietly. "You told me once you'd show me the Malvern Hills and watch the dawn rise over Worcestershire."

"That was a long time ago, Helen, before you married William."

"William is not the man I thought he was."

"You chose him." Jack automatically drew back. The memory that Helen had left him for William still rankled, although he knew Mary was a better wife than Helen could ever be.

"I made a bad choice." Helen seemed to hesitate. "Life here is so dreary. I'd do anything to alleviate the tedium, while William is not an attentive husband. He prefers young servant girls."

Jack remembered the girl in the stable and the straw on William's trousers. "You can go riding," Jack said. "Or meet the other wives of the area."

"They have no life in them," Helen said. "It's an endless round of visits with social tittle-tattle, Jack. I had no idea that life in England was so tedious. I wish I were back in the Crimea with you, or in India, or South Africa." She stepped closer. "I tried not to laugh when you punched William." When Helen smiled again, the years slid away, and she looked like the young woman Jack had once known. "We've been through some interesting times together, Jack."

Jack took a deep breath, remembering the time of the great storm when Helen had stepped from a sinking raft as calmly as if she were shopping in Hereford. "We have, Helen, and now we are both married to other people."

"I wish it were otherwise."

Jack felt a confusion of emotions burst on him. He had thought he loved Helen until she crushed him by rejecting him in favour of William. Only when he met Mary had he realised that Helen had been a passing fancy. Even so, as he remembered the times they had shared, Jack could not prevent some of his old feelings from returning. "We can still be friends," he suggested. He immediately regretted his words.

"Friends?" Helen dismounted, remaining on the opposite side of the boundary wall. "Thank you, Jack. You can't know how much that means to me."

"As long as Mary doesn't mind." Jack knew his hasty amendment was too late. "I'd better be getting back to her."

"Already?" Helen gave a little pout. "After all these years you can only spare me two minutes? I thought you said we were friends." She held her gloved hand across the wall.

"I'm also married," Jack said softly. "There will be other times, Helen."

"Yes," Helen said as Jack turned away. "There will. I'll make sure of it." She waved her fingers, smiling. When Jack looked back, she was still standing in the same place, watching.

CHAPTER TWO

Horse Guards, London, October 1865

"Make no mistake, Windrush, the Fenian movement is the most serious domestic threat that Great Britain has faced for the last half-century, more serious than the Chartists, and they were peril enough. If we can't depend on the army, what hope have we of keeping order in this country, let alone maintain the Empire?"

Jack nodded. When Colonel Hook had asked him to drop into Horse Guards during his home leave, he had thought it was little more than a courtesy call. Instead, an officious clerk had immediately ushered him into a quiet office on the upper floor where a dapper, intense man invited him to sit.

"My name is Smith." The man wore elegant civilian clothes but spoke with the clipped, authoritarian tones of a man used to command. "I expected you last week."

"I did not know you required my presence with such urgency," Jack said, "or I would have come the day our ship docked."

"Quite so. Now, Windrush." Smith sat straight-backed on his chair with his gaze never wavering from Jack's face. "You will wish to know what this is all about and how you can help rectify the situation."

"I had no idea things were so dire, sir. Please remember that I am on leave from India."

"I am aware of your current circumstances, Windrush but, as I have indicated, the situation is extremely serious." Mr Smith did not smile. "Our newspapers mock these Fenian people, and our Members of Parliament pretend not to take much notice, but behind the scenes, Windrush, behind the scenes, there are worried people in this country." He lowered his voice slightly. "Why, Windrush, Palmerston himself has spoken to me at length on this subject, and I believe that even Her Majesty is concerned."

Jack shifted uncomfortably in the hard chair. If Queen Victoria and Viscount Palmerston, the Prime Minister, were involved, he was dabbling in very deep waters. "I know very little about the Fenians," he admitted. "I have been away from this country for some years."

"I am fully aware of your activities, Captain Windrush." Smith spoke in flat tones. "You joined the 113th Foot as an ensign in 1851, fought in the Burmese Campaign, then throughout the Russian War as a lieutenant and served in the Indian Mutiny with your present rank."

Jack nodded. Smith spoke from memory, without recourse to notes.

"After the mutiny, Colonel Snodgrass disapproved of your choice of wife, and you left the 113th Foot." Smith's eyes did not waver as he continued the story of Jack's career. "Colonel Hook sent you on a mission to find gun-runners on the Frontier, which mission led to you doing some useful work among the Pashtun tribes in the late rising."

"Yes, sir," Jack agreed. "As you see, I have spent my entire career abroad. I know little about conditions at home."

"Then allow me to educate you, Captain," Smith said. "Tell me what you do know about the Fenians."

Jack considered for a moment. "I have read brief pieces about them in the newspapers," he said. "If I am correct, they are disgruntled Irishmen who want an Irish republic."

"They are a bit more than that," Smith corrected him. "The original Fenians were a semi-mythical force of Irish warriors some thousands of years ago. This new incarnation began in Ireland around 1857 and boasts a strong following among the Irish who emigrated to the United States and British North America. It appears to be a very formidable mass movement dedicated to – as they see it – freeing Ireland from British control."

"Yes, sir." Jack frowned. "If you'll forgive me, sir, but I am not political. I have scant knowledge of British and even less of Irish politics."

Waiting for Jack to finish, Mr Smith continued: "I am aware of your lack of political knowledge, Captain, as I am aware of every aspect of your life."

Jack felt increasingly irritated. "Why are you telling me all this, sir?" he asked.

"The Fenians are mostly of the lower orders." Smith ignored Jack's question. "They are labourers, small tradesmen, factory workers and the like. I doubt there are half a dozen gentlemen in the entire organisation and, as such, they can never gain any political advantage in Great Britain." Smith tapped his fingers on the desk as if emphasising his points. "Such people, as you are aware, could never stand for parliament."

"Do these Fenians seek political advantage in Britain? I thought you said they sought an Irish Republic, which would, therefore, be outside the United Kingdom."

"However, it is not the masses of Irishmen that concern us," Smith continued, again ignoring Jack's intervention. "We can discount the ramblings of the illiterate and semi-literate classes. We are facing danger from two diverse but related fronts. One is overseas, and the other is in your territory."

"My territory? India?" Jack hazarded. "I am not aware of any major threat in India since General Chamberlain dealt with the Warriors of God and the Bunerwals."

"As I just indicated, the overseas threat is in North America," Smith said. "Tens of thousands of Irishmen and men of Irish descent have joined the Fenian movement in the United States of America. There are threats to invade Canada, which our military people in North America will take care of." His eyes remained disconcertingly direct. "The other threat is in your domain."

"India?" Jack repeated, thinking: *How will Mary react if I tell her I'm being posted back already?*

"The threat is in the army itself," Smith said.

Jack sat back in his chair with an overwhelming sense of relief. The room was small and stuffy, with a single small window to break the monotony of panelled oak walls. There were no books, no pictures, not even a map to dilute the sameness. There was only the clean oaken desk behind which Smith sat, with two armless, straight-backed oak chairs. Nothing else.

"I don't understand," Jack said. "How could the army be a threat?"

Smith's expression did not alter. "Even since the time of King Charles II, Captain, the British Army and Navy have never been political. The officers and men swear allegiance to the reigning monarch, whoever that happens to be."

Jack nodded. Apart from his oath of allegiance to the queen, he had no political attachments whatsoever. He could happily ignore whichever party wielded political power, Whig or Tory.

"The Fenians are interfering with the military being free of politics," Smith said. "They have already infiltrated many regiments of the army and are fomenting mutiny." His expression did not alter. "You may be wondering why I am telling you all this, Windrush."

"I presume because a mutiny in the army could affect us all," Jack said.

"Broadly, Captain, you are correct. On a more particular level, you have worked for Colonel Hook in the military intelligence branch in India and have experience of similar activities in the Crimea."

"I am on leave, sir," Jack reminded.

"You have seen the result of mutiny in the East India Company's army, Windrush. That mutiny cost the country a great deal of money."

"There was a good deal of suffering as well, Mr Smith." Jack thought it best to remind this chilly, dry man that people mattered more than money.

"That is another reason then, Captain, to ensure such a mutiny does not occur in the British Army."

"I have served in the army for more than a decade, sir, without even being aware of any inclination to disloyalty among soldiers from Ireland. Indeed, sir, I have found them to be among the best men we have."

"The officers of the mutinous sepoy regiments said the same about their men." Smith's tone was dry.

Jack grunted, knowing that Smith was right.

"You will be aware that in 1797 mutiny spread across the Royal Navy, putting this country in considerable danger of invasion from France."

"I am aware of that, sir."

"Then you will be aware that only the actions of one man, Admiral Duncan, with intervention from the Admiralty, saved us."

"Yes, sir. I am aware of the Battle of Camperdown." Jack was growing impatient with this precise, cold-blooded man. "Could you tell me where I come into this situation, sir?"

Smith pressed his fingers together. "You are on leave, I believe."

"Yes, sir." Jack confirmed. "I have accumulated 17 months' leave from the army. I intend to show my wife around the country and settle some of our private affairs."

"I am sure you will place your duty before your private pleasure," Smith said. "To expand on my previous statement, it is fortunate you have experience in the less savoury aspects of military endeavour."

Jack shifted uncomfortably in his chair. "I prefer the more conventional aspects, sir."

"Indeed?" Smith raised his eyebrows. "In that case, Captain, you should have remained with the 113th Foot. You had a choice between remaining a regimental officer and marrying a woman of whom your colonel disapproved."

When Jack did not reply, Smith continued. "I want you to continue with your plans, Windrush. Take your wife on your tour of Great Britain by all means, but while you do so, I want you to visit various barracks to judge the feeling among the men. I will give you a list."

Windrush sighed. "I'm not a natural spy, sir. I'd prefer you asked somebody else."

"I'm not asking you, Captain. I am ordering you," Smith said. "Your experience in clandestine work is highly unusual in the army, and impossible for a more conventional British regimental officer."

"I could refuse," Windrush said.

"You could," Smith replied, "if you wished to rot as a half-pay captain for the remainder of your life."

Windrush took a deep breath. "That's a direct threat."

"Refusing a direct order is a court-martial offence, captain. Whatever the result, your career would be at an end."

"My honour is at stake," Jack said.

Smith's expression did not flicker. "I rather think that your honour is a precarious possession at best, captain. You acted the spy in the Crimea and India and married a Eurasian. In performing these actions, you sacrificed your honour."

"I had little choice in the matter of spying in Crimea and India, while the choice of a wife is nobody's business but my own."

"You also have little choice now," Smith said. "You will act as a guest in the barracks to which I send you. You will locate any Fenian sympathisers, note the atmosphere in each place, speak to the men as well as the officers and send me a full report the following day." Smith's expression remained unchanged. "If you are successful, Captain Windrush, you could be this century's Admiral Duncan."

There is no help for it. "Yes." Jack dropped the "sir". He had lost all respect for Mr Smith, whoever he might be. "With the difference that people do not consider spies as honourable as fighting admirals."

"We have already arrested several dozen soldiers who have joined this nefarious organisation," Smith said. "Some we caught after they deserted, others were boasting while in drink."

"Soldiers tend to talk when in drink," Jack said. "Mostly it's just hot air and braggadocio with young Johnny Raws trying to act as they think old soldiers should."

"We have arrested non-commissioned officers with years of experience," Smith countered. "These were solid men who have served with the army in various campaigns yet who still pledged allegiance to the Fenians."

"That's a little unsettling." Jack thought of Sergeant O'Neill, a man he had fought beside through Burma, the Crimea and the Indian Mutiny. He had trusted

O'Neill with his life a score of times. "What are the Fenians offering, to turn such men away from their duty?"

"As I already said, the Fenians seek an Irish Republic." Smith spoke without emotion.

"Is that even possible?" Jack wondered aloud.

"Less than 100 years ago, the United States of America was a disparate collection of squabbling colonies, and France a respectable monarchy." Smith reminded him. "Now look at them. Anything is possible in the world of politics. Your job is not to think of the possibilities. Your job is to help prevent a mutiny in the British Army." For the first time, Smith changed his stance, leaning forward on his hard chair. "How many Irishmen do you think there are in the British Army, Captain?"

"I have no idea, Mr Smith. Many thousands, I should think." Jack thought of the Irishmen he had come across, from General Gough of Sikh Wars fame to the daredevil redcoats who fought in the ranks.

"In 1830, before the Famine, 42.2 per cent of the army was Irish, and nearly 14 percent was Scottish." Smith shook his head. "Not only did we have 15 regiments that were almost entirely Irish, but also so many Irishmen in regiments nominally from Scotland, Wales and England that they made up a significant proportion of their numbers. Even today, Irishmen comprise about a quarter of the army's strength, Windrush, and this disease of Fenianism seems to have affected many of them. The Prime Minister has mentioned the possibility of preventing any more Irish recruitment until we cure this sickness."

"That's impossible!" Jack spoke without thought. "Some of our best soldiers and finest officers are Irish! What would we do without them?"

"We would do very badly, Captain Windrush. Very badly, indeed. That is why we are sending you, and others, to ensure that this nonsensical notion does not affect any officers."

"Do you suspect that officers are affected, sir?"

"We do, Captain. Somebody must be organising things, and I cannot think that a mere sergeant, however good he may be in battle, has the ability to contact men across the regimental divide." Smith leaned back again. "I'll have the list of barracks sent to your hotel with your written orders."

"We're staying at Durrants Hotel."

"I know where you are," Smith said. "Goodbye, Captain Windrush." Smith remained seated as Jack left.

* * *

The document was waiting for Jack when he returned to Durrants Hotel.

"Captain Windrush, sir!" Bowing obsequiously, the hotel clerk handed over a sealed package. "A gentleman left this parcel for you."

"Thank you, Mr Blackley." Jack lifted the thick parchment with its plain red seal. "When did it arrive?"

"You had hardly left the hotel, sir," the clerk began, with another low bow, "when a gentleman handed it in. He said I was to hand it to you and nobody else, not even your wife."

Smith sent that to me before our meeting, Jack reflected. *He knew that I could not refuse his order.*

"Is my wife in?"

Mr Blackley smiled. "Mrs Windrush is out with your son, sir."

"Did she say when she would be back?"

"She did not say, sir."

"Thank you, Mr Blackley." Tucking the package under his arm, Jack made his way to their room. As always with Mary, everything was immaculate, so he threw himself into one of the two leather armchairs and broke the seal of the packet. There were two documents inside. One was a single sheet of paper on which a neat hand had written a list of barracks. The other was a short note. Jack looked again at the list.

Littlehampton Fort
Albany Barracks, Isle of Wight
Hereford Barracks
Berwick Barracks

He had expected more than only four and was grateful he could fit them into their itinerary without disrupting Mary's tour. At least Hereford was within a few miles of Netherhills. Sighing, Jack placed the list to one side and read his official orders, which repeated in brief form what Smith had said, with a small addition.

"Windrush

By now you will have some idea what I wish you to do. Visit every barrack in the enclosed list and write me a report on the general atmosphere. You have seen mutiny in the army and know the signs. Pay particular attention to the Irish officers and officers of Irish extraction. When you reach Berwick, report to Colonel Snodgrass of the 113th Foot. He will expect your arrival as a replacement for an officer who has transferred elsewhere.

Smith."

The 113th Foot. Jack lowered the note. He had never expected to see them again, and now his leave was being curtailed before it had properly begun. What the devil would Mary say? Leaning back in the chair, Jack reached for a cheroot. It was only fortunate that Grandfather Baird had left him a second small property in Berwick. With luck, Mary would settle there while he was on regimental duty. With more luck, the regiment would remain in Britain rather than being sent to India or South Africa or some hell-hole such as Aden or Hong-Kong. Jack sighed again. He did not look forward to giving Mary his news.

CHAPTER THREE

England, Autumn 1865

"On duty?" Mary's eyes were as acidic as Jack had ever known. "What do you mean, called back to the colours? You're meant to be on leave." Her long dress rustled as she stood up, with the crinoline brushing against Jack as she stalked past. She stopped at the window, with her back turned.

"We can combine both," Jack said. "I have only four barracks to visit, and we do have a house in Berwick."

"*Only* four barracks to visit." Mary's emphasis on the first word could not have been more explicit.

"And Hereford is near Netherhills."

Mary was having none of it. "It's too much, Jack; it really is. Can your precious army not leave us alone to enjoy some time together without sending you on more missions? I thought we were finished with all that nonsense when we left India."

"It won't be as bad as all that." Jack tried to mollify her. "We'll still have our tour of England and Scotland. We'll have time to get Netherhills up to scratch and visit the house in Berwick. We can decide which house we wish to have as our home, and my work will be no more than an unpleasant diversion. Why, Mary, when I'm on duty, you can tour on your own, with David."

Mary rounded on him. "I didn't travel thousands of miles on a leaky ship to tour on my own! I travelled to be with my husband! And have you tried touring on your own as a Eurasian woman in England? They treat me as a curiosity, as something to gawp at, as if I was the bearded lady in a circus."

"Do they indeed?" Jack felt his anger rise. "By God, they won't do that if I'm around!"

"No, Jack." Mary put venom in her voice. "But you won't be around, will you? You'll be on duty for your soldier friends, not with me!"

"I'll spend as little time as possible on army matters." After six years of marriage, Jack had not yet learned that trying to appease Mary only inflamed matters.

"Last time you tried to go on leave, you ended up in Afghanistan for months."

"I wasn't in Afghanistan. I was on the North-West Frontier," Jack pointed out. "We're in England now, hardly the same thing."

"I want to go to Scotland, too." Mary reminded him. "Not just your precious England!"

"We'll certainly go to Scotland as well," Jack promised. "Why, Mary, the Scottish Border is at Berwick, where we have Grandfather Baird's second house. We can live there and visit all the places that Sir Walter Scott wrote about."

"So what are you not telling me?" With her back to the window, Mary stood in silhouette. She put her hands on her hips, waiting. "I know you, Jack Baird Windrush. You always hold something back."

Jack took a deep breath. "I'm not telling you that I have to report to Colonel Snodgrass of the 113th in Berwick. I am back on regimental duty again."

"Oh."

Jack could not see Mary's expression. "We'll travel slowly," he assured her, "and regimental duty in Great Britain is not trying, maybe one parade a day and the occasional spell as duty officer. I'll have plenty of time at home. Besides, we won't be living in barracks, remember. We can stay in our own place."

"If Colonel Snodgrass grants permission," Mary rasped.

"He will."

"I would not be so sure," Mary said. "Snodgrass is a most unpleasant man."

"That is true," Jack admitted. "But he also dislikes me so intensely that he'll be glad to have me outside his regiment as much as possible."

"Sometimes," Mary did not face him. "I can understand how he feels."

Jack set his mouth in a hard line. Army duty could be hard, but so could married life. At least when he was on campaign, things were black-and-white, with a clear enemy to fight and defeat. Skirmishing with Mary might be less physically dangerous, but much more emotionally draining because, even if he won a round, he hated to hurt his wife.

Striding over to the window, Jack stared at the busy streets below. This homecoming was not quite what he had hoped.

* * *

The officers at Littlehampton Fort and Albany Barracks could not have been more welcoming when Jack explained his mission. "There are no Fenians here," they said, ushering him into their respective messes.

"I'm sure you are right," Jack said. "Could you give me a list of Irishmen in your regiment?"

"Including me?" The adjutant at Albany Barracks asked with a smile.

Jack closed his eyes. "I don't like this duty any more than you do," he said.

The adjutant nodded. "You have free access to the regimental records," he said, "and when you've wasted sufficient time, you'll be my guest in the mess."

Jack checked the regimental documents, seeing where the men were recruited and trying to judge by names and religion. He toured the barracks, spoke to the officers and NCOs, listened to their comments and woes and could not find anything out of the ordinary. He entered the barrack-rooms and talked to the men, openly mentioning the Fenian Brotherhood and getting little more than blank stares.

"I've heard of them, sir" one man from County Clare admitted, standing to attention. "They want an Irish republic."

"That's the lads," Jack said. "What's your name, and where did you hear about them?"

"Private Sullivan, sir. There was a fellow in the Diggers mentioned them, sir. The Diggers is a public, sir, that's a public house."

"I am aware what a public is. Do you know this man's name?" Jack was aware that other men in the room were listening.

"No, sir."

"Would you recognise him if you saw him again?" Jack wondered if he should search for this mysterious man in the Diggers.

"Yes, sir. He's got a broken nose and busted teeth."

Jack sensed laughter in the room. "Tell me more, Sullivan."

Sullivan could not help smiling. "I hit him, sir, and some of the boys joined in."

"Very good, Sullivan." Jack had difficulty keeping his face straight. "Well done." He left the barrack-room in a better mood.

"I can't see any problems with your regiment, sir," Jack reported in both cases and moved on.

Leaving a still-disgruntled Mary in Netherhills, Jack mounted Cedric and rode the few miles to Hereford, where the Royal Malverns were based. He had not been looking forward to this visit, for he had once intended to join the Malverns, as the Windrush family regiment.

The Royal Malverns were in temporary accommodation in the Militia Depository in Harold Street, a relatively new building of many windows. Squaring his shoulders, Jack entered as if by right, returned the salute of the sentry and asked for the duty officer.

"Lieutenant Fairfax is in the Officers' mess, sir. That way." The sentry was as immaculate as would be expected in an elite regiment.

Lieutenant Fairfax was a young man with laughing eyes. Chewing an apple, he stood under the cased colours and beside a plaque that boasted the regimental motto "Always Victorious" above the inscribed "Heroes of Malplaquet". Jack knew the story of that plaque and the captain who had carved it with a rusty nail during the siege of Quebec in 1759.

"Fenians in the Royals? I'd be surprised, Captain Windrush." Fairfax said. "We're selective here, don't you know? We're meant to be guarding Fenian prisoners, though, until the government decides what to do with them." He took a large bite of his apple. "I say; you're not related to our Major Windrush are you?"

Jack nodded. "I am," he confirmed but said no more.

Fairfax came to sudden attention. "Sorry, sir, I had not realised."

"Easy, Fairfax – I said we're related. We're not the same man." Jack said. "Could you take me around the barracks?"

"Of course, sir."

"The name's Windrush," Jack reminded. "Or Jack, if that is easier. Is my brother here?"

"Yes, sir," Fairfax slammed to attention again as William Windrush strode into the mess.

"What the devil are you doing here, Captain?"

"I am checking up on your regiment, William." Jack faced him down. "Horse Guards believes there are Fenians here." He smiled as William vehemently denied that any Fenians could enter the Malverns.

"That's good, William. In that case, you won't mind me interviewing the men. I'll tell Horse Guards how co-operative the Malverns were." Without waiting for a response, Jack left the mess, brushing past William in the process.

As Jack had expected, the Malverns were smart and efficient, with the usual quota of Irishmen in the ranks. The men that Jack spoke to were quiet and respectful, claiming no more knowledge of the Fenians than that given by the press.

"Thank you for your time, gentlemen," Jack said as he left.

"Where are you going next?" Fairfax asked.

"Berwick." Jack expected the sympathetic looks from the Malverns. "And the 113th."

"Right on the edge of the world," Fairfax said. "Good luck, Windrush."

* * *

Rain sheeted in from the North Sea, hammering at the Elizabethan walls of Berwick-upon-Tweed, weeping from the slate roof of the barracks and bouncing from the cobbled streets. Jack squared his shoulders and marched toward the barrack gate. After 14 years spent abroad, he found the British weather damp and depressing, although the rain lacked the bite of Crimea and the surroundings the danger of the North-West Frontier.

Recognising Jack as an officer, the guard jumped to attention as he approached, with the corporal throwing a smart salute.

"At ease, corporal," Jack returned the salute as he looked around the impressive interior of the barracks. "Where could I find the officer of the day?"

"Over there, sir," the corporal pointed out an open door. "It's Lieutenant Flynn today."

Nodding, Jack eyed the corporal up and down, not recognising the face "You haven't been in the 113th long, have you?"

"Six years, sir," the corporal replied.

Six years. Was it that long since he left the 113th? Jack smiled. Now he was growing maudlin. A regiment was a dynamic institution, always changing as men left and new men joined. He had to prepare himself for many alterations since his time. "Thank you, corporal."

Lieutenant Flynn was an eager young man who regarded Jack with initial suspicion and then with delight when he realised who he was. "You're Fighting Jack Windrush!" The hint of an Irish accent confirmed the ancestry that his freckled face and his name suggested. "I've heard about you, sir!"

Pleased that his name was remembered, Jack allowed Flynn to enthuse for a few moments. "Is Captain Elliot still in the regiment, Lieutenant?"

Flynn frowned. "There is no Captain Elliot, sir."

Jack had served and fought with Elliot for years. He had looked forward to renewing their friendship. "Elliot has left? I had not heard."

"We have a Major Elliot. Perhaps that's who you mean?"

"Major Elliot?" Jack could not restrain his smile. "Major Arthur Elliot?"

"That's the fellow!" Flynn said. "As good a man as you'll ever meet."

"Did somebody say my name?" Elliot marched into the office, even broader of shoulder than the last time Jack saw him. "Good God! Jack!" His hand was out at once while his grin could not have been wider. "You did tell me you were coming home on leave, but what brings you here?"

"I'm back on the strength." Jack took his hand. "Temporarily at least. Congratulations on your promotion. Should I address you as sir?"

"Yes, you should. Call me sir, bow three times and remove your hat when you talk to me."

They grinned at each other until they realised that Flynn was watching, and dropped the handshake.

"Being a major suits you," Jack said. "You look dignified and important, not like your old self at all."

"That's you as duty officer for the next month, you blackguard," Elliot said. "Does the colonel know you are back?"

"Not yet, but I think Horse Guards has informed him that I am coming. I'd best toddle along and report."

"Oh, there's no rush. He's up in Edinburgh at present. Come on, I'll give you the tour and introduce you to the new lads. How's the lady wife? How's Mary?"

Jack shook his head. "Mary's not at all happy that I'm back on duty. We had planned a long, leisurely tour of Britain."

"Oh." Elliot frowned. "Beware the wrath of the lady scorned. You'll be safer with the regiment than with an angry Mary. I remember she was a very doughty lady."

"Aye." Jack remembered Mary's closed face as he left her that morning. "Doughty is one word for her. Bloody dangerous are two others. Show me your barracks, Arthur."

Berwick Barracks was one of the earliest built in Britain, created in the early 18th century to protect England from any possible invasion from the Jacobite Highlanders of Scotland. "It can hold up to 600 men," Elliot explained. He had clearly studied the history of the place thoroughly. "And 36 officers, although the regiment is a bit understrength at present."

"How many do we have?" It felt quite natural for Jack to slip back into the regimental mould.

"There are 453 other ranks, 20 officers." Elliot smiled. "One-and-twenty officers, including you. Recruiting has been slow." He lowered his voice as they stood on the parade square with the three-storey blocks on two sides, the store block on a third and the gatehouse on the fourth. "Do you recall how bad the regiment's reputation was when you and I first joined?"

"I remember," Jack said. "We were the infamous Baby-Butchers, the worst regiment in the British Army."

"That's right. You and I hauled the 113th up by blood and toil in the Crimea and through the Mutiny. Well, since you left, Jack, its reputation has sunk again, so recruiting has slumped. The colonel is a tyrant, men are deserting, and officers are sending in their papers or looking for a transfer."

Jack nodded. "Aye; I can't see Colonel Snodgrass being a benevolent old man."

"We are in barracks most of the time. You're fortunate just now as most of the lads are out on drill. They'll be back soon. As you see, we have two accommodation blocks, with the men sharing eight to a room and us privileged officers having a room to ourselves, Two rooms to majors and above." He grinned. "Sorry old man – you'll have to slum it with one room. Very Spartan after India, eh?"

Jack smiled. "I'll survive, although I was hoping to live outside barracks."

"That depends on the whim of the great Snod."

Jack nodded. "Aye."

"As you'd expect in a building of this age, sanitation is poor, with wells and basic latrines," Elliot said. "After all, we're only the queen's guardians and as such count for less than the servants in any well-run house. But we do have a hospital." Elliot pointed it out. "And an officers' mess there, just inside the main gate, which is where we are heading now."

The mess was comfortable, with solid chairs and a view over the parade square and the mess servants hurried to serve them brandy and soda. Jack sank into a chair, feeling relaxed in Elliot's company while apprehensive about his future meeting with Snodgrass. He looked around the mess, trying to size up the officers, wondering if any of them were Fenians.

"What sort of men are in the regiment now?" Jack asked and shook his head. "Damn it, man, this is all snuff. You know what sort of job Colonel Hook sends me on, and this one is no different."

"I wondered." Finishing his brandy with a single swallow, Elliot signalled for another. "What's to do, Jack?"

"Fenians." Jack explained what his mission was about as Elliot listened, nodding encouragement.

"Does this Smith fellow believe the Fenians have infiltrated the 113th?"

"He seems to think the Fenians are everywhere, just waiting to rise and set the world on fire."

"Maybe they are," Elliot said. "Where do we come in?"

Jack looked around the quiet room, trying to imagine it as a scene of horror like he had witnessed when the sepoy regiments mutinied in India. He shuddered. "Smith sent me to look at three other barracks, but I suspect he thinks the Fenians are entrenched in the 113th. You always have your finger on the pulse, Arthur. Do you think there are any Fenians in the regiment?"

Elliot swirled his brandy around the glass. "I know we have at least one, Jack, Corporal Riordan. He got himself drunk one day and was boasting about establishing an Irish republic."

"What happened to him?" Jack asked.

"General court-martial. He's to be demoted, drummed out of the regiment and given two years' confinement with hard labour."

"That sounds a bit harsh for a drunken rant," Jack commented.

"You'll see how harsh it is soon, Jack. Corporal Riordan is undergoing the first part of his sentence the day after tomorrow. I think our colonel is scared stiff of another Indian Mutiny." Elliot's smile had lost some of its brightness. "Welcome back to the 113th."

* * *

The regiment formed a hollow square around the parade ground, with the officers in front and Colonel Snodgrass astride his white horse in the centre. Jack could nearly taste the tension in the air as the men waited to see one of their own being publicly humiliated. Concentrating on Lieutenant Flynn, Jack wondered how an Irish officer would view the discovery of a Fenian among his men. However, Flynn stood without expression, seemingly no different from any of his colleagues.

The tapping of the drums signalled the start of the ceremony. Jack had heard these same drums encouraging this regiment to battle from the ridge of Inkerman to the walls of Lucknow. Now they were signalling a far different display. Jack altered his position slightly, searching the ranks for familiar faces. He saw Sergeant O'Neill there, his weathered features as hard as flint, while Coleman and Thorpe stood behind him, both old Burma hands, with Thorpe proudly wearing the ribbon of his Victoria Cross. Riley was a few yards away, with the diminutive, ugly figure of Donnie Logan at his side. Jack could almost sense the aura of menace that Logan gave off from where he stood.

The 113th stood in hushed expectancy, with tension so palpable that Jack felt as if he could cut it with an axe. He took a deep breath as Riordan appeared. The corporal was in his early thirties, a fair-haired, erect man with a long face and the stripes of his rank prominent on his sleeve. With his hands manacled in front of him, Riordan marched three steps in advance of two drummers, bare-headed and without any sign of the disgrace he should have been feeling. Jack vaguely remembered Riordan's face from his time in India, although he had never had the man under his direct command.

Led by a burly lieutenant Jack did not know, Riordan and the drummers marched slowly around the parade square, ensuring that every man in the regiment witnessed the proceedings. Except for the constant tapping of the drums, there was no sound, with even the colonel's horse seeming awed by the occasion. After their ponderous circuit, the lieutenant called a halt on the inside of the main gate.

"Attention!" The lieutenant snapped.

His years of drill forced Riordan to automatic attention and he stood erect as the lieutenant stepped up to him, still with the drummers tapping their monotonous beat. As the regiment watched, the lieutenant produced a small knife, cut through the top of Riordan's corporal's stripes and ripped them from his sleeve. Jack felt, rather than heard, the suppressed gasp from the 113th, although Riordan appeared unmoved.

"Slow march!" The lieutenant ordered, and the shameful procession moved again. They halted at the main gates, where the sentries stood at attention with only their eyes mobile, watching the drama unfold.

"Halt!" The lieutenant's voice seemed to crack as they reached the gate. Within the gate was the ordered world of the regiment and the military. Outside the gate, civilian life beckoned with all its chaos, cares and freedoms. However, there was no freedom for ex-corporal Riordan, for a hatchet-faced sergeant and two privates from a fusilier regiment waited to take him into custody.

"Private Riordan," the lieutenant addressed him with a soft Irish accent. "You have disgraced yourself and your regiment. You have broken your oath of allegiance to the queen. You are a disgrace to Ireland." Without another word, the lieutenant took hold of Riordan's shoulders and turned him to face away from the 113th, stepped back and delivered a hefty kick to Riordan's backside that propelled the man outside the gate.

Riordan staggered, but recovered and turned to face the lieutenant and the regiment. Raising both manacled hands above his head, he shouted: "Long live the Fenian Brotherhood! Long live the Republic of Ireland!"

The words seemed to float above the barracks, a chilling threat to the security of Great Britain.

"Come on, you!" The fusilier corporal grabbed Riordan by the scruff of the neck. "It's Greenlaw jail for you, you dirty Fenian bastard."

There was silence for a moment as the 113th waited for something to happen. The regiment had spent a hard decade campaigning in the Crimea and India to win a respectable reputation; now it seemed to have returned to the abyss.

"Form up 113th !" Colonel Snodgrass shattered the hush. "Columns of four." Flicking the reins of his horse, he rode through the gate, with the regiment following in a long scarlet snake. It was common practice in the 113th to perform a route march after an unpleasant parade, such as a hanging, and it seemed that Colonel Snodgrass considered the treatment of Corporal Riordan something best eradicated from the minds of his regiment.

Marching beside Elliot, Jack tried to gauge the mood of the men. They moved well enough, with the veterans setting the pace and the younger keeping up, but there was a certain reserve he did not like. The men crashed down their boots, taking out their anger and humiliation on the road, ignoring the stares of the people of Berwick-upon-Tweed.

From the barracks, Colonel Snodgrass led them across the bridge to Tweedmouth on the south side of the river, scattering the traffic and disregarding any cries of protest from carters or farmers. The men marched stolidly, prepared to shoulder aside anybody who got in their way, welcoming any confrontation. As a captain, Jack was glad he marched on foot with the men, able to share their anger, while officers ranked major or above rode their horses, unable to show their solidarity.

The 113th marched in silence, with only the rhythmic crash of studded boots on the ground and the occasional grunt to accompany the clop of horse's hooves and the steady grumble of the sea to their left.

When they reached the coast opposite Lindisfarne, Colonel Snodgrass rode his horse on to the causeway to the island, while the men splashed uncaring through the shallows as the tide receded. Jack watched the long column toiling under the weak English sun, remembered the regiment at Inkerman and Lucknow and shook his head. Memories were for old men, not for him.

"An hour's rest," Snodgrass ordered when the 113th halted among the dunes of Lindisfarne, "and then we'll head back to barracks."

Throwing themselves to the ground, some of the men produced tobacco or sipped at canteens that held anything except water. Jack watched Coleman and Thorpe cheat two Johnny Raws at cards, while one or two of the more intellectually inclined even spoke about the ruined castle.

"Sir!" Sergeant O'Neill snapped to attention beside Jack. "I heard you were back, sir. Welcome."

"Thank you, O'Neill." Jack felt a surge of affection for the sergeant beside whom he had fought in three wars.

"Are you here permanently, or just visiting, sir?"

"Stand at ease, O'Neill, for God's sake, we've known each other for years! That's rather a strange question, isn't it?"

"Yes, sir." O'Neill remained at attention. "Colonel Snodgrass doesn't like other ranks to relax with the officers, sir. His orders are that we've to stand at attention when talking to an officer."

"I see." Jack nodded. "I'm going for a stroll behind these dunes, O'Neill. I'd be obliged if you would accompany me."

Jack moved away from the main body, with O'Neill marching a step behind him. "Now relax, O'Neill."

"Yes, sir." O'Neill stood at ease. "Some of our boys were wondering what you're doing here, sir."

"I'm a regimental officer, Sergeant, doing what regimental officers do. How are the lads?"

O'Neill relaxed further. "They're still with us, sir. Parker had a pet dog, but the colonel had it shot and then promoted him to sergeant. Coleman and Thorpe are the same as ever, Riley's still a blackguard, and Logan is Logan. Permission to speak freely, sir?"

"Yes, Sergeant." Jack was intrigued by O'Neill's attitude.

"Thank you, sir. You're more than a regimental officer, sir. We've known each other too long for you to fool me."

Jack said nothing. A sergeant in the British Army was a fount of knowledge, cunning and perspicuity. O'Neill had all three in spades. He would know when something was wrong with the regiment before any officer, even an intelligent, experienced man such as Elliot.

"Are you here to investigate the colonel, sir?"

The question took Jack by surprise. "No, Sergeant. What made you ask that?"

"All the lads know you work for the intelligence people, sir."

"What makes you think I should investigate the colonel, O'Neill?"

O'Neill was quiet for a moment. "Sorry, sir. I spoke out of turn there."

The crash of surf on the dunes acted as a reminder that they were on an offshore island. At that minute, Jack felt outside the regiment as well as outside the mainland. "Out with it, man!"

"I don't think the colonel is quite sane sir." O'Neill flinched as if expecting Jack to strike him.

Jack took a deep breath. "I would advise you to keep that thought to yourself, O'Neill."

"Yes, sir." O'Neill stiffened to attention. "Sorry, sir."

"So, tell me why you say that, O'Neill. Between ourselves."

"He's treating us all like first-day recruits, sir," O'Neill said. "He's got the sergeants checking everything the men do, and the officers checking everything the sergeants do. He's got every piece of equipment stencilled with the men's name and number and ordered daily inspections of barrack-rooms and kit."

"The colonel is tightening discipline, then."

"He's got a down on the older soldiers, sir. He hounds them." O'Neill struggled for words. "It's as if he's trying to remake the regiment with youngsters."

"Colonel Snodgrass grew up with the old 113th, O'Neill. He was with the regiment during the Sikh Wars, before my time. Perhaps he is worried about this Fenian nonsense." Jack left an opening there for O'Neill to step in if he wished.

"Perhaps that's what it is, sir." O'Neill sounded more guarded than Jack liked.

They waited as a flight of screaming seagulls passed overhead. "How about you, O'Neill? Have you heard about these Fenians?"

O'Neill nodded. "I've heard the rumours, sir. The boys have been talking about these Fenian people."

"Do you know who's been talking?"

O'Neill shrugged. "Nearly everybody, sir. The Irish lads have been getting some abuse from the rest. I've had to step in now and then to keep the peace."

"Has anybody tried to recruit you?"

O'Neill's expression could have frozen lava. "No." His omission of the customary "sir" was significant.

"If you hear of anything, let me know."

O'Neill nodded. "Is that why you're here, sir?"

How far can I trust O'Neill? Jack pondered. *I've fought with him through three gruelling wars and have had no doubts about his loyalty. But he is Irish, and other Irish NCOs have joined this organisation. But damn it! This is O'Neill!* "Yes, O'Neill." Extracting two cheroots from his pocket, Jack handed one over.

"Thank you, sir."

Jack was not sure if O'Neill was thanking him for the cigar or the trust.

"There's another whisper going about that might be important, sir."

Lighting his cheroot, Jack held the lucifer for O'Neill to light up. "What would that be, O'Neill?"

O'Neill inhaled before he spoke, with smoke dribbling from the corners of his mouth. "I heard that there's a mutiny planned for some regiment over in Ireland, sir. It could be complete moonshine, but after India..." O'Neill shrugged. "After India, sir, I don't trust anything any more. Or anybody."

"Aye," Jack said. "After the Mutiny in India, anything that once seemed impossible could be possible now. Thank you, O'Neill. Did you hear which regiment?"

O'Neill shook his head. "No, sir. It may be no more than the usual barrack-room gossip."

"That's more than likely, O'Neill. Keep me posted, if you hear anything else, will you?"

"Aye, sir." O'Neill looked at Jack through narrowed eyes. "I'll do that."

Jack paced along the coast of the island, drawing on his cheroot until Elliot sauntered up to him.

"Well, Jack, how are your enquiries progressing?"

Jack passed him a cheroot. "I'm not sure, Arthur. Sergeant O'Neill heard a rumour about a possible regimental mutiny in Ireland."

Elliot pulled on his cheroot. "It would be a good place to start."

"Aye," Jack agreed. "The Fenians will be at their strongest over there, and opposition to British rule is commonplace, even expected." He stared at the crashing surf, thinking that there was nothing between him and India except miles of water. The sea was a highway, rather than a barrier. "When I was an idealistic youth, Arthur, life seemed so simple. Great Britain was always right, Johnny Foreigner was always wrong, and the Union Flag symbolised truth, freedom and justice."

"It still does, Jack," Arthur said. "The world would be a much worse place without us fighting to suppress slavery and piracy, ending the rule of tyrannical potentates and putting justice and the rule of law wherever we go."

"The Pashtuns may not agree," Jack argued. "Or the Pandies, or even the Irish, it seems. Now that I am older, and I've helped defend the Empire," Jack was not sure if he was talking to Elliot or trying to unravel the tangled threads within his mind, "I see that things are more complex. I see that imperial powers such as Great Britain are not always benevolent father figures, not all Britain's wars are justified, and not everyone views the Union Flag with favour."

"You might be joining the Fenians if you're not careful, Jack," Elliot said. "I would not say such things too loudly, if I were you."

Jack nodded. "I know," he said. "I've been thinking about these things for some time, so I am unsure where I stand now."

"Keep it simple, Jack," Elliot said. "You've sworn an oath of loyalty to the queen; keep your word, do your duty and you preserve your honour." Lifting a pebble, he tossed it out to sea, watching the resulting splash. "That's what I do. It doesn't pay to think too much."

Jack nodded. "That's probably good advice, Arthur." He sighed. "There's our call to duty now." He lifted his head as the brassy notes of a bugle floated over the dunes toward them, followed by the barks of NCOs.

Jack threw his cheroot into the ripples Elliot's pebble had caused. It floated for an instant and then sank. Jack sighed. Philosophising was all very well, but it did not help at all.

"Come on, Jack," Elliot said. "Enough prosing. We have work to do."

CHAPTER FOUR

Berwick-Upon-Tweed, England, Autumn 1865

"Well, Windrush." Colonel Snodgrass had greyed with age, and the whiskers that covered much of his face could not conceal the red nose that betrayed excessive drinking. "I can't say I am pleased to see you back."

"Yes, sir." Jack decided to be as diplomatic as he could.

"Are you still married to that Eurasian woman?"

"Mary is still my wife, yes," Jack said.

"I'd be obliged if you would refrain from introducing her to the other officers' wives. We have no time for such people in this regiment."

"I am sure my wife shares your sentiments, sir," Jack said.

"What?" Snodgrass stared at him. "Naturally, you must find accommodation outside the barracks. There is no question of you living alongside the other officers."

"Yes, sir. I've taken care of that."

"I don't want you here, Windrush, let me make that perfectly clear."

"You have made that clear, sir." Jack kept his patience. He had never liked Snodgrass, and promotion to lieutenant-colonel had only increased the man's snobbery and bigotry.

"However, Horse Guards, in their infinite wisdom, has sent you and I must abide by its decision." Snodgrass looked up. "You will be with my regiment until I find sufficient reason to be quit of you, which I suspect won't be long, given your history."

Jack allowed Snodgrass's words to drift past him. The colonel was evidently trying to provoke him into saying something untoward, thus giving an excuse to kick him out of the regiment. *Dismissed from the 113th!* Jack gave a wry grin. That would be a first as the 113th once had the reputation as the worst regiment in the British Army.

"Do you find something amusing, Windrush?"

"Not at all sir, I am just glad to be back in the regiment where I started my career."

When Snodgrass snorted, Jack could smell the brandy on his breath. "Career! You've been in the army since 1851, been through three wars and you've not advanced beyond the rank of captain, and that's as far as you will go, Windrush. You're a poor soldier and a poor excuse for a man."

"If you say so, sir."

Snodgrass nodded. "I say so." He opened a drawer of his desk, looked inside and closed it again. "Horse Guards has asked me to send a company over to Charles Fort. I'd been wondering who to exile until you came along." Snodgrass gave a bleak smile. "Maybe you'll be useful after all, Windrush, my worst officer leading a company of misfits. You're dismissed, Windrush. Go and take charge of F Company. I'm sure you'll feel at home with them."

"Yes, sir. Thank you for your consideration." *Charles Fort? Where the devil is Charles Fort?* Jack thought.

* * *

Every regiment had its awkward squad, and F Company was as awkward as any that Jack had encountered. He found them on the parade square, floundering with the basics under the frustrated eye of Sergeant Parker, a man Jack remembered as a private in India.

I've to take these unwanted misfits to Charles Fort, wherever that may be, he mused.

"How are they shaping up, sergeant?"

"They're horrible, sir, just horrible." Parker's Liverpool accent had thickened rather than softened in the years since Jack had last known him. "They can't tell their left from their right, so I've stuck a bit of hay on their left boot and a wisp of straw on their right, and found out they don't know the difference between hay and straw either!" Parker shook his head and raised his voice to a bellow.

"Right! We'll try again. You march by putting one foot before the other. After me! Follow what I do!" Parker lifted his left foot. "Look! Hay foot! Then straw foot! Hay foot! Straw foot!" He shook his head and turned back to Jack. "I heard we're off to Charles Fort, sir. Is that true?"

"It is, Parker."

"We'd better get this lot up to scratch then. I don't like to think of them loose in Ireland." Parker shook his head.

"Ireland?"

"Yes, sir. Charles Fort is in County Cork," Parker said.

"So it is," Jack said, his mind racing. Colonel Snodgrass was sending him into the lion's den.

Parker shook his head ruefully. "Some time, sir, I'll request a transfer to B Company. That's the place to be."

"Why is that, Sergeant Parker?"

Parker shrugged. "I don't know, sir. B Company seems to attract the best soldiers."

"How about our lads from the old days, Parker? Riley, Logan, Thorpe and the rest?"

Parker grinned. "They avoid B Company as if it's got the cholera, sir. They're old enough soldiers to keep out of trouble, mostly."

Jack watched F Company shambling as Parker grew increasingly frustrated. "I'll take over for a few moments, sergeant."

"Thank you, sir." Parker stepped smartly aside. "Good luck, sir."

"Right, lads." Jack surveyed the 63 men of F Company. "Stand easy." He kept his voice conversational. "I don't know you, and you probably don't want to know me, but we'll soon put that right. I am Captain Jack Windrush, your new company commander."

Some of the men glanced up at the name while others continued to look blank. They were the usual collection of Johnny Raws and the hopeless, a mixture of very young boys from the city slums, village ne'er-do-wells, dull-eyed country labourers, men escaping poverty or an unwanted woman and old soldiers soaked in drink and broken by painful experiences.

"Those of you who are recruits will be wondering what you've got yourself into. Well, let me tell you that you've joined the finest regiment in the British Army." Jack saw the surprise on a few faces. "Ah, did you think the Guards were the best? Or the 93rd Highlanders of the Thin Red Line? The Royal Malverns, perhaps?" Jack laughed to show his scorn for such ideas. "Let me ask you some questions."

The men stared ahead, confused.

"Who held the line at Inkerman, when we threw back five times our numbers of Russians?"

Nobody answered.

"The 113th did," Jack told them.

"Who outfought the Cossacks outside the walls of Sebastopol?"

Again there was silence although one boy hesitantly held up his hand as if he were still at school.

"The 113th did!" Jack answered his question. "Who was among the first into Cawnpore and Lucknow?"

"The 113th?" The boy with the raised hand hazarded a guess.

"That's right, Private! The 113th was!" Jack pointed at the man on the extreme left, and gradually moved until he had indicated each man in the company, ensuring they all met his gaze. "The 113th left the Crimea and India as heroes and you men are the next heroes. You are the next to win the Victoria Cross, you are the next to have women flocking to you on your return from a campaign."

Jack walked around F Company, adjusting a tunic here, pulling back a man's shoulders there. "You are new, raw and untested, as we all were when we first joined the army, as I was and even as Sergeant Parker was, once. Every day, every hour, you will gain experience, you will get better at your chosen profession until one day you will be in the firing line as soldiers of the 113th Foot, and then, by God, then you will show the Russians or the Afghans how British soldiers fight. You won't just be part of the 113th, lads, you'll be the best company in the best regiment in the British Army, and that means in the world."

Jack stepped back. Although he did not expect spontaneous applause for his speech, he had hoped for some reaction, rather than the blank stares he received. Army recruits were usually bewildered and lost but this group seemed to lack even the basics of human communication.

"Right, sergeant," Jack turned to Parker, hoping his words might encourage the men, "take over these fine soldiers." He wandered back towards the officer's mess. The Irish officer who had ejected Private Riordan was there, talking to a young and slightly diffident ensign.

"Jack Windrush," Jack introduced himself. "Fresh from India."

"Lieutenant Byrne." The Irishman held out a welcoming hand. "Your reputation precedes you, Captain Windrush. Major Elliot has told us all about your exploits at Lucknow and before Sebastopol!"

"All highly exaggerated, I'm sure," Jack said. He nodded to the ensign who coloured bright scarlet and stared in response. "And you are?" Jack prompted.

"Ensign Peter Snodgrass, sir." Ensign Snodgrass put out his hand, retracted it again, decided he had been correct the first time and thrust it out so quickly that he jabbed his fingers into Jack's stomach. "Oh, God, I'm sorry, sir."

"It's all right, Ensign, There's no harm done." Jack tried to calm the boy down.

Ensign Snodgrass opened and closed his mouth twice before he spoke. "Major Elliot told us about you, sir. Major Elliot said you had fought all through the Crimea and the Mutiny."

"Major Elliot was with me every step of the way, Ensign, and so were most of the 113th and tens of thousands of others." Jack said gently. "There is no need to call me sir in the mess, Snodgrass. We're all equals in here, all officers of the 113th Foot."

"Yes, sir," Ensign Snodgrass said.

"Yes, Windrush," Jack corrected him. "Or yes, Jack, if you prefer." He withdrew a step before the boy collapsed in hero-worship. "Byrne, a minute, if you please."

With Ensign Snodgrass sitting in a corner still staring, Jack propelled Byrne to a table. "I wish to talk about that little scene we witnessed yesterday."

"You mean Riordan the Fenian?"

Jack sipped at his whisky. "Exactly so, Riordan the Fenian. Have you found any other Fenians in this regiment?"

"Very few, Windrush." Byrne spoke with confidence as he accepted a brandy from the mess waiter. "That's only the second case this year."

"What happened to the last fellow?"

Byrne shrugged. "Two dozen of the cat and a year's hard labour. He was caught trying to convert others."

"I've heard of similar cases in other regiments," Jack said "Men of the 4th Dragoons and two men of the 58th in Dublin in December last year, a drum-major of the 2nd Queen's and a sergeant of the 99th in September this year," he shrugged. "The Fenian Brotherhood is a dangerous group."

"It's all of that." Byrne leaned back in his chair. "It's a worrying trend, Windrush. I've heard a rumour that the Army of the Potomac in the United States is sending 50 officers to Ireland to train up discontented men to fight against us." He took a sip at his brandy. "If that weren't bad enough, there are said to be more than 200,000 Fenians in the United States."

Jack noted Byrne's use of the term "us" to describe Britain. "As many as that! That's a fair number of fighting Irishmen. I don't suppose anybody has ever approached you, though."

"Why should they?" Byrne asked, lifting his chin. "I'm a British officer."

"Why, indeed? Nobody's asked me, either!" Jack became aware that Ensign Snodgrass was still staring at him. "Come and join us, Ensign."

"Thank you, sir." Ensign Snodgrass scrambled over. "Sorry, I mean thank you, Windrush."

"That's better," Jack said. "Don't worry; you'll get there. What did you think of that little ceremony with Private Riordan, Ensign?"

"It was terrible," Ensign Snodgrass exclaimed. "Imagine a Fenian in our regiment. We should have shot him, sir!"

Jack grunted. "You have no Fenian notions then, Ensign?" He winked at Byrne. "You don't wish to join the Brotherhood?"

"No, sir! I'm not even Irish, sir!"

"I am," Byrne said dryly.

"Yes, sir, but you're loyal. I mean, you're an officer."

"I like to think so." Byrne said.

"I heard that Lieutenant Flynn was equally loyal." Jack spoke casually, nursing his whisky. "And equally Irish."

Byrne's smile weakened. "I hope you are not insinuating that officers can't be trusted if they are Irish."

Jack forced a smile. "Some of the bravest and best men I ever fought alongside were Irish," he said. "I was with the Connaught Rangers at the Redan."

"Not all Irish are Fenians." Byrne stood up abruptly. "Excuse me, Captain Windrush."

Jack watched Byrne stride out of the Mess. *I dislike this spying business, being suspicious of anybody of any rank. The sooner I'm back to being a regimental officer, the better I will like it.* He sipped at his whisky, hating himself for what he had to do.

"Sir," Ensign Snodgrass said. "Captain Windrush."

"Speak, fellow officer," Jack said, "or for ever hold your peace. What troubles your young mind?"

"Is it true that you're going to Ireland, Captain Windrush?" Ensign Snodgrass asked.

"Yes, Snodgrass. I am taking F Company to Charles Fort in County Cork."

"Sir, Captain, Windrush." Ensign Snodgrass hesitated. "Could I transfer to your company, sir?"

Jack stopped with his glass halfway to his lips. "F Company is raw, Ensign. The men can be difficult to handle. Would you not be better learning your trade with a more established company? B Company, say?"

"I want to be a real soldier, sir. I don't want to sit in an English garrison town all my life. Why, Captain Windrush, when you were an ensign, you shipped right out to the Burmese war and captured Rangoon."

"A few others were involved, Ensign." Jack gave a grave nod. "There was some stiff fighting before we won that war." He remembered the humidity along the rivers, the men dying of fever and dropping from heat exhaustion in the jungle. "War isn't all glory and triumph, but if you put in a transfer request, Ensign, we'll see what we can do."

Now I'm away to Ireland with the worst company in the regiment. What the devil will Mary say about that?

CHAPTER FIVE

Boston, United States, June 1865

The tall man entered without knocking and stood inside the door. "Call me Walsh." He kept his hands deep in the pockets of his greatcoat. "Patrick Walsh."

"Good evening Mr Walsh," the bearded man at the head of the table said. "My name is General Thomas Sweeny. Close the door as you leave – this is a private meeting."

"I know it is." When Walsh spoke, the scar above his left eye visibly pulsated. "You are holding a meeting of the Brotherhood of Fenians."

"The purpose of the meeting is not a secret." Sweeny lifted a finger, and two men closed in on Walsh.

"Call off your dogs," Walsh said. "I wish to join the Brotherhood."

"Why?" Sweeny lifted his hand, stopping the progress of his men. They halted at once, one with his hand inside his jacket.

"I'll show you why." Walsh removed his hands from his pockets and placed two long Colt revolvers on the table. As the other men watched, he shrugged off his coat, then unfastened his shirt, peeled it off and threw it on to the ground, followed by his trousers, so he stood naked before them. The scars were visible on his shoulders, neck and chest, and when Walsh turned around, even the hard-bitten war-veterans sitting at the table gasped. Walsh's back, from his shoulders to his calves, was a mass of white ridged weals. "The work of the British in Dartmoor Prison," he said.

"What did you do?" Sweeny asked.

Walsh faced the gathering again. "I am Irish."

"There would have been another reason." Sweeny was nobody's fool.

"To some British, being Irish is reason enough." Still naked, Walsh lifted one of his revolvers and spun the chamber. "And to me, being British is to be an enemy."

"What you say may be true," Sweeny said dryly. "However, the British judicial system has checks and balances to ensure against such partiality. What did you do?"

Walsh hesitated for only a minute. "That is not your concern."

"Come, come, Walsh. You seek to join us. You must tell us everything." When Sweeny lifted his finger again, his two men took another step forward.

"I chose the wrong side in a war," Walsh said. "They called me a traitor."

"Which war?" Sweeny stopped the advance of his men.

"The war in the Crimea," Walsh said. "I fought for the Russians."

"Where about?"

"The Alma and Inkerman." Walsh began to dress.

"That experience could be useful," Sweeny allowed, "although we have many Civil War veterans in our ranks. What rank did you hold?"

"I was a major in the intelligence branch."

"Impressive. What do you wish to do with us?"

"Kill Englishmen," Walsh said, "and destroy the British Empire." He sensed the approval of the men at the table.

Sweeny lifted Walsh's revolvers, reversed them and returned both. "Welcome to the Fenian Brotherhood, Major Walsh. Now all you have to do is take the oath of allegiance."

Walsh's smile did not reach his eyes. "Good." He slipped his revolvers back inside his coat. "Let's kill Englishmen."

CHAPTER SIX

Berwick-Upon-Tweed, England, Autumn 1865

"I miss India, and I miss Ayah," David said. "When are we going home?"

"This is your home now," Mary told him softly. "This is your home as long as Daddy is based in Berwick."

David looked around the stark rooms of the house and pulled a face. "But I don't want to be here. Ayah told me once that the captain's little son will be an officer in the army. When can I be an officer and go back to India?"

Jack had a vision of his own ayah from 30 years before, with her sari and blouse, her nose rings and the tinkling brass bangles on her wrists and ankles. He understood how David felt.

"Where's Monga?" David asked, referring to his pet mongoose, invaluable for hunting snakes.

"Monga's back in India, where he belongs," Mary said. "We gave him to the snake charmer to look after. He would not like this cold country where there are no snakes for him to chase."

Jack remembered that snake charmer who once sat cross-legged for seven hours without a break, playing his flute to charm a six-foot-long king cobra from under the floor of their bungalow office. There was no need for such professions in England. Compared to India, England was a featureless country without character, where everybody complained about the weather and strove not to be different from their neighbours.

"I understand how David feels," Mary said. "I miss the festivals." She sat on one of the uncomfortable wooden chairs that had come with the house. "Even though they are anything but Christian, I miss the Hindu spring festival of Holi and the Muslim Mohurram when men dress as horses and dance around the gardens outside the British cantonments."

"How about Kali?"

"I never liked Kali. She scared me." Mary replied with a smile. "That's why I've ordered a statue of her for Netherhills. I want to give your charming step-brother the chills every time he sees her staring at him."

"I've married an evil woman. Do you know what I miss?" Jack leaned back in his chair. "I miss watching the sun rising, pale pink and then red, on the great Indian plains, with the grass whispering for ever to the horizon and the scent of woodsmoke in the air." He closed his eyes, briefly back in the land of his birth. "I miss the space and distance."

"I miss travelling by elephant," Mary said, with a slow smile. "A post chaise seems dull in comparison. And lying in bed here with the traffic whirring past is so dreary, compared to listening to the jackals." Licking her fingers, she smoothed down David's blond hair. "Can you remember what the jackals said when they howled?"

"Yes, Mummy," David snuggled closer. "They said: 'I smell the body of my next full meal! Where? Where? Here! Here!' "

They both laughed although David did not understand the meaning.

Jack took a cheroot from his case and lit up. "I don't miss the hot season, though, and the prickly heat when you woke up drenched with sweat, everybody was irritable, and you'd give anything for a cool breeze."

"There were some compensations," Mary lifted David and stood him on the floor. "It's bedtime for you, young man. Off you go." She waited until David left the room. "There was one occasion when I was a senior at the Mission School, and we were out for a walk in the hot season. We came across an entire British regiment bathing naked in a river."

"That's shocking." Jack remembered that Helen had first met him in similar circumstances in the Crimea. He shook away the thought.

"Mrs Cartwright, our teacher, thought so." Mary was still smiling. "Don't look, girls," she said. "Don't look – they're all males."

"Did you look?"

"Of course I did," Mary said. "Everybody looked. Poor Mrs Cartwright was going demented. "If anybody looks," she said, in a very squeaky voice, "I'll give them a jolly good spanking."

"Did she?"

"Yes she did," Mary replied, "but it was worth it. It was the first time I had seen a naked British man, and there they were, hundreds of them all at the same time. The sight was better than any Christmas present."

Jack grinned. "Good for Mrs Cartwright! You deserved all you got, you brazen hussy." He glanced out of the window at the estuary of the River Tweed and the lights of Tweedmouth beyond. "I doubt you'll see anything like that in this river. The chill would freeze bits off the lads."

"Now you're becoming crude, Jack Baird Windrush," Mary admonished with mock severity. "But everything here seems so small in comparison to India."

Jack remembered his impressions of India when he travelled across the country as a young subaltern. He had immediately felt at home with the immense sky and the ever-receding horizon. He remembered the scarlet splash of the gold mohur tree that gave invaluable shade to the village elders who passed their days beneath the branches. "I miss the nearly horizontal streak of smoke from the village fires at sunset and the tramp of cattle returning to the village through a film of pale gold dust."

Reaching across, Mary took Jack's cheroot and drew quietly. "It's the smells I miss most," she said, "the smell of the dying day. Do you remember the Sind plain at evening? Did you ever smell the salty land cooling and the ammoniac scent of tamarisks?"

"I can imagine myself there." Jack closed his eyes. "I'm in an Indian village, smelling the woodsmoke, seeing the brief, sudden twilight and then that blue mist rising from the fields all around." He sighed as the wind rose, sending a spatter of rain against the multi-paned window.

Where do I belong? he found himself wondering. *Here in England, the land of my ancestors; or India, the land of my birth and my grandmother?*

"I best remember the spicy, peppery smells from the bazaar, and sleeping out at night under the scimitar moon, and reading forbidden books by starlight." Mary smiled again. "Until Mrs Cartwright caught us. You can guess what happened next."

"She gave you a jolly good spanking," Jack said with a smile. "And served you right. You must have been a troublesome child. Now you're a troublesome wife instead."

"Well, you chose me!"

"I know. Do you regret my choice?" Jack was suddenly serious. "Do you regret marrying a man who brought you to this cold grey land?"

"No." Mary shook her head. "There was a saying among us Anglo-Indians: 'If you marry the drum, you have to follow it.' "

"Aye. If you can."

"Mummy." David looked up from behind the chair where he had been hiding. "What's a jolly good spanking?"

"It's what you'll get if you don't get back to bed." Mary stood up. "Come on, be off with you." She chased him, clapping her hands, as David scampered away, giggling.

Jack smiled as he watched, but he knew that it was hard for wives when their men were in the army. With every line regiment spending some time in India or other overseas postings, officers' wives had to make a terrible choice. They could remain with their husband in India, or depart to Britain for the sake of the children's education. *I still haven't told her about Ireland. I'll wait until I know the date.*

Mary was laughing when she returned. "That's him settled for the next five minutes." Stooping over Jack, she kissed him briefly on the forehead, slid a hand inside his breast pocket and extracted another cheroot.

"People will say it's not ladylike to smoke one of these," Jack commented as Mary lit up and blew aromatic smoke into the air.

"People can go and jump," Mary responded pleasantly. "Since they call me a blackamoor or a blackie-white, and many shun me altogether, Jack, do you think I care if they approve of me smoking or not?"

"Probably not." Jack inhaled deeply. Even the scent of tobacco smoke could not cover Mary's perfume of jasmine that still excited him after years of marriage. He eyed her up and down, smiling.

"I know that look, Captain Jack," Mary blew a perfect smoke ring. "Later, if you behave yourself."

"I'll hold you to that, Mrs Windrush, and I always behave myself. Sometimes I behave well, other times, I behave badly, but I always behave." Jack frowned as he heard raised voices from the street at the back of the house. "Can you hear that?"

"I can't hear anything. It will be cruel hard to say goodbye to David," Mary said abruptly. "I've told him that he'd stay at school here if we return to India."

"How did he take it?"

"Better than I thought he would," Mary admitted, "and I don't know how I feel about that, either. He said that all boys have to go to school and he'll be back in India when he grows up. I thought there would be tears and tantrums."

"Our David doesn't have tears and tantrums," Jack said.

"No," Mary agreed. "He doesn't." Her smile was a little forced. "But I'll be having both the day we leave him behind. Are we going to send him to the same school you attended?"

Jack shook his head. "No. Brother William has his brat there, and the family knows the headmaster."

"Is that so bad?"

"It means David will be bullied." Remembering his early days at school, Jack shivered. "We're lucky he's blond and fair; there is less chance that bullies will pick on him for his ancestry. We'll send him to quite a different school, one with no Windrush connections."

Mary pulled at her cheroot. "Do you have one in mind?"

The noise in the street was quite distinct now, a disturbance with raised voices and the crash of breaking glass. "I have two possibilities, one near here and one in Herefordshire." Standing, Jack strolled to the window and looked out. All was quiet at the front, where the house faced the roadway around the city walls. "I'm going to have a look around the back," he said casually.

"Be careful, Jack."

"I shall." Jack grinned. "This is England, not the Frontier of India. No Afridis are waiting to cut us up here."

"Take your pistol," Mary said.

"I'll take this instead." Jack lifted his walking cane and tapped the weighted end in the palm of his hand. "It will be quite adequate for any trouble there may be in Berwick."

Even after weeks back in England, the crispness of the air shocked Jack when he first stepped outside. The noise was increasing, a constant roaring punctuated by breaking glass, the shouts of men and the more high-pitched screams of women.

"Get the Fenian bastards!"

The phrase rang out clear above the general din. *So the Fenians are here too, are they?* Gripping his cane firmly, Jack strode forward, to come across a scene of uproar. Scores of men and women were struggling in the centre of the street, with soldiers' uniforms splashes of scarlet amid the general drabness. As only the 113th were in garrison here, the soldiers must be from Jack's regiment.

"113th!" Jack raised his voice in the old stentorian roar. "To me, 113th!" He wished he had taken Mary's advice and carried his pistol. A weighted cane was not of much use against so many rioters.

Some of the soldiers looked up. Most were too busy kicking and punching, or avoiding being kicked or punched. Swinging his cane, Jack caught a stocky civilian a shrewd blow on the back of the head and stepped into the middle of the crowd, still shouting. "113th! Rally to me, 113th!"

"Kill the Fenians," somebody shouted. "The lobsters are all Fenians!"

Cracking a bottle-wielding man on the hand, Jack stood still. "113th!"

The smallest and ugliest of the soldiers moved to Jack's side. "Here, lads! It's Fighting Jack!"

Despite the situation, Jack could not restrain his smile. "Logan! I should have known you would be at the centre of any trouble!"

"Halloa there, sir!" For one mad second, Jack thought that Logan was going to try and shake his hand in the middle of a street brawl. Instead, he leapt high in the air and crashed his forehead against the face of one of the attackers, sending him staggering to the ground.

"Where's Riley?" Jack fended off a wild swinging fist with a sharp prod of his cane to the man's groin. The man collapsed, retching.

"Here I am, sir!" Riley was Logan's rear-rank man and constant companion, although the two could hardly have been more different. While Logan was a short, uncouth Glaswegian, Riley was a gentleman ranker with a background as a skilled cracksman. "We didn't start this, sir."

"Tell me later!"

Two more soldiers staggered up, one bleeding heavily from a wound in his temple. He lashed out at a drunken porter as a bottle spiralled past Jack, to explode in a hundred shards of glass. Jack stood still as the soldiers formed around him, familiar faces and unfamiliar faces amid a mob gathering itself for a charge.

"How many of us are there?" Jack asked. "I see eight."

"There were 10 of us, sir. Somebody felled O'Mara with a brick and I dunno where Jenks is."

"And how many of them?"

"A couple of hundred, sir, maybe more." Riley was as calm as if he was commenting on the weather.

"Here they come!" a gaunt-faced private shouted.

"Back to back, 113th!" Jack yelled. "Form square!"

The mob was gathering itself for a charge, roaring men and wild-eyed women, some with staves, pokers or bottles, encouraging each other with drunken shouts. Jack flexed his cane and sighed. Just 10 minutes earlier, he had been happily talking with Mary, now he was facing a shrieking mob. How quickly things could change.

The mob moved forward, circling the soldiers, with the women at the back urging on their men. A couple of bottles flew. Logan caught one, deftly turned it and threw it back. Grinning, he unfastened his belt and whirled it in the air with the metal buckle a potentially lethal weapon.

"Come on, you Berwick bastards!"

The sound of the shot made Jack start. *That was a pistol! That alters things!* Men and women stopped shouting to see who had the firearm.

"Go home, all of you!" The clear female voice sounded in the shocked silence. "Go on!" Mary strode to the crowd, pushing the nearest men away. "Move! You're acting like children and keeping my son awake." The pistol looked huge in her right hand, but less out of place than the cheroot she also carried. One by one, the crowd began to disperse. "The next bullet goes into somebody's leg!"

"Stand fast, 113th, that's my wife!" Jack had never felt prouder as Mary strode towards them. "What's to do, men? What was that all about?"

"Never mind that now, Jack! You can't have these men filling the street," Mary handed him the revolver. "Either send them back to barracks or bring them into the house. The police will be here soon."

"Into the house, men," Jack said, "and don't wake my son."

Mary waved the men past her. "It's too late for that, Jack. David's watching from the window." She stooped and picked up something from the ground. "That fellow you hit dropped this." She showed a golden sovereign, smiling. "At least we got paid for our trouble."

The soldiers, brave enough to face a mob a few minutes before, were subdued in front of Mary. Knowing her from the Mutiny days, the veterans greeted her shyly, while the Johnny Raws mumbled and looked at their boots. All crowded into Mary's living room, standing awkwardly as David stared at them, wide-eyed and delighted at this new excuse to stay out of bed.

"Right, you men. What's this all about?" Jack took charge. "I heard somebody shouting about the Fenians."

As the men stood in silence, Jack singled out Riley. "You used to be a relatively sensible man, Riley, tell me what happened."

"I'm not sure, sir," Riley spoke slowly as he tried to work out the sequence of events. "Logan and I were having a quiet drink when some local lads began to shout at us, calling us Fenians. We had a slight disagreement and left the public, sir."

"How many of them did Logan hit?"

"Just the one, sir."

Logan's frown made his face even uglier. "He was a right forward bastard, sir..."

"Quiet, Logan, and watch your language in front of my wife and son. Carry on, Riley."

"We left that place, sir. And we met another couple of our lads, so we banded together, sir."

That was understandable. "Where did the crowd come from, Riley?"

"It was strange, sir. Crowds normally gather in small groups and merge. This one seemed to come ready-made as if somebody organised it in advance. They were all shouting that we were Fenians come to blow up the town." Riley stopped, glanced at Mary and looked away again.

"It was that bloody woman," the gaunt-faced private said.

"Mind your bloody language in front of the lady, Johnny Raw!" Logan dug a hard hand into the gaunt soldier's ribs. "Did you not hear Captain Windrush?"

"Thank you, Logan," Mary said, keeping her face straight. "I have heard worse."

"Yes, Mrs Windrush," Logan continued to glare at the offending private. "The captain knows some good words."

"Pray keep silent until Riley has finished his account, Logan," Jack said. "Tell me what you know about this woman, Riley."

When Riley continued to hesitate, Mary leaned forward from the chair on which she had been sitting. "Come along, Riley. You've known us for a long time. Please tell us everything you know, or what you think you know."

"I don't know about a connection, sir, but I saw the same woman in the public."

"Who else saw her?" Jack asked. Riley and the gaunt-faced man lifted a hand. "Anybody more?"

"I saw a woman urging the crowd on," the gaunt-faced man said quietly. "She stood at the back."

"Could she not have joined in to watch?" Mary asked.

Riley shook his head. "No, Mrs Windrush. She was different from the others."

"What was she like?" Jack asked.

"Better dressed," Riley said at once. "She wasn't one of the usual women you'd see in a public house."

The gaunt-faced man shrugged. "She was tall," he said, "tall for a woman, with a bonnet."

"She had a long coat on," Riley added. "And she stood straight, like a soldier."

Jack filed away the information. "All right, that could mean anything or nothing." He nodded. "You lads get back to barracks; stay together and stay out of trouble. Don't react to any provocation and when you get back, report to the duty officer and tell him exactly what happened. And say I've already seen you."

"Yes, sir." Riley saluted.

"I liked these men," David said solemnly as he emerged from behind the sofa. "I think it was that bloody woman, too."

Jack waited until Mary had removed David with suitable motherly words and actions. "What do you think of things then, Mary?"

"I think you're worried."

"I'm concerned rather than worried. I was told to watch out for mutiny within the 113th and here we have people calling us Fenians, just one day after we kicked out Private Riordan for shouting Fenian slogans."

"They must have heard there were Fenians in the ranks." Mary examined the stub of her cheroot. "I don't know what small towns are like in England, but in India, once gossip takes hold, it spreads around in minutes, with everybody adding their own little tale until what started as an argument between two children ends up as a full-scale war."

Jack nodded. "That's probably all it is," he said. "All the same, I'll have a look for this mysterious woman." He sighed. "Women seem to be at the back of so much trouble. Do you remember Jayanti in India?"

"Be careful now, Captain Jack! I can deal with you as easily as I dealt with that crowd outside!" Mary narrowed her eyes, making growling noises.

"Hmmm." Jack leaned back in his chair. "I'd best get you to bed, I see, and calm you down."

"Oh, I'm anything but calm, Captain Jack, as you'll see." Stubbing out the glowing embers of her cheroot, Mary put out her hand. "Come with me. It's time you did your husbandly duty."

Jack sighed deeply. "The things a man has to do." He dodged Mary's slap, lifted her bodily and carried her, laughing, to the bedroom.

* * *

Colonel Snodgrass stared at Jack. "You want permission to what, Windrush?"

"I'd like your permission to visit Private Riordan, sir."

"What the devil for, Windrush? Don't you think you should be getting F Company ready for Ireland?"

"I have instructed Lieutenant Byrne to do that. He's a good man. I want to question Riordan, sir." Jack remained at attention in front of Snodgrass's desk. "I should like to find out who persuaded him to join the Fenians."

Snodgrass grunted. "I knew you'd be trouble, Windrush."

"Yes, sir. Riordan was in F Company, sir. I want to ensure there are no more Fenians recruiting our men. The people in Berwick might not be the only ones doubting the army."

"You have three days, Windrush." Something in Snodgrass's look warned Jack to be careful.

CHAPTER SEVEN

Greenlaw Military Prison, Scotland

Autumn 1865

Greenlaw military prison stood a mile outside the village of Penicuik, south of Edinburgh. After being built as a camp for French prisoners during the Napoleonic War, the army had retained the buildings for a less honourable purpose Now it held those soldiers who had fallen foul of military law, from drunkards to malcontents and thieves. Jack reined in Cedric, savouring the scented breeze and the sight of the green ridge of the Pentland Hills. After the mighty mountains of the North-West Frontier, the Pentland Hills were low and tame, yet he could not help but appreciate their quiet beauty.

The fusilier standing sentry came to attention when Jack halted at the gatehouse.

"Captain Jack Windrush," Jack introduced himself. "Here to see the commandant." He waited until the sergeant of the guard hurried up to escort him inside. Even as a visitor, the sound of the gates closing was forbidding, while the grim timber-built prison did nothing to lighten Jack's mood.

"This used to be a prisoner-of-war camp." The commandant, Captain Johnston, was old for his rank, with deep grooves of disappointment around his mouth and grey hair at his temples. "It held thousands of Frenchmen when we were fighting Boney." He looked around. "Many of them escaped, as well."

"Did they, by Jove?" *Why is the commandant telling me that?* Jack wondered.

"So has your man Riordan."

So that's why he told me. "How did Riordan manage to escape?" Jack felt a surge of anger at the thought of the time he had wasted coming up here.

"I think he had help," Johnston said. "I can't think of any other way."

"Help from whom?" Jack stood up. "Do you mean help from the guards or the other prisoners?"

The commandant shrugged. "I don't know." It was clear that the man had lost any ambition or pride in his command he might once have possessed.

"I take it you organised a search?"

"I notified the local police and sent out three parties of men, Captain Windrush."

"Did they find anything?"

"No." Johnston shrugged again. "Riordan was long gone. He'll be halfway to Ireland by now."

Jack held his temper. "How many searchers did you send?"

"I sent 12 men, all I could spare. I need all my men to guard the prisoners."

Jack fought the angry words that came to his mouth. He did not know what frustrations Captain Johnston had experienced before he ended as a glorified jail turnkey. "Have you ensured that there are no Fenians among your men?"

For the first time, the commandant drew himself erect. "I am confident in the loyalty of my men."

"I heard these very same words during the Indian Mutiny, Captain Johnston, before the sepoys rose up in fire and slaughter."

"My men are British, not Indian."

Jack thought of the impeccable loyalty of the Guides, Sikhs and Gurkhas he had fought with on his last campaign. Once more, he bit back his anger. "May I speak to your men, Commandant?"

"Who the devil do you think you are, Captain?"

That's better; at least the fellow is showing some spirit. "I am an officer of Her Majesty, Commandant Johnston, just as you are," Jack said. "I have the advantage that your men do not know me. I think it would help both of us if I speak to them. Do I have your permission?"

The commandant sighed and looked away with his momentary defiance already gone. "Yes, Captain Windrush, if you think it might help."

"You can lock the prisoners in their cells in the meantime," Jack said.

After leaving a minimum of men to guard the prisoners, the garrison gathered in the square. Behind them stood the jail, a symbol of dishonour and confinement. Before them rose the slopes of the Pentland Hills and, in between, the figures of Commandant Johnston and Captain Jack Windrush, nutmeg-brown from long service overseas, with his sword at his belt and pistol in its holster. The men stood to attention, uneasy under Jack's steady scrutiny, some badly shaved, and others with dirty equipment. Jack understood their disgruntlement – these men wanted to be soldiers, not prison guards. They were the usual mixture of the intelligent and the slow-witted, the old soldier steeped in drink and the Johnny Raw who wondered why he had volunteered.

After a few moments of scrutiny, Jack slowly paced the length of the ranks, counting the men without saying a word. Up above, a parliament of rooks winged past, to land on the field immediately outside the prison, their black plumage seemingly fitting for this dismal place.

"Well, my lads." Jack broke the uneasy silence. "I came here to talk to one of your prisoners, and you've let him go free."

Some of the men stiffened, others wavered a little. Jack paced back again, allowing the tension to mount until he suddenly shouted: "Give three cheers for the Irish Republic!" While most of the men stared at him in confusion, two opened their mouths to respond, closing them abruptly when they realised what they were doing.

Jack indicated the two men. "You two remain. The rest, dismiss."

Waiting until others had gratefully returned to its duties, Jack walked to the two men. One was a youth still in his teens, scarred by acne, the other a dark visaged old soldier with the marks of alcohol in his swollen nose. "Follow me." Jack led them to one of the storehouses at the side of the square, his boots crunching on the hard ground. "In here." He opened the door and motioned them inside. The interior was cool and gloomy. "Stand there." Jack pointed to a space between piled-up boxes.

The two men stood to attention, with the youth clearly terrified and the older man stony-faced.

"I suspect both you men of being Fenians," Jack said. "At ease!"

The old soldier responded at once while the younger man hesitated before obeying.

"What's your name?" Jack asked the older man.

"Stoakes, sir." The accent was Cockney.

"And yours?"

"Freer, sir." Sweat trickled down the young man's face as his eyes darted to Stoakes and back. "I'm not a Fenian, sir!"

"Silence! Get down on the ground! Face first!" Jack roared, and again Stoakes obeyed at once, while Freer hesitated.

"Stand up!" Jack ordered. "Attention!"

The men again stood in front of Jack, with Stoakes staring ahead and Freer trembling slightly.

"Sing God save the Queen!" Jack ordered and Stoakes began to sing, with Freer joining in a moment later.

"What part of Ireland are you from, Freer?"

"I'm English, sir."

"What part of Ireland are your parents from?" When Freer said nothing, Jack continued. "How did you help Riordan escape, Freer?"

Freer gave a little start. "I never, sir."

"You, did, sir," Jack said. "Only two men responded to my Fenian order, you and Stoakes here. Private Stoakes is an old soldier who obeys every order without question, including my command to cheer the Irish Republic, while you are a Johnny Raw who hesitates after an order as you think what to do. You did not hesitate when I ordered you to shout for the Fenians."

When Freer glanced at Stoakes as if for support, Stoakes remained impassive.

"You may go, Stoakes." Jack waited until Stoakes left the storeroom. "All right, Freer. I can have you shot for treason or sent to penal servitude for 20 years. Or you can do yourself a favour and tell me everything you know about Riordan."

"Shot, sir?" Freer looked ready to faint.

"If you're lucky," Jack lied. "After a few weeks penal servitude you'd wish the army *had* executed you." After living through the horror of the Indian Mutiny, Jack had no desire to see another mutiny of any sort, so terrorising one unfortunate young soldier was a small price to pay. "Be kind to yourself, Freer. Tell me all you know."

Freer was visibly shaking now, looking around for help that would never come. Jack moderated his tone slightly. "Come now, Freer, I've caught you. I'm trying to make things easier for you."

"He said that we were to free Ireland from the British." Freer spoke through the tears that were suddenly rolling down his cheeks.

"Who said that?" Jack asked.

"Why, Private Riordan, sir."

"I see." Jack nodded. "What else did Riordan say, Freer?"

"He said that if I didn't help, all Ireland would loathe me as a traitor." Freer swallowed hard, trying to avoid Jack's unrelenting gaze. "He said the Fenians would hunt me down and murder my family."

Jack nodded. He had expected threats of this type. "Are you a Fenian?"

"No, sir." Freer shook his head. "I'm no more a Fenian than I'm a Frenchman." That was probably the most potent negative Freer could devise.

"How did you help Riordan escape?"

Now he had started, Freer seemed unable to stop talking. "He told me to light a fire, sir. The buildings are wooden, sir, and in all this dry weather, they burned easily. When the smoke got thick, the commandant ordered all the prisoners out, and I opened the clothing store and hid Riordan inside. When the commandant ordered search parties out, Riordan was in uniform, and nobody said nothing when he walked out of the gate."

"I see." Jack made a mental note of the prison's lax security. "Can you read and write, Freer?"

Freer started. "I'm no scholar, sir."

Jack nodded. "How old are you, Freer?"

"Eighteen, I think sir."

"Do you know where Riordan is now?"

"No, sir."

"All right, Freer. Come with me and keep your mouth shut. Let me do the talking and for God's sake don't contradict anything I say." Jack led Freer to the commandant's office.

"This young lad has been most helpful, Captain Johnston. He told me that he might know something about Riordan," Jack said.

The commandant glared at Freer. "Why did you not come forward before, Private?"

Jack spoke again. "He's scared to talk, Commandant, in case there are more Fenians in here. He told me that Riordan escaped during the recent fire, and that when you opened the gate for the search parties, Riordan slipped out." Jack was putting the blame firmly on the commandant.

"How does he know this?"

"He heard the rumour in the barrack-room, Commandant. It may be common knowledge in the ranks."

"What's your name, Private?"

"Freer, sir." Freer could hardly speak.

"Are you a Fenian, Freer?"

"No, sir."

"Commandant," Jack said. "This lad is no more a Fenian than I am. He cannot even spell Fenian. Listen. Spell Fenian, Freer."

Freer stared at Jack through big eyes. "I can't sir," he whispered. "I told you; I'm no scholar."

"You see, sir?" Jack said. "I doubt that Private Freer can even define a Fenian."

"What is a Fenian, Freer?" the commandant asked.

Freer shook his head. "I dunno, sir. An Irishman, sir."

"I suggest Private Freer needs lessons in reading and writing, Commandant."

Jack said. "He's guilty of being young and impulsive and nothing else." He felt Freer's grateful eyes on him. "In the meantime, I suggest we continue to look for Riordan."

"Dismissed, Freer." The commandant waited until Freer had left the office. "All right, Windrush, how do you plan to recapture Riordan?"

Jack gave a slow smile. "I worked with the Guides along the North-West Frontier, Commandant. Riordan has only been gone for a day, so I am sure I can track him in these low hills."

"He may have gone into Edinburgh," the commandant said.

"He may intend to do so," Jack said, "but I think he'll lie low for a few days until the hue-and-cry is over."

That's what I would do. As Riordan will know the authorities expect him to run for Edinburgh, only a few miles to the north, he will move in the opposite direction. He'll hide in the hills.

* * *

Ignoring the area immediately outside the barrack gates where soldiers and tradesmen had trampled the ground, Jack began his search for Riordan's trail. He was fortunate that the weather had been dry and there were no animals kept near Greenlaw, so, within a couple of hours, he found three distinct trails leading in different directions.

The first Jack followed led him a mile into the swelling hills before he found a distinct print of a boot. Kneeling to examine it, Jack shook his head. The impression was not of a military boot and could not be Riordan. The second trail led northward, crossed the Logan Burn and ended in a shepherd's cottage. Keeping one hand on the butt of his pistol, Jack knocked on the door, stepping back from the sudden barking of what sounded like a dozen dogs.

The woman who came to the door was younger than Jack had expected, with a pleasant face. "You must be from Greenlaw," she said at once. "My husband is up the hills just now."

"I am sorry to bother you," Jack eyed the collie dogs that stood at the woman's side. "I am Captain Jack Windrush. Have you seen any strangers in these parts lately?"

The woman shook her head. "No strangers." She gave a bright smile. "Except yourself. Who were you looking for?"

"A prisoner who escaped," Jack said.

"Is he dangerous?" The woman looked at her dogs.

"He won't bother you." Jack gave a small bow. "I am sorry to have disturbed you."

With two of the possible tracks having proved false, Jack followed the third. To judge by the deep impressions and length of stride, the man had been running in heavy boots, which was precisely what Jack would expect. He had travelled in a south-westerly direction, the opposite from where the search parties had concentrated. At one point, something must have troubled him, for Jack saw an area of flattened grass where the fugitive had lain down and a broad stretch where he had crawled on his stomach before rising again. Nodding, Jack moved on, knowing that here, unlike on the North-West Frontier, he had time to inspect the ground without some happy Pashtun taking pot-shots at him with his terrifyingly accurate jezzail.

Hearing the hollow thud of boots on the ground, Jack slid beside a wind-twisted rowan tree to survey his surroundings. The man did not attempt to hide as he stalked towards Jack with a Border collie at his heels and a long staff in his hand. "You'll be the Windrush fellow searching for the escaped prisoner," the newcomer said.

"That's right," Jack said.

"Aye, my wife told me about you. I'm Wullie Todd, the herd." The shepherd's face was as tanned as any Frontier Pashtun. "Your man's at the Loganlea Waterfall."

"Where is that?"

The shepherd nodded forward. "You can see his trail, plain as anything. I can get the dogs to round him up if you like."

"Thank you," Jack said, "but I have plans for this fellow."

"Aye, no doubt. Loganlea's a double fall, with your man on the level ground between."

"Thank you." Jack strode forward, thinking that Scottish shepherds were as adept in hillcraft as the Guides. The shepherd had probably known every movement of Riordan, but as it was none of his business, he had not informed the army.

Jack heard the waterfall as he rounded the shoulder of a hill, with the burn gabbling over a shallow bed on his left. The fall lay ahead, a thin thread of water pouring into a pool, with the rocky sides furred by lichen and decorated with ferns and grass. Noticing the new scuff marks on the grass beside the burn, Jack checked his revolver, took a deep breath, and began to climb the banking beside the fall.

"Riordan! Is that you? It's Captain Jack Windrush of the 113th."

The answer was a hail of stones thrown from above, one of which bounced from the ground a yard from Jack's foot. "Bugger off, Captain Windrush, or I'll split your skull wide open."

"Don't be a damned fool, Riordan! You're already in trouble, don't make it worse for yourself."

"Keep back!"

The next rock missed Jack by a finger's width, to fall with a loud splash in the pool beneath. Swearing, Jack took his pistol from its holster and hauled himself up the slope, slipping on the spray-wet grass. Riordan waited at the top, where the burn ran between the upper and lower falls.

"If you come any closer, I'll kill you." Riordan lifted another rock.

"I have a revolver," Jack said, "you have a stone. You're an old enough soldier to know you can't win."

Riordan's voice altered. "Did you say you were Captain Windrush? Are you Fighting Jack Windrush?"

"That's right." Jack shifted aside as Riordan threw the stone. It rattled from the side of the gorge and splashed noisily into the pool. Jack threw himself up the next section, slid, recovered and found Riordan waiting for him.

"I've heard about you." Riordan held a rock in his hand as he stood beside the burn with the top fall a few yards behind him and the second at his feet. "Is this not small beer for you, chasing an escaped prisoner? You were a hero once. You nearly won the Russian War all alone."

"I was never a hero," Jack lifted his revolver. "Come with me, Riordan."

Riordan grunted. "Now you're working for the screws." Running forward, he swung a wild punch, which Jack avoided with ease, cracking Riordan on the side of the head as he rushed past. Riordan fell at once.

Perching himself on a rock with the burn roaring beside him, Jack kept his pistol trained on Riordan's head. "Now we know our positions, Riordan, you can answer some questions for me."

Sitting up, Riordan spat at him. "Not a chance."

"I thought you might say that," Jack said. "We used to hang mutineers in India. We strung them up by the dozen and watched them choke to death."

"You're a bastard, Windrush."

"That's for sure," Jack said. "Tell me, where are you heading? What did you hope to gain by joining the Fenians?"

"A free Ireland," Riordan replied at once.

"Do you think that is possible?"

Riordan grinned, showing misshapen teeth. "The very fact that you are asking means you think it could be possible." He settled down on a rounded boulder, his eyes narrow and watchful. "It worked for the United States. Anyway, you'll hear what the Fenians can do soon enough, Captain Windrush."

"What do you mean?"

Riordan smiled. "We have men and women working for us all the time, Captain. You believe your bright scarlet regiments can intimidate with their massed rifles. Well, what if there were hundreds, thousands more like me? What if your pretty soldiers did not do as you ordered?" He leaned closer to Jack. "What if your own men rose against you?"

Jack shrugged. "If you mean the 113th, Riordan, I don't care." Sitting back, he holstered his revolver. "They're nothing to me." He watched an array of expressions cross Riordan's face as the man tried to work out what he meant. "Did you not hear about me, Riordan?"

"Hear what?" Riordan struggled into a sitting position.

"Evidently, you didn't. Here, have a smoke." Jack lit a cheroot, passed it over and lit another for himself. "Colonel Snodgrass has no time for the likes of me." He knew that the entire regiment would be well aware of Snodgrass's antagonism towards him, and of the reason.

"Because your wife is a nigger."

Jack fought his surge of anger. "Because my wife is a Eurasian."

"Call her whatever you like, you're still lying." Riordan calmly puffed at Jack's cheroot. "You fought with the 113th in Russia and India." He pointed the lit end of the cheroot towards Jack. "That's why they call you Fighting Jack. I know all about you, Captain Windrush."

Jack pulled on his cheroot. "Why would I lie to you, Riordan? I have you at a disadvantage. I could kill you here and now and nobody would question me. No, Private, I need your help." *Something will happen in the 113th, so I must squeeze information from this man before I hurry back.*

"Why should I help you?"

"Because we're both outcasts. You're from a country that is essentially a colony of Great Britain, and I'm not wanted because of my choice of wife." Jack gave a sudden grin – he was physically safe here. After days in solitary confinement on bread and water, followed by a couple of days in the hills, Riordan was weak as a kitten.

Riordan's eyes narrowed. "Why should I believe you?"

"Why shouldn't you?" Jack exhaled smoke. "Where were you going, Riordan?"

"America."

"How did you intend to get there?"

"I'll get there." Riordan was immediately defiant.

"Oh? Do they pay you well in solitary confinement now?" Jack shook his head. "Unless you can work your passage, Riordan, you'll get no closer to America than Penicuik. Now, I have a proposal for you. I'll help pay for your passage if you help me."

"Why would you help me?" Riordan asked. "And why should I help you?"

"Call it a mutual understanding."

"What do you want?"

Jack forced a grin. "I want to join the Fenians," he said. "I want to pay Snodgrass back for his treatment of my wife and me, and I want to get even with the British Army."

"Do you indeed?" Riordan flicked the remains of his cheroot into the burn and watched the water carry it away down the fall. "And I ask again: 'Why should I believe you?'"

Jack shrugged. "It's your choice, Riordan. I'm trusting you by telling you. All I'm asking is for you to put in a good word for me, and tell me who recruited you into the Fenians." He tapped the butt of his revolver. "If you refuse, I can shoot you."

"That's not much of a choice," Riordan said.

"No," Jack agreed, "but I can hardly take you back to Greenlaw after what I've told you. I've killed many men, Riordan, men as brave as you and who fought for just as worthy causes." Drawing his revolver, Jack cocked, aiming at Riordan's face.

"I don't know his name," Riordan did not flinch as he faced Jack's pistol. "He said he was Irish, but there was something not right about him."

"In what way?" Trust a British army corporal to know when a man was wrong.

Riordan screwed up his face in thought. "The fellow was too glib, sir. He knew all the answers even before I asked them. He seemed over-eager to tell me and not a word of humour about him. When an Irishman can't crack a smile, something's wrong."

"What was he like?"

Again, Riordan considered before he replied. "Fairly tall, with neat mutton-chop whiskers."

"How old?"

"About 35 at a guess, dark-haired." Riordan shrugged. "Nothing special."

"Was he a British officer?"

"No." Riordan shook his head. "I know that stamp."

"All right, Riordan. I'll look out for him." Extracting a sovereign from his pocket, Jack handed it over. "That should help you out. Where are you going?" He asked the question naturally, as if to a friend.

"The Shamrock in Leith." Riordan bit the coin to test the purity of the gold. "I'll hole out there until I can ship for America."

"Good luck," Jack knew he could be court-martialled and cashiered for aiding a Fenian and a prisoner to escape, but he had taken worse risks in the past, and now he had the description of a Fenian recruiter and an address where the Fenians might gather. On an impulse, he passed over another sovereign. "I might see you later, under the green flag."

"I'll look out for you." Riordan's eyes were as narrow and suspicious as ever. "Remember to duck when the bullets start to fly." Riordan's mouth twisted into what might have been a smile. "It's your company, after all."

CHAPTER EIGHT

Boston, Winter 1865

Walsh sifted through the papers in front of him. "Recruitment is going well," he said.

"It's going better since you became intelligence liaison officer," Sweeny said. "Your other operation is also showing promise."

Walsh nodded. "I still have some influence in the Imperial Intelligence Department."

"I'm surprised the Russians remember you," Sweeny said.

"Mother Russia has not forgotten Sebastopol." Walsh studied his papers. "We haven't finished with Great Britain yet."

"We?" Sweeny picked up on the word. "I thought you were Irish."

"I am, but I worked for Russia for some time." Walsh handed over one of the documents. "I recommend we use this woman as much as we can."

Sweeny read the description of the woman. "Can we trust her?"

"As much as we can trust any woman of her type."

"She would appear to be extremely unsettled," Sweeny commented. "Perhaps even unstable of mind."

"It is that very instability that we exploit." Retrieving the document, Walsh pointed to a paragraph of the text. "You will see that she has a connection that could be extremely useful to us."

"I noticed her connection," Sweeny replied without emotion, "although I am unsure how it could benefit us."

"We can use her to help unsettle his regiment."

Sweeny grunted. "That is certainly one of the regiments on which we intend to concentrate." Sweeny tried to hide his expression of distaste. "I don't hold with these methods of subterfuge, Walsh. I'm a soldier, not a spy."

"Would you prefer to leave the details to me, sir?"

"That would be my preference, Walsh. You seem to have a flair for this kind of thing."

"We both have the same objective, sir. Only our methods differ."

"I understand the importance of your work, Walsh," Sweeny said. "I don't wish to become involved. I'll leave you a free hand."

"That suits me very well." Walsh did not attempt to hide his satisfaction. "I've already set the wheels in motion, so we would see some results soon."

Sweeny could hardly meet Walsh's gaze. Even although he was a veteran soldier, the cold madness in Walsh's eyes sent a chill down Sweeny's spine. He disliked using such men, but the cause was too great to allow minor details to distract him.

"I also found a spy in our ranks, sir," Walsh said.

"A spy? From the Federal authorities?"

"No," Walsh said. "From British intelligence."

Sweeny leaned back in his chair. "They've caught up with us, have they? I hope he hasn't discovered anything about your operations."

"I have questioned him," Walsh said. "He had nothing of consequence to say."

"That's fortunate." Sweeny decided he would not wish to be questioned by Walsh. "Release him, and send him back."

"Yes, sir." Walsh nodded. "I'll do that right away." Taking his leave, he closed the door quietly, ignored the guard who stood outside and left the building. Signalling to a pair of waiting men, he strode to a nearby warehouse with a heavily padlocked door. "Dermot, open the door."

The larger of his companions unfastened the padlock and they entered, ignored the litter of discarded crates and descended a flight of stone stairs to the basement.

"Here we are, spy," Dermot called. "Did you miss us?"

"Get us light, Cormac," Walsh ordered.

The second man lit a lantern, with yellow light pooling around the basement. The man who lay in a corner was naked, with blood marring his features. He looked up through badly swollen eyes.

"General Sweeny ordered us to let you go," Walsh told him.

The prisoner tried to stifle a groan as Dermot lifted him by his hair.

"Take him upstairs," Walsh ordered.

With Dermot dragging the prisoner by the hair and Cormac pushing from behind, they took him up three flights of stairs to the top floor of the warehouse, where broken windows faced a narrow alley.

"You know what's going to happen," Walsh said. "We're going to obey orders and let you go."

Hawking, the prisoner spat a mouthful of blood and phlegm at Walsh, who stepped aside as his two companions responded with an array of punches and kicks that reduced the man to unconsciousness.

"Out he goes," Walsh watched without expression as the two men lifted the prisoner, dragged him to the window and threw him out. They watched his body fall into the darkness below.

"Goodbye," Dermot said, with a little wave.

"Go and make sure he is dead," Walsh ordered. "I don't want him to survive to spread tales." Glancing at the fresh blood that speckled his jacket, he shrugged and walked away.

CHAPTER NINE

Berwick Upon Tweed, Autumn 1865

Leaving Cedric at Greenlaw with instructions that he would send a man for the horse later, Jack caught the train from Edinburgh to Berwick-upon-Tweed. Despite the number of times he had travelled by rail, he still found this mode of transport a novelty, with the thick smoke from the engine sometimes obscuring his view of the countryside. Jack leaned back in his seat, trying to appear as impassive as a British officer should as he tried to work out the implications of Riordan's words. What the devil had Riordan meant with his, "It's your company after all"? Was he hinting that F Company would mutiny? Or was he only causing trouble? Jack found that he was tapping his fingers on his knees as he stared out of the window. If the Fenians had something planned, the quicker he got back to barracks, the better.

Jack glanced at his watch; with his mind focusing on the possible trouble in the 113th, he was astonished how much distance the train had covered. In amazingly quick time they were easing into the station in the shadow of Berwick Castle ruins, and Jack alighted, swinging his cane.

Everything seemed normal when Jack entered the barracks. The sentry saluted as he passed and C Company at drill on the parade square were performing no better and no worse than any similar body of soldiers. Relieved that there was no sign of murder or mayhem, Jack marched to the colonel's office.

"Colonel Snodgrass," Jack began, saluting. "I have information about an intended mutiny in this regiment."

"The devil you have!" Snodgrass stared at him.

"May I have your permission to counter the insurrection?"

"You are extremely fanciful, Windrush. You are not in India, and these are not Sikhs!" Snodgrass looked away.

"If they were, sir, I would never doubt their loyalty. I ask again, could I ask your permission to counter the insurrection?"

Snodgrass breathed heavily. "There will be no mutiny in my regiment, Windrush."

"Yes, sir. That is something I also hope to avoid. It would look bad for the reputation of the 113th if we failed to stop a Fenian attack."

Snodgrass's hand hesitated above the drawer of his desk. "I take it your spying has discovered something, Windrush?"

"I have been informed that there may be something untoward happening in F Company, sir." Jack hoped he was giving accurate information.

Snodgrass's smile may have been genuine. "I might have known it would be F Company, Windrush. Well, you're responsible for them. You will find them halfway to Ireland by now. I sent them away when you were wasting your time up in Scotland." He leaned back in his chair. "You'd better hurry if you want to catch them. You don't want to be remembered as the man who commanded the only company to mutiny in the British Army."

Damn, damn, damn! How am I going to tell Mary that I'm off to Ireland for an unknown length of time?

"Yes, sir." Jack stalked out of Snodgrass's office, shouting for Micklethwaite, his soldier-servant.

"What's to do, Jack?" Elliot emerged behind the panting Micklethwaite. "You appear more than agitated. Have the French landed, and nobody's told me?"

"You know the regiment better than I do," Jack calmed himself down as he explained the position to Elliot. "What's your opinion, Arthur? Is my company on the verge of mutiny?"

"Lieutenant Byrne's with your men," Elliot said. "He's a solid man, with his finger on the regimental pulse. Ensign Snodgrass, I'm less sure about." Elliot frowned. "He's British to the core, but green as grass, keen as you like and the opposite of his father. Now you go and tell Mary what's happening and ask if she'll go over with you. I'll see to your horse and send your bags and baggage after you."

"Thank you, Arthur."

"That's thank you, sir, and don't you forget it." Elliot's grin was as infectious as ever. "Good luck with Mary, Jack. I'd prefer to face 100 Fenians than your wife out of temper!"

"So would I," Jack agreed, feelingly.

CHAPTER TEN

Ireland, Autumn 1867

Bowing his head before the rain, Jack reined in his steed outside Charles Fort. Situated outside Kinsale, south of Cork, Charles Fort was a 17th-century *Trace Italienne* star-shaped fortress with cannon grinning from the walls and sentries glowering at the gate. Water glinted on three sides, as the sea surged around the base of low cliffs.

"So this is to be my home for the foreseeable future," Jack murmured to himself. Mary had decided to stay with David, saying she would bring him over later. Jack had not needed to sense her anger – Mary was not a woman to hide her emotions. *Maybe you chose well, Mary. After India, I don't wish to involve you in another mutiny.*

"Captain Jack Windrush," Jack announced himself to the sentries. "Of the 113th Foot."

Both sentries were from a local militia regiment. They viewed Jack with more suspicion than welcome as they came to reluctant attention, blinking in the rain. Jack walked his horse inside the fort, which was larger than Berwick Barracks.

"I'll take your horse to the stables, sir," a serious-faced NCO offered. "The colonel's office is over there." He nodded to an imposing stone building. "And the officers' mess down that way."

"Thank you, corporal." Dismounting stiffly, Jack handed over the reins and looked around the interior of the fort. "That will be the main barrack block?"

"Yes, sir." The corporal had a pleasant Cork accent. "F Company of the 113th are there now, and some of our boys."

"Thank you." Jack shook the rain from his face. "I'll pay a visit to the 113th right away."

The militia corporal showed no surprise. "As you wish, sir. I'll get a man to guide you."

"It's all right, corporal, thank you. I'll manage."

Soft-footed, Jack toured the barracks where the men of his company lived and slept when not on duty. Surprisingly large, the barrack-room was more airy than most he had known, with the men sitting or lying on their bunks, cleaning their equipment, playing cards or talking together.

"Officer present!" Sergeant Parker bellowed.

"At ease," Jack ordered as men jumped to attention.

"We didn't know you were coming, sir." Sergeant Parker hurriedly adjusted his uniform. "I thought you were in Scotland."

"Are you settling in all right?" Jack asked.

"It's not much different from Berwick, sir," Parker said. "Seen one barracks, seen 'em all."

Jack permitted himself a small smile. "You could be right there." Peacetime life for the ranking soldier alternated between countless hours of routine boredom and spells of intense discipline on parade. Yet for most private soldiers, it was probably a better life than they had outside the army. They had accommodation, comradeship and regular food and clothing, where many of them would have been verging on the edge of starvation in civilian life. "How are the men?"

Parker looked over the barrack-room before replying. "They're the same as always, sir, some trying their best, others a bunch of lazy scoundrels fresh from the publics or the wrong end of a plough, and a few homesick for their ma."

Jack smiled. That description would fit just about any collection of Johnny Raws in the British Army or, he suspected, any unit in any army in the world. "Has there been any trouble, Sergeant?"

"Not a whisper, sir."

Jack nodded. Either the Fenians were very good at covering their tracks, or Riordan had been lying. Jack had served with Parker through the Mutiny and knew he was a steady man.

Lieutenant Byrne smiled when he saw Jack. "Glad you could make it, sir. We left at very short notice."

Can I trust this man? Jack wondered. *Is he a Fenian?* "Show me around the fort, Byrne." Jack barely listened as Byrne walked around the ramparts, talking about the history of the fort in guarding Kinsale. "It was built to defend the harbour from a seaward attack," Byrne explained, "so when the Williamite forces came by land in the late 17th century, it fell after a short siege."

Trust an Irishman to know his history. Remembering Riordan's doubts about the man who recruited him, Jack asked: "Which part of Ireland are you from, Byrne?"

"County Cavan," Byrne said. "Do you know Ireland at all?"

"This is the first time I've been here."

"Oh, it's a wonderful place, Windrush, but sorely troubled. If the people and the landowners could only pull together, it could be the finest country in the world."

Jack passed over a cheroot as they paused to look over the battlements at the harbour, with chimney smoke joining the rain that hazed over the town of Kinsale. "Now there's a splendid view."

"It is that," Byrne agreed.

"How's young Snodgrass getting on?"

Byrne lit his cheroot and inhaled. "He's a very keen young lad," he said. He glanced sideways at Jack. "Permission to speak freely, sir?"

Jack nodded. "It's Windrush unless we're on parade or campaign."

Byrne nodded his thanks. "Ensign Snodgrass is better away from the colonel, Windrush. He might blossom over here. I have hopes for that young lad."

"I'll keep an eye on him." Jack ignored the rain that blasted into his face. "Somebody told me that the rain in Ireland is soft and mild."

Byrne grinned. "Aye, whoever told you that had never stood sentry at Kinsale harbour. People have strange misconceptions about this country."

"Some people believe it's on the verge of rebellion."

"Some people believe that Ireland is always on the verge of rebellion," Byrne said. "That's why there is always such a large military presence on the island."

Jack wondered how much of Byrne's conversation was bitter humour and how much was just bitter. "Will the Fenians cause trouble?"

"Undoubtedly," Byrne said, "but nothing we can't handle."

Noting the use of the word "we", Jack was satisfied that Byrne was no Fenian. Now he had to watch for any suspicious movements among the men. Once again, Jack hated the part he had to play, acting the friend and officer while always assessing, probing and looking for clues. Taking a final draw on his cheroot, he examined the butt and threw it over the battlements, watching the tiny red glow disappear and then he walked away.

"Best get on," he said. "Duty calls."

"It always does," Byrne agreed.

* * *

"You look happy," Jack said as Ensign Snodgrass almost danced into the Mess.

"I've met the most wonderful girl," Ensign Snodgrass told Jack, and everybody else who was within hearing. "She is everything I've always wanted."

"You're too young for a girl," Byrne admonished, winking at Jack. "You've barely left your school books."

"She's perfect,." Ensign Snodgrass looked decidedly smug.

"I hope you won't bed her and leave her." Byrne kept his face straight. "You know the rules. Ensigns mustn't marry, lieutenants shouldn't marry, captains may marry, majors should marry, and colonels must marry. I'm sure your father would make an exception in your case. When do we meet your intended?"

"Marry her?" Ensign Snodgrass looked startled for a moment. "I wasn't thinking about marriage."

"I thought you were a moral gentleman," Jack said, joining in the teasing. "If your girl's perfect, snap her up now, before somebody else grabs her. It would be good to have a nice Irish girl in the regiment. I take it she is a nice girl and not one of the other kind?"

"She's lovely," Ensign Snodgrass said, clearly not understanding Jack's point.

"A nice Irish girl is the best kind there is," Byrne said solemnly. "She'll keep you on the straight and narrow."

"Oh, I don't know if she's Irish," Ensign Snodgrass said. "Do you think I should marry her, Captain Windrush?" Now he thought about marriage; the idea obviously appealed to Snodgrass.

Leaning back in his chair, Jack sipped at his whiskey. "In all seriousness, Peter, no, I don't think you should consider matrimony quite yet. You could not afford to keep her on your salary, and women take a lot of keeping, believe me." He smiled, missing Mary more than he would ever admit. "You're far too young for marriage, and, I'd hazard to guess, so is she. No, Peter, wait until you're promoted to captain or lieutenant at least."

"She's older than me," Ensign Snodgrass said.

"In that case, Snodgrass, she'll expect more than an ensign can provide," Byrne said. "Keep your mouth closed if she so much as hints at marriage."

"I never thought about the money." Ensign Snodgrass sounded crestfallen. "I don't have a farthing to scratch myself with."

"We know that," Jack said. "We were ensigns, too, remember."

"You had other thoughts in your mind, young Snodgrass." Byrne sipped at his brandy, looking up at the whitewashed ceiling. "Carnal thoughts that do you no honour at all." Again he winked at Jack. "I am shocked."

"We are both shocked." Jack kept his face solemn. "Wait until you are married, young Snodgrass, before you think of that sort of thing."

Ensign Snodgrass looked from one to the other, not sure if they were teasing him or not. "I wasn't," he said, and stopped.

"You weren't?" Byrne repeated. "You were not thinking carnal thoughts? In that case, young Snodgrass, I wonder if this girl is right for you."

"We've got the young lad confused." Jack checked his pocket watch. "Before you contemplate marriage, Peter, check the men are all right."

"He's a good lad," Jack said as Ensign Snodgrass walked away. "He'll do well if he keeps clear of any distractions."

"Aye." Byrne nodded. "Keen and honest. All he needs is some experience in the field to salt him a little, and he'll have the makings of a decent soldier."

Unlike his father, Jack thought, and wondered at the strangeness of family life.

* * *

Rising before reveille, Jack stood in the parade square as F Company, 113th Foot rose to greet another day. He watched them form up, most still dazed from sleep, some with their tunics wrongly fastened, others badly shaved and the old soldiers erect as guardsmen but dull of eye.

"Right, men," Jack began cheerfully, ignoring their shortcomings, "you've lazed about in barracks far too long, merely playing at soldiers. Today, we're going to get to know the countryside." He allowed the men a few minutes to signify their displeasure. "Lieutenant Byrne will take half the company eastward, while I take the other half northward through Kinsale and show the local population that they have real soldiers garrisoned here. Sergeant Parker, you're senior sergeant, I want you to stay with Lieutenant Byrne. Ensign Snodgrass, you are with me."

The men formed up in ragged lines, with Ensign Snodgrass strutting around with great pride and Byrne looking weary as he coaxed his men.

"Right lads," Jack said, "keep in step and march at attention until we are clear of Kinsale. Show the civilians how smart you are."

It was good to be in charge of men again, to stretch his legs marching and see how the 113th reacted. As Jack's men entered the narrow streets of Kinsale, the barking of dogs brought much of the population to the doors and windows. The usual collection of bare-footed urchins followed the soldiers, shouting and hooting, with some gathering at the tail to march in step, laughing at the fun of copying the redcoats.

As Jack had expected, the 113th enjoyed the attention. The men marched more erect, keeping in step, squaring their shoulders as more women appeared in the streets.

"That's the way, lads! We're the 113th!"

Jack halted them beside the harbour, where fishermen were working. "Attention, 113th!"

The half-company slammed to attention.

"That's better." Jack praised them. "Now tell me, who beat the Russians?" He grinned at the half-hearted response. "I didn't hear that. We beat the Russians. Who beat the Russians?"

The reply came with more volume. "We beat the Russians!"

"Who beat the Pandies?"

"We beat the Pandies!" The men were louder now, as the fishermen and a group of women watched curiously.

"We are the 113th Foot. Who are we?"

"We're the 113th!" Now the men were shouting, with one or two of the younger taking off their hats and waving them in the air. Again, Jack ignored the lack of discipline. He wanted to instil a sense of regimental pride first.

"Right, so let's see how good we are." Jack saw Ensign Snodgrass staring at one of the watching women, shook his head and lowered his voice. "This isn't the time for mooning over woman, Ensign. March the men away at the double. Take the lead."

"But sir…"

"Move, Ensign!"

Ensign Snodgrass coloured and saluted. "Yes, sir!" He ran to the head of the men, piping shrill orders to follow him. Jack waited until the ensign had the men formed up then loped to the head of the column.

"We have a busy few days ahead of us, Ensign. We'll be taking a route march every morning, and drilling the men in the afternoon." Jack thought back to his early days with the 113th when he had learned his trade in the Burmese jungle. "We're lucky we have time to train them, Ensign."

"Yes, sir." It was clear that Ensign Snodgrass wanted to tell Jack something.

"What is it, Ensign?"

"She was here, sir," Ensign Snodgrass gabbled the words. "She was in Kinsale, sir, watching us!"

"Who's in Kinsale, Ensign?"

"My girl, sir! My lady."

Jack smiled. "That's good, Ensign. It seems that she is as infatuated with you as you are with her."

"I hope so, sir!" Ensign Snodgrass was the picture of sincerity. "I met her in Berwick, and again last night and she was watching me this morning."

Leaving the men to march on, Jack took Ensign Snodgrass aside. "Are you certain?"

"Yes, sir." Ensign Snodgrass was the picture of sincerity.

"Right, Ensign," Jack said. "Thank you for telling me. Let me know if you see her again." He hesitated for a second. "Be careful, Ensign. Be careful."

As Jack returned to the head of his men, he was frowning. Something was wrong here – young women did not follow penniless ensigns across the British Isles.

* * *

"Mutiny," Jack said quietly to Byrne and Ensign Snodgrass, "usually occurs when men are bored or bullied. I mean to drive these men hard, so they become good soldiers, but I want no bully-ragging."

Byrne nodded. "I was in India," he said. "I saw the Mutiny there."

"You were with John Company's army, weren't you?"

"That's right," Byrne said. "The Second Bengal Fusiliers. I fought on Delhi Ridge."

Jack's eyes narrowed. "That was the toughest fight of the whole war." He raised his glass in tribute. "A toast."

The officers stood, with Ensign Snodgrass looking pleased to be included.

"To the men who cannot be here," Jack said. "Whatever their nationality and race; British, Sikh, Pashtun, Gurkha, Bengali, Madrasa or anything else."

Byrne raised his glass right away, with Ensign Snodgrass fractionally later. "Should we be drinking a toast to the Indians?"

"Nobody deserves it more." Jack held his gaze. "As you will find out if you ever have the honour of fighting beside them."

"To the men who cannot be here," Byrne repeated, met Jack's eye and grinned. "Especially Irishmen."

Jack nodded and repeated: "Especially Irishmen." He tossed back his whiskey, savoured the flavour and continued. "Right. Next on the agenda; I heard a rumour there is to be a mutiny in F Company, so be alert for anything unusual. We're going to be on duty most of the time, gentlemen, so we'll be tired. I want the men drilled and kept busy as well. I'll make up a duty roster, and we'll all do our bit." He turned to Ensign Snodgrass. "This is not the soldiering you hoped for, Ensign, but I'm sure you'll do your duty."

Now I must trap a possible traitor from among these men I pretend to trust. I despise this devious false friendship.

* * *

Jack looked around the assembled officers as they sat in the flickering lamplight of the mess. He had ordered all stewards and other ranks away to ensure it was a select gathering, with a rising wind battering at the windows and a loose shutter banging somewhere outside.

Jack took a deep breath before he spoke. "Gentlemen," he began, "you will be wondering why I have collected you together with such a display of secrecy."

The officers nodded solemnly, some sipping at their drinks, others watching, waiting for Jack to talk before they revealed their thoughts. Byrne looked inscrutable, Snodgrass nervous, eager to make a good impression.

"It's quite simple," Jack said. "You all know about the Fenian threat that hangs over every regiment in the army. Well, I aim to ensure that F Company is prepared to meet it. I aim to have a surprise live firing drill."

Byrne lifted his tumbler of brandy. "Is that such a secret, sir?"

"In these extraordinary times, I see no reason to let the men know what we plan," Jack replied, "in case one of them is a member of the Fenian Brotherhood."

"We can't colour them all as Fenians because we suspect one might be," Byrne said. "There's nothing worse for soldiers than to be distrusted." He sipped at his brandy.

"They don't need to be told," Jack said. "I want the men ready. The Fenians may plan to attack this fort, and men who have never fired a live round will be at a significant disadvantage." When Ensign Snodgrass give a small nod, Jack knew he had at least one ally in the company.

"May we have details, sir?" Byrne asked. "Or is that a secret from us as well?"

Jack accepted the criticism without comment. "The drill will take place on Monday next," he said. "We'll march a few miles along the coast. Is there anybody here who's familiar with the terrain of the area?"

"I am, sir." Byrne lifted his glass.

"Where is most suitable for live firing?"

"Tradoney. That's a little cove a few miles away with no houses nearby. The men can shoot out to sea, or over a stretch of moorland."

"That sounds ideal. Show me."

The officers crowded around a map Jack spread open on one of the tables, with Byrne pointing out the local landmarks.

"Tradoney appears most suitable. Are there any questions?" Jack asked.

"Yes, sir." Snodgrass looked nervous.

"Well, speak up, man!"

"It's nothing to do with the drill, sir." Snodgrass hesitated.

"Is it about your girl, Ensign?" Jack tried to hide his smile.

"Yes, sir," Snodgrass confirmed, scarlet with embarrassment.

"Have you proposed yet?" Byrne asked, lifting the mood.

"No, sir, of course not!" Snodgrass sounded indignant. "I just wanted permission to see her again when I am off duty."

"You don't need my permission for that, Snodgrass," Jack said. "When you are off duty, your time is your own."

"Yes, sir. Thank you, sir." Snodgrass gave an embarrassed smile when Byrne clapped him on the shoulder.

"Just make sure that any resulting little Snodgrasses join the regiment," Byrne said. "We need all the keen young men we can get!"

"Good advice." Jack watched the officers file out, and wondered if any of them would carry news of the drill to the Fenians. He had laid his trap, and now he had to wait to see if he could spring it. He closed his eyes, remembering the horror at Gondabad when the sepoys mutinied and knew he would do anything to prevent such a thing happening in the 113th.

* * *

A scimitar moon seeped faint light on to the serried buildings of Charles Fort, glinted from the ranked windows and deepened shadows in the corner where Jack stood. Schooled in patience by service along the North-West Frontier, he barely noticed the passage of time as he waited, watching the slow slide of the moon. The scream of a seagull nearly masked the stealthy scuff of feet on the ground.

Jack stiffened, curling a hand around the butt of his revolver. He saw the lithe man leave the main barrack block and creep around the outside of the parade square, moving slowly and keeping to the shadows. Jack waited until the man opened a door in the southernmost block before he followed.

What are you up to, my fine fellow? Jack wondered. *What's in that block? Clothing stores, boot stores, the hospital and the armoury.*

The man moved furtively for a few steps before he halted and opened the shutter of a bull's-eye lantern, sending a narrow beam of light slicing through the darkness. He stopped outside the door of the armoury, put down the lamp, fumbled in his pocket and produced the two separate keys that opened the door. He swore softly when the door jammed, pushed harder and stumbled inside.

Jack moved closer, watching the intruder step to the racks of rifles that adorned the interior walls, each with the number of its owner stencilled above, as Colonel Snodgrass's standing orders required. Jack had expected the intruder to steal some of F Company's rifles, but instead, the man was tampering with them.

What the devil is he doing?

Jack stepped back into the darkness, taking note of the intruder's face as he passed. As he had feared, the man was a private of F Company, a quiet, serious-faced soldier who had not given any trouble since Jack took command. However, Jack was thankful it was not one of the men he had served with in past campaigns. Waiting until the intruder relocked the armoury door, Jack gave him five minutes to get clear before sliding through the shadows back to the main barrack block. It was the work of a few moments to collect a lantern and keys and return to the armoury, with the familiar perfume of gun oil greeting him as he stepped inside to check the rifles. They were all in place on their racks, with no visible sign of any damage until Jack inspected them more closely. He found a tiny piece of sponge on the nipple of the first three rifles. It was a straightforward device, yet sufficient to prevent the weapon from firing.

The intruder had left the fourth rifle alone, and the fifth, while the next six all had pieces of sponge on the nipples. Checking each rifle in the company, Jack removed the obstructions, replaced the sponge in the nine previously unaffected weapons and noted the names of the owners.

Nine men! Does that mean there are nine Fenians in F Company alone? If so, how many are there in the entire regiment, and how many in the army? And just as important, who alerted this fellow to the forthcoming drill? Only the officers knew, so one of my officers is undoubtedly a Fenian.

Jack was worried as he paced the interior of the parade square, working out what best to do. When he came to a decision, he checked the sentries before walking into the officers' mess.

"You're up early, sir." The mess steward greeted him with a tired smile. "Shall I pour you a drink?"

Jack glanced at the clock. About to say, "Not at three in the morning, thank you," he felt a momentary temptation. "Whiskey, please."

"Kilbeggan, sir? Or Bushmills?" The steward raised his eyebrows. "We also have some moonshine, sir – locally produced whiskey that the Excise men have not got their grips on."

"I'll wager that's raw stuff."

"It's as smooth as mother's milk, sir."

Jack nodded. "I'll take your word as gospel, steward, and try some of your whiskey-milk."

"You won't regret it, sir."

Irish whiskey is slightly different from Scotch whisky, but the effect was similar, warming Jack up before he retired to his quarters. He knew his servant would wake him in only three hours, so slumped into a chair for the remainder of the night.

"Sir," Micklethwaite was a sturdy, bland-faced Yorkshireman with a healthy sense of his importance. "I've been looking for you everywhere, sir." He glanced reprovingly at the glass in Jack's hand.

"Well, now, you've found me." Jack eased himself up, scratched his unshaven face and groaned. "I'm going to get washed and dressed. Have a clean uniform ready for me."

"Yes, sir," Micklethwaite said.

Washed, dressed and feeling much better, Jack took care to load his revolver and checked his sword slid easily out of its scabbard. *I hope I don't need this,* he thought, *but if I do, I'll need it desperately. I don't want to fight my own men. Jack took a deep breath. Oh, God, I don't want to fight my own men.*

Checking his appearance in the mirror, Jack thanked Micklethwaite for his help and marched to the parade ground. He watched as F Company formed up, with Sergeants Parker and Corbyn checking each man, Byrne giving orders while Ensign Snodgrass scurried around looking enthusiastic. Jack scanned the company, noting the position of the man he had seen the previous night.

"F Company, we're going for another march followed by live fire drill this morning. I want every man to collect 15 rounds of ammunition. You men," Jack ordered, indicating the last section, "fetch the targets."

It was a brusque introduction to the morning, but Jack had determined to force the issue. He had warned the officers about the drill and tried to counter the Fenians' attempt at sabotage. He had told nobody, not even Lieutenant Byrne, of his expectations, although he expected that the news of the drill would be all over the neighbourhood within 10 minutes.

All right, Fenians. Let's see how dedicated you are. Riordan hinted that the 113th would mutiny and I'm giving you the opportunity.

When F Company formed up, Jack led them out of the gate, setting a fast pace towards the cove at Tradoney. Rifles at the slope, F Company marched away with the sound of their boots echoing from the ground and their left arms swinging. The countryside was fresh after the recent rain, sweet-scented, with the swish of the sea an ever-present in the background.

"How are the men this morning?" Jack approached Byrne, who marched alongside the men.

"They seem in good spirits, sir," Byrne replied.

Did he sound guarded? Jack nodded. "That's what I thought." He looked around. They had passed through the fertile belt and were marching through bleak countryside, with small, bare fields scoured by the wind. "We'll see what today brings."

Byrne frowned. "Are you expecting anything, sir?"

"I have a suspicion that something may happen today," Jack said. "That fellow Riordan gave me a warning, remember."

"Yes, sir."

"Now, if you'll take the lead, I want to watch the men."

Byrne nodded. "Very good, sir. If you'll excuse me." He hurried to the head of the column as Jack studied each face, trying not to concentrate on the man he had watched the previous evening. Somewhere among these men were another eight Fenians, awaiting their chance to mutiny, to spread death and dishonour in his regiment. Even worse, one of his small band of officers was passing information to the Fenians. Jack could not prevent the anger from spreading through him. He had helped drag the 113th from the worst regiment in the army to a disciplined fighting unit, and now some malcontents were going to destroy it in the most dishonourable way possible.

No! Jack exclaimed inwardly, studying the men as they filed past. *I'll lead these men to battle and see us all killed before I'll give in to mutineers. I'll shoot the bastards myself and sleep easy afterwards.* He frowned as the man who had sabotaged the rifles muttered something to his companion. *So that's the face of the enemy. I'll be watching you closely, my lad.*

"Sir!" Ensign Snodgrass's voice was high-pitched. "We're being followed, sir!"

Jack had been subconsciously aware of the men who dogged them. "Units of infantry are always followed when they're on the march," he said. "People want to know what's going on."

"They might be Fenians, sir."

"They might be," Jack allowed. "They might also be curious civilians. You keep an eye on them for me, Ensign, and let me know if they attack us." *That should keep Ensign Snodgrass occupied.* "Make sure it's not more women after your body."

"It's not, sir," Snodgrass replied, flushed, added, "Yes, sir," before moving to the rear of the column.

"Keep up the pace, men," Jack marched alongside the leaders, confident in his fitness. "Double as if we were marching across the plains of India."

This landscape of southern Ireland could hardly be less like India, Jack thought. It was cold with the threat of winter, with a steady wind spreading fine rain from the sea.

The fields became smaller and wilder, the cottages further apart. Jack nodded. If there was to be a confrontation with the Fenians, he wanted it in a quiet place away from civilians.

"Sir," Byrne said quietly, "Tradoney is around the next headland."

"Thank you." Hurrying ahead, Jack stood at the entrance to a sheltered cove, where a flock of herring gulls sheltering from the wind was the only sign of life.

"Halt!"

F Company halted. Some of the men were panting, evidently unfit. Jack sought out the saboteur, who faced forward, stony-faced.

"This will be a fine place for a live firing exercise," Jack said. "It's lonely enough." He nodded to the south, where the land descended to a pebble beach, and the sound of breakers carried to them. "We'll set up marks along the beach to ensure no civilians are at risk."

Jack's mind buzzed with activity even as he organised his men. *The Fenians must intend to strike today, or they would not have tampered with the rifles but nine men, even with working firearms, will find it hard to face 70. Perhaps the men following us are not innocent?*

When the seagulls took reluctant flight, Tradoney beach was bare except for the 113th, a couple of bedraggled seals on an isolated rock and a score of oystercatchers where the sea met the sand.

About to warn Byrne, Jack held his peace and altered his stance to observe the lieutenant. As an Irishman, Byrne was the most likely to have informed the Fenians.

"Sir," Ensign Snodgrass whispered. "Those men are still following us."

Jack swore silently. "Thank you, Ensign. Keep an eye on them, will you? And keep your revolver loose in its holster."

"My revolver, sir?" The ensign was trembling with excitement.

"Yes, Ensign." Jack raised his voice. "Sergeant Corbyn! Take two men and ensure no civilians stray into the danger area." He would have chosen Parker but wished to have an experienced NCO handy in case of trouble.

"You men!" Jack indicated the end section. "Set the targets up on the edge of the high tide mark." He sent Parker to supervise, not satisfied until the targets were spaced correctly, waited for something to happen, and tried to watch everybody.

"Line the men up, Byrne," Jack tried to sound casual as Byrne gave crisp orders that saw the men line up as on parade, each man facing out to sea. If the Fenians were to act, it would have to be now. Jack unfastened the button that held his revolver secure in its holster. "Load!"

"Up the Irish Republic!"

Jack did not see who shouted. He only saw a surge from within the company as nine men broke away from the rest. "Up the Irish Republic!" another shouted as they formed a tight group, pointing their rifles towards Byrne.

"What's happening?"

"You Fenian bastards!"

The company broke up in disorder, with men staring at the Fenians, some hefting their rifles, others waiting for orders.

Stepping forward, Jack unholstered his revolver and fired in the air. The report caused a sudden silence, and three of the supposed Fenians turned towards him, with one aiming his rifle and squeezing the trigger. When nothing happened, Jack strode up to him and grabbed the barrel of the rifle with his left hand.

"You've failed, private. Check the nipple of your rifle. You'll find a piece of sponge there."

The man stared at Jack in evident dismay.

"The rest of you, drop your rifles," Jack ordered. "The game's over. Your rifles are useless, and the loyal lads are fully armed. Disarm these fools, Parker!"

"Did you know about this, sir?" Byrne's voice was brittle as he unholstered his pistol.

"I knew something could happen," Jack said. "I could not warn you as I did not know what it was." *And you might have been a Fenian.*

The spatter of musketry took Jack by surprise. He swore, turning around. "Down, lads!"

"It's the Fenians!" Wildly excited, Ensign Snodgrass shouted. "Sir! The Fenians are attacking us!" Hauling out his pistol, he turned toward the gunfire.

"You young idiot!" Swearing, Jack grabbed the ensign, but Parker was first, pulling Snodgrass to the ground and holding him down.

"If the captain says down, sir, you get down," Parker snarled.

In the momentary confusion, the nine mutineers took the opportunity to run inland, some dropping their rifles. Still reluctant to fire on his men, Jack aimed and then lowered his revolver. The unknown attackers fired again, with the bullets spattering around F Company.

Jack looked inland, trying to count heads and wishing he had his veterans rather than this bunch of Johnny Raws and broken old soldiers. "Byrne, take Number Two platoon to the left and outflank them. Snodgrass, take Number One platoon to the right. Sergeant Parker will go with you – listen to his advice." Jack gave rapid orders. "Keep your heads down"

"Right boys." Jack waited until the flanking platoons were away and spoke to the men who remained. "Fix bayonets. We're going straight for their throats."

One of the older soldiers looked pleased. "Just like Inkerman, sir."

"You weren't with me at Inkerman," Jack said.

"I came up in support, sir, when you had the 113th colours flying."

Jack nodded at the memory. "Good to have you aboard, private; what's your name?"

The man's grin was reassuring, despite his drink-dazed eyes. "Nixon, sir."

"Right, Nixon, look after the young lads when we go forward." Knowing he would be an immediate target, Jack rose to his feet. If he were commanding veterans, he would have kept low, but most of his men were young and needed the reassurance of an officer's presence.

"Up lads! Show them the bayonet!" With the familiar mixture of excitement and apprehension, Jack ran forward, not knowing how many men opposed him or how well-armed they were.

Most of his men followed. One or two lagged; he could deal with them later. The ground was uneven under Jack's feet, with a dry-stone wall 50 yards inland, behind which he saw a dozen heads bobbing, with irregular spurts of smoke. A bullet hummed past him, the sound frighteningly familiar. Another burrowed into the ground between his feet, with a third ricocheting from a rock.

On the left, Byrne led his platoon in a wide outflanking manoeuvre, the men's red tunics like smears of blood against the grey-green landscape, while Snodgrass and Parker were on the right, making heavy weather of their attack as some recruits held back.

"With me, men," Jack shouted. "Come on F Company!" He saw the powder smoke ahead and heard the sharp crackling of rifle fire. Something tugged at Jack's leg as he stumbled on rough grass and reached the wall, with white-faced defenders recoiling before him and the cheers of his men at his back. As always, once he was in action, all Jack's nervousness evaporated, allowing him to focus on the task in hand.

For one moment, Jack clearly saw the Fenians. About 20 strong, most were dressed in ragged or very rough clothes. They carried a selection of weapons, from modern rifles to Brown Bess muskets and simple pikes, with his mutineers spread among them, desperately trying to fire their Enfields. Deliberately aiming at the man who had attempted sabotage the previous evening, Jack fired his revolver. The man flinched as the bullet passed close, raised his rifle, fired a single shot, dropped the weapon and ran.

As F Company climbed the wall, the Fenians fled, running across the small fields. One or two stopped to fire a final shot.

Waving his men on, Jack followed. "I want prisoners," he shouted. "I want the mutineers captured alive."

Dead men were no good, Jack thought. He needed to find out who was organising this movement. If he could find who was recruiting soldiers into the Fenians, he could stop that part of the Brotherhood.

As F Company advanced, the Fenians scattered. Jack moved faster, aware that his men were not of the standard he would like. He heard a few shots and a lot of shouting.

One of the mutineers paused beside a ruined cabin, turning to face Jack and struggling to fix his bayonet.

"Up the Irish Republic!"

The man's eyes were wild and unfocused as he lifted his rifle and thrust at Jack, screaming something incoherent. Jack dodged sideways to avoid the mutineer's bayonet and clubbed him on the side of the head with his revolver. The man roared, dropping his rifle. Jack hit him again, sending him to the ground. He lay there, holding his head; he could not have been more than 18 years old.

"You two!" Jack lifted the discarded rifle and pointed to the two nearest privates. "Hold this man secure!" He moved on, with the bulk of F Company a few yards behind. "Form a line," he ordered, drive them on." Few things in the world were more intimidating than a line of British infantry advancing with bayonets fixed.

Jack could see few Fenians now, only the odd man running into the distance, but when one of the less ragged shouted something in Gaelic, half a dozen of the mutineers and some civilians turned to fight, firing a ragged volley at F Company.

Once again, bullets whined and spattered around Jack. "Capture these lads," he ordered. "I want prisoners."

A man behind him gasped and fell, clutching at the red stain that spread on his upper chest. "They got me!" He sounded more surprised than pained.

"With me, boys," Jack strode forward.

The mutineers fired another volley and turned away, to see Byrne's company moving in on their flank and rear. When the leading man shouted an order, they withdrew to a small, stone-built cottage a few yards away. The cottage's glazed windows and chimney suggested the tenant was a person of some prosperity.

"Form around that building," Jack ordered. "Keep under cover. Byrne, take Number One and Three sections. Create a defensive perimeter facing out, in case any more Fenians try to help their companions. Snodgrass, keep your men under control. Send Sergeant Parker back to round up the stragglers."

"They Fenians are going to fight, sir," Nixon said.

"Aye. Keep your heads down, boys." Jack saw a thin wisp of smoke coming from the chimney of the cabin. *There might be people living inside.* "We'll get them out of there. Fire at them lads; keep them away from the windows." He watched as a dozen hens scattered in panic. "We'll smoke them out of there."

"This is better than live firing practise, eh?" Nixon shouted.

Using the covering fire of F Company, Jack jinked forward, to haul himself on to the turf roof of the cottage. Blinking in the smoke, he could see his men formed in two concentric rings, one facing inward toward the cabin, the other outward to block any Fenian counter-attack. His wounded man had crawled to the shelter of a boulder and lay there alone and bleeding.

Voices sounded from the cabin, speaking Gaelic, the tones high-pitched. When somebody shouted an order, the Fenians began to fire again, uselessly, for a handful of untrained men, however brave, would never defeat a company of British infantry. Ripping up a section of turf from the roof, Jack blocked the simple chimney to prevent the smoke escaping. With the chimney smoke added to the powder-smoke and F Company's bullets, conditions within the cabin would soon be intolerable.

Jack waited, ignoring the odd shot from the cabin below. He did not know Byrne well, but Parker had sufficient experience to keep his men under cover, while what he had seen of the Fenians' skill at arms did not worry him unduly. After a few moments, Jack heard the cabin door burst open and saw smoke billow out. Voices sounded from below.

Removing the turf from the chimney, Jack pulled back from the smoke, pulled out his revolver and fired two shots down the chimney. The Fenians replied with a ragged volley, with few shots penetrating the turf. As Jack had hoped, when two of the Fenians ran outside to see who was on the roof, the inner ring of F Company opened fire, forcing the Fenians back inside. Jack flattened himself to avoid the stray shots that whined past his head.

"You in there!" Jack shouted down the chimney. "You can't escape. You can either die or surrender!"

"We won't surrender to you!" The reply came, so Jack fired three more shots down the chimney and rolled away to reload before the Fenians replied.

"Come on, lads!" Jack waved his arm in the air, and the inner ring of F Company moved forward. As the Fenians opened fire, Jack again fired down the chimney. He could only imagine the result inside the house as his bullets ricocheted around, distracting the defenders from the approaching infantry.

Rather than stay, the Fenians rushed outside to meet F Company, and the fight lasted only seconds. Jack slid down from the roof, stopped Nixon from plunging his bayonet into a cowering Fenian civilian and took control as the hens moved back towards the hut. Panting, Jack looked around. No more of his men had been wounded, with one dead Fenian and three wounded. The remainder stood in a sullen group, glowering at him with eyes filled with a mixture of loathing and fear.

"I want prisoners," Jack said. "Take our mutineers to one side and the civilians to the other. Sergeant Parker, my respects to Lieutenant Byrne and pray could he come here on the double."

"Sir." Parker trotted away.

Byrne eyed the prisoners, shaking his head. "You bloody fools," he said.

"I'm keeping Number One platoon here, Byrne. I want you to take the rest and escort the mutineers back to the fort."

"Yes, sir," Byrne said. "Shall I take the Fenian prisoners?"

"No," Jack said. "Leave them with me." He watched Byrne march the bulk of F Company away.

"Right you men," Jack addressed the half-dozen prisoners. "I don't know who you are, or what your purpose was in attacking British soldiers on British territory, but I'm going to find out."

"The prisoners stared at him, wordless. One spat on the ground between Jack's feet.

"What's your name?" Jack indicated the man who had spat. He noticed that Nixon was waiting with his bayonet poised and a new light behind his eyes.

The Fenian muttered something in Gaelic.

"Can you speak English?" Jack asked. The Fenian glowered at him.

"You may have a just grievance," Jack said. "I don't care at the moment. You shot one of my men. In return, I shall kill two of you." He looked for a reaction. The tallest of the Fenians said something in Gaelic. Jack slowly reloaded his revolver, taking his time for maximum effect.

He pointed to the oldest of the Fenians. "Take that one around the back of the building," he said. "Ensign Snodgrass, you stay here. Nixon, come with me."

"The Fenian tried to run until Nixon cracked him over the head with the butt of his rifle and nearly dragged him around the building. Jack followed, deliberately moving slowly.

"This will do," Jack lifted one of the hens by the neck. "Tie that fellow up, will you, Nixon?"

Already stunned by Nixon's blow, the Fenian barely resisted when Nixon roughly tied his wrists and ankles.

"And gag him," Jack said.

When Nixon complied, Jack wrung the hen's neck. "Now bayonet this unfortunate creature and yell loudly."

Catching on at once, Nixon thrust his bayonet into the hen and screamed at the top of his voice. The Fenian prisoner writhed in his bonds.

"You stay there," Jack advised as he and Nixon returned around the building.

"That man told us nothing," Jack said. "Who's next?" He pointed to a sturdy-looking man with red hair. "Take that one, Nixon, and for God's sake, clean the blood off your blade. If you've got a rusty bayonet, I'll have you on extra drill!"

"Yes, sir!" Nixon ostentatiously wiped his blade.

The red-haired Fenian lifted his chin, spat straight at Jack and said something in Gaelic, adding: "Bad cess to you, Redcoat."

"You've got spirit," Jack said. "We could do with men like you in the 113th when we next face the Russians. Tie him up, lads." Jack anticipated that the red-haired man would struggle, so pointed his revolver at the other Fenians. The youngest, a boy who could not be older than 14, whimpered in fear. Jack guessed he had been brought up with scare stories about brutal redcoats.

As the red-haired Fenian began to curse, Jack ordered him gagged. "Take him around the back, Nixon!" he said. "You know what to do."

Wiping the blade of his bayonet on a tuft of grass, Nixon grabbed the now-bound red-haired Fenian by the collar and dragged him around the back of the hut. Jack followed, deliberately taking his time. He kicked the dead hen across to Nixon, winked at the red-haired Fenian and smiled as Nixon plunged his bayonet into the fowl, giving a long-drawn-out scream.

"He's not dead yet." Jack pitched his voice high so the prisoners could hear it. "In the heart, Nixon, not in the guts."

"Yes, sir!" Nixon said happily and gave a realistic gurgle. "Can we do the young one next, sir?"

"Why not?" Jack wanted to end the prisoners' sufferings.

The youngest Fenian was clearly terrified, backing away as Nixon approached with his bloody bayonet. Surprisingly, it was the other, older Fenian who stood up.

"Take me," he pleaded. "Spare the boy."

"Why?" Jack asked. "Why should I spare him? He's a traitor to the Crown, and he shot at my men."

"He shot at nobody." the Fenian had a long face and steady brown eyes. "He never had a gun."

"I've only your word for that," Jack said. "Take him away, Nixon."

"He's only a boy!" The older Fenian stepped forward. "Leave him alone, for Christ's sake. Take me instead."

"Kill the boy slowly, Nixon," Jack ordered. "Bayonet him in the guts."

"Yes, sir," Nixon said.

"I can help you," the older Fenian suddenly said, sounding desperate.

"The only way you can help," Jack said, "is by telling me who is behind all this Fenian nonsense. Who recruited you and who told you to come after my regiment? How did you know there would be trouble today?"

Nixon had been listening. "I'll cut him up slowly, sir." He hauled the young boy around the back of the cabin.

"For God's sake!" The older Fenian started forward until one of F Company thrust his bayonet under his throat. "I'll tell you all I can if you spare the boy."

The remaining prisoners glared at the older man, shouting at him in Gaelic. He replied in the same language.

"Wait, Nixon!" Jack roared. "Come with me." He stepped away, with the long-faced Fenian following. "What's your name?"

"Regan. James Regan."

"Right, Regan, tell me why I should not execute that young man. Tell me who heads this Fenian thing and who recruited you."

"A fellow called Stephens heads the Fenians in Ireland," Regan said at once. "That's no secret, Captain Windrush; all the newspapers speak about him all the time."

Jack was aware of the name. "And did this fellow Stephens recruit you in person?"

"No." Regan looked toward the cottage, behind which Nixon and the young boy remained. "What's happening with that boy?"

"His future depends on you," Jack said easily. "Who recruited you?"

Regan was quiet for a while. "Will the boy be all right? Do I have your word?"

"The word of an English gentleman." Jack smiled. "The English you don't want in your country."

"I want you to tell me that you won't harm my boy."

"Your boy? Is that young man your son?" Jack sighed, visualising David. "You should be ashamed of yourself putting your son in such danger."

"He's my son," Regan admitted.

"I won't kill him," Jack promised. "You have my word, Mr Regan, as long as you help me. Who recruited you?"

Regan hesitated, looking towards the other Fenians.

"Think of your son," Jack encouraged.

"You're a bastard," Regan said.

"My middle name has the initial B," Jack agreed. "Who recruited you?"

When Regan hesitated again, Jack shrugged and raised his voice: "As you were, Nixon! Get that bayonet ready."

"You filthy bastard, Windrush," Regan repeated, clearly near to tears as he struggled between loyalty to the Fenians and love for his son.

Jack took out his watch and opened the cover. "One minute, Regan, and then we carve up your boy." He watched the seconds tick away. "You have 30 seconds... 15..."

"There were two of them," Regan said. "If you hurt that boy..."

"What will you do, Regan? Swear at me? 10 seconds."

"One man and one woman."

Jack snapped shut his watch and raised his voice. "Spare the lad, Nixon." He put the watch away. "Describe this man and woman."

"He was tall and smart; the woman was also tall."

Jack frowned. "Were they locals? Or from America, maybe?"

Regan shook his head. "Not locals. He might have been American. I had never seen them before, and the man's Gaelic was like nothing I've ever heard before."

"Dublin Gaelic?" Jack hazarded.

"Not even Irish," Regan replied, shaking his head. "As I said, he might have been American, or maybe something else."

Jack remembered the Gaelic-speaking Highlanders in the Crimea and India. "Was he Scottish?"

"No. I know Scottish Gaelic." Regan screwed up his face. "He was more foreign than that."

Jack felt a prickle of unease. "French? Russian?"

"Maybe. Maybe he was French-Russian. I dunno." It was evident that Regan had said all he could about his recruiter.

"And the woman? Was she foreign as well?"

"She never spoke to me," Regan said.

"Did she speak to the foreign gentleman?"

"Yes, in English," Regan said. "Educated English."

"And she was tall. Was she plump, fair, dark..?"

"My boy…"

"Your boy is safe. Describe this woman."

"She was tall and dark, and she clung to his arm like they were lovers."

"Right." Jack realised he would get no more from Regan. "Nixon! Bring the prisoners back." He watched Regan's face as the supposedly dead Fenians returned from behind the cottage. "The British Army does not kill prisoners," he said softly, remembering the aftermath of the Indian Mutiny and knowing he lied. The image of scores of men, mutineers and others, hanging by the roadside, haunted his nightmares. *Please, God, we never bring that horror to Ireland.*

"Let the youngster go," Jack ordered. "We'll take the others back to barracks with us until we can hand them over to the civilian authorities."

CHAPTER ELEVEN

Charles Fort, County Cork, Ireland

"Somebody warned the Fenians that we were arranging a live firing drill," Jack said flatly.

The assembled officers stared at him, wordless.

"There are two ways in which that could happen," Jack continued. "Either somebody spoke by mistake, or somebody warned the Fenians deliberately. At present, I don't know which happened."

"Are you accusing us, Captain Windrush?" Byrne sounded angry.

"You will remember that I called an officers' meeting to inform you about the live firing drill," Jack said. "I specifically prevented any other ranks from attending. The night before the drill, I kept watch on the armoury and witnessed Rawlins, one of our pet Fenians, sabotaging the rifles of the loyal men. I corrected that, but somebody sitting here informed the Fenians. They knew about the drill and where and when it would take place."

The officers shifted in their chairs, looking at one another in suspicion and denial.

"I don't know who it was," Jack pressed his point. "Indeed, I don't even have a suspicion, but one of you knows."

"You'll be thinking it was me," Byrne said, "as I am Irish."

"I'm not thinking anything," Jack said. "I am going to appeal to your honour as gentlemen and British officers first, and if that does not work, then by God, I'll hunt the traitor down. His actions..." Jack looked at each officer in turn. "Your actions, whoever you are, could have resulted in all our deaths and lit a fire of rebellion right across Ireland."

Jack's anger built as he remembered the scenes in India. "Some of you know the fruits of rebellion. The others are fortunate never to have seen a land where every tree held a hanging man, where wild dogs gnawed the bodies of raped and murdered women, where men distrusted even their brothers." Jack stopped. "I'll not permit that monstrosity to come to Ireland." When he stood up, Jack found he was shaking. He had never recovered from the horror of the Indian Mutiny.

"I don't take kindly to being accused of treason, sir." Byrne was on his feet, straight-backed, with his eyes like stones.

"Nor would I, Lieutenant Byrne." Jack held his gaze. "So the sooner this affair is cleared up, the better for us all."

"What do you want us to do, sir?"

Jack looked over his officers. They were white-faced, some angry at being accused, others avoiding his gaze. Snodgrass looked on the verge of tears. "This is a new state of affairs for me," Jack admitted. "I want each of you to search his conscience. Find out if you could inadvertently have told somebody, anybody, about the firing drill. If you think you have, then come to see me in my quarters, or drop me a note and we'll meet privately. I hope we can resolve this affair amicably."

"And if not?" Byrne asked.

Jack put a steely edge to his voice. "Then, by the living God, one man here is knowingly passing information to the Fenians. I will root out that traitor and see him hanged."

* * *

Jack expected Byrne to approach him, so when somebody flung open the door of his office, he leaned back in his chair with the best appearance of calmness he could conjure. "Yes, Byrne?"

"You've got a damned cheek, Windrush," Byrne started.

"Are you here to confess your sins, Lieutenant Byrne?" Jack asked mildly.

"You know damn well I'm not!"

"Then take a seat and tell me why you have come." Jack produced his most disarming smile.

"I've come to register my distaste at your attitude and comments," Byrne did not sit.

"Good. Now you have done that, Byrne, you can tell me if you suspect any of our officers of disloyalty. Quite frankly, I can't see any of them helping the enemy."

"What?" Taken by surprise, as Jack had intended, Byrne could only stare.

"Well?" Producing two cheroots, Jack offered one to Byrne. "Have a smoke, sit down and talk to me."

Byrne stiffened. "I came to protest, sir, not to share a cheroot with you."

"I note your protest, Byrne."

"Do you suspect me, sir?"

"Not in the slightest. Is there anybody you think might have passed information to the Fenians?"

"Nobody, sir."

"Good. Thank you for confirming my thoughts. Are you sure you won't accept a cheroot?"

"I will not, sir."

"Then I can only thank you for your time. I see that Ensign Snodgrass is hovering outside waiting to see me next. Please usher him in as you leave."

Ensign Snodgrass nearly pushed past Byrne. "Can I speak to you, sir?"

"Have you also come to register a complaint about my attitude and comments?" Jack asked.

"What? No, sir." Snodgrass shook his head violently.

Jack saw the ensign was nervous. "In you come, Snodgrass. Why do you wish to see me?"

Snodgrass pulled himself to attention. "It was me, sir."

"What do you mean, Snodgrass?"

"I informed the Fenians about the live firing drill."

Jack felt his heart beating fast in his chest. Snodgrass had been one of the least likely suspects. "That is quite an admission, Ensign. Tell me more."

"If you recall, sir, after the meeting when you informed us about the drill, sir, I asked if I could meet my girl."

Jack nodded. "I remember."

Snodgrass remained at attention. "Well, sir. I told her about the drill."

"For heaven's sake, man, why?"

"She asked me to," Snodgrass replied.

"Did she indeed? That puts a different complexion on things." Jack shook his head. "What did she say?"

Snodgrass mumbled something that Jack did not catch.

"Speak up, man! You're a British officer, not a schoolboy up before the headmaster. What did this woman say?"

"She asked me to tell her anything that happened in the regiment, sir."

Jack shook his head, wondering if the woman was merely being curious, or was an active member of the Fenians. "For God's sake, man! As soon as she asked that, you should have told me."

Snodgrass looked away again. "Yes, sir. She never mentioned the Fenians, though, or anything like that. She was always so friendly." He looked up. "I love her, sir."

"Oh, nonsense, man! She was using you, that's all. Luckily there's no major harm done, our casualty will recover, and we've managed to bag a few Fenians." Jack began to pace the length of his room. "We'll have to catch this woman."

"Sir!" Snodgrass shook his head vehemently. "No, sir. I'm sure she's innocent."

"I'm not so sure," Jack said. "Tell me about her. What's her name?"

"Helen, sir. Helen Maxwell."

"What?" Jack stopped abruptly. Maxwell was Helen's maiden name before she married William. "Describe her. What's she like, Snodgrass?"

"Tall and dark and lovely, sir," Snodgrass said.

That described Helen perfectly and was close to Regan's depiction of the woman who helped recruit him. "How old?"

"I don't know, sir," Snodgrass said. "I never asked her age."

"Well, guess, man!"

"Older than me, sir." Snodgrass sounded miserable. "Maybe 25 or so."

"Jack felt a prickle of hope. Helen would be 31. Perhaps there was merely a coincidence of names, or was Snodgrass viewing his woman through the distorted glass of romance? "Does this Helen Maxwell woman have any distinguishing features? A scar perhaps, or a wooden leg?"

"No, sir." Snodgrass pulled himself even more erect. "She is perfect." He hesitated before continuing. "She wears a queer piece of jewellery, like a triangle on a chain. It doesn't look costly."

Helen's Tartar amulet. Jack felt his hopes slide away. Snodgrass's woman was Helen. But why would she help the Fenians?

"Where can we find this Helen Maxwell?" Jack asked.

"She has a small place in Kinsale," Snodgrass said. "That's where we met."

"We'll go there and pick her up."

"Sir! She may be innocent!"

Jack sat back down at his desk. "Listen, Snodgrass. Nobody but the officers knew about the live firing drill. You told this woman and, shortly afterwards, the Fenians tried to sabotage our rifles. Do you still think she is innocent?"

Snodgrass shook his head in evident confusion. "Perhaps not, sir."

"Very well." Jack fought his rising anger. "Good God, man! She's about as innocent as Eve's snake!" *All the same*, he thought, *I hope there is some rational explanation.*

"Micklethwaite!" Jack roared and turned as his servant entered. "My compliments to Lieutenant Byrne, and could he report to me as soon as is convenient."

Byrne still looked resentful as he greeted Jack with a formal salute. "Sir?"

"Organise a picket, Byrne. I'm going into Kinsale to pick up a suspected Fenian."

"Yes, sir."

"You take charge here."

"Yes, sir." Byrne nodded.

"Sir!" Snodgrass spoke loudly. "I am to blame for the Fenian attack."

"That is yet to be proved," Jack said. He gave Byrne a quick summary of what had happened.

Byrne nodded. "I see, sir."

"I deserve a court-martial." Snodgrass remained at attention, with Byrne listening intently.

"You deserve no such thing," Jack said. "You acted like a stupid little love-sick boy. I'll put you as duty officer for a month, and that'll be the end of it."

"No, sir!" Snodgrass protested. "I put men at risk and besmirched my honour."

"Don't be a bloody fool, Snodgrass!" Byrne said. "Captain Windrush is helping you here. You may have a bright sense of honour, but no sense in women, which is normal for a boy your age." He slapped Snodgrass on the shoulder. "Come along, Snoddy; we'll snatch this fickle woman up. It's a good lesson for you never to trust a woman's smile."

* * *

Leading a picket of Sergeant Parker and a dozen men, Jack and Snodgrass doubled into Kinsale. After the late encounter with the Fenians, some people resented this military activity, with some throwing clods of mud or shouting Fenian slogans. The majority watched in silence from behind part-opened shutters. As usual, a group of children followed the picket, copying the movements of the soldiers.

"This way, sir." Snodgrass took them along a narrow street to an isolated two-storey house at the waterfront, with an excellent display of late roses in the front garden and doors painted bright green.

Trust Helen to find such a picturesque little love nest, Jack said to himself. "Sergeant, take four men around the back and post two at each side. Snodgrass, you and the rest follow me." Taking a deep breath, Jack approached the front door. He did not like to think of Helen as a traitor, but the evidence suggested nothing else.

"Open up!" Jack banged on the front door. "It's Captain Windrush of the 113th Foot!"

"She's not in," a young boy said helpfully from the group that was gathering behind the picket. "She's gone away to Americay."

"I doubt that," Jack said. Lifting his foot, he booted the door open and stepped inside. There was nothing remarkable about the house except its extreme tidiness. Helen, he remembered, had been obsessed with cleanliness. When Jack took a deep breath, Helen's perfume brought a whole host of memories. He raised his voice. "Is anybody here?"

Nobody answered. "Wait here," Jack ordered, "except you, Snodgrass. Come with me." He took the stairs two at a time, stopped at the first floor, where four doors opened from a square landing. "Which one is her bedroom?"

"This one, sir," Snodgrass indicated the door on the right.

"Looking over the sea," Jack murmured. "I should have known." Striding across the faded Axminster carpet, he shoved open the door.

As he expected, Helen was not in the room, although the scent of her perfume was strong. Either Helen or some maid had made the bed, while a beflowered pitcher and ewer on a cabinet, plus a collection of books, made up the only decoration. The oval mirror on the wall looked forlorn. Jack lifted the books: Irish history and a volume in Gaelic he could not translate. "Is this where you spoke to her?"

"Yes," Snodgrass confirmed miserably.

Glancing out of the window, Jack saw the ships in the harbour and the growing crowd of children surrounding the garden, with the soldiers talking to them. He nodded; that was normal. There was no threat to his men. Searching through the drawers, Jack found a pad of notepaper, a few quill pens, with ink and a penknife.

"I'll take the books and the notepaper," Jack said. "Search the house, Snodgrass, in case she is hiding somewhere." He knew she was not. Helen was not the sort of woman who would hide from anything or anybody. Jack wondered what game Helen was playing. He refused to believe that she was a true-green Fenian dedicated to the cause of an Irish Republic – Helen had never shown any political or religious inclinations. Jack shrugged; he would make his report to Mr Smith and leave him to decide what to do.

"I told you she was in Americay," the small boy jeered as Jack led the picket away.

* * *

Jack struggled with his report, wondering how to state what happened without landing either Helen or Snodgrass in significant trouble. Despite his chequered history with Helen, he had no desire to accuse her of treason, while Ensign Snodgrass was only a misguided boy who lacked judgement. The possible foreign involvement with the Fenians was equally disturbing, so Jack pondered for a long time before penning a cautious letter to Smith. He mentioned that one of his ensigns might have inadvertently let his girl know about the live firing drill, before moving on to Regan's information.

Sighing, he signed and sealed the letter and leaned back in his seat. He had drawn a fine line between duty and friendship, but it was the best he could do. Jack looked up as Byrne tapped on his door and stepped in.

"I'm sorry to disturb you, sir. Could I have a word?"

"What is it, Byrne?"

"It's young Snodgrass, sir. He's gone over your head and written to the brigadier to request a court-martial."

Jack took a deep breath. "The little idiot! They'll crucify him, an officer acting like that."

"It's his notion of preserving his honour, sir," Byrne explained.

"Has he sent the letter?"

"Yes, sir."

"Then it's out of my hands," Jack said resignedly. "He may come to regret his impulsiveness. This notion of honour has cost more lives and ruined more careers than it's worth."

"The honour of a British gentleman," Byrne said slowly. "The colonel will take it badly if young Snoddy is found guilty."

"That's so," Jack said. "Thank you for telling me, Byrne; we'll have to hope things work out for the best. Could you organise another live firing drill? The last one was interrupted."

Byrne nearly smiled at this sign of trust. "Of course, sir. Do you want it in secret?"

"That's your decision, Byrne," Jack handed over his letter to Micklethwaite. If Ensign Snodgrass had already contacted the brigadier, all Jack's care not to name names was pointless.

CHAPTER TWELVE

London, Autumn 1865

Smith's face was as expressionless as before as he stared at Jack across the width of the desk. "So you believe there are foreigners behind the Fenian movement."

"I believe there are some foreigners involved," Jack said. He had been surprised when Smith had ordered him to London from Ireland. "We know that Irishmen in the United States started the movement, and a fellow called Stephens seems to be the leader in Ireland."

"That much is no secret," Smith said. "It is the foreign connection that concerns me. Tell me what intelligence you have, Windrush."

"The fellow Regan told me that he was recruited by a tall man who may have been a foreigner, as well as a woman." Jack chose not to mention Helen.

"She's probably some local woman the recruiter's picked up," Smith said dismissively.

"My lads in Berwick said there was a woman behind the riot there, too," Jack reminded Smith.

Smith pursed his lips. "I think you'll find a woman behind any riot and much of the crime in Britain," he remarked drily.

"Maybe so, sir, but I think we should watch out for her."

"Concentrate on the essentials." Smith looked up. "I don't want you wasting your time chasing after irrelevant women."

"I won't waste any time, Mr Smith," Jack replied.

"I'm glad to hear it. Now, Windrush, you told me that Riordan was taking a ship at Leith for the United States."

"That's right. He's probably long gone by now."

"He's not; the only ship leaving for the United States from Leith has been delayed for weeks," Smith said. "There was a major problem with its documentation and then the captain found that the cargo was badly stowed."

Somehow Jack guessed that Smith had used his position to delay the ship. "Is that right, sir?"

"That's right, sir. I want you to go to America."

Jack started. "I know nothing about America, sir. Any competence I have is in India." *That little boy in Ireland told me that Helen had gone to America.*

Smith ignored Jack's words. "You can join Riordan in Leith, sail with him and infiltrate the Fenians over there. Leave the foreign recruiter to us. With the situation so fluid, we may need your expertise across the Atlantic."

"I may be getting somewhere hunting down the recruiters, sir. I'd be better following that up over here."

"You'd be better following orders, Windrush. The thrust for this Fenian nonsense comes from the United States," Smith said. "I have also heard whispers that they intend to attack Canada. You will find out how and let us know. As you are interested in following your previous line of enquiries, see if you can find out about this foreign gentleman, Windrush, if he exists."

"He exists," Jack said, "but I'm much more likely to find him in the British Isles than in North America."

"Perhaps. If you find this fellow, I want you to kill him." Smith spoke without emotion.

"I'm not an assassin," Jack said at once. Killing soldiers in battle was one thing; hunting men across continents to assassinate them in cold blood was something else.

"You're a British officer. You will do your duty and obey orders."

Jack tried to use Smith's words against him. "I'm a British officer. How can I join the Fenians? They can check my name is in the Army List, while some may remember me from the Mutiny."

When Smith looked up, his eyes were gimlet-sharp. "You won't be a British officer when you infiltrate the Fenians, Windrush. You'll be a former British officer with a grudge. You already used that story with Riordan – now you will have more proof to back you up. The Fenians will welcome your expertise, bitterness and knowledge."

"*Former* British officer?"

"I've arranged to have Colonel Snodgrass remove you from the 113th. That should not be difficult, given your history there and the fact his son was under your command when he went astray. I'll ensure that the newspapers broadcast your disgrace, so the Fenians hear about it. I'll even have your statement printed saying how unfair it is."

"I haven't made a statement, Mr Smith."

Smith leaned back in his chair. "I'll make one for you. By the time I've finished, you'll be the British Army's number-one enemy."

"It won't do my reputation any good, sir."

"Oh, we'll print a retraction when this affair is over, Windrush. We'll have you back as a respectable officer, never fear." Smith's smile was as bleak as everything else about him. "We'll have to get you cashiered first, though, and that will mean a court-martial. Two court-martials in the 113th simultaneously! Even the most hardened of the Fenians will think they have a most valuable ally."

"Indeed," Jack said.

"One last thing," Smith said, "your code word is Wolfe."

"Wolfe?" Jack repeated. "What does that mean?"

"General Wolfe defeated the French at Quebec and paved the way to conquer Canada," Smith explained. "If you send a message to me or the British authorities in North America, mentioning Wolfe, we'll know it's from you."

"How do I do that?" Jack asked.

"I'm sure you'll think of something," Smith said. "Now, we'd better get you dismissed from the service."

* * *

Jack had never liked Edinburgh, despite Mary's love for Sir Walter Scott's books. The old part of the city was too rumbustious, with neither order nor beauty in the morass of pestilent closes and wynds that clawed out from the Royal Mile – it reminded him of the native quarter of Gondabad without the friendliness. The famous New Town with its Georgian elegance was as cold and precise as the people who lived there, classic formality hiding a multitude of secret vices, in Jack's opinion. Now, under arrest in Edinburgh Castle, he had cause to further his dislike.

Had he been a ranker, Jack knew, he might have been confined in one of the dark dungeons deep in the bowels of the castle. As an officer, his treatment was immeasurably better, with his own quarters and even a soldier-servant, although the armed guard at the door was reason enough to give him pause.

Although Jack had been expecting it, the actual arrest had still come as a shock. It was worse because Colonel Snodgrass sent Elliot to arrest him, with the Provost Sergeant and two nervous young privates as an escort. Jack had seen Elliot ride up to the gates of Charles Fort and guessed his mission. Sighing, he sat on the hard chair in his quarters, lit a cheroot and waited.

"Come in!" He shouted in response to the sharp rap on his door. He waved Micklethwaite away. "You'd best be elsewhere."

"Jack..." Elliot began, and then straightened to attention. "Captain Jack Baird Windrush. It is my duty to place you under arrest." Elliot's eyes were unreadable.

Jack had looked up from his chair and blew out blue smoke. "Have you come all the way from Edinburgh to say that, Major Elliot?"

"Yes, sir." Elliot produced a set of handcuffs. "I am ordered to put you in these, sir, but if you give me your word of honour not to try to escape, I shan't use them."

"You have my word, Major Elliot." Jack nodded to the escort, who gripped their rifles in white-knuckled fingers. "You won't need these lads, either."

"Colonel's orders, Captain Windrush." Elliot's expression pleaded for Jack's understanding.

"Of course, Major." Jack stretched and stood up. "Will you allow me a few moments to gather my things?"

"Yes, of course, Captain." Elliot looked relieved that Jack had not tried to retaliate or run.

After an uncomfortable journey from Ireland to Edinburgh, now Jack sat in his quarters, waiting for the court-martial with its pre-ordained verdict and the inevitable disgrace that would follow. He paced the room, thinking of the glory days when he led his men into action against the Russians and mutineers. In 100 years, if anybody ever remembered Captain Jack Windrush, it would be as an officer cashiered and disgraced. What would Mary think? Jack sighed ruefully. Mary would shake her head, blame the Army for stupidity and carry on with life.

That was his Mary. Whatever happened to him, Mary would be there, shaking her head and holding out her hand to help.

The door thrust open, and Major Hepburn stepped in. "It's time, Captain Windrush," he announced. He spoke in the clipped tones Jack had come to expect from officers of the Royal Scots, the oldest line regiment in the British Army. "I'm your defending counsel."

"Yes, sir." Jack stood to attention, as Major Hepburn expected from all officers junior to him.

"We don't need an escort," Hepburn snapped as two privates slammed to attention. "We're British officers." He nodded to Jack. "Let's get this nonsense over with, Captain Windrush."

The ever-present Edinburgh wind whipped at Jack as he marched from his quarters in the barracks block to the great hall of the castle, where the army was holding his court-martial. He had barely time to register the history of the place, which had hosted dark deeds of treachery as well as Scottish royalty, before the officers who were to judge him marched in, followed by the president of the court. Above him, the oak-beams of the superb roof frowned down, while a small fire in the massive stone fireplace struggled to compete with the chill of the Scottish autumn.

Lieutenant Colonel Lancelot Snodgrass took his position as judge, treated Jack to a disdainful glance and nodded to the other members of the court. The Victoria Cross gleamed bronze on his chest, a reminder of his supposed bravery in the Crimea. "Let's get on with this. On your feet, Windrush."

Jack stood, listening to the opening address of Major Bright of the 18th Foot, the Royal Irish, a regiment he had known in the Crimea. Bright seemed a decent enough officer, nearly apologetic as he fulfilled his assigned role as prosecutor. His words were fair as he described Jack's actions in hunting for Riordan, tracing him to the Pentlands and finally letting him go free.

"Are you saying that Captain Windrush knowingly allowed this man, Private Riordan, a known Fenian sympathiser, walk free?" Snodgrass sounded indignant.

"That is so." Bright glanced at Jack.

"This man, who holds the Queen's commission, and an officer of my regiment, aided a known deserter and traitor?" Snodgrass said each word slowly and distinctly, giving the court the full benefit of the facts.

"That appears to be what happened," Bright said.

Jack stood, expressionless, aware that Snodgrass was enjoying every moment of his degradation, knowing some of the officers present would already be viewing him as a man sympathetic to the Fenian cause.

"Do you have any witnesses to call, Major Bright?"

"I have, sir." Bright called on William Todd, the Pentland shepherd, who swore on oath that he had seen Jack hand a sovereign to Riordan.

"Are you certain of that?" Major Bright asked.

"I swear it on the Bible." Although the shepherd looked uneasy in such company, he spoke with quiet sincerity.

When Major Hepburn tried to cross-examine, the shepherd struck to his story. Jack sat unmoving, knowing that the shepherd spoke the truth.

The atmosphere in the court hardened, with the officers staring at Jack as though he had led the Russian attack at Inkerman.

"Please present your case, Major Hepburn," Colonel Snodgrass invited. "If you have one."

Hepburn looked at Jack. "Are you sure, Captain?"

"I'm sure," Jack said.

"Captain Windrush wishes to plead guilty," Major Hepburn said. "However, I would like to remind the court of this officer's fine record in three brutal wars and along the North-West Frontier, as well as his more recent success in preventing a mutiny and attack on F Company, 113th Foot in Ireland."

Snodgrass snorted sceptically. "This court is only concerned with Captain Windrush's actions with the Fenian Private Riordan, not with any previous actions he may or may not have done, or his supposed subsequent movements in Ireland." Snodgrass faced the court. "In Ireland, this officer allowed the Fenians to infiltrate the company I entrusted to his command, with the result that the Fenians, a bunch of ragged labourers, shot a British soldier."

Jack held Snodgrass's gaze, fighting his dislike for this man.

Snodgrass allowed his words to register before he continued. "Windrush's admission of guilt saves us all time. I order that he should be cashiered and sentence him to 20 years' penal servitude." He leaned closer to Jack. "You may consider yourself fortunate, Windrush. If you had wasted any more of my time, I should have ordered you to be shot for treason." He looked up. "Take him away under armed guard and lock him up securely."

The trial had lasted less than an hour, Jack realised. He had stepped into the Great Hall as a British officer and left as a disgraced traitor. Two privates of the 113th took up position on either side of Jack as he was marched from the Great Hall down to the dungeons beneath the castle.

"In you go, Captain." Major Bright had taken it on himself to escort Jack. "I don't like this any more than you do."

"You were doing your duty," Jack reassured him. "No man can do more than that."

"Why?" Bright asked. "Why help a Fenian? You're not even Irish. Are you a Roman Catholic?"

"Church of England through and through," Jack replied.

"I don't understand," Bright said. "You have a good record; the men call you Fighting Jack."

"Not any more," Jack said. "Now they'll call me Fenian Jack."

"Well, good luck," Bright said, stepping back. "I'm sure there was a reason. Men with a record such as yours don't become traitors overnight."

Jack heard the door slam shut behind him and sat on the wooden bench that was the only furniture the dungeon possessed. He swore softly and buried his head in his hands. He had not reckoned on penal servitude. The idea was to be cashiered, not locked away for years. Jack swore again, stood and tested the door. It was solid oak, about two inches thick and studded with iron. He could never break free of that, while the only window was 12 feet above his head and heavily barred.

It was not the first time Jack had been locked up. He had suffered in a Russian cell during the Crimean War and in an Indian fortress in the latter stages of the Mutiny, but being jailed for treason was far more serious than being captured by the enemy. Once again, Jack wished he could return to being a regimental officer rather than acting in a capacity for which he was temperamentally unsuited. He began to pace the dungeon, three paces one way, turn, and three paces back. The light coming through the window faded, darkened, and the temperature dropped.

No blankets or food? Even Jayanti treated me better than this when I was her prisoner in India.

The darkness deepened, so Jack had to feel his way along the cold stone wall to find his sleeping bench. He heard bagpipes as the resident garrison ended its day, thought of the other occasions he had listened to the music of the pipes, lay on the plank and tried to sleep.

When the door opened with a slight creak, Jack turned, hoping to see a soldier with something for him to eat.

"Captain Windrush?"

"I know that voice." With no light coming through the small window, Jack peered into the dark.

"Yes, sir. It's Riley."

Only Riley could open a dungeon door without any problems. "What the devil are you doing here, Riley?"

"Getting you out, sir." As Jack's eyes became accustomed to the gloom, he saw that Riley had somebody beside him. "If you want to come."

"I do want to come. Who's that with you, Riley?"

"It's me, sir, Logan."

Despite his situation, Jack smiled. If Riley was there, Logan was with him. The two had been inseparable since the early Crimea campaign, the debonair gentleman cracksman and the diminutive Glaswegian with the hair-trigger temper.

"How the devil did you get up here from Berwick?"

"Berwick sir? Oh, no. Three companies of the 113th are in the castle, sir."

Jack stored that information away. "Thanks, lads."

"Aye, time for that later. Come on, sir." Logan was not known for his diplomacy. "Before another of they guards come to bother us."

Jack could not imagine anybody giving Logan any bother. "Another?"

"Oh, aye. One tried to stop us." Pushing the door open, Logan dragged in the unconscious body of a British soldier. "This is Private Landers. He was one of they Birmingham sloggers."

Jack asked no more questions as Logan gagged Landers and tied his wrists and ankles.

"Come on, sir, and we'll get you out of here." Riley gently pushed Jack out of the door. "Just follow me and keep quiet, sir."

From the dungeons, Riley led them up a flight of stone stairs to the battlements of the Half Moon Battery, where a semi-circle of black cannon pointed over the Grassmarket. Even up here, Jack could hear the sound of merriment from the many publics below. "I hope you're still fit, sir."

"Fit enough." Jack stretched his legs.

Riley's teeth gleamed through the dark as he grinned. "Follow me then, sir. We're doing some scrambling."

Jack took a deep breath when he saw that somebody had fastened a rope around the trunnion of a cannon, snaked it through an embrasure and dropped it into the darkness outside the castle walls. Knowing that the castle stood atop a volcanic rock nearly 300 feet high, Jack paused. "Do you mean we have to go down there?"

"Yes, sir," Riley said. "Hold on tight to the rope and walk down the rock."

"Come on, you two!" Logan urged from the rear. "The sentries will be back soon."

"I'll go first, sir, you follow and then Donnie, I mean Logan." Riley slid away without another word.

Taking a deep breath, Jack took hold of the rope, turned his back and slid through the embrasure. The drop sucked at him, inviting him to release his grip and fall to the ground far below. He looked up, where Logan was a few feet above. "How far down is it?"

"Quite a way, sir." Riley answered. "I'll warn you when we near the ground."

Jack's feet scrabbled for purchase on the smooth rock as his hands burned with the friction of the rope. "Has this ever been done before?" he asked anxiously.

"Oh, yes, sir," Riley said. "Some of the French prisoners-of-war did this back in the Napoleonic War."

"That's good. Did they succeed?"

"Some of them did, sir."

"Some?"

Riley avoided the question. "Careful here, sir. There's a bit of an overhang."

Feeling very exposed, Jack clambered outward and then hung free for a moment, holding on only by the strength of his arms as he could not find purchase.

"Scramble down, sir," Riley advised. "Use your hands."

After a few terrifying moments when he dangled, feet flailing into nothingness, Jack felt rock under the soles of his boots and eased the pressure on his aching arms. He could hear noises from below as some late-night drunk reeled across the cobbled Grassmarket. The shout from above came as no surprise. "Here! You on the rope! Halt, or I'll fire!"

Jack hurried down the rope, expecting to hear the crack of a rifle. Instead, his feet thumped onto solid ground.

"Here we are, sir!" Strong hands grabbed hold of Jack's arms. "All safe and serene."

Private Coleman grinned into Jack's face. "Thorpey and I will take care of you now."

"What the devil is this?" Jack glanced upward, expecting a bullet to come flying towards him.

"It's all right, sir. They can't see us for the overhang," Riley replied calmly.

"You lads will get into serious trouble," Jack said.

"Only if they catch us, sir, and they won't do that," Thorpe said. "After dodging Burmese dacoits and Russian Cossacks, these Johnny Raws won't come close."

"Why are you doing this?"

"We're the 113th, sir," Coleman said. "We're the real, fighting 113th, not this pipe-clay and scarlet unit that Colonel Snodgrass wants." His grin was evident even in the dark. "What's to do anyway, sir?"

"What do you mean, Coleman?"

"I mean, what's to do, sir? You're no more a traitor than I'm a bluebottle." He inched closer. "Come on, now, sir! What's happening? We're with you if you need help."

"Thank you, Coleman." Jack wished he could tell his men what he was doing. He would feel far happier having men such as Coleman, Riley and Logan with him. "I can't say any more, and it would be better if you kept your opinion to yourself."

"Yes, sir."

At that moment, Logan landed. "There we are, sir. Let's get away. There's a sentry up there shouting something."

"How about the rope?"

"It's only a rope," Riley said. "They can't trace it. It's from the castle stores anyway."

"Thorpey and I are going back to barracks, sir," Coleman said. "We've brought this for you – civilian clothes and some food. I doubt they fed you in the chokey." He handed over a bundle of rough but clean clothing. Riley and Logie will get you safe."

"I don't know how to thank you," Jack lifted the clothes.

"You can thank us when you get back to the regiment." Coleman grinned. "You can let us off when the provost sergeant marches us before you for being drunk."

"That can't happen," Jack said. "You must have heard that the Army cashiered me. I'm a convicted traitor."

"Aye, we heard that nonsense," Riley said. "What are you up to, sir? You're no traitor."

"The court-martial said I was."

"Aye, right," Logan gave his considered opinion. "Are you taking us with you?"

"What?"

"You're on one of your intelligence missions," Logan said.

Jack sighed. If his men guessed he was on a mission, the Fenians might do the same.

"We're here if you need us, sir." Riley said. "Now let's get you somewhere safe. I know a man who can smuggle you anywhere."

"Thank you, Riley." Jack heard voices from above. "I have to get to Leith Walk."

"What for?" Thorpe asked. "We know better places, sir."

"I'm sure you do, Thorpe, but it's Leith Walk, I'm afraid."

"Follow me, sir," Riley said.

Riley led them at a run, through Princes Street Gardens and into Leith Street that led into Leith Walk, the broad road that stretched from Edinburgh to the port of Leith. "It's getting near morning, sir, the town will be waking soon."

"I'll leave you here, lads," Jack said. "I can't thank you enough."

Riley passed over a small pocketbook. "This might help."

Jack had not thought about money. "Thank you, Riley. Thank you, Logan."

Riley nodded. "We miss the old days, sir. Good luck."

Jack held out his hand. He knew that officers did not shake hands with rankers, but he considered Riley as a friend.

Riley hesitated before responding. "Thank you, sir."

"You too, Logan," Jack said. Logan's fingers felt like iron bars.

"You two get back to barracks." Jack turned and walked away. He might meet them again some time in his career, and he might not. Military life was a mixture of intense experiences and sudden departures. Now he had a mission to fulfil, somehow.

CHAPTER THIRTEEN

Leith, November 1867

Edinburgh's port of Leith was busy, with wagons and pedestrians jamming the road from the warehouses to the docks. Jack stepped aside from the early-morning omnibus that carried workers from Edinburgh and searched for the Shamrock, the public house named by Riordan. Moving into a dark corner, Jack opened the heavy pocketbook that Riley had given him. A host of gold sovereigns clinked among silver and copper coins, with a small folded piece of paper.

Thinking it was a note from Riley, Jack unfolded the paper, then shook his head and smiled as he saw what the paper was. It was a bill from a tailor in Edinburgh to Colonel Snodgrass. Riley had stolen the colonel's pocketbook and handed it to Jack.

Well done, Riley, Jack thought. *You send me to jail, Colonel, and I'll pick your pocket.* "You're some man, Riley," Jack said to himself. He extracted a threepenny bit and bought a *Caledonian Mercury* newspaper. Leafing through the pages, he found the paragraph he sought and tucked the paper under his arm.

The Shamrock was a public house with a couple of rooms above the bar, tucked away off the Shore where the Water of Leith ran into the Firth of Forth. Behind the bar, a large green shamrock decorated the mirror that stretched the full width of one wall, with an array of bottles in front. In one corner, a one-legged man in a faded scarlet tunic played Irish tunes on a tin whistle. In another, Private Riordan sat with his legs stretched out before him, nursing a nearly-empty glass of beer.

"Riordan," Jack greeted him, sliding in beside him.

"Captain Windrush." Riordan did not look surprised to see him.

"No longer captain, it's just plain Jack Windrush now," Jack threw down his copy of the *Caledonian Mercury.*

"What?" Riordan looked up, his eyes narrow with suspicion.

"I'm ruined, Riordan, cashiered. I'm out of the regiment, out of the army and on the run." Jack pointed to the second column on the front page of the *Caledonian*

Mercury. "Read that! Captain Jack Windrush of the 113th cashiered for Fenian sympathies and sent to prison."

"Why?" Riordan only glanced at the paper. Jack wondered if he could read.

"Because I did not bring you back to jail," Jack said. "Or that's the excuse Colonel Snodgrass used." He slumped in the seat beside Riordan. "The real reason was that I married a Eurasian woman."

"Tough luck, my friend."

"Bastards," Jack spat as he caught the barman's eye to order a pint of Leith ale. "Dirty bastards."

"What are you going to do, Captain?"

Jack took a deep draught of the ale. "I'm going to get my own back, Riordan. I want my revenge on the bastards."

"You want revenge on the entire British Army?" Riordan asked as he sipped at the dregs of his beer. "That's a tall order, Captain."

"Is it? I saw the Mutiny in India, remember. I know how to hurt them. I know the weaknesses of the Empire. I'm joining you, Riordan."

"You're not Irish."

"It's not just the Irish who have cause to despise the Empire."

Riordan raised his eyebrows. "The famous Fighting Jack Windrush, the saviour of the Empire, hero of Lucknow, joining the Fenians! Now there's something." He placed his glass carefully on the much-scarred table-top. "I don't believe you."

Banging his glass beside that of Riordan, Jack glowered around the room. He had heard that some of the pubs in Leith could be mildly dangerous and wondered if it would help his cause to start a fight in here. Looking at some of the men, brawny dockers, seamen from the Baltic and Mediterranean trades and collier hands who did not fear man, God or the devil, he decided that it was best to keep quiet. An officer with a reputation for success was one thing, a brawler who came out second best in a Scottish pub something else. "Let's find our ship, Riordan."

"She's been delayed," Riordan said. "There was some trouble stowing the cargo."

"She's sailing on the first tide tomorrow." Jack pointed to an advertisement in the newspaper. "Come on."

Yorktown was a long, lean, three-masted barque over which the United States flag hung in quiet pride. Captain Martin glowered at Jack and Riordan from under a slanted nautical cap.

"Are you on the run from the law?"

It was not a question Jack had expected. "I am not," he lied.

"You may not be, but he," Martin nodded to the half-shaven and unkempt Riordan, "undoubtedly is. Five sovereigns passage money for you, 10 for the Fenian."

"What makes you think I'm a Fenian?" Riordan asked.

"You've got British soldier written all over you," Martin said, "an Irish accent and the haunted expression of a fugitive on your face. Ten sovereigns."

"I don't have that much," Riordan said. "I'll work my passage."

Jack shook his head. "You drive a hard bargain, Captain Martin." He fished for Colonel Snodgrass's pocketbook. "Here are eight golden boys." He dropped the coins on the captain's desk and slammed his hand on top. "I'll give you the other seven when we arrive safely in Boston."

"I want 15 in advance."

"In that case, Captain, we shall bid you farewell. There are other ships departing from Glasgow, Greenock and Liverpool."

Captain Martin growled, with his attention on the gold that Jack's hand covered. "If either of you gives me any trouble I'll drop you both overboard."

"Agreed, Captain," Jack said. "Where do we bunk?"

"In the orlop," Malvern said, sweeping the sovereigns into his hand. "We set sail on the next tide."

The orlop was the lowest deck of the ship, a dark place of foul smells and scurrying rats. The cabin they shared had barely enough headroom for a child to stand upright and a stench so thick Jack thought he could cut it into chunks.

"Why are you helping me?" Riordan asked as they grew accustomed to the dark.

"We're helping each other," Jack said. "You know where to go once we arrive in the USA."

Riordan snorted. "I don't know as much as you think I do."

"You know more than me, and that's something." Jack forced a grin. "Anyway, I'll need you to vouch for me. The Fenians might not believe I want to join them."

Riordan swore. "They'll want anybody with an insight into the British Army," he said.

"We'll see." Jack looked up as he heard a thunder of feet on the deck above. "It seems that we're only just in time. We seem to be on the move."

Within a few moments, a tug eased *Yorktown* into the Firth of Forth, the great body of the sea on which Leith sat.

"Now we endure the sea," Jack said.

"Aye." Riordan lay back on the narrow bunk. "Let's hope it's a fast passage." He gave a sour grin. "This will be harder for you than for me, Captain. Soldiers are used to bad conditions in barracks, while officers live off the fat of the land."

"Ex-officers don't." Jack tried to fit his nearly-six-foot frame on to the five-foot-six plank bunk. He sighed. He was a long way from Durrants Hotel now, let alone Netherhills House.

However mercenary Captain Martin might have been, he was a superb seaman, pushing *Yorktown* around the north of Scotland, through the treacherous Pentland Firth and across the Atlantic Ocean in 17 days flat. Jack endured the crossing as he had endured so much in his military career, ignoring the discomfort as he tried to befriend Riordan and extract as much information from him as he could.

"So what made you join the Fenians, Riordan?" They stood at the rail with *Yorktown* heeled over in the wind and the sails bellied out full.

Riordan said nothing for a while as spray lashed at them. When he faced Jack, his eyes were bitter. "I lost three of my family in the famine, Captain. I saw my sister waste away to a human skeleton, and I scratched a hole in the ground to bury her. My mother died of fever and my father of grief." He held Jack's gaze. "During that time, what did the British authorities do to help?" Riordan said the word British as if it were a curse. "They did nothing and less than nothing. They let us die by the thousand, and did nothing."

Jack wondered how he would feel if Mary and David were starving. "It must have been terrible," he said.

"Aye," Riordan said. "It must have been terrible." He turned to face the sea again. "I didn't join the army through any love for Queen Victoria and her minions.

I joined to put food in my belly. Now we must ensure that nothing of the sort happens again in Ireland."

Jack gave Riordan a few moments to think before he spoke. "Do you think an Irish Republic could manage that?"

"It could not do any worse," Riordan said. "I saw human skeletons walking by the hundred, begging for food; I saw ditches crammed with the dead. I saw things worse than any nightmare." He stopped again, took a deep breath and continued. "Unless you are Irish, you will never understand how I feel. Pray to your God that you never find out."

Jack nodded. "I see."

"No you don't," Riordan said. "Now listen, Windrush, I neither like you nor trust you. I am going along with you because I have to." He spat into the sea. "Once I've taken you to the Fenians, you're on your own."

"That suits me," Jack said. *It seems that Smith has set me an impossible task. Gaining the trust of the Fenians may be a lot harder than he imagined.*

* * *

"Boston," Martin said curtly. "You owe me, mister."

"Seven sovereigns, Captain." Jack handed over the gold as soon as they docked.

Martin counted the coins, biting each one to test their purity. "Fenians, eh?" He shook his head. "You're a pair of bloody fools. Sweeny has you in the palm of his hand."

"Jack noted the name. "It's Sweeny we're going to meet," he said casually.

Captain Martin grunted. "He killed a man in a duel, don't forget, and by foul play, if I recall." He shrugged. "I don't care if you're meeting Sweeny, John O'Neill or the good Lord himself. You've paid your passage, now get off my ship."

"We're off," Jack said. Armed with the bonus of two names, he led Riordan from *Yorktown* to the packed streets of Boston. "Do you know where to find this Sweeny fellow?"

Riordan took a deep breath before he replied. "I have an address." He looked around the busy streets. "So this is what freedom tastes like," He said. "Being English, you don't know what it's like having another nation, people with a different religion and philosophy of life, being in charge of you."

About to say that the English were not all bad, Jack remembered the part he was now playing. "I don't think I realised how hard it was until I married Mary."

"Aye, you'll see things from a different point of view now." Riordan pushed on, trying to hide the tears in his eyes. "We'll have something to eat and then find Sweeny." He glanced at Jack. "You'd better be genuine, for what I've heard about the general, he'll shoot you like a dog without any compunction at all."

"Oh, I'm genuine," Jack said. "I've got a score to settle, particularly with Colonel Lancelot bloody Snodgrass." *That last part*, he told himself, *was genuine.*

* * *

General Thomas Sweeny retained traces of the Irish accent he had brought with him from Cork more than 30 years before. Heavily bearded and with receding hair, he glared at Jack and banged his one remaining fist on the table that lay between them.

He had lost his right arm at the Battle of Churubusco during the United States War with Mexico, a fact that had not impeded his career or his fighting ability through the civil war that had fractured the United States of America.

"You're not an Irishman," General Sweeny said. "How can I trust you?"

"Nor are you Irish." Jack had made some discreet enquiries about Sweeny as soon as he heard the name. "You emigrated from Ireland in 1833. You've been in the United States Army since 1846 and have fought in three separate wars."

Sweeny grunted, glaring at Jack through narrow eyes. "How can I trust you?" Sweeny repeated. "How do I know you are who you say you are?"

Taking the now sadly-battered *Caledonian Mercury* from inside his coat, Jack passed it over. "That's me," he said. "Former Captain Jack Windrush, married to a Eurasian woman and a man who helped a known Fenian escape justice. The British Army cashiered me, sir, and tried to throw me in prison. I know nothing except soldiering."

"So you will turn against the army for whom you have fought in India."

"In India, Russia and Burma," Jack confirmed. "The army for whom I have collected half a dozen wounds and who rewarded me by passing me over for promotion in favour of lesser men with better connections."

"You're a bitter man," Sweeny said.

"You're damned right I'm bitter," Jack said.

"He helped me, sir." Riordan had been a silent observer, standing at the back of Jack. "He helped me escape from military jail and paid for my passage from Leith to Boston."

"There's no doubt that you're Irish at least, Riordan," Sweeny said. "You're a trained British soldier, then."

"Yes, sir." Riordan smartly came to attention. "I'm a Cork man, same as yourself and I fought through the Lucknow campaign in India."

"And you've taken the Fenian oath?" Sweeny's eyes were friendly above high cheekbones as he spoke to Riordan.

"Yes, sir."

"Have you taken the oath, Ex-Captain Windrush?"

"Not yet." Jack had never heard of the Fenian oath.

"You will," Sweeny said, "and on your honour as a gentleman, I'll expect you to keep it or I'll blow your brains out."

Honour as a gentleman? Gentlemen with honour do not work for people such as Mr Smith. "My honour is my affair."

"Swear the oath now," Sweeny said, "in front of witnesses." He rang the small brass bell that stood on the table in front of him, and two burly bearded men entered the room. Both carried long revolvers thrust through their belts and stepped behind Jack.

"This gentleman is Captain Jack Windrush, late of the British army," Sweeny said. "He is about to swear his loyalty to the Fenian cause."

The men said nothing. One touched his pistol butt and smiled slowly.

Reaching into the drawer of his desk, Sweeny produced a piece of stiff card and a Bible.

"Take the Bible in your left hand," Sweeny ordered, "and raise your right hand."

Jack did as Sweeny ordered. *An oath made under duress is meaningless*, he told himself, *and having two armed men behind me is undoubtedly duress.*

"Now repeat after me." Sweeny read the words on the card: "In the presence of Almighty God, I do solemnly swear allegiance to an Irish republic now virtually established, and take arms when called upon in its defence and integrity, and I also swear implicit obedience to my superior officers. I take this oath in the spirit of a soldier of liberty, so help me God."

Jack repeated the words, slowly and carefully, with one eye on Sweeny, who nodded encouragement.

"Good." Sweeny seemed to accept Jack's word. "You are now a member of the Fenian Brotherhood. We have tens of thousands of dedicated Fenians ready to fight the British in Canada, or sail over to Ireland to free the country from Britain, but we have relatively few officers with military experience."

Jack nodded. "I have some of that."

"I will send you to an active unit where you will do the most good for our cause." Sweeny held out his left hand. "Welcome to the Fenian Brotherhood, Captain Windrush."

Jack shook his hand.

"I'll appoint Dermot and Cormac here to guide you," Sweeny said. "They'll make sure you don't get lost. Mr Riordan, you can tag along, too. I'm going to put you to work right away, Captain Windrush."

"What am I doing?" Jack asked.

"Training men," Sweeny said. "Ready for the attack on England. In the meantime, I'll spread the news that one of England's finest young officers has joined us." His smile nearly reached his eyes. "It furnishes further proof that the British Empire is crumbling under the strain of keeping its subject peoples down."

Dermot and Cormac closed on either side of Jack and escorted him out of the room.

"Stay with us," Dermot growled. "We don't want you to get lost."

When Cormac gave a high-pitched laugh, Jack knew that Sweeny had set these two bruisers to watch him. The general did not trust him.

* * *

The carriage was waiting outside, dark painted with a tall driver and a burly guard riding shotgun at his side. Dermot, the taller of the escorts, opened the door for Cormac to push Jack inside.

"Settle back, Captain," Dermot said. "We're due for a long ride."

"Where are we going?"

"You're a terrible man for questions." Despite his Irish name, Dermot's accent was North American.

"I am a terrible man," Jack agreed. "Where are you taking me?"

"Somewhere you can be safe," Dermot replied, "and somewhere you will stay while we check out your story."

Shrugging, Jack leaned back into the leather seats. When he tried to flick back the curtains that covered the windows, Cormac gripped his wrist.

"You'll sit quiet," Cormac pressed the muzzle of a Colt Army model 44 revolver against Jack's chest, "or you'll be the late Captain Windrush, if that's your real name."

The carriage moved off, smoothly at first as it negotiated the streets of Boston, with the driver taking the corners with skill. Knowing there was no help for it, Jack leaned back and closed his eyes. Rest was precious because a tired man could not function efficiently. There was no point in trying to trace his journey by sound alone, as he did not know the geography of the area. So he might as well look relaxed and ignore his present company.

After a while, the street noises faded and the movement of the coach became more violent, so Jack guessed they were out of Boston and into the countryside. They stopped once to change horses, but with Cormac's Colt at his breast, Jack did not even try to look outside. Remembering the patience of the Pashtun tribes on the North-West Frontier of India, he waited, wondered what would happen and trusted to luck.

"You're a cool one," Dermot commented as they changed horses again.

"Cool?" Jack echoed. "It's quite comfortable in here."

"You've hardly said a word for the past five hours."

"I can talk if you wish," Jack said. "What part of the States are you from?"

"No questions," Dermot said, and Jack lapsed back into silence again.

They spent the night in the coach, with Dermot and Cormac taking turns to watch Jack. He slept as best he could, knowing that they would grow progressively more tired as the journey progressed. "How far are we going?" Jack asked.

"No questions," Dermot said.

After three days and nights and frequent changes of horses, the coach pulled up.

"Here we are." Dermot sounded quite jocular. "Journey's end."

After so long confined in the coach, Jack relished the freedom to stretch his legs. He was so cramped, he nearly fell as he stepped outside and looked about him. Dawn was glorious, with light snow falling on broad-leafed woodland around a mansion house as grand as any gentleman's abode in England.

"In you go," Dermot pushed Jack in the back. "Colonel O'Mahony will see you now."

"That's very kind of the colonel," Jack said.

"This way." Cormac thrust his Colt into Jack's back.

"I'm a volunteer, remember," Jack said. "I want to be here. You don't need the pistol."

"In here. Colonel O'Mahony is waiting."

O'Mahony stood at the window of a luxuriously furnished room, looking outside with his back to Jack.

"Come in, Captain Windrush," O'Mahony invited. He spun around quickly. A stern-eyed, high-cheekboned Limerick man, he had taken part in the 1848 Rising against British rule in Ireland and had seen much action during the US Civil War. "I am aware of your exploits in the Crimea."

Jack nodded. "I am also aware of yours, Colonel." He studied this man who seemed to have dedicated himself to removing Britain from Ireland. He should think of him as an enemy, but instead saw only a proud man involved in a near-hopeless struggle.

"However," O'Mahony said, "I am not sure that you are the real Captain Windrush." He stepped towards Jack, halting six feet away as he ran his gaze from the top of Jack's head to his boots and back. "You fit the description all right, but the Fighting Jack Windrush I have heard of would never betray his country. You may be an agent of the British government. That's why we brought you here, Captain, so we could have you positively identified."

"Well, here I am," Jack said. "Positively identify me."

"Not by me," O'Mahony said. "I have somebody who knows you personally." His smile had all the charm that Jack associated with Ireland. Lifting a small brass bell from the desk, he rang it, still holding Jack's gaze.

Who knows me personally? Jack did not have long to wonder as the door opened.

"Hello, Jack." Helen stood there, smiling at him.

CHAPTER FOURTEEN

United States, November 1865

"Helen?" Jack stared at her in some confusion. "What the devil are you doing here?"

"I could ask you the same." Helen was smiling. "Last I heard you were in Ireland."

"It's a long story," Jack said, shaking his head.

"Is this gentleman Captain Jack Windrush?" O'Mahony asked.

"This is Captain Jack Windrush," Helen replied seriously. "I have known him for many years."

Opening the top drawer of his desk, O'Mahony pulled out a bundle of newspapers. "I have read the reports of your court-martial in half a dozen British newspapers," he said. "You helped a Fenian escape."

"That would be Corporal Riordan," Jack said.

"You got rather a harsh sentence for that act."

"Yes," Jack agreed. "I have no great love for the British army."

O'Mahony nodded. "I can appreciate your sentiment. Can you commit to our cause?"

"I have no Irish blood," Jack said, "but I can commit to anything that damages the British Army."

O'Mahony grunted. "Would that include fighting against them?"

Jack nodded. "I have more than one score to settle with Colonel Snodgrass of the 113th Foot," he said, "and with the Royal Malverns."

O'Mahony glanced at the top newspaper. "It was Colonel Snodgrass who sentenced you to penal servitude, I see. Well, Windrush, you won't be the only renegade Englishman in our ranks. As soon as you find out about the historic Fenians, I'll set you to training men."

Helen remained in the room, smiling, with lamplight reflecting from the triangular Tartar amulet around her neck as Dermot and Cormac escorted Jack from the room.

Helen is the traitor. Dear God in Heaven, why?

* * *

The Fenians stood in ordered ranks before him, some wearing the worn remnants of military uniforms, both Federal and Confederate, others in civilian clothes. Some carried rifles, others old shotguns or long-barrelled muskets of ancient vintage, while many held staffs, swords or nothing at all.

"Right lads," Jack began, addressing them as if they were recruits for the British army. "I am here to give you the skills to help free Ireland from oppression."

They cheered at that, with shouts of, "Long live the Irish Republic," and, "Hooray for the Fenian Brotherhood."

Jack smiled. Without an experienced British NCO to keep them quiet, he allowed them their head for a few moments and then began to teach the rudiments of drill. The veterans followed without difficulty, the others tried their best, and after a few days, Jack had them marching in step and obeying simple commands.

"They're good material," he said to O'Mahony. "They'd fit into any line regiment in the British Army."

From time to time, Jack had seen Helen watching from the balcony outside her window, for his makeshift parade ground was in the grounds of the house. Twice she had lifted her hand to wave to him, and once he had waved back. On a third occasion, Jack saw a tall man standing beside her, with his arm around her shoulders.

What the devil are you doing here, Helen, and who is that fellow? Is he the same man who was recruiting Fenians in Britain?

Despite himself, Jack focused on the tall man, noting the neat whiskers on an otherwise clean-shaven face, and the familiar way he placed his hands on Helen's shoulders. *Riordan mentioned the man who recruited him was tall with such whiskers,* Jack mused. *Now I have to find out why Helen is involved in all this nonsense.*

When his military duties permitted, Jack searched for Helen in the rambling house. As the days passed, Dermot and Cormac relaxed their vigilance, even answering some of Jack's questions.

"Where are we?" Jack asked casually.

"Don't you know?" Cormac responded with a smile. "The 23rd state, Limey. You're in Maine."

Jack nodded his thanks. That helped, although he knew that Maine was larger than Wales. "Which part?"

"The North-West," Cormac said. "Don't worry, the Limeys can't get you here, even although we're not far from New Brunswick in British North America."

"Thank you," Jack forced a smile. "I do have a fear that one night a British raiding party will kick down the door and drag me back over the border."

Both Cormac and Dermot laughed at the idea. "I hope they try," Dermot said. "That would bring war between the United States and Great Britain, and then an Irish Republic would be a whole lot closer."

"And I'd probably be hanged," Jack said, which made Cormac laugh.

"It's worth the price to free Ireland," Dermot said gravely.

With the ice broken, Jack found his guards more relaxed, and a few nights later, he left his comfortable quarters to wander around the house.

Rather than hide in corners, Jack strode along the corridor, whistling to show he had nothing to hide. As he passed the door to the barracks, a snatch of a song came to him.

*"We've won many victories
Along with the boys in blue,
Now we'll conquer Canada because there's
Nothing left to do."*

Jack paused. Conquering Canada might not be as easy as the Fenians supposed, but with a long, virtually undefended border with the United States, Canada was undoubtedly vulnerable to raids. That was another snippet of information to pass to Smith if he only knew how.

The laugh took him by surprise. He recognised Helen's voice and climbed up a flight of stairs, resting his hand on the walnut balcony and taking the steps two at a time. The stairs led to a long corridor, deeply carpeted, and brilliantly lit with a dozen oil lamps, hung with portraits of people he did not recognise.

As Jack stood at one end of the corridor, he saw the tall man who had been with Helen. Jack lifted a hand in acknowledgement, only for the man to turn away.

Are you the recruiter? Jack strode forward, his feet sinking into the carpet. Acting on a hunch, he approached the door that the tall man had left and heard soft singing from inside the room.

*"Always victorious
Glorious and more glorious,
We followed Marlborough through battle and war
We're the Royal Malverns, the heroes of Malplaquet."*

The singer mispronounced the last word, tried it again and swore softly. "Oh, damn," she said. "I never get that right."

"Neither you do, Helen," Jack said, and tapped on the door.

"Who is it?" Helen asked.

"It's Jack Windrush," Jack said.

"Jack!" The door opened a crack, and then Helen threw it wide. "Come in, and hurry!"

Sliding inside, Jack waited until Helen closed the door. "What's to do, Helen?"

"I could ask you the same!" Helen looked five years younger than she had in England. Her eyes were as bright as they had been in the Crimea and the spring was back in her step.

"The army cashiered me," Jack said. "You, however, suffered no such fate. Does William know you are here?"

"Certainly not!" Helen snapped and smiled. "Does Mary know you are here?"

"No." Jack shook his head.

"Good." Helen put her back to the door. "Then we are free, are we not?"

The conversation was not going as Jack would have wished. "We are free to talk," he said. "I was surprised to see you here, Helen."

"I was surprised to hear you were coming. Is it true about the court-martial?"

Jack nodded. "When Colonel Snodgrass added 20 years' penal servitude, I thought it best not to remain in Britain."

Helen's eyes widened, then narrowed thoughtfully. "Twenty years! That's a bit much! How about Mary?"

Jack forced a casual shrug. "I'll bring her over by and by. What are you doing here? Who was that man who left your room?"

"Isn't he the handsome one?" Helen's eyes were bright with mischief. "He's the reason I left William."

With her passionate nature, Jack would expect Helen to have illicit encounters with other men, but he was surprised she had taken such a drastic step. "You've left William?"

"Yes," Helen confirmed. "He was chasing the servant girls and had no time to show me any affection. I told you I was bored at Wychwood Manor."

"You did say that," Jack agreed. "But why join the Fenians?"

"Why not? My mother was Irish and anyway," Helen smiled again, "I met Walter."

"The tall fellow with the side-whiskers?"

"That's the man. I met him in Hereford the day after you told me you only wanted to be friends." Helen looked Jack up and down. "He's exciting, Jack. He's got the same sort of edge that you have, except he's not married."

"I don't have an edge," Jack argued.

"You have something indefinable." Helen was no longer smiling. "You attract women, Jack."

"I haven't noticed."

"I know, and that's also attractive," Helen said.

"Are you helping the Fenians? I didn't know your mother was Irish." Jack remembered Helen's mother as a very redoubtable lady who had survived the tribulations of the Crimea without a complaint. If anybody wished an example of Irish grit, they need look no further.

"She's from Donegal," Helen said.

"Are you a Fenian?"

Helen shook her head. "Not a bit of it."

"You're not a Fenian, yet you inveigled information from young Snodgrass in Ireland and passed it on to the Fenians." With Helen, it was best to be direct.

Helen's attempt at innocence was unsuccessful. "He was the sweetest of boys. What a contrast after William." She touched Jack's arm. "Now don't look so jealous, Jack; you said you don't want me. Compared to my husband, young Peter Snodgrass is a true gentleman."

"Your actions got him into trouble," Jack said softly.

"My actions? I only asked him what was happening with his regiment. It was hardly stealing the crown jewels or blowing up the houses of parliament."

"To whom did you pass on the information?"

"A very handsome Irishman who treats me like a princess," Helen said. "The fellow you saw leave my room a moment ago." Her smile was intended to taunt Jack.

"That would be Walter. Does he have a surname?"

"Carmichael," Helen's smile broadened. "He is Walter Carmichael."

Jack nodded. "I'm a bit confused."

Helen hesitated. "Walter's different from anybody I've met before. I enjoy the excitement of being near him." She edged closer until her hip pressed against Jack's. "I still prefer you, though."

"So you claim," Jack said. "One man at a time should suffice, Helen."

"Why?" Helen's smile was as innocent as the serpent in Eden as her hand strayed on to Jack's leg.

"I'm still married." Jack did not remove Helen's hand. He knew me might need her help later.

"Mary's in England," Helen said. "I'm here now. Unless you tell her, she will never know." Her hand moved slightly higher up his thigh.

The knock at the door saved Jack.

"Helen, it's me, Walter."

Jack stepped to the centre of the room. "Let Walter in, Helen. I wish to meet my rival for your affections." For some reason, he grinned as a surge of excitement ran through him. Rather than looking ashamed or at least apprehensive, Helen met his smile.

"This should be interesting," Helen murmured. "Come in, Walter," she called.

Tall and elegant, Walter Carmichael strode in and hesitated when he saw Jack standing in the middle of the room.

"Good evening, Carmichael," Jack said evenly. "I am Jack Windrush." He held out his hand.

"Good evening." Carmichael took Jack's hand. "Walter Carmichael." His eyes were light blue and more wary than Jack had expected.

"You know Mrs Helen Windrush of course," Jack said.

"Mrs Windrush?" Carmichael dropped Jack's hand and reached inside his jacket. "Are you..?"

"No, I'm neither Helen's husband nor her brother," Jack said. "You won't need that pistol you're reaching for."

Carmichael dropped his hand. "Who are you then? Is Windrush a common name in England?"

"I've known Mrs Windrush for years." Jack avoided the question. "Is Carmichael a common name in Ireland?" He noticed that Carmichael's hand was resting on his belt, still close to the bulge inside his jacket.

"Common enough."

Jack could see Carmichael's eyes move from him to Helen and back. "Was there some reason you wished to see my sister-in-law?" he enquired mildly.

"Your sister-in-law?" Carmichael echoed.

"Jack!" Helen slapped his arm. "Stop teasing the poor man! You've got Walter so confused he doesn't know if it's Monday or Christmas." Taking hold of Jack's arm, she pushed him towards the door. "Now thank you for visiting, and it's time to go away. Walter and I have things to discuss."

"I'm leaving," Jack said. "It was a pleasure to meet you, Carmichael, however briefly. I can sense that Helen wants to be alone with you." He opened the door and stepped outside, lingering in the corridor to hear what was said.

"Is he genuinely your brother-in-law?" Carmichael asked.

"He is. When I married his half-brother, Jack married a half-breed Indian woman." Jack knew that Helen was forcing her mocking laughter.

"I don't trust him," Carmichael said. "What did you tell him about me?"

"I told him you introduced me to the Fenians," Helen said. "Now come here and stop wasting time."

When the silence extended for five minutes, broken only by the odd giggle, Jack realised that he would learn nothing useful so, feeling like a Peeping Tom, he walked away, trying to assess all that he had learned.

Helen had left William to be with this Walter Carmichael fellow. Given his last conversation with Helen at Netherhills, Jack was not surprised, for Helen was given to impulsive actions and would follow whatever whim entered her head at the time. More importantly, Jack knew there was something not right with Carmichael. Riordan and Regan both had doubts about his nationality, and now Carmichael had taken Helen under his wing. But why? Jack had no illusions that a recruiter for the Fenians would fall under Helen's charms, evident though they were. The sort of man who put his life at risk every day would be too dedicated to his cause, whatever it might be. Carmichael had another reason for befriending Helen apart from her femininity; presumably to use her to dredge information from young dupes such as Ensign Snodgrass.

Leaving the house, Jack walked around the nighttime grounds with his hands behind his back and his head down. If Carmichael was the foreign recruiter for the Fenians in England, why was he now in the United States and for whom was he working? Jack paused. After the suffering in Ireland, Carmichael might even have genuine sympathy for the Irish cause.

Jack looked up as somebody emerged from the house carrying a lantern, no doubt to see who was perambulating the grounds. He waited for the man to approach. He had succeeded in infiltrating the Fenians but Helen added a complication to his task. Now he had to contact Smith to inform him what was happening. To do that, he needed more freedom, and that meant winning the trust of these people.

"Hey!" The man with the lantern approached. "Who are you?"

"It's me, Cormac." Jack did not attempt to hide. "Jack Windrush. I think we'll have to work on making this place more secure. I've been wandering around for 15 minutes without once being challenged."

* * *

After that evening, Jack altered his strategy. Rather than merely drilling the men, he began to train them properly, although never to quite the same standard he had in the 113th. As winter drew in, the weather deteriorated and the campaigning season closed, Jack knew that there would be no invasion of Canada or anywhere else until the spring.

"You're driving them hard," O'Mahony said as Jack drilled the men on a day of driving snow.

"We fought in worse conditions in Crimea," Jack said. "If these lads have to face the British Army, they'll need to be good."

O'Mahony gave a sad smile. "Many are veterans of the war here. They're aware of the reality of combat."

"Aye, I know that," Jack said. "But facing ill-equipped and half-starved Confederates is one thing. Fighting trained and experienced British infantry is something else."

"Are the British good?" O'Mahony asked seriously.

Jack considered the question. "Trained British infantry is as good as any in the world," he said. "When well-led, I'd say they were the best," he smiled, "but there again, I would, wouldn't I?"

"What are you doing today?" O'Mahony asked.

"Rifle drill." Jack held up the Springfield rifle. "This is a decent weapon; it's not as good as our Enfield, but not bad."

"We're getting better weapons," O'Mahony said. "There's a shipment of Spencer repeaters coming tomorrow."

Jack nodded. "I've read about them."

"Read more. You'll be training the men in their use." Nearly smiling, O'Mahony drifted away, humming a song that Jack did not recognise.

The Spencer impressed Jack. "This is a seven-shot, .52 Calibre Spencer repeater," he said, holding it up for his men to see. "There are two models, carbine and rifle. I will train you in both, with the lighter, younger men as light infantry or skirmishers with the carbines and the older men using the rifles."

The Fenians nodded, accepting his word. Jack knew that they trusted him.

"The rifle is 47 inches long, with a weight of 10 pounds, and uses a rim-fire brass cartridge. You'll like that." Jack waited for the nervous laugh. "The carbine is shorter, at 39 inches, and nearly two pounds lighter so better for skirmishing and light infantry work. You load both through the butt," Jack continued, demonstrating, "which is far faster and easier than ramming balls down the muzzle."

The veterans nodded, each man reliving memories of frantically reloading a rifle under fire. The recruits tried to look knowledgeable.

"One last thing; we still have to cock the hammer before every shot." Jack grinned. "I know that sounds like hard work, but I'm sure you will manage it." He expected the resulting laugh and tried to prevent himself from liking these men. They were the enemy, Fenians who could soon be facing British soldiers, yet when he looked at them, he only saw Irishmen very similar to those he knew in the British Army.

Splitting his men into line infantry and skirmishers, Jack made them march, trained the recruits and wondered if his actions made him a traitor. He also wondered how these men would stand against the 113th Foot. The Spencer repeater gave them an advantage in firepower, and some of the Fenians who had grown up in rural areas were excellent skirmishers with a natural eye for cover.

"These lads could give anybody a run for their money," Jack reported to O'Mahony.

"Good." O'Mahony nodded. "Even your famous Guards?"

Jack smiled. "Perhaps. I haven't seen them march, though," he continued. "Oh, they can walk around the grounds of this house, but so could a group of schoolboys. Soldiers need to march to get anywhere." He grinned. "I think the French Foreign Legion has a motto: 'March or Die'."

"How far do you want to take them?"

"Five miles the first time, 10 miles the next and then increase the distance."

O'Mahony contemplated Jack before coming to a decision. "You'll need a map, then, or you'll get lost."

"Where are we?" Jack tried to sound casual. "I know we're somewhere in Maine."

"That's where we are," O'Mahony said with a grin. "We're in Presque House, only a long spit from the border with New Brunswick, British-owned territory."

Jack nodded. "Handy for an invasion."

"That's the idea," O'Mahony said. "I'll find you a map."

They were about five miles from the New Brunswick border, with the house eight miles from the nearest town of Baring. Jack studied the map, making a circular route for his men to march, taking them as close as possible to British territory. He wondered if he should break away and run for the border to report all he had discovered so far.

No, he decided. Not yet. He had to find out more about Carmichael and, God help him, try to get Helen away. He still felt something for that woman, despite their uneasy history. He would leave when he had more specific information about O'Mahony's plans.

Smith's words came to him. *"If you find him, I want you to kill him."*

Jack paused for a second. Could he assassinate Carmichael? He shivered at the thought. What would Mary think of him? He could not tell her. How would Helen react if he murdered her lover?

Jack shook his head. Helen would possibly believe he had killed Carmichael out of jealousy. She might even be thrilled. Shaking away what was a disturbing thought, Jack returned to training his men.

"Right, you scoundrels! Let's see how well you can march. We can't fight unless we can reach the Limeys; let's cock a snook at the British Empire!"

The men laughed, with some making high-spirited comments, as Jack would expect from an Irish regiment.

As he left the grounds of the house, he was aware of two men following his unit and grinned. That would be Cormac and Dermot, his guard dogs. That was fine. They were large, muscular men, but now he would see how fit they were. Glancing at the house, Jack saw Helen watching from her window, with Carmichael hovering behind her.

Yes, Carmichael, you watch real men while you canoodle with shapely women. Jack felt a surge of dislike. He glanced over his command. *I much prefer these Fenians – they may be enemies of the Crown, but they are honest. More honest than me, by heavens.*

"Come on, lads!" Suddenly angry, Jack led his men into the thick forest that surrounded the house, forcing them to march through the snow. "Keep up with me."

As always, the cold weather made the old Burmese wound in Jack's thigh ache, but he enjoyed the freedom of being away from the house. After a couple of miles, he halted the men in a clearing and split them in two, pushing the skirmishers on to the flanks.

"I want to see how good you are," Jack was aware of Cormac and Dermot hovering 100 yards behind, trying to hide in the trees. "Load," he ordered, suddenly reckless. "Live bullets, lads!" He raised his voice. "British patrol has come behind us! Three rounds rapid-fire!"

Jack watched as the Fenians turned and fired, with the loading ragged but much faster than with single-shot rifles. Although he did not expect them to hit Cormac or Dermot, he hoped the demonstration taught his watchers to keep their distance.

"Well done! I want more precision next time, though. We'll need more training shooting at marks."

After the shooting display, Jack led his men on a fast march through the trees and back to the house. "Tomorrow 10 miles, lads," Jack told them as he marched them back. He saw O'Mahony watching, "and we'll have a look at the enemy as well."

"Where are you taking them?" O'Mahony asked.

"Right to the frontier," Jack replied cheerfully. "There's nothing better for blooding the pups then letting them see the enemy."

"You're getting them prepared," O'Mahony commented approvingly.

"I am," Jack agreed. "I've been on campaign with Johnny Raws before. They're five times the work of veterans and have a tenth the capability. The more the lads see before the fighting starts, the better." He glanced over his shoulder as Cormac and Dermot emerged through the trees, shaking the snow off their boots.

"Well done," Jack shouted over to them. "You kept up like heroes!" He did not look at Helen, who stood at the door, holding a shawl over her shoulders.

* * *

"According to the map," Jack said, "New Brunswick is across the St Croix river there." He indicated the 100-yard wide strip of ice and water that glittered under the thin sun.

He had 30 men with him, the skirmishers of his Fenians. Some stared across without expression on their faces while others looked willing to march on Fredericton without delay or support.

"I want five volunteers," Jack said.

"What are we going to do?" A long-faced man asked.

"We're going to invade British North America," Jack said. "Who's game?"

"I'm game!" the long-faced man replied immediately, with others surging forward eagerly.

"What's your name?" Jack asked.

"Murphy, sir, Sean Murphy," the long-faced man answered with a grin.

"Right, Murphy, you're my corporal."

Jack picked five men from the dozen volunteers and probed the river. Although the ice near the banks held their weight, the centre of the river was deeper than he expected.

"Look for a boat," he said. "Anything that floats."

An hour-long search found an isolated house with an open boat, barely large enough to hold five people. Jack tested the hull, found it sound and had his men drag it to the edge of the ice.

"In we go boys; let's show the Limeys."

Murphy raised a cheer and began to sing:

"We've won many victories
  Along with the boys in blue,
  Now we'll conquer Canada because there's
  Nothing left to do."

"We're not conquering it today," Jack said. "We're only having a look at New Brunswick."

"That's better than marching around Presque House." Murphy had a strange accent, Irish overlaid with New England.

Jack nodded. "Come on, then." He pushed them off from the ice, grunted as the current caught them, and steered for the New Brunswick shore. *I hope I don't precipitate a war,* he thought.

The ice on the New Brunswick shore was as thick and the countryside very similar to that of Maine.

"Congratulations, lads," he said. "We are now on British soil." He waited for the words to sink in. "We will march to the nearest settlement and show them that Ireland has not forgotten what the British did."

Kennedy, a red-haired, freckle-faced man with a fund of jokes, grinned and tapped the stock of his rifle. "Kill the English."

"We're killing nobody!" Jack said. "We're not here to start a war. Not today, anyway." Unfolding the map he had brought, he pointed to a small settlement that lay a bare mile away. "When we reach Glosterville, we'll post a note on the church, just to let them know we've called."

Most of his men looked pleased with the idea. Kennedy did not.

Jack led them on a fast march until they came to the settlement, a group of houses clustered around an unpretentious wooden church. "Can any of you lads read?"

Kennedy was one of the two men who claimed to be scholars and Jack handed over the poster he had written. "Read this out."

Looking happy to be singled out, Kennedy read slowly. "People of New Brunswick. This notice is a friendly warning from the Fenians of America. We wish to gain the freedom of Ireland from British control. We will not make war on the peaceful citizens of New Brunswick so you may sleep safe in your beds. It is only the authorities and the military who need fear. Even Wolfe cannot save you from the wrath of Ireland. Long Live the Fenian Brotherhood! God save the Irish Republic!"

If that did not warn the authorities of the Fenian threat, Jack thought, then nothing would. He had included the name Wolfe, as Smith had ordered. Now he had to wait.

The Fenians nodded in approval as Kennedy shouted the final words. By that time a small group of locals had gathered, some listening, others holding agricultural tools. One heavily bearded man cradled a baby. They did not look like the sort of people to oppress Ireland, or anybody else.

Jack nailed his poster to the church door, reread it for the benefit of anybody who failed to hear the first time and called across the local pastor.

"Could you see that this notice gets to whoever is governor of this part of the world?"

"I will do that." The pastor was a young, man swathed in furs. "Now please get your armed men out of my parish. You are unsettling my parishioners."

Jack did not need to force a smile as he pressed a note in to the pastor's hand. "You're a good man, Reverend. We're leaving."

"We showed the Limeys," Kennedy said. "We warned them!"

Jack's men were in high spirits as he led them back over the river, ensured the boat was returned to its proper owner and marched back to the house. They were singing, convinced they had struck the first blow for Irish freedom. Jack hoped that his mention of Wolfe and the letter he had handed over to the priest reached its intended destination and that his little incursion served as a warning to the Canadian authorities how vulnerable the border was.

As midwinter brought snow deeper than Jack had ever seen, O'Mahony seemed to have trusted Jack and left him alone for days at a time in the lonely house near the border, so Jack relaxed more as he trained his men. He kept the drill basic, unwilling to bring the Fenians near the standard expected of British soldiers while knowing he had to ensure he retained the trust of the Fenian leadership.

"Jack." Helen had taken to watching him when the weather was good, standing outside the house, dressed in layers of clothes and waving whenever she caught his eye.

"Stand easy!" Jack ordered. The Fenians obeyed, with their boots thumping down on frozen snow. "Ten-minute break, boys!"

Lifting her skirt to keep the hem out of the wet, Helen walked towards him. "You've been busy, Jack."

"I have to get these men in shape," Jack said. "Where's your friend?"

"My friend? Oh, Walter is only here from time to time. He roams around the countryside, travels to England or Ireland and all sorts of places leaving me all alone."

Jack shook his head. "Poor old you! And you leaving William for his company, too."

"I'd have left William anyway," Helen said. "You know that." She allowed her eyes to roam the length of his body. "I'd have left him for you any time."

"Where is Walter now?" Jack could see Dermot and Cormac watching him.

"He doesn't tell me," Helen said.

"That's not very friendly of him," Jack said. "At least you'll see him when he's here." He smiled. "You sounded very happy together."

"He makes me laugh, and he's exciting to be around," Helen said.

"Does he share your room?"

"Oh, no," Helen said. "He calls in only occasionally. He has a room on the same floor as you."

Jack nodded. "I see. I thought you were closer than that."

Helen shook her head. "He's exciting, Jack. Nothing more. I would have left William for young Ensign Snodgrass, or you. Especially for you."

"Be careful, Helen," Jack said. "I do not think that Mr Carmichael is all he seems."

Helen's smile did not falter. "Neither are you, Jack. I know you too well. You're playing a double game."

* * *

Riley had taught Jack the basics of lock-picking, and the rooms in Presque House had not been designed to keep out cracksmen. It only took Jack a few moments to break into Carmichael's room.

Lighting his lantern, Jack adjusted the shutter until it emitted a thin beam of light, closed the door and looked around the room. He felt the reassuring pressure of the revolver thrust through the waistband of his trousers and hoped he would not have to use it.

The same size as Jack's, the room was stark in its simplicity, with a bed, chest of drawers, roll-top desk and two chairs. Pushing open the desk, Jack flicked through the contents; pad of paper, pens, ink. Nothing of interest and the drawers were empty. This man Carmichael was too sensible to leave incriminating evidence in such a prominent place.

Jack pondered; what else had Riley taught him about searching? He checked the usual hiding places, with the light from his lantern bouncing around the room, casting weird shadows. There was nothing under the pillow or the bed, and when he shone the lamp up the flue, he saw only the blackness of residual soot. Only the rug remained, and under there, Jack saw a slight bulge.

Carefully rolling back the rug, Jack shone the lantern on the slender leather packet beneath, opened the two small buckles and peered inside. There were two rectangular sheets of paper, both in Russian, a language Jack recognised by sight but could not read.

Russian. I have to tell Smith somehow.

As Jack prepared to leave the room, he saw a single ragged scrap of paper in the fireplace. The paper seemed to be the all that remained from a larger sheet that Carmichael had torn and burned. Lifting it, he saw a confusion of letters that meant nothing, followed by the words English HQ. Jack copied the letters: *Cto alpla*

Now that is undoubtedly a code. But where is the English HQ, and the headquarters for whom?

Jack puzzled over the words, frowned, and swore as he heard footsteps thudding in the corridor outside. Returning the two sheets of paper under the carpet, he rolled to the curtains and remained down.

The footsteps halted outside the door. Somebody tapped. "Walter?"

Jack swore softly.

"Walter? It's me, Helen. Are you there? I thought I saw a light in your room."

Jack kept silent as Helen rapped on the door again. He waited for a few moments until her footsteps sounded and returned to the documents. Tempted to take them away, he knew that would immediately end his usefulness as an agent of the queen, so he retrieved both sheets, selected a pen and paper from the desk and copied down as much as he could, struggling with the unfamiliar words and script.

We were right – Carmichael is Russian. Now why the devil are the Russians involved with the American Fenians?

Jack heard voices, checked his watch and swore. Copying out the Russian script had taken much longer than he thought. Hastily tidying the packet back where he had found it, Jack moved to the door. Now he had to contact Smith. How the devil could he do that?

* * *

Jack saw the horseman trot up to the front door of Presque House, dismount and throw the reins to a servant before striding inside, as confident as if he were coming home.

So you are back, Walter Carmichael.

Jack kept his light off and door ajar, listening to the sounds of the house and watched Walter stride along the corridor to his room. Even before he reached the door, Helen arrived with her arms outstretched, waiting for him. Jack watched, unsure of what he thought.

Are you a traitor, Helen? Or are you merely what you seem, a flighty woman annoyed with her husband and seeking a romantic adventure to alleviate the boredom of married life with an inattentive spouse.

Jack remembered Smith's words. "If you find him, I want you to kill him," and his immediate response that he was not an assassin. Yet now, knowing Carmichael was Russian, and seeing him with Helen, Jack's previous resolution faltered.

Yes, Mr Smith, I could kill the man who calls himself Walter Carmichael. I am not acting as an English gentleman, so I could descend a further rung of the ladder and become an assassin.

* * *

As Jack's Fenians became more restless through the winter, Jack increased the length of their marches and the frequency of their drills. When the bad weather closed in, Jack sent them back to their makeshift barracks and walked around the grounds of Presque House, wondering why he was there.

"Wolfe." The voice was little more than a murmur, like a variation of the breeze, and so low that Jack thought he had imagined it until it came again. "Wolfe."

"Wolfe," Jack repeated.

"Captain Windrush."

Jack couldn't see where the voice was coming from. Reaching for his revolver, he turned around. "I'm Captain Windrush."

The man emerged from behind a tree. He was swathed in furs and wearing snowshoes and a deep hood and a thick beard covered the lower half of his face.

"Donald Fraser." The man threw back his hood, removed one of his mittens and held out his hand. "Pleased to meet you." His accent was educated, with a pleasant Canadian twang.

"How do you do." Jack shook hands, thinking it strange to meet a Canadian on the borders of Maine.

"Wolfe," Fraser said as if that were sufficient explanation for his presence there. "We got the note you left."

"Oh?" Jack was not yet ready to admit who he was. "Which note?"

"Mr Smith was very interested." Fraser had Smith's habit of not answering a direct question.

"I'm glad you got in touch," Jack said "I may have other things to interest you."

"Come and tell me." Fraser replaced his gloves and led Jack into the forest. "Your two shadows are in the house; I think they've given up following you."

"Cormac and Dermot?" Jack nodded. "They're dangerous, if not the sharpest men in the world."

"I've been watching you for a while." Fraser led them to what appeared to be a pile of snow but which proved to be a small hut well camouflaged by a covering of snow and ice. "Brush over our trail." He handed Jack a tree branch to conceal the tracks they had left.

"Coffee?" Fraser had the interior of the hut surprisingly comfortable and poured out two cups of coffee. "So what do you have to tell us?"

Jack explained what he had seen and heard, ending with: "He calls himself Walter Carmichael but Corporal Riordan was convinced he was not Irish and I am nearly certain he is Russian."

Fraser looked up sharply, with his coffee cup halfway to his mouth. "Russian? Are you sure?"

"I recognised and copied the Russian script," Jack said. "But I don't know what the documents say."

"Do you have the copy with you?"

"No." Jack shook his head.

"Leave it in the trees," Fraser said. "I'll see it gets to the proper place." He grinned. "I'll be watching you."

"There was something else, too. A garbled scrap of code and something about an English HQ."

"Code?"

"It said Cto alpla," Jack remembered.

"That means nothing to me," Fraser agreed. "Leave it with the rest." he pointed out a distinctive stand of white birch trees. "Under the third tree there."

"I'll do that," Jack said.

"As soon as you like," Fraser said. "Now you'd better get back before Dermot and Cormac get worried about you."

After they shook hands, Jack moved away, with Fraser smoothing the snow behind him to remove any trail. When Jack looked back a moment later, Fraser was gone, and only the trees remained, with the snow falling softly between them. Jack nodded. Although he could not see Fraser, he no longer felt abandoned and alone.

All that winter, Fraser brought news to Jack about conditions in Canada. There were small murmurings in various places and several Fenians arrested in Toronto, while angry Orangemen met to pledge their loyalty to the Crown.

"The colonies are bristling with rumours," Fraser said, drinking his coffee. "Either the Fenians are going to launch a full-scale attack with American aid, or the Orangemen and regulars will squash them without mercy."

"Did you get the letters translated?" Jack asked.

"They are Russian, as you thought," Fraser said. "Your fellow seems to be a Russian agent, but what his objective is, we don't know. The documents are fairly routine, with consular addresses and some details of the Russian presence in Alaska."

"Were they useful?"

Fraser shrugged. "That's for the men at the top to decide."

"And the coded message?"

"That meant nothing to us," Fraser admitted.

"Best make sure Peshawar and the Khyber are well guarded," Jack said. "If Russia is causing trouble in Canada, their real objective will be somewhere completely different."

Fraser smiled. "I'll pass that little nugget on. Have you much experience of the Russians?"

"I fought through the war in Crimea," Jack told him. "Including some clandestine work against the Plastun Cossacks."

"Aye." Fraser sipped more coffee. "You'll know them, then." He paused as if wondering what to say. "I passed your letter to your wife along."

"Thank you," Jack said. "Mary will be worrying about me."

"Wives are like that." Fraser spoke with long gaps between his sentences. "There is one more thing." He handed a sealed letter to Jack. "I was to give you this. Make sure you destroy it." He held up a hand. "No, don't open it when I'm here. I don't want to know the contents."

Jack tucked the letter away. "I'd like a method of contacting you in an emergency, say if I find anything of importance, or if I need help."

Fraser shook his head. "I can't guarantee anything," he said. "I travel between here and elsewhere."

"Where?" Jack asked.

"Best you don't know," Fraser said. "In case you're discovered. I do have other agents to meet, you know."

"Who?" Jack asked and smiled. "I know, it's best I don't know. Can I contact you?"

"I'm here every Wednesday, at or near the stand of birches. That's the best I can do." Fraser tapped Jack on the back of his hand. "Go, now, and see what Smith says. Don't tell me."

Nodding, Jack retraced his steps to Presque House, concealing his trail as he always did and holding the package under his coat. Breaking the seal outside the grounds of Presque House, Jack pocketed the ten silver dollars and read the simple note.

"Capture C and hand to F. S."

* * *

Capture C? That must mean Carmichael, while F was Fraser and S must be Smith. Jack shook his head. *Why did these people have to talk in riddles? How the devil am I to capture Carmichael? As in any military campaign,* he thought, *I must neutralise his strengths and strike at his weakest point.*

The ancient Chinese philosopher and military strategist Sun Tzu said, "Attack their weaknesses," and Jack knew what Carmichael's weakness was.

Jack burnt the note in his fire, watching the ashes crumble away. He was glad he did not have to murder Carmichael, although capturing him might prove more difficult. *Sorry, Mary; you won't like what I have to do.*

"Cormac." Jack approached the large man. "I must ask you to look the other way for a while."

Cormac looked instantly suspicious. "Why's that?"

"A woman," Jack said.

Cormac and Dermot exchanged knowing glances. "That little redhead from the cookhouse?"

"Indeed no." Jack knew the woman; bright and bubbly, the redhead was popular with the few Fenians who remained at the house. "The dark-headed one."

"Oh." Cormac looked disappointed. "Helen. She's moody."

"She never talks to me," Dermot said. "She treats me like dirt."

That sounds about right, Jack thought. Helen would see no profit in meeting either of these two men with their limited intellectual ability.

"You go right ahead, captain," Cormac said with a grin.

"Thanks lads," Jack tossed a dollar to them. "I'll see if she treats me better."

Helen answered the door to Jack's knock without hesitation. "Helloa, Jack." She looked slightly dishevelled as if she had been sleeping. "What do you want?"

"Your company," Jack said. "Are you alone?"

Helen's smile could not have been broader as she stepped aside. "Not while you're here, Jack. Come on in."

The room was tidy except for the bed, which Helen hurriedly began to make. "I was having a nap," she said. "It's so dull being trapped here all winter." She ran her fingers down his arm. "I'm glad you came."

Jack allowed Helen's hand free play. "You knew I would, eventually."

"I hoped you would," Helen said. "Sit down, Jack." Bouncing on to the bed, she hugged her knees between her hands and nodded to the armchair beside the window. "Shall I ring the maid for coffee, or would you like something stronger, or nothing at all?" Her eyes laughed at him.

"I'd like to talk," Jack said, sitting down. "I'd like to talk about you and the danger you are in."

Helen's smile did not falter. "Danger is the spice, Jack. It alleviates the tedium of life. You are so lucky that you're a man."

"Walter Carmichael is more dangerous than you realise," Jack said.

"Perhaps I know him better than you do," Helen countered.

Wondering how much he could trust her, Jack took a deep breath. "You do realise that he's a fraud, don't you?"

"A fraud?" Helen frowned. "What do you mean?"

"Walter Carmichael is not Irish." Jack watched Helen closely as he spoke. "And I don't think he is American, either."

"Then what is he?"

"He may be Russian," Jack said. "Using the Fenians, as he is using you."

"I'm using him," Helen pointed out. "Just as you are trying to use me. What do you want Jack? What do you really want? And it's not my company – I know you too well to believe that."

"I want your help," Jack said. "I believe Carmichael is working for the Russians, and I want to capture him to find out."

Helen sat up on the bed. "I knew you were not here for my sake." She jumped off the bed and began to pace up and down the room in much the same way as Jack did when thinking. "That will be fun," she said finally. "How do we do it?"

"I haven't worked that out, yet," Jack said. "Tell me, Helen, if Carmichael had asked you to help capture me, would you have agreed as easily?"

Helen stopped to kiss Jack lightly on the forehead. "Oh, Jack, how could you think such a thing of me? Of course not." She walked away again, turned and smiled. "I don't think so, anyway, but we'll never know for sure, will we?"

"No," Jack replied softly. "We'll never know for sure."

CHAPTER FIFTEEN

Presque House, Maine, January 1866

Once Helen decided on a thing, she put her heart and soul into it, Jack thought, at least until something else attracted her attention. Ever since he had mentioned his intention to capture Carmichael, Helen had come up with a succession of plans, each one more audacious than the last, from enticing him into the woods so Jack could hit him on the head to drugging his drink.

"He's a clever man," Jack said. "We'll need something more subtle."

"No," Helen argued, shaking her head. "Straightforward is best. Come on, Jack, we've been at this for a week and resolved nothing."

"I'll think of something," Jack said.

"That will be a change," Helen retorted sharply. "You used to be so resourceful, Jack."

The words stung as Jack walked away. It was hard to make plans to capture a man whose appearances were unpredictable. Carmichael was away more often than he was at Presque House, and when he arrived, he might be there for a few days or only a few hours.

* * *

"Jack!" Helen pushed into Jack's room without knocking.

"Who's that?" Jack sat up in bed, groping for his revolver.

"It's me!" Helen stood in her nightdress without even a candle to light her way. "I've got him."

"What?" Struggling up, Jack lit a candle by the dying embers of his fire.

"Walter! He's asleep in my room, drunk as a lord and snoring fit to frighten the French! Come on!"

Helen was absolutely right – Carmichael was unconscious on the bed, wearing only his shirt and with his mouth wide open.

"Was this your doing?" Jack asked.

Helen's smile was more self-satisfied than Jack expected. "Perhaps a little. I did slip some spirits into his beer."

"What the devil do I do with him? I can hardly carry him out of the house," Jack said.

"No." Helen grabbed at a pile of Carmichael's clothing. "Help me dress him, Jack. I've got an idea."

"You had this planned," Jack said, surprised at how adroitly Helen slipped Carmichael's clothes on his unconscious body.

"Days ago!" Helen admitted cheerfully.

"You're a cunning little minx," Jack said almost admiringly as Helen pulled Carmichael's trousers over his hips and fastened them.

"Why thank you! Coming from you, Jack, I'll take that as a compliment." Helen's eyes were bright with excitement. "Now, Jack, you must trust me. I'm going to put Walter," she slapped the unconscious man's backside, "on his coach and tell the driver to take him to the usual destination."

"Where is that?"

"I don't know," Helen said. "I've heard Walter," she slapped him again, "say that to his coachman."

"Did you ask?"

"Frequently." Helen shook her head. "To no avail." She smiled. "No matter. I'll tell the coachman to go to the usual destination. You must follow the coach without being seen and kidnap him or whatever you have in mind." Helen pushed him toward the door. "Now go, Jack. If anybody sees you with him, Cormac and his pal might suspect you." She pushed again. "Go!"

As Jack left, she heard Helen shouting: "Cormac! Dermot! I need your muscles. This stupid man's fallen asleep when he's due to be away!"

After waiting so long, Jack found he was ill-prepared for the reality of capturing Carmichael. Slipping out of the side door, he watched Cormac carry Carmichael as if he was a sack of potatoes, with Helen giving brisk orders. Dermot had fetched the coach, with the driver looking disgruntled at having to drive in thick snow, although the road to Presque House was clear.

"It was late afternoon, with the shadows already merging with oncoming dark, so Jack had no difficulty in running across unseen and slipping among the nearby trees. He heard Helen's voice floating on the still air and, looking back, saw her breath condensing like smoke around her face.

"He told me he needs to go to the usual destination, driver, wherever that is."

"At this hour?" the driver grumbled. "It'll mean travelling through the night, and the offside front wheel needs attention!"

"Then attend to the wheel and travel through the night!" Helen said, sharply, pulling a shawl close against the bite of the cold. "That's what Mr Carmichael said, so you'd better be off, and smart's the word, or I'll lay your whip across your shoulders."

Growling at Helen, the coachman cracked the reins and pulled away from the house.

Moving quickly through the trees, Jack was out of the grounds and into the forest before the coach appeared. With no real plan, he had nothing in mind except to hold up the coach and drag Carmichael outside so, checking his revolver was loaded, he pulled a scarf across the lower half of his face, took a deep breath and swore as the coach slewed to a halt a few hundred yards outside the main gate of the house.

"What the devil is happening now?" Jack murmured to himself.

Climbing down from from his seat, the driver gave the front offside wheel a mighty kick, swore loudly and crouched beside it, muttering to himself. As he did so, the coach door opened and Carmichael staggered out, vomited copiously behind the coach and wandered drunkenly into the trees.

"Good man," Jack said. "You keep coming towards me."

"Helloa!" Concentrating on his damaged wheel, the driver had not noticed the antics of his passenger until Carmichael was gone. "Where are you off to?" Following the zig-zag trail of footprints into the forest, he continued to shout. "Helloa! Mr Carmichael!"

"Right, driver." Rising from behind a tree, Jack grabbed the man in a headlock, pulled off his hat and cracked him with the butt of his revolver. Knowing the driver would die of exposure if left in the snow overnight, Jack dragged him back to the coach and bundled him inside.

"Now for you, Carmichael, or whatever your name is."

The Russian had left an easy trail through the snow, allowing Jack to locate him in minutes.

"Who are you?" Carmichael slurred the words. "What are you doing here?"

"Saving your life, like as not," Jack said. "You'll die out here in your present condition. Come on."

"Who are you?" Carmichael's eyes were unfocused, yet Jack could not smell alcohol on his breath.

"That's not your concern," Jack said. "I thought Russians were hard-headed when it came to alcohol."

"I'm not Russian," Carmichael slurred, staggering, so Jack slid a hand under his arm and guided him through the forest toward the stand of birch trees. Glancing behind him, Jack saw the distinct trail they were leaving and cursed. The Fenians could follow that without difficulty. He'd have to obliterate that quickly. "Come on, Carmichael. If you're not Russian, what are you?"

"I'm Irish." Carmichael began to sing.

"O Paddy dear, and did ye hear the news that's goin' round?
The shamrock is by law forbid to grow on Irish ground!
No more Saint Patrick's Day we'll keep, his colour can't be seen
For there's a cruel law ag'in the Wearing' o' the Green."

Jack winced. "Keep quiet!"

"Why?" Carmichael asked loudly. "I can sing if I want."

Jack sensed rather than saw the movement ahead of him, and then Fraser was beside him. "Is this the Russian fellow?"

"I'm glad to see you," Jack said. "Yes, this is he."

"Let's get him somewhere safe, then," Fraser said and, without hesitation, produced a small bag from inside his coat, opened it and pressed a pad of cloth over Carmichael's mouth and nose. Jack watched in fascination as Carmichael struggled for a moment and then relaxed into unconsciousness.

"It's a medical thing called chloroform," Carmichael explained. "Help me carry him."

Two men carrying a insensible body was much easier than one struggling with a lively man so, within 15 minutes, they deposited Carmichael inside Fraser's small hut.

Gasping slightly, Fraser looked down at the man. "Well done, Windrush. I'll have him transported to England for questioning."

"It was fortunate you were here at just the right time," Jack said.

"Nothing to do with fortune," Fraser said. "Now, a short message from S. Stay put until the Fenians move. Let us know what they do."

"Is that it?" Jack could not hide his disappointment. "I had hoped I could go home now."

"Not yet," Fraser said. "Your wife will have to wait a little longer. I'll be in touch."

CHAPTER SIXTEEN

Boston, April 1866

"We are agreed." Sweeny spoke quietly. "Colonel John O'Byrne will lead the raid. He will have a battalion of some 700 men across from Maine to seize Campobello Island in New Brunswick. Some of the men you trained will be among them, Windrush."

Jack slowly lit a cheroot and blew smoke into the air. "Once he has control of Campobello, sir, what will he do with it? There's not much there to scare the British."

"Do with it, sir? Why he won't have to do anything with it." Sweeny's smile had all the charm of a sleeping tiger. "That's the beauty of the scheme, you see. Even if we lose, we win. This border between the United States and Canada is hundreds of miles long and as porous as a sieve. I believe you know India's North-West Frontier, Captain?"

"I've served there," Jack admitted.

"There you are, you see," Sweeny said triumphantly. "You've seen a heavily defended frontier. How much wealth do you think that drains from the British Empire?"

Jack thought of the garrison at Peshawar, the Guides base at Mardan and all the frontier outposts, with the scores of expeditionary forces that Britain had to send out to keep even relative peace. "A great deal, I should think, sir."

"I should think so, too," Sweeny said. "Now, imagine what it would cost to maintain garrisons along the full length of the border between Britain's North American possessions and the United States of America."

With another eight men in the room, Jack knew that Sweeny was addressing his audience rather than asking a genuine question. All the same, he drew a breath and considered. A posting to North America was one of the most popular for the British army. The people were friendly, the location healthy, and there was little chance of action. Horse Guards knew that well and kept only a token handful of regulars in

North America, backed by local militia. If Britain had to maintain a garrison all along the frontier with the United States, the cost would be astronomical.

"Britain would have to raise taxes to maintain a large garrison." Sweeny answered his own question. "That would make the empire even less popular than it is now. London might expect the North American colonies to pay for their own defence, and we all know where that could lead, don't we?"

Jack forced a smile. When Great Britain taxed her North American colonies to pay for a British garrison in the late 18th century, 13 had revolved and formed the United States. The initial minor civil disturbances had spread into a near-global war that culminated in Britain opposing a formidable alliance of European powers that included both France and Spain.

"You see? If we win, and the Fenians in Canada rise in support to push out the British, then we have gained a massive victory." Sweeny faced the gathering of earnest, bearded faces. "If we can hold Canada or even part of it, we will offer the British a deal; we will give them back Canada in return for Irish independence."

Jack listened intently. What Sweeny proposed was very bold and, to him, outlandish. Canada was a vast country, and whatever the size of the British garrison, the population was unlikely to welcome a Fenian-American invasion. As the Canadians had already repelled American attacks in the 1770s and 1812, Sweeny was attempting a dangerous venture. The other men at the table seemed not to agree. They clapped, and one sang a few lines of a Fenian song.

> *"Hooray for the land which an Emmet reclaimed*
> *Which the blood of our sires strove to render a nation*
> *With the foul taint of slavery forever he stained*
> *Forward ye Fenians to die or to save*
> *No more shall your land be the home of a slave."*

If songs could win wars, Jack thought, Ireland would have been independent centuries before.

Sweeny was talking again. "I read the report of a British officer," he said. "This officer said that Canada would be easy prey, notwithstanding all the fine talk there is of defending it."

Most of the men at the table clapped. They all listened, while Jack wondered who the nameless British officer was and if he ever even existed.

"The British know that the people of Lower Canada are very lukewarm towards them and there are many Fenians among the Roman Catholic population. There has been much talk of confederation recently, with which New Brunswick and Nova Scotia do not agree."

Jack listened, taking mental notes.

"Indeed," Sweeny continued, "newspapers in New Brunswick are discussing the advantages of the United States annexing them – they will welcome us with open arms!"

The men cheered again, with more singing.

Sweeny stood up, lifting his arms high. "We are going to make history, gentlemen. The British think the Canadians will rise against us. They are wrong! Oh, some volunteer companies will oppose us, but our men are better armed, and most are veterans of real war, not of sham fights with other amateurs."

Jack knew that Sweeny was at least partially correct. The American repeating

Spencers gave the Fenians an advantage over the Canadian Volunteers with their single-shot rifles, and the experience of fighting through the US Civil War made many of the Fenians veterans. Jack listened to Sweeny's words, sorting the wheat of truth from the chaff of encouraging propaganda. Although they were no Pashtuns or Sikhs, these Fenians might give Britain a scare before this game was over.

"Even if we don't win, we will still have twisted the lion's tail, with who knows what results." Sweeny sat down with a heavy thump and leaned back in his chair. "And all the time that Great Britain is expending men, money and energy over here, the real war will take place on the other side of the Atlantic." Sweeny's cigar seemed swamped by the size of his grin. "I see you understand, Captain Windrush. All this, successful or not, is only a diversion. The more trouble we cause for Britain here, the more we divert them from Ireland. If we win in Canada, we have Ireland. If we only draw the British Army into a long war on the Canadian prairies, we can bleed their finances until they sue for peace."

Jack nodded. The Fenians' strategy sounded plausible, provided they had the finances and resources to maintain an army within a foreign nation. They certainly possessed the rhetoric.

O'Mahony, sitting quietly in a corner, lifted his chin from his chest. "I agree," he said. "Let it be so. If we are fortunate, the United States will act with us and push the United States border to the St Lawrence."

"That would show Britain they don't rule the world," one of the two men at the back of the room said, as his companion scribbled notes in a small black pad. He glanced at Sweeny, then at Jack. When he rose to speak, Jack noticed that even Sweeny listened.

"I've been travelling around Britain and Europe, as most of you gentlemen are aware."

Sweeny nodded. "We know, Mr Walsh."

Mr Walsh? Jack focused on the speaker. *Who the devil are you, Mr Walsh?* Although he spoke in quiet tones, Walsh exuded an authority that Jack had seldom encountered before. His face was gaunt, with prominent cheekbones, and the scar on his forehead highlighted deep-set, haunted eyes filled with latent violence. Jack had seen such eyes before, on men damaged by combat or other extreme hardship. This Walsh was a man to avoid.

"I have planted discontent in a dozen British regiments," Walsh said. "One sign of Fenian success in Canada will bring a mutiny in these units, gentlemen. Britain will be unable to rely on its army." Walsh sat back down.

You have planted discontent? Jack studied Walsh from the side of his eyes. *Who are you? Are you the man I should have been searching for, rather than Carmichael?*

"Thank you, Mr Walsh," Sweeny said. "For those of you who do not know, Mr Walsh heads our intelligence department."

Dear God in heaven! He's the man I should have been after.

Sweeny continued. "Our secretary of war has created a plan of attack. We will have multiple invasions from the United States. We will cross from Vermont and Malone and Potsdam in New York to capture the Canadian towns of Cornwall and Prescott before we strike north to Ottawa and Montreal. We will cross Lake Michigan and Lake Huron, capture Stratford and London and take over railway terminals to disrupt Canadian communications, while other Fenian armies occupy Toronto and every important waterway and railway centre."

Jack listened without comment. Although he knew that Britain had only a tiny garrison in Canada, he could not imagine the authorities standing idly by while foreign armies invaded at will, whatever Sweeny and his optimistic followers believed. The Fenians' plans for large armies striking simultaneously at several points in a thinly populated land called for sophisticated logistics and communications that Jack doubted they possessed. All the same, he had to warn the British authorities of the danger.

"I'd like to go with O'Mahony," Jack said. "I'd like a crack at the Empire myself."

"Face me," O'Mahony said.

Jack met his level, sharp eyes as the room became quiet. Jack was aware that Walsh was studying him as carefully as he had scrutinised Walsh.

"You've taken the Fenian oath," O'Mahony said.

"I have," Jack agreed.

"And you give me your word, as an officer and a gentleman, that you are loyal?"

"I am loyal," Jack said.

O'Mahony extended his hand. "I know you have already led a raid into New Brunswick." He raised his voice slightly. "This gentleman is Captain Jack Windrush, who has personal reasons for disliking the British Empire. God bless the Republic of Ireland."

"God bless the Republic of Ireland," Jack said even as he mentally composed his message to Fraser. He felt Walsh's eyes burning into his back.

* * *

After a winter of training, the Fenians were a handy-looking bunch. Jack surveyed them, as he had inspected thousands of recruits in the British Army. Many seemed very young, mere boys with the bright hope of enthusiasm in their eyes and slogans to free Ireland on their lips. Others were veterans of the American Civil War, cynical, hard young men who had seen action at Shiloh and Bull Run, Vicksburg or Antietam. Many were Irish-born, others the sons of Irishmen and women who brought bitter memories of the famine of the 1840s when they emigrated to the United States. Jack saw Riordan's face in the ranks, as well as Murphy and the eager Kennedy. These men would be as willing to fight as any British soldiers and, being of Irish stock, would let nobody down.

Jack thought of the last message he had sent via Fraser, asking him to contact the Royal Navy in Halifax and hoped it would get through in time.

"Here we go, then." Murphy spoke through a mouthful of tobacco. "Our first blow at the Limeys."

"Dirty English bastards," Kennedy said. "I hate them all."

Jack said nothing; he had heard it all before. O'Mahony walked up, his eyes searching. Although Campobello Island, one of the Fundy Islands, was in New Brunswick, it lay off the coast of Maine. It was a beautiful, wooded island that exuded peace as Jack and the Fenians looked across the short stretch of water.

"It's almost a shame to spoil it," Riordan commented.

"Compared to what the British did to Ireland," Kennedy rubbed his hand over the stock of his rifle, "we'll leave it fresh and healthy."

The veteran Fenians checked their weapons, others stamped their boots on the ground in a manner so like the 113th that Jack felt instant nostalgia for his old regiment. Before battle, all armies were probably similar, he thought, with a mixture of apprehension, excitement and fear, as the old soldiers hid their memories and the youngsters strove to prove their worth.

Jack looked around for the Royal Navy. If his message had got through, surely the navy would respond. An early check to the Fenians' hopes might save the hundreds or thousands of lives that a later war would undoubtedly cost. He watched the Fenians. He knew his own company by name and habit. He knew the lazy and the keen, the veterans, and the raw men desperate for others to regard them as old soldiers. Despite their being the Queen's enemies, he felt an affinity towards them. But, at the same time, he could not condone their cause. Bringing war to the peaceful colonies of Canada because of presumed injustices in Ireland made no sense to him.

As evening fell on the collection of islands that made up the settlement of Eastport, Maine, a chill wind bit from the north and ice lingered at the shadowed corners of the buildings. Jack kept his men drilling on a sheltered beach as long as he could, aware of his divided loyalties between his company and the aims of the Fenians.

Opposite them and within comfortable artillery range, the islands of New Brunswick appeared a mirror image of Maine.

"I can see the bloody flag," Kennedy pointed across the intervening water.

"Stand to attention," Jack roared. "You're here to drill, not to sightsee!"

"Look, boys." Ignoring Jack completely, Kennedy pointed across to a small, wooded island, where the Union Flag hung above the substantial Customs House. "There's the flag of repression!"

"We'll get that tonight, boys," Murphy said, with his face looking longer than ever. "That place is called Indian Island."

Jack glanced at O'Mahony. "I think we'll call it a day there," he said.

"Aye," O'Mahony agreed. "These men are more free-spirited than your British redcoats. They won't accept your orders so readily, even after all your training."

"Hmm," Jack agreed. "I could do with a few experienced British sergeants. My Sergeant O'Neill would ginger them up."

"O'Neill?"

"As Irish as any man here and as good a soldier as any I have ever met."

O'Mahony nodded. "He'd be an asset to us. Best get to bed, Captain."

Jack saluted. "Yes, sir," he said. But he knew he would not sleep – he seldom did before an action, however small. Pulling off his boots but otherwise fully dressed in case of emergencies, he lay on the simple cot in his tent. Despite himself, Jack felt himself drifting away to dream of Mary in Netherhills, with Helen riding up singing a Fenian song.

The sound of scurrying feet woke Jack. He sat up in his tent and peered outside. Kennedy, Riordan and Murphy were leading a score of Fenians towards the beach.

"Here! What the devil are you doing?"

"Getting the flag!" Kennedy shouted over his shoulder. "We'll show these British!"

"Don't be stupid!" Hastily hauling on his boots, Jack followed, but too far behind to make any difference. He swore, knowing that a man so filled with unreasoning hatred as Kennedy was liable to do anything.

Pushing out two boats, the Fenians began to row clumsily towards Indian Island, with the blades of their oars splashing in the water and Kennedy urging them to greater effort.

"Don't be stupid!" Jack called. "You'll alert the British that we're coming!"

"What's happening?" O'Mahony emerged from his tent, hauling on his jacket and bleary-eyed from sleep.

"Some fools are rowing across to Indian Island to haul down the British flag," Jack informed him. "Shall I bring them back?"

"Yes," O'Mahony said. "There's no British garrison on Indian Island, and we're not making war on civilians."

The Fenians were a good 100 yards away before Jack managed to push the nearest boat into the water and row in pursuit. It was years since he had last been in a boat, so he struggled to find his rhythm, splashing louder than the Fenians and falling behind them by the minute. He pulled up on a muddy beach in time to see the Fenians running towards the Customs building.

"Stop!" Jack shouted.

"You can't give us orders," a youthful Fenian yelled back. "Limey bastard!"

"He's one of us," Murphy pulled the youth away. "He's no longer a Limey."

Jack chased after them, with his boots crunching on the frost-brittle ground and clouds streaking across a pale moon in a sky brilliant with stars.

The mob surrounded the Customs House, shouting to be let in. Jack heard Kennedy's voice above the general din. "Give us the Limey flag, or we'll burn the house down!"

Candlelight flickered in the nearest window of the house as the noise awakened the residents, and Jack fancied he saw a face peering behind the tiny flame.

"Enough!" Grabbing the nearest Fenian, Jack dragged him back. "We're not here to steal flags from civilians."

"You keep out of this, Limey!" As the Fenian fell, the volatile youth and one of his companions edged forward. While the youngster produced a pistol, his companion levelled his rifle. "You've no right to be here."

With two wild-eyed men pointing weapons at him, Jack withdrew a pace. "I'm your commanding officer!" He felt for his revolver and swore when he realised he had left it behind.

"You're a Limey bastard," the youth's companion was dark-visaged, with neat whiskers. Jack did not know him. "I can tell by your accent."

"He's all right," Murphy said. "Leave him be."

When the door opened, a sleepy-eyed native Canadian stared out. "What's all this? Who are you, people? Get away! I have a woman in labour here!"

"Leave these good people in peace." Jack tried to help as the Fenians crowded around the civilian. "Didn't you hear? There's a woman with child inside the house."

"An English woman," Kennedy said with a sneer.

"Who are you?" Tired of insulting Jack, the long-haired Fenian now pointed his pistol at the Canadian's head. The youth was unshaven and long-haired and his accent was from the southern states of America.

"I am James Dixon," the Canadian faced the pistol without flinching. "My wife is in labour, and you are not helping her."

"We'll shoot you first and then her," Kennedy announced, acting as spokesman.

"Why are you here?" Dixon blocked access to his house and his wife.

"We want that flag!" The long-haired Fenian waved his pistol around so wildly that Jack thought he might shoot one of his colleagues.

James Dixon shook his head. "You can have the flag if you wish," he said. "It's only a flag."

Cheering as though they had won a famous victory, the Fenians clambered to the roof. Jack watched as Kennedy grabbed the Union Flag and slithered back to the ground, with the Fenians baying and hooting. They gathered around the symbol of Britain's dominion, holding it up in front of Jack and sneering as they sang their most popular song.

*"We've won many victories
Along with the boys in blue,
Now we'll conquer Canada because there's
Nothing left to do."*

Five minutes later, the Fenians were crowding back to their boats, laughing, some spitting on the Union Flag, boasting of their victory as they retreated to Eastport. "We'll send this to headquarters in New York," one man said. "The first British flag captured in our conquest of Canada."

Feeling the frustration of failure, Jack lingered at the house and apologised to James Dixon. "I hope it goes well with your lady wife," he said.

Dixon gave a slow smile. "Thank you. I don't think you belong with these men. You may stay with us if you wish."

"I have my duty to do." Jack touched his cap in salute and walked away. He hoped the little display on Indian Island was not a foretaste of the Fenians' behaviour when they invaded Canada. If so, there would be bloodshed on both sides.

Sighing, Jack followed the cheering Fenians, wondering what the morrow would bring, wondering if the messages he sent had reached their destination and wondering if Canada stood at the crux of a full-scale Fenian war. Suddenly he felt drained of energy.

* * *

"Here we go."

Some 700 Fenians boarded boats and set out for their invasion of British North America with the magnificent islands of Passamaquoddy Bay in the Bay of Fundy spread before them, a vision of green and blue. Jack sighed; he had seen the exquisite beauty of the town of Balaclava destroyed by war. Was the same to happen here? Would the Fenians' invasion turn peaceful New Brunswick into a shattered battleground? Jack looked right and left. No sails graced the water – the Royal Navy was not hurrying to defend New Brunswick.

"Right, you Irish patriots," O'Mahony shouted, emphasising the Irish in his accent to appeal to his audience. "You know why we're here! We'll capture Campobello from the Limeys and use the island as a base to attack British shipping. We'll disrupt their trade and show the power of the green flag."

The Fenians cheered, waving hats, pistols and rifles in the air.

"Not only that," O'Mahony said, "If we are here, the British will have to increase their garrison in North America, and bring in ships as well. The more Limeys are here, the fewer will be in Ireland when the revolution starts."

The Fenians cheered again, louder, with some shouting, "Long live the Irish Republic," or, "Hurrah for the Fenian Brotherhood!"

"Remember," O'Mahony raised his hands to calm the noise. "If the Limeys capture any of us, we are citizens of the Irish Republic, so we are neither traitors nor freebooters to be hanged, but legal combatants to be treated as prisoners of war."

Jack thought of Ireland's bloody past and the many hopeful, hopeless attempts the people had made to throw off British rule. Despite his latent sympathy for a people who wished for self-determination, Jack hated war as only a soldier could. He did not want the horrors of war to descend on this most peaceful part of the empire.

"Also remember," O'Mahony altered his tone. "If we capture any British, military or civilian, they are our prisoners-of-war, so treat them decent. Don't give the Limeys any reason to revert to atrocities."

Jack was surprised that most men cheered the words, with only a few, such as Kennedy, appearing to disagree.

"Come on lads; let's strike a blow for Ireland!" O'Mahony gave his final words to another cheer from his Fenians.

Jack stepped into the leading boat, aware of the bustle of the men around him. Some held their rifles like the veterans they were, others giggled nervously, or sang their Fenian songs.

In the bow, O'Mahony surveyed the island through a pair of field glasses. "This will be a contested landing," he said, handing the binoculars to Jack. "Now we'll find out the temper of our boys."

Bright against the green trees, the scarlet tunics looked like a streak of blood. It was the first time that Jack had viewed British infantry as an enemy, and the sight chilled him. He knew what kind of men filled these uniforms, what they thought, how they acted and of what actions they were capable. However brave these Irish and Irish-Americans were, they had never faced professional British soldiers before or even New Brunswick Volunteers.

"Canadian Militia, I think." Jack handed the binoculars back.

"Will they fight?" O'Mahony asked.

"Aye, they'll fight." Jack tried to keep the satisfaction from his voice. The invaders would not get things all their own way. He could sense the unease growing among the Fenians. The veterans would remember the carnage that disciplined firepower could wreak among an advance and the Johnny Raws would be nervous about their first experience of battle.

Murphy stood up in the boat. "Up the Republic of Ireland!" He shouted. "Let's show these redcoats. Remember Oulart!" He was talking about a victory by the United Irishmen against loyalist militia in County Wexford in 1798.

The men responded, some waving their caps or rifles. "Oulart!" they shouted. "We'll Oulart them!" One or two of the wilder spirits fired shots in the air.

While the Fenians concentrated on Campobello, Jack continued to scan the waters around them, so was first to see the sails approaching from the east. They came rapidly, appearing from the shelter of the islands and then surging towards the Fenian fleet. "We may have more to worry about than a few dozen Canadian Militia." He tried to hide his relief. "Look over there."

O'Mahony swivelled around, levelling his binoculars. He swore once, softly, and then again. "What do you make of them, Windrush?"

The ships were not large as they emerged from the shelter of the islands, but there was no mistaking their intent. The white ensign that hung from their masts left no room for mistake.

"That's the Royal Navy!" Jack said.

"The news spread rapidly through the Fenian ranks, with men gesticulating and pointing towards the approaching warships. The flotilla of armed Fenians, which had seemed so powerful as it approached a supposedly undefended island, was now exposed as vulnerable. Not all the men, however, were cowed.

"Fight them!" Murphy levelled his rifle. "Shoot the Limeys as they come close."

"Don't be a fool!" O'Mahony knocked Murphy's rifle barrel down. "That's the Royal Navy, not some gaggle of uniformed civilians! They can blast us out of the water long before we're in range!"

"Then why don't they fire? Eh?" Another man asked. "They're scared of us, I tell you. They're scared of us."

"They won't fire as long as we're in United States waters,"Jack explained. "If we cross the line into New Brunswick waters, they might consider us a threat and open fire."

While some Fenians continued to shout their defiance, the majority watched the advance of the Royal Navy in silence. A few looked back to the shore of Maine, perhaps wondering if they should return.

As the ships drew closer, Jack could see splashes of scarlet on the decks, either of Royal Marines or British soldiers. "They've brought the British Army," Jack said. "I don't know which regiment."

The sight of the soldiers augmenting the Royal Navy and the waiting Canadian militia killed the remaining martial ardour of the Fenians.

"We're caught between two fires," Murphy said. "They've trapped us."

"Get back!" The cry became universal. "We can't fight them!"

"No," Jack shouted, knowing that the invasion was already doomed, but intent on enhancing his reputation as a fire-raising Fenian. "We're not retreating. Keep rowing; let's show these redcoats what Irishmen can do!" Raising his revolver and aware he was well out of range, Jack fired at the distant ships. One or two of the men followed suit until O'Mahony ordered them to cease fire.

"I commend your enthusiasm," O'Mahony growled, "but save the ammunition for later. We can't stand against the Royal Navy, damn their tarry hides!"

Either Jack's message or local information had reached the British authorities, and Major General Charles Hastings Doyle had called up the Royal Navy. Probably pleased to see some action, a small flotilla sailed from Halifax, arriving at Passamaquoddy Bay in time to overawe the Fenians. Believing their own propaganda, the Fenians had not expected much resistance and something like panic seized them.

"Keep together!" Jack's military mind was offended as the Fenian flotilla scattered, oars flailing as they turned to return to United States soil. "You're soldiers, not some rabble of civilians."

"They've defeated us without firing a shot," O'Mahony said gloomily. "Now it's all up to Sweeny."

* * *

Disconsolate, with their small army drifting away or sitting along the beaches of Maine, the leaders of the abortive invasion smoked, drank and watched the Royal

Navy cruising unchallenged in Passamaquoddy Bay. The white ensign, recently adopted as the sole flag of the Royal Navy, taunted the Fenians as it flapped 100 yards off the shore of Maine.

Jack watched the lean man stride towards them across the beach. "Here comes Patrick Walsh," he said. "I'm not sure what part he has to play in all this."

O'Mahony's smile was short and bitter. "Nobody is sure what Walsh's part is, Windrush. He's a man of mystery, is our Mr Walsh. We call him our intelligence officer, yet he wants to fight the British even more than you do."

Jack studied Walsh as he strode past the lounging Fenians. "I have the impression that he's dangerous."

O'Mahony stood up. "So have I, Windrush. The wind blew him in one day, and he made himself useful."

Walsh looked around the forlorn ruins of the Fenian army. "The invasion did not go well, then."

"It did not, Mr Walsh," O'Mahony gestured to the Royal Navy. "The British got wind of it."

Walsh glowered at the ships. "Damn them to hell and back. What are your plans now, General?"

O'Mahony pondered for a moment before replying. "I think the British in Canada are more ready for us than we believed. We'd be better employed in raising money for the boys in Ireland."

Walsh grunted. "You'll give up after one reverse?" He glowered at Jack through his mad, pale-blue eyes. "How about you, Windrush. I hear the British kicked you out of their little scarlet army."

"They did," Jack agreed.

"You'll want revenge." Walsh spoke sharply.

"I do," Jack said.

"Then come with me," Walsh said. "There's no place for you in a defeated army."

CHAPTER SEVENTEEN

New York, Spring 1866

Over the next few weeks, Jack learned more about the Fenians. He learned that there were two separate groups known as the Presidential faction and the Senate faction. While James Stephens and O'Mahony led the more pacific Presidentials, a man named William Roberts led the more aggressive Senate faction, backed by General Sweeny.

As Jack gathered information, he passed it on to Fraser, who seemed to have a knack of appearing in odd places, wherever Jack happened to be.

"I keep an eye on my people," Fraser said.

"How many of us are there?" Jack asked.

"Not many," Fraser said. "Enough to keep me busy."

"Is there anybody else near me?"

Fraser winked. "Best not to know too much," he said. "The less you know, the less you can reveal, either inadvertently or under duress." His grin was unexpected. "You'd be surprised, though. I guarantee you'd be surprised."

Jack nodded; he understood the danger, although he would have liked to know with whom he might be working. "Is there anything else happening in this cloak-and-dagger campaign?"

"There are many rumours and much speculation," Fraser replied, "usually wildly inaccurate."

"Tell me," Jack said.

Fraser told him about gunmen in Dublin who tried to shoot a private of the 8th Foot, and the excitement at St John in New Brunswick when three Fenian ships were rumoured to be approaching the harbour. Fraser shrugged. "The whole of Canada seems to be in a ferment, with bank clerks in Toronto carrying loaded revolvers, refugees from the Southern states of America swearing to help defend Canada and stories of Fenians acquiring torpedoes to sink British ships."

Jack shook his head. "It's unbelievable that things could come to this. Do the Irish hate us so much?"

"Many do," Fraser said, "and not without reason, perhaps, given our mutual history. That's why we have 47 British infantry regiments, and six of cavalry, based in Ireland, ready for an uprising."

"Things are bad, then," Jack said.

"Maybe, or it could be smoke and bluff." Fraser shrugged. "Mostly barrack-room gossip and pub tales. The Fenians are well organised. Their overall head man is James Stephens. The Fenians call him the head centre, with provincial centres under him, then there's a pyramid of groups known as centres, sub-centres and captains they call Bs and beneath them Cs."

"Are they as numerous as they claim?"

Fraser nodded. "On paper they are, but how many are just full of bravado and how many will turn up when the bullets fly is a different thing. There are said to be 184,000 Fenian supporters in the United States alone."

"That's more men than the British Army has in total."

"Yes," Fraser said. "There was a threat to shoot the Prince of Wales that seemed genuine enough, but lone murderers are a long way from a general uprising." He stood up. "But thanks to you and others like you, we know what they are doing. Keep passing on whatever intelligence you can gather."

"I will," Jack promised. "You've left me a lot to think about. Was there any further progress with that code I found in Carmichael's room?"

"Not that I've heard." Without another word, Fraser slipped away.

* * *

All that spring, the Fenians discussed tactics, with Jack among them. At times, the Fenians argued fiercely between themselves, splitting into mutually antagonistic groups, each demanding vastly different methods of gaining Irish independence. Jack noted that only Walsh mentioned Carmichael's disappearance and wondered if the two men were connected. Of all the Senate section, Walsh was the most aggressive, demanding action against the British, pounding his fist on the table to prove his point and even pointing a threatening finger when others tried to moderate his views.

"There is no profit in merely playing with the British Empire," Walsh said. "We must give them war, 10 deaths for one death; we must burn cities to avenge the Irish towns they have destroyed; we must make the Lord weep with the cry of mourning widows. Kill everybody who does not agree with our aims, man woman and child."

General Sweeny resolutely opposed Walsh. "No," he said. "We are soldiers, not murderers. We do not make war on civilians."

"A ruthless war brings a quicker peace," Walsh protested.

"As Secretary of War," Sweeny pointed out, "the final decision is mine, and I say we do not harm the civilians." He moderated his tone. "If we start to kill innocents, Mr Walsh, we will soon lose any support from the Canadian, British or American public, and our funds will soon dry up."

"We want war, not public support." Walsh stormed away as Sweeny again turned him down.

During this period, Jack wondered where Helen was, wishing he'd had time to thank her properly for her help with Carmichael. *Maybe it's for the best*, he told himself. *That woman is only trouble.*

After weeks of tedious debate, the Senate faction came to a decision that was fundamentally the same as that with which they had started. "Gentlemen," Sweeny said, "we will continue with our march on Canada."

Jack saw Walsh nod vigorously in agreement.

"We will not try to hold the whole of the British colonies there," Sweeny said. "It will be sufficient to occupy only a part and disrupt British communications. We will invade on many fronts, in Canada West and Canada East and cut these two colonies off from each other."

"At last!" Walsh fingered the long Colt revolvers that never left his waist. "When do we move?"

"Soon, Mr Walsh," Sweeny said. "The whole plan hinges on one thing – an attack on Fort Erie that will make the British believe we intend to attack the Welland Canal. The British will hurry their men from Toronto, leaving other sections of the frontier bare, ready for us." Sweeny raised his head. "The thrust towards the Welland Canal must be prolonged as long as possible to keep the British and Canadians occupied."

He paused for a long minute. "We cross from Buffalo in New York in two weeks."

"War!" Walsh exclaimed, his voice full of satisfaction.

CHAPTER EIGHTEEN

New York State, June 1866

Jack breathed in the crisp air of the early morning and listened to sweet bird-call and the rush of the Niagara River. Behind and beside him, General Sweeny's Fenians were busy preparing to cross once more into Canadian territory.

"O'Mahony told me how enthusiastic you were in his raid on New Brunswick," Sweeny said. "I admit that I distrusted you when we first met."

"That's not surprising," Jack said, "considering my background."

"You led a raid into Canada and took part in two more," Sweeny said. "That's more than anybody else, I think, and you were ready to take on the Royal Navy with only a revolver."

"I got a bit carried away," Jack admitted.

Sweeny nodded. "The smell of powder smoke can do that."

Jack nodded. "I did not participate in the second raid. I was trying to moderate a few hot-heads at the time."

"So I heard," Sweeny said. "It's one thing to try to fight the Royal Navy, and something else bully-ragging civilians. You did well in both cases. Now, let's get these men loaded up and over the river."

"Come on, lads!" Jack shouted encouragement. "Get a move on; we want to be there before dawn."

Even after the previous abortive raid, the men were enthusiastic, singing about invading Canada and freeing Ireland. Jack noticed that not all the accents were Irish or American. A sprinkling of Europeans had eased into the ranks, men who knew no other profession but soldiering, or vagabonds and adventurers who sought loot in Canada.

"Are you leading us, sir?" Jack asked Sweeny.

"No," Sweeny replied. "You are only a diversion, remember. When you draw the British, I'll lead the main force to take Quebec."

Jack nodded. The Fenian plans seemed to alter each time he heard them. "Who's in charge here, sir?"

"Colonel Owen Starr will be in command of the advance force," Sweeny said. "John O'Neill is in overall command. He knows that you have experience in the British military and will be looking to you for advice about British tactics."

"This day will go down in history," Patrick Walsh shouted. "In future, Friday, June 1st 1866 will be lauded like July 4th and November 5th. It will be a great day for Ireland and the beginning of the end of the British Empire."

Some of the men cheered. Others paid him no attention as they pushed the Fenian fleet of four scows into the river. Jack watched a pair of tugs steam up, with busy mariners attaching lines to the bows of the scows to tow them across the Niagara to Canada. By now Jack could identify the various accents, from the pure Irish of the homeland to men from Indiana and Cincinnati, Ohio and Illinois. He knew the Fenian regiments, from the 13th Tennessee to the 17th Kentucky and the 7th New York, men who had spent the previous few nights billeted in the homes of Irish sympathisers.

Jack was pleased that his own company was more disciplined than the rest, quieter, with cleaner weapons and less inclination to shout and yell, except for Kennedy, who stared, wild-eyed, across the river.

I've trained them well, Jack thought.

Cormac and Dermot remained close to Walsh, who watched Jack, his eyes musing and his usual two large Colts thrust through his belt. When he met Jack's gaze, Walsh lifted a hand in acknowledgement before speaking to Cormac and Dermot, with frequent glances in Jack's direction, making it evident that he was the subject of the conversation.

Well, let them talk, Jack thought. *I've fought Afridis on the Frontier, Burmese in the jungles and Cossacks in the Crimea. A few stray malcontents in the United States won't concern me.*

With about 1,000 men, this raid was more significant than the previous attempts. Although each man had a repeating Spencer or a Springfield or Enfield rifle, they lacked artillery and cavalry, with no commissariat, no wagons, stores or even knapsacks or uniforms. Jack hid his smile. However ambitious and numerous the Fenians might be, they were going off half-cock. This invasion force did not have the resources to be any more than a raid.

Just wait until you meet British regulars, my lads. Then we'll see if your battle songs help you.

It was still dark when Colonel Owen Starr led the initial force across the Niagara River from Buffalo, landing at the small town of Fort Erie.

"You're with me, Windrush," Starr said. "General Sweeny told me you could be useful."

"Yes, sir," Jack agreed. He slipped into the small boat filled with Fenians, heard Kennedy's excited voice and took a deep breath as they pushed across the river. "Up the Irish Republic," Kennedy shouted until Starr snarled at him: "Hush your fool mouth."

"Look, Colonel." A sober-eyed veteran with a Kentucky accent pointed to the fishing boat that emerged from the gloom. "They've seen us."

"Let them," Starr said. "They can't do much about it now."

Jack saw the white bow wave as the Canadian fishing boat sped across the river. He touched the butt of his revolver.

"There might be some resistance," Starr said quietly. "Have your weapons ready, boys." Blooded by the Civil War, the young Fenians looked to their rifles and readied for a firefight. Landing at Freebury's Wharf, they ran ashore, dodging and weaving in case of Canadian sharpshooters. There was no need of the precautions and no shooting as only a few residents of Fort Erie bothered to watch the arrival of these Irish-Americans.

"Establish a perimeter," Starr ordered quickly. "Windrush, take a picket forward."

Jack obeyed, leading a dozen men into the streets and posting sentinels in strategic places. "Here's the telegraph station," he shouted. "I'll destroy it so the Limeys can't send for help."

An elderly man, the telegraph operator was still in bed when Jack burst into his office. "Quick!" Jack dragged him to his feet. "I'm going to destroy your equipment. Send a message to the nearest military garrison."

"What?" Only half awake, the man reached for his equipment. "Who are you? This is most irregular."

"Send: Colonel O'Neill and a thousand Fenians at Fort Erie. Wolfe."

"What? Why?"

"Send it!" Jack lifted his revolver. "Hurry, man!"

Seeing the armed Fenians scurrying outside, the operator obeyed, and Jack set about smashing his equipment.

"You can't do that," the operator protested.

"Keep your head down," Jack advised, "and you'll be safe."

"Well done, Windrush." Starr beamed approvingly as he saw the wreckage of the telegraph station. "Now get back across the river and guide Colonel O'Neill over. Hurry, man; we want to get this town secured before the British arrive."

Not sure if he was acting the traitor or the patriot, Jack took the boat across the river.

"We have a foothold in Fort Erie," he reported to Colonel John O'Neill, an imperious ex-US cavalryman with a stern eye, veteran of campaigns in Ohio and West Virginia. "Colonel Starr requests that you join him, sir."

"And so we shall, Captain." O'Neill shouted orders that set the tugs plying across the river, each one pulling two scows full of eager men, some with green jackets, and others with ordinary civilian clothes or scraps of uniforms from both sides in the late US Civil War.

Dear God, Jack thought. *Will Britain have to fight the United States next?*

As soon as he set foot in Canada, O'Neill took charge. "Get to the railroad! Rip up the track!"

The Fenians obeyed, frustrated when the railroad workers escaped with the rolling stock.

"No matter. We'll disrupt their communications," O'Neill said with satisfaction. He pointed to a flagpole, where the Union Flag hung limp as if hiding its face from these invaders. "Haul that damned flag down and raise our Irish flag."

Jack watched as a flag rose slowly over Fort Erie. It was similar to the United States flag, but in green and white, with gold stars. As it reached the top of the flagstaff, a fortuitous gust of wind caused it to flutter in defiance.

"Dear God," Riordan muttered, staring at the flag. "We've done it; we've actually done it. We've declared war on the British Empire. God defend Ireland."

When Jack saw tears in Riordan's eyes, he realised what this expedition meant to some of these men. He could not imagine the feeling of belonging to a conquered country that existed under the command of another.

"God defend Ireland," Jack repeated softly. "And God save Ireland from another tragedy."

"Windrush," O'Neill said. "Take your company forward; look for any British response."

As Jack secured the perimeter, O'Neill sent men to arrest the town officials, ordered the local hotels and bakery to feed the invaders and read out a proclamation about a free Ireland to the bemused citizens.

"Scour the place for horses," O'Neill said. "Build trenches around the town."

O'Neill knew his job. The defences were crude, simple trenches that, at best, would delay any attack yet, as soon as they were complete, O'Neill marched the Fenians out of the town and along the Niagara River.

"Windrush, lead the way."

"Yes, sir." Jack's company moved into the skirmishing formation he had taught them while others looted what they could, so the invading army marched with plucked chickens and raw-boned farm horses. Above them, the green Fenian banner cried defiance to Queen Victoria and all her armies.

"We might be better to leave a garrison in Fort Erie, sir." Jack's military mind rebelled against having his route unguarded. "In case we need to withdraw."

"We'll leave some men at Newbiggin's farm," O'Neill said. "And anyway, the British don't know we're here yet. They'll have to get past us to reach the town."

"As you wish, sir." Jack nodded.

They stopped at Black Creek, where the river ran flat and fast beside beautiful trees, while the vast expanse of Canada seemed to brood on the horizon.

"Windrush!" O'Neill called Jack over. "I heard that you were adept at scouting in India."

"I did a bit," Jack agreed.

"Take one of the horses and ride around. See if you can see any British forces." O'Neill glanced at his men. "Do you want an escort? A few men in case of trouble?"

"No, sir. They'd only slow me down."

"I can find many good horsemen, Captain," O'Neill said with a smile. "In the United States, men are born in the saddle, not like England with its city dwellers and plodders."

"No, I'm better alone." Jack patted the Colt revolver he wore at his belt. "We'll see what I can find." He grinned to O'Neill. "In case I get lost out there, sir, where are we headed?"

"Port Colborne on the Welland Canal," O'Neill said. "It's also a station of the Welland and Buffalo and Lake Huron Railways so it's an important communications centre. We can disrupt trade there, and we all know how England loves trade, commerce and profit."

Jack's horse was a skewbald, brown and white, with a calm temperament. Jack mounted, patted the horse's neck and sat deep in the saddle.

"What's his name?" he asked.

"Titan," a capable-looking local lad told him. "Please look after him."

"I will," Jack promised as he urged Titan on. He waved as he passed his company. "Cheer up, boys! Ireland for ever!"

They cheered back as Jack trotted forward, past the outlying pickets and into the flat Canadian countryside. Now he had to find some official, Canadian or British, and pass on the intelligence he had.

The area was fertile, with neat farms and well-tended fields. Some of the farmers lifted a friendly hand as Jack trotted up.

"I'm looking for a police post or an army garrison," Jack asked.

The farmer scratched his head. "I don't know of any such. I heard shooting that way." he pointed in the direction Jack from which had come.

"The Fenians have landed," Jack said. "I'd advise you to hide all your valuables and get your family out to safety. Pass the warning on to your neighbours." The more people were on the move, the more likely the authorities were to learn about the Fenians' arrival.

Jack pushed on, spreading his warning until he saw the mounted man approaching.

The rider arrived at the gallop and panted: "Who are you?" Sweat was streaking dark lines down his face and his horse was a lather of sweat and foam. "What the devil's happening over there?"

"The Fenians are happening, that's what," Jack said. "Who are you?" The rider was evidently a figure of authority.

"I am Lieutenant Curran of the Queen's Own Toronto Volunteers."

"Good," Jack said calmly. He scribbled a short note and handed it over. "Pray give that to your commanding officer, Lieutenant, and look sharp."

"Who are you to order me around?" Curran demanded.

"Captain Jack Windrush of the 113th Foot," Jack replied.

"What?" Curran frowned. "I know that name – you're the cashiered traitor, by God."

"If I were a traitor, I'd have killed you by now." Jack revealed the pistol at his belt. "Now turn around and deliver that message to your commanding officer, Lieutenant."

Curran pulled back as though Jack had struck him. "What?"

"Don't question my orders, Lieutenant Curran! Move!"

"Yes, sir." Curran had lost his bounce as he turned, kicking in his spurs.

Jack watched Curran canter away, wondering if he would ever redeem his reputation after this strange campaign.

"Hey, Windrush." The voice was familiar.

"Yes, Dermot." Jack saw both of Walsh's enforcers riding up to him, their expressions full of suspicion.

"We've been following you. Who was that redcoat you were talking to?" Dermot had a hand on the butt of his revolver.

"That eager young man was Lieutenant Curran of the something-or-other Volunteers," Jack said mildly.

"You were talking to him."

"I was," Jack agreed. "I warned him to run and run fast because the Fenians were coming." He grinned. "Did you see how fast he spurred? Like the devil was after him."

"You should have shot him."

"My dear fellow," Jack said. "We are soldiers, not brigands. We don't murder every stray off-duty part-time soldier we meet! We send them away to spread alarm and despondency among their fellows." He laughed. "There is more to soldiering than just firing our little guns, you know. You have much to learn, however brave and bold you might be." He touched a hand to his hat. "Now, if you will excuse me, I have my duty to perform."

"Jack saw that his warnings had taken root, with the local farmers beginning to evacuate, bringing with them their families and property. He watched, knowing that every horse removed and every penny saved deprived the Fenians of a small gain, while every Canadian he warned could inform the authorities and bring retribution that much closer. He was doing his duty to the Queen.

"Come on, Cormac," Jack shouted over his shoulder. "It's time you two did something to earn your corn apart from following me around like shadows. Let's see if we can find some real British soldiers." *Aye, the ones that shoot back.*

Jack trotted away, aware that Dermot and Cormac were following a score of yards further back. Pushing three miles into the countryside, he saw no more redcoats until he returned towards the Fenians, where a small body of mounted men hovered beside a deserted farm.

"Over there," Jack reported to O'Neill. "Canadian Scouts, while the Queen's Own Toronto Volunteers are ahead. The British are watching us."

"I thought they might be," O'Neill said, "but we've done well. One day's work and we command the frontier from Fort Erie to Black Creek with not a single casualty on either side. Tomorrow we can march to the Welland Canal, and we'll control the only nautical route between Lake Erie and Lake Ontario. That should bring the British running." He gave a bleak smile. "I'll have intelligence reports from Mr Walsh soon, and they'll tell me what the enemy are doing."

Jack was unsure how he felt about treating the British as the enemy. He spent the night in the open, with the sound of merriment all around as the Fenians celebrated their successful foray on to Canadian soil. Three times, Jack saw riders approaching the solid building that O'Neill and Walsh had commandeered. When he tried to discover more, he noticed Cormac standing sentinel at the house door and decided to remain where he was. There was nothing to be gained in seeking trouble.

Saturday morning broke bright and warm, with the sense of space reminding Jack of the Indian plains.

"All officers," O'Neill called. "All officers."

Jack joined the others in a huddle around O'Neill, with the Fenian other ranks watching, spitting tobacco juice and huddling around small cooking fires. O'Neill looked serious.

"Mr Walsh has found out that the British have two separate forces marching towards us," he reported. "A Colonel Booker leads a Canadian Volunteer force, while a Colonel Peacocke is bringing British regulars with artillery."

"We can defeat both," Walsh said.

"They aim to link up at Stevensville, a few miles away," O'Neill said, "and if they do, they will outnumber us."

The thought of artillery blasting their men sobered the Fenian officers. "What do we do?" Starr asked.

"We push on," O'Neill said. "We can smash the volunteers before they join the regulars." he paused for a significant moment. "Half-trained volunteers won't stand against our veterans."

The officers gave a faint cheer, with Walsh nodding and fingering the scar above his left eye.

"Break up the camp!" O'Neill ordered. "Bring in the outposts. We're marching towards Port Colborne."

The Fenians moved at some pace, if in a careless fashion, with skirmishers ahead and on the flanks. The men were cheerful, some singing the Fenian songs, others smoking or talking, with most of the accents so familiar that, if Jack closed his eyes, he could almost be back in the Crimea or India, except the British might shoot him as a traitor. That thought chilled him, as did the realisation that the Fenians could also shoot him as a spy.

"Get up ahead, Windrush," O'Neill ordered. "You know better than anybody how the British could act. Inform me the minute you see the Canadians."

"Sir." Jack pushed ahead, riding past the Fenian scouts to a barrage of cheers and whistles. He had gone barely a mile when he saw a smudge of scarlet and heard the rattle of drums.

That's the British response. Jack pushed forward to see which regiments were involved. As he closed, he knew at once that O'Neill was correct and the defenders were part-time soldiers, Canadian volunteers rather than British regulars.

"I thought O'Neill would send you." Fraser appeared from the shelter of a farmhouse and rode up to him. "You're the best man for the job."

"Maybe so," Jack watched the approaching volunteers. He estimated them to be about 800 strong, marching in column with scouts or skirmishers 100 yards ahead. "These lads could do with an experienced man to lead them."

"No," Fraser said flatly. "Mr Smith has another job for you."

"For God's sake! I've sent messages to tell him what's happening here! Now I can help defend Canada."

"The volunteers will do that, and there are a couple of regular British infantry regiments on the march as well."

Jack looked again at the volunteers as they marched solidly onward. When Fraser passed over his field glasses, the men jumped into focus. "They look very young," Jack commented.

"They are. Some are only boys," Fraser said.

"So it seems," Jack said. "Many of the Fenians are veterans of the American Civil War, and some have Spencer repeating rifles. An experienced man with the volunteers would equalise the odds a bit."

"Orders from Mr Smith," Fraser said. "You've to stay with the Fenians and continue to send us reports. Colonel Booker outranks you anyway, Captain, and I don't think any Canadian colonel would give way to a mere captain, especially a declared traitor."

Jack reluctantly nodded. "You're right there, Fraser. What's Booker like as a commander? Is he experienced?"

"Not in battle," Fraser said. "Lieutenant Colonel Alfred Booker is an auctioneer in Hamilton and commands the 13th Battalion of the Royal Hamilton Light Infantry. He's in his early 40s, with a force of college students and such like."

"Who else is coming?"

Fraser grinned. "Tell O'Neill that Booker has the 13th Hamilton, the Queens Own Toronto and the Caledonia and York Companies."

Jack frowned. "I don't like giving information to the enemy."

"He'll find out soon enough anyway," Fraser said, "and the intelligence will enhance your standing with him. If you want to impress him, you can tell him they gathered at Port Colborne, and Booker left by the Grand Trunk Railway, only to disembark about four miles from here and continue on foot," Fraser added. "Booker's got orders not to engage the Fenians until he meets up with Colonel

Peacocke's regulars, but," he continued with a shrug, "Booker may wish to prove himself."

"I'm sure that will interest O'Neill," Jack was watching the volunteers march purposefully toward them, drums encouraging the painfully young men to give their all.

"I'm sure O'Neill already knows. You'd best get back." Fraser lifted a hand in farewell, turned his horse and galloped away.

"British ahead," Jack reported to O'Neill, feeling like a traitor. "About 700 Canadian volunteers, including the Queen's Own Toronto, the Caledonia and York companies and the Hamilton volunteers. Colonel Booker is in command."

O'Neill focused his binoculars forward. "How far?"

"Maybe two miles."

"Any artillery, cavalry or British regulars?"

"No." Jack shook his head. Trust a veteran to ask the right questions. "Not with these lads, but Colonel Peacocke is on his way with a couple of battalions of British regulars plus artillery."

"So I heard," O'Neill said. "Right then." He grinned through his beard as he looked around. "We're on a fine position here at Lime Ridge. We'll leave half our men here and push on with the rest." He raised his voice. "Starr! You remain here and make a defensive position. We'll bring the Limeys to battle on the ridge. Think of New Orleans, by God, or Concorde."

"Sharpshooters and skirmishers to the front! The British are coming. We have twice their numbers," O'Neill said, "and they're only volunteers, part-time weekend soldiers. We're veterans of the greatest war in American history – let's show them that the Fenians are coming."

Moving more slowly, the Fenians continued their advance, with Riordan and Kennedy in the van and the Canadian volunteers now in view. When the Fenians reached a spot known as the Smuggler's Hole, a desolate place of swamps and dying trees, Jack heard the flat crack of a single Spencer rifle and checked his fob watch – it was eight in the morning. The battle had begun.

Rather than halt, Colonel Booker sent sharpshooters from the Queen's Own Toronto Regiment forward. Any doubts Jack may have had about the part-time soldiers fighting vanished as the firing intensified. Although the Fenians were about equal in numbers to the volunteers, and many had repeating rifles, the volunteers more than matched them in the rate of fire.

"Get forward, Windrush. See if you can delay these Canadians until Starr creates his defences." O'Neill ordered.

Jack dismounted and moved down a wooded slope into the swampy ground of Smuggler's Hole, with his feet sinking deep into the mud and mist immediately gathering around him. For all their bombast, the Fenians did not seem so happy under fire.

What the devil do I do now? Jack asked himself. *Lead these men forward against Canadian infantry and be a traitor, or lead them badly and get shot by one side or the other?*

Jack did not have long to ponder, for the Fenian sharpshooters began to retreat, splashing through the mud under the volunteers' pressure, while wisps of mist curled around the trees. "Stand fast!" Jack bellowed. He had no need to feign his anger. "Fight them!" He had never been with men who retreated from a less experienced force.

The Queen's Own pressed forward, keeping immaculate formation despite the conditions and forcing the Fenians back at an ever-increasing speed. The volunteer fire was continuous but not accurate and, more than once, Jack saw a Canadian soldier struggle with his rifle, as if unsure how it worked. All the same, Jack had to duck from Canadian bullets. As the Fenians withdrew and the Canadians pushed forward, Jack also retreated, swearing at the his men's lack of resolution as he sank up to his knees in muddy water. The volunteers pushed on, moving from tree to rock or any cover they could find, with the white gunsmoke drifting across the boggy ground to merge with the mist.

"It seems as if this invasion is over before it's begun," Jack later reported bitterly to O'Neill.

"Not yet." O'Neill was more composed than Jack had expected. "We're drawing the Canadians on to my main body on Lime Ridge, where I have an idea in mind to unsettle the Limeys." His teeth gleamed white through his beard. "Brooker is a conventional commander, without the guile of a veteran."

Jack nodded. "Aye; what's your plan, General?"

"Lure them on, stop them dead and, when they're bogged down, hit them in the flanks with something they don't expect." O'Neill watched the advance of the Canadians through his field glasses. "They're keen enough; I can't fault them for that."

As the Fenians retreated out of the boggy land, they ascended Lime Ridge, leaving the misty marshland and entering a wooded area. They withdrew step by step, still firing, with the raw young volunteers following behind a white cloud of smoke. A man fell here and there, the bodies remaining as a smudge on the landscape or a crumpled scarlet bundle.

Jack realised they were already among the trees, scattered at first but increasingly dense as the ground rose to the main body of Fenians on Lime Ridge. The fighting reached a crude picket fence, once the result of somebody's hard work, now sadly neglected but a definite boundary, with the remaining Fenians waiting behind makeshift defences.

"Halt!" O'Neill's order rang across the battlefield. "We stand here, fellow Irishmen, and we hold the Limeys back!"

Some of the Fenians cheered, others looked over their shoulder to the road back to the United States. At about the same time, the volunteers' fire began to falter.

"Ammunition!" Jack heard the desperate cry. "Has anyone got more cartridges?"

"I've only three left myself."

The leading company of the Queen's Own drifted to the rear, with men of the 13th Hamilton Battalion taking their place in the firing line.

"They're still coming," Jack tried to discourage the Fenians, but O'Neill turned the situation to his advantage.

"If we don't stop the advance of the Canadians, they will hang us all," O'Neill shouted. There was a temporary lull in the firing as the Fenians digested that unwelcome thought. "Better to die honourably by a bullet than dishonourably by the rope."

O'Neill's words put new vigour into the Fenians. They lined up behind the picket fence and opened a terrific fire at the volunteers. For a while, the two sides exchanged musketry, with a haze of smoke pressing down on them, the constant crackle of rifles and the occasional scream of a wounded man.

"We're holding them now," O'Neill said with satisfaction and gave orders for both wings to extend. "We'll see how the weekend soldiers react to being outflanked."

The Canadians refused to panic, but found cover and met the advancing Fenians with controlled volleys.

"They're holding well, the devils." O'Neill sounded surprised. "I could have done with a few regiments of these Canadian boys during the late war." He did not disguise his admiration. "But they are amateur soldiers. Let's see how they cope with the infantryman's nightmare."

"You men!" O'Neill addressed the mounted Fenian officers. "You are now the cavalry of the Irish Republic. Make yourself known – ride up to the Canadians with noise and bluster. Put the fear of God into them!"

Jack nodded. it was a simple plan that could be effective against raw troops, however brave. He watched as the newly constituted Fenian cavalry cantered around the hillside, shouting and waving swords until the volunteers reacted as O'Neill had hoped. Jack heard the near-panicked call of, "Cavalry!" together with the brassy blare of a bugle and watched as the volunteers formed a square, Waterloo-style.

"Got them," O'Neill said. "The Limey's love that formation." He raised his voice. "Push forward the flanking companies. Shoot that square to pieces."

Jack knew that a well-disciplined square of infantry was almost impervious to cavalry but offered an excellent target for riflemen. As the Fenians moved forward, firing, Colonel Booker realised his mistake and ordered his men to break formation once more.

O'Neill waited until the volunteers were in confusion. "Now, my Irish lads! Fix bayonets and charge!"

While the Queen's Own refused to retire and even advanced towards the Fenians, the companies in the rear, unable to see what was happening, hesitated and moved back, with some men running in near panic. Jack heard the hoarse shouts of the officers as they tried to regain command of their young soldiers.

At last, the Queen's Own realised that they were isolated, outflanked and outnumbered. Major Gillmore who commanded the regiment, ordered a withdrawal.

"They're fighting well," O'Neill said as the Queen's Own withdrew in good order, turning every few yards to fire. Occasionally they hit rough ground that broke their formation, reformed on the far side and continued their disciplined retreat. Jack noted that one company was particularly stubborn. He watched them for a while, shaking his head. *The Caledonian Company, of course. Bloody Sawnies. Old General Campbell might approve of that!*

* * *

"You fought well." Jack stopped beside a wounded volunteer.

"We'll do better next time." The boy's smooth face grimaced in pain. "I've never fired live ammunition before. Next time we'll flatten the Fenians."

"Come on, son." A hard-eyed Fenian hurried to help. "You can't fight any more. We'll look after you now."

Leaving behind a few men, O'Neill pushed on until he reached Smugglers Hole when he called a halt to watch the volunteers' steady withdrawal. Standing beside a crooked tree, Jack could only admire the bravery of the half-trained volunteers. "You did Canada proud, boys," he said quietly.

"Chase them," Walsh snarled, firing both pistols at the volunteers. "Chase them back to Toronto!"

While a few of the more hot-headed Fenians obeyed, the bulk decided they had done enough fighting for the day and stopped for a smoke, or to pick up souvenirs of their famous victory.

"Officers, gather to me," O'Neill said. "We'll discuss the situation."

Standing on a slight rise with the immense space of Canada stretching before them and the abyss of the sky above, Jack again thought it very strange to be in the middle of a small army that was trying to topple the British Empire. He stood as the Fenian leaders gathered around, some bearded, intense men, sincere in their belief of a free Ireland, others younger, some foreign mercenaries who knew no other trade except soldiering. Walsh glared towards the volunteers, loading his revolvers.

"Here is the position," O'Neill reminded. "We've repelled the Canadian volunteers, but there are two battalions of British regulars and a battery of artillery on its way towards us."

The serious men nodded, calculating the odds, while the hotheads made wild statements about fighting to the death and twisting the British lion's tail. "We're come here to fight," Walsh said. "We can ambush them, kill as many as possible and encourage the Canadian Irish to rise."

"Colonel Peacocke is a good fighting man," Jack pointed out, hoping the Fenians would retreat rather than fight regulars, with the resulting casualties on both sides and martyrs for the next conflict. He had seen enough of Irish soldiers to know they were formidable whatever the circumstances. He saw Walsh turn those pale, mad eyes towards him.

O'Neill looked from one to the other as *The Wearing of the Green* drifted to them from the Fenian ranks. "There we have both sides. Do we fight, gentlemen? Or do we withdraw? We can still reach the canal and hold out there."

"We fight!" Two of the younger men shouted, with Walsh nodding his agreement.

"We'd lose if we did," Jack said. "I have no doubt that our men are brave, and we've just seen them push back a force of redcoats, but the soldiers coming towards us are professionals. Have any of you ever seen British infantry in action?"

Nobody had. Even Walsh was silent.

"Well, I have. I've led British troops in Burma, India and Russia and they won't heed casualties, or be fooled by a few men on horseback. I'll tell you what Peacocke will do. He'll throw out companies to block our retreat and hammer us with artillery until we either break or charge, right into the massed volleys of British infantry." He let the image sink in for a few moments. "When we've taken hundreds of casualties, the redcoats will advance with the bayonet and finish the job."

"We'll take some with us," Walsh said.

"Yes. We will, if Peacocke allows us to get in range. He has rifled Armstrong artillery, the most accurate cannon in the world. They can dice us long before our rifles can reach them. Imagine the blow to Fenian morale in the States if the British destroy this force with few casualties to them."

O'Neill glanced at Jack. "You know the British Army, Windrush. Tell me honestly; what chance do we have in a straight fight?"

"None," Jack said flatly.

"That's what I thought," O'Neill said. "If we fight, I'd be condemning these men to slaughter. We'll occupy the town of Ridgeway to show the flag, and then we'll return to Fort Erie."

Jack felt Walsh's gaze on him as the Fenians turned around, some happy to get back to America, while others grumbled their disapproval. Kennedy bit off a hunk of stolen tobacco. "We lost nine men defeating the British," he said. "We should be chasing them, not running away!"

* * *

Ridgeway was a quiet little community where the people watched as the intruders paraded around for a while, shouting Fenian slogans. The occupation was short and bloodless until O'Neill gave the order to destroy the weapons they had brought to arm the expected flood of Canadian Fenians recruits.

"We're returning to Fort Erie," O'Neill said.

"We're retreating from shadows," Riordan said, glowering at O'Neill.

Some Fenians cursed as they broke the spare Springfields, while others enjoyed the act of destruction. Moving to the company he had trained, Jack barked them into formation and ensured they marched as a disciplined unit. His professional pride dictated that, enemy or not, his men would look like soldiers when they arrived back on United States soil.

"Windrush," O'Neill said. "Find out if the Canadians are following us."

"Yes, sir." Happy to leave the discontented army, Jack pushed behind the Fenians and trotted cautiously in the direction of the volunteers, to see them withdrawing in good order, with sharpshooters out to watch for any possible Fenian advance. He tailed them for a while, saw they were heading in the opposite direction and hurried back when he heard the crackle of musketry.

Kicking in his heels, Jack galloped forward, to find the Fenians halted in confusion outside Fort Erie.

"What's happening? What's the firing for?"

"It's the Limeys," O'Neill said. "They've occupied the town. We can't get back to the USA until we capture it. We're trapped!"

CHAPTER NINETEEN

Fort Erie, Canada, June 1866

"How many men?" Jack peered over at Fort Erie. "They're using the trenches we built, the rascals!" He focused on the Union Flag the Canadians had raised. "I can't see many men there at all, but they might be in hiding, waiting to ambush us."

"They're blocking our return," O'Neill said. "We'll have to drive them away."

Once again, Jack had mixed emotions. Part of him hoped there were sufficient British soldiers in the garrison to end the Fenian incursion here and now, while he did not wish the Fenians to suffer. Ireland and the Irish had endured too much already.

"Ready, boys," O'Neill said tersely. "Get the sharpshooters forward."

The Fenians moved like the veterans many were, advancing in short rushes under covering fire. The Canadians responded with volleys of musketry that howled and screamed around the Fenians. From the onset, it was evident that the Fenians had 10 times the manpower and 20 times the firepower of the defenders. Jack saw sailors among the Canadians, while men in scarlet fired muzzle-loading muskets against the repeating Spencers of the Fenians.

"They're falling back!" O'Neill ordered his sharpshooters forward, with the bulk of his men following behind as the ill-armed Canadians fought desperately. Some were wounded, others surrounded and forced to surrender, throwing their outdated weapons to the ground in frustration. Once again, Jack noted how well the Fenians treated their prisoners as soon as the fighting ended. Those Canadians who escaped retreated to a small tug for their withdrawal to Port Colborne, a few miles to the west.

"There were fewer than 80," Murphy said. "Navy volunteers and artillerymen without their guns. I thought the Canadians wouldn't fight us."

"They killed four of our boys," Kennedy said, "and wounded dozens. We should shoot them all!"

"Look after the prisoners," O'Neill said. "They're soldiers like us."

"That's twice we've captured Fort Erie," Riordan cleaned and reloaded his rifle. "Once more and we get it to keep."

"I don't think London would swap all of Ireland for one small Canadian town." Jack holstered his revolver. He had not fired a shot in the entire skirmish.

"No, and I don't think we'll be getting any reinforcements over this river." O'Neill pointed to a United States gunboat that cruised off the town. "It seems that we are as unpopular with the Federal authorities as with the Canadians."

With British regulars marching on their position and the US Navy blocking any reinforcements, the Fenians' invasion had come to a dead stop. That night, the Fenian numbers fell as men began to desert, some drifting into the Canadian countryside and others finding small boats to try to cross back into US territory.

"We may get arrested on our return, gentlemen." O'Neill addressed his officers. "But at least we'll be in an American jail and not a British one." He raised a smile. "Let us hope that our exploits on Canadian soil have ignited a fire for Irish freedom."

The men cheered.

"Although the outcome was not what we wished, we have demonstrated our desires and made the Limeys sit up. They know they have another frontier to guard." O'Neill made the best of his hasty retreat. "Now we can withdraw to America, or try again in Canada." O'Neill grinned. "I'm going to try again. Are you with me, boys? Ireland for ever!"

"Ireland for ever!" With O'Neill's suggestion restoring their confidence, the Fenians cheered as the general signalled for a tug and scow from the Fenians on the US shore.

"I will leave some pickets behind," O'Neill said. "Hold the town until we pull the British away and then reinforcements will flood in. I'm looking for volunteers."

Jack was surprised when about 30 men volunteered to return to Fort Erie.

"Take us to Lower Black Rock," O'Neill ordered the tug's master. "While the British are marching to Fort Erie, we will outflank them and show them that the Irish know how to use the water as well."

Boarding the scow, the Fenians cheered, waved their rifles and raised the green flag.

"Ireland for ever!"

"You're playing a losing hand," Jack said as the tug headed along the river.

"Halt right there!" The metallic voice of a speaking trumpet sounded as the US gunboat approached them. "This is USS *Michigan* of the United States Navy. You are all under arrest."

"Keep moving," O'Neill ordered. "They won't do anything. The US authorities support our cause."

The sound of the crack of naval artillery, followed by a tall pillar of water suddenly rising a few yards ahead of the tug proved O'Neill's words to be false.

"Jesus and Mary!" Kennedy pointed his rifle at USS *Michigan*. "We're Fenians!" he shouted. "Don't fire on us!"

"They know who we are," Jack told him. "This invasion's over boys. We're going back to the States."

As USS *Michigan* showed her eight guns, the last of the Fenian objections faded away. There was no resistance as US seamen fastened a hawser from the bows of the scow to the gunboat. Two US Navy cutters sat a few yards away in the river with armed sailors watching the now-quiet Fenians.

"Come on, lads! We've done what we set out to do!" O'Neill sounded cheerful. "The British won't dare attack us when the navy is here."

As the night eased into morning, British troops arrived in Fort Erie, and soon the Union Flag once more soared above the little riverside town. Lifting his binoculars, Jack could see some British regulars watching the drama off their town, while others took prisoner those Fenians who had remained.

"The English will hang them, like as not," Kennedy roared, waving his fist.

"I don't think so," Jack said. "They're US citizens, mainly, so there will be some diplomatic solution."

"They're citizens of the Irish Republic," Riordan glared at Jack. "They took the Fenian oath, same as you and me."

Unwilling to argue the point, Jack only nodded as the US authorities towed the Fenians back to American soil.

"They don't know what to do with us," Riordan said. "If they go against us, America might have another civil war as 100,000 Fenians rise, and the South might join in."

"We want to fight the British Empire," Walsh pointed out, "not the United States."

With a minimum of fuss, the US Navy ushered the Fenians back on land, relieved them of their weapons, and escorted them to an enclosure. They separated the known officers from the rank-and-file, with Jack, as an unknown, thrust in with the latter. The men huddled into small groups, boasting of their part in the late battles or contemplating their next move, depending on their natures. Finding a spot where he could listen to the conversations, Jack sat on the grass and leaned back.

"Wolfe."

Jack looked around, trying to make out the voice amidst the babble of sound. "Fraser?"

"Windrush, follow me."

Jack eased away to one of the few quiet corners, where Fraser sat, dressed in a faded green jacket.

"I'm glad you survived the battles," Fraser said.

"That was a kind thought," Jack said. "What do you want?"

"I have a message from Smith."

"I thought you might have." Jack sighed. "Does he say I can return home now?"

"Here it is." Sliding off his left boot, Fraser extracted a small square of paper from under his heel.

"Why the subterfuge? It would be easier to tell me."

"I am not to know what it says," Fraser said.

Jack sighed. "All right; what happens now?" He looked up, saw Fraser drifting away to merge with the Fenians, and opened the note.

"Stay with the Fenians and follow W. If you need assistance, contact Colonel Ferguson at Fort Erie and mention F. S."

Jack sighed. He had hoped to slip back to Canada. W must be Patrick Walsh, whom the US Navy had also kept with the rank and file Fenians. With no uniforms to identify rank, the Federals had only held the well-known faces as officers. F must be Fraser and S was Smith. But who the devil was Colonel Ferguson? Jack shook his head, again wishing he was back as a regimental officer, with simple decisions of life, death and battle to make rather than these codes and false identities.

***

The smart uniform of the young US Navy lieutenant contrasted with the shabby garb of the Fenians as he addressed them.

"All right, Irishmen," the lieutenant began, "you are leaving us. The government is giving you free passage to your home states without pressing any charges." He looked around. "You are lucky men, for personally, I would charge you all with breaking the neutrality laws and trying to bring this great republic into a war with Great Britain." He turned away to a chorus of jeers and whistles.

After three days of waiting, Jack was glad to be on the move again. He joined in the queue for the train south, keeping Walsh in sight as they boarded the carriages. Some Fenians were laughing, others drinking, with so many smoking that visibility was impaired. Jack estimated there were 2,000 Fenian soldiers crammed into the trains that rattled along the Hudson River Railroad and three out of four men were puffing on either a pipe or a cheap cigar. Fenian songs echoed around the corridors, sung in a variety of accents ranging from New England Yankee to the Southern drawl and the lilt of Connaught and Clare. Meanwhile, Jack kept his eye on Walsh, who was talking with a group of Ohio veterans, while Cormac and Dermot kept close.

The train stopped in a featureless plain, with a group of men lurching noisily off, to the waves of their fellows and a rolling blanket of tobacco smoke.

"We've been watching you, Windrush." Cormac slid beside Jack.

"All the time," Dermot arrived at his other side with a cigar thrust in his mouth.

"That must have been interesting for you," Jack said casually.

"Mr Walsh wants to speak with you," Cormac said.

"Good," Jack said. "Let's go to him."

A crowd of Fenians began to bawl out an Irish song, with the Gaelic words lost on Jack and the fighting of a few moments before having ended in a flurry of good fellowship and handshakes for all.

"Well met, Windrush," Walsh greeted Jack. "I doubted your sincerity until I saw you fighting. The British Army cashiered you, I believe."

"That's right," Jack said.

"You'll want to get back at them," Walsh's disturbingly pale eyes fixed on Jack.

"I do," Jack agreed.

"Yet you argued for a retreat," Walsh said.

"If we had fought and lost," Jack said, "the cause would have ended there and then. Now we can fight again."

"Stay close," Walsh stepped to the head of the compartment. A shaft of weak sunlight illuminated his face, playing on the scar until Jack thought it dominated all else. "Listen to me, anybody who wishes to continue the fight against our real enemies, the British."

There was movement in the carriage as some men moved closer and others, who had seen enough fighting, quietly shifted away. Jack remained where he was, watching and listening.

"That was a poor end to a lacklustre invasion," Walsh said. "We spent a few days in British territory, shot a few militiamen and slunk away with our tails between our legs."

The gathered men listened, some nodding agreement, others showing their disapproval.

"I say we go back," Walsh thundered. "I say we return over the Canadian border and show the British what angry Irishmen can do in a real war."

This time there was more of a reaction, with most of the audience drifting away and a few others sliding into the carriage. Jack observed the ebb and flow of the crowd and noted the calibre of the men who gathered around Walsh. He had seen the type too often in the British army not to recognise them. They were the roughest of the Fenians, the wild men that other, decent, men tended to avoid. Kennedy was among them, grinning fiercely, while Riordan listened with a cynical twist to his mouth.

One tall, lean man with a long Colt revolver hanging low on his hip raised his voice. "I'm with you, Walsh. My name's Butler, and I rode with James Lane."

Walsh raised a hand. "You were a Kansas Jayhawker, were you?"

"I was that," Butler said. "And Kennedy here was at the sacking of Osceola."

Jack knew that the sacking of Osceola in Missouri was one of the worst atrocities in the early years of the American Civil War, leaving the town a smoking wreck.

"That's the sort I want," Walsh said. "I want men who are not afraid to fight and men who are not afraid to kill."

Jack grunted. He had heard about Lane and the Kansas Jayhawkers, irregular riders who fought a guerrilla war along the Kansas-Missouri border. If all Walsh's followers were of that calibre, Canada could experience a much rougher time than they had so far.

Walsh looked directly at Jack. "Are you with us, Windrush?"

"I'm with you."

"Me also." The accent was German, the man squat, with long blonde hair and a flowing moustache. "I am Becker. I fought with the French in Algeria and Sherman in Georgia."

Walsh's grin was among the most evil that Jack had ever seen. "That's my sort," he said. "Stay with me, boys."

* * *

They slipped away from the main body at the next station, 50 of the most hard-bitten Fenians and mercenary soldiers, joined by Jack Windrush, ex-captain in the British army, with Patrick Walsh in command.

"Get horses," Walsh ordered. "I don't care how. Our cause is more important than the complaints of a few civilians. Beg, borrow or steal." He raised his voice further. "We might be Fenians, but as from today, we'll also be known as the Green Company. Now go and find horses!"

Such an order appealed to the Green Company. They scattered around the small town of New Horizon, yelling slogans that belonged to the late Civil War or earlier conflicts on the opposite side of the Atlantic. Jack watched them for a moment before searching for a stable where he could buy a horse. Whatever part he was playing, he was still a British gentleman. Choosing a spirited chestnut gelding with the name of Destiny, Jack carefully calculated how much to pay the dealer, advised him to lock the stable door before the Fenians could get away with the remainder of his stock and purchased a serviceable if worn, saddle.

"Rough times, mister." The stable owner looked at Jack through weary eyes. "I thought we were finished with wars for a while."

"So did I," Jack agreed. "Keep safe."

Not all the Fenians had bothered with saddles – the wildest of the Jayhawkers rode bare-backed, galloping around the town whooping and yelling, showing off their trick riding and firing pistols into the air. Becker stood outside the church, smoking a long pipe as he cleaned his rifle.

God Help Canada when this lot are set loose. Jack thought of the settled, peaceful Canadian communities, totally unprepared for an eruption of battle-hardened badmashes such as these mounted Fenians. With Walsh in charge, there would be little or no restraint.

"With me for Ireland!" Walsh shouted as he gathered the Green Company in New Horizon's small central square. "To Canada!"

"To Canada!"

Some of the riders had hung bags of biscuit or meal on their saddles, others had appropriated new boots, hats, bottles of rum or whatever else they fancied. Walsh led them north in a cloud of dust, a wild bunch of 50 riders intent on causing as much mayhem as possible, and, Jack suspected, more intent on violence than on any political conviction about Ireland or anywhere else.

Jack remained with them for the first day, until they were 30 miles north of New Horizon in a sparsely populated area of woodland and small secret lakes.

"We'll stay here tonight," Walsh ordered, "and tomorrow we'll strike out for the Canadian border and teach the British what an invasion means. We'll set the frontier alight like in the old days of the Kansas-Missouri border war." His laugh was loud and coarse. "We'll give them 100 Osceolas!"

The Green Company camped beside a dark lake in the shadow of a group of tall trees, with the men passing around their rum, singing Fenian and other songs and growing progressively louder as the evening wore away.

"I'll take first watch, Walsh," Jack volunteered.

"First watch?" Butler laughed. "We're in friendly territory, you Limey bastard."

"He's right, Windrush," Walsh said. "There's no need for precautions until we're in Canada. Get some sleep – we have busy days ahead of us."

Jack waited until the last of the revellers lapsed into drunken slumber before he rolled away from the camp and led Destiny into the trees.

I have to warn the Canadian authorities, Jack told himself. *That's more important than sticking with Walsh.*

Within 10 minutes, Jack suspected that somebody was following him. Within 20 minutes, he was certain – no man could survive on the North-West Frontier of India without being aware of every unusual sound and movement. Slowing his horse, Jack allowed his pursuer to close the gap, then rode in a circle to come up behind him. Drawing his revolver, he hid it under a fold of his dust-coat.

"What the devil do you want?"

There were two of them, Dermot and Cormac, with pistols loose in their holsters and Spencer repeating rifles cradled in the crook of their arms.

"You're deserting," Dermot said, raisng his rifle. "You're a dirty Limey deserter." Cormac grinned, patting his revolver.

Jack knew he had to act quickly, or these men would kill him or drag him back to Walsh. He had no intention of ending his career at the wrong end of a Fenian's rifle. "You two men had better return to the Green Company," he said.

"You'll be coming with us, Limey." Dermot lifted his rifle until the muzzle was levelled at Jack's chest, "or we'll drop you right here."

Jack fired on Dermot's last word. Even as he saw the bullet crash into Dermot's stomach, he was wheeling Destiny around, anticipating Cormac's attack. He heard the bark of the rifle before he completed his manoeuvre and felt the wind of the shot as it whistled past his head.

Cormac forced a bullet into the breach of his rifle, swivelling the barrel to aim. Jack extended his arm and fired in the same movement. He saw his shot crash home, saw Cormac stagger in the saddle and heard him curse.

With blood seeping from a wound high in his chest, Cormac lifted his rifle again. "You Limey bastard."

"That's right," Jack said. "That's exactly what I am." Deliberately aiming at Cormac's head, Jack fired again. The bullet smashed between the man's eyes, jerking his head back and killing him instantly. His horse bolted, carrying its dead rider along with it.

Dermot was slumped in his saddle, bleeding heavily. For a moment, Jack contemplated killing him outright. *No! I am still a British officer and gentleman.*

"Down you come." Easing the man from his saddle, Jack removed his rifle, pistol and a long knife. "I'll dress your wound and leave you here," he said.

Dermot glared at him through pain-dulled eyes.

"You might live, and you might die," Jack said, "and quite frankly, I don't care either way." Dressing the man's wound as best he could, Jack propped him against a tree and left him there. "Thank you for your horse," he said, and rode away northward, towards Fort Erie. It would be a long ride.

***

"What do you mean?" Colonel Ferguson was a Canadian officer with grey in his black hair that matched his grey eyes. "We've repulsed the Fenians. We chased them back over the border to the United States. The American authorities are dealing with them."

"There are others," Jack said.

Ferguson eyed Jack up and down. "And who do you say you are?"

"I am Captain Jack Windrush of the 113th Foot."

"The devil you are," Ferguson said. "I know that name. Captain Jack Windrush was court-martialled and cashiered for helping the Fenians." Ferguson stood up, reaching for the revolver that hung in its holster behind his chair. "You're a damned Fenian yourself, man!"

"I'm working for British Intelligence," Jack tried to explain. "If I were a Fenian, I'd hardly come here to warn you about another Fenian raid, would I?"

Ferguson paused. "Perhaps," he allowed, still with one hand on the butt of his revolver. "Or you could be raising a false alarm to lead us in the wrong direction."

Jack remembered the note that Smith had left him. "Perhaps the names Wolfe or Fraser might help."

Ferguson looked up sharply. "Tell me about Fraser."

"No." Jack shook his head. "You know who I mean."

"Wait here," Ferguson ordered. Abruptly standing, he strode from the room, to return a few moments later with a man Jack struggled to recognise until he realised it was none other than Donald Fraser, now clean-shaven and smartly dressed.

"Do you know this man?" Ferguson asked him.

"I can vouch for him," Fraser said. "This gentleman is sound. Do you have intelligence for us, Captain?" He listened as Jack explained about Walsh and the Green Company.

"A company of 50 men, you say?" Ferguson shook his head. "I can call up the volunteers and round them up."

"Are the volunteers mounted?" Jack asked.

"They're mostly infantry."

"The Green Company are all horsemen," Jack said, "hard-riding Jayhawkers, veterans of the Kansas Border War and the US Civil War, bitter Fenians and the rag, tag and bobtail of all nations. I have nothing but admiration for the courage of the Canadian volunteers, but the Green Company would ride rings around any volunteer infantry."

Ferguson glanced at Fraser and then at Jack. "What do you suggest, Captain Windrush?"

"Meet fire with fire." Jack thought as he spoke. "I want a few dozen desperadoes. I want as many frontiersmen and mounted men as you can raise, the more ruffianly, the better. I'm going to play the Green Company at their own game." He knew his smile would have disgraced a long-dead skull. "On my last campaign, I dodged Pashtun tribesmen in the mountains north of India. I doubt the Jayhawkers are any less friendly or more skilled."

"I know some of the very men. How long do we have?" Fraser asked.

"Hours rather than days," Jack said. "I hope to God we can stop them in time. See what you can raise, Fraser, and as quickly as you can."

CHAPTER TWENTY

Louisburgh, Canada, June 1866

The settlement of Louisburgh was not much of a place. Named after its founder, Louis de Ville, it had never grown past the size of a hamlet, despite its antiquity. Centred on a solid church with an ornate wooden spire, and with a cobbled square, on which a monthly market attracted local farmers, Louisburgh boasted fewer than 30 houses, mostly of timber. The town's only claim to fame was a rumour that General Wolfe had passed through, although others scoffed at the notion, asking why the great general should visit such an out-of-the-way place. Apart from that vague legend, there was a story of a marital scandal involving a woman with two husbands at some point during the last century. Apart from these semi-legendary stories, nothing significant had ever happened in Louisburgh, which suited the citizens.

So there was consternation when the half-hundred riders appeared from a fold of ground that morning in June, riding hard and yelling fit to raise the dead. Old Mr Riel, 70 years old, was leading his ancient horse across Main Street when he heard the drumming of hundreds of horses' hooves. He looked up in surprise, lifting a hand as if to ward off the oncoming horde. The last thing he saw was a tall man with a scar pulsing on his forehead before the bullet took him between the eyes.

Mary and James Brown were leaving the general store with their monthly supply of goods for their small farm, bickering happily as long-married couples do. James Brown was lifting a keg of molasses onto his wagon when the riders erupted into the street. "Stand back, Mary," he said. "This could be trouble." He was reaching for his shotgun when Butler the Jayhawker lifted his revolver. The first two shots missed; the third hit Brown in the left leg, smashing his shin. He yelled, falling sideways but still holding the shotgun.

"Jim!" Ignoring the bullets, Mary Brown ran to her husband of 23 years.

"Get back, Mary!" James screamed the words as he levelled his shotgun. Another bullet hit him in the left arm, breaking the humerus bone.

"Jim!" Mary screamed. Mary dived forward, trying to cover her husband's vulnerable body with her own. "Leave him alone!" Others of the Green Company reined the horses in, firing.

Two bullets hit Mary simultaneously, one in her lung and the other breaking her left knee. She collapsed on top of James, choking on her blood as James squeezed the trigger of his shotgun. The pellets sprayed in a wide arc, with one nicking the arm of a rider.

"You bastard!" Kennedy snarled, and fired the remaining rounds of his pistol, with his laughing companions doing the same. James and Mary died together without ever knowing why.

Patience Forster was running an errand for her mother when the Green Company rode into town. In all her 15 years she had never been more than five miles from Louisburgh and had only spoken to strangers on market day. Patience had thought her life dull and often talked about going travelling with her young man, Matthew, whom she had known all her life. She dreamed of venturing as far as Toronto or even Montreal. Patience stared in excitement as the horsemen galloped in, whooping and shouting. Waving, she followed one of the riders, asking who they were and what they were doing.

"Come with me, and I'll show you." Becker bent from the saddle, scooped Patience up in a single movement and threw her face-down across his horse.

"No!" Patience screamed, kicking her legs, but her struggling was in vain as Becker kicked in his spurs and galloped to a barn.

"You're mine, little lady," Becker said, laughing as he halted his horse and kicked open the barn door. Grabbing Patience by her newly-washed hair, he dragged her off the horse and into an empty stall.

Jean Le Mesurier was the descendant of one of the earliest French settlers in Canada, although he had no connection with France except his ancestry and his name. Now he ran the local store, attended the parish church and hoped some day to marry the middle-aged Widow MacAlister. All Louisburgh smiled, knowing that the widow played Jean against his great rival, Donald Vincent, a younger man who ran the stables and was set to become one of the richest men in town. That day Jean had just served Mary and James Brown and heard the commotion in the street.

"What is happening out there?" Jean asked Widow MacAlister, who was sitting comfortably in the small room behind the shop, sipping a cup of the finest imported Indian tea.

"It sounds like somebody's shouting," the widow said. She was not an inquisitive woman and preferred to allow the world to leave her to spin her webs of romantic intrigue with Jean and Donald. "Best leave them to it, Jean."

"No, that's gunfire," Jean replied. "No doubt about it." Loading one of his stock of hunting rifles, Jean walked to the door, just in time to see James and Mary Brown die under a torrent of revolver bullets. A quiet man, Jean was also one of the best hunters in Louisburgh. Shouting to the widow to remain inside the store, he aimed his rifle and shot dead Butler the Jayhawker. Jean was reloading when Kennedy drew another revolver and fired five shots at him. Despite the close range, the first three bullets missed, but the fourth and fifth crashed into Jean's chest, throwing him back against the window of his store. The widow ran out, stared in incomprehension at the crumpled, still-living body of her favoured intended, and screamed as the gunman fired a fatal shot into the storekeeper's head and pushed the widow inside the store.

Young Mrs Greenthorpe was asleep in her house when the bullet smashed through her window and killed her. Her death was merciful as it meant she did not witness the fate of her three children after Walsh ordered the Green Company to set fire to her home. Abraham Greenthorpe was less fortunate as he was working in his blacksmith's forge at the time. Hearing the screams of his children, he ran into the flames to rescue them and died knowing that everything in his life was gone. Walsh watched dispassionately, not sharing the glee of his men.

"Loot whatever you wish," Walsh ordered. "Kill everybody and burn the place down. I want Louisburgh to be a warning to the entire British Empire."

Walsh watched as his Green Company completed ravaging the small settlement that had never before seen any trouble. He watched as his men hunted out the women for their pleasure, not caring about age or condition. He watched as the Louisburgh men were gathered together and shot, and the young children thrown into the flames.

"This is better," Kennedy laughed, with innocent blood speckling his face.

"Kill them all," Walsh ordered.

He watched as the Green Company systematically looted the houses of anything alcoholic or valuable, drove out the horses, killed the pet dogs and cats and finally gathered in a roaring, drunken, rabble in the cobbled square. Smoke and flames arose from what only two hours previously had been a quietly prosperous town.

"We ride in five minutes," Walsh noticed that two of his men still held terrified, weeping women. "Get rid of the women. They'll only slow us down."

The first man obeyed immediately, pressing the muzzle of his revolver against the head of his captive and blowing out her brains. The second was more reluctant. "This one's fun," he said. "She'll keep me warm at night."

"Get rid of her," Walsh said. "I won't repeat my order a third time."

"I'm not in the army," the man said. "I'm not here to answer to you."

Without another word, Walsh drew his pistol and shot the man. The woman fell, silent and shocked, from the saddle. As she lay whimpering on the ground, Walsh lifted his hand. "Ride out," he said. "We head eastward."

Yelling, driving their captured horses before them, the Green Company trotted away from the burning settlement. Walsh saw them all away, circled and shot the woman who still lay sobbing on the ground. After a single glance around, he stepped his horse over the corpse of the Fenian he had killed and followed his men. Patience twitched, moaned once and lay still.

CHAPTER TWENTY-ONE

Fort Erie, Canada, June 1866

Jack surveyed the dozen men that Fraser had gathered for him. Weather-beaten and hard of face, they gazed back at him, unflinching. "My name is Windrush, Captain Jack Windrush, late of the 113th Foot and the Corps of Guides."

"I read about you." The speaker had an Irish accent and a deep white scar across his face. "You were cashiered for supporting the Fenians."

Captain Ferguson pushed himself away from the wall against which he had been leaning. "Captain Windrush is working with me."

The scarred man looked Jack up and down. "Are you the same Windrush who fought at Inkerman?"

"I am," Jack said.

"Aye," the scarred man nodded. "You and the 113th held the ridge until support came up."

"That was us," Jack agreed.

"I was in the 8th Hussars," the man touched his scar. "I got this at Balaclava."

Jack held out his hand. "It is a privilege to shake hands with one of the Light Brigade."

"Troop Sergeant Doherty. I was a year in a Russian prison," Doherty grinned. "So I missed what seems to have been the worst part of the campaign."

"Nothing could have been worse than that charge," Jack said. "I saw part of it from a distance."

Doherty suddenly smiled. "So you're Fighting Jack Windrush. What do you want us to do?"

"There is a band of some 50 or so mounted Fenians about to raid Canada," Jack explained the situation as his audience listened.

"Where are they?" Doherty asked.

"They hit Louisburgh yesterday." Fraser had been a silent spectator. "They wiped the place off the map and killed most of the residents." He waited for a few moments as the horsemen digested the information. "There was one survivor, a young woman named Patience Forster. When I spoke to her, she told me that some of the men shouted Irish slogans. They called themselves the Green Company."

"Telegraph every town in a radius of 200 miles," Jack drew on his experience in the Indian Mutiny. "Tell them to watch out for these raiders. Call out the local militia and Volunteers and have them guard the main settlements and bring in everybody from outlying farms and isolated hamlets."

Fraser nodded. "I'll see to it."

"Raise as many mounted men as you can and have them scout for signs of these raiders. Don't let them ride alone – order them to watch and listen."

Ferguson took scribbled notes. "I'll notify the military garrisons."

Jack raised his voice. "Right, lads, I want every man to take two spare horses and enough food and water for three days at least." He waited for the nods of acknowledgement. "Each man to carry a rifle with 100 rounds of ammunition, plus a knife and blankets. We are hunting the hunters, lads, and the odds are on our side."

"What's the plan, sir?" Doherty asked.

"We head towards Louisburgh. We'll ride in extended order across the countryside, look for the smoke of burning buildings, call at every settlement we come to and when we meet this Green Company, we will herd it towards the nearest defended town."

"When do we start, sir?"

"We ride in two hours. Gather what you need."

They left in an extended line, scouring the land ahead, with each man keeping sight of his neighbour. Even with the best maps that Fraser could get hold of and his men's local knowledge, Jack barely expected to find any trace of the Green Company in the vastness of Canada. He was not surprised when the first day brought no success.

Fraser had passed on the warning, with most of the farms and small hamlets deserted or on alert, so that men watched Jack's riders from behind shuttered windows, and gun barrels protruded from hastily made loopholes in barn doors.

They camped for the night on a small, wooded knoll, with men posted on sentry duty and the horses knee-haltered to prevent them straying.

"This does not seem right for Canada," Doherty commented, puffing on a stubby pipe. "It's the most peaceful land in the world."

"Aye," Jack agreed. "But it only takes a few angry men to turn quiet into chaos."

An hour before dawn, Jack climbed the tallest tree on the knoll, to survey the surrounding countryside for fires.

"Over there." A tall, lithe Canadian named Barton had joined him. "There's a glow on the sky just beyond the horizon."

"So there is, by God," Jack said. "Something's burning. Rouse the men."

Riding in column with outriders on each side and Barton scouting ahead, Jack's men trotted towards the fire. A band of grey across the eastern horizon heralded encroaching dawn, with the strengthening light dimming the fire-glow.

"Smoke!" Barton galloped back to report. "I can smell smoke, Captain."

"It could just be a household fire," Jack said. "Or somebody burning rubbish."

"It could be." Barton did not sound convinced.

"Which direction?"

"Somewhere over to the east, Captain."

Jack pondered for a moment. "All right, extended formation, as we were yesterday. Barton, lead the centre of the line."

They rode forward slowly, breaking to cross fences and skirt copses of trees. After a few moments, Jack also smelt smoke, and urged Destiny forward, speeding up the rate of advance.

The farm had been prosperous, with a generous farmhouse surrounded by barns and storehouses. Now it was a charred wreck, with smoking timbers fallen inwards into what had been a family home.

"Search for bodies." Jack had seen too many such tragedies during the Indian Mutiny to become emotional. Reining up at the highest point of the farm, he scanned the area with his field glasses, looking for smoke, fire or any unusual movement.

"No human bodies," Doherty reported after a few moments. "Only animals."

"It could have been an accidental fire," Barton said.

"Too many hoofprints," Jack said at once. "Somebody raided this place, so my guess would be the Green Company. Are you a local man, Barton?"

"Born and bred," Barton replied proudly.

"If you were raiding here, where would you head next?"

Barton creased his forehead as he considered the question. "The DuProis place," he said at last, "about five miles to the northeast."

"Lead the way," Jack said.

They smelled the smoke a minute before they saw the orange glow of flame through a screen of trees.

"Spur, lads!" Jack ordered. "We might catch this Green Company in the act. Scout ahead, Barton."

"Right, Captain," Barton spurred his mount forward as Jack organised his men in a column. He halted them a quarter of a mile from the DuProis farm, wary of ambush, and pushed Destiny forward. He heard the shouting as he closed.

"Captain." Barton emerged from a copse of trees. "The Green Company is there."

"Right, Barton." Jack stared ahead. "Did you see any sentries? Any lookouts?"

"Not one, sir," Barton answered. "They're too intent on looting the place."

Jack nodded, thinking fast. "Good."

Returning to his men, Jack gave brief instructions. "We don't know how many of the enemy there are, or how they will react. Stay together, shoot anybody who shows resistance but make sure we don't shoot any civilians. Our password is Victoria, with a counter of Canada."

Some men nodded, with others repeating the words. When Doherty ran a hand down his scarred face, Jack wondered if he was thinking of the valley at Balaclava.

"Follow me." For a moment, Jack wished he had his Guides with him, men who were born and bred to this type of warfare. But he shook away the thought. These Canadians were good men. All they lacked was some experience. "Make sure you're loaded and ready."

As the familiar combination of excitement, fear and exhilaration swept through him, Jack pulled Destiny around. It did not matter if the enemy were Russian Cossacks, Pashtun tribesmen or Fenian irregulars, the sense of danger always affected him in the same way.

They rode into a spectacular dawn with bands of silver and orange brilliant to the east as Jack led his men at a fast trot. As they advanced, the flames became more visible, rising behind a screen of tall trees, with smoke coiling blue-brown into a lightening sky. Drawing his revolver, Jack dug in his spurs and raced forward, ready to fight. He heard his men behind him, the noise of the horse's hooves a constant drumming on the hard ground.

Silhouetted against burning buildings, the Green Company did not hear Jack's horsemen approach until they were only a few yards away. One bearded man turned, his mouth open in surprise, shouted something and fell as Doherty shot him from the saddle. The others scattered, some firing at these unexpected attackers, while the majority fled without a second glance.

"They're on the run!" Barton yelled.

"Aye!" Jack had to shout above the crackle of flames and roar of collapsing buildings. He noticed a couple of his men pulling away in pursuit. "Keep your formation, lads!"

Riding on, Jack circled the farm, flushing three more raiders, all of whom spurred into the surrounding countryside. "That's only nine. Where are the others?"

Sudden flames from a neighbouring farm answered him. "They've spread out," Doherty said.

Jack nodded. "We'll hunt them farm by farm."

With the brightening daylight, it was not hard to follow the column of smoke to the neighbouring farms. Angered by this attack on innocent civilians, the Canadians lost their quiet demeanour, firing the instant they saw the raiders.

I'm turning these men into soldiers, Jack told himself. *They are superb raw material, hardy, amenable to discipline and good shots.*

Riding from farm to farm, leaping over fences, and driving the Green Company before them, Jack's men heard concentrated musketry ahead.

"Listen, sir," Doherty said. "That sounds like a skirmish."

"Maybe the Volunteers have found them," Jack said, "or even one of the regular battalions." He coughed in the acrid smoke. "Come on, lads; keep your formation! Let the redcoats see we're not some rabble like the Green Company."

With the sun surprisingly warm above them and smoke drifting through the once-peaceful countryside, Jack trotted towards the sound of the guns. The firing increased in volume before it died away to an intermittent splutter.

"That's not regular British infantry," Jack said. "There's no volley fire."

"Canadian Volunteers, perhaps?" Doherty hazarded.

"Perhaps," Jack allowed. "Barton! Ride ahead!" After their skirmishing, there was no need to warn him to take care. These Canadians were fast learners.

Barton was back within minutes. "It's a farmhouse," he gasped. "The Fenians are attacking a farmhouse."

That explained the lack of disciplined firing. Some stubborn farmer had refused to abandon his home and was trying to fend off the raiders.

"We'll hit the Green Company in the rear," Jack said.

"The farmer will think we're reinforcing the Fenians," Doherty said. "We've no uniforms to show we're British."

Jack swore, knowing that Doherty was correct. "I wish I had the foresight to bring a union flag." Well, it was too late now. He thought rapidly. "When we get close," he decided, "shout out God save the queen. I don't want anybody shot by mistake!"

"Right, sir!" Doherty replied. "We'll do her majesty proud."

"Make sure your rifles are loaded!" Jack pushed in front of his men. Not knowing how long the civilian defenders could hold out, he decided that a direct attack was better than a more cautious approach.

"Hard and fast, lads!" Jack said. "Keep together, shoot any of the enemy and good luck to all of us."

"Good luck, Captain," some of the men called out.

The farmhouse was smaller than any they had encountered so far, a square, stone-built structure, two storeys high with shutters over the windows. Surrounding the building, the Green Company were firing intermittently, with the occasional rush forward. As Jack watched, a defender thrust his rifle between two shutters and fired a single shot.

"Run, you Fenian bastards!" the defender roared. "You'll get nothing here! No surrender!"

"No surrender!" The words were echoed by others inside the house, with both male and female voices joining in.

"They're not surrendering," Barton said, with a smile.

"Right lads!" Jack shouted. "After me!"

Yelling, "God save the queen," Jack's men charged forward, taking the attackers in the rear and scattering them. Jack kicked in his spurs, had a glimpse of a lean, sun-browned face pointing a rifle at him, fired and galloped on without seeing the result of his shot. He heard his men chanting, "God save the queen," behind him as he led around the outside of the house, firing at any of the Green Company they saw.

"God save the queen!" The words came from inside the house. "No surrender!"

Faced by a stubborn defence and without knowing the strength of the force that was attacking them, the Green Company ran, leaving three of their number on the ground.

"Doherty! Barton! Follow them; see where they go. Everyone else remain with me." Jack dismounted and approached the farm.

The defenders emerged from the front door, still holding their weapons. One middle-aged man and two men in their late teens or twenties held rifles, with a younger boy carrying a pistol. Two women, each brandishing a large knife, peered over the shoulders of their men.

"Captain Jack Windrush, late of the 113th and the Guides," Jack removed his hat and gave a little bow to the women. "Your family did very well, sir."

"No surrender," the middle-aged man replied. "I'm Simon Armstrong. We're Orangemen, you see." He grinned. "We held Londonderry against the Fenians in 1690, and we'll defend the Boyne today." He indicated his farm.

Jack nodded. Here was another example of a centuries-old conflict continued in another continent. Would people ever learn to put aside their arguments, allow the past to remain in the past and move into the 19th century?

"Quite so," Jack said. "I congratulate you on a brave stand, whatever the historical reason." He replaced his hat. "Now I must leave you, for I have raiders to pursue."

"Good luck, captain."

Without another word, Jack applied his spurs and trotted in the direction the Green Company had taken. Following their trail of flattened grass and broken branches, it was only a matter of minutes before he caught up with Doherty and Barton.

"They're riding fast, sir," Doherty reported. "There are about 20 of them, as far as I can make out, so there must be more ahead."

"Given the casualties they've taken," Jack said, "I'd estimate that Patrick Walsh, or whatever his real name is, has around the same number."

Doherty grimaced. "That's 40 Fenians then, more than three times our numbers."

"That's right," Jack agreed. "Let's hope that Walsh doesn't realise that. If we keep pushing, we might panic them into flight. I want Walsh alive, if possible."

"Why is that, sir?" Doherty asked.

"I want to find out who he is and who's behind all this mayhem."

"If you tell me what he looks like, I'll ask the boys to look out for him."

"He's tall and gaunt, with a small scar on his forehead."

"I'll pass that on," Doherty said. "I wonder who gave him the scar."

"Captain!" Barton pulled up his horse with a flourish. "The Green Company have gathered together. They've halted about a mile ahead."

"Thank you, Barton." Jack looked around for a defensive position. "We'll make a temporary camp at that knoll there." He led his riders to a small rise, crowned by three tall trees. "Doherty, you are a sergeant again. Form a defensive ring, post sentries and wait for my return."

"Yes, sir." Doherty threw an automatic salute. "Can I ask where you're going?"

"Barton and I are going to scout the Green Company's positions."

"Yes, sir." Doherty accepted Jack's words without visible emotion.

Riding slower, Jack followed Barton away from the picturesque area of small farms into an area of denser woodland, with fewer clearings and many streams and lakes of various sizes.

Jack sniffed. "Can you smell that?"

Barton frowned. "No. Wait, yes, it's tobacco."

"Stop here." Jack halted Destiny in the shadow of a tall tree. "Something's wrong."

Barton came beside him, sliding his rifle ready to fire. They waited as a faint breeze stirred the branches of the trees around them. A bird called, with its notes unfamiliar to Jack. He felt the hairs on the back of his head rise.

"There!" With his eyes trained on the North-West Frontier, Jack saw the movement between the trees. "And there."

The men were moving slowly, sliding from tree to tree, using the undergrowth for cover.

"I see them," Barton levelled his rifle. "Have they seen us?"

"Maybe." Jack felt his heart beat a little faster. He could see at least a dozen men now, vague shapes through the forest, some upright, others crouching. "Fire a single shot and withdraw."

"Yes, Captain." Barton fired on his final word with the sharp crack of his rifle shocking in the still greenness of the forest.

Aiming his rifle, Jack squeezed the trigger and turned his horse. The smoke of their discharges hung acrid as the Green Company returned fire, with the bullets hissing through the branches, cutting off twigs and stray leaves.

"Don't head directly for our men," Jack ordered as they neared the edge of the woodland. "Try a more southerly approach."

Barton nodded, ducking as a bullet slammed into a tree trunk a yard to his right. "Sorry Captain," he said. "I've never been under fire before."

"It doesn't get any easier," Jack told him. "You're doing well. I've seen veterans cope far worse than you are."

Jack's relief at reaching the edge of the forest belt ended when he saw a body of horsemen to the south. A dozen strong, they were strung out along the fringe of the trees, and immediately cantered towards Jack and Barton.

"More of the Green Company, by God," Barton said.

"Walsh is cleverer than I thought," Jack commented. "He must have expected me to go looking for him."

"They flushed us out," Barton said.

"Impudent devils!" Jack swung his horse around. "Come on, Barton! It's a point-to-point race!"

Some of the pursuing riders began to fire as they rode, with the bullets flying well wide. Knowing that it was almost impossible for a mounted man to shoot with any accuracy while riding at speed, Jack ignored the gunfire, concentrating on guiding Destiny over and around obstacles.

Turning in his saddle, Barton fired two shots from his revolver. "There are more of them," he shouted.

"Aye," Jack agreed. From being the hunter, he was now the hunted, with about 40 feral men on his trail.

The Green Company spread out, with half a dozen of the most active riders pushing forward. "They're trying to break us," Jack shouted. "Those lads will chase us until we're exhausted, then the others will go for the kill."

If we're lucky, Jack thought. *If we're unlucky, they'll capture us and torture us to find out where the rest of my men are, and I don't care much for Walsh's mercy.*

"Spur," Jack shouted. "Ride for your life!"

Not knowing the terrain, Jack had to concentrate on every yard he rode, with Barton sometimes at his side or a few yards in front.

"You're a better rider than I am," Jack shouted. "Could you make your way back to the men without getting caught?"

"Yes, Captain."

"Go, then. Tell Doherty to take the lads back to the nearest military post."

"How about you, sir?" Barton hesitated.

"I'll lead Walsh's men astray for a bit," Jack said. "I've been in worse situations." He hardened his voice. "Go! That's an order!"

Jack watched as Barton spurred ahead, jinking on the uneven ground. *Now I'm alone with 40 enemies on my trail.*

This area was empty of people, with recently abandoned small farms scattered among the low hills. Looking behind him, Jack saw the nearest of the Green Company only quarter of a mile away, with the remainder strung out in a line to prevent him from doubling back.

I can only ride and hope, Jack told himself. Feeling Destiny flag beneath him, he knew the horse could not last much longer. Glancing over his shoulder, Jack saw the fastest riders of the Green Company were closing, so his capture was inevitable. He could only delay them as long as possible, or stop and fight.

All right, Jack said to himself. *I'm a soldier, not an athlete. I'll die fighting and see how brave you are when men fight back.*

With Destiny slowing by the minute, Jack cast around for a suitable defensive spot. The first bullet whistled past his head a full second before he heard the sound of the shot. Glancing over his shoulder, he saw that two of the Green Company had dismounted to fire while the remainder galloped forward. Jack saw Walsh giving orders.

Walsh knows my horse is tired.

The small building must have had a purpose at one time, although Jack could not imagine what it might have been. Some 15 yards from a solitary tree, it nestled into the flank of a hill, with a single entrance and a small, square window, both facing downhill. As a defensive position, it was far from ideal, but Jack could see nothing better. Guiding Destiny across the broken ground, he dismounted, took his water bottle, rifle and ammunition and slapped Destiny on the rump.

"Run, boy," he said. "You deserve some freedom."

Ducking the bullets that slammed into the walls of his would-be sanctuary, Jack pushed at the door. He swore when it did not budge, threw himself against it and nearly fell inside when the door burst open. There was not much to see. A single square room empty of everything except dirt, the building provided only shelter.

Slamming the door shut, Jack peered out of the window. The Green Company was only a couple of hundred yards away, with the fastest riders surging forward and the rest now bunching up, knowing they had treed their quarry. Jack half expected to hear hunting horns as they closed on him.

"So here we are," Jack murmured. "Come on then, boys. Let's see how good you are."

Half a dozen of the attackers were firing, with shots thudding against the door or walls, or kicking up fountains of dirt around the hut. Searching for Walsh, Jack saw him astride his horse in the shelter of a tree. It was an impossible shot so, instead, Jack aimed at one of the dismounted Green Company marksmen. His bullet took the man high in the right arm, sending him spinning backwards. Before the marksman hit the ground, Jack ducked back from the window to reload, ignoring the hammer of shots against the wall.

Bobbing back, he took quick aim at a horseman, fired, missed and withdrew. The Green Company had spread out around the hut, with some firing and others advancing from cover to cover.

"There's only one way in, boys, and only room for one man at a time," Jack spoke to himself. "You'll pay to take this house. The closer you get, the better targets you make for me. The longer I delay you, the more chance that the volunteers arrive to round you up."

But Jack knew that Walsh would also have calculated the odds. With one eye on the door in case the Green Company tried a sudden rush, he loosened his revolver in its holster, reloaded his rifle and rose at the window. The attackers were noticeably closer, creeping on all fours up the grassy slope. Sighting on the nearest, Jack took careful aim and fired. The man yelled, jerked backwards and rolled away, cursing, to thrash, moaning, on the grass.

"That's you out of action my boy." Jack bobbed back down. "And then there were 38."

Reloading quickly, he stood up, ducking as a dozen rifles fired, with the bullets splintering the window frame and spattering inside the hut.

"Aye, you're learning, Walsh," Jack said. "It's only a matter of time now." Stepping to the back of the room, he cautiously peered outside. Even from his restricted view, Jack could see some of the attackers were only a few yards away. Determined to fight to the end, Jack raised his rifle, waited until he had a clear shot and fired. Knowing he had hit his man, Jack ducked back before the expected retaliatory fusillade. "And 37…"

"You're a dead man!" The shout came from outside. "If you come out with your hands out, we'll make it quick and easy but if you make us come for you…" the rest of the threat was left unsaid.

"Come and get me!" Jack roared back. "If you dare!"

The reply was only laughter from a score of throats.

"They'll rush the door next," Jack told himself. "I'll shoot two, maybe three and then it'll be all over." He sighed. "Goodbye, Mary and David – you know that I did not choose this end, but soldiers rarely live to a hoary old age."

The shooting was constant now as the Green Company concentrated on the window and door, with the sheer volume of fire preventing Jack from taking time to aim. Twice he rose and fired blindly out of the window, not knowing if he even came close to hitting anybody. The Green Company replied with a score of shots that smashed into the door, sending splinters of wood inside the hut.

After five minutes, the firing stopped. Jack wondered at the sudden silence. Tempted to look outside, he realised that Walsh could be baiting a trap, and remained crouched at the back of the room with his revolver pointing to the door. He smelled the smoke before he heard the crackle of flames.

"They've set fire to the place!" Jack swore, took a deep breath, coughed and swore again, forcing himself to think straight. Although the hut was stone-built, the door and window-frames were of wood, with a turf roof. Walsh might have set some combustible material around the walls, or merely fired the door. Jack knew he would not burn to death, but could die of asphyxiation; Walsh intended to smoke him out. Ripping off the tail of his shirt, Jack emptied half the contents of his water bottle on top and wrapped it around his mouth. He had a choice now: stay and suffocate or leave and allow the Fenians to shoot him to pieces.

Well, he told himself, *I'm a soldier – best to die a soldier's death as so many of my ancestors did.*

Checking that his revolver and rifle were fully loaded, Jack nerved himself for the end. Closing his eyes, he mouthed a brief farewell to Mary and David, hooked open the smouldering door and rushed forward. As he had thought, Walsh had piled branches around the hut, creating a burning barrier. Kicking his way through, Jack emerged onto the open hillside, rifle in hand.

The Green Company waited for him, lying behind rocks or crouching in the shelter of trees. Jack fired his rifle, dropped it, drew his pistol and fired again. He did not see the men who came behind him until they dropped a horse-blanket over his head and held him tight.

* * *

"Well, now, Captain Jack Windrush." Walsh eyed him as lay on the hard ground, tied hand and foot. "It seems that you are a traitor to the Fenian Brotherhood."

Jack looked around at the circle of predatory faces. Most of them were in their late twenties or thirties, bitter-eyed men with lines of hardship etched in their features and not a trace of mercy. Some chewed tobacco as they surveyed him, others sipped from bottles that did not contain water, or merely glared. Kennedy sharpened a large knife, while Riordan merely watched, expressionless.

"I am Captain Jack Windrush of the 113th Foot and the Guides," Jack said.

"That much is true." Walsh stood with his thumbs hooked in the waistband of his trousers, "but you swore allegiance to the Fenian Brotherhood."

"You people are no Fenians," Jack said. "I doubt that there is a drop of Irish blood in even half of you. You're murdering hounds jumping on the Fenian cause purely to murder, loot and rape."

Some of the Green Company laughed at Jack's words, others growled at him.

"This is a court to decide your guilt or innocence," Walsh said. "We could have shot you like a dog, but decided that this way is better." He stepped closer. "Do you deny that you took the Fenian oath and turned against us?"

Jack straightened up as best he could. "I do not deny that. I am Captain Jack Windrush…"

"We know who you are," Walsh interrupted him wearily. "You were cashiered by the British Army, joined us and broke your oath. What do you say, boys, guilty or innocent?"

"Guilty!" The cry was unanimous.

"You have been found guilty," Walsh said pompously. "The penalty is death. Take him to the tree!"

A dozen men grabbed Jack and dragged him to the nearby tree, where a single branch thrust out at right angles 20 feet above the ground.

"You chose a good spot to hold out," one of the Green Company said. "Right handy for a hanging tree."

The others laughed. "The only thing more cheerful than a good lynching," a one-eyed man with a Southern accent said, "is the lynching of a Limey officer."

Jack felt hunger among the comments and a genuine pleasure in anticipating watching him hanged. Unable to resist, he could do nothing as three men untied his legs, hoisted him astride a ridge-backed, saddleless horse and thumped him down as painfully as they could.

"A hangman's knot or a slipknot?" somebody asked.

"Slipknot," Walsh replied at once. "I want to see him strangle slowly."

There was more laughter. "Ready to die, Limey?"

The one-eyed man threw a rope over the inviting bough and expertly tied a loop before sliding it over Jack's head. The hemp was rough against Jack's throat.

"You've done that before," somebody shouted.

"Only for bluenoses," one-eye said. "Never for a real Limey officer."

The laughter was harsh and forced.

"I bet he'll strangle in five minutes."

"Five dollars says he'll snuff it in three!"

Listening to men gambling on how long he would take to die, Jack vowed to go with as little fuss as possible. He had witnessed a few hangings in India during the Mutiny and knew it was an undignified death, with the victim struggling, kicking and squirming in the noose as his bowels and bladder emptied. He would try to avoid giving these men the pleasure of watching him squirm. That at least would be a small final victory.

"Say goodbye, you dirty limey bastard!"

"Goodbye." Jack tried to sound calm although he was shaking at the prospect of a humiliating death. "In a few days, all of you will be where I am now, with the British authorities watching you die for the murdering vermin you are."

Grinning, the one-eyed man slapped his hat against the bony rump of the horse, which bounded away. Jack felt the sudden jerk as the rope tightened around his neck. He had hoped that the Green Company had made a mistake so he would die quickly of a broken neck, but instead, the noose tightened, with more pain than Jack had expected. He felt the pressure increase, realised he was kicking to try to alleviate the agony and forced himself into stillness.

As if from a long way away, Jack heard the voices as the Green Company commented on his execution, although he could not make out the words. The pain was acute, accompanied by panic and a terrible tightness in his chest. *I never got a chance to say goodbye to Mary.* The blackness was a relief as he drifted down into a never-ending abyss where peace awaited him. He felt welcome here. He was home.

***

Light forced back the dark. Pain replaced the peace. "No!" Jack fought the bright renewal of life.

"Here! Are you all right, mister?" The voice was rough, the accent Canadian.

Jack coughed, writhed, and coughed again.

"Who are you?" The voice continued as somebody shook Jack's shoulder and forced something between his teeth. Jack choked as raw spirits burned his throat.

"He's coming to!" The voice seemed to come from a great distance away.

"Who is he?"

"Somebody the Fenians didn't like."

Jack spat out the whisky, tried to sit up, coughed again, choking.

"Easy there, man – you were as close to death as I've ever seen a live man."

"What happened?" Dazed and confused, Jack stared upward into a circle of concerned faces.

"Somebody tried to hang you, boy." The speaker wore the scarlet uniform of a British soldier, but with facings that Jack did not recognise.

"That was Walsh's Green Company." Jack found speaking intensely painful. "Who are you?"

"Lieutenant Peebles, Canadian Volunteer Cavalry." The speaker was tall, with a small moustache.

"I am Captain Jack Windrush of the 113th Foot." Jack thought it best not to enter detailed explanations. "Help me up." He heard his voice emerge as a croak. "And pass over more of that whisky, for God's sake."

The volunteers laughed, helping Jack to his feet.

"Did you see which way they went?" Jack asked.

"They ran when we appeared," Peebles said.

As he leant against the tree, Jack could see the trail. "Follow them," he ordered. "Don't give them a minute to reorganise." He glanced around. "You should find my men somewhere, a dozen of the best."

"That will be Sergeant Doherty's command." The lieutenant was quick on the uptake. "I sent them to the right flank."

"That's them." Jack took command. "I want them in the centre, right behind the Green Company and pushing hard."

"Will do, sir," Peebles said.

"Do you have a spare horse for me?"

"Are you fit to ride, sir?"

Jack frowned, not used to lower-ranking officers questioning him, but these Canadians had minds of their own. "I'm fit," he said. "Bring me a horse and a weapon of some sort."

Back in the saddle with a carbine in his hand and hiding the weakness that made him sway as he rode, Jack sent two scouts ahead. "Follow them up, boys. Don't give them space." When Doherty cantered up with his men, Jack greeted him with a wave and led them in front of the Canadian troops.

"I'm glad to see you again, sir," Doherty said, as Barton gave a brief nod of acknowledgement. "I heard you had a rough time."

"Aye, rough enough," Jack croaked.

The Green Company had ridden too fast to make any attempt to cover their tracks. Once again, Jack assumed a hunter's role, reading the trail, searching for riders breaking away from the main body. There were 50 volunteer cavalrymen, mostly very young, all excellent horsemen and enthusiastic soldiers, if untested in war.

When they reached a small hillock, they found signs that the Green Company had split up, riding in a dozen different directions.

"Good tactics," Jack commented with grudging approval as he called up the lieutenant. "Now they will either double back to get around our flanks, or they'll have a prearranged rendezvous somewhere. Spread your men out and shout if you see anybody that should not be there."

"Yes, sir." Lieutenant Peebles understood. "My men will hunt them down!"

"I'm sure they will, Peebles. I have every faith in them."

Sending Barton ahead with two of his best riders, Jack increased the pace of the pursuit, pressing the Green Company hard while retaining cohesion with his inexperienced troops.

"Keep in sight of one another," Jack ordered.

When the crack of a rifle sounded from the left flank, Jack spurred towards it, hoping the rest of the line kept formation. "Who fired?"

"I did, sir." The volunteer could not have been more than 17, a smooth-chinned boy with steady grey eyes.

"What did you see?"

"An armed horseman resting beside that tree, sir." The volunteer pointed to a stunted oak. "He didn't respond to my challenge."

"Did you hit him?"

"No, sir. As soon as he saw me, he jumped on his horse and rode away."

Jack nodded. "You did well. Better luck next time."

If the man had been resting, others of the Green Company would also be tiring, Jack reasoned, peering ahead. The ground stretched on for ever in undulating farmland, patches of woodland and small rivers. What would he do if he were Walsh?

He would have arranged a rendezvous for his men, gathered them together and thrust back to break through the thin Canadian line. Where? Where could the Green Company collect? It would have to be somewhere easily recognisable for men who did not know the countryside – a prominent feature, perhaps, or a village, small enough for the Green Company to dominate.

"Lieutenant Peebles." Jack still found speaking painful. "Are there any habitations around here?"

The lieutenant screwed up his face in thought. "There are a few farms, sir, but only one village. Menzieshill, it's called. It takes its name from a settler named Menzies."

"Where is it?" Jack interrupted.

"About two miles in this direction," Peebles replied.

"Thank you," Jack said. Sending a horseman after Barton, Jack ordered him to ride hard for Menzieshill to see if Walsh was there. "Don't get into a fight," he cautioned.

"The fight's already started, I think," Peebles said. "That's musketry!"

The firing came from ahead, an intermittent crackle that broke the silence of the Canadian afternoon.

"You're right," Jack said. "Take your men towards the firing. Keep in formation in case Walsh is trying to trick us."

Increasing the pace from a fast walk to a trot, Jack took the lead, with his dozen riders at his back and the volunteers stretched out across the landscape 100 yards behind.

"Captain!" Barton shouted as he galloped towards them. "The Green Company are collecting at Menzieshill, but I saw redcoats already there!"

"Now we have them!" Jack said. Some smart Canadian officer had placed a garrison in the village. Even as he spoke, Jack heard the sputter of musketry again, and the wild yells of the Green Company. "Lieutenant Peebles! Sound the advance. I don't know the local terms, so have your bugler sound whatever it is that orders the men forward at speed."

"Yes, sir!" Grinning, the lieutenant snapped an order to the bugler. When the shrill notes rose, the volunteers increased their speed, converging on the tiny settlement of Menzieshill where it nestled on the southern slope of a low hill. Smoke spurted from a dozen rifles on the perimeter of the village, repulsing the advance of a swarm of horsemen.

"Ireland for ever!" The cry came to Jack, high-pitched above the musketry as at least one of the Green Company yelled defiance.

"After them, boys!" Jack tried to shout, with his injured throat strangling the words before they emerged. He heard the bugle of the volunteers somewhere behind him and glanced over his shoulder. Peebles must have given an order he had not heard, for every volunteer holstered his carbine and drew his sabre, with the sound of steel clearing the scabbards bringing back vivid memories of the Crimea and the Mutiny.

The Green Company hesitated, horses rearing, turning as their riders were unsure which way to ride. Jack sensed their confusion; with a stubborn defence in front and an unknown number of cavalry in the rear, they were in a bad situation. Walsh was prominent in the middle of his men, shouting as the Green Company fragmented. Some fired at the approaching volunteers; others kicked in their spurs and fled, while a desperate few charged towards Menzieshill.

Ignoring the rank and file, Jack galloped straight for Walsh. Shouldering aside the wild-eyed Kennedy, Jack levelled his carbine. "Surrender, Walsh, or I'll blow your brains out!"

Glaring sideways, Walsh shouted something Jack did not hear before galloping away with a dozen of the Green Company forming around him. Jack fired, missed and spurred forward as his men followed, firing into the mass of the Green Company.

On the south, the volunteers closed the gap, but the Green Company riders were desperate. When some turned to fight, the volunteers cut them down, the long sabres glittering in the sun. Jack saw two or three men with their hands high in surrender.

"They're getting away!" Doherty cried.

"Follow!" Jack's voice failed him again, so he pointed forward, hoping that his borrowed horse had the stamina to continue. The defenders of Menzieshill fired a final volley at the rapidly retreating Green Company and then Jack was galloping past.

The volunteer cavalry made a final surge, rounding up another two stragglers before the Green Company surged through the gap with Walsh in the van and the remnants of his men streaming in his wake. Unable to urge his horse to more speed, Jack saw the Green Company racing away. The volunteers were behind them, while in front the vast entirety of Canada offered almost limitless space in which Walsh could hide.

"Night's coming on." Doherty nodded to the sinking sun. "We'll lose them, sir. Permission for Barton and me to ride ahead and get Walsh?"

Jack was about to give his consent when he saw the flash in the distance. "Wait, Doherty. That's sunlight on steel – something is happening over there."

Walsh had led the Green Company into a shallow, westward-facing valley, dotted with small apple orchards. As they galloped on, a line of men rose from an area of dead ground at the west. Even from half a mile away, Jack recognised the scarlet uniforms of British, or Canadian, soldiers. Walsh hesitated, with his horsemen rearing up or altering direction to try the heights to north or south. Jack nodded as more scarlet-clad figures appeared on both ridges, with the dying rays of the sun reflecting on naked bayonets.

"It's Balaclava all over again." Doherty fingered the scar on his face. "Except this time the enemy is trapped in the valley."

Jack agreed. Walsh had led his command into a trap, with the redcoat infantry on three sides of the valley and Jack's horseman closing up the rear.

"Charge forward!" Walsh's voice was loud and clear as he spurred forward to try to burst through the infantry at the head of the valley. Most of the surviving Green Company followed his lead, thundering towards the scarlet line in front. Jack saw the long roll of smoke as the infantry fired a volley, then they calmly stood to receive the charge. Sunlight glittered on bayonets as a second line supported the first.

The Green Company charged on, losing men as the flanking infantry opened fire. The infantry closed the trap, advancing part-way down the hill slope, to halt, reload and fire again.

"Walsh's beat," Doherty said as men and horses tumbled and fell. Some turned to run, only to discover Jack's horsemen blocking their retreat.

"He is," Jack agreed. "Bugler, give the call to advance at a walking pace, picking up prisoners."

"I don't think we have that one, sir."

"Well, do it anyway," Jack croaked.

Some of the dismounted Green Company raised their hands in surrender as the Canadian infantry alternatively fired and advanced, with the wicked bayonets glittering in front of them. Only a few men remained with Walsh when the final handful of horses reared up at the hedge of bayonets. Jack distinctly saw Walsh come off his mount, with a section of infantrymen surrounding him. With the fall of their leader, the surviving men of the Green Company surrendered.

"Come on, lads," Jack said. "Let's go and collect prisoners. It's over."

And thank God it's over. Now I can get back to Mary.

CHAPTER TWENTY-TWO

Canada, June 1866

Fraser sipped from his silver hip-flask, smiled and offered Jack a drink.

"Thank you," Jack accepted gratefully. "I needed that. Was the ambush your idea?"

"Not mine," Fraser said. "That was Colonel Ferguson. He knew the Green Company would come this way, so he prepared accordingly." Taking back the flask, Fraser sipped again and returned it to an inside pocket. "Local knowledge is invaluable in this sort of business."

"That's true." Jack surveyed the prisoners as they sat in a disconsolate group under the watchful gaze of the volunteers. "Well, if the Fenian threat is all finished now, I can get home. My wife will be missing me."

Fraser nodded. "That may be so. In the mean time, we'll extract as much intelligence from the prisoners as we can." He shrugged. "Although I doubt we'll learn much. This bunch seem to be the dregs of the dregs. The only man of any interest is Walsh."

"If that is his name."

"Aye. I have my doubts about that man." Fraser sighed. "He's over there if you want to talk to him. I must say, Windrush, I don't know how you can soldier for a living. I can agree with the man who that the only thing worse than a battle won was a battle lost. There was far too much human suffering in this encounter, so God knows what Inkerman was like."

"It was hell on earth," Jack replied quietly. "I'll speak to Walsh."

* * *

"You bastard Windrush." Bloody faced and tightly bound, Walsh glared at Jack from the wreckage of his plans. "That's twice you've crossed me."

"Aye, and now you'll face a fair trial and the noose." Jack lit a cheroot, trying to disguise his shaking hands as reaction set in. "You're finished, Walsh; your raid was the last throw of the Fenian dice, and it failed. The Canadians defeated every invasion. You'll never conquer Canada."

"Conquer Canada?" Walsh gave a harsh laugh as the blood coursed down his cheek and dripped from his chin. "You still don't understand, do you? Canada was only a pawn in a different game."

Jack stiffened. For a moment he remembered Jayanti's game of chess during the Indian Mutiny, where British soldiers were the pawns. "Aye, you want an Irish republic, or so you say. Is that your objective, Walsh?"

Perhaps the stress of battle or sheer exhaustion had dented Walsh's self-control for he swore in a language that Jack had hoped never to hear again, adding in English: "We'll destroy the whole British Empire."

Jack took a deep breath. "Even if you do establish an Irish Republic," he said carefully, "the British Empire will survive."

"Ireland is only another pawn," Walsh said.

Jack stored the words away. "Your Fenians are finished, Walsh."

"Canada is one piece on the board." Walsh returned to his chess analogy. "Ireland is another. We'll strike again and again. Like the Hydra, we have many heads."

"Aye, and we can cut them all off, one by one."

"Two will grow for each one you cut off." Walsh sneered and looked away. "You might win a battle or two, Windrush, but ultimately you'll lose the war. The British Empire is too fragmented, with too many pieces spread over too much of the planet for you to defend them all. As soon as one piece falls, others will follow."

"Not in my lifetime, Walsh," Jack said. "Not as long as we have the Royal Navy to connect the pieces. The sea is our highway, not a barrier."

Jack stepped away, paused and lit a cheroot. "*Ты далеко от святой россии* – you are a long way from Holy Russia," he said casually, using almost the only Russian phrase he knew.

"*Россия со мной всегда*," Walsh replied without thought. "Russia is with me always."

Jack moved away without another word. He had found out what he wished to know. He had suspected there was something not right about Walsh – now he knew the man was Russian.

* * *

"Russian? Are you certain?" It was the first time that Jack had seen Fraser look shaken.

"I suspected something when I found he was friendly with Carmichael, the Russian agent who recruited for the Fenians. I knew he was false but when he was exhausted, he muttered in Russian."

"Does that mean the Russians are behind the entire Fenian movement?"

"You can ask that when you question him." Jack remembered Walsh's mention of the Hydra, the multi-headed monster of Greek mythology. "I don't think Mr Walsh is finished with us yet. I believe he has something else planned."

"You could be right," Fraser said.

"Have you had any luck with that code of Carmichael's yet? Cto Alpla?"

Fraser gave a small shake of his head. "I passed Cto Alpla on to our experts with no success at all. Nobody has any idea what it may mean." He looked up sharply. "I didn't know you spoke Russian."

Jack shook his head. "I know only a few words. I wonder if Sergeant Doherty could help. He was a Russian prisoner of war after Balaclava."

"Bring him," Fraser ordered.

Pleased to try to help, Doherty gazed at the scrap of paper for a long time but finally shook his head. "No, sir. I know some Russian, but not much. These words mean nothing to me. They look like gibberish."

"Maybe that's all they are." Jack hid his disappointment. "Thank you, Doherty. Now it's back to you, Fraser. You'd better question Walsh."

"We'll send him back to Britain for that," Fraser said. "He'll join the important Fenians prisoners the government is holding." Standing up, he held out his hand. "Well, it was good working with you, Captain. With the capture of Walsh, your work here is done –you can cut along home now."

Jack nearly gasped with relief. "It was good working with you, too, Fraser, or whatever your name is."

"It's Fraser. My ancestor was Simon Fraser, whom the British government executed for treason."

"Oh? My father was a Windrush who bedded an Indian." Jack wondered if he had said too much.

They shook hands. "I've got a woman to pick up, then I'll find a passage to England, home and beauty."

"I've never been there," Fraser said. "Maybe one day"

* * *

"What happened to your neck?"

They sat in Helen's large room in the Queen's Hotel in Toronto, with the cheerful noise of traffic seeping in from the road below.

"People have always said I'd live to be hanged," Jack said. "They were nearly right."

Helen pulled down Jack's collar for a closer look. "It's a bit of a mess. You have a whole collection of scars, as I recall." her eyes were bright with mischief. "I might wish to count them again some time."

"Mary wouldn't like that." Jack did not mention that he had many more scars since Helen had last seen them.

"That woman always spoils our fun," Helen said. "What have you been doing, Jack Windrush?"

"My duty," Jack said.

"You always put your duty first," Helen said. "That's what put us apart last time, Jack. We'll have to ensure that we put ourselves before duty this time."

"There is no this time," Jack said. "I'm taking you back to England and leaving you there."

"Oh, Jack, after everything we've been through!"

Jack was never sure whether Helen was mocking him or being serious. "I'm going back to Mary. I strongly advise you to try to reconcile your differences with William."

"Helen pulled a face and mimicked him. "I strongly advise you to try to reconcile your differences with William. How formal, Jack. Surely you can be easy with me."

Jack looked away, trying to hide his emotions. Despite his love for Mary, Helen still managed to unsettle him. "Let's get back where we belong."

"Jack." Helen's hand closed on Jack's arm. "We are where we belong, you and me together. The geography doesn't matter; only the fact we are together."

"We're not together," Jack said.

"No?" Helen glanced around the room. "I could swear that only you and I are here, and nobody else."

Removing Helen's hand from his arm, Jack backed away. "I'm going to the shipping office to buy tickets for home. You sit here and be good."

Helen laughed. "Would you not prefer that I were not good?" She shifted her stance slightly, sufficient to draw attention to her shape without being blatant.

"Start packing what you have." Jack put a hand on the door handle.

"I'm not going back to William with his perpetual chasing after women," Helen said, "and singing that damned song of his." She began to sing the regimental march of the Royal Malverns.

"*Always victorious*
Glorious and more glorious,
We followed Marlborough through battle and war
We're the Royal Malverns, the heroes of Malplaquet."

Stuttering at the final word, Helen overemphasised the middle syllable.

"Say that again," Jack said as the words jarred in his head.

"Do you like my singing?" Helen swayed toward him.

"Just sing the last line again," Jack stepped closer to her.

Helen smiled, thrust out her hand in a dramatic pose and repeated her final line, once again stumbling over the word "Malplaquet". "I can never pronounce that word," she said, smiling.

"Helen," Jack said, "you are a genius."

"I know," Helen agreed.

"I could kiss you," Jack said, and did so, surprising both of them.

"I can sing it again if you like," Helen offered, smiling, "if it has that effect on you."

"Look," Jack produced his folded scrap of paper. "Cto alpla."

"Cto alpla," Helen repeated. "What does that mean?"

"You just told me," Jack said. "The cto is from victorious, and the alpla is from Malplaquet, the word you found hard to pronounce."

"Oh, I see," Helen said. "But what does it mean? How are these words significant?"

"I don't know yet," Jack admitted. "I found the bits of words in some charred notes your man Carmichael left behind."

"What would Walter want with the regimental song of the Royal Malverns?" Helen wondered. "I doubt my old Russian friend wanted to join the regiment!"

"He might want to attack it," Jack said, "or try to cause a mutiny as he did with the 113th." He sat down, lighting a cheroot to help him think. "Fortunately, he can't do anything at present."

"Not from a British jail."

"He'll probably be sentenced to hang as a Russian spy," Jack said soberly.

Helen nodded, seemingly unconcerned about Carmichael's possible execution. "I doubt we'll ever know, then."

"I'll telegraph a warning to Colonel Ledbury of the Malverns when I buy our tickets," Jack blew smoke into the room, "although I think the threat is lifted with Walsh also out of the way."

When Helen smiled at him, the years rolled back and once more Jack remembered her in the Crimea, a vivacious, laughing girl with all the world before her. On an impulse, he reached out.

"I wish things were different," Helen gripped his hand. "Do you remember that time you saved us during the great storm?"

"I remember." Jack could not help smiling. "I thought then you were the bravest, boldest woman in the world."

Helen's thumb stroked the back of Jack's hand. "You were always the bravest man." She stood up. "Let's start again, Jack. Come on! We're in a new land with new opportunities; let's get back together. Please, Jack."

Helen looked so eager that Jack felt a sudden desire not to hurt her. "Oh, Helen," he said softly, releasing his hand from hers. "We can't alter what we are. We are both married, and I love my wife."

"You love me, too," Helen countered, desperation in her voice. "I can see it in your eyes. I can feel it."

"I like you, certainly," Jack admitted.

"I want you," Helen stepped closer to him, with the subtle scent of her perfume wafting around him. "I want to make the most passionate love to you, Jack, to make up for our past mistakes and show you what the future could be like."

Jack took a deep breath, inhaling Helen's scent as his mind danced with images that were both delightful and disturbing. He turned away, hating himself. "No, Helen! I love Mary." Opening the door with sudden anger, he spoke over his shoulder. "I'll be back in an hour or so. Get packed."

Cursing his weakness, Jack took the hotel stairs two at a time and nearly missed the cavalry cornet who stood beside the reception desk.

"Captain Windrush?"

"That's me." Jack knew it would not be good news.

"I have a message for you," the cornet said, handing over a surprisingly weighty package.

"Thank you." Breaking the seal, Jack emptied a stream of sovereigns on to the desk before scanning the enclosed note.

> *Captain Windrush*
>
> *W has escaped and is believed to be heading for England on SS Glen Moray. Follow and act accordingly. F"*

CHAPTER TWENTY-THREE

Canada June 1866

Follow and act accordingly? What the devil does Fraser mean by that? Am I to kill him, capture him or merely prevent him from doing whatever he has planned? The Royal Malverns! Walsh is going after the Malverns!

Hurrying to the nearest shipping office, Jack asked for passage to Britain on the next available ship.

"Sorry, Captain. We're all booked up."

"Anything will do," Jack said, "even steerage."

"Sorry Captain. We have nothing. It's because of this Fenian nonsense."

After trying a further two shipping companies with the same result, Jack learned that none of the steamboat lines sailing to Britain had any space, so contacted the Navy, in the hope they might take him.

"You're a cashiered army officer." A supercilious commander looked down his aristocratic nose. "The Royal Navy has better things to do than transport failed lobsters around the globe."

When Jack protested that he was working on national security, the commander beckoned to a hefty petty officer who lumbered up with two bluejackets at his back, each man eager to toss this upstart soldier into the street. With Fraser seemingly vanished on some business of his own, Jack was left fretting.

What the devil do I do now?

At her best in a crisis, Helen gave practical advice. "Well, Jack, how did you cross the Atlantic in the first place?"

"By a sailing packet," Jack said.

"We can return the same way."

"That means a trip to Boston first," Jack said. "And that's 500 miles away."

"We'd better get moving, then," Helen said. "I'm already packed." She nodded towards the single carpet bag that stood beside the bed.

"Is that all you have?"

"I'm a soldier's daughter, remember," Helen said. "I'm used to travelling light."

"God bless you, Helen." Jack fought off his impulse to kiss her again. "You're the best of women."

"I'm glad you realise that," Helen replied dryly, reaching for her coat.

* * *

Boston waterfront was as busy as always, with ships arriving and departing, loading and unloading their cargoes while seamen filled the waterside taverns and made lewd comments at any passing woman. Helen smiled at the remarks, waved to the more forward of the men and clutched at Jack's arm as he enquired after the first ship leaving for Great Britain.

"There's the very vessel." Jack immediately recognised the long, lean *Yorktown*. "Come on, Helen."

Captain Martin glowered at Jack from under his slanted cap. "I remember you," he said. "You were with that Irish fellow, both keen to join the Fenians."

"That's right," Jack said.

"Aye, and a right blasted mess you made of that, didn't you? The Limeys chased you from Monday to Christmas and back again."

"They did." Jack thought it better to agree than to argue.

"You've changed the Irish lad for some extra cargo, I see." Captain Martin nodded towards Helen.

"We're travelling together," Jack said, "and in a hurry."

"Aye, running from the law no doubt," Martin said. "I have one cabin vacant with the same rates as last time." He glowered at Helen. "The lady may not find the accommodation up to her usual standard."

"The lady is used to living in camps and tents." Helen held out her hand. "I am Mrs Helen Windrush, and this is Jack Windrush."

"Oh, you're married. are you?" Martin said sourly, taking Helen's hand with surprising gentleness. "Pleased to meet you. Pay in full, in advance, and we sail on the next tide. You can carry your own baggage."

"Thank you, Captain." Helen dipped in a graceful curtsey. "We are immensely grateful for your kindness. Pay the gentleman, please, Jack. There's a good chap."

Martin's grimace could have passed as smile as Helen followed a crewman down below. "Aye, it's easy to see who wears the trousers in your marriage."

Opening his mouth to speak, Jack closed it again without saying a word. Sometimes it was better to let life take its course without comment.

"We'll be snug in here," Helen commented as she surveyed the tiny cabin.

"I'll keep my clothes on," Jack told her.

"You'll keep your clothes on for the entire journey?" Helen held her nose. "You'll be stinking. I intend to bathe as often as possible."

"In here?" Jack had to stoop to avoid hitting his head on the deck beams above, while the bulkheads crowded so close he could not stretch out even one arm. "There's hardly room to swing a mouse, let alone a cat." He looked at her sideways. "I suppose you could bathe on deck and entertain the crew."

Helen's look could have frozen a live volcano. "You're always so clever, Jack Windrush."

"I know," Jack said, pleased that he had managed to draw a reaction.

Yorktown sailed without ceremony, easing into the long swells of the North Atlantic without resorting to the expense of a pilot.

"Clap on all the sails she can carry," Martin ordered the moment they hit clear water. "I want to be in the Mersey in 10 days! Hell or Liverpool, by God!"

"That's the spirit," Jack said softly. "Push her hard, Captain."

"Stunsails!" Captain Martin roared, "skysails and moonrakers! By God, I want more speed out of this tub! Mrs Windrush! Hang out your blasted washing if it helps! Mister Blackrock, padlock the sheets and shoot any lubber who tries to take in sail!"

Standing at the break of the poop with his thumbs in his waistband and a model 1861 Navy Colt revolver thrust through his belt, Captain Martin cut a formidable figure.

"If there are many more like him in the States," Jack said, "Britannia had better look to her trident."

"Why's that?"

"The Americans will take hold of it," Jack said.

Helen shook her head. "The Americans are too busy fighting each other and scrabbling for the lands to the west. Have you heard their phrase, manifest destiny? They think it's their right to occupy all the land from the Atlantic to the Pacific. First, they have to grab the land from the Indians; then they have to settle it. It might take decades for the Americans to build their empire in the west."

"Aye, maybe you're right." Jack narrowed his eyes. "I'd forgotten how genuinely clever you are, Helen, when you're not flirting with anything in trousers."

"Not anything, Jack." Helen took hold of his arm, staring at the grey seas. "Only men with spirit and edge."

"You're flirting again." But Jack lost interest in arguing with Helen when he saw a smudge of smoke on the horizon. "There's a steamship ahead."

"So I see," Helen said. "I'm sure that wasn't there a few moments ago."

"It wasn't." Jack stepped up to the poop, where Captain Martin stood. "Captain, in which direction is that steam vessel heading?"

"East," Martin said at *once*.

"Are we catching her?"

"In this wind, mister, *Yorktown* could catch Saint Michael sitting on Mercury's shoulders."

Returning to his quarters, Jack brought up his binoculars and focused on the steam vessel. "That's a passenger liner!"

"Aye, one of Grant's Glen Line vessels." Martin was inclined to be garrulous. "They carry emigrants from Liverpool to Boston and general cargo and passengers back to Boston."

"Could it be *Glen Moray*?"

Martin shrugged. "It could be. I heard she was delayed before sailing. We'll see when we overtake her."

Glen Moray was delayed? Was that more of Fraser's work?

With all her sails taut, *Yorktown* powered down on the Glen Line vessel, so that Jack could soon make out details, although steam and smuts from her funnel helped conceal her name.

Martin shouted something that had the hands trim the angle of the sails by a fraction and gave *Yorktown* an extra surge of speed until she drew level with the steam vessel. As they closed, the steamship's name gleamed yellow on her black counter.

"That's her!" Helen read the name. "That's *Glen Moray*!"

"Could you send a message to her master?" Jack shouted to Martin.

"Why the devil should I do that?" Martin asked.

"She has a Russian agent on board," Jack explained hurriedly. "He plans to create trouble in England. I want him arrested."

Grunting, Martin altered the angle of his cap with a jerk of his hand. "That's a tall story, mister, and it's not my affair. My job is to sail *Yorktown* across the Atlantic, not to order ship's masters to arrest their passengers."

"There are 10 golden boys in it for you, Captain. The Russian goes by the name of Walsh."

Martin glowered at Jack, adjusted the angle of his cap again and grabbed the speaking-trumpet from its bracket on the mizzen mast. "Ahoy, *Glen Moray*!"

The answering hail came immediately. "You have a fast ship, Captain!"

Jack saw the master of *Glen Moray*. Tall, erect and dressed in a blue uniform, he stood beside the helmsman, studying *Yorktown*.

"I have," Martin agreed. "It seems you have an imposter on board your ship, a foreign agent posing as an Irishman named Walsh."

"I'd wager half my passengers are imposters, Captain."

"The British have asked me to have you arrest him," Martin shouted.

Jack saw the master of *Glen Moray* consult with one of his officers, who disappeared below. "Wait," he shouted as *Yorktown* and *Glen Moray* raced side by side, a bare two cables-length apart with the sea surging silver, green and white between them.

"I haven't time for this," Martin handed the speaking-trumpet to one of his officers and rattled off a string of commands that saw *Yorktown* edge slightly away from the steamship. A stray gust of wind blew smoke over *Yorktown's* poop, making Helen cough. When it cleared, *Glen Moray* was a further cable's length away and falling back in the race.

"Wait!" Dashing up the companionway to the poop, Jack grabbed the speaking trumpet.

"Master of *Glen Moray*!" He felt his still imperfectly-healed throat protest as he shouted. "I am Captain Jack Windrush of the British Army. Do you have a man named Walsh on board?"

The master lifted his speaking trumpet. "There is nobody of that name on our passenger list. Have a safe voyage." Putting down the speaking-trumpet, he turned away.

"There he is!" Helen had been examining *Glen Moray* through Jack's recently acquired binoculars. "On the deck there."

Grabbing the binoculars, Jack focused on a small group of men who stood amidships. Walsh was among them, staring intently at Jack. For one second, Jack saw him clearly, and then smoke blew across the ship, and he was gone.

"Damn it to hell and back," Jack swore. "Captain Martin, have you any weapons on board?"

"You owe me 10 sovereigns, mister," Martin reminded him. "You'll get no more favours until you pay your debts."

Jack swore. "Helen! Run down to the cabin and fetch my pocketbook! Hurry now!"

Obeying without hesitation, Helen lifted her skirt and scurried away. She returned in minutes, smiled and passed Jack his pocketbook, from which he extracted 10 sovereigns. "There you are, captain," Jack said quickly, glancing at his diminished store of gold. "Do you have a rifle on board?"

"I have," Martin's hand closed on the sovereigns, "but it's not for hire. I'm not having any Limey soldier loose on my ship with a rifle. God knows what damage you might cause. Now get off my poop."

Knowing the range was too long for his pistol, Jack could only watch in frustration as *Yorktown* pulled further away from *Glen Moray*. Walsh casually strolled to the bow, from where he studied Jack and Helen on the American vessel. As the light faded and *Yorktown* eased ahead, Walsh raised a hand in ironic farewell and walked away.

"Damn you, Walsh, or whatever your name is," Jack muttered.

"It's all right, Jack." Helen patted his arm. "We'll get to England before him and tell the Royal Malverns to be on guard."

"We'll do better than that," Jack said. "I'll have him arrested the minute he steps ashore." Ignoring the pain, he raised his voice. "Captain Martin! Can't you get any more speed from this old tub? We're waddling here like a fat duck in a village pond!" He enjoyed Martin's responding glower.

Only later that night, as he lay in his cramped bunk, did a thought come to him. "Are you awake, Helen?"

"If you wish me to be." She stretched an arm across to him.

"How did you know what Walsh looked like?"

Helen sighed. "Can't you think of anything other than your duty? He came to Presque House to see Walter." She patted his arm. "It's all right, Jack; he's not another of my lovers. I'm reserving that position for you." She laughed softly. "I don't think he likes women – we never met."

* * *

Liverpool was as grey and uncompromising as when Jack last saw it, with the docks filled with the usual assortment of the unsavoury, the hard-working, prosperous ship-owners, down-at-heel seamen, pimps, crimps and prostitutes. Even so, it was good to be back in England, despite the grey drizzle that soaked them on arrival and awakened the dull ache of the wound Jack had picked up in Burma 14 years earlier.

"Right now, Helen. I'm going to leave you here while I notify the police about Walsh."

"And I'm coming with you." Helen took hold of his arm.

"I haven't the time to argue," Jack said. "If you're with me you'd better keep up, although you should contact your husband and see if he'll take you back."

"I don't want William," Helen said. "I want you." She looked sidelong at Jack. "Maybe you'd better ask yourself if Mary will have you back after you've spent so much time alone with me."

"Don't try to sow discord now." Jack did not admit that the thought worried him. As soon as he had warned the police about Walsh, he scribbled two letters to Mary, sending one to Netherhills and the other to their house in Berwick-upon-Tweed. Jack pushed that concern away. He had to concentrate on his duty.

***

"*Glen Moray* is due in on this tide," the harbourmaster said.

"Good," Inspector Rafferty of the Liverpool Dock Police said. He nodded to the squad of grim-faced detectives among the uniformed police. "My men are ready for this Russian fellow. Captain Windrush, I'll need you with me to identify him."

"He's a dangerous man." Jack ensured his revolver was fully loaded and ready for use in case Walsh tried to resist. "There might be somebody to greet him. Fenians or the like."

"We're ready for whatever happens," Rafferty said. "Don't you worry, Captain."

"I'm sure you have things organised, Inspector." Helen stood at Jack's side, smiling.

"You'd best stay out of the way, Mrs Windrush," Rafferty advised. "It might get hectic here."

"I shall," Helen promised.

"I'll be happier when Walsh is back in custody," Jack admitted. "Here's somebody coming now, Inspector." He waited for the approaching constable's report.

"*Glen Moray* is entering the Mersey wearing a distress flag," The constable said calmly.

"This way, Windrush." Rafferty sounded equally calm. "We have the police launch ready for just such an emergency."

"You stay on land, Helen," Jack ordered as he boarded the steam launch behind Rafferty, with half a dozen uniformed men and two detectives following. The crew took her out quickly, coming alongside *Glen Moray* within 15 minutes of getting the message.

The captain greeted them. "Murder," he said at once. "One of my crew has been murdered."

Jack looked along the length of the ship's deck, where a dozen passengers congregated. He did not recognise any of the faces. "Have you checked your passengers?"

"I have," the captain confirmed. "One man is missing, a Robert Emmet."

"That's our man," Rafferty said at once. "The real Robert Emmet led the 1803 rising in Ireland. Our Mr Walsh is using a false name. Search the ship, lads," Rafferty ordered. "Heave to, captain. I don't want *Glen Moray* to dock until we locate the missing man."

"That won't do, Inspector." Jack felt infinitely weary. "You won't find him. I'll put 100 sovereigns to a false sixpence that our Mr Walsh is long gone."

"We've been at sea," the captain said. "He'd have had to jump overboard."

"Then that's what he's done," Jack said. "He'll either have swum for land, or he'll have a prior arrangement with some small boat to pick him up and bring him ashore. Your murderer is off the ship."

"I'll still search the ship and question the passengers," Rafferty said. "I might find something of interest."

"You might," Jack conceded. "Take me to this fellow Emmet's cabin."

The tiny cubicle that Walsh had occupied was stark. The single bed was neatly made up, the bookshelf empty and the bulkheads bare of decoration of any kind. Rafferty found the single sheet of paper pinned to the underside of the bed. "See you later, Windrush," he read. "Walsh must have known you would search the ship for him."

"Aye," Jack said. "He's a clever man, and a dangerous one. I'll have to get ashore now, inspector."

"If he's already ashore," Rafferty said, "he'll be hiding out somewhere along Scotland Road. That's where the criminal classes congregate."

"He's not in Liverpool," Jack said. "I think he's heading south to Hereford."

"Hereford? That's a queer destination," Rafferty said. "It's a bit of a backwater, isn't it?"

"He's heading for the barracks." Jack was suddenly desperate to get ashore.

Rafferty raised his eyebrows. "No need to rush, then, Captain. I'll telegraph the local police, and they'll warn the garrison. The soldier boys will take care of him. Which regiment is it?"

"The Royal Malverns," Jack replied. "Take me ashore."

CHAPTER TWENTY-FOUR

Hereford, England, July 1866

Hereford bustled with activity as Jack pushed his horse through the accumulation of farmers' carts, coaches and pedestrians. Thinly sprinkled among the civilians, the scarlet tunics of soldiers showed the continuing presence of the Royal Malverns. Ignoring everybody, Jack rode to the barracks, where a solemn-faced sentry stepped across to deny him entry.

"Halt!" the sentry was young and nervous, evidently a recruit. "Where are you going?" He levelled his rifle.

"Well done, Private," Jack said. "I am Captain Jack Windrush with an urgent message for Colonel Ledbury."

The sentry blinked, looking confused. His training had not included this type of situation.

"It might be best if you called for your sergeant," Jack suggested. "My mission is rather urgent."

The sergeant marched up at the double, sent the sentry back to his post and stood to attention. "Excuse me for asking, sir, but are you related to our Major Windrush?"

"Vaguely," Jack admitted. "Could you take me to Colonel Ledbury?"

"The colonel is not here at present, sir," the sergeant said. "Major Windrush is in command. Shall I take you to him, sir?"

Jack swore silently. His half-brother was the last person he wished to meet. "Yes, Sergeant."

Major William Windrush leaned back in the colonel's chair and surveyed Jack for a long 30 seconds. The Victoria Cross he had gained in the Crimea hung at his breast, proclaiming his heroism to the world. He bit the end from a cheroot, scratched a lucifer to light it and blew the smoke towards Jack. "I heard you further disgraced the Windrush name, Jack. Cashiered for helping a Fenian, for God's sake, and I thought you could not stoop any lower."

Ignoring the barbs, Jack leaned across the desk. "Your regiment is in danger, William."

"You call me sir." William Windrush stood up. "And I won't listen to your lies. I'm putting you in the guardroom where you belong."

"This goes beyond personal dislike, William," Jack said. "The Royal Malverns, your regiment, your responsibility, is in danger."

William shook his head. "This is England, Captain, not some primitive outpost of Empire. The Royals are in no danger here." He snorted. "Why, man, we have half a dozen Fenians held securely in our cells and not a whisper out of any of them!"

"I assure you, sir," Jack began, nearly choking on the term of respect, "there is a Russian agent loose in England, acting with the Fenians, and he intends to attack the Royals."

William was silent for another long minute. "A Russian working with the Fenians! Really, Captain, that's too rich, even for you. The Fenians are a bunch of illiterate dreamers without any idea what they are doing. Working with the Russians indeed! What nonsense! I can't think of any reason why I should listen to the ramblings of a half-caste traitor married to a nigger. Sergeant!"

Until that point, Jack had managed to control his temper, but William's insult to Mary tipped him over the edge. Lunging forward, he took William by the throat, just as the sergeant entered the room.

"Sir!" The sergeant saw a man in civilian clothes holding the commanding officer of his regiment by the throat and reacted accordingly. Grabbing Jack by the head, he hauled him backwards.

"Enough of that, you!"

Dragged away, Jack lost his balance and fell to the floor, where the sergeant, vastly experienced in quelling unruly soldiers, landed a couple of hefty kicks before applying an arm-lock. "What shall I do with this fellow, sir?"

William nursed his throat for a moment before replying. "Throw him in a cell, Sergeant, and don't be too gentle about it. This man is a cashiered officer and a traitor." Stepping closer to Jack, William punched him hard in the stomach. "You'll be in good company in our cells – we seem to be collecting disgraced officers from the regiment you once tainted. Take him away, Sergeant."

"Yes, sir." Twisting Jack's arm painfully behind his back, the sergeant pushed him out of the office. "Guard!"

Four privates hurried up, their bayonets glittering in the light of hanging lanterns.

"This man is a traitor," the sergeant said, "and he attacked Major Windrush."

"Yes, sergeant," one of the privates levelled his bayonet at Jack. "Do you want me to stick him, sir?"

"Not yet, Bryant. Maybe later."

"Yes, sir." Bryant sounded disappointed.

"Your regiment is under threat, lads!" Jack shouted. "The Fenians are planning to attack you."

"Take that man away, Sergeant," William ordered, emerging from his office, "and do something about the noise he's making, for God's sake."

"Yes, sir! Come on, you!" Grabbing hold of Jack once more, the sergeant stuffed a handkerchief in his mouth and fastened it around the back of his head, ensuring the knot was tight. "Double!"

With Bryant adding encouragement with jabs from his bayonet, the sergeant marched Jack to makeshift cells below ground. "In you go with your friend."

Opening the door, the sergeant pushed Jack inside, while Bryant added colourful threats.

"Bloody Fenian-loving bastard! I hope they hang you!"

Falling on his face, Jack rolled on to his back as the cell door banged shut, leaving him in complete darkness. He lay there for a moment, gathering his wits. *This is the second time the army has thrown me in a cell. I hope it's the last.*

After a few moments, Jack rose to his feet, aware that he was not alone.

"Welcome to the hospitality of the Royal Malverns." The voice was soft and familiar.

Jack unfastened his gag. "Ensign Snodgrass? What the devil are you doing here?"

"The same as you, sir, by the looks of it."

As Jack's eyes became accustomed to the gloom, he realised that faint light was seeping into the cell from a grilled opening far above their heads. Snodgrass was sitting on a plain plank bed with the wall supporting his back.

"It's good to see you again, sir, despite the unfortunate circumstances." Snodgrass's face was heavily bruised, with his left eye nearly closed, while his uniform was torn and dirty.

"Have they been mistreating you, Ensign?"

"No worse than expected, sir," Ensign Snodgrass said. "I did act the traitor." He sounded resigned to his present state.

"What sentence did the court-martial give you?"

"They cashiered me, sir, plus 10 years' penal servitude." Ensign Snodgrass gave a twisted grin. "The president of the court said they were treating me leniently because of my youth."

Jack sighed. Ten years of the living hell they called penal servitude was anything but lenient. While locked away in solitary confinement, Ensign Snodgrass's guilt would eat at his thoughts, as was the intention. If he survived, he would emerge with his physical health permanently damaged and his mind broken.

"My advice is to do exactly as the wardens say, ensign, but don't dwell on what's happened. You cannot alter the past. All you can do is think what your life will be like when you're free again."

"Free again?" There was a new cynicism in Ensign Snodgrass's voice. "I'll never be free again, sir. I might survive the jail, but all my life I'll know I betrayed my country and besmirched my honour." His voice dropped to a whisper. "And I let my father down."

"Try to put that behind you, Ensign," Jack said. "Yes, you made mistakes, but you are young. We all make mistakes that we regret. God knows I've made plenty!"

"You never betrayed your country over a woman, sir!"

"You have your whole life to make amends for what you did, Peter." Jack tried to ease Ensign Snodgrass's despair. "Some time, you will have an opportunity to salve your conscience. I know you will." Jack slid to the cold stone floor and immersed himself in his thoughts. The army must be keeping keep its Fenian prisoners in Hereford before sending them to Dartmoor or some other secure prison. That would make the barracks a prime target; no wonder the Fenians intended to strike here.

"Why are you here, sir?"

Jack felt himself smile. "That's a long story, Peter. Suffice to say that I am also a cashiered traitor, according to the army. Now let's make the best of things while we can."

"There's not much to make the best of, sir."

"You have your youth, Peter. That's more than many people have."

There was silence for a while, broken by Snodgrass's intermittent sobbing. Jack left him, knowing he could not help. Honour was the most precious commodity for an officer, more precious than life.

"I wish they had shot me, sir," Snodgrass said, after a long pause.

"No, Peter. If you are alive, you could have a chance to redeem yourself."

"In jail, sir?" Snodgrass sounded desperate. "How can I do anything if I'm locked up?"

Jack felt the thump before he heard the sound. "That was an explosion," he said.

"Was it, sir?" Ensign Snodgrass asked without interest.

"Yes, it was." Jack got to his feet. "By God, the Fenians are attacking the barracks already!" *Walsh must have moved fast.* He raised his voice. "Guards! Let us out! We can help!"

Another explosion shook the building, bringing down a trickle of dust and plaster from the ceiling. Ensign Snodgrass lay still as Jack hammered on the door.

"Guards! Let us out!"

When nobody responded, Jack kicked the door in frustration. "I can help! I know these people."

A third explosion sounded, louder than the previous two, and more dry plaster descended from the ceiling, accompanied by a few small stones. "If this carries on there won't be anything left of the cells," Jack said. "We'll be able to walk out over the rubble."

"Walk where?" Ensign Snodgrass said. "We're both condemned men."

"None of that!" Jack snapped. "You're a British officer! Act like one."

"They cashiered me," Ensign Snodgrass said. "I'm nothing."

"Then make yourself something." Jack kicked the door again. "Let us out!" He was surprised when a key turned in the lock.

A round-faced man in civilian clothes peered into the cell. "Identify yourselves!"

"Captain Jack Windrush and Ensign Snodgrass," Jack said at once. "Who are you?"

"Are you the British officers jailed for aiding our cause?"

This man's a Fenian. Jack thought quickly. "Yes, that's us. Captain Windrush and Ensign Snodgrass, both bound for Dartmoor." He shook his head to stop Ensign Snodgrass from speaking.

"Out you come, then; we're breaking the boys free." The round-faced man was genial as he moved to the next cell with the same question. "Identify yourselves!"

That must have been the plan, Jack thought. He had guessed wrongly – rather than an attack on the Royal Malverns, the Fenians intended to free the prisoners.

"We're with you," Jack shouted, dragging Ensign Snodgrass with him. "Up the Irish Republic!"

"I'm no Fe..." Snodgrass began until Jack clapped a hand over his mouth.

"Shut up, you fool!" Jack snapped. Holding the ensign close, Jack dragged him out of the cell. A dozen armed civilians surrounded them, some shouting Fenian slogans as they crashed open the remaining cells to release the prisoners.

"Come out, boys! Up the Irish Republic!"

Ensign Snodgrass struggled as Jack pushed him away from the Fenians. "Stay with me," Jack hissed. "Let's find the leader of this raid."

Hereford Barracks were in confusion, with parties of the Royal Malverns running around, some fully dressed, others only in their shirts or wearing trousers and a tunic. Jack heard another explosion and saw a sergeant leading a section of men in the direction of the noise.

"They're bombing the barracks," Ensign Snodgrass said.

"So it seems." Jack could see no casualties, nor hear the cries of wounded men. "Let's find a weapon."

A young private ran past, clutching a rifle. "We've got to beat them," he muttered, "we've got to beat them!"

"That man!" Jack pointed to him. "Halt!"

The young soldier stopped, staring at Jack in evident confusion. "Who are you?"

"Captain Windrush," Jack said. "Lend me your rifle and whatever ammunition you have."

"You're not in uniform," the private pulled back. "How do I know you're an officer?"

Jack conceded the private had a valid point. Drawing himself erect, he adopted his most imperious tone and glared down at the boy. "Look at me!"

The private looked up at Jack. "Yes, sir." He handed over his rifle.

"Thank you," Jack said. "Now find your sergeant and tell him the Fenians are releasing the prisoners. Tell him that Captain Windrush says to bring as many men as he can find to the cells and shoot any Fenians. Have you got that?"

"Yes, sir." Sweat coursed down the youngster's face at the responsibility Jack was handing him. "I've to find Sergeant Fletcher and tell him to bring men to the cells because the Fenians are freeing the prisoners."

"That's right. Off you go, lad."

"What happens now, sir?" Imprisonment and despair had robbed Snodgrass of his initiative.

Holding his rifle, Jack nodded to the cells. "Now we go back, Ensign, and do our duty."

"Sir! We're no longer officers."

Jack checked and loaded the rifle. It was an 1860 pattern two-band Enfield. Trust the Royal Malverns to have the best weapons. "We are by inclination and training, Peter."

"The bombs, sir. Should we not help there?"

"No." Jack shook his head. "The explosions are a diversion from the prisoners. Whoever planned this attack knew what he was doing." *That would be Walsh,* Jack thought.

Ignoring the various groups of confused soldiers, Jack headed back to the cells. Flame licked skyward to his left, either the result of an explosion or a further refinement to the Fenians' diversionary tactics. Jack was not sure. Pushing Snodgrass behind him, Jack watched an armed civilian emerge from the cell-block. Without shouting a warning, Jack aimed and fired.

The man spun around, roaring. Reloading quickly, Jack fired again, seeing his target stagger against the wall of the building.

"One down." Jack reloaded.

"What's happening, sir?" The NCO was steady-eyed with neat whiskers.

"Sergeant Fletcher?"

"Yes, sir."

"I am Captain Windrush, and this is Ensign Snodgrass."

"Are you not prisoners, sir?" Fletcher held his rifle with professional skill.

"We're British officers taking charge of the situation," Jack said. "We can discuss the details later."

"Begging your pardon, sir, but are you related to Fighting Jack Windrush?"

"This is Fighting Jack Windrush," Snodgrass said, giving the first indication of returning confidence.

Fletcher's grin was visible even in the dark. "What do you want us to do, sir?"

"Follow me in, Sergeant, and shoot anybody carrying a weapon, unless he's a British soldier."

"Yes, sir." Fletcher passed on the command to the men at his back.

"And watch for a tall, thin fellow with a scar on his forehead. He's dangerous, he's Russian, and I want him kept alive if possible."

"Russian, sir?"

"I'm not sure of the connection, sergeant. Were you in the Crimea?"

Fletcher nodded. "Yes, sir."

"Then you'll know how dangerous the Russians can be."

"I do, sir." Again, Fletcher passed the information on to his men. Jack spared them a glance. They looked an intelligent bunch compared to the average British soldier – an elite regiment such as the Malverns could pick and choose their recruits. Even so, Jack still wished he had his old command from the days of the Indian Mutiny. With Logan, Riley and Thorpe, he knew he could do anything.

"Follow me, men." Holding his rifle ready, Jack stepped towards the stairs.

The Fenians fired first, charging up from the cells and erupting into the barracks. The first volley blew the head off a private.

"Fire!" Fletcher shouted. "Blast the bastards to hell, lads!"

The exchange of fire was intense but short. Not expecting to meet any resistance, the Fenians fired only a few shots before they scattered, with some running towards the barrack gate while the majority retreated hurriedly back to the cells.

"Is there another entrance to the cells, sergeant?" Jack asked.

"No, sir," Fletcher replied as he reloaded his rifle. "They are just adapted storerooms with one entrance."

Jack glanced over his shoulder, where the escapees were nearing the gates. "Keep them confined, sergeant, until another officer arrives to take command. If any Fenian shows his face, shoot him flat."

"Yes, sir," Fletcher said. "Where are you going, sir?"

"I'm going after the ones that got away," Jack said. "I'll be back."

"Yes, sir." Fletcher hesitated for a moment. "It was a pleasure to meet you, sir."

"You too, Fletcher." Jack nudged Snodgrass. "Come on, Ensign. I'll wager that our Russian fellow is among that lot there."

"They've got the major!" Jack heard the shout before a flare of firelight revealed a tall figure struggling amid the fugitives at the barrack gate.

"That's William," Jack said. "That's Major Windrush." For one betraying moment, he wondered if he should leave his half-brother to whatever fate the Fenians and their Russian allies intended, but he knew he would not. It was always his duty to help a fellow British officer.

"Come on, Snodgrass!"

Jack heard a burst of firing behind him as he raced towards William. Although he shouted for support, there was so much noise that he did not expect anybody to hear.

"Come on, Snodgrass!" Jack ran to the main gate with the fugitives a good 50 yards in front. Riordan was one of the two who frog-marched William, with another in front and two in the rear.

"Somebody's planned this," Jack said. "These men intended to free the Fenian prisoners and grab William, Ensign Snodgrass."

The barrack gate leaned open, with the sentry lying in a crumpled heap as the fugitives dashed outside, where three dark broughams waited. The coach drivers huddled into concealing coats, with low-crowned hats pulled well down over their faces.

"Damn them! They've planned this well," Jack said. Increasing his speed, he grabbed at the nearest brougham just as the last of the fugitives dived in. For one moment, Jack stared straight into the man's face.

"I know you," he said, and then the fugitive slammed shut the door, and the coach driver cracked the reins across the rump of his horse. The brougham lurched into motion, dragging Jack with it. "Stop!" He held on with his left hand, with his right still gripping the Enfield. When the driver lashed backwards, the tip of his whip caught Jack's fingers, forcing him to release his hold. Jack staggered, ran a few awkward steps and stumbled to a halt, watching the broughams rumble into the night-dark streets.

That was Walter Carmichael. We must have held him prisoner here.

"Will we follow them?" Ensign Snodgrass asked.

"They're faster than we are," Jack said. "We'll need horses." He thought rapidly. "You chase after the broughams to see in which direction they take; I'll find a couple of horses." He pushed Snodgrass as he hesitated. "Go!"

With the barracks in confusion, Jack found it easy to open the stable that held the officers' horses. Choosing two of the best, he hastily saddled them, grabbed a couple of revolvers from the unattended armoury and left, cursing the time the operation had taken. Harold Street was busy with people hurrying to see what all the noise was, but Jack pushed through, leading the second empty horse.

"Snodgrass!" He shouted above the roar of the crowd.

"Sir!" Sensibly, Snodgrass had climbed high on a building on the corner of Harold and Green Streets. He waved to Jack. "Over here!"

"Which way did they go?"

"Northward, sir." Snodgrass mounted the horse with ease. "They were moving fast."

"Lead on," Jack ordered.

With the burning barracks lighting up the southern sky, Jack and Snodgrass trotted through Hereford and into the countryside, listening for the sound of the broughams' wheels as they peered into the fading dark.

"We've lost them," Snodgrass said.

"Not yet." Jack did not accept defeat so easily. "Look for somebody to ask. Country people notice anything out of the ordinary."

The ploughman was already at work, guiding his horse over the fertile soil. He looked up when Jack hailed him.

"We're looking for three coaches," Jack said.

"I saw coaches, but I don't know how many there were," the ploughman said in a rich, unhurried, Herefordshire accent.

"More than one?" Jack asked.

The ploughman considered the question for a long 10 seconds. "Oh, yes. There were more than one."

"That will be them." Despite his impatience, Jack knew there was no point in trying to hurry this man. "Did you see which direction they took?"

"Yes." The ploughman was about 30, with steady brown eyes. "They took the Worcester Road." He waited a moment to contemplate the sunrise. "Then they left the highway for that side road there." The ploughman nodded. "They'll get lost unless they're from Herefordshire."

"Thank you." Lifting his hand in acknowledgement, Jack kicked in his heels, with Snodgrass a horse-length behind. The side roads in this part of Herefordshire were narrow, winding between high hedges that frustratingly restricted visibility. Guessing his route in a multiplicity of lanes, Jack knew he would be lucky to see anything. After half an hour, Jack knew he had lost the broughams.

"Stop here." Jack reined his horse in beside a tall elm. "Climb up there, Snodgrass and look for the coaches."

"Yes, sir." Snodgrass clambered up faster than Jack expected. "I can't see anything, sir."

Jack swore. "Climb higher! Look for the glint of the sun on the coach roof."

"Yes, sir." Snodgrass pulled himself up a further few feet. "I think I might see them, sir!"

"I'm coming." Older and more cautious, Jack hauled himself on to the bough that Snodgrass occupied.

To the north, the long ridge of the Malvern Hills rose like an old friend while, to the east, Jack could see the convoy, three dark vehicles against a silver-grey dawn, with patches of mist clinging to the bodywork.

"They took a different route from us, damn them," Jack said.

"We can catch them!" Snodgrass said.

"No. Follow at a distance. I want to see where they're heading." Jack passed over one of the revolvers he had picked up. "You might need this."

"Thank you." Snodgrass thrust the revolver through the waistband of his trousers.

Stopping every few minutes to check on the coaches, Jack and Snodgrass followed the side roads in a manner that would be bewildering to anybody not familiar with the Herefordshire countryside. Jack pushed closer, but far enough in the rear to be out of sight as he watched the broughams rock and lurch over the ruts.

"Where are they headed?" Jack murmured to himself as the broughams took the road leading to the Malvern Hills. "There's nothing in Malvern except spa hotels."

As the sun burned away the early morning patches of mist, Jack realised the coaches' route would take them to the west of Malvern and towards the southern hills of the Malvern range. *Where the devil are you going, Walsh?* he thought. *That's disturbingly close to Netherhills.*

When the convoy stopped at the end of a cart track, the passengers jumped out. Carmichael led the five Fenians up the track, pushing William before them as the broughams rolled away. Riordan acted as rearguard, with an Enfield rifle comfortable in his hands.

"What do we do?" Snodgrass asked. "Who do we follow? The coaches or the escapees?"

"We follow the fugitives," Jack said. "The carriages are unimportant – they're only for transport."

After Jack's experiences on the North-West Frontier, following half a dozen men across familiar English countryside was simple. "Stay behind me," he whispered to Snodgrass, "and if I tell you to do something, obey immediately."

"Yes, sir," Snodgrass stiffened to attention.

"And for God's sake don't get all regimental with me," Jack said.

"Sir, I'm not an officer!"

"Shut up and follow orders!" Jack tried to shock Snodgrass to his duty.

They're heading for Netherhills. Thank God that Mary is safe up in Berwick.

The fugitives kept to the shelter of the hedgerows, with Riordan occasionally turning to look behind him, rifle at the ready. As Jack had thought, they entered the grounds of Netherhills House.

Netherhills must be their English headquarters, Jack told himself. *And why not? Isolated and empty, yet not far from Worcester with its connections to London and Liverpool.*

"Wait." Jack put a hand on Snodgrass's shoulder. "We'll have to watch them first and see how many there are. I wish we had some means of getting help."

"I saw six, sir," Snodgrass volunteered helpfully.

"There might be more inside," Jack pointed out.

The fugitives slid into the main house by a side door, with Riordan lingering to check behind him before joining the others.

"This way." Jack ran across the still-unkempt grass to the house. "There's a window that doesn't shut properly."

"How do you know that, sir?"

"This is my house." Jack eased inside the house, wincing as Snodgrass's boots thumped on to the wooden floorboards. "Try to keep quiet, Snodgrass! We don't have to announce our presence to the Fenians."

Moving quickly through the dim rooms, Jack recalled the mess left by the men he had suspected to be poachers. Now he realised that had been the Fenians using his Netherhills as their base. *I should have known! How could I be so stupid?*

Jack heard rough laughter from ahead, with the snatch of a Fenian song. "They must believe themselves very safe here," he murmured to Snodgrass.

"Yes, sir," Snodgrass said. "Where are they, sir?"

Jack pointed along a short corridor with four deeply inset doors. "I think they're in that room at the end."

"We can surprise them," Snodgrass lifted his revolver. "We can kill them all."

"You bloodthirsty little devil," Jack said. "That's the spirit!"

Snodgrass shook his head. "If it weren't for them, I'd still be an officer. I hate them more than anything."

"We might not get your commission back," Jack said, "but we can retrieve your honour."

"I want to kill them."

"I want the Russian, Carmichael, alive," Jack said. "I want to find out their connection to the Fenian Brotherhood and if he can lead us to Walsh." He glanced at Snodgrass. "We need more firepower than a couple of revolvers. You stay on watch here."

Although Jack had not spent sufficient time in Netherhills for the house to feel like home, the corridors and rooms were familiar as he hurried to the gun room. On his previous visit, he had left a shotgun for rabbits and carrion crows and a fowling-piece for any interesting game. Loading both, he grabbed a handful of cartridges for each and returned to Snodgrass.

"Is anything happening?"

Snodgrass was visibly shaking. "They sang for a while, sir, and then they began to talk. I couldn't make out what they were saying."

"You wait here," Jack positioned Snodgrass in a recessed doorway with a field of fire the length of a corridor. "I'm going to go outside and burst through their window like the Sikhs attacking the Kaiserbagh. Hopefully, they'll think I am a whole company of men, and they'll run out that door to escape."

Snodgrass nodded. "Right, sir. What do you want me to do?"

"You are Campbell's Highlanders at Balaclava. You hold the line, whatever comes out. Make so much noise the enemy think there are scores of Ensign Snodgrasses, all attacking them. Shoot the enemy flat, Snodgrass."

"You wanted prisoners, sir."

"Only one." Jack handed Snodgrass the shotgun and a handful of cartridges. "Have you fired one of these before?"

"Yes, sir. I used to shoot on my Uncle Bob's estate in Leicestershire."

"Good man. Do you remember the tall, handsome fellow the Fenians hustled out of the gate?"

"Yes, sir. I think so."

"That's the Russian who calls himself Carmichael. Try not to kill him, but don't worry if you do. Blast the rest to kingdom come."

"Yes, sir." Snodgrass checked the shotgun was loaded. "What about your brother, Major Windrush, sir?"

Jack considered for a moment. "He's a soldier. He has to take his chances like the rest of us." *Anyway, it will be better for William to be killed in action than to live as a prisoner of the Fenians.*

"I won't let you down, sir."

"I know you won't, Ensign Snodgrass." Jack said. "Now do your duty."

Slipping outside by a side door, Jack circled to the window of the Fenians' room. The shutters were open but the Fenians had drawn the curtains, enabling Jack to creep up unobserved. With his revolver ready in his belt and the fowling-piece to hand, Jack eased up the window. The murmur of conversation inside the room blanketed the resulting creak as Jack heard the clink of glasses and a long moan, followed by somebody laughing. Waiting for a moment, Jack rolled through the now-open window and crouched behind the curtain, rifle in hand.

"I wanted Colonel Ledbury!" That was Walsh's voice, as authoritarian as ever, "not some underling."

So you're here too, Walsh, Jack felt a surge of satisfaction. *Whatever else happens, you're dead or captured before this day ends.*

"The colonel wasn't there. This officer was in command," somebody answered, the accent from Connaught.

"He's only a major!" Walsh said. "A man of no rank or importance. The British won't care about him."

Another voice intervened, laced with pain. "I am Major William Windrush! My name is well known."

Jack could feel the sudden tension in the room. "Windrush?" Walsh spoke again, his tones smoothly persuasive. "Are you related to my good friend Captain Jack Windrush?"

"He's my brother," William said desperately.

"In that case, we'll kill you slowly, major, and send your head to decorate your officers' mess, minus your eyes, ears, tongue and nose." Jack had heard enough. "Come on the 113th!" He roared, "follow me!" Shoving aside the curtains, he fired his fowling-piece into the mass of startled occupants, dropped it and drew his pistol.

Jack did not count the men in the room. He saw William, spread-eagled naked on an oval table, tied wrist and ankle. Around William was a circle of faces, some familiar, others that Jack did not recognise. Walsh sat at the foot of the table, holding a brandy glass with a nervous-looking Carmichael at his side, while Riordan leaned against the door, nursing his rifle. The others must have been the local Fenians, one of whom had a lit cigar in his hand; Jack saw several burns on William's chest and guessed the Fenian had been torturing him.

Jack took in the situation without conscious thought. "Come on the 113th!" he shouted. Aiming quickly, he fired at the cigar-wielding Fenian. "Follow me!"

"Windrush!" Throwing his glass at Jack, Walsh pulled a pistol from inside his jacket.

Jack saw the cigar-wielding Fenian stagger backwards, then shifted his aim to Walsh. Most of the other men dashed for the door, getting in each other's way as they tried to escape the supposed attack by the 113th.

The boom of Snodgrass's shotgun stopped the Fenians' flight. The blast caught one man squarely in the body, propelling him back into the room in a welter of blood and shredded flesh.

"At them, the 113th!" Snodgrass shouted. "Fire at will!" The rapid crack-crack of his revolver added force to his words. Another Fenian fell, with the remainder either running back into the room or throwing themselves on to the floor.

Walsh was the first to recover. "It's a trick! There are only two of them," he shouted. "Kill them!" While some Fenians charged at Snodgrass, two lunged at Jack, swearing. He shot the first, sending him spinning across William on the table, quickly altered his aim and tried to fire at the second, cursing when the revolver jammed.

"Damn and blast the thing!" Jack tried again, with the same result, and staggered as the Fenian grappled with him.

"Kill him!" Walsh shouted.

The Fenian grabbed Jack by the throat, with his fingers wrapping around the red marks the hangman's noose had left. Jack gasped, crashed the barrel of his revolver on the man's head and raked the muzzle down his face. When the Fenian yelled, loosening his grip, Jack rammed a knee into his groin. The Fenian gasped in agony and doubled up. Pushing him aside, Jack looked for Walsh.

The Russian had hardly moved. He stood at the foot of the table with his pistol aimed at William, as calm as if he had been in a gentleman's club.

"You can watch your brother die, Windrush," Walsh said, "and then I'll kill you."

With his revolver jammed, and the table between him and Walsh, Jack could do nothing as Walsh straightened his arm.

"No!" Bleeding from a gash on his face, Ensign Snodgrass pushed through the fleeing Fenians to enter the room. He fired at Walsh and missed.

Turning at once, Walsh fired two rapid shots. The first missed but the second hit Snodgrass in the stomach, knocking him backwards. As Snodgrass crumpled with his face twisted in agony, Jack jumped on the table, trod on William and leapt on Walsh.

The Russian slammed an elbow into Jack's face, fired a shot that missed and ran out of the open door. Jack looked around. Save for the dead and wounded, he and William were the only people in the room. *Where did Carmichael go?*

"Cut me loose," William shouted.

Ignoring him, Jack crouched over Snodgrass. "You'll be all right," he said. "It's not serious."

"It is," Snodgrass said calmly. "I'm dying. I can feel it." He writhed in a spasm of agony. "Jesus, that hurts. It's sore, Captain."

"You did well, Ensign," Jack said. "You acted like the true British officer you are."

Snodgrass nodded, coughed bright blood and gasped. "Could you tell Father that I'm sorry?"

"You can tell him yourself," Jack said.

"I'm dying, Jack," Snodgrass said. "Please tell Father that I'm sorry." His anguish was evident. "Please, Windrush?"

"I'll tell him," Jack said. "I'll also tell him that you died with honour and bravery, like the true British officer you are."

"But the court-martial," Snodgrass said.

"They'll rescind the judgment," Jack said. "They'll reinstate your rank."

Snodgrass writhed again, coughing up blood, gasped in pain and died with his hands clutching at Jack's arm.

"Poor little bugger," Jack said. "You had so much promise and so much potential."

"Never mind him," William said. "Cut me free, for God's sake before the blasted Fenians come back."

"They were Russians." Lifting a knife from the belt of a dead Fenian, Jack sliced through William's bonds. "Get some clothes on, William and let's hunt them down."

Reloading his revolver, Jack left the room. Judging by the bodies, dead and wounded, in the corridor, Ensign Snodgrass had put up a good fight. Cursing that neither of the Russians was among the casualties, Jack ran along the corridor.

If I were Walsh, what would I do? I would head for Ireland, where I have friends. Jack paused. Walsh would go to the stable for a horse. When he found the stable empty, he would run for the nearest town to hire a horse or a carriage.

The pistol shot took Jack by surprise, with the bullet gouging a chunk of wood from the panelling at his shoulder. Ducking instinctively, he wheeled around, revolver in hand. A second shot tugged at the sleeve of his jacket, tearing the cloth without hitting him. This time he saw the muzzle-flare and the jet of powder smoke from a doorway a few yards along the corridor.

"Don't run, Walsh! I'm coming for you." Stepping carefully, Jack moved along the passage, weaving from side to side to disrupt Walsh's aim. He knew how difficult it was to snap-shoot with accuracy, but the closer he came to Walsh, the easier the target he would present.

"Windrush!" The shout came from behind him. Jack jumped to the side as the revolver crashed out, with the bullet passing uncomfortably close. He saw

Carmichael duck away, fired an instant too late and saw his bullet punch into the door frame.

Mary will kill me for destroying her house, Jack told himself, and controlled his laugh, recognising it as the onset of hysteria. His nerves felt so stretched he wondered if they might break, leaving him a gibbering wreck. He had seen it happen after battle in the Crimea and India when strong men collapsed with nervous strain. Jack took a deep breath; *I have a Russian in front and a Russian behind me. Which one is more dangerous?*

If I show myself, either of them can shoot me, but on the other hand, if they attempt to leave the room, I can shoot them. We are all equally trapped.

"Windrush!" That was Walsh's voice. "You can surrender now."

"Surrender?" Jack forced a laugh. "You're stuck in England with your allies dead or imprisoned. The authorities know about you while the police and army are now hurrying to arrest you. You can give yourself up for a fair trial, or fight me and die like a soldier."

Walsh's laugh sounded genuine. "You have things inverted, Windrush. You're trapped in this house between two armed men. Your young ally is dead, you are a hunted fugitive, a cashiered officer and neither the police nor your army knows where you are." He paused for a moment. "Furthermore, Windrush, we have your woman. Will you surrender? Or shall I kill her, slowly?"

"What?" Jack shuddered at the thought of Mary in Walsh's hands. "I don't believe you."

Walsh laughed again. "That's your choice, Windrush. Wait!"

Backing into a recessed doorway, Jack looked up and down the corridor. A woman's scream rang through the house, and then Walsh's voice sounded once more.

"Do you want to hear her again?"

Shaken, Jack gripped the butt of his revolver, fighting the desire to rush into the room where Walsh waited. He knew that would be suicide. "If you harm one hair of her head, I swear to God I'll make you suffer, Walsh."

"One hair of her head?" Walsh laughed and again, there was a prolonged woman's moan.

"Do you recognise this, Windrush?" He threw something from the door of his room, not appearing long enough for Jack even to attempt a single shot.

The length of black hair appeared to have been torn out by the roots. Stooping, Jack lifted the hair, pressed it to his nose and recognised the scent. He swore softly.

"I'll kill you, Walsh, or whatever your name is."

"Throw down your pistol and come out, Windrush, if you value your woman." Another scream followed Walsh's words, and then a woman's voice.

"Don't you dare surrender, Jack Windrush! Fight!"

The next scream was more prolonged.

When Jack started forward, Carmichael fired twice. The first shot lifted splinters from the wood panelling while the second nicked Jack's left thigh. He gasped, staggered and fell back into his doorway.

"Are you still alive, Windrush?" Walsh taunted him. "So is this pretty little thing. Shall I make her less pretty?"

As a professional soldier, Jack knew he should not allow frustration to overcome his caution. All the same, he lunged forward again, this time expecting Carmichael to fire. Falling to the floor, Jack crawled down the corridor, closer to Carmichael, and fired three shots the instant the Russian appeared.

The first shot scored a lucky hit in Carmichael's arm. Gasping, he dropped his pistol, which skidded across the wooden floor, far out of Jack's reach. The second shot hit the panelling, and the third crashed into the door, slamming it against its stopper. It bounced back, cracked into the retreating Russian, sending him staggering into the corridor.

Jack's fourth bullet caught Carmichael square in his handsome face, smashing his nose and exiting out the back of his head. Giving a prolonged gasp, the Russian collapsed backwards.

Jack emptied his revolver into the Russian.

"That's you dead, you bastard," Jack gasped. Keeping low, he rolled into the shelter of the room, with powder smoke thick in the corridor and his injured leg stinging. *Now I have Walsh to kill.* He fished in his pocket for cartridges. There were none.

"Good evening, Captain."

Jack looked up. Riordan sat on a wooden chair, with his Enfield rifle pointed directly at Jack's head.

"Your gun's empty, captain, and at this range, I can't miss." Riordan said. "I've been waiting to get you."

"I helped you escape," Jack said.

"You used me to infiltrate the Brotherhood," Riordan said, "and now we have you." He raised his voice. "I've got him, Walsh!"

"His name's not Walsh," Jack said. "He's not even Irish – he's a Russian using Ireland for his own ends."

"I don't care," Riordan prodded Jack with the muzzle of his rifle.

"Bring him here," Walsh shouted. "He can meet his wife."

"You can die together," Riordan gave a little smile. "How romantic. Turn around and walk out slowly."

With the muzzle of the Enfield pressing hard into his spine, Jack stepped over Carmichael's body and along the corridor. He contemplated sudden flight, but knew Riordan had been right; a trained veteran could not miss at that range.

"Bring him in," Walsh was waiting at the entrance to the room with his revolver pointed at Jack. "Now I have you both."

Riordan pushed Jack into the room. "Here's your husband, Mrs Windrush," he said.

"That's not my husband." Helen was sitting on a chair, tied hand and foot with one eye bruised and her lips swollen.

"You've got the wrong woman," Jack said. "That's not my wife."

"I'd like the honour, though." Helen lifted her chin with the spirit that had always characterised her. "Hello, Jack. I'm sorry, I can't greet you properly."

"That's all right, Helen," Jack gave a little bow. "Circumstances seem against us at present."

Helen's smile seemed genuine. "We'll be together in death, Jack, although we could not be together in life."

Jack gave another little bow. He tried to think of something comforting to say, but the words did not come. "I never stopped liking you, Helen."

"I know," Helen said. "I'm happy with that."

"Enough of this," Riordan said. "Can I shoot him now, Walsh?"

"Oh, ladies first." Walsh pressed his revolver to the side of Helen's head.

Lifting his chin, Jack held Walsh's gaze. "You're a brave man, Walsh, murdering an unarmed woman."

"See you on the other side, Jack," Helen said.

"Not yet, I think." The voice came from the doorway.

Jack started as Mary entered the room with a pistol in her right hand and a cheroot in her left. She fired once, sending Riordan staggering back as Walsh turned to face this new threat.

Grabbing the Enfield as it fell, Jack swung it, catching Walsh on the arm. Unbalanced, Walsh fired, with the bullet smashing into the wall behind Mary, who fired again and missed, as Jack reversed the rifle and pressed the trigger. The bullet crashed into Walsh's chest, propelling him backwards into Helen, clattering both to the floor. Stepping over Helen, Jack smashed the rifle barrel against Walsh's head.

"We want him alive," he said.

Standing in the doorway, Mary took a long pull at her cheroot and passed it over to Jack. "What about her?" She pointed at Helen with the muzzle of her revolver. "Is she going to cause trouble for our marriage? If so, I can end it now and say she died in the fighting."

"No." Jack drew on the cheroot. He could feel himself beginning to shake as reaction set in. "She won't cause any trouble."

Mary did not lower the pistol. "If you do, Helen, I'll be ready for you."

Jack took the revolver from Mary. "There's no need for that. Where did you spring from?"

"I was upstairs all the time," Mary explained. "This is my home, after all. I had to wait until I could get a pistol."

Jack stared at her. "You're a cool one." He imagined Mary listening to the alien voices in her house, planning her move. "What have I married?"

"Me," Mary said, with her eyes fixed on Helen.

"Listen!" Jack said. "Can you hear that?" Stepping to the window, he looked outside. "Your husband is back, Helen, and he's brought help."

Half dressed, William sat astride a black horse, with a troop of cavalry behind him.

Helen snorted. "I hoped the Fenians would kill him."

CHAPTER TWENTY-FIVE

London, August 1866

Smith peered at Jack, sighing. "Well, Windrush, you were moderately successful. You exposed the Russians and disposed of their men, but also revealed yourself as an agent."

"Yes, sir," Jack agreed.

"Naturally, that compromises your usefulness with us. Now that everybody knows what you've been up to, we can no longer send you on any similar expeditions."

"Yes, sir." Jack felt no disappointment. "Did you find out Walsh's and Carmichael's real names?"

Smith glanced at the open file on his desk. "Walsh is a Russian named Markovic. We captured him in London during the Crimean War, when he tried to blow up a Royal Naval ship. He joined the Fenians in jail and escaped from Dartmoor some years ago. We think imprisonment unhinged him because he still seemed to believe he was fighting the Crimean War."

"He was a victim of the late war, then," Jack said.

"Quite," Smith said. "Carmichael wasn't even Russian. He is a Pole called Bajek. As far as we can ascertain, he worked for Russia because they hold his family hostage. The world is a wicked place, Windrush."

"Indeed, sir."

Smith closed the file on his desk. "Because I can no longer use your special talents, I have decided to return you to regimental duties. As it's no longer a secret you have been working in the secret service, I have advertised that fact, to negate the previous stories of your court-martial and restore your reputation as a British officer."

"Not all British officers will look kindly on my acting the spy," Jack said.

"That cannot be helped," Smith said.

"My brother?" Jack asked. "What happened to him? He must have lost prestige, with the Fenians capturing him during their raid on the Royal Malverns."

"Quite the contrary," Smith said. "Major William Windrush could land in a cesspit and come out smelling of lavender. He's getting the credit for recapturing the escaped prisoners and fighting off the Fenians."

"The Fenians captured him," Jack reminded Smith.

"He resisted torture." Smith gave a little smile. "Then he escaped and brought help. Your part will never be fully known. That's part of the price of being an agent of the queen, you see. You work in the shadows, while others get the glory."

Jack shook his head. "When I first joined the army, I was after glory. Now?" He shrugged. "Now I know it for a false mistress. There was nothing glorious about young Snodgrass dying before his life had properly begun or the slaughter on Inkerman Ridge."

When Smith looked up, there was no humour in his eyes. "Poor men join the army because they are hungry. Wealthy men join because of a sense of duty or hunger for glory. We need glory."

Jack nodded – he knew that Smith was had a point. "I'd prefer some advancement, sir. I have a wife and family to support."

"You should be thankful you're not in jail for treason, Windrush. After all, you did help Riordan to escape."

Jack nodded, knowing Smith was right.

"There is one more thing." Reaching into his top drawer, Smith produced a small bell. When he rang it, Helen walked in.

"Good morning Jack." Dressed modestly in a dark crinoline, Helen did not look like the woman who had shared Jack's adventures.

Jack hid his surprise. "Good morning, Helen." He stood up and Helen took his chair as if by right.

"Mrs Windrush has been working with us," Smith said quietly. "You may have guessed she was the woman in Berwick, laying her snares for Bajek and Markovic."

"You caused that riot in Berwick?" Jack asked.

"It was fun," Helen said. "I didn't expect to see you there, though."

"You led young Snodgrass astray and encouraged mutiny in my company."

"I knew you could deal with it." Helen's smile did not falter. "It was a shame about Peter, though. He was a nice young boy."

Jack looked away. "Aye. Well, Helen, for the life of me, I cannot think of anybody more suitable for the position of a spy. What does William say?"

"He and I are irreconcilably apart." Helen gave a little curtsey. "His opinion is of far less interest to me than yours."

"It seems that William is a man going places. He is destined for high rank. You could be a general's wife."

Helen shrugged. "He has no edge at all."

Smith cleared his throat. "To return to business. You're going back to the 113th, Captain Windrush. No more adventuring for you, only the life of a normal regimental officer."

Jack nodded. "That suits me, sir."

"I wonder." Smith fixed him with a steady gaze. "I wonder if you will miss the excitement."

"I won't, sir. It's a quiet life for me from now on."

"All right, Windrush." Smith handed over a sealed packet. "Report to the 113th at Berwick."

"Yes, sir. I'll be glad to get back to honest regimental soldiering again." Jack hesitated. "Although Colonel Snodgrass won't be pleased to see me."

"Ah," Smith said, "you haven't heard. The good colonel was asked to resign his command due to his son's activities. He's retired on half-pay, gone to some dismal seaside town or other to eke out the remainder of his life, poor chap. I'm afraid the disgrace might prove too much for him."

Jack nodded. "He and I never got along, sir, so I can't say I'll worry overmuch about his feelings."

"Good luck, Windrush." Smith managed a smile. "It's been a pleasure working with you. Come with me, Mrs Windrush."

Smith and Helen walked away, leaving Jack alone in the austere office, knowing that part of his life had ended for ever. He sighed, wondering when the next train for Berwick departed.

* * *

"We're under siege, old boy." Elliot leaned against the front of Jack's house, looking over the parapet of Berwick town wall to the lights of the nighttime harbour. "We see ourselves as an expanding empire, yet all the time we're defending it from external and internal enemies. The Empire is constantly under siege." He pulled on his cheroot. "I suppose that's all good for men like you and me. It gives us employment and the opportunity to advance our careers."

"Sometimes, Arthur," Jack exhaled a thread of blue smoke, "sometimes I wonder what it's all about."

"Best not to think too much, Jack," Elliot said. "We're soldiers. We go where the government sends us and fight the Queen's enemies. That's enough for me."

"Maybe so," Jack said, "but don't you wonder why, sometimes? When I was at school…"

"Many years ago," Elliot murmured.

"When I was at school," Jack continued, "the teachers taught us that Boadicea and Caractacus were heroes for resisting the Roman Empire, and here we are, spreading our Empire by putting down rebellions by people who frankly, view us as alien invaders. We are fighting against the Boadiceas and Caractacuses now; whether they are Pashtun, Maori or Fenian, they all view us as the alien invader."

"That's true, old boy," Elliot said. "But we're also doing good. We're spreading enlightenment and civilisation, ending slavery, bringing education, the rule of law and Christianity."

"Do you think that's enough?" Jack asked. "We're forcing our culture on people who are quite content with their own."

"We have to think that's enough, Jack," Elliot was suddenly sober. "We wouldn't do it otherwise." He threw away the end of his cheroot, watching the faint red glow spiralling into the dark. "We'd go mad if we considered the rights and wrongs of everything we do." He sighed. "Consider the alternative. If we were not in India, or Ireland, or New Zealand, do you think the other powers would leave these places alone? They are all vulnerable and ripe for conquest. Do you think Russia say, or France, would sit back and allow these places to exist?"

Jack shook his head. "No. Russia would be through Afghanistan and into India like a shot."

"Aye; they're pushing that way already. Would you like to see Ireland all alone and unprotected with France on the prowl? Or Russia? Or even Prussia?" Elliot lit another cheroot. "Mark my words, Jack, the countries of our empire are better under our protection than being occupied by anybody else."

"France might move into Ireland," Jack agreed. "I can't see Prussia, though. They're a land-based power."

"So far," Elliot said. "That Bismarck fellow has ideas above his station. We may have to slap him down yet, and the Russians hate us for Crimea, as you well know." He sighed. "I don't know the answers, Jack; I just know that the Lord doesn't do things or allow things for no reason. He's allowed the British Empire to grow, so there must be a reason for it. I think there is a great evil coming and we're here to stop it." He grinned. "After that, there will be no more use for us and the British Empire will crumble to make way for something else."

"When will this happen?"

Elliot shrugged. "I don't know, Jack. Maybe in our time; maybe in our children's time, or maybe even our grandchildren's. The Lord knows best, while we puny little pawns can only plod on. We're here, we have a job to do, and that's the end of it."

Jack nodded. "Do you think there is a reason for all this? Do you honestly believe we are a tool for good?"

"We must believe that, Jack," Elliot said. "Otherwise, all this death and suffering is for nothing." When he met Jack's gaze, Elliot looked weary. "We must do our duty, Jack, and pray to God we're doing the right thing."

"Here, you two!" Mary appeared at the front door, smiling. "Do you intend to stand there talking all day? Dinner's on the table."

"Coming." Jack stood up. "Come on, Arthur, Colonel Mary has given her orders."

"Colonel Mary? That lady would be a general, at least!"

Jack nodded. "On that, Arthur, we can agree."

HISTORICAL NOTE

Although this story is fictitious, parts are based on historical fact. The Fenian Brotherhood was an Irish-American organisation that menaced Great Britain from time to time from 1865 onwards. Their methods included inciting mutiny in the British Army, bombings throughout the British Isles and raids into Canada from the United States. The majority of the Fenian participants in the invasions were either Irish or men of Irish extraction who were veterans of the late American Civil War.

The Fenian invasions of Canada had one positive outcome. Made aware of their vulnerability to attack across the long border, most of the colonies of British North America, New Brunswick, the United Provinces of Canada and Lower Canada combined into the Dominion of Canada. In attempting to create the Republic of Ireland, the Fenians had unwittingly helped create Canada.

For a while, the Fenians hoped to provoke a war between Great Britain and the United States, but in June 1866 President Andrew Johnson declared that the USA was neutral in the dispute. The Canadians coped well with the Fenian invasions, which were both short-lived and abortive. The major encounter was at Ridgeway, Ontario, where the untried Canadian Volunteers lost nine men killed and 33 wounded, with four more men subsequently dying of wounds or disease. Fenian casualties were around the same.

The Russian connection, Patrick Walsh, Walter Carmichael and the activities of the Green Company are entirely fictitious.

Malcolm Archibald

WINDRUSH - THE CITY OF DREADFUL DEATH

JACK WINDRUSH BOOK 8

We could not move in that city of dreadful death without coming across signs of human sacrifices and suffering.
Sergeant J. Flynn, Rifle Brigade

Wha saw the Forty Second?
Wha saw the Forty Twa?
Wha saw the bare ersed buggers
Coming frae the Ashanti War?
Traditional

ACKNOWLEDGEMENT

I would like to thank Dr Zachary Beier of the Department of History and Archaeology, University of the West Indies for clearing up a couple of historical points.

PRELUDE

Denkyira, West Africa, Summer 1800

The family sat together in the courtyard of their house with the wind rustling the leaves of the palm tree in one corner and the food set up before them. Kodzo knew that with the first harvest of the year successfully gathered, there was plenty for everybody, plantains, yams and manioc, together with sweet potato and gourds of beer.

Koshiwa Badu sat at the head, joking with her family, chiding where necessary, allowing the children all the freedom of childhood while keeping them from danger, as was the Denkyira tradition. Beside Koshiwa was Yawo, her daughter, and Kofi and Fifi, her sons. Further away, Kwabena and Kodzo, her grandsons, played happily with the fowls, not caring about the conversation of their elders. They were at home and life was as it had always been.

Koshiwa looked up when she heard the frantic barking of a dog. She glanced at Kofi, who pulled a face and continued to eat, while Fifi reached for his second gourd of beer. A shift of wind rustled the palm leaves and brought the sound of a man shouting in the distance.

"That's Kwasi Bekoe," Kofi said. "He's probably drunk again." He laughed, with his family joining in. Kwasi Bekoe was something of a standing joke in the village, always getting drunk and falling out with his wife and anybody else who had the misfortune to meet him.

When the dog's barking ended in a high-pitched squeal, Fifi lowered his gourd, wiped the beer from his chin and smiled. "Kwasi has kicked the dog!"

"I wish he would shut his teeth," Koshiwa said, as the shouting continued. "Kofi, go and tell him to keep quiet. Either that or I will."

"You would start a quarrel," Kofi said. "I'd better go." Taking a sip at Fifi's gourd, he stepped outside the courtyard, walked through the open front room and into the village. He saw Kwasi running towards him, his legs blundering as if he were exhausted, and blood sliding down his face.

"Kofi!" Kwasi said. "Run! Run now!"

"What is it?" Kofi dropped his smile as he saw what was behind Kwasi. "Edwesu Asanti slave hunters!"

"Mother!" Kofi only had time for one word before the rush of men overpowered him. Knocked to the ground, he struggled for only a moment as two men held him, and a third cracked a heavy stick on the back of his head. Other men rushed past him and into Koshiwa's house.

Koshiwa rose from her seat, screaming as the Edwesu warriors charged into her courtyard. Naked except for white loin-cloths, each man had two white stripes painted down each side of his face, and carried a heavy club in his hand.

Fifi was first to react, throwing his gourd at the first man and leaping for the long spear in the corner of the courtyard. The gourd caught the striped man square in the face, sending him staggering back. His companions blocked Fifi's path, swinging their clubs, knocking him to the ground. The white striped Edwesu circled the courtyard, grabbing everybody, smashing their clubs on the heads of those who tried to resist.

Only Kodzo managed to escape, ducking under the long arms of one Edwesu warrior and side-stepping another to run into the street outside. Panting with fear, he saw more of the white striped warriors all around the village, gathering together the Denkyira people and shoving them under the fetish tree in the small village square. Sliding into a patch of bushes, Kodzo watched the Edwesus grab the Denkyiras and manacle their ankles and wrists, hugged his knees to his chest and lay still, sobbing in fear.

As soon as night came, Kodzo slid free from his hiding place. By that time the Edwesus had marched the Denkyiras away, leaving the village deserted. Wiping away his tears, Kodzo ran home to search for food. He did not notice the man with the white stripes until it was too late.

"Another for the slave market!" The Edwesu said. "Come with me, little slave."

Kodzo began to scream. It was a sound he would grow used to in the long, bitter years ahead.

CHAPTER ONE

Atlantic Ocean, June 1873

"The barometer's falling fast." Harry Young, mate of the three-masted barque *Lady Luck,* tapped the glass, swore softly, and checked the set of the sails.

"Aye," Captain Hobson glanced aft, where dark clouds piled up from the darkening horizon, and a greasy sheen tinted the sea. "We're in for the very devil of a blow, I reckon, Mr Young."

"Best get below, Mary." Lounging by the rail, Jack Windrush had been listening to the conversation. "If the captain thinks there's a storm coming, I don't want you swept overboard."

Mary smiled. "It's not stormy yet, Jack. All we have is a fresh breeze."

Jack grunted. "Aye, but a fresh breeze can soon turn into a howling gale."

"If that happens," Mary said, "I might go below." She stepped along the deck with the wind whipping her long hair around her shoulders and threatening to lift her straw hat. "I can't stand being cooped up in that tiny cabin, Jack. I'll stay on deck as long as I can."

"You're a stubborn hussy, Mary Windrush!"

Mary gave a small curtsey, with a stray shaft of sunlight reflecting from the silver Celtic cross she wore around her neck. "Why, thank you, Captain Jack. Coming from you, I'll take that as a compliment."

"That's Major Jack, hussy, and I'll thank you to remember it!"

Mary laughed. "You've been Captain Jack to me for too long to change now, *Captain* Jack!"

The wind increased, coming from the south-west, cracking the canvas against the spars and whistling through the standing rigging. Jack put a protective arm around Mary, who shook it away. "I can stand on my own two feet, thank you!"

"All hands aloft!" Captain Hobson roared. "Make fast the skysails, royals and royal staysails!"

Mary watched the seamen scramble aloft with the wind flapping their loose clothing and shirts and threatening to blast them from their precarious hand-and-foot-holds. "Brave men up there," she said, tucking her purple-and-gold scarf around her neck.

Jack tapped the glass. "The barometer is still falling."

"Aye," Harry Young glanced at the gathering clouds. "We'd better shorten all sail before we're caught out here." He watched the seamen return to the deck, some to slip below to the foc'sle.

Captain Hobson grunted, paced the deck for a few moments, checked the sea and made his decision. "All hands!" he roared. "All hands shorten sail!"

"Time for us to get below," Jack said as a rush of nimble-footed seamen filled the deck and once more swarmed aloft.

"It is getting blowy!" Mary grabbed at her hat a second too late as the wind finally whisked it from her head and tossed it overboard. She watched as if floated for a moment then was lost in the rapidly rising waves.

"The lads are struggling up there," Jack gestured aloft, where the seamen balanced on the footropes fought with the gaskets. Unfurled, the heavy canvas of the sails billowed and bellied as the wind rose. One bald seaman momentarily lost his footing and wrapped both arms around a spar as the rising gale blasted the sails from the gaskets, thrashed the canvas to pieces and hurled the ragged remnants into the heaving sea.

"Mary!" Jack grabbed his wife as the deck heeled to starboard. After stripping the canvas from the masts, the wind pressed down on *Lady Luck*, forcing Jack and Mary to hold onto anything solid. The bald seaman slipped and nearly fell until one of his mates hauled him back to comparative safety.

"I can hardly breathe!" Mary gasped as the wind clutched at her.

"Get that woman below!" Jack could hardly hear Captain Hobson's bellow above the howl of the wind that was now forcing the ship further and ever further over. Waves leapt up the side of *Lady Luck*, reaching for the frail life on board.

"She's broaching to!" Harry Young yelled as *Lady Luck* tilted onto her beam ends, with her lower yards dragging in the frothing white water to leeward. Her seamen held on with white-knuckled hands, while their feet scrabbled for purchase on ropes that were no longer taut.

"Hold on!" Jack held Mary, who had wrapped both arms around the mizzen mast. He saw the white faces and gaping mouths of the helmsmen, both unable to move as the wind pressed them against the wheel.

"Dear God help us!" a half-shaven seaman yelled.

"Aye, Peter," a rough voice replied. "I knew you were a Christian at heart. I told you before that there are no atheists in a storm."

After that, there was no speech as the gale mounted, and the waves broke green and white over the heeling deck. Unable to speak, scarcely able to breathe, Jack fought to see through the curtain of spindrift and driving rain. The light had died, with the occasional burst of lightning the only illumination, each flash revealing a nightmare of leaping dark water topped with crests of foaming white. Looking aloft, Jack saw the storm had carried away the main topmast, while the mizzen topgallant hung in the rigging, threatening to fall with every fresh assault of the wind.

Sodden, with her dress and hair slicked close to body and head, Mary wrapped her fingers around Jack's thumb. He met her gaze, saw no fear in her brown eyes, and tried to muster a smile.

Then the wind died. A great sea broke over the stern, sweeping up the length of the ship, carrying away the steering and standard compass, splintering the ship's longboat into a thousand pieces and breaking the cover of number two hatch. As that wave receded, *Lady Luck* dipped by the head, thrusting her bowsprit underwater.

"Are we going to sink?" Mary asked with surprising calmness.

"No," Jack said. "The storm's easing. I can hear you talk."

Mary nodded. "So you can." Her smile did not look forced. "I can hear you as well."

Although the wind had receded, *Lady Luck* still wallowed in a tremendous sea, with waves around her higher than the broken mizzen.

"Sound the well!" Captain Hobson ordered the carpenter. "See how much water we're making."

"I tried, sir," the carpenter was a balding, middle-aged man with a worn-out face. "There's too much water slopping in there to get an accurate reading."

"Try again." The captain stepped aft to examine the damage aloft, holding onto the rail to keep his balance on the heeling deck. "You're still with us I see, Major and Mrs Windrush?"

"We're still here, Captain," Jack confirmed. "How's *Lady Luck*?"

Captain Hobson grunted. "Deserted us, Major, deserted us." He continued his scrutiny of the masts and rigging. "The cap of the lower masthead is broken," he said to the mate, "and the storm's wrenched the masthead around. The main yard and both topsail yards are also down." He nodded to the splintered spars as they lay across what remained of the rail, "and the topmast, topgallant mast and all the upper yards and their gear are floating to leeward, hammering at our hull."

"Yes, sir," the mate nodded to the ten-foot-high tangle of broken spars, cordage and various pieces of ship's timbers that lay across the main deck. "There's that, too, and the mizzen topgallant mast and yards could fall at any minute." He raised his voice slightly. "Major Windrush, you and the missus would be better moving elsewhere. If that raffle falls, you are right underneath."

Jack looked up at the mess above, with only the straining lower rigging holding it in place. He shifted further along the deck as Captain Hobson watched, unsmiling.

Brushing wet hair from her face, Mary looked around *Lady Luck*. "What happens now, Captain? Can you repair your ship out here at sea? Or do we continue the voyage with only half our masts and no sails?"

The captain glanced at the mate, who screwed up his face.

"We'll set up a temporary jury rig," Captain Hobson said, "but we're making too much water to sail right to London. No, Mrs Windrush, we'll have to head to the nearest land to fix her up. I'm sorry, but your journey home will be delayed by a few weeks."

"Sir!" the carpenter appeared from below, "we're making water fast. About two feet since I checked below. I reckon we're stove in below the waterline."

"Well, that confirms it," Captain Hobson said. "We head for the nearest sheltered anchorage."

"That would be somewhere in West Africa," Jack said. "Over there beyond the horizon."

"Aye," the captain said. "The Gold Coast; Cape Coast Castle if we can make it, although it's not the best anchorage in the world."

"And if we can't make it?" Mary was still calm. "We don't seem to have many boats left."

"We make for Elmina."

"I don't know that place," Jack said.

"It's part of our Gold Coast colony," the captain's eyes were never still, checking the rigging, the set of the masts, the actions of his crew and the slowly decreasing swell of the sea. "It used to be Dutch, but we took it over last year. I'm surprised you haven't heard about it."

Jack frowned. "Our regiment has been in Ireland, dying of fever in Hong Kong and doing a little soldiering in Penang. I've not had much interest in politicians redrawing maps in West Africa."

"Well, Major, you'll see it for yourself soon, if the old *Lady* holds out until we get there." Captain glanced looked aloft as another line parted. "I believe the anchorage at Elmina is more sheltered than Cape Coast although I've no charts."

"No charts?" Mary began to look worried.

Jack glanced at the waves, marbled grey-and-white and still as high as the mizzen-mast, their tips white and curling, with the remnants of the storm flicking spindrift onto *Lady Luck*. "We'd best leave you to carry on."

"Jack?" Mary clung to his arm as they inched along the deck. Pieces of loose gear rattled above them, with a block swaying precariously a few feet above the deck.

"It's as bad below," Jack said. Their cabin was a wreck, with seawater swirling three feet deep through a smashed porthole.

"All our possessions are in there," Mary gripped Jack's arm.

"The sea chests are water-proofed," Jack held her tight as the ship rolled from side to side. "Everything will be fine."

Captain Hobson shouted orders which saw the crew working aloft, clearing the worst of the mess and tossing cordage and splintered spars overboard. As the wind kicked up again, *Lady Luck* lurched, with seawater surging over the port quarter.

"Come on, old *Lady*!" Captain Hobson revealed a tenderness towards his ship that surprised Jack. "We'll get you sorted out."

With the south-west wind driving her on, *Lady Luck* plunged over the sea, raising clouds of spray as the crew worked frantically to save the ship. Captain Hobson and Harry Young nursed *Lady Luck* towards the shore, chasing the hands from difficulty to crisis as spars broke and water surged through holes in the hull.

"We won't make Cape Coast," Harry Young shouted. "We'll be lucky to reach Elmina."

"We'll be lucky to reach anywhere," Captain Hobson said.

With the waves only gradually decreasing and the masts creaking ominously, Mary lifted her head. "Can you smell that?"

"I can," Jack said.

"It's like the Indian jungle," Mary said, "yet different." She drew a hand over her head, pushing back her long black hair. "It's wilder."

"Aye," Jack peered eastward, trying to see through the curtain of spray.

"Have you ever been to Africa?" Mary asked.

"Never to stay," Jack said. "I passed through Egypt on my way to India back in '52, and touched at Cape Town a couple of times, but that's all."

"We're both strangers here, then," Mary said.

Battling against the offshore wind, *Lady Luck* limped closer to the shore, hour by wave-battered hour until Jack heard the call from the wreckage aloft. "Land ho!"

"We're going to make it," Jack said.

"I've never doubted it." Mary had somehow rescued Jack's sole remaining dry cheroot and lit it with a salvaged Lucifer. Waving the match in the air to extinguish it, she drew on the cheroot. "So that's Africa."

"That's Elmina," Captain Hobson said. "Thank you, Lord, for small mercies. If we can cross the bar, we might find the river there a better anchorage than Cape Coast."

"It's not what I expected." Borrowing the mate's telescope, Jack studied the large white building that dominated the town of Elmina. "It's like a mediaeval castle." He checked to ensure that it was the Union flag that hung from the flagpole. "Aye, it's British, thank God."

"It's charming. I'd like to visit that place." Shifting the cheroot to the corner of her mouth, Mary relieved Jack of the telescope. "I wonder if the captain will allow us to land."

"How long will repairs take?" Jack asked.

"Weeks," Harry Young said. "You'd be as well taking Mrs Windrush ashore as letting her remain here in a flooded cabin."

"We're making water fast," the carpenter looked even more worried than he had with his previous report. "There are more planks stove in."

"Let me see." Without hesitation, Captain Hobson swung down a length of rope to inspect the hold. He emerged swearing and sodden a few moments later, and in that short space of time, Jack saw the ship had settled further into the water.

"She waited," Mary murmured, still studying Elmina.

"Who waited?"

"*Lady Luck*," Mary said. "She waited until we were close to shore before she decided to sink. She was looking after her crew and passengers."

"Aye," Captain Hobson said. "The old *Lady* would do that." He gave Mary an approving nod before raising his voice. "Get the hands together! Salvage all that can be salvaged and then abandon ship."

CHAPTER TWO

Elmina June 1873

The news spread through *Lady Luck* in seconds. Most of the seamen looked over the side and towards the land, calculating how far they could swim.

"Are there sharks?" The carpenter asked.

"Not that I am aware of." The mate raised his voice to a roar. "Come on, lads; get what you need from the foc'sle and off we go."

"Wait here," Jack said and splashed down the companionway to the tiny cubicle he had shared with Mary for the past three months. Seawater lapped nearly to the deck above, ruining the bedding and any loose clothing. Fortunately, both he and Mary were experienced travellers and had packed their essentials into two seachests, with the remainder of their possessions travelling separately. Both chests were floating, chest-height in the cabin, washing back and forth with the movement of the ship.

Calling on a reluctant seaman to help, Jack hauled the chests on a deck which was now nearly on a level with the waves.

"Major Windrush," Captain Hobson said. "Take your wife ashore at once. You're no good to us here."

"How the devil do we get the chests to land?" Jack stared at the heaving sea between *Lady Luck* and the shore, and the white line of surf that crashed on the beach, a quarter of a mile distant.

"These men may help." Mary pointed the stump of her still smouldering cheroot at the half dozen canoes that came out from the shore, their prows rising high with the waves. "They seem to know what they are doing."

Propelled by two grinning, near-naked men, the first canoe came alongside, with the men handling their paddles with unconscious skill.

"Kroomen," Harry Young said. 'They're everywhere on this coast."

"Are you going ashore, my lady?" One youngster asked Mary.

"Yes," Mary said. "Our ship is sinking. Have you room for two people and two sea chests?"

The young Krooman said something to his companion, who swarmed on board without hesitation and helped Jack lift the chests into the canoe as if it was something he did every day.

"Your ship is sinking fast," the younger Krooman said. "Better hurry, my lady."

The second paddler waited until Jack helped Mary into the canoe before he joined them. "Sit in the centre," the paddler said, still smiling. Jack noted that his teeth were filed to sharp points, and close to he looked older than he had appeared from the deck. The Kroomen pushed off without another word, guiding the canoe through the waves to the beach beside the castle where tall palm trees waved in the breeze, and the surf boomed like thunder.

"Hold on," the leading paddler steered the bow of the canoe up the next wave. The muscles in his back shone like oiled ebony as he dug in the paddle, then abruptly changed hands and paddled from the other side. For a minute the canoe rode the surf, with growling waves on both sides of them and the beach approaching at a terrifyingly fast pace, and then they were hissing onto the sand with the roller breaking around them. The whole operation from boarding the canoe to fetching up on the beach had taken less than fifteen minutes.

"Welcome to Africa," Jack said.

"Elmina," the leading paddler said, as he leapt from the canoe, nimble as a youth although the more Jack saw him, the more he realised the Krooman was well into his middle age.

"Elmina," Mary repeated, stepping clear of the canoe into knee-deep water without turning a hair. She curtseyed to the paddlers. "Thank you, gentlemen. My husband will pay you."

Jack fumbled in his pocket, produced a silver crown and pressed it onto the first paddler's eager palm.

"Five shillings for twenty minutes work," he said. "That's good wages."

"Yes," Mary said absently. "I am not so sure I like this place, now I am close to it. There's a sinister atmosphere."

"Maybe so," Jack agreed.

The castle loomed above them, its white walls reflecting the sunlight while the snouts of cannon poked menacingly toward the sea. Whoever had built this place knew his job, for it stood securely on an outcrop of black rock at the end of a peninsula of sand. Jack saw the scarlet splash of military uniforms on the walls, and the multi-crossed Union Flag alternatively straining at the rope or hanging limp against the pole, depending on the vagaries of the wind.

"It's very impressive," Jack said, watching as the Kroomen unloaded the chests and carried them above the high-water mark. "I wonder what it was for, and who built it."

"So do I," Mary said. "Look, Jack, the ship's going. The old *Lady*."

As Jack looked out to sea, the last of *Lady Luck*'s masts dipped underwater, leaving only a litter of wreckage. A dozen canoes ferried most of the crew towards the land.

"Nobody has drowned, at least." Jack watched as an unmistakable Royal Navy ship pulled alongside the canoes, and bluejackets shouted out to the survivors. Captain Hobson and Harry Young were last to be rescued, clambering on board the naval ship as a host of bluejackets clustered to help.

"Jack," Mary nudged Jack with her elbow. "We have company."

"Halloa!" The man wore a uniform that reminded Jack of the French Zouaves he had seen in the Crimea. "Castaways are you?" He glanced at Mary. "Venus rising from the waves, no less!"

"How do you do?" Jack extended his hand.

"Welcome to Elmina and all that." The man was about twenty-five, with an open, freckled face and the voice and bearing of an officer however unfamiliar his uniform. He wore baggy blue trousers below an open scarlet jacket, while on his head he wore a turban wrapped around a red fez. His handshake was firm and vigorous. "You'd better get off the beach and into the castle." He glanced at the chests. "I'll have some of the lads bring your kit up. I'm Walter Hopringle by the by, or Lieutenant Hopringle, 2nd West India Regiment if you're interested."

"I thought the uniform was unfamiliar," Jack said. "I've never met your regiment before. I am Major Jack Windrush, 113th Foot."

Hopringle's smile vanished. "Major!" He straightened to attention. "My apologies, sir. I had no idea."

Jack glanced down at his civilian clothes. "There is no reason to apologise, Hopringle. You could not have known."

"Thank you, sir." Hopringle gave an awkward bow to Mary. "Mrs Windrush."

"Lieutenant Hopringle." Despite her sodden clothes and sand-stained boots, Mary still managed to make an elegant curtsey.

"This way, if you please," Hopringle spoke over his shoulder. "You might have chosen somewhere quieter to be shipwrecked, sir, and Mrs Windrush. We expect all sort of excitement here over the next few days."

"What sort of excitement?" Jack's military eyes noted that the fort had a river on one side and the sea on the other. It would have been a secure defensive position except for the ramshackle village that straggled along the spit to within pistol-shot of the castle walls. A curious crowd gathered at the edge of the settlement, watching the drama offshore.

"Oh, the Ashantis, of course."

"The what?"

"The who," Hopringle corrected. "The Ashantis are the dominant people of the Gold Coast area."

"The local tribe," Mary said.

"The Ashanti are a bit more than a tribe," Hopringle led them to a flight of steps ascending to a gateway in the white wall of the castle. "This is the Door of No Return," he said, "from the old slave trading days."

Mary lifted her head. "Slave trading?"

"Yes, Mrs Windrush. This castle, St George's, was a major slave trading post for the Portuguese and the Dutch."

Mary looked around her in disgust. "I knew I didn't like this place."

"I'll have your baggage brought in." Hopringle lifted his voice. "Sergeant Wickham! Bring four men!"

They entered a long chamber, dimly lit by flickering lamps. The arched ceiling seemed to press down on them. Mary shivered as the echoes of their voices seemed to waken memories of past suffering. "I like this place even less," Mary said.

A file of a sergeant and four West Indian soldiers clattered into the chamber, all wearing the same Zouave uniforms as Hopringle. The sergeant saluted Hopringle while the men looked sideways at Jack and Mary.

"Go to the beach, Sergeant Wickham," Hopringle said quietly. "You'll find two sea chests there. Take them to the officers' quarters."

"Yes, sir." The sergeant was a broad-shouldered man with two scars on his left cheek. He glanced at Mary as he hurried past, with his men as smart as guardsmen.

"This chamber is where the Dutch and Portuguese held the slaves," Hopringle said. "Some of them may have been the ancestors of my men."

"I can feel them," Mary shivered. "Their sorrow is still here." She felt for Jack's arm.

From the slave dungeons, Hopringle escorted them to the sun-blessed castle courtyard, from where tall white walls, punctured by shuttered windows, rose all around. Stairways led to defensive platforms, wrought iron railings, partly rusted by the salt air, eased around balconies and soldiers of the 2nd West India Regiment spoke to blue-coated Royal Marines. Jack was relieved to escape from even that brief visit to the dungeons.

"That's the church," Hopringle nodded to the most significant building within the fort.

"Shackle the slaves and pray for forgiveness," Mary did not hide her distaste.

"And up there," Hopringle said, "is where you will be staying." He led them up a flight of wooden stairs to the upper stories where the rooms were lighter and airier, with an onshore breeze ruffling the cane curtains.

"I hope you're comfortable here," Hopringle opened a heavy door to a surprisingly fresh chamber. "I only pray you have time to get used to it."

"Why is that?"

"The Ashantis," Hopringle's grin merged his freckles into an orange mass. "They don't want us here."

Jack grunted as his mind took stock of the situation. "You have an impressively strong fort here. How big is your garrison?"

"We can rustle up a couple of hundred on a good day, including Hausas, that is native police from Lagos, further up the coast, plus bluejackets, Royal Marines and my own Wests."

Jack nodded. "Two hundred men behind the walls of a strong fort. How many men can these Ashantis muster?"

Hopringle stepped aside as the Wests bustled up with his men and the sea chests. "We estimate around fifty thousand."

"So many?" Jack did not hide his surprise.

"So many," Hopringle said. "And they also have allies and friends among the neighbouring tribes." He nodded to the small window. "If you look out there, sir, you'll see Elmina village."

"I noticed it when we arrived," Jack said.

"The Elminas are staunch allies of the Ashantis." Hopringle said, "which could be awkward as they're so close to the fort."

Jack became aware of Sergeant Wickham listening at the door.

"You'll have duties to attend, Sergeant," Hopringle acknowledged Wickham's salute with a nod.

Jack felt Wickham's gaze as the sergeant left the room. He raised his head and stared back until Wickham dropped his eyes and withdrew.

"Why allow the natives so close to the fort if they are hostile?" Jack surveyed the native village, estimating the numbers. "There must be a few thousand people there."

"The village was there long before we took over Fort St George," Hopringle said.

"I see." Jack accepted the explanation. "How effective are your men, Hopringle? I confess I know nothing about West Indian soldiers."

Hopringle's smile was back. "They are about the best in the business, Major. Loyal and brave to a fault."

Watching as Mary inspected the room, Jack invited Hopringle to sit on one of the three cane chairs. "I have not heard anything of them, Hopringle."

"No," Hopringle suddenly sounded defensive. "As they are black troops, they don't get the credit they deserve. Our lads serve in the worst conditions and have the toughest and most thankless tasks in the British Army."

"Where do they serve?" Jack sank into a second chair.

"In the fever jungles of West Africa, the White Man's Grave," Hopringle's smile had vanished as he spoke of his regiment, "and across the West Indies and Central America. My lads did a lot of good work against the French and Americans last century, and Private Hodge of the 3rd Wests won a Victoria Cross in the Gambia only a few years ago."

Mary had stepped closer to listen. "Why are these things not better known?"

Hopringle shrugged. "Either because we're a regiment of black soldiers, or because British newspapers don't write about regiments where there is no local interest." He leaned back in the chair. "Newspapers exist to make money, and where there is no interest, there are no sales. So my Wests are destined to work without recognition."

"Except by their officers and the men who fight alongside them," Jack said. "A bit like the 113th Foot or the Sepoys from what they call non-martial races."

"Quite so," Hopringle said. He rose from his seat. "Now, if you'll excuse me, sir and Mrs Windrush, I am sure you'll want to get settled in. Colonel Festing will no doubt wish to see you later."

"Thank you, Lieutenant Hopringle," Mary said. "It was very kind of you to help."

Jack heard the distant thud of a musket but said nothing. A shipwreck and a slave station in one day was sufficient drama for Mary.

CHAPTER THREE

Elmina, Gold Coast Colony, June 1874

The setting sun brought the drums. Mary heard them first, lifting her head and frowning as she walked to the window.

"Can you hear that, Jack?"

"I hear them," Jack said. He remembered the drums beating out their warning along the North-West Frontier of India. "There is something ominous about drums at night. They sound more menacing when you can't see the drummer."

"I wonder what they are saying." Mary stood at the window for a few moments with her head cocked to one side.

The drumming increased in volume, seeming to penetrate the walls of the fort and creep into Jack's head, so they became part of his mind, rhythmic, alien and intrusive. Lying on the hard bed in the heat of the night, he swatted at the circling insects, listening to the insistent beat.

"I can't sleep either," Mary threw herself on the bed.

"The drummers are trying to unsettle us," Jack said. "Don't allow them."

"I'd be unsettled even without the drums," Mary said. "This is a bad place, Jack, worse than any we've been in."

"The slave chambers?" Jack asked.

"I can feel the slaves, Jack," Mary said. "I can feel the despair down there. The people have gone, but they left something behind them. It's as if a part of them never went away."

Jack pulled her closer. "It's nearly seventy years since we stopped the slave trade. It was all a long time ago."

"How much time doesn't matter, Jack. That depth of hurt doesn't disappear. It haunts the place," Mary said. "Some people can sense the tragedy on places of distress. Others, such as you, Captain Jack, are cold-blooded Englishmen with no sense of the spiritual at all."

"Not all Englishmen are cold-blooded," Jack said quietly. "Anyway, I'm part Indian, remember?"

"You know what I mean!" Mary moved to the edge of the bed and sat up.

Aware of the effect the idea of slavery had on Mary, Jack decided it was best to say nothing.

"I've had a recurring nightmare ever since I was small," Mary spoke so softly that Jack had to strain to hear her words. "I dreamt I would be a slave, being led away in chains. I used to wake up crying and in a terrible state. I can't imagine anything worse."

"It won't happen," Jack assured her.

"It happened here," Mary said. "It happened to hundreds of thousands of people right in this building."

"It's stopped now," Jack said.

"No, it still happens," Mary contradicted him. "The Arabs still have slaves and so do some tribes up there," she jerked her head towards the interior of Africa. Rolling over, she clung to him. "Promise me something, Jack."

"What's that?"

"Promise me that you'll never let anybody take me as a slave."

"That's an easy promise to make, Mary. You know I wouldn't let that happen."

Mary nodded. "I know, but that place scared me. I could feel the anguish of these poor people."

The drumming continued, a resonant throb that seemed to echo around the room, rattling the pitcher and ewer on the dressing table, making it difficult to think.

"I thought I'd sleep after all the excitement of the day," Mary rolled back to her side of the bed and lay back, watching the stars through the open window. "I was wrong."

"Maybe you're overtired," Jack said.

"I don't like this place, Jack. I hope we can get a ship home soon."

"So do I," Jack realised that the drumming had stopped as suddenly as it started. Somebody shouted, high and clear, and then there was silence except for the distant crash of surf.

Mary was asleep, with both hands behind her head. Smiling, Jack rearranged her to be more comfortable, eased out of bed and stepped to the window. In the open ground on the other side of the Benya River, beyond a suburb of Elmina village, Jack saw moonlight gleam on something. Although he could not be sure, he thought it looked like an umbrella, but why anybody should be walking in the night under a yellow umbrella, he could not imagine.

Pulling the shutters closed, he lay down beside Mary. He was an old enough campaigner to grab sleep whenever he could, for the morrow could bring unpleasant surprises. In his head, he still heard the drums.

* * *

"Major Windrush!"

"Sir." Jack drew himself to attention, with the air already stuffy in this small room.

"Lieutenant Colonel Francis Festing, Royal Marine Artillery." Heavily bearded, the colonel stood erect beside his desk. He surveyed Jack through level grey eyes on either side of a straight nose. "I heard you were shipwrecked here yesterday."

"That's correct, sir." Jack knew that Festing was a veteran of the Baltic and Crimean campaigns and the Chinese War. Festing knew his business.

"Well, that was a piece of damned bad luck for you, but could be opportune for us." Festing remained standing as he spoke, forcing Jack to do the same. "You have some experience in action, I believe."

"Yes, sir, Burma, Crimea and the Mutiny, as well as the North-West Frontier."

"I remember hearing about a Windrush in the Crimea. Royal Malverns was it not?"

"No, sir," Jack said. "That was my half-brother. I was with the 113th Foot."

"I don't know them," Festing dismissed the subject. "What do you know about Africa?"

"Not much, sir. I've never served in Africa."

"Well, now is your chance. I am requisitioning you for my little army. Do you know of the situation here on the Gold Coast?"

"Only what I've picked up since we came ashore, sir. We bought Elmina from the Dutch a few years ago, and now the Ashantis are massing to attack us."

Festing managed a small smile. "I suppose that's all a soldier needs to know. However, I'll give you a little more background information. Sit down, Windrush."

It was an hour before dawn, and they were in a small office on the upper floor of St George's Castle. From the window, Jack had a view to a starlit beach, festooned with waving palm trees and a few canoes, while a line of phosphorescence marked the crashing surf. Successive occupiers had furnished the room with a very ornate desk that looked as if it had been in the castle since the Portuguese were in charge, a heavy Dutch armchair and half a dozen cane-chairs. Jack settled on one of the latter, feeling the structure creak under his weight. Festing positioned himself behind the desk.

"The Portuguese built this fort back in the fifteenth century," Festing said, "and the Dutch grabbed it, either by agreement or war, I don't know or care which." He shrugged his shoulders to show his contempt of other European nations. "However the Ashantis – I'll come to them later – claimed the place, and rather than fight, the Dutch paid them about £9000 a year rent or tribute. That suited both parties, for the Ashantis were the chief suppliers of slaves, so the Dutch were guaranteed a steady supply and the Ashanti, a regular customer."

Jack nodded. "Thank God we stopped that hellish business."

"Aye," Festing looked up. "Thank God we did, but in doing so, we made some dangerous enemies. When we ended the Slave Trade back in '07, the Ashantis, and other tribes who had made a good living supplying European states and others with slaves, got a rude shock. The Ashantis had expanded their empire at the expense of neighbouring tribes partly to capture slaves; it became the reason for the Ashantis' existence."

Festing fixed Jack with a long look. "As you can imagine, the Ashantis were displeased when we stopped the slave trade and instituted anti-slavery patrols along the coast."

"I imagine so, sir," Jack said.

"We've had a few difficulties with them, including a war back in the twenties when the Ashanti killed our Sir Charles McCarthy, cut off his head and made the skull into a drinking cup."

"Charming people," Jack murmured, wondering where Festing was leading.

"Oh, absolutely delightful," Festing said. "Just the sort you wish to bring home to tea with mama."

Jack decided he could smile.

"We had another Ashanti war in the 60s, and then, a few years ago, the Dutch transferred Elmina to us. King Kofi Karikari of the Ashantis, or the Asantahene, as they call him, claims he owns the place and wants us to continue the payments that the Dutch made."

"And will we pay them?" Jack asked.

Festing visibly stiffened in his seat. "Her Majesty will not pay a penny to people who use the heads of British generals as drinking cups."

"No, sir," Jack said. "Of course not." He paused for a few seconds. "Although paying the rent might save the treasury a fortune. Wars tend to be expensive in currency and lives."

"National prestige is more important than mere money," Festing said. "If one foreign potentate gets away with it, who knows who'll try it next? Perhaps Spain will demand tribute for Gibraltar, or Prussia for Heligoland." He shook his head. "No, Windrush, Great Britain cannot go along that road. We don't want war, but we'll draw a line in the sand. If the Asantahene wishes to co-operate, then we can all be friends. If he chooses war, then war it shall be."

"I believe we only have a few hundred men in the colony, sir," Jack said.

"The bulk of the Second West India Regiment is coming from Bermuda to reinforce us." Abruptly standing, Festing walked to the window. "Ah; that's what I like to see. Come here, Windrush and I'll show you Her Majesty's response to demands."

The ships sailed past the coast in line astern. Even without the White Ensign at the masthead, there would be no mistaking them for anything except Royal Navy warships, with the neatness and precision that Jack expected from the Senior Service. There were only two warships, a sloop and a gun-vessel, with their size hardly impressive by navy standards, but each towed several ship's boats from which a cannon or rocket-trough projected, and they joined another sloop off Elmina.

"HMS *Decoy*, *Druid* and *Argus*," Festing indicated each vessel in turn, "towing boats from the squadron we have at Cape Coast Castle, eight miles up the coast."

"Yes, sir."

"You must have noticed the native town beside the castle wall," Festing said.

"I did, sir," Jack said.

"The men of Elmina have openly supported the Ashantis, and they want the Dutch back here," Festing explained. "The Ashantis store weapons in the town and the Ashantis strut around with great arrogance as if they rule the roost. Now that the navy's here, I can do something about it."

"Yes, sir. What do you wish me to do?"

"I want you to go along with the 2nd West India," Festing said. "A man with your experience could be a steadying influence." He looked at Jack. "I am well aware that you have never worked with West Indian soldiers but the more British officers, the better."

"Yes, sir." Used to army life, Jack accepted the command without expression although internally he felt the old familiar slide of mixed dismay and excitement.

"Captain Brett is in charge of the West Indians; report to him and offer your services." Festing sighed. "I hope there won't be any awkwardness because you outrank him."

"None at all, sir," Jack said. "It is his regiment."

* * *

From the battlements of St George's Castle, Jack looked down on Elmina, a village of brushwood and timber houses that had grown up in the lee of the castle. While the larger section of the town, the King's Quarter, was on the same side of the river as the castle, the smaller, the Garden Quarter, was on the opposite side, across a low, broad bridge. Jack watched the navy's boats take up their positions on the river, with their cannon pointing toward the King's Quarter.

"What about that part of the town?" Jack indicated the Garden Quarter.

Captain Brett was a steady, sober man with the lines of responsibility etched deeply in his face. "The people there are friendly to us."

Jack nodded, noting that the Garden Quarter had some decent stone-built houses.

"And there?" Jack indicated a smaller fort further inland.

"That's Fort St Jago. We don't have the manpower to occupy that." Brett shrugged, "we've scraped up all our reserves for this little operation today, let alone garrisoning anything inland."

"What's out there, Brett?"

Brett screwed up his face. "Past St Jago, there is a lagoon and a chain of small hills; I've never been out there, but I hear the local people are hostile. They preferred the Dutch, who did not interfere with their quaint local customs such as slave-owning and human sacrifice."

Jack grunted. "I see."

"Here we go," Brett said as Festing stepped into the courtyard of the castle, where a score of the local chiefs and dignities had gathered. Some sat on elaborately carved stools, others sheltered under elaborate umbrellas and two had little boys at their feet, either their sons or for purposes that Jack did not wish to consider.

"You are all welcome," Festing said. "Her Majesty, Queen Victoria, who owns this castle and this town, is displeased that some misguided people in Elmina have been openly aiding the Ashantis."

The chiefs and dignities looked at him without expression.

"Some foolish men in this town have been giving the Ashantis arms, ammunition and gunpowder, with the Ashanti have been using to kill, terrorise and enslave Her Majesty's subjects."

A few chiefs nodded sagely, although Jack was unsure if they agreed that such events had taken place, or the opposite.

Colonel Festing continued: "I will shortly fire a cannon. You have one hour after that signal to hand your weapons to St George's Castle, or I will bombard the town."

"Well, that was short and sweet," Brett said as the chiefs turned and left, most without saying a word. "They won't believe the colonel, though. The Dutch were forever making empty threats."

Jack remembered Festing's level gaze and fighting experience. "I think they'll find that Colonel Festing is no Dutchman." He nodded. "Now, Captain Brett, where do you want to place me?"

"This is most awkward as you outrank me, sir."

"I am here by mischance, Captain. You know your regiment best, so where would I be most useful?"

Brett looked embarrassed as he spoke. "If the Elminas don't hand in their weapons, Major, could I prevail upon you to take half a company and hold that bridge?" He pointed to the bridge across the Benya River that linked both quarters of Elmina town.

"I'll do that willingly," Jack said. "Although we could be bolting the stable door after the horse has carried away the hay." He watched a trickle of men and women cross the bridge, most carrying household goods and some with bundles that looked suspiciously like firearms.

"Aye, that's so," Brett said, "but we've given a time, and we must stick by our word." He gave a twisted grin. "After all, we are British officers."

The bang of the cannon echoed across the castle and town, setting a score of dogs barking and causing some women to scream in alarm. White powder smoke drifted from the castle out to sea, where the Royal Naval vessels floated as a reminder that Britain's power extended everywhere there was salt water, and many places there was fresh.

"That's Colonel Festing's signal. We have one hour to wait," Jack watched the trickle of people across the bridge increase to a steady flow. "By that time there won't be many people left in Elmina."

"As long as the women and children are safe," Brett said. "We don't want to war on innocents."

Hopringle glanced at his watch. "I'll check on our men," he said. "They might be getting restless."

"I'll come along," Jack wanted to see the unit he was going to command.

The Second Wests looked like any other regiment that Jack had served with, except for the black faces. The sergeants barked them to obedience the same way; there was the same mixture of old soldiers with greying hair and young recruits desperate to prove themselves, confident men and men who jumped whenever a sergeant barked. Jack looked them over, aware that they were also inspecting him.

"We might be called upon to go on duty soon," Jack said to his half-company. "If so, we'll be holding the bridge against gun smugglers." He watched their faces, looking for the eager and the trouble-makers, marking his men.

One man looked particularly enthusiastic, nearly stepping forward when Jack passed.

"What's your name?" Jack asked.

"Private Samuel Stair, sir! Are we going to fight the Bushmen?"

"He means the Ashantis, sir. That's the rankers name for them," Hopringle explained.

"Good man, Stair. You'll get your chance. We'll all get our chance." Jack nodded to Sergeant Wickham. "Carry on, Sergeant."

"Sir!" Wickham gave a smart salute.

"They seem a decent bunch," Jack said as they returned upstairs.

"None better!" Hopringle was enthusiastic about his regiment. He checked his watch. "That's the hour about up."

"Give them another hour before we open fire," Festing had his binoculars trained on the town. "They seem reluctant to comply." One elderly man tottered up on matchstick legs, dropped off a broken Tower musket and wandered off, duty done. A young boy followed, threw a stick against the gate, lifted the Tower musket, sighted against the castle wall and dropped it in disgust.

The first hour passed, then the second. A second broken musket joined the weapon at the castle gate, but still, Festing hesitated to give the order to fire. He sighed, checked his watch, and shook his head. "I'll give them until noon."

"I'll get off to the bridge." Ensuring his revolver was loaded, Jack marched downstairs where his half-company of West Indians were waiting in the courtyard.

"Right lads! Are you all set?" Out of habit, he checked their rifles, noting that they were the old pattern muzzle-loading Enfields rather than the newer breech-loading Sniders. "Keep together now. Don't be too eager, Stair, trouble will come whether you seek it or not."

"Yes, sir!" Stair bellowed.

Jack nodded to Sergeant Wickham. "How are the men, Sergeant?"

"All set, sir." Wickham stood at attention.

"Stand easy man; we're not on parade." Jack faced the fifty men, noting the nervous eyes of two of them. "Right lads, you don't know me, I don't know you, and none of us knows what this day will bring."

The men watched him, expressionless except for Stair. Jack noted the smell of rum and wondered who had been drinking.

"In a few moments, we'll be marching out to guard the bridge between Elmina and the mainland. Our duty is to ensure that nobody carrying arms tries to leave, and no Ashantis enter." Jack recognised the excitement that ran through him. "I've heard that the 2nd West is as good a regiment as any in the British Army so we should get on fine."

"Sir," Sergeant Wickham spoke as if he was addressing a deaf man thirty yards away. "Permission to speak, sir?"

"You're my sergeant, Wickham. You don't have to ask permission. Speak, man!"

"Thank you, sir. Are you the Captain Windrush who fought through the Crimea War and the Indian Mutiny?"

"That was me," Jack said.

"I thought so. Thank you, sir." Wickham said.

"Right lads; follow me!" Jack led the way, wishing he led men from his 113th rather than these unknown West Indians. However, both Hopringle and Brett claimed the Wests were good soldiers when well-led, which could describe any regiment in the British Army or any other army, Jack guessed.

The Wests filed after Jack, each man with his Enfield at his shoulder. They looked smart enough, Jack conceded, yet he hoped he never had to fight the Ashantis with these raw troops.

Although Jack had spent much of his twenty-one years in the army in India, the tropical sun felt different in Africa. It was a damper heat somehow, less friendly. As he marched through the castle, he saw the Royal Marine artillerymen working on the castle's guns, training them to aim at the town. The artillerymen were sweltering, dripping drops of sweat onto the stone slabs.

Clattering from the castle, Jack led his men onto the wooden bridge. "Halt! Stand at ease! Stand easy!"

The Wests stood across the entrance to the bridge, Enfields in hands, sun shining on the red jackets and waving turbans. To Jack, they were unfamiliar, foreign-looking soldiers, and he wondered if he would ever get used to them.

Beyond the Garden Quarter, on a plain between the coast and the fringe of what appeared to be a never-ending forest, Jack saw a large number of men gathering, all carrying firearms, mostly muskets but a few with more modern rifles. They were bare-chested, some with kilt-like clothes of multi-coloured stripes, others with long white robes from the waist down. He frowned as he saw a group of men standing under a bright yellow umbrella.

I saw that umbrella last night, Jack told himself. *You were walking in the open, examining the castle of St George.*

"Sergeant," Jack nodded to the umbrella. "Do you know anything about that?"

"An umbrella is the sign of a chief or a nobleman," Sergeant Wickham said at once. "The Ashantis use umbrellas as we use regimental colours or flags."

"Do they indeed? Thank you, Sergeant." Lifting his binoculars, Jack focussed on the men beneath the umbrella. There were four. One held the umbrella; tall and muscular, he had the dull eyes of a menial. Jack ignored him. The next carried a long Tower musket and wore a bandolier across his shoulder. He was a foot soldier, a bodyguard perhaps, tough-looking and handy to know. Jack nodded and slid his attention to the next man, a slim, wiry young man with a strange cap on his head and a gold hilted knife at his waist.

"Now, you are somebody who matters," Jack said. "I'll watch for you."

When he focussed on the fourth man, Jack knew he had found a chief. Half a head taller than any of the others, he stood proud, nearly haughty, with a broad face under a leopard-skin cap adorned with ram's horns and eagle-feathers. A multi-coloured robe decorated in geometrical shapes descended from his shoulders, while around his waist, a gold –hilted sword hung almost to his ankles.

"'Sergeant Wickham." Jack passed over the binoculars. "What do you make of that fellow?"

The sergeant took the binoculars gently, as if afraid to damage them. He put them to his eyes and looked away until Jack showed him how to focus.

"The men under the yellow umbrella are of the Edwesu tribe of the Asante, the Ashanti as you call them," Wickham said. "Asante means 'because of war'."

"I thought the Ashanti was one tribe," Jack said.

"They are a fusion of many tribes of the Akan people," Wickham explained. 'The Oyoko and the Edwesu are the most warlike. I don't know that man's name." He handed back the binoculars.

"He's important, then," Jack said. "Thank you, Sergeant."

"He's a chief or perhaps a minor king."

Jack studied the group below the yellow umbrella again until the crowd surged and a score of men blocked his view. The umbrella remained in place, dominant above the mass.

Jack checked his watch. Noon: That was the final deadline. "Load, lads. Sergeant, check the rifles." He could nearly taste the tension in the air. The Ashantis had threatened war by invading the British colony, and now the British had retaliated. The next few moments would decide if this game of dare and bluff would escalate into war, or if Colonel Festing would back down.

"Sir," Wickham said. "The enemy is collecting."

"I see them, Sergeant," Jack said. "We may have to fight on two fronts here. Number the men from one to fifty, with the even numbers facing the town and the odds the plain." He watched as Wickham obeyed. "Make sure every man has his rifle loaded."

Jack looked up as a pair of vultures flapped clumsily past the castle to land on the ground a hundred paces beyond the bridge. With their long bald necks and predatory eyes, they looked like the scavengers they were.

Further to his right, a hundred and fifty of the Hausas lined the riverbank, their red fezzes distinct. Their officers seemed to have them well in hand, although Jack thought the men were excitable, like recruits on their inaugural Field Day. He glanced over his Wests, growling unnecessarily.

"Keep steady, men. Show these Hausas how real soldiers behave."

"Hausas are not soldiers," young Private Manning said slyly. 'They're Bushmen in uniform." He laughed, relapsing into silence when nobody else joined in.

Despite expecting the sound, Jack started when the cannon from the fort fired, with great tongues of orange flame and jets of dirty white smoke erupting across the town. The gunboats were next, fifteen seconds later, sending a storm of shot crashing into Elmina. The iron cannonballs smashed through frail walls, ripped at thatch roofs and cascaded along now-deserted streets.

We're at war, Jack said to himself. *My fourth official war and I should not even be here. Now the Asantahene will know that he cannot treat the British with the same contempt as the Dutch. I only hope I can send Mary to safety before this thing expands.*

CHAPTER FOUR

Elmina, June 1873

"Steady now, lads," Jack spoke above the bark of the artillery and the sharp orders of officers and NCOs. For a moment, he wondered how Mary was faring, told himself that she was familiar with army life and had lived through far worse than a minor native war, and watched the progress of the bombardment. The smoke already formed a white bank around the boats, so they fired blind, shot after shot and shell after shell howling into the King's Quarter of Elmina.

Within a few moments, a house exploded, with a sound louder than any of the British cannon. Broken pieces of timber and burning palm-thatch rose high above the smoke, hovered for a few seconds then drifted back down, setting fire to other thatched roofs.

"There must have been gunpowder stored there," Jack said, as his men openly wondered. Young Private Manning backed away until Sergeant Wickham roared him back to his position.

"You're a soldier, Manning, remember? Not a Bushman in uniform."

Jack wondered if Manning appreciated the dark humour as his initial doubts about bombarding what he had thought to be an innocent town faded a little, and vanished altogether when a second house erupted in fire and smoke, and then a third. "The colonel was right," he said above the crack of cannon fire and crackle of flames. "The Elmina men are storing arms and powder for the Ashantis."

"The Ashanti and Elminas are waiting to fight us, sir." Sergeant Wickham gestured to the men who continued to mass on the plain.

"Our duty is to guard the bridge, Sergeant," Jack said as Wickham moved forward as if to challenge the entire enemy host. "Keep vigilant in case the Elmina people try to storm the bridge."

There was no sign of movement from Elmina. Jack saw one of the boats fire a rocket, with the fiery trail glowing through the smoke before the missile exploded against the wall of a stone-built house. By now, most of the town was ablaze as fire from the burning powder-stores spread to the other buildings. Smoke rose in choking clouds, with the gunfire and rockets from the castle and Royal Navy adding to the confusion.

"Sir," Sergeant Wickham was tense, moving from foot to foot as he stared at the village and then at the mass of men standing in the clearing.

"The enemy is firing back, sir."

Peering through the smoke, Jack saw the flashes from the massed Elmina men and Ashantis as they fired at the naval vessels and the Hausas who lined the river bank. Although the yellow umbrella had advanced to the Ashanti front rank, the smoke was too dense for Jack to see the men beneath. He started when something struck the parapet of the bridge beside him, ricocheting away with a vicious whine. The bullet had left a raw scar in the wood and bent the top of a nail.

"The enemy's firing at us," Private Daley, a handsome young man, raised his rifle. Jack saw the beads of nervous sweat on his upper lip.

"Don't fire yet," Jack was not a believer in blooding his men by allowing them to take casualties, but that might have been a stray shot. By firing on the enemy, he would invite retaliation by a vastly larger force. "Lie down on the ground, aim at the enemy and wait for my orders. Nobody fire yet."

Jack looked up as something cooled his cheek. An offshore breeze was stirring the smoke, shredding it to increase visibility. He could see the wreckage of the village and the dull green of the forest. Two more vultures had arrived, waiting for the fresh meat that fighting humans always provided.

"Sir!" When Private Edward Ogston nodded to the enemy, Jack smelled the rum on his breath. "Over there."

As Jack watched, warriors filed from the forest to join the more ragged ranks of the Elmina men, with one entire company forming up around the yellow umbrella.

"Ashantis!" Sergeant Windham nearly hissed the words as he brought his rifle to his shoulder.

The Ashanti warriors moved in disciplined formations, most carrying long, old fashioned muskets while a few held more modern weapons. War captains, older men with long robes and an elaborate close-fitting head dress, stood in front of each formation, clearly giving orders. One of these war captains approached the group at the yellow umbrella and then moved his company to the far flank of the Ashanti horde.

"They look a formidable bunch," Jack ran his experienced eye over them. "And the fellow with the umbrella appears to be in charge."

"The Ashanti are the best forest fighters in Africa," Windham's eyes were intent on the enemy as more emerged from the forest, including a man under a scarlet and black umbrella. "And they have royalty with them."

"Royalty?"

Yes, sir." Windham aimed his rifle.

"You're out of range, Sergeant," Jack said. "If they come closer, you can have a pot at them."

Jack glanced behind him. His half company of Wests was the only barrier between the Ashanti army and the castle. On one side of the river was the now fiercely burning town and on the other, the Garden Quarter, where the more loyal inhabitants watched proceedings from the doors of their houses or huddled in small groups. *They'll be praying to their ancestral spirits that the British can protect them from the Ashantis,* Jack thought.

As the boats continued their bombardment, the Ashanti army and their Elmina allies moved closed and opened a terrific fire. The slugs barely reached the navy boats, but the Hausas wavered and looked towards the bridge.

"I told you the Hausas are only Bushmen in uniform," Private Manning sneered. "We'll be shooting them soon." He lifted his rifle in readiness.

"Settle down, Manning," Jack said. "The 2nd West doesn't shoot our friends."

A bugle sounded, high and shrill above the barking of the guns and crackle of flames. Within minutes the castle gate slammed open, and the garrison marched out, with the Royal Marine Light Infantry, the Jollies, in front, followed by the bright colours of the 2nd West Indians and the more sombre Hausas. Amongst the troops, the bluejackets, the Royal Navy landing party, stood out with their peculiar rolling gate and the cutlasses hanging from their belts.

"Stand ready, men," Jack said.

"Windrush, isn't it?" Freemantle, the Royal Naval captain in command, stopped for a second beside Jack. "Leave half your men here, Major and bring the rest with us. You'll be eager to join the fun."

"Yes, sir," Jack said. "Sergeant Wickham! Remain in charge here."

"I'd prefer to come, sir." Wickham stood at attention, looking every inch the professional soldier.

"Not this time, Sergeant," Jack said. "I need you here. Don't worry; you'll get your chance." He frowned when he saw Wickham about to protest and closed off any possible insubordination with a quick. "Guard the bridge. That's an order."

Years of discipline snapped Wickham to attention. "Yes, sir."

"Fleet Marines and bluejackets," Captain Freemantle gave quick orders, "take the right flank. Marines of the garrison, 2nd West India and Hausas, take the centre and left." He led the way with a long lope, his sword dangling at his side.

"Come on, lads!" Jack marched towards the enemy, pulling his revolver from its holster. A glance over his shoulder revealed his Wests marching forward resolutely. Private Coffin was singing under his breath, Daley looked nervous, while Ogston was impassive. At their side, the garrison Marines had already fixed bayonets. On average the Marines were smaller and lighter than the 2nd West, lithe men with a swing to their step, hurrying forward towards the enemy.

"Halt!" Freemantle ordered.

The British force stopped amidst the smoke from the burning town. They remained static as the Ashantis fired at them, the deep thuds of muzzle-loading muskets sounding like artillery but most of the shots dropping short. Jack saw a single Hausa stagger and hold a hand to his chest as if in wonderment.

"Aim!" Captain Freemantle ordered.

Jack ran his gaze over his Wests. They lifted their Enfields handily enough, although some held them loosely, rather than cuddling them close to their shoulders. He pushed down the barrel of Private Stair's rifle. "Aim at the Ashantis, Stair, not at the sky. The clouds are not your enemy."

"Yes, sir," Stair said with a smile.

"Fire!" The Marines' Sniders and Wests' Enfields cracked out with jets of white smoke. As Stair stepped back with the recoil, Jack made a mental note to ensure the men cleaned their rifles later.

The front rank of the Ashantis wavered as the rifle bullets slammed into them, although the yellow umbrella remained proud above the smoke.

"Reload!"

The Marines inserted cartridges into the breech, with the sun reflecting on the brass. Armed with the muzzle-loading Enfields, Jack's half company were noticeably slower, with Private Daley fumbling the percussion cap, dropping it and stooping to pick it up.

"Advance!" Freemantle snapped, pacing forward five steps. The Wests moved without hesitation, with the powder smoke shredding around them.

"Halt!" The British line halted. Two deep, the British looked vulnerable against the mass of Ashantis and Elminas. Every yard they came closer to the enemy, the British bullets were more effective, passing through men in the dense mass of the Ashantis. Yet every step also brought them closer to the far more numerous Ashanti muskets. Gunsmoke rolled between both forces, with the deep roars of the Ashanti war-cry sounding as background noise, aided by the rattling thunder of the drums. Behind the warriors, Jack thought he saw a horde of women in bright dresses, urging their men on, and then Freemantle lifted his arm.

"Fire!"

Another British volley crashed out, with the 2nd Wests firing steadily, although Jack saw some of the Enfield barrels were still too elevated. *I'll sort out their marksmanship after this affair is completed.*

The smoke hid any results of the volley, and the Ashantis replied, their muzzle flashes showing as orange spurts.

"Load!"

There was another rattle of brass from the Marines, another flurry of percussion caps from the Wests. Jack saw his men knocking the butts of Enfields on the ground to drop the bullets down the barrels.

"Advance!"

Advancing and firing, the Marines and sailors of the centre and right faced the bulk of the enemy. Jack's Wests were on the left flank, slightly further back, slower to load but every bit as ready to take on the enemy. Jack watched his men; they were fighting well, although their marksmanship was shocking. It was relentless, this advance and fire against the enemy.

"Halt! Fire!"

Again the bullets smashed into the Ashanti ranks, shivering their morale, knocking down the warriors. Jack heard a Marine laugh. 'If you get two directly behind each other, Joe, you can bowl them over together.'

"I like to see the beggars jump when the bullets hit them. Make them dance for King Kofi!"

Seen closer to, even behind a blanket of powder smoke, the Ashantis looked frighteningly dangerous. They were big men, as tall as the Wests, taller than the Royal Marine Light Infantry, and held their muskets with the confidence of long practice. However, the Marines, West Indians and Bluejackets were more disciplined and had more modern weapons, with the Ashantis beginning to waver as their casualties mounted. They withdrew, step by step, towards the forest, still firing, but outranged by the British guns. Few of the Ashanti shots took effect although Jack saw one of the West Indians crumple to the ground and lie still while others fell, groaning or writhing with wounds.

The men under the yellow umbrella remained in the centre of the Ashantis, with the black-and-red umbrella slightly further back.

"Right lads," Jack shouted. "When we fire again, I want everybody to aim at the group under the yellow umbrella. Whoever these men are, they are organising the enemy."

Even as he spoke, Jack knew he was wasting his words. The Wests were such poor shots that targeting the men with the yellow umbrella was probably making him the safest man in the Ashanti army.

Behind the Ashantis, Jack saw the women again, urging their men on, cracking sticks over the heads and backs of any who turned away, pointing to the advancing British and yelling.

"Lieutenant Quinn!" Freemantle's voice carried even above the intermittent thunder of the Ashanti musketry. "Take your Marines and clear the bush running parallel to the beach. Windrush; your Wests go in support!"

Quinn was a young man, as eager as all these Marines seemed to be. He grinned at Jack. "Come along, sir! My lads will do the work, and your Wests can watch and learn."

Jack met Quinn's smile. "When the Ashantis chase you back, we'll be here to stop them."

The bush was thicker than Jack had realised, with a mixture of shrubs, plants and flowers intertwined beneath trees that soared up to 200 feet. Creepers barred the passage of anybody not equipped with a long knife while the atmosphere was stifling, with the air so dense Jack found it hard to breathe. He felt the sweat burst from his pores the second he stepped off the beach onto the narrow path, with its twists and turns and clouds of flying insects.

"Come on, men," Jack checked his revolver and strode, on with his Wests a few yards behind.

Facing the Ashantis in the forest was utterly different from fighting them in the open. When the Marines attempted to extend into skirmishing order, with two yards between each man, the thick bush impeded their vision, and they instinctively closed their files. The officer's orders echoed through the trees.

"Open your ranks, Marines! Skirmish order!"

Quinn remained on the path, giving sharp commands to his men as they pushed through the foliage. Thirty paces behind, Jack arranged his men, waiting for the first sign of the Ashantis.

"They've all gone, sir!" A Marine shouted in the hard accents of Northumberland. "They've run."

The response came almost at once as half a dozen Ashantis opened fire. They hid behind trees and bushes to fire their long muskets, but for every shot they fired, the Marines, with their faster-loading Sniders, could fire four, and British bullets were more potent than the slugs of the Ashantis. The British moved on, blasting at every gush of powder smoke and gradually driving the Ashantis out of the woodland. Jack followed the Marines, with his Wests hardly firing a shot, ensuring the Ashantis did not try to ease around the British flanks to take the Marines in the rear.

"There's one!" Private Stair lifted his Enfield and fired, with three more Wests following his example.

"Don't fire unless you're sure of your target," Jack shouted. "We don't want to pot a Marine. Their heads would be ugly decorating our wall."

Some of the Wests smiled, others looked puzzled, not understanding the humour.

There was a flurry of activity to the left as the Marines dealt with a nest of resistance, and a single Ashanti warrior ran toward them. Private Ogston knelt and fired, with the shot clipping a tree branch ten feet above the man's head. Private Daly tried next and missed by about three feet, so Jack aimed his revolver and fired three rounds, knocking the man backwards.

"We're doing target shooting once we've cleared away the Ashantis," Jack promised. "I've never seen such poor marksmanship."

As the British advanced on two fronts, the Ashantis melted into the main forest, only for a large formation to appear behind the British ranks.

"Bugger that!" A young Marine said as the Ashantis ran up an area of high ground beside the beach. "They're persistent buggers, aren't they?" He looked exhausted, with his face brick-red and his sweat-dark uniform clinging to his slight body.

"Clear them off, lads!" Thankful for something constructive to do rather than following Lieutenant Quinn's men, Jack led his Wests toward the high ground.

"Volley fire on my command," Jack said, stepping back to see how the men reacted. Their first volley was reasonably controlled, with a few shots finding their target, but after that, they lost cohesion and began to fire wildly, without aiming. The bullets whistled in all directions, including towards the other British soldiers.

"Right, that's enough!" Jack had to grab Private Jackson's rifle to prevent him from firing again. "Cease firing!"

The musketry had not dislodged the Ashantis from the high ground. They stood there with a colourful green-and-yellow flag flying, drums beating and, Jack noted with interest, the same two groups of chiefs standing together under the shade of umbrellas. High above the group, a man taunted the British with a Dutch flag.

"Bayonets, lads! And follow me." Reloading his revolver, Jack strode forward. As always in action, he felt a surge of elation, tempered by the dread he could be wounded and left a faceless, mewling cripple.

As soon as the Ashantis saw Jack's men marching forward, they began a fire that kicked up sand or hummed through the air around the Wests. Jack saw a slug burrow into the sand a few feet in front of him, like some fast-moving insect. Stepping over the little mound, he calmed his nerves with a deep breath.

"Come on, lads, the quicker we get there, the less time we're under fire!" Jack increased his pace, hoping that his men would follow. Instead, they gave a yell and charged forward, some overtaking Jack in their enthusiasm to reach the Ashantis' position.

"Damn your eagerness! Keep in formation!" Jack swore, realised the Wests did not listen to his words, swore again, and ran with them.

The Ashantis faced the West Indians for a few moments, still firing, with the flags waving and the nobles beneath the umbrellas standing firm. Only when the Royal Marines came in support did the Ashantis drift back towards the forest. Rushing forward, a Marine and a Hausa reached the Dutch flag together. As the Marine bayonetted the Ashanti, the Hausa grabbed the flag, only for the Marine to snatch it back. By that time the rest of the Marines, with the Hausas and Jack's Wests, pursued the retreating Ashantis into the fringe of the forest until the shrill notes of a bugle ordered them to return.

"Come on!" Jack dragged a snarling Private Stair back from the trees. "The Ashantis will be waiting for us!"

One by one, his Wests withdrew from the forest, with Manning taking a final shot and Private Coffin singing a quiet psalm as he reloaded his Enfield in the shade of a giant banyan.

"Form up!" Jack ordered. Pushing his men into a column of fours, he counted them. "One man wounded."

"Hargreaves, sir." Coffin said. "He's gone back to the castle."

Jack noted that some of the Marines encouraged captured Ashantis back at the point of a bayonet, while a blue jacket wiped the blood off the blade of his cutlass.

"Back to the bridge, lads." Jack stopped Private Stair from pursuing the entire Ashanti army into the forest and watched the orderly withdrawal of the Marines and Naval Brigade. Except for the litter of Ashanti bodies and the drift of powder smoke, nothing seemed to have changed.

"You did not bad," he said as they took up their former position guarding the bridge. "Except for your marksmanship." He nodded, grimly pleased. "We'll soon get to work on that."

* * *

"I wonder if anybody back home will ever hear of that battle." Mary watched the Naval Brigade and Marines from the fleet board the boats that took them back to their ships. In the few days since her arrival, Mary had altered their room to make it more comfortable, cleaned it of cobwebs and dust and put out a few of their possessions to look more like home.

"I doubt one man in a thousand could point to the Gold Coast on a map, let alone realise we have a colony here," Jack looked through the window at the dark forest. "I don't know why we are in this God-forsaken place."

Mary pulled on a cheroot and exhaled blue smoke into the room. "The name should give a clue," she said. "The Gold Coast. Gold is the local currency, Jack, with an ackie of gold worth half a crown and a periguin about ten shillings. There is gold inland, and I am sure the Ashanti use slaves to mine it." She pulled a face. "I truly despise slavery. Imagine people owning a fellow human being. What sort of mentality is that? I can't think of anything more despicable than tearing somebody away from their home and making them a permanent chattel, yet it was a way of life and still is," she pointed to the forest with her cheroot. "In there."

"Aye," Jack nodded. "I once thought that only Europeans and Americans took slaves from Africa. I had no idea the Africans used slavery too."

"Aye, Jack, we were heavily involved." Mary glared at Jack as if he had been personally responsible for the slave trade. "But there has been slavery in Africa forever."

"I hope we can get away from here soon." Jack knew better than to challenge Mary when she was laying down her law. "I'll talk to Colonel Festing tomorrow, and if he doesn't need me, we'll hitch a lift on the first Royal Navy ship going back to Britain."

"The British and African Company has regular mail steamers that stop at Cape Coast Castle," Mary told him. "I'm sure we can get a couple of berths on *Loanda* if we can get to Cape Coast."

"Cape Coast Castle?" Jack said. "That's only eight miles away. We might manage that."

"We can walk that in a few hours," Mary blew out more smoke. "Hire some porters to carry our baggage, and we'll be there by this time tomorrow."

"There are about 50,000 Ashantis out there," Jack reminded. "They might not let us pass them."

Mary's look could have melted cheese. "Let them try," she said, "just let them try."

A bugle blared again, insistent, accompanied by the urgent shouts of officers and the drumbeats of boots.

"It looks like I'm needed again," Jack kissed her gently on the forehead. "Don't stray far, Mary. The Gold Coast is a dangerous place."

Mary nodded without looking round. "Take care of yourself, Jack." Only when Jack left did she take a deep draw of her cheroot to calm her suddenly trembling body. "And may God protect you, Captain Jack. Please bring him back safe to me, Lord. Don't let anything happen to my Jack in this terrible place."

CHAPTER FIVE

Elmina June 1873

Colonel Festing stroked his whiskers as he spoke. "The Ashantis are back in force, gentlemen. It seems that we did not teach them a sufficiently severe lesson earlier today."

Looking around the gathering of officers, Jack saw the tired, wan faces and wondered if these men could fight for long in this tropical climate. West Africa seemed even unhealthier than India.

"Our friendly natives report that an Ashanti noble called Kumi Okese boasts he will burn the Garden Quarter of Elmina and capture Fort St George. I intend to stop him."

Kumi Okese. Jack repeated the name. He recalled the men beneath the two umbrellas, the black satin and the yellow, and wondered which one had issued the threat.

"Will the navy help again, sir?" Lieutenant Hopringle asked.

"I believe so, Hopringle," Festing managed a faint smile. "Otherwise they will have no fort to defend and no anchorage to call their own."

Jack thought of the handful of Hausas and West Indians, plus the few hundred bluejackets and very young Marines. They were brave enough, but when pitted against tens of thousands of Ashantis who were fighting for what they believed was their property, it was hardly a fair contest. The British would have to maximise their advantages of better discipline and superior weapons.

"The Ashantis are coming in force, gentlemen, and fast. They are about two miles north of the town near the salt ponds in the plain and heading towards us."

"Can we hold the fort, sir?" Hopringle asked.

"I will fight the Ashantis in the open," Festing said. "I don't intend to let them near Elmina. This Kumi Okese fellow promised to kill the white men and enslave the white women in the town."

Jack stiffened. "Did he now?" He thought of Mary's abhorrence of slavery. "I don't think we'll allow that."

Festing fixed Jack with a steady look. "No, Major Windrush. We won't allow that."

"Captain Freemantle, I want your Marines and bluejackets to remove any Ashantis from the Garden Quarter."

Freemantle nodded. "We'll do that." There was no hesitation in his voice.

"Windrush, you seem to have a bit of a roving commission. Go with the West Indians; they have a shortage of officers." Colonel Festing said. "You'll have to take a command beneath your rank, but in the present emergency, I am sure you will understand."

"Yes, sir." Jack nodded.

"Right, off you go and the best of British luck to you all." Festing managed another smile. "Shoot straight, gentlemen."

Once again, Jack felt the strange mixture of apprehension and excitement as he marched out with the West Indians. Sergeant Wickham marched with great determination, glaring at the Ashantis as if they were his personal enemies, while Ogston swayed slightly.

"Ogston," Jack stepped beside him, "lay off the rum."

Ogston's eyes were huge as he stared at Jack.

"Shoot straight," Jack said, marching ahead.

The Naval Brigade trotted out of the castle with their cutlasses bouncing at their hips, beards on their chins and straw hats at jaunty angles. Jack thought they were almost a throwback from an earlier age. He could imagine these men fighting alongside Nelson at Trafalgar, Duncan at Camperdown or even with Hawke or Anson.

"Come on, lads! We're not guarding a bridge this time," Jack said. "We're chasing the enemy back to his forest." He caught Sergeant Wickham's eye. "You'll get your chance to fight now, Sergeant."

Wickham nodded, fingering his Enfield. He looked very intense.

As the Naval Brigade and Marines spread into the houses and trees of the Garden Quarter, the Ashantis and Elmina men opened fire from behind a wall. The deep thud of their muskets echoed from the buildings, with the crash of slugs against stone a second later.

Led by a young midshipman, the sailors and Marines gave a loud cheer and charged forward, with the sailors leaping over the wall, cutlasses flashing in the evening sun as they leapt down on the Ashantis. One sailor fell back, doubled up as a slug hit him.

Sergeant Wickham edged toward the fighting, his face contorted.

"Don't be distracted, Sergeant," Jack said. "There are plenty more Ashanti for us!"

Stiffened by a sizeable body of Royal Marines, the Wests and Hausas advanced against the Ashanti army. Ashanti drums sounded non-stop, with flags fluttering above the chanting warriors. When Jack swept his binoculars over them, he saw again that most carried long muskets with exquisite gold decorations, while umbrellas sheltered the captains and chiefs. As before, a group of women stood in the rear, singing and carrying powder horns and sticks.

"That's new," Jack passed his binoculars to Hopringle. "There's a bunch of lads right at the back."

"They're carrying whips," Hopringle said after an examination. "I wager they're to ensure nobody runs from the fight."

"That could be right," Jack said.

The main Ashanti army had split, with one section advancing in front of the main body and a third, ragged group of ill-armed men pushed to the van.

"Skirmishers," Jack said.

"Bushmen slaves," Sergeant Wickham grunted. "Musket fodder."

"You seem to know a lot about the Ashantis, Sergeant," Jack examined the enemy, searching for weaknesses.

"I know too much about them," Wickham said.

Jack spared him a glance. "After this battle, Sergeant, you can tell me more. In the meantime, keep the men in order."

"Yes, sir." Wickham continued to glare at the Ashantis.

Although Jack outranked Lieutenant Quinn, he was experienced enough not to interfere in other units, so he concentrated on his Wests and gave Quinn free rein with his Marines.

"Keep in formation, Wests," Jack said for the fifth time. "Don't break ranks even when the fighting begins. That means you, too Stair!"

"Yes, sir!" Stair responded with his usual smile.

When they were three hundred yards away, the Ashanti skirmishers opened fire on the British with a huge volume of smoke and noise.

"Never mind the shine, Wests!" Jack knew how alarming the first taste of action was for inexperienced men. "It's all noise and smoke. They're well out of range!"

The drums began again, joining the high-pitched singing of the women. The warriors increased the noise with a deep-throated chant that crossed the space between them and the British.

"If noise won battles, the Ashanti could conquer all Africa," Jack said. "I wonder what the words mean."

Wickham spoke quietly. "The Ashantis are saying: 'If I go on, I shall die; if I stay behind, I shall be killed. It is better to go on.' "

Jack glanced at the sergeant. "You're a man of hidden depths, Wickham."

"It is the Ashanti tradition," Wickham said. "If they run away, the chief's policemen will kill them, or the women."

"Interesting concept," Jack said, as the Ashanti fired another ragged volley, this time with some of the shots landing among the British.

"Keep in line, men!" Jack shouted. "Don't fire until I give the order."

The British moved on, mostly ignoring the torrent of slugs from the Ashantis, whose advance force had joined the skirmishers. When they were about 250 yards from the still advancing enemy, Lieutenant Quinn ordered the seamen and Marines to open fire. As the Sniders cracked viciously, the Wests looked hopefully at Jack.

"Wait," Jack said, acutely aware of the low standard of marksmanship among his men. Marching them on another twenty paces, he gave the welcome order. "Aim low and drive into the smoke, lads!"

Jack saw a pair of Hausas crumple to the ground without a sound. The British line marched on, halted to fire, loaded again, marched, halted to fire, loaded and marched on. Each volley felled a dozen or a score of the enemy without seeming to reduce their numbers or the volume of fire they returned. The hammer of the drums continued, with the blare of horns and the high screeching of the women.

Bedlam, Jack thought. *We are at the sharp end of soldiering, marching towards an enemy in an alien land.*

"I hope these Ashanti lads break before we reach them," Quinn said to Jack. "There are thousands of them. We must be outnumbered twenty to one, and I don't fancy charging them with the bayonet."

"It's not as bad as that," Jack said, checking his Wests, "here are our supports coming now."

After clearing the Ashantis from the Garden Quarter, the bluejackets and Marines hurried to the right of the main British body.

"That's much better," Quinn approved. "Now the odds are only ten to one."

"Advance!" When Colonel Festing gave the order, the British moved forward again, marching and firing in a succession of volleys that tore into the Ashantis, whose main force now merged with the advance guard, with the umbrellas visible above the smoke. Jack saw the familiar yellow umbrella prominent in the centre-right, with the red-and-black umbrella at its side.

Kumi Okese, he said to himself. *I'd wager my pension that's you under that umbrella. I thought you were going to capture Elmina! Not today, my friend; not today.* Beside him, Jack could feel Sergeant Wickham edging forward.

"Stay in formation," Jack shouted. "We have to meet them as a cohesive force."

"Yes, sir," Wickham growled.

The Ashantis withdrew a few paces, still firing until the yellow umbrella lifted high above the smoke.

"They're making a stand," Jack said as the Ashantis halted beside a large pool of salt water. The light was fading fast, eroding visibility, enhancing the muzzle flares of the Ashantis' muskets.

"Halt!" Festing ordered. "Fire three volleys. Fire!"

"Steady boys!" Jack said as his Wests began to rush to keep pace with the Marine's breech-loaders, going for speed rather than accuracy. "Keep the men in order, Sergeant!"

"Yes, sir!" Wickham said, and snarled at his men.

With British bullets tearing into their ranks, the Ashanti army began to disintegrate. As a rising wind cleared some of the smoke, Jack saw first one, then two Ashantis, and then groups of a dozen or more, turn away from the Sniders and withdraw into the thick forest. Only the men around the umbrellas remained, firing in disciplined volleys that would have done credit to any infantry in the world.

"You're a good soldier, Kumi Okese," Jack said, "whatever else you might be." He watched as Sergeant Wickham knelt to fire, aiming each shot and grunting with satisfaction when his chosen target crumpled to the ground. As he fired, he mumbled something in a language that Jack did not understand.

Lieutenant Quinn stepped across to Jack as the Marines took up position beside the Wests. "We're pushing them back, except for that group around the yellow umbrella. They're a stubborn bunch and no mistake."

"That's Kumi Okese, I believe," Jack said.

"It could be King Kofi himself, for all I know," Quinn said. "I don't believe in finding out about the enemy. It's easier to kill them when they're only targets."

"I like to know my enemy," Jack said. "The more I find out about them, the more I can work out their tactics." Lifting his binoculars, Jack studied the men beneath the umbrellas.

With the onshore breeze continuing to shred the powder smoke, Jack saw the two captains standing side by side. The man under the red-and-black umbrella was less tall than Kumi Okese, younger and festooned with golden jewellery. The warriors around the umbrellas remained static, each man sporting vertical white lines down his face and each arm.

"These must be the Ashanti equivalent of the Guards," Jack said, knowing the image would always remain with him.

Without saying a word, Wickham dropped a ball down the barrel of his rifle, rammed it home and carefully placed a percussion cap in place. Kneeling, he aimed at the younger captain, took a deep breath and squeezed the trigger. Jack knew immediately that the shot would go home. He saw the Ashanti captain stagger, saw the tall man beneath the yellow umbrella jump to his aid as a collective shiver ran through the Ashanti ranks. The man with the yellow umbrella seemed to stare directly at Windrush and Wickham, and then the breeze died, and smoke closed around the Ashantis.

"You got him," Jack said.

"I did," Wickham reloaded hurriedly. "I'll get that other fellow, Kumi Okese, now."

"Everybody aim beneath the yellow umbrella," Jack ordered. "That's where one of their chiefs stands."

As Jack spoke, the Ashantis fired in a torrent of smoke and flame. The slugs pattered around the West's ranks, hitting two men. One gasped, writhed and stood up, while the other felt the lump of ironstone that had lodged in his forehead.

"Thank God these Ashantis don't have modern weapons," Jack said.

"And they can thank God we don't have more men," Quinn said. "Or we'd burn their whole blessed country to the ground."

The Wests aimed and fired, and had time for a second shot, but the yellow umbrella remained in place, standing firm through the smoke. The black-and-red umbrella vanished.

"Some of them are running," a Marine with a Devon accent said, and Colonel Festing ordered the bugle to call cease fire. The bluejackets led the cheering, with the Royal Marines next and the Hausas and West Indians joining in enthusiastically.

"There goes the last umbrella," Quinn said.

Bright through the smoke, the yellow umbrella withdrew with a final blare of horns. The drumming continued for a few moments, slowly diminishing to a single beat that also stopped. Only the harsh breathing of the Wests and the soft moaning of wounded Ashantis disturbed the silence.

"By George's wig," Quinn said. "I rather think we've beat them."

"I rather think we have," Jack said.

Wickham reloaded his rifle, staring through the smoke. "I hope we got Kumi Okese, sir."

"So do I, Sergeant," Jack said. "Do you have some personal animosity towards the man?"

Wickham hesitated before replying. "No, sir. I only wished to test my shooting."

"Well, that's a damned lie," Jack said. "You're a good shot, the best shot in the company by far. What's the real reason?"

"There is no other reason, sir." Wickham remained impassive except for a single bead of sweat that ran down his temple.

Jack grunted. "Let's have a look then. You other Wests stand easy. We'll be back directly."

Scattered bodies showed where the Ashantis had stood, many with the white stripes down face and arms. One wounded warrior raised his musket and fired a last defiant shot at Jack, with the slug going nowhere. Wickham kicked away the weapon and allowed the man to die.

"I can't see Kumi Okese's body," Jack said. "Or the body of the man with the gold jewellery."

"The Ashantis retrieve the bodies of their nobility," Wickham said. "We may have killed these two chiefs.' He turned over one of the corpses with his foot. "Or they may be alive and well."

"I hope we've killed enough to persuade King Kofi, not to attack British territory again," Jack said.

Wickham shook his head. "No, sir."

"No, sir?"

"I know of the Ashanti, sir," Wickham spoke with perfect sincerity. "Unless they are utterly defeated, they won't give up. They will come again and again until they have swept every last British man, woman and child into the sea, and then they will enslave and slaughter every other tribe in the area." When he looked up, Wickham's eyes were clear. "They'll chop down the Fanti fetish trees – the sacred trees - to show they've defeated the Fanti gods, enslave the white women, decapitate any white prisoners and display their skulls on their war drums."

"Are they that bad?" Jack studied the forest edge. It was too dark to be sure, but he thought he saw movement there, as though the Ashantis were watching him.

"They are the devil's brood, sir; worse than anything you can imagine."

For a moment the forest leaves parted and Jack saw a man standing under the trees. Kumi Okese was staring directly at him, and without a word, he lifted his right hand and pointed. Jack felt himself shiver; he knew that the man had singled him out. Raising his binoculars, Jack stared back at the Ashanti, and even at this distance, he recognised the malevolence in Kumi Okese's brooding eyes.

Then the leaves closed and he was alone with Wickham, the bodies of the Ashanti and the drifting smoke.

CHAPTER SIX

Cape Coast Castle June 1873

"So this is Cape Coast Castle," Mary said. "I think I preferred Elmina." She looked in distaste at the castle that rose from the shore, with the lines of high surf marking the beach. A ridge of reddish-brown clay stretched in both directions, with scrubby plants fighting for space under a weeping grey sky. In the centre of the ridge, crushed into a gorge, was the settlement of Cape Coast Castle. Three hills thrust up, each surmounted by a square-built fort, while the most significant feature was the castle itself, with the union flag hanging limp from its staff.

"Do the British deliberately choose situations with the most awkward places to land?"

"Of course," Jack said. "That's how we test British pluck, don't ye know?"

"No, Jack, that's how we test British stupidity," Mary was not in the best of tempers. "How do we get ashore? Will the navy take us?"

"I think we land by canoe again."

Mary sighed, looking at the heaving waves that ended in crashing silver-white surf. "If we must. Come on then, Jack. Let's get this over with."

A collection of canoes bobbed alongside HMS *Druid*, the wooden screw-corvette that had carried Jack and Mary from Elmina. Most were the native fish-canoes, little more than hollowed-out tree trunks, while a few were the more sturdy craft known as surf boats. Mary chose one of the latter and charmed a couple of seamen to lower their chests into the eager hands of the Kroomen paddlers.

"Hello my lady! Hello, sir! Thank you!" The Kroomen grinned as they helped passengers into the surf boats.

The closer they came to Cape Coast Castle, the less Jack liked it. There seemed to be a high number of decayed buildings with sagging roofs, and far too many people milling hopelessly on the shore. He was too intent on watching the town to realise that they were near the shore until the boat gave a massive lurch, her bow rose nearly vertically, and they were speeding with frothy surf on each side of them and the roar of a breaking wave in front. They beached with a crunch of sand, and Mary stepped unaided into the shallow water.

"That's us ashore again," Jack helped the Kroomen pull the surf boat further up the beach, where they unloaded the chests. "Now we'll see about getting you a ship for Britain."

"I'm not leaving without you," Mary said. "We're going on leave to visit our son, and I'm staying until your duty is done. There is no argument, Captain Jack."

People packed the streets, some evidently locals while most were refugees fleeing from the Ashanti invasion. They stood in huddled groups, staring at nothing, talking together or trying to beg food from equally unfortunate people.

"Look at that," Mary pointed to an emaciated woman carrying an ancient man on her back, "and that," a baby sitting in a puddle in the road, ignored by everybody.

Mary lifted the child. "Who's in charge here, Jack?"

"The Governor," Jack said, "whoever that may be."

"Why isn't he doing something about these people? They've starving!"

"I'm sure I don't know," Jack said.

"I'm sure you can find out and get something done," Mary said, with the light of battle in her eyes. "I won't see people suffering like this."

"We've only arrived," Jack said.

Mary shook her head, holding the baby close to her. "I know that, Jack Windrush. Find the governor and get him told."

"I will, as soon as we're settled." Jack looked up as a harassed Marine lieutenant rushed towards them.

"Major and Mrs Windrush, isn't it?"

"It is," Mary answered for them. "Who is looking after these people?"

The lieutenant looked at her. "Looking after them?"

"That's what I said."

"I've come here to take you to your accommodation," the lieutenant was about thirty, with a skin yellowed by fever. "I don't know about anything else."

"This gentleman is not the man to ask," Jack felt a mixture of pride for Mary's concern and embarrassment as her verbal assault on an evidently harassed officer.

"Where is the Governor?" Mary moderated her tone slightly.

"Colonel Harley, the Administrator-General might be in his office in Government House," the lieutenant gestured vaguely towards the town.

"Then that's where I'll see him." Mary stalked away, still carrying the child.

"Mary!" Jack shouted after her, knowing he was wasting his breath. Once Mary set out on a crusade, she let nothing stand in her way. Jack pitied Colonel Harley with an animated Mary crashing through his door.

The lieutenant glanced at Mary, decided to say nothing, and gestured to a group of watching Kroomen. "You, men! Take these chests."

Jack watched the Kroomen lift the chests as if they were feathers. "Where are we going, Lieutenant?"

"Green Lettuce Lane, sir. I'm afraid there is no suitable accommodation in the castle for a married couple."

"I am sure Colonel Harley will be pleased about that."

"Quite, sir! This way, if you please." The lieutenant led the way at a brisk pace that the Kroomen matched easily, despite the heavy chests. Refugees crammed in every street, staring at Jack with dull eyes and the occasional hopefully outstretched hand. Jack could taste the fear in the air. It was worse than the atmosphere in India during the Mutiny, for then there had been defiance and the anger of revenge. These people lacked even hope.

"Can we not band these men together?" Jack gestured to the staring refugees. "Arm them and train them to fight the Ashantis?"

"They wouldn't fight, sir," the lieutenant said. "They run at the first sign of the Ashantis. They need us to protect them."

"Surely some of them can be trained." Used to the sepoy regiments of India, Jack found it hard to believe that so many fit, strong young men would not wish to fight back. "They're a fine-looking people."

"They're cowards, sir," the lieutenant said. "It's as simple as that." He halted at the end of a street of flat-roofed, stone-built houses. "Here we are, Sir. Green Lettuce Lane. It's not the most salubrious area in the world, but the best available at present."

Jack could see nothing green in the street and not a sign of a lettuce. "I've lived in much worse," he said as the Kroomen hefted his trunks into the house, laid them down with a thump and waited hopefully. Sighing, Jack passed over half a crown, knowing he was over-paying.

"A shilling is the going rate, sir," the lieutenant advised.

"Aye, but these lads might be paddling the canoe taking my wife out to the next ship," Jack said. "I hope to give a good enough impression that they take care of her."

"Yes, sir.' The lieutenant said no more.

The house had four rooms and a kitchen, with windows on the upper storey that afforded a view of a lighthouse. Jack had barely settled in when Mary came to the door.

"Colonel Hartley wishes to see you," Mary said as she entered. "His official title is the Administrator-General of the West African Settlements, and he's very proud of his position."

"I hope you haven't upset him too much, Mary," Jack looked around for the child.

"Hardly at all. I handed over the baby to the local church; it's the best I could do." Mary smiled. "I'll get this town organised Jack, once I've cleaned up our house. Now go, and sugar talk the colonel. He's in Government House, top floor."

***

The Royal Marine on duty slammed to attention and called for the sergeant, who conducted Jack to a very airy room. Jack entered with a feeling of trepidation, wondering if Mary had angered Harley or if there was another reason the Administrator-General should want to see him.

As soon as he stepped inside the room, Jack knew there was trouble ahead. Three men stood in a small huddle amidst a cloud of blue tobacco smoke. One was Colonel Festing, who gave him a cordial nod, the second a man he did not know but guessed to be Harley, and the third advanced towards him with a broad smile and his hand outstretched.

"Windrush! Jack, my dear fellow! How good to see you again!"

"Colonel Hook," Jack felt the sick slide of dismay as he took Hook's hand. "I did not know you would be here." Jack had known Hook as the Head of Intelligence in India and later in Britain.

"Major General Hook, now, Windrush." Hook said. "As soon as your wife spoke to Harley, I knew you were in West Africa, and I thought to myself: Jack Windrush! The very man!"

Thank you, Mary, Jack thought.

"I'm a regimental officer now, sir," Jack reminded. "I haven't been involved in anything political since that Fenian business in North America."

"I know," Hook ushered Jack to one of the four seats that stood around a central table. "Cheroot? Drink? Whisky was your tipple, was it not?"

"It still is, sir," Jack admitted cautiously. He liked Hook well enough but knew that when any senior officer expressed such delight at a meeting, there was trouble in the wind.

"I understand you two know each other?" Colonel Harley was a tall, dignified man with straggly whiskers and hard eyes. In common with so many British on this coast, his skin bore the yellowish tinge of fever.

"Oh, we go back a long way," Hook said. "As far back as the Mutiny. Isn't that right, Jack?"

"Yes, sir," Jack said cautiously. "General Hook, or Colonel Hook as he was then, sent me on some political missions in India and along the Frontier."

"In North America too, old fellow," Hook murmured.

"North America, too," Jack said. "But now I am a regimental officer and thankfully no longer involved in such matters."

Harley and Festing looked at one another before Festing spoke. "I saw you in action at Elmina, Windrush. You are a fighting soldier who leads from the front. I had no idea you were also talented in other directions."

Jack sipped his whisky, watching a beam of sunlight seep through the window to highlight the amber liquid within the crystal of the glass. It was strange to think that a spirit distilled beside the Spey in the far north should glow with strong sunshine in West Africa. "I have little talent, sir."

"I've met your wife, Windrush," Harley said with a slight smile. "If you can control her, you have immense talent."

Jack smiled. "I have never managed to control that woman, sir."

"Fighting Jack Windrush, his men call him," Hook said, "and he's just the man for the job, although he'll deny it."

Jack sighed. "What job is that, sir? I'm only passing through Africa. My ship was driven in by bad weather, my uncontrollable wife is in a rented house in the town, and our son is waiting for us back home."

Hook smiled. "And how is the redoubtable Mary?"

Jack noted the oh-so-casual use of his wife's Christian name. "Mary is looking forward to going home to see our son, sir. We both are."

"Ah, David, isn't it? He'll be a fine young man now. I'll arrange for Mary to be on the next steamer, in a first-class cabin, paid for by Her Majesty's government. That should keep her happy and ease any worries you have on her part. If everything goes well, you'll be able to join her within a few weeks. I'll ensure you have passage on the first available steamer."

Acutely aware that three senior officers were watching him and assessing everything he did, Jack took his time with the whisky. *Is it worthwhile kicking against the pricks? No; they would only turn a request into an order, with bad feeling on all sides.* He had been a soldier for twenty years, long enough to know it was better to accept the inevitable with good grace.

"Thank you, sir," Jack said. "Mary will enjoy travelling first class after being squeezed into a tiny cabin in a sailing ship." He mustered what he hoped was a convincing smile. "What is it you wish me to do?"

Jack felt the atmosphere in the room relax.

"Good man, Jack. I knew we could rely on you. Tell me, what do you know about the Ashanti Empire?"

"Only what I've learned here, sir."

Hook nodded. "I'll try and keep this brief. The Ashanti are Akan people from further west and moved to this part of Africa about two hundred years ago. They started as a minor tribe, paying tribute to the then larger Denkyira nation until around 1700 a priest named Anokye summoned a golden stool from heaven."

Jack sipped at his whisky, raised his eyebrows and waited for signs of scorn from the other officers present. When they gave no indication, he took another sip and listened, aware that Hook would not talk of such things unless he thought them essential.

Noticing Jack's scepticism, Hook gave a small smile and continued. "The Golden Stool drifted down onto the knees of the then king, Osei Tutu. Anokye, the priest, claimed the stool held the spirits of the Ashantis' ancestors and as the king was its guardian, he was also the guardian of all the Ashanti tribes."

Hook paused for a moment. "In case you are unsure, Windrush, the Ashantis, like all the tribes in this area, worship their ancestors. That is their religion."

"I see, sir," Jack said.

Nobody else in the room spoke. Jack heard a sergeant's voice from the courtyard outside, and the crisp marching of a Royal Marine guard.

Hook continued. "The Ashanti kings used the Golden Stool to unify all the Ashanti tribes. It was not only a link between the king and his people but also a link to their ancestors."

Jack fidgeted on his seat, acutely aware of the importance of symbols to any nation.

Hook lowered his voice. "Unless you understand their beliefs, you can never understand a people. If we are to defeat the Ashantis, we must first know what we are fighting."

Jack nodded.

"United under the Golden Stool, the Ashantis began empire building. They imported guns and gunpowder from the Dutch who they saw as a tributary nation and conquered a host of Akim tribes, the Sefwi, Banda, Wassaw, Gyaman and others. They invaded the plains to the north of the forest belt and eventually controlled everything from the River Volta to Assinie, which is the westernmost port on the Gold Coast. Naturally, each victory brought them territory and slaves."

"Slavery seems to be endemic here." Jack sipped his whisky. "With us part of it."

Hook nodded. "What we did was appalling and utterly disgusting. We encouraged tribes such as the Ashanti who captured tens of thousands of slaves and sold them to the European and American slavers. It was supply and demand: the Ashanti wanted European goods and supplied slaves in return." Hook paused for a moment, staring at Jack. "The Ashantis also kept slaves for mining gold, clearing land and other purposes including human sacrifice."

Jack nodded; he did not wish to think about the slave trade.

"When Britain led the way in ending the slave trade in 1807, we immediately became unpopular in West Africa. Nations like the Ashanti and Dahomey had built up a culture based on catching and selling slaves."

"Yes, sir." Jack fidgeted in his seat. Not naturally a patient man, he wondered what this history lesson had to do with him.

"Nearly done, Windrush," Hook read the expression on Jack's face.

"When we outlawed the slave trade in 1807 the Asantahene, the High King of the Ashanti tribes, sent his army to the coast. They smashed the local tribe, the Fantis, and we agreed to pay the Ashantis rent for our forts and trading posts.' Hook paused for a moment. 'Remember the context, gentlemen. We were in the middle of a war with Bonaparte at the time, so a minor colonial skirmish in Africa was hardly important."

"Yes, sir,' Jack finished his whisky.

"That situation continued until the 1820s when the first crown governor, as opposed to a commercial trading company, took over the forts. Our man, Sir Charles McCarthy, refused to pay bribes to the Ashanti and tried to protect the Fanti chiefs. He brought a small army inland, but when he faced the Ashantis, the Fantis ran away. The Ashantis killed and decapitated McCarthy."

"Yes, sir."

"I have already given Windrush the background," Festing said.

Jack nursed his empty glass, hoping somebody would offer to refill it. Nobody did.

Hook continued. "The Fantis have constantly proved too terrified to fight. They know the Ashantis of old as slavers and killers."

"Yes, sir," Jack said. "I saw hundreds of young men in the town and wondered if we could form them into a regiment."

"We'd be as likely to find a regiment of abstainers in the British Army," Hook said. "Now then, you are wondering where you come in."

"Yes, sir," Jack said.

"Since Colonel Festing pushed the Ashantis back from Elmina, they have settled in a town called Effutu, about 10 miles inland. Their advance parties have occupied villages about six miles from Cape Coast. We estimate they are about fifteen to twenty thousand strong, so not quite the fifty thousand of rumour, but far too many for our handful of men to tackle, with or without the doubtful help of our native allies."

Jack felt the tension in the room rise as everybody looked at him.

"We might be able to defend Cape Coast and Elmina, and perhaps mount some limited attacks along the coast, where the Royal Navy gunboats will offer support. However, at present, we have given up control of the interior to the Ashantis. In effect, despite Colonel Festing's gallant victories, their General Amanquatia has won the first campaign."

Jack nodded. "We often lose the first battle sir, yet still win the war."

"We intend to win the war, Windrush." Hook leaned back in his chair. "We cannot allow such a dangerous enemy loose in our lands. Now, what I am about to say will not leave this room." He paused for a moment before continuing. "The government is so concerned about the situation here that they are sending out one of our best young generals. You may have heard of Sir Garnet Wolseley?"

"I met him in the Crimea, sir, and I heard he did great things in North America."

"That's the fellow. He's our brightest up-and-coming general." Hook passed over the whisky decanter, with the sunlight glittering on the crystal. "We also have the remainder of the 2nd West on their way from Bermuda."

Jack poured himself a generous tot of whisky, knowing that Hook was about to reveal what his duties were to be.

"Well Windrush, I want you to go to Effutu as our ambassador, see what's happening there and talk to them, palaver as they say here. Delay them until our reinforcements arrive. We could only defend Elmina by stripping Cape Coast and the fleet of every available man. If the Ashantis attacked both towns at once, we wouldn't have sufficient men to hold them."

Jack swallowed the last of his whisky in a single gulp. "I am no diplomat, sir, and I don't even speak the language."

"That's all right," Hook said. "We'll supply you with a translator and an escort of some of the 2nd West. Every day you gain will be invaluable as we strengthen our defences and await reinforcements." He paused for a moment. "Wear your medals and take your best uniform. That sort of thing might impress the Ashantis; they seem to go in for show."

"I might be better with a large umbrella," Jack said. "The Ashantis seem to like them, too."

"Very good, Windrush, I'm glad to see you've retained a sense of humour. The climate here drains that sort of thing."

"Yes, sir."

So I am being ordered to go to a village and palaver with the Ashantis, a people who practise human sacrifice and slavery, and try to persuade them not to attack until we can build up a decent force to fight them. Why me? Why a man with no African experience?

Because I have no official position, I am an extra man and therefore expendable. My loss would not weaken any British unit here.

"I can see you are thinking how best to proceed," Hook said cheerfully. "Oh, one more thing, Jack. Some European missionaries are being held in Kumasi; see if you can free them as well, or at least find out if they are still alive."

"How many missionaries, sir?" Jack asked, trying to gain time.

"We are aware of three, from the Society of Basle, worthy people who educate the youngsters as well as preaching the Bible. More importantly, they train masons, blacksmiths, and carpenters."

"I've never heard of them, sir." With Mary being Mission-educated in India, Jack knew what good work missionaries could do.

"They are among the best of people," Hook said. "And a great civilising influence wherever they are." He managed a brief smile. "I wish they could come into some of the back slums of London, but I suspect that would be too wild even for them."

"Yes, sir. I see you've retained your sense of humour as well."

Hook smiled. "These unfortunate missionaries have been held hostage since June 1869. We don't know what conditions they'll be in."

Without asking, Jack poured himself another glass of whisky. He had worked in some dangerous places before, but even the North-West Frontier of India had a veneer of civilisation. This King Kofi, with his slavery and human sacrifice, was something beyond his experience. He took a deep breath.

"When do I leave, sir?"

CHAPTER SEVEN

Cape Coast Castle, June 1874

"That's another alert." Mary stood at the window, listening to the pandemonium in the streets outside. Shouts and wails reached the house, with one woman sobbing hysterically. "One only has to whisper the name Ashanti to cause a panic. If the Ashantis ever come, these people will be too petrified to put up any resistance."

"Aye, they're scared right enough," Jack gestured to the orange glow on the underside of the clouds. "Maybe with reason. That's the reflection of a large fire, probably the Ashantis burning a Fanti village."

"I've heard it's been like this for weeks," Mary sipped at a cup of tea. "The Ashanti general Amanquatia controls all the interior.' She faced Jack. "I hate this place, Jack. I hate all the memories of slavery. We did terrible things here."

"We did," Jack agreed.

"Now we have to do something to redress the evil to which we contributed," Mary said. "God knows I don't approve of wars, Jack, but the townsfolk and the Fanti people are terrified of the Ashantis, and we should protect them."

Jack nodded slowly. "I think we're going to."

"You must win this war, Jack, for me."

"I'll do my best," Jack said.

"I know you will," Mary came closer. "You always do. And I'll persuade General Harley to help the people in Cape Coast." She smiled. "He'll soon get so sick of me that he'll be glad to help them."

"That poor man," Jack said. "I feel sorry for him already."

Mary touched his arm and turned away. There was no need for any more words between them.

* * *

Sergeant Wickham threw an immaculate salute. "I am to lead your escort, sir."

"Glad to have you with me, Sergeant," Jack said. "I can't think of anybody in Africa I'd rather have."

"The good sergeant volunteered," Hook was puffing on a thin cheroot. "As soon as he heard what was happening."

"Sergeant Wickham fought at my side outside Elmina," Jack said. "He's the best shot in the company."

"I've detailed five privates of the 2nd West to accompany you," Hook indicated the men who stood rigidly to attention within the courtyard of Cape Coast Castle.

Jack nodded. "I know these lads: Privates Stair, Manning, Daley, Ogston and Coffin. They're veterans of the fight outside Elmina. We'll get to know each other even better on the journey to Effutu."

"They're only a token, of course," Hook said. "If the Ashantis decide to kill you, six soldiers or sixty won't make much difference." He gestured to a group of local men who sat or lay around a pile of baggage. "Those are your porters. They carry your tents, food, water purifying tubes and so on."

"I don't need the porters," Jack said. "I'm used to travelling light in India. Porters will only slow us down and give us extra mouths to defend."

"You'll take them," Hook said. "It's expected here. You know the old rhyme, 'beware and take care of the Bight of Benin, where one comes out for forty goes in? Well, it's as bad here'. If the climate doesn't get you, the fever will, and if the fever doesn't, the Ashantis will." He paused. "We have the dangers of night-dews, soil-exhalations, unwholesome nourishment and heat exhaustion. Shall I order the porters to leave?"

"I'll take them then," Jack decided. "They might make me look more important."

"Making a show matters here," Hook said. "Show and noise. You'll have heard the drums already."

"I have," Jack said.

"Well, good luck, Windrush," Hook said. "Remember, you are there to stall, to play for time, nothing else. I don't want any heroics, no taking on the entire Ashanti army on your own."

"I won't do that," Jack promised.

"They know you are coming," Hook said. "And here is the interpreter. Akron Bekoh."

The interpreter was in his early thirties, with the bearing of a warrior and gold bracelets on both wrists, He gave an elaborate bow to Jack, ignored Wickham's hostile stare and waited politely for orders.

Having said his goodbyes to a staunchly cheerful, Mary, Jack felt self-conscious as he marched out of Cape Coast Castle with his tiny West Indian escort and a dozen Fanti porters balancing loads on their heads. *All I need now is a fife and drum, and I'd be completely ridiculous.* The castle garrison watched them leave, with the West Indians and Hausas saying nothing while the Marines gave cheerful advice and black humour.

"Good luck, sir," a Marine sergeant said. "Don't trust them Shantees. Leave an escape route back to the coast."

"Keep your gun handy," a young midshipman with basilisk eyes advised. "If in danger or in doubt, hoist the anchor, get off out."

"We'll watch for you coming back without your head," an Irish voice said. "I heard King Kofi likes souvenirs of his visiting British officers."

"Thank you, all," Jack lifted a hand in farewell and headed northward into the interior. He knew that Mary would be watching but refrained from turning to see her. Jack could picture her on the battlements, holding her straw hat on her head, lifting her chin and refusing to cry. Goodbyes were always the worst part of life and, God willing, he would only be a few days, a couple of weeks at most.

One hundred yards from Cape Coast, Akron stepped in front as if it was his right.

"Get behind me!" Jack ordered.

"I will have to speak to any Ashanti or Fanti we meet," Akron explained, smiling.

"You can speak to them from behind me as well as from the front," Jack said.

Akrom gave another little smile and slipped behind Jack, where Wickham pushed him to the side.

Aware that the Ashantis could be watching every step, Jack led his men on the short march across the open plain and into the first patch of forest. Almost immediately the path narrowed and deepened, with trees soaring on both sides and creepers coiling around their trunks like watchful serpents.

"Load your rifles, men," Jack said, "and make sure your bayonets are loose in their scabbards."

Well used to the forests of India, Jack expected the stifling heat and the green tinge to the light, the slanting sun-beams and the hum of insects. It was the atmosphere that was different. Even during the Mutiny, Jack had never experienced such foreboding, as if some great evil waited to unleash itself. He shook his head to clear away such fantasies. He was a British officer, not an impressionable Johnnie Raw.

He heard the regular thump of boots as the West Indians continued their parade-ground march. They remained at attention, with rifles shouldered and eyes firmly fixed in front of them.

"Break your formation, lads. We don't know if the Ashantis are waiting in ambush or not. Watch the trees for movement and if anybody fires, shoot the buggers flat." Manning and Stair grinned at that, as Jack had intended.

Behind the Wests, the porters moved with a regular rhythm, making light of the packs balanced on their heads. Jack gave them a few words of encouragement, nodded to Akron and returned to the front of the column. Moving slower now, they walked into steadily increasing heat with a shower of insects tormenting them.

How much time had passed since they entered the forest? An hour? Two hours? Three? Jack did not know. He could not work out time within the denseness of trees. He could only march, swat insects and watch for ambushes.

The Ashanti warrior stepped out of the forest in front of them with his long musket held butt up and muzzle down as a sign he came in peace. Bare-chested, he wore a patterned robe around his waist and a green turban on his head.

Jack halted his men, knowing that things were about to get interesting. "Akrom, go and do your stuff. Ask that fellow what he wants."

Stepping forward, the interpreter gave a broad smile before hurrying forward to speak to the Ashanti.

"Keep the lads alert, Sergeant," Jack looked around the trees. Where there was one Ashanti, there could well be more, hiding among the sheltering trees, probably with their muskets trained on the Wests as they stood on the path.

"This Ashanti warrior is a friend," Akrom said. "He says that the people in Effutu are waiting to welcome the brave Major Jack Windrush."

"Thank him, Akrom and tell him that we are looking forward to talking to Amanquatia as a representative of the Ashanti people."

There was an exchange of conversation for a few moments before Akrom spoke to Jack again. "This warrior will lead you to Effutu."

"Thank him kindly, Akrom, and say we will follow." Jack glanced at Wickham. "Make sure the men are alert, Sergeant."

"Yes, sir," Wickham said. "I'd like to speak to you, sir, where these two can't hear."

"We can't show mistrust on a diplomatic mission, Sergeant," Jack said. "Don't make it obvious."

"This way!" Akron said as the Ashanti warrior trotted along the track for another fifty yards before turning to his left, pushing aside a screen of palm-leaves and stepping onto a side path. They moved on for another ten minutes before they reached a village in a clearing. Jack looked around, for it was the first purely African village he had seen. Set on a slight rise, a score of houses lined both sides of a broad street, with a single mangrove tree in the centre. Half a dozen white-haired men sat under the tree, idly chatting, while bones and other objects hung above their heads. Dogs and children ran around, with hens scraping at the dust and the smell of cooking fires pleasant in the air. There was not a single warrior in sight, only a few brightly-dressed women and a dozen children. It all looked so peaceful that Jack felt himself relax.

"Bring up the porters," Jack said.

"They won't come, sir," Wickham said. "They're scared."

"Let me talk to them," Jack stepped back.

"Sir," Wickham spoke in a low tone. "Don't trust the interpreter. He's only telling you half what that Ashanti is saying."

Jack grunted. 'How much of the language do you know?"

"We spoke it at home as much as English. My mother insisted."

"You're an interesting man, Sergeant. Not many soldiers can speak two languages."

"Yes, sir." Wickham opened his mouth to say something else, changed his mind and looked away.

"Keep your skill to yourself, Sergeant. It might come in useful." Jack felt the change in the atmosphere a moment too late.

"Shantee!" One of the porters cried. "Shantee!"

"What the devil?" Jack looked up at the exact moment the first porter dropped his load, turned, and fled in the direction he had come. Without waiting for an explanation, the other porters followed, dropping their baggage on the path as a score of Ashanti warriors appeared from the forest. Tall men with impressive physiques, they stood around the Wests, fingering their muskets. Each one sported white stripes down their face and on both arms.

Kumi Okese's men. That is not good. Jack felt for the butt of his revolver.

Akron smiled. "Here is our escort, Major Windrush. Now we are safe from any unwanted incidents."

"You scared my porters, damn you!" Too angry to heed his safety, Jack strode to the warrior who seemed to be in command of the Ashantis. "What's the meaning of this?"

Seeing Jack's indignant advance, the Ashanti stepped back, pointing his long musket, which had Wickham calling the West Indians to ready their rifles.

"Back to back!" Wickham snapped.

For a moment, it seemed that Jack's mission would end there until he calmed himself down.

"Lead on then, Ashantis, and pray carry our baggage." He exchanged glares with the Ashanti leader, a man he judged to be in his mid-twenties, with a healed star-shaped bullet wound on his shoulder and gold inlays around the lock of his musket.

"Leave the baggage," Akron was still smiling as more warriors appeared until thirty Ashantis surrounding Jack's little band. "It will be safe here. Amanquatia has given orders that nobody will touch your possessions."

"You seem to know a lot all of a sudden," Jack said. "All right men, it seems that we have an escort. Shoulder arms and we'll go with the Ashantis. Be prepared for treachery."

"The Ashanti are known for treachery," Sergeant Wickham said. "Deception and lies are how they wage war. That is how they have managed to conquer their neighbours, deception, lies and savagery."

With the Ashanti warriors all around, Jack felt more like a prisoner than a diplomat as they hurried on narrow forest tracks to Effutu. After half an hour, one of the Ashanti began to beat time on a small drum he carried around his neck, and the others chanted, repeating the same refrain again and again until the rhythm felt imprinted on Jack's brain. The Ashantis increased the speed, with Jack's Wests keeping pace with them while the sweat beaded on Jack's forehead and rolled down his chin.

"How far is this place, Akron?" Jack asked.

"Not far now," Akron looked as uncomfortable as Jack felt. He was a translator, not a superbly fit warrior.

The number of Ashanti warriors surrounding them multiplied as they moved on until there were a couple of hundred, all carrying long muskets and looking askance at Jack and his handful of red-coated soldiers. The white-striped men kept closer to the Wests, glancing at them every so often.

"We'll be there soon," Akron promised. "Then you'll get a nice rest."

Not sure what to expect, Jack was surprised when their escort slowed to a walk. They climbed up a short slope, passed a cleared area that had once been used for agriculture and reached Effutu. Expecting a small village, Jack looked around at a town of three main streets that met at an open space in which stood a large tree. *That will be the fetish tree.* The roads were broad and clean, with large, square-built houses with an open frontage and roofs of overhanging palm leaves that provided shade from the sun and shelter from the rain.

Lining the streets, crowding every house and camping around the central tree, Ashanti warriors looked up curiously when the striped men escorted in Jack and his men.

"Keep your heads up, lads!" Jack said. "Remember you are soldiers, men of the 2nd West India Regiment! Show these Ashantis what that means!" Glancing over his shoulder, Jack saw that, despite the heat and the stifling dust raised by thousands of feet, his Wests were marching at attention, with their rifles at the slope and eyes facing forward.

Well done, lads.

Among the warriors were several chiefs or captains, sheltering under enormous umbrellas, every colour of the rainbow and decorated with dangling tassels, with gold figurines of various animals festooned across the peak.

Women emerged from the houses, pointing and shouting, yet without any overt hostility. Scores of Ashanti warriors kept pace with them as Akron led Jack and the Wests to the largest house in the town, opposite the fetish tree.

"Here we go, lads," Jack said.

Two massive umbrellas stood side by side outside the house. One was of scarlet silk, with gold elephants parading across the top, and the other was ominously yellow. Under the scarlet umbrella sat a very dignified woman who eyed Jack with curiosity from narrow eyes, taking in every detail of his dress and appearance. Under the yellow umbrella, seated on an ornately carved chair, was the man with whom Jack had exchanged glares outside the walls of Elmina.

"Major Jack Windrush of the 113th Foot, British Army," Akron said with elaborate politeness, "may I introduce Yaa Asantewaa, a lady of the royal household."

Jack gave a polite bow, "your ladyship," he said as Yaa Asantewaa responded with a slight nod.

Akron seemed pleased with the response. "And under the yellow umbrella, may I introduce Kumi Okese, the commander of this section of the army of the Asantahene, King Kofi Karikari."

CHAPTER EIGHT

Effutu, July 1873

Kumi Okese pushed aside the young slave who sat at his feet and stared at Jack through curiously clouded eyes. He was even more impressive than Jack remembered, a tall, broad-shouldered man with the horned leopard-skin cap and vertical white lines somehow enhancing the strong bones of his face. When Kumi Okese spoke, his voice was deep and crisp, with Akron translating almost instantaneously.

"That white man Windrush fought against us at Elmina. That man killed the nephew of the king!"

Jack knew that Okese referred to the man embellished in gold that Sergeant Wickham had shot. "I did fight against your army, Kumi Okese," Jack spoke directly to the Ashanti warrior. "As for the death of the king's nephew, well, he was a soldier, as you and I are, and dying in battle is part of the soldier's bargain."

When Akron translated, Kumi Okese stiffened and reached for the gold hilted sword at his waist. Jack put a hand on the butt of his revolver, knowing that if he shot this chief, the hundreds of Ashanti warriors would massacre him and his men. He held the Ashanti chief's glare, aware of the rising tension, and then Yaa Asantewaa spoke. Kumi Okese relaxed his grip on his sword, and Jack released the butt of his revolver.

"There is no need for killing, yet." Akron translated Yaa Asantewaa's words. "We need to hear what the British officer says."

"I will remind you," Jack strove to keep his voice calm although he could feel his heart racing, "that I am on a diplomatic meeting to ease our differences and free the hostages in Kumasi."

While Akron translated as quickly as before, Jack saw Yaa Asantewaa listening intently.

"There are no hostages in Kumasi." Kumi Okese was still on his feet, with his hand remaining close to the hilt of his sword. Around them, a score of Ashanti warriors waited to attack, while Sergeant Wickham and his men were equally prepared to fight.

Yaa Asantewaa spoke again, with Akron translating her words with genuine humility.

"Yaa Asantewaa says that neither she nor Kumi Okese has the authority to deal with such important matters." Akron nearly prostrated himself to the woman, hardly raising his eyes to meet her.

"You told me Yaa Asantewaa was of royal blood," Jack reminded, "and that Kumi Okese is the commander of this division of the army."

Akron turned mournful eyes on Jack. "They don't have the king's authority, Major."

"I can shoot them both, sir," Sergeant Wickham said softly. "Just give the order."

No; then they'll kill all of us. We have a mission here, Sergeant."

"They'll kill us all anyway."

"Don't fire, Sergeant. That's an order." Jack felt the tension rise further. He sensed that Wickham would willingly sacrifice his life to kill Kumi Okese. "Ground your rifle!"

Yaa Asantewaa spoke again, with Akron translating in a quiet tone. "Yaa Asantewaa said you have to go to Kumasi."

Jack started. "That's the Ashanti capital, right in the heart of Ashantiland. I am here to palaver with the commander of this army, not with the Asantahene."

Yaa Asantewaa listened to Akron's translation and gave a little smile. "You wished to discuss what you call the hostages, Major Windrush. We prefer to think of them as our guests."

"Discussing the hostages was one reason I am here," Jack agreed.

"Then you must come with us," Yaa Asantewaa said. "Our guests are in Kumasi, under the Asantahene's direct care."

"Will my men be safe?"

"If your men do not threaten us, then they will be safe." Yaa Asantewaa said, with Akron translating immediately.

Something in the woman's tone told Jack she could be trusted. "I am going nowhere until you give your assurance that my men and I will be permitted to return to Cape Coast Castle." Jack forced a smile. "I don't wish to add to the number of your guests in Kumasi."

Yaa Asantewaa nodded slowly. "If your men do not cause trouble in our land, they will not be harmed, and will return to the coast once your palaver is completed."

"Thank you," Jack said. "In that case, we are happy to accompany you to Kumasi."

Yaa Asantewaa lifted one finger. "Kumi Okese will take you." Moving with great dignity, she left Jack and his escort in the middle of the street, with her scarlet umbrella proud among the crowds. Kumi Okese and the white-striped Ashanti warriors stepped towards the Wests.

"We can fight! We can kill some of them," Wickham slid his hand closer to the trigger of his rifle.

"We'll accept the lady's word," Jack said. "Shoulder your rifles, lads."

"Don't trust them, sir," Wickham shouted as Kumi Okese yelled orders. A crowd of warriors closed on the Wests. Dozens of hands grabbed them, snatching their rifles and Jack's revolver.

"This wasn't part of the agreement!" Jack roared. "Tell them, Akron!" He saw Kumi Okese push Akron aside as the translator tried to speak.

"What the devil?" Jack thrust away a tall Ashanti who grabbed at his wrists, only for a warrior to pinion him from behind as a burly man fastened heavy metal shackles around his wrists.

"Thank you," Kumi Okese said.

"Thank you?" Jack lunged forward until a warrior cracked him over the head with a heavy stick. He winced, swung his manacles in the hope he might make contact and fell as two warriors pushed him to the ground. Within seconds, the same practised hands were snapping iron manacles around his ankles.

"Who the devil are you?" Jack glared at the burly man.

"He is a policeman," Akron spoke rapidly, his eyes wide. "He ensures the men don't run from battle and he looks after the prisoners."

Kumi Okese stared at Jack, his eyes smokier than ever. When he stalked away, two of his warriors hooked a stick through the shackles around Jack's wrists and hauled him upright. The Wests had been similarly treated and staggered behind the Ashantis, stumbling as they tried to keep their balance. The chains around their ankles clanked as they moved.

"We're slaves!" Wickham said in a tone of infinite horror. "The Ashantis have taken us as slaves!"

"Keep your head up, Sergeant!" Jack snapped. "You're a British soldier!"

"They'll sell us to the Arabs," Wickham said. "Or sacrifice us to one of their fetishes."

"They won't," Jack noticed that Manning appeared to be in shock, staring ahead of them without a word. "We're British soldiers. If we are maltreated, the British army will exact such revenge that the Ashantis will never recover."

I hope so, anyway. Not that it will help us much.

"We're the 2nd Wests!" Jack shouted. "Heads up, men! We'll get through this."

Akron appeared, wringing his hands. "I did not mean this to happen," he said. "I did not know."

"Tell Kumi Okese that he is foolish," Jack stumbled on the rough track. "Tell him that our queen will be displeased that the Ashantis are maltreating her subjects."

"I can't," Akron looked close to tears. "He is sending me away. I have to go with Yaa Asantewaa."

"Tell him!" Jack said, trying to kick out as the Ashanti policeman appeared, brandishing his whip.

"I can't!" Akron was near to tears as a press of warriors ushered him away.

"Tell him Queen Victoria will not be happy!" Jack's voice was lost in a roar of noise as the Ashantis surrounded the prisoners. The warriors pulled and pushed them onward, disregarding the shackles that rubbed the skin from their ankles and chafed their wrists.

"Thank you!" That phrase seemed to be the only English the Ashantis knew as they propelled the Wests along the track. "Thank you!"

Within an hour, Jack realised that even wearing shackles was torture that restricted movement and made every step painful. After two hours, he was breathing heavily, cursing the flies attracted to his raw flesh, and forcing himself to remain cheerful for the sake of his men.

"Keep your heads up, lads. We're the 2nd Wests. This situation won't last forever."

Jack was drooping with weariness when evening found them at a small village. Thrown into a filthy hut with his men, he checked their condition, thrust palm leaves between their wounds and the rusty iron manacles before he did the same for himself. The Ashanti policeman threw a mess of some vegetable stew onto the floor and watched dispassionately as the Wests scrambled to eat it.

"Officers first!" Sergeant Wickham roared.

"No," Jack shook his head. "Equal shares for all."

Unused to sharing with an officer, some of the men backed away.

"Come on, Daley," Jack urged. "You have to eat as well."

"It's not right," Daley said.

"It is right," Jack contradicted. "Eat, man."

Slowly, lying on their face in the filthy hut, the men took their share of the stew.

"Now sleep," Jack ordered. "We don't know what tomorrow will bring, so get whatever rest you can."

Lying on his side with the manacles biting into his flesh, Jack tried to sleep. He heard the rustling of rats in the hut, the clanking of iron every time one of his men moved, the stifled groans, and Coffin's quiet voice as he sang a psalm. *I can't help them. I'm their officer, and I've led them to humiliating captivity, perhaps slavery or worse. How can I make amends?*

Jack was not sure which was worse that night, the torment of the irons, the nibbling of the rats or the mental agony of knowing he had led his men into captivity. He lay as still as he could, aware he had made the only rational decision, and after a night of discomfort, rose bleary-eyed and unshaven to see two Ashantis at the door of the hut.

The warriors dragged Jack and the Wests outside and shoved them along the narrow forest path, with the brawny policeman slashing any who straggled with a hippopotamus hide whip.

"Keep moving men!" Jack swore as the whip curled around his shoulders. He stopped to stare at the policeman, remembering his broad face in case he ever had the opportunity to retaliate, however unlikely that seemed at present. When the man gestured with his whip, Jack turned away and limped after the others, dragging his feet with their heavy chains.

Every time they crossed a river, Jack and the Wests risked the whip to scoop up handfuls of water. Once, Manning delayed too long, and the policeman landed two heavy blows before Jack hustled him away. The Wests moved on, gasping with the heat, tormented by insects, drooping with exhaustion.

"We should have fought them," Wickham said.

"If we had, we'd all be dead now," Jack pointed out. "This way, we are alive and have a chance to survive."

"It's better to be dead than to be a slave of the Ashantis."

Jack did not reply to that. He kept moving, harbouring what strength he could. Each step was an ordeal, each hour seemed to stretch forever and the sun, green-tinged through the forest, beat on their heads with callous unconcern.

That second night, Jack and the Wests collapsed without thought into another hut. Heedless of the rats and other vermin, they slept, waking only when the burly policeman wielded his whip. The third day was worse than the second, and after that, life was only a torment of effort and pain until they reached the river.

"The Prah," Sergeant Wickham said. "Once we're over that, everything we see is Ashanti. No enemy army will dare to cross."

Jack nodded. The river was around seventy yards wide, hardly impressive, with the water sluggish and a dirty brown colour. "Don't give up, Sergeant."

With the police urging them on with their whips, the captives stepped into the river. Jack hoped there were no snakes or crocodiles, or whatever other predatory animal lived in this country. The Ashantis were all around, talking together, their faces devoid of pity or concern and the vertical white stripes somehow making them even fiercer.

The water was barely waist-deep, the current manageable, yet Jack felt he had crossed a significant barrier when he struggled up to the northern side of the Prah. Now he was in the territory of the Ashantis proper. Not even the most thrusting of British administrators could claim this land for the queen.

"Thank you." The policeman cracked his whip, pushing them on.

Wickham looked around him. "I've often dreamed of being in this land, but not as a slave."

"You've dreamed of this, Sergeant?" Jack asked. "Why?"

Wickham looked away. "Not as a slave," he repeated in a whisper.

"We're prisoners, not slaves," Jack said. "Colonel Festing will already be negotiating our release." He thought of the missionaries, held for years, and wondered what Mary was thinking. *Do the British even know we are prisoners? Or does General Hook think I am engaged in a long palaver with Amanquatia?*

Once across the Prah, the forest became denser, if anything, although the Ashantis relaxed a little. Kumi Okese visited the prisoners, prodding at them as he spoke to his warriors.

"What will happen to us?" Daley asked.

"I don't know, Daley," Jack said.

"Keep faith in the Lord," Coffin said. "He will get us through this."

"We're British soldiers," Ogston reminded. "We defeated Bonaparte at Waterloo. We can defeat the Ashanti Empire as well."

Jack felt a surge of pride for his Wests. "Well said, Ogston. We're British soldiers. Keep your heads up!"

After days of toil, the country altered, rising into a series of hills. Walking along the level was hard, walking up a slope was nearly impossible, particularly since the Ashanti road thrust in a straight line, whatever the gradient. Jack and the Wests, taking tiny steps with the constraints of the shackles, constantly under attack by flying insects, inched their way up the slope, gasping.

"Thank you!" The policeman plied his whip as young Private Manning collapsed.

"Leave him alone!" Jack snarled.

"Leave him!" Ogston stood over Manning, glaring defiantly at the policeman.

"Come on, Ogston, help me here!" Taking one of Manning's arms, Jack hauled him upright, gasping as the whip slashed across his back. "You'd better be careful, my man," he said to the policeman. "Once I'm free of this, I'll be coming for you."

Helping each other, dragging young Manning behind them, the prisoners ascended the hill, to find a much gentler slope descending northward, and then another steep hill rising behind.

"Keep going, Wests," Jack said, although his legs felt like rubber and his heart was thundering within his chest.

A crowd of warriors surrounded them, prodding with the barrels of their muskets, laughing, jeering.

"We're slaves," Sergeant Wickham said again. "You've led us into slavery, Major Windrush!"

"Keep your discipline, Sergeant!" Jack snapped, although he could understand Wickham's point of view. *I've failed these men. They trusted me, and I've failed them.*

Moving more slowly by the hour, the prisoners dragged themselves up the next hill, and then Manning dropped again.

"I can't go on, sir."

"You must," Jack said. "The Ashantis will kill you."

"Let them." Manning's face was grey with fatigue. He shook his head. "Leave me."

"No." Jack looked upwards, where the path cut directly upward. "I'll carry you."

"We'll carry you," Ogston corrected.

"No." Manning shook his head.

Working together, Jack and Ogston lifted Manning and carried on, fighting the slope, with their muscles screaming at every step. They reached the summit with the blood seeping over the shackles on Jack's ankles and Manning's weight pressing down on him.

"There are no more hills, lads," Jack was hardly aware of the sweat beading on his forehead and soaking through his uniform jacket. The Ashanti warriors stopped, with one man pressing the muzzle of his musket at the base of Jack's spine, shouting something that Jack took as an order to halt. A pleasant breeze up here kept the insects away and cooled the Wests, while a short distance away, a scarlet umbrella told Jack there was another group of Ashantis.

Lying on the ground, Jack wondered if he could walk any more. Between the ache of his muscles and the agony of his torn ankles, every step was a nightmare. He looked around. They were in a small clearing, with a group of three trees together, hung with low creepers. Behind them, the path undulated downwards toward the distant and unseen coast. In front was a deep forest, mostly hidden beneath a thin mist, through which forested hill-crests protruded like islands in a grey-green sea.

I'm in the heart of Ashanti-land, Jack said to himself. *As dark and mysterious as anywhere I have ever been.*

"Cheer up, lads," Jack croaked through a thirst-parched throat. "That's the hills behind us now. Better days ahead."

When three people left the shade of the scarlet umbrella, the warriors stepped aside to leave a distinct passage to the Wests. Yaa Asantewaa had returned, walking with dignity through the warriors, who reversed their muskets as a sign of peace and respect.

When Yaa came closer to Jack, speaking rapidly, Kumi Okese stood in her path. Yaa pushed him aside, evidently angry, and Kumi Okese reached for his knife.

For a second, Jack thought there would be a stabbing, until Yaa yelled at Kumi Okese, adding a full-blooded slap on the face, which resounded around the clearing. The Ashanti war captain recoiled, his eyes wild and murder in his face until Yaa's sharp order brought two policemen from the mass.

Yaa pointed to Jack's shackles and spoke sharply. The broad-faced policeman produced a key and opened the manacles around Jack's wrists, then the shackles on his ankles. When the policeman made to step away again, Jack shook his head and grabbed the man around the wrist.

"No," Jack said. "Free my men as well."

The policeman looked at Jack in total incomprehension. Pointing to his men, Jack repeated his words louder, wishing he had even a few words of the local language. Tempted to ask Wickham, he bit back the order, knowing the sergeant wanted to hide his knowledge of Ashanti.

As the policeman reached for the knife at his belt, Yaa stepped forward, gesturing behind her. Akron hurried through the ranked warriors, his eyes worried. Yaa spoke sharply, pointed to Kumi Okese and then to the West Indians.

"Yaa Asantewaa wishes to know what you said, Major Windrush."

"Tell Yaa that I want my men freed. They are British soldiers, not slaves. They are my escort on a diplomatic mission, and I demand that the Ashanti treat them with respect!"

Yaa spoke to Jack and gave a sharp order.

Akron translated. "Yaa Asantewaa said she did not wish you to be shackled. Now you will all be released."

The policeman immediately released their shackles, smiling obsequiously.

Jack stood, rubbing his ankles. As soon as his men were freed, he stepped up to the policeman and threw an uppercut. It was not the best punch he had ever landed, but Jack could think of few that had afforded him so much satisfaction. The policeman staggered back, astonished, with a hand to his jaw and murder in his eyes.

Although Yaa Asantewaa watched without saying a word, Jack suspected he saw a glint of humour in her eyes. He bowed to Yaa. "Thank you, Ma'am," he said. "I will return the favour if I ever have the opportunity."

Without a word or change in her expression, Yaa gave another order, turned around and walked to her umbrella. A moment later, three stony-faced Ashanti warriors brought fruit to the prisoners.

"I said things would get easier," Jack said as they began to move again, with Yaa's scarlet umbrella in front and Kumi Okese's yellow a hundred yards in the rear. Putting an arm around Manning, he helped him along the track.

"It's not right," Manning said. "You're an officer."

"We're all British soldiers," Jack checked his men. They looked more alert, watching the guards as they kept together. Only Sergeant Wickham walked apart, with his shoulders erect as befitted a soldier but his eyes fixed on the scarlet umbrella.

CHAPTER NINE

Kumasi July 1873

They heard the noise from nearly a mile away, a cacophony of horns, drums and human voices raised in either welcome or defiance, Jack was not sure which.

"They must know the 2nd Wests are coming," Jack said as Daley and Stair started. "They've never met such soldiers. Heads up, lads!"

"They're going to surrender to us." Manning's joke was feeble but welcome. He had recovered quicker than Jack had expected.

"That's what it must be," Stair agreed.

Akron approached them, with a body of slaves. "You must change."

"Change?" Jack looked at his much stained and battered uniform. "I have no other clothes."

Akron snapped an order, and the slaves hurried away, to return with the baggage Jack had thought long lost. "Well, that's a cheering sight." He noticed Yaa Asantewaa watching, stony-faced as he changed. Only when Jack was in his best uniform did Yaa walk away.

"Yaa Asantewaa wanted to see if white men were different from Ashanti men," Akron said. "We are approaching Kumasi."

A few moments later, they moved on, with the noise increasing with every yard. As they splashed through a shallow swamp, they saw a slope rising ahead, with a scattering of trees.

Coffin glanced upward. Two tall poles soared upward with the body of a dead goat suspended between them, wrapped in red cloth. "Good Lord, preserve us."

"What's that?" Jack asked.

"It's a fetish," Sergeant Wickham said. "The people worship such things either because it is magical, like a god, or because they believe a spirit lives inside it."

Jack raised his eyebrows without saying anything. He was familiar with the deities of the Indian sub-continent, but this was different from anything he had encountered before. *I am glad Mary is not here to witness such things.*

"And those," Wickham pointed to a pair of human skeletons, tied to the top of two separate trees. "Those men were slaves. The king must have ordered them fastened to the trees to die of starvation."

"Why?" Jack asked.

Wickham shrugged. "The Ashanti priests would study their deaths to work out the outcome of the war."

Jack grunted. "It makes our gipsy fortune tellers look innocent."

The noise rose to a frenzy as thousands of people banged drums, blew horns, shook rattles and clanged gongs. The instant Yaa Asantewaa entered Kumasi, scores of warriors added to the commotion by firing muskets into the air.

Thick powder-smoke and the dense crowd prevented Jack from seeing much of the town, although he noted a broad street of well-built houses before the mob rushed towards him.

"What the devil is this?" Jack asked as a group of colourfully-dressed men approached, amidst a riot of colourful flags, with the Union flag beside that of the Netherlands and Denmark. As the incoming column wound through the main street, the men within the flags began to dance.

"Those are the war captains welcoming Yaa Asantewaa back into Kumasi," Akron spoke with pride.

"I've never seen anything quite like them before," Jack said.

Like Kumi Okese, the war captains wore caps adorned with gilded ram's horns that thrust out from their heads, while plumes of eagles' feathers waved sideways above each ear. From waist to neck they wore a jacket of red cloth, adorned with dozens of objects that must have been sacred fetishes, while embroidered boxes rattled against their chests as they threw themselves around in wild dancing. Brass bells, animal horns, shells and cow tails completed their decoration in front, while behind, a profusion of leopard tails bounced in time with their movements. Below the waist, their cotton trousers ended at tall boots of red leather covered in shells and more brass bells.

Jack wondered if the captains wore such finery when they fought in the forest. He hoped so, for British soldiers could find them distinctive targets.

The bearer of a yellow and green flag waved it over the heads of the warriors as they fired a welcoming volley. When the muzzle flares set light to the flag, the bearer dropped it immediately, with a dozen sandaled feet eagerly stamping out the flames. "Nicely done," Jack approved as the procession continued. Surrounded by thousands of people, Jack still could not make out details of Kumasi, except to see the houses were large, with palm-leaf thatch.

More umbrellas appeared, some of them huge, rising and falling in time with the band, making an incredible spectacle as the sun reflected from the ornamental figurine on top of each umbrella. Some were animals; others abstract shapes without apparent meaning.

After ten minutes of walking through the crowd, the drums altered their beat to a slow rhythm.

"The drums are talking to us," Akron said.

"Talking to us?" Jack repeated.

"Yes, Major," Akron spoke with pride. "The drums send messages as fast as your telegrams, and more efficiently."

"You have an interesting culture," Jack said. "What are the drums saying?"

"They say that the king is coming. The Asantahene," Akron sounded awed. "There's King Kofi. He's under the black and red umbrella."

Jack squinted up the street, where the sun reflected from what he thought was a massive mirror.

"That's the king," Akron said.

As Jack's party moved through the crowd, Jack realised that his imagined mirror was the sun reflecting from a mass of gold ornaments that every man around the king wore.

"What do you think, Major Windrush? Is the Asantahene not the most majestic of kings," Akron asked, "with the most dignified of noblemen?"

Sitting under his red-and-black umbrella, the king was half-hidden, although the ministers and nobles around him were prominent.

"He is undoubtedly the finest king I have ever seen," Jack said solemnly. "Tell me, who are these people, these gold-encrusted noblemen, around the king?"

Akron looked pleased to educate Jack. "The tall man is the chamberlain, a very important personage. The man with the golden horn in the Gold Horn-Blower and, beside him is the Captain of the Messengers."

Jack tried to concentrate through the cacophony of horns and bells, with the hammer of drums a constant distraction. Anything he learned about the Ashantis might be useful in the forthcoming campaign if he managed to return to Cape Coast Castle before the Ashantis killed him.

Akron was still talking. "The Captain of the Messengers makes sure the drummers send the right messages." He gave a small laugh. "After all, it would not do to say the Asantahene was coming when all the time it was a British army at the sacred Prah River."

"No, indeed," Jack snatched at the words. "Is the Prah sacred?"

Akron gave a solemn nod. "Some say it is the outer border of our Empire. Sixteen years ago the British Governor Benjamin Pine failed to take his army across the Prah."

"Why was that?" Jack asked.

"Our priests cast a spell on him. He became confused and ran in circles before throwing away all his supplies and fleeing back to Cape Coast Castle."

"Ah," Jack said.

"No British Army will ever cross the Prah," Akron boasted. He continued, shouting above the discordant medley of sounds. "That gentleman there, the fellow with the golden wristband, he is the Captain for Royal Executions."

"That's an interesting title," Jack said. "I'll try to keep on his good side."

"And that gentleman," Akron was positively glowing with enthusiasm as he indicated a massively muscled man who sported an impressively large golden hatchet on his chest. "That gentleman is the Royal Executioner."

Remembering a similar man in Jayanti's realm in India, Jack repressed his shudder. However impressive and dignified a monarch, there was always an iron fist beneath the velvet glove. The gleam of gold could not hide the sinister threat of the hatchet.

As Akron continued to list the Asantahene's officials, Jack realised that the Asantahene's officials were men of responsibility and this kingdom was organised with some skill, indeed better than many European nations. Ashantiland was far more than a grouping of iron-age forest tribes, as he had imagined, but a sophisticated and complex society. He looked up as Akron raised his voice in excitement.

"There are the Linguists, Major Windrush! See? The Asantahene's Linguists!"

Three men sat under yet another splendid umbrella with a bundle of golden rods in front of them.

"Linguists? Are you not one of the king's Linguists?"

"I am not," Akron spoke in hushed tones. "The Linguists are the men who can bridge the gap between the dead and the living."

Jack nodded. "They are a sort of priest, then?"

"Yes. The Linguists have great powers." Akron looked away as one of the Linguists glanced in his direction.

"And you, Akron," Jack said quickly, aware that King Kofi was coming closer. "What are you?"

"A humble translator," Akron said.

The Asantahene was looking at them. The scarlet umbrella was no longer moving.

"Did King Kofi send you to spy on us?" Jack asked quickly.

"I am an interpreter," Akron said.

While the king waited under his umbrella, Jack realised that a troop of muscular slaves carried the king in an ornate cradle, like the body of a coach. The slaves looked sleek and well cared for, while leopard-skin and red velvet lined the cradle. The king wore a long leopard-skin cloak, with a necklace of silver bullets.

"Why is the necklace only silver and not gold?" Jack asked softly.

"The bullets are a sign the nation is at war," Akron said. "Please don't talk any more, Major, unless at the Asantahene's request."

A body of chiefs or sub-kings stepped clear of their crimson hammocks and approached the Asantahene, each chief with his bodyguard of captains, each with a gold-handled sword.

Jack estimated King Kofi at around 40 years old, sitting in great dignity with a thin gold band around his head and the silver bullets prominent around his neck. Beside the king was a tall man holding a sword with a gold handle, and then one of the nobles stepped in front, blocking Jack's vision.

Shift, damn you, Jack said to himself, but the moment was passed.

Behind the king, a group of royal females was also present. Slender women with a dignity equal to the king's and with necklaces of fine gold, they looked over the assembly with calm eyes, ignored Jack and the 2nd West entirely and spoke only to each other.

The king lifted a single finger towards Akron, who approached immediately. When the king pointed to Jack and the West Indians, Akron launched into a long speech, evidently explaining who Jack was and his purpose in Kumasi. King Kofi lifted his hand, and Akron returned. The King gave a soft order, and a few moments later, a body of Kumi Okese's white striped warriors separated Jack from his men.

"Keep your heads up, lads!" Jack shouted as the warriors hustled him down the street, with the crowd parting before them.

"Yes, sir!" That was Private Coffin. "The Lord will look after us!"

Glancing over his shoulder, Jack saw Wickham call his men to attention as a company of warriors escorted them in the opposite direction. "Good luck, 2nd Wests!" Jack shouted, and then his escort pushed him inside one of the large houses. A warrior cracked him over the head with a musket butt, another poked him in the back, and he sprawled on the floor.

CHAPTER TEN

Kumasi July 1873

Jack's first impression was of a large open chamber, with a tall Ashanti warrior staring down at him, and then Kumi Okese stepped close, with Akron at his side.

"These are Kumi Okese's words, Major Windrush, not mine," Akron sounded almost apologetic.

"Just translate honestly," Jack rose to his feet, dusting himself down. When two white-striped warriors levelled their muskets, Kumi Okese gestured them back.

"Kumi says that if it were up to him, he would decapitate you right away and decorate the walls of his house with your head," Akron said. "You are fortunate that the king wishes you to live."

Jack nodded. "Tell Kumi Okese that I appreciate the kindness of the Asantahene and his loyalty to the king's wishes."

Kumi Okese glowered at Jack as Akron translated the words.

"Kumi Okese says that if you try to escape, he will personally cut off your head."

Jack forced a smile. "Tell Kumi Okese that if he chooses to disregard the wishes of the Asantahene, that is his choice. Tell him that my sovereign Queen Victoria, expects her subjects to be well treated and will be displeased if you abuse my men or me."

When Akron passed the message, Kumi Okese touched one hand to the gold hilt of his sword, leaned closer to Jack and stormed from the house. The two warriors took hold of Jack, dragged him from the front room into a back chamber and tied him to a bolt on the wall. Landing a few parting kicks, the warriors left Jack lying on the ground and walked away.

"Don't you harm my men!" Jack shouted, knowing the Ashantis would not understand his words. He struggled with his bonds, while a single rat emerged from a corner of the room to explore his feet. Outside the house, the singing, intermittent musket shots, blaring of horns and the constant thunder of the drums continued. Jack knew that for the remainder of his life, he would remember these Ashanti drums.

* * *

Jack did not know how much time passed as he lay in the gloomy hut. The drumming died away and stopped, rats explored his legs, and the light faded. He tried to sleep, dozed fitfully, fought the cords around his wrist and worried about his men. It might have been ten hours or two days when somebody entered his room.

Jack looked up. "What's happening?"

Akron looked nervous as he unfastened Jack's bonds. "Get up slowly, Major Windrush. You have a visitor."

Kumi Okese was wearing the full ceremonial clothes of an Ashanti war captain, from the cap and feathers to the baggy red trousers and gold-hilted sword. A group of warriors had followed him into Jack's room.

"Kumi Okese wishes you to watch the ceremony," Akron said.

"Which ceremony is it this time?" Jack heard the blowing of horns and the inevitable tapping of drums.

"The British killed one of the king's nephews during the battle outside Elmina," Akron reminded. "And four chiefs. This ceremony is for one of the chiefs to ensure he has slaves to look after him in the afterlife."

"Oh?" Jack did not resist when three stalwart Ashantis dragged him to a front room and held him secure, with one clamping a firm hand across his jaw. It was the first time Jack could see the street in its entirety, with elegant substantial houses with palm-thatched roofs, stately banyan trees for shade and cleanliness that would do credit to any town in Europe.

Growling something, Kumi Okese stalked away, with his eagle feathers bouncing beside his head and his sword hanging from his waist. Akron remained in the room, although he kept his distance from the warriors.

Hundreds of people filled the street, children, women and men of every rank from the lowest to the royal officials. The Ashanti nobles were dressed in their finery as they gathered, with their followers and warriors surrounding them. Both men and women wore bright costumes, talking animatedly as if on some public holiday. Remembering the starvation in Cape Coast, Jack pondered on the difference between the flamboyance of the aggressor and misery of the victims.

"You see," Akron spoke as if three men were not holding Jack rigid, "when people enter the next world, they retain the same rank they did in this one. That means that a king will be a king, and a slave will still be a slave, and a king will need his wives and slaves to look after him."

"Ah,"' Jack nodded as best he could. "That's interesting." He remembered the Islamic belief that when a man died a martyr, seventy-two virgins and a palace awaited him in paradise, while the ancient Norse thought they would ascend to Valhalla, a place of feasting and battle. Every religion had its beliefs and traditions. Jack watched as the nobles drank from a gourd, pointed their muskets upwards and fired a volley, to the delight of the crowd. White smoke coiled around the street. After a few moments, the nobles moved to the next house and repeated the whole drinking and firing procedure.

"This is a sign of respect for the dead man," Akron said. "They are only firing powder, not ball ammunition."

The nobles continued along the main street, drinking and firing in front of each house. With so much beer consumed, the warriors became increasingly inebriated so that Jack wondered if somebody might load with ball and kill one of the bystanders. *If I'm lucky, they'll blow Kumi Okese's head right off his shoulders.*

When they reached a house diagonally opposite to Jack's, the procession halted, with the gun smoke slowly lifting. Four drummers walked slowly down the street, each leading a burly man with a large black cap. The drummers beat a slow, sinister rhythm that Jack guessed was the precursor of something more extreme than a drunken celebration. When the black-capped men joined the head of the procession, they spoke together for a few moments before moving into the crowd.

"They are the executioners," Akron said. "They're searching for the correct people to accompany the king's nephew into the next world."

"I see," Jack said. "Does that mean they're going to find people to murder?"

"Those the executioners choose are called the ochres of the deceased," Akron spoke in hushed tones, as befitted a funeral.

Jack struggled with the warriors holding him. "Can you get these lads to let go of me? I'm not going anywhere."

After a few words from Akron, the warriors released Jack and moved aside, although they still watched him from the corner of their eyes.

"Do the executions know who they are choosing?" Jack asked. "Or is it a random selection?"

"I don't know," Akron said. "They will choose which slaves they think best for the dead chiefs."

The crowd's chatter rose when the executioners dragged out a struggling young man. The executioners tied their victims' arms behind him, with the crowd watching in tense excitement. The youngster protested violently, screaming for help until one of the executioners thrust a knife through his face, in the right cheek and out the left. War-hardened though he was, Jack could not repress a shudder of horror as the executioner added a second knife in the right cheek, pushing it right through until it came out the left, with bright blood flowing from the ochre's face.

"Oh, dear God," Jack said as the crowd watched in apparent approval, with a few horns blaring against the constant hammer of the drums.

Working slowly, the executioners looped the youngster's lips over the point of each knife, then cut off his left ear and carried it, dripping blood, in front of him. A second executioner slashed at the ochre's right ear but failed to sever it, so it hung on a flap of skin.

As Jack watched in sick horror, one of the executions bored a hole through the ochre's nose, passed a thin cord through and pulled him along, while others pushed a long blade under each of his shoulder blades and, seemingly at random, slashed his back.

"Is this part of the ceremony?" Jack asked.

Akron nodded, seemingly unable to look away from the ongoing horror. "Yes, Major Windrush."

The executioners found a second man, and a third and then a woman, until a row of prisoners, male and female, stood, bound, knife-gagged and bleeding in the centre of the street. The crowd shouted at them, some jeering or making loud comments. When Jack tried to look away, two of the Ashanti warriors took hold of him, forcing him to watch every second.

After a few moments, the executioners grabbed the nearest ochre and, to the intense interest of the crowd, forced him to his knees. While one man held him, another lifted his large, clumsy-looking sword, and hacked at the victim's neck. Although he must have had a good deal of experience, the executioner took three attempts to remove the man's head. The struggles of the second victim proved unavailing as two of the executioners held him secure while a third wielded the sword.

"Dear God in heaven," Jack said. He noted that his Ashanti guards watched avidly.

"It's a sign of respect for the deceased," Akron explained, without diverting his gaze from the executions. "The higher the rank, the more slaves should accompany them. It would be very disrespectful not to provide slaves for the afterlife."

"There appear to be hundreds of slaves in Kumasi. Where do they come from?" Jack was grateful for anything that provided a diversion from the executions.

"The slave market," Akron sounded surprised that Jack should ask such a question.

"Who brings them there?" Jack pressed further. "Are they criminals to be made into slaves?"

"The army captures them, Major Windrush," Akron said. "The Ashanti raid all around for slaves to ensure a ready supply for work and sacrifice." He paused for a moment. "Unlike your terrible societies, men here are not born into slavery."

Jack made no reply. *Akron has confirmed what we thought. No wonder the Fanti are afraid of the Ashanti.* He looked up as Kumi Okese strode into view, with half a dozen of his striped warriors at his back. Kumi Okese stared deliberately at Jack before clapping his hands and giving a rapid order. Jack felt Akron stiffen at his side.

"What's happening, Akron."

"Nothing," Akron's voice was strained. "It would be best if you closed your eyes, Major Windrush." When Akron said something to the warriors, they again gripped Jack.

"What's happening, damn you?" Rather than withdraw, Jack stepped forward. "What did Kumi Okese say?"

"Look away, Major Windrush," Akron pleaded. "Look away."

The crowd shifted, looking up the street as the executioners trotted away. Umbrellas rose and twirled, with people talking in high, excited tones until the executioners returned, dragging another victim with them.

"That's one of my men," Jack saw the West's uniform. "Oh, dear God," Jack said as the executioners hauled Private Manning to Kumi Okese. Jack raised his voice to a shout. "Leave that man alone! He's a British soldier, damn your murdering hides! He's escorting a diplomatic mission." Jack struggled to escape his guards. "Tell them, Akron. For God's sake, tell them they can't murder a British soldier."

With the sweat running down his face, Akron shook his head. "I dare not."

"You dare not? That's Stanley Manning! That's one of my men!" Jack scraped his nailed boots down the shin of a guard and broke free when the man yelled and jerked backwards. Taken by surprise, the second warrior's lunge was ineffective, and Jack leapt for the door, only for the third guard to crack the hilt of his knife over Jack's head, temporarily stunning him. Jack fell swearing.

Grabbing him, the guards dragged Jack back to the window, forcing him to watch. Two executioners held the struggling Private Manning.

"Manning!" Jack shouted. "Stanley! We are the 2nd Wests!"

For a second Private Manning looked up. "2nd Wests!" He saw Jack at the window. "God save the queen!"

"Good man," Jack whispered. "Good man indeed." He straightened to attention as two executioners thrust Manning onto his knees and a third poised his sword. "Make it quick," Jack said softly. "Please, God, make it quick."

Mercifully, the executioner swung his sword. Private Manning's head sprung from his body to roll on the ground and lie, eyes open, staring at the impassive Kumi Okese. Jack's guards relaxed their grip, stepping back now the entertainment had finished.

"You're a murdering hound Kumi Okese," Jack shouted into the sudden hush. "Tell him, Akron, tell Kumi that he's a dirty murdering hound and I'll see him dead for murdering one of my men."

"I dare not."

Grabbing Akron by the front of his robe, Jack crashed him against the wall of the house. "Tell him, Akron, or by the living God I'll kill you here and now."

The guards hauled Jack roughly away, shouting at him as they rammed him against the window.

"Kumi Okese!" Jack roared. "You murdering bastard! Come here and fight me!"

When Kumi looked over, Jack was sure he had a faint smile on his face. He looked directly at Jack, said something to the executioner and lifted Private Manning's head by the hair before striding to Jack's house.

"Come here, Kumi Okese!" The guards stopped Jack's lunge for the door, holding him secure as Kumi Okese stepped inside, still with Manning's dripping head hanging from his fingers. "You're a dirty murdering hound!" Jack said. "Translate, Akron, tell the bastard what I think of him."

"I am sure he can tell what you think of him," Akron said.

"Tell him anyway!" Jack shouted. "He murdered one of my men!"

As Akron spoke a few halting phrases, Kumi Okese stepped closer to Jack, and Akron translated again.

"You are alive only because the Asantahene wishes it, Major Windrush. When the Asantahene tires of you…" Kumi Okese did not need to complete the sentence. The head he deposited at Jack's feet was completion enough.

Jack grunted. "Your time will come, Kumi, I promise you that." He prodded Akron. "Tell him what I said."

Looking at his feet, Akron said something, and Kumi Okese gave a short, barking laugh. "If you try to leave Kumasi," Kumi Okese spoke through Akron. "I will hand all your soldiers to the executioners." He stalked away, with his warriors and Akron at his heels, leaving Jack alone in the house.

Across the road, the executioners lifted what was left of Private Manning and threw him with the other bodies. Already the vultures were busy, their beaks tearing at the eyes and bellies of the dead.

"I'm not leaving you there," Jack spoke to himself as he stalked outside, ignoring the dissipating crowd. "Come on, Stanley," he lifted Manning's head. "I can't do much for you except give you a decent burial." Walking over to the pile of bodies, Jack lifted Manning, balanced him over his back and carried him to the outskirts of the town, holding the head under his arm. A squad of Ashanti warriors followed, muskets ready in case Jack tried to escape.

The earth beside the marsh was sufficiently soft for Jack to scrape a hole with his hands, with the Ashantis watching him curiously. Knowing they would not kill him without the king's permission, Jack turned his back and continued to dig. He looked up in surprise when a little girl joined him, delving into the earth with a small hoe.

"Thank you," Jack gave what he hoped was a smile.

"Are you digging a grave?" The girl spoke in nearly perfect English, albeit with an accent Jack had never heard before.

"Yes," Jack said. "For my friend."

"I'll help." The girl was on her hands and knees, digging energetically.

"Where did you learn to speak English?" Jack could not hide his surprise.

"Mrs Ramsayer taught me," the girl said. "Is that deep enough?"

"It is," Jack looked at the hole. It was only a shallow pit, but better than nothing.

Carrying Private Manning over, Jack laid the body down and placed the head where it belonged. When he began to push back the earth, the little girl joined in.

"Are you going to say a prayer?"

Jack stared at her. "Did Mrs Ramsayer teach you about prayers as well?"

"Yes." The girl waited for Jack's reply.

"I'm not very good with prayers." Jack had seen soldiers buried from Burma to Berwick and from Canada to the Crimea. Each death was a personal tragedy, yet he felt worse over Private Manning's murder than any of the others.

"I know some," the girl said.

"I am sure Stanley would appreciate that," Jack said.

"Was that his name?" The girl did not look disturbed about the presence of a corpse. Living in Kumasi, Jack reasoned, had probably conditioned her to such sights. "My name is Abena." The girl stood beside the grave, closed her eyes and bowed her head. "Go with God, Stanley and Jesus will take you in his arms; Amen." She opened her eyes. "How was that?"

"You did very well," Jack said. "Thank you, Abena." He looked up as a sharp female voice sounded from the outskirts of Kumasi.

"Abena! What are you doing here?"

CHAPTER ELEVEN

Kumasi July-Aug 1873

"I am sorry if Abena is causing you concern." The woman was blonde and too sun-bronzed to be even remotely fashionable, while her clothing was patched beyond recognition. Jack could not begin to guess her age.

"Abena is helping me," Jack said. "You must be Mrs Ramsayer."

"I am Elda Becker." The newcomer said, slightly coolly, Jack thought. "Abena! Off you go!"

"Yes, Miss Becker!" Giving a small curtsey, Abena scampered away.

"I am sorry about the death of your soldier," Elda said. "The execution ceremony was not an edifying sight, was it?"

"It was repulsive," Jack said.

Elda nodded. "Not all the Ashanti culture is like that. They are very advanced in other matters. I won't give up trying to change them." Her smile was unexpected. "You are Major Windrush, aren't you?"

"Major Jack Windrush, 113th Foot, attached to the 2nd West India Regiment, at your service, madam." Jack gave a polite bow. "I am sorry to see a woman in such circumstances."

Elda's accent was heavily German. "The Lord sent me here for a purpose, Major. I am alive, as are you, unlike these poor unfortunate people we saw killed today."

"That is true," Jack said. "May I ask how the Ashantis are treating you?"

"Tolerably well, Major," Elda said, then looked away. "Most of the Ashantis are kind, despite the executions and there is one man who helps me." She lifted her chin as if expecting Jack to criticise her.

Jack nodded. "It is good to have a friend in a strange place."

Elda gave a small smile. "Not everybody would agree with my choice of friends, Major. His ideas are different from those in Europe." Again, she lifted her chin.

Jack did not take the bait. "I hope he can keep you safe after you while you are here."

"I also hope that," Elda said. "What brought you to Kumasi, Major?"

"My original mission was to try and gain your release." Jack gave a wry smile. "I did not expect to become a hostage myself."

"Man proposes," Elda said, "but the Lord disposes. Are the authorities in Cape Coast Castle in touch with the Asantahene?"

Jack patted her arm. "Now don't you fret, the Ashantis have attacked the British at Elmina and are threatening Cape Coast Castle. That's a declaration of war if I ever heard one so we could see a British army marching through Kumasi before long."

"You haven't seen the power of the Ashantis," Elda said. "You have not seen the number of men they can muster, or how they fight. They're unbeatable in the forest."

"They have never met British infantry," Jack tried to calm her down.

"You can't beat them," Elda repeated.

"I've had my share of forest fighting," Jack said. "In Burma and India. The British soldier is the most adaptable in the world." He tried to sound confident.

"Are you going back into Kumasi?" Elda asked.

"Soon. I'll put a cross on Private Manning's grave first." Jack looked at the human skeletons on the tree nearby. "It will give him some protection."

Elda nodded. "He's in the Lord's hands now. The Ashanti won't allow a cross to remain."

"I'll know I've placed it," Jack said, "and so will Manning." *Mary would wish me to*, Jack told himself. Why was it that he always felt more religious when in these terrible places, yet when he was back in safety, he rarely attended church? The old seaman on *Lady Luck* was right, there were no atheists in a storm, either in a storm of waves at sea, or a storm of blood and horror in this forest.

At least Mary was safe. She might even be home now, back in Herefordshire or Berwick, with David, unaware of the troubles her husband was enduring.

The Ashanti warriors watched as Jack made a simple cross out of two tree branches, and then, shouting, they grabbed him.

"I'll look for you, Elda," Jack said as the warriors hustled him back to Kumasi. "Don't give up hope."

The warriors half guided, half dragged Jack to a small house in a side street, where they threw him into the front room and left him there.

* * *

"This is the man," Abena's small voice sounded in Jack's ear. "He's a soldier."

Jack looked up to see a circle of people around him. One elderly, bearded man helped him to his feet.

"You are welcome to our house," the elderly man said in a thick German accent. "Although the Lord knows we have little to offer in the way of hospitality."

"The fact you are here is sufficient," Jack said. "I am Major Jack Windrush, 113th Foot, temporarily attached to the 2nd West India Regiment. You must be the missionary hostages."

"Yes." The elderly man nodded. "I am Mr Kuhne, one of the Basle missionaries." He seemed eager to speak. "Are you here with good news? Are the British trying to release us from this dreadful place?"

"The British are aware of your plight," Jack said. "I was sent to try and persuade

King Kofi to release you." He looked down at himself. "I was not very successful, as you see."

"We are the Ramseyers," a calm-eyed man said, gesturing to his wife and the two children who stared, wide-eyed, at Jack. "There is also a Frenchman named Bonnet. The Ashantis hold him in a different house."

"I didn't know about the Frenchman," Jack said.

The missionaries glanced at each other before Mrs Ramseyer spoke. "He was a gun dealer," she said. "He was bringing the Ashantis a consignment of muskets when they seized him and his guns."

Jack grunted. "I've no time for gunrunners," he said, "but it seems like the Ashantis have killed the goose that lays the golden eggs."

The missionaries crowded around, asking a dozen questions about the latest developments on the Gold Coast. They all looked haggard, with shaded eyes and lined faces. Jack could only guess what horrors they had witnessed in their years of confinement, never sure when the Ashantis might decide to sacrifice them.

"Major Windrush, will the British come to rescue us?" Mr Kuhne stroked Jack's uniform jacket as if it were a talisman.

"Soon," Jack said. "They will be here soon. General Wolseley, one of the best generals in the army, is coming to Africa, and reinforcements are already at sea. Once they arrive, General Wolseley will be in a better position to pursue the war. Hold on to your faith; only a few more months."

Mrs Ramseyer could not hold back her tears. "A few more months!"

When Mr Ramseyer put an arm around her, speaking in German, Jack turned away. "Does Elda Becker also live here?"

"No." Kuhne was almost abrupt. "She lives elsewhere."

The missionaries glanced at each other. "We don't like to discuss Elda Becker," Mr Kuhne said quietly. "She is different from us."

"Are you not all Christian?" Jack asked.

"We are." Mrs Ramseyer put her arm around Abena. "I am not sure if Miss Becker is."

Jack nodded without understanding. "All right," he said. "I have no intention of waiting here to be executed, or for a British army to maybe come sometime. We seem to have an element of freedom. Are we allowed to go into the streets? Or are we shot on sight?"

"We have freedom," Kuhne said, "as long as we don't leave Kumasi."

"How are they treating you apart from that?" Jack asked.

"Well enough by their lights," Kuhne said. "The king allows us a monthly allowance of gold dust to buy food, while the mission at the Gold Coast sends us money and clothes from time to time."

Jack nodded. When he first heard about the hostages, he imagined much worse confinement with chains and tiny cells. "When I get back, I'll let the people in Cape Coast know."

Kuhne shook his head. "The Ashantis won't let you go, Major. They will detain you here for years."

Jack grunted. "Perhaps. Do any of you know where the Ashantis hold my men?"

"I do," Abena held up her hand like a schoolgirl.

Jack smiled. "I thought you might, Abena. Can you take me there without getting into trouble?"

"Yes!" Abena seemed pleased to help.

"Come on, then." Jack held out his hand for the little girl.

"Major Windrush," Kuhne said. "What are you going to do?"

"Get out of Kumasi. Somehow."

As Abena led him from the missionaries' house, Jack was surprised how attractive Kumasi was. Sitting in the middle of a gloomy forest, he had expected only a large village with ramshackle huts with thousands of near-naked people. Kumasi, Jack allowed, was nothing like that. The town was as sizeable as many in Britain, with brightness and vitality everywhere he looked. Each nobleman seemed determined to outdo his neighbours, wearing colourful clothes similar to the Roman toga. The women looked sophisticated, with necklaces of aggry beads, gold ankle rings, bright sandals, and gold bands around their knees, while handsome slave boys followed them.

Although the people stared as Jack walked past, nobody tried to stop him. He had experienced more unfriendliness in many English towns.

"Your men are along here, Major Windrush." Abena tugged Jack into a side street, quieter than the main thoroughfare although still busy with people. Men laughed together, women walked, balancing burdens on top of their head and a single nobleman strode under his umbrella with his gold-handled swords thrust carelessly into a leopard-skin sheath. Behind him, his entourage of shapely young women walked as if in a missionary school crocodile, except for the last in line, who stared at Jack.

"Your soldiers are up here," Abena pulled at Jack's sleeve.

"How far, Abena?"

"Not far, Major Windrush." Abena stopped at the smallest house in the street. Even if Abena had not shown him, Jack would have known his men were inside, for there were two Ashanti guards at the door, each armed with a musket and sword.

Jack stood outside, trying to peer in the small window. The guards looked at him with a mixture of boredom and suspicion.

"Halloa! Second Wests!" Jack shouted. "Are you in there?"

When one of the sentries gestured angrily, Abena shouted at him, waving her hand. After a few moments, Sergeant Wickham appeared at a small window beside the door. "Major Windrush?"

"Is everybody all right in there?"

"Yes, sir." Other faces joined Wickham's. "Except for Private Manning, Sir."

"I know about Manning," Jack said. "How are they treating you?"

"Well, sir."

"Don't give up," Jack said. "Things will get better."

"Major," Abena pulled at Jack's sleeve. "Look."

A dozen warriors were marching toward them, white-striped faces set into ferocious scowls.

"Thank you, Abena," Jack said. Raising his hand in quick farewell to the Wests, he moved away.

Now I know where my men are held. I have to work out how to free them and get back to Cape Coast Castle, though a hundred and forty miles of Ashanti-controlled forest, with no map and a single track.

* * *

"Major Windrush," Mr Kuhne spoke quietly. "Please come here. You may find it interesting."

Jack stepped to the window beside Kuhne. The yellow umbrella moved slowly up the street, announcing to all the world that Kumi Okese was coming. As well as the umbrella bearer, there were two bodyguards, one with a long musket, and the other with a long, gold hilted knife at his belt. Behind them, beyond the shelter of the umbrella, a small train of slaves walked, heads down. Kumi Okese strode in the shade of the umbrella, straight-backed and proud, with his leopard-skin cap on his head and his colourful robes covering him from neck to knees. At his side, wearing a simple Ashanti robe and with a thin gold chain around her neck, Elda walked with all the grace and dignity of an Ashanti noblewoman.

"What the devil?"

"That is why Elda Becker is not with us," Kuhne said. "She has gone native. She has left our community to live with that Ashanti chief."

Jack nodded, trying to control his anger. "That's Kumi Okese."

Elda's husband or not, I am going to kill him the first opportunity I get.

"I would have no objection to Elda's man being African," the missionary said, "except that Elda has rejected Christianity to adopt fetish worship." He dropped his voice. "She has even bought a slave from the slave market."

Jack shivered at that. "I did not know that." He watched Elda walk past. She did not look healthy, and he wondered if she had chosen Kumi Okese out of self-preservation rather than affection. How genuine was she?

"They are coming here." Kuhne's voice rose in alarm.

The Ashanti warriors burst through the door in a body, pointing their muskets at the missionaries.

"Major Windrush," Akron stepped to the front. "You are greatly honoured. The Asantahene wants to see you in the Bantummah."

CHAPTER TWELVE

Kumasi August 1873

"Thank you!" The warriors formed around Jack, pushing him out of the house and up the street. "Thank you!"

Kumi Okese watched, unsmiling, then marched in front, with his followers at his back.

"You are greatly honoured," Akron repeated. "Very few foreigners meet the Asantahene."

At that moment, Jack only felt apprehension as he stumbled through Kumasi towards the Bantummah, the king's palace, at the northern side of the town. Jack's escort propelled him down a narrow street with a foul odour that may have emanated from the deep ditch that ran down the centre until they came to a large, flat-roofed building.

At first glance, Jack thought the palace gates appeared like the entrance to some Lancashire factory, except for the gaudily-dressed sentries. The fence was of bamboo, somewhat imposing but not threatening. The palace itself was fairly large, with shutters open on an array of windows.

Akron stepped back. "What do you think?"

"It's an impressive building," Jack watched as the escort spread out, some evidently in awe at their surroundings.

"The Asantahene has many uses for his palace," Akron enthused. "As well as living here, he has some of his wives, his royal treasury and an armoury."

"Some of his wives?" Jack queried. "I have enough trouble with one! How many does King Kofi have?"

"Three thousand, three hundred and thirty-three," Akron said. "It is a magical figure to protect the life of the king." He lowered his voice as they entered the outer courtyard. "Most of the king's wives live at a palace called Barramang."

"We would call that a harem," Jack said. "It must be a large building."

"It is," Akron said.

"Have you been there?"

Akron shook his head. "No. I have heard it is built of stone, with a lot of big rooms."

"I see." Jack thought it best to say no more.

They moved on, inside the palace gates as Jack surveyed his surroundings. He knew that any scrap of information might help him escape, although he could not think how to get through the forest between Kumasi and the coast. *The Ashantis don't need to imprison their hostages,* Jack told himself. *The jungle is a greater barrier than shackles and stone walls.*

To Jack's eyes, Bantummah was not a single building, but a group with a well-built two-storey stone tower in one corner. In common with the best houses of Kumasi, the palace was composed of several courtyards, all beautifully worked in painted stucco, with diamond and scrollwork on the red-and-white walls. One courtyard led to another, some with rounded, others square columns with pediments and capitals, but all with alcoves filled with various items.

"Is that the king's treasure?"

"His treasury and his stores," Akron replied.

Some of the alcoves held European swords, others held gold ornaments, carelessly piled together as though they were of less value than the ivory horns or colourful silk umbrellas. Jack stopped involuntarily at the alcove that held a collection of war drums, each one dark with blood, while human jaw-bones and skulls decorated the sides. It was an image that remained with Jack as Akron ushered him into the stone tower where the king had his private chambers. As he hesitated, two guards stepped closer, each with a sword at his belt, while a third prodded the muzzle of his musket hard into Jack's spine.

"Better to come this way, Major Windrush," Akron headed up a flight of stairs, with Jack a few steps behind.

The upper storey of the tower was like a cornucopia of everything the royal family had collected for generations, from Persian rugs to silver dinner services, gold masks to necklaces of aggry beads.

Akron pushed Jack in front. "Hurry, Major Windrush. The king is waiting."

The guards stepped closer as Jack approached the chamber in which the king waited. He could feel Akron's reverence when they entered the room.

"Very few foreigners are allowed into the palace," Akron spoke in hushed tones. "You are very privileged."

Jack thought of his long line of ancestors, most of whom had achieved a higher rank than he ever would, yet he doubted if any had met an African king. Whatever happened next, he would have something to boast about to his grandchildren, provided he survived.

King Kofi Karikari sat on a carved throne, with a bevy of noblemen at his back, Yaa Asantewaa in the corner and a second throne at his side. On the second throne sat what Jack guessed was the famous Golden Stool. He studied it for a moment, seeing a squat, highly carved piece of dark craftsmanship, adorned with golden plates and ornaments. It was like nothing he had seen before, yet he could feel the power emanating from that ornate piece of furniture.

As Jack looked, he became aware that in the centre of the nobles, Kumi Okese stood, with his smoky eyes glaring at Jack. Kumi Okese's fingers tapped the hilt of his sword, and he thrust his head very slightly forward.

King Kofi looked Jack up and down. "Who are you?" Akron translated the king's words.

"Major Jack Windrush of the 113th Foot, attached to the 2nd West India Regiment, Your Majesty." Jack bowed politely.

King Kofi half rose from his throne, with his mild voice at odds with his stern eyes. "Why are you in my kingdom?"

Aware that his life, and the lives of his men, depended on his answers, Jack gave a direct answer. "Your army brought me into your kingdom, Your Majesty. I had not intended to cross the Prah."

"You came to my army, which was in my territory. The Ashantis own all the land as far as the coast."

Jack knew it was not the time to dispute the boundaries of the Asantahene's kingdom. "I was sent to talk to General Amanquatia, to ask about the captive missionaries and ask if Your Majesty will release them."

"And if I do not?" King Kofi gave the hint of a smile, without a trace of humour.

Jack took a deep breath. "My sovereign, Queen Victoria of the United Kingdom of Great Britain and Ireland, will be displeased," Jack took it upon himself to expand upon his original mission. "She may decide to send an army across the Prah."

King Kofi gave a bark of laughter, which the gathering chose to mean they should laugh as well until the Asantahene raised one hand. Instant silence descended. King Kofi leaned slightly closer to Jack, with Akron still translating his words. "The people of your queen have occupied my fort of Elmina without paying tribute."

Jack had anticipated that statement. "My queen bought Elmina and the adjacent land from the previous owners, the Dutch. There was no mention of payment to your Majesty." Jack waited until Akron translated his words before he continued.

King Kofi smiled. "You say your queen may send her army against me. Do white men know how to travel to fight? You need black men to carry you."

Jack thought of the fever-ravaged traders in Cape Coast who had the local men carry them on litters as if they were either invalids or too important to walk.

"British soldiers can march anywhere," Jack said boldly. "From the snows of Canada to the mountains of Afghanistan. I have fought the queen's enemies in the Burmese forest and the plains of Russia."

King Kofi nodded solemnly. "So you say, Major Jack Windrush, yet I can see the marks of Ashanti shackles on your wrists. It is only by the kindness of our women that you are free."

"Yaa Asantewaa is indeed a generous lady and a true friend to Great Britain. Her counsel is wise." Jack floundered for words.

King Kofi laughed again, with the nobles joining in as if Jack had said something uproariously amusing. "You know little about Ashanti women, Major Jack Windrush."

"What man knows anything about any woman?" Jack countered. "I barely understand my wife!"

The king spoke again in his soft, polite voice, with Akron bowing as he translated. "Elmina is mine, and I will come and retake it by the sword. My ancestors ate and drank at Elmina, and they got whatever they wanted there. Tell your queen to pay tribute for my fort of Elmina, or I will send my armies to destroy that fort and Cape Coast Castle."

Fully aware that Colonel Harley had no intention of paying anything to King Kofi, Jack knew he could only play for time, which had been his original mission.

"I will take his Majesty's message back to my superiors," Jack hinted that he expected to get back to Cape Coast Castle soon. "Will your Majesty restrain his armies until he receives a reply?" He saw Kumi Okese inch forward, with his fist closing on the hilt of his sword.

King Kofi said something that made Kumi Okese glance at Jack with something like triumph. Akron hesitated before he translated. "The Asantahene has asked Kumi Okese to show you the power of his tribe as a warning to your queen."

What the devil does that mean? "Tell the Asantahene that I will be honoured to review Kumi Okese's warriors," Jack watched the king's face as Akron translated his words.

When King Kofi snapped an order flicked his fingers, the guards hustled Jack away, with Akron hurrying beside him and Kumi Okese a few paces behind, still gripping his sword.

About five minutes' walk from the palace, they came to an area of tall rushes around a misshapen tree, where scores of birds fought in ear-piercing disharmony. The sickly-sweet stench warned Jack there were dead bodies nearby.

"What's this?" Jack asked. "Does Kumi Okese intend to kill me, now?"

"This is the fetish tree," Akron said. "Kumi Okese wished to show you where we leave the bodies of the sacrificed."

"Oh, dear God in heaven." Jack gasped as he parted the reeds. The tree looked even uglier when Jack knew its purpose, with scores of strange fetish objects dangling from the branches. Uncounted dead bodies were scattered around, some recent, all in various stages of decomposition and many mere skeletons, with skulls lying in untidy, sun-bleached heaps. The stench was appalling, and the birds, vultures prominent among them, continued to tear at their feast despite the presence of the humans.

Kumi Okese spoke, pointing to the birds. Akron shook his head until Jack said: "Tell me what he said, Akron."

"Kumi Okese said to tell you that if he had his way you and all the hostages would end up here."

Jack faced Kumi Okese. "Tell him that we are enemies after he murdered my soldier."

Akron took a deep breath before he related Jack's words. Kumi Okese nodded grimly, growled something and stepped away.

"Kumi Okese says that if the British invade his country, he will personally feed the hostages to the birds," Akron said.

Jack forced a grin. "Dead men can't do that," he said, "and I promise that I will kill him the first chance I get."

"We have to go to the central square," Akron took hold of Jack's sleeve. "Please Major. The Asantahene ordered it."

Jack nodded. "Take me," he said.

War-hardened as Jack was, the remains of dead men did not bother him unduly. Rather it was the manner and futility of their death that sickened him. Only when the rattle of drums caught his attention did he look up.

Kumi Okese stood under his yellow umbrella with rank after rank of white-striped warriors behind him.

"How many of Kumi Okese's Edwesu warriors are there?" Jack asked.

"Some say two thousand," Akron said. "Some say five thousand."

At a word from Kumi Okese, a pair of drummers began a slow beat, with two horn-players blasting at their side. The entire force began to march, company after company of warriors, each man painted with white stripes, and each man carrying a long musket, some beautifully inlaid with gold.

Staring straight ahead, the warriors were uniformly tall and surprisingly silent for African troops. Kumi Okese watched, wordless, as his men marched past, not in step but undoubtedly disciplined until Jack reckoned that 2,500 warriors had passed him. Behind them came half a dozen policemen. Distinctive figures with their half-shaved heads and a fringe of hair over their foreheads, the policemen carried either a short lance or the whips Jack remembered from the journey from the coast. The hairstyle stirred a memory from Jack's school days when he had toiled over Homer's *The Illiad* where,

The sprinting Abantes followed hard at his heels,
Their forelocks cropped, hair grown long at the back.

Pushing the memory away, Jack glanced at the hundred women who followed the warriors, carrying powder horns and large staffs. He thought they looked every bit as formidable as the men. When they had all passed, and the drumming and blare of the horns faded away, Kumi Okese faced Jack again, spoke a few words and followed his men.

"Kumi Okese said that he will wash his warrior's feet in the blood of the British," Akron said.

"That may be so," Jack replied. "That may well be so."

Tonight, Jack promised himself. *I'll see if I can get the men out tonight and head for the coast. If we get a decent lead, I defy the Ashanti to catch us, however good they think they are.*

* * *

"Yaa Asantewaa wishes to see you." Akron's voice sounded through the darkness of the room. Jack heard the missionaries stirring in the house. He was already awake, ready to leave the house to try and rescue his men.

"I'm coming," he called.

"Hurry, Major Windrush!"

"I doubt I have any choice in the matter." Jack looked down at himself, wishing he had a candle. "Give me a minute, and I'll put on my dress uniform." He fumbled to change his uniform.

"Hurry!" Akron said. "Yaa Asantewaa is waiting!"

Dressed in his crumpled and soiled best, Jack followed Akron out of the house. Two guards fell in behind them, long muskets and knives prominent. Starlight illuminated the night-time streets, with a small patrol of police staring at them until they recognised Akron and looked hurriedly away. Somewhere a dog barked, the staccato sound echoing eerily.

"This way, Major." Yaa Asantewaa's house was at an intersection of two streets, square-built, with the shutters open and a light behind the windows. The guards hesitated outside until Akron snapped at them and they took position on either side of the door.

"I told them that you are an English gentleman," Akron said. "You do not hurt ladies."

Jack nodded. "Thank you, Akron."

Yaa Asantewaa greeted Jack with great courtesy at the open front room. "Welcome to this house," she said. "I do not normally live here, you understand." She waited for Akron to translate, "Kumasi is not my home."

Jack bowed deeply. He respected this woman, although he suspected she had no liking for him.

"This way," Yaa Asantewaa led Jack to an inner courtyard, where a banyan tree soared upward. "There is more privacy here." Her stern face relaxed in a smile. "We can talk without prying ears."

When Jack glanced at Akron, Yaa Asantewaa shook her head. "Akron occupies a very privileged position here. He will say nothing. Will you, Akron?"

"I never reveal any conversation," Akron said.

"If you did, I'd have your head," Yaa Asantewaa said without any change of expression on her face.

"I know that." Akron was equally expressionless.

"I also have a guard with us." Yaa Asantewaa indicated a broad-shouldered sentinel who appeared from the shadow of the banyan. "He knows his orders." Sitting on a beautifully carved stool, she gestured that Jack should do likewise. "I know you have spoken to the king, but I want you to tell me what the British want in our lands."

"Peace and trade, my lady," Jack said as Yaa Asantewaa's steady gaze scrutinised his face.

"Peace, trade and conquest," Yaa Asantewaa corrected. "And money. Europeans, white men, think of everything in terms of how much money they can make. They would sell their souls for money and take our Golden Stool for its monetary value."

Jack shifted uneasily, knowing there was truth in Yaa Asantewaa's words. British businessmen would sell their mothers for half a sovereign and think the bargain worthwhile, while Britain was notorious for appropriating the national symbols of other nations.

"You look askance at our dress and culture," Yaa Asantewaa spoke like a school teacher lecturing a backward pupil.

"Your ways are different from ours," Jack said, warily. He thought of the murder of Private Manning and the horror around the Fetish Tree.

"Perhaps not so different as you imagine," Yaa Asantewaa said. "We have bands to welcome our royalty. Does your Queen Victoria not have music to welcome her?"

Jack thought of the military brass bands, the flutes and drums and the highland bag-pipers. While the Ashanti soldiers had fired muskets in the air, the British and other Europeans fired 21-gun salutes; there was little difference. He had to admit Yaa Asantewaa had a point. "She does," Jack said.

"We are an empire that absorbs people and makes them into Ashantis," Yaa continued her reasoned discourse. "The British Empire also absorbs people and makes them British, as we see with your West Indian soldiers. What is the difference?"

Jack thought of the components of the British Empire; from the Inuit of Canada to the Aborigines of Australia, all were subject to the same queen. Britain itself had been formed by the union of Scotland with England and Wales and had attached

Ireland in 1801. "You have a point," he admitted. He thought of his grandmother, Indian by birth, who had contributed her blood to the Windrush line, and of Mary, his Eurasian wife, mother to his quarter-Indian son.

"You do not approve of our religion," Yaa Asantewaa pointed to the fetishes that hung from the banyan tree in the courtyard.

"I do not," Jack said.

"Yet you worship a man who the Romans executed, and the very symbol of that execution is holy to your religion."

Jack could not argue. One of the principles that senior officers hammered into him when he was an ensign was to respect the religion of the people of the empire. Yet the British had crushed Thugee, an Indian religion based on killing travellers, and had ended the practice of Sati, where widows were burned on their husband's funeral pyres. Where did humanity end and religious tolerance begin?

"Our war captains wear colourful uniforms," Yaa Asantewaa said. "Don't yours?"

Jack thought of the plumes, gold braid and tassels of British officers on parade and decided that there was not much difference in military finery. He smiled. "If you saw the officers of a Highland regiment in all their glory," he said, "you'd wonder how they are ever able to fight."

"Our king and his officers of state wear gold to prove their status," Yaa ignored Jack's comments. "Does your Queen Victoria not have a crown adorned with gold and jewels?"

Jack nodded. "She has two," he said. "One in London and one in Edinburgh."

Yaa Asantewaa gave a small smile, her point proven. She shifted slightly, leaning closer to Jack. "And you think us barbaric for having a Captain for Royal Executions and an Official Executioner."

"It would be thought unusual in Europe." Jack tried to be diplomatic.

"Is the Lord Chief Justice of England not the same as a Captain for Royal Executions? He has the power to order executions or to lock up men and women for all their lives, which is torture that endures for years."

Again, Jack had to admit that Yaa was correct. "There is a similarity, Yaa Asantewaa." He held his patience, wondering why Yaa had summoned him. Akron translated diligently, standing at the side.

Yaa Asantewaa continued, pressing home her points with undeniable logic. "You also have a chief executioner, although you hide him away and pretend he is something abhorrent, yet on him depends the ultimate sanction of your law."

Jack remembered William Calcraft, only the latest in a line of official English hangmen that stretched back to the Elizabethan Jack Ketch and no doubt much further. Jack had never witnessed an execution in England but knew that public hangings had only ended a few years before, partly out of official moral indignation over the crowds of thousands who considered the spectacle to be free entertainment. Jack thought of the fetish tree. It was a repulsive sight, but not much worse than the merry old English practice of gibbeting, placing executed men in a metal frame and leaving them to rot at crossroads and other public places. It was only forty years since that monstrosity ended.

"The Golden Stool," Yaa said, smiling as she realised she was winning her argument. "Do you find that strange?"

"It is outside my experience," Jack said, cautiously.

"Yet your Queen Victoria is anointed by God, and sits on the sacred Stone of

Destiny." Yaa waited a second. "A stone that one of your many aggressive kings stole from a neighbouring country."

Once again, Jack could not disagree.

"You see?" Yaa Asantewaa said, "we are more alike than not. Except the Ashantis do not have the same lust for conquest and money as white men do."

"You have slaves," Jack said. "We abolished slavery decades ago."

Yaa Asantewaa shook her head. "We treat our slaves well," she said. "Many men marry their slaves and have them as honoured wives. In your country, are there not children and men who work in dark underground mines all their lives? And women, children and men work in mills and factories, kept away from daylight and the sounds of nature?"

"There are."

"That is worse than any slavery that even our prisoners of war have to endure," Yaa said. "We would not make our children suffer in that manner."

Jack kept his temper, reminding himself of his original mission. He was here to delay any Ashanti attack on Cape Coast Castle, and to find out about the hostages. "We're not all bad," he said.

Some soldier's instinct made him turn around an instant before somebody kicked over the lantern, plunging the room into darkness. Jack saw the blur of movement, the flash of steel and the dark shape wielding the knife and then the guard was writhing on the ground with blood pumping from his throat. He heard Yaa Asantewaa gasp as the intruder jumped on her, knife held blade upmost.

"Enough!" Jack launched himself forward.

Blocking the blade with his left forearm, Jack jabbed a fist to the intruder's chin, rocking him back. The man was strong and agile, recovered quickly and tried to push Jack aside. In the dark, Jack could only see the flash of bared teeth and the glint of wide eyes. He slammed the man onto the floor, saw him roll away and leap to his feet, still holding the knife.

There was no sound except the harsh gasps of Jack and the attacker, and little whimpers from Akron, who had stepped back with both hands to his mouth.

The intruder tried to shoulder Jack out of the way, lunging at Yaa Asantewaa with the knife until Jack jabbed at the man's elbow with the heel of his hand, deflecting the blow. From the corner of his eye, he saw Yaa lift a heavy gold figurine from the back of the room and step forward.

"Keep back, Yaa!" Jack snapped, landing another punch that rocked the intruder and sprayed blood across the room. Following up with a kick from his steel-shod boots, Jack saw the intruder scramble away to the door from where he had entered. Throwing himself forward, Jack reached the door at the same time as a guard carrying a blazing torch.

For a fraction of a second, Jack and the intruder stared at each other, both panting for breath. Sergeant Wickham's eyes were narrow, with blood dribbling from his mouth where Jack's fist had cut his lip, and then he dashed away, pushing past the guard as though he was not there.

Yaa Asantewaa was breathing hard as she joined Jack, still holding the golden figurine. She pointed to Akron, who translated in a shaky voice. "Did you see who that was? Did you see his face?"

"Not clearly enough to identify him," Jack lied. "Are you all right."

"He meant to kill me." Yaa Asantewaa sat down, cradling the ornament on her lap.

"I believe he did," Jack said.

"You saved my life."

Jack nodded. "Perhaps."

"Why did you save me?"

"I don't believe in killing women," Jack said truthfully. "I am here on a diplomatic mission to try and bring peace to our empires, and I was a guest in your house."

Yaa Asantewaa gave Jack a sideways look. "Many British soldiers would have allowed that man to kill me."

"Some, perhaps. I think that most officers would have acted as I did."

Nodding, Yaa Asantewaa pushed past Jack, stepping over the body of the guard. She gave a string of orders that saw a score of warriors appear outside the house and spread out on the streets. One or two stared at Jack until Yaa waved them impatiently away.

"Yaa Asantewaa has ordered a search for the intruder," Akron said. "When they find him they'll kill him and enslave his family."

Jack nodded, expecting no less. *If the Ashantis catch Sergeant Wickham, they'll likely murder all my men.*

Yaa Asantewaa watched as a captain appeared with a squad of men behind him. "If you had not helped me, Major Windrush," she said, "I would have suspected the British had ordered me killed."

"We don't operate like that," Jack recalled that his superiors in London had once ordered him to assassinate a foreign agent. This unexpected visit to Africa was forcing him to face some uncomfortable truths.

Yaa Asantewaa gave him a sideways look. "I think the British are capable of anything if it furthers their cause. They will convince themselves they are right, whatever they do." When she leaned closer to Jack, he saw the deep intelligence in her eyes; this woman understood the British mentality far too well.

"I know the history of your people, Major Windrush," Yaa said quietly. "I know how you arrive with promises of trade and friendship, then expand and take over, always with a plausible excuse and a smile to hide the gunboats and bayonets."

"As far as I am aware," Jack said carefully, "Great Britain has no intention of taking over the Ashanti lands."

Yaa Asantewaa's eyes narrowed slightly. "You say the words Great Britain as if you were not part of it, yet you are a British officer, Major Windrush." She gasped with sudden shrewd insight. "No! You are not wholly British, are you?"

"I am as British as anybody can be," Jack said.

Shifting away from Jack, Yaa Asantewaa paced the length of the chamber with her hands working at her sides. "What are you, Major Windrush?" She turned abruptly to face him again. "You don't burn in the sun as other British do."

"My mother was half Indian," Jack felt his chin lift as if in defiance.

"I knew it!" Yaa Asantewaa said. "I knew you were different from the other cold-eyed Northerners." She gave one of her rare smiles. "Because you saved my life, Major Windrush, I'm going to send you back to Cape Coast Castle with a message from the Ashanti people."

Jack felt a lift of elation, quickly tempered by worry. "If you free me, you must also free my men," Jack said. "And the hostages."

"We have no hostages," Yaa Asantewaa said. "We do have some white guests, who will remain with us."

"And my men?" Jack wondered about Sergeant Wickham.

"They will go with you," Yaa Asantewaa said.

"Thank you." Jack did not press for the release of the hostages. He had seen them, they were reasonably safe and well, while freeing them was probably beyond Yaa Asantewaa's power.

"Here is my message," Yaa Asantewaa still spoke through Akron although Jack knew by the tone of her voice that she was sincere. "You may add it to anything that the Asantahene says. The Ashanti lands may be small to you, but they are our home, and your ways are not our ways. You are occupying our lands and interfering with our trade."

Jack nodded. He expected that scores of native tribes and small kingdoms around the globe had thought the same when the British, or the Dutch, or the Americans, Burmese, Moghuls or even Ashantis had encroached on their territory. "I will pass your message on."

Yaa Asantewaa continued. "Then also tell Colonel Harley, your Administrator-General this, Major Windrush. Tell him that we will fight to hold our lands, and fight to preserve our freedom. We have thousands of men and a barrier of forest through which white men cannot penetrate." Yaa Asantewaa stepped closer and lowered her voice so that although Akron translated in a monotone, her words still carried sincere intent. "And if our men will not fight, then I will gather the women of Ashanti together to fight for our land."

Jack had met warrior queens before, notably Jayanti during the Indian Mutiny, but Yaa Asantewaa impressed him with her sincerity. For a minute, he felt like applauding her, and then a whiff of the decaying bodies from the fetish tree came to him, and he recalled the horrific scenes of execution. *Be careful, Jack, and get your men out safe.*

"I will relay your message to my superiors," Jack said. "If we get safely to the coast."

"I will arrange for a party of warriors to escort you," Yaa Asantewaa said. She stepped back inside her house. The sun was rising now, tinging the tops of the trees and sending near-horizontal shafts of sunlight along the streets. "I do not like you, Major Windrush. I do not like the British. You do not belong in the land of the Ashantis, and you do not belong in Africa."

Jack nodded. "If the Ashantis did not raid the Fantis, the British would not make war on the Ashantis."

"The British make war on everybody," Yaa Asantewaa's tone altered. "They make war on their neighbours, and everywhere their ships can sail." She stepped back. "Although I will permit you and your men to leave, Major Windrush, I will give one warning. If you return, I will hand you over to the executioners."

"I will endeavour to avoid that," Jack said.

CHAPTER THIRTEEN

Kumasi August 1873

Sergeant Wickham called his men to attention when Jack entered their house.

"We're going back to the coast, lads," Jack saw that Wickham's lips were swollen and knew one of his blows had taken effect, "under an Ashanti escort, so don't do anything to antagonise them."

"What about our rifles, sir?" Private Daley asked.

"We'll be lucky to get out with our heads," Jack said. "I don't think we'll see our weapons again." He nodded to Wickham. "I need to speak to you alone, Sergeant. You lads get yourselves ready."

Jack took Wickham outside. "Explain, Sergeant?"

"Sir?" Wickham tried to look innocent.

"Don't play the old soldier with me! Why did you attempt to murder Yaa Asantewaa?"

Sergeant Wickham opened his eyes wide as if surprised by the question. "I am a British soldier, sir. Yaa Asantewaa is the enemy. It's my duty to kill the enemy."

"Don't take me for a fool, Sergeant. Why?"

When Wickham dropped his eyes, Jack took hold of his jacket. "Tell me why, Sergeant!"

Wickham straightened his shoulders. "It's a long story, sir."

"Give me the short version."

"Yaa Asantewaa is Ashanti of the Edwesu people, as is Kumi Okese. I am of the Denkyira."

Jack frowned. "And?"

For a moment, Wickham's eyes registered something like contempt, and then he resumed the habitual blank stare of a ranker talking to an officer. "The Denkyira are the true tribe of this area. We were the dominant people before the Ashanti moved in. We are enemies."

"I see." Jack knew that Wickham was not telling the whole story. "Was that not a long time ago? Are you not all the same now?"

"Do you think we are all the same because we are all black African?" Wickham had a bite in his voice. "Are white men all the same because they are from Europe? Are the French the same as the Dutch and the Scots the same as the English?"

Jack conceded that point. "You are not African, Sergeant. You are from Jamaica."

"My ancestors were carried over to Jamaica as slaves," Wickham was fighting to control his emotions. "They were slaves in the British plantations for decades before emancipation."

Jack nodded. "Your ancestors experienced rough times, Sergeant, but now you have a career in a fine regiment."

"You don't understand what it's like to be treated as an inferior all your life."

"Perhaps better than you think," Jack murmured. "Why try to kill Yaa Asantewaa?"

Wickham stiffened. "It was an Edwesu slave party of the Ashantis that raided our village and sold my ancestors to the white men as slaves."

"Ah." Jack nodded, thinking about the decades of degradation Wickham's family must have suffered as British slaves. "I understand, Wickham, but Yaa Asantewaa was not involved. She was not born then."

"It is about blood, sir."

Is it not always about blood and family? The wars between nations are only part of it. The real rivalries, the real hatreds are between families and within families.

"All right, Wickham. Your actions put your men in danger." Jack pondered for a moment. He had intended to strip Wickham of his sergeant's stripes, but he would need his expertise on the journey back to the coast.

"Yes, sir," Wickham said. "Sir, in Africa, I'd prefer to be known by my real name. I am Kwabena Badu."

For a moment, Jack was unsure of what to say. "That may well be so," he said at last, "but you enlisted as Albert Wickham, and that is the name I shall call you."

"I am more than just a sergeant in the Second West Indians," Wickham said. "I am also Kwabena Badu of the Denkyira."

"When you're time served," Jack said, "let me know. I will help you return here if that is what you wish."

Wickham's eyes were wild. "The Edwesu Ashanti are the enemies of the Denkyira people."

"If you had succeeded in murdering Yaa Asantewaa," Jack tried to keep his voice level, "the Ashanti would have killed all your men. Whatever your ancestors were, you are a sergeant in the British Army, with your primary responsibility to look after your soldiers." Jack's anger overcame him, and he raised his voice.

"You put some ancient feud before your duty, Sergeant! When we get back to Cape Coast, I will order a court-martial to see what becomes of you, but no NCO under my command will put his men in danger over a private dispute. Dismiss!"

The privates looked up as Jack and Wickham returned, neither hiding their anger. Jack took a deep breath. "Steady, lads. We'll be leaving this hellish place soon."

The Ashanti escort lined up in the street, twenty men with long muskets, twenty men who did not look in the least pleased at their task. They hurried Jack's party out of Kumasi and onto the track that led back to the coast.

"Thank you," they said, pushing the Wests along. "Thank you!"

"Major Windrush!" Abena stood under a tall tree. "Come back and see us."

Jack only had time to give Abena a wave before Mrs Ramsayer hustled her away.

As they crossed the area of marshland on the southern border of Kumasi, Jack paused for a moment to look behind him. He felt an overwhelming sense of relief to leave Kumasi. Although he had visited many terrible places in his career, none had worshipped death in such a fashion. Jack shivered, thinking of the awful end of Private Manning. As Abena had warned, somebody had removed the cross he had placed on Manning's grave.

The wave of hatred was so intense that Jack felt dizzy. Manning had been his man, and Kumi Okese had ordered him butchered for some warped religious ceremony. That had not been a soldier's death.

"I won't forget you, Stanley," Jack promised, 'I'll make Kumi Okese pay for your murder, I swear. Somehow, I'll make him pay. Yes, Abena, I'll be back, and I'll bring a whole blasted army with me!"

"Thank you!" the Ashanti escort shoved Jack in the back. "Thank you!"

"I'll see you later," Jack warned with the anger still hot inside him.

The Ashanti pushed him again, digging the butt of his musket into the small of Jack's back. "Thank you!"

Jack moved on, splashing through the marsh to the rising ground beyond, knowing he would remember Kumasi with a shiver of horror. The escort set a fast pace, which Jack was pleased to accept. *I'll write you the moment I return to Cape Coast Castle, Mary*, he said, willing himself to march along the horribly familiar road.

"Straighten up, lads," Jack snapped. "We're British soldiers, not Bushmen in uniform!" That had been Manning's phrase, and again Jack felt the twist of anger within him. "Get these feet moving! Show these Bushmen how real soldiers can march."

The Wests responded with a will, banging down their feet on the damp path as they overtook their escort, so the Ashantis had to jog to keep pace with them.

"That's my men," Jack stared at the gap where Manning should be. "That's my 2nd Wests!"

On the third day, Sergeant Wickham vanished. Jack did not see him leave. One minute he was at the rear of the Wests, the next he had gone.

"The forest took him." Private Daley said, with his eyes wide. "It swallowed him up."

Jack looked around at the forest. "Sergeant Wickham was a good soldier," he said. "Hopefully he will join us at a later date." *He's deserted,* Jack thought. *I should not have told him about the court-martial. Rather than face the disgrace, he has run. That's two men I've lost to the Ashantis. That's two scores I have to settle.*

* * *

As soon as the West Indians waded to the southern bank of the Prah, the escort turned back to Kumasi. Only then did the drumming begin, as if the entire Ashanti nation had waited until the invaders had left.

"This way Wests," Jack led his men south, still forcing the pace, thinking as much of Mary as of his duty. "Only a few days now. Keep alert for stray Ashantis."

Banging down their boots, partly relieved that they were safe but angry and guilty at the loss of Manning and Wickham, the Wests nearly double marched towards the coast.

"Halloa!" The sound of a British voice was welcome.

Jack looked up to see a shirt-sleeved man with a Havelock hanging from his forage cap, and sweat beading his face. "Halloa; what the devil are you doing so near to Ashanti land? You look like a civilian."

The man wiped the sweat from his forehead with the back of his hand. "Civilian yourself! I am Lieutenant Gordon, 98th Foot, surveying a road for the infantry. Who are you? And who are these scarecrows?"

"Major Jack Windrush, 113th Foot, with Privates Stair, Coffin, Ogston and Daley of the 2nd West India Regiment," Jack said, "returned from Kumasi in Ashantiland."

"Good God, man! What were you doing there?"

"Just talking to the king," Jack tried to sound nonchalant, "watching a few human sacrifices, the usual sort of thing."

Gordon lifted his head as the sound of voices travelled from down the track. "There's my boys now. Have to get them to work. Glad you're back safely, sir although you look awful."

Jack grinned. "Thank you, Gordon. I wouldn't cross the Prah if I were you, the Ashantis don't like visitors."

Gordon lifted a single eyebrow. "What the Ashantis want and what they're going to get are two different things, Sir."

Jack nodded, looking over his men. "Aye."

The further south Jack moved, the busier the road became as parties of workmen laboured under the direction of harassed engineers. He kept the Wests moving, fighting his fatigue, forcing himself to keep marching, thinking of Private Manning, thinking of Mary, thinking of revenge.

CHAPTER FOURTEEN

Cape Coast Castle September 1873

As Jack led his men into Cape Coast Castle, a fitful breeze flapped the union flag against a grey sky. With their stained uniforms hanging on emaciated bodies and their faces drawn and haggard, the Wests looked like men returning from the other side of hell. Yet when Jack inspected them, he was intensely proud; they marched with their backs straight and heads up, their arms swinging and eyes level. *They may be disarmed and battered*, Jack thought, *but by the Gods of War, these are men, and as good soldiers, as any I have known.*

"You lads get along to the hospital, get examined, and get some food and rest." Jack watched them march away, smiling as he contemplated a hot bath and writing a letter to Mary.

"Good afternoon, sir." Captain Brett looked tense. "Welcome back. Colonel Harley requests your presence."

"He can wait," Jack refused to lose his dream of a hot bath.

Brett shook his head. 'Sorry, sir. He's insistent." He put his hand on Jack's shoulder. "I'm sorry, Windrush, I really am."

"Sorry?" Jack said, but Brett was already three steps in front, heading for the Administrator's office.

* * *

Colonel Harley sat in a deep chair with his beard unkempt and deep lines around his eyes and nose. He looked up, unsmiling when Jack entered.

"Sit down, Major Windrush."

Jack sat on a hard chair, hoping that the Administrator-General did not keep him long. That bath was more appealing by the minute, while if he wrote a letter today, he could catch the next ship for Britain. He could imagine Mary's expression as she read about his adventures in Kumasi.

"I imagine you have had some interesting times, Major Windrush." Colonel Harley spoke formally.

"I would agree, sir," Jack said cautiously.

Harley looked away for a moment. "I won't ask for a report, yet, Major." He hesitated again. "I am afraid I have some bad news for you."

"Indeed, sir?" Jack straightened in his chair.

"It is your wife," Harley held Jack's eyes in an expressionless gaze. "We had a message about her."

"Mary?" Jack felt sudden concern. "She will be safe in England now."

Harley took a deep breath. "I am sorry, Windrush. I only wish that were the case."

Jack could only stare at the Administrator-General as the fear mounted within him. "What has happened, sir? Where is my wife?"

"Oh, my dear fellow," Harley changed from a stuffy, straight-faced official weighed down with responsibility to a caring human being. "I am so sorry."

"Sorry?" Jack could only repeat the word. He felt sick.

"Oh, my dear fellow," Harley repeated.

"What's happened to Mary?" Jack half rose from his seat. At that second, he could not have cared less about the fate of the Gold Coast Colony. The Ashantis could have it, and all the rest of Africa, as long as Mary was safe.

"There was a severe water shortage in Cape Coast Castle while you were away and some unfortunate people, the Fanti refugees, were in a bad way."

Jack nodded. "Mary got involved," he forced all emotion from his voice. Mary would have been the first to help.

"Mrs Windrush got involved," Harley confirmed. "She badgered me to send a section to fetch water from one of the small rivers." He gave a small smile. "Mrs Windrush is the most persistent of ladies."

"She is," Jack agreed. He grasped Harley's use of the present tense. "Is? Is she still alive?"

Harley gave a brief nod. "I believe so, Major Windrush."

Immediate apprehension replaced Jack's surge of relief. "You believe so? You're not sure?"

"Let me finish, Major." Harley held up his hand. "I sent out men to fetch water, and Mrs Windrush accompanied them herself, to supervise, as she said."

"I can imagine Mary doing that," Jack could not hide the pride in his voice even as he hated the dangers to which Mary exposed herself.

"The first trip was a success, but the Ashantis must have been watching. They ambushed the second patrol."

Jack stiffened. "And?"

"The Ashanti captured two men and Mrs Windrush." Harley looked away. "The Ashantis took their prisoners into the bush. I sent out strong patrols to search as soon as the news reached us."

Jack waited, unable to say anything.

"One of the patrols found the two soldiers, both decapitated," Harley spoke so quietly that Jack could hardly hear him.

"And Mary?" Jack had to struggle for breath.

"We heard nothing until this morning when one of our spies told us that Mrs Windrush had been held captive at Effutu and was now with the other hostages in Kumasi."

Jack flinched. "Held in Kumasi? Dear God, I've just left that place! If I had known that!" He thought of the human sacrifices and the fetish trees. Kumasi was the last place on earth that he wanted Mary to be.

No; the missionaries there are decent people. They will look after her. She is alive and in no immediate danger.

"Don't you fret, Windrush. We'll get her back. I'm a married man myself; I know how you must be feeling." Colonel Harley leaned back in his chair. "I have made it a point to demand the release of all King Kofi's hostages, and Mrs Windrush will be included."

Jack stood up. "Sir; give me a company of good men. With a hundred Wests and Royal Marines, I'll hammer through to Kumasi and free the hostages!"

"And get yourself and your men killed in the process," Harley said, shaking his head with a sad smile. "I can't allow that, I'm afraid, not against such redoubtable forest warriors as the Ashanti. No, Windrush. Careful planning is the way to defeat the Ashanti, not a madcap dash through Africa."

Jack took a deep breath, knowing he had allowed his emotions to control his sense. Harley was correct; the Ashantis would destroy anything less than an army. "When are we attacking Kumasi, sir?"

"I cannot answer that, Windrush. As you may be aware, I am being replaced. Major General Wolseley is on his way to Cape Coast, and he has his own ring of officers."

"If he does not want me on the expedition," Jack said. "Then I'll hand in my papers and go as a blasted war correspondent. I'm damned if I'll let Mary stay in that hellish place one hour longer than necessary."

"Calm yourself, Windrush," Harley said. "I am sure General Wolseley will always find a use for such a resourceful officer as you have proved to be."

Jack took a deep breath. "Thank you, sir."

"In the meantime, keep yourself busy. I am sure the Wests would appreciate your help. Go home, get some rest, write your report and in a day or so I wish you to resume your duties. The 2nd Wests are short of officers so I'll officially second you to them."

Jack knew Harley was trying to be kind, although at the minute he could not think of anything except Mary in Kumasi.

* * *

Jack viewed the company he now commanded, nodding to the familiar faces and wishing that Sergeant Wickham was still with him. A good NCO was worth his weight in gold in any military unit. Private Stair greeted him with a very undisciplined grin, while Coffin looked as professional as any Guardsman. Jack did not approach Ogston in case the rum fumes should knock him down.

"Right, lads. In a few weeks, we'll be going up against some of the fiercest and most experienced forest fighters in Africa in their domain. They know the forest, and how it works, so we have to be better than them."

C Company, 2nd West Indian Regiment listened intently, with the veterans nodding agreement. Daley was shaking slightly, either with fever or nervousness.

Jack spoke slowly, allowing the men time to absorb his words. "The Ashantis have the advantages of knowing the terrain and how it works. We have the advantages of better weapons, better discipline and," Jack paused for effect, "we have the advantage of being the 2nd West."

While a British regiment might have cheered at those words, the West Indians remained silent, with only the men who returned from Kumasi allowing even a smile to crease their faces. *I'll have to do something about esprit de corps*, Jack thought.

"Until today," Jack said. "You have used the muzzle-loading Enfield Rifle. Today I'll introduce you to the breech-loading Snider," Jack said, "and when you are all familiar with it, we'll practice skirmishing and bush warfare."

Again, the response was muted. Daley looked decidedly nervous as if he lacked the confidence to learn anything new.

"I have managed to obtain sufficient Sniders for us," Jack beckoned to a corporal, who handed him a rifle.

"The Snider will be your weapon for the remainder of the campaign. It is 54 inches long and weighs nine pounds three ounces, so it is slightly longer and heavier than the Enfield. It has a range of 1000 yards, although when you're fighting in the bush, you'll be much closer to the enemy. I want you all to take a few moments to familiarise yourself with the weight and feel."

As the West Indians examined the weapon, Jack explained the technical details. "Unlike your old Enfield, the Snider is breech-loading, so your rate of fire will be faster. Once you gain experience, you'll be able to fire perhaps ten rounds a minute compared to two with the Enfield." Jack held up a Snider cartridge. "The bullet has a detonator cap within the base, dispensing with the need for a percussion cap." Jack watched his men. "These are major advantages. You can fire five shots to the Ashanti's one, and your bullets are infinitely more powerful than his slugs. You don't need to fear him, even in the forest."

"We don't fear him, Sir," Ogston said, with the rum working in his system. "The Ashantis murdered Stan Manning and Sergeant Wickham. I want to get back at them."

"So do I Ogston," Jack said, waving back the shocked corporal who wanted to blast Ogston into silence for his impertinence. "And the more skilled we are with the Snider, the better chance we'll have of victory, so pay attention!"

"Yes, sir!" Ogston shouted.

With the men settled down, Jack demonstrated the use of the rifle, noting the West Indians were quick to understand the new procedure of loading through the breech rather than the old way by the muzzle.

"We'll have a few practise rounds." Jack glanced over his men. "As I explained, with the Snider, we already have an immense superiority in firepower over the Ashanti. With better skirmishing, we will be able to meet them in their own forests. I have heard good things about the fighting ability of the 2nd West, and I have seen some of you in action; I want us to be the best company in Wolseley's army!"

Private Stair grinned at Jack's words. He opened his mouth to speak, thought better of it, and said nothing.

"Target practise," Jack said. "We start now."

Leading his company to the beach, Jack set up a row of sand-filled sacks as targets.

"These sacks are about the size of a man's body," he said. "We'll practise shooting until every man of you can hit them eight times out of ten at a hundred yards, and then we'll try at a hundred and fifty yards, and so on."

As the men lined up to fire, Jack walked behind them, correcting the angle of their rifles. "Aim low," he said. "If you can see your target, aim for the broadest part of their body, where the belt buckle would be. If you can't see a belt aim where you think one should be."

When they fired, only the veterans were close to the target, with the others jerking at the triggers as if they could force out the bullet by sheer force. One by one, Jack corrected the faults, although, by the time he had the majority of them hitting the target, daylight was fading.

Jack wiped the sweat from his forehead. "Not bad, lads. You're a lot better than you were this morning."

The men looked at him, some smiling, others tired.

"Daley, you did very well." Jack encouraged the most nervous man in the company. "Carry on like that, and the Russians would run away from you, let alone the Ashantis."

"They'd run because he so ugly, sir." Stair said.

"I not ugly!" Daley said. "You ugly, man!"

Lieutenant Hopringle sauntered up. "Good evening, sir."

"Evening, Hopringle," Jack said.

"I wondered what all the noise was," Hopringle said. "Excuse me for saying, sir, but is training musketry not an NCO's job?"

"I like to keep myself busy," Jack said. *If I don't, I'll be worrying myself to distraction over Mary.*

"Yes, sir,' Hopringle said. "I was sorry to hear about Mrs Windrush, Sir."

"Thank you," Jack said curtly. "I think my lads are tired of shooting for now. I'll show them some skirmishing tomorrow, how we did it against the Plastun Cossacks."

"I'm sorry to be the bearer of bad tidings, sir, but you won't be skirmishing tomorrow."

"Why is that, Hopringle?"

"General Wolseley is arriving at Cape Coast soon, sir, and Colonel Harley has appointed you to command the guard of honour."

"What?" Jack looked around in alarm. "I want my men to be fighting troops, not parade ground soldiers. When does Wolseley arrive?"

"The day after tomorrow, sir, so you'd better curtail your shooting and skirmishing drill and get your men ready for something much more important, like looking pretty for the commander."

CHAPTER FIFTEEN

Cape Coast Castle October 1873

"I don't have time to mount a guard of honour, sir," Jack tried to control his frustration. "I need to train these men, so they are fit to fight the Ashantis."

"You'll have time, Windrush," Colonel Harley said. "I can't see General Wolseley landing on Monday and attacking Kumasi on Tuesday. He's a methodical man. In the meantime, we need to welcome him to the Gold Coast, and you'll be the first officer he sees."

Jack took a deep breath, thinking of Mary under the Ashantis' power. "I'd rather get the men ready for fighting, sir."

"I have given my orders, Windrush."

"Yes, sir. You mean I have to provide the guard of honour at the landing stage and Government House?"

"That's right old boy. We don't have sufficient men for both." Colonel Harley smiled. "If the Ashantis knew we only held this territory by bluff and smoke, they would waltz right in and depose us tomorrow."

"It's the same in many of our colonies," Jack spoke to calm himself down. "We hold Canada with a handful of regiments and a half-trained militia, Australia with less and I doubt we have enough fit men in all West Africa to fill one full-strength battalion."

"Quite right. We rule half the world by brazen cheek, and the navy." Harley said. "And you'll have to use that same strategy to provide two guards of honour with one company of Wests. I simply don't have enough men to spare you more, and the general will expect all the trimmings."

"I was hoping to train my company in skirmishing," Jack said.

"I selected your company because you train them so assiduously," Harley said. "The general arrives on *Ambriz* the day after tomorrow." He nodded to the door. "That does not give you any time to waste."

***

"Right, men," Jack addressed his company. "Colonel Harley has chosen us to be the Guard of Honour for Sir Garnet Wolseley in two places in succession. That is impossible for any regiment, except for the 2nd West India."

The men looked pleased with the praise. Stair nodded as if he was giving his approval.

"We'll have to look our best, lads, and move quickly."

For the full next day, Jack drove his company hard, having them stand at attention at the landing stage, then double to Government House and parade again. In the evening, he ensured their uniforms were at their best, brushed, pressed, and clean.

"You'll do," Jack was nearly dropping with weariness when, at last, he believed them ready. "It's an important day tomorrow, lads. Make yourselves proud."

Only when he returned to Green Lettuce Lane did Jack think of his own dress uniform. Dragging it from the cupboard, he sighed at the damage and set to work as best he could.

***

Through his binoculars, Jack saw a seagull perched on the masthead of the African Steamship Company's *Ambriz*. "Ready men,"' Jack said softly. "If I heard right about General Wolseley, he'll have his telescope trained on us to note every defect in our uniform and bearing."

As *Ambriz* eased closer, Jack watched her progress towards Cape Coast Castle. Knowing the strain of standing at attention for prolonged periods, Jack waited until he could see the crown superimposed on the red cross of the company flag before he called his men to attention. Only a few of the crowd bothered to look at the West Indians as they lined the landing-place, for the arrival of the new governor was more interesting than a company of soldiers.

"Here he comes, men!" Hoping Wolseley did not inspect his battered dress uniform too carefully; Jack called C Company to attention. Major General Wolseley disembarked with a core of selected 'special service' officers around him. Thin faced with a neat moustache, the general marched past the West Indians with an appreciative glance. He stopped at Sergeant Mathews at the end of the line. "Good show," he said. "Very smart," and moved on to Government House with his entourage following.

The moment Wolseley was out of sight, Jack ordered his men to move at the double, avoiding the general's route as they nearly ran through the narrow streets of Cape Coast to Government House, where Colonel Harley waited anxiously at the head of the long garden.

"Same routine, men," Jack said, noting some of the Wests were panting with exertion. "The general will be here in a minute. You're looking fine, Daley. Ogston, try not to breathe too hard, we don't want General Wolseley reeling drunk before he's properly arrived. Stop smiling Stair."

"Here he comes, sir," Sergeant Mathews said.

Once again, Wolseley spared a few moments to inspect the West Indians before entering the house. Once again, he stopped before the immaculate Sergeant Mathews. "Excellent turnout," he said and stepped inside the large building. "Your 2nd Wests are a credit to the army in dress and appearance," he said to Jack.

"Thank you, sir."

"It's a pity your uniform lets your men down," Wolseley said quietly. "I'd get a better servant, Major."

Jack had known Wolseley as a young officer in the Crimea, but promotion had been rapid, and now Wolseley arrived as major-general and Governor of the Gold Coast while Jack was only a major.

Leaving Jack feeling foolish, Wolseley greeted Harley with a handshake and entered the wide doorway of Government House. A heavily moustached captain stopped briefly beside Jack.

"Don't take it hard, sir. Sir Garnet always hates sea voyages. They bring out the worst in him."

"You'd best come inside, Windrush," Colonel Harley said. "Dismiss your men."

Still irritated at the loss of time on what he considered a pointless exercise, Jack entered Government House with all its opulence as his men returned to their austere barracks.

Even before all the officers and officials filed into the great hall, Wolseley read his letter of appointment, with the Chief Justice of the colony looking suitably self-important in his barrister's wig and gown, so unsuitable for the climate. Near the back of the gathering, the captain who had spoken to Jack introduced himself.

"Redvers Buller," he said. "60th Rifles."

"I know the name," Jack said. "You were with Wolseley in the Red River Expedition."

"I was," Buller was about 35, with a bluff appearance and a slight West Country burr to his voice.

"Jack Windrush," Jack said. "113th Foot."

Buller looked at Jack with his head on one side. "Fighting Jack?"

"That's one name they called me."

Buller nodded. "Careful, the general is coming." He stepped aside.

With the ceremony complete, Wolseley immediately became business-like, pushing past the civilians to speak to his circle of officers.

"Buller," he said, "I want you in charge of intelligence gathering."

"Yes, sir," Buller nodded as if he expected nothing less.

Wolseley pulled Jack aside. "You were the officer with the Guard of Honour."

"I was, sir." Jack waited for more criticism.

"I noticed the same faces on guard at the landing stage and here," Wolseley said.

Jack nodded. Sir Garnet Wolseley was a vastly experienced fighting man and nobody's fool.

"Are we that short of men, Major? How many fighting men do we have in the colony?"

"Less than a thousand, sir," Jack replied. "Including the West Indians and Marines."

"Good God." Wolseley frowned. "I know your face. Who are you?"

"Major Jack Windrush, sir, 113th Foot."

"That's right," Wolseley nodded. 'I remember you from the Crimea. How many men exactly, Major?"

Jack had already ascertained the number. "Seven hundred soldiers of the 2nd West India regiment, sir, with only 398 fit for field service and 102 in Cape Coast

Castle. Captain Thompson of the Queen's Bays informs me he has ten fit men of the Fanti police fit for service."

Wolseley raised his eyebrows slightly. "And our native allies?"

"I don't think there are many, sir. Colonel Glover has some up-country, with the Hausas."

"I'll speak to you later, Windrush," Wolseley ordered. "I'll send for you when I want you."

I have an unknown length of time to train my company.

CHAPTER SIXTEEN

Cape Coast Castle October 1873

"All right, men," Jack paced in front of C Company. "I've led some of you in your first action, and your lack of experience showed."

The men looked at him, some sullen under his admonishing tone, others expressionless. Daley looked as if was he was about to burst into tears.

"Outside Elmina, you did better than the Hausas, but not as well as the Royal Marines, and they are mostly children, and part-time sailors, not professional soldiers like you."

Jack paced the length of the West Indian line and returned, aware that every man was watching him, waiting for his next words.

"Now you have met the enemy; some few of you have seen their capital city with all the horrors of human sacrifice." Jack paused beside Ogston. "You know the Ashantis murdered Private Manning." As he hoped, his words brought a low growl from the men. He waited until the sound ended before he continued.

"You also know how the Ashantis fight and you know you are better than them."

Some of the men looked a bit brighter at those words. Stair tightened his grip on his Snider.

"I intend to make you better than the Royal Marines, better than any of the regular British regiments that may land here and, by God, better even than the Brigade of Guards. When I have finished, in times to come, men will say with pride that they marched and fought beside the 2nd West India Regiment!"

Now even Daley was smiling.

"But first we have to work at it," Jack said. "Sergeant Mathews, I will need your expertise."

Jack knew he had to push them to their limit, for although they were brave as any men he had fought beside, they knew little about skirmishing, their firing, although improved, was not as good as he wished, and their discipline was poor.

"You have a lot to learn," Jack said. "And I am just the man to teach you." He also had to work himself hard, for the moment he stopped, he thought of Mary trapped inside Kumasi, and in constant danger. Acutely aware that worrying did not help anything, Jack concentrated on training his company. The harder they trained, the better soldiers they would be and the more effective in fighting the Ashanti and therefore in rescuing Mary.

I'm not going into that forest with a company of half-trained soldiers. I will drill these men and train them until they are as good as any soldiers in the world.

After ensuring his company could fire at stationary targets, Jack asked for two volunteers.

"Why, sir?" Coffin asked.

"You will be pulling moving targets for the others," Jack said. "I'll show you." Fastening a long rope onto a six-foot-long log, he hauled it across the beach. "The log is the target, not the men pulling." He knew that Stair would step forward. "You and me then, Stair."

"Aim at the logs," Jack ordered. "Pretend it's an Ashanti!"

Nobody hit the target at the first attempt, Jack rotated the men pulling, demonstrated what he expected and kept the men working. The Wests fired by sections and then individually until they could all hit the target four times out of five.

"Better," Jack said as the echoes of the firing faded with the last of the sun. "You can hit your mark and no casualties. Tomorrow we'll progress to the next stage, avoiding being shot."

The Wests watched him, listening, all aware of the spectators who had gathered to watch Jack's novel ideas of training. "Dismiss."

Nights were the worst, when Jack lay awake, worrying about Mary. He tried whisky, which made him feel worse and tried pacing the ramparts until the sentries grew used to his company. Leaving his house, he lived in the Officer's Mess, sleeping on a cane chair and growing morose and ill-tempered, living only to train his men.

"If the enemy can see you, he has a better chance of shooting you," Jack said as the skies greyed with the dawn. "So you have to learn to take cover."

The Wests listened, slowly learning the skills that Jack had garnered over two decades of soldiering.

"Forget the parade ground soldiering," Jack said. "The Ashantis don't fight like the French at Waterloo. Fight to survive; fight to win." He paced the ranks, "I don't want you to defeat the enemy. I want you to destroy them."

With Colonel Wood of the 90th Foot mounting patrols to keep away any prowling Ashantis, Jack had space in which to train his men. He gave them instructions in the Ashanti way of fighting and showed them how to counter ambushes, either firing from behind cover or charging forward. The men responded with a will, although Jack still thought their fire discipline was poor.

Recruiting a hundred local Fanti tribesmen, Jack had them cut battle-paths alongside a local forest path and gave each man a captured musket with powder but no ball. Speaking through a local Krooman, he gave the Fantis orders.

"You men are to be the enemy," he said. "You are armed with blanks so you can't hurt anybody. Ambush my company."

The Fantis stared at him in complete confusion.

"Tell them they are to try to ambush my men without being seen," Jack told the translator. When the Fantis got the idea, they grinned and scampered away.

Allowing the Fantis ten minutes to arrange themselves, Jack addressed C Company.

"Ready, lads?" Jack led his men to the closest patch of forest where a narrow path sliced between the trees. "You have blank ammunition in case you fire at each other." Without mentioning the Fantis, he gave his orders. "Keep apart as I trained you, and march along the path. React to any surprises." Jack issued instructions, divided his men into sections of ten and sent the first section into the bush.

As soon as the Wests were fairly on the path, Jack joined the Fantis. Recalling fighting the Mutineers and Cossacks, Jack walked slowly, avoided twigs and loose branches, and slid beneath creepers. He followed the Fantis' battle path, stopped behind a brightly flowering bush and watched his men.

As he expected, the first section of Wests had bunched together as soon as they rounded the first bend. They were laughing and talking as they walked, not taking the exercise seriously.

"Right you Fantis," Jack spoke through his translator. "On my word, fire at the men."

Waiting until the section was level, Jack had his Fantis fire a volley, with the powder-smoke nearly filling the track. As the Wests recoiled in confusion, Jack leapt out, grabbed the last man and dragged him into the forest. Before Private Adams had time to react, Jack stuffed a gag in his mouth and had two grinning Fantis tie him up.

"Keep alert next time," Jack growled in Adams' ear.

By now, the section was firing wildly and shouting orders to each other. Leaving them to it, Jack led his Fantis and their reluctant prisoner away, crossed the main path higher up and waited in a second ambush site.

When the section eventually stopped firing, they moved on in better discipline although shaken by the loss of one of their men and not sure what was happening. Jack lay low, holding a loop of rope. Again he waited until the last man was passing, threw the loop over his trailing leg, tripped him and dragged him, yelling into the forest. Now thoroughly alarmed, the section again opened a wild fire as the Fantis fired a volley and scampered along the battle path.

After a quarter of an hour, the section was firing at every movement, so Jack carried his prisoners back to the starting point, released them and had Sergeant Mathews bring the discomfited men back to the beach.

"You see what happens when you disobey orders?" He railed at the shamefaced men. "Next time, stay in skirmishing formation, each man watching over his mate. Watch for ambushes and only fire when you're sure of a target." He pointed to the next section. "Now Sergeant Mathews will lead you in."

Jack stood back. Throughout the training, he had one overriding idea; he wanted to ensure these men could out-march, out-shoot, and out-fight the Ashantis. Every Ashanti they killed was one less to harm Mary.

With the example of the shamed section before them, Mathews' men fared better, obeying orders to stay apart and responding to the ambush with controlled fire.

"Now the next section," Jack said, and doubled the number of ambushes, varying his technique each time to keep his men guessing.

For three days, Jack hammered his company in fighting off ambushes, then on the fourth, he marched them to the beach, firing from various positions, standing, kneeling and lying.

"Look for whatever cover you can," Jack said. "If the enemy can't see you, he can't shoot you." He watched them stare across the sandy expanse. "Aye, it's easy enough in the forest, but not here, eh? Look for dead ground, dunes or anything that can keep you alive."

"We were always taught that soldiers stood straight and proud," Private Ogston sounded confused.

"In this campaign, and under my command," Jack said, "I want you to hide behind trees or rocks or bushes. Immerse yourself up to your nose in a swamp if you need to, as long as you can kill the enemy before he kills you. The Ashantis have developed a technique of fighting that works in their forests, so we'll use it against them, but better." He stepped closer to Ogston until their faces were nearly touching. "I want you to stay alive, Edward!" He doubted that any officer or NCO had ever called Ogston by his first name before.

I want you to stay alive, Edward Ogston, so you can help me get Mary back.

"I want you to live to tell your grandchildren about the days you fought and defeated the Bushmen, the savage Ashantis."

When the men gave a nervous grin at that, Jack knew he was training them harder than they had ever worked in their lives.

He continued, driving them on when they wanted to collapse, training them in concealing themselves by making them take cover and throwing stones at any part of them that he could see. Every evening he had them post sentries, and checked each man, then sent small parties out with orders to sneak up to the sentinels without being seen. He stopped that particular exercise after Private Stair fired his rifle, called out the guard and woke half the Cape Coast Castle garrison. When half a dozen irate senior officers returned to their bed, grumbling about being awakened by "damned uppity majors and damned jumpy sentries," Jack sought out the abashed private.

"Well done, Stair," Jack said. "You did exactly what an alert sentry is supposed to do. Any fault lies with me, not you."

Stair gave a wide smile. "I've never seen a colonel wearing a night-cap before, sir. It was worth it just for that."

Jack hid his grin. "Yes, Stair. It was." *You'll go far Stair. I only wish privates in the Wests could earn commissions. You'd brighten up any officers' Mess.*

After a week, a servant delivered a small booklet to Jack's house. Entitled *The Soldier's Pocket Book*, General Wolseley had written it especially for the forthcoming campaign. When Jack read through the notes, he nodded at the advice, and the next day passed the best on to his men.

They stood on the beach with the offshore breeze pleasant and the usual gathering of spectators waving to the Wests.

"Ignore your admirers," Jack said. "Especially you, Stair. I can see three young women who want to make you their own."

Jack paraphrased Wolseley's book, adding modifications from his own experience. "We'll divide the company into four sections, with an officer or NCO in command of each. Once Lieutenant Hopringle recovers from the fever he'll have One Section; I'll take Two Section, Sergeants Mathews and Roberts will take Three and Four." *That made sense when fighting in such close country. Wolseley knows his job.*

"These sections will remain together and perform all details, except pickets, which half-sections will perform."

Jack looked around the men. They were paying attention, some nodding at all the correct places.

"When we are in action," Jack spoke slowly to press home his points. "Three sections of the company will be extended, with the fourth in support of the skirmishing line. All fighting against the Ashantis will be in skirmishing order with the files two, three or four paces apart, as we have been practising this last week."

Some men nodded, with the veterans beginning to understand what Jack had been trying to drive home.

"Remember, when in action, with the smoke and noise confusing you, and wounded men lying on the ground, the support section must not lag. Stay in sight of the skirmishing line, even in thick bush. You will be in two-man files, and always keep together to support each other."

As Jack had expected, the men looked at their opposite numbers, to check they had not suddenly run away.

"Two more things, men," Jack said. "You know that the Ashanti fight with ambushes in the bush. When they ambush us, and they will, find cover and aim low where you see the smoke. Don't waste ammunition. The bearers will have to carry every bullet we fire."

From the beach, Jack led them on another drill in the forest, with platoon against platoon and section against section, pushing deeper into the bush to familiarise his men with the environment.

"Sir!" Private Coffin gestured with his head. "I can see something ahead."

"Halt!" When Jack gave the quiet order, the company stopped at once, waiting. "What can you see, Coffin?"

"I'm not sure, sir." Coffin spoke quietly. "There's something ahead, off the path."

Drawing his revolver, Jack instinctively checked it was loaded. "You men find cover and keep alert. Coffin show me."

The instant Coffin pointed ahead with his chin, Jack saw the flash of gold. He stepped carefully forward and removed the purple-and-gold scarf from the bush in which it had become entangled.

"You are right, Coffin," Jack said. "This does not belong here." He held it close, remembering Mary buying that scarf from a bazaar in Gondabad. Either the Ashantis had taken her this way, or they had stolen her scarf and dropped it. "Well done, Coffin."

Jack held the scarf for a long minute before tucking it inside his tunic. Taking a deep breath, he turned to his men. "That's us for the day, Wests." He knew he could not concentrate on his duty at that moment.

I cannot sit in the castle, waiting for something to happen. If I am not active, I will go crazy with worry. I'll continue to train my men, but they need battle experience.

With C Company safely inside Cape Coast Castle, Jack turned to face the forest. The sun eased in the west, gloriously orange, then slid away as velvet darkness spread across Africa. Jack held Mary's scarf in both hands.

"Hold on, Mary," he said. "I'm coming for you. I'm training my men so nothing will stand in our way. Whatever happens, stay alive."

The darkness was sinister, silent except for the hush and suck of the surf and the distant rustle of trees. Only when Jack turned away did the drums start with a slow, repetitive beat.

CHAPTER SEVENTEEN

Cape Coast Castle October 1873

"Ah, Major Jack Windrush!" General Sir Garnet Wolseley held out his hand.

Wolseley was young for his rank, with a small moustache enhancing his eager face, but it was his cheerful demeanour that attracted men to him.

"Yes, sir."

They were in Government House, with a cool breeze easing through the window and two busy secretaries at the other end of the room. Lieutenant Wood, Wolseley's aide-de-camp, stood at attention behind the desk, looking every bit the aristocrat that he was.

"We were in the Crimea together twenty years ago," Wolseley remembered. "You were a good soldier, Windrush. I don't understand how you have not advanced beyond your present rank."

"I couldn't say, sir."

"Perhaps this campaign will be the springboard." Wolseley nodded as the door opened and Hook walked in. "You know General Hook, I believe."

"I do, sir."

"Oh, don't mind me, you fellows." Hook took a seat, crossed his legs and lit a cheroot. "Pretend I am not here."

Wolseley continued, addressing Jack. "You were in Kumasi, Windrush."

"I was, sir."

"And returned with most of your men." Wolseley gestured to Jack to sit opposite him.

"I lost two men, sir." Jack kept his voice level. "The Ashanti executed Private Manning, and Sergeant Wickham disappeared on the journey home."

"Executed?" Wolseley raised his eyebrows.

"They sacrificed him, sir. They chopped off his head."

"Did they, by God? A British soldier." Wolseley's expression sharpened. "You'll want to return to Kumasi then, Major."

"Yes, sir. My wife is there."

"I know," Wolseley said softly. "We'll get her back, Windrush, don't you fear."

"Yes, sir," Jack said.

Wolseley smoothed his moustache. "I plan to march my army from Cape Coast Castle to Prahsu, about 70 miles inland, cross the Prah and continue to Kumasi."

"Yes, sir," Jack said. "When do we start?"

Wolseley gave a small smile. "Not until I am ready, Windrush. In this part of the world, the organisation is everything. I will raise a force of natives, stiffened with British officers, and whatever men I have here." Nodding to Wood, Wolseley said. "Take notes, Lieutenant while Windrush tells me about the road, the conditions our troops are likely to face, if you think the Ashantis will fight and what sort of warriors they are."

Taking a deep breath, Jack gave details of his enforced journey to Kumasi and what he had seen of the Ashantis.

"Tell me of the Ashantis battle tactics, Windrush." The general listened as Jack explained about the war captains and the umbrellas, the ambushes, muskets and few modern rifles.

"Ambuscade, then," Wolseley ensured that Wood scribbled more notes. "They form a horseshoe around their enemy and hit the flanks. That tallies with my previous information. Continue, Windrush."

"Yes, sir. When we were fighting in the bush outside Elmina, I noticed that the Ashanti seemed to appear and disappear at will." Jack noticed that Wolseley was listening carefully, as was Hook. "The warriors had made small paths through the forest, only big enough for one man to use at a time, running parallel to the road."

"Is that how they ambush their enemies?" Hook asked.

"Yes, sir."

"Clever." Hook said. "Did you learn anything else?"

"Yes, sir. I have a message from an Ashanti noblewoman," Jack said. "A lady named Yaa Asantewaa."

"A woman?" Wolseley half-smiled. "Is she important?"

"The Ashanti are a matrilineal society, sir," Jack said. "Their royal line descents from the female side. Yaa Asantewaa is the equivalent of a duchess of the royal blood in Britain."

"Oh," Wolseley did not look impressed. "What does this Yaa woman have to say for herself?"

Jack brought Yaa Asantewaa's words to his mind. "She said that the Ashanti lands might be small to us, but they are their home, and our ways are not their ways. She said that we are occupying their lands and interfering with their trade."

"Did she indeed? This woman has strong opinions." Wolseley nodded. "Carry on."

"Yaa Asantewaa also said that the Ashanti would fight to hold their lands, and preserve their freedom." Jack could sense that Wolseley was not impressed. "She said they have thousands of men and a barrier of thick forest through which white men cannot penetrate."

Wolseley looked up. "The Ashantis greatest defence is the forest, climate and disease. That is why I intend to raise a local army. Only if that proves impossible will I have to prove that white men, or British soldiers at least, can penetrate their forest and fight them in their heartland."

"Unless we do, sir, they will never feel defeated," Jack said. "We beat them on the plain outside Elmina, but they believe they are invincible in the forest."

"Yes, indeed," Wolseley said. "If I must use British soldiers, I'll march to Kumasi in the dry season, between December and February. With or without tribal help, I'm going to invade Ashantiland, Windrush. I have the Rifles, the 23rd Foot and the 42nd Highlanders standing by. Will the Ashanti warriors fight British regulars?"

"Yes, sir, they'll fight. They don't have a high opinion of us as soldiers."

Wolseley pondered for a few moments before replying. "You'll know I have brought out several special service officers, including young Wood here, Viscount Halifax's son, don't you know."

"Yes, sir."

Wolseley smiled. "The press calls them the Wolseley Gang. Well Windrush, if you acquit yourself well out here, you may join us."

With Wolseley as the rising star of the military establishment, being included in his immediate entourage would mean almost certain promotion. "Thank you, sir.'

Jack heard Hook clear his throat and scrape a boot across the floor.

"Did Yaa Asantewaa say anything else?" Hook asked.

"Yes, sir. She said that if the Ashanti men did not fight, then she would use the Ashanti women."

Jack expected Wolseley to ridicule the notion of Ashanti women fighting regular British soldiers. Instead, the general raised his eyebrows, with Hook bending forward.

"Is she as determined as her words sound, Windrush?" Hook asked.

"I believe so, sir. The Ashanti are a proud people."

Wolseley drummed his fingers on the desk. "You have experience of fighting the Ashantis, and you know them well. I'm going to use you, Windrush."

"Thank you, sir." Jack had a mental vision of the executioner slicing off Manning's head, and of Mary struggling in the hands of two white-striped warriors.

"It will be a hard fight, Sir. Can you guarantee the lives of the hostages when we invade?" From the corner of his eye, Jack saw Hook shake his head in warning. Special Service officers were there to support the general, not put obstacles in the path of his plans.

"There are no guarantees in war, Windrush."

"No, sir," Jack said.

"Even if I cannot raise local levies here," Wolseley continued, "I'll have Captain Glover and Captain Butler leading native forces from different directions to split the Ashanti army." He looked up. "The coastal kings hope to sit down quietly with their rum bottles and yams, while Queen Victoria's soldiers defeat the Ashantis. Well, Windrush, I won't let that happen."

Again, Jack said nothing. He could not guess what the local kings thought.

"Thank you, Windrush. That will be all for the present." Wolseley said.

It was an abrupt dismissal that left Jack feeling vaguely uncomfortable. "When are we attacking, sir?"

"When I am ready, Windrush," Wolseley said, "and when I have some experience of defeating the Ashanti." When he lowered his voice, Jack saw the steel behind this methodical soldier. "With only have a few weeks in which to reach Kumasi, Windrush, I must leave nothing to chance."

"Jack," Hook rose from his chair. 'Never fear. We have not forgotten your wife. Her predicament is in my mind. We will endeavour to free her."

"Thank you, sir."

"Oh, Windrush," Wolseley looked up from his papers. "It's best if you employ yourself rather than fret over your wife, so I'll endeavour to keep you busy. I'm calling the local chiefs to a palaver. Once that's complete, take your Wests and have a look at the road building, will you? Lieutenant Gordon was complaining that the Ashantis were harassing his men."

"Yes, sir." *Thank God. I'd go crazy doing nothing when Mary is in danger.*

CHAPTER EIGHTEEN

Cape Coast Castle October 1873

Moving with impressive speed, Wolseley called together the chiefs and kings to a palaver the next day. Rather than squeeze the kings into Government House, Wolseley had ordered the servants to erect a large marquee on the grounds.

"It's a bit like the umbrellas of the Ashantis," Jack remembered the colourful gatherings at Kumasi. *Perhaps we are even more similar than Yaa Asantewaa thought.*

"On this coast,' Wolseley said, "They call such a gathering a palaver. Old India hands such as myself know it better as a durbar, where we meet the local kings, rajahs and whatnots, listen to their points of view and then tell them what we're going to do."

Jack thought that Wolseley seemed very sure of himself for a man so new to the coast. "I've attended a few durbars myself," he said. "Mostly on the Frontier."

Wolseley gave Jack a sharp look. "We must treat these people with respect and dignity," Wolseley said. "Remember, they were here long before us."

Meeting Jack's eye, Hook winked.

In mid-afternoon, the kings arrived from all around, each with his entourage of followers. Some had sword-bearers or men with gold-topped canes. Many sheltered under the umbrellas which denoted their status, and others marked their approach by beating drums. All filed into the marquee and perched on beautifully carved stools, pompous with self-importance like the senior class at a public school or newly appointed politicians in the House of Commons.

Some chiefs were too intent on their own affairs to notice anything else, while others studied the raised dais where Wolseley waited with Lieutenant Wood pristine at his side.

"Bring them up," Wolseley stood up. "One at a time."

As a mere major, Jack stood in the background as the kings ascended the dais to shake Wolseley's hand. The general greeted each with great cordiality, smiling as the translator repeated the king's words. Wolseley remained on his feet until all the chiefs had returned to their seats before he addressed them. Speaking slowly through the translator, Wolseley reminded the chiefs of the continuing threat from the Ashantis and asked them to call up their men for mutual defence.

"May as well ask them to whistle down the moon," Buller whispered.

Nodding politely and giving promises of co-operation and help, the kings accepted Wolseley's gifts of gin, traditional for West Africa and filed away as noisily as they had arrived.

"And that's the last we'll see of them," Buller lit a cheroot, passing one over to Jack. "All smiles and promises."

"Aye," Jack agreed. "I don't think they'll raise their men. Why should they fight for themselves when we're here to do the fighting for them?"

"They are very divided," Buller said. "The native peoples here are split into hundreds of small clans, tribes and nations. In the east, there are Awoonah, Krepe, Akeamu, Accra, Akim and others. To the north or west are Wassaws, Amanaheas, Denkyiras and Assins, with Fantis and Kroomen along the coast." He puffed on his cheroot, "and that's only the tribes I know about."

"I've heard some of these names," Jack said.

"Exactly so. Each small clan thinks of itself only, knowing it cannot face the mighty Ashanti Empire, so why should it try? The Ashantis don't stay on the coast long, so the tribes run away or hide and hope the Ashantis attack somebody else."

"Aye," Jack did not care about local politics. He only wanted to rescue Mary.

"Ashanti land is about the same size as Scotland," Buller said. "It extends northward from our coastal fringe to about three hundred miles inland."

Jack nodded. "I've been there, remember."

"I know you've visited," Buller said. "I'm hoping you can correct any gaps in my intelligence gathering."

"Oh, my pleasure," Jack said. "Carry on, Macduff."

"I have it written that the river Prah divides the country in about the middle, which flows east to west in its upper reaches, then at a place called Prahsu, it alters course towards the south and reaches the sea to the west of Cape Coast Castle."

"That sounds accurate, as far as I know," Jack said.

"My people have been feeding me information about the Ashanti," Buller said, "and I send it to your fellow Hook as well as to General Wolseley."

"Indeed?"

"They have a very experienced general in Amanquatia and an up-and-coming chief named Kumi Okese. He seems to be the Ashanti equivalent of our Sir Garnet, a man destined to go places in the Ashanti world."

Jack stiffened. "I've met Kumi Okese."

"Tell me about him." Buller took out a notebook. "Any detail, however insignificant could be useful."

Jack related all he knew of Kumi Okese and his Edwesu warriors as Buller scribbled notes. "Thank you, Windrush," Buller said. "I believe that when we invade, and we will, Amanquatia and this Kumi Okese fellow will be defending."

"Kumi Okese is a dangerous man," Jack said.

"You want another crack at him, do you?"

"He ordered one of my men murdered," Jack did not give more details.

"Ah," Buller nodded understandingly, adding to his notes. "I heard that." He paused reflectively. "Do you realise that we're making history here? When these

Fanti fellows refuse to fight, as they will, Sir Garnet will call in British regulars. We'll be the first European army ever to land on the west coast of Africa."

Jack thought of the dense Ashanti forest and the number of men already sick with fever. "Let's hope we all come out again."

"Amen to that," Buller dropped his smile. "Amen to that."

* * *

As Wolseley attempted to raise local levies, Lieutenant Gordon of the 98th foot continued to work. To secure the security of Cape Coast Castle and Elmina, he built a couple of defensive redoubts a few miles inland, garrisoned them with whatever men Cape Coast Castle could scrape up and began work on the road to the Prah. Using local labour, good humour and bad language, Gordon had already widened the old track northwards from Cape Coast to the village of Mansu, where Jack met him.

"Good afternoon, Gordon!" With Hopringle back with them, although still weak after a bout of fever, Jack marched C Company along the new road.

"Is that you again?" Gordon gave a grin, wiping away the sweat from his forehead. "You're in better shape than last time I saw you."

Jack nodded. "So is your road, Gordon."

"Aye, but I've heard a shave that Sir Garnet intends bringing in a genuine Royal Engineer to replace me." Gordon shrugged. "Until then, I'll carry on."

"Were the Ashantis giving you trouble?"

"They were unsettling my people," Gordon said. "They appear from time to time, watch, fire the occasional shot and vanish again. They've never hit anybody yet, but I'd appreciate a military presence."

Glad of something active to do, Jack divided his men into their sections and had them patrol both sides of the road.

"Keep in skirmishing formation," he said, "and remember what I taught you. Hopringle, you take your men on the east side. Sergeants Roberts and Mathews take the west."

"Sir."

"I'll go ahead with my section." Jack moved off at a fast pace, following the route that Gordon had surveyed. *I want to meet the Ashantis. I want to destroy the men who kidnapped my wife.*

Twice Jack heard movement in the bush on either side of the path, and each time he extended his section, hoping for a confrontation, wanting to kill. He had never felt this eager to fight since he viewed the Well at Cawnpore, where the Mutineers had massacred British women and children. *Come out. Show yourselves!* He led Number Two Section into an area of thick bush, with low vegetation below tall trees, where creepers swung over the cleared path, and a cloud of insects hung as if suspended from slanting beams of green-tinged sunlight.

"There's somebody ahead, sir," Ogston said. "I can smell them."

"Ashantis?"

"Yes, sir."

"Find cover." Jack did not have to emphasise the words. Sliding behind a tree, he glanced around him, looking for his men. He saw sunlight gleaming on scarlet. "Coffin! I can see you!"

Coffin moved a fraction until vegetation covered him. Jack nodded, vaguely satisfied. "Load. Don't fire until I give the word."

Drawing his revolver, Jack checked it was fully loaded, controlled his nerves and waited.

The first Ashanti warrior appeared at a bend in the path, carrying a long musket and with a bandolier of ammunition across his shoulder. He moved confidently, with a score of men at his back, nearly trotting between the trees.

Jack waited until the leading man was parallel with Coffin. "Fire!" He squeezed the trigger of his revolver, missed with his first shot, saw his target, a lanky warrior in the middle of the Ashantis, swing his musket to his shoulder, and fired again. The Ashanti staggered as Jack's bullet crashed into his hip-bone. He fell, trying to balance on the ground with his forearm. Jack fired a third time, with the shot taking the warrior in the top of his skull, smashing the bone and spraying his brains over the ground.

Taken by surprise, few of the Ashantis had time to respond before the Wests fired another volley of .577 bullets, felling more men to add to the six casualties from the initial attack.

"Keep firing!" Jack shouted. Although these were not the white striped men of Kumi Okese's tribe, Jack still wanted to dispose of as many as possible. He cursed when he saw a Snider bullet knock a splinter from an overhanging branch. "Fire low! Don't waste ammunition!"

The Ashantis were reeling, some lying down, a few turning to run and the bravest aiming at the bush to return fire from this invisible enemy.

"Finish them off!" Jack ignored the slug that thumped into the tree in front of him. He emptied his revolver at one of the more stubborn of the Ashantis, saw Stair take deliberate aim at a running man and knock him clean off his feet, reloaded, and then it was over. The road was empty except for dead and wounded Ashantis.

"Anybody hurt?"

With no casualties among his Wests, Jack had them take the weapons from the enemy, dragged the wounded into the shelter of the trees and left them there. "Good work, men."

That was it. A successful ambush that had disposed of eleven of an enemy that numbered around fifty thousand, and wounded four more. The skirmish would not even dent the fighting power of the Ashantis, but it would raise his men's morale, it proved the Wests could defeat the enemy in their own forests and may help defend the road engineers.

Gordon looked agitated when Jack led his men back. "I heard firing."

"We found an Ashanti patrol," Jack indicated their haul of muskets.

"I see." Gordon looked relieved. "I was a bit concerned."

Jack raised his voice to enable all his men to hear. "No need for concern, Gordon. The 2nd Wests are here. We can handle a few Bushmen."

The road-building continued steadily, mile by slow mile as the engineers progressed toward the Prah. With every yard, the invasion of Ashantiland and the rescue of Mary became more of a possibility.

Jack continued with the patrols, each time probing further north, closer to the Prah. Sergeant Mathews had another brush with the enemy two days later, again with no casualties among the Wests and a few Ashanti dead. After that, the Ashantis left the engineers severely alone. Felling trees, Gordon's men built bridges and created camps at regular intervals, so when the army eventually arrived, the men could have proper shelter.

"The Romans called them marching camps," Gordon said. "If they are already in place when we invade, the lads won't be so tired and fewer will succumb to heat exhaustion."

Jack approved. "Wolseley has things well worked out."

As well as broadening the path, the engineers placed tree trunks across the worst of the marshes like a corduroy to give marching men sure footing. Jack watched one team of workers manoeuvre a log into position.

"You're using women as labourers," Jack said.

"Yes," Gordon said. "Only as far as Mansu, which used to be the Fantis slave market."

Jack watched Private Coffin jump to help as a slender Fanti woman staggered under her load.

"Good man, Coffin!" Jack forestalled Sergeant Mathews' rebuke. "Sergeant; our men can help these ladies as long as we are here."

"Yes, sir."

"Why are you using women, Gordon? Where are the men?"

The engineer shrugged. "As far as I can see, the men are anywhere except where they might meet the Ashantis. It makes me wonder what we're fighting for."

"I often wonder that," Jack said. "Is it the politicians who cause these wars or the businessmen who want to make money?" He watched Coffin hefting a log as if it was nothing.

"Did you hear the latest shave, Windrush?"

"What was that?"

"King Kofi has said that if the British ever cross the Prah, he will sacrifice all the hostages."

Jack felt nausea rise in his throat. "No,' he said. 'I had not heard that."

"It might only be a rumour," Gordon said.

"It had better be," Jack looked north with his fingers curling around Mary's scarf. At that moment, he felt further apart from Mary than he had ever done in his life and utterly useless.

CHAPTER NINETEEN

Cape Coast Castle November 1873

As the days passed without any gathering of Fanti warriors, Wolseley became frustrated. "The women in this land have more courage than the men," he said.

Thinking of Yaa Asantewaa and the women building the road northward, Jack nodded. "That may be so, sir."

Wolseley rose from his desk, scattering the piled papers across the floor. "All right then, we'll call a palaver with the women, and see if they can encourage their men." He swayed slightly but pushed away Jack's helping hand. "I'm all right, Windrush, damn it!"

You're catching fever, General. You don't know the signs yet, but the Gold Coast is fighting back.

It was perhaps the most unusual meeting that Jack had ever attended as Major General Wolseley presided over scores of wives and mothers of Fanti chiefs and kings. The women arrived with fewer attendants than their men had, yet with equal solemnity. All had paid strict attention to their hair, all wore a profusion of gold rings and most had shawls and robes adorned with golden ornaments that would have put a European princess to shame.

They listened attentively to Wolseley, promised to send their men to war and returned home.

"Now we'll see," Wolseley said, as Hook lifted a glass of brandy to his lips, smiled his slow smile and walked to the window.

"You'd better get the British regiments ready," Hook said. "You're going to need them before this is over."

"Oh, ye of little faith," Wolseley said.

"Little faith?" Hook said quietly. "I never had much and lost that many years ago."

After a few days, Jack knew that Hook was correct. There was no surge of warriors eager to fight the Ashanti. Wolseley's gamble in trying to recruit the Fanti women had failed. As so often in the past, Britain had to turn to the underpaid, hard-used men in scarlet.

* * *

They stood on the wall of Cape Coast Castle, smoking cheroots and looking northward into the interior of Africa. Buller sighed, pulled on his cheroot and blew out a ribbon of blue smoke.

"There is no gathering of the clans, then."

"No," Jack said. "Perhaps we should send out the fiery cross?"

Buller grinned. "It looks like we'll have to fight these people's war for them with what we have, and whatever force Sir Garnet can manage to scrape up back home."

"Aye, but it's a bad country for white men," Jack said.

Buller laughed. "When I asked people's advice on what kit I would require for the Gold Coast, one old West Africa hand gave me a dirty look. 'Take a coffin,' he said. 'It's all you'll need'."

Jack pulled on his cheroot, raised his eyebrows and said nothing.

Buller nodded. "We've no choice now, Windrush if we've to cane King Kofi. Sir Garnet has failed to raise any sizeable force among the coastal Fantis, despite threats and promises. Now he's sent Captain Nicol of the Hampshire Militia up the Rivers Bonny and Opobo on a recruiting drive."

"That would be a change from Hampshire," Jack said.

"I would imagine so," Buller said. "Nicol was successful though, and brought back some decent warriors, while Lieutenant Bolton of the 1st Wests did the same at Winnebah."

Jack stared to the gloomy north. "The more we recruit, the better, although I doubt the levies will stand for even a single Ashanti volley."

Buller smiled. "Wolseley formed these new men into two regiments, one with Colonel Wood of the 90th in command, and the other under Major Russell of the 13th Hussars."

"God help us," Jack said, "a major of a crack cavalry regiment commanding irregular African infantry. Wellington would turn in his grave."

Buller suddenly cleared his throat, dropped his cheroot and stood at attention. "Sorry, sir, I didn't know you were there."

Wolseley stood a yard away, with Hook at his side.

"I've just arrived, Buller. What's that you were saying, Windrush?"

Jack stubbed out his cheroot. "I hope we are attacking the enemy soon, sir."

Wolseley gave a faint smile. "All in good time, Windrush."

"Perhaps Major Windrush is becoming frustrated at waiting," Hook said smoothly. "According to Buller's reports," he nodded to Buller, "General Amanquatia still has some twenty thousand Ashanti warriors in the field."

Wolseley did not look even slightly concerned at the news. "I'd better do something about it then, hadn't I?"

"Give me a resume of the present situation, Buller." Hook said. "A brief resume."

Buller stood at attention. "The Ashantis are obtaining help from a chain of small villages on the coast near Elmina. The villagers send food and supplies to Essaman, about four miles inland amidst pretty dense jungle, where Amanquatia boasts about building a town as a base for the next invasion."

"Does he, indeed," Wolseley said quietly.

"That's what their General Amanquatia said, sir, according to my spies."' Buller gave a small cough. "I think it was Napoleon who said an army marched on its stomach."

"I believe it was," Hook said.

"Well, if we cut the supplies, the Ashanti army won't be secure," Buller said. "They'll have to withdraw to Ashantiland."

"Thank you for your opinion, Buller." Hook's voice was ominously quiet. "Stick to the facts, if you please."

"Yes, sir. Colonel Wood demanded that the chiefs report to him at Elmina. Rather than obey, they asked Amanquatia what they should do."

"The small villages are caught between the devil and the deep blue sea," Hook said. "Between the Ashanti Empire, that they fear, and the British Empire, which to the best of their knowledge is a handful of West Indian infantry and some sickly European civilians."

"You've developed an efficient intelligence service, Buller," Jack said.

"Bribery helps," Buller said.

"What was Amanquatia's reply to the village chiefs?" Hook returned to the main topic.

"Amanquatia ordered the chiefs not to attend. He said the Ashantis would protect the villages as the white men would not go into the forest."

"We keep hearing that," Wolseley murmured.

Hook nodded. "We do. What did the Fanti chiefs say to Colonel Wood, Buller?"

Buller frowned. "I wrote all this in my report, sir."

"Remind me, Captain." Hook's voice was like silk.

"Yes, Sir. The Ampenee chief did not reply at all," Buller said, "while the Amquana chief told Colonel Wood that he had smallpox that day, but he would come the next."

"The insolent beggar!" Hook smiled. "Did he come the next day?"

Buller shook his head. "No, sir. He fled to the Ashantis. The chief at Essaman was worse. He challenged Colonel Wood to come and fetch him, adding the usual taunt that white men don't dare to go into the bush."

"Cheeky blighter," Jack said, although he had a sneaking admiration for a petty chief who challenged the British Empire.

Wolseley paced away with his hands behind his back and his fingers intertwining. Hook met Jack's eye, winked and gave a small shake of his head.

"Sir Garnet is thinking," Hook said.

Wolseley stopped as if he had reached a decision. When he returned, his face was animated. "You have given me much to consider, Captain Buller."

Buller nodded. "That is my job, sir."

Wolseley smiled. "Gentlemen, you will agree that the Ashanti are growing bolder, day by day."

"They are," Hook agreed.

Wolseley nodded to Jack. "Windrush here has daunted their attacks on our engineering parties cutting roads, but now we have Buller's intelligence about the chiefs at Essaman and such places." Wolseley's smile was unexpected. "Gentlemen!" He rubbed his hands together. "It is time we gathered the press. I expect you all to attend."

Jack shook his head as Wolseley marched away, closely followed by Hook.

"What the devil is Sir Garnet planning? He detests the press," Jack grunted. "All us old Crimea hands detest reporters. They told the Russians all our moves before we made them.' Jack kept the bitterness from his voice as he recalled the chaos of the Crimean campaign. "I'm surprised that Wolseley even allows reporters into the colony."

* * *

Henry Morton Stanley was the first journalist to enter. The Welshman who had discovered Livingstone, he strode to a seat near the front of the room. Winwood Reade, a minor African explorer, was next, looking as if he wished to tell Wolseley his job, while the bearded George Henty of the *Standard* already scribbled notes as he took his seat.

"Here they are," Buller said, "parasites all, hoping for death and suffering to fill their columns. Let's pray that Sir Garnet gives them a swift kick up the trousers."

"Gentlemen of the press," Wolseley said, with some of the Irish accent still in his speech, "you will be aware that Colonel Glover is leading a force of native levies up the flank to menace Ashantiland."

The journalists nodded, taking solemn notes as Jack and Buller glanced at each other.

"I have some rather unsettling news, I am afraid."

Jack felt the ripple of interest as the journalists scribbled on their pads.

Wolseley continued. "I regret to say that the Awoonas, allies of the Ashantis have trapped Glover at Addah, on the right bank of the Volta River. I am going to lead a force to Glover's rescue." Wolseley glanced around the room. "Are there any questions?"

"Yes, Sir Garnet," Stanley stood, looking around to ensure everybody could see him. "Why are we taking such a passive stance? We know Ashantis are hovering around in British territory. Why do you not attack them right away?"

Wolseley looked slightly annoyed at the question. "Until reinforcements arrive, Mr Stanley, I have only a limited number of men available to defend the colony."

"You have sailors and Marines on the Royal Navy ships," Stanley said.

"The naval personnel are only available if the Ashanti attack the settlements," Wolseley explained. "I must use my small force to the best effect I can." He raised his voice slightly. "I trust you all not to release the intelligence I have just given you."

When the journalists raced out to write their copy, Wolseley smiled. "Now they will spread that news out to all and sundry, and the Ashantis will hear and hopefully act accordingly. Prepare your men, gentlemen, for we are leaving for Elmina this evening. He glanced at Jack and Captain Brett. "Windrush, I want your C Company to embark on HMS *Bittern* at six. Brett, you take A Company."

"I presume we are not going to help Colonel Glover, sir," Jack said.

"Why would we do that?" Wolseley asked, innocent as a baby. "He's in no trouble."

CHAPTER TWENTY

At Sea November 1873

As the tropical light faded and the surf crashed silver onto the beach, Jack chivvied his men onto HM gunboat *Decoy*. The Wests filed on board, chattering happily, finding spaces below deck and preparing for a voyage into the unknown. Once they settled, Jack stood on deck to watch the bustle, with boats conveying the Royal Marines and Royal Marine Artillery to HMS *Barracoutta*. With its usual efficiency, the navy sent Captain Peel and a landing party of fifty sailors ashore to man the outlying posts of Cape Coast Castle.

"Sir Garnet's taking a risk, denuding Cape Coast of all its defenders except a handful of tarry jacks," Hopringle sounded nervous.

"Aye," Jack agreed. "But he knows what he's doing."

"Does he?"

"I've never known such a meticulous planner," Jack said. "He's one of the best commanders I've served under."

Hopringle sipped from a pewter hip flask. "I've heard men say that Sir Garnet is the best general since Wellington."

Jack considered for a while. "Not in my experience. I think Colin Campbell, Lord Clyde, was the best, but Wolseley comes close. He is undoubtedly well organised."

Hopringle moved aside as a sailor rolled forward. "You were in the Mutiny weren't you, Windrush? How about Havelock?"

Jack remembered those desperate days when Havelock led his 113th to the relief of Lucknow. "Havelock would have attacked by now,' Jack said. "He'd have taken every man in the colony, soldier, sailor, Marine, policeman and Uncle Tom Cobley and all, and charged straight for Kumasi. He was the right man in the right place in the Mutiny." Jack considered for a moment, "I don't think these tactics would work here."

It was nine in the evening before Wolseley, and his staff boarded *Barracoutta*, where the journalists were already waiting. Never having met this breed of man before, Jack examined them through his binoculars, watching them drinking naval grog before settling down under an awning for the night.

Hopringle grinned. "Watching the writers are you, Windrush? Making sure they don't signal our supposed plans to the Ashantis?"

"I don't trust them," Jack said.

"There are Ashanti spies everywhere," Hopringle said. "So I heard."

At half-past one, with the stars brilliant above, the flotilla weighed anchor for the short voyage to Elmina. A heavy swell rocked the ships from side to side, which did not bother the island-bred West Indians, who understood the sea as well as anybody.

"I say, sir, could you ensure your Wests are off the deck for a while?" Jack did not know the officer who spoke.

"Why is that?"

"I want to train my Hausas," the man was young and eager. "They've never fired an Enfield before."

"Good God!" Jack was genuinely startled. "We'll keep the deck clear for you." He watched as the Hausas lined up on deck, chattering happily as their officers holding up Enfield rifles.

Dear Lord, Jack thought. *What chance have these unfortunate Hausas got in action? No wonder they made a poor showing at Elmina if nobody had trained them.*

The Hausas looked clumsy with the Enfields, although they were keen to learn. They copied the officers' movements, repeating the words by rote as they squeezed days and weeks of training into a couple of hours.

"Good luck, lads," Jack said as their training finished and the Hausas clumped off below. "Aim low and shoot straight."

With the deck clear, Jack checked his men and lay on the deck to sleep. At three o'clock in a dark morning, with an onshore breeze flicking spindrift from the sea and moaning through the rigging, they arrived at Elmina, and the men began to disembark. Jack loaded his revolver, felt his tension rising and watched as Wolseley and Captain Freemantle were first ashore, with half a dozen seamen rowing their gig into the entrance of the Benya River.

"Right, lads," Jack had shaved by lantern light with a mirror propped on the sea-knife of a grinning sailor. He dabbed at the blood that seeped from a cut. "We're marching inland soon. Don't leave any kit behind. Sergeants, make sure your men are ready."

As the Wests queued on deck to board the shore-bound boats, Jack checked their equipment: Rifle, 70 rounds of ball ammunition, greatcoat, haversack, water purifier and water bottle. They filed past him, the men he had trained, the young faces and older faces, the brash and the nervous, his men going to war. *Good luck, lads; I hope my training helped keep you alive.*

"Make sure your water bottles are full!" Jack roared as *Decoy* rose and fell alarmingly with the swell. "If we have to fight, you'll need water desperately. There is nothing more thirst-inducing than powder smoke."

The men swung onto the ladder, ready to descend into the boats, with the swell so high that one minute they were ten feet above the sea, then the next thigh-deep in the water.

"Keep your rifles dry!" Jack roared. "You'll need them later!"

The navy had provided steam launches that towed the boats, with fifty soldiers crammed into each vessel and sailors wielding oars to help the engines. Private Coffin sang a spiritual song that Jack did not know, and others joined in as they jerked and soared toward the coast, dimly seen as a line of white surf against the dark background. St George's Castle' lights seemed to float in the sky like an ethereal construction on the coast, a tenuous European fingerprint on a hostile continent. High above, the stars were bright in a moonless sky, Jupiter and Venus prominent. Jack looked up briefly, knowing that Mary would be watching the same stars, only a hundred and sixty miles away yet in a different world.

The steam-launch eased toward the bar at the narrow mouth of the Benya River, with the familiar bulk of St George's Castle loomed to port. Supporting the 2nd West, boats from *Barracoutta* carried Marines and bluejackets, together with a rocket tube and a cannon. Jack could smell a whiff of tobacco from the sailors, although in the dark, he could not see their bearded faces. More obvious were the white helmets and puggaries of the Marines, and Jack wondered if the Ashantis would relish the excellent targets that splash of light made in the green gloom of the forest.

As the boats hovered offshore, a small flotilla of boats rowed up to them, with local Kroomen paddling beside the bluejackets.

The sailors' voices sounded clearly through the night. "On you come, lobsterbacks! We'll take you ashore! You'll have to change boats now. It's low water here, and if you try the bar fully loaded, the surf will capsize you, sure as eggs is bacon."

Once again the West Indians proved their skills as they leapt from boat to boat, laughing and joking as the larger flotilla headed for the breakers. With the water hissing around them and spilling inboard, Jack shouted orders.

"Keep your rifles and ammunition dry, lads! Hold them up! We don't know how many Ashantis are waiting for us." Following his own advice, Jack took off his pistol belt and the fifty rounds he carried, holding it clear of the water that splashed inboard. The surf lifted his boat high, carried it forward and deposited it with a grinding crash on the sand, still waist-deep in water.

"Stay here, lobsters!" The sailors shouted cheerfully as they and the Kroomen jumped overboard to haul the boat to shallower water.

"Off we get, lads!' Forming C Company up, Jack marched them up the hill to St George's Castle, acknowledging the salutes of the Hausa policemen who guarded the entrance. "Check your ammunition," he ordered, "make sure your rifles are dry and oiled." He walked along the ranks, inspecting each man, giving a word of encouragement to the young, calming down the nervous, exchanging jokes with the old soldiers and the men who had been with him in Kumasi.

"Are we going to avenge Stan Manning, sir?" Ogston asked.

"We will, Ogston, we will," Jack promised.

The night eased away; the stars faded and a wan band of light filtered into the eastern sky. Birds called in the trees to the constant background of surf hammering on the shore.

"Marines! Leave your greatcoats behind!" A stentorian roar temporarily silenced the birds.

Jack saw the Royal Marines thankfully drop their heavy coats. He gave the same order to his West Indians. If twenty years of military experience and four wars had taught him anything, it was that the less burden a soldier carried, the faster he could move and the higher his chance of survival.

The bluejackets of the Naval Brigade gathered in small groups, their bearded faces laughing, short cutlasses prominent at their belts. Jack had met their like in the

Crimea and India and knew them to be the most willing of fighting men. The Hausas in their blue serge and scarlet fezzes swapped anecdotes with the seamen, each speaking in their native language yet seeming to make themselves understood.

Wolseley appeared in the courtyard, erect and dapper, with Lieutenant Colonel Wood at his side. Jack had never met Wood but knew him as a fighting officer, if unlucky with wounds. The Colonel was in nominal command of the column, which must have been hard with Wolseley overlooking everything he did.

When Wood snapped an order, the small army formed up, with Lieutenants Richmond and Woodgate in command of the Hausas. The Hausas looked well, but Jack remembered their far-too-brief training with the Enfields. As they had only come over from Nigeria a few days ago, they had hardly acclimatised to the Gold Coast. *It's unfair to bring these unprepared men to fight the Ashantis.*

With an old wound troubling him, Wolseley was hardly able to walk, so four men carried him in a hammock.

"That will make Sir Garnet a target for every Ashanti with a musket," Hopringle murmured.

Jack lit a cheroot, wishing they were advancing on Kumasi rather than skirmishing around the fringes of the colony. "Aye; it won't be healthy around the general."

"Windrush," Wood said, "take half your company and follow the Hausas. The rest can join the main body of the 2nd in the rear guard."

"You'll be with the rear guard, Hopringle." Jack hurried forward with two sections of Wests, while a ragged group of Fantis clustered around.

"These Bushmen look fierce enough to scare off the devil himself," Daley said.

"We'll see if they are fierce when the fighting starts," Ogston tapped the breech of his Snider. "I'll put my faith in old Snidey, here."

Immediately behind Jack's Wests came a group of local volunteers and sailors with the artillery, a solitary seven pounder plus two rocket tubes with rockets and ammunition. Captain Freemantle of *Barracouta* commanded the Naval Brigade, who swaggered along, joking with brawny native labourers who carried broad-bladed axes.

Behind the axemen marched Captain Crean's Marines. A solid block of blue, they moved with a determined stride as if nothing, not Russians, Frenchmen and definitely not Ashantis, would stop them.

The porters were next, near-naked natives with great bundles balanced on their heads containing ammunition, some food and hammocks for the expected wounded. Finally, Captain Brett and the remainder of the 2nd Wests made up the rearguard. Hopringle trotted up to Jack.

"Captain Brett said I've to stay with you, sir, if you send Sergeant Mathews to take my place."

"Off you go, Mathews," Jack said.

"Brett says I'll be more useful here," Hopringle explained.

"You may well be. This is a long column," Jack knew he would be happier with more fighting men and fewer porters. "Single file lads, and keep alert."

As the dawn light strengthened, the little army began to march along the coast, with every step sinking ankle-deep in sand, the sky clear above and birdcall sweetening the air. Jack remembered the landing in the Crimea and how that ended in carnage and chaos. *Here we go and may God help us.*

CHAPTER TWENTY-ONE

In The Bush November 1873

Ten minutes later, the column headed inland, past the lagoon, with a good view of St George's Fort and the bridge that Jack and the 2nd West had held. Then it was over marshland with a stink that made the men gag. On either flank, the Hausas searched clumps of bushland, with the shouts of the officers as clear as their Elwood helmets and white puggarees.

"Here's the first village," Colonel Wood said. "It's deserted now, but the Ashanti used it as a base only a few weeks ago."

By now, Jack was familiar with the local villages. The brushwood huts were flimsy, offering protection from the sun and little else. When the inhabitants fled, they left only a few odds and ends on the ground. "Not even a gold nugget," a Marine grumbled. "I thought this was the Gold Coast, not the Mosquito Coast."

The column marched on, deeper into the bush. After another fifteen minutes, Jack looked behind him, where smoke smudged the treeline, and the occasional orange flame raised high.

"Somebody's set the village on fire," he said.

"No bad thing." Hopringle scratched at his leg, "I'm sure I caught fleas there."

They strode over a plain of thin scrubland intersected by occasional dense bush that cut visibility to only a few feet. "Careful here, lads," Jack said as he heard the deep boom of an Ashanti musket from ahead. "Remember your skirmishing drill if we go into action."

"We will, sir,' Stair said. "Shall we join the Hausas?"

"Don't be too eager, Stair. Trouble will find us when it wants to."

As they entered an area of thick forest, Jack ordered the men into skirmishing formation, had them watch all around and probe the bush. He knew he was making himself unpopular as he slowed down the column, but the safety of his men was paramount. With shrubs at head height and creepers coiled around the trees, the forest could be deadly, despite the melodious bird sounds all around. Jack breathed deeply when they emerged without any incident.

"No Ashantis this time," Jack said.

"I'm sorry, sir," Ogston said, "but it wasn't a bird calling to us."

"What do you mean?" Jack asked.

"We didn't see any Ashantis," Ogston said, "but they saw us. They are watching everything that we do."

Daley nodded, licking his lips. "That's right, sir. I sensed them in there. And they're here too, hiding in the grassland."

The track was wending through shoulder-high grass, yellow under the sun, and specked with areas of forest and enlivened by bright flowers. It was undoubtedly beautiful but could conceal all kinds of predators.

Mary would love these flowers. "Come on!" Jack snarled at his men. "Pick the pace up!" He loosened the pistol in its holster. "I'll give a half-sovereign to the first man to sight an Ashanti warrior!" Thinking of Mary had rekindled his anger, awakening a desire to kill. He closed his eyes, struggling with the images that raced through his mind. He seemed to hear the throb of Ashanti drums and share the bloodlust of that terrible city.

"Push on!" Jack forced himself to stride ahead, with the grass swishing on both sides and his men looking around, Sniders poised.

Hold on, Mary. Hold on. Do anything you can to stay alive.

Despite the promised reward, none of his men saw an Ashanti as they left the tall grass for an area of swampland, where black ooze clutched at their feet and legs. They plodded on, step after sucking step, with Jack dreading the thought of water snakes, and insects clouding around their heads.

Colonel Wood called a halt when they left the swamp, and Jack posted sentries at hundred-yard intervals around his half-company. "Keep your eyes open," he said, altering the angle of his pith helmet, so the brim shaded his eyes from the now burning sun.

"We're approaching territory where the Ashantis are known to operate," Wood said. "I'd like all the Hausas in skirmishing order."

Jack waited hopefully for the order to deploy his men. It did not come, and after a hurried breakfast, they moved on.

With the Hausas and the Fanti tribesmen fanned out around the column, they moved forward with more caution, surrounding each patch of dense bushland and carefully probing as they advanced. Jack extended his Wests further, each man covering his neighbour.

"Sir!" Private Coffin lifted an arm. "I think I saw somebody up there." The hill rose from the surrounding bushland, with the summit cleared for agriculture.

"Stair, run back to Colonel Wood. Tell him, with my compliments, that there may be Ashantis on that hill."

Willing as always, Stair hurried to the middle of the column, returning ten minutes later with his usual smile. "The colonel says it's in hand, sir."

Within a few moments, Lieutenant Woodgate and a dozen Hausas left the column. While they doubled around the back of the hill, Lieutenant Graves led a further twelve Hausas to the base.

"Where's your Ashanti, Windrush?" Colonel Wood pushed through the column to speak to Jack.

"There's a village there," Jack studied the hill through his binoculars. 'I see it a couple of hundred yards to the right of the clearing, in the jungle. I can't see any movement at present, but this is Ashanti country, and one of my men saw somebody hereabouts."

"Can you trust his word?" Wood asked.

Jack knew his men were listening. "Implicitly, sir."

"Very good," Wood said. "Richmond," he spoke the commander of the Hausas. "Take the rest of your Hausas and inspect that village. Windrush, you and your Wests jog along in reserve."

"Yes, sir. Come on, lads. Form a skirmishing line and follow me." Feeling his old familiar mixture of excitement and trepidation, Jack advanced with his men in extended order, rifles ready.

The Hausas were in front, too bunched up for Jack's taste. He knew that on the North-West Frontier, the Pashtuns would have cut them down with ease and he suspected the Ashantis were as dangerous.

"Keep spread out," Jack ordered, as the Wests also began to creep closer together. Jack knew it was natural to seek company, but that it was false security that increased the target area for enemy marksmen. Reaching the base of the hill, they began to climb, with the tension rising when they entered the trees.

"The village is empty!" Lieutenant Graves reported. "The Ashanti have left."

"They're watching us," Ogston said. "What's that on the ground?"

It was the body of a man, stark naked, with a sword wound to the chest. "He's a Hausa," Ogston said at once. 'Not one of our men. The Ashantis must have had him as a slave and killed him for fetish."

Jack viewed the dead man for a moment, seeing him as a mute reminder of the tragedy of human existence. He wondered how the Hausa had come to be a slave, and who missed him in his homeland.

"Set fire to the village," Colonel Wood ordered, and soon orange flames and blue smoke smudged the sky. The explosion took everybody by surprise, with men ducking or crouching down. Two of the Hausas fired without aiming, and Hopringle's section knelt, slamming their Sniders into their shoulders.

"Hold your fire," Jack shouted. "That's a barrel of gunpowder exploding! The Ashanti must have stored it in the village as they did in Elmina."

Slightly shame-faced, the Wests clambered back to their feet. "Better luck next time, lads," Jack said.

Leaving the village in flames behind them, the British moved on, still without having seen a single Ashanti.

"They're all around us," Ogston said. "Watching us every step of the way."

Jack felt the eyes on him before he saw the grass move against the wind. The Ashanti stood still, with his striped face and arms perfect camouflage amidst the tall grass, and then he stepped back, the grass closed and he was gone.

"I saw him too, Windrush," Wood said quietly. "Where there is one, there will be more."

"That was one of Kumi Okese's Edwesus," Jack said. "They're the best warriors the Ashanti has."

"Royal Marines!" Wood ordered. "I want a section of Marines skirmishing on either flank. The Ashantis are here."

To their left, the open land altered as the patches of forest became more extensive and more frequent, perfect country to hide Ashantis. The column moved slower, with the native levies checking the bush and Jack's men spread out, ready to fire. On the flanks, the Marines held their rifles at the high port as the sun reflected from their white hats.

Good luck, lads.

As the Marines passed an area of tangled jungle, Jack heard a single thud, deeper than a Snider.

"That's an Ashanti musket," he said. 'Skirmish positions, men, ready your rifles!'

A second shot followed, with the sound echoing against the forest, and then a third, with white powder-smoke rising to the left and in front.

"It's an ambush!" Ogston yelled.

"Fire!" Wood gave the first order, which officers repeated along the column, like an echo.

The Marines fired a volley, the sharp crack of the Sniders contrasting with the deep, ugly thuds of the Ashanti's Tower muskets.

"Steady, Marines!" A young officer shouted. "Take your time! Don't throw away your shots!"

A hundred yards in front, the Hausas also fired, their musketry wild as they shot into the trees or anything that might be an Ashanti warrior.

Lieutenant Graves lifted his voice. "Don't fire at random, Hausas! Pick your targets!"

"Come on, lads!" Jack led his Wests forward. "Stay with me. We're supporting the Hausas." The Marines were mostly very young, but Jack had more faith in their steadiness than he had in the Hausa police. White smoke jetted from Jack's right, with the wind of a slug hissing past him. An inch to the left and it would have struck him in the right temple. Shrugging he carried on; it was only another miss.

"Marines!" Graves shouted again. "Take ground to the left!"

"Put the gun on its carriage!" A calm officer said. "Load and bring it forward. Give the lads some support."

The Ashantis had adopted their favoured horseshoe formation, firing on the British column from the front and both flanks. Jack watched his men, knowing that it was the first time most had been in action and no amount of training could prepare them for the real thing. They retained their formation, lying or crouching behind cover as they fired steadily.

"Aim at the smoke," Jack walked along the skirmish line, letting his men see him and fighting his desire to duck. "Don't waste your bullets." He flinched as something slammed into the tree beside his head, saw the gleam of the metal slug against the bark, and walked on. "Make sure you don't fire at your own men. The Marines are out there."

Stair was shouting something, his Jamaican accent thickening with excitement as he stood up for a clearer shot.

"Take your time, Stair!" Jack pushed him back into cover. "Keep your fool head down!"

The concentrated fire of muskets, Sniders and Enfields echoed around the forest, with bullets and slugs hissing and crackling in all directions. Gunsmoke coiled between the branches, writhing around the creepers, stinging the eyes and noses of all the men. Above the hammer of musketry, Jack heard the yells of the wounded, but whether friend or enemy he could not tell.

Colonel Wood stepped forward, with Wolseley at his side, as calm as if they were on the parade square at Aldershot. "Over there, I think," Wood indicated a piece of rising ground a little to the left of their present position.

"Take the high ground!" Wolseley ordered. "Hold it until we see what's happening out there." He glanced at Jack. "Windrush, you and your Wests push back the enemy."

"Yes, sir. Up you get lads! Let's show the world how good we are."

The Wests rose, some taking a parting shot at the Ashantis, others loading. Coffin was muttering a prayer as he thumbed a cartridge into the breech of his rifle.

"Maintain your discipline," Jack said, "no running. NCOs, keep your men in formation." He saw some of the Hausas charge forward, while others fired wildly at the trees.

"Aim before you fire, Jackson!" Jack grabbed the rifle from a yelling young soldier. "You're wasting ammunition!'

Keeping his men as a cover for the main British force, Jack led them to the front of the rising ground, where thick, shoulder-high bush offered shelter for any Ashantis.

"Halt!" Jack ordered. "Form a firing line." He peered through the smoke, ensuring that his men obeyed, pulled back two of the most eager and checked his surroundings.

To the left of the Wests, an area of tall grass extended for about three hundred yards, ending in a steep bush-covered ridge. Jack's Wests and the Hausas were in an extended line in front of the British force, firing at the puffs of smoke in the trees. The Hausas were yelling in excitement, yanking the triggers, so their bullets endangered everybody except the Ashantis.

When the jets of smoke from the forest lessened, Jack raised a hand. The deep booming of Ashanti muskets had stopped entirely.

"Cease fire!" Jack shouted. "Cease fire!"

One by one, his men stopped, looking at each other in evident pleasure, satisfied that they had shown their martial prowess and forced the Ashantis back. Jack grunted; some had acted like the untried recruits, many of them were excited and ill-disciplined, but not a single man had run. They had the makings of soldiers, once they learned to control their zeal.

The Hausa officers were busy stopping their men from firing so gradually silence descended on the slopes. Jack swore, as one of the rearguard shouted "Ashanti," and the firing started again.

"Hold your fire!" Jack snarled to his men. "Only fire if I give the order."

The noise ended, and silence returned, with gunsmoke drifting from the British position towards the surrounding woodland. A bird called, and another as nature recovered from the disruption. Jack saw a single leaf fall from a tree, to drift slowly to the ground, unheeded by everybody except him.

Colonel Wood scanned the forest with his binoculars before giving quiet orders that saw Captain Freemantle with the Naval Brigade drag the rocket tubes and seven-pounder toward the trees beyond the grassland on the left flank. At the same time, the men of the Royal Marine Artillery headed for the right.

Jack saw the movement behind the leaves. "It's not finished yet, boys. The Ashantis have shifted their position, that's all."

The Ashantis proved Jack right when they replied to the threat to their flanks by firing ineffectual volleys from the trees.

"You're out of range, you lubbers!" A tattooed seaman jeered.

One of the seamen was cracking jokes, with his mates laughed, adding lewd comments that spread the humour, while a section of Hausas began to chant Islamic verses. Hearing the words of the Koran, Coffin retaliated with a psalm, so it was a strange medley of sounds that greeted the Ashanti ambush.

There are no drums, Jack thought. *Why are there no drums today?*

"They're at extreme range for their muskets," Jack said. "Number One section, fire when you see a target. Number Two Section, hold your fire."

The firefight continued for a few moments, with the Ashanti fire gradually diminishing.

"Lieutenants Graves and Woodgate, take a platoon of Hausas each and skirmish lower down the slopes." Wolseley gave rapid orders. "The rest of the Hausas and Windrush's West Indians, follow the main path into the valley past that hill."

We're the bait, Jack thought. *Wolseley is sending us along the path to tempt the Ashanti into attacking so the rockets and artillery can catch them.* "Come on, boys! You heard the general! Follow me!"

As the British moved, the Ashanti fire began again, with the forest fighters concentrating on the flanking parties.

"These Ashanti know their stuff," Jack said to Hopringle. "They recognise that the main threat comes from the flanks."

In his first real action, Hopringle gave a nervous grin, ducking as an Ashanti slug whizzed past his head.

"You'll get used to it," Jack said. "You'll never get to like it, but you'll put on a mask, as the rest of us do."

The Wests were becoming noisy, shouting threats at the Ashanti and bunching until Jack ordered silence. "Skirmishing order," he reminded. "Keep apart and don't offer yourselves as targets for the enemy."

The firing from the trees increased, and Jack felt a tug on his jacket. He looked down to see an ironstone slug embedded in the fabric on a level with his ribs. *If that had been a bullet, I'd be dead,* he told himself. "Keep moving forward, C Company! Only fire if you are sure of your target!"

Judging by the response from the Wests, many were very sure of their target. They fired, loaded and fired again, moving forward from cover to cover as Jack had trained them. Jack grunted, knowing the psychological strain of being under fire without hitting back. It was better to retaliate, even if the possibility of hitting the enemy was remote. Only the best-disciplined troops could receive fire without responding. Slipping his hand inside his tunic, he touched Mary's scarf for luck.

"Keep moving!" Seeing movement in a bush ahead, Jack fired two rounds, side-stepped as something buzzed past him and stepped on. Knowing that he was a conspicuous target in the scarlet uniform of the 113th, he had to fight his nerves. *Once this expedition is over, I'll see if Wolseley allows my men to wear something more neutral.*

Jack flinched as one of the Hausas staggered under the impact of a slug, then a second smashed into the man's face. As the Hausa crumpled, two more Ashantis fired, with the Hausas body jerking at each strike. He lay, groaning on the ground, trying to pluck something from inside his jacket.

"Lie still, man," Jack stepped to the wounded man. "The bearers will take you back."

The Hausa looked at Jack with the light fading from his eyes, still reaching inside his jacket.

"What do you want?" Jack opened the Hausa's tunic. When a small copy of the

Koran slid out, Jack pushed the book into the man's hand. "Rest easy, Hausa," Jack said, patted his shoulder and stood up.

C Company had advanced fifteen yards while Jack had been with the wounded man. Stepping across a trailing branch, Jack moved forward. The Hausas and his Wests were firing, with the sharp crackle of musketry marking their route. With so many Ashanti warriors around them, the British seemed to be moving through a tunnel of smoke so dense it nearly hid the trees.

The Hausas ahead were erratic, running in all directions, loading and firing without taking aim and ignoring the frantic orders of their officers. *That's not surprising, with their lack of training.*

"Keep moving!" Jack said. "Aim and fire only when you have a target! Don't waste ammunition!"

He saw a small clearing in the forest, with a sizeable village under the pall of drifting white smoke. *That must be Essaman.* The palm-leaf roofs looked very peaceful amidst the din of battle, and Jack hoped the woman and children had escaped to safety. He grunted as a score of Ashanti warriors emerged from the houses, firing towards the advancing British. *These Ashanti lads are game.* Suddenly aware of movement to his left, Jack saw the Hausas retiring, one by one and then in a great body of open-mouthed men. Half a dozen discarded fezzes remained, red against the green bush, to show how far the Hausas had advanced. The sharp notes of a bugle tried to recall the Hausas, failed and tried again.

"Stay with me, C Company!" Jack lifted a hand to Hopringle, who stood erect amidst his men, daring the Ashantis to fire. "Hopringle! Keep your fool head down!"

Glancing behind him, Jack saw the Hausas Lieutenant Woodgate retiring with only his bugler, swearing like a Marine on a drunken binge.

"These Hausas don't have your training," Jack shouted to his men. "Come on, 2nd West! Show them how true soldiers behave!"

All around him, Jack heard heavy firing, from the deep thuds of the Ashantis' muskets to the regulated, sharper crack of the Sniders. Behind the musketry, he heard the shrilling of British bugles and the throbbing of Ashanti war-drums and blare of their horns. Powder-smoke filled the air, the hoarse shouts of men and the occasional shriek as a shot slammed home. *This is getting hot, but my lads are holding up well.*

A sinister whoosh intruded into the sounds of battle. Jack looked up to see Captain Freemantle's rocket fly over the palm-thatch roofs of the village, trailing a ribbon of smoke and sparks. He had heard that rockets unsettled the Ashantis, but evidently, nobody had told that to the defenders of Essaman. They stood their ground, loading and firing from the shelter of houses as rockets soared past.

As the rocketeers and the Ashanti exchanged fire, Captain Freemantle pushed forward the nine-pounder, with Captain Bullen of the Marines at his side and the seamen and Kroomen struggling with the weight. A group of Ashantis emerged from the forest and opened a steady fire on the gunners, momentarily exposing themselves.

"Get these men!" Jack pointed to the Ashantis.

Captain Bullen staggered as a slug hit the compass case around his neck, while a bullet passed through Captain Freemantle's arm, spinning him in a complete circle.

"Force them back, lads! Hopringle! Your section is closer, protect the gunners."

Even as he directed his men, Jack admired the skill of the enemy. *Good tactics of these Ashantis, targeting the officers.*

With blood seeping from his arm, Freemantle tore a handkerchief from his pocket, wrapped it around his arm, tied it with his teeth and carried on.

"Hopringle! Defend the artillery. We'll press on here." Jack's section and the remaining Hausas advanced steadily. Again the Ashantis aimed at the officers, with another spent slug winding Jack as it struck him under the breast bone, and a bold warrior stepping clear of the forest to shoot Colonel McNeill. As the colonel collapsed with blood gushing from his lacerated arm, Ogston took steady aim and shot the Ashanti marksman.

"Well done, Ogston!" Jack praised. He saw the flash of white teeth as Ogston grinned at him through the smoke.

With many of the officers down, Wolseley took direct command, ordering Jack's Wests to attack Essaman in front as the Marines closed in on each flank.

"Both your sections, Windrush!"

A frontal attack against steady infantry was one of the most perilous manoeuvres, so Jack knew he had to set an example to his inexperienced troops. "Come on the Wests!" Loading as he marched, Jack advanced in front of his men. "Come on, C Company!"

Immediately aware that the pincer movement would squeeze them in a crossfire, the Ashantis fired a final farewell and fled into the jungle, leaving Jack dizzy with relief. He gripped Mary's scarf. *We survived that action, Mary.*

"We've captured Essaman!" Somebody shouted in a broad Devon accent as the Marines' flanking sections met in the centre of the village. "Stand and fight, you beggars!"

"Well done, Wests!" Jack praised as his company grinned at each other. "Make sure you're loaded in case the Ashantis return."

Throwing off any final shred of discipline, the Hausas ran into Essaman, yelling and shrieking, as they began to loot the village of anything they could carry. Jack realised that some of his men were looking at him hopefully. He shook his head. "We're the 2nd Wests," he said, "not Bushmen in uniform." He knew that looting had been a soldier's perquisite since time immemorial, but he wanted his Wests to maintain their discipline until he knew it was safe.

"Torch it!" The word spread. "Put Essaman to the flames."

"Not yet!" Coffin yelled. "There's somebody inside that house!"

"Hold!" Jack shouted as a bearded sailor lifted a blazing torch. "Check inside, Coffin. Cover him Ogston."

Holding his rifle ready, Coffin dived inside the hut, emerging a moment later with a terrified little boy. "What do I do with this wild Ashanti warrior, sir?"

"I'll take that beggar off your hands, soldier," Captain Crean said, lifted the child and promptly handed him over to a group of eager Marines. "Here, men, do something with this little chap."

"A recruit!" The Marines welcomed the youngster with grins and extended arms.

"My missus always wanted a little boy," a grizzled sergeant said. "If she sees this little tyke we'll never get rid of the blighter."

"Now can I burn the house, sir?" The bearded sailor asked plaintively, with his torch dripping sparks.

"Yes, on you go," Jack said.

When the flames took hold of Essaman, with the now-expected explosions from casks of gunpowder, Wolseley ordered the buglers to blow assembly, and his small army gathered in a nearby clearing, some laughing, others quiet, as the officers checked the casualties. "Thirty-two wounded, one dead."

Jack had two of his Wests injured, none seriously. "That's your first action, lads," he said. "You did well." His men grinned to him, with Daley shaking with reaction as Ogston put an arm around him.

The Marines looked exhausted, some lying flat on the ground, others in a state of shock. Except for the NCOs, Jack doubted if any of them were twenty years old, and many much younger. They were little more than boys, first-year recruits who had proved themselves in this very alien environment. Now some were severely wounded and may die before they had properly matured.

"I heard they were dragged from Devon and sent here before their training was complete," Hopringle noticed Jack studying the Marines. "I wonder how many regret taking the Queen's Shilling now."

"I think most soldiers have regrets after their first action," Jack said. "Then it becomes part of life. Regrets are part of the soldiers' bargain. And the Marines' bargain."

Although Jack had taken part in much bloodier expeditions, he wondered if the results were worth the casualties. The British had destroyed a couple of villages that the Ashantis could rebuild in a few days and had killed a few dozen warriors from an army of many thousand.

"That's a good day's work so far, Windrush." Colonel Wood did not agree with Jack's assessment. "We've proved that British soldiers can face and defeat the Ashantis in their own forests."

Jack nodded. "It's a start, sir." He was more interested in the behaviour of his West Indians, and the safety of Mary. If he was going to Kumasi, he wanted his men to be thoroughly trained and better disciplined. *They are not ready yet. I need a crack company to fight the Ashantis. I need to get my company into action again.*

CHAPTER TWENTY-TWO

In The Bush November 1873

With a section of Wests escorting the wounded back to Cape Coast Castle, Wolseley ordered the column to march on. Jack adjusted his pith helmet, ensured his men were loaded and led them across a plain where patches of scrub and forest could give the enemy plenty cover. Now aware how stubborn the Ashantis' defence would be, Wolseley sent skirmishers in front, with Jack's company supporting the Hausas.

"Don't shoot unless you see an enemy," Jack emphasised. "Remember that the porters have to carry every cartridge, and the further we march, the more scarce ammunition will become."

He thought of Mary and that hellish fetish tree. "Aim before you fire," he said for at least the fiftieth time, "and make every shot count. We are not here to loot the enemy's villages. We are here to destroy their empire and free the hostages."

After an hour of slow progress, Wolseley called a halt outside another small village, from which the inhabitants had fled. A quick search revealed no women or children, only a couple of kegs of gunpowder and a vintage French musket, abandoned by a fleeing warrior.

Jack glanced up. Although there was no sound of drums, he could feel the menace all around.

"Torch the place," Wolseley spoke from his hammock. As the flames rose, he called the officers together. "We've marched far enough inland to make our point, gentlemen. The Ashanti now know we can defeat them in the forest. It's time to remove the enemy from our coast."

The column left the village blazing behind them and plunged into an area of forest so dense that Jack could hardly see two yards on either flank.

"Wait here, lads." Borrowing a cutlass from a seaman, Jack hacked into the bush beside the track.

"What are you doing, sir?" Hopringle asked.

"Searching for an Ashanti battle path," Jack said. "They cut them parallel to the main track to ambush us." After a few moments, with sweat bursting from every pore, he knew that not even the Ashanti could cut a secondary path in such impenetrable jungle.

"We're safe from ambush here," Jack told his waiting Wests, "but don't relax. Keep alert, keep in extended order and keep your rifles loaded. There might be a stray Ashanti, somewhere."

The path narrowed further, forcing the column into single file, a long line of men all wondering if the Ashantis had infiltrated the thick trees on their flanks. Shortly after, they had other worries, for even walking was difficult. With this track the only route, thousands of travellers had worn a deep cleft in the ground, which nature had filled with a particularly glutinous mud. Men cursed as the mud sucked the boots from their feet and insects clouded around their heads.

"It's bloody hot," a flame-haired young Marine took his helmet off to wipe sweat from his face. "I never knew it would be this hot."

"Put your helmet back on!" Jack snarled. "The sun is as deadly as any Ashanti bullet." He looked up as a shift in the wind carried a low rumbling to them. "That's gunfire," he said. "Heavy stuff, not musketry."

As they staggered and limped along the track, starting at every hint of possible Ashanti ambush, the booming of heavy guns became more distinct.

"What's happening, sir?" Hopringle sounded nervous.

"I'm blessed if I know," Jack said.

"Don't you lobster-backs worry," a smiling Navy lieutenant said. "The navy's here to look after you. That noise you hear will be *Argus* and *Decoy* shelling the enemy." He looked southward as if he could see the sea through miles of forest. "I know the sound of British gunboats anywhere, even in the middle of the African jungle."

"Thank you, lieutenant," Jack nodded, thinking that Wolseley was the most organised general he had ever met, ensuring that the navy bombarded the enemy in conjunction with an attack by the army.

"Oh, always happy to oblige, old chap. Any time you lobsters need educated, just ask a sailor."

"Pick the pace up!" Wolseley shouted from his hammock. "We want to reach the villages soon after the Navy has finished with them."

Hopringle looked confused. "I thought we were returning to Cape Coast. Which villages did the general mean?"

"Amguna, Akimfoo and Ampeenee," Jack said. "They've been helping the Ashantis."

Hopringle shrugged. "We'd best have a look, then."

After a few hours inland, it was a relief to come to the freshness of the coast, although a fringe of cocoa-not grass and palm trees blocked any view of the sea. The cannonade grew louder as the column marched to Amguna, with the regular boom of naval artillery an alien intrusion into the natural sounds of Africa.

Colonel Wood lifted his voice. "Windrush, take a section ahead, ensure there are no Ashantis in Amguna."

"Come on, lads," Jack jogged ahead, with his men at his heels. "Skirmishing order!" They moved at a fast pace across the sand, with the wind pleasant on hot faces and palm trees rustling beside them. Always aware the Ashantis would target him first, Jack forced himself to stand tall, encouraging his men.

Amguna was similar to the villages inland, except for the belt of cocoa- nut trees and the fresh sea breeze. Jack saw a flicker of movement across a doorway. "Careful, lads, in case there are musket men."

Now veterans, the Wests obeyed at once, stretching into a line that outflanked Amguna on both sides. As they approached the village, a dozen people fled, taking their children, animals and some household possessions with them. There was no musketry and no sign of any Ashanti warriors as the bleating of goats gradually faded.

"Follow me," Jack moved cautiously between the houses, kicking open doors to see if anybody was inside. After ten minutes, he ordered Ogston back to the column. "My compliments to General Wolseley," he said, "and Amguna is clear of the enemy."

"Burn the place down," Wolseley ordered from his hammock.

Moving away a few hundred yards from the burning village, the British halted, with coconut trees protecting them from the worst of the afternoon sun. Again, the young Marines collapsed on the greyish sand, seeking shade as sweat eased from faces already burned brick-red.

"Look up there!" Stair pointed upwards, where green coconuts bunched under the leaves.

"Get some down, Sam!" Ogston urged, lifting a fallen branch.

Grinning, Stair climbed part way up the tree, reached up with the branch and dislodged a dozen nuts.

"What's this?" A young Marine lifted a coconut curiously. "What's it do?"

"It's a coconut, Johnnie," Private Coffin explained. He showed the Marine how to open the shell, using his bayonet to slice away the green rind and gouging a hole in the nut.

"Drink the milk, Johnnie," Ogston demonstrated. "It's good."

At first hesitant at this novel food, the Marine tasted the contents, nodded and swallowed the contents before passing the news on to his mates. Within a few moments Marines and bluejackets joined the West Indians and Hausas in drinking coconut milk, laughing together under the swaying palms with the sound of the surf in the background. Jack thought it could be an Elysian scene, except for the smoke from the burning village, the grumble of naval gunfire and the preponderance of weapons.

"You, men." Jack pointed to Number Two section. "You're on sentry duty. Go a hundred yards outside the camp and watch for Ashantis."

"The Marines aren't on picket," Jackson protested, with coconut milk dripping from his chin.

"You're better than them," Jack said. "You're the 2nd West." He looked at the Marines. Despite the refreshing coconuts and the sea-breeze, most of the young men lay supine, sweat-streaked and exhausted. Some were sleeping, others just lying prone, trying to draw deep breaths of air. *These lads won't go much longer.*

Wolseley and Colonel Wood seemed to come to the same conclusion. "The youngsters are about done," Wolseley said.

"Best leave them here for the navy to collect, I think, sir," Wood said. "The Hausas and the 2nd West are better acclimatised to the conditions."

"I'll see if there are any volunteers," Wolseley said. "You never know with Royal Marines. They always have the capacity to surprise."

When Wood said he was "looking for twenty Marine volunteers to continue the march," he was nearly knocked down in the rush. Smooth-faced boys who had been prone with exhaustion a moment before declared their willingness to continue.

"Take me, sir! I'll show these Shanties what for!"

"I'm your man, sir," said a boy who looked as if he should still be in school.

"I'm tough stuff, Colonel! I'm coming!"

Wood smiled. "Good boys," he said, visibly moved, "brave, brave boys." Selecting twenty of the fittest, he ordered the surgeon to examine them and sent the remainder as an escort for the dozen hammocks of wounded men. "Take them to Elmina," Wood pointed along the coast. "It's only a few miles away."

Jack's Wests marched with the main body in the opposite direction, with each footstep sinking and sliding in soft sand and the sun glaring above, reflecting from the sea as the breakers crashed beside them. After an hour, HMS *Decoy* came close inshore and sent her boats full of fresh bluejackets and Marines.

"You couldn't do without us, could you?" Captain Luxmore said, grinning as his men swarmed ashore through the surf. "Typical army, full of colour and shine until things get difficult and then what is it? Send for the navy!"

"Not quite," Jack shouted back. "My 2nd Wests wanted to show the bluejackets how real warriors fight, not shellbacks who spend all night in comfortable bunks and all day swanning about in cool breezes." He felt, rather than saw, his men's pleasure at his words.

"We've brought water," Luxmore's smile did not fade, "and a case of claret for the Marines. Can't have the lads going thirsty, can we?"

"Well met, Captain," Jack said, as the newly arrived bluejackets and 2nd West sized each other up.

A bugle blared, bringing the men back to the ranks and they marched on, sometimes with the sea in view and the navy patrolling as if in a different world, and at other times with tall trees screening them on both sides. When they approached another village, the inhabitants fled, some carrying household goods, others driving fowls or goats before them.

"Shall we torch the houses, sir?" An eager midshipman asked.

"Not this time," Wolseley said. "They have not fired on us, and we've had no reports of this village supporting the Ashantis." He raised his voice. "No looting here and no souvenir hunting! We do not hurt our friends."

Blinking away the sweat that dripped into his eyes, Jack marched on, until they reached another, larger village that a stretch of coconut grass, twelve feet high, had protected from the navy. Even naval gunners could not bombard a target they could not see.

"What's this place called?" Hopringle slumped down with his back to a tall palm.

Jack checked his notes. "I'm not sure."

"Burn it," Wolseley said without hesitation, "and march on."

Once again, the flames rose, orange-red and ugly, while dirty smoke smudged the bright sky.

"They'll remember us on this coast," Hopringle said.

"Aye." Jack took a pull at his water bottle. "For all the wrong reasons. We're the men who destroyed their homes." He ignored Hopringle's curious look, for this work of destruction depressed him.

"They can build the houses again, sir," Ogston must have understood Jack's thoughts. "Better burning houses than enslaving the inhabitants."

Jack trudged on, head down, hating himself. *I should be rescuing Mary, not burning huts scores of miles from Kumasi.* "Pick up your feet, C Company!" He roared. "This is not a blasted picnic!"

They forded an ankle-deep stream, with the water muddy and foul as it flowed from a lagoon, and with insects hovering near the surface.

"Don't drink that," Jack snarled as some of the Marines scooped up water with their helmets. "God only knows what diseases it harbours."

"God knows everything," Coffin said quietly.

"Windrush," Colonel Wood gave a quiet order. "Take your Wests and scout ahead, for Ampanee."

Glad to be active, Jack led his men forward, all his fatigue forgotten in the energy of movement. After another quarter-mile, Stair gestured ahead.

"Sir," Stair said, "a flag."

Green, black and yellow, the Ashanti flag hung from a tall flag post in defiance of General Wolseley, Queen Victoria and the entire British Empire. Jack drew his revolver. "They would not display that flag unless they intended to fight. Skirmishing order, lads, and be prepared for an ambush."

The Wests moved on, more warily now, tense, expecting trouble, with their heart-beat increasing and the breath harsh in their throats. Ampanee huddled behind tall grass, with thick forest fifty yards to the rear. As he came closer, Jack saw the village was a collection of simple huts no different to all the others on this coast, except for the flag.

"Take One Section ahead, Hopringle." Jack knew it would do the lieutenant good to lead his men in action.

The group of Ashanti warriors that clustered beneath the flag were too intent on watching a coastal gunboat to notice C Company's advance. Jack pushed his section in support of Hopringle, who had taken to cover a hundred yards from the village.

"Extended skirmishing formation, lads!" Jack ordered.

"Sir!" Coffin pointed to the figure on the base of the flagstaff. "That's a man."

Stark naked, the man was spread-eagled upside down against the staff. He lacked his head, which lay on the sand a few yards away. Whether he had been sacrificed to a fetish or killed because he sympathised with the British, his death would have been terrifying.

Once again, Jack thought of Mary in the hands of the Ashanti and choked on his next words. He was tempted to charge straight in, killing, but twenty years of military experience tempered his ardour with caution.

"Hopringle, notify Colonel Wood what we have here." Jack fingered the chamber of his revolver. "Watch over these Ashantis, lads." He posted his men in the best places he could, having to push three into cover.

"Sir! We're soldiers," Jackson protested. "We're not scared of the Bushmen. We stand in the open to fight! We don't skulk behind trees!"

"Do as you are ordered," Jack snarled. "A dead soldier is no good to anybody." He slammed Jackson behind a tree. "Stay there and obey orders!"

Jackson's movement had alerted the Ashanti, with some moving in single file towards this new British threat on their flank.

"Right, boys. Fire when they get in range. Make sure of your target and aim low." Jack cursed when more of the enemy appeared. Rather than a dozen warriors, there were scores, in the village or emerging from the forest fringe. "Ampanee must be one of the Ashantis' main bases!"

"Shall we withdraw, sir?" Hopringle asked.

"No!" Jack snarled the word. "We stand fast and hold them."

With some Ashantis giving covering fire from the village, scores of others advanced towards Jack's thin line, ducking into cover like trained soldiers and coming steadily closer despite their casualties.

"Fire at will, Wests!" Jack flinched as something thudded into the sand beside him. *That was a bullet from a Snider or an Enfield. This is not pleasant.*

The whoosh and fiery trail was welcome as Wolseley put three rockets into the village and then sent forward the Naval Brigade. At the sight of rockets, the Ashantis faltered. "Rapid-fire, boys!" Jack roared. "They're wavering!"

The Naval Brigade passed through the 2nd Wests' position with the usual exchange of banter and a genuine request, "don't fire at us, Wests! We're on your side!"

"Cease fire!" Jack shouted. "Let the tarry-backs do their work!" He grabbed Jackson's rifle. "You too, Jackson!"

Drawing their cutlasses, the sailors charged forward, chased the Ashantis out of the village and took up defensive positions facing the bush.

"Follow the sailors, boys," Jack led them into Ampanee, "the Bushmen aren't done yet."

After a few moments of relative quiet, the Ashanti opened a heavy fire from the trees, with slugs hammering against the huts and scarring the trees.

"Get around their flanks," a beefy naval lieutenant ordered and the seamen moved in single file to the left, when a horde of Ashantis burst from the trees, yelling and waving muskets and long knives.

For a terrible second, Jack thought the Ashantis would massacre the seamen, but without waiting for an order, the sailors dropped to their knees and opened rapid fire. The Snider bullets felled the first wave of Ashantis, while the rest wavered.

"One Section," Jack said, "be prepared to support the seamen." He could not fire for fear of hitting the sailors. "Fix bayonets!" Although he had not had time to train his company in bayonet drill, he hoped their natural aggression would be enough. He saw Stair inch forward. "Wait for my order, damn it!"

Miraculously surviving the hail of Snider bullets, a tall, rangy Ashanti with a long white cloak ran for a petty officer with his knife. The petty officer fired, missed, dropped his rifle and drew his cutlass. Without a word, he squared up to the charging warrior, feinted left, cut right and thrust straight for the Ashanti's throat.

"And that's done for you, my lad," the petty officer said, wiped his blade on the Ashanti's cloak, sheathed his cutlass, picked up his rifle, loaded it and carried on as if nothing had happened.

"Hold!" Jack said. "The navy doesn't need us this time."

As the surviving Ashantis retreated into the forest, a second group charged at the British right flank.

"Here they come again, boys,' Jack shouted. "Keep calm, shoot low and take your time." He heard Captain Crean give his Marines similar instructions. The initial volley from the British staggered the Ashanti charge, and when Jack ordered independent firing, the volume of bullets increased in direct proportion to a decrease in accuracy.

"Remember your training! Take your time, men!" Jack admonished again. "Aim before you fire!"

The concentrated fire of Wests, Hausas, Marines and the Naval Brigade forced the Ashantis back, still firing but with their long muzzle-loaders giving them a significant disadvantage when facing breech-loaders in the open. Leaving a scatter of bodies on the ground, the Ashantis retreated to the forest and continued to fire.

"Lie down," Jack ordered as two of his men staggered under the impact of Ashanti slugs. "Get behind cover!"

Jackson looked at the blood seeping from his shoulder. "We're soldiers, sir. We fight in the open!"

"You'll be dead soldiers if an Ashanti slug hits you in the head! Get under cover! I'm not losing good men!"

Eventually, the firing died away. Gunsmoke drifted out to sea as Marines, seamen and West Indians grinned to each other as comrades in arms. A sailor passed over a twist of tobacco to Ogston, who responded with a smile.

"Have a swig, Jack," Ogston handed over his water bottle.

The sailor took a drink, gasped and took another. "By God, lobster, that's better than water! Where did you get it?"

"Jamaican rum!" Ogston said. "We make it!"

"I'll have to get a transfer to your mob," the sailor said in pure Somerset.

Ogston grinned. "Bring your tobacco with you."

"Burn the place down," Wolseley ordered from the hammock.

When the seamen thrust torches into the thatched roofs, hundreds of rats and bats swarmed from the huts and around the column. The seamen made game of them, competing to see who could kill most with their cutlasses as the Wests watched, cheering on their favourites. It was just another minor incident in a campaign that Jack wished would end. He could not see this process of skirmishes and village burning, defeating King Kofi or freeing Mary.

"That was a good start, gentlemen," Wolseley said. "We have shown the Ashanti that we can fight in their terrain and punished some of their villages." Gathering his staff, he sailed back to Cape Coast Castle on *Decoy*.

"Sir Garnet has his life well organised," Hopringle said.

"His life is all Sir Garnet," a navy lieutenant said.

"Everything is well then," Hopringle said. "All Sir Garnet."

"We're heading back to Elmina!" Colonel Wood said cheerfully. "Step along, men!"

"Come on, C Company!" Jack roared. "You're veterans now! You faced and defeated the Ashantis."

That may be so, Jack told himself, *but we're no closer to rescuing Mary and every day in Kumasi is dangerous for her. When are we going to march?*

CHAPTER TWENTY-THREE

Cape Coast Castle November December 1873

"That's all Sir Garnet, then,' Hopringle said. "The chiefs of Essaman and Amperee have sworn allegiance to the queen. We're turning the tide."

Jack nodded. The phrase "all Sir Garnet" was entering slang, meaning that everything was perfect. "I heard as much. Might is right, and the chiefs do what they must to protect themselves. If the British seem to be the stronger, they'll attach themselves to us. If the Ashantis are in the ascendancy, the chiefs will be cheering on the Asantahene." Jack lit a cheroot as he stared over the wall. "We can't blame them for seeking self-preservation."

The defection of the two chiefs was not the only success of Wolseley's raid, for Buller's spies reported that Amanquatia had ordered a withdrawal to Ashantiland. Jack was unsure if Wolseley's expedition was the direct cause of the Ashanti retreat, or if sickness in Amanquatia's army was the real reason. Whatever the truth, the people of the Gold Coast breathed a collective sigh of relief.

"Amanquatia has retreated to Mampon," Hopringle said. 'Sir Garnet should gather every man he can and hit him now. Smash the Ashantis when they are in retreat!"

"What with?" Jack blew smoke into the air. "Sir Garnet has no more men now than he had a month ago."

"We defeated the Ashantis at Essaman," Hopringle said.

"We defeated a small local force," Jack said, "after some pretty stiff fighting. Wolseley's trick with the journalists worked, or Amanquatia would have reinforced his army at Essaman. Amanquatia has the cream of the Ashanti army, thousands of seasoned veterans including Kumi Okese's Edwesus. I have no doubt our scraped up few hundred would fight well, but…" Jack shrugged. "Remember McCarthy? The Ashantis defeated him and used his skull as a drinking cup. I have no desire for King Kofi to slurp his Earl Grey from my head."

"Your wife is in Kumasi," Hopringle said.

"I know that," Jack whispered savagely. "You'd better be getting on with your duties, Lieutenant, or I'll knock you down."

He turned away, considering the implications of Amanquatia's withdrawal. With the Ashanti army concentrated in its homeland, Kumasi would be better defended. Remembering the forested Adansi Hills that lay between the coast and Kumasi, Jack thought of the difficulties of pushing a British army through miles of Ashanti ambushes. It may have been better to keep the Ashantis less concentrated near the coast, where the British could thin out their numbers in a series of encounters rather than risking everything on a single push into the Ashanti homeland.

Jack fingered Mary's scarf that he wore around his neck. *Stay alive, Mary, that's all I ask. Stay alive, and I'll come for you.*

* * *

"I don't normally agree with interfering with the religious beliefs of other people," Wolseley faced Jack across the width of the desk. "However, in the case of the Ashantis, I am prepared to stretch a point. For health and climatic reasons, we cannot risk a prolonged campaign in West Africa, so I must think of some way of augmenting our military superiority."

Jack guessed what was coming next.

"You may know that the Ashanti kings each have a stool in which they hold their ancestral spirits," Wolseley said. "I will retain you as commander of C Company of the Second Wests, Windrush and when we go to Kumasi, I wish you to find King Kofi's Golden Stool. If I have that, the Ashanti people will know that Great Britain is their master in spiritual as well as military matters." Wolseley shuffled the papers in front of him. "I have chosen you for this task, Windrush, because you know Kumasi better than any of my officers. I want you to make the capture of the Golden Stool your priority."

"My wife is also in Kumasi, sir," Jack reminded.

"I have not forgotten, Windrush," Wolseley said. "I have sent numerous messages to King Kofi demanding that he release all the hostages, including Mrs Windrush."

"Thank you, sir," Jack said. "Are the British regiments on their way?" He felt his heartbeat increase. If King Kofi released the hostages, his emotional nightmare would end, and he could concentrate on his duty.

"I expect them to arrive in early December," Wolseley said. "One battalion each of the Rifles, the 23rd Foot and the 42nd Highlanders, with Royal Artillery and Royal Engineers."

Jack nodded. "It's a full-scale war, then."

"It's war." Wolseley looked up. "Kumasi will burn, depend on it."

"That's good news, sir. I hope your diplomacy works and the hostages are released."

"The Golden Stool would be a fitting prize for this campaign, Windrush. I rely on your discretion to keep the mission to yourself." Wolseley nearly smiled. "General Hook told me you were the best man for this sort of work."

"Thank you, sir." Jack could hardly think of capturing the Golden Stool. He thought of Mary in Kumasi and hoped that Wolseley's diplomacy, on top of the success of the recent expedition, could bring her back.

***

Despite all Wolseley's best efforts, the Fanti chiefs failed to provide warriors in either quantity or quality. Only a few hundred turned up, and to Jack's eyes, used to the superb fighting men of the Indian sub-continent, the chiefs had sent their dregs.

"The Ashanti warriors will eat these men for breakfast." Jack watched Colonel Wood trying to train the recruits, while the Wests laughed with unhidden scorn.

"Oh?" Buller raised his eyebrows. "I didn't realise the Ashanti were cannibals." He grinned. "One more reason to destroy them."

"We'll not destroy them with that bunch," Jack pointed to the Fantis. "They'll run at first sight of a proper Ashanti warrior."

"It's all up to us then," Buller said. "As usual."

"Aye," Jack said. "As usual."

As Jack continued to train his men, Wolseley used what forces he had to harass the retreating Ashantis. He sent Colonel Wood on a reconnaissance from Elmina, while he arranged an expedition inland.

"The Ashantis are retreating," Wolseley said. "I want to hurry them along. Bring a half company of your Wests, Windrush."

"Yes, sir." Jack was already fretting to do something rather than waiting in Cape Coast.

Although some of his men were down with fever, Jack selected Numbers One and Two sections, filled the gaps with volunteers from Three and Four sections and joined the expedition. The engineers had improved the road beyond compare, so the column made good time, stopping at wayside stations where well-built huts sheltered them, and military police kept order.

"We're already civilising the country," Buller said.

"We are," Jack agreed. "The quicker, the better."

The Marines already looked more mature than on the previous expedition, while the sailors were the same willing warriors as ever. Russell's regiment of men from half a dozen tribes took the van, with Jack's Wests watching them with the suspicion of professional soldiers eyeing amateurs.

"Are we attacking Kumasi?" Stair asked.

"Not this time," Jack told him.

"Oh," Stair looked disappointed. "The women there were gorgeous."

They marched through the night, with a full moon throwing nearly ghostly light on low scrubland, while the occasional patch of tall forest plunging them into sudden darkness where sounds and smells prevailed. When the night eased, they marched through the hottest day Jack had yet experienced in Africa, with two Marines collapsing through sunstroke.

"Isn't this fun, Windrush?" Buller wiped the sweat from his forehead as they halted in the evening. "Wandering across Africa chasing shadows."

"Any more intelligence?" Jack had not seen a single enemy yet. His men were bored with marching without reason, and he felt the same.

"I am here with a report for Sir Garnet," Buller tried to sound important.

"Damn Sir Garnet. Have you any news of Mary, of the hostages? Has King Kofi released them, yet?"

"Not yet," Buller shook his head with genuine sympathy. "I'll contact you the second I hear anything, Windrush." He lowered his voice. "Getting information from within Kumasi is not easy. King Kofi has a new man in charge of internal security there, and he executed one of my spies."

Jack could picture the scene. "Do you know who?"

"A man you already know," Buller said. "Kumi Okese."

Jack felt his stomach churn. "That's unfortunate," he said. "He's a most efficient man and a fine fighter, the Sir Garnet of the Ashantis. He'd be an asset to any army."

Buller lit another cigar. "Is that so? Maybe we'll recruit him after we complete this business." He grinned. "We seem to get out best soldiers from the ranks of ex-enemies, Sikhs, Gurkhas, Highlanders *et al*. Why not a regiment of Ashantis?"

"Maybe," Jack could not smile, "although I doubt Kumi Okese would join us. He's an Ashanti to his bones and as dangerous an enemy as we will ever face."

"We're moving again," a young midshipman said with great excitement. "General Wolseley sends his compliments, Major Windrush, and could your West Indians take the rearguard, please."

"It's a chase now, Windrush," Buller said. "We've got Amanquatia on the run."

"We're like a terrier dog chasing a lion," Jack said. "The Ashanti have split into several armies, each one much larger than ours. Wolseley wants to catch one of them on the flank around our garrison at Abrakrampa."

Their march took them across a plain with patches of forest and scrub, to a deep forest broken by areas of knee-deep swamp. Although Wolseley's old wound had prevented him from marching on the previous expedition, the creepers and low branches on this track negated the use of a hammock. Wolseley had to walk, disguising the pain of his injured leg. Jack's old Burma wound also played up, so he limped, fought the pain and curled Mary's scarf around his fist.

Hold on, Mary.

With around 300 houses and huts, plus a Wesleyan chapel at one end of the town, Abrakrampa was sizeable by local standards, with a static garrison of mixed British and native defenders. Wolseley arrived as moonlight glowed behind static clouds and nervous sentries sent a challenge.

"Who goes there?" The words hollow in the dark.

"General Wolseley!" A brass-lunged naval lieutenant replied.

"Enter, sir!"

Although cleared of Ashantis, the inhabitants of Abrakrampa were in dread, jumping at small sounds and continually checking the surrounding forest. "They think the Ashantis are all around them," Buller said, "blocking the roads."

Wolseley's little force rested for an hour and set off again, heading for an Ashanti gathering at the village of Assanchi. Clouds shrouded the moon, so the British patrolled in the dark, with lantern-light bouncing against the surrounding trees and casting weird shadows.

"The Ashantis are waiting for us," Daley said.

Jack felt the same. He could taste the men's nervousness, smell the fear in their sweat. Wolseley's recent successes had only given a temporary respite; the dread of the Ashantis was too deep-rooted for one victorious skirmish to remove. Night passed into day, and the sun rose in glorious dawn that turned into a stiflingly hot morning. The men marched on into Africa, waiting for the dull thud of Ashanti muskets or the ominous hammer of the war drums.

They reached the village of Assanchi, to find the Ashantis had already left. The heat and conditions drained the Marines' strength, so they lay in the shade, gasping for breath. Even the Wests reached for their water bottles and cursed the sun that beat down upon them.

"The Ashantis are leading us into a trap," Daley said. "They'll draw us deeper and deeper into Africa and then cut us off and kill us."

"The officers are too stupid to see their plan," Jackson glowered at Wolseley, nursing his still aching arm. "We should run the army, not them."

Jack ignored the grumbling. Soldiers had groused since armies were invented and would continue to complain until the ploughshare drove the sword from the globe. Like looting a captured town, it was one of their perquisites. Grumbling was a safety valve that did little harm unless it spread and deepened. Jack had no reason to believe that would happen in the 2nd Wests, but he kept his ears open, ready to squash any persistent complaints.

After a fruitless night chasing empty rumours, Wolseley lifted his hand. "I think that's sufficient marching for the day. The Ashantis are well gone now." He rubbed at his sore leg. "Back to Abrakrampa."

It was early morning when they passed the clearing around Abrakrampa, to find Buller was waiting for them, surrounded by a bevy of his native spies. "No luck then, Windrush?"

"Not a whisper of the enemy," Jack watched as dozens of the Marines slumped to the ground, overcome by the heat or suffering from their ill-fitting boots.

Buller shook his head. "You were with the wrong column, old man. Colonel Festing took out 700 men and clashed with the Ashanti at Iscabio. I don't know the enemy casualties, but Festing had five killed and 47 wounded, including himself."

Jack nodded. "I fought under Festing at Elmina. He's a good man." *All the same,* he thought to himself, *these encounters are only pinpricks that do nothing to free Mary.* Every day that passed, Mary was in danger, and if these small defeats annoyed King Kofi, he might well decide to sacrifice the hostages in revenge. The sooner the British regiments arrived, the quicker they could attack Kumasi.

"If the general had more men, he could follow up his successes," Buller said.

"Aye, and if wishes came true, I'd have been born a belted earl," Jack retorted. "You are right, though, Buller. Given a couple of regular British regiments and some artillery, Wolseley could chase Amanquatia back to Kumasi. He could squash the Ashantis before they had time to organise their defence."

"Thank God for the Navy," Buller said. "So far we've fought this campaign with untrained natives, a part battalion of West Indians, Marines who should still be with their mummies and sailors on land. If King Kofi knew how weak we were, he'd whistle up all his men and sweep us into the sea."

"All the more reason to keep pressing him," Jack said. "King Kofi must have spies in Cape Coast and Elmina. Keep him on the run, or he'll regroup and come back at us. We'll just have to manage with what we have until then."

The British regiments aren't due until late December, Jack thought. *Even if they marched as soon as they arrived, the British regiments could not possibly reach Kumasi until early February. Kumi Okese had weeks to organise his defence.*

Jack heard the firing at seven that morning. He was on his feet in a second, buckling on his revolver and shouting for his men.

"Stand to, Wests!"

Bugles blared the Alarm as Jack's men ran to their posts, some fully dressed, others in a state of near-nudity, but all carrying their rifles and ammunition, which was the mark of a soldier.

The musketry continued for a few moments, sputtered up again and died out. Silence returned, save for the usual sounds of the bush.

"Only skirmishers," Buller said.

"They're still out there," Ogston said. "Waiting."

"I can feel them," Jack said. The menace was palpable, the sensation of thousands of fierce forest warriors within a mile or so of the village.

Limping heavily, Wolseley toured the defences. "Windrush, you reinforce Abrakrampa with your Wests. I'm hunting Amanquatia." The general gave crisp orders as he led his column away.

The defenders watched Wolseley march out, and then silence descended, except for the croak of circling vultures.

* * *

Abrakrampa baked under the sun, with the defenders knowing they were all alone. If the Ashanti decided to attack, there was no sizeable army to come to their aid until the British regiments finally arrived. Jack lifted his head as he heard drums muttering in the distance. They beat for half an hour and stopped, leaving a silence that seemed to press down upon them.

"They know the general has gone," Jack said to Lieutenant Gordon, who had strengthened the defences of the village.

"We have a good position," Gordon said, quietly, "with Captain Grant and ninety men of the Wests, Lieutenant Wells and 50 Marines and bluejackets, 100 Hausas, assorted Fantis, Sierra Leone Volunteers and Kosoos, plus the local king with a few hundred Ambras."

"Will they fight?" Jack knew that numbers mattered less than spirit when the battle started.

Gordon shrugged and smiled at the same time. "Time will tell."

Gordon had transformed the chapel into a small fortress by removing the thatched roof and strengthening the upper story to support the weight of a rocket trough and an ancient cannon. "The Marines and sailors garrison the chapel," Gordon said. "It's like their ship in the forest." He grinned, a likeable man in an unlikely situation. "The cannon is Dutch and probably as reliable as a snyde shilling, but the bluejackets call it Nelly and keep it polished."

Jack looked over the chapel, noting the sandbags that fortified the windows and the Marines and seamen lounging inside, smoking pipes, chewing tobacco and exchanging jokes that would blister the ears of any respectable chapel-goer. "That place is in good hands."

A wooden palisade surrounded most of Abrakrampa, with defensive trenches along the sides, while determined men guarded loopholed houses. Gordon had created a killing ground around the village by clearing away the trees yet leaving sufficient low bushes to hamper any attempt at a full charge.

"You've done a good job, Gordon," Jack approved.

"If the Ashantis come, they'll break their regiments against our defences," Gordon said, "providing the men hold firm." He lowered his voice. "I'd give a hundred guineas for half a battalion of British regulars, though."

Major Baker Russell, the garrison commander, greeted Jack cordially. "You've been under siege before, I hear, Windrush."

"Yes, sir. At Lucknow."

"Well, place your men wherever you think best. Your experience will be useful." Russell hesitated. "Do you know our local fighters?"

"Not well sir, except for the Ashantis."

"Permit me to enlighten you. The Hausas are Mohammedans, brave soldiers, but a bit undisciplined. The Kossoos are fierce swordsmen from the Sherbro River, courageous to a fault. You'll like them."

"I'm sure I will," Jack said.

The drums started at noon, distant yet menacing, throwing their threats over the garrison of Abrakrampa.

"Our neighbours are bidding us good afternoon," Russell said. "They're at Anasmadi, about a mile away." He grinned. "My Kossoos like to catch any stray Ashantis and chop them up."

The drums muttered away in the background all day, unnerving until Jack grew used to the sound, and then he ignored it. Village life continued. Using the opportunity, Jack trained his men in the rudiments of defensive warfare, with the Kossoos and Hausas watching, and the seamen giving bawdy advice. The tension mounted in Abrakrampa as people awaited the inevitable attack.

On the 2nd November, Russell sent out Jack with a mixed party to reconnoitre Anasmadi. With Winnebah tribesmen in front, Kossoos acting as scouts and the Hausas marching eagerly, Jack ordered his Wests to keep alert.

"I have no idea how these tribesmen will behave if we meet the enemy."

"I can hear the Bushmen," Ogston said. "I can smell them."

"Where?" Jack fingered the butt of his revolver.

A musket boomed ahead, quickly followed by the crack of a rifle. A moment later, the Winnebah tribesmen rushed back, nearly flattening Jack in their panic to escape from the Ashantis.

"So much for our allies," Jack said. "Stay with me, men." Sliding behind a tree, he waited for the Ashantis to appear. After five minutes, when the Hausas fired in every direction, things calmed down without a single Ashanti approaching them.

"Let's have a look," Jack said. "Ogston and Stair, you're with me." A hundred yards deeper into the forest, they found the Ashanti camp. Cooking fires were unattended, huts left vacant and bits of clothing scattered. "It looks as if our scouts met their scouts and the Ashantis ran as fast as the Winnebahs," Jack said.

"Bloody Bushmen," Stair said. "They must know the 2nd Wests are here."

Jack nodded. "That's what it must have been. There's nothing here for us, so we'd better return to Abrakrampa."

"Sir," Ogston said. "Can you hear that?" He lifted his rifle. "It sounds as if something's dragging on the ground."

"I hear it." Jack half-crouched, watching for some Ashanti trick. The silence was oppressive as if Africa waited to pounce.

"Sir!" Ogston pointed his rifle at the woman who crawled towards them, hauling a six-foot-long log. "The Bushmen left a slave behind."

"Cover me," Jack crouched beside the woman, who stared at him through wide, terrified eyes. "The Ashanti have clamped the poor woman to this log."

"I'll get it, sir." Drawing his bayonet, Ogston prised the clamp from the wood. "There we go, my pretty."

"Bring her with us," Jack said as the woman broke into a long speech in Fanti. "She might have some useful information."

"How about the Winnebahs, sir?" Ogston asked.

Jack grunted. "They can make their own way back."

* * *

"What have we here?" Using his working knowledge of Fanti, Major Russell listened to the woman's story. "This unhappy woman is Amba Firitumba. She was in her village outside Cape Coast a few months ago when the Ashanti enslaved her and her three children. She hasn't seen her little ones since."

"Poor woman," Jack said.

"One of many, I'm afraid," Russell said. "She is a reminder of why we are here. Of more immediate concern, Amba told me that Amanquatia is going to attack Abrakrampa."

"Amanquatia is still around, is he?" Jack glanced at his surroundings. "I hoped he was halfway back to Kumasi by now."

"So did I." Russell shook his head. "No matter, we'll keep the defences up to scratch," Russell said. "Although we can discount the Winnebahs."

The Ashantis returned that evening, remaining within the forest as they circled Abrakrampa, talking in loud voices, occasionally showing themselves to the sentries, laughing and immediately withdrawing to the shelter of the trees.

"They're trying to unnerve us," Jack said. "Letting us know they're there, tempting the frightened to desert and weakening our resolve."

"Well, Windrush," Russell said, "Sir Garnet has weakened us without any help from the Ashantis. First, we lose the Winnebahs, and now the general has ordered our Naval Brigade to Esseboo."

"They're some of our best men," Jack said. "After the 2nd West."

"Aye," Russell gave a wry smile. "We'll miss them."

The Naval Brigade took the news phlegmatically, with Lieutenant Wells ordering them to pack up their gear and prepare the artillery for transport. The seamen and Marines worked with a will, squaring away all their kit within an hour.

"I'll send a section of Wests to defend the church, Russell," Jack said. "If you can persuade the Navy to leave Nelly the cannon behind, I'm sure we can work out how to fire the blasted thing."

Russell grunted. "Thank you, Windrush."

The firing came without warning, hundreds of muskets in a great arc around the west side of the village around the church.

"Well now," Russell drawled the words as a hail of slugs rattled around Abrakrampa. "It looks like our Naval Brigade is going nowhere. The attack has begun."

CHAPTER TWENTY-FOUR

Abrakrampa November 1873

Without waiting for orders, the seamen and Marines raced to their old positions. Backing the Ashanti musketry, drums and war horns sounded all around Abrakrampa, with a chorus of the chilling Ashanti war song.

"What the devil," Jack said as a lone defender left the village and stepped into the clearing, half-seen in the fading light. "Who is that idiot?"

"That's no idiot," Russell said. "That's the King of Arbra, the local tribe."

"Is it indeed? Well, he's either going to desert to the enemy with all his men, or surrender."

"No, Windrush," Russell said. "Have a little faith."

Raising his hands, the king shouted something, with Russell translating to Jack. "I am the king of this country; come on if you are coming!"

"Brave man," Jack altered his opinion of the king.

Less impressed than Jack, the Ashantis responded with a volley that kicked up the dirt and grass around the king, who turned and withdrew with a dignity that Jack could only admire.

"Well, he tried," Russell said. "Naval Brigade, show these Ashanti what you can do."

"Aye, aye, sir!" A seaman bellowed, and the Naval Brigade immediately fired Nelly. The sound was like nothing Jack had heard before, a stupendous bang that shook the church as a cloud of blue-white smoke enveloped the sailors.

"That's from the navy, boys!" The seamen yelled in evident glee.

The Ashanti musketry continued, with the defenders replying, Sniders and Enfields cracking all around the village perimeter. As so often in Africa, the moon glowed strongly, highlighting the surrounding trees and casting wavering shadows on the cleared space. The Ashanti drums throbbed incessantly, with war horns blaring to the sky.

"Don't' waste ammunition," Jack snapped as Stair began rapid fire. "Don't shoot unless you're sure of your target."

"It's all right, old man," Russell said. "I made sure we're well supplied." He laughed as a slug landed at his feet. "The enemy will run out of men before Abrakrampa runs out of ammunition."

The seamen were in their element, loading Nelly with handfuls of bullets and firing them at any concentration of the enemy. "Give them a broadside, lads, the bloody land pirates!"

"Away you lubbers! The navy's here!"

Every so often, a group of Ashantis would venture from the forest onto the clearing, when the Navy would fire one of their scarce rockets. The group would scatter, yelling, to the cheers of the sailors and Marines. On one occasion moonlight fell squarely on a particularly bold group, revealing the white stripes down their faces and arms.

"Pot those men," Jack ordered. "That's Kumi Okese's Edwesus." Taking the rifle from Daley, he took careful aim for the tallest, fired, rode the kick and saw his target stagger. "That's one less," he said, to the cheers of the Wests. He felt no satisfaction in his little victory as he reloaded and fired again. The Edwesus melted into the bush, a second before a rocket hissed over where they had stood.

"Only fire when you see their gunsmoke," Jack walked behind his men, knowing the Ashanti would aim for him but hoping the darkness and distance would minimise their accuracy.

"They're not very good," Ogston said. "If they were the French at Waterloo, they would have attacked by now. We beat the French, and we'll beat the Bushmen, too."

"Good man, Ogston," Jack said. "If the Wests were at Waterloo, we'd have beat the French all the quicker!"

"That's right, sir!" Ogston aimed and fired. "I wish the Ashanti would show themselves."

"So do I, Ogston." Jack agreed. It was unnerving fighting an invisible enemy.

At about four in the morning, the drums altered their beat, and the Ashanti fire suddenly ceased. As the moon waned, Russell ordered lanterns lit around the perimeter of the village, each one casting an arc of yellow light into the clearing, with the forest a dark smudge on the periphery.

"Now what are the Ashantis up to?" Russell asked.

"I'm blessed if I know, sir," Jack said.

"Maybe they've run."

"Not these lads," Jack shook his head. "These men won't run." He stepped over to his Wests. "I want every third man to remain on sentry," he said. "The others grab what sleep you can."

The pre-dawn dark intensified, with the sounds of night slowly diminishing. Jack patrolled his section of the perimeter, peering across the clearing. *If this was the Frontier*, he told himself, *the Pashtun would be massing to attack our most vulnerable spot. In Crimea, the Plastun Cossacks would use the dark to crawl across the killing area. What are the Ashantis planning?*

"The Bushmen are scared to come," Ogston said.

"Can we attack them, sir?" Stair asked.

"We sit tight," Jack said. "At least until daylight."

"What do you think, Windrush?" Captain Grant's Scottish accent was somehow reassuring in the dark.

"I think you and I should get some rest while we can," Jack said. "Tomorrow might be a long day."

* * *

Dawn was majestic above the trees, creating a sense of peace that Jack always relished. He lay on the ground, stretched, listened to the bird calls and fell back asleep with his fist curled around Mary's scarf.

"Windrush." Grant leaned over him. "Your men need you."

"What time is it?" Jack pushed himself upright, remembering where he was. He pushed Mary's scarf out of sight within his tunic.

"Breakfast," Grant said.

Still sleep-confused, Jack ate, washed and shaved while watching his men change the guard with as little fuss as veterans. Coffin was nearest to him, humming a hymn as he peered over the plain at the dark smear of the forest beyond.

"There's a weakness in our defences," Jack said, after another circuit. He pointed to a slope beyond the church, yellow grass illuminated by the rising sun. "If the Ashantis occupied that hill, they could fire onto our gunners."

Russell nodded. "Captain Grant said the same. Could a section of your men hold the hill in the open?" Both ducked as the Ashanti opened fire, the slugs pattering onto Abrakrampa's houses like hail on a window. "Here we go again!"

By now used to being under fire, the Wests acted coolly, only responding when they were sure of their target.

"Here they come!" Ogston pointed to a group of Ashantis mustering opposite C Company, just outside the forest. "They're going to rush us."

"Bayonets, boys," Jack checked his revolver was fully loaded. "Let's show them West Indian steel! Two Section come with me. Hopringle, stay here with One Section, provide covering fire if the Ashantis drive us back." He waited until the Ashantis were well into the clearing, then vaulted the parapet and ran forward, cheering, with the Wests at his back.

Not used to seeing men run at them, the Ashanti attack faltered at the sight of a score of determined West Indians behind long glittering bayonets.

"At them, Two Section!" Jack fired his revolver as his Wests slammed into the Ashantis, bayonets stabbing, men roaring, gasping, fighting their fear as they lunged into the kill. Jack shot at the leading warrior, ducked the slash of a sword and saw the Ashantis almost immediately recoil. Rather than face the Wests, they turned to run.

"After the Bushmen!' Stair shouted, bounding five paces in front of his colleagues.

"No! Get back, Stair!" Jack knew that the Ashantis might be waiting in ambush among the trees. "Get back! That's an order, Private!"

As the Ashantis retreated, Jack's men were left vulnerable in the open plain, with the warriors within the trees having an excellent target. Even before the last Ashanti slid into the forest, the firing began. Jack saw Ogston stagger, clutching at his chest. "Back, lads!"

Stair stopped, shouted at the hidden warriors and joined the withdrawal, with Number One section providing covering fire. The entire affair had only taken five minutes and left four Ashantis lying on the ground. Ogston rubbed at his chest. "That slug surely stung," he said.

"Let me see," Jack opened Ogston's tunic. The bruise spread across the left side of Ogston's chest. "Nothing's broken," Jack said. "You're made of tough stuff."

"I'm from Jamaica!" Ogston said.

"That explains it," Jack closed the tunic. "Take care of yourself, Ogston."

The day continued, with the defenders keeping behind cover and the Ashantis firing from the trees. When the Ashantis launched an occasional rush into the clearing, the defenders responded with a counter-attack that pushed them back. In mid-morning, the Ashantis finally occupied the hill above the church and targeted the Naval Brigade.

"I can take a section and remove them," Jack offered.

"That's in hand, Windrush," Russell said. "You can't have all the fun."

At two in the afternoon with no warning, Captain Grant led his section of Wests in a mad assault at the Ashantis.

"Charge!" Grant roared, drew his sword and ran uphill with his men behind him.

"Bloody crazy Sawnie," Jack said, shaking his head. "Thank God they're on our side."

As soon as the Wests closed, the Ashantis turned to run, with Grant slashing at them with his sword, chasing them to the forest. His Wests took no prisoners, stabbing their bayonets into any Ashanti who tried to fight.

"You see?" Russell said, smiling, "Captain Grant has it all in hand."

After Grant's attack, the Ashantis remained within the forest wall, never venturing into the open. The firing continued until the evening, sometimes sporadic, sometimes intense but seldom effective against the barricades and houses of Abrakrampa.

"We've held them off," Hopringle sounded surprised.

"Somebody is coming," Ogston said, still rubbing at his chest where the slug had hit him.

Jack had learned to trust his men, so was not surprised ten minutes later when Wolseley marched into the village with a body of seamen and Marines, and a company of native levies.

"Aye, come now the fighting's over, Sir Garnet," Grant said.

Jack nodded. "As long as he came," he said.

It might have been the arrival of Wolseley that persuaded the Ashantis to retreat, for there was no firing that night. Next morning, cautious patrols found only the dead and wounded in the forest and on the road.

"Follow them up, Windrush," Wolseley ordered. "Dog their rearguard, harass them back to the Prah."

"Yes, sir," Jack said. "Come on, boys; we're on the road again."

Marching in the wake of the Ashantis, Jack found the track and surrounding countryside a litter of discarded gear. As well as powder-kegs and muskets, there were brass pans and beautifully carved stools, a chicken coop complete with chickens that Coffin swore belonged to Amanquatia himself, and flasks of rum that Ogston appropriated.

"Sir," Coffin pointed to the bodies that lay beside the road. Most were Ashanti warriors, dead or dying from wounds or disease; others were Fanti slaves, killed by the retreating army.

Only once did the Ashantis throw out a rearguard, firing their muskets too early to do any damage.

Jack grunted at the familiar drift of powder smoke. "Hopringle, take your section and engage them on the road. Number Two Section come with me."

Moving into the forest, Jack hacked a passage a hundred yards deep and then moved towards the Ashanti. As soon as they saw the Wests menacing their flank, the Ashantis withdrew, as Jack had intended.

"Right boys, on we go! If you see the enemy, fire at once!"

There was something deeply exhilarating in moving at speed along the track, passing the occasional Ashanti casualty or escaped Fanti prisoner. For the first time in weeks, Jack began to feel optimistic. The Ashantis were on the run; he was in command of half a company of quality infantry, and the road to the Prah was clear. All he had to do was press on, hope the British reinforcements arrived soon, and this war would be over.

On the third day of the pursuit, a messenger ran to Jack as he strode onwards at the head of his men.

"Major Windrush!" The midshipman was heavily perspiring. "I have urgent news."

Jack opened up the paper the midshipman handed to him, read the contents with disbelief and swore. All his high hopes vanished like snow on a warm day.

General Wolseley is ill with fever, the message said. *You are ordered to discontinue any offensive actions until the position is clarified. Return with C Company, 2nd West Indian Regiment to Cape Coast Castle.*

"Is there a reply, sir?" The messenger asked.

"No, no reply," Jack said. He looked onward up the track, where the debris of the retreating Ashantis covered the ground, crumpled up the note and threw it away. "No reply at all."

CHAPTER TWENTY-FIVE

To The Prah January 1874

Two months. It was two months since the siege of Abrakrampa and the short but exciting chase that followed. Two months of frustration, waiting for Sir Garnet to recover and gather sufficient bearers for the march. Two months more for Mary to languish in captivity in Kumasi.

Jack stood on the beach at Cape Coast Castle, clenching his teeth on the butt of a cheroot as the British regulars arrived. They sat in ordered ranks in the broad-beamed surf boats as the Kroomen guided them through the rollers and onto the white sands. Rather than the traditional bright scarlet that had made British soldiers such good targets on campaign, the men wore uniforms of neutral grey, which would be far more suitable for action in the African forests. Jack nodded, *well done Wolseley, all Sir Garnet indeed.*

"You know,' Windrush," Buller spoke around his cigar, "if that beach were in England, it would be crowded with holidaymakers, every summer."

"That might happen once we civilise the place,' Jack watched as the 23rd Foot disembarked, each man staring at the unfamiliar scenery, the bright sand and the white Cape Coast Castle. Although some were young, they looked more mature than the Royal Marines with whom Colonel Festing had defended Elmina. The 23rd carried themselves like professional fighting men, confident, slightly arrogant yet wary. "I can't see many people coming here from Birmingham or Glasgow if it's full of human sacrifice and fetishes. Margate is bad enough in all conscience, but the Gold Coast is beyond the pale."

"Aye, maybe," Buller puffed out a perfect smoke ring. "Although for some, it may even be an attraction. Get rid of the mother-in-law, don't you think? Hand her over to King Kofi's executioners and have her head hung from the old fetish tree? That would be a change from music halls and publics."

Jack forced a smile. "That might be an attraction, indeed." He watched as the soldiers marched up the beach, their uniforms drab, baggy and unsightly under the bright sun. "I must be getting old,' Jack said. 'When I started soldiering, everybody except the Rifle Brigade wore scarlet. Now we're wearing grey and khaki, looking like workmen rather than soldiers. It's more sensible, yet it detracts, somehow."

"Aye, you're right," Buller said. "There's no glamour left in this profession. We should all wear bright uniforms, march towards the enemy in dense columns and die gloriously as they shoot us to pieces. Wouldn't the Ashanti just love that?"

"I'm sure they would," Jack had already ordered grey uniforms for his company. He watched the 23rd Foot, the Royal Welch Fusiliers march past, with the goat at their head looking very confused. "A couple of weeks ago these men were in a British winter and in another couple of weeks they'll be fighting in the middle of a tropical forest. No wonder we lose so many men to heatstroke and disease."

"Disease has hit half the officers who arrived with Wolseley," Buller looked at Jack from the side of his eyes. "I imagine you're better equipped with your half-Indian mother."

Jack stiffened. "That must be it," he said. "I didn't know you knew."

"It's common knowledge, old boy," Buller said, returning his attention to the landing infantry. "Fighting Jack Windrush from India."

Unsure if Buller was insulting him, Jack said nothing.

"Others just call you Fighting Jack, the lucky major with the charming wife." Buller smiled. "How did you land such a beauty?"

"That beauty is still in Kumasi," Jack said.

"I know," Buller said softly. "You're taking your company to Prahsu on the Prah River very shortly, Major. Then you'll be in striking distance of Kumasi."

"How do you know that?"

"It's my job, old boy, it's my job."

* * *

Once again on the road north, Jack felt a new purpose as he marched his men onward. With no baggage train, he had to rely on porters, who became more unsettled with every mile. However, the state of the road more than made up for a few disgruntled porters, for the engineers had completed the route from Cape Coast to Prahsu. Jack thought the road was probably the best in sub-Saharan Africa, broad and well-surfaced, with nearly 240 newly-constructed bridges and eight carefully designed camping grounds complete with huts and a hospital.

Jack watched his men swing along in their new Norfolk grey uniforms, with pith helmets replacing the turbans, Sniders on their shoulders and pocket filters to cleanse the river water. Jack was impressed by these new devices, simple tubes of charcoal, but having experienced the foul water in the forest, he knew the filters could be as essential as a rifle.

They're looking good, Jack said to himself. *My company of Wests are looking very good.*

"Here we are, lads," Jack said when they reached Accroful. "Our first stop."

Day after day, they moved on, eating well and as fit as any soldier in West Africa could be. For the first four stages, the road strode over scrubland with few trees to break the impact of the sun, and then they were in the forest, with massive trees on either side and interlaced branches filtering the rays of the sun. It took six days to march the 74 miles to Prahsu, and when they arrived, Jack could hardly believe the difference. Where once had been virgin forest, the engineers had created a formidably large camp, with military quarters, solid huts for men and officers and a flagpole from which the Union flag draped.

Jack grunted, as a crudely painted notice caught his attention. *The Forlorn Hope*, it read, above the doorway of the hospital. Shaking his head, Jack strode to the river. He had crossed the Prah twice already, once in each direction. It may be the sacred river of the Ashantis, but now there was a British camp on its banks and British, African, and West Indian voices echoing across its dark brown, somehow sinister water.

"We're crossing the Prah tomorrow," Jack told his men. "We don't know how the Ashantis will act, but I'll guarantee they won't greet us with open arms and bottles of rum. Not even you, Ogston."

"I don't need their rum, sir," Ogston said. "I got my own."

"Well, don't tell the sailors, or they'll want some," Jack replied.

"We trade regularly," Ogston said, laughing.

As Jack looked across the swirling river, the Naval Brigade gathered around the campfire, utterly careless of any Ashanti, Russian or anybody else as they roared out songs born on ships from the Arctic to Cape Horn. The seamen had built a massive fire, adding entire tree trunks to keep the blaze alight, fighting the dark, forcing away any fears of what tomorrow might bring.

As the last of the bawdy nautical songs died away, a lone Marine stood up and sang in broad Cockney.

"Vith the fair sex, bless 'em, need I say
That I am number Von
It's really quite a bore to me
The way the girls do run
Not away from me, but after me
Hah, you may laugh and scoff
But I can tell yer that the girls
Think me Immensekoff."

Girls, Jack thought. *Girls or drink; that's the mainstay of military men, and I am no different.* He returned to the side of the Prah.

"I'm coming for you Kumi Okese. You murdered Private Manning, and I'm going to kill you." He fingered Mary's scarf. "And I'm coming for you, Mary." For a second, he pondered the possibility that Mary could be dead, then shook his head. No. No; he would have felt something if she died. A final log fell on the fire, scattering sparks, and the ember-glow faded until the night was as dark as Jack's thoughts.

"I'm coming, Mary," Jack wrapped Mary's scarf around his fist. He felt closer to her than he had for months, although he knew the Ashantis would fight and had been granted months in which to prepare a defence.

"Aye, you'll be waiting for us," Jack said as he peered across to the northern forests. "But you've never met British infantry before." He did not move when an Ashanti warrior emerged from the trees a few hundred yards on the northern side of the river. As the man approached, Jack saw that he wore the full uniform of a war-captain, except for the eagle feathers.

"Kumi Okese!" Jack said and reached for his revolver.

Three more Ashanti warriors stepped from the trees, all with the white stripes of

Kumi Okese's Edwesus. They formed around Kumi Okese, as the war captain returned Jack's gaze, unflinching.

"Sir!" Hopringle trotted up to Jack. "Jesus! That's an Ashanti!" Without a thought, Hopringle pulled out his revolver, but by that time, Kumi Okese and his bodyguard had gone.

"That was Kumi Okese himself," Jack remained where he was, staring north until Buller sauntered up in a cloud of tobacco smoke.

"Come along, old boy. You'll wear out the trees, glaring at them like that." Buller lowered his voice. "You'll get her back, never fear."

"Aye," Jack realised his hand was tight around the butt of his pistol. "Aye, I will."

General Wolseley sat outside his hut as Jack returned. "Ah, anything happening, Windrush?"

"Nothing of note, sir," Jack said. "Kumi Okese was looking us over, so we know the Ashantis will defend the road to Kumasi."

"Splendid," Wolseley said. "That way we can smash them and prove that British soldiers are a match for the fiercest warriors in West Africa."

* * *

The army crossed the 200-foot long bridge over the Prah by stages, with Russell's Regiment and Lord Gifford's Scouts probing first. On the 13th January, the 2nd Wests crossed, leaving behind a camp hospital already full of fever-struck men.

Meeting no opposition, the British gradually moved north, investigating each village as they approached the Adansi Hills.

Hopringle gave a small laugh. "It looks like King Kofi is not even going to fight. We've crossed their blessed Prah and not an Ashanti to be seen."

"They'll fight," Jack produced two cheroots, handed one to Hopringle and lit both. "We think the Prah is the boundary of Ashantiland, but north of these Adansi Hills is their real homeland. To the south, the land we are on now belonged to the Assin, a tribe the Ashanti conquered."

"What's beyond the hills?" Hopringle stopped for breath, and to ease his aching muscles.

Jack recalled the route. "Forests and mud swamps," he said. "Half a dozen villages, then the small town of Amoaful, and the Ordah River. The Ashantis might contest any or all of them, and finally, there is the marsh around Kumasi where I buried Private Manning, and the city itself."

"The city of gold," Hopringle whispered.

"It is a city of death," Jack replied. "A city of dreadful death."

As they came closer to the hills, the drums began a deep throbbing from the surrounding forest, punctuated by the blare of Ashanti horns.

"I detest that sound," Jack said. "When I leave Africa, I will hear these drums in my worst nightmares.'

"Sir!' Coffin said. "On the summit of the hill!"

Dressed in the full uniform of a war captain, Kumi Okese stood in front of his three-man bodyguard, with Akron at his side. When Kumi Okese held up his hand, the drums stopped, and the Ashantis looked down on the long British column that toiled up their guardian hills.

WINDRUSH - THE CITY OF DREADFUL DEATH

Kumi Okese said something in his deep voice, with Akron roaring out the words, so his voice echoed through the trees.

"British soldiers! Return home, British soldiers. You will die if you cross these hills!"

The words seemed to linger, a threat in themselves.

"No white man will return alive!" Kumi Okese stood on the apex of the hill, with the sun catching the gold bands around his arms and the long, gold-handled knife at his waist. A breeze rattled the fetish objects that adorned his chest. The bodyguards behind him each cradled an Enfield rifle, possibly the weapons taken from Jack's men when they were prisoners.

"No white man will cross our hills and return alive!"

"Ho! Bushman!" Private Stair shouted back. "How about us? How about C Company of the 2nd West? We are all black men!"

Jack's company laughed at that, with one or two glancing at Jack.

"You're white sir,' Private Stair said, greatly daring. "Maybe we'd best leave you behind on the north side of these hills while we defeat the Ashantis without you?"

Pleased at the reaction of his men, Jack ignored the insolence. "And when I'm with you lads, I am entirely West Indian!"

When the men nearby smiled or cheered, Jack wondered if such a simple statement helped morale more than all his training. Yet it was true. When he was with these men, he was part of a unit; he and his men fought and died together; they were C Company, 2nd West Indians, the best company in the British Army or any other army, damn you!

Jack did not see Kumi Okese move. One moment the Ashanti captain was prominent on the forest track, and the next he was gone.

"Fire!" Belatedly, Jack came to his senses. "Shoot that fellow."

As if awakening from a dream, the West Indians fired a volley, with bullets thudding into trees and flicking leaves from the branches. Stair reloaded hastily, stepped into the bush beside the path and fired again. "I'll get him, sir!"

"Come back, Stair!" Jack ordered. "Cease fire. He's gone."

The column struggled to the summit of the hill, with creepers brushing against their shoulders and the occasional bright flower a reminder of English cottage gardens and a life that was not constant toil and the ever-present threat of ambush. Despite their altitude, the heat was stifling, pressing down on them, squeezing the breath from their lungs, forcing the British soldiers to struggle for each lungful of oxygen.

They toiled up the steep southward facing slopes of the hills with the men gasping in the heat and swatting at clouding flies, slashing at creepers that overhung the path and alert for any Ashanti ambush. Every time they crested a hill, Jack looked north into what seemed a never-ending forest, with mist coiling around the tops of trees, still with an aura of mystery and menace. Yet every step brought him closer to Mary, just as every mile the British advanced put Mary in more danger of retaliation from King Kofi.

Reaching every summit was a small victory, with the northward slopes gentler, easing them downward towards Kumasi. Once again, Jack wondered why the Ashanti were not contesting this frontier.

"If I were the Ashanti commander," a captain of the Rifles said, puffing on a cheroot, "I'd place ambushes on every hill slope. We are most vulnerable when we're climbing up, concentrating on the path rather than the trees."

"Aye," Jack agreed. "I can't help thinking we'll pay for this yet. A few threats and the odd musket shot isn't much of a defence."

"You were in Kumasi, I hear," the Rifleman said.

"I was," Jack admitted.

"What do you think they are doing up there?"

Jack looked ahead. "I wish I knew," he said.

"Maybe they've given up," Lieutenant Wood said. As Wolseley's aide-de-camp, he had no business to be away from his master, Jack thought sourly. "Maybe the Ashantis know they can't stand against the British army and they've all run away." He lifted his revolver. "I hope not! I want a crack at the devils!"

Jack pushed Lieutenant Wood's revolver until the muzzle faced the ground. "Careful of that thing, son. You might blow somebody's head off, and the way you handle it, probably one of my men."

"I want to fight them."

"I think you'll get your chance later. Just now your position is with the general. Trot along to his side now, there's a good chap.!

The Rifles' captain grunted as Wood ran back down the column. "I'm Moore, by the way."

"Windrush," Jack nodded to the Rifles. "Your men look a handy bunch, Captain."

"Some are twenty-year veterans," Moore said. "They've been with the regiment since the Crimea. Others?" He shrugged. "We have far too many young boys in the army now with the short service rules. We hardly have time to train them up before they leave."

"I noticed the Marines were the same," Jack said. "Half grown boys with little stamina or experience in handling their weapons. It hardly seems right pitting them against seasoned Forest fighters."

Moore looked over his men, shaking his head. "When I joined up, the men were ten, twenty, even thirty-year veterans who had seen it all. They were tough as teak. Now we depend too much on children, drill and superior weapons. One day we'll meet an enemy with weapons and discipline to match ours. And then we'll pay for our expectations of superiority."

Jack nodded. "Let's hope it's not on this campaign." He looked northward, thinking of Mary.

"Oh well, best be marching on!" Moore gave a weak smile. "Kingdoms to conquer and all that, don't you know?"

"Aye, kingdoms to conquer," Jack agreed.

At the top of the final hill, they halted, with the older men and youths sinking at the base of trees, reaching for their water bottles. Jack frowned, recognising his surroundings. They stood in a clearing, with a group of three trees together, hung with low creepers and with a group of bright red flowers peeping from a broad-leafed plant.

This spot was where Yaa Asantewaa had ordered my manacles removed on my previous journey to Kumasi. This spot was where I had my first view of the strange land of the Ashanti.

"Last time I came this way I was in chains." Jack rubbed his wrists in painful memory.

Hopringle was breathing hard. "This time you have the best general in the army and thousands of British and West Indian soldiers with you."

Jack compared his situation then as a shackled prisoner, and now as part of a British column striking at the heart of the Ashanti kingdom. Curling his fist around Mary's scarf, he thought of Mary with manacles around her ankles and shivered. *Why am I resting here?* "Pick it up, boys! We've a long way to go yet. I think the Bushmen will be waiting for us."

Kumi Okese has missed a trick, Jack told himself. *The Ashanti should have defended this range of hills. The Afridi or any other Pashtun tribe would have made us fight for every yard we gained in such a territory.* The Ashanti were forest fighters and brave men, of that he had no doubt, but they lacked the tactical and strategical skills of the Pashtun.

Unless, Jack thought, and the idea chilled him unless they were allowing the British column to penetrate so deep into the forest that they could never fight their way out. Unless the Ashanti were already around them in their favoured horseshoe position, watching everything Wolseley and his men did. Unless the Ashanti had them in a trap.

"Keep alert, 2nd Wests," Jack put a hand on the butt of his pistol "If you see anything suspicious, anything that should not be there, let me know at once."

"We always do," Jackson murmured, sotto voice.

"Are you all right, sir?" Hopringle unbuttoned his holster. "Have you seen something?"

"It's too quiet," Jack said. "The Ashantis are too passive. They are bold warriors, and we are in their territory. Why don't they strike? Why are they waiting?" Jack pointed to Hopringle's holster. "Keep that unfastened all the time, and check you don't drop your revolver. If you need it, you'll need it quickly."

"Go back, white men!" The voice floated towards them. "Go back, white men! You'll never see your homeland again."

"Who said that?" Hopringle said, staring all around.

"I doubt we'll ever know," Jack said.

They walked on, easing down the gentle slope until they saw the old woman at the side of the track as if she were waiting for them.

"This could be trouble," Jack said as the woman stepped square into the middle of the path. Jack put a hand on the butt of his revolver as the woman pointed at him with a long-nailed finger and spoke in a high, cracked voice.

"I doubt that's a blessing," Hopringle said.

"More likely a curse," Jack checked the men at his back. Daley looked a little shaken, while Coffin was unruffled.

"Pagan Bushman religion," Coffin said. "We are better than such superstition."

"I hope so," Jack said. "It seems as if the Ashantis are using religion and psychological warfare against us."

"We'll use Sniders against them," Coffin said.

Leaving the old woman beside the path, they marched on, with the summit of the hills protruding above a hazy green-tinted mist and the trees seeming to glower at them with cold hatred.

"Message from Sir Garnet for Major Windrush!" Lieutenant Wood was eager as a puppy.

"Here I am, Lieutenant"

"Major!" Wood jumped to attention and saluted so hard he nearly knocked off his pith helmet. "Sir Garnet Wolseley sends his compliments, sir, and could you take your men and join the Rifle Brigade."

"Thank you, Wood," Jack said formally. "Pray convey my compliments to Sir Garnet and inform him I will be there directly."

Jack had served alongside the Rifles in earlier campaigns and knew their techniques. He signalled to his men "Come on, boys! There's no finer regiment for this sort of terrain."

The sun was half-way to the horizon when Jack led his company to the hard-bitten Rifles. A veteran NCO looked askance as the Wests formed up at their side. "Don't you Wests make us a target," he snarled. "We've no time for Johnny Raws here."

"Yes, sergeant. How long have you been in Africa?" Sergeant Mathews asked.

"Three weeks in Africa, but we've got more battle honours on our colours than nearly any other regiment." The Rifles' sergeant said with justifiable pride.

"Three weeks?" Mathews scoffed. "We've been here for three years! Don't let us down, Johnny Raw in Africa!"

Jack stifled his smile. Regimental rivalry was one of the strengths of the army, and it was good to hear his men holding their own with soldiers of a crack British regiment.

"Windrush!" Hopringle nearly tugged Jack's sleeve with excitement. "Did you hear the news?"

"What news was that?"

"King Kofi has released the hostages!"

"What?" Jack was not sure which emotion was uppermost, elation, relief or disbelief. "What? Where?"

Hopringle could not contain his grin. "I thought you'd be pleased, sir. I don't know the details, Windrush, but they're coming down the path from Kumasi, and there are women amongst them."

"Women?" *It must be Mary.* Not stopping to listen to any more, Jack ordered Hopringle to take charge of his men as he ran up the path.

Oh, God, please let it be true! Let Mary be safe.

CHAPTER TWENTY-SIX

Across The Prah January 1874

With no thought for his dignity as a British officer, Jack ran past the troops, barely acknowledging the salutes of the men, and surged ahead. Buller stood on his own, talking to a group of his spies.

"The released hostage?" Jack asked. "Where are they?"

Buller shook his head. "They're not here yet, Windrush. Sorry old chap. You'll have to wait for them. It's not safe to go on. The Ashantis are a bit treacherous, don't you know?"

"To the devil with the Ashantis," Jack said. "I'm going up the track."

"I wouldn't if I were you," Buller said, as Jack loped ahead, part running, part striding, and unheedful of any possible Ashanti ambush.

Mary, dear God, I hope you are safe! Jack tried to control his rising excitement as he thought of taking his wife in his arms once more and losing his nagging dread.

He saw the group approaching, walking slowly with a small Ashanti escort. "Mary!" Yelling her name, Jack broke into a full run, splashing through a small stream without pause. "Mary!"

On sight of a British soldier running towards them, the Ashanti warriors levelled their muskets, then turned them upside down as a sign of peace. Jack ignored them completely as he scanned the released hostages.

"Mary?" He asked. "Where's Mary Windrush, my wife?"

He knew the hostages from his time in Kumasi. Mr Kuhne and the Ramsayers lifted their heads when they saw him, while an Ashanti ambassador, resplendent with his golden breastplate, hurried past to seek Wolseley. Mary was not with this group. *She must be beyond that bend in the track.*

Mr Ramsayer greeted Jack like an old friend. "Major Windrush! My dear fellow." He held out his hand. "You said you'd be back to rescue us and here you are."

With his mind full of Mary, Jack had little time for pleasantries. "My wife was in Kumasi, Mr Ramsayer. Is she coming? Did you see her?"

Ramsayer's expression altered. "Your wife?" He shook his head. "Oh, my dear fellow. That lovely lady. Of course, Mrs Windrush; I had not thought she would be your wife. Oh, I am sorry."

"Have you seen her? How is she?" Jack grabbed Ramsayer's arms, shaking the missionary in his anxiety. "Is she with you?"

"I've seen her," Ramsayer said. "She is alive." He smiled, trying to soothe Jack's anxiety. "She did not come with us."

"Why not?" Jack asked sharply.

Ramsayer glanced at his wife before he replied. "I cannot say," he said.

Jack knew he was lying. "Why not?" He did not turn around when he heard the clump of footsteps behind him. He knew it was two of his Wests.

Mrs Ramsayer stepped beside her husband. "One of the Ashanti nobles refused to let her go," she said, quietly.

Jack felt as if somebody was squeezing the blood from his heart. "Why?" He almost whispered the word.

"I'm dreadfully sorry to say this, Major Windrush," Mrs Ramsayer placed a hand on Jack's shoulder. "But he wanted a white slave."

Jack felt as near to fainting as he ever had in his life. "What?"

"Kumi Okese wants a white slave," Mrs Ramsayer said. "That was his intention with Elda Becker, but they married, Ashanti style, so now he has your wife."

"Dear God in heaven," Jack whispered. "Mary, a slave? Will this nightmare ever end?"

"I apologise for bringing you bad news," Mrs Ramsayer said.

"Thank you," Jack stood still as the missionaries hurried toward Prahsu. He stared northward, momentarily unable to move. *Mary was a slave of Kumi Okese.*

"Sir?" Ogston stood behind him, with Coffin at his side. "Are you all right?"

Jack took a deep breath of the humid air. "Yes, thank you, Ogston. I'm all right."

"We heard the lady," Coffin said. "We'll get Mrs Major Windrush back."

"Thank you," Jack said. "Please tell Lieutenant Hopringle I will return shortly." Without another word, Jack walked northward, keeping to the middle of the track. After a dozen steps, he pulled the revolver from his holster.

Come on, Ashantis, he pleaded, *ambush me now. I want to kill. I want to kill every one of you and destroy your entire bloody empire! Oh, God, preserve my wife. Whatever else happens, protect my wife.*

CHAPTER TWENTY-SEVEN

Across The Prah January 1874

"We're moving out, Windrush. We're reconnoitring a village three miles ahead."

Jack lifted a hand, acknowledged the order, and rose from his cot. Shouting at his men to wake, he gesturing to them to join him as the Naval Brigade trotted ahead, with A Company of the Rifles jogging in skirmishing order, rifles at the trail.

"Keep up with the Rifles," Jack said, "study them; they're the best in the business at this kind of soldiering."

The Wests nodded, following Jack's lead. By now, every man in C Company knew that the Ashantis held Mary as a slave. They acted with silent sympathy, obeying orders without question, not knowing that Jack understood and appreciated their support.

The figure in white loomed out of the dark with his arms upraised.

"It's a priest," Daley said.

"A false priest," Coffin raised his voice. "May I shoot him, sir?"

"No," Jack said. "He's an unarmed civilian."

The Rifles and Wests marched past the priest, who retained his stance, shouting, until a Rifles sergeant gave him a shove. "Go and bother somebody else, old fellow," the sergeant said. "You're wasting your time with us."

"Sir," Stair pointed to a white thread stretched across the path in front of them. "That's a fetish thread sir, to stop us passing."

Jack grunted. "Is it by God? We're the 2nd Wests, not some superstitious bunch of blasted Bushmen!"

Kicking the thread aside, Jack marched on, as his men pointed out other fetish signs, with various animals sacrificed and left beside the road and once the naked body of a man, castrated, mutilated and impaled.

"Keep moving," Jack ordered, thinking of Mary. "Let's destroy these people."

Dawn arrived at the same time they came in sight of the next village. The Rifles opened into extended order, outflanking the settlement as Jack's C Company and the Naval Brigade advanced towards the front.

"Keep alert, men," Jack held his revolver ready, hoping for resistance. He felt no fear for himself, only a desire to fight, to kill, to destroy.

The orange flash of muzzle-flares augmented the growing light as half a dozen Ashanti warriors opened fire, with the slugs going nowhere, then the defenders quickly retired when the Rifles closed from the flanks.

"Search the houses," Jack ordered as his West Indians pushed forward, side by side with the bluejackets. "Watch out for hidden marksmen," On the North-West Frontier, the Afridi could pretend to retreat while leaving a few men to shoot unwary British soldiers. Jack was sure the Ashantis could be every bit as devious. He watched his men spread out as he had trained them, keeping in pairs, covering each other as they kicked open doors and checked inside.

"The village is empty, sir," Sergeant Roberts gave a smart salute.

We didn't kill a single Ashanti.

"Take up defence positions, in case the enemy return," Jack ordered, watching the men of the Rifle Brigade move outside the village to shelter behind fallen trees. "Watch how the Rifles move and learn from them."

"Now, what, sir?" Hopringle asked.

"Now we wait for orders," Jack said.

The drumming began an hour later. At first, it was only a slight throbbing, and then it increased in volume, minute by minute until every man was alert. The Rifles began to patrol deeper into the forest, moving silently, grey ghosts through the trees.

"Keep alert," Jack felt his palm sticky with sweat as he gripped his revolver. "I've heard that rhythm on the drums before. I'm sure it's a message of some sort."

"Ashanti drums summon men to war, sir," Ogston said. "They also send some messages."

Jack nodded. "Do you know what these drums are saying?"

"No, sir," Ogston smiled. "Maybe they are saying we surrender now that the 2nd West are here?"

"Perhaps they are,' Jack forced a smile. "Keep alert. The drumming might signal an attack on the village."

Taking out his binoculars, Jack scanned the forest, looking for unusual movement, when he saw the man staring directly at him. White stripes down the warrior's face and arms revealed his tribe, while he carried an Enfield rifle. Without hesitating, Jack lifted his revolver and fired, with Stair's Snider cracking out simultaneously. When neither shot took effect, Jack fired again, with Ogston and Jackson joining him. Two bullets ploughed into the warrior, knocking him backwards and onto the ground at the side of the path.

"Cover my back, lads," Jack ordered. "I want that Enfield." Without waiting for a reply, Jack ran across the road, weaving to disrupt the aim of any Ashanti marksman, and slid down beside the injured warrior. The man was severely hit, yet did not make a sound as he lay on top of a creeper.

Jack lifted the Enfield. "Ours, I believe," he said, and stopped as the silver Celtic Cross caught his gaze. "Where the devil did you get this?" The Ashanti had attached the cross to the butt of the rifle, so it hung loose like a pagan fetish charm. "That's Mary's! That belongs to my wife!"

Ripping the cross free, Jack held it tight. He remembered buying that cross from a jeweller outside the priory on the Holy Island of Lindisfarne. Mary had held it up to the light, laughing. "Where did you get it?"

The Ashanti stared at him, uncomprehending as blood from his wounds seeped into the ground.

"Where's my wife, damn you?" Lifting the man, Jack shouted in his face, shaking him until droplets of blood scattered, some landing on Jack. "Tell me, you murdering bastard!"

"Sir!' Coffin was at Jack's side. "Sir, you're making a target of yourself."

"This bastard has my wife's cross! He'll tell me where she is, damn him!" Lifting his revolver, Jack rammed it into the Ashanti's mouth.

"He can't tell you, sir," Coffin tried to ease the Ashanti from Jack's hands. "He's dead. Come away now!"

"Dead?" Jack looked up, suddenly aware of the Ashanti slugs that were bouncing around him. The warrior's head lolled backwards. Jack tried to control the fear that had threatened him ever since he learned the Ashanti had captured Mary. He knew that he was hovering on the edge of insanity, and for a moment, he had crossed that precarious threshold into madness. "Thank you, Coffin."

"Come away, sir!"

The Wests were waiting for him, firing at the Ashanti gunsmoke. Jack held Mary's cross in his hand. "Shoot them," he said softly, as the drums stopped, so for a moment, there was a deadly hush, with even the birds silent. The smoke drifted away, leaving nothing except the crumpled corpse of the Edwesu warrior, and the cross in Jack's hand.

"What are we waiting for, sir?" Hopringle asked.

"Orders, Hopringle," Jack said. "Orders."

* * *

The drums began again, drowning out the music of nature, making thought difficult, dominating everything, the resonance of native, untamed Africa. Watching the great trees all around, Jack thought that the British occupied the land they stood on and could dominate as far as the range of their rifles. Beyond that, Africa remained much as it always had been, watching, waiting, knowing the British presence was as temporary as a footstep in soft mud.

"We've got two prisoners," a patrol of the Rifles returned, with the men looking far more at home in the Forest than Jack had expected. The London accent was reassuring in this alien environment.

A runner panted up, looking over his shoulder. "Colonel Wood's compliments, sir, and could you return to the column."

The withdrawal was without incident, although Ogston saw warriors dogging them just beyond the forest fringe. Jack did not know when the drumming stopped. The noise seemed to fade away rather than ending in a crescendo, and the bird song continued, yet as Jack threaded along the path southward, the rhythm of the drums remained within his head. They were a threat, he knew, a personal threat from Kumi Okese to him. He felt sick heading away from Kumasi as if he was betraying Mary.

Can we push on from here? Can we move quickly now, before it's too late and the Ashantis murder Mary, or worse, enslave her and disappear forever? That thought brought nausea to Jack's throat.

And the rhythm of the drums returned, throbbing through Jack's head as he lay on his hammock that night. He curbed his impatience, checked his revolver, and grasped Mary's cross in his fist, with anxiety fighting his reasoning. He wondered if he should leave the column and head for Kumasi on his own, but shook his head. With unknown thousands of Ashantis between him and Mary, he must stay with the column. A dead man could not help anybody.

He woke without leaving his nightmare, gave automatic orders and roamed around the camp.

"It's all right, sir," Coffin said quietly. "The Lord will look after her." Coffin's eyes were steady. "Mrs Windrush is a good woman."

"Thank you, Coffin," Jack felt the silent sympathy of his men as he stared up the path to Kumasi.

That day was pure frustration as Wolseley ordered C Company, and the Rifles to remain in camp. He could only watch as the Naval Brigade rolled past, chewing tobacco and exchanging banter with the soldiers.

"You have a nice rest, boys, and let the navy do the work," a bearded petty officer said.

"Away you tarry-arsed bastards! We'll be there when the real fighting begins!"

A company of the 23rd Fusiliers were next, led by their regimental goat as they marched northward.

"You're going the wrong way, Welshmen," the Rifles jeered. "There are no sheep up there in Ashantiland!"

"I'll see you later, boy, and you'll not be smart with no teeth in your mouth."

Fighting his frustration as he watched others march to the front, Jack checked his men, ensured their rifles were clean and oiled, and all had sufficient ammunition. He listened as a section of Rifles preparing for picket duty as a youngster voiced his opinion about the campaign.

"These old soldiers moan about the trenches in the Crimea. They weren't in it compared to this."

Jack moved on, remembering the months of misery in the frozen trenches before Sebastopol. These young soldiers might find it hard in the heat and mud of the tropical forest, but this campaign would only last a few weeks, then they would be home. It had to be quick, for when the rains came, every stream would be a river, every river a torrent and every patch of swamp would double or quadruple in size until they were impassable.

I am getting old, he told himself, *reminiscing over past campaigns*. Remembering the jungle in Burma, he wondered how this new generation of soldiers would cope with the swampy bush, humid heat and swarming insects and flies. As he had before, Jack tried to accept the green gloominess as sunlight struggled to seep through the forest canopy.

Push on, Sir Garnet; push on!

It was good to hear the bugle calls resound through the trees, with each company having its call, good to have British Army organisation amidst the primeval chaos of the forest. Jack checked his revolver for the twentieth time, aware he was only trying to distract himself from agonising about Mary. The bugle called again, his company's call.

"That's us, boys!" Jack shouted. "We're with the Rifles again."

They marched, with Jack's men keeping pace with the crack British infantry, the

42nd, the Rifle Brigade and 23rd, one Scottish, one English and one Welsh regiment, a union brigade probing into the forest.

"We cannae fight in the forest, can we no'?" A Black Watch private said, glowering hopefully at the green gloom. "Come on then and see, you Shantees!" With the red buckle on his helmet the only sign he was from the Black Watch, the private thrust on, sweat pouring down his freckled face and determination in the line of his jaw.

Jack nodded. Whatever King Kofi and Kumi Okese chose to believe, the Ashantis would find the British regiments, the most versatile infantry in the world, more than willing to face them in the forest, or anywhere else.

They marched that day, and on the next, the 29th of January. Jack's company and the Rifles set off again half an hour before dawn, with the sound of their boots loud through the forest.

"Hopringle," Jack said. "Send Ogston and Coffin out as scouts, they're steady men."

Where are the Ashantis? Why does Kumi Okese not fight?

They marched on, nearly silent except for the thudding of their boots as they waited for an Ashanti ambush. Ogston trotted back towards them, carrying his Snider at the trail and with Coffin guarding his back. "Somebody's coming down the track towards us, sir."

Jack nodded. "Thank you, Ogston." He could feel the vibrations, the steady tramp of feet that told him that British soldiers, not Ashantis, were approaching. Even so, Jack raised his voice. "Keep your rifles ready."

Five minutes later the Naval Brigade met them head-on, with the 23rd Foot a few minutes behind them, marching in column of four, red-faced and unhappy.

"Nothing to see up there, Westies," the Welshmen of the 23rd said. "Only more bloody trees. The Ashantis have hooked it."

"Where are you headed?" Jack asked.

"Another village in the middle of bugger all,' the Welshman replied. "We've to count the trees and make sure they're not Ashantis in disguise. Some bloody campaign this, marching up and down all bloody day. The Grand old Duke's not in it!"

Now near the front of the straggling column, Jack's West Indians pushed on, finding the road narrowing the further north they marched, and the ground rougher. The drumming continued, now rising, now falling, passing messages around all of Ashantiland.

"They're gathering their men," Jack guessed. "They'll be waiting for us up ahead somewhere." He touched the butt of his revolver. *The bastards are going to try and stop me from rescuing Mary.*

The column marched down a slope and halted at a small clearing. With the ground too uneven for the tents, Jack posted sentries and ordered his men to clear away the bush, as the Rifles, a hundred yards away, did the same. The forest crowded all around, with Jack feeling as though the trees were watching. Twice he thought he saw movement and once he could have sworn a white-striped Edwesu warrior stared at him from the shelter of a bush. The birds were calling, insects humming, and everything seemed normal, yet he could not shake off the feeling that something was wrong.

"The forest demons are there," Daley shared Jack's forebodings.

"Aye, maybe. Double sentries tonight," Jack ordered. "And NCOs to patrol regularly. Ensure each man studies the ground in front of him, so he immediately knows if anything changes."

"You're feeling the same way, then," Captain Moore of the Rifles accepted one of Jack's cheroots. "The Ashantis are out there."

"I'm certain of it," Jack said. "Although I haven't even smelled one and my sentries haven't seen any."

"Nor have mine," Moore said. "I felt the same before the Russians attacked at Inkerman. It was a sort of hush as if the earth knew something was going to happen. In this case, it's the forest."

Jack nodded. "I remember that hush at Inkerman."

Moore gave him a doubting look. "I can't remember the Wests being in the Crimea."

"I was with the 113th Foot."

"Ah, the old Baby Butchers." The Rifleman dragged at his cheroot. "I remember them at Inkerman." His eyes narrowed. "What's your name again? Windrush?"

"That's me."

"Jack Windrush, Fighting Jack." Moore extended his hand. "I did not realise that you were that Windrush. A pleasure to meet another Crimea veteran."

"Likewise," Jack shook the Rifleman's hand. They stood side by side with the sounds of the daytime forest sinking with the light. The infantrymen settled down with murmured conversations.

"You'll be checking your men tonight?" Jack asked.

"I think neither of us will get much sleep," Moore said.

Jack nodded. "Aye. That's all part of the soldier's bargain."

They parted, each with his duty to do as the night closed with that remarkable swiftness of the tropics. Jack took a deep breath. Uncomfortable as it was, waiting for the Ashantis to attack was soldiering that he understood. He much preferred this, with an honest enemy who wished to kill him for an honourable end, to the subtle half-truths and downright lies of diplomacy and spying. Regimental soldiering was the life he chose, and he could accept the hardships and challenges with an easy mind.

Oh, God, Mary, I hope that you are all right. If the Ashantis have hurt you, I swear I will not rest until I have torn their empire piece by piece and tree by bloody, fetish-ridden tree. I'll destroy their golden stool, kill Kumi Okese and burn their towns to the ground.

Jack stopped himself. He knew he could not do any of these things. He took a last draw of his cheroot to calm his nerves and tried to push any thoughts of Mary to the back of his mind. He would need all his concentration for the ordeal to come, for the Ashanti were gathering, of that he was sure.

CHAPTER TWENTY-EIGHT

The Road To Kumasi January –February 1874

"Sir," Ogston whispered. "Something's not right."

Jack squinted into the dark. With dawn at least half an hour yet, he could barely see the edge of the forest let alone anybody moving out there. "What's wrong, Ogston?"'

"I'm not sure, sir," Ogston said. "I've been watching the trees." He looked away, as if afraid to say more.

Jack sighed. "What's wrong with the trees?"

"They're moving, sir," Ogston said. "They say there are demons in the forest."

There are worse things than demons out here.

"Could it be the wind?"

"There's no wind, sir."

Although Jack focussed his binoculars, he could not make out details in the dark. "I'm going forward, Ogston. Don't shoot me!"

Feeling very vulnerable, Jack stepped forward, depending on his night vision as he focussed on one tree that stood behind a darker belt of bush. After a moment, Jack blinked as the tree seemed to have moved further away from the shrubbery.

Forest demons? I don't believe in such things.

"Jesus!" Jack breathed. He was wrong; the tree was not sliding away from the bushes; the bushes were creeping closer to him. He concentrated, watching as the bushes moved again, sliding noiselessly towards the British camp. Backing away, with his heart pounding inside his chest, Jack returned to Ogston.

"Wake the men," he said urgently. He kicked Sergeant Mathews awake. "Mathews! Get everybody into firing positions, as quietly as they can. Don't bother getting dressed, just grab a rifle and ammunition. Hurry man! As quietly as you can!"

Jack checked again. He was right; it was no illusion caused by overwrought nerves. The bushes were undoubtedly closer.

"The forest is alive!" Daley said. "It's coming for us! The Fantis said there were forest spirits and we've angered them by coming here."

"It's not the forest." Fighting his jangling nerves, Jack checked to see his men were coming into position, some fully dressed, others only in their shirts and Stair naked except his rifle and ammunition. "It's the Ashantis hiding behind palm leaves and bushes. Load!"

Even before his men were all in position, Jack gave the order. "Aim for the bushes, boys. Aim low and fire at will."

The sudden crackle of musketry awoke the rest of the sleeping camp, with the Rifles bugler blasting the alert and the Riflemen running to their positions. The Wests' muzzle flares revealed vignettes of the surroundings, with Ashanti warriors frozen in time as they emerged from behind their sheltering bushes to return the Wests' fire, or falling under the searching Snider bullets. White smoke jetted as the Ashantis fired from behind their screens of leaves and small bushes.

"The forest is attacking us!" Daley repeated until Sergeant Mathews shoved him hard down on the ground.

"Shut your mouth and shoot!" Mathews snarled.

Standing tall so his men could see him, Jack felt an Ashanti slug zip past his face. "This is foolish," he told himself and fired three rounds into the smoke-tinged dark. Long jets of flame showed the position of the Ashanti musket men, so many that he could not count them.

"Aim for the muzzle flares," Jack ordered, swearing when the hammer of his revolver clicked on an empty chamber. He reloaded hastily, surprised that his fingers obeyed his brain without fumbling.

When Coffin chanted the first line of a revivalist hymn, others joined in, singing the words in deep, melodious voices, so Christian hymns battled against the din of gunfire and hoarse cries of fighting men.

Jack realised he was shooting at nothing. There was no return fire from the forest. "Cease fire! Cease fire!"

In the excitement of battle, some of his men continued to load and fire until Jack and the NCOs physically stopped them. The Rifles had already ceased fire, so only the dying strains of the hymn and the harsh panting of scared men filled the air. A leaf dropped, landing with an audible rustle that drew two more shots.

"I said cease fire, damn it!" Jack said. "They've gone." He checked his watch, startled to see that they had been firing for nearly an hour. It seemed like only a couple of minutes.

"Casualties?" A calm voice sounded from the Rifle's ranks. "Any casualties?"

Jack asked the same question. One man had been grazed by a slug; another had a minor wound in his leg.

"Keep alert," Jack said. "Sergeant Roberts, take over here; the men not on duty, get back to bed. Stair, there are no women to impress, so get dressed. Ogston and Coffin come with me."

Ensuring his revolver was loaded, Jack inspected the ground in front of the 2nd West's positions. He counted twelve Ashanti dead and judging by the trails of flattened grass and broken undergrowth, others had been wounded, but in the half-light of approaching morning, Jack could not even guess how many. He nodded in grim satisfaction when he saw three of the casualties had the Edwesus' white stripes.

"You did well, lads," Jack said when he wakened his men for breakfast. "The Ashantis won't try another night attack on the 2nd Wests."

But Jack knew that the worst was still ahead. With warriors such as Kumi Okese and inspirational women like Yaa Asantewaa, the Ashanti would contest every yard of territory. The fight for Kumasi was only beginning.

* * *

Jack lifted his head at the unmistakable wail of bagpipes. The sound brought back a host of memories, from the 93rd Highlanders of the Thin Red Line at Balaclava to Campbell's pipes that signalled the relief of Lucknow. Jack remembered what a Highland corporal had told him about the pipes. "The pipes warn the enemy that the Highlanders are coming," the corporal had said. "They tell the enemy how long they have to live."

"Here come the kilties," Jack said.

"Bloody Sawnie bastards," a bitter-faced Rifle private said. "They get all the glory. Bloody Queen Victoria's pets."

When the 42nd Highlanders, the Black Watch, swaggered along the forest path as if they owned the place, Jack was slightly disappointed they did not wear kilts but were in the same grey uniforms as the other regiments. He knew the alteration of uniform was sensible in the forest, but there was something particularly martial about a Highland regiment in kilts.

"All right, lads," Jack said as the Wests cheered the 42nd. "On we go."

They marched on through the swampy bush, now with the Black Watch in the van and C Company further back with the Rifles, swatting insects and watching the flanks. Then Private Jackson vanished without a sound.

"Sir!" Daley doubled up to Jack, slithering on the greasy mud-covered track. "Jackson has gone!"

"Gone?" Jack checked his men; there was a gap in the ranks where Jackson should have been. "When?"

"A minute ago, sir. He was walking and then he wasn't. The forest took him, sir. The forest spirits!" Daley looked over his shoulder as if afraid a tree would reach over to him.

"It was the Ashantis, not the forest. Show me exactly where it happened."

"Over here," Daley guided Jack fifty yards down the trail, eyeing the overhanging creepers with deep suspicion.

Jack saw the trail of broken vegetation where the Ashantis had dragged Jackson into the bush. Unholstering his revolver, he ordered Sergeant Mathews and Ogston to follow and eased into the forest. Immediately Jack did so, the atmosphere altered as the foliage closed around him. Within ten steps, he could have been a mile from the column, and after twenty, the entire British Army seemed like a different world. He stopped to examine the trail. A trio of colourful butterflies rose from the ground, where Jack saw scuffed earth and flattened grass.

"The Ashanti dragged Jackson here." Jack followed the spoor until he came to one of the Ashanti battle paths parallel to the main track. Scores of footprints headed north.

"The Ashanti are moving beside the column," Jack increased his speed, hoping to overtake the Ashantis before they killed Jackson. The battle path ran in a series of curves, then turned abruptly to the left at a patch of mahogany trees.

With sweat dampening his palms, Jack motioned for Mathews and Ogston to wait. He listened for the enemy, wondering if they were watching him. When he heard nothing, he moved forward, step by cautious step, following the trail that stretched as far as a fast-flowing stream and then disappeared altogether. Mathews and Ogston followed, silent as creeping night.

A drift of conversation came to Jack and he held up his hand. His men halted, rifles ready, as a group of Ashantis entered a clearing on the opposite side of the stream. Jack counted them, reaching fifteen before the last man appeared.

Fifteen Ashantis against three Wests. A sudden attack might panic them.

"There's Jackson!" Mathews gestured with his chin.

When Jack saw Jackson's body lying underneath the largest of the trees, minus his head, his anger mounted. *That was one of my men*! A sudden sound made him turn around, to see Coffin and Stair behind him, with Sergeant Roberts and three more Wests.

"What the devil are you doing here?"

"We thought you might need help," Roberts said.

Jack bit back his angry retort. "These Ashantis have killed Jackson. Form a skirmishing line and on my word, shoot the bastards flat."

That was the kind of order the Wests understood. Spreading out, they lay behind cover, extended their rifles and waited.

"Fire," Jack said when the Ashantis bunched up.

The fusillade ripped into the unsuspecting Ashantis, scattering those who were not immediately hit. Jack emptied his revolver, reloaded and emptied it again before he realised the enemy had vanished. The Ashanti casualties lay in the undignified postures of death, some with expressions of surprise on their face, others with a frown. Jack counted them. Seven, of whom five wore the Edwesu white stripes. Seven deaths to avenge a private of the Wests.

"Retrieve Jackson's body," he said. "We'll bury it here and now. Dig a grave with your bayonets. Coffin, I want you to say the appropriate words. Sergeant Mathews, you and Ogston stand guard."

Jack felt cold. Apart from sorrow at Jackson's death, he felt no emotion at having killed seven men. There was neither elation nor guilt. This skirmish had been only another incident in a war in which he should not be involved.

* * *

On the morning of 30th January, Captain Moore appeared with intelligence. "I hear that the Ashantis are massing. They have warriors beside the track all the way to the town of Amoaful."

"Amoaful," Jack remembered the place. "That's a sizeable settlement on the north side of a steep-sided gulley. If I were Kumi Okese or Amanquatia, I would make my stand there."

Moore grunted. "We'll soon see if they agree with you, Windrush."

As the track ran along level ground, the column moved faster, with the soldiers stopping to fill their water bottles from the numerous streams of bright water.

"Don't forget to filter the water before you drink," Jack warned. "It might look clean, but you don't know what impurities it contains." Ensuring the NCOs enforced his orders, Jack walked around his men, talking to them one by one.

Sergeant Mathews saw the object before anybody else. It was stuck on a pole in the track, with the eyes open and staring at them.

"That's Private Jackson," he said.

"It is." Jack took the head down at once, in case it unsettled his men, yet the word spread within minutes. Where he expected superstitious fear and a loss of morale, he found a surge of anger and a desire for revenge instead. Jack could feel the tension rising. When Coffin sang a soft psalm, others joined in, until Stair began a chant of "blood, blood, blood," which spread through the ranks.

"Sir," Sergeant Roberts said, "the men want to march at the head of the column. We want to get back at the Ashantis for what they did to Jackson."

"I feel the same way," Jack said. "We'll obey orders though, and remember Hubert Jackson when next we fight. And we won't forget Stanley Manning."

"Yes, sir," Roberts saluted. Jack heard the news circulate C Company.

Jack wrapped Mary's scarf around his fist, looked at the silver cross he had fastened to his pistol holster for luck and marched on. He knew that the Ashantis would fight at Amoaful. Jack did not doubt that. He only hoped the British could inflict a sufficiently signal defeat to end the war.

We're coming, Mary. Every day brings us closer.

CHAPTER TWENTY-NINE

Amoaful 31st January 1874

"Check your ammunition," Jack said. "There will be a battle today. Make sure your rifles are clean and oiled, and your water bottles are full of filtered water." He walked the ranks of C Company as they stood at ease.

"You are as good as any regiment in the British Army," Jack said, "and better than most, so I know you will fight well."

The men listened, straight-faced but proud.

"General Wolseley has issued his order of battle," Jack said. "It is nothing less than the traditional British regimental square."

"That's the one we used to defeat Napoleon," a hopefully anonymous voice from the ranks said.

"That's correct, Ogston," Jack said. "But in our case, the square will be inside the forest. The general has arranged the army into four columns, with Brigadier General Sir Archibald Alison commanding the first column, which will be the front of the square. Colonel McLeod of the 42nd has the left flank, Lieutenant Colonel Wood the right flank and Lieutenant Colonel Warren of the Rifle Brigade the rear."

The Wests listened. Jack knew that few officers ever bothered to explain tactics to the men, whose duty was only to follow orders, but he remembered how it felt to fight without knowing the full picture.

"At present, we are with the Rifles," Jack said. "There is no knowing where the fortunes of battle may send us. Wherever it is, I know you will add lustre to the name of the 2nd West Indians."

For once, C Company cheered, with Jack responding with a wave. He remembered his military history studies, when Publius Flavius Vegetius Renatus, 1500 years earlier recommended forming a square when the troops were superior in morale and quality to the enemy. Jack did not doubt that the British soldiers held both cards, while the Ashantis had the advantage in numbers and knowledge of the terrain. The coming day would decide who held the aces.

The 42nd Highlanders led the column. They started marching with the breaking dawn, the splashes of red on their helmets reminders of past glories and the swagger of their shoulders a warning not to oppose them. Jack's C Company was next, with the Rifle Brigade immediately behind.

"The Ashantis are out there," Sergeant Mathews said. "I can smell them."

"You and Manning came from the same island, didn't you?" After four months in their company, Jack knew his men.

"Yes, sir. We're Bajans, from Barbados, the pride of the West Indies." Mathews said.

"Then you can avenge him, today," Jack said. Both men lifted their heads when they heard the spatter of musketry.

"That's it started," Jack checked his watch. "Nearly eight o'clock. Lord Gifford's African scouts will be clearing the village of Egginassie."

At the sound of gunfire, the Highlanders quickened their step. "Come on, lads!" A Perthshire voice roared. "Hurry it up, or there'll be nane left for us!"

A couple of wounded scouts staggered past and made their way to the rear, dripping blood.

"Pick it up!' A Black Watch lieutenant shouted, and the Highlanders increased their pace until they were doubling as they came to Egginassie, a wretched place beside the road. Lord Gifford, slim and dapper, was there with his wild-looking tribesmen. He waved to the hurrying column.

Passing through the village, the British nearly trotted along the forest path with Sergeant Mathews growing more eager by the yard.

"I hope the Ashantis fight, sir," Mathews patted the lock of his Snider.

So do I. I want to smash them. "Amanquatia and Kumi Okese command them," Jack said. "They are both fighting men."

"I knew the Bushmen would cause trouble today," Sergeant Mathews said as the Ashanti battle cries sounded without the accompaniment of war drums.

"Make sure your rifles are loaded!" Jack ordered. They were still marching along the narrow track with the forest pressing on both sides. With a hundred trees overhanging the path, Jack felt as though he was travelling through a long green tunnel.

"Skirmishing order," Jack shouted, and the Wests spread out like the veterans they now were. As the left flank pushed into the forest on either side of the path, it stumbled into what had been the Ashantis encampment, with small huts thatched with plantain leaves. "Be careful of ambushes," Jack ordered, but the huts held no warriors, only low bamboo bedsteads and cooking pots.

"Sir!" Mathews said. "Listen to the firing! They've started the battle without us."

An unmistakable volley sounded, with the deep boom of the Ashanti muskets echoing in the green gloom of the trees. After the gunfire came the singing, thousands of voices chanting the Ashanti war-song, a noise that lifted the hairs on the back of Jack's neck. He had heard British regiments singing on the march, and the Warriors of God on the Frontier shout "Allah Akbar," but he had never heard anything as impressive as the Ashanti chorus that day. The sound came from all around them, a theatre of music with the British as the audience.

After a few minutes, the horns joined in, all with different tones, a weird accompaniment and then, finally, the roar of war drums, with the three sounds combining in an unnerving harmony.

The silence, when it came, seemed to paralyse the British advance as the men stood in their ranks, staring at the trees. The red hackle of the Black Watch looked like miniature spots of blood against the sombre green of the forest.

"Well, bugger this, lads, eh?" A Dundonian voice sounded. "Come on, let's get intae they Shanty bastards, eh?"

The Ashantis responded with a tremendous volley that ripped into the British ranks, knocking down a dozen of the 42nd. Jack saw Highlanders stagger back, holding faces, arms and chests as the slugs smashed at them from close range.

Colonel McLeod of the Black Watch roared above the chaos of battle. "The 42nd will fire by companies, front rank to the right, rear rank to the left!"

The Highlanders moved on, firing as men dropped. "A Company, front rank, fire! Rear rank, fire!"

"Advance!" Major Duncan MacPherson shouted. The Black Watch responded, crashing through the trees. They fired a volley of their own, the painful crack of the Snider meeting the deep boom of the muzzle-loaders as the Highlanders loaded, fired and advanced, heedless of casualties.

The Ashanti's fire continued, erupting from the trees all around the 42nd as thousands of muskets fired together.

"Amanquatia has gathered every Ashanti in the world here," Hopringle said, staring at the clouds of smoke, through which orange muzzle-flares gleamed.

"Advance!" Major MacPherson shouted again, then crumpled as a slug smashed into his leg.

"The Shanties have got Big Duncae, eh?" The Dundonian voice sounded again. "Ye've hud it, noo, ya Shanty bastards!"

Major MacPherson rose, tied a handkerchief around the bleeding gash in his leg and shouted again. "Advance!"

Jack saw a piper with the 42nd, encouraging the men as the thin wail of his pipes rose above the hellish racket of battle.

"Double," Jack ordered. "We're the 2nd West! If the Sawnies need us, we'll be there."

"Who are the Sawnies, sir?" When Sergeant Mathews looked confused, Jack remembered his company had never fought alongside regular British infantry before. "The Sawnies are any Scottish regiment. The 42nd is also known as the Black Watch, or the Forty-twa." He moved on, "Never mind, just follow my orders, sergeant."

The Ashanti army held the heavily wooded slopes that slid down to a swampy valley and then rose again to the sizeable village of Amoaful. As Jack led his company forward, he saw white powder smoke wreathed both slopes, with myriad muzzle-flares all around. Standing exposed on the path and extended into the trees, the Black Watch was firing back, volley after volley of Snider bullets that hissed and crackled through the trees, with every so often Major MacPherson shouting "advance" and pushing the men forward. Casualties were everywhere as the Highlanders, necessarily exposed as they moved, fell to the concealed Ashanti marksmen.

"Now we'll see if British soldiers can face the Ashanti in the bush," Hopringle said.

"That's the Black Watch," Jack said. "I saw them at the Alma and in the Mutiny. They'll face anybody, anywhere."

"Advance!" Major MacPherson said, and the Highlanders moved again, ignoring their casualties as they fired and pushed forward into the dense undergrowth.

"They're all around us!" Sir Archibald Alison had fought under Sir Colin Campbell in the Indian Mutiny, where he lost an arm. Now he commanded the advance, where two companies of the Black Watch were in action. "Bring up another company!"

"It's how they fight, sir," Jack came beside the colonel. "They adopt a horseshoe formation to ambush their prey."

"We're the 42nd, damn them. We're nobody's prey." Sir Archibald stroked his whiskers, evidently wanting to draw his claymore and charge forward with his men.

"Yes, sir. I've brought a company of the 2nd West in support. Where do you want us?"

"Support the Forty-twa, Major! Take the left flank of the frontal assault and keep out of the Highlanders' path."

Nodding, Jack returned to his men. He did not know Sir Archibald, so could not compare him to the many splendid Scottish soldiers he had met, from Lord Clyde to Hugh Rose. Jack did not doubt the man's courage, for nobody could command Scottish infantry unless they were brave, but on first impressions, he thought Alison blinkered and tactically naïve.

The Ashanti fire was increasing as a third company of Black Watch arrived, with the pipers playing as they doubled forward. The sound of the pipes heard through the crackle of musketry, the incessant thunder of the drums and the harsh shouts of fighting men, was one of the strangest things Jack had ever heard.

"The Ashantis are trying to turn the flank," Jack said.

Sir Archibald nodded to Jack. "So I believe, Major." Without a qualm, he nodded to a stocky major. "Baird, take two companies along to the left, will you? The Royal Engineers will go along with you to widen the path." Despite Jack's misgivings, Sir Archibald was as calm as anybody there. "You know the general's instructions."

The fighting intensified, with some Ashanti waiting in the branches of the tall trees to fire down on the advancing British.

"Wests," Jack said. "Aim for these men, and for God's sake don't hit the Forty Second!" Now was the opportunity to test his musketry training.

As he moved slowly forward, Jack could see the virtue of Wolseley's classic square, for the Ashantis were unable to outflank the British. Whichever the Ashantis advanced, they faced a wall of Sniders and determined men. Three hundred yards out on each flank, engineers hacked out forest paths in the manner of the Ashantis, along which the infantry marched, under constant fire.

Wolseley had collected the reserve ammunition, the hammocks and the bearers within the centre of the square, where the infantry could protect them. Jack's appreciation of Wolseley as a commander increased; in Jack's estimation, Wolseley was proving himself the best Irish-born general since the Duke of Wellington. He had countered the Ashantis' battle tactics, now all depended on the steadiness of the troops.

Jack had no doubts about the British regiments, with the Black Watch, the 23rd and the Rifles amongst the best soldiers anywhere, and he knew his company of the 2nd West would hold their own. He was less sure about the Hausas and hoped they were not in the line if the Ashantis launched a serious attack.

"Advance," Major MacPherson ordered yet again, staggered from loss of blood, grabbed a stick to support him and moved on with his men.

"Listen to that bloody tune!" The Dundonian voice sounded again, distinct above the battle. "The pipie's playing *The Campbells are Coming*! Does he think we're the bloody Argylls?"

One heavily bearded lance-sergeant grunted as an Ashanti slug hit him. He looked at the blood soaking through his chest, grunted again and pushed on into the trees. "Come on, lads!"

"Good man, Sergeant McGaw," Major MacPherson said, limping on with his stick.

Jack nodded. "Aye; you were wrong, Amanquatia. British infantry can face your Ashantis in the bush. Come on, C Company!"

As the British cut through the forest to form Wolseley's square, Jack led his Wests to the front left, where the 42nd continued to advance on either side of the track. The Black Watch had pushed the enemy down the slope, so Jack saw wounded Highlanders amidst a host of Ashanti dead and injured. As he slid downhill in the wake of the 42nd, Jack noticed that many of the Ashantis had white stripes down their faces. Kumi Okese's Edwesus were resisting bravely, as expected.

Fighting all the way, the Black Watch reached the ugly swamp at the bottom of the gully. The fringe of bright flowers seemed out of place in this scene of slaughter and strife.

Beyond the swamp, the ground rose to a heavily wooded ridge, curling towards the British left flank. Gunsmoke from the ridge proved that the Ashanti musketeers were there in numbers.

"Come on, men," Major Baird shouted. "The enemy on that ridge is blocking our advance." Leading from the front, he splashed into the swamp with slugs kicking up mud all around. With Sergeant McGaw and the cheering Black Watch a few steps behind, Major Baird began the ascent of the wooded slope.

"Come on, the Wests!" Jack shouted, following in close support.

As the Highlanders and West Indians crossed the swamp, Jack realised there was a river as an additional barrier, while the Ashantis were reinforcing their numbers by the minute. He shuddered; Amanquatia had chosen a position similar to the Russians at the Alma, forcing the British to cross a river and climb a slope in the face of defensive fire.

The stream at the bottom of the ravine was shallow, reaching only to Jack's knees, but as soon as he burst from cover, half a dozen Ashantis fired, with the slugs tearing the surface of the water all around.

"Come on, 2nd West!" Jack fired his revolver at the nearest musket smoke. "Skirmishing order! Open your ranks, fire at the smoke and support one another!"

Somewhere to his right, Jack heard the pipes screaming above the constant fusillade of Snider fire and the thuds of Ashanti muskets. Looking to left and right, he saw the 42nd advance, company by company and section by section, never halting for long, but still in too close formation for his liking. "Open their ranks, for God's sake," Jack pleaded, but the Highland officers kept their men together, offering targets for the thousands of enemy marksmen. In the thick bush, entire sections of the Highlanders vanished from Jack's view, with only the crackle of the Sniders, the hoarse orders of officers and NCOs and the wailing pipes signalling their presence.

The sheer volume of enemy fire showed that the Ashantis far outnumbered the 42nd. Jack saw Highlanders fall in ones and twos, most to rise and stagger onward, some with horrendous facial wounds from the Ashanti slugs, others holding limbs or trunk where dark blood seeped through the sweat-stained grey cloth. Despite the casualties, the remainder never faltered, pushing the Ashantis back yard by hard-won yard.

"Follow my orders, C Company!" Jack beckoned to the bugler. "Listen for the regimental calls." He inched forward, checking his men, firing whenever he thought he saw the enemy.

A new outbreak of musketry erupted from the left. "The Ashantis are still trying to outflank us!" A hard-faced highland major shouted.

The 42nd companies on the left flank immediately shifted their attack to the front. "We cannae get through the bastards that way," one tousle-haired corporal roared, tying a handkerchief around an arm that streamed with blood. "So let's go right down their throat! Come on the Forty-twa!" Hefting his rifle, he plunged into the bushes, snapped a shot, loaded, swore when a slug sliced at his leg and carried on with the red hackles of his men bobbing in his wake.

"That's the way, Rab!" Sergeant McGaw roared, ignoring the blood that soaked his uniform. "Show them your cap badge, Forty-twa! Take the bayonet to them!"

"Keep going, 2nd Wests!" Jack shouted. "Follow the Highlanders!" Taking a deep breath, Jack plunged forward. He knew his men were behind him, saw a flicker of movement to his right and left as the Black Watch forced their way on, stepped over the slowly-writhing body of a wounded Highlander and shouted again.

"This way, the Wests!"

Jack knew the British musketry must be taking effect, but for every Ashanti the Highlanders and West Indians shot, half a dozen took their place, so resistance stiffened as they pushed up the hill. Jack swore as a slug hammered into a tree he sheltered behind, ducked as something hummed through the air above his head and fired at a gush of smoke a few yards to his left. He had been in a score of battles from Pegu in 1852 and Inkerman to the Ridgeway fight Canada, but he swore he had never experienced such a volume of fire as in that African forest.

Even when Wolseley sent a company of Rifles to reinforce the 42nd, the British were losing men for every five yards of ground they gained. The advance stalled, with panting Highlanders glaring uphill and the Rifles and Wests exchanging Snider bullets for Ashanti slugs as the battle reached its crucial point.

"We're losing too many men," Hopringle said.

"It's not finished yet," Jack ducked as a dozen shots screamed overhead. "Those were Snider bullets. We're firing at ourselves."

"Here's the artillery coming!" Captain Moore of the Rifles said.

"Give the gunners covering fire," Jack ordered.

Although the 42nd and Rifles had advanced a considerable distance up the slope, the Ashantis still managed to harass Rait's artillerymen. Busily firing at the enemy, Jack had little time to watch as the Hausas, and Royal Artillerymen manoeuvred their steel nine-pounder across the swamp and river. The men struggled, sweat trickling down their faces as they pushed the cannon, flinching as Ashanti slugs rattled off the gun barrel, swearing to manoeuvre reluctant wheels through clinging mud.

"That's hard work for the gunners," Moore said.

"Support the artillery!" Jack yelled. "Keep these blasted Ashanti musket men down!"

When he reached a relatively flat area, Rait stepped clear of the gun, ignored the Ashanti slugs, and scanned the hillside. Noting a dense patch of forest where the Ashanti gun smoke was thickest, he aimed his nine-pounder. The Hausa gun-crew were smart, loading in seconds and firing at once. Jack saw the case-shot rip into the trees, again and again, as Rait altered the angle of aim slightly each time. When the artillery fire ceased, a company of the 42nd charged forward, bayonets fixed and the pipes screaming in support.

"Come on, 2nd West," Jack rose from his cover. "Follow the Black Watch!"

The West Indians advanced without hesitation, scrambling up the slope as slugs tore leaves from the trees and hammered into the ground.

"Go on, the Westies!" A wounded Black Watch private shouted encouragement. "Give them hell!"

By the time Jack's men arrived, there was nobody left to fight. The bayonets of the 42nd had completed the artillery's work, with shattered Ashanti bodies scattered around and a lone Black Watch private sitting against a tree, smoking and muttering to himself, tears in his young eyes.

"They're breaking," a Black Watch lieutenant shouted as the Ashanti firing began to ease. "Push on, the Forty-twa!"

When the 42nd penetrated their centre, the Ashanti on the flanks crumbled. Too preoccupied with his own fight, Jack had no time to watch the action elsewhere. On the left, the British had cut through to the crest of the ridge. Once there, the artillery fired rockets at an Ashanti encampment, forcing them away. On the right, Colonel Wood and the Naval Brigade had made progress until heavy Ashanti fire pinned them down. Too careful of his men's lives to engage in a frontal attack, Wood ordered his men to lie down and fire back, depending on the superior firepower of the Sniders to overcome the Ashanti numbers.

"Come on!" Jack followed the Black Watch over the ridge, where the Ashantis were now fleeing from their camp. For the first time that day, Jack saw a live Ashanti as Amanquatia formed up his battered regiments in the village of Amoaful. Kumi Okese was there, prominent under his yellow umbrella as he addressed his white-striped Edwesus.

This time the British did not allow the Ashantis to form a proper defence. Rait's artillery blasted case shot into Amoaful, sweeping into the Ashanti ranks like a broom, felling dozens and scattering the others. Panting with effort, Jack watched. "Form up, C Company," he ordered. "Take a roll call, Hopringle."

"Capture that village," Sir Archibald Alison ordered, and the Black Watch, angered by their casualties in the slogging advance, gave a cheer and charged in with the bayonet. Jack's Wests followed, with the Rifle Brigade company soon after, scattering the remaining defenders and firing at the warriors as they fled into the trees. The battle for the village was short and fierce, ending in the Ashantis total rout.

"We've done it," Sergeant Mathews said, rubbing at his chest.

"We've broken through and captured Amoaful," Jack checked his watch. One thirty. It had taken the British five and a half hours to press the Ashantis back, yet he still heard heavy firing from the British right flank and further down the column. The Ashantis were not done yet.

"They're devils, these Ashantis," Captain Moore leaned on a tree, wiping sweat and blood from his forehead. "But they're brave devils."

"They're as persistent as the Pashtun," Jack said.

"The 42nd took heavy casualties," Moore said. "Their tactics were all wrong, advancing in sections as they did."

Although he agreed, Jack did not comment. Criticising any regiment's tactics was a sure way to create bad blood, and the Highlanders had fought with their customary bravery.

Sir Archibald Alison looked over the men in Amoaful. Some were lying exhausted, others drinking from water bottles. A few men tied makeshift bandages around wounds, while others checked their ammunition or swapped stories about the fighting. Sergeant McGaw was checking his section, ignoring his bloodstained tunic.

"Windrush," Alison spoke in an educated Edinburgh accent. "How are your Wests?"

"They did well, sir," Jack said.

"How many casualties?"

"I have three wounded, one seriously. I sent the badly hurt man back." Jack said.

"So few?" Alison raised his eyebrows.

"I taught them to fire from cover, sir, rather than expose themselves needlessly," Jack defended his men, feeling that Alison was attacking them for not taking more casualties.

Jack looked back down the hill as heavy firing broke out. "What's happening down there?"

Captain Moore joined them. "The Ashantis are attacking the column, trying to break the supply lines,"

"They're resilient; I'll grant them that," Alison said.

"Shall I take my Wests down and help the column out, sir?"

"Stay put," Alison said. "I may need you here."

It was nearly three in the afternoon before the last sputter of fire died out, and relative peace returned to the forest. The British had four killed and 173 wounded, mostly from the 42nd, who had taken the brunt of the fighting. Jack leaned against a tree in the middle of the village and lit a cheroot, surprised he was not shaking with reaction.

"How many men did the Ashantis lose?" Hopringle asked.

"We'll never know," Jack said. "The bodies will be out there in the forest. If you want to go and count them, help yourself."

"I'd say we shot thousands," Hopringle said. "We taught them no end of a lesson."

"You may be right," Jack said, "although my estimate would be about five or six hundred if we're lucky. The Ashantis are expert at keeping behind cover. Now go and check your section, ensure your men are fed and watered and have sufficient ammunition. We won a battle, not the whole war."

"Yes, sir," Hopringle injected a little resentment into his reply. Although Jack knew the lieutenant wanted to talk about his first action, he had no desire to listen to a Johnny Raw's ideas. He wanted to be alone. No, Jack corrected himself as he curled Mary's scarf around his fist. That was not true. He wanted to be with his wife.

The remainder of the Rifles and the baggage entered Amoaful later that afternoon, tired and glad to have somewhere to rest. Wolseley set up a field hospital in the village, where busy surgeons treated the casualties before an escort took them back to the coast. Towards evening, Wolseley sent two companies of the Rifles and a section of the Wests to a nearby village, leaving Jack's men where they were.

"Bed down, lads," Jack ordered. "Three section, you take the first watch." Crawling into a hut, he lay down. As always after a battle, a hundred scenes and incidents crowded into his mind as the day's events unfolded. He closed his eyes, mentally and emotionally drained, yet sleep evaded him. Sometime after midnight, he heard the sputter of musketry as the Rifles and Wests combined to repel an Ashanti attack on the village.

"Come on, lads," Jack ordered as his men emerged with rifles in their hands. "Defensive positions."

After half an hour, the firing died away, without a serious attack on his men. "Number Three Section, get some sleep. Two Section, take their place."

Remaining outside the hut, Jack lay on his back, staring at the sky and hoping that Mary was all right. It was always worse at night, for during the day he had a host of problems to keep his mind occupied. At night, when he lay alone, he had time to worry. The images of the battle no longer troubled him. Now, he only saw Mary in chains, with Kumi Okese leering at her through his smoky eyes.

CHAPTER THIRTY

On To The Ordah February 1874

Jack awoke with a slight ache in his head and a bitter taste in his mouth from the previous day's powder-smoke.

"Are we pressing on to Kumasi?" He asked hopefully, watching Wolseley give orders.

"It seems not," Captain Moore said. "I think Wolseley is consolidating first."

"What is there to consolidate?" Jack asked. "We beat them fair and square on ground of their choosing! Now is the time to double march to Kumasi."

Moore grinned. "Shall I go and tell the general your opinion? I'm sure Sir Garnet will listen to your advice."

Biting back his impatience, Jack checked his men, ensured they all had full water-bottles and got their fair share of provisions, set out sentries from One Section and tried not to think of Mary. While the Rifles patrolled two miles southward to ensure the baggage came through safely, the 42nd and a few of the 23rd engaged in punitive expeditions, Jack and the West remained in Amoaful, baking in the heat.

"One thing's for sure," Captain Moore said. "The Ashanti won't be starved to death."

Cunning hands had woven palm leaves into large containers, which held a mixture of flour and maize. The British soldiers tasted the contents cautiously, some thinking they may have been poisoned.

"It's fresh as a Sunday morning," Coffin said, smiling. "Far better than army rations."

"Well done, lads!" Jack approved. "Dig in!"

As Jack watched his Wests enhance their rations with this free food, the Rifle other ranks discussed Kumasi.

"It's true, I tell you," one private said. "King Kofi pays his men in gold, and solid nuggets are lying about the streets."

"You're talking nonsense, man," another said.

"I'm telling you!" The first soldier shouted to prove his words. "That's why this place is called the Gold Coast! The king has a great gold crown and sits on a golden stool. And all his wives, he's got thousands of them, all his wives wear great gold chains and nothing else."

"Nothing else?" A quiet man showed sudden interest. "Nothing at all?"

"Only gold chains."

Shaking his head, Jack walked away. The soldiers were in for a disappointment if they expected to pick up lumps of gold from the streets of Kumasi.

"Ah, Windrush," Buller appeared, cigar in hand and looking as immaculate as if he were squiring women in Hyde Park rather than facing Ashantis in the African forest. "Did you hear the news? No, then I'll tell you. We disposed of your old adversary in the late battle."

"Who? Kumi Okese?"

"Oh, no, the general himself, Amanquatia. Your Okese fellow must be in charge of the Ashanti army now." Buller drifted away, waving a languid hand at soldiers who saluted him.

Kumi Okese in charge? Jack pondered. If so, he was not with Mary, which could only be good. *If I see him, I will kill him*, Jack promised, wrapping Mary's scarf around his fist.

After a day's frustrating rest, Wolseley ordered the army to march again. With Russell's local levies scouting ahead, Colonel McLeod commanded the advance guard, while Rait's men transported the nine-pounder.

"We're at the head today," Captain Moore trotted past with H and C Companies of the Rifle Brigade, who moved further back after their exploits at Amoaful.

"We'll support you, Moore," Jack said. "Come on, C Company! We're travelling light. Take your rifle, ammunition and three days rations in your haversack. Nothing else."

The Wests obeyed without question.

"No tents?" Hopringle asked.

"It looks like we're finally dashing for Kumasi," Jack said. "Three days, maybe even two, and we should be there." *Hold on Mary; I'm coming.*

* * *

Even after their defeat two days previously, the Ashantis showed their spirit. Only an hour after leaving Amoaful, Jack heard the first deep thuds of Ashanti musketry. *Here we go again.* He touched the silver cross on his holster.

"Keep in formation, boys!" Jack said. "Make sure you're loaded and ready." He did not alter the speed of the march as he heard the slow spatter of aimed rifle fire and knew the Rifles were responding. Within a few moments the firing died away, and a quarter of a mile up the track they passed a bullet-scarred tree trunk with the dead body of an Ashanti warrior crumpled on top. The Wests barely paused to look; they had all seen dead warriors before. Jack noted the man's white stripes. *Kumi Okese is not finished yet.*

There was more musketry half an hour later, and again the column barely paused.

"We're pushing them aside now," Jack said. "Maybe we'll have a rapid march to Kumasi." *Two days, stay alive, Mary!*

This time two Ashanti warriors lay dead beside the road, while another with a splintered leg glowered at the marching column.

The rain started then, easing through the canopy above to patter on the road, drip on men's heads and quickly turn the hard-packed earth into mud.

"This rain might swell the rivers," Jack said, worrying.

"We'll get her back," Hopringle tried to reassure him.

Another hour of hard marching found them in a small deserted village. The only living thing was a half-starved dog, which one of the Rifles immediately fed with a biscuit. Jack saw a cooking fire outside a hut, with maize-meal bubbling in the pot on top.

"Not bad!" Coffin said, after a quick taste. "What a waste to leave it here."

"The Ashanti must be rattled now to leave in so much of a hurry," Hopringle said. "We've beaten them."

"They're on the run, for sure," Jack said.

Hold on, Mary, Jack thought. *Not long now. I'm coming for you.*

An outbreak of firing ahead halted the column, denting Jack hopes. "Front rank face right," he ordered. "Rear rank face left."

The Wests swung around, ready to repel any ambush until Colonel McLeod ordered them up to support the Rifles.

"With me, lads!" Although Jack marched C Company at the double, by the time they reached the front, the Rifles had already cleared away the Ashantis.

"You're not needed, after all, Windrush," McLeod said. "The Rifles did the job. Good skirmishers, these men."

"Yes, sir," Jack said. "If the Forty Second had adopted the Rifles' fighting style, they might have taken fewer casualties at Amoaful." He ignored McLeod's hard glare, for he disliked seeing unfortunate leadership waste good soldiers.

There was another deserted village a few miles further on, and two streams of clear water running across a bed flecked with iron pyrites.

"Gold!" A young Rifle said, to the jeers of his companions.

The column continued for half an hour and then halted, sweltering in the heat. The Rifles' adopted dog slowly wafted its tail, enjoying its unaccustomed popularity as Jack looked ahead, calculating the distance to Kumasi.

"What's happening, sir?" Jack felt his frustration mounting, knowing that Mary was only a few dozen miles ahead.

"We're waiting for Sir Garnet," Colonel McLeod said, "and the rest of the column."

"I could take my Wests and push on sir," Jack offered. "We're used to this sort of terrain."

"Stay with the column, Windrush," McLeod said. "The Ashantis may have more ambushes ahead."

Knowing McLeod was correct, Jack nodded. "Yes, sir."

"Rest while you can, fill your bottles and remember to filter the water," Jack said. The Wests scattered to find shade from the sun, except for the unlucky half-section Jack posted as sentries. Insects buzzed around the men, irritating everybody. A cloud brought light rain, which increased as the day wore on.

Wolseley arrived with four stalwart men carrying him on a litter, while his Black Watch bodyguard exchanged pleasantries and insults with the Rifle Brigade. "Feed the men," Wolseley descended from his perch, gasped as he put his weight on his wounded leg and limped around the village, "and the Rifles will advance to the next village."

Jack looked up. "Permission to accompany the Rifles, sir?"

Wolseley nodded. "Yes, Windrush. Take your Wests."

Gathering his men, Jack followed in the wake of the hurrying Rifles without encountering a single Ashanti warrior. A solitary woman sat under a tree in the village of Aggemmamu, pointing to the British soldiers as they splashed through the spreading puddles.

"King Kofi is a bad man," she said in English, repeating herself three times as laughing porters gathered around her, brave in the presence of British soldiers.

Captain Moore ordered the woman to be taken to a hut and guarded. "If we don't look after her," he said, "either one of these bold lads will put a knife through her, or she'll cut somebody's throat and disappear into the bush."

"Aye," Jack said, remembering the women along the North-West Frontier. "Like as not, Moore."

By evening the rain had eased away. The Wests collected dry wood and built a fire in the centre of Aggemmamu, with most removing their clothes to dry them. Some had disappeared into the huts to sleep when somebody shouted: "Ashanti!"

Jack did not see who started the panic, but within seconds all the porters and many of the native levies were on their feet, yelling "Shantee" and running down the path, southward, towards the far distant coast. The Rifles sergeant on guard tried to stop them, and half the Rifles and Wests poured out of the huts, Sniders in hand, to see a disorderly mob fleeing in panic.

"Now we have no porters," Jack told his men. "We'll have to travel without anything except what we can carry."

The Wests nodded. Daley lifted his chin. "We don't need these bloody Bushmen." He looked at Jack. "We're the 2nd Wests."

Jack looked upwards as the sky wept again, large drops of rain dropping from unseen clouds.

* * *

Jack peered into the rain that bounced from the track and dripped from the trees, hoping the weather would not slow their progress. His company marched immediately behind the Rifles, sloshing along the muddy path, miserable yet determined.

"We're nearing the River Ordah," Jack said. "That's the last major obstacle before Kumasi, so watch for ambushes," he gave the order to his men, knowing they were veterans now and needed no warning.

"Maybe the Ashantis have all run," Coffin said hopefully, a moment before the deep thud of a musket proved the opposite.

"No. They're still there," Sergeant Roberts said, immediately firing at the jet of powder smoke.

"Front rank face right," Jack ordered, "rear rank face left. Fire."

The Wests fired a volley, waited to see if the Ashantis retaliated and marched on. Nobody commented, such small scale ambushes were part of the routine of the column and seldom did any harm. Birds called unheeded from the trees as insects continued to plague the column. When they came to a rise, one of the few remaining porters carrying Rait's gun stumbled so the wooden framework on which the nine-pounder sat tipped to the left. An artillery corporal rushed up to straighten things up, and they continued, step by step along the narrow track on a march that seemed never-ending.

The rain ended suddenly as if God had turned off the tap of heaven and the Wests lifted their shoulders slightly. Coffin hummed a hymn, stumbled, recovered and marched on.

Frequent firing ahead proved the Rifles were in contact with the Ashantis, but the column continued at the same pace, the Sniders clearing the way. Jack felt the sweat soaking his tunic, thought of Mary and scanned the trees on either side of the path. The desultory firing continued, culminating in a sharp outbreak that, for once, slowed the column.

"Number One section," Jack shouted. "You're with me!' He was about to hurry forward when the firing ended, and a Cockney voice shouted.

"Who's that?"

Flicking away the sweat that beaded on his eyebrows, Jack ordered Sergeant Mathews to take command of the section and hurried forward to the Rifles position.

"It's a flag of truce!" Captain Moore passed the news down the column. "The beggars are surrendering!"

"Not them," Jack said. "It's some sort of ruse." He joined the Rifles' officers at the front of the column, with the native levies looking scared and the Riflemen fingering their triggers as they stood or crouched behind cover.

The elderly Ashanti stood on the path, with an ambassador's gold breastplate on his chest, and apprehension on his face. Beside him, a familiar figure carried a flag of truce.

"Akron," Jack said quietly.

"I know the fellow in the breastplate," Captain Moore said. "He's an ambassador from King Kofi. We gave him a guard of honour back in Fomanah."

"I know his companion," Jack said quietly.

"Send them to the general," McLeod took charge." "They're ambassadors! Treat them with respect." He glanced at Jack. "Major Windrush, take a section to escort the Ashantis."

"This way, gentlemen," Jack said, forming Number One section around the two ambassadors. "Akron; how is my wife?"

Akron looked astonished. "Your wife, Major?"

"Your people hold her prisoner in Kumasi," Jack said. "How is she?"

Akron and the ambassador struggled to keep paste with the Wests. "The Indian woman? Kumi Okese's new slave?"

"Is she well?" Jack asked.

"She is well cared for," Akron said.

"Where is she held?"

"Kumi Okese has her in his slave quarters," Akron said.

"Where is that?"

"Behind his house."

About to ask more, Jack stopped as Wolseley, imperious on his hammock, demanded the letters the ambassador held. Wolseley scanned the paper, grunted and gave a small snort of impatience. "King Kofi wishes me to halt my advance. What do you say, Windrush? You're the only man here who has met his Ashanti Majesty."

Jack glanced at Akron, who stood impassive as if he did not understand a word. "I'd say push on harder than ever, sir. I would not believe King Kofi's if he told me it snowed at the North Pole." Jack looked up as another shower of rain spattered them. "The rainy season is due, sir. The longer we delay, the more chance there is of a constant downpour, and we have the Ordah River to cross, and the swamp that guards Kumasi. If they are swollen, they will delay our progress, and seriously impede our withdrawal."

Wolseley smiled. "You speak with great eloquence, Windrush. Do either of these gentlemen speak English?"

"Yes, sir. Akron, the man with the flag, is fluent."

"Then, Mr Akron," Wolseley said, "pray tell the Asantahene that we will not halt. That is all."

"Thank you, sir."

"You have not forgotten the charge I laid upon you, Windrush," Wolseley said.

"No, sir. I have not." *But your blessed Golden Stool can wait until I've found Mary, Sir Garnet.*

As the ambassadors returned up the column, the Ashanti started firing again, with slugs whistling from the forest. "So much for the flag of truce, Akron," Jack said. "I want to speak to you before you return."

"Yes, Major." Akron ducked as a slug ripped into his flag. His companion with the gold breastplate gave a little whimper and began to hurry along the path, shouting something. The firing intensified, with one Rifleman grunting and falling, to rise shortly after, looking at the slow spread of blood on his leg. He swore, lifted his Snider, aimed and fired back.

"I'm Joe Briggs!" he shouted. "You'll not see me die in a hurry! We're tough stuff in Whitechapel!"

Despite the situation, Jack gave a grim smile. He knew the Ashantis were capable warriors, but British soldiers could hold their own against anybody. At the next shot, the ambassador backed away, and Jack was sure he would have fled to Wolseley if a Rifles' corporal had not ushered him to the front of the column.

"There you go, chum," the corporal said. "Go and join your mates." He looked at Jack, "can I boot him up the backside, sir? Help him on his way, like?"

"That's not very diplomatic, corporal," Jack placed his hand on Akron's arm. "Could you imagine doing that to a British diplomat?"

The corporal considered for a moment and his grin widened. "Oh, yes, sir. It would do them a world of good. They start the wars and beggars like us, and these Ashanti lads do the fighting."

Jack nodded. "That's very true." He swore as Akron slipped, twisted free and ran up the path as though his life depended on it. "Come back!" he shouted in vain, watching as both Ashantis revealed an amazing turn of speed.

Well, now I know that Mary is alive and where the Ashantis hold her. This time tomorrow I could be with her.

The firing sputtered away and then increased all around the advance guard. "The devils are stubborn today," Captain Moore said.

"They don't want us to cross the Ordah," Jack fired his revolver into a patch of woodland, ducked behind the trunk of a tree and hastily reloaded. 'It's the last barrier before Kumasi."

"Good," Captain Moore said. "All the sweeter when we cross."

As the firing grew even more intense, the Rifles sent patrols into the forest to seek for the Ashantis. Jack watched them leave the path, exchanging dark jokes as they slid under the leaves.

"Sir?" Sergeant Mathews sounded hopeful. "Can we not hunt the Ashantis too?"

"No," Jack said emphatically. "I'll need all of you when we get to Kumasi. I don't want unnecessary casualties."

"Yes, sir." Mathews looked disappointed.

"Get into cover," Jack said. "Only fire when you are sure it's an Ashanti. Remember that the Rifles are out there too." He heard the tussle in the bush, the deep thuds of the muskets and the returning crackle of the Sniders and then the Rifles' patrols returned with wounded men.

"We got three of the devils," one long-faced sergeant said, sending his two wounded back down the column. "Maybe four. Big beggars with white stripes down their faces. They thought they were facing parade ground soldiers, not the Rifles!"

Jack nodded agreement. The common perception of the British soldier was the scarlet-coated Guards, with their spit-and-polish and immaculate drill. The reality was here, the men from London slums and the back-streets of Dundee, men brought up in the harsh climate of Highland Scotland, or with the tyranny of the soil in English shires. These men faced adversity with a curse and dark humour. Death might claim them, but nothing could defeat them. Jack felt a sudden surge of pride, tinged with a shame he did not understand.

The column moved on again, with the Ashantis contesting every yard, so the British marched through drifting powder-smoke, with slugs pattering around them. At one stage, where a swamp spread at the base of a wooded rise, the Ashanti fought behind a barricade until the artillery and the Rifles forced them out. A quarter of a mile further back, Jack's Wests listened to the battle in growing frustration. Only when the Rifles cleared the route could the march continue, with Jack aware of growing dampness burdening the atmosphere.

"The rains are gathering," he said. "We'd better get a move on."

"This is still the dry season," Hopringle protested.

Jack grunted, saying nothing as they rounded a bend, and the column came to a halt.

"There's the Ordah." Excitement tinged Hopringle's quiet voice as he pointed to the slow brown river that slithered between dipping green trees.

Jack nodded. Once across that river, Ashanti resistance should either stiffen or collapse. The column halted, with the Rifles' skirmishers taking up defensive positions along the banks.

"Number One Section, face your front, extended order," Jack snapped. "Number Two Section, front rank face right, rear rank face left. Number Three and Four Sections, you're in reserve."

"I thought they'd have put up a better defence here," Jack said, as the musketry died away. "I thought they'd have at least a screen of musket men." He stepped to the river bank, very aware a score of Ashantis could be aiming at him.

"So did I," Hopringle stood slightly further back, holding his revolver. "I was expecting a contested river crossing."

At thirty yards wide, the Ordah was as more of a psychological as a physical barrier, with the water not sufficiently deep to halt a determined advance. "King Kofi bathes here once a year," Jack remembered something that Akron had told him. "The Ashantis think the Ordah is sacred."

"The Ashantis seem to think that every river is sacred," Captain Moore said grimly. "Here comes the general."

"Camp here," Wolseley ordered. "The engineers can build a bridge. That will be easier for the porters and wounded to cross, and when the rains come, a swollen river won't delay our return."

Biting back his frustration at the thought that Mary was only a few miles down the road, Jack took C Company to form a defensive perimeter. He watched the engineers felling trees with a controlled frenzy as they constructed the first bridge the Ordah had ever seen. Despite his desire to charge ahead, Jack knew that Wolseley was correct. If they had to withdraw at speed, having a rain-swollen river behind them would be dangerous, especially if Ashanti musket men filled the woods.

"I don't think I've ever properly appreciated the engineers before," Captain Moore said.

"Nor have I," Jack admitted. "They're a Godsend."

"Aye, or a Wolseleysend!"

As the day eased, the rain began again, with the Wests and Rifles using tree boughs and leaves to build shelters while the Engineers toiled by torchlight. At eight in the evening, a supply officer brought up a keg of Jamaican rum, which proved popular with the men.

"That's not bad stuff," Ogston said.

"You should know, Oggy," a Rifle corporal said. "You make the best there is."

After creating a guard rota for the night, Jack tried to sleep, although the rush of the river and thoughts of Mary restricted his rest. He woke before dawn, realised he lay in a muddy puddle, swore soundly and rose to check the sentries. The rain teemed down over the new bridge, pattered in the river and dripped from the surrounding trees.

"Welcome to Africa," Jack pulled up his collar and hauled his pith helmet over his head.

"That's Kumasi joined to civilisation for the first time in its history," Captain Moore joined Jack, a wet cigar between his teeth. "I can hear the Ashantis celebrating already."

The sound drifted towards them, a myriad voices, the monotonous grumble of the drums and an occasional yell.

Jack nodded. "Aye." He said no more as he checked his revolver was loaded. He did not feel like talking that morning. *By tomorrow evening*, he told himself, *I will be with Mary, or I'll be dead.*

CHAPTER THIRTY-ONE

Across The Ordah February 1874

The Wests moved an hour before dawn, thundering across the bridge as the rain eased to a reluctant stop. Water dripped from the overhanging leaves, the only sound in the ominous hush as if the country was shocked at this foreign army invading the empire that had caused so much fear.

"Orders from the general!" Lieutenant Wood shouted. "The advance party is not to fire first! King Kofi might want to negotiate."

Jack watched the young officer run back, all his dignity gone as he passed on what he must have considered a critical order.

"Bugger that," one of the Riflemen said.

"Did you hear that boys?" Jack said to his men. "If you see an Ashanti pointing his musket at you, don't fire. Greet him nicely and say how do ye do?"

When only Sergeant Mathews smiled at the irony, Jack continued with a warning. "Keep alert, lads. The Ashantis won't be happy today."

Jack had barely finished speaking before the muskets roared. Once again, Jack had his men take cover and fire back, blasting every jet of smoke and muzzle flash with bullets as Russell's Bonny natives and the Rifle Brigade led the advance, firing and moving, pushing slowly forward.

"Is that the Ashantis negotiating, sir?" Hopringle asked.

Behind Jack's company, the 42nd lined the length of the road to keep communications open and guard the baggage, with musketry continuous and the occasional casualty as Ashanti slugs found their mark.

"Maybe we should invite the politicians here," Jack said. "Show them the reality of Imperial diplomacy."

The track rose towards the village of Ordahsu, which the Ashantis seemed determined to hold. The firing increased with every yard, forcing the column to halt and return fire.

Jack grunted. "This is getting hot!" confined to the road, the column fired into the forest, taking casualties, aiming at spurts of smoke, men cursing, groaning, shouting, helping their colleagues and performing acts of unrecorded heroism.

"Keep moving!" Still carried on his litter, a target for every Ashanti musket within range, Wolseley gave orders without flinching from the slugs that whistled past him. "Press on!"

Walking amongst his men, Jack beckoned them forwards. "Come on, lads! Support the Rifles!"

Heading the column, the Rifles surged into Ordahsu. The Ashantis met them with a torrent of musketry, making every hut a strongpoint and every house a redoubt. In an unfamiliar town gritty with concealing smoke, the Rifles fought through the streets, kneeling to fire, finding cover where they could, cursing as they met the Ashantis head-on.

"With me, boys!" Jack pushed up his Wests, charging towards a hut where two musket men were reloading. Firing as he ran, Jack's first two shots missed, and only his third caught an Ashanti in the stomach. The man doubled up, while his companion lifted his musket by the barrel and swung it at Jack.

Stair leapt past, thrusting with his bayonet as he shouted: "Second Wests!" He turned to Jack with the Ashantis blood spattered over his face. "That Bushman's dead sir," he casually bayonetted the wounded man and ran on to the next hut as Jack reloaded his revolver.

The crack of artillery made Jack flinch as the nine-pounder added to the noise, with the gunners targeting the most stubborn areas of Ashanti defence.

"You!" Colonel McLeod pointed to a Rifleman who sheltered at the corner of a hut to fire at the Ashantis. "Are you afraid of the enemy that you must hide from them?"

The Rifleman turned around, surprise on his face. "No, sir. I am not afraid, but if I did not take cover, I should expect to be marked for extra drill."

"Good answer, Rifleman," Jack encouraged as McLeod stormed away. "Come on, lads!" Revolver in hand, he led a rush towards the right side of the village, where a group of Ashanti were sheltering behind the doorway of a substantial house, firing up the main street at the Rifles.

Bullets kicked up dust at Jack's feet, and a slug cracked against his jacket, temporarily winding him. He gasped, sinking to his knees as he struggled to catch his breath.

"Sir?" Sergeant Mathews stopped at his side. "Sir?"

"I'm all right," Jack said. "Go on! Take that hut."

Rolling onto his side, Jack recovered his breath, stood up and staggered forward. The Wests and Rifles had cleared the village and were searching the houses for any stragglers. Rifle and West wounded sat side by side in the shade, while a score of dead Edwesus lay in their own blood, mature warriors killed defending their country, the white stripes bright in the sunlight. A dozen native porters also lay on the ground, some whimpering in fear.

"Well done, lads," Jack recovered his breath. "Now we'll have to wait and see what happens next."

As the British consolidated their hold on Ordahsu, the Ashanti launched a surprise counter-attack, yelling as they rushed from the forest. For a few moments, the position was precarious as the outlying Rifle pickets withdrew.

"Force them back!" Jack fired and reloaded as his men joined the Rifles. The high crack of Sniders drowned all other sounds as the Ashanti attack faltered before it reached the village. They fell back, sullenly. Silence descended, save for a few isolated shots that did no harm.

"They're getting desperate," Hopringle said.

"They knew we've got them beat." Jack counted his revolver cartridges. He had twenty left and no way to replenish until nightfall. He waited, with the tension mounting inside him. Although Jack knew the British had mauled the Ashanti army, Kumi Okese might have some nasty surprises yet. Now that he was no close to Mary, he did not want to die in a sordid ambush.

"Why are we waiting?" Hopringle echoed Jack's thoughts. "We've got the Ashantis on the run; we should push them hard."

"Didn't you hear?" Captain Moore had dried blood down one side of his face. "Sir Garnet, in his wisdom, has decided that the 42nd should have the honour of being first to enter Kumasi."

Jack swore silently. "So we have to wait until they march to the front of the column."

"That's right, Windrush, we wait while the Ashantis gather their forces again."

Jack fretted with impatience, wondering if he should leave his men and strike off alone to find Mary. With the Ashanti army in retreat, the danger would not be as great. He calculated the odds. He knew where Kumi Okese held Mary, so once he entered Kumasi, he could find her. However, a lone white face in an enemy capital city would make him vulnerable. With scores, possibly hundreds of disgruntled Ashanti warriors in the streets, it was unlikely he would survive for long. It would be better to wait. A dead husband was no good to Mary, and getting her killed while trying to rescue her, was not intelligent. However… Jack was still deliberating when he heard the sound of pipes.

"Bloody Sawnies," a Rifles sergeant said. "We've led the advance for three days. We should be first into Kumasi, not the Forty-bloody-second."

Jack listened as the Rifles greeted the 42nd with insults and jeers, to which the 42nd responded in kind. For a moment, Jack thought there would be a full-scale inter-regimental brawl until things simmered down into mutual glowers.

"Take us into Kumasi, 42nd," McLeod ordered, and the Black Watch marched ahead.

"Windrush!" Wolseley beckoned him forward. "You have a mission to accomplish."

"Yes, sir," Jack said. "Come on, lads, we'll follow the Forty-second!"

For the first mile, the British met no opposition, but after that, the Ashantis had recovered. Their first volley wounded seven men. The 42nd returned fire, hammering the trees, bushes and all that hid behind them, so they forced a passage along the road, marching with the pipes screaming defiance. Colonel McLeod strode to the front, shouting orders as the Ashantis tried ambush after ambush.

"A Company, front rank, fire! Rear rank, fire!"

One private stepped ahead of the column, level with the colonel, daring the Ashantis to shoot him.

"Who's that man?" McLeod asked.

"That's Tam Adams, sir," A Fife accent came in reply.

"Good man, Adams! The Forty-second will fire by companies!"

"For old Scotland!" The Highlanders cheered as they forced the road, ignoring casualties, blasting through ambushes. Jack grunted; perhaps there was a reason that Sir Garnet put the Black Watch in the van. Their unique *elan* was better for this sort of advance than the more cautious approach of the Rifles. Accepting casualties, they powered along the road to the scream of the pipes, smashing through each Ashanti ambush.

Can you hear the pipes, Kumasi? Can you hear the Highlanders coming? Then you're going to die. The 42nd is advancing, the Black Watch, Queen Victoria's Highland furies. You can run, or you can die.

Jack began to recognise landmarks. "Six miles to Kumasi," he said, wrapping Mary's scarf around his fist. "If the 42nd keep this speed up, we'll be there in two hours, ambushes or not."

After the weeks and months of waiting, it was exhilarating to march along in the wake of the Highlanders, brushing aside Ashanti ambushes, passing empty kegs of gunpowder and the Ashanti dead and wounded.

I'm coming, Mary!

After four miles the landscape altered, with the scrub and forest giving way to waving grass higher than the tallest man. Alert for possible ambushes, Jack ordered his Wests to spread further out even as he increased his pace. *I'm coming! Hold on, Mary, I'm coming.* Splashing through the final swamp without a care for the depth, Jack automatically replaced the cross the Ashantis had knocked from Manning's grave.

"We've not forgotten," Sergeant Mathews saw the name Jack had carved on the wood.

"Nor have I," Jack said.

They ascended the rise to the main street of Kumasi with the Highlanders before them and the wail of the pipes warning the Ashantis to keep clear. Jack looked around, seeing the familiar houses as if in a dream. After so much effort, he was back, yet it felt unreal. He wanted to run ahead and shout for Mary, yet knew he could not.

"Keep in skirmishing order," Jack said as the Wests spread out, rifles ready. He had wondered if the Ashanti warriors would make a last stand in the streets of their capital, but instead, they had joined the crowds that gathered to watch the British enter. Most warriors stood with their muskets held butt-upward as a sign of peace, while a few even offered gourds of cool water for the soldiers. It felt like an anticlimax, as though a proud empire had collapsed with a whimper. There was not even a single drum beating, not a horn sounding and no umbrellas in sight.

Was that it? No final flourish? No gallant heroes?

"Sergeant Mathews," Jack led his men away from the main streets to a quieter square, where a group of women and children watched curiously from under the dripping leaves of a banyan tree.

"Yes, sir." Mathews' eyes were never still as he surveyed his surroundings, looking for the enemy.

"I have two things to find in Kumasi."

"I know, sir," Mathews said. "The Golden Stool and Mrs Windrush."

"How the devil do you know about the Stool?" Jack knew he should not be surprised. Sergeants in the British Army had a knack of finding out everything. There was no reason that a sergeant in the 2nd West should be different.

Mathews smiled. "I hear things."

"Well, sergeant, take Number One Section and try to get into the palace; search for the Stool; it was in the upper storey of the tower when I saw it last. I am going to find my wife."

"Yes, sir." Sergeant Mathews hesitated a second. "Good luck, sir."

"Thank you," Jack said, ordered Hopringle to take over C Company and without another word, headed for Kumi Okese's house.

You had better be right about Mary, Akron. Groups of Ashantis watched him, civilians and soldiers, yet Jack knew if anybody challenged him, he would shoot without compulsion.

Jack's heart raced as he ran through the streets, trying to remember where Kumi Okese lived. When a curiously shaped banyan tree caught his eye, he knew he was on the right track, ran into the side street, and stopped with a curse.

A hundred men were milling around, pushing and shoving at each other as a section of Rifles was arguing with a large group of Ashanti warriors. Desperate to find Mary, Jack would have avoided them, but they were directly in his path.

Looking past them to Kumi Okese's house, Jack swore again "What the devil's all the commotion, Corporal?"

The corporal was Irish, severely sunburned and with a mouth like a gin-trap. "The general wants us to disarm the Shantees, sir. This bunch doesn't want to be disarmed."

"So I see." Jack saw that the Ashanti warriors were already disappearing. "Take what you can, corporal, but if any Ashanti objects, don't argue." The last thing the British needed was a mass brawl when the column was scattered about the streets and vastly outnumbered.

"Yes, sir!" The corporal stared as Jack grabbed an Enfield and a bandolier of ammunition from a surprised Ashanti.

"I'll have these, fellow!"

With the situation resolved, Jack moved on, feeling his tension mount as he neared Kumi Okese's house. "Mary!" He raised his voice, loading the Enfield in case any Ashanti showed fight. "Mary!"

There was no reply. Jack ran inside, shouting. He ran from room to room, booting open doors, holding his rifle at the ready. There was no sign of Mary and nothing to say that she had ever been there.

"Mary!" Jack felt panic surging through him as he yelled himself hoarse, peering desperately into alcoves and courtyards. Only echoes replied.

Swearing, Jack sped from the house and headed for the street where the Ashanti had held the hostages, ignoring the comments of the British soldiers he passed.

"You're in a rush, sir."

"I say," a plump major tried to stop him. "You, fellow! What's the hurry?"

The hostages' houses looked as if Jack had left them the previous day, with everything so familiar, it was hard to believe he had been involved in three expeditions since he was last here. Rushing forward, Jack entered the open front room where he had spoken to Elda.

"Mary!"

"Who are you looking for?" Elda sounded as calm as if she was in a drawing-room in her native Bohemia.

"Oh, thank God it's you, Elda!" Jack could have collapsed with relief. "I'm looking for Mary Windrush. The Ashanti took her hostage. Is she here?"

"The half-caste woman?"

"My wife," Jack belatedly remembered Elda's relationship with Kumi Okese. "Do you know where she is?"

Elda shrugged. "Yes, she was here."

"Was?" Grabbing Elda by the shoulders, Jack shook her. "What do you mean was here? Where is she now?"

"I don't know." Elda looked away.

"Yes, you do!" Abena burst into the room, her young face crumpled with anger. "You do know Miss Becker! Kumi Okese took her with him as his slave!"

"Oh, dear God in heaven!" Pushing Elda aside, Jack crouched beside Abena. "Do you know where they are now?" He tried to calm his panic. The thought of Mary in Kumi Okese's hands made him feel sick.

"Kumi Okese took her north, to his village I think," Abena said.

"You'll never find her," Elda said. "Never."

CHAPTER THIRTY-TWO

Kumasi February 1874

"Which village? Why? Tell me!" Terrified for Mary, Jack nearly shook Abena.

"It's called Nkaben," Abena said.

Jack stepped back. "Why has he taken her away, for God's sake?"

Elda rose from the floor, brushing herself down. "He's either going to keep her as a slave, or sacrifice her."

Jack felt the iced hand of shock grip him. "'Oh, dear God in heaven. Where is this place, Nkaben?"

As Elda gave a small smile, Abena took hold of Jack's sleeve. "I'll take you, Major Windrush."

"Hurry," Jack said. Leaving Elda standing in the middle of the house, Jack lifted his Enfield, scooped up Abena, and stormed away.

"Is there a path, Abena?"

"I'll show you," Abena said. "Past the palace, Major."

Jack nodded, rushing northward through Kumasi. He had a glimpse of Wolseley staring at him and moved on. Sir Garnet Wolseley, the British army, the war, the Golden Stool, and even the 2nd Wests, would have to do without him. Mary was more important than anything else.

"This way, Major Windrush, I think."

Following Abena's directions, Jack pushed through a crowd of Ashanti civilians and ran to the northern outskirts of Kumasi where a confusion of tracks led in various directions.

"Which one, Abena?"

Abena stopped, staring around her before she shook her head. "I don't remember," she began to cry. "There are too many roads; I don't remember."

"You!" Jack grabbed the nearest Ashanti, a warrior with a musket draped across his back. "Where is Nkaben?"

The man looked confused for a second, then his face cleared as Abena translated Jack's words.

"Nkaben," the Ashanti said, indicating one of the tracks.

"Is that where Kumi Okese is?" Jack asked, aware the man could not understand his words until Abena translated again.

"Nkaben," the warrior was about twenty years old, with clear eyes. Powder stains on his clothes and arms showed he had taken part in the recent fighting. He said something else.

"The man does not know if Kumi Okese is there," Abena said.

"Take me!" Shoving the muzzle of his Enfield into the man's chest, Jack repeated: "Take me to Nkaben!"

The warrior set off at a fast trot across the muddy ground. Jack followed, with his boots splashing through puddles and his head brushing against creepers that unleashed showers of lukewarm of water. After a few minutes, the Ashanti increased his speed and darted into the forest, leaving Jack floundering on the path and Abena a few yards behind.

"Come back!" Jack shouted, knowing his entreaties were futile. He aimed the Enfield in the direction the warrior had taken but did not fire. Taking a deep breath, Jack tried to calm himself down. He was an experienced soldier, he told himself. If he was tracking anybody else save Mary, what would he do? He certainly would not dash unheeding into the forest after an unknown number of enemies as if he were a young ensign on his first campaign.

Jack considered his position. He was alone in the Ashanti forest except for a child, chasing an enemy who had his wife and might kill her. He had no support, and he did not know the strength or position of his enemy.

Very well then, check my surroundings and see what they tell me.

"Stand still," Jack said to Abena. The ground underfoot was muddy, with falling rain deepening the puddles. Jack scouted around, looking for footprints. There were many, mostly of bare feet or sandals, yet he saw, quite distinctly, the pointed toe of a European-style boot. Kneeling, Jack put his hand against the smudged print to judge the size; it was a woman's boot, and he knew without a doubt, it was Mary's.

"Abena." Jack instinctively put out his hand and lightly squeezed when Abena responded in kind. "I'm sorry. You'd better get back to Kumasi. It might get dangerous here." He waited for her protest, but Abena only nodded, turned around and ran back the way she had come.

Hefting the Enfield, Jack strode along the track, searching for any further evidence. Twice more, he saw the impression of Mary's toe, as if she had been running. Jack speeded up, long-striding while still searching for spoor.

He was so intent on looking for Mary's footsteps that he nearly failed to notice the abrupt bend in the path. Halting at the banks of a fast stream that crossed the road, Jack saw Mary's footprint pressed into the mud and crossed over.

Nkaben squatted on a slight rise in the bend of the river. As with many African villages, a collection of well-built houses spread around a central tree, while smaller huts straggling northward and eastward to a cleared area of small fields. Jack heard the soft throbbing of the drums from three hundred yards away and slid behind a tree to watch.

The yellow umbrella was in plain sight, with Kumi Okese standing beneath it and one of his bodyguards at his side, sporting a bandage on his left arm. Around the umbrella, a hundred Ashanti warriors gathered, some brandishing muskets, others with rough bandages. These were the remnants of Edwesu fighting men who had resisted the British advance into Ashantiland, pushed back but still defiant, still undefeated. These were the warriors who had contested a modern army with outdated weapons and raw courage. Despite his situation, Jack could feel respect for them as warriors.

That feeling altered as he saw Mary, standing with shackles on her wrists and ankles. A group of men pushed her back and forward. Every time they shoved, Mary stumbled, recovered and straightened her shoulders.

"Right, you bastards," Jack said. "That's my wife you have there." He wondered if he should have brought his Wests, knew there was no time, and aimed the Enfield. "I'm going to whittle you down," he said, "and free Mary. You first Kumi Okese."

Aiming at Kumi Okese's head, Jack took a deep breath and squeezed the trigger. The Enfield gave a loud crack and bucked violently against his shoulder. *When was this thing last cleaned?* He saw a man next to Kumi Okese jerk upright and spin as the bullet took him in the shoulder. By the time the crowd had worked out what had happened, Jack had loaded. Again aiming at Kumi Okese, he adjusted for his previous miss and pressed the trigger.

"Damn!" Jack swore when another warrior stepped in his line of fire. At three hundred yards, the bullet took the warrior in the head, blowing a mess of blood and brains over Kumi Okese.

"Come on the 113th!" Jack roared, hoping that Mary would hear and understand he was there. "Cry Havelock!" He used the old slogan that the 113th had adopted during the Indian Mutiny. "Cry Havelock!"

Jack fired again as the yellow umbrella shifted, and Kumi Okese gave orders that saw his warriors fan out towards Jack's position.

Loading as quickly as he could, Jack moved to his right, outflanking the village and heading diagonally towards Mary. He could see her clearly now, standing erect, refusing even to bow her shoulders before her captors. Jack was never more proud of her than at that moment. *Show them, Mary!*

Throwing himself down behind a fallen tree, Jack aimed and fired, reloaded without waiting to see the result of his shot, yelled "113th Foot! Come on the 113th!" and ran on, still skirting the village, trying to unsettle the Ashantis so they would leave Mary unattended, trying to make the Ashantis believe a British regiment surrounded them.

The Ashanti warriors were closer now, some firing at the places Jack had already vacated, others shooting at shadows as Jack slid through the forest, using all the bushcraft he had learned in two decades of soldiering. His route had taken him closer to Mary, so now they were only separated by a hundred yards. Mary remained standing with her head high.

"Cry Havelock!" Jack roared.

"Let loose the dogs of war!" Mary joined in. "Come on, the 113th!"

Aiming, Jack fired again, knocking down a young Ashanti warrior. "Come on the 113th!" He reloaded desperately, wishing he had a breech-loading Snider rather than the old muzzle-loading Enfield. Mary would know the 113th were not part of the campaign. She would understand he was alone and unsupported. Jack fired again, rolled on his side to reload and swore when two Ashanti warriors spotted him. While one knelt to fire, the other drew a long knife and ran forward, yelling. Fumbling his reloading, Jack swore as he dropped the percussion cap, rolled away, drew his revolver and shot the charging man. The second Ashanti fired, with the slug passing so close that Jack flinched with the wind of its passage, and then the Ashanti was on his feet, hefting his musket like a club.

Waiting until the warrior was only ten paces away, Jack fired two shots. Both hit the Ashanti in the chest, knocking him back. He crumpled with an expression of surprise on his face as Jack reloaded the Enfield and his revolver. *I'm coming, Mary!*

Jack had lost sight of Kumi Okese and the yellow umbrella. Mary stood about ten yards from the fetish tree, with a shaft of sunlight reflecting from a human skull swinging from a branch. At the base of the trunk, two vultures feasted on a dismembered human body, barely pausing as the echoes of the gunfire died away. Jack could not see the bodyguard anywhere. *Now! Move now!*

"Stand fast, the 113th!" Jack shouted, took a deep breath, and ran towards Mary.

"Good evening, Captain Jack," Mary greeted him with a small curtsey that rattled her manacles.

"Good evening, Mrs Windrush," Jack said. "I don't approve of your new jewellery."

"They are rather heavy, don't you think?" Mary lifted her wrists. "I intend to hand it back at the first opportunity."

"They do look a little clumsy." Now that he was close, Jack could see the lines of strain on Mary's face and the worry in her eyes. "We'd better remove them, I think."

"Jack!" Mary screamed as Kumi Okese's bodyguard leapt from behind the tree, with his knife bare in his fist. Lifting the Enfield, Jack shot the man through the stomach, leaving him to lie, writhing on the ground.

"We only have a minute before the warriors return," Jack said. "Pray excuse my lack of manners." Ducking down, he placed Mary over his shoulder, straightened up and headed towards the forest.

Tired after days of campaigning and months of stress, Jack found Mary heavier than he expected. "You must have put on weight. Tell me if you see any Ashantis following us."

"Not yet," Mary said. "We're all right so far."

When he had first come to Africa, Jack had considered the forest a hostile place, but now it seemed a welcoming refuge as he ran over the open ground. Splashing across the river, Jack slipped on a loose stone, nearly dropped Mary and staggered into the trees. After only a few steps, he slumped down in the shelter of a tall palm and eased Mary to the ground.

"I might keep you like this," he said. "It's easier to control you."

"It's damned uncomfortable." Mary's use of bad language proved her agitation.

"Lie still and I'll try to get the shackles off you."

The manacles around Mary's wrists had a simple bolt to pull, while her ankle shackles were more complex, with a screw.

"Jack," Mary whispered as he worked the mechanism.

"We're nearly there. Be patient."

"Jack!" Mary injected more urgency into the word.

Jack looked up. "What is it?"

"Over there."

Jack saw the movement in the trees, the flicker of white cloth and the glint of sun on metal. He slid down beside Mary, still working on her shackles. "Only a few more twists, Mary."

"Jack!"

The Ashantis arrived suddenly, thrusting the muzzles of their muskets into Jack's back. Rolling over, he reached for his revolver until a hard hand grabbed his wrist and Kumi Okese snarled an order. Half a dozen Ashantis pulled Jack upright, with Mary at his side. Jack punched at the nearest warrior, felt a surge of satisfaction when the man staggered back, and then gasped as somebody cracked him across his head.

"You could have lived, Major Windrush," Elda slid beside Kumi Okese. "You could have left the woman and lived, but you had to be a hero, and of course I told Kumi you were coming." When she smiled, Jack saw the madness in her eyes. "Now Kumi will sacrifice you both."

Jack glanced at Mary, struggling between two brawny warriors. "Tell Kumi he does not need to kill the woman. I will willingly go if he sets her free."

"It's too late for that," Elda said.

"Set her free, you bastard!" Jack struggled against his captors as Kumi Okese watched, expressionless. The warriors dragged Jack and Mary to the fetish tree, with Elda following, clapping her hands. The vultures hopped further away, waiting, with blood dripping from their cruel beaks.

"Sorry, Mary," Jack said. "I failed you."

"No, you didn't," Mary tried to sound calm. "If I had not been stupid enough to get captured, we would not be in this mess."

The executioner from Kumasi stood under the tree, holding a large, slightly curved sword. He looked dispassionately as the warriors hustled Jack and Mary to him.

"Kumi Okese is sacrificing you to his ancestors," Elda explained, "and to the ancestors of his tribe." She was laughing, and Jack wondered if her long captivity in Kumasi had unhinged her mind.

Jack fought hard to retain the phlegm of a British officer. "Tell him that he can kill me if he wishes, but if he murders my wife, a British woman, Lord Wolseley will burn all of Ashantiland. Tell Kumi Okese the British Army will hunt him down and hang him like a dog."

Jack saw Elda pale at the words and speak to Kumi Okese, who shrugged and said a few short words.

"Kumi will take that chance," Elda said.

With two Ashanti warriors forcing him onto his knees, Jack tried to grab Mary's hand, but she was just out of reach. He was aware of Elda watching, her eyes bright.

"Goodbye, Mary, old girl," Jack said. "I'll see you on the other side in a few minutes."

"Goodbye, Captain Jack. I love you." Mary began to intone the 23rd Psalm, her voice quavering at first but strengthening with each verse.

"The Lord is my shepherd; I shall not want.
He maketh me to lie down in green pastures."

Never a religious man, Jack tried to join in, then reverted to something he knew far better. "Cry Havelock!" He could see the executioner approaching, with rainwater dripping from the blade of his sword. "Come on the 113th!" He was back in India again, leading his men towards Lucknow. Then he was on Inkerman Ridge with the great grey masses of Russian infantry rolling towards him through the mist and his handful of the 113th waiting under the dripping colours.

Mary's voice strengthened as the Ashantis pushed her to her knees.

"He restoreth my soul: he leadeth me in the paths of righteousness for his name's sake.

Yea, though I walk through the valley of the shadow of death, I will fear no evil: for thou art with me; thy rod and thy staff they comfort me."

The crack of the rifle meant nothing to Jack. It seemed part of his memories until his soldier's brain analysed the sound. *That was a Snider*, he thought, *except they didn't have Sniders at Inkerman.* He heard the thump of the bullet hitting its target and saw the executioner staring in amazement at the small hole that had appeared in his side. The Snider cracked again, and the executioner's head snapped back, with blood spraying out the back of his skull.

"Thou preparest a table before me in the presence of mine enemies: thou anointest my head with oil; my cup runneth over.

Surely goodness and mercy shall follow me all the days of my life: and I will dwell in the house of the Lord forever. Jack?" Mary stopped her singing.

With the Ashanti guards distracted by the unknown marksman, Jack made a sudden lunge up and barged into the men holding Mary. "Run, Mary! Run!"

"Jack," Mary hesitated, waiting for him.

"Run!" Jack pushed her away, landed a punch on the jaw of the nearest Ashanti and scooped up the executioner's sword. Although it was heavy and poorly balanced, it was better than nothing. As the second Ashanti stared, Jack chopped him down. Another shot sounded, and then a roar as fifty warriors ran from the forest.

"What the devil?" Jack looked for Kumi Okese, gripping the sword as blood dribbled onto his fingers.

Mary grabbed his left hand. "Come on, Jack!"

"No! You get away, Mary!" Jack swung the sword, missed the nearest man and tried again, stepping forward to shield his wife.

The mob of men charged into the village, carrying an assortment of weapons, from swords and spears to muskets. The man at their head held an Enfield rifle with a fixed bayonet. Jack stared at him. "Sergeant Wickham."

The newcomers were attacking the Ashanti with great gusto, hacking with their swords and spears, or firing their muskets and using the butts as clubs. Sergeant Wickham stopped in front of Jack. Out of uniform, he looked every inch the African warrior. "I answer to Kwabena Badu now, Major Windrush."

"I'm glad to see you're alive, Sergeant," Jack said. "Who are these men?"

"Men of my tribe," Wickham said. "Denkyira warriors."

Jack watched two of the Denkyiras dispose of two Ashantis without difficulty, leaving the white-striped men sprawled on the ground. Yelling, Kumi Okese slashed aside three Denkyiras and strode towards Wickham. Three warriors followed their chief. Jack felt for his revolver, swore at the empty holster and hefted his sword.

"I want him, Major," Wickham said.

"So do I," Jack said softly. "He was going to murder my wife, and he murdered one of my men."

"One of my friends," Wickham drew his knife as Kumi Okese came closer.

Kumi Okese's Edwesus charged first, with the Denkyiras meeting them before they reached Jack and Wickham. Kumi Okese feinted at Wickham, sidestepped, and attacked Jack, swinging his knife at Jack's throat. He was fast and fierce, but clumsier than Jack had expected. Used to the Pashtun with their long Khyber knives, Jack dodged Okese's slash and hacked his sword at onto the Ashanti's head, splitting it in two. Kumi Okese crumpled to the ground.

That's Private Manning avenged. Yet inside, Jack felt hollow.

"Nicely done," Wickham approved.

"I thought your people were scared of the Ashanti and could not fight," Jack said.

Wickham smiled. "We fight when we want to and when we have a reason. Whatever you may pretend, the British war with the Ashanti is not our war. You want control of this part of Africa, nothing else."

Jack dropped his sword. "I suspect that you are not returning to the regiment?"

"No," Wickham said. "For three generations, my family has wanted to come home. I am home." He spread a hand to indicate the tribesmen who stood around the village, some leaning on their weapons as they watched Jack, others finishing off the Edwesu wounded. "These are my people."

Jack nodded. "I posted you as killed in action," he said. "That is accurate as Sergeant Albert Wickham no longer exists. You killed him, Kwabena Badu, and you saved our lives. Live in peace."

"I did not save your life," Kwabena Badu pointed to Abena, who appeared from behind the fetish tree. "That little girl told me what was happening." He smiled. She is Denkyira and was a slave of the Ashantis; now she will be my adopted daughter."

Mary smiled to Abena. "Thank you, Abena."

Jack looked at the bodies of Kumi Okese's warrior, lying in crumpled heaps on the ground. For a moment he thought of the proud regiment Kumi Okese had paraded through the streets of Kumasi. They were all gone now, their pride broken by Highland bayonets and the bullets of Snider rifles, their regiment destroyed at Abrakrampa, Amoaful and Ordahsu, with the survivors scattered with the taste of defeat bitter in their mouths. They had been brave men, fighting for a culture that had no place in the late 19th century.

Elda Becker body lay prone, separated from the rest. Jack did not know who killed her or why. He shook his head; she had come to Africa to do good, but Africa had proved too much for her.

Stooping, Jack lifted the yellow umbrella from the ground. For months it had been a symbol of his enemy, a thing of dread. Now it was only an umbrella, nothing more. "I've been watching this all through the campaign," he said. "'I was going to take it for the officer's mess." He handed to Kwabena. "I think you deserve it more than me."

"Keep it," Kwabena said. "I may get more."

Handing the umbrella to Abena, Jack watched as Kwabena led the Denkyiras away. "Oh, Mary," he said, "I have something else for you." Sliding a hand inside his tunic, he produced the scarf he had carried for so long and placed the Celtic cross on top.

"I wondered where those had got to." Mary tried to hide the catch in her throat. "We bought that scarf in Gondabad two days before we got married." Turning away to hide her tears, she tied it loosely around her neck. "And we bought the cross in Lindisfarne when you were based in Berwick."

"Come on, Mary," Jack heard the roughness in his voice. "We have a golden stool to find."

"I don't care about the Golden Stool or a hundred golden stools," Mary said. "We're together again, and that's all that matters."

CHAPTER THIRTY-THREE

Kumasi February 1874

When Jack walked into the house Wolseley had requisitioned, the general was with Lieutenant Wood, both of them admiring the lieutenant's booty. Augmenting King Kofi's state umbrella of black and crimson velvet, Wood had a beautifully carved stool with silver ornamentation. Jack knew that as aide de camp to Wolseley, Wood could be relied on to be first to the loot. Aristocrats always were; in Jack's opinion, that was how they had obtained their titles in the first place.

"I found the stool with a sergeant of the Wests," Wood said. "The beggar refused to give it up to me. I had to put him under arrest."

I'll have Sergeant Mathews free before this day is over.

"Ah, Windrush," Wolseley looked up from his study of the stool. "I ordered you to locate the Golden Stool of the Ashantis, did I not?"

"You did, sir," Jack said.

"Yet despite my direct order, you went swanning around on some personal mission, delegating your duty to a sergeant, of the West Indian Regiment at that."

"Sergeant Mathews is a good man, sir. He was good enough to fight for the queen and put his life on the line, and the West Indians are excellent soldiers."

"You put your personal interest before your duty, Windrush," Wolseley said. "I had hopes for you. I wondered why a man with your fine fighting record had not advanced beyond major, and now I see why. You neglect your duty, sir. I am not surprised that you are only a major; indeed, I am surprised that you reached that exalted rank." Wolseley was working himself into a rage. "I hope you enjoy your majority, Windrush, for you will climb no higher for the remainder of your career."

About to retaliate, Jack thought of Mary. "Yes, sir, you're probably right."

"Fortunately, Lieutenant Wood here located the stool. Dismissed, Windrush."

"Yes, sir." Jack glanced at the stool, smiled and left the room.

Yaa Asantewaa was outside, standing close to a circle of Ashanti warriors. "Your general does not approve of you, Major Windrush."

"It would appear not," Jack said.

"We have a saying in our land," Yaa said. "*Enne ye medea okyina nso we dee*. It means, today is mine, tomorrow is yours. That means one day one person has a victory; the next day, his enemy will win."

Jack nodded. "Aye, Yaa, that is the way of the world."

"Today your general has won his victory over us, and you." Yaa was not smiling. "Tomorrow he may find out he does not have our Golden Stool but another. Will you tell him?"

Jack shook his head. "Not I. As far as I am concerned, the Ashanti are entitled to their Stool. They fought hard for it. I've got my wife back so I'll call the bargain square."

Yaa smiled. "You are a strange man for a British soldier, Major Windrush." She looked into his eyes. "I will guard our Golden Stool in case another British soldier wishes to steal it, and your day will come."

Jack looked over to Mary. "I think it already has," he said.

HISTORICAL NOTES

The slave trade was one of the most despicable events to disgrace humanity, with British slavers playing their ignoble part.

In the three centuries of European participation, an estimated six million slaves were transported from West Africa. The numbers captured in East Africa during 1800 years of Arab slaving must be staggering.

From 1807 onward the Royal Navy instituted anti-slavery patrols off the coast of West Africa, with 150,000 slaves freed from 1810 and 1864. This figure is impressive but pales into insignificance with the estimated 100,000 a year carried across to the Americas. The Royal Navy paid a high price for this humanitarian service. In 1829 alone, over 25% of the men in the West African squadron died from disease. Ships could spend up to five years off the West African coast.

The West Indian Regiment

The West Indian Regiment was part of the British Army from the late eighteenth century and has never received the publicity or recognition it deserves. The regiment participated in many expeditions against the French in the Caribbean and fought in Central America and West Africa. The senior officers who knew the soldiers had nothing but praise for them.

The Wests played a prominent part in the Ashanti Wars. Although I have included them in the occupation of Kumasi in this fictional account, they were denied that opportunity in reality. Of their bravery and devotion to duty, there is no doubt.

Yaa Asantewaa (1840-1921) is one of the most significant female figures in African history. She led the Ashanti against the British in the war of 1900 when the then British governor of the Gold Coast demanded the sacred Golden Stool so he could sit on it. Although the British eventually won the fighting, the Ashanti retained the sacred stool.

HISTORICAL NOTES

Amoaful: The deciding battle of the Ashanti War, where the British defeated a very determined Ashanti defence. Lance Sergeant McGaw won the Victoria Cross and gained promotion to sergeant. He died in Cyprus four years later.

Kumasi. Wolseley's occupation of Kumasi was astonishingly short. The British remained only a few days, looted the palace, set fire to the town and withdrew, struggling over the swollen rivers as the rains came. The Ashantis did not attack the coastal settlements again.

ABOUT THE AUTHOR

Born in Edinburgh, Scotland and educated at the University of Dundee, Malcolm Archibald writes in a variety of genres, from academic history to folklore, historical fiction to fantasy. He won the Dundee International Book Prize with 'Whales for the Wizard' in 2005.

Happily married for 35 years, Malcolm has three grown children and lives in darkest Moray in northern Scotland, close by a 13th century abbey and with buzzards and deer more common than people.

* * *

To learn more about Malcolm Archibald and discover more Next Chapter authors, visit our website at www.nextchapter.pub.

Printed in Great Britain
by Amazon